ARTILLERY OF TIME

BOOKS BY CHARD POWERS SMITH

PROSE

Artillery of Time
Annals of the Poets
Pattern and Variation in Poetry

VERSE

Along the Wind
Lost Address
The Quest of Pan
Hamilton—a Poetic Drama
Prelude to Man

ARTILLERY OF TIME

BY

Chard Powers Smith

WILDSIDE PRESS

To the Memory of my Mother
who was a Yankee

In grateful acknowledgment:

To Nannette for daily encouragement and criticism, and months of research;

To Maxwell Perkins for his unfailing sympathy, patience and affirmative helpfulness of a great editor;

To Doctor Douglas Southall Freeman for invaluable assistance in my study of the terrain of the Seven Days' Battle;

To Colonel Beverly Ober for his hospitality in entertaining me during a tour of the officers of his 110th Field Artillery across the same terrain, conducted by Doctor Freeman;

To Mark Kiley, Librarian of the University Club, for instant provision of all manner of sources throughout the years of composition;

To Doctors Frank Glenn and Theodore W. Oppel for surgical and medical details;

To Theodore E. Knowlton for much of the engineering and manufacturing data;

To Allen M. Bailey of Oberlin College for material on the village and college of Oberlin in the period covered by the book;

To Mrs. T. H. Benedict for recollections of Yankee domestic life in the nineteenth century;

To Anne Powers and Ivan Beede for reading the manuscript carefully and making valuable suggestions, many of which found their way into the final draft.

In apology, I must add that the material and suggestions offered me by these friends have often been varied in the text, and that no one but myself is responsible for any statement as it finally appears.

C. P. S.

CONTENTS

Part I

DANDY

CHAPTER I

I K E L A T H R O P , second son of the Squire, awoke as planned to the sound of the big clock below stairs striking five. From the scratch of a squirrel's claws scampering over the roof, he knew it had frozen in the night. From the absolute darkness and a snug oppressiveness in the silence, he sensed that it was snowing. In the little rope bed beside his big one, his young brother Benjamin rolled over in sleep, and Ike's mind stirred to his duties as the nineteen-year-old, senior member of his generation in the house.

It was a Friday, thirteen days before Thanksgiving, in the year 1850, and Ike was to drive the four and a half miles down to the Falls to meet his elderly cousins Joel and Alvina who would arrive on the Utica stage at 7, along with Uncle Brandon, a lawyer in Utica and a frequent visitor, and probably sister Agatha and her husband from Oberlin, Ohio. The elderly cousins were coming all the way from the old homestead in Connecticut to visit the new homestead in northern New York. It was an important event for the family, and Ike's mother had asked him particularly to look nice when he met his cousins. Privately he considered it a piece of danged nonsense to rig up like a dude on a work-day, but he didn't want to disappoint his ma. "Clothes ain't but a custom," he considered as he lay in the darkness. "Best do the proper thing and not stew about it."

Ike nevertheless decided not to get into his new store suit. Best save that to cut a figure on Sunday. For today he'd pick out some old duds that had been dress-up once, though they might be a little patchy and too tight for him now. He'd put on his big brother John's one-time best buff pants; his own every-day boots; one of his new, plaited shirt-fronts; the new-fangled bow tie John had brought him from New Haven last summer and which John had tied for him the once he had worn it; his old pink waistcoat and brass-buttoned green coat he could still squeeze into; and brother John's coonskin cap which was now virtually discarded and, though torn in the lining, less frayed externally than Ike's own.

He wished John were coming on the morning stage too, but by the last letter he wouldn't be home for ten days yet, most likely on the Monday before Thanksgiving. Ike would rather see John than all the cousins in the connection, though he did think he was too danged extravagant since he'd gone off to Yale. He didn't see any sense in rigging out every day in fancy clothes that cost as much as a cow. Ike hoped sister Agatha would be on the stage, even if she did have to bring that show-off husband of hers. Next to John, Aggie was Ike's favorite relation. She'd written Ma that she thought they would catch the same stage as the Connecticut cousins, but to expect them when she saw them. Homer had just been elected to Congress and was "very much occupied." Lying there in the dark, Ike gave a sniff of contempt at his brother-in-law, Homer Hislip. He'd wager he was "occupied"—likely hadn't stopped palaverin' in three months.

Realizing that his sartorial plans would take some doing, Ike stepped out of bed onto the cold floor. He groped for his wool stockings on the chest and pulled them on. He walked unerringly through the dark to the closet, picked up his every-day boots and, carrying them in his hand, tiptoed down the front stairs, through the little hall where the big clock beat in the darkness, and into the keeping-room. He kicked a chair that Octavia must have left there, and the agony of his big toe forced a "Consarn it" from him. "Good-morning, son," came his father's quiet voice through the door of the master's bedroom at the rear. Ike found the latch and opened the door noiselessly. "Mornin', pa—sorry I woke ye."

"It's right fresh out, Isaac, and you should take along a drop of spirits for your cousins Joel and Alvina. You will find the flask in the cupboard in the north parlor." "Yes, sir," said Ike, much dignified by this assignment of authority in the mature matter of alcohol. He heard his father dismiss him by rolling over in bed, and so closed the door. The house was his again.

He tip-toed into the big kitchen where a single ember showed him the hearth. Balancing on one foot and then the other, he pulled on his boots. Then he took the hearth-rake from its hook on the casing of the huge fireplace and delicately raked back the ashes from last night's embers. Hastily he piled on the pine kindling that Ben had left by the hearth the night before, gave it a few soft puffs with the bellows, and laid on a couple of four-foot maple sticks from the wood-box. As the kindling began to crackle and the flames curled up round the bigger wood, he took down the candle lantern from the mantel, stooped on the hearth and lit it with a piece of kindling, unconscious of the splendid and diabolic image he made as the dancing fire lit up his red flannel night-shirt and golden mane of hair, and threw his crouching shadow immense on the opposite wall. As the light from the fire increased, the copper and iron utensils came out of the upper darkness like grotesque stalactites hanging from the beams of the ceiling amid festoons of dried apples and nutshells already strung up for Thanksgiving decoration.

Having lighted the lantern, Ike rose and, swinging it, strode out through the summer kitchen and so down the passage at the end and into the horse barn attached. One of the barn cats streaked away in the long beam of the lantern, and Mol, Pol and Dandy looked around at the light as he walked behind their stalls.

In spite of the horses' warmth it was cold in the barn; but Ike held to his plan of doing the early chores now so as to keep his clothes clean once he was dressed for the trip to the Falls. As he swung back and hooked the big door in front of the little family coach the blast of chill on his legs, the light snow falling, and the sight of his breath in the lantern light raised the hope that they might have sleighing for Thanksgiving, still almost two weeks away.

He took two leather buckets from their pegs and crunched over the thin snow and frozen grass out to the well in front of the house. The snow was falling fast in no wind, and Ike figured there must be near ten degrees of frost. He wound up the well rope on the new windlass, caught the slobbering, big black oak bucket, and set it on the stone sill of the well. Being in a hurry, he spilled water on himself in filling the horse-buckets and muttered another "Consarn it," only to slop more water on his drenched legs as he returned with his load to the barn, carrying the lantern in his teeth.

"Git over, dang ye," he grumbled to one horse after another as he crowded in past them and held up the buckets to their steaming muzzles; but as they drank he stroked their necks each in turn, and called them his "beauties," and calculated the time had come to blanket them nights. Then he crowded out and in again, threw a big scoop of oats in each manger, and finished the horse chores quickly with a few passes of the brush, for he wanted time to dress as he had planned and he was shivering with his wet nightshirt sticking to his legs.

Hurrying back to the kitchen, he took the two big tin pails, one from the wooden sink and one from under it, and, opening the kitchen door, went through the courtyard with its woodpile looming in the lantern-light and out to the well again. His teeth were chattering while he filled the buckets, and an idea tempted him. "I mustn't take cold," he rationalized as he returned to the kitchen. Putting one bucket in its place in the sink beside the washbasin, he filled from the other the pot on the crane over the fire, set the bucket under the sink, swung the crane back over the fire, and paused in the throes of a moral decision. "I'm shiverin', ain't I," he thought, "right here by the fire?"

Although he figured his pa wouldn't mind, yet instinctively he listened for sounds from the master's bedroom or from the back stairs whence Octavia the hired girl might emerge any minute now. Then, convinced of the reasonableness of his intent, this six-foot-one, red-night-shirted youth seized the lantern, walked determinedly into the north parlor, opened the cupboard over the little fireplace, took out the big pewter flask, slid off the elliptical cup that fitted over it, unscrewed its stopper, poured himself out a minute drink of rum and swallowed it.

Although Ike had had his glass of grog on festive occasions for years, this was the first drink he had ever taken except as proffered by Pa, and it was his first taste of neat spirits. Unable to breathe, he rushed back into the kitchen, snatched the piggin and gulped water from the pail. When he stopped gasping he remembered an axiom of Master Lane the hired man —"A gentleman don't swill liquor like a hog." "Serves me right," said Ike in a dramatic whisper, then poured himself out a larger drink, filled it up with water and drank again, in nonchalant and solitary dignity.

Too late he heard the click of a latch. The door of the back stairs swung open and down stepped Octavia Samson, holding a candle high so that her billowy golden hair glittered, waving out from the part and down behind her ears, framing the long, flat cheeks, the pointed chin, the short, full mouth, the brown eyes wide apart and shining in the firelight like ebony.

Ike had often seen the dove-gray dress swelling out from the trim waist that needed no stays. But he hadn't seen the gold hair released from the mesh that usually confined it, nor the gay ribbon with the lilac rosette at the ear, nor, as she came down the last high step, the white silk stockings with black needlework, and the lilac rosettes on her slippers. Nor had Octavia ever seen Ike in the guise in which she now surprised him, the unstopped flask beside him, the empty evidence of guilt in his hand, and his strong long legs as good as naked with the wet, red night-shirt plastered against them. Each stood for a moment speechless, jaws dropping in astonishment.

Ike found his tongue first, his sense of guilt vanishing in admiration. "Tavie, ye're pretty as a picture!" he said, and colored faintly, for he was inexperienced in the matter of girls and this was his first compliment to womankind outside his ma and sister. Tavie dropped her eyes, then flashed up at him, "Ike, aren't you ashamed? What are you up to?" Manliness and rum restored the young sinner's composure. "It's colder'n blue crickets out this morning," he said casually, replacing the cup on the flask and screwing down the stopper. Then with the utmost bravado he walked to the row of wraps hanging on their pegs above the table on the south wall, carefully selected his own greatcoat, deposited the flask in its pocket with an air of authority, and strode magnificently into the darkness of the keeping-room.

Immediately Tavie heard a chair falling and a full-spoken "god dang it." She seized the lantern he had left on the sink and rushed after him. "Here, Ike, you forgot your light. And you'd better hurry. It's almost five already." "Keerect, Tave," he said, then pressed a finger to his lips, and they both listened. Behind his door they heard the Squire snoring calmly. The big clock in the front hall announced five-thirty. Ike tip-toed up the front stairs two steps at a time, possessed by a combined sense of guilt and a tendency to giggle. Tavie returned to the kitchen, hesitated, reached a decision, ran to Ike's greatcoat, and carried something into the darkness of the north parlor. Then she went back to the kitchen, bore her candle into the north pantry, took down a plate, cup, and a tin of tea, slipped a ham from its hook, and began to slice it violently. "Tavie Samson, you're a silly little fool," she said aloud.

Tavie was twenty-one and a graduate of Oberlin College, one of the few hundred women in the whole United States to be dignified by an A. B. degree. Indeed she had been second in her class, and was only helping her family's neighbors, the Lathrops, until her application for a teaching position in Oberlin should be honored. "Oh, why doesn't a letter arrive?" she thought desperately. During her summer vacation two years ago she had attended the Women's Rights Convention at Seneca Falls, where Mistress Lucretia Mott and Mistress Elizabeth Cady Stanton, especially the former, had elicited her worship, both leaders having corresponded with her since, and Mrs. Stanton having recently intimated that there might soon be a paid position for her somewhere in the ranks of the Cause. The Temperance lecturers at Oberlin, too, had taken an interest in her and she had sat on the platform in some of the Ohio villages. Oh, why didn't a letter arrive?—from anywhere! She had thought everything out, and her pa approved. America was the greatest country in the world, and in a few years every abuse would be swept away. Time enough after women were free and alcohol subjugated and prisons reformed and even slavery abolished, time enough then to think of marrying. Oh, why didn't a letter arrive? Slicing the ham, she narrowly missed cutting herself. "You're a silly girl," she said in an angry whisper— "Marrying forsooth!" Gradually she smiled a little, twisted smile. Her long face settled into its accustomed, tense calm, and Ike faded into the problem of breakfast.

In his room Ike, feeling the alcohol throbbing in his veins, held up the lantern and looked at himself long and searchingly in the mirror. "Steady, old man, steady," he said with solemnity. "What say, brother?" asked seventeen-year old Benjamin, sitting up suddenly in his bed in the corner. Ike stiffened and said lightly with a wave of his hand, "Was saying it's right smart out this morning. Ye'd best lay good fires in the north parlor and the loom-room." "Laid 'em last night," said Ben. He sniffed the air and watched his older brother with amazed and admiring suspicion.

With laborious precision Ike began to array himself as projected. The only mishaps were when one of the brass buttons on the sleeve of the green coat caught on the latch of the closet as he snatched it out and was left dangling; and when, being fully dressed and inspecting himself in the mirror, he threw out his chest for better effect and split his waistcoat up the back—but that wouldn't show under his coat.

He was proud of his achievement in neckwear. Having affixed the plaited shirt-front and attached the lofty "swaller-choker" collar without accident, he tied round the latter his new and modish black satin bow tie which, being long enough to encircle his neck twice but now circling it only once, hung in two long loops and two long ribbons down inside his pink waistcoat.

The effects of his drink were wearing off. "There," he said, giving himself a last approving look, and a few more stitches gave way in the back of his waistcoat. Tavie came to the stairs and spoke softly, "Ike, what are you doing? You ought to be harnessing by now. Don't you want any breakfast?" Ike clumped down stairs. Benjamin jumped out of bed, retrieved the lantern his brother had left, snatched *The Plays of William Shakespeare* from the corner shelf, and climbed back into bed.

Tavie had set out the table before the fire, with a candle in the center of it and at Ike's place a thick slice of broiled ham and an enormous wedge of his favorite hickory nut cake. As he stepped into the room she shovelled the fried potatoes from the spider onto his plate, returned to the fireplace and lifted the tea-pot from the trivet. She glanced up and saw that he had struck an attitude for her appraisal, one hand propped against the door-frame and dangling the torn button, one foot thrown out over the other, the toe on the floor. She restrained a gasp at his array. His brow puckered between his big blue eyes that opened wide. She saw the essential combination that was Ike, in that pucker between the eyes the gentleness and sweetness that wanted her approval, and behind the eyes something at once lonely and frightening, something hard and challenging that she knew no woman would ever reach. She slopped the tea pouring it.

"Now hustle," she said, and, setting back the tea-pot on the trivet, ran up the back stairs with the lantern. Ike dumped some tea into his saucer to cool, and attacked the ham. When Tavie came back his cheeks were swollen with cake. She had needle and thread and knelt quickly beside him, sewing the dangling button on the cuff of his coat-sleeve. He finished the cake and the tea with his left hand.

"Now stand up," said Tavie. "That's a nice tie but you don't know quite how to manage it." As she untied his foolish knot she said, "When John tied it for you he wound it round twice, and I suppose he knows. Here, hold this." And while Ike held one end down she walked round him twice with the other, adjusting the satin band so a thin border of it showed above the green coat collar. While she looked up at him tying the bow she saw his big, gentle features lift into the quiet, long-dimpled smile that always seemed to understand everything and made him a person without age.

She gave the tie a final pat and stepped back, letting herself smile richly for once. Then she saw that pucker between his eyes and stiffened in panic. "Tavie," said his rich baritone as if from miles away, "I guess there'd be no wrong in my kissing ye." She felt suddenly strong and looked straight up at him from her glittering brown eyes. "You'll be sorry if you do, Ike." But he kissed her all the same, taking her by the shoulders and touching her lips so gently that she relaxed for an instant and found herself leaning against him. Then she drew back in fury at her weakness, and when she stared up at him his boyish face was flushed red.

"Guess I'd best be off," he said lamely, and Tavie rushed to the wraps on the wall—"Here's your coat"—she threw it at him—"I put sugar for the horses in the pocket— Here's your tippet— Here's your mittens— Here's"— she paused with his wool cap in her hands—"I suppose you want John's coonskin—get out to the horses—I'll fetch it— I was going to mend the lining." She rushed up the backstairs. The clock in the front hall began to strike six.

Ike grabbed the lantern and ran out through the summer kitchen where in the second of his passing every familiar detail—the stove, the churn, the barrels of flour and meal, the sap-pails hanging from the ceiling, the three muskets on their pegs—seemed fresh and wonderful and important. The first thing he knew he had Dandy in place across the pole of the little family coach. As he was leading Mol out of the stall he suddenly stopped dead still. "Crimus, I kissed her," he thought. "I kissed a girl."

CHAPTER II

I K E slewed the coach dangerously as he swung out into the road, then stood up on the high box to throw a fine wave of the coonskin cap back to Tavie where she stood in the barn door holding the lantern. Still standing like an exultant charioteer, with his cap stuck on the back of his head, he let the horses trot the half mile down to the corners. As he neared the pike, and the Wren church tower came filmily through the dim twilight and snowfall, he saw Jehu Jones leaning on his barnyard gate with a package in his hand, the heads of his four cows hanging over the bars beside him, the five sets of jaws all equally busy. Jehu had on the enormous, varnished straw hat which was his everyday headgear winter and summer, and the thin homespun shirt which did him from April till December. He was the thinnest, one of the tallest, and probably the oldest man in Lathrop Hollow, and had a sparse, silky beard which waved gracefully as he chewed.

"Whoa," sung Ike, pressing the brake gently with his foot and leaning back a little on the reins as the horses squatted into their breechings and slid, snorting to a stop on the ice-filmed grade.

"Morning, Jehu Jones." "Mornin', Ike. When I heern ye comin' full chizzle down the slant I figgered I might have to hop one o' my critters to catch ye. Thar ye be"—he tossed up the little bundle of out-going mail tied up in a string. "Welcome t' the cousins from back east, and if ye're o' mind to, ye might set up a notice touchin' the special cotillion two weeks tonight. Benefit fer them two-dozen lights we're bound to git onto the church windies afore winter, else we'll all be a-settin' in snow t' meetin'. Special occasion, uncommon fine send-off fer them youngsters leavin' fer Californy day follerin'. Spryer'n customary. 'Cordeen player pertic'ler from Center Sand'ich in 'Trury Township. Gents ninepence, ladies sixpence. Two bar'ls first-class cider bunged since Febr'y, new sweet cider fer the ladies—all tupence the glass. Gen'l ticket fer dancin' and ciderin' t'yer fancy, one shillin', and paper of all the county banks acceptable. I'll thank'ee fer tendin' to it. And now let's see ye pull the bungs o' them beauties and let'm rattle."

Ike touched his cap to the sexton-postmaster-social organizer of Lathrop Hollow, sat down, clucked to the horses and trotted off through the Corners; on the left the church, the little parsonage, the long low hall close to the highway and, as he clattered across the bridge to the opposite bank, the square red brick school house where he had graduated five years before. Across the stream the highway turned northward under tall maples, passing Jehu's cider mill—another of his local responsibilities, the grist mill of Elisha Stone, and the saw mill of Jared Oxbow. As Ike expected, young Jared was already busy hammering on one of the two big, boat-like Conestoga wagons he was building for the departure for California the Saturday after Thanksgiving. "Morning, Jared." "Morning, Ike." They waved to each other as Ike trotted past. In a moment the little coach emerged from the trees, passed the Oxbow farm, and from there on the snow-covered road was unmarked by tracks.

Ike slumped into a mood of sadness, his elbows on his knees, thinking of the eight friends who were pulling out for the West only two weeks off: Jared and his wife Roxanna, Savillian Stone and his wife Lucinda, and the young bachelors Hosanna Birdseye, Emanuel Swift, Sam Emmens, and Constant Oaks, none of them more than five years Ike's senior, all his boyhood friends, all people he had counted on, and still did, as permanent members of the community. The thought hadn't occurred to him, or to anybody else in the Hollow, that they wouldn't all be back in a few years, but in the meantime it would be lonesome without them, comprising as they did about half of the local folks of Ike's generation. "Can't figger out why they want to go gallivanting to California," Ike ruminated, "along with all the other sheep in the country. If they're so consarned set on making money, there's surer ways of making it right here in Byzantium, plenty of ways, as I see it." Coming out of his reverie, he realized that Dandy and Mol had jogged down to a walk.

This raised an important issue in his mind. He ought to let them walk about a mile, especially Dandy. The big, dappled gray gelding was the show horse of three counties, the only Arab north of the Mohawk. He was Ike's own horse, a present from his pa five years ago, and for the first three of them he had carried off all the prizes at the Bloomington Fair. But for the last two years his wind had been growing short and his breathing was sometimes noisy. Ike, the acknowledged horseman and horse trader of the family, had stopped showing him. They used him now only for light riding and driving.

As things stood at this moment, Ike had four miles to make in less than thirty minutes. He shouldn't do it, especially with the coach, but he'd have to risk trotting as far as the toll gate at the Center. Then he ought to have time to walk the horses down the two-mile hill to the Falls. He spoke softly to Dandy and Mol and they moved out. Mol was a good lively bay mare, but she was lighter than Dandy, half a hand shorter, and had nothing like the air the big gelding had in the carriage of his head and in throwing his front feet forward when he trotted. As now, they always stepped nicely together, and Ike was very proud of them.

He glanced up to the right, in the direction of Lathrop Hill, whence Tavie might have seen them from the summer kitchen window but for the half-mile-thick curtain of snow between. Thinking of Tavie, he grinned with satisfaction at his recent conquest and felt impelled to confirm his manliness by indulging in a chew of tobacco—something contrary to his pa's wishes, though not expressly forbidden. He slipped off his mitten and fumbled deeply in his greatcoat pocket for the little, paper-wrapped mark of manly maturity. Instantly he stiffened, then slapped the other pocket of his coat. "By Crimus!" he exclaimed aloud. "By Jimminy Jeepers!" The plug of tobacco was there all right, but the flask of rum was gone! "By golly dang! Tavie, the prying tupenny little flibbidigibbet!" Tavie and her danged temperance, meddling in other people's business! He'd show her! He laughed with lofty contempt. Well, anyhow he'd kissed her, hadn't he? And she hadn't minded, had she? He guessed it was while he was upstairs dressing that she'd swiped the flask. By Crimus! He'd show her. He slapped the horses into a smarter trot, bit off a chew of tobacco with a jerk, and returned the plug to his pocket.

Quite suddenly it stopped snowing, and soon the sun was glittering on the wide white hills, checkered by stone walls and snake fences into pastures, meadows and woodlots, dotted at intervals with white or gray, unpainted houses, each releasing its column of white smoke straight up into the blue, windless air. It was a heatless winter sun, and the inch of snow on the road showed no sign of melting.

The brightened landscape dissipated for Ike the ignominy of the stolen rum. He had had enough of his quid and hove it away with relief, thereafter hocking and spitting for some minutes to clear his mouth. The emotional reverberations of the recent kiss quieted down. But the energy it had aroused remained and now turned into well patterned channels in his mind. Clucking to the horses from time to time, he began to ponder his future. By next summer, when John would graduate from Yale, he must settle on the plan of his career.

If Ike at nineteen was little experienced in matters of the heart, he was in practical affairs a grown man and respected as such in the township. It was

well known that for two years now, ever since his graduation from the
Kamargo Literary and Religious Institute at the Falls, it had been young
Ike who had suggested the policies of the Lathrop farm. It was he who, first
appreciating the importance of the western grain trade now flowing eastward by rail and the Erie Canal, had persuaded the Squire to give up raising
wheat and rye for the down-state markets and to build up a larger herd than
anyone else had thus far dared to carry. In consequence the Lathrops had
been making a good thing of shipping cheese to Utica, Albany, and even
New York, and recently the Squire, by giving Ike joint control of the farm's
bank account, had virtually turned the management over to him. It was Ike
who exclusively handled the purchase, sale and swopping of the Squire's
cattle. And when it came to horse-trading, there was not a hard-bitten old
Yankee in Blackwater County who didn't squint his eyes when young
Lathrop drove or rode into market behind or upon some horse-flesh that
nobody had seen before. Because of his family's standing and the warmth
and kindness of his own manners, no one entertained any sinister suspicions
of him, and he had the reputation, not universal among horse-traders, of
never having been taken in a direct lie.

   Ike's thoughts, as he now rumbled along the highway, were not on horse-
trading. Rather he was preoccupied with a bigger kind of trading which he
had been watching for several years in the village where he would be in
twenty minutes. The Falls in 1790 had been only one of five cross-roads in
Byzantium Township and of less consequence than Lathrop Hollow. But in
spite of the fact that it wasn't nominally or geographically the "Center," its
situation on the three cataracts of the big Kamargo River had gradually
given it pre-eminence. Town meetings came to be held there instead of at
the Center. In 1805 it became the seat of Blackwater County. In 1816 it was
independently incorporated as the village of Byzantium Falls. And in Ike's
own nineteen years it had grown from two to five thousand inhabitants.

   Ike's interest in the Falls was not social. He certainly did not want to
live there, with everybody looking in your windows. What preoccupied him
was that in his pa's life-time a dozen men had grown rich there while his family had plugged along, having until recently a harder time each year to make
ends meet. He didn't have much faith in the cheese business he had inaugu-
rated. It would last only so long as the westerners with their big farms didn't
take it up on a scale that would get them cheap rates from the canals and
the railroads that were getting to be everywhere. And when that happened,
where would the Lathrops be?

   Ike's family had always been educated people, with one or more ministers
or lawyers in every generation way back to the beginning. But he puckered

his brow now, recollecting his pa's and his brother John's assumption that their position in the town depended on education alone. Ike knew that they were an educated family because they'd had the means to educate their sons. He knew that his pa had sold two hundred acres to put John through college, and that he planned to sell more to put Ike himself through. Those acres weren't coming back, and he couldn't make out that pa or John had any plan for getting back the money they represented.

Ike figured that the world had changed in his pa's life-time, and somebody in the family had best change with it or there wouldn't be any family left worth hauling together on Thanksgiving, or for that matter any homestead to haul them to. For years he had read daily every word in the week-late *New York Tribune*. While his mother and elder sister, Agatha—now married and living in Oberlin, Ohio—had still spent most of the winter in the loom-room, he had read of the growth of big cotton and woollen mills, not only at the Falls but in New England and all over the East. While he and Master Lane, the hired man, were hammering out tacks and nails at the little kitchen forge on winter evenings, he had known that factories in New England were turning them out to be bought for money that could be earned at the Falls in less time than it took to whang them out at home. And so of tools, and finished store clothes, and hats and shoes.

In his own nineteen years he had read of the invention of the Colt revolver, the telegraph, the sewing machine, the reaper and harvester, and of the spread of "iron horses"—though he had never seen one—from a few hundred miles of rails to over ten thousand. Two years before he had persuaded his pa to buy the only mowing machine in all of northern New York, and he figured it had already half paid for itself by saving the wages of two men for two years' harvesting. Just recently he had been reading with particular interest of the new stationary steam engine that might grow to replace water power in factories. It seemed that if run at high pressure, they would be economical for commercial operations, but that, so far, boilers heavy enough to carry the high pressure would be too costly.

"Crimus," thought Ike as he jogged along, "I figger right enough, like Tavie and John do, that America's the coming country in the world. Only where they see it in everybody's getting reformed and entering some sort of heaven on earth, I see it in everybody's first getting rich and comfortable, with plenty of leisure. Then they'll have time to make a first-rate job of their reforming and book-learning, and the more of it the better. Question's simply whether folks with some sense are to come out on top, or whether we're going to hand over everything to those ignorant skin-flints at the Falls who hain't the decency to get in a neighbor's hay when he's down with the rheumatism. Problem, as I see it, is to stay out in the country where we can call our souls our own, and at the same time have the spunk to push off in this new current of money and machinery that's got the future in it. Why, dang it!"—he set his big jaw—"I ain't scared to swop horses with those cutthroats, am I? Why should I be scared to swop bigger critters with them?"

Ike was just coming in sight of the Center with its old tavern and the little cluster of farm-houses on the five-corners beyond. The horses were still trotting smartly, just climbing the little grade in front of the ruins of the old tavern. Ike recalled his grandfather's telling how they used to hold town meetings there in the early days before the Falls got so populous. Looking at the naked, rotting rafters and the door hanging slantwise on one hinge, he was thinking, "If we don't watch out the Lathrop Homestead'll look like that one of these days," when suddenly a strange, wheezing rhythm came into his consciousness. As if somebody had doused him with spring-water he came out of his reverie.

"By Crimus!" he murmured, leaning forward, "By Jumpin' Jehosophat!" Then, "Whoa, beauties," he shouted, leaning back on the reins, and when the horses had slowed to a stop he set the brake, jumped into the road and ran forward, pressing his ear against Dandy's throat whence the gasping roar continued with every jet of steam from his nostrils. "By Cracky, my Dandy, I've broke ye," said Ike, patting the big sweaty neck, while Dandy rolled the whites of his eyes at him and tossed his handsome head, jangling his bridle and throwing foam over Ike and Mol indiscriminately.

Immediately Ike's thoughts became practical. A hundred yards ahead was the five-corners where more than one pair of eyes might be looking at him this minute. If he was lucky he guessed he might gain a couple of minutes' rest for Dandy, standing at the toll gate. After that the only house for a mile was Judge Longcoat's, above the plank pike where it cut down through the cliff at the crest of the big hill. Likely the fat old Judge wasn't up yet. If he was, he'd have to come way out to the cliff to see him. And even if he did, being a cousin of Ike's mother's, he might see fit to keep his political mouth shut. Ike decided to chance it and not stop for a real rest till he was down in the cut. Otherwise the whole town would know before night that something was amiss with the Lathrops' gray.

He made a great show of business around Mol's bridle and, when Dandy's gasping had calmed to normal, fast breathing, he performed other passes around his bit also. Then, while Mol tried to edge over toward the snowy grass on the left of the road, he brought the blankets from under the box of the coach and strapped them over both the sweating horses. He climbed back to the box, released the brake, and said softly, "All keerect, beauties."

Dandy jumped into the collar. "Hooo, beauty," said Ike, drawing back and holding a tight rein. Mol settled into a slow walk and Dandy danced a little way, then came down to Mol's gait, still tossing his head.

At this pace they proceeded to the corners where, as Ike had expected, one of the inhabitants opened his front door to greet him. "Morning, Hi Hastings." "Mornin', Ike. Been runnin' a piece, have ye?" "Too much lather fer a cold day," said Ike as they walked on by. "Chafed a bit, too. Should have known better." To his relief they reached the toll gate without further evidence of Dandy's broken wind. He "whoa'd" the horses and waited, looking in at the gate-keeper's house from time to time as if he were impatient, while watching Dandy's sides that continued to heave, though his breathing was now quiet.

After two or three minutes, fat Elijah Harris appeared from his door and stumped out to the road on his peg leg. He was the local jew's-harp player and general artisan of the order of Jehu Jones, his wooden leg, a memento of the Battle of Round Harbor in 1814, being of his own manufacture. "Mornin', Ike," he squeaked. "Cal'late I'm gettin' hard o' hearin' and ye have to holler right sharp. Hope I hain't delayed ye, bein's I see ye been a-runnin' the hosses. Aimin' t' ketch the mail coach, be ye?" Ike allowed he was and that he figgered he'd make it. He handed the penny toll down to Elijah, and the fat old man lifted the gate from its socket and swung it back.

This time Dandy started as quietly as Mol, and at a sedate walk they went thumping off down the pike, Dandy's sides still heaving. Then, as ill luck would have it, just as they were approaching the cut down the limestone cliff at the top of the hill below Judge Longcoat's house, the Judge's famous Great Dane bitch burst into angry bellows from back at the barn. Ike knew she was chained, but he knew also that if she kept it up long enough the Judge or his housekeeper Miss Patience would come out to see what was up. Also, every ear in the Center would observe that he had stopped, a suspicious circumstance when he had said he was trying to meet the stage at the Falls. Dandy began to wheeze—no doubt partly in nervousness at the dog—but Ike decided he'd have to go on. He set the brake a notch and slumped tensely forward on his knees as the coach started scraping down the two-mile hill. In the midst of the empty landscape he felt uncomfortably on show, not unlike the time two years before when he had found his pants unbuttoned in the middle of his graduation oration at the Institute.

The hill was in two long steps with a short level stretch between. When he reached this the danged Dane bitch had stopped bellowing and Judge Longcoat's house was out of sight behind the crest. Ike decided on a course that, if it was observed, might yet pass without remark except on his pride in his horses. It was certain Dandy must quiet down and start all over, even if Cousins Joel and Alvina did have to wait a spell at the Liberty. Ike stopped the team, headed them into the wall, and sat tensely, listening for hoof-beats.

When half a minute had passed with no sign of anyone approaching, his mind turned on that old scalper Gamaliel Stark, proprietor of the Liberty whither he was bound, whose seventeen-year-old daughter his brother John was so danged sweet on. Ike recollected that Stark had a good-looking gray mare, dappled like Dandy, but without the quality Dandy had. He also recollected that it was common knowledge, since an accident at the Bloomington Fair three years ago, that Dandy, having been cut late, could strike and bite like all caution, and wouldn't have anybody round his head but the members of the Lathrop household. "Well," Ike ruminated, "before God A'mighty I don't give a continental dang what he does to Gam Stark, so long as the old pole-cat has fair warning."

Ike looked absently out over the village a mile below, for here he was just above the level of the trees, with the church towers protruding through them. As usual it was warmer at the Falls than up in the hills. Instead of snowing there, it had rained and frozen in the night, and the leafless tree-tops were a sea of glassy lace, shimmering with spectra in the morning sun. Whatever else the village might be, no denying it was pretty.

Guessing that five minutes had passed, Ike climbed down and looked Dandy over. His sides had stopped heaving and his breathing was quiet. Ike felt under the blanket and found him partly dry. Then he threw it off, took the curry comb and brush from the box and went over him quickly and as thoroughly as he could in harness. He threw off Mol's blanket, gave her a few passes for good measure, put the blankets away, petted both horses, mounted the box, and started at a slow walk down the second dip of the long hill.

Ten minutes later the coach walked down Washington Street into the edge of the village that in outward appearance was still like any big Yankee agricultural center. At the corporation limits the even rows of elms and maples, now coated with ice, closed in a lofty arcade, and as Ike entered this long, glittering, fairy tunnel its rapidly thawing roof spilled a rain of diamonds and isinglass on driver and horses that made Dandy fidget and snort. A few men were hastening down-street along the muddy foot-paths, touching their caps, beavers or wide brimmed felt hats as they overtook one another or met at street corners. From their haste Ike gathered that it was almost seven. But he had not yet heard the coach horn and knew he was in time. A peddler of glittering tin-ware, piled high like a knight in grotesque armor, went crying by, making Dandy rear a little till he had passed. A milk-vendor was working his route into town, ringing his bell at the house of each customer, whence the housewife emerged with her pitcher and received her quota scooped out with a wooden ladle from the big gray crocks. Carts and buggies rattled by with increasing frequency. The planking was here doubled on the widened street, and the blows of the hoofs, breaking the night's film of ice, shot out bow waves of mud that splattered the picket fences and made pedestrians step from the foot-path to the cover of trees.

At the First Presbyterian church—built of cut limestone, with a columned, classical façade and soaring Wren belfry and steeple—the plank road ended. Dandy, Mol and the coach slumped down into the slithering, clay quagmire of the South Mall, two long blocks of magnificent avenue bordered by parks with double rows of primæval trees and having a corner on the fine mansions of the village, each set well back from the park behind its low fence of pickets or stone, surrounded by its now drab garden, and shaded by its own grove. All of these big houses were on the old massive lines, either in clapboard or limestone, except one at which Ike glanced with an indulgent half-smile as he started down the South Mall.

This was a high, square, flat-roofed pile only a year old, built of brick painted bright red, with a profusion of glaring white trimming, including a cupola, and it stuck up there on the right quite literally like a sore thumb. It was the property of a young and successful paper miller whom his atheist father, one Hercules Tanofly, had defiantly christened Beelzebub, and whom Ike instinctively liked, in spite of his loud vulgarity and apparent intent to live up to his name. There was something strong as well as garish about this new house, standing as it did too close to the park on the highest corner of the South Mall, actually topping most of the trees and glowering down on them, as if it didn't give a damn for their antique dignity. Most startling of its external features was an awesome portico over the front door whose heavy, white sides, curving back from the roof and out again on the stone steps, gave it a gaping appearance like the maw of some heathen god, and justified its popular name of "the gates of hell." It was in fact the last word in modern mansions, for "Bub" Tanofly, still only twenty-five, had said to his wife that if she wanted a house, by God he'd build her a good one. So he had sent to New York for an architect and had told him, by God, to spare nothing. As Ike glanced at the house now he estimated that the common rumor was correct, that Bub had spent nigh to five thousand on his "devil's den," what with its new-fangled, running water system, including a copper bath tub and a water-closet.

Ike was roused from these calculations by a sudden clatter from the cross-street alongside the house, followed by galloping hoofs, and he looked around to see Bub slew down into the South Mall, standing on the box of his brand new little brougham, the only carriage of the sort in town, himself hatless and coatless, his modish blue claw-hammer tails flying out behind him, his bulging forehead and pink face held up stiffly by the last word in "swaller-chokers." "Danged little show-off," thought Ike, "coaching to work." But he smiled all the same and waved in greeting. "Hi, thar, young Lathrop," shouted Bub in his rich tenor, and all of his conversation thenceforth could be heard for blocks around.

Pulling up his brougham beside Ike's coach, Bub bawled, "What ye up to so early? Bet ye didn't pull yer critters' tits this mornin'. Say, by God's holy britches, when are you stuck-up Lathrops goin' t' move t' town and live like gentlemen? Ye're a likely young 'un yerself. When y' goin' t' decide where yer bread's buttered and come over and help me t' the mill?" "Just as soon as I slick up so I can lick ye and take the whole shebang away from ye," said Ike. "All keerect, young feller, I'm ready any time you be. Say! What ye swoppin' the big gray fer? What's the matter on him that ye been slickin' 'im smooth as a baby's ass? Wal, it's nigh seven and I'm late t' the mill a'ready. Speakin' o' trimmin', I'll run ye t' Perkins Corner just as we be." And without waiting for reply he gave his team a slap with the reins and started off at a gallop, the horses' hoofs heaving up black gobs of the road in every direction.

Seeing that Ike held his pair in when they danced to follow, Bub stopped his with brake and bit, and waited where Hamilton Street crossed, halfway down to the main Mall or market, two blocks below. "What ye scaret of?" he squawled. "You farmers losin' yer ginger, be ye?" "Ain't figgering to plaster the coach with mud just when I'm down to meet the folks," said Ike, gloomy that Dandy's condition had prevented his giving Bub the trimming he needed. "Ho-ho-ho," roared Bub, starting once more to walk his coach alongside Ike's. "Meetin' the folks, be ye? Ike, m' boy, ye've got too god danged many folks tied t' yer galluses. Cut loose, say I, and one o' these days ye'll be doin' less Thanksgivin' t' God A'mighty and more thankin' of yerself." "I'll think over what ye say," said Ike, smiling his big smile.

"Ye got t' learn t' take care o' yourself in this world, my boy. Ye'll learn to some day, but so fer, says I, ye ain't got yer diapers off. Well, I gotta skedaddle. Stop in any time and I'll give ye something to wake ye up proper." And with that he slapped his horses again, plunged full tilt down the sharp drop into the main Mall at Perkins Corner, galloped over to Wheeler Corner and disappeared down Court Street, throwing mud on pedestrians and shop windows. From the other end of the Mall, around Perkins Corner, the Baptist Church's cracked basso began to announce seven, followed immediately by the soft alto of Trinity Church down Court Street.

"Ain't got my diapers off, eh?" thought Ike. He had an impulse to follow Bub right then and give him a lickin' in his own mill. But again he thought of Dandy, and the mail coach being already overdue. So he only drew the horses back into their breechings as they went down the short, sharp grade in front of Perkins' Hotel, turned the Corner eastward into the main Mall, and, listening for the coach horn from out the State Road, let Mol and Dandy gallump along at the same slow walk.

The Mall was almost treeless, a sort of natural theater, sloping inward from the south, east and west, these three sides being marked by steep little bluffs, ten to thirty feet high, from the top of which the buildings looked loftily down on the business of the central forum. Each business block, tavern, bank, house or church was reached by a flight of from ten to fifty steps, while the occasional alleys between, leading up to the rear of the buildings, mounted precipitously through cuts in the embankment. The west end was a solid block of trim little business buildings, all three stories high and of unpainted brick, except the Wheeler House which was frame with unpainted clapboards. The south side and east end were more open, with separate buildings, most of them frame, beginning with Perkins' Hotel on the corner Ike had just turned and ending with Gamaliel Stark's Liberty Tavern in the northeast corner, official stage station whither Ike was bound. The north side was at street level and free of buildings. Here the downward slope was resumed, giving an open view over the roofs of the houses on River Street below to the edge of the gorge of the Kamargo River whence the Middle Falls sent up a rolling cloud of mist and livened the Mall with continuous, low thunder, and sometimes with perceptible vibrations of the underlying limestone.

This wide, unshaded forum where eight roads met, almost identical in dimensions with that of ancient Rome, had for Ike the same significance that its classical predecessor might have had for any country citizen driving in from his villa in the hills. Here there were always crowds of people, always something going on. Here, in the three banks, beat the financial pulse of empire. Here, in three elliptical islands in the central mud marked off by hitching posts, were the markets reserved for the farmers on Thursdays. Here was the endless roar of the falls, the expression of irresistible, imperial power and the promise of authority in the world for those who could learn to turn that power to their uses.

Here, too, was the physical filth that recalled the swamp the Roman

Forum had been before the great sewer. Here Dandy, wading almost knee-deep in mud, had already reared at the corpse of a cat and was now shying against Mol to avoid a colorful heap of domestic garbage. Beyond the central market islands, on the north side, a veritable slough was made perpetual by the spring which spilled out of the log watering trough near the west end of the great market-place. This region was the open dump for the garbage of the neighborhood, and the haunt of some two score pigs of the abutting owners, which animals, sometimes invading the southern side of the Mall, were treated with all the respect due to the official scavengers of the community.

Watching the pigs now, Ike recollected that most of them were Gam Stark's, and this reminded him that he had business with that sharp tavern-keeper. He was already half way down the Mall, with no more than fifteen rods to go to the Liberty. Even if old Stark wasn't peeking out his front curtains, there were plenty of other folks watching the gray from the wide foot-paths and from office windows. Dandy was the smartest trotter in the north country and this was no time to let him poke along as if he was wind-broke. Ike sat up straight on the box and clucked the horses into a slow trot. Dandy looked all the prettier for pitching up clods like a mad bull. Without slowing down, Ike rattled through the covered drive into the Liberty yard, "whoa'd" the horses softly without pulling the reins, walked them into a free place in the long shed, and hitched them. He blanketed Mol first, then Dandy, patted both of their necks, observed that Dandy's breathing was easy, and scratched their foreheads, all the time observing Gam Stark's chestnut which his septuagenarian stableman, once the Lathrop's hired man, was leading out to the watering-trough. Then Ike walked back to the tavern across the muddy yard where the coach should arrive any minute now.

CHAPTER III

"MORNIN', Ike Lathrop," said the host of the Liberty as he opened the tap-room door and stood with his sour smile, his head dangling forward in his perpetual stoop, his hands loosely in the pockets of his well-tailored brown clothes, spreading the coat to reveal the gorgeously flowered waistcoat. In physique he was a scare-crow draped with fine feathers; a tall, lanky man, with unkempt hair, a hawk nose, lusterless brown eyes, sunken cheeks, and a leathern complexion—a finely cut face if you caught it in repose, but usually distorted by some furtive emotion. "I'll wage ye it be chilly back in the hills," he said with forced geniality as Ike approached the door. "Yes, it's a deal warmer in the Falls," replied Ike, shaking the lean limp hand, "and a deal dirtier, too." "What be the matter?" asked Stark with sarcasm appearing around his nose. "Did ye spatter the big gray?" Then, smiling again, "I'll send Henry t' clean him fer ye." "Don't trouble," said Ike. "We never let anybody touch him outside the family." Then, as he stepped into the warm room with the fire crackling, "He's a mean customer, is Dandy, if ye don't know him. Can bite and strike like all natur—" Ike wanted to clear up these matters of legal warranty before any bargaining began, and he looked around the room hoping for witnesses to his remark.

Three strangers, eating their steak breakfasts, were paying no attention, but little Postmaster Loyal Hall was there with his sack, awaiting the coach, and four farmers whose names Ike remembered. "Good morning, Isaac," said the Postmaster, and the rest nodded greetings. In the far corner Ike saw old Lemuel Grabbot staring at him, squatting over a deck of cards and a tumbler of grog like a fat spider in homespun. The cards meant that he and Stark were already at their daily pinochle. Though mutually contemptuous of each other, they were cronies, being the two richest men in town and suffering the same ostracism, even by the leading industrialists, for their unrelenting cupidity.

"Cal'late ye ain't figgerin' t' dispose of the gray if he's sech a wildcat," said Stark, smirking, while Ike hung his wraps on a peg and crossed the room to stand with his back to the enormous fireplace. "No, he's a sort o' pet o' mine, if he is wind-broke and ten years old." Ike knew that every man in three counties knew the outstanding facts about Dandy, that he had taken both carriage and saddle blue ribbons at Bloomington the three times he had been shown, that he was six years old and had always had the best of care. He figured that to make merely the usual denial that the horse was for sale would be as good as putting him up to auction, while by mingling a little truth with a little obvious hyperbole he would at once dispose of the warranty matter and might convince such as Stark and Grabbot that he really didn't want to sell. He had decided to rely, not on ordinary bargaining, but on Stark's vanity, on the fact that he already had a dappled gray mare and was eager to impress the community these days, on his hatred of the educated families and probable ambition to humble them. It might be he could whet the miser into an arbitrary determination to buy just to put the stuck-up Lathrops in their place.

"What d'ye mean by sayin' the critter's wind-broke?" snarled Grabbot, piercing Ike with his black, gimlet eyes. "Well, if he ain't he will be before long," said Ike lightly. "I figger in another year he'll be no use but to poke around the farm on." Ike knew this would cause the usual sneer at the highfalootin' way the Lathrops babied their horses. He realized he was on thin ice, but gambled that these traders would see no farther than to accredit him with more sense than to confess a horse's faults if the faults actually existed.

Old Grabbot half saw through him and growled, "I'll give ye five hundred fer the animal." There was a general turning of heads, a spitting into big cuspidors, and a shuffling around on benches to get a better view as the game really opened. There was also a general smile at Ike in recognition of the absurdity of the offer. Stark shot a moment's fierce stare at Grabbot, then lowered his eyes and grinned. "Lem, ain't ye heared the boy say he ain't sellin' the gray? Ain't ye satisfied with a fair answer?"

Now five hundred was all Ike had hoped to get for Dandy, but on the other hand fifteen hundred would have been a fair price for him if he had been sound. Also he saw Stark's angry stare and diagnosed it correctly. Incidentally, he heard a vanishing rustle of skirts in the ladies' parlor behind him to the right, and guessed that it was Stark's daughter Prudence who had been listening. He suspected she would like to see their gray mare matched and knew she was Stark's greatest weakness. So he merely took part in the general smile, then changed the subject.

"Gam Stark, there's to be a specially fine dance at the Hollow two weeks this evening, day after Thanksgiving. Occasion's some of our young folks setting out for Californy and a mountain of gold marked special with their names." Everybody chuckled. "Uncommon fine dance—church benefit—

accordion player particular from Center Sandwich. Hope you won't mind if I tack an announcement on your board." Stark waved absently at the clutter of notices on the wall by the bar, threw another fierce look at Grabbot, and slipped out through the door to the office at the opposite end of the fireplace from the door to the ladies' parlor.

Ike walked to the bar, took paper and quill from the maid and wrote out his notice. He heard Stark clump up the front stairs whither he suspected his daughter Prudence had preceded him. He was aware of Grabbot's eyes on his back, aware likewise of the whispers and general tension in the company, each of whom recognized this as the usual shift at the beginning of a trade. As he tacked up his notice he heard Stark coming down stairs again, and as he turned the host stood once more in the office doorway doing his best to look casual.

"Gam Stark, may I speak to you on a private matter?" said Ike, crossing the room. Stark made way for him into the office, threw a leer at Grabbot, and closed the door. He walked over to the high ledger desk and, as if to assume authority, climbed up on the stool behind it.

"Gam Stark," said Ike, "is it true you hold Lawyer Solon Samson's note for two hundred?" "Wal, what if it be?" said Stark, glowering at Ike's necktie. "Ye may think it's none of my business, and perhaps it ain't, but I'd like to make it so. What do ye value that note at?" "Hundred cents on the dollar, one way or t'other." "By 't'other' way I figger ye mean the law, for I happen to know ye sent Lawyer Samson a letter intimating as much." "Danged shame I couldn't throw the good-fer-nothin' varmint in the stocks like we used to do." "Well, ye know the law don't permit that any more, and I suppose ye know that if ye sue Lawyer Samson ye hain't a chance of getting your two hundred, let alone the twenty-five or fifty dollars Joel Kirkwood would charge ye."

"Got a farm, hain't he?" Stark met Ike's eyes for a second. "Well, if ye don't know who's really got the Samson farm ye'd best go down to the Clerk's office and find out. Fact is ye've nothing to attach but two cows, a few old tools, and a little furniture. There's plenty of other creditors Solon Samson's bound to honor before you. I'm telling ye the honest truth when I say that ye'll never get more than fifty cents on the dollar on that note, and lawyer's fee to come out of that." Stark was looking at his ledger cover, thinking of that danged little midget Banker Sherwood, supposing he held the mortgage if there was one.

"Now I'll tell ye what I'm up to," continued Ike. "Lawyer Samson is my pa's near friend and he'd like to do him a turn if he's able. Also, being a neighbor and my pa's lawyer, there are ways he could work off the debt to us that he couldn't do for you, ways not involving any property. We don't figger, of course, to get more out of Solon than we pay you for the paper but, he being an honest man, I reckon he'll square up anything we're out of pocket. In other words, we figger to pay ye all or more than ye'll ever get for your two hundred, to save Solon from a lawsuit, and eventually to get value received. I'll give ye a hundred flat for the note. You'll want to go down to the Clerk's office before accepting that figger. But the offer stands open, and I hope ye'll consider it."

Ike knew that Stark had scalped the note, but he didn't know for how much. Stark's mouth had pursed up in a sneer, through which he was trying to smile. "Wal, young feller, I'll think it over," he said, glancing at his iron-bound safe. Ike wanted to lambaste him through the window into the street, but instead he bowed perfectly and went back into the tap-room. Stark sent after him a splendid look of hatred, swearing he'd fetch down them god danged Lathrops soon or late, and thinking of the older brother, John, who was sweet on his daughter. He knew they were a long way from as well off as they used to be.

In the tap-room Ike sat down on the bench beside Postmaster Hall, his one-time school-teacher at the Institute. Everybody looked up as he entered, and he was relieved to feel that the iron wasn't cold. He was just giving the bundle of post from the Hollow to Master Hall when Grabbot growled from his corner. "Young Lathrop, ye ain't give me an answer to my proposition." Everybody spat again, turned round, and settled to listen. "I'm sorry, Master Grabbot, but ye know as well as I do it don't deserve an answer." Ike looked with feigned impatience at the mantel clock that already stood at twenty minutes of eight.

"If there's any joking going on," said Loyal Hall, laughing, "I'll gladly give you seven-fifty for the gray." "Well, by Jimminy," said one of the farmers from Camilla Township, "if that hoss be wuth seven-fifty he's wuth eight hunner, on sheer specc] ulation." Ike beamed on the room with his full frank smile. "Gentlemen, this is all nonsense. I hope I ain't tooting Dandy too much if I tell ye we've refused fifteen hundred for him three times in the past year. If anybody offered me better'n that I'd be bound to consider it, but short o' that ye're only playing at swoppin'."

"If it ain't askin' too much," drawled one of the strangers over his breakfast plate—he was a rough-looking man with a long shock of black hair, a leather shirt, and a pistol on his belt—"would ye show a stranger this piece of valuable hoss-flesh?" "Well, there's no harm in looking at him," said Ike, rising and opening the door for this suspicious-looking prospect.

During the five minutes Ike and the stranger were absent, not a word was spoken in the tap-room. As they re-entered, the stranger was saying, "Hand-some critter, no denyin' it—ten-year-old, ye said?" "Fact is he's six," said Ike *sotto voce,* but so everyone heard him. The stranger stood a few seconds looking out the window, then sat down, saying, "I'd give a thousand fer that hoss-flesh if he's sound, after I've jogged him round a spell. I'd have to give ye a note, though, havin' no more specie on me than's needful fer my trav-ellin' expenses."

"I'll give ye a thousand cash," snarled Grabbot, glaring at the stranger as if to say, "You keep out of this," then glaring at Ike as if to say, "You im-poverished stuck-up, I guess that'll take ye down a peg!", and finally throw-ing a triumphant leer at Stark who was shuffling in through the office door. Stark looked Grabbot straight in the eye and half-shouted, "I'll give ye a thousand and my chestnut to boot." "What about that paper we were dis-cussing?" demanded Ike with sudden arrogance. Stark sniffed. "The paper o' that polecat Samson? Aye—I'll throw that in fer good measure."

"Sold," snapped Ike in the presence of six or eight credible witnesses, then —breaking the delighted hush that followed—"and I'll ask ye to take back those words about Lawyer Samson or I'll lay ye out flat as a squashed snake."

Stark straightened up to his possible six feet two and smirked. "I didn't mean nothin' by it. If he's a friend o' yourn I guess he be all right in his way. Come along, I'll give ye yer money an' yer paper." During this last altercation no one in the room noticed that the stranger who had bid on Dandy glanced up at the mention of Samson's name, then gazed casually at Ike.

Ike followed Gam Stark into the office where he opened his safe, took out packages of bank-notes, personal notes, and blank bills of sale, made out one of the latter for the chestnut, handed Ike the quill to make out one for the gray, and while Ike wrote, found Solon Samson's note and counted out a thousand dollars in local bank notes and handed them over. "Want a rub-ber?" asked Stark. "Thanks," replied Ike. Stark handed him a rubber band which Ike put around his roll of bills and stuck them, with Samson's note, in his breast pocket. "Penny fer the rubber," said Stark. "Oh, of course," said Ike, fishing out the coin.

There was a rustle in the front hall. "Am I intruding?" said the softest possible voice. There, in the doorway to the front hall, stood seventeen-year-old Prudence Stark, with the blue saucer eyes, the round face with bright pink cheeks, the glossy black hair smoothed back from the central part, and the forest of dancing little curls all around her ears. "Good morning to you, Miss Prudence," said Ike, bowing very low, and startled, in spite of his prejudice, by the increasing beauty of this girl who had his brother John dancing in circles. But before he bowed he was not too startled to note an imperious flash of her eyes toward her pa who sent back a sly smile of subservient affection and victory. Prudence lowered her eyes. Ike knew his guess had been right.

Stark started to shuffle out of the room, wagging his head. "Master Stark," said Ike, "will you be so good as to set up yourself and all present to anything they like? Please make my apologies." Ike bowed at Stark's disappearing back, then turned with a forced smile to this other Stark, this prettiest and richest girl in town, this valedictorian of her class at the Kamargo Literary and Religious Institute, this presumptive bride of his brother whom he loved.

"Why do you dislike me so, Isaac?" asked Prudence abruptly, looking straight up at him with a direct, blue-eyed candor that had nothing of old Gam in it. "Is it that I have done something you disapprove of, or is it simply that everybody hates Papa and you are afraid John will make an unsuitable match?" Ike was flabbergasted and confused, brought down slam bang from his exultation in victory in the world of men's affairs where he had felt at home.

He parried awkwardly. "Hadn't ever noticed I disliked ye, Pru." "Fiddle-sticks and fol-de-rol, Ike Lathrop. Didn't I see you glower at me when John led me out at the September cotillion? And would *you* ever lead me out? Not you! I'd sooner expect you to lead out one of your heifers with a wreath of daisies around her neck!" And she giggled so genuinely and contagiously, shaking her curls, that Ike chuckled too, and Pru dropped her eyes, giving her buckram-stiffened green merino dress a pat so it swayed like a bell backward and forward twice, then settled into place. Then she crossed her hands at the waist-line and looked up at him with humor and consciousness of her prerogative of acknowledged beauty.

"Come now," she continued, her face growing serious again. "Is it I? Or is it Papa?" "One thing is sure," said Ike, thoroughly disarmed. "It ain't you." "Thank you," said Pru, her delicately arched nose drawing up into the shadow of a sneer, then relaxing into her earnest expression again. "Then do you want me to stop seeing John? If you say so, I'll do it." "Now I guess it's my turn to say fiddle-sticks and fol-de-rol," laughed Ike, but her candid look held as he continued. "It'll be some time yet before John's ready to marry. If when the time comes he settles on you and you settle on him it won't be any of my business what ye do." "But you wouldn't like it, would you?" she asked almost plaintively, a tiny furrow appearing in her forehead.

Her beauty invaded Ike suddenly like warm poison. His face bloomed into its inclusive smile, then his nose puckered between the eyes in that boyish, appealing look of his, while his eyes were as big and blue as Pru's looking up at them. She disregarded the appeal, being accustomed to some such look in all men. As Tavie had done two hours before, she saw something cold and rigid behind that sudden warmth. But where Tavie had feared the icy specter, it intrigued Pru. Her face settled into a proud, china-like serenity. A little haughtily she repeated her question, "You wouldn't like it, would you?"

Ike came slowly out of his trance. "Indeed I would," he said absently, but the appeal was now gone from his look. Pru walked to the window, then looked back over her shoulder, swaying her dress. "When are you going to college, Ike?" "Ain't sure I'm going—that's a dead secret—Pa and John don't know it. I figger to make some money." "Good," said Pru to herself, almost audibly.

An aversion came over Ike. He wanted to get away. Suddenly Pru switched around, bent forward, pressing down her dress with both hands, and looked up at him playfully. "Ike, what *do* you think of bundling?" Ike was more uncomfortable than ever and grew very solemn. "Don't know much about it, I guess. I guess in the old way—question of staying warm in winter—it's well enough. But this gadding around in the bushes like—they say—some folks do, it don't seem right to me." Pru, still with her playful look, shook her head very solemnly. Ike thought of a way of escape. "Is your—do you suppose I could see your ma?" "Yes, of course," giggled Pru. And, picking up her dress with the tips of her fingers, she turned, ran into the hall and rose up the stairs like a rustling green balloon. In a moment she called down, "Ike, Mama says come on up."

The Starks used the second story of the main part of the tavern for their living quarters. Ike climbed the narrow stairway and turned into the south front room, now Mistress Stark's parlor, overlooking the Mall. She was sitting on the little hair-cloth sofa, dressed in a brown cashmere dress with a wide old-fashioned lace kerchief, her slim hands busy making a *petit point* chair-seat. Pru vanished through the rear door. "Good morning, Isaac," said Mistress Stark, extending her hand. "It is always a happy occasion to see a Lathrop in the village." Ike bowed over her fingers, smiling warmly. "It's always mighty nice to see you too, Mistress Stark. Ma says she wishes you'd drive out more often. She specially sent you her love today and hoped you would come out any afternoon during the season." Susan Stark sighed and took up her work again. "Oh, I do wish I might, but I can't promise anything for this busy time in the village—so many doings for the young people it keeps the old folks occupied chasing round after them. Enjoy yourself while you're young, Isaac. I suppose I needn't tell you that things will be different when you're ten years older. Do sit down." She indicated the other end of the sofa.

Ike adored pretty little Mistress Stark. Pru took after her in round face and big blue eyes and in sense of humor. But Pru's dominating vitality, the arrogant arch of her nose, and her air of calculating, faintly hostile detachment, all these qualities which alienated Ike from her came from the old man and were not found in the mother. Susan Stark had a saint-like, and almost apologetic self-effacement, the result, folks said, of years of hard slavery under the sarcastic lash of her husband. Because of his ostracism by the men, they never went anywhere as a family except to public dances, sociables and other benefits. But the ladies all loved Mistress Susan, visited her, and had her to their houses to visit and sew over tea or cordial and biscuit. She was perhaps the only woman in the village for whom no one had anything but kindly words.

Pru floated back into the room, handed her ma a cylindrical package, and sat down, a trifle stiffly, in a low rocker. Ike was aware of the fine new furniture of the Starks—all walnut or mahogany veneer—and its contrast with the stiff pine pieces of the Lathrop homestead.

"Isaac, please tell your ma this is that squash relish we talked about when we last visited. The recipe's inside—you tied it to the jar, didn't you, Prudence?" "No, I didn't Mama," said Pru, looking faintly astonished. Mistress Stark gave her daughter a tired look. "Please copy it then, and give it to Isaac." Pru sailed out of the room.

"Well, Isaac, I suppose you'll be going to college next. I am glad for you. Master Stark wanted our Jonathan to go straight to work, though I confess I would rather see him free a little longer. You probably know he's in the West now. It will be a disappointment if he settles away from home."

There was a short silence. Then Ike said, "I'm not sure I'm going to college either, Mistress Stark. Seems to me I'm plenty old to go to work, and—" lowering his voice "—times, you know, ain't what they used to be for farmers."

Mistress Stark sighed without looking up. "I think you'll be sorry, Isaac, if you don't see the world while you can. Three or four years are not much. There will be plenty of time to work in the future, and once you are tied down you'll never get away." "Seems to me there's plenty to learn right here in Byzantium," said Ike earnestly. Mistress Stark leaned forward and put her light hand on his big one, "Just money, Isaac—just how to make money. You have too fine an inheritance to throw away. Some day you will understand what I mean when I assure you that even if you get rich as Crœsus it will mean nothing to you unless you have something else to live for—as your father has, and your grandfather, and your brother John will have."

Ike's mind turned inward upon deep and warm resources. Mistress Stark, glancing up, saw on his large face a calm and inclusive look which made her love him. She squeezed his hand, then resumed her work. "You are sure of yourself now, Isaac, but you may not always be so. You have something that money can't give you, but"—she looked up and her eyes glistened—"money might take it away."

Hardly hearing her words, Ike felt a surge of affection. He leaned forward, his eyes big with honesty, and murmured, "Excuse me, Mistress Stark —but I wish you—I—well, I wish ye were single and I—you—we might get married." He drew back and looked at the sofa in exquisite embarrassment. "You're a dear boy, Isaac, and I thank you. I shall always remember what you have said."

Ike's embarrassment vanished and he leaned forward again, murmuring eagerly, "Well, we can be real friends, can't we? I guess there's no wrong in that." But from the bowed face before him a full-sized tear fell into the needlework and he drew back, amazed and uncomprehending. Susan Stark took a handkerchief from her blue bead bag, dabbed her eyes and smiled up at Ike like sunshine. Downstairs in the tap-room the company was whooping the nautical drinking song, "Charge the Can Cheerily," and Ike wondered if it wasn't time for him to go down and join them.

Pru marched in airily and dropped the recipe on the sofa. "There, Isaac," said Mistress Stark, "give that to your ma with my love."

As Ike was stuffing the recipe under the string of the package, there was a bang of the knocker on the front door below. Shortly someone opened it and a panting boy's voice called, "Telegram fer Postmaster Hall."

Ike rose. "Excuse me—maybe it's about the coach." Mistress Stark gave him her hand and Ike held it a moment. "It was good of you to come up to see me, Isaac. I hope you will do it often." "Sure as shootin' I will," said Ike, effacing a sense of embarrassment by clicking his heels and making a stiff bow. He gave Pru the same courtesy and ran downstairs.

"He's a lovely boy," said Mistress Stark. "Has horse sense too," replied her daughter. "Says he isn't going to waste his time on Greek and Latin." Susan Stark sighed and resumed her work in silence.

CHAPTER IV

WHEN IKE re-entered the tap-room each of those present, except Grabbot and the telegraph boy, raised glasses or cans toward him in thanks for the grog or ale they were enjoying. But attention was now on the Postmaster who read his telegram aloud: "Axle broke Paris delay likely three hour"—signed by the coach driver. "Comes from drivin' them hencoops fer coaches," growled Grabbot, rising and waddling out to the front door. "Three hour!" snorted an irritated farmer from Camilla. "Plain they're too shiftless to carry a spare ex." "Drink on the house?" smirked Gamaliel Stark, leaning on the bar, now returned to his rôle of host with duties of mollification in such crises. The bar-maid switched about among the guests, collecting the cans and tumblers and taking the new orders.

"Likely pull in about ten," said one of the Camilla farmers. "If it don't fall to pieces," said the irritated one. "Wal," said their fellow-townsman who had bid on Dandy, "no use t' git yer dander riz cause o' no God's accident. Sissy, fetch on that ar chain lightnin' and I fer one am thankin' A'mighty I'm settin' here place o' chasin' greasers or pokin' my nose west'ard into no bees' nest o' Injun arrers." Then, as he got his pony glass, "Here's t' peace an' the Union an' the greasin' o' the only kind o' railroad as is aimin' at human liberty."

This reference to the "Underground Railroad" caused quick glances at the three strangers in the room, and the toast was drunk hesitantly. The leather-shirted man who had bid on Dandy did not participate in it, but as the cans and glasses were thumping back on the boards he leaned forward on his table and addressed the room in a weary drawl. "Speakin' o' th' Railroad," he said, "I may as well tell ye hereabouts that I'm a gov'ment marshal up here on pertickler business. I ain't cal'latin' t' take no advantage o' no evidence not got reg'lar, but I'd thank ye t' avide danglin' too much bounty money afore my nose, bein's I'm a man with a family."

There was an uncomfortable and hostile silence, broken at last by the talkative farmer who had bid on Dandy. "Wal, stranger," said he expansively, "I guess ye're plowin' a straight furrer, and I figger ye're o' the gen'l view of us fellers that this law, passed fer a compromise an' not 'cause the majority of Congress wants it, jest ain't no law 't all. Same's the potash law back forty year. Same's this nigger law now. Fer us here, I guess there ain't one on us could tell ye the whereabouts of a nigger station. But come the Railroad in gen'l, I'm fer it, and I'm speakin' fer plenty o' my neighbors. It's the first time since that potash war we've been put to it strong atween our dooties as law-abidin' citizens and our doubts as t' whether this here be a law enacted constitootional. If I understand yer remarks we're thankful to ye fer the tip-off and we'd like fer t' see ye skim off plenty o' bounty cream s'long's ye don't skim it off'n no human critter's freedom an' s'long—" here he looked straight at the marshal—"'s ye don't ask no single soul in this county to go nigger-ketchin' like this god danged law says ye kin."

There was a taut silence while the marshal looked out the window. Then the farmer relieved the situation he had created. "So with that thar leetle proviso, welcome, sonny, an' th' wust o' luck t' ye, an' here's to Whig Millard though I preferred Old Zack that I fit unner and voted agin." This toast went off jovially, bottoms up, and the government agent signalled for another round on him. Postmaster Hall went out with his sack, saying, "I'll be back at ten, Gamaliel Stark." One of the farmers started again the song, "Charge the Can Cheerily," the company taking it up and continuing it, banging their cans on the tables. The clock on the mantel stood at a quarter-past eight.

After putting Mistress Stark's package in the pocket of his greatcoat, Ike walked over to the host at the bar and asked the rental of a saddle for his new chestnut. "Twopence an hour, tenpence a day," said Stark. Ike started for the door, then came back. "Where do ye want the gray lodged?" he asked. "Tell Henry t' put him up in the lot fer now," said Stark with a faintly sly look. "Don't forget," said Ike in a quiet voice, "what I told ye about Dandy's striking and biting. I figger ye recall he put one of those grooms to bed at Bloomington three years back. If ye'll treat him gentle and slow he'll serve ye pretty, but once he takes a dislike to somebody I wouldn't warrant him coming round."

"Young feller," snarled Stark out of the corner of his mouth, "I was a-twitching mean horse-flesh afore ye wuz dreamed on an' I guess I ain't scared o' no late-cut gelding as has had too much babyin' an' not enough tannin' onto 'im." Ike had an impulse to buy Dandy back, but he figured things would go as he had planned and he guessed he could trust the gray to take care of himself for a short spell, specially out in the lot. He took the coon cap from the peg, went out and closed the door on the singing in the tap-room. It was now a mild, gray day with the thermometer above fifty.

Ike walked across the yard to the stable to take a look at his new chestnut.

He found old Henry Hawks in the stable with its dozen stalls, half of them occupied by Stark's horses and half by the relay horses of the coach company. Henry was the stableman to Stark and coachman to his family whom Ike had seen leading the chestnut out to water when he first arrived. He looked like a five-foot-tall hickory sliver split off by lightning. "Mornin', Master Ike. They tell me ye swopped th' gray fer th' chestnut, and I tell ye I'd sooner tackle a mean bull 'n' an elephant in one critter than that ar beauty o' yourn—or ruther o' his'n," pointing his thumb at the tavern. "I seen him paw that poor feller t' Bloomington and I ain't rarin' t' take no sech mortal punishment, come a fair way o' 'vidin' it. Man an' boy I been nussin' hosses sixty year come Easter when I started helpin' yer great gran'ther. I seen plenty o' bad eyes in my day, but by Jimpers afore yonder man-eater I hain't never seen a wusser."

"Well, Henry, you're wise to be scared of Dandy, though if ye weren't scared of him I'd say ye were one man might handle him. He ain't precisely a one-man horse, seeing all of us at home can manage him. But he's either your friend or he ain't, and he may be too old now to make new acquaintances. Since ye say ye're scared of him, likely it wouldn't be amiss to make up your mind whether ye're hankering to hold your job at the Liberty."

"Fact, I ain't, 'twixt you'n me'n the manure pile. I been here on a year now'n this Stark's the slitherinest cattle I ever tried to fetch a salary onto. They ain't a spark in the Falls but'd set me on his coach, if it is me says it, and once I kin git ketched up of my wages I cal'late t' skedaddle. Matter o' confidence 'twixt you'n me, Master Isaac."

"Feeling as ye do, Henry Hawks," said Ike, "I'd advise ye to refuse point-blank to meddle with Dandy. I warned Stark about him, before I sold him and after. He's a'mighty certain he can manage him, but I wouldn't wager a penny he could, or anybody else either. If ye get in a fix cause o' the horse, be sure to let us know and we'll see ye settled."

"Fact, Master Isaac, if I had my fingers onto a little cash I'd quit th' varmint quicker'n a weasel an' sue 'im fer the nigh hunner he's into me. Truth is, if ye're o' mind o' hoss-swoppin' I got an ol' bay mare in yonder stall's fer sale at a low figger. Ain't much fer looks'r fer fancy trottin'. Twelve year old. Gentle's a daisy. Draw a load with yer best ox and a tarnel sight more sartin. Cheap, say I, at three fifty."

Ike walked into the stall and gave the heavy draft mare a lookover. He wanted to try out a horse in place of an ox for plowing, but didn't want to sink much in the experiment. He untied Nancy—that was her name, by the ticket on her post—and led her out around the yard, her big unshod feet clumping in the swale. "First class draft hoss," said Henry as Ike turned her back to him to tie up. "New style t' plow with, puttin' their value higher'n a kite. Good carriage hoss too, team or single. Wouldn't part with her sooner'n I would my sister, only's I'm kind o' toggled t' th' village'n got no more use fer a draft animal."

"I'll give ye twenty-five for her," said Ike as Henry came out of the stall. "Sorry ye ben't interested, Master Ike. Drop in some time if ye figger on makin' a purchase." "Make it fifty," said Ike, turning away and eyeing his new chestnut in one of the other stalls. "Well, Master Ike," said Henry, "that's a leetle mite under my askin' figger, but arter all, say I, what's three hunner to a true grit hoss-trade? Sold, say I." Ike gave him the cash. "Could ye get her shod for me right quick, in return for a good seegar?" "Surer'n shootin'," said Henry, pocketing his fifty dollars.

Ike decided to get the present business over before trying out the chestnut. "Gam says to put the gray up in the lot," he said, "and all in all I figger it's a good notion. If we stabled him now there ain't the ring he wouldn't pull out when I left him." "Wonder how he figgers t' ketch 'im," said Henry. "That ain't my concern," said Ike. "I guess I'd better lead him up. If ye'll fetch me a halter I'll tend to it before Gam changes his mind."

Five minutes later, having unharnessed Dandy, Ike led him out the side entrance of the Liberty yard into the State Road, now generally called State Street, the regular highway by which the Utica coach would arrive. As he trudged up the street in the mud, holding Dandy short, he felt grim and nervous over the sale and wanted to get this last phase of it over. He was irritated by the wise smiles people gave him as he passed, the news already having spread through the village. As if sensing Ike's unquiet, Dandy danced and sidled more than usual, and before Ike got him up to the lot he had fed him most of the chunks of sugar he carried in his greatcoat pocket. As they approached the bar-way Dandy snuffed the horses inside, whinnied, and stood expectant as Ike took down the heavy bars. But once Ike had closed the bars and climbed back outside, Dandy neglected the other two horses that trotted up to him and stood looking at Ike, dilating his nostrils.

As Ike scratched Dandy's nose through the bars he thought how this ten-acre tract of Gam Stark's was the most valuable property in the village that hadn't been built up. He wondered how much he'd take for the central acre that he used as a paddock for his horses, it having been the close of the original Stark homestead, and Gam having kept its wall in repair. The old hay-barn still stood, in partial ruin, and gave the horses some shelter, but the house had burned down—with insurance—soon after Gam bought the

Liberty. Gazing absent-mindedly at the old cellar-hole, it occurred to Ike that a new house might well be built on the same site, using the old foundation stones. No, Ike thought, he'd never want to live in the village—but all the same—just as a speculation——

This diversion of his thoughts made it easier for Ike to give Dandy one last rub on the nose and start down-street. But by the time he was passing the big, red Kamargo Literary and Religious Institute, he had a lump in his throat and forced himself to reason sensibly about what he had done. Yes, he reassured himself, it was certain he'd get Dandy back before long, at a low figure. Stark couldn't handle him, and even if he could he'd learn he was wind-broke. As Ike saw it, he'd given the old skunk a good trimming, and there was no harm done. By the time he walked into the Liberty yard, his sadness at leaving Dandy was gone.

He found Henry Hawks sitting in the stable door, whittling. "Now for that chestnut," said Ike cheerfully. "Is he worth his keep? Will he drive in a team?" "Wal, I wouldn't put no val'able dash-board behind 'im, an' I ain't yet seed the trace he wouldn't kick over. But he's good ridin' if ye can git the better o' his bitin' and sudden rearin' notions. Can't never tell when he'll uncork one o' them jumps o' his'n. Ain't ornery. Just a leetle might twirly. Like as not a mite o' decent treatment'll fix 'im."

During this instruction Ike had taken off his coat. "I'll try saddling him now," he said, "and ride him round till the coach comes. And I'll ask ye to hitch Nancy into the gray's place in the team after she's shod." "Sure grit," said Henry.

Ike hung up his greatcoat and walked in beside the tall, long-barrelled, skinny chestnut. Instantly he reached round and snapped at Ike who gave him a full blow on the nose. Then, as he raised his head, Ike leapt up and caught his ear and hung on as the chestnut tried to rear. Slowly the horse's head came down till Ike stuck his thumb and two fingers in his nostrils. When he tried to rear again, he dug his nails in till the blood came. When the horse stood quiet Ike let go his ear and patted his neck, calling him his "Chesty." In less than a minute he felt the horse relax, released his nostrils and reached up to scratch his forelock. Chesty lowered his head and seemed to enjoy the scratching, his teeth still bared, but making no further effort to bite. Ike took the last of the sugar from his pocket and fed him.

He spoke quietly to Henry. "Fetch me a rental saddle and bridle and hand them over the stall." As Henry complied he said, "Ye're an a'mighty wonder fer a youngster. No fear ye're a good hoss-trader." "I guess most chestnuts are like that," said Ike. "Sartin they be," said Henry. "They like to act mean, but they like to be bossed if'n ye know how t' do it. I allus cal-

'lated a chestnut was like a woman, that a-way." "All hosses are," said Ike with a superior air as he set the saddle on gently, recollecting his conquest of Tavie that morning. "Even that ar big gray?" "Yes," said Ike, "only ye don't want to try bossing him like ye'd boss this chestnut. If I saw ye trying to put your fingers in his nose, or doing anything to hurt him, the first place I'd run for would be the undertaker."

Henry handed in the bridle. Ike held an ear cautiously as he slipped it on. But the precaution wasn't necessary. Chesty seemed anxious to be off. Ike put on his coat, led him into the yard, and mounted, throwing himself forward for a rear. But there wasn't any rear. He trotted out into Factory Street and let Chesty out into his long slow stride. He was just indulging vainglorious thoughts of how he'd got a better utility horse than Dandy when Chesty sidled from a big pool of mud-water so quickly Ike almost went off. Immediately he drew him in, turned him, circled back and, leaning forward on his neck, kicked him hard and drove him straight into the water. Once his front feet were in, Chesty relaxed and put on speed. From behind Ike heard a cheer for him. He didn't know a little audience of passers-by had been watching.

Factory Street was the oldest street in the village, connecting the Mall with Factory Square which had been the original village green but was now entirely surrounded by mills. Ike had two reasons for riding up Factory Street now, instead of going directly to Howell Sherwoods' bank on the Mall and depositing the $950 he had in his pocket from the sale of Dandy. For one thing, he wanted to get the hang of Chesty in a less populous region before braving the eyes of the main market-place. And besides, Factory Square always fascinated him anyway, both as a rumbling display of machinery and as the symbol of that new industrial wealth in which he believed his family must share if it was to maintain its position of leadership in the town. As he trotted slowly along, touching his cap to pedestrians, he watched the big, brownish black Kamargo that flowed parallel to Factory Street close on the left, here deep and slow-gliding between the Upper Falls at Factory Square and the Middle Falls below at Fleet's Island where it plunged into its cañon. Ike recollected that every water-power site for twenty miles was already pre-empted by somebody who knew its value, and how a fellow who wanted to get into manufacturing now would likely have no choice but to go into the employ of one of the new-rich industrialists whom he detested.

A little ahead on the left was the first building on the river side of Factory Street, the new, brick station of the veteran Neptune Hose Company, now officially called "Fire Company Number One," recently presented by the village with a fabulous, horse-drawn pump which Ike had already inspected with awe. As he approached and passed the station-house now, he thought of the newly invented steam fire-pump, a drawing of which he had seen not long since in *The New York Tribune*. This suggested to him the general possibilities of stationary steam engines, a new source of power for manufacturing that might one day put the water-power factories on the back seat. "Why," thought Ike, "a feller could set up a steam-driven factory clean out at Lathrop Hollow, with all the surrounding forest for fuel!"

Beyond the fire house Ike entered the last block before Factory Square, a solid series of one-story shops on both sides of the street, known as Mechanic's Row, where the remaining artisans of the old, agricultural civilization still worked paradoxically in the shadow of the big factories that foretold their doom. Here flourished the hand craftsmen the factories had not yet replaced and in whom the standard of excellence in workmanship still dominated the motive of gain—the old-fashioned mechanics, blacksmiths, wagoners, wheelwrights, tanners, saddlers, cabinet-makers, carpenters, woodcutters, gunsmiths, tinsmiths, distillers, coopers, masons, stone-masons, tailors, weavers and spinners. Among these a certain tanner, saddler and wheelwright was a favorite of Ike's, as he was of every other young man in town. Yielding to a whim and a pretense of business, Ike now turned Chesty across the street and pulled up in front of the long, one-story stone shop.

The artisan in question was one Jerusalem Stone, universally known as "Old Jerry," eccentric and best-beloved patriarch of the village. Thirty years back Old Jerry had caused to be carved in wood an enormous bull's head which glared down on the street from under the peak of his roof fifteen feet above the foot-path. This massive idol, painted a fiery red and livened with real glass eyes, held in its mouth an iron bell whose weight and voice would have done honor to any church in town. By alternate pulls on the ends of a chain cogged over a pulley and hanging to the ground between the two sets of double doors, the great bull—known as "Jerry's Bashan"—could be made to roll his head from side to side and to send his melodious bellow echoing beyond the village into the surrounding hills.

This mobile minotaur had three civic uses which had already become traditional. The first was ostensibly to wake Old Jerry's flock of 'prentices each morning, but in effect to notify the whole village that it was six o'clock and time to be up and doing. The second use was official, to serve as the fire bell for all that eastern part of the village whose first alarms were responded to by Neptune Company Number One. The third use was social and more far-reaching than either of the others. Jerry's Bashan was the recognized challenge to youth, the pagan god who presided at the ritual by which boys were tried for admission to the fraternity of the stalwart and the brave. The boy who had not challenged Jerry's rage by stalking the bull Indian-like in the adjoining alley, rushing out for a yank at the chain and a flight over fences and through barnyards on the wings of convulsing terror, that boy knew in his heart he was a coward, yea, knew it throughout his life with a conviction which no deed of daring, and pugnacity, no act of self-sacrifice or patriotism ever fully expunged from his conscience. Twelve and thirteen years later there would be heroes decorated for valor at Antietam and Gettysburg who still carried in their bosoms the guilt of failure in their crucial hour; while deserters, buried in hay, trundling westward in covered wagons across Nebraska, would remember in their hearts that once they had been men.

There were ways and ways of meeting your test of yanking Bashan, but the initiation of highest degree, the final accolade into greatness, was to do it in broad daylight. That was usually to be seen by Old Jerry himself, to be caught either in the act or not long thereafter, to be tanned handsomely with raw-hide, and then to be given a slab of ginger candy from a box kept for the purpose, to be shown through the mysteries of the shop, patted on the shoulder and invited to become a 'prentice when you were older. And, whether you accepted this offer or not, thenceforth you would be one of Old Jerry's boys, which meant that by the most indirect and unaccountable ways, you would be encouraged and helped in your early efforts in the world.

What consciously led Ike to stop by at Old Jerry's was the fact that the old man was sitting now in one of the big open doorways and Ike had in mind to make a purchase from him. But the real reason he stopped, perhaps the real reason he had taken this ride up Factory Street, was a subconscious desire at this moment just to see the laconic old oracle, to enjoy the reassurance always to be found in his presence. Ike pulled up Chesty under the sign of the bull's head and lounged forward on his neck, full of feelings at once shy, contented, humorous and touched with regret. For the first time in the four years, since a certain afternoon during his second year at The Institute, he was in easy reach of the chains of Bashan. There was something he had always wondered whether Old Jerry knew.

As usual, Old Jerry gave no sign of recognition. As usual he was sitting on a stool near the open double doors, his leather apron dangling on the floor between his spread knees, his stubby fingers now busy at sewing a horse-collar. As usual his face was bent close to his work, so he presented to Ike only his bald pate with its halo of scraggly white hair. But Ike knew he knew he was there, so he said nothing and waited, relieved that Chesty showed no interest in the head of the red god that glowered down on them.

At the forge in the rear of the shadowy shop two 'prentices were warping on a white-hot tire, while a dozen others sat around on benches, sewing leather with awls, needles, and collar palms, and glancing at Ike or Jerry as they paused to clip their thread.

"What ye up to, young Lathrop?" said Old Jerry without looking up. "Cal'latin' to give another yank t' Bashan?" Ike's heart pounded with delight, and he could say nothing. The priest of youth looked up with a fierce scowl round his kindly blue eyes with their oblong steel-rimmed spectacles. He was the wrinkledest man in town, and the right side of his mouth drooped harshly in a circular opening long shaped for either spitting or chewing a cigar. Getting no answer from Ike, he now spat a thin stream ten feet over the foot-path into the street and looked down to his work again.

"Figgered ye hadn't seen me," said Ike shyly. "Humph," said Old Jerry. "Why didn't ye tan me, Old Jerry?" persisted Ike. "Humph," said the priest again. "Had a hot iron if I remember rightly. Figgered ye kind o' outside the range o' my leather, livin's y' do up yonder in the hills. Didn't know rightly whether there was that in ye was worth my tannin'." He continued his work in silence for half a minute, then looked up fiercely again. "What ye up to? Figger ye're still due that hidin' and come back t' collect it?" "Mebbe," said Ike with an uncertain smile, wondering what Old Jerry meant by saying he didn't know whether there was that in him was worth tanning.

Casually Ike swung down from Chesty, hitched him to the stone post, and stood leaning against the door-frame. Old Jerry turned the collar round and round on his knees, examining the stitching, then got up and hung it on a peg. "Understand ye're too big fer a hidin' and ginger candy from the likes o' me." And the old man turned abruptly and walked back into the shop. At this clear rebuff, little as Ike then understood the reason for it, he had a momentary sense of having been tried by a competent court and found wanting. He felt superfluous and resentful, and was just unhitching Chesty when the old tanner returned with a pewter can. "Have a drink o' sweet cider—'t's better'n common this autumn."

Ike took the can with a bow and enjoyed the long cool drink. Old Jerry, having been made a drunkard as a 'prentice through being sent daily for buckets of ale by his master, had given up alcohol abruptly when he steadied down forty years back and opened a shop of his own—"figgered it wa'n't no kind of example fer the 'prentices," though he had no patience for the current temperance movement.

"Thanks, Old Jerry," said Ike, finishing the drink and handing back the mug. "Best I ever tasted." "Figger ye ain't losin' no sleep over not gittin' that hidin'," said Jerry. "From what I hear ye're a man grown and don't need no nussin' from no old coot that's more consarned with makin' good leather than he be with swoppin' it. Did ye have any further business in yer mind?" he added, with a tone of dismissal.

"Wanted to ask the value of these new Mexican saddles," said Ike indifferently. Jerry glanced at the chestnut. "Wal, ye can pay up t' thirty dollar fer'm t'a store. Figger I could make ye a better one fer ten or better. If it's that chestnut yer thinkin' on, as I hear ye jest swopped off'n Stark, my advice'd be that ye don't need no fancy contrapshun. Nothin' wrong with the animal only that gawd damned skin-flint beat 'im into skittishness. Treat 'im human fer a month an' he'll do ye well's that fancy gray ye just turned over t' the butcher."

Suddenly Ike understood the old man's apparent hostility. "Look here," he said angrily. "I'm a-lookin'," snapped Old Jerry like a steel rod. "I'll bet ye a dollar I'll have the gray back in two weeks." "An' if ye do he won't be the same hoss ye sold fer money. If ye ask me I'd sooner knock a critter on the head than git him in range o' that yaller-bellied hellion, an' if ye ask me, my opinion o' you ain't riz no more'n a batch o' sour dough. I wa'n't figgerin' on givin' ye no tongue-lashin', but thar she be an' ye can value 'er great er little as ye see fit." And the old artisan walked back into the shop again and didn't return.

Ike mounted Chesty and walked him slowly up the street. As when Stark had referred to his violent methods with horses, he had an impulse to go back to the Liberty to see if he couldn't reverse the trade. Perhaps Old Jerry was right and he'd done wrong in giving Gam Stark a chance to hurt Dandy. He suffered a moment's uncomfortable prescience of how his brother John at least would most likely disapprove the sale. He'd talk it over with Pa. Dandy would be safe enough for a day or so out in the lot.

Ike was now entering Factory Square, and the composite roar of heavy machinery, hundreds of spindles and the Upper Falls pre-empted his attention and obliterated for the moment his stirrings of conscience. On the left the Square opened back like a bay of massive, limestone temples of industry, the biggest buildings in town: the printing house and bindery of Fulton and Price whose paper mill was a half mile down the river, the Kamargo Woollen Company, the Byzantium Cotton Company, Wycomb's Machine Shops, and, visible across the bridge on Factory Island, the Ludlow Woollen Mill. Ike pulled up Chesty for a moment, fascinated as always by the rush, the roar and the clang of this outpost of the new, money civilization, the endless parade of carts across the Square, the frequent flitting of human figures across windows, figures impersonal, moving with a speed unknown to the old, intellectual time, figures enviable to Ike as being already part of a secret he wanted to learn.

Thinking of the owners of these mills most of whom he despised, and of their financial power that, through their newspapers and politicians, was supplanting the old-fashioned leadership of his pa and his pa's friends, Ike lounged in the saddle, letting Chesty nibble at the rotten, November grass by the roadside. But slowly, as his ears grew accustomed to the roar of the mills, Old Jerry's insult about selling Dandy to "that butcher" rose in his mind to plague him and sully the glamor of the scene. Old Jerry might be wrong, but Ike was still boy enough to respect his utterances as presumptively oracular. He'd have to figure it out again, he thought, but this was no place to do it, in the middle of all this racket. Best first ride back to the Mall and across the Middle Bridge out into Camilla where he'd be able to think a few minutes and still have time to deposit his money and meet the coach. Incidentally, Ike wanted subconsciously to get back past Old Jerry's biasing influence before trying to think clearly. He pulled up Chesty from his cropping and made no objection when the horse, now headed homeward, teetered into a canter as he approached the gauntlet of those omniscient eyes. There the wrinkled old man sat in the door as before. But this time as Ike approached he looked up and stared at him with a sort of blank violence that defied interpretation. Ike saluted politely and let Chesty canter by.

CHAPTER V

A S I K E approached the Liberty he realized the absurdity of trying to get Stark to reverse the trade before he'd had a set-to with Dandy or learned for himself that he was wind-broke. Nevertheless, he wanted to get his thoughts clear before facing his pa, and he decided to continue his plan to ride out into the country in the time he had to spare. When Chesty sidled at the entrance to the Liberty yard, he yanked him past with an impatience unusual with him. Then he turned right on Mill Street and descended the slope to Fleet's Island.

Here Byzantium's second cluster of mills took their power from the Middle Falls. On the Byzantium side, Ike passed the long paper mill of Fulton and Price with its big flume occupying the whole of the south channel. After crossing the little bridge to the Island he was engulfed in the thunder of machinery and waterpower more closely than he had been in the open area of Factory Square. Behind was the rumble of the big cylinders of Fulton and Price's mill; immediately around him the clang of Forman and Bowen's Sash and Butter Tub factory, Watchful Smart's Foundry, and Judah Lowell's Foundry and Plow Factory, besides several small and relatively silent shops; ten rods ahead, the main bridge and the mist and earth-shaking roar of the Middle Falls; and across the bridge, on the Camilla bank, the Union Mills and the foundry of Horace Gadston.

Here the mingled thunder of man's power and nature's failed at first to dispel Ike's moral determination to think over the propriety of his sale of Dandy. But as he walked Chesty out on the long wooden bridge where the crash of water obliterated the rumble of machinery behind him, the spectacle of the falls as always made him catch his breath with wonder, while the power of it soothed his worries and filled his subconscious with a deep, unspecified faith in impersonal nature that made his problem of personal conduct seem negligible and small. The might of the falls effaced at once all consciousness of himself, Dandy, Stark, Old Jerry, his pa, and his plan to ride out into Camilla and think. Instead, he dismounted in the middle of the bridge and leaned on the rail, luxuriating in the sight of tons of six-foot-deep, brown water rolling over the brink into its forty-foot, crashing drop to the chaos of the whirlpool below, the ceaseless trembling of the bridge, the clouds of mist spouting up and spattering over him and Chesty like rain.

The sight, the sound, the irresistible motion embraced him completely. There was something in his spirit, something he had never recognized or puzzled about, that surrendered to that natural power and became one with it. He felt alone, detached from the world and its moral dilemmas. Then he felt companioned in his loneliness, exalted by identification with the falls. Without any thought, without any sensation but one of relaxation and ease, he became one with nature, one with a universe wherein he, his problems, his family, all questions of policy, all questions of right and wrong, all needs of body and mind, were transcended and drained out of consciousness. Half a dozen people crossed the bridge without Ike's knowing it, though each of them shouted his loudest to him against the thunder of the falls.

Several minutes, a measureless time, passed over him. Then slowly, as if waking from sleep, he became aware of his elbows bearing his weight on the wooden rail and remembered where he was. He looked round to the left at the Camilla shore, and the first thing his eyes focussed on was a hat-less stranger entering a double door under the number "29," painted in white on a gray-painted, brick wall. It was a little building nestling under the eaves of Gadston's Foundry, a building Ike had never noticed before and which seemed suitable for a machine or blacksmith shop.

Having stared vacantly at this building for a moment as if it were the whole of the unfamiliar world, he looked around at Chesty who had low-ered his head to get the shelter of Ike's body from the spouting mist. He had no notion how much time had passed and it occurred to him that he'd best be getting back or he might be late for the coach. As from a great distance the image of Dandy at the bars of Stark's ten-acre lot swelled into his mind. He looked back at the falls, and his love for Dandy grew large and one with the indescribable emotion that united him to that plunging power. "There's the real Dandy!" he shouted aloud and could not hear his own voice for the roar. "That's the main thing to remember!" And in the light of this mysti-cal truth the question of whether Stark might hurt Dandy, or whether he had done wrong in selling him Dandy, seemed remote and petty matters whose solution was not of great importance and must therefore be easy. He turned round, put his elbows backwards on the rail and resolved these questions with a practicality that was altogether clear and satisfying to him. Then, luxuriating in affection for the whole world, as inclusive as the power of the falls and as unrelated as they to moral action, he led Chesty off the bridge, mounted, and rode back across Fleet's Island.

For a few seconds, as Ike rode between the rumbling factories, they impressed his half-mystical mood no more than the questions he had just been considering with relation to Dandy. He was happy in the subconscious awareness that the falls, the "real Dandy," would always be there whenever he needed to escape from the world or any of its petty affairs. Then, as he pressed Chesty up the grade past the Fulton and Price mill, his mind lapsed easily into immediate business. Ahead of him at the end of the Mall, the Baptist Church clock struck half-past nine. He still had half an hour to deposit his nine hundred and fifty. For the first time he became aware of the responsibility of possessing so much money, more than he had ever had except in the general account which was really Pa's. Even after he bought Dandy back he'd have at least four hundred and fifty left, and that was enough to think about seriously investing, in the way Gadston and the rest of the rich did. He felt exhilarated, as at the beginning of some game or a hoss-swoppin', as he faced the prospect of figuring out what to do with his wealth. It did not occur to him to wonder why this particular kind of practical problem was so much more inviting, so much less petty in comparison to his feeling about the falls, than the moral questions related to the sale of Dandy which he thought he had settled.

Posting up the Mall through the mud and the mid-morning traffic of riders, carriages, carts, pedestrians, dogs, hogs and chickens, Ike touched his cap and waved cheerfully to passers-by, most of whom smiled broadly at him, being appraised of the recent trade. Suddenly, as he neared Perkins Corner, the composure of his half-mystical experience at the falls gave way to the dry-throated shyness he always felt on approaching Howell Sherwood's bank. More than any man in the Falls, Ike revered the trim little financier, originally from New York, who possessed the double status of being personally a member of his father's intellectual oligarchy, and professionally the banker of several of the leading industrialists of the town. Subconsciously as yet, Master Sherwood figured in Ike's own ambitions and, instinctively wanting to impress him above all men, he always felt as awkward and resourceless in his presence as he used to feel five years before in the presence of some pretty little school girl he was being sweet on. So now, as he rounded Perkins Corner and headed for the stone building that contained the great bank, along with a grocery store and Staunton's Book Store, all of his recent self-confidence vanished. With a great show of worldly dignity he straightened in the saddle and posted over to the bank in his best form, holding the reins high in his right hand, his left straight down at his side, and occasionally bending forward stiffly from the waist to glance down at Chesty's legs as if appraising his obviously unimpressive gait.

He was just nosing Chesty up to one of the empty hitching-posts in front of the bank when with a convulsion of his stomach he recognized the very god of his dreams coming across Daw Street, immaculately clad in black as usual, picking his way over the archipelago of stepping stones that were the only islands in the street's foot-deep river of mud. Reaching the foot-path in front of his bank, Master Sherwood looked up, recognized Ike and, turning toward him, swung up his gold-headed cane in preliminary greeting, whereat, quick as a jack-rabbit, Chesty squatted and leapt head-foremost into the air in a sort of standing high jump—Ike felt a soft thud and fetched up looking up into the classical face of the banker who, inclining toward him in a civil bow, was just saying, "Good morning, Isaac," to which Ike, sitting in a pool of mud water, grinned up foolishly, touched his brother's coonskin and replied, "Good morning to ye, Master Sherwood."

Dimly around the fringes of his blinding humiliation Ike became aware of a blur of people—familiar faces, strange faces, sounds, laughter, insulting comments—"Burlington Fair"—"Big gray fer it"—"Mud harder'n customary this mornin'?"—"Name's Larrupin' Lathrop"—"Circus hoss—does it three times a week till his pants is wore out." When detailed consciousness of his surroundings had returned, Ike had already tied Chesty to the hitching-post. Master Sherwood had him by the arm, leading him toward the door of the bank, and was inquiring whether he had hurt himself. "Not in the least, thank ye, sir," said Ike. "I'm a'mighty ashamed—" Master Sherwood clapped him gently on the shoulder, laughed in the most friendly fashion, and bowed him into his awesome precinct.

Instinctively Ike removed his cap in those sacred walls, so dim that on this gray day the red-headed clerk had lighted the kerosene lamp in the fancy iron bracket over the long desk where he stood bent over his ledgers. Another similar lamp at the rear lit on each of the three tall safes the three identical semi-circles of golden letters that spelled the words of power, "Howell Sherwood." Deferentially Ike hesitated, but Master Sherwood touched his arm again and led him back along the counter just as two men rose from waiting chairs at the rear. Both were middle-aged and expensively dressed, one of them tall, bulky, pasty-faced, with a slight twist in his nose and a set, jovial expression; the other older, short, rotund but solid, his face rosy even in the dim light, but wearing a perpetual scowl and being disfigured by a wall eye which squinted up and outward and may or may not have been of service to the other in the function of sight. Ike recognized the pasty-faced man as Ostrum Applemore, State Senator and Democratic leader of the District, small stock-holder in most of the factories and one-time lawyer for many of them, now occupied solely with politics and his weekly newspaper, the *Blackwater Democratic Union*. The squint-eyed man was familiar to Ike as Horace Gadston, Applemore's chief financial backer, third richest man in the village, but first in power of his wealth, for Stark and Grabbot were ostracized from the local councils. With the possible exceptions of Master Sherwood and Squire Fulton, another close friend of Ike's pa, these were the two most influential men in town, the leaders of the industrial group for whom Ike felt personal contempt, coupled with practical respect and fear. Obviously they were waiting for the great banker, and both touched their hats as he and Ike approached, Applemore with a cheery, "Good-day to ye, Masters Sherwood and Lathrop," Gadston with a surly, "Mornin', Howell."

The banker led Ike out the back door to the shed where a pail of water stood on a rough bench, with a basin, a slab of soap, a clean towel and a mirror. "This will take the worst of the mud off," said Howell Sherwood. "And did you wish to see me, Isaac?" "No, thank ye, Master Sherwood," said Ike. "Fact is, I stopped by to make a deposit. Pa sends ye greetings and hopes ye'll stop by after church on Thanksgiving, if not sooner." "Indeed I shall," said Master Sherwood. "Thanksgiving at Lathrop Hollow is too long-established and happy a custom to be in danger of being broken now. And now, Isaac, if you will excuse me, Philip will take care of your deposit." "Thank ye, sir," said Ike as Howell Sherwood bowed and went back into the bank.

As Ike busied himself with the mud on his boots, his brother's buff trousers and his own green coat, and finally stood washing his hands, his humiliation vanished and a new kind of self-confidence came over him, not unlike the assurance he felt in approaching a business deal. It had nothing to do with his having nine hundred and fifty dollars in his pocket, nor yet with his recent experience at the Middle Falls. He felt reassured by the conviction that Howell Sherwood was interested in him, and by the fact that under his wing he had for a moment been in a position superior to Horace Gadston and Ostrum Applemore. Here they were, the leaders of the new age, dancing attendance on Howell Sherwood, compelled to wait while he helped Ike clean up. As Ike dried his hands, an idea came up out of his unconscious mind and took its place among his notions about the necessity of the Lathrops making money. As he looked in the mirror to smooth back his hair, his blue eyes exchanged a glance of understanding with their reflection.

When he came out into the bank, Master Sherwood was sitting sideways at his desk, deep in conversation with Gadston and Applemore. Ike made his deposit with Philip the red-haired, red-cravatted, facially expressionless clerk. Then in walking rapidly out the front door, he almost collided with Old Jerry Stone who came waddling in with a money-sack in his hand. "Excuse me, Old Jerry," said Ike, stepping aside. For a moment the tanner stood blocking the door, blinking his eyes to accustom them to the dimness, then peering to the rear. Abruptly he turned on Ike, seized him by the lapels, and shook him till the money-sack rattled. "Look here, young feller," he growled, "you stay clear o' them hyenas and stick t' yer knittin' on th' farm. If ye don't ye'll be a sorry boy one o' these days." And he waddled off into the bank. Ike walked slowly out to the hitching post, feeling suddenly let down.

But as he unhitched Chesty this uncomfortable feeling changed to one of resentment, then to a sense of inner security that was deeper than Old Jerry could reach, something compounded of the Middle Falls and Howell Sherwood. Faintly, from far off to the eastward out the State Road, came the long, musical wail of the coach horn. Ike vaulted onto Chesty and kicked him into a run, heaving up gobs of mud thirty feet in the gray sky. Every recent event left his mind. Perhaps Aggie would be on the coach! —Aggie, his big sister whom he loved almost as much as John, and whom he hadn't seen since her marriage three years ago! That was something of consequence! What did all this amount to that he'd been stewing about?

CHAPTER VI

I K E needn't have hurried to meet the coach, for it was still a good mile out the State Road and would be ten minutes yet in arriving. He hitched Chesty in the shed, saw that Henry Hawks had harnessed the broad-backed mare Nancy, freshly shod, in beside Mol, and paused to pat both of the new team-mates. Then he went into the inn, bought a ten-penny cigar for Henry, and returned to the yard as the old stableman was leading out and hitching the harnessed relay team for the stage. "Shoeing two shillings, was it?" asked Ike. "Yep," said Henry. Then, "Much obleeged," as Ike handed him the money and the cigar. "I'd sure grit thank ye," said Ike in a confidential tone, "if ye'd send me out notice of any particular doings about Dandy." "I'll ride out myself if need be," said old Henry out of the side of his mouth. "Thank ye kindly," said Ike. From the tap-room window Stark saw the money, cigar and quiet talk pass between Ike and Henry. Though he knew of the shoeing, he filed in his mind the suspicion that those two were somehow in cahoots about the big gray.

The company in the tap-room was the same as before. The fire had been replenished and puffed up, and the bar-maid, one of the veteran harlots of the village, was busy slicing a hot roast of beef and a cold loin of pork and pouring out the bases of a half-dozen grogs, in anticipation of the business that would follow the arrival of the coach. Ike remained impatiently at the door, warmly hoping for Aggie's arrival when, through the door to the ladies' parlor, his indifferent eye fell on Prudence seated on the little corner sofa. When he looked at her she smiled and crooked a finger in summons. Ike felt a wince of annoyance, not wanting to be interrupted in the pleasure of anticipating Aggie. But when the finger was crooked a second time and the smile was even sweeter than before, he felt he had no choice, and so walked into the parlor a little stiffly.

"Ike Lathrop!" trilled Pru, rising, and her pretty forehead lifted in distress. "You're just a sight. Come upstairs this minute." Mechanically he followed her up to Mistress Stark's parlor where she took a long, straw whisk from the cupboard over the fireplace and began a sedulous brushing of his

48

muddy coat-tails. At first irritated at her officiousness, Ike now became carnally aware of her brush strokes on his person, then experienced that same sense of revulsion he had felt earlier in her presence, and finally composed himself in the thought that at least he would now make a better appearance before the Connecticut kin.

"Now hold up your coat-tails," the seventeen-year-old beauty commanded, and Ike held them up, while they both snickered, and vigorously she had at the mud-caked seat of his pants, and so down one leg after the other. "I hope Papa didn't trim you with the chestnut," she said as she worked. "He's awfully sharp, you know." "I'm satisfied," said Ike. "I wonder what John will think," said Prudence, lingering too long on a ticklish spot behind his knee. This was something Ike wondered himself, but he said lightly, "Oh, I guess he'll be pleased, being as it's you got Dandy." "They'll make a sparky pair, Dandy and our other gray." "Ought to," said Ike enigmatically, and as she took a rag from the cupboard and knelt rubbing his boots he could not help looking down at her and indulging delicious sensations of desire.

"There," she said, jumping up, putting the whisk and the rag away and flouncing her voluminous dress into shape. "I could fix you better if I had time and my way, but you'll have to do for now." She surveyed him gravely, then jumped forward and stood on tiptoe, straightening his tie, while her curls danced. Ike remembered Tavie's similar attention five hours earlier, and was relieved to find that the instant Pru's little bosom touched him his feeling of revulsion replaced the voluptuous impulses he had felt a few moments before. "My, you look fierce," said Pru, backing away. "You might at least thank me, even if you do hate me." They both smiled quite genuinely, and their eyes met in a sort of challenging understanding. "Indeed I do thank ye," said Ike, "and if you're bound I'm to hate ye I'll do it, so long as you'll give me a polishing now and then."

Close by, out on the State Road the coach horn sounded three short blasts for arrival, and Ike turned toward the door. "Just one thing, Ike," said Pru, touching his sleeve with her fingers and looking up at him with pretty concern. "I do wish you'd tell me how you want me to act toward John. I will do whatever you tell me, I promise."

This touched something deep and complicated in Ike. For the moment he forgot even Aggie, turned his back on Pru and gazed out on the Mall. He wanted to reply flatly, "Let him alone"; but knew instinctively that was the worst thing he could say. He was almost wholly inexperienced in fencing with women, but he sensed that somehow this was a sort of game, like a hoss-trade, and the last thing you must do was to say exactly what you meant. He turned round with his brow puckered and said candidly, "Pru,

I honest don't know. The plain thing is, I've no call to interfere." "But," plead Pru, clasping her hands prayerfully, "you're the only person I can advise with who really knows the big darling. You'd talk frankly with *him*, wouldn't you?" "Likely," said Ike. "Then why not talk frankly with me? At least we both want the best for John, and we ought to be able to talk honestly together—even if we do hate each other;" and she arched a desperately appealing eyebrow. Ike felt her beauty swim through him again, enhanced by the flattering suspicion that she was really quite helpless and dependent on him in this business. "We'll see," he said with his big Lathrop smile and started down the stairs, feeling strangely important and authoritative. The coach horn wailed from the inn yard and Ike knew he had missed the arrival. Consarn the little minx!

As Ike ran out the tap-room door another wail from the powerful coach horn struck him as it were straight in the face, and there on the box by the driver he saw his pesky brother-in-law, Homer Hislip, standing in a bright green greatcoat showing a flaming orange stock, and obviously aiming the blast at him. At the same moment he recognized Aggie's mitted hand with the long fingers waving at him from the coach window, and ran forward through the mud. But Homer jumped down first and, thrusting Gam Stark aside from this customary office, opened the coach door and handed down his wife and two-year-old child, at the same time looking at Ike—whom he had not troubled to greet but with the blast of the horn—and saying loudly, "Precious sack o' eggs, I'll tell ye, and fresh as the day they was laid. Haw! Haw! Haw!" And he gave the little crowd round the coach an enormous wink.

Clad in a blue bonnet and long cape to match, Agatha stepped down, carrying her child, ran to Ike, pulled his head down with her free arm and gave him a long kiss. Nothing was said, for Agatha was both the most sympathetic and the most silent of the Lathrops. Being five years older than John, she had the status of old nurse to all three of her little brothers. Ike looked like her, and he was her favorite. She stood by him now, taller than he in her bonnet, her arm locked in his, her face shining like an angel, watching the others descend, watching the changing of the horses, the unbuckling of the great baggage sack at the rear of the coach and all the goings on of the inn yard, as if everybody here were her child and her special joy and devotion.

After her came down old Cousin Joel, a little unsteady on his tall, gilt-headed walking-stick, a little corpulent, and very stately in his old-fashioned, mulberry greatcoat with wide collar and wrist-length cape, mulberry beaver to match, and tight-fitting gray pantaloons. He shook Ike warmly by the hand and chuckled, "Ain't you feeling a mite tall today, Isaac? I declare, you're a weed. I can remember, back at the old place, how you used to crawl through a knot-hole in the barn whenever I chased ye out of the oat-bin. Before long you'll be going the way of your big brother John, getting a Yale education like the rest of the Lathrops, a sinful education in porter and grog like all the Lathrops from the beginning even unto the end." And he shook his head as it were with great sadness.

In the meantime Cousin Alvina, in her stylish little bonnet and shawl, had been standing in the coach door, unconsciously impeding the other passengers, vaguely awaiting her husband to hand her down the steps, and near-sightedly ignoring Gam Stark who stood offering his services with bow after bow and an unctuous smile. Discovering her tardily, Joel sprang to her with a bow and flourish. "Step right down, Vinnie," he said, taking her hand. "Step down, and as lightly as you did on your bridal night." And as she stepped down he kissed her mitted hand, which she continued thereafter to hold out near-sightedly as if offering the same civility to many others, a little doubtful whether she or someone else was hostess here, whether this was a ball or supper party, whether in fact she was in Hartford, New Haven, or just at another stage station. At last, finding no takers and seeing a tall figure beside her whom she took for some young cousin or other, she turned to Gam Stark, laid an affectionate hand on his arm and said, "How do you do, my dear boy."

At this Ike stepped into the breach and kissed her on the lips, saying, "Cousin Alvina, it's a great joy to see ye again." Whereat, seeing her error, she giggled and slapped Ike playfully with her fingers. "You know I'm such an old fool," she whispered loudly. "Joel says if I found a stranger in my bed I wouldn't know him from my husband. He calls me a silly old goose. Now do you think I ought to put up with such language?" And she went off into a merry trill of laughter that ended in a sneeze.

Meanwhile the other passengers had bundled out, last of all Uncle Brandon, lawyer in Utica and frequent visitor, who greeted Ike with, "How do you do, my boy. I fear we have caused you great inconvenience by this delay. I doubt not you have been here since dawn." "Not quite, Uncle Brandon," replied Ike. "And I have managed to occupy my time. But I am indeed glad ye have arrived safely."

Slowly, with many jokes and whisperings and blockings of other travellers, the Lathrop party made its way through the mud to the side door, where the ladies were bowed into their parlor. Instead of procuring a room for the ladies to rest, Ike had planned to have Agatha seek this directly from

Susan Stark and now whispered to her to do so, and if possible to appraise Prudence whom she hadn't seen in three years during which the girl had discarded pantalettes for the long dresses of young ladyhood. Accordingly, Aggie now went upstairs to greet her ma's friend, and the men repaired to the tap-room and fell upon a light refreshment of pork, hot roast beef and grog or porter. In a moment Ike saw Aggie return with both Mistress Stark and Pru, and together they conducted Cousin Alvina upstairs.

It was almost ten-thirty before Ike got his little cavalcade assembled, Uncle Brandon to drive, with Homer beside him on the box, Cousin Joel and the ladies bundled warmly inside the coach, and Ike astride Chesty as outrider. As they walked out of the covered drive into the Mall, Ike looked back, saw Pru waving at the upstairs window and touched his cap to her. Then Stark himself opened the front door and raised his hand in farewell. This was a civil enough gesture, yet Ike knew Stark was gloating over the reduced splendor of the Lathrop equipage. He gripped Chesty with his knees and leaned forward. At least he mustn't come a cropper now.

Brandon snapped the long whip and Mol and Chesty danced, but the new mare Nancy only leaned sturdily forward and pounded the mud in the strong walk of a draft horse. Before Cousins Joel and Alvina, Ike was specially chagrined at the absence of Dandy, above all when numerous pedestrians stared as they passed, with something between amazement and pity. But Ike solaced himself with the fact that he had nine hundred and fifty dollars in the bank, a good farm horse, a good utility mount, the note of a needy friend in his pocket, the likelihood that Dandy would be back before this visit was over, and above all the fact that he was bringing Aggie home. She hadn't even inquired about Dandy. Aggie wouldn't!

As they started up Washington Street Ike rode in close to the coach and said, "Knot the lash short, Uncle Brandon, and pass it to me." When Brandon complied Ike, gripping Chesty with all his knees' might, began to flick Nancy's legs, till she lunged into an elephantine trot up the little grade, and Mol kept easy pace with her.

After what seemed a long time they emerged from the arcade of trees onto the open pike, and Ike as usual was glad to have the village behind him. In front of them the wide hills piled back like titanic steps, and at that moment the sun came out of the grayness and glittered on the limitless reaches of snow. Cousin Joel beckoned Ike in beside the coach and exclaimed, "Ah, Isaac, my great uncle John was right. This is a wide country, a country where a man can breathe." "O Ike," called Agatha suddenly, leaning out of the coach and seizing his hand. "O Ike." And he saw she was weeping.

CHAPTER VII

I K E'S departure from home soon after six that morning had left Tavie almost an hour before the family breakfast. With three or five special guests to come back in the coach, there was plenty to do. In a daze of combined exaltation and panic at her helpless behavior with Ike, she walked back from the barn to the kitchen, extinguished the now superfluous lantern, and went hectically at Ike's breakfast dishes.

Master Lane came rheumatically down the back stairs. "Good morning, Octavia." "Good morning, Master Lane"—everybody called this little old hired man "Master"—nobody of the young generation even knew whether he had a first name. He dipped some water into the basin and spluttered as he threw it on his face. "Ye're looking like an angel, my child," he said through his gums. "Ye're looking like your grandma, Miss Octavia. And as an old man that's the prettiest compliment I can pay ye." Master Lane— who knew a thing or two—took the lantern and went out the kitchen door. Tavie heard the clatter outside as he picked up the milk pails and the yoke from the snowy bench and went up the slope to the cow-shed. She saw the ancient cow-dog, "Tippie," trot out from his kennel beyond the barn. Tippie lived an independent life out-doors, and Master Lane was the only member of the household he recognized as his peer.

Tavie washed Ike's dishes and put them away in the north pantry. As she re-entered the kitchen, young Ben came in, Ben the dwarf of the Lathrop family, the only one under six feet, and afflicted with a flattened nose, bulbous at the end, which suggested no kinship to either of his parents. Just now Ben was wide-eyed. "Say, Tavie," he murmured excitedly, "I know a secret." "What is your secret, Ben?" "Don't you tell, don't you tell Pa!" "Well?" Ben came over and whispered, "Ike took a real swig of something this morning!" At first Tavie turned away indifferently. Then a look of terror came on her face and she stiffened. "Ben," she said icily, "since Ike's gone to the Falls you'd better hurry to help Master Lane with chores." "Oh, I know it," said Ben loftily. "You've no need to be bossing me all the time." He opened the door and looked back. "Don't you tell." "I won't—no fear."

Ben went out, and Tavie walked over and leaned tensely on the sink, looking out the window. It was daylight now and still snowing. So that was it! That was it and all of it! Of course! "Ike took a swig of something!" And you a temperance worker! You're just a silly fool! She laughed hysterically, clenching the edge of the sink. Then she smiled her tortured smile, and turned violently to the business of the day.

First she lit the fire already laid in the domed brick oven beside the fireplace, leaving the charred, maple door open for draft. Next she laid the breakfast for the family, setting out the usual apple pies, doughnuts, cucumber pickle, mustard pickle, butter and syrup, and mixing the molasses into the round-nozzled jug of buckwheat batter. Then, fetching from the barrels in the pantry a big bowl of flour and another of white sugar, she carried them out into the chilly summer kitchen and launched into Sarah Lathrop's recipe for gold and silver cake. From the buttery she fetched two dozen eggs, three pounds of butter and a quart of milk, and set them on the wide mixing table with the other ingredients. Putting half the butter in a big bowl, she began creaming it with a wooden spoon, adding the sugar from time to time. Having adjusted the tilt of the bowl and settled down to beating, she glanced out the north window in front of her at the suddenly bright day.

The snowfall had stopped abruptly and the sun, fully risen, was glittering on the snow-covered slopes of the steep-sided little valley called Lathrop Hollow. Through the bare trees Tavie could see all the houses in that part of the cup in the hills: a quarter-mile below in Jolam's Glen, the house of her own family, the Samsons; behind it, her grandfather Jolam's tiny stone retreat, once a smokehouse, and his forge on the stream just below Jolam's Falls; farther up the stream at the Upper Falls, Lem Oaks's tannery, with his big house beyond on the Upper Road, and the new house of young Hate-evil Haddock intervening; to the right the house of "Professor" Thomas Lathrop, the Squire's eighty-one-year-old father; still farther to the right the house, grist mill and store of Eliphalet Emmens; to the left of Lem Oaks' house the ruin of the house where her father Solon Samson had been born and reared in poverty; still farther to the left the Wilcox's and, clear down on the main highway to the Center, the house and forge of Solomon Sloan who divided the smithy business of the Hollow with Tavie's maternal grandfather. Beyond Solomon Sloan's the highway and the little Lathrop River cut through an imposing gap in the hills northeastward. It was in that direction that Tavie, as she mixed, kept glancing each time with a little jump in her stomach, for that was the direction to the Center and the Falls, by which Ike had departed and by which he would return.

The butter was just beginning to stir easily when she heard a step outside in the snowy court-yard. Looking around, she saw Constant Oaks through a window, dropped her work and ran to meet him as to a familiar haven in the storm of her feelings about Ike. Constant was Tavie's age, her childhood playmate and by all odds her closest and most trusted friend among men. He came now on the pretext of bringing Mistress Sarah Lathrop a present from his ma, a jar of Felicity Oaks's famous blackberry preserve. He had purposely finished his own chores early and picked this time for his errand when he knew that all the members of the Lathrop household except Tavie would be either in bed or at the cow-shed.

"Come in, Constant," she said, opening the summer kitchen door, "I'm creaming butter for gold cake. Want some?— Sure to give you hiccups." She turned away and he followed her in with his slow, lounging gait, furtively wagging his big head and mop of black hair to the right and left to see if anyone else was there. He set down his jar and came over to Tavie, who had turned her back to him and gone back to her beating. "Tave, I just had t' come over and kiss ye once, thinkin' how quick now I'll be settin' out fer Californy."

Tavie put down her spoon and turned candidly into his too desperately strong embrace. He gave her half a dozen smacking kisses on the mouth, whereat she said quietly, "Connie, you're breaking me in two," and pushed him away. He loosened his grip, dropped his head on her shoulder and sobbed. "Two weeks from tomorry I'll be gone fer good. Maybe never see ye again." "Yes, you will, Connie," said Tavie, patting his head, while she adjusted her hair with her other hand. "I've been West and it's not as far as it seems. You'll come back, or maybe I'll get that job in Oberlin." "Oberlin!" said Constant, releasing her. "Oberlin ain't nuthin' t' me—'lessen you'd marry me—then I'd settle anywhere you said. Likely wouldn't set foot out o' Byzantium 'lessen you wished it. As things stand I'm goin' clean t' Californy, and there ain't no assurance o' gettin' back—ever—what with injuns and deserts and Gawd knows what."

"Yes, California *is* a long way, that's certain," said Tavie, returning to her work, scooping a little flour into the butter and beginning to stir again. "Maybe you won't ever get there, Connie. There are plenty of chances to buy fine land cheap, right in Ohio. You must do as you see fit, but I'd be more comfortable if you'd settle nearer home." Tavie meant this, for Connie was a sort of anchor she didn't want to lose, even if she wasn't in love with him. Also, there was a kind of impulsive and naïve violence about him which she dreaded to think of being at large among bandits and cardsharks in the Far West, a kind of violence that was all the more danger-

ous for being coupled with the most uncompromising and selfless moral
integrity.

"O Tave," he was saying, standing against the table where she was now
adding milk to the butter, "figger how different things 'ld 'a' been if you'd
'a' give into me just one o' them times, when we was youngsters out ber-
ryin', or down in the hemlocks by the falls, or even last year when yer pa
let us bundle up by the fire. 'Member all them times, Tave? T' me it's like
they was all yesterday." "Me too, Connie," she said, stopping to smile over
her shoulder at him, then to gaze a long time out the window.

How comfortable it would be, after all, to marry Connie! How different
from Ike who would ruin her career! Connie'd let her do as she wished. He
could get a farm or a store in Oberlin. She'd teach in the College and go
on with the Reform work and pay a hired girl out of what she earned. Perhaps she'd never have such another opportunity. Constant guessed that she was
considering him and put his great clumsy paw on her long, slim hand. She
looked up at him intently, her forehead wrinkled. Too quickly he leaned to
embrace her, and with too abject worship in his black eyes. "It's impossible,
Connie," she said, with tears in hers, and she went back to beating the butter with concentrated speed. "G'by fer now, Tave," he said softly. "Likely
I shan't bother ye any more. Master Lane's coming."

They kissed each other tenderly, then Connie opened the door to the
court-yard. Master Lane was coming down the snowy slope, carrying the
usual four pails of milk—well over a hundred pounds—suspended on ropes
from the yoke. By grasping the outer two ropes in a crucifixial attitude and
pressing his biceps against the inner two, the little man expertly kept all
four pails from swinging and slopping their contents. In the court-yard he
stomped gingerly on the flagstones, then sidled in through the door with
his heavy and delicate load.

"Mornin', Master Lane," said Connie. "Looks like sleighin' early."
"Stone-boat sleighin' if ye've a mind to it," said Master Lane, crossing the
summer kitchen. "Stay on wheels, say I, while ye can, and be thankful."
After emptying his pails in the skimming pans and five-gallon crocks in the
buttery, he hooked them empty on the yoke again and shuffled out through
the court and around to the well, muttering about folks' outlandish notions
of riding in sleighs in November.

Close after Master Lane, Ben likewise came down from the cow-shed with
a similar four-pail load on a yoke, but he carried it less adroitly than the
old man, and had to halt every few steps to stop an incipient swing. As he
came in side-ways one of the pails hit the door-post and slopped. "Consarn
it," he said. "Mornin', Connie. What you doing over here so early?"

"Thought ye might need a hand with yer yokin'—here, gimme the inside pails." "Hush ye and stand away from me," retorted the seventeen-year-old, getting his load in hand again and proceeding slowly to the buttery. "If folks would let me be perhaps I'd learn to handle this rig." He set his pails down without mishap by the buttery door, unhooked them from the yoke and stood it in the corner. "If the pans and two crocks are full," Tavie instructed him, "take the rest up to the cheese room." "Oh, I know my affairs, don't I?" grumbled Ben. "How would you like it if I started teaching you how to mix that mess you're fussing with?"

He went into the buttery, returned, leaving the door open, picked up two pails in his hands, crossed to the opposite corner and disappeared up the stairs to the cheese room. Without comment Tavie closed the buttery door and went back to her beating. Presently Ben came down again and went out with the yoked pails to join Master Lane in sousing them at the well. Tavie and Constant looked after him and smiled at each other. Tavie had the gold cake batter ready for the eggs, so she took another bowl and started creaming the butter for the silver cake.

Quite suddenly Tavie glanced at Constant, then beat faster. Telepathically Constant knew that their visit was over, though he wondered why. The fact was that without any sound reaching her Tavie knew that Squire Lathrop had come out of his bed-room. She had hardly imposed silence when they heard his slow step cross the kitchen, and there he stood, filling the door with his broad-shouldered, six-foot-two figure, immaculate in brown broadcloth, flowered waistcoat, plaited shirt, lofty collar and stock, his enormous head, with its swirl of whitening blond hair, inclined in a half bow. "Good morning, John Lathrop," said Tavie, turning toward him with a curtsy. "Good morning, John Lathrop," said Constant, dipping his head. Instantly Squire Lathrop possessed the room, and both young people felt secure, ready to face easily whatever was in store for them.

"Ah, my dear," said the Squire, advancing to Tavie with both arms extended and the universally understanding smile with which he and all his children habitually disarmed the world. "Ah, my dear, you grow lovelier every day, and that lilac bow was made specially to set off the gold of your hair." Taking her by the shoulders, he gave her an affectionate shake and touched her forehead with his lips. "Ah, Constant," he said, looking over at the youth, "it was such a face as this that launched those famous ships." "Yes, sir," said the embarrassed boy, and, seeing his blush, the Squire went over to him and took his hand in both of his.

"So you are indeed leaving us, Constant? Really going after this myth of the golden fleece in a country so far away it is hard to imagine the distance?"

"Looks that way, sir," said Constant, trying to smile. "And what's to come of the Hollow twenty years hence when we old folks have passed on, and you six young men ain't here to succeed us?" "It's 'tarnal hard to go, John Lathrop," said Constant Oaks, and from his earnest look, his presence here at this hour, and Tavie's sudden preoccupation with her beating, the Squire guessed the reason for his departure. "Yet, it's a great adventure you're bound on," he said, changing his tone, "a nobler enterprise than remaining to the performance of routine duty at home. You are setting out not only to test your own strength but to found a civilization in that great new state now admitted with a charter of freedom—a new civilization to be perhaps the wonder of the world. Never forget that we at home believe in ye, and whether you succeed or whether you fail our love goes with ye all the same."

The Squire heard Tavie stifling a sob behind him and in Constant's glowing eyes saw determination emerging through despair. He was glad to hear the rustle of his wife's approach, for he knew he had said enough. But, not wishing to look at her until she was well into the room and composed for his appraisal, he continued to hold Constant's hand with one of his while resting the other on the boy's shoulder and looking tenderly into his eyes.

Tall Sarah Lathrop came into the room with her swift, silent, long-legged, competent gait, and stood with her hands folded at her waist, appreciating her husband's tact and addressing his back with a direct stare of her dark blue eyes and an arrogant lift of her wide, lean, triangular face, the forehead faintly lined, the chin exquisitely pointed, the nose short and delicately arched, with large, sensitive nostrils. Her dark brown hair was slicked down from a central part, and she had a cluster of curls before each ear, with a rose—clipped from the pot in the bed-room—behind one of them. Her arrogant look was defensive, a sign of momentary shyness or uncertainty. Just now it was due to suspense, awaiting her husband's reaction to her new dress, brown and blue, with a tight-fitting, buttoned waist and a wide, buckram-stiffened flare to the voluminous skirt.

After the Squire had heard Sarah stop and exchange greetings with Tavie, he turned, and his wife's face lighted as he advanced to her approvingly, kissed her hand, then her lips, as ceremoniously as if he hadn't left her bed twenty minutes before, and whispered, "You are fresh as that rose, my dear. Indeed, it's as if I had never seen ye before." Sarah's cheeks glowed like her rose, for she secretly prided herself that never in thirty-three years had her husband twice paid her precisely the same compliment. So there was a glance of love between them, and Sarah whispered back, "Indeed, sir, it seems I have never seen *you* before. And who may *you* be?" Then the

Squire, backing off, said aloud, "Here is Constant come to pay court to ye so early in the morning."

"Mornin' to ye, Sarah Lathrop," said Constant, advancing and bowing over her hand. "Ma says thanks fer the sweet-pickle relish and she's savin' it fer Thanksgivin' and she wants ye should try this blackberry I come over to fetch ye." "Thank you, Constant, and thank your dear ma for the most famous conserve in town. And please tell your pa and ma that our cousins from Connecticut are arriving today and we hope that all of you will stop by." "Indeed I will, ma'm," said Constant, looking down and shifting his feet in confusion, for Sarah Lathrop in her finery, for all her fifty-one years, was altogether something formidable for a tense young man to face.

She lowered her eyes to relieve him and prepared to say something to put him on his own ground. But the Squire, still admiring her, wouldn't let her surrender her moment of self-intoxication in the awareness of her beauty, a moment which came to her rarely enough and which was appropriate to the opening of the festive Thanksgiving season. He clapped his hands once, lifted his Sally's hand high, pointed his well-oiled Wellington boot, and together they did half a dozen minuet turns in the most stately and flirtatious fashion, while Connie drew Tavie away from her mixing and did the same in his clumsier, more earnest way.

This passage being over, Constant took his departure. Master Lane came in and kissed Sarah's hand with the courtliness of his generation, followed by Ben who kissed her cheek, murmuring, "Ma, you look like those great ladies in Shakespeare." And Sarah had to hum and skip like a girl as she went over to Tavie, whispered in her ear that the lilac rosette and ribbon in her hair were a complete success, tried the two batches of cake batter, found them right and said they might stand until after breakfast. Then together they went into the kitchen, took down two spiders from the ceiling, and started respectively the buckwheat cakes and the ham. Immediately, as they leaned over at opposite corners of the fireplace, the gala spirit of the last few minutes vanished, for Sarah observed that Tavie avoided her eyes and divined that something had happened with Ike that morning.

For three minutes the two women leaned in silence over the fire, Tavie tending severely to her business of frying the slabs of ham and afterwards the potatoes in the grease, Sarah unconsciously wearing her arrogant look which meant uncertainty—for, fond as she was of Octavia, she doubted whether, with her interest in Reform, she was the proper wife for Ike. When the ham and potatoes were ready and Sarah had the first two dozen buckwheat cakes piled up, they went round filling the plates, and afterwards the big cups from the steaming tea-pot. Sarah looked into the roaring oven and closed the door. Then she clanged once the bell on the mantel, and the men filed in. The Squire asked the blessing, requesting the Lord to "watch over those on the highways and bring them safely to their destinations." The chairs scraped and clattered as they all sat down. The pies, doughnuts, pickles, butter and syrup went around, and the light meal of the day began.

CHAPTER VIII

AFTER breakfast and prayers Ben went to his endless chores of wood and water, then joined his pa and Master Lane in the barns. The house was left to the women. Having donned full length, long-sleeved aprons and done the dishes hurriedly, they separated to their several duties. Tavie went upstairs, made Master Lane's bed and prepared her own room for Brandon who was to occupy it, she to go home nights during the season. Then she returned to the summer kitchen, separated the two dozen eggs and started the long beating of the yolks for the gold cake, the whites to be whipped later for the silver cake. Sarah meanwhile fetched from the buttery a leg of mutton, already sewed in linen, and put it in the simmering pot on the crane with peppercorns and bay leaf. This done, she opened the oven door to a blast of heat, poked the glowing sticks together with the long peel, closed the charred door again, and started a final inspection of the house. It was almost eight and the guests should arrive in little more than half an hour.

The house, indeed, was ready, not only for its guests, but for Thanksgiving still two weeks off, Thanksgiving that was the object and consummation of the work of the year. For two months, barrels, cart- and wagon-loads had poured in from the fields, the barns, the mills, the orchards and wood lots. From the cellar with its swollen bins, its dozens of barrels, its hanging tables with scores of jugs of wine and cordial, its sacred, remaining barrel of last year's cider, its ten barrels of new cider with their bung-holes sizzling and plopping in the darkness, from the cellar upward through the shelves, barrels, crocks, tins, jars and meat hooks of pantry, buttery and summer kitchen to the back attic with its heaps of nuts and spreads of peas and beans, from cellar to attic the house was a three-story larder, heavy with tons of food for Thanksgiving and the months to follow. The long summer of labor was over, and the winter of enjoyment was about to begin.

The house was stored for the winter, and it was scrubbed from garret to cellar in preparation for the Thanksgiving season. The kitchen, where Sarah now started her final inspection, was gay with festoons of dried apples and nutshells hanging from the ceiling with grape-bunches for tassels, and spot-less with its pewter glowing in the courting-cabinet, its galaxy of brass, cop-per and tin glittering among the heavier, iron utensils round the fireplace, or hanging from the walls and the blackened beams of the ceiling. The final straightening here must follow the preparations for dinner, so Sarah first made the maple four-poster bed in the master's bedroom, then provided herself with a dust cloth, a bottle of vinegar-of-the-four-thieves and whisk broom for flicking it, and proceeded, room by room, through the rest of the house.

The keeping-, or general living-room, with its reek of tobacco, its dark mulberry panelling and wood-work, its pale mulberry walls stencilled round the line of the ceiling, its big cherry desk, corner book-case, settle and other home-made furniture, and its orderly piles of newspapers on the long table, was essentially the Squire's domain. Sarah took from the mantel a big, var-nished and brass-bound steer's horn, carried it out to the pantry, filled it with hulled nuts, dried blackberries and cherries, and returned it to place, leaving an inviting overflow. Then she proceeded to the little front hall just as the big clock there began striking eight.

Here she was busy for some minutes, opening the wide front door, sweep-ing the snow from the stone steps, arranging sprays of bittersweet around the fan- and side-lights, and finally hanging a sprig of mistletoe brazenly from the door lintel. Then she opened the door into the north parlor.

This room, with its French blue panelling, walls, woodwork and shell corner-cupboard, its French gray damask curtains and deep-matted, rose-designed carpet, its gilt harpsichord, fireplace and delicate Louis XV furni-ture, its portraits of the first Squire and his wife, was sacred to the fastidious Thomas, the present Squire's father, eighty-one-year-old school-master emeritus of the Hollow, who now lived half a mile away on the Upper Road, beloved and supported by the community, respected for his scholar-ship, generally known as "The Professor," but never honored with the in-formal title of Squire. All the furnishings of this room but the corner-cupboard, harpsichord and portraits he had purchased in New York in 1790 out of money provided by his father for an extended wedding tour—he had had to draw on his pa to get home, and his practical wife, Samantha, was disillusioned forever. Sarah now whisked about a little vinegar-of-the-four-thieves to freshen the air, glanced at the golden-manteled little fireplace to see that Ben had laid the fire properly, set out on the corner-cupboard the punch-bowl, ladle, pewter cans and decanters of rum and cordials, sat down impulsively at the harpsichord and rippled her fingers the length of the keyboard, then left the door open and ran up the front stairs—the north parlor always made her feel that way.

The loom-room, above the north parlor, was Sarah's own citadel, the place where she had spent about half of her waking hours during the thirty-three winters of her married life. The front wall was low under the sloping roof, but the other three walls were normal height and adorned with a cyclorama Sarah had painted, a winter evening scene in the Hollow, centering on the church on the back wall whither the recognizable figures of her early married years were gathering to service in the glow of a red-orange sun setting over the fireplace. Entering the room on this day when she expected Agatha home for the first time since her marriage, Sarah felt carried back to that day, now almost four years ago, when in the midst of a terrible February storm her daughter had suddenly turned from her weaving, fallen on her knees and confessed her love for the loud-spoken young adventurer, Homer Hislip, who—at least by his own tell—had accompanied Coloniel Fremont to Oregon, and whom some ill-fated political mission had brought to Byzantium that winter to see Ostrum Applemore. Aggie's little loom, along with both spinning-wheels and the lighter chests, had now been carried out to the back attic and replaced by a spare four-poster, a commode and tall mirror for the reception of Cousins Joel and Alvina. Sarah flitted about some of her refreshing vinegar, lighted the fire Ben had laid, straightened the geranium plants in the low front windows, and spread on the made bed her favorite quilt, a huge rose in the center with rose trees growing in from the corners, all her own design.

Across the little upper hall and over the keeping-room, the boys' room was unadorned but for whitewash and the jack-knife and pen-and-ink vandalism of three generations of young Lathrops. The plain furniture was now augmented by the family cradle which Sarah fondly made up with diminutive bedding last used to cover a baby of her own who had died. Then she carried the bedding from the two full-sized beds into the back attic, made up the double—normally Ike's and John's—bed afresh, and placed on it a brand new infant's coat and bonnet of wool, silk and rabbit's fur. She looked with resignation at the young masculine confusion of the corner-cupboard and closet, sighed, realized that Aggie would understand, and passed hurriedly on.

In the back attic—dim, unfinished catch-all of the house, open to the garret—she made up a double mattress for Ike, which John would share with him later, and a single one for Ben. Ignoring Master Lane's room that let off one end of the back attic, she glanced into Tavie's at the other, to see that she had cleared the room and made the bed fresh for Brandon. Faintly she heard the front hall clock strike half-past eight. Joel and Alvina might arrive any minute now! Sarah heaved a short, nervous sigh, went down the darkness of the back stairs, opened the door and stepped down into the kitchen.

Tavie was still busy beating the egg yolks for the gold cake, but for Sarah there could be a short hiatus here. It was now that she had expected her guests to arrive and had planned to take out time to receive them, before getting down to the serious and dishevelling business of cooking. She heard the men coming down from the barns and opened the kitchen door for them with the command, "Boots off today!" She sent Ben to sweep off the flagstones from the front door to the mounting block. When Master Lane and the Squire stepped in, carrying their boots, she sent the latter to the pantry to select the ingredients for the grog and put them in the punch-bowl in the north parlor. When these operations were finished, Sarah caused the men to carry in from the summer kitchen the long, square-legged, oaken table whereon the feasts of the next two weeks were to be spread. She dispatched Ben down cellar to fetch up a bucket of onions, three cabbages and a half bushel of potatoes. Afterwards he would go upstairs, take down his bed and store it in the back attic, clear the boys' closet and sweep the room very gently so as to raise no dust.

Sarah went out to the hall and looked at the clock. It was almost nine. She could not afford to be idle any longer, and strode back to the kitchen as if marching into combat. Tavie had already tinned the gold cake. Sarah opened the oven, found the bricks everywhere white hot, shovelled out the embers with the peel, pushed the cake under the center of the dome, and closed the door. Tavie went back to whip the egg-whites for the silver cake. Sarah inspected the simmering mutton with a fork, then went out into the summer kitchen and lost herself in one of her special arts, pumpkin pie. She mixed and rolled the crusts for a half-dozen pies, smoothed them into the crockery plates, cut them and scalloped the edges with the ivory scalloper, and set them in the buttery window to keep cold. Then she mixed her highly spiced and brandied batter, first beating the eggs thoroughly to give it a shiny crust.

When Sarah had finished the pumpkin pie batter, Tavie had finished and tinned the silver cake, and they replaced the gold cake with it in the oven, setting out the latter to cool. They cut up the cabbages, put them in a pot with a big chunk of salt pork, hung it on the crane to boil, and sat down to the tedious and lachrymose peeling of onions and potatoes.

Meanwhile Ben had swept the boys' room, and he and Master Lane were changing their clothes. In the keeping-room the Squire sat reading in his walnut, hair-cloth rocker, a recent gift from Ike to his pa, the only modern piece in the room but for a low, mahogany veneer rocker, a gift of the Squire to Sarah on their silver wedding. He finished all of the last *New York Tribune* and the current weeklies, the *Byzantium Eagle,* the *Blackwater Democratic Union,* and the *Albany Argus.* Laying them aside, he sat for a few minutes, seething with ideas for replies to the hot-heads who were advocating open defiance of the new Fugitive Slave Law, enacted two months before as part of Clay's great Compromise. It had been passed as a trade with the South for the admission of California with a free constitution, and the Squire thought the Abolitionists ought to be satisfied with the bargain. He could not start writing now, for the travellers should arrive any time. He looked at his big turnip watch and wondered why the coach company troubled to announce a schedule when they obviously had no intention of keeping it. He took down a copy of the sermons of his great-great-grandfather who had been the minister of the First Church of Somerset, Connecticut, in the days of Jonathan Edwards. From time to time he scowled in irritation at the stiff-necked orthodoxy of his ancestor.

At ten o'clock Master Lane came downstairs in his ancient, dark blue, shad-belly coat and knee-breeches, with laced shirt and neck-cloth, lace at the sleeves, black worsted stockings, and big-buckled shoes. To the Squire's own recollection this suit was fifty years old, and it wasn't Master Lane's oldest or best either. The old man had combed back his gray hair carefully, but, like his best suit, he would save for Thanksgiving his final touch of antique tonsorial splendor. He walked through the north parlor, cast an inquiring look at the punch-bowl, crossed into the keeping-room, sat down on the settle in the corner, threw one leg stiffly over the other, placed both rheumatic hands on the upper knee, and notified his young employer that Congress would accomplish nothing in the ensuing session.

Soon after Master Lane, Ben came down in his new tan store suit with the pantaloons strapped outside the boots—not too well oiled—and the black tie, a present from John like Ike's, but which Ben, unlike Ike, had tied into a passable bow round the painfully high collar. Conscious of his fine feathers, Ben bowed excellently to his pa and Master Lane, then proceeded to the kitchen and kissed his mother's hand, she pausing to stand off and appraise her youngest with love and approval.

At ten-thirty Sarah and Tavie had the potatoes and onions ready. The silver cake was done, and they replaced it with the six pumpkin pies in the now slow oven. Tavie put on her carpet slippers and set out to give the kitchen, summer kitchen and buttery their final wet sweeping and mopping.

Sarah performed the delicate business of upside-down cherry pudding, the batter of rich, sour milk, the reserved juice of the preserved cherries to be cooked separately in sugar and later beaten into thick cream. She poured the batter into a dozen custard dishes and put them in the oven among the pies. Then she went to setting the table. From the corner-cupboard in the north parlor she brought her second best set of china; from the courting cabinet in the kitchen, twenty-two heavy tumblers, eleven sets of pewter cutlery and miscellaneous ladles and spoons; from the pantry in increasing profusion, jars and plates of currant jelly, chili sauce, chopped pickles, cucumber pickle, mustard pickle, spiced peaches, doughnuts, cookies, bread and two castors of condiments. The table, already covered, stood ready to receive the major offerings of crane and oven.

It was now after eleven, and Sarah still proceeded on the assumption that the guests would arrive for dinner at noon. She hung the potatoes and onions on the crane and stirred the fire, then went out to the summer kitchen and mixed the journey cake batter, covering the two big boards with the little cakes, each pressed into shape with her fingers. When the journey cake was done, she went back to the kitchen, tried the pumpkin pies and cherry puddings with a straw, and left the oven door open. Tavie was finishing her sweeping. Everything but last-minute preparations was now done. Sarah and Tavie went to their rooms to tidy up. The hall clock struck half-past eleven. From far off the household heard the deep, pompous tone of the Lathrop coach horn. "Ike can't blow that for sour apples," thought Ben to himself.

In the room she was about to vacate, Tavie impulsively dashed to the window and saw the coach trotting slowly along the highway in the Hollow almost a mile away. One figure was standing up on the box waving, and Ike was riding separately in front. Tavie felt her knees weaken with sudden emotion, then stiffened up with resentment. As if impelled by authority stronger than her will, her eyes sought the little mirror and her hands went up, flouncing her golden hair and adjusting the lilac rosette and ribbon. With a last look of high scorn at the image of a girl so silly as to indulge this vanity, she turned and, for no explainable reason, took pleasure in pointing one slippered toe after the other as she descended the gloom of the back stairs.

CHAPTER IX

TEN MINUTES after the coach horn was heard far down in the Hollow the fires in the keeping-room and north parlor were crackling with fresh wood. Pitchers of recently boiling water, covered with cloths, were waiting in the loom-room, the boys' room and Tavie's room. In the north parlor, whose door was closed, a bottle of Napoleon brandy, with brandy glasses, stood with the other potables on the wide shelf of the corner-cupboard, and Tavie was stirring a quart of rum in the punch-bowl where the Squire had previously deposited spices to his taste. "What of it?" Tavie was saying to herself against the pounding of her heart. Ike had kissed her that morning!— "In Heaven's name, what difference does it make?" Sarah, having put a fresh rose in her hair, strode into the keeping-room and, leaning on the table, peered out the south window, while behind her Master Lane took a pinch of snuff from a silver box and stood watching in bent dignity.

The Squire and Ben stood in the open front door. The horn sounded beyond the crest of the hill—like Ben, the Squire wondered how Ike or Brandon could blow it so badly. He heard the beat of walking horses. The horn sounded again and continued to blare, to the annoyance of the Squire, for he knew it must bother Joel. The coach came round the turn from behind the barns, Brandon driving with young Hislip beside him puffing his cheeks to blow the horn and laughing between blasts at the way it made Ike's horse side-step—a strange chestnut, the Squire observed, no doubt a livery horse— which Ike was riding in front of the equipage. With some astonishment the Squire observed also that a heavy bay was in Dandy's place beside Mol drawing the coach—had they had an accident?

Immediately these thoughts were lost in a cheer as Brandon and Homer stood up on the box and Ike in his stirrups, all waving and joining in a prolonged "*Yeaaaaaaa*," while Agatha and Joel likewise waved from the coach window. In accordance with custom the Squire and Ben walked out to the mounting-block and raised their hands in salute. Master Lane kept his dignified position in the keeping-room, while the women-folks stood in the open front door, Sarah's arm around Tavie who deplored the fact that she was trembling and that Sarah would notice it.

Brandon negotiated the turn into the drive and the horses shuffled to a trot, Mol foreseeing oats. Brandon reined them back strongly and pushed down the brake to make a good stop. Ben ran to the horses' heads and also took the reins of the chestnut as Ike dismounted and ran to open the coach door. "Thank God, you've arrived," said the Squire, extending both hands through the open door. "What a tedious journey you must have had! Pray God, you've had no misadventure on the way?" "None at all, John," came Joel's cheerful voice from inside, "nothing worth relating."

Brandon from the box was waving to his sister-in-law, and Ike, holding the door back, was looking haughtily at Tavie, but, aware of the ceremonious import of the occasion, all kept their places, Homer having been tactfully coached by Ike and now being restrained by Brandon with difficulty. Very carefully Joel handed out Alvina to his cousin, the Squire, she giggling softly and protesting, "Not really arrived? From all that tooting of horns I thought we must be racing with another coach. John Lathrop, my dear!"—this as the Squire kissed her first on one cheek and then on the other. "Vinnie, my beauty," he said, still holding her hand, "I see that ten years can't take the bloom from a pretty girl." "John Lathrop, you haven't changed a bit," she whispered, and made a little pass at him with her lace-mitted hand.

At this Ike appeared at her side, for Cousin Joel was getting out of the coach. "At last, Joel," said the Squire, while they shook hands and looked at each other with affection. "It is the victory of thirty-three years to see ye at last at my doorstep." "Ah, my boy," said Joel, his hand on the taller and younger man's shoulder, "it is a happiness to come here before it's too late. This will be our last journey." "Nonsense," replied the Squire. "Forgive me," said Joel, who seemed suddenly older than his seventy years. "Here I am keeping ye from someone who will surely come back many times." The Squire turned to Agatha, who had left her baby inside and now rose into her father's full embrace with a hardly audible "Pa." For many seconds she kept her eyes closed, then released him without a word and stood dazed among the familiar sights, the big house with its once red paint faded a little nearer to lilac, the new windlass well which had replaced the sweep since Aggie left, the tall, stone gate-posts, the two gigantic maples in front that they said had been there before Columbus discovered America.

Meanwhile Homer Hislip had descended by the other side and came around the coach. "How do you do, Homer," said the Squire, shaking his hand with enthusiasm, "and congratulations on your election. I am more than happy to see ye again, happy and proud." "More proud than last time, mebbe, eh?" asked Homer with a faint sneer in his voice. The father-in-law paused for an effective second while he scotched his irritation. "Yes," he said, still holding the young congressman's hand and looking straight into his eyes. For once Homer Hislip was nonplussed. "Thank ye, sir," he said simply, and turned away.

"Well, Brandon," the Squire now took the hand of his lawyer younger brother who had climbed down from the box, "how was the trip?" "Disgraceful, Jack—worse than ever. I understand some of your sharp friends—Stark among them—have taken over the line. If they don't have a suit for damages they'll be lucky. A broken axle, forsooth, on a bump no bigger than a walnut!" "Broken axle, eh? Well, cheer up, Brandon. We'll make it right to ye some way."

Seeing that Sarah was advancing to meet the cousins, the Squire leaned shyly into the coach, plucked out a heavily shawled bundle that was his sleeping grandson, contrived to uncover the fat little face, then covered it again and walked after the others, feeling very pompous and a little silly.

Joel had recovered his spirits at the sight of Sarah and was delivering an oration on her rose. She turned from him to hold Agatha while they both shed quiet tears, then broke away to kiss Alvina on the cheeks and murmur, "Cousin Vinnie! At last!" Seeing her husband bringing up the rear with his bundle, she turned from Alvina and with an authoritative bound took their grandson from him and uncovered his face. Auspiciously he awoke, gestured in the direction of Sarah's rose and said, "Flower," to general applause. His grandma kissed his forehead, held him close for an instant, handed him to the blushing Agatha, and proceeded with her duties.

Tavie was still standing in the doorway. "Cousin Joel and Alvina," said Sarah, "this is our neighbor, Octavia Samson, who is helping us during the season." Tavie and Alvina curtsied and Joel bowed low. Ben ran up to kiss Agatha with an exuberant, "Hi, Sis." He greeted the other new arrivals with a shy, junior form of the big Lathrop smile, then excused himself to go and help Ike, who was already leading the horses and coach back toward the coach-shed alongside the barn.

The Squire and Sarah stepped up into the door to welcome their cousins across the threshold, and each man stole a kiss and a little scream from the other's wife as they passed under the mistletoe. "Joel and Vinnie, follow me," said Sarah, starting up the stairs and glancing at Tavie with a nod at the closed door of the north parlor. From the first little landing she called back, "Homer and Agatha in the boys' room, and Brandon you-know-where." Joel and Alvina followed Sarah up the stairs, Alvina in a fluttering panic at their narrowness. Being abnormally narrow in the hips, she affected unusually heavy and wide stiffening in the sides of her dresses, and suffered from chronic nervousness lest it be deranged. Tavie followed the guests up with a tray of cakes and steaming grog. In the loom-room, Joel cast an expectant eye in the direction of the commode, then bowed Sarah and Tavie out with some impatience.

Fifteen minutes later the luggage was all fetched in and the horses put away. All the men except Joel were congregated in the keeping-room, and the recent cases of defiance of the Fugitive Slave Law in Boston, Springfield, Syracuse and throughout the West were leading the talk away from the inefficiency of the coach company. Ike drew his pa aside and told him he would prefer to await a more leisurely moment to explain the absence of Dandy, but assured him that there was no cause for concern about the horse. Then he sauntered in to Tavie in the north parlor and whispered to her, "Let me know when ye figger I'm old enough to take a swig of something," whereat she turned away from him in anger and joined Sarah in the kitchen. Agatha was sitting quietly in her room beside her baby, awaiting a grave event concerning which Sarah, knowing Alvina's idiosyncrasies, had cautioned all the members of the immediate family.

Suddenly, as by some telepathy, silence descended on the house. Each person paused, in suspended animation, as if awaiting an avatar. The house was so still that above the hissing of fires the gurgling of water could be heard running into the trough of the barnyard two hundred feet away.

Upstairs, the door of the loom-room opened a cautious inch, then swung slowly back. Joel stepped out, saw the door of the room opposite closed, listened for a long moment, heard no sound, and came boldly out on tiptoe. The floor creaked under his steps, and the treads of the stairs likewise as he descended. When he reached the lower landing he saw to his relief that the doors to both downstairs rooms were closed. Then he wondered at the silence in this house that was strange to him. Where was everybody? Were they preparing some trick on him? To jump out at him to his humiliation? John wouldn't permit that. But where was John? That ruffian of a Hislip man! He could hear his heart beating louder than the clock and felt as if he were in the midst of some dangerous, youthful escapade. He looked up through the stairwell, cupped his hands in the direction of his bedroom door and uttered a soft "Pssst."

Alvina emerged with dignity, clad in a rich maroon silk dress with deep white lace 'kerchief and cuffs, her gray hair wound high under a ribboned lace cap and two gray curls dancing before each ear. With cautious tread and lips set in desperate determination, she proceeded to the head of the narrow stairs, extended her arms forward and down, picked up in a bundle before her her four-foot spread of dress, lifted it well over the confining barrier of the bannisters and, while Joel discreetly contemplated the maples through the side-lights of the door, descended the stairs in the shameless glory of long lace drawers which slid up at every downward step to reveal her chubby calves, of which, at sixty-eight, she was in fact unashamed. When she had completed the descent, she smoothed herself down with sedate care and touched her husband on the shoulder. Joel was still confused. Which one of the three doors should he open? Like a bomb-shell, his good wife solved the problem by sneezing loudly. In the keeping-room they heard the Squire striding over to the door. As he opened it he greeted them with an exclamation— "What? Down so soon! And no rest! I see they still make them sturdy in Connecticut!"

Instantly the house stirred with activity again. From the kitchen Tavie rushed into the north parlor, emptied and stirred a quart of boiling water into the base of rum and spice in the punch-bowl. The Squire complimented Alvina's dress and cap, and as they entered the keeping-room presented Master Lane to his cousins. "My father," said Joel, "used to speak of a Repentance Lane of Wethersfield whom he first knew at Yale and with whom he kept up a correspondence until this Master Lane went West with his family, a witty man, by my father's account, a tanner, as I recall it, and a great fellow with the harmonica." "From which, sir," said Master Lane with a bow, "we may assume that our fathers were friends, and let me welcome ye as I may to this my adopted home. Of my pa's qualities ye mention, his music proves to have lasted longest, for I have his harmonicas yet, and there are no such instruments made today." "Ah, the world moves on," sighed Joel. "Let us rather say, sir," replied Master Lane, "that the world don't change."

The Squire now squeezed behind Alvina's spaciousness into the hall, opened the door to the north parlor and bowed the company in. "By gad, John," exclaimed Joel, "this room exceeds your account of it. I have seen many fine rooms in Hartford and in Boston, but I have never seen the equal of this." Through her near-sightedness Alvina was catching the flavor of the French blue and gilt and was sighing, "Exquisite, exquisite." "Yes," said the Squire. "Though we often feel that our house is small, we always think of this room with pride. It is our vanity, our burden of worldliness that will keep us all outside the gate of the heaven of orthodoxy. I have already expressed to my sons the wish that, come what may, this room should be preserved." "When Pa talks like that," whispered Ike to Uncle Brandon, "do you figger he means this room *in this house?*" "Of course," said Brandon, and he gave Ike a quick, faintly suspicious look.

"But come," the Squire was continuing, seeing Sarah signalling to him from the kitchen to get on, "I want all of ye to drink a toast with me—Ike, Ben, Tavie and all." Standing at the corner-cupboard, he filled eleven little glasses with Napoleon brandy, and the boys passed them round, Sarah, Tavie and Aggie coming in from the kitchen for the ceremony. "Now I want ye all to drink with me to our cousins, Joel and Alvina, a toast of gratitude to them for coming so far to visit us, a toast of welcome to them to this house which is henceforth as much theirs as ours, and above all a toast to long life and continual happiness to them who have already known happiness but still have a long life ahead." The Squire clicked his glass with Sarah's. Everybody except Joel and Alvina clicked glasses with somebody, Ike maliciously seeking out Tavie for the purpose. The women sipped their brandy and set it down. The men tossed theirs off in a gulp, after which Ike and Bén swiftly and silently retreated to the pail and piggin at the kitchen sink.

When they tiptoed back, Cousin Joel was responding. "Cousins, we feel, as John has said, at home, and we accept your hospitality with great joy. As you know, this is an important occasion for us, important at least in terms of that worldly vanity with which I fear we Lathrops have always been pleasantly cursed. Because of the presence here of these three strong boys— I count upon young John as already here—we have felt that the center of our clan henceforth should be here, and that what we have always called the New Homestead should become simply *the* Homestead. As I have just said to Master Lane, the world moves on, and our New England is spreading westward to cover the whole country, at least the northern part of it. And as Master Lane said to me, the world in reality don't change much. Here, three hundred miles to the west, we are the same people we were back in Somerset, and before that in Wethersfield, and before that in Newtown. Our ideas may change some, but our ways of life hain't changed, and whatever strength has brought us here will carry us forward through centuries to come. Our country is only beginning, and I think that the Lathrops are only beginning. Our first phase of the little Rome of Italy is over and I think we are expanding perhaps to rule the world, by right of the example of our national virtues but not by way of military conquest. John, we accept your hospitality and we likewise wish ye and Sarah long life and happiness, and long life and strength to all the Lathrops in what is henceforth the Lathrop Homestead. Long life to the master and mistress of this house and all their family. And," lifting his glass to his cousin, "God bless the new head of the Lathrop family."

His hand trembled as he drank but he gulped it down, and Alvina sipped

hers, handed it to anybody and clung to her husband's arm. Sarah came forward and kissed them both. "By God, Sarah," said Joel, "that's the first
oration I've made since they sent me up to the General Assembly in 'fifteen.
How d'ye like it?" "Joel, I'm afraid your memory is failing. For my part
I've heard you make a score of orations. But this, I believe, was your best
one, and I hope you know how deeply John and I appreciate it, both for
what it means to you and for what it means to us." "Heaven bless ye, girl,"
said Joel, patting her on the shoulder, and the emotional tension was
relieved.

The clock in the hall struck twelve. Master Lane was the first to go to
the bowl of grog, and, after ceremoniously offering Alvina a can which she
refused, he unceremoniously tossed it off himself, bottoms-up, and poured
another to dispose of at greater leisure. Behind him came the other men,
except Ben. Ike looked inquiringly at his pa and received a nod of assent,
and presently lifted his mug to Tavie to punish her further. In five minutes the atmosphere was rosy and noisy with mirth in which every remark
seemed witty and profound.

Meanwhile, as ever since the arrival of the guests, Sarah, Tavie and Aggie
were busy in the kitchen and summer kitchen. The little journey cakes had
come in on their two big boards that were slanted up on their hinged props
before the fire. Sarah had made the sour cream biscuits, and they were baking in a tin Dutch oven close to the flames, while a coon pie and a venison
pie, brought in from the buttery, were warming in another Dutch oven.
Tavie swung out the crane, forked out the mutton onto a pan and went to
snipping off the linen. Sarah slowly poured the broth from the pot into a
big saucepan where a dozen eggs were already beaten, added her treasured
capers and leaned over the fire, holding the pan over the hottest coals and
stirring constantly.

By the time this prized gravy was thickened, Agatha and Tavie had the
mutton on a platter at the Squire's place, the vegetables heaped into serving
dishes, the journey cakes and the biscuits shovelled onto plates, the hot venison and coon pies set on the table. The long board was buried from end to
end with the output of the morning, to which was now added two gallons
of milk, two pitchers of cider and two decanters of blackberry wine. Steaming tea from the trivets went round into the eleven cups. Only the cherry
pudding and the pumpkin pies still waited in the now cool oven, through
whose partly opened doors their rich aroma dominated the symphony of
fumes from the table. Sarah placed the pewter salt-cellar, the mark of office,
at the Squire's place, then rang the dinner-bell with zest. " 'Roast-beef,' "
shouted the Squire.

All crowded laughing into the kitchen, and Sarah disposed them to their places. There was a hush of bowed heads while the Squire raised his hand in the laden air: "Father, we thank Thee for sending to us these Thy children who are here gathered together. Bless them and bless this family. May it continue industrious and humble in Thy service, and deserving of the bounty Thou hast bestowed upon it. Bless Thy children everywhere, in this country and over the earth. Give them courage under anguish of whatever kind, and peace of soul according to their consciences under the guidance of Thy wisdom. In Jesus' name we ask these things." "Amen," boomed the response. The chairs scraped, and eleven good appetites pounced down with enthusiasm upon the blessings of the Lord.

CHAPTER X

THAT EVENING, after the household had retired, the Squire gave Ike a cigar, which meant he wanted to talk with him, and Ike knew the time had come to account for the absence of Dandy. Standing with his back to the keeping-room fireplace, he recounted every detail of the sale, from the original breaking of his wind to the reaction of Old Jerry Stone. The Squire did not look at him as he listened, which was unusual, but sat in the big hair-cloth rocker with his legs crossed, gazing at the home-made book-case opposite and smoking his cigar slowly without flicking it, till the ash dropped on his waistcoat. Only once, when Ike mentioned his getting the Solon Samson note as part of the bargain, the Squire looked up, murmured, "Very good," then resumed his rapt attitude.

Feeling his pa's disapproval, Ike ended his report in a defensive vein: "Ye see, Pa, I'd be willing to wage ten dollars we'll have Dandy back in two weeks, keeping the chestnut and Solon's note, and something like five hundred in cash to boot. When ye come to think of it straight, Gam Stark ain't going to damage what he considers a valuable animal, even if he is a rough customer. And if he tried even to put a twitch on him, I'd gamble 'twould be Gam would suffer, not Dandy. After thinking it over, I ain't concerned on that score. The only thing that bothers me is Old Jerry's being put out with me, and wondering whether you and John will feel like he does about it. If you did, that would bother me plenty."

After a long silence, while Ike re-lit his cigar, the Squire said, "As I understand it, Isaac, the virtue of this transaction to you is that within, say, two weeks you expect to have Dandy back, in addition to some money and other property which previously belonged to someone else—in this case, Master Stark. Is that correct?" "Yes, sir," said Ike. "And your only doubt about the propriety of the sale lies in the fact that Master Stone, and possibly other persons of whom you are fond, may disapprove of it? Otherwise, you have no private misgivings of your own as to whether you have done right or wrong?" "Why, no, sir," said Ike without hesitation. "If Dandy comes back all keerect, and nobody goes against me, and I turn a few hundred dollars and a new horse, and do Solon Samson a kindness, I can't see I'd have any-thing to complain of."

The Squire was so appalled and shaken by this revelation, the worst blow he had ever received from any of his children, that he dared not speak quickly. It was the more severe because he had a secret preference for Ike, thought him the most promising of his sons, the most original in his interest in the new mechanics, the most practical in his notions of farming, the most tolerant, sympathetic and free from prejudice, at nineteen more mature than John who was a year older and would graduate from Yale next sum-mer. Never until now had Ike's cleverness in trading struck the Squire as specially significant, for swopping or barter was one of the fundamental functions of the only economy he knew, and to be adept at it was like being adept at milking or any other part of the day's work.

But suddenly now, in this sale of Dandy and Ike's manner of defending it, the Squire saw, or feared he saw, all of the boy's practical concerns in a new light, evincing a tendency to which drunkenness or wenching would have been far preferable. In Ike's attitude toward the act more than the act itself, there was a clear and conscienceless violation of the strongest single taboo in the Squire's two-century-old tradition, the taboo upon the lust for gold, "the root of all evil," the tradition of scorn for money beyond the needs of a respectable subsistence, and of contempt for those who sought it. In the light of this violation of the basic principles of social existence, it was inci-dental to the Squire that the subject of the sale was a pet of the family, beloved by the Squire himself almost as much as an adopted child.

But his impulse to say all this to Ike was checked by another deep-rooted conviction, this one not so much a part of his traditional code as the result of his own living and thinking. At the cornerstone of his Emerson-like per-sonal philosophy was the belief that every grown man's moral conscience, like his relation to God, was his own; and he considered Ike so near a grown man that he thought he should make his own decisions in such matters in-stead of conforming himself, like a child, to the decisions of others. To seek to rescind this transaction because someone asked him to would involve no growth but a weakening of Ike's character. In the long run the boy's happi-ness must depend upon his reaching his own convictions in his own way and then applying them courageously, without regard for the opinions of others.

So, having got his first emotional revulsion in hand, and his mind cleared of personal bias, the Squire looked up and said quietly, "Isaac, I would pre-fer not to sit in judgment on what you have done. I will ask ye to do only one thing. I will ask ye to think this thing over by yourself during the next few days, during the next two weeks if that is the term you are putting on this transaction. And in thinking of it I will ask ye to put out of mind the two criteria you have mentioned, the immediate practical advantages of the deal and the effect it may have on anyone's opinion of ye."

"Pa," interrupted Ike, "excuse me. It ain't anybody's *opinion* that bothers me. It's their *liking* of me, their *friendship*. Nothing is worth coming between me and you or anybody else in the family."

"Well," said the Squire, "you may have a distinction there. But I'll ask ye just the same to try to forget all about the effects of what you have done. Set your mind clearly on your action as a thing by itself, and decide for yourself whether it was right or wrong. What you settle upon will be right for you, and therefore right for everybody who knows and loves ye. Don't worry about me or anybody else standing by ye. You know you can count on that." With that the Squire rose, shook Ike's hand and said goodnight with a look of deep affection. Then he turned abruptly and went into his bedroom, where Sarah was sound asleep, she having failed to listen to the conversation through the door.

Ike stood for some minutes with his back to the fireplace, his brow puckered in distress. His pa's last straight look had not quite struck true. If he wanted him to go back and rescind the sale, why didn't he say so in plain words? As for thinking it out, he'd done that already, and he had seen no wrong in it.

CHAPTER XI

BY THE next day, Saturday, the snow had melted and there began a week of typical, raw, dank, gusty, November weather, with alternating squalls of rain, sleet and snow, the latter never staying on the ground more than a few hours. Cousin Alvina came down with a cold and stayed in her room throughout the week, Ben and Cousin Joel keeping the little fireplace there blazing night and day, and Sarah and Aggie ministering with steaming-hot mustard foot-baths, flaxseed tea and ipecac. All the near neighbors called, on Saturday, old Thomas and Samantha, the Samsons, the Oakses, Doctor and Mistress Swift, and afterwards, Jehu Jones, the young minister Nathaniel Norcross, the Emmenses, Stones, Oxbows, and others. But, excepting only old Samantha who went up to her room, poor Cousin Alvina saw none of them. Sarah cancelled the parties she had planned and went a little shame-faced to Mistress Oaks' quilting bee and the Swift's apple-paring bee, both of these having been planned in honor of the guests.

On Saturday afternoon when the Samsons called, Ike compounded with Solon the scalped note he had taken from Gam Stark as part of the consideration for Dandy. In spite of his best diplomacy he failed to avoid insulting the severe lawyer when he first offered to cancel the note in payment for legal services already rendered. Afterwards, with the greatest difficulty he got Solon's consent to value the note at the $100 he figured he had paid for it instead of the face value of $200—Ike agreeing that if Master Samson felt he owed the remaining hundred he should pay it to Master Staunton, the bookseller from whom Stark had scalped the note. They finally reached a settlement involving a bull calf of Solon's out of the Lathrops' bull Xerxes and the Samsons' only cow, Clover, altogether, Ike insisted and believed, the most promising bull calf he knew of anywhere. The calf was to be delivered and the present veal price of $10 written off the note. The Lathrops would raise the bull and have the use of him. At any time in the future, or if the bull died, either party could demand a valuation of him, and the Lathrops would pay Solon his then value, less the $90 due on the note, Solon in the meantime to pay interest. Ike was delighted to get this much settled. Whatever else might happen, Gam Stark would never see that note again. In

78

doing this kindness for a friend, Ike's impulse was perfectly clear, for there were no nice moral distinctions involved. Solon fetched up the calf that evening.

But outside of this small satisfaction, the period from that Saturday until the following Thursday was a trying one for Ike, between his pa's attitude and his anxiety for news of Dandy. For the first time in his life he felt uneasy in the house, confused and uncomprehending in the beginning, then gradually resentful and alienated from those he loved. He felt that all of the family except Aggie—also Homer, but he didn't count—were against him, and that things were being said behind his back. Pa was too nice to him. He sometimes caught Ma looking at him strangely. Uncle Brandon was formal with him. The worst of all was Tavie, toward whom he at first felt mighty sparky because of the kiss and having put her in her place by drinking openly with the family. But he never could get her alone, and whenever their eyes met she ducked hers as if he were poison to look at.

He spent most of his nights thinking about the sale of Dandy as Pa had told him to, lying on his mattress in the cold back attic. But he always got back where he started from. The only question he could see in it was whether he'd hurt Dandy or not. Dandy was up in Stark's lot and well enough off now, though likely not being fed proper. Henry Hawks would let him know if anything out of the way was going on, and if it was he'd go in and take pleasure in laying out Stark so he wouldn't forget it. Sooner or later Gam was sure to learn Dandy was wind-broke, and then he'd get him back. Putting aside, as Pa told him, the fact that he had turned everybody against him, he couldn't see anything askew in his figuring.

He never felt so alone in his life or, finally, so independent. He spent Monday and Tuesday evenings going over the farm accounts more closely than ever, sitting at the desk in the keeping-room while the family chattered behind him. He found that, for all their sending cheese to New York, they were just breaking even. He checked over the results of several new kinds of manure he had tried and sent unfavorable reports about all of them to the *New England Farmer,* the forum where the thousands of experimenters from all over the nation exchanged views on these matters. Having thought as far as he could about Dandy and settled his own mind, on Wednesday evening he went to bed early, taking the current *Tribune* and a lot of back numbers, and kept his thoughts off the subject by re-reading the places he had marked referring to the unperfected and dangerous stationary steam engine. They all seemed agreed that what they needed was some new kind of boiler. In Ike's restless dreams, exploding engines and Dandies pawing Starks were all mixed up together.

The next morning, Thursday, after breakfast, Ike harnessed Pol to the wagon and loaded a dozen cheeses for market. Before going he found Ma and Pa alone and asked them straight if they wanted him to buy Dandy back. The Squire merely put his hand on his shoulder and said, "Not unless you think best." Ma gave him a nice kiss, but she didn't say anything. Ike clattered off in the wagon so mad he could have cried, then stiffened up in a mood of defiance as he crossed the Four Corners. Presently, the daily rain and sleet began, and the rest of the way in Ike sat hunched over on the seat, thinking with disgust how they were all slaving to make ends meet at the homestead while Grabbot and Gadston and such were coining money out of their mills. As he passed Judge Longcoat's the Dane bitch bellowed at him as usual, and he wished she was loose so he could come her one with the whip.

The first thing he wanted to do in town was to see Dandy. So after he had run his wagon in amongst the hundred and more round the islands in the center of the Mall, unharnessed Pol and tied her to a hitching-post, he postponed business and walked down to the Liberty, first filling a pocket of his greatcoat with sugar. Pru waved to him from the upstairs parlor window, but he merely touched his cap, walked through the covered drive into the yard, and didn't see her all that day.

He found Henry Hawks leaning against the stable door-post whittling. "Mornin', Master Ike. Come fer yer gray?" "How is he?" "Ain't feedin' proper. They ain't grass enough up yonder t' give him a day's breakfast, even 'f he would eat it, which he won't. I got Gam t' let me fetch up some hay and spread it in the old barn, but he wouldn't go nowise nigh it and the other hosses et it. He's lookin' peakéd." "Gam tried to catch him yet?" Ike asked. "Don't know rightly. He went up yesterday and come back with the other two hosses, leavin' the gray up thar by himself. No place fer him this weather, with summer comin' no nigher a spell yet. Figger he misses ye."

Ike went into the tap-room and managed to talk in friendly fashion with Gam. "I can't help still feeling sort of personal about Dandy," he said. "If ye'll let me fetch him into the stable and ask Henry to feed him particular, I'll pay for the extra forage." "Still cal'late he's sort o' yourn, do ye?" asked Gam in his most artificially genial vein. "Likely always will," replied Ike. "Don't blame me, do ye?" "Go fetch him in if ye're o' mind to," said Gam with a leer.

Ike heard Dandy cough as he climbed the bars of the lot, but a moment later he came trotting to him whinnying and with his tail up. As he fed him handfuls of sugar and rubbed his ears, Ike looked him over. He was thin and his nostrils were a little snotty, but Ike figured he'd come round in the box stall Henry had agreed to bed down for him. He danced in his old way all the time Ike was putting the halter on him and letting them out the bars. Instead of leading him down as he had planned, Ike vaulted impulsively on his back and rode him at a run bare-back down the State Road, patting him and talking to him all the time. Dandy's breathing began to rasp, but Ike didn't care if Gam found out about his wind now. The sooner the better. He sidled at the entrance to the Liberty but went in easily to Ike's clucking.

As Ike led him into the box stall he noticed the two-inch oak planks of walls and door, and thought they might last a spell. When he was currying him a lump rose in his throat and he kept murmuring, " 'Twon't be for long, old feller—'twon't be for long, old feller," while Dandy kept rolling his eyes back at him as if asking what was expected of him next. When Ike closed the door and put up the bar Dandy suddenly squealed and reared like a dog, striking at the door with great splintering sounds. Ike talked to him through the bars and rubbed his nose till he was quiet. Then he walked round behind, and hayed, grained and watered him through the slot, Dandy watching him and trembling like a pople in a wind. The moment Ike left the stable the screaming and thumping began again. Henry Hawks closed the stable doors, so they were only faintly audible in the tavern.

The ordeal was too much for Ike and he walked straight up to Gam Stark who was sitting on his stool behind the high desk in his office. Ike's face was flushed and boyish and he spoke rapidly and on impulse. "Gam Stark, I've to tell ye that I trimmed ye in selling ye Dandy. I told ye before we started swoppin' he was wind-broke and he is, bad, got to wheezing now just with the little run down from the lot. I'm telling ye the truth, and if ye doubt me we'll harness him right now and I'll take ye out on the road and show ye. He ain't worth a penny to you or to anybody, except to look at in a stall or out in the lot. But my family's uncommon attached to him, and me more'n the rest. I'll give ye five hundred cash back for him, and that's five hundred more'n ye'll ever get from anybody else. Ye don't need to worry about what folks 'll say. I'll give out that I gave ye back your thousand, and paid ye cash for Solon's note and the chestnut."

Stark merely looked at Ike's cravat with a sneer in one corner of his mouth, his head sometimes vibrating in little nods in simulation of a wise chuckle. Wind-broke or no wind-broke, money or no money, he wasn't going to let the Lathrops get that horse back. He'd put them in their place and he'd keep them there.

Ike grew angry and his blue eyes darkened. "Ye're making a danged big mistake, Gam Stark, and don't forget I told ye. And don't figger ye can get this present of five hundred any time ye're o' mind to. I'll leave the offer open till a week from tomorrow, the day after Thanksgiving. That's two weeks from the sale last Friday. I'll ride in then to see if ye hain't settled to accept it. After that I ain't promising what I'll give ye for the horse, ain't promising I'll give ye anything for him. And in the meantime, get one thing straight—if I hear of your so much as laying a whip on that animal, let alone a club or a twitch or an iron, I'll come in and paste ye into mincemeat if I go to jail for it." And Ike thumped the desk-top with his fist so hard he cracked it, and walked out the front door, slamming it, leaving Gam looking at first a little awed, then leaning forward on his desk with a look that became fiendish in its cruelty and cunning.

Ike's truculent mood was not dissipated by his experience at market. The buyer from New York who came round every month or so and who had written Ike he expected to be there today, had not appeared. Instead, Ike found a letter from him at the Post Office, saying that for the time being they were buying cheese in bigger lots from Ohio. This put the finishing touch on Ike's recent study of the condition of the homestead. From now on, if the Lathrops were to make ends meet, they must get cash income from some source not yet tried, either some new use of the land or some enterprise in the village. Ike disposed of his cheeses to the local stores at two cents a pound less than he had been getting from down-state for a year.

He had in mind to have a talk with Banker Howell Sherwood some time today, but when he went into the bank to deposit the proceeds from the cheeses, the great little man wasn't there. Having made his deposit with Philip the red-headed and red-waistcoated clerk, he came out on the footpath and looked at his watch. It was almost noon, time to go back to the cart and eat the half-dozen mutton sandwiches, the quart of milk, the quarter of cake and the pickles Ma had put up for his dinner. He remembered that he hadn't bought Ben anything for months, and was starting into Staunton's book-store, next door to the bank, when a loud tenor, "Hi, thar, Ike Lathrop!" echoed through the noon crowd from the direction of Wheeler Corner. It was Bub Tanofly, and Ike turned and waited, recollecting the insult about not having his diapers off and making no move to go and meet him.

Bub came running up, characteristically dressed to kill but hatless and coatless in spite of the drizzly day. "So here ye be again, ye god danged country sharper," he bawled. "Figgerin' t' trim the village folks some more, be ye?" "Yep, here I be," said Ike quietly, his eyes darkening.

"Say," Bub beamed with a patronizing smile, "they tell me ye swopped the big gray with Stark last week fer a thousand 'n a skinny chestnut rat 'n a useless note. Say, what's wrong with yer ears? Didn't ye hear me a-warmin' up t' a swop when ye was pokin' down street that mornin'? I'd a' give ye a thousand 'n a half cash, same's I offered before. What's the matter, farmer boy? Ain't my money good as Stark's?" "Had my reasons," said Ike.

"Had yer reasons, did ye? Haw! Haw! Haw!" roared Bub. "And what were yer reasons that Stark should have a hoss 'stead o' me, 'n fer less money?" "None o' yer business," said Ike. "Say," sneered Bub, "grow up and talk sense. Ye ain't swoppin' hosses now with no ignorant louts back in the hills. Ye're talkin' t' a business man that's got some brains in his head. Why don't ye wake up an' git yer diapers off like——"

"Look here," snapped Ike, squaring off. "Ye'll apologize for that or ye're in for a thrashing right now." Bub looked up at the bigger youth with no fear, but a widening smile of admiration. "Well," said Ike, "are ye apologizin' or ain't ye?" "Sure grit, I apologize, Ike, m' boy," said Bub. "I guess if I didn't like ye I wouldn't pester ye. Will ye forgive me?" Ike had to look away and kick the mud to calm down. Then they shook hands, and Ike knew he had a real friend—a friend, by God, who wouldn't judge him harshly for the sale of Dandy!

CHAPTER XII

B U B took Ike home for dinner with his pretty wife Patience in their big red and white monstrosity on the upper corner of the South Mall. Afterwards, when they were walking down-street together, Ike told Bub the truth about Dandy. When they parted in front of the bank, Ike felt suddenly shy at the prospect of interviewing Howell Sherwood. He recollected that he was to buy a book for Ben and stepped into the bookstore of Master Henry Clay Staunton, whose pa was Byzantium's leading statesman and the lifelong friend of the great Kentuckian for whom he had named his son. After conference with the slightly effeminate mentor of local literary taste, Ike bought Ben a book called *Omoo,* by one Melville. Emerging with the book in his pocket, he hesitated in front of the bank, subconsciously seeking other excuses for delay. But he had none, so at last he set his jaw and slipped into the dim, kerosene-lighted temple of finance.

He was at first relieved, then a little put out, that none of the four personages in the bank even saw him come in. Philip the clerk was as usual bent over his tall desk under the kerosene lamp. Master Sherwood sat sideways at his desk exactly where Ike had last seen him the Friday before, his classical features and fine swirl of dark gray hair—as imperturbable as if cast in iron—silhouetted against one of the rear windows. As then, he was in conference with two men, and as then the one in the center was old Horace Gadston, his silk hat tilted back from his forehead releasing a tangle of gray hair, his odd eye surveying vacancy off to his upper left, his right fixing the person with whom he was conversing, and his cigar undulating slowly as he chewed.

The third member of the group, however, was not Ostrum Applemore, but a black-haired young man little older than Ike himself, who seemed dimly familiar. Facing Master Sherwood, his face was also in profile, the head large and the features delicate and mobile even in that dim light, and he frequently ran his slim hand nervously through his dishevelled bush of black hair. He had on a greatcoat that had once been sparky, but it was now worn and wrinkled, and his dirty white stock was askew. Ike sat down

84

in one of the waiting chairs, all the time looking curiously at this young man. All of a sudden the number "29" came into his mind. Then he remembered. This was the feller he had seen last Friday when he was on the bridge at the Middle Falls thinking about Dandy. Just as he turned back from looking at the falls he had seen him go into that little building next to Gadston's foundry, the little building that looked like a blacksmith shop and had its number on Mill Street, "29," painted in white over the double doors. Ike was curious about the young stranger, wondered what he was up to and how long he had been in town without his meeting him.

Being no more than a rod and a half from the conferees, Ike did not scruple to listen to their talk. "Young feller!" Gadston was saying, "ye're a smart young un and ye can have a situation in the shop whenever ye ask fer it. All I got to say is, I need the property and I'll give six hundred fer it, which is a fair price and ye'd best take it, fer as fer's I kin jedge ye're bound to lose it purty soon anyhow, one way or t'other."

"For my part," said Master Sherwood in his rich baritone, "I confess I am embarrassed through being in a dual position. As a banker whose interest is in arrears and whose mortgage is already too large, I ought to compel you, on threat of foreclosure, to accept this fair offer. On the other hand, as your adviser and your father's friend, it is my duty to see that you exhaust every possibility before giving up your venture. I feel that if it is possible we should consult your father before taking any step in the matter."

"But you know as well as I do," said the young man, running his fingers through his hair, "that Pa won't give me another penny. He bought me the property on the understanding that you would give a mortgage to purchase the equipment. That was the end as far as he was concerned. He approved of the thing even less than you did. Why, he'll even be glad that I have failed and that he can compel me to come back to New York and start over in his bank where my future is assured. Feeling as he does, he has helped me handsomely and I am grateful to him. To ask him for more would be both ungrateful and useless. Oh, don't you see," and he began to run his hands through his hair with excited regularity, "I need only a little more money and I'm bound to succeed? Six months isn't a fair trial, especially when everything has cost double what it was quoted. There are only four other people in the country working to improve steam engines, and my patents are far better than theirs. With three hundred dollars and living expenses for another six months I will build an engine that will revolutionize industry and make this town famous the world over." Ike's stomach jumped and he stiffened in his chair.

" 'Death warrants,' they call 'em in New York," growled Gadston. "They

tell me there's a factory somewhere in Mass'chusetts's been at .'em fer better'n thirty year an' they've killed two dozen men in their own shop, let
alone anybody bein' fool enough to buy one and commit suicide all by
himself."

"Don't you see," plead the young man, "their trouble is in trying to use
the old type of boiler under high pressure? I have tested my water-tube
boiler to eighty pounds, and all that I shall recommend it for is forty." Ike
wanted to cheer for him. "Humph," interposed Gadston. "And now," continued the young engineer, "I have just finished my model with full diameter tubes and I will give you a demonstration any day over in my place.
Now all I've to do is to build a full-sized engine and, doing all the work
myself, it couldn't cost more than three hundred dollars. Why, Master Gadston, right in your foundry I could do the heavier turning and casting I
haven't the facilities for in my shop. You'd charge me no more than a hundred dollars and make a good profit at that. And then—" "And then where'd
ye be?" asked Gadston. "Who'd buy yer contraption, once ye had it?"

"Why, any saw mill, any grist mill, any spinning mill would buy it. It's
cheaper to install than a water wheel and you can set it up anywhere—
you're not bound to a few places where you can find water-power. I tell you
the stationary steam engine holds the secret of the whole future of industry
in this country and in the world." "Ye mean business is goin' to blow up
again one o' these days? Mebbe ye're right," said Gadston, chuckling. The
young inventor slapped the desk in disgust.

"No, Alexander," said Sherwood in a serious and kindly tone. "As a
banker with a duty to his depositors, I think it's a bad risk, and as an individual I make it a rule never to commit myself to anything I would not
support as a banker. Personally, I hope you can raise the money and that
you will make a great success. I have been wondering whether the three of
us could not come to some informal agreement to last, say, two months.
During that period I would neither foreclose nor press you for the interest
due on the mortgage. Master Gadston would hold his offer open. You,
Alexander, would give him an option to purchase for six hundred dollars
at the end of the period, unless in the meantime you had fully carried out
your obligations to me and had raised the further three hundred dollars you
say you need to proceed. Is that reasonable, Master Gadston?"

"Wal," said the industrialist, "I want to see the young feller have a chance,
though I'm itchin' to git goin' enlargin' the shop and there's another piece
downstream I guess I could buy. Suppose I add another condition that if
ye don't make out ye'll sell me the patent on the boiler ye speak of at a fair
price, with Howell here fer referee if we can't agree on a figger. Though I

don't give yer patent much value, I oughtta git at least a long chance at some return fer delayin' my plans." "That's a hard condition, Master Gadston," said the young man, "to give an option on a patent I have been working on since I was a boy. I would certainly refuse it unless Master Sherwood made it a condition of his deferring foreclosure for two months."

"I agree," said the banker, "this is a hard condition. If your patent is to be at stake I would incline to reduce my demand on you to the minimum that is consonant with the security of my depositors. Let us say that instead of being bound to settle all your indebtedness at the end of two months you will be required only to pay the interest to the then date and to reduce the mortgage from four hundred to two hundred dollars."

"You mean," the young man replied, "that if I can raise two hundred and twelve dollars in two months you will let the balance of the mortgage stand and will give me further time to raise the additional three hundred dollars I need to build the engine?" "I'll give you an additional six months, at least." "Oh, thank you, Master Sherwood," said Alexander, jumping up and seizing the banker's hand. "I'll raise the money, no fear—and perhaps if I can show Master Gadston my model he'll be the one to help me out. We might form some kind of a company, eh—?" "D'ye think we'd best put this little agreement in writing?" interrupted Gadston. "I shall be glad to see to that, if you will both drop by just before supper," concluded Banker Sherwood.

As Ike listened to this conversation, the timidity with which he had entered the bank gave way to the hard, clear-thinking detachment that characterized him when he was trading. He now saw the three men rise and shake hands and the young Alexander take his leave, Gadston delaying to discuss something further with Sherwood. As the inventor approached with his long, energetic stride, swinging the skirts of his rumpled but finely cut greatcoat, Ike rose to meet him.

"Excuse me, could I speak to ye a minute, though I ain't had the pleasure of meeting ye? My name's Lathrop, Isaac Lathrop." The other smiled. "Is your father the gentleman they call Squire Lathrop—lives somewhere outside the village?" Ike nodded. "Yes, I've heard Master Sherwood speak of all of you, and I'm delighted to meet you. My name's Mathiesson, Alexander Mathiesson. I've been here six months, but I've stuck pretty close to business and have hardly met anybody."

They shook hands and walked forward to the front windows where they paused, looking out on the street. "What I wanted to say," said Ike, "was that I've made a sort of study of stationary engines myself—don't sure grit know much about 'em—just what I've read in the *New York Tribune*." "Yes, I know. Greeley believes in them," Mathiesson interrupted, then added, laughing, "If my experience is worth anything, they're pretty good things to keep away from."

Ike noticed how pale he was and wondered if he was getting enough to eat. "If ye don't mind," he said, "I'd like to ride over and see your steam engine, if it wouldn't be too much trouble." "Delighted, any time," said Mathiesson. "Where's your place?" asked Ike, though he knew already. "Number twenty-nine Mill Street, next to Gadston's foundry on the Camilla side." Ike looked out the window. He couldn't count on having any free cash till after the Dandy business was settled, might yet have to give back the whole thousand. "Hardly figger I'll get over today," he said slowly. "Maybe not for quite a spell yet—fact is, likely not till after Thanksgiving. But, say,—" Ike looked at him and their eyes met and held in a kind of easy mutuality—"I'd like to ask ye, since I know something about engines already, not to try over-hard to raise that money I overheard ye talking about until after, say, Monday following Thanksgiving. Likely it's asking plenty for a stranger, but I'd be glad to give ye a consideration for say, a two weeks' sort of option."

The young man flickered his eyes, then looked at Ike again, and laughed nervously. "Well, if you heard the talk I guess you know there isn't much of an option necessary." "I mean what I say," persisted Ike. "All right," said the other. "I'll tell you. Let's not make it one of those awful, legal options, but I'll just promise to do nothing about it until after you've come over to the shop. How's that? No consideration necessary, and you don't need to worry about the rush of people anxious to lose money on my ideas. Only, do please come soon—a week from next Monday, you say?—I mustn't delay about this business, you know—it means everything to me." "No fear," said Ike. "I'll be there."

"By the way," Ike resumed after a short silence, "if you hain't other plans, Pa'd be mighty pleased if you'd drive out for flip Thanksgiving Day after church. Neighbors make it a kind of habit to drop in on us then, that being a time when a lot of folks come back to the Hollow Church that's the oldest in the township. Fact is, it's likely your friend Master Sherwood will drive out. I'll ask him to fetch ye, eh? My brother John'll be back from Yale and ye might enjoy talking to him." "Indeed I would," was the reply, "for I went to Yale myself not long ago. I am most grateful to you for the invitation." Over Alexander Mathiesson's shoulder Ike saw old Gadston and Howell Sherwood walking forward from the rear of the bank, and through the window he saw Ostrum Applemore coming in with Theophilus Bostwick, the editor of Applemore's *Blackwater Democratic Union.*

"Afternoon, gentlemen," said Applemore, chuckling with senatorial joviality as the older men saluted each other. "We've had great news for Byzantium and bad news for Howell here. Theophilus has decided to try a new press for the *Union,* finest press in the world—what d'ye call it, Theophilus?" "Napier," said the editor with a bow. "Don't need it more 'n a cat needs two tails," continued the statesman, "and can't pay for it either. So we've settled that poor old Howell's to perform the high public service of coming down for—how much is it, Theophilus?—three thousand dollars, much as the finest house in Byzantium." "Excuse me," said Alexander Mathiesson, stepping up to the older men, "but isn't the Napier a power press?" "Believe it is—ain't that so, Theophilus? We're figgerin' to move the whole shebang into a corner of somebody's factory on the River, or maybe we'll build a place next to some factory or other where we can borrow a little water-power." Mathiesson glanced round at Ike, and their eyes understood each other.

Master Sherwood left the main group to come over to Ike, who was now alone. "Good afternoon, Isaac," he said heartily as they shook hands. "Have you been waiting long? I failed to see you until you got up to speak to Alexander." "Hope you'll bring him out to flip on Thanksgiving, Master Sherwood," said Ike. "Indeed, I shall be delighted," said the banker, looking at Ike with a smile wrinkling around the corners of his eyes. "And now, come. Let us go back and visit a little while, for I haven't seen you in months, except once when you were sitting in the mud."

Ike glowed with importance as he followed the broadcloth back of the banker to his desk at the rear and obeyed his wave to sit down where Mathiesson had sat before. "I shan't take a moment, Howell Sherwood," he said. Then, "Likely I'd best come back another time when ye ain't quite so occupied." "Not at all," said Master Sherwood with the kindly wrinkles appearing round the corners of his eyes, and composed himself in an easy, attentive attitude.

"Well, sir," said Ike, "fact is—that is, I've been sort of thinking about what I'm to do with myself, and I sort of thought I'd like to talk over with you—that is—about the possibilities of my—maybe—working for you in the bank—sort of learning the business—kind of apprentice, or whatever ye call it in a bank." And he dropped his eyes in confusion and relief at having got out the momentous declaration.

"Ah, that is a subject which interests me very much," said Howell Sherwood with enthusiasm. "Your father has told me of your enterprise and your sound judgment in helping him run the farm for the last two years, and I suspect that your innovation in making cheese for commercial purposes is going to have its effect on the country generally. We indeed have great hopes for you, and if ever it seems best that you should make your start in the banking business, I can assure you that I will make every effort to find you a good position, here or elsewhere. I am delighted that you have mentioned the matter of your own volition. I shall certainly keep you in mind, though of course we can't do much in the matter until you are through college, and that will be three or four years off."

"But suppose I don't go to college?" said Ike, looking at Master Sherwood challengingly out of his big blue eyes. "I think your father is planning to send you," replied the banker, looking away and fingering the sandbox on his desk. "But suppose he changes his mind?" "If he does, then what I have just said still holds good—provided always that we have his complete consent. You realize, of course, that it's a serious matter with him. I doubt if he will spare you from the farm for a while, unless it is to send you to college. But—if he does change his mind—you may count on me. And—in the meantime—I hope you will not continue to neglect me as you have these recent months. You must always stop by when you are in the village, either here or at my house. Alexander Mathiesson lives with me, you know. You and he should be acquainted," this last with a repetition of the smile in the corners of the eyes.

"Thank you, Howell Sherwood," said Ike, rising. "Thank ye more than I figger I could ever make ye understand." They shook hands and Ike walked rapidly out of the bank, saluting Messrs. Gadston, Applemore, Bostwick and Mathiesson as he passed, while Howell Sherwood—who had no son—still stood at his desk, watching him with a look of tenderness.

Ike walked over to the market where Pol was tied, swinging his coonskin cap in his hand, unconscious of the rain, forgetful of Dandy, hardly conscious of where he was. If his pa could at that moment have looked into his favorite son's soul he must have admitted that the requirements of his individualistic philosophy were fulfilled that this step Ike was proposing to take was for him right, conformable to his own peculiar nature, to the demands of his conscience—or whatever it was in Ike that was the equivalent of conscience.

CHAPTER XIII

DURING the next few days the weather, Cousin Alvina's cold, and Ike's relations with the family all improved. Although he still had misgivings on the score that his pa disapproved of the sale of Dandy, he felt so secure now in the sympathy of Howell Sherwood and the prospect of a position in his bank that he lost his recent sense of isolation and resentment of the family's silence and was his normal, sympathetic, cheerful self. As for the Squire, he was now certain that, one way or another, Isaac had worked out his problem to a solution that was sincere and, therefore, best for him. With his own philosophy of individual moral standards, that was all he could ask of his almost mature son.

Ike decided to say nothing to his pa of his talk with Master Sherwood till after the trouble about Dandy was out of the way and the Thanksgiving season was over. The only one he talked to was Aggie, who merely smiled at the whole business and said, "Well, Scamp, I guess none of it will seem very important to you in a few years when you've got the main things of life settled." At this, Ike had a moment of something like insight which he could not have put into words. He looked at his big sister's eyes, that were identical with his own, and said, "Likely, Ag."

The one person in the house who seemed to retain a grudge against him was Tavie. As his spirits rose, hers seemed to go down, and if she was alone in a room when Ike came in she actually skedaddled from him. Once he cornered her and asked good-naturedly what the matter was—did she figger he'd taken another swig at chore time? But she gave him a look at once so angry and so appealing that Ike was taken aback and wanted to apologize for something. But for what? Something he had done had upset her more than just taking a drink, or even selling Dandy. Dandy was nothing to Tavie. Was it kissing her? But she hadn't minded at the time. Women were funny.

On Saturday the weather turned clear and cold. It was general baking day, the oven giving forth batch after batch of cookies and apple and mince pies that filled the house with their reek of cinnamon, lemon, clove, nutmeg and brandy. Master Lane and Ike slaughtered a beef, a mutton and a hog, dressed them and added them to the three slabs of jerked beef, the dozen smoked hams, the half dozen mutton hams already hanging in the buttery. Homer Hislip went up on Titus Mountain and got two rabbits and a buck, still-hunting—Ike figgered Aggie'd never hear the end of it. On Sunday, in a light snow, they all walked to church, including Cousin Alvina. She held an informal reception in the vestibule afterward and delighted everyone, catching every name correctly and applying it to the wrong person.

The snow was all gone by dinner time, but before supper it set in again in earnest. At ten o'clock, before the family retired, the Squire opened the kitchen door. There was nearly two inches on the doorsill and the falling flakes drifted down into the candle-light in the easy, confident, goose-feather way of winter. That gave everybody an excuse to stay up longer and have a nip of brandy. It was a good start for Thanksgiving week. Might mean sleighing.

On Monday morning John was to arrive, and Ike got up at four to meet the coach as he had done for the others. Although Aggie wanted to get his breakfast, Tavie had insisted, a little defiantly, that it was her duty and she would do it, though it involved walking up from the Samsons' in the dark and the snow. She came in while Ike was upstairs dressing, and was violently busy when he appeared. He was in the highest possible spirits at the prospect of John's return and caught her by the shoulders, wanting to kiss her, but she jerked away. "What's up, Tave?" he asked in real confusion. "Are ye so mad because I sold Dandy? Or is it what I did the other morning?" Tavie gave him another piece of salt pork and a swift look of scorn.

At half-past five Ike set out for the Falls in the dark, squeaking in the cart through the now six inches of snow, the fall having begun to lessen. As usual when he was excited, he stood up and kept Pol at a trot, slapping her with the reins. The big Lollapaloosa, as he called John, was coming, and that would put an end to all this nonsense about Dandy. He and John were closer to each other than to anybody else in the world. The Lollapaloosa could commit rape, murder and arson, and Ike wouldn't care a dang. Naturally, he assumed John would feel the same about him and the sale of Dandy —even if he disapproved of it. They both would say what they thought, and that would be the end of it. Things would be easy again.

By the time Ike passed the toll gate at the Center, it had stopped snowing and was near daylight. He bethought him of divers commissions he had to invite folks out for grog on Thanksgiving, among them Judge Longcoat, who was his ma's distant cousin, though he had nothing in common with her but a fatted version of the McLeod hawk beak. As he turned up the drive of the Judge's house at the top of the big hill, the Great Dane bitch burst into bloodthirsty roars from the front of the barn, and when he went up and tapped on the kitchen door, plunged the length of her chain and fell back as it snubbed her in mid-air.

The kitchen door opened sedately and the monstrous judge filled the opening, his flushed, apoplectic head and expanding rolls of chin sitting like a vast red bee-hive on the mountainous mass of his white night-shirt. Seeing Ike, his fat-enclosed eyes opened wide and blue and he puffed a tremendous exhalation through lightly closed lips. "Good morning, my son, and welcome," he roared, extending his pumpkin of a hand which Ike half enclosed with his own big one. "Come in, come in," continued the Judge, stepping back against the partition, which trembled, and bending forward minutely from the thighs.

"Forgive me, Cousin Ezry," said Ike, "but I can't stop just now. I'm on my way to the Falls to meet John. Stopped to say good morning, and Pa and Ma specially hope you will honor us at flip Thanksgiving noon. Our cousins, Joel and Alvina, from Connecticut are visiting us, you know."

The Judge's eyes opened again till the whites bulged, and he planted his hands firmly on the sides of his great paunch before him. "Thank the Squire very much," he bellowed. "It happens that His Honor Justice Twiggin of Rome is to honor me for the season. May I assume it proper that he accompany me on this enjoyable occasion?" "Indeed, Pa would be delighted, sir." "We shall be honored, I am sure, greatly honored," said the Judge with another attempt at a bow. "And be so good as to convey our compliments to the cousins from Connecticut, Jonah and Albina, persons of great parts, I have no doubt, whom it will be a signal honor to meet."

As Ike bade Cousin Ezry good morning and backed away, the Dane bitch started roaring. The Judge's eyes swelled and he bellowed, "Peace, Lucille." Lucille roared again, and again the Judge bellowed, "Peace." So they alternated, "Wow"—"Peace"—"Wow"—"Peace," while Ike untied Pol from the hitching-post, got in and drove down the dip to the pike. He was glad to have this over. The Judge was the ex-law partner of Ostrum Applemore, his creature on the Federal bench, and the bitter enemy of Solon Samson, who, five years before, had publicly despaired of an administration that could make such an appointment.

As Ike walked Pol through the covered drive of the Liberty, his excitement at the prospect of seeing John was suddenly eclipsed by a pang of sadness and terror on Dandy's account. Without a word he stopped Pol in the shed, stepped down in the mud, hitched her, and started across the snowy yard as quietly as if Dandy were a child sleeping yonder in the stable whom he mustn't wake.

But it was no use. Like a pail of ice water in his face, Dandy started to scream and thump, and Ike hurried toward the tap-room like a thief. Glancing round, he saw Henry Hawks come out of the stable door with a lantern which he blew out, then unhook the big doors and close them. As Ike reached the tap-room door, Gamaliel Stark stepped out in obvious irritation and summoned old Henry to him. "Stop that critter squealin'," he commanded. Ike grew tense. "Can't do it, Gam," replied Henry, taking aim and spitting on a chip floating in a pool of mud water. "Ye heered what I said?" continued Stark in a threatening tone. "Yep, I heered ye," said Henry. "He's more'n I can handle." "I could stop him," said Ike ineffectually, "but it'd only be worse when I left him." "Don't trouble yerself," said Stark with his arrogant glance that faded quickly into his servile smirk. "We'll get the best o' him." With a glare at Henry Hawks he turned back into the inn. Ike followed him, closing the door to keep out the sound.

He was so unnerved that he failed to return greetings in the crowded tap-room, but walked over to the fireplace and stood staring up at the mantel clock as if he didn't know how to read it. The stage was due in ten minutes and he prayed it would be on time. For the Thanksgiving traffic they ran a special through coach ahead of the regular, and John would certainly be on the special. When Ike turned from the clock to face the room he met the half-accusing smile of a man sitting alone at a table by the window. It was the Federal Marshal who had bid on Dandy and as good as said he was up here after people in the Underground Railroad. He had finished his breakfast and had on his broad-brimmed felt hat and his long, faded blue cape. "Wage he can hear Dandy there by the window," thought Ike, then dropped his eyes and walked away.

In the ladies' parlor, he saw Pru and she smiled invitingly at him. For the first time in his life he voluntarily walked in to see her, one subconscious reason being that the ladies' parlor was farther from the stable and another that he was really glad to see her—she was someone who was indirectly involved in the sale of Dandy and who would not criticize him for it. It was not until they greeted each other with real warmth and had exchanged a little banter that Ike realized that of course her reason for being there was to meet John. Then his features hardened a little and John began to edge Dandy out of his mind. "Let's go upstairs till the horn," said Pru, and Ike followed her, now with reluctance.

Mistress Stark was not in her parlor, and the moment they entered Pru turned round and backed off, bending forward and clapping her hands to-

gether with delight. "Oh, Ike," she said, "I do wish you had sat down in the
mud again so I'd truly have an excuse to tidy you up as I did last time."
"Let's pretend," said Ike, with his big easy smile, for her beauty was warming him at the same time that he was now hating her normally for stringing
John along when she didn't give a dang for him. "But you know," said Pru,
shaking a warning finger at him and taking the whisk from the chimney
closet, "this time it will really be a spanking for having been here last Thursday and never coming near me." "Had business with your pa," said Ike a
little sourly, and at that moment they heard the coach horn not far out on
the State Road.

Immediately Pru, Dandy and everything left Ike's mind in favor of his
brother, and he started for the stairs so thoughtlessly that he collided with
Pru in the doorway and drew back with a laughing apology and inward
resentment that she was going down to make a show of herself before John.
As if guessing his feelings, Pru suddenly drew back and looked up at him
seriously. "You know, last time I begged you to tell me how to behave
toward John. Now I beg you to tell me straight—would you rather I stayed
up here like a lady?" "Yes," said Ike quite simply. "All right," said Pru, giving him an arch, half-triumphant smile. "Tell John I'm here." "Keerect,"
said Ike, and he went down the stairs feeling a strange and momentary
sense of comfort and authority, exactly as he had felt after the similar conversation at the arrival of the coach with his other relations ten days ago.

Once Ike was downstairs, the effect of Pru vanished in exultation at the
prospect of John's arrival, and as he ran through the tap-room and pushed
with the crowd through the door into the yard, he could feel his heart beating like mad. Dandy was not screaming, but he wouldn't have known it if
he had been. There was an eternal suspense of half a minute. Then out on
the State Road the coach horn sent three short, melodious blasts of arrival
echoing away across the village. A pounding of heavy-shod feet and the
loud rasp of a brake rolled rapidly nearer. With a tremendous jangling of
equipage and rustling of the festive cornstalks with which it was adorned
for the season, the big four-horse, special coach swung into the wide lane
behind the Baptist Church and down the grade into the yard. On the box
beside the driver, spreading both arms and waving his gray silk hat in general greeting, sat John Lathrop, Jr., till, discovering Ike, he stood up and
shouted, "Hi, Scamp," then, as the driver, also standing, leaned back on
the reins whoaing the lathered horses and Henry Hawks ran to the heads
of the leaders, he jumped clean over the wheel down into the snowy mud,
where Ike fairly caught him. For a moment the two brothers stood embraced, with tears in the eyes of each, while beside them the coach still oscil-

lated in its straps and the footman came down from his high rumble seat, opened the door, and released the general bustle that ensued.

"Hi, Lollapaloosa," said Ike almost inaudibly through his joy, looking up into the eyes of his almost six-foot-three brother who now stood back to survey him, still holding him by the shoulders in his big, gloved hands. Then, with their arms around each other's shoulders, they started for the inn. Above the clatter and shouts of arrival they heard a horse's scream from the stable. "What horse is that?" asked John. "Come on in," said Ike.

In the tap-room, as everywhere he went, young John Lathrop was a dominating figure, in stature, in feature and in force. Everybody in the crowd looked at him now and all the local men greeted him with unfeigned deference. From the ladies' parlor, which the female passengers were now entering by the side door, numerous glances fell on him, though they instantly shifted and rested a longer moment on the shorter and stockier giant who walked behind him with the coonskin cap stuck over his left ear. Having been accustomed to the public gaze from childhood, and not being of an introspective turn, John was beautifully unaware of drawing special attention to himself, here or anywhere. Beaming on everybody the universally inclusive, seemingly omniscient, Lathrop smile, he pushed through the crowd while Ike walked close behind him, his hands on his big brother's sides and tickling him through his greatcoat so that John frequently giggled in the face of someone he was greeting or said, "Quit it, drat you," into a stranger's ear, or lunged back with his elbows, unbalancing his tall, shiny gray hat that moved majestically close to the ceiling beams, all to Ike's chuckling delight as well as his own. At length they reached the table in the far corner where Grabbot had sat in the bargaining for Dandy ten days before. John swung off his long tan coat with its cape, and revealed an immaculate gray tailored suit, a tan and pink striped waistcoat and a tan bow tie round a lofty "swaller choker" that would have put even Howell Sherwood to shame.

But the brothers had no eyes now for each other's apparel. John hung his coat and hat on a peg and sat down opposite Ike, who still wore his coonskin. One of the extra bar-maids hired for the season had taken her station in this corner of the room and kept glancing at John till she caught his eye. "How do you do, John Lathrop?" she said shyly. "Oh, hello, Mathilda," said John, jumping up and bending over her hand. "How have you been since we graduated? Can you spell as well as ever?" "Not much chance to spell nowadays," said Mathilda, dropping her gray-blue eyes. "Pa lost the farm, ye know. He's workin' for Master Applemore, and I'm second barmaid for now at the Liberty. Seems like old times, don't it? I guess you boys are old enough to drink and—well, here I am servin' ye." "I'm all fired sorry to hear you've lost the farm, Mattie," said John, "but one thing's sure, you're prettier than ever." "Thank you, John," she said, dropping her eyes again. "To be sure, the village is fun—sometimes. Well," looking up with an artificial smile, "can I bring ye anything?" "I'll have a light grog," said John, sitting down again, "though I shouldn't before breakfast." "Me, too," said Ike, winking at John on this the occasion of their first public drink together.

The tragedy of Mattie Spencer evaporated in the pleasure of the brothers at being reunited. They sat facing each other, their elbows on the table, smiling identical smiles into each other's not quite identical eyes, content to say nothing. "Well, Scamp?" said John at length. "Well, 'Paloosa?" retorted Ike, and they beamed again in long silence, as if this exchange were some tremendous joke.

Facially, their resemblance stopped with the wide brow, the large blue eyes—John's slightly darker, the rosy complexion. John's hair was darker than Ike's, and where Ike's nose was long and straight and fleshy, John's was arched and shorter and delicately modelled around the nostrils. Both of their mouths were large, but where Ike's lips were full and loose, John's were relatively thin and capable of a steel-like compression. Where Ike's chin was long and wide and his cheeks and jowls fat, John's jaw-line contracted to a narrowly rounded, shallower chin, while his cheeks were flat, and all the lower lines and planes of his face sharp and severe. Physically, Ike was a close replica of the Squire, John a masculine version of their ma. One observer, watching the brothers, might have called John's a strong face and Ike's a weak one. Another would have called John's an active face and Ike's a contemplative face. Still another would have seen Ike's as a face bespeaking tolerant, humane understanding, and John's as the face of a devotee and a fanatic.

Mattie Spencer brought the tumblers of grog and they clicked them with the apparent casualness of hardened drinkers, lifted them solemnly, exploded together at their own pompousness, and set the glasses back on the table. "Does Pa know you take a swig outside?" whispered Ike. "Yep," whispered John. "How about you?" "Well, the other day he told me offhand to take the flask in for the relations on the coach and, it being chilly and he not saying I shouldn't, I took a good swig. And Tavie, when I wasn't looking, stole the whole shebang out of my coat." "The little squirt," said John, airing his college slang. "The pernickety bobcat, says I," countered Ike, not to be outdone. "Well, here's to the broad highway to hell," said John, lifting his glass again, and they both took a sip with dignity, being much relieved when they glanced around and saw that nobody was observing them. "Tavie's a good girl," said John. "She's a silly little fool," said Ike, "trying to run the world and meddle in other people's affairs." He took a big swallow of his light grog.

"That reminds me," said John. "I wonder if Pru's upstairs." And he started to rise. "Hold your hosses," said Ike, feeling his drink and growing serious. "Sit down. I've to tell ye something." He dropped his eyes to his glass and rolled it between his thumb and fingers, then looked up. "I sold Dandy ten days back." Pause, while John's brow wrinkled and his eyes darkened. "Why did you do that? He's like our brother. "When ye see how things stand with Pa ye'll get the idea. Dandy was wind-broke, no use to anybody any more, not worth a red cent. I got a thousand for him from Gam Stark, beside a good chestnut and a two-hundred-dollar note of Solon Samson's." John scowled, his lips thinned, and he said slowly, with controlled emotion, "You mean you—cheated Stark—besides selling Dandy to a man with his reputation?" "Trimmin' is what they call it in hoss-swoppin'," said Ike, smiling uneasily. "I figger to get him back Friday, saving Solon's note, the chestnut and four or five hundred to boot." Ike dropped his eyes for a moment, then lifted them. The brothers looked at each other level, with strong trust and love, but there was something like horror round John's eyes as he said through tight lips, "You should not have done it, Ike."

And when John said that, something came over the brothers that each was powerless to prevent or explain. While they continued to look hard into each other's eyes, each felt the stir of something new in the depth of his being, something of ultimate pain only incidentally related to this question of Dandy, something very different from the old rages when they used to go at it with their fists until pa or their now dead older brother Tom appeared with a horse-whip, or ma stood beside them stamping her foot and ordering them both to bed. There was no anger now, rather something between wonder and fear. For a few seconds they remained so, looking into each other's eyes in intolerable and uncomprehending recognition of a thin curtain rising between them.

Then their youthful buoyancy triumphed. John put his hands behind his head, tilted back and said, "Well, let's forget it for now." "All keerect," said Ike a little hoarsely, and for the first time in his life he gave his brother an artificial smile. Against both their wills the spell of meeting was broken. "I wonder if Pru's upstairs," said John. "Yep," said Ike as they both rose. "Suppose I send Mattie up with some breakfast for ye." "All right," said John, "unless I come right down." He walked through the office to the front stairs. Ike summoned Mattie Spencer and told her to take John a plate with some of everything from the refreshment table.

John ran up the front stairs, stepped into the open parlor door, then froze as he saw Pru coming toward him, and for a moment the world went black. The next thing he 'knew he was holding both of her little hands, his head lifted and his eyes closed because he didn't dare look at her again.

Meanwhile Pru stood before her giant with head lowered in conventional modesty and genuine confusion. When their eyes finally met, John was pale and his smile was sickly with tender appeal, while Pru smiled back mechanically and patted his hands, hardly knowing what she was doing. At last she said weakly, "It's nice to see you, John." He managed to smile more normally, touched her soft, round cheek with his hand, and released her. She sat down a little awkwardly, and he did the same.

Immediately there was that excruciating tension between them which had been growing for the last two years, since the Starks had taken their daughter to the larger dances and had permitted a few favored youths to call at the tavern. On John's part, he was completely possessed by her beauty, possessed far beyond the possibility of any consideration of her actual qualities, while at the same time his code negated every sensual impulse, and put it utterly out of the question that he should make even the most formal articulate love to this girl of seventeen. On Pru's part, though she could not quite put out of mind her pa's warning that the Lathrops weren't as well off as they used to be, nevertheless, she was mindful of their fine qualities, particularly John's exquisite courtesy, his courage and idealism, the high scholastic standing he was making at Yale, the opinion of everybody but her pa that he was the coming young man and—a few putting him second to Ike—the catch of the town. Altogether, between the passionate love he must not express, and the flight from him which she was not yet ready to indulge, they had no mutuality at all.

So now Pru found herself plying him with obvious and polite questions, to all of which he responded with the utmost eagerness and seriousness. Yes, he was enjoying his last year at college, but he was all fired glad to get home—and to see her. Yes, he was a member of the honorary society of fifteen seniors, but he was under oath not to name or discuss it—not even with her. And how did she feel to be graduated from the Institute and out in the world? And he supposed there'd be no use asking her pa to let him take her to any dances there might be between now and Monday, when he'd have to leave—he got this special vacation, he said, only because he was leading his class and he'd have to make up for it by missing the winter vacation. Pru admitted that she was looking forward joyfully to a dance at the Hollow on Friday evening, but she shook her head gravely over the possibility of her pa's letting anybody take her to a dance alone. "Not till I'm eighteen," she said. "They're getting very strict in the village, you know. I'm to ride out in the Gadston's party, either a hay wagon or a sleigh." Pru dropped her eyes and John looked away. Nat Gadston, son of old Horace, was one of his rivals. The old man was making him work in the foundry two years before sending him to college.

Mattie Spencer brought up a plate of ham, beef, pies, miscellaneous pickles and a cup of coffee, which John devoured while Pru chattered the gossip of the town, feeling easier in a monologue than when they were talking together.

"Oh, I can hardly wait for the year to be over," said John as he put down his plate, "so I can come home and set out to make my mark." "I thought you were going to Divinity School." "No, I believe I can get enough of that by staying in New Haven during the winter and spring vacations. Ah, it seems hardly believable that next August I shall really be home for good!" "It does, indeed," said Pru, feeling a little frightened.

"Friday, then, if not sooner!" John exclaimed with a glad smile as he rose. "And at least you will dance the first set with me?" "I should love to," Pru replied, and gave him the tips of her fingers. He stumbled a little on the threshold as he backed out. Pru walked away to release him and he went downstairs slowly, glowing, the ruler of the world.

"Well, 'Paloosa, did ye swallow the canary?" laughed Ike, who was waiting in the office. John hit him softly in the chest, they scuffled a little, then stood at the window looking out along the Mall, John's arm around Ike's shoulder. "Oh, Scamp," he said, "it's great to get home. Every time it's better than before and worth the price of going away." "The Falls ain't exactly home, though," said Ike. "That's right," said John. "Why, there's old Pol out in front all ready for the prodigal son! I thought she'd be in the shed." "Figgered to save time while ye were upstairs," said Ike. "Got Henry Hawks to put in your trunk and fetch her out here." "I must say hello to old Henry," said John, starting back. "He ain't there," lied Ike. "Get your things and we'd best start. I've to invite a few folks out to flip Thanksgiving."

There was the remote scream of a horse from the stable which neither was sure the other heard. They exchanged a glance with that same uncomprehending pain in it. Then John got his greatcoat and hat and followed Ike out the front door. In the cart they went squeaking through the snowy mud down the Mall, while John held his hat high in greeting to Byzantium generally, and individually to everyone they passed.

CHAPTER XIV

JOHN'S reception at the homestead was not ceremonious, through the front door, but enthusiastic, with the family running together through the snow like chickens, from barn, sheep-cote, kitchen and summer kitchen. Everybody from the Squire down felt that John's arrival would ease the little tension that had arisen over the sale of Dandy, so he came not only as the beloved eldest son but as a peace-maker, the one who would help Ike to a solution of the problem that would be satisfactory to everybody.

During the general kissing and embracing, Tavie stood with a self-conscious smile on the outside of the little circle. When John spied her he did what she had foreseen. With forced enthusiasm he shouted, "Greetings, Tave," then paced up to her and gave her an ostentatious kiss on the cheek. Tavie and John were of an age, and their mutual moral slant and interest in Reform made them fundamentally congenial. But, their parents being the closest friends, they had unfortunately been proclaimed in their cradles as "made for each other," and in consequence had been disqualified for each other by mutual embarrassment throughout their conscious years.

After dinner John said he would walk over to see Grandpa and Grandma and the Samsons, Solon Samson, the great political idealist, being his idol almost beyond his more moderate father. Ike had plenty of work to do, but the little rift of the morning made him want to stay close to John till it was certainly closed. So he said he'd walk over with him. The sky was graying to snow again, and they put on their hats and coats. Once outside, they felt happy and close as ever in that mutual world where both knew the shape of every stone in every wall and almost every fold in the bark of the big maples and elms whose still snowy upper twigs closed in black and white lace over the road.

Ten rods north of the gate, where the Upper and Lower Roads forked, they decided to go down to the Samsons' first and set off down the grade with the northern part of the snow-covered Hollow spread below them. Under the dull November sky and through the leafless trees, the familiar roads, unpainted houses and enclosing slopes stood close in clear and detailed perspective as if seen through one of the new stereopticon glasses, and remote sounds were sharply audible in that sounding-box of hills. A mile ahead and below, the Wilcox cattle were standing in the barnyard, and Ike and John saw Hannah Wilcox come out and throw a pan of slops to her pigs. The Four Corners a half mile behind them was hidden by the little crest of Lathrop Hill, but they could hear young Jared Oxbow hammering on the wagon he was finishing by his father's saw-mill in preparation for the departure for California, now only five days off. Like a pulse feeding the life of the community, the rush of the two cascades of the Lathrop River sounded softly before and below them as they turned down the Lower Road.

"Jared all settled on California, is he?" said John. "So he claims," said Ike, "and Sam Emmens, and Manuel Swift, and Savillian Stone and Hosy Birdseye. Likely Connie Oaks too. Pack of nonsense, I tell them, risking death for a little gold when there's certain money to be made right in Byzantium for anybody who'll go to milling with modern machinery." "It isn't just money they're after, Scamp," said John, "not if they're like the boys from college who went out last year." Then he added in a conciliatory tone, "Of course, if they are going after gold it is a year late for it. Perhaps California being admitted as a free state is sending a lot of folks out who were dubious before."

After a pause John asked, "Tave given Connie the cold shoulder for good, has she?" "Looks so," said Ike. "Can't figger any other reason he'd be lighting out." John thought a moment. "She certainly has the bit in her teeth to follow her pa, hasn't she?" " 'Tain't natural," said Ike, and decided this wasn't the moment to tell John about the kiss. John pursued his thought. "It's as if Solon had fought so hard to live down the shiftless reputation of his pa and grandpa he's got a sort of righteous momentum in the blood that they're bound to follow even if they're girls." "Yet," said Ike, "seems he ain't all ways so different from his family." "Sort of rebel, you mean?" said John. "Yep," said Ike. "His grandpa broke the whisky law, claiming it was unconstitutional, and his pa did the same with the potash law. They both went to jail for it, and I'm mighty afraid Solon 'll end there himself." "The difference is," said John, "that his pa and grandpa had something to gain out of breaking those laws, where Solon's alleged slave-running is pure idealism." "Likely," said Ike, seeing no practical value in the distinction.

They were getting down toward Jolam's Glen now where the trees were mostly chestnut, pine and hemlock, and the road was corduroy and steep along the course of a rill. The logs were damp and a little icy and they walked gingerly. Beyond the wall on the top of the low bank on the left, they

could hear the bells of the Lathrop cattle who were making a tentative trial
of the snowy meadow before returning to the barnyard and the certainty of
hay. On the slope up to the right was the little, low-walled, Lathrop cemetery, where the first Squire and his wife, their great-grandparents, still
asserted themselves in the dignity of wide, erect limestone slabs, Great-uncle
Ben stood a little askew and to one side, two maiden great-aunts barely
peeked over the wall with their chaste, cut marble markers, Brother Tom
stood alone near the upper left corner, and numerous other children were
invisible from the road.

John leading, they walked up the little grade and stood looking over
the wall. John gazed a moment at the marker of their older brother, Tom,
who had died seven years before at the age of nineteen. "Remember the day
Tom died?" said John. "Yep," said Ike. "And you went up to the hayloft
by yourself," said John, "and came back to Ma and me and said, 'No use
crying, Ma. Tom ain't dead.' And I said, 'Of course not, but he ain't here
any more.' And you said, 'That don't matter to us, does it, Ma?' Do you
remember?" "Yep," said Ike. "Never understood what you meant," said
the older brother. "Do you still feel it doesn't matter that Tom isn't with us,
isn't going to grow any older than you are now?" "I miss him plenty, if
that's what ye mean," said Ike, "but I don't figger the way I feel about Tom's
any different from what it would be if he was here. Sometimes when I get
to thinking about him I figger he's around just the same as ever. Whether I
see him or not's another story—not so important as I see it."

"Ground hogs getting after Great-uncle Ben again?" asked John, turning away and starting down the road. "Yep," said Ike, following. "I've to do
a good job next time, though I hate spading round too close to his skull."
"Won't Master Lane tend to it?" "No. Says he knew Ben too well, though
he was ten years older than Uncle Ben was. Claims he sees him sometimes
down here in the moonlight. I just pried out of the old feller, not three
weeks back, how it was he figgers Uncle Ben blighted his life—though, says
Master Lane graciously, he don't hold it against him. Never told ye, did
he?" John shook his head, and their progress was slow during Ike's account
of the incipient local legend.

"It seems," he said, "that Uncle Ben just happened to be at the tannery
one night, about forty years back, when Charity Samson's ma, Mistress
Jolam, came to Master Lane through the snow and asked him to take her
West away from old Malachi Jolam. Uncle Ben being there and old Jolam
being Master Lane's friend, his conscience got the best of him, so they just
kept her there all night and took her back to Jolam's in the morning. And,
two weeks after, she took pneumonia and died. Master Lane never got over

it—made him take to drink worse 'n old Jolam, and sell the tannery to Lem Oaks the minute Uncle Ben died, and come to work for Great-grandpa."

"Funny old Jolam don't die," continued Ike after a pause. "He's eighty-eight, they say, and drives a horse-nail as true as ever. Won't live in his own house with his daughter—says he figgers one woman's life was enough to ruin. But I'll wage ye he fetches more cash into the Samson family than Solon does with his lawyer's shingle." "Fine people, all of them," said John.

They were talking quietly and John, not watching his footing, stepped on a loose corduroy which came up, and, as he caught himself, fell back with a loud thump. At the sound there was a croak from the direction of the cemetery, a rustle, and a shadow rocketed across the road in front of them. "That's that owl," said Ike. "Seems to have taken up residence in the cemetery." "Gave me a start," said John. Suddenly they both paused, hearing the far-off gallop of horse's hoofs, and gazed straight down the Hollow more than a mile to the forge and house of Solomon Sloan, who divided with old Malachi Jolam the smithy business of the neighborhood. As they watched, a rider, a blueish, moving object on the white landscape, pulled up in front of the stone forge, and they saw Solomon, a darker object, come out and stand as if talking with him.

In a moment the blacksmith's voice reached them faintly and clearly between the confining hills—"Solon Samson!" it called slowly. "Can't tell ye rightly!" "Old Sol's using his lungs," said John. "Hush ye," said Ike. "Solon Samson!" came the far, faint shout again, and they saw the blueish object dismount and stand close to the blacksmith as if in argument. In a moment it mounted again and moved along the highway toward the Corners.

"Can't be certain," said Ike, "but I think I've seen that feller at the Liberty. If that's the one, he's a Federal Marshal, and he's here tracking the Underground." "Come on," yelled John, and they started at a dog-trot down the corduroy which was levelling out now, a hundred yards short of Solon Samson's house. "Sol wasn't hollering that way for fun," said Ike as he ran. "We ought to have twenty minutes before he gets here," said John. "Specially if Sol throw him off the scent, as is likely," said Ike.

At the Samsons' gate stood a split cedar post, bearing a crossbar which dangled a piece of plank painted white and neatly lettered in blue, "Solon Samson—Attorney at Law." The house—a small one, previously the Jolam house—stood on a steep little knoll two rods back from the road on the right. Another two rods behind it loomed an irregular, shadowy cliff, varying in height from six to a dozen feet. Against this cliff nestled the Samsons' small outbuildings and Jolam's Forge, and on top of it, as well as all around the house, rose a magnificent stand of hemlocks which kept the place in shadow at all hours and all seasons and gave the little homestead a sort of cavernous, underground atmosphere, at once snug and eerie. The mystery of the place, known as Jolam's Glen, was enhanced by the ceaseless, soft rumble of Jolam's Falls that, unseen, tumbled over the ledge a little way above the forge and supplied a changeless undertone to the varying moans and whispers of the wind through the needles of the lofty hemlocks. In full summer midday it was a romantic, elfin retreat. At any other hour or season it was a place of dark portent which children dreaded to pass.

The drive that ran up to the house continued thereafter as a lane leading up around the cliff that flattened down at the right, thence up the grade past the former smokehouse which old Malachi Jolam had transformed into a dwelling, and so on up along the Lathrop River to Lane's Falls, Lem Oaks's tannery, and the Upper Road about a hundred rods above the Lower. It was up this byway that Mistress Jolam, now forty years dead, had fled on the February night when Master Lane was tried and found wanting. It had become a public way by long usage, being the normal means of access for the inhabitants of the Upper Road to Jolam's forge or to Lawyer Samson's august presence.

Solon must have been looking out of his office window, for as John and Ike ran up the path to the wide flagstones that rose in steps to his entrance he opened the door and stood filling it with his lofty, lean stature and his penetrating gaze. His eyes were set almost monstrously wide apart and they were of a fierce, coal-black, passionate brightness that made some people claim they shone in the dark. His left cheek was disfigured by a long, slanting scar whose origin had been nothing more sinister than a fall upon a scythe-blade when he was a youth. As if to conceal this scar, or for whatever reason, he carried his head habitually bent to the left with the chin drawn in, the slightly receding chin with its imperfect covering of thin, straggling, brown beard. His clothes were always neat, shiny to threadbare, and five to ten years behind the mode, representing always a fee in kind.

"Welcome to ye, John," he now said with the scowl and increased glitter of his eyes that was his smile, and extending both his hands with a graceful, senatorial gesture. "It was indeed good of ye to call on your neighbor so soon after arriving. How d' ye do, Isaac? It is always good to see ye. I trust your pa and ma are well and prepared for a happy Thanksgiving, and that your cousin Samantha is now over her indisposition." "I am afraid, Solon Samson"—John all but interrupted him—"that our business at this time is more pressing and perhaps more important than we intended when we set out. Did you hear—?" "Do come right in," said the lawyer, stepping back and extending his long arm graciously toward the open door of his office on the right. "Come right in and make yourselves easy." And he bowed them into the little room with its Franklin stove burning merrily, its home-made, flat-topped desk variously littered, its three office chairs and its walls completely lined with books in all stages of losing their backs and bindings.

Without sitting down, John continued, "Did you hear Solomon Sloan shouting your name from his place scarce two minutes ago?" "No, John, I did not. Because of the enclosure of the trees and the slope at this point, few sounds reach us but the natural ones of the stream and the wind. Even my father-in-law's hammering on his anvil, though close by, sounds muffled to us and remote, hardly breaking the quiet of our situation." "Well, sir," broke in Ike, "as we were coming down the corduroy a man rode up to Solomon Sloan's forge from the direction of the Center, and in the course of their talk Master Sloan twice bellered your name as he certainly had no need to beller it in ordinary talk. Pretty soon the man rode on toward the Corners. If I ain't mistaken I've seen that feller twice at the Liberty and he's a Federal agent here for the purpose of investigating the Underground."

"And you thought you ought to warn me ere he arrives?" asked Master Samson in a tone of noncommittal austerity. "Figgered it wouldn't do any harm," said Ike, turning away to look out the window; "not that we know anything about such things." "I hope you will forgive us," added John hastily. It was in the current code that no one actually knew who was in the Underground Railroad, or would have admitted it under oath if he had. So this hasty approach, even to their father's friend, was at least irregular on the part of the Lathrop boys, if not positively impudent.

"Thank ye both for your interest," said Solon Samson calmly, putting a hand on the shoulder of each and directing them gently toward the door. "And now I must appear inhospitable and return to certain business which I have undertaken to finish before tomorrow." John faced him and met his eyes with a gaze almost as black and stern as his own. "Solon Samson," he said, "we know nothing but unreliable rumor as to your having anything to do with the Underground. But if it is true that you know something of it, then I implore you to let us serve with you, now or at any time. I believe it is the noblest cause in the country today."

Solon continued to bow them toward the door. "You must understand," he said, "that even if I had some knowledge of the systematic evasion of the so-called Fugitive Slave Law, it would be highly improper for me to impart it to ye without your pa's consent, for any participation in this business must, I daresay, involve some danger of arrest and criminal prosecution."

"Solon Samson," said John, still holding his ground, "I must confess what

I have confessed to no one before, that in view of the savage inhumanity of this new law, I am already engaged, along with many other Yale students, in the work of the Underground." Ike looked at his brother with his forehead puckered in astonishment. "Already," continued John, "I have transported several fugitives on their way, and twice have narrowly missed arrest." "Does your pa know of this?" asked Solon. "No," admitted John. "Then I regret that I could not participate in any deception of him. And now I must beg ye to leave instantly," said Solon. "Please continue along the Lower Road or up the lane as you choose. And kindly walk rapidly, and do me the favor not to look behind. Later in the afternoon—perhaps in half an hour—I shall be at liberty. I would be happy if you would both return then."

"Come on, 'Paloosa," said Ike, "ye're wasting time. That feller must be at the Corners by now." With a lofty toss of his head John followed Ike out into the little hall, and just at that moment Charity Samson opened the door from the parlor opposite. "How do you do, John," exclaimed Charity, with an animation that belied her lusterless, gray eyes.

"I am so glad—" "Excuse me, my dear," her husband interrupted her with a tone unusually severe for him. "I must tell ye that John and Isaac are in some haste to be gone. I have asked them to return to us later in the afternoon." "Forgive us, Charity Samson," said John, as they stepped out. Solon closed the door unceremoniously behind them.

As they started briskly up the lane toward their grandparents' house on the Upper Road, old Jolam stepped out of his cabin and stood awaiting them. "How d' you do, Malachi Jolam," called John to the prophet-bearded patriarch, then added softly, as they drew near, "we can't stop now, for Solon Samson had some reason for asking us to be off in a hurry." Master Jolam lifted his heavy white eyebrows, and the boys hastened past without looking back. The old man remained in front of his door, looking down the lane.

A few rods above, a big deer had recently crossed the way going uphill to the right. "Let's follow him," said John. "Keerect," said Ike, and they left the lane to walk alongside the fresh track. Ten rods up the hill it crossed the wall between the Jolam and Lathrop properties, just below a point where old Jolam's privy and a big maple stub, a famous bee-tree, stood close on one side of the wall and a pile of hemlock planks lay along the Lathrop side.

They mounted the wall, and as Ike was stepping down backwards on the opposite side he could not avoid seeing, out of the corner of his eye, Solon Samson, coatless and hatless, coming up the lane leading by the hand a figure with its head completely covered with a shawl. John also saw the apparition and, true to Solon's orders, turned away and continued on the trail of the deer. Ike, however, delayed for a moment, until he saw Solon deliver his charge to old Malachi, then turn back down the lane, placing his steps carefully so as to efface the tracks of the Negro. Immediately old Jolam started up the slope with his charge toward the privy and the bee-tree. Ike glanced up at the old stub, and as he ducked back out of sight, saw the end of a ladder protruding from under the top board of the pile of planks.

Ike ran and overtook John, following the deer-tracks into the ten-acre lot of half-grown pines their pa had set out thirty years before. "Did ye see the ladder?" whispered Ike, as he came up behind. "Yes," said John without looking round. "I thought," continued Ike, "it sounded fishy last summer when old Jolam told us there were no more bees in that tree—I figgered then he was afraid we might swipe 'em."

John's eyes were still black as Solon Samson's, his jaw set, and his thoughts on loftier matters than the evidences of a Samson-Jolam station of the Underground. "You know, Scamp," he said aloud, "this is the peskiest thing we have to do. I've often thought the hardest part of being a soldier must be to obey orders to march *away* from the fight." "What bothered me most," replied Ike, "was leaving Solon by himself when we could as well have slipped off with his darky and left him to meet the marshal comfortably."

They followed the deer trail in silence, thrusting through the pine boughs that spilled their light powder of snow over them. Presently the tracks curved round to the Upper Road and crossed it just above Emmens' grist mill, not far from their grandfather's house. "No use following that track any farther," said John. "Let's go call on Grandpa and Grandma now." "Keerect," said Ike, then suddenly, "Hush ye!" As they stood listening, still concealed in the pine thicket, there was no near sound but the breathing of the falls behind them. Snow began to fall softly in slow, floating feathers. Remotely they could still hear young Jared Oxbow hammering on his wagon. Somewhere down in the glen a bluejay called. Then from behind Lathrop Hill they heard the trot of a horse approaching. It came rapidly nearer, then the steps slowed down, and presently sounded muffled as if striking on corduroy. They looked at each other and nodded. Each felt his mouth dry and swallowed, and each could hear his heart beating. "Come on," whispered John, and they walked casually out onto the road and headed for their grandfather's.

CHAPTER XV

AFTER closing the door on John and Ike, Solon led Charity quickly back to the kitchen where seven-year-old Numa Samson was lying on the floor, deep in Pope's *Iliad*. Solon spoke to his wife hurriedly and in Latin. "A Federal officer comes. To lead the boy upstairs. To retain him there till I shall return. To sweep the steps of the entrance and a path down to the lane in order that you may obliterate the footprints of John and Isaac."

Charity led the frowning Numa upstairs, explaining that she must mop the kitchen. Solon clomped down cellar with a candle, and immediately clomped up again, dragging a trembling young Negro clad in a torn overcoat and a shawl. Without ado Solon wrapped the latter garment over his entire head, tucking the ends into his coat collar, then led him out through the back door and closed it.

Charity returned from upstairs and proceeded swiftly to her second mission, the sweeping of the steps and a track down to the lane to efface the tracks of the Lathrop boys. This finished, she paused in the front door, heard no sound, noticed that the sky promised snow, and re-entered the house. As she reached the kitchen her husband was opening the back door. She handed him the broom and he swept his boots carefully before coming in. He kissed her gently, and she whispered, "Have no fear, husband. All will be well for a time yet"—for Charity Samson was generally accredited with second sight. Solon returned to his office and sat down to the Theocritus he had been reading before the boys came.

In the kitchen Charity went to mopping. She was worried about her husband, wished he was not always so exact, so extreme in the performance of what he saw as his duty, particularly in breaking this new Fugitive Slave Law, now only three months old. Under the old law the work of the Underground involved only the inconvenience of succoring the poor fugitives and carrying them on their way toward Canada without the slightest danger of arrest. But this new law carried heavy penalties, and by all accounts it was being rigidly enforced. Charity knew her husband would willingly march to the gallows for his convictions on this or any subject. She sometimes even feared that he anticipated and courted some such martyr-

dom. Although she took less stock in her second sight than did some of her
neighbors, she had indulged in many long gazings into her crystal respecting her husband's and son's futures. The remote future she had seen as
bright, but there was darkness and confusion not far ahead. Now, as she
mopped, she paused every few strokes to listen. The house was absolutely
quiet but for the hiss of the fire. Once she heard Solon cough. That showed
he was nervous, she thought. When she had finished one end of the kitchen,
she called little Numa downstairs and told him he might read by the fire
if he chose, but he mustn't lie on the floor till it was dry.

In his office Solon Samson was glaring at his Theocritus with a fury that
might well have frightened those playful nymphs and satyrs from the page,
and from time to time he coughed in irritation, and shifted the position of
his long legs, one over the other. What disturbed and angered him was the
necessity of lying for purposes of expediency. If his own welfare alone had
been involved he would have told the truth to any officer or court in earth
or Heaven. But if he did this now he would not only violate a duty to a
fugitive who was in his care, but he would jeopardize the whole organization of the Underground in that part of the state. He was compelled to act
like a liar, a thief and a coward.

When five minutes had passed, by the slow-ticking clock on the mantel
over his stove, Solon began to suspect that the boys had made a mistake. He
closed his Theocritus, rose, and at that moment saw through the window
a man in a long, blue cape ride up to his gate and rein in to read the shingle.
Solon made no effort to conceal himself, but stood in full view peering out
the window. The officer rode in as far as the hitching-post, to which
Charity had swept a passage clear of snow, dismounted there, tied his horse,
looked straight at Solon without making any sign, and walked around to
the rear of the house with his eyes on the snow-covered ground. Solon paced
through to the kitchen, nodded to his wife and went out the door just after
the officer had passed it and was pausing to look at the outside cellar-way.

The promised snow was falling rapidly now, and Solon had neither coat,
hat nor very much brown hair on the top of his head. "To whom," he inquired, "am I indebted for the honor of this visit?" The marshal looked at
him as blankly as if he had been a cow, proceeded to walk back and around
the little horse barn, privy and chicken house that stood so close to the cliff
as barely to leave passage behind them, reappeared and continued his circle
of inspection out of sight around the corner of the house. Solon re-entered,
paced slowly through to his office again, and stood with his back to the
Franklin stove, his brows knit in consideration of the degree of force that
might be justifiable in the ejection of a trespasser.

In a few seconds the front knocker banged. Solon waited until the summons was repeated several times, each time with increasing force. Then he walked leisurely to the front door, opened it and stood quietly glaring. The man nodded to him as impersonally as he had looked at him before and took a step forward as if to enter. Solon stood his ground, blocking the door.

"I perceive," he said, "by your cape that you are, or pretend to be, a Federal officer. I observe by your conduct that you are a very unmannerly young man." "Aw, why don't ye write President Fillmore about it?" grumbled the visitor, curling his lip. "It happens," said Samson, "that is just what I intend to do. If you are not an officer, I will be grateful to ye if you will leave my premises at once. If you are, will you be good enough to show me your badge?"

The young man threw back his cape, revealing no uniform beneath, but an ordinary leather shirt and wool pants, and, on his belt, a big holster with one of the new Colt revolvers. Unbuttoning his shirt, he revealed a proper marshal's badge pinned to his undershirt, and Solon made a mental note of its number.

"Yer name Solon Samson?" asked the marshal, buttoning his shirt. "The same," said Solon with a little bow. "And have you any explanation to offer of your peculiar manner of approaching my house?" "Didn't cal'late ye was any more anxious to palaver with me than I was with you. Routine to walk round a place afore ye search it and arter, specially with snow on the ground, just t'make sure nobody stepped out t' take the air while ye was callin'."

"You say you propose to search my house? Kindly show me your warrant?" Wearily the young man fished in a pocket in his cape, pulled out a document and handed it to Solon, who read it carefully, noted with contempt that it was signed by Judge Longcoat, also the name of the marshal, folded it carefully and handed it back.

"You realize, I suppose, that you are operating under a void statute, one that will be held so when it reaches the Supreme Court." "Lawyer, be ye?" asked Marshal Day. "I have the honor," said Samson. "Wal," the officer continued, now in a loud tone, "I've heered all that talk plenty o' times. Mebbe it's keerect. Mebbe it ain't. Fact is, Lawyer Samson, I don't like this kind o' dooty any better'n you do. All I know is I got my orders and it's fer them as issues 'em to scratch their heads about the law. Come now," he continued more sharply, looking straight at Solon for the first time, "be ye resistin' me or ain't ye? If ye be I'll have to arrest ye. If ye ain't I'll trouble ye to stand one side." Solon bowed him in, the man kicking the snow carefully from his boots, but keeping his big felt hat on.

"If ye'd care to foller 'round with me I'd likely discommode ye less," he said in a decent tone. "Allers start with the cellar." Solon led him back to the kitchen where Charity straightened up from her mopping and looked with an inquiring smile at her husband, as if expecting an introduction. "Sorry t' bother ye, ma'am," said Marshal Day, removing his hat. "Got any niggers in the house?" "Assuredly not," replied Charity with a chuckle. "Ever have one, ma'am?" "Improper question, Marshal," Solon broke in, and the officer sneered in his bored way. "Proper or not, the answer is 'No,' " said Charity with a flash of light in her gray eyes. "Like yer story, sonny?" he said methodically to little Numa, who was sitting by the chimney look- ing up at him gravely over his big book. "Yes, sir—I am reading of Ulysses and his proposal of the ruse of the wooden horse." "Ever see a nigger, sonny?" "I must beg ye—" began Solon. "What's a nigger, papa?" asked Numa with a puzzled brow. "Got him well trained, ain't ye?" Marshal Day turned to Solon with a professional smile. "Now if ye'll get a light we'll start with the cellar. Don't concern yerself, ma'am," he continued as Solon lit a candle with a fagot. "This is my business, ye know, and part of it's to do no damage lessen it's necessary. Cal'late t'ain't goin' t' be necessary here."

Solon led him down to the little cellar which was under only the rear part of the house. In the process of a perfunctory inspection of the walls, the dirt floor, and the bins and barrels, the marshal came on a plate and fork under the stairs showing signs of a freshly finished meal. "Mighty considerate o' th' missus," he said as he set the plate down, "supplyin' a fork fer the cat." A tension in Solon's nerves relaxed, and thereafter the officer grew surlier than ever. Curtly he ordered Solon to lead him upstairs and through the rest of the house, ending with the tiny garret reached by a ladder through a trap door in one of the two bedrooms.

As part of his routine Marshal Day peered under beds, poked into closets and thumped the wall for secret chambers. When he had finished he led the way downstairs again and opened the back door. "Don't need t' come out with me," he growled as he closed the door and made a hasty inspection of the outbuildings. Then he repeated his circuit of the property, knocked at the front door again and Solon admitted him promptly.

"If ye don't mind, Lawyer Samson," he said in a genial tone, "I may as well fill out my return right here." "By all means," said Solon, and bowed him into the office. "May I bring ye a glass of brandy? It might be right smart outside before long." "No drinkin' on duty," said the marshal, paus- ing in his laborious manipulation of Solon's big goose quill and looking out the window. "Yes, sir, looks like a chilly night ahead. Got three places to visit yet, and afterwards got to patrol all night and next night round a corners they call Field Settlement. They say," he continued significantly, looking down at his paper again, "that's a mighty bad place fer the Underground—niggers goin' through there nigh every night." And he g'anced up at Solon, who nodded sternly and said, "Ummm?"

Having finished his return and signed it with a flourish, Marshal Day tilted back in his chair and grew familiar. "Ye know, Lawyer Samson, you folks up this way's got the wrong slant on us fellers. They ain't one on a hunner o' us in the Northern districts as tries overly hard t' catch a nigger. 'Tain't none o' my business, but I may as well tell ye that yerself and half a dozen others missed gettin' arrested this time by the skin on a calf's eye. Changed my orders this mornin's post jest t' search yer premises fer three niggers come up this way less'n a week back. 'S long as our section's doin' the work ye ain't gotta set back so purty on yer laws o' evidence and all that. I ain't sayin' ye're in it, mind ye, but I may as well tell ye they're cal'latin' t' enforce this 'ere law mighty close, and if ever they send a batch o' them Southern marshals up here, them as is interested personal had best den up in a mighty tall tree and keep mighty still. Them fellers does business."

"As you must know," replied Solon, "there is scarcely a citizen between Utica and Canada who isn't prepared at least to shut his eyes to the infraction of this statute which we believe will be found unconstitutional sooner or later. If, as you say, they start really enforcing this so-called law it is possible that these marshals might find a small rebellion on their hands."

"That's just the time," replied Marshal Day, "when us fellers wants t' be a long way off. They ain't nobody likes a fight better'n Zach Day, but when it comes to that I want t' be fightin' fer somethin' I believe on."

"Well, sir," continued Solon, "and this in turn is none of my business— but might I ask why, feeling as you do in the matter, you made such an improper and discourteous approach to my premises? Our people up here are independent, and they're not used to Federal officers—haven't seen any since the potash days. I can think of some men who would have taken down their musket if they had seen ye walking round their house and you refused, as you did with me, to answer a fair challenge."

"Gotta keep up appearances," replied Day indifferently. "Also I might say, fer myself, that you folks easterly are greater sticklers fer propriety than we be out where I hail from. Out t' Indiany a spade's a spade and, lessen where women's involved, yer bowin' and scrapin' don't change it none. As fer's niggers is concerned I figger we pretty much agree, but when it comes t' yer fine manners I guess we're a kind o' different race, and if ye don't like our way o' doin' things we don't like yourn none better. When ye mentioned a drink o' brandy jest now ye made me feel like home,

but when ye says t' me out younder, 'T' whom am I indebted fer the honor
o' this visit,' I felt like spittin' in yer eye an' lookin' sharper into them
tracks goin' up the road, one o' 'em takin' no injun t' figger it's bein' double. Wal"—he rose abruptly—"I'm mighty glad to a' made yer acquaintance. Say good-by fer me t' the missus and I hope the little feller grows up
t' be as smart a lawyer as his pa. Drop in when yer out Indiany way an'
we'll have that nip ye mentioned." He shook Solon's hand violently and
slammed out the front door without giving him a chance to reply. Solon
opened the door after him and stood watching as he buttoned up his cape
against the snow and unhitched his horse. As he mounted, Solon raised his
hand in salute, but Marshal Day turned on him only his blank, impersonal
look and trotted back to the road. Solon's severe expression grew more
severe in what was his smile.

CHAPTER XVI

SOLON and Charity Samson sat in their parlor on the stiff little empire settee, an inheritance from Charity's ill-starred mother, while he made his whispered report. He told of the officer's tip about danger on the Field Settlement Road tonight and tomorrow night, and said he believed the man had been frank with him. This meant he must defer driving the Negro to Round Harbor till Wednesday night, Thanksgiving Eve. He then proceeded to reassure his wife as to their personal situation. "For the present," he said, "the Northern marshals are lax in enforcement of this supposed law, a condition which I deplore, the inevitable result of a law which is contrary to the well nigh unanimous sentiment of the people. Indeed, I propose to write the President, requesting rigid enforcement, for the sooner that is done, the sooner a test case will reach the Supreme Court." Solon's eyes glittered and Charity sighed. "But for the inconvenience to others," he continued, "I would welcome the opportunity of carrying this case up and establishing its unconstitutionality. That would be a privilege to do the nation a signal service, an enviable privilege that will fall to but one man in our time." "Would it not involve going to jail?" asked Charity. "Probably not," said Solon, taking his wife's hand, "though if it did, then to be jailed for this purpose would be the loftiest legacy I could leave to our son."

When they had talked for ten minutes in this vein they heard steps at the front door and Solon opened to John and Ike, their hats and shoulders well powdered with snow. "Come in, John and Isaac," said Solon. "I am glad to say that I am now at liberty to receive ye, and I hope you will forgive my brusqueness before." The boys stamped their boots on the flagstone step, entered the hall and shook the snow from their coats. "Do take off your wraps and visit a while," said Charity, who had also risen. "Looks like sleighing for Thanksgiving," said Ike as they hung their coats and hats on pegs opposite the door.

John asked to see Numa, who was summoned into the parlor and duly recited the first ten lines of the *Iliad* in the original, after which he was permitted to return to his English version in the kitchen. John was asked the appropriate questions about college, and when they were all answered he begged Charity to bring out her crystal and tell their fortunes. They fetched out a small table from the wall and set chairs so the prophetess and the subject might sit opposite each other, both gazing into the many-lighted sphere of prevision. "The plaguyest thing about this," said Charity, "is that some folks believe what ye say, and that's the last thing I want them to do. Like as not all the nonsense I tell them comes right out of my own head. So you must both promise me not to remember anything I tell ye, no matter how dark or bright it may be." Charity said all this very lightly, though actually she was as excited as the boys, since the future of either of them might be mixed up with that of her nervous, brilliant daughter. Ah! If only one of these boys would marry her and put an end to her impractical passion for Reform!

Ike insisted that John be first, and he and Charity sat down with the table and crystal ball between them, both gazing intently into the mysterious depths, while Solon and Ike stood by in silence. Solon was not wholly persuaded that his wife's prophecies were spurious, having seen some of them, especially those respecting their daughter's fortunate education, fulfilled with remarkable accuracy. Ike observed how tense Charity grew, how her normally delicate white skin seemed gray, how her long, soap-cracked hands on the table looked like dead and detached members, how the sinews stood out on her neck where he could see the barely perceptible, slow pulsing of the jugular. He could not see her eyes, but John could see them, large and cavernous, with heavy, black circles of shadow beneath them.

"I see a great bird," she began presently in a sepulchral, masculine voice, "an eagle, flying very high over the earth, so high I can see only fields and houses, but no people on the ground. I see smoke on the horizon and the eagle is flying that way. Now there is flame through the smoke and it is rolling up near as high as the eagle is flying. The whole earth is on fire, like a forest fire only much bigger. Now the eagle swoops down into the smoke, and the flames are whirling around him. The flames are crowded with the faces of men, all whirling around, all red and black in the fire and the smoke. Their mouths are open as if they were shouting, and many of them are in pain, their faces twisted in awful expressions. They are all turning round the eagle, who seems to be flying forward all the time with the whirl of faces following him. Now the fire and the smoke and the faces seem to be going back to the earth. The eagle is still flying and now there is blue sky above him. Now the fire is gone and the earth is green again. The eagle swoops again and is approaching a white house on a low hilltop. He seems to be hanging in the air just in front of the house. The door opens and——"

Charity paused and Ike saw her color·rise until her whole face and neck were as red as a Baldwin apple. She lifted her eyes from the crystal and John watched them as they seemed to move forward to normal position out of remote eaves. The flush vanished as rapidly as it had come, and she smiled. "That is all," she said in her normal voice. "After the door opened I could not make out anything more. Isn't it absurd?" she giggled. "Not at all," said John. "And thank you, Charity Samson. After reading about those Rochester rappings, I believe your gift is a genuine and great one." "Fiddlesticks, John," said Charity, but she was now fully recovered and beaming, obviously pleased with what she had seen.

"Now, Ike," said John, rising; and Ike sat down opposite the prophetess. "Perhaps that is enough for now," he suggested with genuine solicitude. "Oh, no, indeed," laughed Charity. "That was very short. I should love to try just once more." Ike felt suddenly that he was looking at Tavie, who looked like her ma except for her dark eyes which were Solon's. Ike consciously wished that the daughter had some of her ma's lightness. "Stop smiling at me with such condescension," said Charity, reaching across the table and patting his cheek. "If you don't take any stock in this, no more do I. But you've got to indulge me all the same. Now grow serious and look intently into the ball." "The indulgence is of me," said Ike, growing very solemn and lowering his eyes as directed.

Charity sank into her tense, self-hypnotized state again, and there was a long pause. "I see," she began at last in the unnatural, masculine tone, "a large stone building—it seems—on the Mall at the Falls. I see a man approaching one of three doors in the building. He looks somewhat like Isaac Lathrop, though he is an old man with a white beard, and his shoulders are bent forward, and I cannot see his eyes. A—young woman comes from the door, smiling, to greet him. He— He——"

She paused as abruptly as she had in reading John's future, but now she continued to gaze silently into the crystal, and all three men saw her trembling. Her breath began to come in gasps, and Solon stepped forward and put his hand on her shoulder. Suddenly she screamed and leaned back on her husband, covering her eyes and panting hysterically. Solon half-lifted her from the chair and supported her to the settee, where they sat down and he held her strongly. Her panting lapsed into sobs, and very slowly she became calm.

Meanwhile John and Ike stood troubled and uncertain. Ike signalled to Solon that they had best be going, and they were putting on their coats when Charity rallied with a forced smile. "I must have fainted," she said. "The last thing I remember was sitting down to the crystal with—Ike—" she swallowed hard—"sitting opposite me. Do forgive me, boys. I assure you it is nothing." "I beg you to forgive *me*," said Ike, "for imposing on you so thoughtlessly." She gave him a very artificial smile and avoided his eyes. "Are you fully recovered ma'am?" asked John. "Quite," she replied, and in addressing him her strength did seem to come back to her, for she rose easily and smiled up at him with something of her usual vivacity. The boys took their leave, and as soon as the front door closed, Charity flew into her husband's arms— "Solon, we must take Octavia out of that house. I am terribly frightened. I must tell you everything at once!" And they sat down again on the settee, Charity now trembling again but in full possession of herself.

John and Ike walked in silence up the corduroy. The snow was falling fast now in no wind, and it was growing dusk. "Ye know," Ike said at last, "I'll wage ye Tave was in both those visions. Seems like you did her a good turn and I did her a bad one." "Maybe," said John. "Anyway, I'm danged sorry it happened." "Me, too," agreed Ike, "though I don't take any stock in it." "I do," said John, and they walked silently again. Finally Ike said, a little self-consciously, "Maybe I'm wrong about Tave. I guess she's kind o' on my mind, being as I kissed her one morning a spell back—first girl I ever kissed—really kissed, I mean—she and I alone at chore time—hadn't figgered on anything o' the sort—first thing I know I just up and kissed her."

"Well," said John, "you've the start of me—at least as far as good women are concerned." "Don't mind, do ye?" asked Ike, looking away at Uncle Ben's tombstone, dimly visible through the snow as they passed the cemetery. "I should say not," said John. He was enjoying an exhilarating sense of lightness and escape, thinking how ideal it would be to have Tavie for his sister-in-law, Ike's wife. "At least," he added, "I don't mind if you know what you're about." "Oh, I figger it don't amount to much," said Ike slowly. "She's been avoiding me like poison ever since."

John walked silently, while a faint wave of resentment or jealousy rose and fell away, leaving the sense of exhilaration again. The image of Pru came enticingly into his mind, and in a waking dream he enjoyed liberties with her person. Then he squelched these impulses, came back to earth and felt happy to be with Ike. As they approached the house he slipped his arm through his brother's. "There's that owl," said Ike, and they walked on silently, listening to him whoo-whooing softly behind them down by the cemetery.

In the house John helped the women set out the supper dishes, and Tavie, finding him easier with her than she had ever seen him, had to suppress an impulse actually to flirt with him.

CHAPTER XVII

ON TUESDAY a thaw carried away all of the recent snow. Hope of sleighing for Thanksgiving waned, though the frost was now deep enough in the ground so that any further snowfall would remain if the air was not too far above freezing. On Tuesday morning six chickens, a goose, two twenty-pound turkeys and a young pig were killed and added to the beef, venison, mutton and pork carcasses hanging in the buttery—Homer Hislip in the meantime having failed to provide a wild turkey, for he missed a big cock which temporarily joined the domestic flock for erotic purposes. Besides this slaughtering and the ensuant plucking of feathers and scalding of the pig, this was a day of supplementary baking, the output being bread and cookies. In the afternoon John took Pol and the cart and delivered some thirty jars of jelly and conserve to all the neighboring houses, along with full baskets, including a chicken each, for the three old couples who were on the town. All day Ike worked with the Squire on the new sheep-cote. It was natural that they should talk little while at work, but it was also clear that one subject was avoided by tacit agreement.

Because of festivities planned for the morrow, Cousins Joel and Alvina, Uncle Brandon and Master Lane retired soon after supper. Realizing that this gave their pa his first opportunity for a real talk with John, Agatha persuaded Homer and Ben, both unwilling, to go to bed, and Ike gave her an understanding nod. Sarah cautioned the Squire that it would be a long day tomorrow, then said good night to the boys. As Ike kissed her he saw a look of troubled appeal in her eyes, suspected it had to do with Dandy, and gave her back a look of tender reassurance. "Why don't you sit and talk a while, ma?" John asked. "No, my dear," said Sarah. "I'm tuckered out, But I'll thank you boys if you'll come in when you're through visiting, and wake me and say good night again as you used to do." She looked with patronizing pride from one to the other of her enormous babies, then strode into the master's bedroom and closed the door through which all of their conversation in the keeping-room would be audible to her if she chose to listen.

The Squire lit a fresh cigar from the table, settled himself in his hair-cloth rocker, and motioned to both of the boys to sit down. John likewise lit a fresh cigar from the candelabra and sat down on the high-back settle in the corner, but Ike remained standing with his back to the mantel. In the short silence that ensued they heard the wind moaning in rising gusts in the flue, and each wondered if it had changed to northerly, for on that would largely depend the hope of snow and sleighing.

Ike spoke first. "I don't figger to stay but a minute," he said, "for it's after nine and I'm to be up for chores. But I want to tell both of ye that I've been thinking some more about Dandy and I've concluded to get him back if I have to take a trimming for it. A week back I told Gam Stark he was wind-broke and offered him five hundred cash back—said the offer was good till Friday after Thanksgiving. Friday morning I figger to ride in, and if he stays pernickety I'll give him back the whole thousand, the chestnut, the full value of Solon Samson's note and, if needful, some extra cash to boot. I wanted to tell ye both this, so we can all feel easy about it."

When Ike first began his announcement both John and the Squire looked at him with obvious pleasure. But when he had finished the Squire grew thoughtful, looked straight ahead instead of at Ike, and presently said, "May I ask ye, Isaac, how you arrived at this decision?" "Well, Pa," said Ike, "from the start-off I figgered this sale didn't suit ye. But, with your telling me to hold on to my own notions, I did, figgering the straight of it was we'd get Dandy back and save some profit, like I said. But after John came home and made his notions plainer than you did, I wanted to go farther and give ye both some assurance that I'd get Dandy back no matter what, profit or no profit. The short of it is that this sort of misunderstanding just ain't worth the money to me—" "But, Scamp," broke in John impatiently, his eyes near as black as Solon Samson's, "that isn't the point. It's a question of right or wrong." "That is true, John," said the Squire slowly, "but it must be right or wrong as Isaac himself sees it. He is the judge of his own actions, not you or I." John looked intensely, almost defiantly, at his pa, for he could see nothing in this modern individualism, having debated the matter many times at Yale.

The Squire looked back at Ike and spoke with the utmost gentleness. "I asked ye before, Isaac, to consider this matter on its own merits, irrespective of what John or I or anyone may think, and I can do no better than to ask ye now that before taking action you be indeed certain that you have done this. If, after reconsideration, you are aware of having done no wrong in the sale itself, then my advice would be that you let it stand. But if, after consideration, you find that, quite independently of what anyone else may think, your conscience is not clear, that you are not at peace with your soul, then I believe you should do as you say."

"I ain't at peace, Pa," said Ike simply, "for the reasons I told ye. If I were all alone in the world, I'd likely settle it on the common sense of whether Gam Stark was likely to hurt Dandy"—John's lips set in a thin line and he ran his fingers through his hair. "But," continued Ike, "I figger the folks I'm fond of are more to me than common sense, not, as ye put it, what they *think* of me, but whether they are sure grit friendly to me or whether they have some kind of doubts about me that stand between us. Maybe"— Ike's brow puckered and he spoke slowly and softly—"some day something might come up where common sense would seem more important—for all of us. But that certainly ain't the case here."

Ike waited for his pa to speak, and, when he remained silent, said, "Well, that's all I had in my bonnet, and if ye don't mind I'll go up to bed. See ye later, Lollapaloosa. Good night, Pa." And he walked over to shake hands with the Squire. "Wait a minute, Scamp," said John, who had been looking at Ike with something like suspicion. "I've something to ask Pa that concerns you, and it won't take two minutes." Ike paused beside the Squire's chair, and they both looked at John, hearing the wind that was now whining in the flue and making the fire flicker.

"I just wanted to ask," said John, "if it's all settled that Ike is to enter Yale next fall. There are a few things I should like to arrange for him through the year." "Yes," said the Squire, "I believe it's all arranged. Isaac has managed to lay us by a few hundred dollars in the bank, and Eliphalet Emmens tells me he'll give me three hundred dollars for the ten-acre pine lot any time. If we continue to sell cheese as we have been doing for the past two years it may not be necessary to sell the pine lot at all, eh, Isaac?" "Thank you," said John, "that's all I wanted to know."

As soon as John had asked the original question Ike had sat down on the desk chair and put his elbows on his knees with his hands clasped in front of him. "Well, Pa," he said, "I was going to put this off to another time, but since it's come up now I may as well give ye my notions on the subject. It begins to look—what with Dandy and all—like I'm setting out to be the black sheep of the family. I've about concluded—for my part—that I don't want to go to college. I ain't much on learning except for science and invention, and they tell me ye don't get much of that at college. John and Ben are the booky ones in the family, and if anybody's to go beside John, Ben's the feller."

. "What's to prevent both of you going?" asked John. "There's plenty, 'Paloosa. This farm has come to a point where we've got to settle a few things right now—I mean in the next year or so, and my going to college is one of the things bearing on the farm. This place, and for that, any place in the county, ain't ever made much more'n enough cash to buy coffee, tea, salt and pepper and a store suit now and then—at least not until the past two years, and what with those fellers out West following us into the cheese business I ain't sure we're going to keep up like we've started. Anyhow, if we are it'll take a lot of doing, and it looks like I'm the feller has the hang of the new way of doing things."

Ike glanced at the Squire to see if he was talking too much, then continued. "To go back—farming ain't ever been a cash paying business. All of the Lathrops have gone to college and they've done it in just one way, by selling off a little more land, until from the thousand and more acres Great-Grandpa had, we're down to a little better'n four hundred, and if we're to keep up having much for market we need every chain of it. We've come down more'n any of our neighbors for the simple reason that more of us have gone to college. Most of them have sent one son in a generation. A few of 'em hain't sent any. We've sent everybody. If I stay in town it's a gamble we can lay something by and send Ben, come another year or two, without disposing of any land—for I've notions in my bonnet I hain't even mentioned to Pa. But if I go to college the chances are the time'll come we'll have to sell the old place. That would hardly be worth the education of one member of the family, specially a member who ain't hankering after the education anyhow."

Ike sat silent, looking at his hands. The wind roared in the chimney and they could hear it outside in the maples. The breath of the three was becoming visible. John glanced at the Squire, then said quietly but through compressed lips, "The important thing for the Lathrop family is to keep up its tradition of moral and intellectual leadership in the community. We might keep that up in poverty, in Solon Samson's way, but if we lose it we might as well all go and drown ourselves in Lake Ontario."

"Just a minute, 'Paloosa," Ike broke in abruptly, for here he was on ground he had thought clean through. "There's two ways of looking at that. In the first place, you've got the education, and ye're danged well going to have more if ye want it and I can any way help ye to it. You're the feller's going to take on the leadership ye're speaking of, and maybe Ben to boot. Meantime somebody's got to haul the supply cart, and it happens I'm the feller that has a hankering to do that part of it. I'm the feller that's to take the place of all the fine acres that have been sold to put five Lathrops through college. Your leadership will go on a mighty sight better for having a tap-root in the ground to keep ye from having to scratch your head about getting enough to eat."

John started to speak, but Ike looked straight at him and held the floor. "And nowadays there's a deal more to it than that, more'n just having plenty to eat. Ye may not have observed it, but there's a whole new lot of rich people rising up all over the country, people who are making their money in various ways, but most of them in manufacturing." "I'm glad you recognize that," put in John with sarcasm in his voice. "Well," continued Ike, "if by and large these people are like Gadston and Applemore and a few more at the Falls, they're a mighty pernickety crew, and I don't like 'em."

"So," said John, with his jaw set, "you are planning to become one of them?"

"Fact is," Ike went on, "they're the fellers are getting hold of your leadership, and they're doing it right now. It's anybody's guess now'days who's really running the show in the Falls, and, for that, in the Town and the County, whether it's Squire Staunton, Squire Fulton, Judge Van Wyck, Judge Van Sanford, and the rest of Pa's friends, or whether it's Applemore, Gadston, Slocum, Wycomb, Ludlow, and their crew. While the old, respectable families that never worried about money and never had much are sitting back feeling superior, these rich fellers with their hell-fire orations and their newspapers and torch-light peerades are creeping up on 'em mighty fast and a'ready are laughing up their sleeves at folks like us. If the Lathrops can't keep up to 'em—like Howell Sherwood and maybe Squire Fulton and Perez Price are doing—we're going to wake up one of these days to find ourselves just poor farmers and leading nobody but an old three-quart cow."

"Do you mean to say," asked John, his forehead wrinkling in positive pain, "that you plan actually to go into competition with these money-grubbers on their own ground, that you are thinking of going into industry or finance or something of the sort? How do you think I would feel if, as you imply, I were to accept help from any such source? It would be one thing to accept help from my brother, but it would be something else to be dependent on someone who was the associate and competitor of men like Applemore and Gadston."

"Competitor, keerect," said Ike, "but not associate. On two points I figger we see alike. We're both working for the good of the family and we don't like those hyenas. Only you figger that virtue alone's going to trim 'em, that ye can sort of walk 'round 'em and leave 'em to rot in their own manure. But I claim that if ye try that they'll stab ye in the back surer'n shootin'. The only way's to meet 'em head on at their own game, and play it just a little foxier'n they do. Like Pa read me the other day, Napoleon figgered God was on the side of the strongest legions."

"And so," said John, "you are adopting that philosophy which is precisely the philosophy of your Gadstons and your Applemores. It's an ancient question, and you can find plenty of evidence in history to support both sides, and never reach a conclusion. It all comes back to a matter of private inclination or, at best, opinion. Some are born to follow truth, and some to follow expediency. The latter sometimes win temporary glory, like Napoleon, but, in my view, they always end up on St. Helena. There is no profit in debating the point. What distresses me is that you are starting out to belong to the opposite school. You propose at best to compromise with evil, and to compromise with evil is always to surrender to it in the end."

Something in this speech touched Ike at once on his traditional and human side, and both boys were silent, feeling acutely wretched, with their eyes on the rag rug in the center of the floor. But the emotional pot stayed boiling in the silence, like the driven snow they could now hear hissing against the kitchen window. John simmered over first. "You are implying, of course, that I am virtually unable to make my living, that I shan't be able to make enough to carry out my aims of statesmanship?" "Not enough to compete with Applemore plus Gadston's money," said Ike. "You may be right as July cider, but he'll buy the votes with his newspaper and his torch-light peerades and his hypocritical weeping about the welfare of the people." "And you plan," said John, "to supply the money for these spurious practices by means of some enterprise the nature of which you haven't revealed; but I take it you are thinking of manufacturing of some kind, some business where all your attention is centered on making money."

"Most of it, likely," said Ike, "though my real aim'd be to keep the homestead going and the Lathrops on the map."

"And what good do you think financial aid would be to me from such a source? It would be nothing to you, I suppose, that I would have to break my principles to accept it. But from your *practical* point of view"—a sneer came into John's voice—"what good would it do me? What kind of position would I have if I stood up to attack the rich and their methods, and everybody knew I had a brother who was supporting me by the same—dishonest methods?——"

"That's a lie, John Lathrop," said Ike quietly, looking straight up at John, "and you'll take it back or I'll beat your big empty head in." John snorted.

"Boys," said the Squire suddenly with a quiet resonance in his voice which neither of them had heard for years. "What are you thinking of? Do you realize you're getting angry over one of the eternal questions of moral philosophy to which no one has found an answer satisfactory to all? As John well said a moment ago, it comes down to a matter of individual personality and opinion. It would be well, John, if you would take what you said as a living truth and not as a phrase you got from a book. It would be well for both of ye to take a less high-handed attitude and to realize that there may be profound sincerity and conviction in the point of view of the other. At least I will say for Isaac that he made no personal criticism of you, John, as you just did of him. He was right in resenting it, and I'll ask ye to apologize as he properly demanded."

Both boys had felt immediately relieved by the entrance of their father into the argument, and both were desperately ashamed. "I'm sorry, Scamp," said John from the depth of his soul. "So'm I, Lollapaloosa," said Ike, also rising. They shook hands, embraced impulsively, and both turned away, ashamed to weep in their father's presence. Neither of them observed that he was having a similar struggle of his own.

When they had seated themselves again, the Squire resumed quietly. "In the first place, John, when you spoke of Isaac's intentions as being 'dishonest,' I take it you did not mean to question his personal integrity?" "Assuredly not, sir. I merely meant that the pursuit of money is incompatible with the highest moral law as I see it." "In that you are assuredly entitled to your opinion, and in that my own instinct, and the instinct of most of my friends, is similar to yours. But I am convinced that Isaac has shown us that his concern about money and the economic status of the family conforms with truth as he sees it. It is possible that he may change his view in the future, perhaps in the not far distant future. But if he does not, we have no choice but to encourage him in the way he has chosen for himself. If I may say so without criticizing you—for I am glad to see that you are also clear and sincere in your convictions—I think that both you and I are a little old-fashioned—and that is nothing against us. You are interested in the Reform Movement, and that is something that looks to the future. But this economic change you have indicated is one of the two chief trends of our times, the other being the unprecedented emigration to the West. You and I are aware of these movements and have both apparently made some study of them."

"I have sometimes thought of going West—just to travel," put in John.

"You and I," repeated the Squire, "are critically aware of these movements, but we see them from the negative side. Instinctively we disapprove of them. Isaac, on the other hand, feels one of them affirmatively and deeply. He does not care to study the industrial tendency in order to criticize it. He wants to enter into it. He is modern in this respect, and you and I are of the old time, reactionary as they say.

"It is quite impossible," the Squire continued, "for us to foresee where this tendency will lead or to appraise it finally. It is certainly not for us to condemn wealth because we do not understand it, because it is new, and because we are unsympathetic to those who possess it at present. Many of the greatest movements of civilization started among ignorant folk. Later, men of wider outlook join the movements and give them universal application. The presence of Master Sherwood and Master Marshfield in finance, and especially of Squire Fulton in manufacturing, are hopeful signs. It may be that thousands of young men in Isaac's position are minded as he is, and that in another generation men of the highest education and integrity will be found everywhere in the possession of wealth and at the head of banks and factories. I confess that I feel apprehensive at Isaac's entering upon a course where the experience of none of us can be of help to him. But at least he will have access to Master Sherwood and Squire Fulton and Master Marshfield. Had it ever occurred to ye, Isaac, to discuss your intentions with one or more of them?"

"Yes, sir," said Ike. "I talked with Master Sherwood last Thursday. He said he couldn't advise me without knowing how you felt, but he as good as told me that if ever I was looking for a position in a bank, with your permission he'd find me one—sort of gathered he meant he'd consider giving me a position himself. I was figgering—if ye'll give your consent—to ask him for a position after Thanksgiving season's over. I'd be here for chores, and out of my salary I'd figger to pay a man to do my other work here through the winter—woodin', icin' and all. Fact is, I've already sounded out old Henry Hawks."

"Banking?" asked the Squire, confused. "Knowing your preoccupation with steam engines and machines generally, I supposed that if you had anything specifically in mind it would be in manufacturing." "Yes, sir," said Ike, "that's what I figger on in the long run. But it's a good idea to work in a bank first. If ye're to do much about manufacturing ye've first to know something about finance. I've an eye on something for the future, but it's kind of doubtful yet, and anyway, even if I had a choice, which I haven't, I'd figger 'twas best to start in a bank."

"Does that mean leaving the farm?" asked John. "No, not in the long run. If I can once get a good concern started, I could spend most of my time on the farm and just ride in once or twice a week." "I am afraid," said

John, "you underestimate the amount of time that industry demands. If you really get into it I'll wage you'll have to move into the Falls." "If I do, it won't be for long. Once I can lay by a few investments to stand behind us, I'll come back here quick enough. Then, of course, there's always the chance of the farm making more money on its own. If it does, I'll quit industry, except as sort of side issue, and move back here as a steady job. I ain't quitting the old place, that's certain."

After a pause the Squire said, "If you want to take a position with Master Sherwood for the winter, I shall make no objection. The only thing I ask ye is that you make clear to him that it is not necessarily permanent. Try it there for the winter, and I have no doubt you'll learn a deal about finance and industry. Postpone your decision about college till June. Perhaps you'll change your mind by then, and there will still be time to register. Eh, John?" John nodded, and Ike leaned forward and put his hand on his father's. "Thank ye, Pa," he said. "I won't disappoint ye."

"And now," Ike continued, rising, "I figger I've made enough trouble for one evening and I'd best go up." "I daresay it's time we all turned in," said the Squire, for he had been more shaken by Ike's announcement than he had acknowledged. Ike took a candle, and they all went out to the barn through the summer kitchen that was trembling every few seconds under the rumbling blows of the wind, while the mullions of the windows on the north side were already deep in snow. "Real nor'wester," said Ike as the three of them stood in the stalls beside the horses. "Here to stay," said the Squire with satisfaction. They blanketed the horses, returned to the keeping-room and the Squire reminded them to go in and say good night to their ma as she had asked them to do.

Sarah had overheard most of the conversation, and when Ike approached her, holding up the candle, she sat up in bed and stared at him with a look of terror. Then, as he leaned forward to kiss her she seized him by the shoulders and gave him a little shake. "Isaac," she whispered, "do you know what you are doing to your pa? Are you sure in your heart that you are doing right?" "No, Ma," said Ike, looking at her very intently, "I ain't sure what's right and what's wrong. I only figger that's the kind of work I'm cut out for, and it's the best way I can help the family along. Also, I ain't so sure Pa disagrees with me." "Yes, he does," she whispered, drawing him close. "Don't you understand that he'd rather cut off his hand than stand in your way? But if you actually went into competition with those—those —peculiar men at the Falls—I think it would kill him."

But to Ike, looking straight into his ma's steel-blue eyes, the prophecy she had uttered was insignificant—he hardly even heard it. To him the importance of the moment lay in the fact that, even though there was a surface disagreement, emotionally they were together again. The aloofness of the last ten days was over. Far from diverting his intentions from the direction they were taking, the sense of emotional closeness to his ma only strengthened his nature and reinforced his vitality to continue its own way. Taking her tenderly by her flannel nightgowned shoulders, he beamed on her with his big smile, whispered in her ear, "Don't worry about me, Ma," kissed her good night, and stepped back to make way for John.

Silently Sarah drew John down and pressed her head into his shoulder. Then she looked up, kissed him, patted his cheek, kissed him again, smiled and murmured, "Good night, my big boy."

Upstairs, for half an hour John and Ike had it out in whispers on their mattress in the back attic, while Ben slept soundly on his smaller mattress beside them, the rafters creaking and the blizzard whipping the roof over them like a titanic flail. There was no more quarrelling, for each above all things wanted to transcend the difference between them. At last John said, "Scamp, I just can't see things your way, though I shall keep on trying." "For my part," said Ike, "I can't see that agreement's so pesky important." "Perhaps not," said John. But his soul remained troubled, torn between his moral sense and his devotion to Ike. It was well below frost in the back attic, and they snuggled closer together as they settled into sleep.

CHAPTER XVIII

THE BLIZZARD of Tuesday night let up before dawn, and the day before Thanksgiving was shining blue, gold and white, the first real winter day. All that was needed now to make perfect sleighing for tomorrow would be the noon thaw, followed by a hard freeze tonight, both of which were certain.

The men's work of the day was limited to chores, the unveiling of the three-seater sleigh in the carriage shed, the scraping of rust from the runners, rubbing off oil from the winter harness, combing out the cream-colored horsehair plumes, and thereafter generally co-operating with the women in the preparations not only for the junket planned for the evening but for the elaborate festivities of the morrow. Sarah was the tyrant of the occasion, allotting her three subordinate females to their responsible tasks and attaching to each a committee of males to act as beasts of burden, bearing up from the cellar a sack of Irish and a sack of Indian potatoes, two buckets of turnips, half a dozen winter squash, as many pumpkins, and a bushel of onions. The turkeys were stuffed with sage, savory, marjoram, onions, bread moistened in milk, and butter; the pig with sage, saltish moist bread and onions. Cuts of pork, beef and venison were prepared. Two lemon pies were baked as a special delicacy. The kitchen and summer kitchen were decked with cornstalks, pumpkins and squash, and candles were put in the windows of keeping-room and north parlor. Finally, the whole house was cleaned again from back attic to buttery.

Among Tavie's duties was the preparation of the apple butter, a common delicacy which Sarah Lathrop had raised to the dignity of a specialty, and which she always postponed making until the day before Thanksgiving because of the rich aroma it spread through the house. It was a two days' process: on the first day, to boil ten gallons of cider down to five on the little stove in the summer kitchen; then, on Thanksgiving morning, to add the spices and stir expertly during the thickening to avoid the grave danger of sticking to the pot and burning. The work of the first day was elementary enough, being no more than to fetch the cider and keep a hot fire in the stove. So Tavie delegated this duty to her attendant committee of males, which was John and Ike.

Ever since Monday afternoon, when Ike had told John about having kissed Tavie, a change had been occurring in the relations of these three. John's self-consciousness seemed to have suddenly disappeared and he hovered around Tavie with eager and genuine attentiveness. Responsively, Tavie became vivacious and easy, not only with John but with the household generally. Fortified by this new attention from a source whence she had never expected it, her concern about her responsiveness to Ike evaporated. Her tense attitude toward him, extreme since he had kissed her, relaxed. She permitted herself to exult a little in what appeared to be the rivalry of the two brothers, and did not scruple to flirt playfully with both of them.

For Ike's part, he now stepped into the rôle of self-consciousness previously borne by John. By Wednesday morning it was plain that Tavie had come round to a friendly attitude again and, while he figured that the change had something to do with his announced intention to get Dandy back, he found himself too much affected by it to think about its causes one way or the other. Without analysis, he was obsessed by the notion that now Tavie was willing he should kiss her again, and, what was more important, he found himself wanting to kiss her more than he had ever specifically wanted anything of the kind in his life. The sudden intensity of his feelings troubled him, for there was nothing in the world to prevent their leading to serious developments. Consequently, he put himself on guard against possible commitments for which he was certainly not ready, grew self-conscious and artificial with Tavie as John had been before, as evasive in his glances at her as she had been with him for the past two weeks. But at the same time he hovered round her equally with John, and sought to help her in her duties in what he fancied was a thoroughly impersonal and unrevealing manner.

So there was indeed a sort of rivalry between the brothers, as to whether more wood was needed in the stove under the boiling cider, who should put it in, how the drafts should be set, who should bring Tavie another quart of milk from the buttery, who a slab of pork, who a measuring cup, who this or that tin of spices from the pantry, who should fetch the water for the final mopping of the summer kitchen, who should wield the one extra mop. And in all, while this competition was going on under a surface of pleasantry, there was a streak of edged feeling on Ike's part to which John, all the time slyly favored by Tavie, never failed to defer with some laughing observation to the effect that he was wrong again, that he guessed the only effect of a college education was to addle the brains for usefulness around the house.

Soon after sunset, at four-thirty, the work of preparation was completed. Master Lane and Ike went up to chores, and the women turned to the easy preparations of supper, at which old Thomas—"The Professor"—and Samantha were to be the only guests. The chill of winter evening crept into the house and Ben heaped up the fires in kitchen, keeping-room and north parlor till they roared and crackled against it. The sky grayed over the first stars. It began to snow lightly. The twilight deepened quickly into darkness, and the candles were lighted.

Just after the hall clock had struck half-past five, Cousin Joel in the keeping-room called, "Hark ye," and all rushed to the front windows to enjoy the year's first music of sleigh bells approaching through the night. In a moment Grandpa and Grandma jingled into the drive in the famous little cutter of the first Squire's, the lantern on the dashboard silhouetting its graceful shape of a shell and the lofty curve of the runners sweeping upward with the dashboard, then backward and forward again into the heads of two swans that seemed to be swimming on the snow.

Ike, who delighted in his grandmother, ran down from the barn through the darkness and snowfall, and John and Ben joined him from the house. The boys helped the octogenarian and his seventy-six-year-old spouse out of their bear robe and handed them to the kitchen door. Ike returned to milking, leaving John and Ben to tie and blanket the horse in the open barn and haul the cutter in backwards to be ready for hitching again.

On entering his son's house the Professor, with his lofty, deferential stoop, his long, slightly aquiline nose, gentle blue eyes and kindly smile, immediately filled the little mansion with an air of genial elegance, as if the north parlor had expanded to include the entire house. Samantha, on the other hand, with her snapping eyes in her broad, pale, heavy-jowled face, at once livened the air electrically and drew everybody's attention to herself, whether in apprehension or in mirth.

"Well, Sarah, my dear," she said, as her daughter-in-law took her heavy cloak and she gave herself an enormous, hen-like shake to settle into her elegant, puff-sleeved, wide-flaring, medium low-cut, heavy purple silk gown, "Well, Sarah, here we be in full regalia, makin' a powerful effort to impress the finicky folks from Connecticut. How do ye like me, Joel?" she demanded, turning full on her second cousin-in-law, her broad bosom, neck, ears and fingers aglitter with the Lathrop diamonds, her gray head surmounted with a many-colored squirrel's nest of lace cap, flowers, ribbons and feathers. "As for my Thomas," she continued, waiting for no reply but Joel's preparatory smile, "they tell me he's a little scrawny and ten years older'n you be. But for me, I still favor his leg, if it is good for nothin' but chasin' down gerundives and Sanskrit roots." And she gave her Thomas a reassuring pat on his lofty, shrunken cheek, he being in fact the most striking figure in the room in his lace-ruffled shirt and light blue velvet coat and knee-breeches of the old time, his silver-buckled shoes, and his white, silk-stockinged legs that were slim but gracefully modelled and not shrunken at all. He beamed silently down on his wife in the habit of sixty years, and she returned the smile as perfunctorily, then switched abruptly back to Joel.

"Ay, Joel, we're still holdin' our own, and ye're just as pretty a boy as ye were in 'eighty-nine when Tom fetched me to yer house on our weddin' trip, and ye were no bigger'n a grasshopper and ye whispered to me as we were leavin' that I was the beautifullest lady ye'd ever seen." "Well I remember, Samanthy," replied Joel, taking her hand and kissing it. "I have carried that image of ye till this day, and now I find it altered and dulled no whit, not by the shadow of a shadow."

"Don't distress yerself, Cousin Alvina," said Samantha. "I hain't stolen a lady's husband now these many years. Though I wouldn't mind," she added in a stage whisper, "sort o' borrowin' him fer a minute—some night that was dark enough so he couldn't see me too plain." And she gave Joel a playful bat on the head with her fan. "Ah, son," she said, turning toward the Squire, who had been standing patiently behind her with a glass of cordial, "ye're a thoughtful boy and just in time to save yer old mother from disgracin' ye fer good and all. Here's to ye, Alvina and Joel, and now I'll hush me and try t' behave like a lady."

Alvina, who was far too rarefied for jealousy, put her hand on Samantha's arm, whispered in her ear and tittered softly, whereupon Samantha guffawed, tossed off her cordial at a gulp, and both snickered again as they turned and walked arm in arm away from the rest and into the keeping-room. Homer Hislip, who had been laughing loudly at every gesture of Samantha, followed them, and presently the rest of the men, leaving Sarah and Tavie and Agatha to set supper.

Master Lane and Ike came stamping in, Master Lane stepping into the keeping-room and bending over Samantha's hand with a grace which the Squire could hardly have equalled. "Evening, Samanthy," he said; then, "Evening, Thomas," taking her husband's hand and exchanging with him an equally perfect half bow.

So far it was clearly the old people's party, and the rest stood aside indulgently and began discussing the weather with one another. Only Homer Hislip kept intruding noisy remarks into the circle of five seniors standing by the desk, until Alvina, with the vaguest politeness, asked him if he would do her the courtesy of telling her again his relationship to the family, whereupon he retired with an attempt at congressional dignity and asked the Squire how much corn he had put in that autumn.

At six o'clock Sarah summoned them to the kitchen, old Thomas said grace, and they all sat down informally to a pick-up meal of two cold hams, two cold legs of lamb, a pyramid of doughnuts, with cookies and cakes to match, a ten-pound cheese, a paltry two gallons of year-old cider, and relishes and jellies to suit. The men were just rising, having lighted their cigars, when they heard wheels whining on the snow in the drive. Looking out at a lantern moving busily in the dark, they made out Solon Samson hitching his horse and spring wagon to the post under the big maple.

He blanketed the horse, took little Numa from Charity on the seat, handed her down, and walked round to the kitchen door. The Squire opened it and they came in, kicking off the snow on the step and doorsill. "Good evening, John," said Solon, holding his sleeping boy in his arms. "I took the liberty of coming early because I am unfortunately required to leave at nine." All knew this meant duty for the Underground. John had an image of the Negro he had seen with the shawl over his head and wondered if he was shivering now up there in the old bee tree.

Sarah came forward and kissed Charity who turned from her to hold Agatha in a long, snowy embrace. Sarah brushed off Numa's cloak and led Solon, still carrying him, upstairs to the boys' room, now Aggie's and Homer's, traditionally the temporary orphanage during the entertainment of parents. The Squire performed the introductions all round in the keeping-room, while Tavie bore thither a bowl of steaming grog and deposited it on the long table by the window.

The kitchen door opened again and in walked the dark, leather-faced tanner, Lemuel Oaks, with his equally dark-haired but fair-skinned wife, Felicity, their equally dark-haired and dark-skinned son, Constant, and two more sleeping infants to go up on Aggie's and Homer's bed.

After them came Dr. Swift, jovial, rotund-bodied and rotund-headed physician and tombstone poet-laureate from up the hill. With him, his tall wife with the one-time doll-like, infantile face, now heavily furrowed; their pretty, slightly awkward, marriageable daughter, Diodema, who had been told, somewhat unfortunately, that her charm lay in her vivacity; and, finally, the tall, powerful, thirty-year-old minister, Nathaniel Norcross, dark-eyed, dark- and wavy-haired, sensitive and eager in manner, death to all ladies, protégé of the Squire's, boarder with the Swifts and supposed suitor to Diodema, modern minded young divine who had already created a schism in the Hollow Church.

Last of the guests came Jehu Jones, tall, skin-and-bones Nestor of the community, spry and of incalculable age, jack of all the usual trades that every citizen had, plus those of sexton, stone mason, cider miller, musician, dancing master and master of all ceremonies, silken bearded, adept at stowing a secret quid long before the practice became fashionable, incongruous in the elegance of his manners and rusticity of his speech, though he was easy as most with his Hebrew and Greek Testaments; Jehu Jones, ancient and professional bachelor, possessed of only two sartorial outfits, both of which he had inherited from his pa who fought at Bunker Hill, was afterwards a colonel of Massachusetts militia, and came west to York state with the general emigration in the 'nineties when Jehu was already a man grown. Tonight he had on his black cocked hat and the long faded, blue, revolutionary officer's cape which had been smart in its day and which Jehu could still swing with a fitting swagger. As he entered the kitchen he bowed to the room with a handsome sweep of his hat and, as the Squire stood by him waiting to take his cape, he took his time in carefully removing the clean but colorless gloves from his marvellously long, skinny fingers. "On such a snowy night ye should have driven up, Jehu Jones," said his host. "No, John, them little snowflakes a' been a-pepperin' at me fer nigh on ninety year, and they hain't as much chance o' hittin' me as ye'd have a-settin' in the top o' one o' them maples o' yourn a-shootin' down at a pertickler straight blade o' timothy." He permitted the Squire to lift his cape, walked into the keeping-room and faced the company in a perfectly fitting, dark blue velvet coat and knee-breeches of the end of the century.

Immediately Jehu exhibited that delicate grace of movement which had made him famous in ballroom and parlor, the featherlike gesture of his fingers and the lightness of his long steps which gave him the appearance of floating from lady to lady in greeting. When Alvina felt the touch of those fingers she experienced such a tremor as she thought she had forgotten and came out of her near-sighted vagueness to give him a smile and a droop of her long lashes the like of which she had not bestowed these twenty years. It was something to be in the room with that young Apollo of a minister, but to meet such a beau as this to whom you still were a mere girl—mercy me!—why, it was worth all the trip from Connecticut!

"Madam," he was saying, "I hope before long ye'll do a turn with an old leather strap that ain't lost all its pliancy yet." Alvina felt herself coloring, looked away, and to her astonishment noticed that all the other ladies had left the room. "Excuse me," she giggled to Jehu, rising and dangling her fingers at him from a forearm raised close to her side. "I'm a silly fool, you know. I wonder how long I've been intruding on you gentlemen." And Alvina rustled into the kitchen, joining the ladies, some of whom were helping with the supper dishes and others visiting in the north parlor.

Seven of the fourteen men now left to their grog and cigars were the little senate that, by sufferance of the community, ran the affairs of Lathrop Hollow, those outside the oligarchy being the three Lathrop boys, Joel, Brandon, Homer and Master Lane. All but young Ben filled their mugs or glasses. At the Squire's insistence Joel seated himself in the big haircloth rocker, and Solon Samson in Sarah's low, veneer rocker where he looked all arms and legs, with his knees almost as high as his face. The rest disposed themselves as might be on the settle and chairs, on the table, leaning against the mantel, and the Lathrop boys sitting on the floor.

Being as it were in the President's chair, Joel threw out the opinion that the Clay-Webster Compromise of last summer had settled the slavery problem for good, and with this the conversation was off. The Squire was of the view that the Compromise would be effective only to the degree that the people accepted its two main features. The South must abate its fury over the admission of California with a free constitution; the North must desist from its flagrant defiance of the Fugitive Slave Law. The slavery question would be settled for good only when the Southerners settled it in their own way, most of their leaders deploring it as much as the North did, but being unable to cope with it quickly since their whole cotton economy was bound up in it.

Jehu Jones observed, "It looks like them philosophical and conscientious Southern leaders is a-gittin' less squeamish every day about their 'peculyer institootion.' I jest come from readin' a sermon by some hell-fire artist down t' Mississippi as explains how slavery's a mighty virtuous thing, healthiest condition fer the darkies, and as how we fellers up here is a'mighty sinners fer shirkin' our share towards keepin' 'em in their uncommon comfortable shackles."

Homer Hislip cleared his throat and said sententiously, "Best advice I could give ye out in these parts 'd be to leave these matters to us members o' Congress, likewise t' our Western folks that has nigh the population and more ginger'n any part o' the country. Ye kin set it down fer sartin we ain't a-goin' t' let 'em extend slavery to New Mexicy or Uty, or anywheres else. Furthermore, when Congress convenes in December Senator Clay'll shet up all this gabbin' fer good. Though he's a slaveholder, he's a Kentuckian, and, bein' that ain't fer different from our folk out north o' th'

Ohio, we like him." In response to these insolent and somewhat incon- sistent declarations the Squire and Dr. Swift agreed that any new state- ment from Clay would be of great value. But they likewise agreed that in any new statement he would insist upon strict adherence to the Compro- mise, and therefore rigid enforcement of the Fugitive Slave Law.

This immediately brought forth from Solon Samson the resounding opin- ion that the Fugitive Slave Law was unconstitutional, and so introduced an old and endless argument between him and the Squire and Brandon. Pass- ing through the familiar region of the constitutional provisions regarding citizenship, trial by jury and the return of fugitives from service, it opened out into the loftiest regions of jurisprudence and higher moral law, the Reverend Norcross and young John joining heatedly in support of Solon.

The talk took the inevitable turn toward abolition, and Solon Samson was as categorical upon its unconstitutionality as he had just been upon the unconstitutionality of the Fugitive Slave Law. He went farther and said that even an Amendment abolishing slavery would be contrary to the whole spirit of our Federal Government. And here young John, growing always more heated, parted company with his idol.

"Then, sir," John demanded, his eyes glowing steel black and his jaw setting, "are we to understand that we are not, after all, a Union, not one country that can move forward toward human betterment according to the will of the majority?" "We are a Union for specified purposes only," said Solon. "For all other purposes we are thirty-one sovereign republics."

"If you will forgive me, gentlemen," said John, "I believe that the feeling of the younger generation is otherwise, at least in the North. At college I talk and debate with young men from every state and I believe their views reflect those of their contemporaries throughout the nation. I know of not one young man from above the Mason-Dixon Line who does not believe that we shall and must move forward together, through Reform, toward a more ideal order of things. The liberal thought of the world is looking to the leadership of this nation, and if it fails to fulfill its mission its failure will be that of humanity. We realize with deference that we are young, that our opinions are yet of small weight. But our determination is such that we believe it will survive into the time when we properly assume our share in the direction of events."

The talk ranged on into the South's continuing threats of secession and non-intercourse with the North, because of the admission of California and the widespread belief that the North would not enforce the Fugitive Slave Law. The Squire read a few typical, violent quotations from recent state- ments of the Governors of Alabama and Georgia, from groups of planters in Georgia and Mississippi, from newspapers in Natchez, Montgomery, Jackson, Dallas, Columbus. The Squire said that here, in these threats of secession, lay the gravest danger. If only we would enforce the Compromise and stop meddling with the South, they would work out their own problem. But when Mr. Garrison, Mrs. Stowe and the other Abolitionists fulminated against them, threatened them, and called them fiends, they were being gradually driven into a position of justifying their "peculiar institution," and of considering actual withdrawal from the Union. To this Solon Samson said quietly that secession, of all proposals, was indisputedly unconstitutional, that while the powers of the Federal Government were limited, within those limits they and the Union were perpetual, until two-thirds of the States should agree to alter or withdraw them.

And with this pronouncement there was no disagreement, for it touched one of the deepest convictions of every man there, the conviction of the sanctity of the Federal Union as the best government on earth and the promise to all nations of the early and earthly perfectibility of mankind. It was one of those convictions that, in these modern, liberal minds, had taken the place of the old, orthodox ideal of the perfectibility of mankind in Heaven. It was, therefore, a conviction in defense of which these men, in their inflexible idealism and moral integrity, would be willing to die. With Solon's declaration that secession was unconstitutional there fell a moment of silent agreement. To the rustle of snow outside and the rhythm of the tall clock in the hall they heard time sweeping over them. But they heard no horsemen riding it.

Only the Squire and John foresaw, and they but faintly, a deeper threat in the rage of the Southern extremists. The Squire, continuing his protest against badgering the South with threats of abolition, pointed out that if we did at last force them to secession, however unconstitutional, we might then find ourselves faced with the "difficult alternative of either letting them go or proceeding against them with arms, which would only aggravate the controversy beyond the possibility of settlement in any foreseeable time." He turned to John. "I wish you would raise these questions among your young friends, and suggest to them that patience, rather than action, may be the best method of effecting their desirable ends."

"I am sorry to say, Pa, that we have debated these matters many times, and, with a few exceptions, we have concluded that in defense of the two principles, the equality of all men before the law and the preservation of the Union, it will be preferable, if necessary, to proceed to military measures against the South. It would hardly be a war. The South would capitulate at a show of our strength." "That was what the British thought in 'seventy-five," said the Squire. And he looked straight down at his twenty-year-old son with a vague fear.

"Come what may," continued John, his head lifted defiantly, "the North will not permit secession. This continent must be either all free or all slave. If we can make it all free, it will become at once the first great temple of justice in the world. If it is to be all slave, then we would have done better to have remained slaves under British tyranny. But if we try to remain half slave and half free we shall become the laughingstock of the world."

"Strikes me," put in Jehu Jones, "we might survive bein' a laughin'-stock fer the world if it give 'em any pleasure. What sets kind o' oneasy on my stummick is the suspicion o' our gittin' ourselves up ridiculous in our own eyes, a-bitin' off mebbe a leetle more'n we can chew in tryin' t' tell them sinful southern fellers how t' run their affairs—like some folks I could mention as'd like to deprive the wicked old sexton o' his liquor, or like Deacon Birdseye's mule a-trying t' do a gentlemanly turn by Jed Oxbow's mare and gittin' nothin' but a paste in the ribs fer his more'n kindly intentions."

Everyone saw that young John was pale with rage, and all looked to the Squire to end the conversation. "Ultimately, gentlemen," said the minister soothingly, "these matters will be determined, not by Constitutional Amendment, nor yet by the Supreme Court of the United States, but by the Highest Court of All." All accepted this diplomatic resolution as it was intended except Solon Samson who, still in his legalistic role, took the reference to be to the final court of human disputes and the actual source of all law—namely war. He was about to utter an opinion upon the probable outcome of hostilities, should they arise, when, to the relief of everybody else, the harpsichord began to tinkle in the north parlor and Agatha to sing "Home, Sweet Home." The Squire opened the doors to the hall and to the kitchen. All the men rose, tipped back their heads as one man, finishing their grog, and threw their cigar-butts in the fireplace.

John stayed behind the rest to take another touch of grog and calm down. As he turned round he saw Ike waiting for him and beamed down on him affectionately to show he was all right now. "Why didn't you support me, Scamp?" he murmured good-naturedly, half expecting the answer. " 'Cause I think Pa's right and you're wrong," said the younger brother, looking up at him very straight and very troubled. "I'm danged sorry, 'Paloosa. I guess I ain't thought about it as much as you, but so far as I can figger, it's a matter o' their mindin' their business and our mindin' ours." "Well, don't lose any sleep over it, Scamp," said John, patting his shoulder. "If you think I'm wrong in this, then I guess we're quits, eh?" Ike gave him a dubious smile. "I don't bother much," he said, "about who's right and who's wrong. All that bothers me is not standing beside ye, whether ye're right or wrong." "Me too," said John impulsively. And so, with mutuality restored, they walked out into the kitchen.

Homer Hislip seemed to be waiting for them in the kitchen, all the rest being gathered round Aggie at the harpsichord in the north parlor, just finishing "Black Eyed Susan" and presently beginning, "Where Are You Going, My Pretty Maid?" Homer walked up to John with a smile that had a sneer in it. "If I figgered you young college fellers meant anything more'n talk I'd likely be with ye. But I'll bet ye a dollar ye never do a thing and we'll jog along in some sort o' compromise until them people settle their own problem, like yer pa says." "How long will you give us?" asked John with arched eyebrows and repressing an impulse to knock his brother-in-law down. "I'll bet ye don't stir up anything in twenty year." "If you'll make it a hundred dollars," said John, "I'll take it." "Keerect," said Homer and shook hands, dropping his eyes. His opinion of these people was always being upset by things of this sort. Ike puckered his brow, wondering where the 'Paloosa expected to find his hundred in twenty years.

Tavie came in smiling and went into the pantry for ingredients to replenish the bowl in the keeping-room. She suspected from the flush on Ike's cheek that he had been having several "swigs o' somethin'." When she passed the second time Ike felt her attraction surge in him, and he walked into the north parlor and stood with his back to the kitchen, singing with the rest "Oh, Had I the Wings of a Dove." In a moment he sensed Tavie's eyes on him, but when he turned around very casually as he sang, she was not in sight. His yielding to this illusion annoyed him greatly, and he missed a bar of the song, swearing to himself, by Crimus, that he wouldn't look at her again, not if she came and stood right up against him to be kissed. From the kitchen Tavie indeed had seen him look round at her. She flitted back into the keeping-room and, making as if to stir the grog, concluded—to her distress, as she thought—that Ike must be desperately in love with her. She must of course put a stop to that! She knew she had been playing the minx during the last few days. Wherefore, during the rest of the evening, she rose into unusual gaiety with John, seeming to disregard Ike, and watching him only covertly.

When "Had I the Wings of a Dove" was over Sarah suggested a minuet. The furniture in the north parlor was moved back to the wall and Agatha remained at the harpsichord. Although the Squire had overheard a part of Jehu's flirtation with Alvina, he exercised his prerogative as host and led her out. Joel invited Sarah, Jehu took Samantha, and Thomas led out

Charity Samson. The blue-gray room was alive in its proper period of the Revolution, and the music and the dancers moved with a composed grace which the younger generation had not inherited. When the first figure was over Jehu said that he had "a pertickler smart pain in his heart as he never heered Doc Swift havin' physic fer, bein's it meant imminent death unless Mistress Alvina'd have pity on him." So they did another figure, Sarah and the three men dropping out to make room for the other elders who had not danced before.

When it was over, Solon Samson, whose grace in dancing would have been more appropriate to the floor of the Roman Senate than to a minuet, regretted that they must take their leave. In the meantime the young men had carried the big table out into the summer kitchen and the main kitchen, larger than the north parlor and uncarpeted, was ready for the more sprightly modern dances. Young John rushed forward and begged the Samsons to stay long enough for him to dance with Tavie, or, if they must go now, to grant him permission to escort her home within the hour. Charity Samson besought her husband with a look and he agreed to stay until nine-thirty—curiously to Tavie's disappointment, for when she heard John offer to see her home, his first voluntary gesture of the kind in their lives, she felt a strange strength, a strange sense of repose flood through her nerves, a crystallization of her feeling of release during the last two days. She saw Constant Oaks glaring at John from the kitchen and was sorry for him. She saw Ike and Diodema Swift giggling in the corner and hoped she hadn't driven him to that. But nothing mattered for the moment. For the first time in her life she was at the center of the world, in control of everything—all of which her mother observed, and with no prophetic apprehensions.

Jehu Jones had professionally omitted to bring his fiddle, but Master Lane was up on the modern dances. In a kitchen dance a harmonica was better than a fiddle anyway, and Jehu Jones would be free to prompt. Master Lane took a candle up to his room and returned with his father's most cherished harmonica. When he came down the set in the kitchen was three-quarters formed for a quadrille. John and Tavie, Ike and Diodema, the Reverend Norcross and Agatha. As if conferring on her a mighty favor, Homer Hislip led out his mother-in-law, she protesting that she knew nothing of the modern steps.

"Sets in order," commanded Jehu Jones. He nodded to Master Lane. The harmonica and the whole house broke into sudden, irrepressible life. Standing in the doors to watch, the faces of all the parents, except that of Solon Samson, broke into smiles, in spite of their professed scorn of these jigging dances—lascivious they were called by the orthodox, of whom there were none present. Joel began unconsciously to tap his foot and Alvina—who had had a glass of grog—waved her hands airily. John lifted Tavie's hand high, the other couples did the same, Jehu Jones began to sing, the floor began to vibrate under the rhythm of more than a half-ton falling and rising, and the tenons of the big beams settled another sixty-fourth of an inch into their sockets in the sills:

> "Honors all—
> To great and small.
> Eight hands round and around ye go—
> Eight hands back and not too slow.
> First couple lead to the right—
> Four hands around with all yer might—
> Duck fer the oyster—
> Dive fer the clam—
> Dip fer the home and the happy land—
> Lead to the next—four hands round—
> Four hands round and hold yer ground—
> Dip fer the oyster—
> Dive fer the clam—
> Duck fer the home and the happy land—
> Lead to the next and circle four—
> Four hands round to the open door—
> Dive fer the oyster—
> Duck fer the clam—
> Dip fer the home and the happy land—
> Turn yer own—
> And yer corner too—
> And yer own again if she's dear to you.
> Second couple lead to the right—
> Circle four like a swallow in flight—"

At the end of the second couple's tour Jehu winked at John and instead of calling, "Turn yer own," shouted, "*Swing* yer own," and John electrified the company by seizing Tavie by the waist instead of by the hand and swinging her full twice around instead of the usual single turn, then—"And yer corner too"—doing the same to his sister Agatha and—"And yer own again if ye're able to"—returning to Tavie to swing her so vigorously that she almost left the floor. This was the latest wrinkle, suspected to be of the lowest origins. All the on-lookers gasped, Solon Samson and

Constant Oaks scowled, the other dancers cheered, and at that moment the kitchen door opened abruptly; there was a whiff of cold air and a tall, black, snowy apparition in a broad-brimmed felt hat stood there motionless.

Master Lane and Jehu Jones saved the situation. The harmonica panted more vigorously than before, and Jehu was ready with a rhyme—

> "Third couple lead to the right—
> In Deacon Victory Birdseye's sight—
> Duck fer the Deacon
> That danged old clam—
> Dive fer the Deacon and don't give a damn—"

Meanwhile the Squire had gone up quickly to the new arrival. "Delighted to see ye, Victory Birdseye. Let me take your coat. You've arrived at a gay moment." "Indeed I have, John Lathrop," boomed the Deacon, for it was necessary to shout above the music and the rhythm of the feet. "I must apologize for intruding. I had intended simply to make a friendly call, but I perceive that like Moses coming down from the mountain I would be but a discordant note in your entertainment." "Nonsense, Vic," said the Squire in his most jovial tone. "You know we are always delighted to see ye." "Some other time, Brother Lathrop," said the Deacon with a scowl, for he was just beginning to catch some of Sexton Jones's improvisations. "You know full well of my disapproval of dancing and extreme merriment, though I assure ye that if I had known ye were having a revel I should not have stopped." This the Squire knew was a lie, for the music could surely be heard a quarter of a mile away and the probability was that the old gander had been at the window ever since the dance began, perhaps even longer, for he was not one to inaugurate a call at nine o'clock in the evening.

As these thoughts were passing through his mind he saw the deacon stiffen suddenly. It happened that the figure had just ended, and it also happened that the fourth couple, who had been doing the last tour, to the increasing scurrilities of Jehu Jones, were none other than Agatha and the young Reverend Norcross. Deacon Victory Birdseye perceived for the first time that the minister was involved in this blasphemy, and the wrath of the Lord was rising through his frame and flashing as a fiery sword from his eyes, which were almost all of him that was perceptible between his black tippet and his big black hat. "John Lathrop," he suddenly thundered, injecting a rhetorical quaver in his voice and looking straight at the young minister, "fer you and yer friends I have no word of admonition at this time, fer I come as an uninvited guest and as such I now take my leave. But seein' here this ordained minister of the Lord engaged even as a participant in these heathenish revels, I could not meet my Lord upon my knees this night if I had not admonished him. Sir, I warn ye that ye are engaged in the traffic of Satan, and be doubly warned that there is no fall so profound as the fall of angels, no pit so deep, no fire so hot as that prepared fer 'em. Ye be still young. I call upon ye while there is time to mend yer ways." And he turned and disappeared into the night without waiting for an answer.

There was a silence tense with incipient laughter, resentment, and in one or two cases faint jabs of conscience. Then Samantha spoke shrilly from beside the punch-bowl in the keeping-room. "Trouble with Vic is he never could learn to dance nohow. Jehu, d'ye recall the time he fell down in the money-musk t' the cotilllion? That, I recollect, was in Adams's administration, an' he ain't had the gumption t' try it since." "An' d'ye recollect, Samanthy," said Jehu, slapping his knee with delighted memories, "'t the next cotillion you and I was peekin' at him through a knothole—." Words failed Jehu in his ecstasy, and Samantha took up the account. "He was a-courtin' yer ma, Charity, and all 't once she give that lovely laugh o' hers, like water fallin', and poor Vic he jest strutted off like a rooster." "And next Sabbath," resumed Jehu, gasping and wiping his eyes with his big handkerchief, "an' the next Sabbath he stood up t' meetin' and bore witness to his first vision." "And not long after," continued Samantha, "poor Fanny Oxbow got religion and up and married Vic, and thirty years later, when poor Fanny was already crazier'n a bedbug, along come young Hosanna." "Undoubtedly an immaculate conception," said Dr. Swift gravely, and everybody roared.

Solon Samson took down his coat, wearing his heaviest scowl and the brighter glitter of eye that was his smile. While he went upstairs and returned with the sleeping Numa in his arms, the Squire helped Charity on with her scarf and cloak. Tavie whispered breathlessly to John that she must go, and he helped her with her things. The Samsons said their farewells, the Squire at the last minute holding a spray of mistletoe over Charity and giving her a smack on the cheek. And when the cheers for this boldness had subsided, the rest of the guests began also to put on their things.

In the spring-wagon Tavie, wrapped in a blanket, sat in the straw behind her parents and her little brother. She was happier than she had ever been in her life, recalling with special enthusiasm that John was as ardent a

Reformer as she herself. It had stopped snowing, and light clouds travelling on a fast wind above the earth were veiling and unveiling the moon and patches of stars. Solon, driving, reflected that it was coming off cold and clear and that the crunching of wagon-wheels would be audible for miles. But he felt reasonably secure in the tip-off the marshal had given him, that the road through Field Settlement, having been patrolled Monday and Tuesday nights, would be unwatched tonight.

It was already ten o'clock when, having seen his family into the house and brought in more wood, Solon drove out the lane with his trembling freight. Charity and Tavie sat in front of the fire, discussing the party. It was the first time they had been alone together since the crisis of the crystal on Monday. In a pause Charity took the bull by the horns and told her daughter that she thought best she should leave the Lathrop household for good. Tavie presumed some kind of prophetic vision was involved. "Who is it, Ma?" she asked, playing with the hearth-broom. "Is it John or Ike?" As Charity hesitated to answer her question, Tavie added, "If I left now, you know, it would seem that I was running away from John." "By all means stay on through the season," said Charity. "It is the coming winter I am thinking of."

"But, Ma," said Tavie gaily, jumping up and reseating herself on the floor at her mother's knee, "there is no reason in the world to be concerned about Ike. We are not at all congenial, you know. And furthermore,"—dropping her voice to a confidential whisper—"it is John I like."

Charity was startled and confused. Such a confession implied some kind of emotional commitment, such as hardly could have occurred in the three days John had been home; and if it had been made last September Charity was sure she would have seen some sign of it before now. Tavie—as surprised by her statement as her mother—adjusted herself quickly and dropped her eyes in maidenly fashion. But there were no tears, no flutter of wings in the psychic air, and Charity, although literally accepting her daughter's announcement, was yet somehow unable to envelop her with the maternal blessing which would have been appropriate. Instead, she merely patted her on the shoulder and lifted up her face. "It is John I like too," she whispered, kissing Tavie on the forehead.

CHAPTER XIX

T A V I E was a-flutter when she entered the Lathrop kitchen in the dawn twilight of Thanksgiving, and she felt a sort of disappointment she told herself was a sense of relief when she found that Ike was already up to chores. The kitchen fire was crackling up round its three fresh chestnut sticks, and Tavie knew that Ike had laid it, because of the way he always laid the bottom stick askew to insure the draft. She hung up her wraps and went into the dim summer kitchen where the fire in the stove was roaring up the pipe, but as yet had made no perceptible inroad on the night chill. She saw that in starting this fire Ike had set off the pot of prospective apple-butter, though he needn't have bothered. It still needed an hour or more of boiling before the sugar and spices could be added, and it was only after that that it would need tending to keep it from burning. Tavie set it back on the stove, half closed the draft and the damper, and immediately the heat began to swell out into the room.

She heard John coming down the back stairs and her heart gave a jump. He walked into the summer kitchen with his tall, easy swing, and took her hand in both of his. But all he said was, "Good morning, Tave. How much snow do you make it?" Then he turned from her and looked out doors.

"Near two inches," Tavie replied. She tried to congratulate herself on how much easier John's company was than Ike's, his eyes showing none of that devastating light that Ike's had when they were alone and he looked at her with the pucker in his brow. But she missed that light all the same, and she was annoyed at John's nonchalance now, in contrast with his zest of the evening before. Also he had on his oldest clothes, and they never became him. She started for the kitchen just as Ben came down the back stairs.

"Oh, Ben," she said before he was fairly out of the door. "I suppose," said Ben, walking into the summer kitchen without any greeting, "you wish to remind me of my duty to fetch in some stove wood. Just for that, I'll fetch in wood everywhere else, and you will find three cord of stove lengths on the other side of the pile against the barn." "I wanted to ask you and John," said Tavie, "to carry back the big table into the kitchen, and afterwards to split three squash."

While they carried in the table she rolled the big winter squash on spread newspapers. Ben fetched an ax and, with strokes as delicate as if he were carving, halved, quartered, eighthed and sixteenthed them into chunks small enough for steaming, leaving Tavie to finish them and clean up the mess. In the meantime she lit the fire in the oven, for the pig must be put in early.

John helped Ben with the wood and water chores, then together they started up to the carriage shed to get the sleigh. The gold sun was just rolling up over the tall pines to the right of the Upper Road, and they paused to look back at it. The sky, now clear, swelled rapidly from slate-blue into rich turquoise. The snowy fields to the eastward under the sun sparkled like diamonds, and the white lace on the trees by the road was everywhere bordered in gold. Below them to the north and west the whole Hollow shone dazzling white as the shadow of Lathrop hill contracted toward them, and on the opposite slope it was hard to tell forest from pasture.

"Fine day, Runt," said John. "Indeed it is," said Ben absently. His eye had spotted a fox on the snow-covered sand hill half a mile below them. "Yoo-hoo," he shouted through cupped hands. John then saw the fox too, but Ben saw him lift his foot and his nose. "Yoo-hoo," he sang again, and they both saw the fox turn and vanish over the knoll. "There's a new den down there," said Ben as they walked on up the slope. "I go down sometimes to watch them and they don't mind me any more than as if I were a cow."

They went into the carriage shed where the big, cream-colored, three-seater sleigh had been dusted yesterday, and its dashboard plumes combed out so they seemed alive and eager to toss to the pace of the horses. John and Ben took down the pole from the ceiling, but when they tried to attach it the king-bolt stuck. As Ben tapped it with a stone he said, "I can't figure why folks like to trap things, especially foxes. They don't take two chickens a year and they're death on the ground hogs." "Never was much for it myself," said John, "or shooting either for that matter. Down at Yale I even joined the Connecticut Association for the Humane Treatment of Animals." "Can't understand that any better," said Ben, still tapping the king-bolt; "always having to join some association or other, as if you needed folks to agree with what you'd already settled in your own mind." "It's the only way to get things done, Runt," said John, with a patronizing smile. "Well, what's all this need of doing so much?" said Ben. "Ain't just living chore enough?" This gave John pause before he replied, "I daresay you'll see it differently after you go to college."

Ben got the king-bolt loose, they let in the pole and proceeded to bump the sleigh gently down across the plowed and frost-hardened garden to the horse barn. On the way Master Lane and Ike successively passed them, yoking the milk down to the buttery. They backed the sleigh into the barn, propped it up, and set to greasing the runners with tallow. The Squire came out in his best broadcloth finery, looked over the sleigh, then for the first time walked into Dandy's old stall to inspect Ike's new chestnut. Chesty tossed up his head and rolled back an eye—it was a peculiar fact that in all his life no horse had ever struck, bitten or kicked at the Squire.

Meanwhile in the house the women had foregathered earlier than usual, in order to complete the preparation of the day's banquet before breakfast, that the cooking might start immediately after the midday festivities. Sarah as usual tended to the pumpkin pie, both crust and custard, and stuffed the goose. The rest spitted the two turkeys on one spit, and afterwards the goose on another, and disposed the vegetables in the five pots where they were to be boiled. Last of the preparations, the embers were raked from the now hot oven, and the twenty-five pound, stuffed pig was put on an enormous dripping pan and shut up to bake till dinner at three. Meanwhile, Sarah and Tavie both kept an eye on the boiling apple butter.

It was almost eight o'clock when at last the breakfast bell rang and the household assembled in the kitchen, now more crowded than before because of Sarah's, Alvina's and Aggie's best and most voluminous Sunday-go-to-meeting gowns. The Squire asked Cousin Joel to say the blessing, which took the form of an encomium upon the Lathrop family, past and present, and a somewhat patronizing injunction on the Lord to bless it, with the implication that He would perforce do so if He knew what was good for Him. After breakfast Joel continued in the same vein by reading the boastful Forty-seventh Psalm, and ended the inauguration of this day of thanks with a prayer in which the Lord figured incidentally but in which John, Ike and Ben were especially advised of their distinguished tradition, their high future and their duties respecting it.

By nine o'clock morning chores were finished. Sarah added the sugar and cinnamon to the apple butter and left Tavie to stir it as it thickened, with increasing danger of burning. Master Lane and the boys went upstairs to put on their best clothes, John the gray tailored suit with the striped waistcoat, Ike and Ben their new store suits of broadcloth, Ike's blue and

Ben's tan. John tied Ben's broad black tie for him, but Ike said he guessed he might as well start learning for himself.

Coming down the back stairs, Ike found Tavie for the moment alone in the kitchen, and decided that this was as good a time as any to test his oath of independence of the previous evening. "How'll I do, Tave?" he inquired, as she carried a pail of water to the fire, apparently unaware of him. She looked around casually and suppressed a thrill under a look of calm appraisal—Ike was more boyishly appealing in home-spun, but these new finely fitting feathers set off his strength of body and will and made a man of him. "You're first-rate, Ike," said Tavie artificially, "all except—except for the tie."

"Will ye fix it for me?" he asked coolly. While she untied, unwound, rewound and retied it much as she had done that morning two weeks before, she scowled, keeping her eyes studiously on her work. But when she had finished and backed off to look up at him, she saw in his big blue eyes such a profoundly cold, although smiling, indifference as made her catch her breath. "That will do nicely," she managed to say. "Thank ye, Tave," said Ike, "and now is there anything I can do for *you?*" "No, thanks," said Tavie, picking up the pail again and swinging out the crane. With self-conscious dignity Ike paced through the kitchen and joined the old folks in the keeping-room.

Five minutes later the family got one of its semi-annual delights, reserved for Thanksgiving and Independence Day, when Master Lane appeared in full regalia of two generations before: royal purple velvet coat and knee-breeches fastened with silver buckles, white silk stockings elaborately embroidered, shiny black shoes with silver buckles, white velvet waistcoat with pearl buttons, profusion of lace on shirt-front and wrists, and—triumph of vanished splendor—his ancestral white wig with its rusty black bow. Bowing slightly to acknowledge the compliments of one after another, flourishing his be-laced wrists as he took snuff from his silver box, he proceeded once across the keeping-room and back, then as three mornings previously, sat down on the settle, crossed his legs with dignity, and informed the Squire that times were not what they used to be.

At a quarter of ten John and Ike went out and harnessed Mol and Pol to the sleigh, the back-straps bearing lofty, cream-colored, horse-hair plumes to match the paint of the body and the other two plumes on the dashboard, the breast straps and surcingles melodious with a dominant chord of bells. Walking beside the sleigh, Ike drove the horses out to the mounting block at the end of the path from the front door. Ben brought two foot stoves from the house and stowed one under each

of the two front seats. As the fast ten o'clock ringing began to float up
from the Hollow through the blue and white air, the Squire and Sarah,
Joel and Alvina, Brandon and Master Lane came out the front door: the
Squire in his tall, shiny hat, black cape, fawn gloves, and carrying his
gold-headed cane tucked under his arm; Joel in his mulberry beaver and
greatcoat, with his thin, gold-headed walking stick as tall as his shoulder;
Brandon in his silk hat and dark blue greatcoat; Master Lane in his old
cocked hat and frayed, brown cape; Sarah in a black-velvet-covered, flat-
backed bonnet trimmed with cherries and red ribbons, long, black, braid-
trimmed coat fitted and flaring over her gown, and slightly yellowing
ermine tippet and muff; Alvina swaying in wider stiffening under a blue
silk, quilted cloak with globe-like, puffed sleeves in the old, empire fashion,
a new pair of pink velvet mitts, and a smart new bonnet cut back at the
cheeks, adorned with pink marabou and rouching under the brim and
half a dozen long pink ribbons trailing variously in front and behind her
shoulders.

Ben threw forward the bear robes from the three seats. The ladies were
assisted in first, stepping up and across from the mounting block, and
there was a long flouncing and adjusting of dresses. Brandon and Master
Lane climbed into the back seat, and the Squire and Joel walked round
and sidled into the few inches left them beside their wives. Ben threw
back the robes and tucked in the front two with special care, so that the
heat of the braziers was contained around grateful, silk-stockinged legs.
Agatha and Tavie came to the front door. The Squire took the reins from
Ike and the horses danced a little, livening their orchestra of bells. The
Squire released them and they leapt jangling into their collars, everybody
waved, and the senior Lathrops slid out into the highway to that rich,
rhythmed music of winter, always so like and so much gayer than the
frog-bells of spring. Immediately after them Agatha, Homer and the three
boys set out for church on foot, leaving Tavie to tend Aggie's baby and
the apple butter, to prepare for the large company expected after church,
to take out the pig while giving the oven an intermediate firing late in the
morning, and to complete innumerable other details in preparation for the
feast of mid-afternoon.

The five young Lathrops walked down most of the half mile of Lathrop
Lane to the fast rhythm of Sexton Jones' preliminary summons that filled
the Hollow, rebounding in clashing echoes from all the white, surrounding hills. On the way they were passed and saluted by the Swifts in their
crimson-painted, gilt-trimmed bobsleigh with plumes on the horses to
match and specially deep-throated bells on the thills; by Grandma and

Grandpa in the pink and blue shell cutter, generally conceded to be the daintiest equipage in town; by the Oakses in their home-made blue and silver two-seater whose lofty back was adorned with a silver soaring eagle, the output of Lemuel's jackknife through most of a winter of evenings; by the Emmenses and the Wilcoxes, each in their special extravaganza of home design; and by the Samsons who trotted gravely to service in their simple little one-seated bobsleigh with a utility box behind and a plume on the horse of undyed, white horse hair, this expressing the limit of gaiety to which poverty and Solon's dignity permitted them to aspire.

Agatha had not seen an old-fashioned Thanksgiving gathering for three years, and as the neighbors one after another overtook and passed them with a wave and a falling pitch of the bells as they dipped down the ridge, her excitement rose like a child's on the way to a fair. As the preliminary ringing of the church bell stopped and they came in hearing of the medley of bells in the Hollow, she slipped her mittened hands into the arms of Homer and Ike on either side of her. And when they walked out on the nose of the ridge and looked down over the burying ground of the Corners and the Church like a living white lily thirty rods below, she stopped the procession to drink in the scene of gala confusion. For, like the Lathrop Hollow dances, Thanksgiving service there was still the popular one of the township, many families returning for this one service a year, a practice reminiscent of the time when the Hollow had social precedence over the Falls.

A few rigs were already hitched in the long shed behind the church, the families that had arrived in them walking back to congregate like a reception committee before the front doors, while scores of later arrivals trotted in to noisy stops among near collisions and final spurts for a place in the shed. Cutters, single-runner sleighs, bobsleighs in every shape and every color of the rainbow; a couple of old lumber sledges whose owners were too poor to buy finer conveyances and too lazy to make them; a yoke of white oxen that must have started at dawn from Field Settlement, dragging a big farm sleigh with a noisy family of ten, all wrapped in parti-colored woollen mufflers and mittens; a few single riders galloping in to beat heavier rigs to the stalls; many drivers already contenting themselves with hitching their teams to the stone posts surrounding the church like a fence, or to the rings in the half-dozen maples along the side; the people converging on the front door in ever increasing numbers: altogether a ballet of costumes in every imaginable cut and combination of color, of tenor, alto and soprano sleigh-bells all ringing against each other in shifting chords and discords, of blue incense drifting from three hundred human mouths and the nostrils of a hundred horses; continuous sound, color and motion between bright blue sky above and white snow beneath, combining the glitter of the gayest ballroom with the musical features of a gargantuan April frog-pond.

Now the last arrivals were jangling in from the direction of the Center and the Falls, and the symphony of bells was diminishing. John began to despair of the hope of seeing Pru Stark, while at the same time Ike emerged from a fear he had entertained that Gam Stark might have got the best of Dandy and used this occasion to humiliate the Lathrops. The atheist Bub Tanofly slewed up, cracking his whip, in the fastest cutter in town, so nearly bereft of dashboard and seat-arms to hold the robe that his lovely wife Patience in her ermine hat and neckpiece was visibly blue with cold. Judge Longcoat jogged up in his enormous, yellow-painted cutter, his face under his silk hat wrapped to the eyes in a purple plaid scarf. When his skinny colleague and honorable guest Mr. Justice Twiggin from Rome had alighted from invisibility beside him, the three hundred pounds of local Justice still sat there immobile and helpless till young Jared Oxbow and Savillian Stone ran out from the church steps, pried him upright, and eased him down without casualty. Meanwhile, the rich, deep warble of the last arrival was clearly audible, nearing behind the mills across the stream. In a moment a pair of white horses, their harnesses glittering with nickel and their heads splendid with gray plumes rising forward between their ears, clattered in step across the bridge drawing the wonder of the countryside, a small gray and silver coach on bobs, with a driver on the front box and a footman on the rear. Opposite the door of the church it halted; the footman leapt down to the door and out stepped Howell Sherwood and his young friend Alexander Mathiesson. The arrival was perfectly timed, for at that moment Jehu Jones, hanging with all his meager weight to the rope in the church vestibule, released it: there was a swift rattle of hemp, and the bell—the gift of the first Squire Lathrop—in the open belfry began to toll.

Immediately all worldly activity ceased. The crowd at the triple church doors slid quietly into the vestibule. The ruddy, peg-legged Homer Haddock and the bearded miller Eliphalet Emmens ceased conversing suddenly and walked side by side up to their pews, leaving unanswered the latter's question as to when he should bring over a certain cow to be served. Mistress Swift, who had turned sideways in her pew to inquire of Mistress Oxbow behind her how her sick baby was doing, turned abruptly back without an answer and without thereby giving offense. Outside, the Sherwood horses were led away, their bells warbling softly, and hitched at the side of the grounds. And thereafter there was no sound within or without but the slow toll that at each stroke shook the little building, the soft rattle of the bell-rope, and an occasional remote flutter of bells when a horse shifted position.

All the animals were blanketed and munching the hay provided in mangers or in little piles about the hitching-posts and the trees. All the people except the younger Lathrops were in place in the church as they ought to be. Now Agatha, happy and thankful in the presence around her of the four young men she loved, led them on down the road and up to the delicately traced façade where the slow booming of the bell overhead was like the power of a protecting God speaking welcome down to them. Through reverent silence that seemed to ignore them, the five late-comers went up the aisle to the front-most of the two Lathrop box pews—not an overt sign of recognition, not a smile in that house of prayer, not a turn of a head to greet young John, the returned friend of them all. Through a few male minds there passed simply the thought-wave, "There is young John," and the swiftly fading prescience of flip at the Lathrops' after the service. Through others, of a different school, there shot a moral judgment upon these irresponsible young people who came late to meeting, and upon the Squire who permitted such irreverence—chief among these being Deacon Victory Birdseye who sat at the minister's right with his head bowed diagonally into his palm. Through many female minds there passed a superior judgment upon Agatha's tasteful but too expensive cloak and bonnet of blue embroidered silk. Through others a superior judgment upon a young woman who made a show of her four young men by coming late to meeting. But through most of the female minds there passed no thought, no judgment at all, merely a moment's slow concentrated glance at John or Isaac, the handsomest boys in the church, the handsomest boys in the town.

The young Lathrops settled themselves, and all personal thoughts and impulses evaporated in the common, concentrated calm. Those who had found no seats stood like statues round the rear of the floor and the rear of the little balcony, forcing the occupants of the facing seats behind them to stand up to see. Judge Longcoat sneezed and Agatha caught Ike's eye and ducked her head. The silence continued. There was a faint odor of woodsmoke from numerous foot stoves concealed under voluminous petticoats throughout the unheated church. The Reverend Nathaniel Norcross looked at his watch. The bell continued to rattle its rope and toll. The Reverend Norcross stood up and stepped forward under the sounding-board. The bell ceased tolling. In one motion the whole congregation rose. Mistress Stone trod the scratchy foot-pumps of the organ and struck a chord. Instantly joined by the congregation, Deacon Victory Birdseye began in his cracked tenor:

> "Praise God from whom all blessings flow,
> Praise him all creatures here below. . . ."

There was a march and a throb in that imperfect singing, and in the Deacon's prayer for sinners that followed, and in the Lord's Prayer, and the hymn, and the responsive reading, and the second hymn, in the reading of the lesson from II Corinthians 9, in the long prayer, in the third hymn, and in the passionate amateur rendering of the anthem by the local choir. In that simple ritual there was the moral power of three hundred fiercely individualistic souls united in the one impulse that was common to them all, the impulse to commune with the eternal Truth behind this transient world, a truth to be daily rediscovered by each of them alone on his knees and to be expressed or belied in their outward conduct toward one another. In three-quarters of the congregation the old orthodoxy of damnation had no longer any meaning, but the reverence and the unceasing quest for truth remained. And when they joined together in the celebration of that truth in the name of God, there was a fusion of moral emotion into a power that lifted the little church to a spiritual eminence where all those lives were one, an eminence that was the loftier for being framed in the discipline of those educated minds.

And beyond the concerns of that little congregation, the march and the throb of its service was the song of the two-century-old crusade of Yankee civilization, where individuals and congregations and townships were drops in the greater stream. The aim of the crusade was spiritual truth beyond the errors and the shackles of the visible world; but if ever that singing power should transfer its aspiration to some single truth in the present world, it would continue on its way till the truth was attained or the crusading race with its millions of souls was destroyed.

For half an hour this united power flowed upward through the simple rituals of the service. Then, after a fourth hymn, it returned into its separate sources and they were three hundred individuals again. There was a rustling adjustment of posture and a decorous sliding under pews of numerous burned-out foot stoves. The Reverend Nathaniel Norcross stood behind the carved spread eagle of the lectern that surmounted the pulpit. The sermon, as distinguished from the preceding parts of the service, would be an appeal to the intellects of the listeners, an appeal that would attempt to lay hold of the emotional power already aroused and, by dispassionate logic, to direct it to its appropriate moral ends. The service gave power, the sermon form and significance to the meeting. And, between them, all of the energies of those people came alive.

The tall young minister reversed the glass—today it was the half-hour glass, glanced reverently aloft for God's blessing, settled his hands on the outer edges of the pulpit and repeated in his perfectly modulated baritone the text, taken from the morning's lesson: "Being enriched in everything to all bounteousness, which causeth through us Thanksgiving to God."

It was to be a short sermon, appropriate to Thanksgiving. After the usual brief review of the history of the festival, and the reading of the proclamation of His Excellency Governor Hamilton Fish of New York, the Reverend Norcross launched upon a catalogue of things for which they ought to be thankful, a catalogue that rose and fell in measured periods, so that the recital seemed like a litany, the pauses filled with the unspoken thought responses of the congregation—"Let us be thankful."

"Brethren, let us lift up our hearts in Thanksgiving to Almighty God that He has revealed Himself to us in the person of His Son. Let us thank Him that He has vouchsafed us the power through prayer to kneel at His throne and to hear His voice speaking in our hearts, directing us in the way we should go. Let us thank Him Who permits us to dwell in this land of beauty and fruitfulness. Let us thank Him for the plenty He has showered upon us during the past year. Let us thank Him for the gift of freedom which He has chosen to bestow on this nation above all nations of the earth, where a man may walk proudly under the sky, knowing no interposition of the will of another between his conscience and the God with which it communes. Let us thank Him for that spirit of independence and inquiry which democracy has loosed in the land, for the existence among us of those many who are examining, each in his way, into the causes of human misery and degradation and are proposing those Reforms whose aim it is to bring the souls of all men into closer communion with God. Finally, brethren"—here the minister paused, and continued slowly, for he was introducing the theme of his sermon—"let us thank Almighty God for the revelation, through these same curious minds, of those devices by which our advance against sin and suffering is made easier, for the miracles of communication, the railroad and the electric telegraph, and for numberless machines whose divine purpose it is to lighten the burden of human labor and bring us nearer to that millennium when the spirit shall be freed to its untrammelled joy in eternal worship and praise."

The Reverend Norcross now relaxed the set attitude he had held before, with his hands clasping the rail of the pulpit, and as he delivered his sermon he stepped back and forth, now on one side, now on the other of the lectern, speaking as it were confidentially to his flock all of whom he believed would be in agreement with him in his central thesis:

"Brethren, I say unto you, let us be thankful for all these tokens of God's favor to us, for these signs of progress toward a better world. But in our gratitude let us not relax that eternal watchfulness which is enjoined upon the righteous man. For as the Lord is walking with us in new and miraculous forms, so the devil also is at large in the land, and he is tempting the hearts of men to misuse the very means that have been given us through the Lord's bounty.

"All these new devices and machines, and those great factories by which we are learning to make what is needful with less of human labor, all these are a trust given us from on high, to be used for the betterment of mankind. But there are men among us who already are beginning to use them for their own aggrandizement, and, so used, I declare to you, that they may become the instruments of hell. Whoever uses a mill or factory as a steward of the community, having thought first to the welfare of those he employs, that they may increase in health of body and grace of spirit, and who takes no profit to himself beyond a fair livelihood and the satisfaction that goes with doing God's work in the world, such a man, I say, is a laborer in the Lord's vineyard. But whoever gives thought first to his moneybags, or to his fine house, or his clothes, or his carriage, or the luxuries of his family, or the power in the community which he hopes his money can buy, I say that such a man is given over to vanity and that he is the agent of the devil within our borders."

John was delighted with the sermon, and from time to time glanced furtively at Ike who was gazing up blandly at the Reverend Norcross, showing no outward sign either of approval or disapproval. The minister pointed out that in Massachusetts children were working in factories under conditions more degrading than those of the southern slaves, "while the godless owners of these mills grow rich on the blood of these little ones, building themselves mansions and riding in gilded coaches even as the kings and the nobles whom their grandfathers fought to eject from the land." Without naming anyone, he declared that there were instances "in our very township of Byzantium where the sick and the aged have been uncharitably discharged without future provision, for the sole reason that their feeble efforts were no longer able to satisfy the rapacity of their employers."

John observed that at this last statement Ike's forehead puckered in a troubled, sympathetic expression. But as the minister proceeded, the gentleness left Ike's face. The pucker between his eyes hardened, and his jaw set in defiance as John had never seen it do except in a fist fight.

"I warn you, therefore," the Reverend Norcross concluded, "that while there are many things for which we must lift up our hearts in thanksgiving to God, yet the new wealth that is rising among us is not one of those things. We are offered such an opportunity as few nations have enjoyed in the history of the world to lighten somewhat the burden of Adam and return a little nearer to that state of blessedness where life was lived, and will again be lived, perpetually in communion with the Lord. This is our opportunity, and commensurate with it comes a temptation to use our blessings, not for the betterment of mankind, but for the elevation of ourselves to worldly power. Sooner or later in these days, every one of us here will stand at a fork in the ways, where the blessings of the new age will stand ready like a coach for a journey in either direction. To the right the way leads up through the hills of truth to the throne of God. To the left it leads downward through sloughs and morasses of vanity and greed to the bottomless pit and eternal damnation.

"Let us, therefore, thank God reverently for His numerous bounty bestowed on us. And, each in his closet, let us fall on our knees and examine our hearts and thank God that He has given us this choice to use His bounty for good or for evil, and the power, by His grace, to make that choice to His eternal honor and glory.

"Let us pray."

In the prayer he recapitulated the material of the sermon, but phrasing it in a richer and more heavily rhythmed rhetoric and a reverence of tone which restored the emotional foundation of the service and sent the congregation, after the last hymn and the benediction, filing gravely down the aisle, a united body, bent on the extirpation of the demon of wealth, and believing in the early induction of the Kingdom of God.

CHAPTER XX

A G G I E also had noticed Ike's set expression toward the end of the sermon. During the final prayer she glanced at him and noticed that, though he was properly bowed, he was looking intently up at the Reverned Norcross instead of closing his eyes. At the end of the service she watched him crowd down the aisle more rapidly than was needful to get the sleigh from the shed, so rapidly that he reached the vestibule before the minister and so missed the usual pastoral handshake. Afterwards, while the family was easing through the vestibule, exchanging with neighbors those rapt, pontifical nods expressive of a state of inward grace, Aggie kept glancing at Ike, now out in front waiting with the team. He had the reins looped indifferently through his arm and was not petting the horses as he usually did. Instead, he was kicking a stick that was frozen in the ground and when he had it loose he picked it up, took his jackknife from his pocket and whittled rapidly, occasionally touching his beaver to someone in a detached way.

As they were coming down the steps Aggie whispered to John and Homer and Ben to walk ahead, that she wanted to talk to Ike. When they had bundled off the six old folks toward the Corners, where many of the sleighs were turning right to jingle up the hill toward the Lathrops', the three boys walked off in the same direction. Aggie slipped her hand in Ike's arm and said, "Let's take the old cut-off behind the graveyard up to the lower orchard." Ike gave her a glance of tender gratitude, and they turned off the road up the snow-buried path.

They walked slowly and neither spoke till they were almost past the burying ground. Then Ike said, "Sis, do you figger the place we've always had here is just vanity, or the works of the devil, or some such nonsense?" "No, I don't, Scamp. After all, we've never been rich, and Pa and Ma have certainly done well by the community." "Do you figger, then, that if a pack of hyenas at the Falls are getting rich and doing nothing for the community, but are stealing our influence as sure as shooting, do you figger that if we tried to get rich and head them off and keep our place

157

we'd be doing the devil's work and going down hill to hell, as Nathaniel just put it?" "Are you talking about yourself, Ike?" "Yep." "Well," said Agatha, pressing his arm, "I think I know what Pa'd say. He'd say it depended on how you felt yourself. If you were sure in your heart that you were doing it only for the good of the community, then he'd agree that you might be doing the Lord's work in trying to stay influential in town."

"But how do you feel about it yourself?" Ike insisted. "Don't you see, brother," she said, again squeezing his arm, "that I'm no longer in a position to have opinions as freely as I used to. It's for me to make the best of my own situation and not criticize other people one way or the other. I love Homer and he's made a lot of money speculating in land. I suppose that in my heart I didn't like it, and I suppose that I finally made my feelings plain. I'm awfully glad that Homer's going to Congress where he can feel important and try to do some good."

"What's Homer to do with me?" asked Ike. "You ain't a slave, are ye?" Aggie smiled up at him. "Ask Tavie about that," she laughed. "But if I am, I like it."

They walked in silence for a way, taking slow little steps up the hill in the slippery snow. Finally Aggie said, "No, Ike, on principle I guess I'd hate to see you thrown in with those people at the Falls. It might not hurt you, but then again maybe it might. I'd be afraid you'd wake up years later and find you had lost something you couldn't ever get back. Maybe I'm wrong, but that's what I'd be afraid of."

They walked silently again, and Ike's attention wandered off to an appraisal of the succession of horses jingling their rigs along the ridge above them. "You know, Scamp," said Aggie again, squeezing his arm gently in her characteristic way, "I don't think you're really that kind of a man at all. You've got something very special in you that we never talked about, but I guess we'd best talk about it now. Pa has a little of it, and so have I, but you have it most. Ma and Ben and John haven't it at all. It's a kind of dreamy thing, a thing that has to do with people—probably something to do with what's—up there—something that some day you'll figure out for yourself and call God. You've got a personal sort of power over people, whether you know it or not. You've got it in you to make somebody awfully happy—or awfully miserable."

Aggie hesitated for a few steps, then continued, "If you and I hadn't been brother and sister we'd probably have got married, and I think I would have been good for you. You'd have thought mostly about God, and it wouldn't have mattered whether you or the Lathrops were influential or not, not even whether you did much good in the world or not. We'd have just lived, and you'd have done some job well, and we wouldn't have had any such choices to make. Now, I think that one of these days you will discover somebody who will make you as happy as I could have, perhaps happier. When you've got that you'll begin to think more about your soul and less about your money, or even your family."

"Tavie?" interrupted Ike.

"No, I'm not going to make any prophecies, for if I did they'd be wrong. I haven't anybody but you in mind. I just hope that something of the kind will happen to you before you have to make this decision about the future one way or the other. Once you've found love and God, it will be easier to make it. It just won't be so important."

Aggie clung to his arm as they minced up the steep, slippery grade to the bar-way out to the lane. Suddenly Ike stopped and closed his eyes. An impulse from somewhere in his abdomen seemed to rise and spread till it included all that countryside and the sky above them. He knew Aggie was with him, though her pressure on his arm was now lighter than a snow-flake. For a flash he was at the heart of everything. Then he opened his eyes. "You're right, Sis," he whispered, and they walked on, her eyes on the snow, his on the northern horizon. In a moment they had turned into the lane and began absently to bow to the sleighs and cutters passing them, all speeding up to the Lathrop homestead. Among them was the silver coach of Howell Sherwood, but Ike noticed it and its occupants no more than the rest.

By the time they reached the big lilac-red house, twenty caparisoned teams and sleighs were hitched to the rings in the maples, in the side of the horse-barn, in the tall stone gateposts, or were tethered to hitching weights brought along for the purpose. Sixty-odd people had corrugated the snow with their footprints, walking up to the front door, and a few, having greeted the Squire and Sarah and supplied themselves with flip, were already overflowing the house back into the sunshine.

Ike moved in a detached haze, greeting the guests with mechanical cor-diality as he approached and entered the house. The little front hall was a pile of overshoes, India rubbers and wraps that spilled over into the north parlor, where the ladies were sipping cherry cordial, and into the keeping-room where some thirty men, mostly in blue, black, gray or tan tailcoats, with richly embroidered waistcoats, all smoking cigars, chewing tobacco, or both, crowded the room, jostling and laughing around the bowl of steaming flip.

Thither Ike made his way and, finding a little open space at the end of the table, stood there unhospitably, refilling a can again and again.

This position required him to face most of the men when they squeezed their way back for their second or third can-fuls or slices from the ham or the shoulder of beef that also graced the big table. Most of them, as they came up, made some flippant reference to the sale of Dandy to Stark, with a sly smile or a wink that implied they knew Ike had got the better of the deal. Bub Tanofly, spotting Ike, elbowed his way up to him and gave him a cordial whack on the shoulder. "Worryin' about that sermon, be ye? Say, first thing ye know ye'll have to lambaste me again fer callin' ye a milksop and a baby."

Ike, dreaming alone with the reality in him which Aggie had awakened and which hot ale and rum were keeping awake, heard only remotely this loud intrusion, and, instead of retorting, he simply gave Bub a straight, unseeing stare. Bub, suspecting that he had really hurt him, dismissed as inappropriate an impulse to apologize, and turned away, vigorously mouthing his long cigar.

Vaguely Ike saw the outlines of his pa and Howell Sherwood in close conversation at one of the front windows. In a lull in the general talk he heard his pa mention his name, but even this important cue did not hold his attention. More arresting was the entry of Tavie from the kitchen with a large pitcher and the hot loggerhead to replenish the bowl. All the men she passed greeted her gaily, crowding back to make her room. At first she seemed not to notice Ike, but when she had refilled the bowl and was stirring it with the loggerhead she felt compelled to glance up at him. He was staring at her with a blank expression and a concentrated power in his eyes that made her lower hers and flee back to the kitchen before the flip was properly frothed. Several men who had been standing by looked wisely at one another.

Meanwhile, affairs personal and political, bawdy and sublime, were being bandied about in the two front rooms of the house under a rich aura compounded of alcohol, tobacco smoke and the now heavy aroma of cooking apple butter. Young Mathiesson, having been introduced to the Reverend Norcross, was thanking him earnestly for his splendid sermon, while Jabez Forest, Judge VanSanford, and others from the Falls were trying to approach him for the same purpose. Homer Haddock, buttressed by his wooden leg planted out at a wide angle, was whispering to Jared Oxbow the new one about the old bull, and Savillian Stone was the center of four heads bent together, all chuckling and occasionally straightening up with full-throated guffaws, obviously obscene.

In the north parlor Samantha, being perpetually plied with flip by her grandson John, was entertaining the ladies—all but Samantha sipping cordial—with a loud attack on the Woman's Rights Movement on the theory that it was "too damned unfeminine." Sarah, Agatha and Tavie slipped back and forth between the north parlor, the kitchen and the summer kitchen. Tavie had given the oven a second firing about eleven o'clock, and the half-cooked pig was now shut up again to continue baking. The apple butter on the summer kitchen stove was nearing the proper consistency and needed Tavie's constant watching.

On the front doorstep a stately group, centered around Solon Samson, Thomas Lathrop and Lemuel Oaks, was sipping its liquor slowly, in dignified avoidance of the crowd and boisterousness within. Judges Longcoat and Twiggin, the last arrivals, drove up in the former's big yellow cutter and halted in the drive, just as a bevy of young men of the "California gang" poured noisily out of the house. Seeing Judge Longcoat arrive and sensing the prospect of his need of help and of probable amusement, they all slid to a stop in the snow and stood near the cutter, feigning interest in Howell Sherwood's sleigh-coach nearby. Judge Longcoat rolled an eye at them, sensed disrespect, and his huge, round face purpled to near the shade of his tippet. The wisp-like Judge Twiggin threw back the robe and alighted nimbly.

Jared Oxbow and Savillian Stone, having assisted the fat judge before at the church, felt accredited to step forward to the cutter and await his heavy honor's pleasure. His heavy honor, however, was now urged by a point of apoplectic pride. With a cavernous grunt that made his bay mare start and sent Sam Emmens to her head, he hunched forward to the edge of the seat and with one short leg groped precariously for the snowy ground and found it. Grasping the dashboard and the seat-arm and groaning like a cow's low, he heaved up, and at that moment Sam Emmens' self-control gave way. He released the mare's head to stuff his fist in his mouth against his laughter. The mare took her cue and lurched forward. The arm of the cutter caught the Judge in the flank and in one movement turned him round and toppled him outward upon his back where he lay in the snow kicking with arms and legs like a gigantic, capsized beetle.

At this, Solon Samson and Lemuel Oaks ran forward from the front door and, with the help of the young men thrusting from behind, lifted the fallen magistrate upright. Slowly, like a great ship coming about, he turned and faced the culprit Sam Emmens.

"What is your name, sir?" he demanded with judicial fierceness. "Emmens, sir," replied Sam, lowering his head to control his laughter, "Samuel Emmens." Now, it happened that Eliphalet Emmens, the miller, Sam's pa, was the one supporter of Judge Longcoat in Lathrop Hollow.

"I shall take the matter under advisement," he snorted, rolling his head to one side and the other as if surveying a court-room, and, still half-carried by Messrs. Samson and Oaks, he turned back until he faced the house and began slowly to put one foot before the other in the direction of the front door.

At the doorstep Judge Longcoat for the first time recognized one of his rescuers as Solon Samson. He promptly blew like a porpoise, turned Mr. Justice Twiggin over to John, "my esteemed young cousin," who came out to greet him, then swung away from the house with a gesture of his fat hand, signifying that he wanted to speak to Solon Samson privately.

When they had moved away a few steps he turned slowly toward Solon, opened his eyes wide, and seemed to look up into his face, though actually looking over his shoulder and focussing on nothing in particular, while Solon glared down at him with his single expression that now meant contempt.

"Master Samson," the Judge began, "though I have not yet received a proper return, I have reason to suspect that you were visited recently by a Federal marshal bearing a search warrant issued by me. Am I correct in that supposition?" "Yes, sir," said Solon with a bow. "And may I inquire, without prejudice, whether you submitted to the search or whether you resisted it?" "I submitted to it," said Solon icily. "That, sir," snapped the Judge, blowing out his lips, "was contrary to my expectation."

He rolled his eyes up at Solon, met for an instant that black, gimlet-like gaze, quickly blew through his lips again, and once more addressed himself to outer space. "It may be taken, I believe, as common knowledge— at least I have it on persuasive hearsay—that you hold Chapter 60, Laws of 1850, the so-called Fugitive Slave Law, to be unconstitutional. Wherefore, it was my expectation that you would resist this search. Aye, I may say that I selected you deliberately and with aforethought to make a test case upon this statute. I instructed the marshal upon your resistance to the search, to arrest you formally, to release you upon your recognizance, and to make his return accordingly. Thereafter you might institute a habeas corpus action, or if you failed to do so, you would be subject to prosecution for resisting a warrant. In either case the court would be privileged to hear your argument against the constitutionality of the statute, presumably, I may say, the ablest argument in the matter to be heard in this District."

Again he glanced up at Solon, but did not risk meeting his eyes directly. "Now it is my suspicion," the Judge resumed, "that an action may still be had in this matter, but it must come on your instance. You may bring an action against the officer for trespass upon an improper warrant. Or you may bring an action against me for issuing such a warrant."

"Need I remind you," said Solon, "that before issuing process the court might have required qualified counsel to present briefs and argument upon the validity of the proposed process." "No doubt, no doubt," snapped the Judge, waving his fat hands. "I must beg you, sir, to leave these matters in the discretion of the court."

Again he pursed his lips and blew. "To be brief, sir, will you bring the action I suggest or will you not?" "I will not," said Solon. "May I remind you," rattled the Judge, "that the court may appoint you as counsel to any defendant in this or any other action." "May I remind you," said Solon, "that outside the court-room I need no instruction in my duties as a Federal attorney."

The Judge swung heavily around and addressed the front door. "Shall we refresh ourselves?" he said, with an attempt at a bow. "Thank you, sir," said Solon, "with your permission I must decline further refreshment." The Judge hove himself up the step and disappeared in the house, leaving Solon with an expression of his nearest approach to humor, a faint twist of the mouth, knowing as he did, that this was all a cock-and-bull story, knowing that Justice Longcoat had issued the search warrant because he had expected that he would catch him, subject him to indictment, have him disbarred as a lawyer, send him to prison and ruin him finally with a fine.

Meanwhile many of the men inside the house were getting tipsy and Ike still held his station by the flip-bowl. "I don't give a dang—I don't give a dang," his mind kept saying as the talk and the laughter around him blended into an indistinct hum. "B' God, I'll show 'em—b' God, I'll show 'em," he muttered a dozen times, then broke into a mental oration of which the most emphatic words came out articulately—"Look at 'em—all against me—all 'cept Bub 'n Ag—whole pack of 'em. Why are they here? I ask ye that—why are they here? 'Cause they're decent and 'cause they're well off. Wouldn't be here if they weren't decent—all keerect. Likewise wouldn't be here if they weren't well off—all keerect again. Didn't sell Dandy 'cause I wanted to—sold him 'cause we ain't well off any more—all keerect again—keerect—keerect—keerect."

He swayed a little, picked up his can and set it down again—"Figger ye've had plenty fer now"—he sniffed and giggled to himself. He caught his pa's eye and looked away. "Aggie's the only one's right," his mind said. "Figger there's more to it'n money—b' God, she's true grit—love'n

God—love'n God—love'n God—that's it—all keerect." And he lowered his head, feeling he was about to cry.

At this moment there was a general dislocation in the room due to the entrance of Judge Longcoat, the Squire's going up to greet him, and the subsequent elephantine progress toward the punch-bowl. Somebody backed into Ike, stepped on his toe, turned around and exclaimed, "Beg pardon, Ike, ye old trimmer, ye!" "By God, I ain't a trimmer, I ain't a trimmer," Ike murmured in a passionate whisper. The crowd broke into the drinking song,

> *"A plague on those musty old lubbers*
> *Who tell us to fast and to think,*
> *And patient to fall in with life's rubbers,*
> *With nothing but water to drink—"*

all toasting Judge Longcoat as he reached the table and confronted the bowl that looked like a cup he might pick up lightly and toss off at a draught. Someone handed him a can and he lifted it, while the song continued—

> *"A can of good stuff, had they twigg'd it,*
> *Would have set them for pleasure agog,*
> *And spite of the rules,*
> *The rules of the schools,*
> *The old fools would have all of 'em swigg'd it*
> *And sworn there was nothing like grog."*

Almost crying with rage, Ike forced his way from the shouting room and hurried out through the kitchen to the summer kitchen where, unaware of anybody's presence, he opened the north door and sat down on the step, breathing the cool air. Tavie, giving the apple butter its last stirring before taking it from the stove, was the only person in the room.

At the sight of the open sky and the quiet valley below, Ike's burst of fury passed and his feelings took a warm, sentimental turn, a love of the familiar scene and everything it contained. Part of the muffled roar of the house, the grog song continued far away—

> *"And it set the old codger agog,*
> *And he swigg'd, and mother swigg'd,*
> *And sister swigg'd, and brother swigg'd,*
> *And I swigg'd, and all of us swigg'd it,*
> *And swore there was nothing like grog."*

The song went on through two stanzas more, and ended. Slowly, Ike became aware of the scraping of the wooden ladle in the pot behind him and looked around. Tavie's trim figure and finely cut profile seemed supremely beautiful to him, part of the whole reality of the quiet scene. "Love'n God—love'n God," his mind sang in his veins—then "Tave— Why ain't it, Tave?"

A quick, far-off twinge of caution was drowned in his throbbing mood. "Howdy, Tave," he said. " 'M glad ye're here 'n nobody else." "I'm glad you're glad," said Tavie a little loftily, but hearing none of that hardness in his voice which she had seen in his eyes before church. "Tave, they're all against me in there—all of 'em—'cept maybe Aggie. You 'gainst me, too? Kind o' figger ye ain't. Hope ye ain't, true grit." He looked away again, out over the valley.

Tavie's tense and confused feelings surged to grasp a moment's release. She dropped the ladle in the pot, ran to Ike, leaned down behind him, put her hands on his broad shoulders and whispered in his ear, "Of course I'm not against you. You know I'm not against you." Conscience now spoke clearly to Ike, but it was a remote, thin voice, like a fading call in a dream— " 'Tain't Tavie—'Tain't Tavie."

Ike knew he'd had plenty to drink, but he understood nothing of the consequent psychological dangers. Everything at the moment seemed ultimately clear and real. He put his hand up to his shoulder and covered Tavie's. "Love'n God," he said. "I got to find love'n God—got to find love, Tave." Tavie was whirling in such a vortex of emotion that she felt almost faint, and crouched down behind Ike with her hand still on his shoulder. "Seem's though I got t' kiss ye, Tave, but I'd best not 'cause I been havin' too many swigs o' rum—'twouldn't be just proper, I figger."

Tavie, for all her temperance work, was wholly inexperienced in meeting drunkenness or in detecting its signs. "I'm sorry if you've been drinking, Ike," she whispered, then added, "and I'm sorry too that I stole that bottle of rum—if you haven't forgotten it." This almost overcame Ike, but he only squeezed her hand and murmured, "No, 't wouldn't be right, 't wouldn't be right."

He mused for a moment, then said, "Tave, I figger ye can't find lov'n God just thinkin' about it. Do ye figger ye can?" "No, Ike." She was just able to frame the words. "Don't figger," he went on, "you 'n I could find love—'n God—just thinkin' about it, do you, Tave?"

Taking this for a proposal Tavie dropped her head on his shoulder and wet his coat with tears. In the pause while Ike was fighting a rapidly losing battle with the impulse to turn around and kiss her, a sweet, acrid odor crept into Tavie's nostrils. Horribly she woke from her dream into realization. She leapt up, seized a holder, snatched the apple butter from the stove and set it on an upturned milk pail. But sharp, scorching fumes poured up from it and hurt her eyes. It was burned beyond redemption. In her agitated mood there was nothing to do but to cover her eyes with her hands and try to choke back the sobs. Oh, if Ike would only get up now and come and hold her in his strong arms!

But Ike made no sign. As she left him he had looked around and seen the smoke, then had turned back to gazing down the valley, while a jingle rose in his mind—

> "Burn the apple in the morning,
> Cows and geese and hens take warning."

As he repeated this over and over in his mind he began to find it increasingly funny, and with each line he extended first one hand and then the other in a rhetorical gesture, while he improvised variations on the theme:

> "Burn the apple in the morning,
> Ma 'n Pa 'n John take warning.
> Ma 'n Pa 'n John take warning,
> Burn the apple in the morning.
> Burn the apple in the morning,
> Tave and Ike and Ben take warning.
> Master Lane and Ag take warning,
> Burn the apple in the morning."

Suddenly the back door from the horse-barn opened with a bang, and the four young California roisterers burst in from an inspection of Ike's new chestnut. Seeing Tavie now openly in tears, they rushed around her, seizing her hands, patting her shoulders. "What's the matter, Tave?" "Have ye had bad news, Tave?" "Don't cry, Tave." "We're all with ye, Tave." "There, there, there."

Jared Oxbow, with his arm around her, patting her head against his shoulder, was the first to see the cause of the tragedy. "Say, fellers," he said, "this is serious." And he pointed to the smoking pot. "Don't worry, Tave, we'll say we did it. 'T's natural you'd be upset at seeing it, but you didn't do it, see, darling. You went out to get some wood or somethin', and you asked me to stir it for you and I forgot it."

The sympathy quieted Tavie a little, and just then Sarah Lathrop, having smelled the fatal smoke all the way in the north parlor, came striding anxiously into the room. Jared instantly met his test. "Mistress Lathrop, I have done a terrible thing for which no apology can ever be adequate. Tavie asked me to stir the apple butter for—for—just a minute. I—I—didn't know how quick it was to burn and left it to go—outside, and when I came back with the boys Tavie was here with it off the stove in this shape."

Tavie simply gave Jared a tender smile, laid her head on Sarah's big, bony bosom, and burst into fresh sobs. "It's not true, Sarah Lathrop," she whispered between paroxysms. "I left it myself and I alone am to blame."

"There, there," said Sarah in her big comfortable contralto. "Whoever did it, it's all right. There's plenty more cider in the cellar. Please don't anybody worry about it."

"I did it, Ma," said Ike, standing up and leaning against the doorpost. "Nobody's to blame but me." His mother's entrance half sobered him for a moment, as far as his mind and emotions went. The recent passage with Tavie was already dim and meaningless, a dream of which he could have recalled no details. But the sight of Tavie weeping was more than he could stand, his friend Tavie whom he had kissed a while back. To his shame in his mother's presence, he found, as he started toward her and Tavie, that he couldn't for the life of him walk straight. But he persisted and, reaching the two women, stood swaying a little under his mother's amazed eye, took Tavie's shoulders and said huskily, "Don' cry, Tave. 'T's all my fault, 'n 'm mighty sorry." But at his touch Tavie only pressed closer against Sarah and again sobbed hysterically.

Detecting Ike's condition and something more in the episode than apple butter, Sarah ordered him away with an imperious jerk of her head, and with some difficulty he made his way to the kitchen. As he opened the back-stairs door, John came by. "B' God, 'P'loosa," muttered Ike, "'m drunk, and 'm go'n bed. Tell that feller Math'son—friend o' Sherwood's— tell 'm glad he came—got sick or somp'n—'t's important—tell 'm 'm awful sick." And Ike turned and thumped up the back stairs.

Meanwhile Sarah was pacifying Tavie, while the four boys stood around in concern. Presently she said, "Tavie's all right now. Why don't you boys have a kitchen dance? It may be the last chance we'll have for a long time to see some of you dancing in this house. Come, Jared and Savillian. Try out that new tune about Cal-i-for-ni-a, and if it works we can make a big go with it at the ball tomorrow. Master Lane knows it. Go fetch him, Jared." "You're a brick, Sarah Lathrop," said Savillian. "We were only afraid there were too many people, and your Thanksgiving dinner and all. Come on, fellers. Tavie—" Savillian didn't complete his proposed invitation to dance, for at that moment Constant Oaks appeared, and everybody knew how Connie felt about Tavie.

Jared said he'd prompt, and the other three boys rushed into the main house for partners. Five minutes later Master Lane struck up the new popular tune with its peculiarly slow, heavy rhythm. Immediately a shout went through the house, and everybody was singing before the set in the summer kitchen was well in order—

> *"O Susanna,*
> *Don't you cry for me,*
> *For I'm off to Cal-i-for-ni-a*
> *With my banjo on my knee."*

Jared first joined in the singing to get himself in the mood, then clapped his hands and began to improvise the calls—

> "Eight hands round now—
> And half way round you be—
> Now back to Cal-i-for-ni-a
> And stop right where you be—
> Honors, everybody—
> Then hold your lady free—
> All for'd to Cal-i-for-ni-a
> And back to where you be—"

And so forth and so forth. Jared got the set badly snarled up, at last got it untangled, and ended triumphantly—

> "Prom'nade to Cal-i-for-ni-a
> And take a seat that's free."

By now the crowd of older folks in the front of the house had had their fill of flip and singing. Pair by pair, they began coming out to take their leave of Sarah. She joined the Squire in the north parlor and, it being now one o'clock, the guests departed rapidly in various degrees of hilarity. The bells went jingling away in all directions like expanding ripples, and ten minutes after the exodus began only half a dozen rigs remained, among them the silver coach of Howell Sherwood. The Squire walked out with the trim banker, putting his arm around his shoulder and thanking him warmly for the consideration he had promised to give Ike. Young John walked behind with Alexander Mathiesson, discussing mutual friends in New Haven and New York and explaining that Ike had got pretty keyed up, was ashamed of himself, and had gone to bed, sending his apologies. John urged his new acquaintance to come to the grand ball tomorrow night in the hall at Lathrop Corners and, with some embarrassment, gave young Mathiesson a note which he asked him to deliver to Miss Prudence Stark at the Liberty. The footman handed Master Sherwood and Mathiesson into the coach, and it slid warbling away over the crest of the hill.

Last of all, the young dancers joined their families who were waiting for them in the sleighs outside. As they drove off in three directions, the boys of the California gang stood up and waved back to each other, still singing—

> *"I'm off to Cal-i-for-ni-a*
> *With my banjo on my knee.*
> *O Susanna—*
> *Don't you cry for me—*
> *For I'm off to Cal-i-for-ni-a*
> *With my banjo on my knee."*

The Squire and Sarah stood in the front door till the last of them were out of sight. One by one, the singing voices faded. The jingle of many sleigh bells receded and died away in the distance, and there was silence in the house.

CHAPTER XXI

A F T E R the departure of the guests there was none of the usual gossip and laughter following a party, for Ike's indiscretion threw a temporary shadow over the principal members of the household. Sarah whispered the news of it to the Squire as they closed the front door, and Aggie, having noticed Ike's departure, drew John into the pantry and got the truth from him. Ben, silly on half a can of flip, pestered Tavie in the summer kitchen, demanding to know if Ike had been taking another swig. Joel and Alvina, ignorant or indifferent to Ike's condition, praised the occasion profusely and went up to their room for a nap. Uncle Brandon did the same except for the praise. Thomas slipped unobtrusively into his son's bedroom, took off his blue velvet coat, lay down on the coverlet, and instantly began his gentle, melodious snore. Samantha whispered to Sarah that she was "drunk as a man," and followed her husband into the master's bedroom. Master Lane, who had put away two or three times what Ike had and was dazed only as a result of his musical efforts, sat grumbling for a time on a milk stool in the summer kitchen. Then he informed the Squire that he was going to bed, labored up the back stairs and made his way to his room, ignoring the prostrate form of Ike, for he had seen many drunks in his day, in this and other back attics.

Homer Hislip, in the keeping-room, was difficult to handle, having got himself as drunk as anybody at the party and being less master of himself under these circumstances. He insisted on pawing Aggie while the Squire, nettled by the proceeding, stood looking out the window. After begging him to stop, Aggie at last flared up, "Oh, Homer, please try to behave like a gentleman!"

This squelched his amorousness, but replaced it with an equally unpleasant surliness. "So that's it, be it?" he snarled. "So I ain't a gentleman, eh? Not good enough fer yer stuck-up family, eh? Well, we don' hit women in the West, but outside o' that we do's we damned please, and I'll notify ye, miss pretty, 't I'm the best man in this house, and there ain't a ninc'poop in yer danged family can tell me differ'nt." The Squire looked around in annoyance. "How 'bout it, John—they may call ye fancy names hereabouts, but ye're plain John to me. Stick up yer fists, I says, if ye think ye're boss o' this house." The Squire did stick up an arm to ward off a clumsy blow. Then, pinning Homer's arms behind him, he picked him up, carried him upstairs, deposited him on his bed and held him down. "You stay there, young man," he commanded. "If you get up before I tell ye, I'll take ye out in the barn and give ye such a tanning as you won't forget in a little while. And I ain't anxious to do that, for Agatha's sake." "All right, *Squire*," Homer shouted, "I throw up th' sponge. 'N I 'pologize like Ag'd want me to. Been drinkin' too much o' yer likker. Didn't mean no harm." And as the Squire walked out of the room, straightening his tie, Homer laughed hysterically for a few seconds. Then he sank into dishevelled sleep.

Downstairs the Squire comforted Aggie who was livid with fury and humiliation. "He never did that before, Pa," she whispered, "I swear he didn't. He's told me he thought you were the greatest man he ever knew. But he wouldn't tell you that, wouldn't even admit it to himself when he's East." "I understand, Aggie," said the Squire. "It's really our fault, all our faults, for letting him feel at a disadvantage. He's a decent fellow and he's going to feel awfully ashamed—unless he forgets the whole incident, as he may." They both smiled. Aggie joined her ma and Tavie in the final preparations for dinner, the five pots of prepared vegetables to be hung on the crane over the fire, the spits with the turkeys and the goose to be hung each in a pair of rings on the andirons and turned, miscellaneous meat pies, pumpkin pies and other pastries to join the pig in the main oven or to be baked in Dutch ovens.

John tip-toed up the back stairs to look at Ike, carrying a glass of buttermilk, well salted. In a moment he returned and reported openly and laughingly that the patient was doing well and was expected to take nourishment. This pooling of the subject of everybody's thoughts lightened the atmosphere. Presently John and Aggie and Ma and Pa were gossiping and giggling about the party and the guests in the good old way, while the women tended the three sizzling carcasses on the two spits in front of the fire. When Aggie went out to help Tavie bring in the things for the oven, leaving her ma to tend the two spits-'n-jacks, the Squire told Sarah and John to make a particular effort to make Homer feel at home.

After John relieved the tension about Ike, only Tavie continued to move silently about her duties, more tight-lipped than ever. Aggie now came on her sobbing in the buttery and petted her as best she could, being as yet uninformed of the important fact of Ike's presence with Tavie at the time of the tragedy of the apple butter. "Do you mind so terribly, dearest," she whispered, "Ike's getting drunk?" "No," said Tavie, looking at her helplessly, "not that—though I ought to—that's the worst of it. I—oh—I—," she dropped her head on Aggie's strong shoulder. "I must get away—I must—I must—and yet——."

Aggie had feared as much, and her love flowed out to envelop her over-intellectualized friend. There was nothing to say. As Aggie had told Ike, she and he had the same kind of human warmth. To Tavie it was almost as if it were Ike holding her in those strong, gentle arms. After a few seconds she looked up, smiled frankly, kissed Aggie, and much relieved, went on cutting a slice of salt pork from the slab in the barrel. An un-attended tear dropped into the barrel and she smiled again, snuffling. "If I stay here long," she said, "we won't have to refresh the brine in the barrel." "That'll be a new recipe," laughed Aggie, replacing the heavy stone on the pork, as Tavie wiped her eyes on her apron and began to pick up a stack of things for the oven. As they walked with their loads back into the kitchen Aggie was more worried about Ike than before. Tavie was her best friend, but, like her ma, and for the same reasons, she thought she would make a poor wife for Ike. Until now she had hoped against hope that Ike was not in the dangerous position of having Tavie really in love with him.

By half-past two the long, white damask cloth was spread over the table in the kitchen and places laid for fourteen, with the best china and silver from the north parlor corner-cupboard, and glasses and pewter cans from the courting-cabinet that stood open at the north end of the room. The Irish potatoes were mashed in cream and butter, the turnips and Indian potatoes in butter alone; the squash was scraped from the skin; the onions were mixed with butter; and they all stood steaming in dishes on trivets before the fire. The four meat pies were cooking in Dutch ovens. Miscellaneous gravies, the four pots of coffee and tea were steaming on the stone shelves of the fireplace. Everything that needn't come hot from the oven, the spit, the crane, the fireplace or the Dutch ovens, was loaded on the table or on the drainboard of the sink. On the table, two lofty pyramids of doughnuts and two of cookies; three loaves of rye bread and four pounds of butter; two castors with condiments; two large cranberry jellies removed from their molds and miscellaneous other jellies, upturned and quiver-ing; conserves in china boats; chow-chow, piccallili, mustard pickles, pickled cherries, brandied peaches, and other pickles and relishes in a gay assort-ment of colored glass dishes; gallons of milk, hard cider, sweet cider, cherry cider, blackberry, dandelion and elderberry wine, and heaped plates of hickory nuts, butternuts and dried berries. On the drainboard at the side, covered like the table with a damask cloth, half a dozen mince pies, and half a dozen apple, two lemon pies, pound cake, marble cake and white fruit cake, a whole plain cheese, half a sage cheese, and four decanters containing cherry, peach, blackberry, and chokecherry cordial. The fire was burning evenly and low above its deep bed of coals, and the hot air was rich with the reek of turkey, goose, Indian potatoes, turnips, squash, onions, meat pie, coffee, tea, and the toothsome intimations of pig and pumpkin pie escaping from the main oven. The firelight was stronger than the daylight in the long room with its single window, and the pumpkins piled in the corners and the cornstalks that rose from them to the ceiling glowed orange and gold. Among the black pots, pans, skillets and ladles hung from the ceiling, the festoons of dried apples and nut shells and the tassel of grapes and apples in which they now centered, swayed gently, rustling in the waves of heat from the fire. Sarah took a final look in the oven and left the door ajar. She saw the steam from the roasting turkeys and goose going straight to the fire, and knew they were ready. She told John and Aggie to look to their respective, prostrate charges, and herself went to wake Thomas and Samantha, taking Tavie with her that they both might straighten up.

Aggie found Homer awake, still drunk, but now maudlin and penitent. After she had reassured him, retied his tie, straightened and brushed his coat and rubbed his boots, he went slowly downstairs and found the Squire awaiting him with a broad grin. "I'm tarnal ashamed of myself, Squire Lathrop," Homer said. "Can ye make out to forgive a fool like me?" "Nothing to forgive, Homer," said the Squire, taking his hand and looking surprised. "I've been that way too many times myself. I generally try to stay sober when I'm host. If I'd had as much as you, we'd have had a real set-to, eh?" "Gosh, I'm glad ye didn't," said Homer. "Ye'd have given me an awful trimmin'." "I ain't so sure o' that," said the Squire. "A man'll take risks when he's keyed up, but he hasn't much chance in the long run with a man that's sober." At this Homer gave a powerful hiccough. Instantly the Squire started to laugh and said, "Damn you, Homer. I just got over the hic-cups myself, and now you'll start me off again." Homer hiccoughed again, and the Squire did the same. In a moment they were hiccoughing staccato laughter back and forth at each other. "Wait, Homer," said the Squire, "we'll have to tend to this." With a gesture to stay there, he went out into the kitchen and returned with a cup of warm water and salt. Homer sipped it, soon belched heavily, and handed the cup to the Squire, who repeated the process. They both seemed cured and the Squire patted Homer on the arm. "Ye're true grit, Squire," said Homer, shaking his hand again, and feeling enormously at home.

John found Ike wide awake and was relieved to see he had drunk the buttermilk and had not been sick. "Gosh A'mighty, 'Paloosa," said Ike, "I got a beauty. Were you ever that way?" "Plenty of times," said John. "How do you feel?" "Trimmer'n a whistle. Still drunk, I figger. Hungrier'n a woodchuck in May. Missed Thanksgiving, did I? What time is it, to-morrow morning?" "Dinner's in about five minutes. Came up to see if you wanted any." "Thank Crimus. Figger I can eat that whole pig." He sat up, then sank back. "Hate to get up, though. Been lying here half-awake, dreaming everything was slicked out. Got Dandy back. Selling cheeses faster'n we could make 'em. New mowing machine and threshing machine, and a sewing machine for Ma. Rolling in money. You in Congress. Dreamed about women too—" Ike paused, and volunteered no details of his erotic dreams.

He got up on his elbow. "Gosh A'mighty, 'Paloosa, what 'm I goin' t' say t' Ma 'n Pa? I oughta be a'mighty ashamed o' myself, but the trouble is, I ain't." "Don't worry about Ma and Pa," laughed John. "Homer was drunker'n you and tried to lay Pa out. Pa says to make a special effort to make him feel at home. Come on now. Bell'll ring in half a minute."

Ike got up and stood unsteadily. "Gosh, 'Paloosa, I feel funny—like I was eight feel tall—like I could walk right through the wall—like everything around was just thin air." "Look out you don't act as if everything was thin air," cautioned John. "When you feel that way it's mighty easy to fall downstairs." "Figger ye're keerect," said Ike, chuckling and laboring into his coat. He tapped on the door of Homer and Aggie's room, got no response, went in, straightened himself before the mirror, crept down the front stairs unsteadily, gripping the banister, got hold of himself in the front hall and walked straight to the Squire in the keeping-room. "Pa, I'm awful ashamed of myself. Feel like ye ought to give me one of those old-fashioned thrashin's. I won't be up to it in a hurry again, that's certain." "Don't worry about it, Isaac," said his father. "I hope you had some sleep." "Fact is, Pa, I feel finer'n a fiddle."

At this Homer, whom Ike hadn't noticed leaning against the mantel behind him, came forward and gave him a slap on the back that dazed him. "Cheer up, partner," shouted Homer. "We're both in the same boat. Haw! Haw! Haw! Put 'er thar." As Homer pumped his hand, Ike vaguely recollected John's instructions and smiled back at him. "You drunk too, Homer?" he laughed. "What d'ye say to having a swig before dinner?" "No, boys, if you don't mind, no more," said the Squire.

Ike asked where Ma was, and crossed into the north parlor where she came to him. "Ma, how can I ever make it up to you? Not only getting drunk, but getting drunk before the whole town. Hope I didn't cut up any high jinks." "No, Isaac," said Sarah, taking his big face in both hands and looking intently into his eyes. "You behaved properly enough. But I'm so worried about you, my boy. Why did you want to do it? I'm so afraid something I said night before last may·have driven you to it." Ike's face grew very sober, and his mother added, "But we'll talk that over later when the house isn't full of guests." And she pulled his head down and kissed him. "Thanks, Ma," he said, threw his arm around her and kissed her. "Now, can't I carry the pig, or do something else to help?" "Come along and carry the pig right now," said Sarah gaily.

Going into the summer kitchen to wash his hands, Ike passed Tavie who looked away as he started to speak to her and walked back into the main kitchen. As he spluttered into the cold water, his most recent and very imperfect memories of Tavie in this room began to trouble him. He remembered sitting there in the door, and he remembered Ma coming in and Tavie crying. That was all he could distinctly recall, but he knew there was more. However, he was in too high spirits now to bother with vague qualms. So, having wiped his face and hands on the roller towel, he returned to the kitchen, concentrating his attention on the delicate operation he knew he wasn't fit to perform. But he wanted to do it because it now represented a symbol of reconciliation with Ma. They had already unspitted the goose and the two turkeys on platters on the hearth, and Aggie and Tavie were lifting them to the table.

Sarah gave Ike two pot-holders with which he drew out the twenty-five-pound pig from the oven and set it on the hearth. With two big forks apiece they lifted it onto its platter which it overhung at both ends, looking alive and malicious, crouching on its belly with its cranberry eyes and the apple which Sarah now put in its mouth. After pouring over it the juice from the pan, she stepped back and gave Ike a pontifical nod. With great care he lifted the precious burden and bore it slowly along behind the chairs to his pa's place at the end of the table. His balance was faulty and he had a precarious moment when he side-swiped a chair and the heavy roast careened a little away from him, almost spilling the flood of juice from the platter. But he finally landed it safely at the master's place. Sarah pushed the Squire's chair back into position, and sounded the dinner bell.

While the family was gathering in the keeping-room for the formal entrance, Sarah, Aggie and Tavie transferred the various dishes to plates, platters and pewter containers and heaped them on the table. From the Dutch ovens came two venison pies and two rabbit pies; from the fireplace, Irish potatoes, Indian potatoes, onions, turnips, squash, tall pitchers of coffee and tea and copious gravy boats; from the oven three plate-loads of hot corn meal biscuits and the aroma of the pumpkin pies, completing the feast of smells. The table was buried, leaving hardly room for the individual plates, the vegetable dishes being piled upon one another. Sarah, Aggie and Tavie now joined the family, assembled in the keeping-room. The Squire offered Alvina his arm and moved with ritualistic dignity into the kitchen, followed by Joel and Sarah, with the others pairing off behind, Thomas taking Aggie, John his grandmother, and Master Lane, Tavie. All took their places and stood behind their chairs, like wild beasts about to be released into the arena. Both Joel's and Master Lane's mouths watered visibly, a few drops escaping down their chins onto their neck-cloths.

The Squire lifted his hand and fourteen heads bowed in impatient reverence. "For Thy bounty to us this year and all the years before, for good health and cheer, for the gathering of this family together from widely scattered regions, for peace within our borders, for the continuance of government under liberty of state and nation, for these and all Thine innumerable blessings and with the hope of continuing joyfully in Thy service, O Lord of Hosts, Thy humble and loving servants thank Thee." "Amen," the fourteen voices rumbled together, and there was a pause as before the gun of a horse race. With a slight bow the Squire extended both arms, including all present and the steaming board in a gesture of hospitality. Then he drew back his chair, all likewise broke the disciplined ranks, and the race was on.

There ensued three hours of unrelieved gluttony. At half-past four the sun set, the candles were lighted, and the battle was resumed with fresh vigor. At six o'clock the table looked like the coliseum after the beasts had been driven back to their dens. The skeletons of the principal victims were carried off, the carnage was swept away and replaced by sweets in the ratio of a pie and a quarter of a cake per person.

Slowly the jaws and the stomachs labored on to the end. At last the Squire nodded to Tavie, and she went round with a basin of warm water in which napkins were dipped for the mopping of hands and faces. The Squire rose and, with Alvina on his arm, led the heavy recessional into the keeping-room, followed in order by Joel and Samantha, Uncle Brandon and Sarah, John and Aggie, Ike and Tavie—whose hand Ike felt trembling on his arm, with Thomas, Master Lane, Homer and Ben bringing up the rear. With awful grunts all descended to their knees 'round the Squire who, remaining standing, lifted his hands and once more gave thanks to Almighty God, in commemoration of a time two hundred and twenty-nine years before when a little band of starving Englishmen likewise lifted up their hearts in thanksgiving that half their number had survived on a bleak and hostile shore.

CHAPTER XXII

I T   W A S   chore time when the ravenous and religious rituals of Thanksgiving were finally over, and while the other men lighted cigars and sank into chairs in the keeping-room in varying degrees of pain, Ike and Master Lane went upstairs to change to working clothes. When they were coming back downstairs Ike whispered to Master Lane that he would join him in five minutes, whereto the shrivelled old man grunted and, showing no more effects of his gluttony than he had of his drunkenness, lit a candle-lantern and went up to the cow-shed alone.

Ike feigned to help the women with clearing the table, until Aggie and Sarah were well occupied at the main sink and Tavie went out to the other sink in the summer kitchen. Then he casually sauntered after her, closed the door from the main kitchen, picked up a dish towel and began drying to her washing. He was determined to find out why she had been uppity toward him all through dinner. If he had done something in his cups that put her out it seemed, in his present gay and stupefied mood, an easy matter to set everything right with an apology and a few friendly words.

After wiping two plates in silence, he asked in a confidential tone, "Tave, was I awful drunk?" "I don't know," said Tavie, accelerating her scrubbing. "Is that what ye're mad at me about?" "Didn't know I was mad at you," said Tavie lightly, setting another plate on the dripboard and keeping her eyes on her work.

Ike's flippancy faded. He realized that she was really hurt over something. He stood still, holding a plate, trying to remember exactly what had happened. He knew that he had *felt* amorously toward her when he was sitting there on the steps, but he could not for the life of him recall anything specific he had said or done. "Sure grit, Tave, what is it?" he whispered. "Did I try to kiss ye or something?" Inadvertently Tavie glanced up at him and saw, exaggerated in the candle-light, that troubled, quizzical, fatal pucker in his forehead. Quickly she dropped her eyes to the dishpan. "No," she said, biting her lip, and averted her profile from him.

With returning emotion, Ike now remembered having said something to her about love and God. "Well, whatever it was," he went on earnestly, "whatever I did or whatever I said to ye, I didn't mean a word of it and I wish ye'd forget it. Will ye let me kiss you just once?" he asked tenderly, but at the touch of his hand on her shoulder she switched away so violently that she banged the plate into the wall and nicked both the plate and the plaster.

"Gosh, Tave," said Ike after a long pause, "if it's so serious why won't ye tell me what it is and give me a chance to make up for it?" Ike's attempt to kiss her had awakened the steel in Tavie. She turned on him now without flinching and looked straight into his mild eyes with her blazing black ones. "You just asked me to marry you, that was all," she said with a little hiss in her voice.

Ike was completely astounded, though he knew he had been considering Tavie as the possible answer to Aggie's injunction to find love and God, had in fact been considering her as an answer even now as he had been talking to her. With relief he now realized that the thing was on the plane of honor, and he had no further choice in the matter. "Why, let's get married, then," he said without hesitation. "I was going to ask ye sooner or later anyhow."

Now Tavie felt restored and her fury had power in it. "You silly little fool," she snapped, "don't you know you're the last person in the world I'd marry?" And she flashed a look at him which made him drop his eyes, then turned back to her dishes. "But why not?" pleaded Ike with gallant insincerity. "We've always been fond of each other, ain't we? It's the most natural thing in the world."

"Do you want to do me a kindness?" she asked, pausing and looking up at him candidly. "Of course," said Ike. "Then promise me you will never mention such a thing to me again as long as we live."

If Ike had felt relieved before at the appearance of honor to take responsibility from him, he now felt more profoundly relieved that honor had not led him into a final and ill-considered commitment. But he equivocated manfully and rationally. "That's a foolish thing to promise, Tave. I'll promise for a week or a month if ye say so, but it seems kind of crazy to bind ourselves forever." "Nevertheless," said Tavie firmly, "that's just what I ask. And if you won't promise me right now I'll never step in this house after tonight, and in a day or two I'll leave town for good." "All right, I'll promise," said Ike, knowing that it was all nonsense and suppressing an impulse to smile. "Now you'd better get on to chores," said Tavie quietly, being suddenly terrified by what she had done, and feeling tears rising again.

The immediate issue being resolved, Ike began trying to puzzle out Tavie's conduct, and the minute the thing got into the reasoning part of his brain he simply stood still, looking at the back of Tavie's head in the utmost bewilderment. Why was she mad at him because he had asked her to marry him? He didn't know much about girls, but he never supposed they objected to being proposed to, even if they didn't want to accept. He remembered everything pretty clearly now, and he was sure he hadn't tried to paw her or done or said anything else really out of the way. He couldn't figger anything to it except that he had been drunk when he popped the question.

"Please go along," said Tavie without looking around, for she well knew that if she did she'd confront that hard, calculating look of his. "Well, whatever it is, I'm sorry, Tave," said Ike honestly. He went into the kitchen, lit his candle-lantern behind the backs of his ma and sister, both sedulously occupied at the sink, and let himself out the back door. It was a clear night bright with stars in an almost black sky. Ike stopped for a moment and looked up, wondering if there really was a God somewhere up yonder who would help him if he knew how to ask. Up in the cowshed, when he had settled to milking, Master Lane, two critters away, said, "If ye'll fergive the meddlin', Ike, it ain't wise to concern yourself with women when ye're liquored up." Ike wondered how many other people in the house knew what he'd been up to. "Keerect," he said quietly. There was no further sound but the buzz of milk streams on tin and the thud of them into the half-filled pail.

Meanwhile, Sarah and Aggie had been concerned beyond curiosity over the possible goings on behind the closed door in the summer kitchen. Ike was no sooner out of the house than Aggie rushed out to comfort or bless her friend. She found Tavie gripping the sink with both hands, gazing so fiercely at the black window before her that for some time she didn't know Aggie was there. At last she turned and, without relaxing her set expression, said, "Well, I've done it. He asked me to marry him and I refused him. Made him promise never to ask me again, and I meant it. I've made my decision. Now I shan't marry until I have made my own way."

Aggie knew Tavie's fanaticisms well and, though she sympathized with them in theory, they seemed only theory to her and she could not take them with profound seriousness. What she did take seriously was the almost continuous torture Tavie imposed on herself. Like Ike, Aggie's impulse was to smile at the declaration, but she realized what an awful winter Tavie was laying out for herself. At the same time she hoped her friend would hold to her decision, both for her own sake and for Ike's.

"If you've really made that decision, dear," said Aggie, taking Tavie's cold hand, "why don't you come out and stay with us until you get your position in the college?" "I've thought of that, too," replied Tavie, "but—" "We're right in Oberlin village now, you know, on Lorain Street, not two blocks from the college. It would be a good place to stay even after you got your position. We have two nice guest rooms and one of them could be yours always—that is, until you changed your mind."

Tavie gave her a quick, fleeting smile of gratitude. "No, I've decided to face it out. I see everything clearly. If it isn't Ike it will be somebody else. I might as well fight it out right here where I'm earning a little money instead of spending it." "But, my darling," protested Aggie, "what's the use of deliberately torturing yourself?" "Because wherever I go I'll be tortured just the same. If I run away from it this time, it'll be that much harder to withstand the next one, whoever it is."

After a moment Aggie said, "I'm afraid I'm shocked at your talking this way, as if you were an—an animal, and one man was as good as another, as if love was a sort of general, impersonal thing, like breathing or eating." "What else is it?" demanded Tavie through set teeth. "Do you think you're in love with Homer's—*soul?*"

Now it was Aggie's eyes that blackened in anger. "Tavie, what ever do you *mean?*" she said and, lifting both hands to her hot cheeks, she started to walk away. Immediately Tavie melted and ran after her. "Darling, I didn't mean that—truly—I didn't mean you— I was only thinking about myself— Oh, you must forgive me."

"After all," said Aggie, turning back slowly, "what do you know about this, really?" "Nothing, from experience, but I know my own feelings and they're as promiscuous as a—cow. Ike pays me a little attention and I'm in love with him. John is gay with me and I love him. The only one I seem unable to love is the only one who loves me—Constant." "All of which simply means that you've never been in love at all. I hope, for your own sake, that you don't marry anybody while you feel that way. You're quite right in putting your ambitions above emotions of that sort."

This unmasking of Tavie's pose of nobility in her decision immediately calmed her. "You're right, Aggie," she said simply. "That makes it easier." She fished another plate from the dishpan. "I'm not sure it makes it any easier," said Aggie, "for I credit you with more decent emotions than you allow yourself. I don't think for a minute that you feel toward John as you do toward Ike. The time will come when you'll admit that, and when you do, unless you are willing to marry him, you certainly should leave the house and come to me."

Tavie looked up with real love for Aggie in her eyes. "You're the sweetest person in the world," she said fervently, and stood on tip-toe to kiss her tall friend. "Do you really want me to come?—after what I said?" "Yes, I really do, and the sooner the better." "I'm sure you're wrong—about me," said Tavie, returning to the sink. "But I'll remember that like—money in the bank—a haven I can go to if I get too tired. Would you really want me, dear—no matter what?" "No matter what," said Aggie tenderly. "Even if I loved Ike only—like a cow?" "All the more reason," said Aggie. Tavie looked up with a shy smile, and Aggie kissed her.

"Which means, I suppose," said Aggie, smiling facetiously and starting to wipe dishes, "that you won't go to the ball tomorrow night?" "Oh, yes, I will," laughed Tavie, "and I'm going to have the best time of anybody there. Mistress Haddock owes your ma a sitting in and she's coming over to mind little Homer." "Going to dance with Ike?" "Of course—if he asks me. If he doesn't I'm going to flirt with John and make him dance with me. And anyway, that young Master Mathiesson has already asked me to dance."

"Aha! That's more than he did me," said Aggie, delighted at this new possibility. "He's the handsomest boy the Falls ever turned out, to the best of my knowledge." "From New York," said Tavie. "What's he up to here?" "Haven't the faintest notion." "Do you think that's just proper?" "Of course not," said Tavie. "Drove out with Master Sherwood, didn't he?" Tavie nodded. "Smart suit he had on." "Hadn't been ironed in six months," whispered Tavie. "That means," said Aggie, "that he's an honest man."

They chattered on, Aggie shortly opening the kitchen door to notify her ma that the coast was clear. Presently she came in, inquiring what ever they had been up to. Master Lane and Ike came down with the milk, and, after disposing of it, joined the men in the keeping-room. Half an hour later there was a general exodus, Thomas and Samantha homeward in their cutter, Tavie homeward on foot, and the rest to bed.

While the men were making their final, mass visit to the barn, the Squire told Ike to wait up, that he wished to speak to him. Two minutes later they stood alone in the keeping-room, Ike braced for a reprimand about his recent excess, perhaps also a word about Tavie. The Squire yawned, sat down heavily and smiled at Ike for some moments, sensing what the boy expected and anticipating the pleasant surprise he had for him instead. Presently he said that what he wished was to report the results of his talk with Howell Sherwood during flip that noon. Ike looked puzzled, remembering the party dimly, like something that had happened in another life. Master Sherwood, the Squire said, would give Ike a position in the bank any time, beginning Monday. At the start he would pay him five dollars a week, but would advance him in responsibility and wages as rapidly as he deserved it. He understood fully that the arrangement was experimental, and Ike would be free to leave any time on short notice. It was hoped, however, that the arrangement would last until spring, when Ike would decide whether he wanted to continue it or go to Yale.

When the Squire had finished outlining the plan he smiled broadly, proud at having abetted his son's ambitions in this unfamiliar field. "How does that suit ye, my young banker?" he demanded, leaning forward in his chair and playfully cocking his big head on one side. "It's true grit, Pa," said Ike, smiling back in excitement. "Crimus, I hope it ain't a mistake." "If it is," said the Squire with an expansive gesture, "you'll have five or six months to find out. And while you're down there you can learn something about these engines and factories you're so concerned about." "I'll be here for chores," said Ike, "and for woodin' and icin' I'll hire help out of my wages." "Fix that to suit yourself," said the Squire.

"In the meantime," said Ike, wanting to gratify his pa, "I'm going down after Dandy in the morning, first thing after breakfast." "I'm truly glad of that, Isaac," said the Squire, rising. "I think we'll all feel better with Dandy back in the stall, eh?—even if his wind is broken?" "We certainly will, sir," said Ike. Father and son took each other by the shoulders, gave each other a squeeze and a shake of affection with their strong hands, then without further words separated and went to bed. For the first time in near two weeks, Ike felt completely a member of the family.

CHAPTER XXIII

G A M S T A R K knew he had a mean horse in Dandy. But he was too valuable to risk damaging with the methods he would have used on lesser critters, and he decided to take his time. After young Lathrop brought him into the box stall a week before Thanksgiving, Gam ordered him on a diet of water and a quarter ration of hay, and Henry Hawks had to feed him oats by hand through the bars for fear Gam might find some spilled on the floor.

By Monday before Thanksgiving the gray had quit yelling and Gam calculated it was time to give him a try. But after the coach and special came in—this was when John had arrived—the Liberty was full of guests. Gam didn't want to have a racket in the stable with all these people to laugh at him, especially all these remunerative people. Also, he'd have to keep on his best brown broadcloth all day and he had no intention of wrestling with a bad horse in that rig.

So the day passed, and Tuesday and Wednesday followed, with the same inaction for the same reasons. Gam decided to wait until after Thanksgiving, and kept, as he supposed, the gray's diet down. But on Thanksgiving morning Pru got after him at breakfast with the assumption that they were going that very day to hitch Dandy with their other gray and drive out to service at Lathrop Hollow. "Won't it be lovely, Mama?" she said. "At last we shall have another dapple beside old Jennie? And such a beautiful horse, by all odds the finest in town. O Papa, you are a darling to get him for us." And she put her little hand on his big, red, knotty one, making him chew faster on a mouthful of ham he had stuffed into his mouth when she broached the subject.

Gam scowled darkly, his lightless brown eyes avoiding hers until he had swallowed some of the ham. Then he grumbled, "No pair o' grays today." Pru put her hand to her mouth and looked at her mother in astonishment. Mistress Stark, who knew that whatever position she took her husband would take the opposite, discreetly dipped a doughnut in her coffee and made no sign. "But, Pa," said Pru, knowing his vanity, the hole in his armor, "what will people say? Master Gamaliel Stark buys a fine

183

horse from Isaac Lathrop, and on Thanksgiving day, of all days in the year, he's afraid to drive him. Oh, I know that ain't true," she said sweetly, touching his hand again, "but that's what they'll *say,* or my name's not Prudence Stark."

Mistress Stark, who feared the time when Gam should try to break Dandy, and was hoping daily that Squire Lathrop would have the sale rescinded, now tried a tack which she thought might cook the goose. "Prudence, my dear, they won't say anything of the kind. But," smiling at her husband, "it would indeed be nice to ride out behind the pair on Thanksgiving." Pru, who knew her ma as well as her pa, gave her an imperious look; but Gam took the opposite bait from the one expected. "Yes, by God, that's just what they'll say," he snorted, swallowed the rest of his coffee and strode downstairs into the tap-room.

There he found old Henry Hawks just putting away his last slab of beef. "Come with me, Henry," Stark said out of the corner of his mouth to his hireling, and led him out into the inn yard, now two inches deep in snow, and tracked heretofore only by Henry himself and the horses he had earlier led out from the stable to the watering trough. Gam led the way into the long stable and straight to the box stall the inner planking of which Dandy had already shattered into splinters.

The big gray wheeled round as they approached and stood with his head lifted high, distending his nostrils and blowing suspiciously. "Had him out?" inquired Gam. "No sir-ee, sir," laughed Henry. "Just fed him and watered him through the slot." Stark gave Henry a sneer and a sniff of disgust. "Cal'latin' t' drive out t' the Hollow to church. Figger t' leave in half an hour. Try hitchin' 'im t' the sleigh alongside Jennie."

"No, Gam," laughed Henry. "I ain't riskin' my skin goin' in with that critter, not fer you ner nobody." "Ye're fired," snapped Stark, "startin' tomorrow."

"Figger if there's any startin' it'll be today," said Henry with a grin. "Considerin' the hunner I been into ye fer two months, don't figger I'll git any further hangin' around till t'morry." "Git out afore I kick ye out," bellowed Gam, "and tell young Lathrop that I seen him a-greasin' ye and if he figgers t' git the critter back he's got an a'mighty long figger comin'." "Don't cal'late t' see Ike fer a spell," said Henry, walking away and looking back over his shoulder. "But one feller I figger t' see t'morry's the sheriff, unless ye choose t' pay me that hunner right now." "Don't owe ye no hunner but I'll give ye somethin' t' keep ye from beggin'. Git along into the office." And with that he squared off and looked at Dandy with the utmost scorn, took down the pitchfork hanging on the post by the stall, stuck the handle through the bars and gave him a rap on the nose. "That's just to show ye who's yer new boss," he sneered.

All the beautiful muscles of Dandy trembled for a moment. Then, as Stark walked away he leapt against the side of the stall so hard that he drove a splinter three inches into his shoulder. Stark paid old Henry the hundred dollars he owed him, taking a receipt in full, and he, his wife and daughter walked to the First Presbyterian Church for Thanksgiving service.

Prudence pouted prettily all day, and rose into sarcasm when, about dinner time, she got a note from John Lathrop regretting that she and her parents had not come out for service, and begging her to appear at the ball tomorrow night, at which she had already promised him the opening dance. "I suppose," said Pru to her mother in her father's presence at dinner, "that papa won't be able to take us to the ball tomorrow night either. The chief purpose in buying the gray seems to have been to keep us shut up in the tavern during the whole season." This was not good for Master Stark's disposition, and when numerous townspeople came in through the evening with the covert inference—based on Henry Hawks' gabbin'—that Gam had asked the old man to do what he dasn't do himself, he rose into a fixed rage that made him toss in bed all night. That god danged horse became the symbol of the stuck-up Lathrops, of old Henry, and generally of the citizens of Byzantium all of whom he hated.

The next morning, wearing his working clothes to water and bed the other horses before breakfast, Stark gave Dandy neither water nor hay, but only sly looks as he passed his stall, back and forth in the lantern light. This was Friday, two weeks after the sale, the day young Lathrop had said he'd come in for an answer to his offer of five hundred. "He'll git his answer all keerect," thought Stark, as he left the stable and walked back to the inn.

Mistress Stark and Pru being still abed, Gam breakfasted with the guests in the tap-room, where a considerable company was assembled by seven-thirty, awaiting the Round Harbor Coach which was due at that time, though it seldom arrived before eight. The sale two weeks before was now a legend round the Liberty which every guest who stopped there picked up. Also everybody in the tavern, townspeople and guests alike, had now heard the stories old Henry Hawks had spread, stories that of course had improved with repetition. So Stark knew that he was an object of veiled amusement among those present.

Little Loyal Hall felt his person to be inviolate in the Liberty because of the postal contract he had helped get for Stark and which he could

probably have transferred to one of the other taverns if he wished. Therefore, as Stark was finishing his coffee, it was the Postmaster who broke
the ice that for two weeks had been growing thinner in the anticipation
of every frequenter of the Liberty. In a pause he asked casually, "Are
you planning to exercise your gray today, Master Stark?" "Want the job,
do ye?" asked Stark with attempted joviality. "Not me," said the Postmaster, and everybody laughed and, still smiling, continued to look at
Stark. "What ye all gawkin' at me fer?" Gam demanded, still keeping a
pleasant tone but beginning to lose his host's artificial poise. "Kind o'
hangin' 'round, I figger," said the Camilla Farmer who had bid on Dandy
two weeks before, "t' see if ye've made anythin' yet o' that Lathrop hoss."

The mention of "Lathrop" punctured Master Stark's aplomb, and he
did an unfortunate thing. "Ye don't think I kin get the best o' him, do ye?—
not a danged one o' ye?" "Fer my part, I don't," said the farmer, grinning. "There's a dollar," said Stark, throwing a bill on the table, "I kin git
a bridle and saddle onto him a-fore the stage arrives." "Thar ye be," said
the farmer, also throwing down a bill. "Postmaster Hall suit ye fer stake-
holder?" Stark grunted assent. Half a dozen men pushed forward, wanting to be in on the game— "Here's another dollar, ye can't git the best on
him"— "I'll take another"— "Make her five."

But Stark limited his risk to the original dollar. With his wry smile he
rose and went out into the inn yard, followed by a dozen men eager to see
the fun, certain of excitement and perhaps bloodshed. Wishing to give
Stark a fair chance, they entered the stable quietly and congregated without comment in the empty stall opposite Dandy, the stall that had been
the chestnut's.

Master Stark had his plan, and he set out calmly enough to execute it.
First he went around to the rear, the feeding end of the box stall and,
reaching through the wide feeding slot while Dandy reared and snorted,
succeeded in throwing a light rope over his back and capturing and
drawing back the end with the wooden-tined pitchfork. With this rope he
drew a strong chain over his back and succeeded in hooking it fairly
close to Dandy's throat. He then proceeded to pull on the chain, but at
each pull Dandy only reared back. "Gimme a hand, some o' ye," growled
Stark, and half a dozen men came over and put their brawn on the chain.
By this method they drew the horse in a little, but when the chain was
down to about four feet he simply stood stolidly, trembling, breathing
loudly, and they tethered him with that much play. "Ike told him he was
wind-broke," one of the watchers remarked, listening to those heavy
wheezes. At the sound of them Stark remembered also what Ike had told

him eight days ago when he offered him the five hundred back for the gray. For the first time he realized that he had indeed been done, that he was bound to be a laughingstock now, no matter what happened.

Snarling to himself, he fetched a bridle with a curb bit and adjusted it long. Then, murmuring mechanically, "Now, then, my beauty," he rolled back the door of the box stall and entered. Instantly Dandy screamed, reared, pulled out the ring his chain was fastened to, wheeled on his hind feet and lunged at Stark, striking. Lithe as a ferret, Stark slid out of the stall and closed the door just as Dandy's feet crashed down where he had been.

Stark was game. Sliding back the door enough to give passage to man but not horse, he rushed in again, caught the chain over Dandy's shoulders before he reared and went up with him when he rose. Up and down he rode several times, Dandy now screaming like a bull and pawing the air ineffectually in front. Once Stark tried to mount him, but Dandy went up so far that he felt him going over and slid off, hanging to the chain to pull him down. After two or three more rears, when the horse was near the door, Stark let go as he came down and dove for the exit. Dandy was in no position to strike, but quick as a snake he lunged with his head and bit, and as Stark slid out he left the back of his leather shirt and a piece of his shoulder in Dandy's teeth.

This shattered the last shreds of Stark's control. Everybody was laughing at him openly. The horse, now wheezing like a steam engine, was plainly wind-broke beyond any value. Seizing the pitchfork from the post, Stark shot the door wide open and went at him.

Dandy reared as Stark thrust and came straight down on the pitchfork, which Stark let go in order to duck those deadly hoofs. The handle, coming end down on the floor, first drove the sharp, oaken tines three or four inches into the great muscles of the chest, then broke off a foot above the floor. And so, dangling a chain and a broken pitchfork with blood oozing round the tines, Dandy sprang with a scream out of his prison, and galloped out of the stable, across the inn yard, through the covered passage, and out into the Mall. Immediately a score of dogs and a half dozen riders closed in pursuit. By the time Dandy reached the other end of the Mall he was leaving a trail of blood in the snow.

Stark, meanwhile, having no plan now but to worst that horse by whatever means, threw saddle and bridle on the fastest animal in his stable and galloped out in pursuit. By the time he turned up Washington Street only the rearmost of the riders who had preceded him showed the way Dandy had gone, and the quarry himself had almost a mile start.

CHAPTER XXIV

I K E whistled all through second chores in the cow-shed that Friday morning. At 8:30 he dumped the last load of manure, stood up the wheelbarrow, and said to Master Lane as he walked to the door, "Well, now to saddle the chestnut and see what his legs are good for. Bein's the road's thawing, ought to pull into the Falls soon after nine. Figger to have Dandy back by dinner if it takes all my savings."

He stepped out of the cow-shed and heard a sound like fast-beating, powerful surf coming rapidly up the hill from the Corners. He listened curiously, and a few seconds later heard heavy hoofbeats. Then he knew. Dandy, still running at top speed and his breath roaring, surged up through the little cut, the chain swinging from side to side, the stub of the pitchfork bobbing between his front legs, his mouth, nostrils, chest, legs and belly soggy with foam and blood. Plunging past Ike without noticing him, he charged down to the horse-barn, in through the open door, and clattered into his old stall beside the chestnut who reared, broke his halter-rope, escaped from this colossal attack, and ran confused circles in the snow of the front yard till Ben caught him and tied him up.

When Ike ran into Dandy's stall he was sagging slowly on his front legs, blood pouring from his nose and mouth, and while Ike struggled to pull out the pitchfork he only bore more heavily down on it till he collapsed, the oaken tines finishing their work by piercing his heart and lungs, and in a few seconds the big horse rolled up his eyes and ceased to breathe. Desperately Ike fell on his knees in the blood, throwing his arms across the hot reeking barrel and pressing his forehead into it in an attitude of prayer, identifying himself with that waning life, straining to hold it back with the force of his own.

He heard his own breathing and the beating of his heart, and for a few minutes was possessed by the illusion that they were Dandy's. He was unaware of his pa and John who came running out and stood watching him, then tip-toed away. As if from a great distance he heard his pa's voice outside in the drive, saying to the pursuers as they came up one by one, "The horse is dead. There is nothing further to be done."

Slowly the silence of the great, gray form, the fact of death, penetrated to Ike's sub-consciousness. He lifted his head and gazed intently, without thought or emotion, at the rough head of a nail in the opposite planking of the stall. He heard more voices outside, very far away, meaningless. "Dead, eh?—my experience ye can't always trust these Lathrops. I'll trouble ye . . . " "You will not dismount on these premises . . . " "Mighty brave, ain't ye, Brandon." Long silence, Ike still staring at the nail, his mind and emotions in suspension, paralyzed, dead. Voices again—" . . . check for fifteen hundred . . . I believe it sufficient to cover the items of the sale." Short silence. " . . . That fer yer money—ye kin keep it, bein's the hull world knows ye need it a danged sight more'n I do"— "Stand back, Brandon." Another silence, with hoofbeats fading. " . . . John, you're a bigger man than I am." "Come into the house."

Laboriously Ike rose. Somebody—his brother John—was standing by the stall. Ike walked outside and stood in a daze, his clothes and hands splotched with blood. He saw meaningless bits of paper strewn in the snow of the drive—they were the fragments of the Squire's check Stark had torn up. Ike felt a hand on his shoulder. He knew it was John's, but it gave him an intolerable sense of actuality. "Leave me be, 'Paloosa," he whispered hoarsely from a dry mouth. "Leave me be!" he whispered again in desperate appeal. For the first time a sob broke from him, and in a staggering run he fled up to the hay-barn, closed the big door behind him, and shot the beam-bolt across with a bang.

Then, in that dim solitude, the emotion broke, such a spasm of sobs as he had not known since he was a tiny boy. Leaning against one of the big hayloft posts, he kept crying, "O God, O God," over and over without any meaning, while the disturbed pigeons on the beams rustled in little circles on their squeaky wings or cocked their heads down at him, "whoo-whooing" in curiosity. Dragging himself up a hay-ladder he walked a beam and flung himself heavily face-down on the mow, where he lay silent for a moment while the diversion of the little exercise vanished and the tears returned.

It was not only grief that was shaking him, grief at the loss of the horse that had been his friend, but the first real sense of guilt he had ever known. "O God, I killed him. O God, I killed him," he kept murmuring to the silence, and for almost an hour no thought or emotion but grief, guilt and despair entered his mind.

Then gradually his stricken soul began to grope for its anodyne. The bloody image in the barn passed from his brain and he lay quietly in the hay with eyes closed, remembering the pleasure and the excitement he and Dandy had had together: the time they had chased a deer all the way from the orchard down across the upper pasture, the forty-acre meadow, the lower pasture and the potato field, taking the walls and the snake fences as easily as the quarry, till at last he lost them in the pine woods; the time Pa had lain in a fever two days when Dr. Swift was away, till Ma had said they should get a doctor and he had ridden Dandy to the Falls in the blizzard of '44 when there was no sign of a road and they broke the way back for old Dr. Daw on his bay; the ribbons they had won at the Fair; the races they had won on the highway. These and many more images poured through Ike's brain, punctuated by occasional stabs of present realization, until at length he and Dandy were living in a sort of world of memory that was impervious to change.

As Ike had concluded of his big brother Tom seven years before, when he was twelve, he began now to say in his mind, "Dandy ain't dead— Dandy couldn't die." Then the present would come back; Ike would realize that he would never ride Dandy again in this world; and guilt and grief would surge for a moment stronger than his sense of the permanence of things.

At length his mind began to build a subtler rationalization, and he heard something like a voice whispering, " 'Twas only a mistake—'twas a mistake ye made— Ye didn't do anything calculated to hurt Dandy— 'Twas only a mistake as if he'd had a bad fall when ye were riding him." Then the more valid anodyne returned— "He ain't really dead though, more n Tom's dead— Don't figger his being a dumb beast makes any difference in such matters." So, gradually, Ike got his transcendental imagination separated from his sense of actuality, till at last he reached a point where his mystical perception afforded him consistent relief from the stab of guilt. If only now he didn't have to return to the world, and eat and work and see people, he could be reconciled to Dandy's death.

But he knew he did have to go back, and before long now, first of all back to the family, every one of whom had blamed him for selling Dandy. They had been right and he'd been wrong, sure grit. He'd admit that sure enough now. Then he felt ashamed of thinking that way about the family. He remembered the way Pa and Ma had acted when he came down to dinner yesterday. They'd feel just as bad about it as he did, and they'd all stand together. They'd know this wasn't a time for blaming anybody. The main thing to remember was that Dandy had been alive a little while before and he must still be alive somewhere. He couldn't just disappear. And so, still weighed down by grief and self-blame but possessed of a mystic formula for escaping them, he first sat up in the hay, then climbed back on the big beam, descended the ladder and went out the barn door.

It was snowing lightly and he stood for some minutes looking down at the familiar buildings that were so incredibly still and strange in a world where Dandy had been a short time before and would not be seen any more. He heard voices coming up from the near pasture and saw all the men approaching with Mol and Pol and the stone-boat. He knew what they had been doing, walked down to meet them and passed them with his eyes on the ground, exchanging no word or look of greeting with any of them.

They had dug Dandy's grave and left him lying by it under the north side of an enormous boulder with a clump of cedars growing on its top, a boulder that had been the play castle of all the children of the family. As soon as he saw Dandy lying there, Ike wished he hadn't come. But he knew they had left him there for him to see last, and he had a job to do. Clenching his teeth, he walked up to the big, bloody body, picked up the two pairs of hoofs, and with an abrupt angry effort rolled it over and heard it thud into the deep grave. He looked around for a shovel and found they had left him none. Hurriedly he walked to the horse-barn where Master Lane and Ben were unharnessing Mol and Pol. He picked up a shovel from the corner where they had stood their tools and started back. "Say, Ike," called Master Lane, "ye hain't to do that. Leave the gravin' to me." "Ye can come if ye choose," said Ike over his shoulder. So Master Lane and Ben hurried down after him, and without a word spoken they buried Dandy, trampled the earth firmly down, and restored the frozen sod.

It was dinner time now, and Ike walked into the house with the rest. When he entered no one expected a word from him, but he gave not the faintest gesture or look of recognition to anybody. As he washed his hands and went upstairs to take off his bloody clothes there was that coldness about him, that terrible dignity which not even Aggie could penetrate. Not a word was spoken through dinner, and all the family, especially John, felt a strange respect for Ike in his quiet and icy detachment, as if he had some secret knowledge that set him apart, a little above any of them.

CHAPTER XXV

T H E D E A T H of Dandy was the next thing to the death of a member of the Lathrop family, and if it had been an ordinary junket planned for that evening it might well have been postponed. But the occasion for this ball was the departure for California in the morning of six of the finest young men of the Hollow, six of the finest in the town, with the wives of two of them. Not the death of Squire Lathrop or Dr. Swift could have cancelled that ball. During the day several neighbors who were passing took the trouble to stop and convey to the Squire their sympathy about Dandy. But they went on preparing for the dance just the same, and everybody noted with satisfaction that the afternoon's steady snowfall guaranteed sleighing and a good turnout from the Falls.

By evening the long, one-story, white-washed hall at the Corners was more bedecked with laurel, hemlock and pine, long festoons of calico and strings of dried fruit, heaps of corn, pumpkin and squash, and red and blue painted kegs of sweet and hard cider, altogether more gaily adorned than ever before in its fifty years of housing the festivities and the politics of the little community. In addition to the ordinary decorations there was at the end opposite the entrance, adjacent to the musicians' platform in the corner, a suspicious-looking square of the white-washed plank wall that was completely covered with laurel. One of the covered wagons that Jared Oxbow had finished for the expedition had been rolled up alongside the building so that the back of it was by the main entrance and would serve as a ticket office. The other covered wagon stood in the snow outside the end of the hall toward the main road, the end where the musicians' platform was.

As everyone expected, Ike said to the Squire at supper that he didn't feel specially up to dancing though he'd go down and look in for a spell. At half-past seven John and Ike by mutual wish walked down the road together in the darkness, dressed in their best clothes, their tall hats and their greatcoats, their boots crunching in the snow that continued to fall. "Do ye figger ye can forgive me, Lollapaloosa?" asked Ike in his quietest voice.

They tramped along for ten rods before John replied, "It's all fired funny, Scamp, but there's nothing to forgive now. If Dandy had lived and come back healthy as you planned, I would always have thought you had done wrong and would always have hoped you'd admit it some day. But Dandy's having died makes that all seem—childish."

They walked silently for another hundred yards, each feeling strengthened by the reconciliation, each puzzling to himself over the paradox that they were actually happier as a result of Dandy's death than they would have been had he lived. For the first time since John had come home Ike now felt able to declare what had been bothering him.

" 'Paloosa, I got to tell ye that I hope ye never marry Pru. I just don't trust her, and one way or another I'll wage ye she'll lead ye a song and dance. I just had to tell ye how I feel. It ain't that I'm trying to give ye advice." "I can't see now that I'll ever get over it," said John, "and if I feel this way when I can afford to marry I'll have no choice but to marry her if she'll have me." "Ain't blaming ye," said Ike. "If ye do marry her, I'll likely grow fond of her in the long run. She's smarter 'n a fox in November, no denying that."

"It's funny though," said John after a short silence, "I'd as lief she didn't come to the ball tonight, after all my having come home mostly for the pleasure of dancing with her. It isn't so much her being Stark's daughter as that—somehow—the way I feel about her has nothing to do with the way I feel about—Dandy's dying. As long as I can't get that out of my mind I—I'd hardly know how to behave with Pru. It's an awful thing to say about somebody I'm in love with, but it seems as if a thing of this kind is just—none of her business." "That's my notion to a T," said Ike. And they walked the rest of the way to the hall without speaking.

When John and Ike arrived, and the rest of their family soon after on foot and in the sleigh, only the immediate neighbors were congregated. Two big coach lamps were blazing at the main entrance, with the snowflakes like little moths flying softly down through their light. Half a dozen other lamps and hundreds of candles lighted the gay hall inside. Dr. Swift, dressed in a fringed leather, western scout's costume, was installed as ticket agent, sitting on a chair in the rear of the covered wagon that was backed up by the door. All the men paid their admission, got their little red tags and strung them to their buttonholes. John and Ike, feeling that they were wet-blanketing the party, sauntered around the outside of the hall to inspect the other covered wagon that stood there in the shadow.

Having had nothing to do with the preparation for the ball, they didn't know why it had been rolled up here from Oxbow's mill. They looked it

over as best they could in the half-light, admiring Jared's work, and climbed
up on the seat. John lit a cigar, and Ike took a bite from a plug of tobacco.
"Sometimes I wish I were going out there," said John. "It's the great
adventure of our generation." "It's that, all keerect," said Ike, "and sometimes I'd like to go too. But for me," he added slowly, "it'd be like running away from a job I've to do here—that is, unless I'm to take Dandy's
dying as a kind of warning to quit figgering on going to the Falls and
making money and all that." "You'd best wait a while before basing any
decision on what's happened today," said John. "It'll be too close for a
good while yet."

"Ye know," said Ike, "I can't see yet how there's anything wrong in
trying to make a little money. And I can't see it that there was anything
wrong—in general—in selling Dandy. Suppose, for instance, I'd sold him
to Master Sherwood or Judge Van Wyck where he'd have been well
treated. That wouldn't have been wrong, as I see it. And even if I'd sold
him to Stark and he hadn't been hurt and we got him back like I figgered,
even that, as I see it, wouldn't have been wrong. What was wrong was
that Dandy got hurt, and what I did that was wrong was to make a
mistake, a mistake in judgment. Maybe that's all there is to it. Maybe that's
all there is to the whole business of right and wrong, sin and all that."

"Maybe," said John quietly, for his own direct moral impulses were
stunned for the time being, and he would have been unable at any time
to analyze them closely. They sat silent for two or three minutes, while
the distant sound of singing drew nearer from the direction of the Center—

> *"Go to Jane Glover, and*
> *Tell her I love her, and*
> *By the light of the moon*
> *I will come to her—*
> *Go to Jane Glover, and*
> *Tell her I love her, and*
> ......"

"Well," said John reluctantly, "guess I'd better go round front, in case
Pru's in the first sleigh." And he jumped over the wheel and walked
around into the light.

In Ike's present, half-mystical mood there was no such thing as time
and place or presence and absence. He had been virtually thinking aloud
before and now he continued thinking verbally as if he were still talking
to the Lollapaloosa. "Always two things about anything important," he
thought. "There's the whole meaning of it—that's the fact that Dandy

ain't really dead. Then there's the morals of it—the right and wrong—
the way folks behave about it. If ye do something that hurts somebody,
that's wrong. If ye do the same thing and it don't hurt anybody, then it's
right. All a question of judgment. What I did was to make a mistake in
judgment that hurt Dandy, and I'll be punished for it as long as I live."
As if it were miles instead of a hundred feet away from him, Ike realized
that the first sleigh was arriving and that others were approaching. As in
the morning when he stepped out of the barn, he was startled by the
strangeness, the remoteness of active life, now that Dandy was dead.

Meanwhile, John had been standing restlessly at the entrance among
the little group that was awaiting the approaching sleighs. As the assembly
for church the day before had been a medley of bells, the assembly for
the ball was a medley of songs: "Go to Jane Glover . . ." "Come, follow,
follow, follow . . ." "O, believe me, if all those endearing young
charms . . ." "Drink to me only with thine eyes . . ." "John Anderson,
my Jo, John . . ." Instead of private sleighs and cutters, revellers from a
distance now came in noisy parties lying under bear robes in hay spread
over wide racks on wood-sleighs, the poles sedately wagging a cowbell
against the rhythm and harmony of the voices. As John waited, a dozen
such equipages were bearing in out of the darkness from all directions.
One by one they arrived and whoaed up at the main entrance, discharging
their freight of gaiety in the snow-streaked circle of light from the big
coach lamps. Under the robes furtive hands unclasped. Young men groped
for silk and beaver hats, stood up and leaped from the racks down into the
snow. With squeals and laughter buckram-huge ladies were lifted down
in strong arms, and there was a great stamping and shaking off of snow
in the entrance. Soon, three-score old folks and two or three times that
number of young men and maidens were circulating in the hall, displaying the widest flaring and lowest cut gowns, the most fetching curls and
headgear, the richest silks, ruffles, taffeta and broadcloth, the most spar-
kling ear-rings, finger-rings, brooches and necklaces that the town could
offer.

As the last sleigh of expected guests pulled into the light and stopped,
John perceived, with combined relief and disappointment, that Pru was
not coming. This was the Gadston party, chaperoned by old Horace himself and his red-haired, ceremonious wife. When the ladies were all lifted
down young Nat Gadston, John's principal rival for Pru, walked up to
him and shook hands. "Glad to see you, John, and I'm uncommon sorry
t' hear about the horse. Here's a note Pru asked me t' hand ye when we
stopped t' fetch her and her ma. Mistress Stark gave me another note fer

yer ma. Inside, is she?" "Thanks, Nat," said John. "Yes, Ma's in there somewhere."

When the party had disappeared in the hall, most of them giving John the sympathies he had been enduring all evening, he broke the pretty little blue seal and read by the light of one of the coach lights at the entrance:

My dear John:

You will of course understand how impossible it would be for me to appear tonight after what has happened. The one thing I want to do is to crawl away into a corner of the attic where nobody will ever see me again. Candidly, I don't see how I can ever look you or Ike in the face, though I know how kind you both are. I am almost ashamed to ask you to accept my sincerest sympathy. That goes for Ike too.

Ever Yours,

Pru.

After reading the note for the fifth or sixth time, John put it in his pocket and looked up with a smile that met the sympathetic eyes of Dr. Swift, glancing up as it were casually from counting the gate receipts in the rear of the covered wagon by the door. "Ever yours!" thought John with a sigh and a catch in the throat. He had an impulse to run around and make Ike come and read the wise and tender note. But from inside he heard the accordion player running scales and Jehu Jones tuning his fiddle. For the first time he felt that he might dance a turn or two without difficulty. Almost gaily he walked inside, threw off his coat and hat, and, after accustoming his eyes to the sudden light of the whale-oil lamps and the dozens of candelabras, began to circulate in greeting among the crowded, flaring skirts, like weightless, lacy mushrooms, pink and lilac, crimson, yellow and green, each swaying delicately as breath and supporting an ætherial flower of bare bosom and shoulders and trembling jewels and curls.

The two visiting musicians were seated on the platform, Elijah Harris the jew's-harp player from the Center, and the accordion player from Etruria township with the red strap slung over his shoulder supporting his great, ebony, silver-embossed box with the ivory keys. Jehu Jones, dressed in his resplendent blue velvet coat and knee breeches, and with his white hair swirled back in a commanding pompadour, finished his tuning and resined his bow with a great flourish. Then, nodding and smiling to the right and left, he walked out to consult with Dr. Swift, returned, mounted the platform, and nodded to the accordion player. The latter did a quick sequence of chords, and paused. Jehu rapped with his bow on the side of his fiddle and obtained silence.

"Ladies and gentlemen," he intoned in his clear tenor, "ye're more'n common welcome this evenin', bein's this is a more'n common occasion, not only fer the folks o' Lathrop Holler but fer all the folks o' the township. As ye've no doubt heard, tomorry mornin' six o' the finest striplin's and two o' the fairest young ladies in Byzantium are shovin' off fer Californy and Lord knows where else. Bein's we want t' git 'em back home after they've got the Ulysses out o' their systems, we want ye t' show 'em a celebration tonight as'll not only assure 'em o' yer love but'll stay in their minds and make 'em conclude, after they've loaded their backs with gold, that the best place to settle down and enjoy their fortune is the old town they come from.

"Now as I call yer names I want each o' ye to stand up and remain standin'. Master Jared Oxbow, junior, leader o' the expedition and his wife Roxanna"—a round of cheers and hand-clapping as young Master and Mistress Oxbow arose, bowed and curtsied respectively, and remained standing. "Master Savillian Stone, second in command, and his wife Lucinda"—again cheers and hand-clapping. "Master Hosanna Birdseye—Master Emanuel Swift—Master Eliphalet Emmens—Master Constant Oaks"—they all stood, bowed and waited.

"And now, friends," continued Jehu, "I propose ye three cheers and a toast to Byzantium's bravest and may God A'mighty watch over every one on 'em in their travels and bring 'em back home rich with good fortune and wisdom. Now then! Hip—hip—" "Hooray!" thundered the hall until the beams trembled and the decorations rustled—"Hooray"—"Hooray!" All who had mugs of cider lifted them and the rest simulated the toast.

"And now," shouted Jehu, "lead out yer partners fer the grand promenade." He seized his fiddle, nodded to the other two musicians, and they surged into "O Susanna, don't you cry for me," as the company, breaking into song, formed in line as pre-arranged, the emigrants leading, followed by the older citizens of Lathrop Hollow, then the older citizens of the rest of the town, and finally the long procession of young people, the young men already beginning to cut a few steps individually, impatient for the main ball to begin.

After the grand promenade, with all of its windings, its separatings and returns and its final grand right-and-left was over, Jehu gave them no pause. Rapping on his fiddle, he called, "Lead out yer partners fer the Money Musk. Here ten couple. Ten couple yonder, and ten beyond. Three more sets at the other end. Hi, thar, what are ye up to with eleven couple?

Git along with ye. Are ye ready? Sets in order." And he came down on his fiddle with all his might, the accordion roaring in behind him and the jew's-harp setting up its wavering alto in the strain that New England had danced to for more than two hundred years. And so with a uniform swinging of hands and feet and the swaying of sixty round skirts like colored bells, the great farewell ball began.

Outside, alone in the dark on the box of the covered wagon, and separated from the musicians' platform only by the single plank siding and stripping of the building, Ike was as close to the sounds of the festivities as if he had been in the hall. Yet when the grand promenade started, that Susanna music was not to him an invitation to dance but the rhythm of a change that was coming over the Hollow, the rhythm of the march of his eight friends who were starting westward tomorrow in search of a strange world, the rhythm of a change in himself that was somehow connected with their going away, the change that had made him sell Dandy, that made him interested in machines and was impelling him, like these others, to leave home for a new life. It was the rhythm of all this Reform that John and Tavie were interested in, all for one reason or another discontented with things as they were and as they always had been.

When, following the Money Musk, the dance moved out into the stately Minuet, Ike's mood moved backward into his childhood, back into the security of his pa's world in the time long before Dandy had died, when no one had thought of making money or going West or reforming anything. When they swung into Hull's Victory, everyone inside sang as they danced, and Ike remembered his great-grandfather's stories of the Revolution and the War of 1812, the heroic time when liberty was young and meant only freedom to live one's life in the old places without interference.

Then they did the White Cockade which was Ike's favorite dance, and he beat time on the foot-board as Jehu Jones sang the well-known changes: "Gent by the right and your own by the left—gent by the right and the opposite by the left—gent by the right and your own by the left—sashay clean around that couple." Here Ike felt he was on strong, familiar ground of his own. And so through the Portland Fancy and the Waltz Quadrille— in the certainty of established things he almost forgot that Dandy had died, that Jared and the rest were going West tomorrow, and that he was going to work in the Falls Monday.

An hour of dancing passed without respite. Then there was a pause in the hall, an intermission filled with laughter and singing and the hum of talk. Couple by couple the old folks had been dropping out and taking permanent stations on the benches around the wall. But the young people were just warming to the work. A shout went round for "the Polka," and Ike heard them calling for John, and for George Fulton, Fred Van Sanford, and others of the young men from the Falls who, like John, had been away to college recently. The frolicsome rhythm started and immediately Ike was back in the world of change. He heard them cavorting around the floor in this dance that was not their own, this dance they were bringing back from the cities, this dance that represented everything that was luring people away from the homesteads—machinery, reforms, excitement, all kinds of new ideas, the chance to make money.

Then came a series of the newer quadrilles, with their fast jig-time and their swinging of the ladies by the waist instead of by the hand. Birdie in the Cage. Ladies Bow and Gents Bow-wow. Ladies Dos-Y-Domino. Ike felt an abandon in it, a lack of the certainty and precision of the older dances, only the need to be up and doing something, to be going somewhere. He had an impulse to go in and dance merely because the new music made him restless, because you couldn't sit still and think with it twiddling at you. He jumped down from the wagon, but the figure ended then and he merely spat on the snow and stood leaning against the wagonwheel.

It had stopped snowing and, being out from under the big curve of the hood, Ike saw the stars appearing. This and a short silence inside let his larger mood return. He realized what an enormous gulf there was going to be between the time before and after Dandy died, between the time before and after his best friends went away from the Hollow.

Somebody inside began shouting "Susanna," and others took it up. He heard Jehu calling out the sets. Presently the popular air started once more with a vengeance. Jehu was especially loud in calling the changes which few of them had tried before, and the whole company of watchers around the wall was singing. In this tune alone among the other new ones Ike felt a strange kind of validity and power, something real and compelling behind the restlessness of the new time. To the beat of this rhythm his vision of change became more specific and prophetic, a pageant of the millions marching forward from that night into the remote future.

Slowly that march took on a new significance in his mind. Heretofore he had not thought of his going to the Falls or his friends going West as anything but a temporary adventure. But now he felt the whole change as a final and permanent one, the beginning of a new world. He saw the Falls and hundreds of other such places grown into great cities where the power and the money was, where people stayed and most of them worked in enormous factories or banks. He saw the West as a fabulous country where everybody had bags of gold and the corn grew fifteen feet high and where people also stayed and made new homes. Perhaps, he thought, the eight who were leaving tomorrow would never come back. Perhaps he would never come back from the Falls. Perhaps John would go to teaching or preaching somewhere else and would never come back. Nothing would ever be again what it was before Dandy died. He saw the Hollow as it had been before the white people came, no roads, no houses, only the forest and Indians and wolves.

Then suddenly his own vision angered him. Striking the iron tire of the wagon wheel with his fist, he said aloud to the rhythm of "Susanna," "By God, we'll beat 'em. B' God, we'll beat 'em yet." But he could not have said exactly what he meant, except that somehow the Lathrops would carry on. He could not have said for certain that he meant that the Lathrops would carry on as they had here for more than sixty years, and for a century and three-quarters before that in New England. He only thought of Stark and Gadston and Applemore whom somehow they were going to beat. The rhythm of "Susanna" was in him. He knew that, like the eight inside, he too was going somewhere. But he was coming back, by God!—back here where Dandy was still alive, and where living meant something!

The music ended, but the company kept singing diminishingly. With contempt Ike felt the tire of the wagon under his hand. What was the danged thing doing here? He glanced before him up the road toward the Lathrop homestead. He looked to the right at the church, all dark except for the spire that was silhouetted against the stars all the way to the tip. As the singing ended inside, he heard for a moment the sound of the stream under its ice beyond the other end of the hall. He heard a fox yelp on Swift Mountain and the replying voices of half a dozen dogs, each one of whom he knew. This, by God! was where he lived and they wouldn't take it from him, not with all their Californias and all their factories. He'd learn all about banking and machinery and he'd build a factory right here that would make them sit up and take notice!

The music began again, a tune like "Susanna" that had to do with going away. Jehu's voice began—"Head couples pass right through—and swing that girl behind you—" The dancers and the audience inside joined in the song. Then Ike heard voices and the crunch of feet in the snow.

A group of men came round the corner of the hall and Ike recognized Dr. Swift, Jared Oxbow's younger brother Joshua, Savillian Stone's older brother Lawrence, and three or four young men from the Falls. "Evening," he said as they came up to the front of the wagon. "Well, Isaac, my lad," said Dr. Swift, "we didn't expect to find you here. We've a little surprise for the people inside. Will ye give us a hand?" "Sure grit," said Ike. "Just got to back the wagon up to the end of the hall," said the Doctor. "Suppose you direct us, Isaac. Ye'll see a square cut out o' the sidin' yonder. I'll take the pole and you just direct me so's we get the wagon plumb in the middle of the square."

Ike walked over to the end of the hall and noticed for the first time that a big section of the siding had been sawed out and was held in place only by a few sections of fence-rail for braces. Joshua Oxbow removed the braces and stood holding up the square of siding with his hand. Under Ike's direction and with Dr. Swift swinging the pole, the rest ran the wagon out and back until it was about two feet from the wall at the place designated.

Dr. Swift told Lawrence Stone to go back and give Jehu the signal. Then he said to Ike, "This'll be the last dance, Isaac. After that, if ye care to see the show, I'd step around yonder. If ye don't want to be seen ye could stand in the door and nobody'd step on your toes." Ike not only wanted to see the show now. He wanted to dance. He wanted to dance with his friends here in the Hollow where he belonged. And "The Girl I Left Behind Me" was a good old tune, if it did have to do with going away. He said, "Thank ye, Dr. Swift," spat out his quid, walked quickly around to the entrance and into the hall, deposited his things and made his appearance.

Five sets were dancing and one after another everyone on the floor recognized Ike and raised a hand of welcome. They were all singing, but Jehu's voice was audible above them. John and Tavie were dancing number four couple in a set close by where Alexander Mathiesson was dancing with Aggie. A new change was beginning. John whispered to Tavie, then came over to Ike and told him to go and take his place. Ike was notoriously the best dancer in town, and his entrance livened the room perceptibly, from Jehu Jones down. "Put your lady in front and march right round, and swing that girl behind you— Lady in front once more and march right round, and swing that girl behind you."

Jehu prolonged the dance for Ike's benefit, but at last, against vigorous shouts for more, he sang the usual final command, to "Promenade you know where, promenade to that big armchair." Then he whispered instructions to the accordion player and rapped on his fiddle for attention: "Partners fer the grand promenade and everybody out fer something special fer them as is leavin' us. Will the eight young Cal-i-for-ni-ans be so good as to step up here fer instructions? And the rest of ye form in the usual manner."

Tavie had promised the promenade to Mathiesson whom Ike greeted warmly, with apologies for his "indisposition"—they both winked—of yesterday. Aggie stepped over brazenly and asked Ike for the promenade. The long line of couples being formed and almost circling the hall, and the principals being notified of their duties, Jehu placed them at the head of the procession, the two married couples leading, and the four bachelors paired off behind them, so that the group was intact, with no odd partners who were not "off fer Cal-i-for-ni-a."

Then Jehu whispered instructions to Squire Lathrop, who came next with Mistress Swift, and to young Nat Gadston whom, with his tall sister Gloriana, he judged to be about half way back from the front. Then he waved to the musicians and the final, solemn promenade began. With Aggie's hand on his arm Ike felt once more secure in a world that would not change.

To the stately "Washington Guards March" the company proceeded twice around the hall. Then, at Jehu's command, Jared and Roxanna Oxbow turned at the end opposite the musicians and came straight down the center, leading the little band of emigrants. Behind them Squire and Mistress Swift led off on a diagonal to the right, and when young Nat Gadston and his sister turned they led the rest of the procession to the left, so that when Jehu by raising his bow stopped the music, the guests stood in a great V, with the eight young guests of honor in the center, opposite and facing the square in the siding that was completely covered with laurel.

At this the Reverend Norcross, leaving Diodema Swift, stepped out of the promenade and mounted the platform. "Friends," he said, "it is not customary for a minister of the gospel to take an active part in a ball. But at the urgent request of Master-of-Ceremonies Jehu Jones, and having a mind to the very special nature of this occasion, I have consented to do my part in bestowing our blessing and inviting the blessing of Almighty God upon those who, under His guidance, will be far from us and from their homes by the time another evening has fallen upon the world. Our hearts are too full both of joy and sadness to make any admonition appropriate or necessary at this time. Instead I ask that we bow our heads in a moment of supplication to that God who has blessed us and this nation so far upon our journey, and who will continue to bless us while we put

our trust in Him." He lifted his hands. The eight young people knelt on
the floor and the rest of the company bowed their heads.

"O God, it is not for us to know or to prophesy our future journey. It
is for us only to do courageously the day's task as we see it and to trust in
Thy care and Thy providence for all the future years and for eternity. Not
one of these young people who have seen their course westward and out
of this flock can prophesy where another year will find him. Not a father
or a mother left behind can do more than hope and pray. We know they
are bound upon a courageous journey, an undertaking which the bravest
of us cannot but admire. We know that there is danger in their adventure, we know that there are rewards in a new liberty in a new and vaster
world, a promised land of which we can only dream. Keep each one of
these travellers in Thy love and let them not fail, if trial comes, to pause
and look to Thee, and not to man for guidance. Keep the memory of
home warm in their hearts, and to us who will be deprived of their company for a little season, give courage to walk upright in our loneliness,
knowing that Thou art surely going before these sons and daughters,
these brothers and sisters, these friends whom we shall miss henceforth
in our daily walks and our greetings and our meetings together. And so,
God of our fathers, God of this nation and God of Freedom, to Thy care
we commend them. Let it be unto them and unto us according to Thy will.
Amen."

The minister was more moved than anyone had ever seen him, and
when he finished the prayer there was a prolonged silence, broken by a
few stifled sobs, and not a head was lifted. At the beginning of the prayer
Jehu and the other two musicians had slipped out of the hall, and now,
from outside behind the laurelled square in the wall came the melody of
"O God, Our Help in Ages Past" on a muted violin. No one sang with it
but most of the people, with heads still bowed, hummed the tune and the
harmony. When the stanza was ended there was another pause. Then very
softly the muted violin began, "We're off to Cal-i-for-ni-a-," and one by
one the heads of the listeners rose. The music grew louder and the
accordion and the jew's-harp joined in. Slowly the square of laurel slid
back, revealing the rear of the covered wagon outside the hall, with the
step let down. The music rose to full force and the company joined in the
song. Jehu Jones stepped into the opening beside the wagon and beckoned
to the eight travellers who were still kneeling. Slowly they rose, went forward, climbed into the wagon and turned back, facing their friends.

At this a great shout went up, and with tears still on their faces they

smiled, waved and joined in the singing. Slowly, as they continued to
wave and throw kisses, the wagon was drawn away from the opening into
the darkness, and the square of laurel moved back into place. The music
outside grew softer again until it faded away.

For a minute there was silence, then a gay shout at the entrance and
the eight travellers rushed in again pell-mell, the husbands carrying their
wives. Then the real leave-taking began, gay, passionate, inarticulate but
for mingled laughter and weeping.

This continued for half an hour, during which "Auld Lang Syne" was
sung again and again, every one of the eight was embraced by every one of
the guests, and the covered wagons were piled with hundreds of tender
and useless gifts. Then the big wood-sleighs jangled up and the visitors
from far away took their leave, not singing now but each waving a farewell that was too deeply felt for words. Last of all, the neighbors of the
Hollow kissed all the travellers again, and the crisp winter night was undisturbed by twenty families crunching or softly jingling home under the
stars.

When they reached the homestead John and Ike walked down across
the bright, snow-covered pasture to Dandy's grave. They took off their
hats and stood silent a few moments, then sauntered back to the house,
facing a rising full moon. "No more play castle on the big rock," said
John. "Keerect," said Ike softly. "Do ye know what I was thinking,
'Paloosa? I was thinking it's our boyhood that's buried there."

Part II

THE SQUIRE

CHAPTER XXVI

ON THE Monday morning following Thanksgiving the Lathrop household was up early, for the holiday guests were to depart on the Round Harbor-Utica stage. Instead of going to the Falls, they were going to take the stage at the Field Settlement station, in spite of the inferior appointments of the rickety old tavern there. Uncle Brandon had sworn that he wouldn't enter the Liberty again while Stark owned it, no, by God, not if he had to walk to Utica; and the Squire had said more moderately that he was of the same view. In the interest of the family, young John gave up his leave-taking from Pru Stark, though he hoped that in the bustle of the stop at the Liberty he would be able to slip around and enter by the front door without being detected.

It was a gloomy pre-dawn of mingled rain and sleet, the kind of weather when none of the flues would draw, when the chilly damp seemed to pour in through the walls, and there was no comfort except in intense activity or in bed. Sarah got half a dozen damp candles lighted in each of the main downstairs rooms, but they were weary candles, two-thirds burned down with recent hospitality, and wherever anyone stood or sat it seemed as if their shadows on wall or ceiling were the chief effect of the little light.

Over the twelve figures breakfasting at 5:30 at the long table in the kitchen, the emotional atmosphere also was laden. After a few futile sallies at gaiety Sarah discovered that they all were content to consume their pie, meat and coffee in stolid silence. She took some comfort in the fact that these four branches of the family had achieved in her house a unity wherein they might, when they chose, eschew conversation without embarrassment.

The tragedy of Dandy was still heavy over the members of the immediate household, not only for itself but as an omen, as yet vaguely felt, of other and more radical change. The Squire ate in a detached mood, his mind on the future. On this very day Ike was to embark upon a strange adventure that might one day lead to a shift not only in the geographical center but in the very moral quality of the Lathrop tradition. And reassuring as was the integrity of John, nevertheless, when he came to set up as a minister or a lawyer, the restless spirit of the times might also carry him away from the homestead. Although a long way yet from admitting these things to himself, the Squire was for the moment oppressed by unconscious intimations that the days of the unified Lathrop family were numbered. And at the same time young John and Ike also ate in silence, each sensing some of the reasons for their pa's unwonted quiet, each examining his heart and consecrating himself to loyalty to the family, whatever happened.

Tavie was in an agitated state at the prospect of the departure of John and the rest, filling her with fright at once grim and delicious at the assurance of being henceforth alone with Ike for a while each morning before breakfast—in spite of her professed preference of John to Ike, her ma was going to make her come home nights. As she sat at the silent table she was fascinated with the shadows of Ike and John side by side and enormous on the back door and the wall behind them. She was startled by a specially loud spatter of sleet on the window and, looking that way, saw in the dark pane the reflection of two candles, close together. As she watched, they became eyes and around them she saw the features of Constant Oaks. With a shudder she rose and walked straight to the window. The face disappeared, as she knew it would. There was another spatter of sleet on the panes. In the front hall the clock struck six. "Well, John," said the voice of Joel Lathrop, "all good things must end." Everyone at the table returned from his private thoughts to the present. The Squire rose, followed by the others, and they repaired to the keeping-room for prayers.

Before breakfast the boys had rolled the coach into the horse-barn and stowed the luggage, and the Squire, knowing Ike's eagerness to be off on his business to the Falls, had announced that he himself would act as coachman. Immediately after prayers they harnessed Mol and Pol, and because of the inclemency of the weather the farewells were said by lantern light in the barn. While Master Lane, Tavie, Sarah and Ike were exchanging their last words and kisses with the departing guests, young John lit the coach lamps and the Squire stood by the front wheels in the same air of detachment he had shown at breakfast. When Ike finished his last good-bys and chanced to turn toward him, the Squire, as if awaiting his turn and believing it was Ike who was going away, absent-mindedly took his hand and said quietly, "Good-by, my boy, and the best of luck to ye always." He caught himself with a barely perceptible start, and he and Ike both smiled as if a joke had been intended. Then the Squire turned, climbed up to the box and took the reins. Aggie whispered to Tavie not to forget that she had a home in Oberlin any time she came there, and for as long as she wished. Homer, following Aggie into the coach, was effusive in assuring all present of the same hospitality awaiting them. Last of all John said his farewells in a manner that was tense to the point of violence. "Don't worry about Ike," he whispered to his ma in Ike's hearing. "We're going to show them, aren't we, Scamp?" Then he turned to his brother and crushed his hand. "Sure grit," said Ike, looking straight up into John's face with eyes as darkened with emotion as his own. "Hold the fort, big boy," said John to Ben, embracing him. He startled Tavie by kissing her with fervor, even holding her close for a moment and patting her cheek with tenderness. He hurt Master Lane's rheumatic hand until the old man muttered, "Crimus." He inspected the adjustments in the little coach, over-crowded with Cousins Joel and Alvina, Uncle Brandon, Homer and Agatha and the baby. Then he jumped up to the box beside his pa. The Squire released the brake. Ben, who had been standing by Mol's head, stepped back. And with silent wavings and blowing of kisses the coach moved out and was lost in the sleet-slanted darkness.

Much disturbed by the behavior of his pa and John, Ike put his arm around his ma and walked her back through the barn, the summer kitchen, and the kitchen, and into the keeping-room where he sat her down beside him on the old settle in the corner and held her hand in both of his. As usual under emotion, he was inarticulate. For a few seconds he looked into his mother's eyes with a violence that exceeded John's. She dropped her gaze to his hands, and the silence continued while Ike shifted his troubled stare to a candle on the window sill.

At last Sarah broke the tension— "Did you see, Isaac, what you are doing to your pa?" "Yes, Ma." "Then why do you do it?" She looked up at him again and met his gaze, now suddenly softened but no whit weakened. For the first time in her life she was not frightened by that hard intelligence that looked out from behind the human yearning in the pucker between the eyes, that strange mixture of tenderness and ice. He continued to look straight into her eyes. "Because, Ma," he said gently, "I believe it's right and the job that's cut out for me in the world."

And now Sarah believed that too, because she knew he believed it. The hard, untouchable thing in Ike now strangely reassured and comforted her. She felt no longer in the presence of her little boy but of a man grown, a man older than John, older than Tom would have been had he lived, a man older and wiser even than her husband. She remembered her pa when she was a little girl, something remote but intensely real, a man who knew everything and who was possessed of a humanity in which she could absolutely trust. She took Ike by the shoulders and continued to search his gaze. "Then we must show your pa," she said. "It'll take years," he said grimly. "Then we must show him all the same," she replied.

They both rose and stood confronting each other with their full strengths meeting and coalescing for the first time since Ike was an infant at breast. With a sense of strangely cold consecration Sarah took his face between her hands and touched his lips with hers. Then she walked away into the kitchen, and Ike, still in the same intense, detached mood, went mechanically up to the cow-shed to finish the chores.

For a long time Sarah stood by the kitchen sink. The house seemed strange, as if it were expanded and renewed, as if some god had just been there in avatar, an absolute integrity, an inescapable force, and a force that was part of her. Tavie came in and Sarah, to the astonishment of both, suddenly embraced her. She was no longer afraid of Tavie and what she might fail to do for Ike. What need, after all, did *he* have of her? For the first time she saw that the girl was frightened, and as from a remote height she felt tenderness and pity for her. Sarah went about her work in a haze, not joyful but elevated, full of wonder and lonely conviction, as if she had been admitted behind a veil and had seen mysteries which no one but herself would ever understand.

CHAPTER XXVII

I K E'S mood of desperate concern over the strange detachment of his pa and John lasted until he was out of the Hollow on his way to the Falls. As part of that mood, the ghost of Dandy was strong on him all along the highway. Leaning forward on Chesty, holding his coat-collar closed under his throat and bending his head and leather cap forward into the northeast sleet that was changing to rain, he imagined he saw spots of Dandy's blood from time to time in the mud. He decided that the first thing he must do in the village was to seek out Old Jerry Stone and confess his error, his virtual murder of Dandy. If he was to work in the village, or even if he wasn't, he must be able to look Old Jerry in the eye.

The landscape was at its gloomiest of the year, the snow of last week long soaked away, leaving bare, skeleton trees, bare gray hills, stark with their dun blemishes exaggerated, sodden meadows, muddy fields streaked with long black lines of furrow water ruffling in the wind gusts. Soon after Ike passed Solomon Sloan's forge the sleet and rain let up, leaving solid gray clouds driving over on the wind that was northerly overhead. He could sit upright in the saddle now, and his native buoyancy began to get the better of his worries. "Anyhow," he thought, "Ma's come round to my notions. Between us I guess we can fetch Pa round." As for John—well, Ike guessed he'd to become what he'd never been much of, a letter writer. He'd set all his ideas down on paper and he figured the 'Paloosa wouldn't be able to get around them then. John now was in that safe situation where Ike's imagination could cope with him and perfect their relations again—that is, John was absent in person. Ike's troubles gave way to excitement at the prospect of entering the village, becoming part of its momentous goings-on. He began to make plans for his interview with Howell Sherwood, his inspection of Alexander Mathiesson's engine, his next talk with Bub Tanofly. He was in their world now!

Ike had just paid his toll penny to peg-leg Elijy Harris at the Center when they both looked up, suddenly tense. Intermittently on the gusty wind, but unmistakable in its dread significance, floated up from three

211

miles away across the village the heavy rhythm of "the last trump," the
deep, steady basso of the Court House bell, intoning the fateful, the inescapable word of terror—*"Fire—Fire—Fire—Fire."* "Best take my buckets!"
squeaked Elijy—but Ike was already out of hearing, clattering down the
plank pike at a dead run.

As he plunged down the long hill Ike knew, from its being the Court
House bell instead of Old Jerry's Bashan or the Universalist Church, that
the fire was in the western part of the village, where the summons would
be answered first by Jefferson Hose and John Hancock Hook and Ladder
Company Number Three, while Cataract Company Number Two and the
resplendent red, green and gold Neptune Company Number One would
stand at the alert, awaiting a second alarm. As he entered the village and
Chesty's stride began to send gobs of mud like soft cannon balls plopping
against trees and houses, the tolling of the last trump stopped, which meant
that Company Number Three had arrived and the village was waiting
a-tremble for the dreaded second alarm, the signal that the fire was serious.
None but the citizens of the precinct involved responded, with their
buckets, to a first alarm. It was only at a further ringing of the summons
that general pandemonium broke loose. Ike pulled Chesty down to a walk,
not wishing to show himself ignorant of the sophisticated customs of the
metropolis. Then, as he passed the First Presbyterian Church and Chesty
plumped down into the mud of the South Mall the second alarm sounded.

Instantly the village was a bedlam, men running and yelling, horses
whinnying, doors slamming, women on their porches clasping their babies
and staring wildly while their biscuits burned, in the distance the great
foghorn of horse-drawn Neptune beginning to bellow into action, and
nearer, the snarl of Cataract Company moving down Gadston Street into
the Mall.

Reaching the Mall, Ike charged into the vortex of the maelstrom, the great
plaza a jammed Circus Maximus of milling pedestrians, galloping wagons, carriages, single riders, riders down in the mire, horses that had broken
their halters to circulate aimlessly, barking dogs, snorting hogs and shrieking chickens. In the midst of this pandemonium the horn-blower of man-
drawn Cataract Company Number Two was fighting his way in advance
of the pump, drowning the racket of men and horses with his blasts like
the bellows of a sick steer, while down Factory Street came the awful and
authoritative roar of Neptune Company Number One.

Where Columbia and Court Street debouched from the Mall through
the narrows of Wheeler's Corner, the crush tightened round Ike as he
arrived there abreast of Cataract Company. Pedestrians, carriages, riders

and fire company alike were slowed to a walk where thousands of feet inched their precarious way among hundreds of hoofs and wheels. In the face of danger the crowd became orderly and jocular, each citizen yielding without resistance to the current in which fate placed him. By dint of Herculean horn-blowing, a few minor casualties, and the recognition of its authority by the crowd, Cataract Company got itself detached and loped away up Columbia Street at a fast dog-trot, while the main current, including Ike, continued to jostle its way down Court.

Once past the bottleneck of Wheeler's Corner, the crowd lengthened out in front, and it was possible to let Chesty into a fast walk. When Ike was opposite Trinity Church on the right the melodious bell of that wooden temple sang ten o'clock. Beyond the church the blocks closed solid again and here the crowd, as it came on, smelled smoke and fell silent. From his mounted position Ike presently saw hundreds of people pouring down the lane and open lot from the white-columned Court House to the long, covered bridge over the Kamargo, where they collided with the other crowds debouching from Lower Court and River Streets and the press was worse than it had been at Wheeler's Corner. From this Ike gathered that they were squeezing onto the bridge and that the fire must be on the opposite or Camilla side. In a moment he saw smoke above the near trees and buildings and, coming opposite an open lot, saw flames apparently licking out of the northern end of Bub Tanofly's big stone paper mill. He wondered if Bub carried adequate insurance.

As Ike slowed up perforce with the crowd twenty rods short of the jam at the bridge, he caught glimpses of strange doings there. The respective horns of Neptune and Cataract Companies were converging from River Street below and from the region of the Court House above. On one of two tall stone posts that flanked the end of the bridge the black-clad, shovel-hatted Reverend Tremble Thomas of the Columbia Street Methodist Episcopal Church was gesticulating and shouting, apparently trying to control traffic, while below him fat Constable Hank Haverstraw was heaving people like bags of meal off the road into the open ground at the left. Presently, purposeful shouts rose from the front ranks of the crowd, and Ike helped pass them back to the press behind—"Halt!"—"Whoa, mare!"—"Hold yer hosses!"—"Whoa!"—"Halt!" All up and down Court Street the crowd stopped and stood waiting. Above the horns of the approaching fire companies Ike could hear the respective admonitions of Church and State from the congested point below at the approach to the bridge.

"Peace brethren," intoned the Reverend Tremble Thomas, "for lo, the

avenger cometh!" "Git yer god damned caracasses out o' the road!" roared
Constable Haverstraw. " 'Stand aside,' saith the Lord," called the minister, " 'that my chariot may pass on to victory!' " "Git over or I'll bust yer
god danged heads open!" adjured the police officer. "Aye, ye kings of the
earth," shouted God's vicar, "I command ye to halt and make way for
the engine of mercy!" "That means you, ye snivelling bastard!" bellowed
the constable, heaving aside Senator Ostrum Applemore at whose pleasure
he held office—"And you, ye fat-bellied polecat!"—this to old Horace Gadston—"And you, ye Christ-begotten porcupine!"—this to the Baptist minister. Thus opposed by both spiritual and secular authority, the crowd
cleared the way for the fire companies; and at this juncture a cow, maddened by the horn of Cataract Company from Madison Street behind it,
charged panic-stricken down Court House Hill straight for the bridge.

In this crisis the Reverend Thomas did not quail. He jumped down from
his column and confronted the on-coming cow, waving his arms and shouting—getting his sources mixed in his excitement, "Turn, hell-kite, turn!
Depart ye into everlasting fire, and do no more mischief among us!" Un-
persuaded, the cow came on, sliding down the hill, then cavorting and
snorting along the level. Like a toreador the Reverend Thomas pointed his
swordlike finger and called down ultimate authority, "In the name of God,
I command you, swerve!" And, lo, the cow did swerve and like the Gerge-
sene swine slid down the embankment to the river and broke her hip, and
the village paid the cost of her afterwards. Triumphantly Neptune Company, its great gold and green pump beaked with the head of its titular god,
and its members now gorgeous in red helmets, galloped out of River Street
and did a hairpin skid onto the bridge, followed in a few seconds by
Cataract Company, coming down Court House Hill. Ike joined in the cheer
that accompanied this passage of the couriers of safety. The minister and
the constable suspended their efforts. The press of people moved on. And
the Court House bell ceased tolling.

As Ike, near the end of the crowd, rode Chesty through the smoke that
now hung inside the covered bridge, he could hear, above the roar of the
river, the crackling of flames. When he got off the bridge on the Camilla
side, there a hundred yards down Main Street was the fire, roaring and
vomiting red and black like an angry dragon. It was not in the big, stone
Tanofly Mill, at least not yet, but in a one-story, frame building that nestled
against the near end of it, the windows pouring out smoke and tongues
of flame, but the roof not yet alight. Deputies placed by chief Obid Plum,
of all the fire companies, were directing the crowd up Lasalle Street. As Ike
was hitching Chesty to a sapling and lashing his greatcoat to the saddle

to be ready for action, he learned from members of the crowd that the little building was the drug shop of one Redemption Quin, a name that was strange to him. He hurried around behind the first two houses on Main Street, and pressed his way into the front line of the crowd that stood submitting to the discipline of the deputies.

The activity at the fire was as orderly as the approach had been disorderly. The men at the pumps of the three companies were working grimly in relays, keeping up the walking-beam rise and fall of the long handlebars. Dr. Jephthah Starbuck, the veteran nozzler of Hose Number Three, had carried his line heroically into the front door of the burning building, and nozzler Hezekiah Simmons, jeweler, of Hose Number Two, was lobbing his inch stream stoutly against the flames rolling out one of the windows, while their respective comrades kept each refreshed with wet cloths bound round their noses and mouths. Two bucket lines were at work reinforcing the intake hoses from the river, passing water up the cliffs to pour into the reserve tanks, while other bucketeers were at all the windows on that end of the Tanofly Mill, wetting down the frames against the heat of the fire which was separated from the stone mill only by an alley. The flames were roaring deeply like wind in a pine forest, and every few seconds some of Master Redemption Quin's chemicals went off somewhere inside the raging little furnace. The crowd stood tense, watchful, every man resentful that he hadn't been called on for some deed of valiance, while their cheers were quick to encourage those who had.

As Ike got into place in the front of the crowd, the first step of Chief Obid Plum's major strategy was being effected. Under the direction of old Captain Seth Marlow, general merchant, of the John Hancock Hook and Ladder Company, the overhanging gables of the Tanofly Mill had been sawed off, and Ike watched young Captain George Fulton of Neptune Hose Number One—graduated from Yale last year and John's best friend —mounting the long ladder to do dangerous, volunteer work. Behind him his men carried up the two-inch hose, while down at the pump Captain Emeritus Jerusalem Stone was left in command of doings aground. Young George had just reached the peak and waved for the water to be released when flames broke upward at several points from the eaves of the drug shop on the side of the Tanofly factory and only three feet from its walls. Men at every window started splashing the sills and frames and Captain Fulton on the peak leaned out over the heat sousing down the sawed-off edges of the gable, while relays of wet cloths began to be passed up and down the roof to him and his hose-tenders. The gable being safe for the moment, he peered down at the windows and wherever he saw a spark alight drove down his stream so that window-tender after window-tender was suddenly soused and withdrew, to the cheers of the crowd. Between soaking the gable and the windows Captain Fulton let his stream pound a loud tattoo on the burning roof of the shop.

It seemed to many of the watchers, including Ike, that the fire was now under control. He considered getting away ahead of the crowd. But at this moment Chief Plum came out of the factory with Bub Tanofly, immaculate and hatless as usual, and they conferred in front of the fire, the Chief indicating by gestures the direction of the wind which was fortuitously drawing round to the west, driving the flames away from the mill. Presently Bub nodded agreement to some plan, and as he turned to go back into the mill he saw Ike and gave him a sarcastic and condescending smile. This angered Ike, for with all the goings-on Bub ought to be able to find him something to do. He figgered he'd have to give him a lickin' yet.

Meanwhile there was a new burst of activity around the long carriage of John Hancock Hook and Ladder Company. Under Captain Seth Marlow's direction enormous coils of rope and cable were being unloaded and run out in four parallel lines, each about fifty yards long, stretching away from the fire toward the bridge. On the four ends nearer the fire were great iron grappling hooks. After much sousing and chopping away of clapboards to the cheers of the crowd, one of these hooks was made fast into each of the four corner posts of the burning drug shop, just under the one-story-high eaves. Then Chief Plum strode to the end of the crowd opposite the Tanofly Mill and shouted something Ike couldn't understand above the roar of the flames and the pelting of the water. Immediately about a hundred men broke across the street and lengthened out along the farthest of the four ropes. Then the Chief walked past Ike a little, turned back and called, "Everybody from me westerly on the next farthest line yonder, and *don't pick up no rope till I tell ye.*" Ike ran with the crowd to the second line. In the same way the third and fourth lines were manned.

The Chief now looked over the four lines of about a hundred men each, made some adjustments in their strengths, and addressed the cohorts through cupped hands: "Now, when I order ye to pick up the line, I don't want no yearlin' bull o' ye yankin' on it till I give the word. Just straighten 'er out easy and *stand where ye be*. All right, *pick 'er up.*" This was done quietly, and a member of the Company ran along each line, moving the men back until the ropes were taut without strain. Then Captain Seth Marlow of the Hook and Ladder made a final inspection of the grappling hooks and waved to the Chief, who again addressed the lines of men: "When I tell ye jest heave hard and steady without no jerkin', like ye was a bunch o' cattle pullin' a stone-boat, and don't quit till I say, and then quit quick. *All ready! Pull 'er tail!*" The men leaned back, the lines straightened, the little building groaned, bent, leaned and crashed away from the factory, sending up a roar of flame and sparks so that Ike, walking back on his heels, could see neither the mill nor young George Fulton on the peak. "Whoa! Whoa!" roared Chief Plum, "and skedaddle back to where ye was, every god danged one o' ye."

Ike skedaddled with the rest, then looked back from his former location on the other side of Main Street. The sparks had settled and the flames were not so high, though hotter than ever, curling up round the ends of sections of wall away from the factory and pouring up great rolls of smoke into the wind that bore it harmlessly away eastward. One central post still remained of the wall next to the mill, but a long beam out of a window was battering it and it soon fell, completing the ruin. Dr. Starbuck and Hezekiah Simmons were pouring in water under the sections of wall that lay slantwise on the heaps of ruins, and George Fulton, having let himself down the roof a little, was squirting now one and now the other gable of the factory. Then after dousing all the windows, he joined Cataract and Jefferson in pelting the big bonfire that snarled and crackled like a panther that was down but not dead yet. Ike decided that now was surely the time to beat the crowd to the bridge.

As he walked up through the yard of the house opposite the fire he passed a little man, hatless and coatless, sitting in the mud under a tree, his head forward on his knees and his slim body shaking with sobs. Ike stopped by the pathetic figure, and in a pause between the sobs ventured, "Beg your pardon, sir,—can I do anything for ye?" A delicately wrinkled face, about fifty years old, looked up at Ike, and the hands went out in a shrug of helpless resignation. "Have ye lost something?" asked Ike, his big, gentle face all solicitude. The little man looked surprised, extended both hands toward the fire and sighed, "Everything." Then he dropped his head on his knees and sobbed again. "Are you—are you—Master Quin?" asked Ike softly. The bowed head nodded. "No insurance?" The head waggled a negative.

Ike considered—Bub should own that bit of land—Bub still figgered him a country boy where real business was concerned. "How much do ye figger the piece is worth?" he asked quietly, but his tone now hardening. "I paid two hundred dollars for the shop and equipment five years ago. Two hours ago," his voice breaking, "there was a hundred dollars' worth of stock in it. Now it's all worth as much as a piece of land twenty by forty with a pile of trash on it." From his face hidden in his hands, the little man's despairing voice became almost unintelligible. "Only last week young

Master Tanofly offered me two hundred and fifty for the place, but he'd never give me that for it now."

"Got a clear deed, have ye?" asked Ike unsympathetically. "Excuse me, young man," said Master Quin, looking up with a show of dignity, "but I fear I do not recognize you." "Name's Lathrop—Isaac Lathrop." "Son of John Lathrop?" "Yes, sir." "I grew up in the Center. Used to play with your pa and your uncle." He reached up and they shook hands.

"If ye don't mind my asking agin," pressed Ike, "have ye a clear title?" "Yes," said Master Quin. "Figger ye had three hundred in cash in the place, do ye—besides the value of the business?" The little man nodded again and Ike ruminated. "Do ye figger ye could start over if ye had three hundred now?" "Yes. There's a shop on Columbia Street near Mistress Spencer's where I board that I believe I could get for about two hundred."

Ike saw Bub come out of the factory and stand watching the still infernal bonfire. He'd show him! He leaned down behind Master Quin so Bub wouldn't see him and said, *sotto voce,* "I'll give ye three hundred spot cash for the property."

Redemption Quin looked up at him with mingled incredulity and joy. "Do you mean?— Can you?— Would your father?—" "Yes, sir," Ike interrupted him. "I'm talking about my own money, not Pa's. Only condition is, come right up to the Clerk's office with me now and make a deed. What d'ye say?"

Master Quin cast a long and loving look at the end of five years' conscientious chemistry, then rose slowly and, reassured by Ike's smile, permitted himself to be led as precipitately as possible—for he had a deep limp—around behind the houses out of sight of anyone at the fire who might happen to look that way.

"Fact is, Master Quin," said Ike in a natural tone as they approached Chesty, "I've two or three reasons for wanting to make this purchase quick, but none of 'em's to trim you. While we're walking upstreet I hope ye'll think the matter over and if ye think I ain't offered ye a fair price it's all keerect to call the deal off up to the minute ye've signed the deed."

"It seems to me like more than a fair price, Master Isaac, a price that permits me to set up again in a better location." "Anyhow," said Ike out of a brimming conscience, "think it over careful and don't decide till we've reached the Clerk's office."

Ike had noticed the little man's limp, which would mean twenty minutes walking up to the Town Clerk's. He heard Trinity Church speak once for half-past eleven. "Here's my horse," he said. "Suppose you ride him ahead. I'll follow on foot and by the time I get there maybe ye'll have the deed all ready, eh?" "I fear," said Master Quin, "that I am little of a horseman, not having ridden since I came to the village almost twenty years ago. Shameful, isn't it? I'd be humiliated to come a cropper, but, if you say, I'll attempt it. I do not wish to inconvenience you. Gentle animal, is he?"

"If ye don't mind," said Ike, "just try mounting him while I hold his head. If it don't seem to be working out proper I'll go along beside ye. Been in the saddle all mornin' and I'd greatly appreciate trying my legs for a change." Ike unlashed his greatcoat and put it on, tightened the girth and held Chesty while the little druggist, putting his bad foot in the stirrup, leapt part way up and scrambled the rest of the way into the saddle. Chesty at once tried to rear and Ike decided he must alter his plan for getting his prize out of sight in a hurry. He led Chesty with his mount at a fast walk down Lasalle Street to the corner of Main, where an increasing number of people were streaming onto the bridge. There Ike broke into a run which permitted Chesty to lengthen out in a long, slow trot, but immediately a voice of mild anguish came from behind and above, "I fear, Master Isaac, I shall not long be able to hold my seat at this pace."

Thus in the middle of the busy corner Ike was forced to pull Chesty back to a walk. He peeked under the horse's neck to see if Bub Tanofly was still in front of the fire. He not only was, but he was looking straight at Ike. In a moment his rich tenor rolled up from a hundred yards away, "Hi thar, Ike Lathrop, what'll ye take fer hoss and jockey?" Ike, hiding behind Chesty, heard half the village of Byzantium Falls salute him with a combined laugh and cheer. In his chagrin he did not notice that he was overtaking Messrs. Gadston and Applemore until he was abreast of those worthies on the bridge. He saw Horace nudge Ostrum and they both looked at him with sly smiles. Ike saluted nicely, gave them back his frankest, kindliest smile, and pressed on in the greatest embarrassment of his life. Just ahead he saw Alexander Mathiesson and hurried to catch him at the Byzantium end of the bridge. "Morning, Master Mathiesson," said Ike, coming up behind.

Mathiesson looked aghast at Ike's equipage, but Ike gave him no time to speak. "One reason I'm in such a lather," said Ike as he came abreast, "is that I was aiming to ride over and ask ye to dine with me at the Wheeler, and maybe afterwards ye'll take me over and show me your steam engine. Will ye do me the honor?" "Gladly," said Mathiesson, "but with the proviso that I play the host this time." "Hardly figgered 'twas your turn," said Ike, hurrying on, "after the hospitality I showed ye last time." They both laughed and Ike turned back. "Quarter-past twelve suit ye?" "Sure as shooting," said Mathiesson.

Ike turned away from Lower Court into River Street, anticipating less company there. When he was at the rear of Trinity Churchyard he turned up the lane alongside it, turned left behind the buildings on Court Street, hitched Chesty behind the Town Clerk's office, helped Redemption Quin down from his precarious seat, and entered by the back door just as Bub Tanofly rushed in at the front.

"Thought ye'd trim me, did ye?" said Bub with a smile of admiration, and shook hands with Ike. "Mornin', Master Quin. Little inconvenience we've been havin', eh? Meant to speak to ye a while back, but Chief Obid seemed to figger my place was worth stewin' about. Wal, what's this young feller givin' ye fer the property?" "That, I believe," said Master Redemption Quin, "is a matter of confidence between Master Lathrop and myself." "Wal, whatever he's givin' ye, I'll make her fifty more." "If you will permit me the discourtesy," said Master Quin haughtily, "I ain't interested."

"My humblest apologies," said Bub with a deep bow. Then, "Well, Ike, my boy, you win." And he turned and walked out with a patronizing grin. "A very sharp and unmannerly young man," said Redemption Quin, knitting his brow. "He's the feller I figger to trim," said Ike. "Well, sir," replied the druggist, "I don't wish to seem unfair, but I can't refrain from wishing you luck." They both laughed, shook hands, and addressed themselves to bent, spectacled Town Clerk Blevin, who, being used to such little skirmishes, had not until now looked up from his ledgers.

CHAPTER XXVIII

THE Wheeler House was the oldest tavern in the village. Outside of its shining kitchen and serving ware, it was also the filthiest, the sawdust of its tap-room and dining-room floors having resisted the introduction of cuspidors as stoutly as its kitchen fireplace had withstood the modern threat of stoves. Unlike the Liberty, which was merely a private house with an "L" attached for guests, the Wheeler had been designed as an inn, with a central hall leading back between two parlors to the tap-room with its bar, its shelf of small kegs, surmounted by an enormous chromo of the unfinished frigate *New Orleans,* and its heavy odor of rotting sawdust, tobacco juice, tobacco smoke and rum.

According to appointment, Ike entered the Wheeler tap-room at a quarter-past twelve, and, being unfamiliar with the place, did not immediately notice Alexander Mathiesson waiting for him, standing alone by the window. Among the dozen men at the bar, however, Ike did observe Horace Gadston and Ostrum Applemore in close conversation with the host, Job Wheeler, who was a political power in the district. Job was about fifty years old, a rotund ex-sergeant of the Regular Army and still handy with his fists. He had inherited the tavern, his grandfather having been the first proprietor.

In return to Ike's salute Applemore gave him a senatorial nod, and Master Gadston scowled at him with no other sign of recognition. Job Wheeler came around the bar and shook his hand, assuming at once the double duty of host to one of Byzantium's finest and preceptor to the young. "Almighty glad to see ye here, Ike Lathrop," said Job, taking his coat and cap. " 'N' th' place is yourn but fer one pertic'ler straight furrer this house ain't jumped over since afore yer pa and me was hereabouts." "No liquor for minors?" asked Ike with a smile so easy that Job wondered if the report was true that he was only nineteen. "Keerect," he said, "less'n fer a nip o' ale. Yonder's yer friend a-waitin' fer ye, and do ye like yer slab o' roast thick or thin?" "Make it tolerable thick," said Ike and, leaving Job to slice him some beef from the haunch on the table by the kitchen door, he went over to shake hands with Alexander Mathiesson.

"Hope ye ain't been waiting long, Master Mathiesson," said Ike. "Figger by now it's no secret I was over buying some property." He beamed with triumph. "May I ask what property you have bought?" said Mathiesson, smiling back in response to Ike's exuberance. "Scene of the fire!" said Ike in a stage whisper, then glanced at the bar and noticed vaingloriously that Horace Gadston quickly averted his head as he looked around. "That's fast work, indeed," said Mathiesson, "and—if I may have the privilege—it deserves a toast." "All keerect," said Ike, "only my toast'll have to be in ale." "Ale suits me to a T," said Mathiesson. At this moment Job came up with their plates piled high with beef, potatoes, squash and cabbage, led them into the dining room off the tap-room, and settled them at a small table where they could see the bar through the wide door. At Mathiesson's request he brought them two mugs of ale, and a toast was duly gulped to "Quin's pile of ashes."

Thereupon Ike grew serious and began to explain to Mathiesson his interest in stationary steam engines, not only as marvels of engineering but as a possible bonanza for anyone who got into the manufacture of them before their value was generally appreciated. Having sized up his man for a fine fellow who was only secondarily interested in money, Ike laid all his cards on the table, and Alexander, having learned of Ike's reputation as a hoss swopper, liked him for his frankness. Other parties came into the dining room, and the tap-room was getting crowded and noisy as more and more men returned from the fire. Messrs. Gadston and Applemore departed. At a specially numerous incursion from the Mall with much stamping and shouting, Ike gave up his confidential disquisition and sat back to enjoy his dinner and the mature glory of being present in this favorite haunt of the village of which he was now a part.

The fifteen or twenty new arrivals were under the leadership of Bub Tanofly, who, since the village had undoubtedly saved his factory, considered it his duty on that day to set up the village. Having already performed that office at two other taverns on the way from the factory, and having left instructions with the hosts that they were to be liberal with all and sundry who might reasonably have served in the bucket lines, Bub now led a select band into the more esoteric precincts of the Wheeler. He already had three or four good hookers under his striped green waistcoat, and his usual boisterousness had accordingly given way to a solemnity of manner which was characteristic of him in his cups. Being greeted by a shout from the two dozen drinkers already in the tap-room, he doffed his beaver and said, "Gentlemen, accept my gratitude for having saved the old factory, and kindly do me the honor to consider the balance of this day's festivities as mine." With that he shook hands with Job Wheeler, waved inclusively at the crowd and the bar, bowed in acknowledgment of another shout, and walked away that his guests might be first served. Miraculously Job produced two dozen cold grogs already mixed, and Bub had just spied Ike in the dining room when he was forced to turn back and acknowledge a toast and the song, "For he's a jolly good fellow, For he's a jolly good fellow . . ."

After the song, Bub came into the dining room, followed by Nat Gadston and Tim Slocum, both minors like Ike, and so ineligible for spirits. Bub stood for a long time with folded arms by the little table, glaring alternately at Ike and Alexander Mathiesson. Finally, his severe pop-eyed gaze settled on the latter and, without change of expression, he said through clenched teeth, "Name's Mathiesson, ain't it?" The latter nodded in some bewilderment, having often seen this young man but being now at a loss as to his identity.

"Well, Master Mathiesson, I take it ye're some'at of a stranger in these parts and likely ain't overfamiliar with the snares and pitfalls of this sinful community. Wherefore and whereinafter I find it my pertic'ler duty as host on this very pertic'ler occasion, to warn ye that ye're a-settin' in the company of the wust trimmer, the most dastardly, scoundrelly, scalpin' hoss-trader north o' the well known Mohawk River. Be assured that when ye take off yer breeches tonight, whatever's missin' *he* took it—no doubt on it—not a scintilla of doubt on it. 'N furthermore"—now pointing his finger first at Mathiesson and then at Ike—"whatever he's up to, be sure there ain't no good in it. Whatever he's a-persuadin' ye to, don't do it. Fer if ye do ye'll be sorry as long as ye live. 'N *furthermore*"—pausing and shaking his finger viciously at Ike—"he hain't got his diapers off."

At this Ike, who had been beaming in delight, made a feint to lunge at Bub, who dashed back into the tap-room just in time to collide with fat Fire Captain Emeritus Jerusalem Stone, who, with young Captain George Fulton, Chief Obid Plum and other high officials of the Department, had dropped off Neptune Company Number One on its return journey to refresh themselves.

The shout that greeted these heroes made the glasses and the pewter rattle, and gentle, dark-eyed George Fulton, exhausted and scorched, was picked up on shoulders and paraded backwards and forwards through the hall between the front door and the tap-room to the chorus, "For he's a jolly good fellow," until they bumped his head badly on a lintel and he managed to wriggle down and put away two of the dozen grogs that were thrust at him.

While this was going on and Obid and Old Jerry were receiving ovations in their kind, Bub slipped back into the dining room and whispered to Ike, Alexander, Nat and Tim, "Set over yonder t' the big table and we'll get George and some o' the other young stock in here 'n give 'em a quiet beddin'' down." Two minutes later Bub extricated young Fulton from the adulating mob, likewise the gigantic heavy-bearded Jabez Munson, who had been next to George on the hose of Number One, and both sank gratefully on the benches that all rose to vacate for them as they came in. Fred Van Sanford, blond, Vandyke-bearded son of the Judge and not a member of the Department, sauntered in and sat down with the rest at the big oblong table. There were missing but two or three to complete this chance meeting of the most likely young men of the village between the ages of eighteen and twenty-six.

This group of junior dignitaries was barely settled, and Bub Tanofly and Fred VanSanford had just got them supplied with grog and ale when the round, short-legged figure of Old Jerry Stone filled the door from the tap-room. Immediately all joined in a shout and rose in a toast to "Old Jerry"— "Bull of Bashan"— "Come in, Jerry!"— "Come in and set down with us where ye belong!" His face smiling in wrinkles in every direction, the prophet of youth waddled forward to the edge of the table which his great, leather-vested belly overhung. Suddenly and for the first time he spied Ike, glared at him for a moment, then turned away with a wave, saying genially, "You fellers are gettin' too big fer the likes o' me." "Sit down, Jerry"— "What's the matter, Old Jerry?" came the affectionate chorus. But the wrinkled old artisan waddled out, while the seven young men looked at one another in questioning amazement. Suddenly Ike jumped up, walked on the bench around behind Tim Slocum and Fred VanSanford and ran after Old Jerry into the tap-room. "Looks like Ike had a notion what it's about," said Jabe Munson.

Ike was in an exhilarated and self-confident mood. So it was with politeness but small humility that he touched Old Jerry Stone on the shoulder and said, "Old Jerry, may I have a word with ye?" The old man grunted, hesitated, then backed off to the wall and stood glaring. "I wanted to acknowledge to ye, Old Jerry," said Ike in a low tone, "that you were right and I was wrong about my selling—the big gray—to Gam Stark. I done wrong, just as ye said I did, and I reckon I shan't ever get over it." "Sort o' shov'lin' th' manure out o' yer conscience, be ye?" said Old Jerry, and the wrinkles of his face readjusted themselves to show dubious concern rather than accusation or scorn. "Mebbe," said Ike, his features hardening a little and his eyes continuing to look straight into Old Jerry's. "Pecul'ar slant yer repentance is takin'," said Old Jerry, "a-comin' t' the village and skinnin' that sliver 'v a Quin so quick arter yer other lesson." "Ain't skinnin' him," said Ike, "and that hain't to do with it, anyway. And furthermore," he added after a short pause, "I want to beg your pardon for troubling ye." He turned and started back for the dining-room door.

"Young Lathrop," Old Jerry called after him so decisively that several drinkers looked round from the crowd at the bar. Ike returned and stood stiffly, looking down into the wrinkled old face as Old Jerry said gently, but with his fiercest expression, "Don't figger, young feller, I'm a-passin' jedgment on ye. I took it ye was askin' my notions and I give 'em to ye. But I an't a-settin' up fer no Gawd A'mighty, 'n though I figger ye're gettin' off on the wrong foot I hope ye ain't, 'n Gawd's blessin' on ye, 'n thar's my hand on it." Ike took the hard, old hand, smiled and said earnestly, "Thank ye, Old Jerry, and I hope that one of these days I'll be able to show ye that ye're judging me wrongly."

As Ike returned to the table the heads of the six young men were bent close over it, and Jabez Munson, raconteur of his generation, was telling a story. Ike came up quietly and stood listening, just in time to hear Jabe wind up the tale— " 'And so,' says she, 'now I've got a-holt of the pesky thing, what do I do with it?' " The six young heads straightened up, Mathiesson with a warm smile, Fred VanSanford with his worldly-wise one, George Fulton with his melodious chuckle, Bub Tanofly with his loud laugh, and the two eighteen-year-olds, Nat Gadston and Tim Slocum, with the tense, self-conscious giggle of virginal youth awed by the obscene conversation of its elders.

Fred and Tim stood up to let Ike climb back to his place. Outside at the bar the "General Toast" to the ladies was getting under way and it was impossible to talk for the racket:

> *"Here's to the maiden of bashful fifteen,*
> *Likewise to the widow of fifty;*
> *Here's to the bold and extravagant queen,*
> *And here's to the housewife that's thrifty.*
> *Let the toast pass,*
> *Drink to the lass,*
> *I warrant she'll prove an excuse for the glass.*
>
> *Here's to the maiden whose dimples we praise ..."*

The song went on for three stanzas more, everyone at the table of young men joining in except Ike and Mathiesson, who were eating their dinner, and George Fulton, who sat looking lazily at Ike. George was twenty-one and knew John better than he did Ike, but he couldn't see what this hoss-swoppin' streak had to do with any of the Lathrops. With the detached concentration of fatigue, he let his mild, dark eyes rest on Ike's face while his fingers turned his can idly on the table, till Ike, looking up with his mouth full of beef and cabbage, met the look and gave back his big, dimpled, disarming smile which George, of all people in the village, was able to return approximately in kind.

The "General Toast" ended, and a few enthusiasts at the bar set up,

> *"Amo, amas,*
> *I love a lass,*
> *As a cedar tall and slender.*
> *Sweet cowslip grace*
> *Is her nominative case*
> *And she's of the feminine gender.*
> *Rorum, corum,*
> *Sunt divorum,*
> *Harum Scarum*
>   *Divo.*
> *Tag rag merry derry,*
> *Periwig and hatband,*
> *Hic, hoc, horum,*
>   *Genitivo."*

This song was not strongly sustained, for few knew the words after the first stanza. Urged by Fred VanSanford, Jabe Munson—who was employed with Fred in Judge VanSanford's office—told a story about a broken plow, which got prolonged laughter. When it had quieted down and the bawdy, Latinesque song ended, George Fulton asked Ike why he didn't move into the village.

Immediately the question was pressed by everybody at the table. Ike said he had it in mind, sort of figgered to ride both horses. "Can't do it," said Jabe; "might as well set out t' hold onto the tails o' two steers aimin' t' go east and west respective." In the discussion that ensued, only George Fulton held out for Ike's notion that a fellow could work in the village and still farm it—George's pa, Squire Fulton, still farmed twenty acres on the edge of the village, besides running a book bindery and the biggest paper mill in the county. "Well, just you try law practice, eh, Jabe?" said Fred, looking at George impatiently. He was a little resentful of George for his easy-going ways, his pa having enough and sufficiently varied resources so that George needn't do a day's work all his life if he wasn't o' mind to.

When the general conversation had run about ten minutes, there fell another silence in which George told Ike that his pa had given old Henry Hawks temporary employment, but that he planned to keep him only until Henry found a permanent place. Ike said he was glad to hear it and that he figgered to find something for Henry in a week or two. George pulled out his big gold watch and said, "Well, I guess they'll be keeping dinner for me and I'd best be running along." "Me, too," said everybody except Bub, Mathiesson and Ike, and they all rose.

"Say, Ike," said George as they were shaking hands, "this has been a mighty pleasant little gathering—all thanks to Bub. I for one propose that we aim to repeat it now and again without any fire. All meet here at, say, twelve, and tell our families we won't be home for dinner. What do you say, Ike? What do you say, fellows?"—"Fine notion."—"Good idea."—"All keerect," were the rejoinders. "What about a week from today?" said George. "Eh, Ike? Eh, Fred? Eh, Jabe? Eh, Bub? Eh, Mathiesson? Eh, Tim? Eh, Nat?" They all agreed, and four of them filed out with, "See you come a week"—"See ye next Monday." Bub and Mathiesson and Ike were left alone.

The tap-room and dining room were now cleared of company but for a few chronic barflies. Bub looked at his watch, then said to Ike, "Set down a minute, young feller. You, too, Mathiesson. Ye may enjoy seein' this young Lathrop when he takes off his false whiskers and gits sure grit down to trimmin'." The three of them sat down and Ike and Bub looked at each other with amusement for a few seconds.

"Wal," said Bub at length, "what ye goin' t' stick me fer it?" "Four hundred," said Ike. "Haw! Haw! Haw!" roared Bub, slapping the table. "Can ye beat 'im, Mathiesson, and a-settin' there with a face solemn as any hypocritical meetin'? Come, now, what'd ye give him fer it?" "That," said Ike, smiling, "as my friend Master Quin will assure you, is privileged information." "Wal, I s'pose he told ye I offered him two fifty fer it a while back?" Ike nodded. "Cal'late ye didn't give him a penny over two hundred. I'll give ye two twenty-five fer the lot, and that's twenty-five fer takin' advantage of a friend when he was all brustled up a-tryin' t' decide quick a-tween his factory and his insurance." "Haw, haw, haw," said Ike in quiet derision. "All keerect," said Bub; "make it two fifty." Ike continued to smile.

Thus baited, Bub's egotism got the better of his affection and admiration for Ike. With a sneer he rose and strode out into the tap-room, shouting,

"Job, got a quill handy?" Job looked inquiringly at Ike who chuckled, and Alexander followed suit, not quite understanding what was going on but feeling that he was in excellent company in the presence of this big, gentle youth who was four years his junior.

Presently Bub returned with his hat on and carrying in his hand a quarter of a sheet of foolscap which he threw down before Ike and himself remained standing. It was a cheque for five hundred dollars with the conditional inscription "Purchase price of Quin property." "That's t' show ye," said Bub, "that down here ye're dealing with business men who don't haggle about pennies. And, furthermore, young feller, when I want a thing I most gen'ly git it." Ike's smile showed annoyance as he tore the check in little pieces and dropped them in the sawdust. "Price I told ye was four hundred. An't lookin' fer presents." And with that he rose and glanced at Mathiesson, suggesting departure.

Mathiesson also rose and Ike looked coldly at Bub, being deeply hurt and prepared, upon the least further pretext, to take him out and give him that thrashing he surely had coming. Bub was flushed with rage but, drunk as he was, he knew he was in the wrong. He merely curled his lip, bowed formally, said, "Good day, gentlemen," turned and strode out. Ike followed into the tap-room, where he asked Job Wheeler for the reckoning. The host assured him that all drinks were to be settled for by Bub, and Mathiesson, coming up, begged so earnestly to be permitted to pay for the dinner that Ike deferred to him.

Mistress Wheeler came in from the kitchen and took Ike by both arms with her fat, red hands, looking up at him out of her moon face, so exactly like her husband's that they were usually taken for brother and sister. "Isaac Lathrop, you great big boy! You never saw me in your life before, for the only time you laid eyes on me was when you was just born and, trade bein' slack that winter at the tavern, I come out t' th' Hollow t' help yer ma. Many's the time I've walked the floor with ye a-cattawallin' and, 'pon my word, I don't believe I've seen ye since to know ye."

"Ike kin do his cattawallin' to you," said her husband, leaning over the bar with his round smile and sizing up Ike as political timber, "but if he wants to do a little quiet talkin' he kin do it with me." With that he came around the bar and continued, "Would ye mind givin' me a private word, Ike?" "Not at all," said Ike. "Will you excuse me, Mistress Wheeler, and— I beg your pardon—this is Master Mathiesson, Mistress Wheeler." With that he followed Job into the empty dining room where the tavern-keeper looked straight at him.

" 'Tain't none o' my business," said Job, "but are ye free t' tell me whether or not ye bought Quin's property?" "No secret to it," said Ike. "Anybody can find out by steppin' over t' the Clerk's office." "Well, t' tell ye the truth," said Job, "I don't much like this business o' playin' agent, but I agreed t' tell ye that a certain responsible party I couldn't well afford t' turn down has a pertic'ler interest in the property and 'll give ye five hundred cash fer it. Needn't add that I'm just carryin' a message and ain't takin' no commission from nobody. So thar ye be, 'n I've done 's I agreed to, and ye can take it or leave it." And with that he turned and walked out.

Ike remained behind· and stepped over to the window, more than ever annoyed at Bub. Presently he turned and beckoned Job back to him and, when he came, told him Bub Tanofly had a ten-day option and that if he didn't take it up he'd be glad to talk business with the party making the offer. They returned to the tap-room, Job helped the young men on with their coats, and they went out ·the front door into the Mall.

CHAPTER XXIX

I K E and Alexander Mathiesson walked down the half dozen steps to the roadway at Wheeler Corner and proceeded along the muddy footpath on the north side of the Mall. The west wind had cleared the clouds and the sky was blue, with a clean, dry snap in the air. The footpath was at street level on this side of the Mall, and beyond Applemore's Iron Block there were no buildings, the ground sloping down to River Street and, beyond, to the gorge of the Kamargo. They took a diagonal path down toward Mill Street, Mathiesson leading. Ike could feel the trembling of the earth from the power of the Middle Falls a quarter of a mile ahead of them. It was an exhilarating sensation, and Ike felt himself on the verge of great adventure. When the path widened he came up alongside his companion. "Say, do ye mind if I call ye by your first name?" he asked momentously. "It's a mighty sight handier, and ye ain't a powerful sight older'n I am." " 'Alec' they usually call me," said Mathiesson, "and it would feel like home to have somebody call me that." "I figger ye've caught my name," said Ike.

They walked along in silence, each sure that he was entering upon one of the important associations of his life. Ike needed Alec, someone who had a detailed knowledge of modern mechanics. And Alec likewise needed Ike, someone who was genuinely interested in his inventions and at the same time understood financial affairs instead of being bored and confused by them as Alec himself was. Most important, the two young men felt personally drawn to each other and, being together now for only the second time in their lives, it was as if they had known each other always. As they crossed the Middle Bridge the crash and the billowing spray of the falls revived the mystical intimations Ike had felt there two weeks before and reinforced his faith that he was entering upon some indomitable enterprise. On the opposite bank Alec paused and looked back at the wooden bridge. "Ought to be a suspension bridge here," he shouted close to Ike's ear. "I've a plan for one if only they'd let me build it." "How much would it cost?" Ike bellowed. "I haven't calculated that," Alec shouted. They both laughed and walked along toward Alec's place, passing Gadston's foundry on the left and the Union Mills on the right. "Did you know that place is for sale?" asked Ike, jerking his head toward the Union Mills. "Yes," said Alec as their eyes met.

Number 29 Mill Street had been built as a smithy forty years before and the gray paint was beginning to scale from its brick. It was endwise to the street and had heavy doors opening inward, one of which Alec now pushed back, the door swinging smoothly on an iron wheel he had rigged to run on an arc-shaped track supported by a stone foundation. Inside, the sanctum, with its dirt floor, was not as neat as Sarah Lathrop's kitchen, yet it was neater than any metal-working place Ike had ever seen. There was an order of usefulness about it, an impression that this place was identified with and controlled by a particular, vital personality. Along one side was a pile of bar iron and another of pipe, along the other side a pile of sheet iron. To the left and rear was the forge, swept as clean as a stove, and near it the rollers for turning boiler plate. Along the rear, under the two windows, ran a heavy bench of recent construction, bewilderingly panoplied with vises of wood, vises of iron, a long metal lathe, and scores of hammers, sledge hammers, drills, iron cutters, tongs, files, calipers, crucibles, pestles, and innumerable tools whose functions Ike couldn't even guess. Under the bench were deep drawers, each labelled with the size and shape of nails, screws, bolts, nuts, and rivets it contained. Above it was a long shelf crowded with bottles and vials. At one end stood a large, home-made desk with a sloping drawing board, and above it a case containing design books two or three feet high. And, wonder of wonders, between Ike and the desk there stood the first steam engine he had ever seen, a horizontal cylinder four or five feet long and half sunk in the brick firebox, with an ordinary stovepipe leading from it out a rear window whence a pane had been removed, and alongside the firebox the horizontal steam cylinder, connecting rod and flywheel. To Ike the sight of the engine was like coming into some fabulous country of which he had dreamed but which he had never hoped to reach. As he walked to the rear of the shop he had a fading sense of having been here before.

Ike paused by the machine of his dreams, feeling as shy and bewildered as if he had been ushered into the presence of the President of the United States. At length he ventured timidly, "She's a beauty, but—ain't they sometimes bigger'n that?" Alec laughed and ran his hands through his shock of black hair. "That's only a model—wouldn't pull more than ten or twelve horsepower." "Oh, yes, I recollect," said Ike in embarrassment. "To make a real one," continued Alec, "I shall need $200 in cash and I shall probably have to take out the flooring overhead. It may be necessary to do this for demonstration purposes, but the most economical plan would be to build the first full-sized one in the place where it's to work."

Alec began clawing back his hair. "There isn't any doubt that I can build it if I can raise the two hundred. I could turn the plates of the bigger shell and cast the cylinders either in Gadston's foundry or Smart's. The unique things I have to offer are my water tube boiler that I've already patented and a compound cylinder, a small cylinder taking the steam first, then passing it on to a larger cylinder while it is still expanding. The small cylinder I'm still working on. Here's the casting of it. I've still to turn the separate piston for it. Then I'll put it on the little fellow and see how it works."

"Can ye make your own cylinders?" asked Ike innocently. "Assuredly not," laughed Alec. "They have to be cast." "Who does your casting for ye?" asked Ike. "Master Gadston in his foundry." "Charges ye plenty, don't he?" said Ike, coming down to earth. "Too much," replied Alec, indifferently, hanging up his coat and beaver hat, then picking up a bar of iron and beginning to go over it for flaws. "Ever figger on getting somebody else to do your casting for ye?" "No. Master Gadston's right next door. Friend of Master Sherwood's. Never thought it worth while getting his enmity." "Humph," said Ike, "I figger we can do better'n toady t' Horace Gadston."

Both noticed that Ike said "we" inadvertently, and both fell silent. Alec began measuring off his piston rod with a metal ruler. Ike looked over his shoulder like a little boy entranced by the wonders of a blacksmith shop, forgot Horace Gadston, and slipped once more into his mood of romantic awe. Presently he walked back to the model, reached down gingerly and pushed on the flywheel, which turned a little. "Tough, ain't she?" he asked. "No doubt," said Alec without looking up. "Haven't had him running in a week. Oil's probably caked. Want to see him go? I call him 'Yankee Doodle' because he makes a rattle that sounds like that." "Figger I'll have to put that off," said Ike, subconsciously relieved that genuine necessity prevented him from staying to witness such a cataclysmic and perilous experiment.

"Got one of those safety valves, has she?" asked Ike, trying to sound professional. "The bar with the weight, on the steam drum," said Alec, setting his proposed piston rod in a vise. Ike located the lever, with a chain on the long, unweighted arm. "O.K. if I try it?" said Ike, taking hold of the chain gingerly. "Of course," said Alec indifferently. "It's set for eighty pounds now. Can set it for anything down to five pounds by shifting the weight. That's the steam gauge beside it."

Ike yanked on the chain, and was pleased to see how easy it was to lift the weighted valve with the long leverage. "That tube business inside, is it?" he asked, looking in bewilderment at the boiler. Alec lit a candle from a perpetual lamp, came over and opened the low firebox door. "You'll have to stand on your head to see the water tubes," he said, crouching down and shoving the candlestick into the firebox. Ike took off his hat, got down on his knees and peered in, twisting his head to look up. "See them, do you?" said Alec. "I figger," said Ike. "Revolution in boilers," said Alec. "No question of it. Can make them to stand any pressure, and cheaply." Ike stood up and continued to look bewildered. "She's a beauty, sure grit," was all he could say. Alec went back to his piston rod and began to tighten the vise. Neither spoke for some time.

"Tell ye what I was figgerin'," said Ike in a detached tone, still looking at the engine, and with his back to Alec, who now turned round, leaned back against the bench and resumed slowly his nervous gesture of pawing his mane. "Sort of gathered ye need two hundred and some dollars to reduce your mortgage to Master Sherwood, and on top of that some more for what they call working capital—mebbe to pay off Master Sherwood altogether and get out of that thundering bad agreement ye made with him and Gadston—mebbe just to build your engine and have something in the bank to talk turkey with in case ye can persuade somebody—like the *Democratic Union*—to take a shot at it. Figger ye ought to have three or four hundred lying around easy if ye're going ahead." Ike paused and gave the little flywheel another push. "Figgered it might help some if I put, say, about six hundred into the thing for a starter. Likely can find more when it's needful. My notion'd be not to let any more folks into the deal than's necessary to raise what ye need."

Ike paused, and now it was Alec who was tense and bewildered, his heart beating so loud he could hear it. "And by the way," resumed Ike, still keeping his back turned to Alec, "I figger ye know me well enough to understand that though I ain't precisely a trimmer, I'm in it for what I can make for myself as well as for you, and as a starter I want ye to consult with Master Sherwood before doing anything. Well," Ike concluded after another short pause, "what d' ye think of my notion?"

Alec's head was floating in the realm of money as Ike's had been in the realm of steam engines. He understood nothing except the momentous fact that somehow Ike was going to make several hundred available. He tried to speak and couldn't. Ike looked slyly around. They both laughed, then impulsively rushed together and shook hands. "Great event of my life, sure grit," said Ike. "Sort of thing I've been figgering on for years. Fact is, Alec, I'm gambling my future on ye." "We'll make one of those partnerships or corporations or what-not," said Alec, "with a fifty-fifty interest, eh? You be president." "Alec," said Ike, looking straight at him, "ye're a consarned fool if I ever saw one. Now, as I figger it, we're both putting about six hundred cash into it. Besides that you're putting in the patents and the knowledge and the work, all the real ginger. If ye give me a third interest ye'll be uncommon generous." "Make it sixty-forty," said Alec with a grin. "Suits me, partner," said Ike, and they shook hands again.

Alec produced a flask of rum, took off the cup and poured out a stiff drink, kept it, and handed the flask to Ike. "Here, you're the president, you get the flask." "No, you're the president," said Ike, forcing the flask back on him. "I'm what they call the business manager. Gimme that cup." "Well," said Alec, lifting the flask, "here's to—?" "What?" said Ike. "Lathrop, Mathiesson and Company," said Alec, again lifting the flask. "No," said Ike, "it'd have to be Mathiesson, Lathrop and Company. Makes quite a mouthful, don't it? What about Mathiesson Steam Engine Company?" "No, if your name isn't to be in it, neither is mine. What about Blackwater Engine Company?" "Ye're getting warm," said Ike. "What about Kamargo Steam Engine Company? Sounds kind of powerful, like the falls." Suddenly Alec's face lighted. "Yankee Doodle Steam Engine Company!" he said, again raising the flask. Ike laughed, then shook his head. "Too easy to make fun of," he said, "though, since that's the name you've given the engine, I figger we'll prefer to use it just between ourselves." Alec looked chagrined. "Something simple," said Ike, "like The Byzantium Steam Engine Company. After all that's what it is." "So be it," said Alec. For the fourth time he raised the flask, said gravely, "To The Byzantium Steam Engine Company," and they gulped the toast with such enthusiasm that Alec had to beat Ike's back before he could breathe. At last he straightened up and whispered through near strangulation, "Uncommon suspicious beginning—partner tries to poison me hot off the griddle."

As soon as Ike could talk he said, "If the meeting's adjourned I got to skedaddle up to Master Sherwood's on another matter. What d'ye say to riding out for supper, say, Wednesday, and spend the night? Mebbe I'll have something in writing by then we can mull over." "I should be delighted," said Alec.

Ike stepped out into the street, waved back an enthusiastic salute, and strode rapidly toward the bridge with the world of rum and factories and finance whirling round him so that he felt as if he were floating. Just after he passed the door marked "Office" in Gadston's foundry it opened and Ike heard, as if far off, a harsh voice calling, "Hey, there, Young Lathrop;" and he heard his own voice going back in reply, mingling with the roar of the falls, "Danged sorry, Master Gadston, but I've pressing business and I'll have to see ye later." When he slowed down on the grade up the path to the Mall he thought to himself, "Steady, Ike Lathrop, ye're drunk again and ye've no business sassing Horace Gadston." Then, inconsistently, he said aloud, "Poor old Horace!" and chuckled.

CHAPTER XXX

AS IKE crossed Wheeler Corner the clocks of the Baptist and Trinity Churches were striking two. The Mall was now normally populous and moving at its normal, moderate tempo, under a blue sky that promised cold. Perhaps a hundred mounts and carriages were scattered along its inner palisade of stone hitching-posts. A dozen wagons crept at their heavy pace through the mud, two of them elephantine with loads of hay, the rest miscellaneously laden with logs, lumber, sacks of grain, barrels of vegetables or fruit, hides, bolts of woollen or cotton fabric, ungainly monsters of hardware. Several mounted men, posting in their best form, touched their hats to Ike from the roadway below the footpath, and gaily bonneted and ribboned ladies, just now emerging to their shopping after the excitement of the morning, bowed to him from their smartly drawn carriages.

As he walked along the west end of the Mall his progress was minutely watched by half a dozen merchants who at the moment had nothing better to do than to occupy the doors of their shops and exchange observations on life in the metropolis of Byzantium Falls, N. Y., on that Monday afternoon, December the 2d, 1850. So well codified were these exchanges that Fire Chief Obiḍ Plum, sitting in a chair in the doorway of his shop on the South Mall, had only to sweep his eyes through an arc of forty degrees whereby he struck instantaneous understanding, more than ten rods across on the little bluffs opposite, with the eyes of Goliath Walsh, saddler, Seth Marlow, general merchant, Caleb Carter, druggist, Jerome Small, tinsmith, and Jabez Forest, hatter. There was no external motion but that single flash of eyes so far apart as to be almost invisible to each other. Yet by that single motion those six merchants now said to each other: "There goes Ike Lathrop, son of the Squire of Lathrop Hollow, smart hoss-trader and purchaser of the scene of the morning's fire against all comers. We wonder what he's up to now!"

As Ike passed Seth Marlow's store, bowing over-pompously to old Seth—for his veins were still spinning with rum—he spied Bub Tanofly sitting overhead in a window of the office of Jonah Ball, insurance agent. At the sight of Bub, Ike bristled a little and gave him a peremptory wave to come down. When Bub appeared the eyes of the world settled on them. Instinctively they moved out from the buildings to the edge of the wide footpath, and their talk was in an undertone.

"First off," said Ike unceremoniously, "I don't want any more of your spoilt colt nonsense. I ain't fooling with ye, and I ain't hoss-swopping with ye, and what's more I'm in a tarnal hurry." "Ain't ye talkin' a wee mite big?" asked Bub with his patronizing smile. "Mebbe I am," said Ike, "because I figger it's the only kind of talk ye'll understand. What I'm getting at is I've what looks like a true grit cash offer of five hundred for the Quin property. Got my suspicions it's Applemore and he wants it either to hold you up or maybe for a water-power site for a new power press I heard him talking about a spell back. However that may be, I'm going to accept this offer of five hundred unless ye see fit to give me the four hundred I mentioned this noon."

"Give ye five hundred fer it a'ready," said Bub. "Gave me five hundred to let me know you were my boss," snapped Ike. "That's neither here nor there. All I want to know now is, are ye going to take it for four hundred or ain't ye?"

"Course I am," said Bub out of the side of his mouth. "What's more, I'm a-goin' t' make up that extry hundred to ye in one way or another, and that ain't playin' God A'mighty either. I'm god danged sorry I acted like I did, Ike, and there's my apology." "Sure about the four hundred, are ye?" said Ike unsympathetically. "That's my hand on it," said Bub, "and I'll give ye a check or cash right now." "Hain't time for that," said Ike. He shook Bub's hand. The eyes of the watching merchants agreed that young Lathrop had sold Bub Tanofly the Quin property at a profit.

Bub started back toward the stairway to the insurance office. "Hold your hosses," said Ike, and when Bub came back he again dropped his voice to a confidential murmur. "I'm going to ask ye a favor," he said, "that ye can refuse and nobody'd blame ye. As I told ye I don't mind making a hundred out of you on this deal, being ye had it coming and being ye can afford it. But I ain't calculating to make anything out of Master Redemption Quin, being he can't afford it. What he's concerned with is getting himself set up again in a shop somewhere up Columbia Street, not far from the Arsenal, I figger. Tells me he can get it for two hundred, and a hundred more will set him up again in drugs. That makes just the three hundred I gave him. I'm bound to see to it that Master Quin gets his property all keerect, to the extent, if needful, of putting up the hundred I've made on the deal. It may be I'm going to work in the village before long, and it may be I ain't. Until

I do, what I'm asking you to do is to see that Master Quin gets his new place and his new batch of drugs. Anything it costs up to a hundred ye can take out of the four hundred ye owe me."

This touched Bub on his generous side. "Ye're true grit, Ike, and I'll see the little feller set up if I have to throw in some boot. From what ye say I figger ye ain't settled yet on a job in the village, eh?" "I'm going to see Howell Sherwood now," murmured Ike, and turned away. "Say," said Bub, "I'll lay ye another hundred that if ye settle there ye won't stay six months, you havin' a danged sight more t' teach Master Sherwood than he'll ever have to teach you." "Hell with ye," said Ike, and started off briskly toward Daw Street.

To talk serious business with Howell Sherwood when keyed up with rum was a far call from telling off Bub Tanofly. In front of the bank Ike suddenly stopped, conscious of his condition, and pondered postponing this interview to another day. For a good minute he stood on the edge of the footpath by the post where he had tied Chesty ten days before, contemplating the ring in the post with the deepest concern and muttering over such trial phrases as, "May I have the honor of a moment of your time, Master Sherwood?" "I have the honor to present myself, Master Sherwood, with my father's permission, to apply for a humble position in your employ."

Suddenly he jumped at a tap on his shoulder and turned quickly to confront the great banker himself, smiling up at him from his diminutive height. "Good day to ye, Howell Sherwood," said Ike, touching his leather cap with a flourish and shaking hands. "The fact is, sir, I rode into the village today particularly to see you, but, between the fire and too much company at the Wheeler, I have been in doubt whether I was longer fit to approach ye."

They both laughed. The svelt little banker in his perfect gray suit and lofty collar took big Ike by the arm, led him across the footpath to the door, and bowed him in. The eyes of the six watching merchants met in a flash that said, "Ike Lathrop's a prize worth a bid by Banker Sherwood, and therefore a force to be reckoned with from now on in the affairs of the village."

Howell Sherwood's bank was almost cheerful this afternoon, with the western sun pouring in the two back windows between the three great safes. The kerosene lamps in the fancy brackets were not lighted. As Ike walked along the counter red-haired Philip the clerk gave a perceptible flicker of his eye in his direction, which for Philip was a maximal salutation.

The interview with Master Sherwood went off pleasantly and without disagreement. The employment was to be experimental, leaving Ike free to decide, in May or June, whether or not he wished to go to Yale. He would receive five dollars a week, free dinner and free stable in Master Sherwood's barn a block up Washington Street. His hours were to be from eighty-thirty to four, so as to permit him to perform both morning and evening chores at the Hollow. His employment would start on Monday, the ninth, a week from today.

When they had settled on the terms, Master Sherwood embarked upon what at first seemed to Ike an irrelevant comparison between his own bank and the Blackwater County Bank, much to the credit of the latter. When he had given Ike a lot of information, most of which he already knew, he astonished him by revealing his reasons for the lengthy comparison. He had been discussing Ike's prospects with Master Marshfield, the president of the Blackwater, and, from things Master Marshfield had said, Master Sherwood had gathered that if Ike wished to seek employment there he could have it.

This gave Ike a moment's pause, and he dropped his eyes from Master Sherwood's to stare intently at an iron paperweight on the desk cast in the form of a pelican. The Blackwater was the oldest and most respected financial institution in the county, its depositors including the greater number of the old leading families—the Stauntons, Fultons, VanWycks, VanSanfords—who had always been the associates of Ike's family. He felt a stir of pride at this unexpected opportunity of being employed there, but his mind quickly returned to the practicalities of his situation. His venture in the village was to be an attempt to rehabilitate the Lathrop fortunes in terms of modern industry and finance, and it was in Sherwood's bank, not the Blackwater, that most of the leading industrialists had their accounts. It was here that he would be able to observe their methods, perhaps even be privy to some of their enterprises. He looked up from the pelican to Master Sherwood again and said simply, "I'd rather work for you, Howell Sherwood."

His new employer now pulled a real plum out of the bag. "In addition to this intimation of a position," he said, "and, I am certain, quite independent of it, Master Marshfield asked me to tell you that henceforth you will be welcome on Wednesday afternoons round the cider barrel in the room at the rear of the Blackwater Bank."

In response to this momentous invitation Ike could only stare. The Blackwater cider barrel was the conclave of the elders of the whole county, including Howell Sherwood himself, Ike's pa and Solon Samson. From childhood he had looked on it as a sort of Heaven, hardly to be entered before he had achieved some incalculable age beyond the remote and now seemingly august forties. He could not believe his ears and asked in amazement, "Are ye certain of that, Howell Sherwood?" "Indeed, I am," said Master Sherwood. "George Fulton and the oldest VanSanford boy, Medad, are also to join us. You see, we are in need of young ideas, such as yours, to liven our senile deliberations." "That's sure grit more than I bargained for," said Ike. He managed to thank Master Sherwood warmly for all his kindness, and left the bank in a daze. He was elated, flattered, but at the same time he felt something like disappointment. The Blackwater County Bank! The Blackwater cider barrel! The Falls! They were not so remote and glorious after all. At nineteen he had captured them without a fight. He felt a little let down, a little ashamed for them, less honored than he would have expected.

A few minutes later, Ike was still in a detached mood of combined triumph and disillusion when, starting for home, he rode Chesty out of the Wheeler yard, and found himself abreast of Mistress Stark and Pru in their carriage, both winsomely bonneted and shawled and being driven by the new stable boy of the Liberty. Mistress Stark gave him a nice bow with a faintly tired smile in it, but Pru lifted her gloved hand and called softly, . "Ike!" A little resentfully Ike rode in alongside, with his fingers touching his cap. By crooking a finger, Pru signalled him to bend down to receive grave information, and when he had done so she said in a stage whisper, "I thought you might like to know I made an excuse not to see John when the stage came through this morning!" And she threw him a covert smile such as might have changed the history of eighteenth-century France. Dazzled into a silly smirk, Ike wheeled Chesty, waved his cap and set off across the Mall at a gallop, a precipitate action which the watching merchants were unable to diagnose.

CHAPTER XXXI

IKE forced the conversation at supper through combined enthusiasm over the day's developments and self-consciousness in the suspicion that his pa might not approve his having chosen Howell Sherwood's bank over the Blackwater. Little Ben listened with awe to the account of the fire, and afterwards gave but perfunctory attention. Master Lane only grumbled occasionally, never looking.at Ike, for he disapproved of the whole venture in the village. Tavie, flushed, avoiding Ike's eyes, gay to the verge of hysteria, flitted round the table like a golden sunbeam. Sarah abetted Ike with appropriate laughter, comment and serious attention, observing not only Tavie but more especially her husband, and greatly fearing the effects on him of Ike's plans as they began actually to materialize.

The Squire listened responsively and with mobile features to the account of the fire, but when Ike threw himself with zest into the account of the purchase of the Quin property Sarah noticed that the Squire's smile became set, and he began nodding slowly and regularly in apparent accord, a mannerism characteristic of him when he was listening to a bore. From then on, also, he forgot to eat, leaving a freshly taken slab of pie untouched before him. When Ike carried his account into the Wheeler House, the Squire looked up with approval at the mention of young Fulton and young VanSanford, the sons of his friends with whom he was delighted to have Ike associate. But when Ike gave a solemn account of his confession to Old Jerry Stone, the Squire again began to nod his disinterested approval. At this point Sarah touched his arm, intimating that supper was over. They all retired to the keeping-room for prayers, which the Squire carried off but indifferently. Sarah and Tavie retired to the kitchen, where Sarah left Tavie to do the main redding up, herself tending to the dishes at the sink where she could hear the talk in the keeping-room and, by turning from time to time, could observe her husband.

"Well, Isaac," said the Squire, "you've had a busy day without a doubt," and he gave Ike a somewhat formal pat on the shoulder. "Oh, there's lots more, Pa," said Ike, "and in the long run much more important, I figger, than anything I've told ye so far." With that the Squire motioned Ike and Master Lane and Ben to sit down and, himself sinking into his big, hair-cloth rocker, looked intently and affectionately at Ike in signal to proceed.

Ike glossed over the vinous aspects of the gathering at the Wheeler by saying that they had "a mighty pleasant time," and this statement the Squire accepted with a tolerant smile. But when Ike described as "funnier'n a short-tailed bull in fly-time" Bub Tanofly's attempt to bull-doze him about the Quin property, his pa's attention wandered again and he resumed the slow, rhythmic nodding until Sarah was convinced he was no longer hearing a word Ike said. He seemed to awake from his detached state when Ike began describing a steam engine. Sarah saw him sit up and begin to show genuine interest in young Mathiesson's shop and his inventions, until Ike as it were struck him squarely in his hopes and his prejudices by reveal-ing the arrangement he had made for the formation of some kind of company.

Sarah could fairly see this blow fall at a moment when the Squire was off guard, having been drawn out of the detachment he had determined to maintain toward Ike's conduct. Previously Ike had told how he had put $300 of the sale price of Dandy into the purchase of some real estate or other. Now Sarah saw the Squire wince with troubled amazement when Ike said he had put further $600 into this industrial enterprise. She knew what he was thinking—$900 in speculation in the village! It was more than enough to put him through one year of college!

Impulsively the Squire rose, took a fresh cigar and gave one to Master Lane and Ike. Then he sat down again, and Sarah watched him master himself and retire into his detachment. It was apparent to her that Ike also saw the effect of the blow. From that time on he was always trying either to amuse his pa or to justify himself. He referred to this arrangement with young Mathiesson as "what we figger to call between ourselves the 'Yankee Doodle Steam Engine Company,'" and he greatly embellished an incident of rudeness to old Horace Gadston. He approached seriously and with apparent reluctance an arrangement he had made with Howell Sherwood, and his tone became pleading when he told how and why he had accepted this arrangement in preference to working for Master Marshfield at the Blackwater. But by now the Squire was again far gone in detachment, and Sarah was certain that he was hearing nothing.

Having finished the dishes, she now went into the keeping-room and slipped unobtrusively into a chair. Aroused by her entrance, the Squire looked up at her with such a smile of love and appeal as she had not seen since Tom died. Ike seized the moment to lean forward and address his pa earnestly, narrating the sale of the Quin property to Bub, and he succeeded in holding his attention until he had driven home the fact that he had provided that all profit from the sale should go back to Master Quin. At this the Squire was able to slap the arm of his chair lightly and say, "Very good!" After a pause, Ike took advantage of this momentary approval to say that old Henry Hawks was helping the Fultons temporarily, and that next week, after he went to work for Master Sherwood, he planned to bring Henry out to the homestead and pay his wages and board out of his salary at the bank.

Having completed his narrative, Ike threw his ma a troubled glance, then rose and stepped over to stand with his back against the mantel. The Squire also rose, re-lighted at the candelabra his cigar which had gone out, and stood a few moments gazing out the south window into the now bright starlight. Then he turned back with his big, natural smile and said heartily, "Isaac, I congratulate ye on the number of things you have accomplished today. Though you realize no doubt that the course you are taking is on some accounts baffling to me and on other accounts seems perilous, yet I believe in my heart that you are proceeding as your conscience directs, and in that belief I want you to feel that I am behind ye in whatever you do and wherever your course may lead ye. And since we are in accord, it strikes me that a toast is appropriate, and for my part I propose that we drink it in that good Napoleon brandy."

At this Sarah disappeared, returned with the bottle and the brandy glasses and set them on the big table. The Squire poured a thimbleful for all and passed them round, saying to Ben as he handed him one, "Take care, my son, if you be not more worldly than I think ye. A mere wetting of your lips is enough, and for the rest you'd best take it with water." Standing with his glass half raised the Squire paused and said, "There seems to be someone missing." Then he called, "Octavia, my girl, come into the keeping-room for a serious and pleasant duty."

Tavie came in, flinging aside her apron, and the Squire poured her out a glass. "Oh, John Lathrop," she said quickly, "I beg you to excuse me. I have taken a pledge never to touch alcohol." "Very well, my girl, here's an empty glass, and we'll pretend that it holds, if not spirits in the flesh, then spirits in the spirit, eh?"

Then, raising his glass, he said, "Isaac, my son, if you continue as you have begun, you are taking the most courageous step of any member of this family since your great-grandfather came out to the wilderness from Connecticut. I pledge ye success to Banker Isaac Lathrop and I pledge ye further the success of the—Yankee Doodle Steam Engine Company. . . ."

The Squire apparently intended to say more, but something in the incongruous absurdity of the last phrase caused a catch in his throat which only Sarah observed. All but Ike tossed off the drink, Tavie in pantomime and little Ben wetting his lips as directed. Ike responded, "And I pledge ye that whatever I do, I do first of all for the honor and success of the Lathrop family." With a determination born of recent humiliation, Ike took a deep breath, tossed off the dram, set the glass down on the mantel, let out his breath very gingerly, made no effort to speak, and found to his relief that he could breathe. Ben went to the kitchen, filled his glass with water and finished it, while the Squire tossed off the drink he had poured for Tavie under the jealous eye of Master Lane.

"Sarah Lathrop," said Tavie with a smile and a covert glance past Ike at the mantel, "the sweeping is finished. May I go home now, as Ma wishes me to?" Sarah said indeed she might, and Ike said, "Tave, if ye're going home may I walk with ye, for I've to talk to your pa on business?" "Why, of course," said Tavie, with astonishment, and suddenly having to force her voice above a whisper. "I'm to see Solon Samson," said Ike to his pa, "about drawing up the papers for the steam engine company." "An excellent plan," said the Squire.

A few minutes later Tavie and Ike went out the kitchen door, Tavie in her cloak and Ike in his greatcoat and old coonskin cap. The Squire resumed his stance looking out the south window whence he saw Ike and Tavie walk out the drive arm in arm in the starlight. Sarah went to the chimney closet, took out the cribbage board and cards and motioned to Master Lane and Ben to follow her, which they did. In the kitchen she set the board and the cards on the table in front of the fire and looked significantly at Master Lane, who grunted understanding. Then she went back into the keeping-room and closed the door.

She went up quietly and stood beside her husband with her head bowed. For a long time he seemed not to know that she was there. Then, while he still gazed straight ahead out of the window, his arm went around her and held her strongly, and she half turned to him and looked up at his face with what they both knew was the one love that would surely never fail him. Again for the first time since Tom's death, she saw a tear in the wrinkle under each great eye.

"It ain't what the boy is doing," he said slowly. "It's only that he is failing to do as I planned for him. It's my own selfishness—the last battle of the flesh with the spirit—the last, that is, but one." Sarah lifted his other hand and held it to her lips. "There's still John and Ben," she whispered. "It ain't the boys," the Squire continued after another pause. "It's the world that is changing before us as we grow older. Joel has had his trial, and faced his—defeat. Our trial is just beginning." "Not mine," Sarah murmured, "not while I have you, John."

Not noticing this, the Squire continued, "You know, my girl, it would be good to have children who would still be little ones when we die." "Yes, that would be good," she whispered, and moved around in front of him so that he held her gently with both arms, while she dropped her head on his shoulder, feeling herself trembling as she had that night thirty-three years before in the bridal suite at the old tavern in Bloomington.

"But it's better," he said again, "to face our defeat together. Perhaps I could force the boys—Isaac—to my will, but in the long run—in the long run on earth—it would be Isaac—not I—who would suffer—for at heart he's a gentle boy." "Yes, John," whispered Sarah, looking up at him not less reverently than she would have looked up into the face of God.

Later that night it was not the Squire but Sarah who lay long awake, with her face turned into the pillow, sobbing softly. For sixteen years now she had been childless, and during that time had never ceased to hope. But recently she had felt the time approaching, and now she was sure it had arrived, when she could hope no longer.

CHAPTER XXXII

AS THEY stepped out of the kitchen door into the night Ike took Tavie's arm as naturally as he would have done walking home with any girl of the neighborhood, and his thoughts took the barometric direction that was conventional upon emergence from any house. "Mercury's dropping fast," he said, noticing the clear plume of his breath and the crackle of freezing mud underfoot, then glancing up at the unclouded starlight overhead. "Beautiful night," Tavie murmured as they turned into the road under the big maples. Over Swift Mountain there was the milky shine of incipient moonrise, but the near light was as yet entirely from the stars. There were no shadows, but a diffused, dull silver glow on everything, even the undersides of branches, as if it were twilight in a pewter world.

As they turned down the corduroy Lower Road the rush of Jolam's Falls seemed far off, but little wind gusts began rustling softly through the bare treetops on the right and the bushes on the embankment above them on the left. "Kind o' spooky, ain't it?" said Ike. "Bet ye couldn't get Master Lane two rods from the house a night like this."

Conscious of guiding Tavie, he kept his eyes down on the corduroy that was already filmed with ice, while she, relaxing under his touch and the spell of the night, let her eyes wander about among the silvery images that surrounded them. As they approached the little Lathrop cemetery on the cleared knoll to the right of the road, she first made out the marble slabs of the two great aunts side by side like gigantic arched eyes looking over the near wall. Then, back of them, the square-topped slab of Great-uncle Ben, which Ike had recently straightened. Then, a little lower, Tom's slab. And in the center of the back, at the highest point in the little square, the two big slabs of the first Squire and his wife. All the markers, whether of marble or limestone, now seemed of the same softly glowing gray, indistinguishable in color from the fieldstone of the wall and the trunks of the trees that closed round the lot at the rear.

As Tavie gazed at the little burying ground she was suddenly conscious of motion in the upper left corner where presumably the next dead Lathrops were to lie. It seemed as if something white were rising there and beginning to throw light all round on the trees. A spasm of night terror swam freezingly through her. She stopped, disengaged her arm from Ike's and clung to him with both hands, holding him back. "Look there," she whispered. Ike looked up, saw what she did, and automatically his arm went round her.

The thing continued to rise behind the wall and glowed increasingly white, seeming to light up the whole burying ground and the woods behind as bright as day. Gradually the top of it took a rounded, hoodlike shape, like a white cowl or the arched top of a big marble grave-slab, but shining a thousand times brighter than any marshlight Ike had ever seen. " 'Tain't an earthly light," he thought to himself, and felt the chill of the supernatural run down his spine. He wondered if liquor had bewitched him and he shut his eyes hard. When he opened them there it was, brighter than ever. He heard fast breathing near by, but it was only Tavie. "Hi, there!" he shouted loudly to get hold of his wits.

At that Tavie clung to him so hard that she nearly unbalanced him, and he fancied that the thing ducked down a little behind the wall and paused, as if watching them. One of the little wind gusts made him turn his head quickly and glance up the bank to the left. On its top he noticed that the bushes along the fence were lighted like the woods behind the white thing and, glancing higher, he saw that the treetops were also shining although the lower trunks were still dark, darker even than they had been before. Suddenly he laughed, "We're a pair o' scary cats! Do you know what it is, Tave?"

Tavie by this time had buried her eyes in his shoulder and was speechless with fright, so she only waggled her head against his greatcoat. "It's just that old bent birch behind the cemetery wall we used to pretend was a camel, and the reason for its shining so is the moon's just up." Tavie peeked up. It was all clear now and they both giggled. Ike gave her an affectionate squeeze, removed his arm, took hers conventionally again and started on down the corduroy. At that instant there was a rustle of wings, not so loud as a partridge but louder than a chickadee, and a dull brownish shape shot over them from the vicinity of the ghostly birch to the bank above. Again Tavie turned and seized Ike with a little gasp.

This time Ike was not deceived. "Ain't ye seen that before?" Tavie waggled her head against him. "That's an owl seems aiming to spend the winter here in the glen." "Of course," said Tavie, giving Ike her arm again and starting along. "I've seen him plenty of times by daylight. That birch got me jumpy, I guess."

They walked on, Ike thinking of Tavie's ma's clairvoyance and of the tales of her grandmother's ghost in the glen, and being a little impressed himself by the resemblance of the arch of the bent birch to the top of a curved, marble gravestone, and by the recollection that the owl had flown across the road in just that way when he and John were walking down here last Monday before Dandy died. Ungallantly, he allayed his own creepiness by accusing Tavie of it. "Kind o' spooky, are ye, Tave?" he said. "Assuredly not," she replied. "Even Ma doesn't believe in ghosts and only half believes in her visions. Pa believes in them less than she does. And I don't believe in them at all. Do you?" "Not till I've seen some of 'em come true," said Ike ambiguously.

"I'll tell you what I do believe, though," continued Tavie. "I believe in some sort of a great Spirit of Good over everything, something like a person, to Whom our little troubles are childish but Who, if we try to do right in the world, will some day bring us happiness. Don't you, Ike?" "Mebbe," said Ike, not greatly interested in the moral implications of the supernatural.

They walked on in silence, Ike now conscious of Tavie and feeling very close to her and fond of her because of the recent mutual adventure. He recalled his decision of last week not to try to kiss her any more and his promise to her not to speak of marriage again. His new self-importance as a man of affairs made it easy for him silently to renew those compacts with himself. He guessed he had enough to think about without getting snarled up with a girl, even Tavie, yet awhile.

Having disentangled himself from any possible snarls at the moment, he felt more genuinely friendly with Tavie than he had in some time. He would like to stay out a spell and was glad when she seemed to hang back as they came down into the flat at the bottom of Jolam's Glen and there remained only a few rods to her pa's gate. When they reached it they paused. The great hemlocks rose before them and around the dimly lighted house, their lofty tops gorgeously splotched with moonlight, while all was gloom down in the road. The little rumble of Jolam's Falls over beyond the forge drowned out all other sounds.

"Let's walk on a bit before we go in," said Tavie, and Ike welcomed the suggestion. When they had gone about three rods, Tavie said, "Let's stop here. This is my favorite place, where the knoll shuts out the sound of the falls a little and you can always hear the hemlocks. This is where I come when I have something to think out. This is where I decided two years ago to devote my life to the Reform Movement. It seems as though the Spirit of Good lives here, up in the hemlocks, and He always sings me a lullaby, as if I were a baby and He wanted to assure me that everything will come out for the best."

They were silent for a full minute, listening to the billion-voiced fairy choir of the hemlock needles that was never still here, not even in the dog-days of August, and just now was rising and falling, coming nearer and drawing away in endless variations on the little gusts of wind. "Sort of like the whole earth living here, ain't it?" said Ike softly, and in their different fashions they were both in the approaches to the temple of mysticism.

"Ike," said Tavie after another long pause. "Yep," said Ike as if from a great distance, having now released her arm and standing before her almost invisible in the gloom. "Would you kiss me just once more? You see, with you going into the Falls every day and me coming home every night, it isn't likely that we'll see much of each other from now on. I did like your kissing me the other morning, and I would like you to do it just once more, especially in this place. After that we must stop it for good."

"Guess there'd be no wrong in it," mumbled Ike, deliciously paralyzed of thought by this unexpected provocation. He fumbled for her hand, then joyfully and strongly closed both arms around her as he had never done before, and, drawing her close to him, while she pressed herself against him as eagerly, began kissing her again and again on the lips in a way that was very much more "wrong"—in the sense of being dangerous—than Ike then realized. Tavie relaxed utterly for the first time in her life, having, as she then believed, her fling, feeling all the fierce little nerves lying down as if smoothed by Ike's big hands, and hearing her blood racing round and round with joy.

Presently Ike felt more strength rising in him than he cared to cope with, and, checking it, the power of thought returned. He thrust her gently away, still holding her by the shoulders, and whispered hoarsely, "Now we'd best not do that any more—at least not for a good spell—not until I've done a lot of things I'm figgering on and have got myself so situated that I've a right to think about such matters."

At this Tavie grew rigid and lifted her hand to her forehead in the darkness. "Don't forget your promise," she murmured, with tenderness still in her voice. "Don't worry. I won't," said Ike, remembering his drunkenness more than his promise not to mention marriage, and saying this so casually that it seemed almost insulting to Tavie. She turned away abruptly and started back for the house. "What's the matter, Tave?" said Ike aloud, taking after her. "Nothing at all," she replied, and waited for him. "Well, good-by," she said, and he was barely able to see her face lifted to him. He embraced her and kissed her once more, but now she stood rigid, her arms straight down at her side, and her lips seemed hard. Mechanically he slipped his hand into her arm and they walked back toward the house, having trouble to get in step.

In the house Ike was sedulously attentive to Charity, hoping to dispel the sinister effects of whatever it was she saw about him in the crystal a week ago. She was a little ceremonious at first, but by the time he and Solon retired to the office he felt that he had almost restored himself to her good graces.

It didn't take long for Ike to outline to Solon his plans for incorporating the Byzantium Steam Engine Company, and after that they settled into general conversation. Solon, glowering with special ferocity because the ground was unfamiliar to him, inquired whether it would not be possible, by the use of this stationary steam engine, to erect a factory in or near Lathrop Hollow. Ike replied that it would, indeed, that that was precisely what was in the back of his mind. If, in addition, they could get a railroad through the Hollow—even though it went on to the Falls afterward—factories in the Hollow would be in a better position than those in the Falls because of their greater proximity to the downstate cities. With a railroad it would be possible to reach Utica in six or eight hours. Ike said expansively that he was planning to turn his attention to the matter of a railroad as soon as he could command the resources to make the venture possible.

Solon said that he had had—if Ike would pardon him—the ill fortune of observing the railroad running between Albany and Utica, and that he considered it dangerous. Ike launched into the recent developments of railroad mechanics, and explained how the dangers were being eliminated. He announced largely that he looked forward to the time when railroads would replace horses entirely for long journeys, even for passenger service.

The talk ranged on into the perennial subject of the modern industries; from there to Ike's new job in the bank; his invitation to the gathering at the Blackwater Bank on Wednesdays; politics; the weakness of abolition in the Falls—though they avoided the subject of the Underground Railroad; finally, Ike's dominating notion that the place for folks like them was in the Falls, to prevent the control of the township falling into the hands of the scalawags who controlled industry already. Indirectly Ike was suggesting that Solon would do well to move to the Falls, his implication being that there he could be of greater service to the town, but his real hope being that Solon would locate himself where his law practice would be more remunerative.

It was almost ten o'clock, and Charity and Tavie had retired, when Ike started home, turning back to touch his cap to Solon, who stood watching him from the door till he was on the road. The moon was half way up to the zenith and a few rays penetrated to the depths of Jolam's Glen. The stars were dimmed by the moon and the night was clear, dry, glass-like cold. The higher Ike went the brighter the world became, till at the bend below the cemetery the moonlight came straight down into the road and it was bright as day. Climbing higher, he looked back at the spook of two and a half hours before. He made out the birch, but it was not specially prominent now, being partially in shadow and all the other trees being likewise whitened by the moon.

When he reached the upper road he paused in the magnificent silence, luxuriating in the glorified, cold immensity of earth and sky. He thought there was more of God in a night like this than in how people behaved. This was a reference in thought to Tavie's notion of the great Spirit of Good. But as a person she did not enter his mind all the way home. Nor all that night when he did not dream at all, being content with the great things he had done that day.

CHAPTER XXXIII

T H E week remaining before his employment in the village should begin was one of eager impatience for Ike, as was all too evident to the family. On Wednesday Alec Mathiesson rode out for supper and the night. The Samsons also being invited for supper, Solon brought along the application for articles of incorporation of the Byzantium Steam Engine Company. As previously arranged with Ike, the authorized capital stock was to be two hundred shares of $100 each, of which Alec was stated to be the subscriber of nine and Ike of six. In the morning Alec took in the application and posted it to Albany. He also carried in two notes from Ike, one for Squire Fulton, the other for old Henry Hawks, saying that Henry's place was ready for him whenever he wanted to come out. Henry got a ride out on Saturday, thus returning to the house where he had worked for the first Squire Lathrop fifty years and more before. Henceforth Ike was to have no duties at the homestead except morning and evening chores, and to continue to supervise the marketing and the accounts. He was to pay Henry $2.50 a week, and the Squire 50c a week for Henry's board.

On Monday, the 9th of December, Ike rode into the village splendidly arrayed in his pa's old beaver hat and his own best, his only, store suit, with the requisite lofty collar and smart black bow—today the handiwork of his pa. He turned over Chesty to Howell Sherwood's groom just as the Baptist Church was banging out eight o'clock into the cold morning, and walked out the drive beside Master Sherwood's rambling frame house with its handsomest iron fences, gates and trellises in town. Saluting right and left, he swung down Washington Street, self-conscious in his sartorial splendor and importance as a banker, and duly reported to work almost half an hour early. After greeting him Master Sherwood turned him over to Philip, the now senior clerk who was asserting his importance this day by wearing a flaming red waistcoat and neckpiece that more than offset his almost equally flaming red hair. By noon Ike had mastered the shallower mysteries of checks, deposit slips, personal accounts and savings accounts, and was beginning on the ledgers.

Master Sherwood understood that Ike would be unable to dine with him that day, and transmitted to Ike a message from Alec Mathiesson that he was not coming to the Wheeler because he was too busy on something he hoped to be able to show Ike today or tomorrow. Accordingly, at twelve o'clock Ike walked off to the Wheeler alone, overtaking at the door Fred VanSanford and Jabe Munson, both of whom spit out quids of tobacco before entering. George Fulton, Nat Gadston and Tim Slocum were already in the dining room, and George greeted the newcomers with, "Ah, here's the whole gang!" "Strikes me," said Jabe, shaking hands with George and Nat and Tim, "that'd be a fittin' name fer this august assemblage—the Gang." And so the "Gang" henceforth this Monday dinner club became.

Bub Tanofly came in with coat-tails flying and, greeting no one, started talking to Ike before he was seated. "Lem Grabbot owned the property yer Miss Nancy Quin wanted. Old rapscallion held out fer three hundred. T' stock up yer little friend with drugs, had t' throw in another hundred like ye directed, and yer Missy Quin claimed he was bound t' give ye back this note and mortgage." Bub whipped the documents out of his pocket and handed them to Ike with a flourish. "Thar's my check for the rest o' four hundred," Bub added, taking a folded piece of paper from his waistcoat pocket. "And now, young feller, cal'late I don't owe ye a red, and my commission'll be ye holler fer dinner and set up a round o' coffin-varnish fer the hul—the hul—" "Gang," said Nat Gadston. "O.K.," said Bub, "the hul gang."

Ike went out to the kitchen and ordered the dinner, then returned to the bar in some trepidation. He had never in his life bought drinks for a crowd, and he didn't have enough cash in his pocket to pay for them. Confidentially he confessed his predicament to Job Wheeler, who embarrassed him by roaring with delight in the presence of three or four drinkers. "Pesky little cash goes over this counter, Master Ike, leastwise from folks we know. Payin' fer the round, be ye? All keerect. Down she goes in the book, and ye settle yer account when ye're a-feelin' pertickler frisky." "All keerect," said Ike unenthusiastically, this striking him as a peculiarly unsound method of financing.

Meanwhile Mistress Wheeler was bringing in the plates. Ike returned to the dining room and sat down by Bub, who now grew confidential and monopolized his attention, while the rest carried on their own talk. Bub was unusually serious and polite, saying he hoped Ike wouldn't take what he was about to say as any kind of monkeyshines, but as a piece of straight business. Though Ike had skinned him "a hunner" on the Quin property, nevertheless he'd saved him another hundred by not accepting the other offer. He felt bound to come down for that hundred in one way or another and he'd feel uncommon set up if Ike would accept a little present of a share of stock in the Tanofly Paper Company. "Ye'd be doin' me a kindness t' accept it," he said, "fer I'd a'mighty like t' git ye interested in the business. No obligation. Nothin' t' scratch yer head about. Every now'n again I'll shell ye out a dividend o' five 'r ten dollars, and if ye're o' mind to ye can make me show ye the books o' the shebang. Ye can set it down sartin there's plenty'd give ye a hunner an' more fer the share any day, but I'd take it kindly if ye spoke t' me first whenever ye figgered on sellin' it. Wal, what d' ye say, ye god danged banker ye?"

Ike was touched by this evidence of Bub's decency and esteem. "Why, I'm a'mighty grateful to ye, Bub, and if ever I can do ye a turn, I'll do it sure grit."

He lowered his head and thought hard. Yes, Bub did owe him some sort of obligation. Anyhow, wouldn't he do as much for Bub if the chance offered? For that matter, wouldn't he do as much for anybody here? Weren't they all members of the "Gang?" He felt a surge of affection for this excellent fellowship around him—almost as good as the old days at the Hollow. And yet—his mind took a nostalgic turn—not quite so good. He suddenly remembered that his best friends at the Hollow were already on their way to California. He had a prescient moment—was this, then, to take the place of the old crowd at the Hollow—permanently? He looked up, and the scene seemed strange. George Fulton was watching him with his gentle, big brown eyes. "All keerect, Scamp?" he whispered across the table, knowing this nickname from his friendship with John. George had guessed what he was thinking. Ike felt a lump in his throat. Then he managed to smile, and presently worked himself into the general talk.

The conversation was animated, and Ike acquired the startling intelligence that Bub was an Abolitionist, working tooth and nail for the movement in the county. Also, he was somewhat drawn out of himself by an increasing liking for Jabe Munson, the oldest member of the Gang—he was twenty-six—and the only one besides Fred VanSanford adorned with a beard. But in spite of these diversions Ike could not throw off the feeling of sadness that had come over him at the thought of the "Gang" replacing the old association at the Hollow. The mood followed him back to the bank, where, although it was a bright day with the western sun pouring in the back windows, he felt confined by the walls. The air seemed stuffy, like a dusty haymow when you were unloading—only now Ike wouldn't be able to breathe freely again till he had passed the Center on the way home. "Guess I'm homesick," he thought. "Figger I'll get over it pretty quick."

At half-past three, half an hour before Ike's quitting time, Alec Mathiesson came running into the bank, breathless, uncoated, and with his hair awry. "Ike," he called in a dramatic whisper, waving to Master Sherwood and addressing Ike's back where he stood at one of the tall desks behind the counter, studying a book of old accounts. Ike turned around and Alec continued in his excited tone, "How soon can you come over to the shop? I've something to show you that will revolutionize steam engines in America." Ike glanced at his employer, doubting if these extraneous interruptions were proper. "Get over about ten minutes past four," he whispered. And Alec rushed out as precipitately as he had entered.

At four o'clock Ike left the bank, receiving his employer's congratulations on the progress he had made in one day. Ten minutes later he hitched Chesty outside the incipient Byzantium Steam Engine Company, pushed back the closed door and entered. It was dusk in the shop, but Alec had not troubled to light a candle. When Ike entered he was crouching before the open door of the firebox of the little engine, his sharp-cut features and black hair making a fiendish apparition in the orange light. Although Ike had but a few minutes to stay, he nervously took off his coat and hat and went over and crouched beside Alec, the firelight glinting gold on his blond hair. "Let the steam down to save wood," Alec said without looking at him. "It'll be up again in two minutes."

In about that time there was a rumpus inside the boiler. Alec fetched a candle from the desk, lit it from a fagot in the firebox, and stood watching the steam gauge. Ike watched, too, while the pointer moved in pulsations from fifteen pounds up to twenty. "That will do," said Alec. "Now look here."

He lowered the candle to show Ike the new little cylinder bolted above the larger one, the connecting-rod from the small cylinder being attached to the flywheel a quarter of a turn from the connecting-rod from the larger cylinder. "You see, with this compound cylinder," said Alec, "we use all the expansive power of the steam. Instead of being wasted in the air after it's worked in the small cylinder, it goes into the big cylinder and works all over again." He straightened up and looked triumphantly at Ike. "Do you see, you old banker?"

Ike nodded, at the same time glancing nervously at the pressure gauge, and Alec poked him in the ribs. "Do you realize, scared cat," he said, "that with this compound cylinder we are almost doubling the power per unit of steam and thereby almost halving the amount of fuel necessary! And that between this and the water-tube boiler we have the *first really economical stationary steam engine in America!* The first one suited to wide commercial uses! To really compete with water power and drive a big machine

like a—" "Napier press?" suggested Ike in a tense whisper, for his mouth
was dry. "Exactly," said Alec, "a Napier press for Applemore's *Democratic
Union*. Do you realize, my boy, that *if he works now our fortune is made?*"

"Watch your pressure," interrupted Ike pleadingly. Alec sniffed indifferently, glanced at the gauge and saw it climbing past thirty. "He's tested
for eighty," he said, "and we'll guarantee forty, but without a load even ten
would do the trick. Now watch." He opened the throttle valve. There was
a hissing leak from the small cylinder, then the flywheel moved and accelerated rapidly. Alec shut the throttle, turned to Ike, clapped his greasy hand
on his shoulder, and said, "Do you see?"

"She works, don't she?" said Ike vaguely, really more impressed by the
fact that the engine had gone at all than by the fact that it had these mar-
vellous features. It was the first time a steam engine had been seen in operation in that part of the country, except by the young inventor himself.
"Watch your gauge," begged Ike, for he could see that it was nearing
thirty-five.

"Want to see the safety valve work?" asked Alec. "We'll set it down to
forty and the pressure'll get there in no time." "Sure grit," said Ike with
frightened eagerness. This was a terrific test! It was here, he supposed, that
the engine was likely to blow up!

By means of a screw Alec moved the weight on the safety valve from
eighty back to forty, then led Ike over to the desk and started enthusiastically to show him the working drawings of the new compound cylinder.
"All we have to do now," he said, "is to make a clean drawing and send it
to the patent office with thirty dollars and a blank filled out and—" he
spread his arms to indicate that the world would be theirs.

"What about the gauge?" asked Ike, jerking his head in the direction of
the engine standing not ten feet behind them in the darkness, its firebox
door outlined in red, and heavy gurgling noises coming from the boiler.
Alec walked up to it with the candle and Ike peered over his shoulder. The
indicator was already at forty and Alec stepped back, treading on Ike's toe
and giving him a frightful start. "Squirts steam too much when it goes off,"
said Alec. "Ought to have an envelope of some kind. Very easy to make. If
you've time, I'll knock one out now and hook it on," and he started over to
the bench.

"What about the pressure?" said Ike in a tortured voice. "Oh, it'll go off
in a moment," said Alec, going over to the bench and leaving Ike as it were
alone with this deadly monster. Suddenly there was a seeming explosion
and Ike jumped back so quickly that he tripped over the edge of the pile
of sheet iron and fetched up lying on it. When he sat up the safety valve

was still hissing out steam at a diminishing rate. Alec apparently had noticed neither the discharge of the safety valve nor Ike's panicky tumble.

Cautiously Ike tip-toed back to the engine and stood casually close to it, as if he had been there all the time. Suddenly the valve spit at him again, but less decisively this time and he held his ground. "That's sure grit, Alec," he called casually, "and I give ye my heartiest congratulations. I'm afraid I'll have to be running home to chores. Could ye make the engine go just once more?"

"Of course," said Alec as he walked over to Ike. "You do it this time. That safety valve will stop spluttering as soon as the engine starts. Here's the throttle. Here, use this rag—he may be hot."

Ike turned the throttle a little. There was a hiss of steam and the wheel began to turn. As soon as it was swinging round easily Alec said, "That's enough. No use shaking him to pieces without a load." Ike took his hand off the throttle. The flywheel accelerated a little and settled into a regular, rattling rhythm with a clank to it. "Yankee-doodle-Yankee-doodle-Yankee-doodle-Yankee-doodle," said Alec, and Ike began to keep time with his hands. "Yankee-doodle-Yankee-doodle-Yankee-doodle-Yankee-doodle—," they said together, Alec grinning at Ike's amazed delight, while the engine rattled on.

"Want to hear him shriek?" asked Alec. "I forgot to tell you about the whistle." Ike was entranced and merely waved assent, while he crouched watching the wonderful swing of the connecting-rods and flywheel, and continuing to whisper, "Yankee-doodle-Yankee-doodle-Yankee-doodle-Yankee-doodle." Alec squatted down beside him, holding the end of a leather thong which he had attached to the whistle. "Hold your ears," he whispered. Ike did, and the whistle split the small building. "Yankee-doo-dle-Yankee-doodle-Yankee-doodle," the lively engine rattled on. "Lemme yank that," said Ike, taking the thong from Alec and laughing as the little monster seemed to scream in the middle of his head. He let the whistle go and there they crouched, young inventor and young financier, at the center of their world, grinning at each other and their machine rattling its endless, absurd, prophetic music—"Yankee-doodle-Yankee-doodle-Yankee-doodle."

At last Ike rose, saying he had to skedaddle, and he hurt Alec's hand with his too spontaneous grip. All the way home Chesty trotted to the rhythm of Yankee-doodle-Yankee-doodle-Yankee-doodle, and the whistle screamed in Ike's brain throughout that night.

CHAPTER XXXIV

ON WEDNESDAY noon the Squire and Sarah drove into the village behind Mol and Pol, using the carriage because the recent snowfall had been insignificant. On the Squire's part, the object of the expedition was to accompany Ike on his first appearance at the senatorial gathering round the cider barrel at the rear of the Blackwater County National Bank. On Sarah's part, the purpose was to get Ike a second best utility suit for daily wear in place of his now overworked best. In response to Master Sherwood's invitation, they dined at his house, along with Ike and Alec Mathiesson.

Soon after dinner, and before the men returned to work, Sarah, neatly bonneted, flowingly cloaked and in holiday spirits, launched out into the village alone and on foot. Both her grandmother and her mother had belonged to fabulous sisterhoods whose fruitfulness, it was impudently said, had rendered non-incestuous marriage no longer possible in Blackwater County. Sarah herself declared that she was cousin to most of the decent people and all the scoundrels in the village. Consequently, her visits there were of the nature of progressive family reunions, during the long and enthusiastic course of which the Squire found himself obliged to attend to other matters.

Sarah had barely emerged from Master Sherwood's gate and was starting down Washington Street with her nose high and her cloak swinging when she was first summoned in by Cousin and Mistress Jabez Forest, then, on entering their gate, was called back by Judge VanSanford—husband to her cousin—and, so detained, was quickly surrounded and immobilized by Cousin Lydia Bentham, who chanced to be passing, by Cousin Freelove Price, who ran all the way across the street without a wrap to kiss her and drag her in the direction of her house, and by Cousins Meshack Holman— hired man to Washington Wycomb—and Dan Adams—hired man to Horace Gadston—who came running up with brooms in their hands. At the height of this reception Mistress Mehitabel Gadston, being driven out shopping, passed down the great avenue, and no one noticed the lofty nod she bestowed on the boisterous group.

A few minutes later, when the Squire, Master Sherwood and the two boys started downstreet, the reunion was still in progress, and they were compelled to stop, the Squire dispensing greetings and wearing such a grin as might have been evoked by an incorrigible daughter of whom he was fatuously fond. Promising everyone faithfully to return for supper, Sarah broke away under a shower of kisses and proceeded downstreet, flushed and happy, and for the moment restrained by her bodyguard of four men. At the bank they released her upon the Mall, where, as more and more people returned from dinner, the reception approached such proportions in front of (Cousin) Seth Marlow's store that Constable (Cousin) Hank Haverstraw, at first unaware of the occasion of the hurra's-nest, sauntered up from Wheeler Corner in the interest of the public peace.

At length, having suffered some slight disarray, Sarah worked her way eastward toward the Liberty Tavern, where she aimed specially to reassure Susan Stark (not her cousin) of her affection, after the dreadful incident of the death of Dandy. Later, when she had got Ike his suit and the men had gone to their meeting she would go up to the Fultons'. It was there she really intended that they all should sup.

At three o'clock Sarah, Ike with Chesty, and the Squire with the rig met by prearrangement at Dr. Jephthah Starbuck's "Checkered Store"—so painted for publicity purposes—on Court Street. The prospect of any store suit impressed Ike beyond the possibility of critical judgment, so, during the trial of coat after coat he merely stood up his straightest and awaited the consultations of Dr. Starbuck, his pa and his ma. At length they settled on a heavy brown worsted, built special, so Dr. Starbuck said, for bankers, lawyers and such, having a doubled seat, the patch hidden under the coat-tails and removable when frayed so as to leave the pants thenceforth as slick as new. There followed the purchase of a much-needed silk hat.

Burdened with the bundle and the box, the three Lathrops emerged from the store. Sarah and the Squire climbed into the carriage and, with Ike following on Chesty, trotted through the Mall and up Factory Street to the Fulton Mansion on Fulton Lane. Ike stabled Chesty there and Sarah settled herself for the rest of the day with Lorinda Fulton. The Squire and Ike rode back in the carriage to the Mall, turned up Gadston Street, drove in beside the Blackwater Bank, blanketed the horses in the shed, and entered by the side door for Ike's initiation into the mysteries of the famous cider barrel.

The venerable fellowship was already assembled when Squire Lathrop and Ike entered the rear room of the bank. The tall, central stove was humming. There was fresh sawdust on the floor. On a table at one side rested the social barrel, with an array of tumblers. The air was already streaked with hanging cigar smoke and most of the company was seated in low, tavern chairs in a rough circle between the stove and the barrel.

Outside of the neophytes George Fulton and Medad VanSanford, the only man in this circle still in his fifties was Perez Price, Squire Fulton's partner and not a native of the county. Master Marshfield, Judge Van Wyck and Squire MacLeod of Chalons Township—Sarah Lathrop's uncle—were over seventy. In their sixties were Howell Sherwood, Squire Fulton, Judge VanSanford, Solon Samson and Humility Halleck, proprietor and editor of the *Blackwater Eagle,* venerable opponent of Applemore's three-year-old *Democratic Union.* Outside the circle and alone at the end of the mantel over the boarded-up fireplace, stood arrow-straight, six-foot-three, hawk-eyed, lean-featured Squire Staunton, patriarch of the district, close friend of Henry Clay, himself retired from Congress only two years before at 79, at the end of his tenth term. On a table across the room from the cider barrel, with one knee drawn up in his clasped hands, sat Squire Sample of Round Harbor, fifty years old and the baby of the company. His mother was the daughter of a French count, and he lifted his shoulders and eyebrows slightly when making a point in some tale with which he was now regaling the seventy-year-old Reverend Ira Bentham of the First Presbyterian Church.

It was a group of old men that Ike was now joining, mostly of the generation whose life spanned the great events between the military revolution of 1775, fought under a profession of democracy, and the political revolution of 1828 that made the profession a fact. Most of them had been Jacksonian Democrats, but under the local democratic ascendancy of Ostrum Applemore all had now turned Whig except Squire Staunton, Judge Van Sanford and Squire Lathrop. It was a group of old men most of whose sons had moved away or had demonstrated their inability to carry on the local intellectual and moral tradition against rising industrialism. Squire Staunton's only two sons who remained in town were pottering pedants who kept the bookstore. Master Marshfield's two sons were both clerks in his bank, both fat little bachelors in their forties and never referred to except collectively as the "Marshfield boys." All but four of the rest were childless, sonless, or their sons were good-for-nothing. Only George Fulton, little Numa Samson, the three VanSanford boys and the three Lathrop boys still offered any promise of stepping into their fathers' shoes.

When Squire Lathrop and Ike entered, Master Marshfield, with the aspect of a cheerful, beak-nosed little old woman and manners so gentle it seemed any fair wind might blow him away, came forward to greet them and, with the Squire following, took Ike around for the formal introductions. Though he knew them all well, Ike was greatly impressed by the occasion, and when Squire Staunton offered him his hand, assuring him of his pleasure in seeing him there, Ike took it with a feeling of reverence, as if he were being welcomed to the seat of government by George Washington. The main group, already settled in chairs, greeted him informally, each giving him a nod and a smile and shaking his hand without rising. Only rosy-complexioned Squire Fulton, his pa's best friend after Solon Samson, stood up, patted Ike's hand between his two chubby ones, led him to the barrel and drew him a glass of year-old cider. "Isaac, my lad," he said, as he handed him the glass with a roguish smile round the same brown eyes that were George's, "when our sinful old friend Isaiah Marshfield invited ye hither, he took ye forever from the care of that severe man, your pa, and from now on you are bound to drink all the good cider you're o' mind to. Here's welcome to ye, my lad." He lifted his glass and took a copious swallow. "Thank ye, John Fulton; thank ye, sir," said Ike, likewise lifting his glass, "and I hardly need tell ye what an honor it is to be here in this company." Squire Fulton returned to his chair, and Ike sat down between George and his own pa.

The conversation was now centered round Perez Price, the junior partner of Squire Fulton, the Squire being seldom articulate except in lighter vein, habitually reserving his opinions on all subjects till prepared to announce a decision leading to action. Today Perez Price had troubled the waters with news that the Kamargo Woollen Mill—biggest employer in town, Lemuel Grabbot controlling stockholder—had done a dastardly thing. As Ike sat down and began to listen, Master Price's round, usually smiling face was scowling as he recounted how agents of the Kamargo in New York had hired two hundred recently immigrated Irish who in the spring were to replace as many of their present employees in the mill. Instead of the decent wage of seventy-five cents a day, they were to pay them forty-five cents, and they were to be housed in cheap hovels to be rented to them at five dollars a month, most of these hovels to be erected on the long strip Grabbot owned between Factory Street and the River. These Irish immigrants, Master Price said, were people accustomed to the meanest existence, and were therefore willing to work at this wage.

The reactions to this news were swift and increasingly pertinent. Master Halleck benignly expressed the indignant opinion that this would destroy the pleasant prospect of the River along Factory Street. Master Marshfield feared that it would loose a disorderly rabble on the streets at night. Judge VanSanford prophesied that in the long run it would mean poverty and squalor and a large number of people on the town, a condition that, so far as he knew, had not yet disgraced the county anywhere. Master Price said that two hundred decent citizens would be thrown out of work, with no other employment waiting for them. Moreover, these new Irish laborers, living in rented hovels with little or no ground around them, would be unable to victual themselves as all the laborers did today. They would be dependent entirely on their piddling wages, utterly at the mercy of the Kamargo Mill. If ever Grabbot saw fit to discharge them, they would have nothing to fall back on but charity. Finally, what struck Master Price as the most serious feature was that it set a precedent of profit through immoral behavior.

One positive suggestion after another came up and was tabled. Could the residents of Factory Street claim an easement of prospect and enjoin the erection of the hovels? Could a sufficient fund be raised to buy control of the Kamargo Mill? Could the village pass an ordinance prescribing the specifications of buildings to be erected in given localities? Could the village pass an ordinance placing a minimum limit on wages? Could the village exclude undesirable persons from residence, especially where, as was likely in this case, they were not citizens of the United States?

All these proposals were discussed and discarded. It was agreed that the only course available would be an action for nuisance, and that only after the nuisance had actually arisen. Squire Staunton delivered the final statement of democratic principle applicable to the circumstances. "Gentlemen," he said, "I fear it is improper to attempt any measures to prevent these persons from coming here and seeking their livelihood and establishing homes in any way they see fit. Any other attitude toward them is contrary to the letter and spirit of the Constitution. If they do come among us, it is then for us to instruct them in the duties and privileges of citizenship, to assist them if possible to find more advantageous employment. But it is not for us to dictate to them what they shall do, or to throw prohibitions in the way of their following their own inclinations, unless and until they do indeed prove themselves a nuisance in the community. As for the Kamargo Mill, I believe it is pursuing a short-sighted policy. For a little profit it will bring down on its head the condemnation of the community." "And furthermore," added the Reverend Bentham, "I have no doubt that Divine Providence will shortly put an end to such barbarism."

There was a shifting of positions and a replenishing of glasses. All through the discussion Ike had been fidgety and flushed. He wanted to speak, but was checked by excruciating timidity that dried his mouth, and by the realization that it would be highly improper for a new member and the youngest man there to do otherwise than listen. As the men began to settle back in their chairs and light fresh cigars, George Fulton whispered to him, "If you've something to say, why don't you speak up?" Ike shook his head nervously and shifted his legs for the hundredth time. Then he rose and got himself a second glass of cider.

As he drew it he looked sideways at Squire Fulton, and when he passed him, returning to his chair, leaned down and whispered, "It's no use, is it?" A moment later, as he sat with his eyes on his boots, he heard as from a great distance, and with increasing terror, Squire Fulton's voice: "Gentlemen, I believe that one of our new guests has something to say, and I wish to assure him that it will be entirely proper for him to express himself." "By all means"— "Precisely what we need"— "Let everyone be heard"— came from all round the circle. Suddenly Ike was alone in an agonizing silence. The whole world was waiting for *him!* He dared not lift his eyes. He heard several people shifting in their chairs. He heard a chunk settle in the stove. "Speak up, Isaac," said Squire Fulton's voice again. "That's what we're all here for."

"I hadn't intended to speak," he managed to stammer, "unless privately, to some of you gentlemen, afterwards." "Come, young man," came the voice of Squire Staunton that had been raised its melodious hundreds of times in the Congress of the United States. "We all must make our start some time. If this is your first opportunity, you are fortunate that it comes to you among friends." Ike glanced at his pa beside him, who fortified him with a smile that had pride in it. He looked round the circle, and everyone was giving him the most courteous attention.

"Gentlemen," he said, "I must confess it is hard for me to speak, for I feel deeply honored by Master Marshfield's invitation, and I fear that many of ye—perhaps all of ye—will disapprove what I have in mind. It happens that the problem Master Price has raised is close to one I have been thinking over as long as I could think about anything—and that, of course, ain't very long. It is a problem I'm bound to meet in planning my own life. It is"— Ike's eyes began to darken and the color to leave his face—"it is a question of life or death for all of us folks who believe that our community should continue under the traditions which we represent and which our fathers and grandfathers have represented. If we do not act mighty quick we shall soon see the control of all our affairs pass into the hands of ignorant rapscallions who don't give a continental for the community or anything except getting themselves ahead.

"As I see it, ye'll never meet the threat of this new power of money and machinery by passing laws and bringing lawsuits, nor by talking of liberty to such as these Micks when Master Grabbot is doing everything to make slaves of them. The only way to meet this new power is to take hold of it ourselves and use it in ways we think proper. The only way to beat money is with more money. If Master Grabbot is doing something scoundrelly with his factory, the only way to get the best of him is to build a better factory and take the business away from him."

Ike dropped his eyes and felt himself trembling. He looked up. Master Humility Halleck of the *Blackwater Eagle* was looking at him with a smile of sickly-sweet condescension that infuriated him. But the rest were listening thoughtfully, and Master Marshfield was nodding encouragement to go on. Ike proceeded with increased vehemence across his Rubicon.

"This question of the Kamargo Mill," he said, "ain't but a drop in the bucket; just another little step on the road that leads to the ruin of Byzantium. I want to put a bigger question before ye, a proposition by which ye will be able to control the community for a long time to come—and the only way, as I see it. We all know that in the last campaign Master Applemore promised to get a steam railroad all the way from Uticy. Gentlemen, do ye figger what that would mean? Talk about the Kamargo Mill and their Micks! Just the building of the railroad would employ hundreds of men right away, and as soon as it got started ye'd see new factories going up like crocuses in April. It would mean the opening of all the downstate markets to our products, not just the output of the factories but the cheese and grain and maple syrup of the farmers. It would mean increased wealth and power for everybody.

"But especially"—Ike slapped both arms of his chair in excitement—"it would mean power for the fellers who controlled the railroad. If Master Applemore gets it, it will mean control of the community by Master Applemore and his friends for good and all. If somebody else gets the railroad they'll get the same power. And somebody, *anybody* else can get it if they're willing to jump quick.

"Likely many of ye know better than I do how far Master Applemore has got with his subscription. As I understand it, he has Master Gadston and Master Slocum, and has excused himself for not going farther on the ground that these two, besides himself, are the only public-spirited men in the district. That means he hasn't yet got Master Grabbot, Master Ludlow or Master Wycomb. It means he's failed to raise the money he needs and"—Ike glared challengingly at the smiling Humility Halleck—"the field is still wide open. From what I've read of railroads, $150,000 would do it. Anybody who can put that up can still run Byzantium and keep it decent. Gentlemen"—Ike slapped the arms of his chair violently again—"this is the biggest chance that has come to anyone in this region since Squire Fulton's pa began to develop the water power of the Kamargo."

Ike paused and glanced at the ceiling. The room seemed to be swimming round him. With his head still lifted he murmured, "That's all I've to say, gentlemen."

He dropped his face in his hands and closed his eyes. He began trembling worse than ever and could hear his heart pounding. Otherwise there was not a sound in the room. He felt his pa's hand laid gently on his arm. Without raising his head he dropped his hands, then reached over and laid one over his pa's. It was almost a protective gesture.

Squire Staunton was the first to speak. Ike raised his head and gave him a pale stare of half-frightened courtesy. "Young man, it may be that the picture ye have drawn of the future is true. I have seen many changes in my day, but this, if it takes place, I believe to be the most ominous of all. I am not declaring ye wrong, for I know that at my age there are many new things I cannot quickly understand, many signs of the times I am unable to read. At the moment I can make but one observation, and I pray God it is mistaken. I cannot but regret the fact that young men such as yourself, young men of the finest background and undoubtedly the most liberal intentions, should feel moved to consecrate the splendid energies and imagination of their youth to what, in fine, is no more than a selfish struggle for power."

Ike lowered his eyes again and silence returned. There was a slight stir. Master Halleck had risen and was looking at his watch. But no one seemed to notice him at all, not even Master Marshfield, the impeccable host. Ike felt his earlier panic returning, closed his eyes, and dropped his forehead in one hand. The silence continued. Why didn't they *say* something? Why didn't they *do* something? Did they want him to leave? He wanted to shout, to break that awful silence. But it continued.

At last, when Ike had withdrawn so far into himself that he hardly knew where he was, he heard something he had not foreseen. "I," said Squire Fulton, "will start a subscription for a railroad with $20,000." "I will add $10,000," said Perez Price without hesitation. Everybody knew that that meant almost the full value of the Fulton and Price Mill. Squire Sample crossed the room and casually filled his glass of cider. Standing by the barrel and draining it he said, "I shall be happy to add $30,000." Ike felt his forehead go icy cold. The floor seemed to be rising, and for a few moments he thought he was going to throw up. He closed his eyes, and the talk in the room was blurred and far away. When he mastered himself one of the "Marshfield boys" had been called in and was penning a formal subscription in his beautiful hand on a piece of parchment.

CHAPTER XXXV

D U R I N G the next month, winter and the affairs of the railroad and the Byzantium Steam Engine Company advanced by fits and starts. Besides the original $60,000, a further $4,000 had been raised for the railroad subscription at the meeting where Ike had set off the venture. Thereafter, Ike was to approach Bub Tanofly and the Smart brothers, one a founder, the other a farmer, both Whigs and to be trusted to keep silent. Through Alec Mathiesson Ike was to get in touch with a proper engineer and obtain an estimate of the cost of construction. Squire Fulton was cautiously to approach Jones Ludlow and Washington Wycomb, both rich and nominally Democrats, but both snobs who would like to join the Blackwater fellowship, Ludlow the more decent of the two but talkative in his cups, Wycomb the stronger and less trustworthy but known to have a personal grudge against Applemore. As soon as Squire Fulton had sounded out these two slippery customers he was to set out for Albany, carrying the subscription southward through the towns the railroad presumably would touch between Utica and Byzantium. With him would go Solon Samson, who would see to incorporation at Albany, while the Squire, many times a state senator and narrowly defeated by Applemore in the recent election, would see to getting the charter through the legislature. The utmost secrecy had been enjoined upon all, especially Master Humility Halleck of the *Blackwater Eagle.*

Ike easily landed Bub Tanofly for $10,000 and the Smart brothers promised to contribute $5,000 whenever that sum would bring the total to $150,000. Jubilant over these successes during the first week of the conspiracy, Ike made himself a nuisance in seeking out Squire Fulton almost every day to see if there was any news from Ludlow and Wycomb. But the Squire only told him that good things must come slowly.

Christmas came on and passed. John wrote home ruefully from New Haven that he was going to stick to his plan of sacrificing the winter vacation—probably the spring vacation also—to reading in both the law and divinity libraries, in order to decide whether he should return next year either to law or to divinity school.

On the day after Christmas Alec got a letter from engineer friends in

Albany, saying that a reliable estimate could not be based on so little data, but that it was probable that the railroad he had described could be built for $200,000. Ike hastened to Squire Fulton with this information. Still no news of Ludlow and Wycomb. Ike wondered how long before Applemore would get wind of the plot.

On December 28 Alec rushed into the bank, having got, in the same post, the patent for the compound cylinder and the articles of incorporation of the Byzantium Steam Engine Company. That afternoon, before starting to the Hollow, Ike rode over to the shop at 29 Mill Street and he and Alec held their first "meeting," duly electing Alec President and Chief Engineer, and Ike Secretary, Treasurer and Business Manager.

The following Monday, Ike and Alec revealed to the Gang at dinner the momentous fact of the organization of the Steam Engine Company. Bub got them to promise to let him be the next subscriber to its stock.

After work that afternoon Ike called on Master Humility Halleck at the office of the *Blackwater Eagle* and tried to persuade him of the wisdom of purchasing a Napier press, as the *Democratic Union* was going to do, and a steam engine to run it. With a Napier power press, Ike argued, printing thousands of papers where now they printed scores, the *Union* and Applemore would greatly increase their power in the district. But in order to use the press, they were planning to move to some site on the River. This costly move could be avoided by installing a stationary steam engine. If Master Halleck would install a power press and a steam engine to run it, Ike said the Byzantium Steam Engine Company would deal exclusively with him. This would enable the *Eagle* to get ahead of the *Union* and stay ahead, for the Byzantium Steam Engine Company held the patents that alone could make a stationary steam engine both safe and efficient.

While Ike talked, Master Halleck sat with an elbow on his desk, fondly caressing his forehead with his great quill. When Ike had finished, the little editor's smile of syrupy condescension spread over his face. He congratulated Ike, with gentle sarcasm, on the energy with which he was attacking the affairs of the village. As to the new press, he said he had always suspected that what made a newspaper was *what* was printed in it, not *how* it was printed. And he lifted his little eyebrows in appreciation of his witticism by which Ike must of course be confounded. Ike rose, expressed his regret that Master Halleck rejected his offer, and proceeded to the neighboring office of the *Democratic Union*.

Master Theophilus Bostwick, editor of Applemore's *Democratic Union,* was an earnest but weak man, with some literary fluency, no political convictions, and a genuine interest in modern science and mechanics. He was much interested in Ike's proposal, expressed a wish to publish an article on the new steam engine in the *Union,* and gladly complied with Ike's request to lend him the drawings and specifications of the Napier press, in order that the Byzantium Steam Engine Company might submit an estimate on a stationary engine to run it. He added, however, that Master Applemore was still doubtful of the wisdom of purchasing a power press, and he held out small hope of his adding the cost of a steam engine to the investment. Ike thanked him, and before he rode out to the Hollow, triumphantly delivered the drawings and specifications of the press to Alec.

The days wore by with no news from Squire Fulton about the subscription for the railroad. New Year's passed, with the great cotillion in the Arsenal in the village and the jingling of cutters all over the countryside in progress from neighborly punch-bowl to neighborly punch-bowl. Winter closed down with its two-foot blanket of snow over the village, the township, the county and all that northern country from the Mohawk to the St. Lawrence. The thermometer settled into its normal winter range, between a maximum of forty above at noon and a minimum of thirty below at night. The snow in the highways melted by day under the pressure of runners, then frozen behind them, starting that pavement of ice which would gradually build up to a depth of a foot or two and would remain so till spring. Carriages and shays were put away for good, and runners were fitted on wagons, carts and stagecoaches. Snow lay high over the banks of hay, leaves or manure piled round houses for warmth, and the icicles lengthened from eaves with each midday thaw. Spinning wheels, looms, kitchen forges, awls and harness needles settled into their winter routine, and from thousands of chimneys all over those hills and valleys the smoke rose day and night in pale columns or veered into streamers fraying in the wind.

Chesty, now winter-shod, carried Ike in and out of the village every day. Ike began to lose hope of the railroad and ceased troubling Squire Fulton about it. The Fulton and Price ball, the great event of the year even more than the New Year's Eve cotillion, was announced for Monday, January 13.

On the Wednesday before the great ball, just as the weekly gathering at the Blackwater Bank was breaking up, Squire Fulton began to chuckle and asked, in a tone of mock indifference, whether anyone was still interested in the railroad. If they were, they might like to know that Washington Wycomb and Jones Ludlow were nailed to the mast the evening before to the tune of ten thousand nails each. During the enthusiasm that ensued Master Humility Halleck looked on with a maternal smile, as if all these bad boys were too much for him.

Squire Fulton, Solon Samson and Ike stayed after the meeting to perfect their plans. The subscription was now at $99,000, all they had aimed to raise in the village. The next move was for the Squire and Solon to set out for Utica, to complete the subscription there and in the villages between, then to go to Albany to effect incorporation and get the charter. The Squire asked Solon if he could leave on Thursday or Friday of next week. He said that he himself could not well leave sooner, on account of the ball on Monday.

On Saturday, there began a three-day fall of snow, a fast vertical fall of small dry flakes in no wind, the kind of snowfall that, if you laid a tool down carelessly for five minutes, buried it without trace so that you left it there until spring gave it back to you covered with rust. On Monday, Ike and Chesty had to break trail all the way to the Falls, Ike in his best suit for the ball that evening, but carrying his silk hat in a box and wearing John's coonskin cap bound on with a red muffler. He was to spend the night with the Fultons, his pa and ma to drive in later unless the weather prevented.

That noon Ike went to the Wheeler as usual for the weekly dinner with the Gang. As he entered the front door alone, he recognized in the tap-room at the end of the hall the backs of Theophilus Bostwick and Humility Halleck, great friends—as Ike well knew—in spite of being rival editors representing respectively the warring factions of Applemore and the Blackwater. Just now they were leaning over the bar, their heads close together in typical, alcoholic confidence. Instinctively, Ike softened his tread as he walked down the hall, and as he stepped through the door he caught from Humility the phrases "John Fulton" and "twenty thousand." Ike felt a surge of panic and did something which he afterwards remembered with no pride. He stepped back into the hall behind the jog of the doorway and stood eavesdropping.

The confidential tones of the editors gave him only occasional snatches from their talk—"enthusiasm," "young Lathrop," "Ludlow," "Wycomb." There was not the slightest doubt that Halleck was letting the cat out of the bag. Ike closed his eyes for a moment, trying to think up a plausible way of breaking into the conversation and throwing Bostwick off the scent. When he opened them, something made him glance quickly over his right shoulder, and he looked straight into the eyes of State Senator Ostrum Applemore, that politician having one hand cupped to his ear in an exaggerated, mocking gesture of listening.

Ike's start of dismay was so apparent that, after continuing the dumb show of listening a few seconds longer, Applemore chuckled and whis-

pered, "Hope I didn't startle ye. Figgered if the gabbin' of our literary
friends was so important to you it might likewise be important to me, bein's
ye've joined those grannified Backwaters and are likely plotting the demise
of poor old Ostrum. Anyhow, says I, let's have a drink on it, Isaac, my boy.
If there ain't any honor, at least there can be grog among thieves." And
with that he took Ike by the arm and led him up to the bar a little removed
from the two editors, throwing a salute of greeting to Job Wheeler, who,
through a diagonal mirror he had in the corner, had seen all.

Ike, relieved of embarrassment now that the battle was actually on, said
that Job wouldn't sell him grog, but he'd be honored to drink an ale with
Master Applemore. Job set out their drinks, and immediately the manner
of the local boss became grave and confidential. Looking most candidly into
Ike's blue eyes with equally large, lighter blue ones, he said he was danged
sorry to hear that he had settled in the other camp. He sure grit thought
Ike was taking the wrong tack in lining up with old men all of whom were
fine fellers but whose notions hadn't progressed in thirty years and whose
chief aim was to prevent the village from keeping up with the times. He
said frankly he'd been watching Ike and liked him, wanted to get him in
the organization of the Democratic Party. His pa had always been a good
Jackson Democrat, hadn't he? Master Applemore had no doubt he himself
was making many mistakes. Politics, Ike must understand, wasn't no bed
of roses. But if Ike disapproved of some of the things he was up to, why not
tell him so, and help him set them right, instead of lining up with the other
side, whose chances of getting anywhere were getting slimmer every year.
He always figgered the best way for a young man to butter his parsnips
was first to join up with the party in power. Afterwards, when he'd won
his spurs and had a following of his own, then, if he had some notions of
reform or what-not and couldn't get what he wanted, it might be time to
bolt in some sort of revolt of his own. But if he started in with the minority
party he'd get no experience and likely'd never be heard of at all. That was
horse sense, wasn't it?

Ike saw what he had before been curious about, the personal source of
Applemore's power, this confidential candor, this frank practicality. He
said that, to speak truly, he had no interest in politics for the present, that
he wanted first to learn something about banking—"First-rate foundation,"
interposed Applemore—and that he was almighty interested in steam
engines and the possibility of running machines with them instead of with
water power. He confided the incorporation of the Byzantium Steam
Engine Company, told of the patents it had, reviewed his conversation with
Master Bostwick of two weeks before, and expressed his hope that the

Union would buy a steam engine instead of wasting money by moving its plant to the River.

Senator Applemore gave him the closest attention and Ike began to hope the old fox had really heard nothing of Halleck's revelation to Bostwick. He realized that the "Gang" had all passed behind him into the dining room and were by now well along with their dinner. Nevertheless he felt that this iron was hot. He was just leading up to his main argument of the economies of steam over water power when out of the blue Fate struck him another blow. There was a tug at his elbow and, as he turned, Jones Ludlow, soused to the gills, stretched up to his ear and whispered so that the whole bar could hear him, "Ike, my boy, ye're a true grit lad 'n 'n ind'b't'ble ben'factor t' th' community, t' th' *hul* community"—this with a splendid wave of his arm which upset his glass.

Ike glanced back at Applemore just in time to catch a narrowing of his eyelids before he smiled easily and said, "Friend of yours, is he?" Ludlow, catching not the words but the sarcastic flavor of this, leaned in between Ike and the bar and said, "'N's fer you, Ost'um Ap'more, ye may be 'n a'mighty big tater t'day, but one o' these days this youngster'll give ye yer comeuppance plenty, 'n 'm with ye, Ike, m' boy, with ye clean fr'm th' start-off, 'n I like yer idee top notch—top notch"—this with another swing of his arm which he directed more carefully so as to avoid his glass which Job had replaced.

Ike turned around casually toward Ludlow and gave him a great obvious wink of his off eye as he said, "Thank ye, Jones Ludlow, I look for great things from the stationary engine myself, but I figger it'll take a few years before many people see it." Ludlow caught mistily the significance of the wink and gave way to a drunken chuckle which ended in a hiccough. "Yeah—unnershtan'—unnershtan' p'f'c'ly," he said, then added in another loud whisper in Ike's ear, "we know what kind 'v engine we're talkin' 'bout, eh, Ike, m' boy?" Whereat, catching Applemore's eye, he turned away with another chuckle and addressed himself loudly to Job Wheeler behind the bar: "Great young feller, eh, Job? Finest in town, not a bit doubt 'n it, not a bit doubt 'n it."

At this point, like a hard-pressed infantryman hearing his artillery going into action, Ike heard the voice of Bub Tanofly closing in from behind. "Jones Ludlow, ye god-danged pot-bellied old billy-goat, I told ye t' keep yer dribblin' clam-trap shet about Ike 'n' his steam engine company. I've got a few things t' tell ye that'll be pertickler good fer yer health"—seizing his arm. "Come along out o' here afore I come ye a clout 'n they have t' carry ye out." And with that he swung Master Ludlow out of the tap-room, and along the hall to the front parlor, where he sat him down and began to waken a little sense in his fumy, fifty-year-old head.

"In your engine company is he?" asked Applemore. "Not to my knowing, he ain't," said Ike jovially. "But Bub is"—Ike considered this a reasonable anticipatory statement—"and Bub's a great feller to talk sometimes." "Yer dinner'll be gettin' cold," said Applemore with a nod toward the dining room. "And there's all yer young friends leavin' ye." With that he stepped around Ike, took him by the elbows and thrust him gently into the dining room, where all the Gang, except Alec Mathiesson, were putting on their coats to go. As soon as Ike was out of the tap-room the local boss stepped over to the two editors, who by this time were on the relative merits of *M'Fingal* and the *Columbiad,* and mumbled into his journalistic employee's ear, "Slip out in the kitchen, Bos. I got something to tell ye."

In the dining room the Gang said good-by to Ike, each expressing his gratitude for the pleasure of having seen his back. When all had gone but Alec, Ike sat down with him, and Alec laid before him the estimate he had brought along for the *Democratic Union* engine, some of the figures being tentative. While Alec talked Ike bolted his dinner.

Fifteen minutes later Alec departed and Ike stepped back into the tap-room. Master Applemore and Master Bostwick were again at the bar, Humility Halleck having gone. As Ike came into the room the boss jerked his head at his minion, who thereupon went out with the aspect of a terrier being sent home with his tail between his legs. "Isaac," said Applemore pleasantly but without his political smile, "I cal'late it'd be useful to both of us to continue our little conversation." Ike glanced at the clock, which stood at three minutes of one. "I see it's time ye were back in the bank," said Applemore, "but I promise ye to explain to Howell, and what we've to discuss may be important to him, as it is to you and me." He pointed to the dining room. "Let's go in yonder where there ain't so many ears. Job, tell Mamie to fetch me a plate of victuals."

"First off," said Applemore when they had sat down at a small table opposite each other, "I'd be obliged if ye'd continue where ye left off about the engine and the press. Ye were just warming up to figgers when our friend Jones gave us his little colloquy." Ike knew this was merely a foil for bigger matters to come, but he saw his opponent giving him that engaging, wide-eyed, and undivided attention of his, and he thought that a few points registered now wouldn't do any harm. He launched into the proposition Alec had prepared for the *Union.*

The company could not make a final bid yet, Ike said, because they suspected they could better Master Gadston's figures for certain castings, but the net cost of the engine would not exceed $1,000, might be as low as $900. Applemore interposed with a chuckle that he might have some influence with Horace Gadston. The list price of the press, Ike continued, was $3,000, but that figure included the cost of installation, which was considerable, and the further cost of a demonstrator to operate the press for a week after installation. If the *Union* bought a Byzantium steam engine these incidental costs could be eliminated. Master Mathiesson had studied the latest presses as a part of his engineering training, had been through the Napier factory. He was competent to install the press and instruct in its operation and would do so, as part of the contract, without additional charge; would operate both the engine and the press for a month free if the *Union* wanted him to. The extra charges in the Napier price—for installation and operation—probably ran as high as $500. In other words, the *Union* could buy a press and Byzantium engine for probably no more than $3500, only $500 more than the press alone. The engine would be housed separately outside the main newspaper building, and the Engine Company would give a bond in $10,000 to cover any property damage occasioned by any accident to the engine. In other words the Engine Company took all the risk and the *Union* would enjoy the distinction of owning the first steam engine in northern New York and the first steam-driven press, as far as Ike knew, in the world.

Applemore went out into the tap-room, returned with quill and ink, and wrote down the estimate on the back of a letter—$3500. Then he seemed to be studying it for a long time.

At last he said with the utmost simplicity and candor, "Ye probably wonder what I'm working up to, and it's true I'm working up to something, and though ye may be surprised to hear it, this proposition of yours has something to do with it. As ye likely heard, yer friend Humility upset the cart about yer railroad to my Bos. Don't ever trust them newspaper fellers, Isaac. They don't give a damn for anything but their consarn' literary style. Some day I hope to find an editor's got some sense, but the trouble is the people still want somebody can write like he's been to college. Well, anyhow, Master Humility's upset yer apple-cart, leastwise he busted one side of it wide open. I don't believe ye can put yer scheme through, though it's mighty cute of ye, and I ain't underestimating the influence of John Fulton. What I've to say to you personal is, if ye'll start around with a subscription fer a railroad fer me instead of John I'll give ye a share in it fer every ten ye get, and a good position in the company, with a fat salary, once we've the shebang a-goin'. And besides, I'll take yer engine on the terms ye state, which'll be about $3400, instead of $3500, bein's I'll get Horace to come down the $100 or know the reason why."

He paused and looked at Ike very decently, neither arrogantly nor fawningly, but with a genuine sort of eagerness which Ike couldn't help liking. Ike asked him very casually how far he'd got with his subscription, and Applemore said, with a faint sneer coming into his smile, that he cal'lated Ike had more sense than to ask him that. Ike fell silent for a while, then asked how long he'd give him to consider, adding—what he'd had in mind to throw out ever since he stepped up to the bar before dinner—that Master Halleck had left the Blackwater meeting before plans had been discussed and that things likely hadn't gone as far as he supposed. Applemore paid no attention to this and said, now with a touch of sarcasm, that he was uncommon sorry but Ike'd have to make up his mind right now.

Ike looked long and silently into Applemore's eyes, while his broadest, gentlest smile spread over his rosy face and the older man returned it in his flabby-faced kind, till they were looking at each other with the most complete and friendliest understanding. "Mighty sorry, Master Applemore," said Ike quietly, "I'm uncommon grateful to ye."

Applemore rose, put his hand on Ike's shoulder, and stood smiling down at him. "Figgered ye'd give me the mitten," he said, "but thought ye entitled to a chance to pull out your chestnuts before it was too late. Now ye can have a good laugh on old Ostrum with John and the other Backwater boys. But whatever happens to ye in the future, don't ever say Ostrum Applemore didn't give ye yer chance. And if ye discover from now on—in such little things as buying a piece of property from Grabbot, or a bid by Horace Gadston, or a bill in Congress, or an appointment for somebody, or a little influence at Albany—if ye discover that somehow ye ain't getting the consideration ye figger ye ought—don't be pertic'ler surprised, and don't waste nobody's time running to Ostrum Applemore about it."

Ike continued to beam up at Applemore, till his smile began to nettle the Senator and his lip curled. "And as for your pip-squeak railroad," he began, "ye hain't the chance of a candle in the snowstorm out yonder." At this Ike's eyes seemed to darken a little. Applemore checked his vindictive impulse, and his friendly smile returned. For a moment they looked at each other again with perfect understanding. Then the Senator gave Ike a pat on the shoulder like a pat of encouragement, and walked out to the taproom to get his coat. A moment later Ike followed him out into the blizzard.

CHAPTER XXXVI

W H E N Ike left the Wheeler the wind was rising and the snow was driving level. He hurried to the bank, got Howell Sherwood's permission to take off what time was needful from now on, wrote and sent a note of explicit instructions to Bub Tanofly, walked up to Master Sherwood's stable, saddled Chesty, rode circuitously to Squire Fulton's office, and held a secret and convivial conference with him. At 3:30 he emerged with a note for Solon Samson in his pocket and the scent of Squire Fulton's brandy on his breath.

Because of the blizzard it was already dusk, and Ike and Chesty had a two-hour battle with the drifts, and presently with the darkness, in reaching the Hollow, Ike using lanes and by-ways in order to avoid detection. The only casualty occurred when Ike, floundering through a wood lot, leading Chesty, took a header over a stump and tore his best pants. He arrived about chore time and plowed straight down into the glen to deliver Squire Fulton's note to Solon Samson. Solon agreed to stop for him at the Lathrops' about half-past six.

During supper Ike was so excited about this opening of the real battle for the railroad that he talked too much and missed everybody's reaction when he said he might be held in town a day or so—his pa's beginning to nod in his courteous, detached way, his ma's glances of appeal to him, and Tavie's avoidance of his eyes—he had scarcely greeted Tavie. He did manage to notice that no one was dressed for the ball and showed genuine disappointment when he learned they had decided not to drive in because of the storm. When he had eaten a hearty meal his ma took him up to the loom-room and, while she was sewing up the tear in his knee, asked him if he had forgotten that tomorrow was his pa's sixtieth birthday. "Jumpin' Jehoshafat!" said Ike, "I'd forgot, that's certain!" When they came downstairs the Squire was in the north parlor taking a solitary nip of brandy— an unusual indulgence for him. In the keeping-room Ike led the talk around to how badly he'd feel if he couldn't get out tomorrow of all days, trying to make it appear that he'd known all along what day it was.

At half-past six Solon Samson appeared and sat mounted in front of the barn on his little black horse while Ike saddled Chesty. In the lantern light he cut a gaunt and belligerent figure in his long, black greatcoat, his old beaver hat with the flaps sewn to the rim and now tied down under his chin, his stirrups so long his feet touched the snow, a bundle lashed to the cantle of his saddle, and a stout club in his hand. When they set off in the roaring blizzard Solon took the lead, both he and his horse being accustomed to the night work of the Underground and seeming to know the way by touch. Nothing was said as they waded through the snow at a fast walk except when Solon occasionally turned in the saddle and shouted back into the wind, "Are you following, Isaac?"

When they reached the Center, Solon turned down the pike instead of attempting the by-roads Ike had used in coming out. At his order Ike dismounted to open and close the tollgate, contrary to law. "It is quite proper," Solon boomed to him—for the wind was particularly strong here—"I have a permanent accord with Master Harris and settle the accumulated fees monthly."

As they neared the beginning of the long hill in the cut below Judge Longcoat's house, Solon waited for Ike and bellowed to him to ride by his side for a way, and to be prepared to increase the pace. Not long after, there was a sudden roar in the darkness from the other side of Solon whose horse shied against Chesty, and in the moment of contact Ike felt Solon's body swinging forward and back, until Chesty with a scream leapt sideways into a drift and Ike had to look to his seat. He heard a faint thud and a snarl, then Solon's voice ahead of him shouting, "Now run ye," and Ike kicked Chesty into a gallop that was immediately a series of pitches as he plunged into the four-foot drift in the cut.

"This way—this way—this way, mind ye," shouted Solon, now a good two lengths ahead and his horse throwing back geysers of snow over Ike and Chesty as they labored after him in the darkness. They came out of the cut and galloped on through the shallower snow till they approached the descent of the second hill. Then Solon called back, "Now rein ye in," and as Ike came alongside he thundered angrily, "It's that beast of his Honor, Judge Longcoat, the bitch called Lucille, permitted to roam the highway at night, which is contrary to law." "I never knew her to be loose before," shouted Ike. "Only on tempestuous nights," thundered Solon, "when his Honor doubts there will be credible witnesses abroad. It is for that I carry this club. I am persuaded I struck the animal roundly on the head, which is within the rights of the traveller."

Half an hour later, having skirted the village by lanes unknown to Ike, they stamped into Squire Fulton's barn. A lantern was standing in the door for them, and George ran out to help them with the horses. It was not yet eight-thirty, but Squire and Mistress Fulton had perforce departed to receive at the ball at the mill. In the house George had flip mixed for them, the loggerhead already hot. After two tumblers Solon Samson retired to the bedroom that was ready for him, settled himself in an easy chair by the table and sat reading *The Frogs* without any glimmer of humor in his black eyes. But downstairs Ike was still regaling George with the details of his interview with Applemore and his recent wild ride. By the time they put on their things and started for the ball they were both very merry.

At the gathering in the Fulton and Price Paper Mill no one had noted the absence of Ike and George more quickly than Ostrum Applemore and those of his cohorts who were in on the new game. So relieved was the Senator at their appearance that he strode up to Ike as he emerged from a little room off the office where the men were leaving their things, seized his hand, told him how happy he was to see him, and whispered to him that he'd had a bee in his pants for fear Ike was stealing a march on him. Ike was in fine fettle and whispered back that indeed he had, that he'd just landed Lem Grabbot for fifty thousand. Over Applemore's shoulder he saw Bub Tanofly nodding to him, meaning he'd got Ike's note and was complying with its contents. And behind Bub he observed Joe Kirkwood smiling at all of them, he being the twenty-five-year-old, smart and notoriously unscrupulous lawyer of both Applemore and Gadston.

But Ike was for the dance now, and not at all for business. He whispered to Applemore that he must do the honors, and walked out of the office into the great assemblage. The Senator looked after him till he disappeared, not failing to notice the rumpled condition of his clothes and the sewn tear in his knee.

After greeting both Fultons, Ike made Mistress Lorinda his best bow and invited her to honor him with the Waltz Quadrille, just then being announced by a strain of its music from the violins. There being no new arrivals at the moment, the sixty-year-old hostess accepted, and they joined one of the twenty sets that nowhere near filled the enormous room.

The Fulton and Price ball was numerically and in every other way the big event of the year. Everyone in the county was welcome and it had the aspect of a great family affair, like an impromptu kitchen dance on the grand scale. It was unusually small tonight, there being no more than three hundred people present, for the blizzard had snowbound almost everybody from outside the village. The ballroom was the largest room in the mill, the drying room, and for this occasion the long racks were pushed back into one corner, exactly as chairs and tables would be pushed back for a kitchen dance. Master Fulton, Master Price and most of the other big employers of the village danced with the wives and daughters of their employees, and the workmen in turn led out the ladies of their bosses. Under the social genius of Squire Fulton, everyone felt as easy as he would in his own kitchen. It was the old tradition of the countryside brought to the village, still pure and dominant at the beginning of the industrial age. The music was four fiddles, clarinet, pianoforte and drum.

The Waltz Quadrille being over and Ike having returned Mistress Fulton to her place, he stood for a while giggling with George and Joe Kirkwood who was a blade, though married, and an excellent companion, though dishonest and of the enemy. But even as Ike chatted he found his eye perpetually returning to Pru Stark. Always the belle of the ball, she was tonight in a rich, blonde satin dress, standing with her ma at the other end of the room, a good thirty yards away, while a dozen self-conscious little boys clustered pompously around.

Ike felt an exuberant devil rising in him. When Hull's Victory was announced, he suddenly whispered to his companions, "Here's where I steal a march on John." With an anticipatory skip in his stride he rushed up the middle of the floor before anyone had come out to dance, burst through the cordon of youths before any had made his bow, kissed Mistress Stark's hand with a flourish, bowed to Pru with his irresistible smile, offered her his arm, and led out Prudence Stark for the first time in their lives—the best dancer and the prettiest girl in town—more important to watching eyes, the seller of Dandy and his murderer's daughter, and one brother invading another brother's domain!

Pru was as gay as a butterfly, and even as they were walking out they were already doing little twirls and gig steps that no one in the world but Ike Lathrop could improvise. "This'll give 'em something to gab about," he whispered, and Pru threw back her bejewelled head with a merry little trill. So unanimous had been the astonishment of three hundred seemingly casual glances that even after good manners returned all the eyes to their former concerns, there remained a reluctance on the part of everybody else to come out on the floor. For a moment it looked like a solo, until George Fulton and Joe Kirkwood rushed to the rescue with half-unwilling partners, and thereafter the floor slowly filled.

While they waited, Ike and Pru practiced the new double-time swing by the waist, and, at this, social censure was added to the other meanings of the glances from along the wall. When the reel started in earnest Ike outdid himself, and Pru lost consciousness of everything except what a perfect partner he was and what a joyful time she was having. They balanced, half-turned, and reeled and swung, sashayed, cast-off, right-and-left and swung. And all too soon the music ended and Ike led Pru, swaying her bell-like dress in pretty breathlessness, back to her mama. Ike made his way to the masculine retreat of the office, where his entrance was cheered and Bub Tanofly asked with a sardonic grin, "Liquored up, be ye?" "Figger I am," said Ike with a laugh, and struck the floor with his heel in a conventional caper.

During the rest of the ball Ike was always coming back to Pru. When, long after intermission and supper, he led her out for the White Cockade, for which he was famous, there were shouts of "An exhibition!"—"An exhibition dance!"—followed by a general cheer. The other members of the set were nominated by acclamation,—"Joe Kirkwood!"—"Jabe Munson!"— then a pause. "Squire Fulton!" one of the workmen shouted, and there was another cheer. The Squire held up his hand in laughing negation and proposed, "Tom Sherman," who was one of his foremen and a famous jig dancer. All shouted assent and big Tom Sherman stepped out with little Mistress Freelove Price.

Ike was abashed now and glanced at Mistress Fulton who smiled her reassurances. He was in the soup for sure, and there was nothing for him but to do his dangdest. So he shut his eyes for a moment when the music started, got into the swing with the eight-hands-round and then led off with the audience completely forgotten. As he wove in and out his body above the waist swayed to a rhythm as stately as the minuet while his feet were doing unimaginable, improvised things in perfect quadruple time. He seemed to be floating without effort, but his rhythm at once took the audience and before he had finished his tour with the second couple the whole room was singing and many were clapping his accompaniment. The enthusiasm of the audience subsided a little while Joe and Jabez were doing their more conventional tours, but it picked up again for Tom Sherman who went around with a different step for each couple, always some intricate jig step, noisy and robust and as good of its kind as Ike's more elegant performance.

When they ended, there was a tremendous cheer and Ike and Tom went off the floor with their partners, all arm in arm. "I figger that'll do," Ike whispered to Pru as they left the others and walked back toward her ma. "For *now*, perhaps," whispered Pru, giving his arm a squeeze. "Anyway, you've led me out once," she added, lengthening her step to his, "even if you never do it again." And she glanced up at him with a serious look. "I wonder what John'll think?" Ike said. "What does that matter, silly?" said Pru, and knew instantly she had said the wrong thing. "After all you're his brother, aren't you?" she added, but it was too late. Ike bowed a little too perfectly over her ma's hand, then hers, and took his leave of them. Why had he done it? Pru wondered, realizing that he wouldn't come back that night—if indeed he ever came back.

And of all the people there Ike probably had the least notion of why he had done it. All he knew, as he walked back to the men, was that his old revulsion against Pru had suddenly returned. "Made a danged booby of yourself," he thought to himself, then from another corner of his brain, "Oh, hell—what does it matter?—she's a pretty minx—and we had a first-rate evening." He decided he'd write John all about it in a day 'or so. But in some matters it was characteristic of Ike that a pious determination was sufficient satisfaction of a moral impulse, without the necessity of carrying the determination into action. Strangely enough, it was not from Ike but from Pru herself that John first had a long, written account of this extravagant escapade.

As the house-guest of the Fulton's, Ike was bound to stay out the ball to the final singing of "Home, Sweet Home." He indulged his sense of humor by giving a two-dance rush to tall Gloriana Gadston—whose mother Mistress Mehitabel was wont to give off with an air of erudition that of course everyone knew Gloriana to have been the poetic name of the great virgin Queen. After disposing of Glory, Ike enjoyed himself mightily in the partnership of half a dozen old friends of the Institute days, including Mattie Spencer who had served John and Ike at the Liberty and was now steady bar-maid there. It was near two o'clock when Tom Sherman, the last of the guests, departed with this same Mattie Spencer whom he had escorted to the ball. Immediately the floor was cleared, and while the ladies were still putting on their things, Squire Fulton poured straight rum for himself, Perez Price, Ike and George, and tossed off his own with the uncharacteristic preamble, "Well, that's over."

Outside, the snow was three feet deep on the level, but the footpath along Factory Street had been well trodden down by the departing guests. The blizzard had entirely stopped, both wind and snow, and a few stars were visible. It felt like the coldest night of the year, the mercury likely near thirty below. Squire Fulton was in an unusually detached mood, and no word was spoken as he and Mistress Lorinda crunched home, followed by the two boys.

Three hours later while it was still night and now bright starlight, Squire Fulton's little coach glided out his drive on its runners and turned up Fulton's Lane. On the box was the old hired man. Inside sat Squire Fulton, with the railroad subscription list and gold in the pockets of his calfskin money belt, and Solon Samson, with the application for incorporation, and no gold, in the pockets of his. According to instructions, Mistress Fulton, George and Ike did not come out the front door, but watched the departure, crowded together at one of the parlor windows. The Squire revealed only his hand, which waved farewell from the coach window as its runners squealed away into silence, heading for the State Road.

CHAPTER XXXVII

ALL MORNING Ike was present in the bank not at all in spirit and only fumblingly in body and mind. Not once could he prove a column of figures. He knocked a bottle of ink from one of the high desks and left a permanent stain on the floor. He short-changed several patrons, and over-changed others. At half-past ten he sat down in a chair and put his chin in his hands, determined to will himself fully awake. The next thing he knew Master Sherwood was shaking him laughingly and telling him it was dinner time. For an hour and a half he had been an exhibit to delighted patrons—a picture called "The White Cockade" someone suggested—sound asleep with his head in his hands, breathing heavily.

After dinner Ike revived somewhat, and revised his accounts of the morning. At two o'clock Ostrum Applemore came into the bank, and this brought him fully alert. He saw Bub Tanofly stroll by the front windows a couple of times and knew he was on the job. He made occasion to step next door into Staunton's book store, and there imparted to Bub the great fact of the Squire's and Solon's departure. While there he bought a birthday present for his pa, a new novel called *David Copperfield*.

When Ike came back into the bank Applemore and Howell Sherwood were standing up shaking hands. "A'mighty sorry to do it, Howell," the Senator was saying as Ike came up to them and stopped, as if to enter the conversation. "A'mighty sorry to do it," he repeated, now grasping Ike's arm and smiling, "but your teaming up with this dangerous young enemy of mine is a little more than I can swaller." "Senator Applemore is transferring his account to the Merchants'," said Howell Sherwood to Ike. Applemore and Ike exchanged their frank, mutually understanding looks. The Merchants' was Grabbot's bank. This meant Grabbot had subscribed on Applemore's railroad list.

As Applemore turned to go, Joe Kirkwood strode into the bank with a vicious gleam in his handsome, dissipated eyes. As he came up, his big mouth widened in a laugh at Ike, then he led Applemore into a corner by one of the safes, where they whispered excitedly for five minutes. Finally

Joe nodded agreement, turned, and started back toward the front of the bank. "Don't be late," Applemore whispered audibly after him, and Joe waved understanding with a departing arm. He turned right, up Washington Street, toward both his house and Applemore's, an unusual direction to take in the middle of the business day. Applemore now grew very formal and, after stalling for a minute or two, sauntered out and turned in the same direction. Master Sherwood and Ike exchanged a silent glance, and Ike, with his brow puckered nervously, returned to work.

Half an hour later Bub Tanofly galloped up to the bank on horseback, threw the reins over a hitching-post, and ran in, panting. "Ostrum went home and pretty soon Joe drove down in his own coach. They've gone off on the Center road, which means Howeville by way of Barnes Mills and Berne; means they're givin' up Bethlehem and Paris and figgerin' to beat the Squire into Howeville where old Howe's a sure democrat and richer'n all hell. Take my horse. Every minute's worth more'n a thousand dollars." "I'll take him to Fulton's," shouted Ike in excitement, throwing on his coat. "Mine's there and I'll leave yours in the barn. Howell Sherwood, may I draw a hundred in gold?" "Never mind the draft," said Master Sherwood, counting out the five twenty-dollar pieces. "I'll tend to that," said Bub. "I advise ye to take a money belt," said Sherwood, running back to his desk, producing one from a bottom drawer and buttoning the coins into it. "And here"—springing back to the till with the agility of a sleek, well-tailored monkey—"here are a few notes to carry loose in your pocket."

Ike threw back his greatcoat, undercoat and waistcoat, lifted his shirt, and Master Sherwood and Bub together got the bellyband around him under his shirt, and buckled it fast. "Do ye know yer politics, Ike?" Bub demanded while this was in process. "No, but I'll learn 'em," said Ike, buttoning up again, "and send word to my pa I had to go to Uticy—and send him this book"—taking it out of his pocket —"I got for his birthday—and tell George—and Alec—and otherwise ye don't know where I've gone." He grabbed Master Sherwood's hand, then Bub's, ran out, vaulted onto Bub's horse and was already off when Bub bellowed from the bank so half the Mall could hear him, "And, Ike, don't wet yer diapers." "I likely will," Ike shouted back, and Bub's roan bore him off like a greyhound round the corner at Perkins' Hotel.

The events of the next two weeks passed into the local legends of four counties. How Ike overtook Squire Fulton and Solon Samson just pulling into Paris after a day in Bethlehem. How they laid their strategy during a hasty supper at the big stone tavern: the Squire to proceed directly from rich Whig to rich Whig; Ike to take the Democrats who would be dubious anyway, and Ike's pa being a well-known Democrat; the various points on the route to be called at for messages and telegrams. How that evening Ike had the great Democrat, Squire Howe of Howeville, at his desk prepared to sign for a moderate subscription when His Honor Congressman Applemore and Lawyer Kirkwood appeared; the courtesies that ensued, ending in a substantial subscription for Applemore; and how in the meantime Squire Fulton and Solon had slipped through Howeville to reach the Thurber House at Bloomington at two in the morning. How Ike beat the others out of Howeville on Wednesday, but how Joe Kirkwood bought a saddle horse and equipment at great cost, so that thereafter the forces were about even. How the war worked slowly ninety miles southward on a front of twenty miles, Ike and Joe always out in front, reconnoitering like cavalry and trying to draw each other away from the main advance. How the thing became a game with rules respected by both sides, and in the sport of it the bitterness of the contest for power evaporated. How Ike one day was plowing wearily through the snow up a side road and met Joe returning who assured him on his honor that if he was looking for Master So-and-So that wasn't the road, and how after that they rode together by the right road, and Ike granted Joe the first interview. How Ike once came on Joe in a tavern sound asleep at a table with his subscription list in his hand, but how Ike didn't look at it, merely ordering himself a grog and, when he had finished it, waked Joe and said he thought it was time they were both on their way. How they were forever racing long miles through the snow to remote houses, cutting through back lots and fording streams, the first interview to go to the winner, and to be uninterrupted. How Joe once, seeing Ike behind him, tried to jump his horse over a wall out of deep snow and broke the animal's leg, after which Ike called the nearest farmer who shot the horse and drove Joe into the next village where Ike waited till Joe had bought a fresh mount, Ike trying unsuccessfully to persuade him to take the poorest of the possibilities. How Chesty who had carried Ike through fires and blizzards, one day shied at a rabbit and pitched Ike into a snowbank, Ike letting go the reins and Chesty galloping into the next village where Joe, entering by another road, recognized him surrounded by a crowd, and led him back by his tracks till he found Ike coming on on foot.

How the coaches also raced, and Joe Kirkwood's team was the faster and one day, passing the Squire, crowded him off into a ditch where the coach over-turned without damage; but Ostrum Applemore stopped Joe's driver and sent him back with the horses to help pull the Squire out. How once all five met by accident at supper time at a tavern, supped hilariously together and thereafter spent the whole night playing poker. How each side habitually bribed farmers at crossroads to send the other the wrong way, and how sometimes the farmer rejected the bribe and sent the briber the wrong way. How they lied and boasted and bluffed and locked each other in tavern rooms and did each other good turns. How the subscriptions mounted and with them the fun, for they were all Yankees and hoss-traders at heart and the excitement of the game was worth more than the money. How both sides sent long letters ahead to friends in Utica, each warning of the other "spurious" subscription, so that all the bench, bar and pulpit of Utica were taking sides days before any of the contestants arrived; but Squire Fulton wrote in his most confidential letters that he might not stop in Utica now, though he'd need the subscriptions later, after he got his franchise.

How on Thursday the twenty-third of January Ike and Joe ended by racing two exhausted livery nags neck and neck down the main street of Utica at the dinner hour to the huzzas of the townsfolks on the footpaths, most of them cheering just any horserace but several of the leading citizens guessing who these young bloods were. How Ike and Joe, in the excitement of the race, ignored their actual destinations, raced by "The Busy Corner" with Joe a yard in the lead, and so on thirty rods till suddenly the street dead-ended at an embankment; how Joe's horse leapt for it and fell on top, but Ike's horse balked at it from a dead run and threw Ike clean over it; and how Ike and Joe ended the "railroad war" by sliding out side by side on the clean-swept ice of the Erie Canal, and how Joe, seeing that Ike was going to slide farther, grabbed him, so that they majestically slowed to a stop together ten feet short of the opposite bank. Finally, how that evening, after much railroad business had been tended to—not to mention Joe's dislocated shoulder and Ike's broken ribs—they held a tavern trial in which, Ike complaining that Joe exceeded the rules in grabbing him on the ice, the judgment was given to Ike, and Joe was sentenced to sing "Love and Brandy" and buy grog for the forty-odd members of the Jury.

On the same day the two main armies were executing major maneuvers in the rear. Ostrum Applemore was putting his main hopes on Utica, but Squire Fulton, having pushed his subscription past two hundred thousand just before reaching Henderson, now determined on the final, direct spurt for Albany. Applemore reached Utica late that night, ready for business in the morning. But the Squire put up his whole equipage, including the driver, at Henderson, and he and Solon proceeded at leisure by the night stage, changing at dawn in Utica for the railroad for Albany, thus gaining at least a full day's valuable lobbying at the capitol where the Whigs had a dubious majority in both houses.

What with fatigue, drunkenness, and his painful ribs, Ike was late in carrying out his telegraphed instructions to meet the Squire at the railroad station. He galloped up in the dawn twilight just as the little engine was snorting into its start, chased the slow-moving train down the track, and managed to hand the Squire through the rear coach window his supplementary subscription list which, with what work Ike had done in Utica, amounted to almost $50,000. Before dinner he visited his last two prospects in Utica and, refusing all invitations, returned to the inn. As he hoped, he found Joe there, slumped in a chair, hollow-eyed, his forehead furrowed from the pain in his shoulder, more dead than drunk. Ike said he was done, and Joe agreed that from now on they could let the old cocks fight it out. So after a cold dinner from the bar they went to the room they had taken together, lay down on the bed without undressing, and in perfect accord slept the clock around.

On Saturday afternoon they set out on the return journey, taking three leisurely days to it, the two empty coaches, Ike on a rested Chesty, his ribs not troubling him except at a hard trot, Joe, with his arm in a sling, on the second horse he had bought during the campaign. At the start they solemnly agreed to no skulduggery, but on the last morning out Ike awoke in Paris to find Joe missing from the room. Rushing downstairs in his nightshirt and greatcoat, he learned that he had ridden out an hour before. He pursued without breakfast and found Joe's horse, as he had expected, tied up at the door of a leading Democrat whom the Squire had failed to land. Bursting in without knocking Ike exclaimed, "Joe, that ain't fair!" whereupon Joe laughed and introduced him as "my young friend who is helping me."

Back at the tavern, after they had sent the coaches on, Joe read Ike a lecture while the latter was eating breakfast. "Ike, from now on don't ever trust Joe Kirkwood. Sometimes he'll keep his word and sometimes he won't, you can't ever tell. He likes a good game of poker, but he's out for Joe Kirkwood first. He'll trim ye any way he can, and the devil take the hindmost. His people were like yours not so far back, but it's a rough-and-tumble world now, and I hope ye won't ever trouble again to tell me that something 'ain't fair.'"

From time to time as Ike ate he glanced up at Joe's straight gaze out of blood-shot eyes, the broad smile, at once frank and sinister, revealing the wide, gat teeth, the dark, curly sideburns framing the round, solid, florid face. Listening to him there in the Paris Tavern, Ike could not deny an increasing respect, even a liking for him. And through the rest of that day, as they rode homeward at a walk through the snow-covered hills, Ike was silently reaffirming the decision he had reached before, that in this money game he must always fight this or any particular devil with his own weapons.

It was almost supper time when they reached the village, so Ike spent the night at the Fultons', and did not go out to the Hollow until the following afternoon.

CHAPTER XXXVIII

I K E ' S absence during the last two weeks of January had its reverberations in the feelings of those close to him at the Hollow, especially the Squire and Tavie. On the afternoon of the Squire's birthday, Howell Sherwood's Irish groom brought out the present from Ike and a note from Howell explaining his sudden departure for Utica. This news of Ike's entering into open, financial competition with Applemore threw a pall over the party that evening, the guests being the Squire's parents and Charity Samson with little Numa.

After supper the Squire took his father into the north parlor and raised the question of changing his will so as to leave the homestead to John instead of Ike. Old Thomas countered by raising the question of Ben, who was his own pet and in whom he foresaw a distinguished literary career. When they rejoined the others in the keeping-room, the grandfather pressed home his point by drawing Ben into a discussion of the new poets Tennyson and Longfellow and of the adventure story called Omoo he had read recently. Shy at first, Ben presently warmed to his grandpa's enthusiasm and fell to quoting whole pages, not only of verse but of prose, and doing it for illustration only, quite unconscious that there was anything remarkable in it.

The following day the Squire started woodin', and since it was too early for community woodin' and there were still plenty of winter repairs to tend to, he didn't take the two old hired men with him. Every day he went out with his snowshoes, ax, saw, gun, and a dinner put up by Sarah, and spent nine or ten hours alone on Lathrop Ridge, up back of the Oakses' and his father's house, where he still owned a hundred acres of virgin timber. He diverted himself with all kinds of fancy cuts and difficult fells. He took out a tump-line and enjoyed the strain of hauling together and piling logs that were load enough for a horse. But he couldn't keep Ike out of his mind. He would suddenly stop with a tree half-cut and gaze into the cold distance, while silence repossessed the forest, livened only by the snowy flutterings and busy calls of the chickadees.

On Wednesday the twenty-second he rode in to the meeting at the Blackwater Bank, and got the latest local news:

Master Marshfield announced that, having learned of Humility Halleck's revelation to Bostwick of the secret of the subscription, he had written him a note of regret that henceforth they would be compelled to dispense with his friendly counsel on Wednesday afternoons.

Tuesday morning last week, the morning after the blizzard and the ball, when Judge Longcoat's hired man had been plowing out the cut below his house, he had come on the frozen body of the unfortunate Dane bitch Lucille, the skull broken, apparently by a blow.

Perez Price read a letter from Squire Fulton, posted the day before, chronicling some of the droll events of the railroad war, saying that he had high hopes of raising the full two hundred thousand, and that everything now depended on success in Albany.

Altogether, the company of his friends, their enthusiasm for the railroad and admiration of Ike's enterprise did much to draw the Squire out of his recent depression. He returned to the Hollow that evening in lighter spirits.

Meanwhile, Tavie had been continuing her daily commuting between her home and the Lathrops', now perforce on snowshoes, either in darkness or in the cold twilight of early dawn. Ever since Ike had seen her home that evening in early December she had felt creepier in taking the half-mile walk at night than at any time since her childhood. As she approached the cemetery she always stared boldly in the direction of the ghostly, gravestone-like birch and forced her mind to remember Ike's laughing exposure of the specter. As long as she knew he was up there in the Lathrop house behind her, she had little trouble in downing the eerie terror. But on the very night in mid-January when Howell Sherwood's groom brought the news of his sudden departure for Utica, as soon as she had lashed on her snowshoes, put up the hood of her cottage cloak and set out in the darkness, she was attacked by such a spasm of panic as had never come over her before. Even through the surges of her fear, she knew the cause of it. Ike had gone away, and she was alone. She had submitted to him more than she intended in letting him kiss her down there in the glen. Ever since, she had been drifting self-indulgently. Boldly she tramped on to the fork of the Lower and Upper Roads and stopped, determined instantly to get herself in hand.

And instantly she did. Who was Ike, after all, but a boy who attracted her as many another boy would no doubt do in the future? An irresponsible boy who was shamefully unaware of the great things going on in the country, a boy with whom she had nothing in common at all. She, Octavia Samson, second in her class at Oberlin, friend of Mrs. Mott, the greatest woman of her time. Indeed she was lucky that Ike was not congenial to her, lucky that it was not John who roused in her these irrelevant feelings, John with whom she did indeed have intellectual sympathy. With Ike her battle would be easy, and, having won that, she would thereafter be stronger to combat the more serious temptation that would come later, in the person of someone like John, someone who would really be one with her in devotion to the cause of Reform.

Her trembling had stopped. With proud determination she clumped along on her snowshoes in the darkness, descending the drifts that now buried the corduroy. When she passed the little Lathrop cemetery it was too dark to see the gravestones and the ghostly birch. But she stared arrogantly in their direction, and when she felt a creep start up her spine she stamped her snowshoe with a thump and said loudly, "Octavia Samson!" And thereafter the creep did not return, at least not as it had before.

During the two weeks of Ike's absence, Tavie's recaptured independence was strengthened from other sources. Twice in the first week she got packets of long, pathetic letters from Constant Oaks, letters full of jerks and scrawls, written as the wagon trundled westward, letters written at Abbington, at Roaring Corners, at Syracuse, at Rochester, and at Cleveland, letters of deep, consecrated devotion, homesick, lovesick letters, yet diaries full of the strange new people they were falling in with and full of the little misadventures of this first, mild part of the long journey.

Finally, on the Wednesday the Squire went into the Blackwater meeting, there arrived a surprise letter posted at Oberlin. Constant had decided that California was not for him. He had thought of coming home, but was ashamed to do it. He had gone by coach to Oberlin, because he figured Aggie would be there, because he wanted to see where Tavie had gone to college, because he hoped that before long she would come there again. He had spent New Year's with Aggie and Homer, but had not wanted to write home till he was settled. Aggie and Homer were mighty hopeful that before long Tavie would come and occupy the spare room that had been his. Homer was quite a spark in the village, though he had no dealings with the college. He had just found Constant a first-rate position as clerk in one of the general stores. He would start there tomorrow and had taken a room in a boarding house where the landlady recollected Tavie well, because she had taken her meals there for a spell. So, Connie said, they talked about Tavie, and he felt mighty at home. He hoped Tavie wouldn't mind what he'd done. If she wanted him to go away when she came he would be ready to do it. He felt about her the same as ever, only maybe more so.

As a crowning piece of reassurance Tavie received two days later a most friendly letter from President Mahan of Oberlin College. He wanted to assure her that her application for a position in the Female Department was being seriously considered, although there were no openings at this time and he was unable to give her any definite hope.

Thereafter for five days Tavie sang at her work. She was more independent than ever before in her life, free of self-doubt, free of Ike, free of spooks in the glen. She was ready to do battle with the world. Sometimes the creepy feeling returned when she was plodding home past the cemetery. But now it had nothing to do with the graves or the old birch. It had more to do with sounds, with gusts of wind through the frozen branches. The gusts were voices that seemed to call continuously, "Octavia Samson—Octavia Samson." Sometimes it was the voice of Mrs. Mott or of Mrs. Stanton, sometimes the voice of President Mahan of Oberlin, or of Dr. Finney who had been Tavie's favorite teacher there. Once it was the voice of William Lloyd Garrison, the abolitionist editor of *The Liberator*. More often they were unrecognizable voices that represented the suffering and downtrodden of the nation.

But Tavie was not deceived. She knew these voices were only her own imaginings, that it was only her ma in her. After a few days she decided that she was listening too eagerly to them. They might involve some kind of a temptation she could not understand. Also it was tedious business trudging back and forth over the deep snow, especially going uphill in the morning. So one evening almost two weeks after Ike had gone away she convinced her ma of her independence of him and got her permission to stay up on the hill, at least while there was so much snow. She would come home often but not every night. On Monday, the twenty-seventh of January, Sarah Lathrop reinstalled her in the little north bedroom off the back attic. Henry Hawks would sleep in the loom-room or with Ike in the big bed in the boys' room.

A while before supper the following day Tavie was peeling potatoes at the sink. Behind her, Sarah was stirring broth on the crane. The Squire and Ben were reading in the keeping-room. Henry Hawks was up to chores alone, and Master Lane, in the corner by the outside door, was trying, with some glue and a patch of leather, to mend a hole in the bellows of the little forge whereon he hammered out nails and tacks every evening.

Suddenly Tavie felt a catch in her throat as if her heart had stopped. Then she heard the steps of a horse in the drive, then steps on the planks of the barn, then running feet out in the court. The outside door burst open with a bang against the back of Master Lane's chair, and Ike rushed in like a cyclone. "Mind yer god-dinged knittin'," growled Master Lane without looking up.

Tavie heard Ike behind her embracing his mother to the sound of a muffled "Ma" and a responsive "Isaac," then heard him turn and with equal vehemence embrace his father who had come out to meet him. She knew that her turn would come in a moment and her nerves went into a whirlpool. But she was not unprepared for this, and when Ike spun her around, seized her joyfully in his arms and gave her a great cold-faced smack on the mouth he might as well have been kissing the stone hitching-post out on the drive.

"Well, Pa," said Ike, at last finding his voice in his excitement, "did ye think I'd run off to Californy? All the way to Uticy I was just too danged occupied gallivantin' to write letters, and after I got to Uticy I figgered I'd get home as quick as a letter would. By Crimus! it's never been so good to get home. Have ye a—" he checked himself, remembering that he wasn't in a tavern with Joe Kirkwood.

But his pa caught the inference. "It strikes me," he said, "the return of the prodigal son might be the occasion for a little toast before supper. You must be chilly after your ride." "No, thanks, honest, Pa," said Ike, ashamed of his first impulse. "All I want is just to know I'm home again, if ye can forgive me for running off the way I did. Figger Bub or somebody let ye know, didn't he?" The faces of the Squire and Sarah showed no doubt as to his welcome and his forgiveness.

Suddenly he turned back to Tavie, who had resumed her potato peeling. "What's up, Tave? Ye're glummer'n an old owl. Come on, let's see if ye ain't still good for a turn or two." And he seized her again and spun her round half a dozen times, she assisting with such determined independence that she never got in step with him. As he released her, Ike gave her for a flash that quick, curious pucker of his brow, then turned back to his parents and to Ben, the latter having just come in and standing unnoticed in the corner. "Been taking good care of the old folks, have ye, Runt?" he said, grabbing his little brother by the shoulders and giving him a good shake. "Hey, there, Master Lane, can't ye say howdy to a stranger?" he continued, slapping the seated old man on the shoulder. But Master Lane only grumbled, and the Squire made Ike a gesture of drinking to show that he was in his normal, winter condition.

"Well, where shall I begin?" said Ike, hanging up his silk hat and swinging off his coat. His ribs were giving him fits from all this activity but he decided to conceal the worst for a while. "Let's save it for after supper, eh, Pa, for I want all of ye to listen. It's the biggest thing's ever happened in this town since old Jonah Coughlin cut down the first trees and made his cabin." Ike rattled on, and Ben slipped out to put up Chesty for him.

"He's certainly in his best fettle," Tavie thought, shuddering as if she were hearing voices. For a moment she considered the wisdom of going home after all. But then she mentally sneered at herself for a coward. This was only the beginning. Every victory she won from now on would make the next easier. She caught her breath with a great, sudden sigh and admitted that the battle was on. She carried the colander of potatoes to the crane and dropped them into the ready kettle of boiling water. She was relieved when Ike followed his pa into the keeping-room. When Sarah wasn't looking she closed her eyes and said in her mind, "O God, hearken now to Thy servant's prayer."

After supper Ike insisted on waiting until the dishes were washed and put away before telling his story, so that Ma and Tave could join the men—all the men except Master Lane who returned to his pottering. As Tavie pretended to listen, she kept her eyes on the rag-rug, on the desk, in her lap, anywhere but on Ike's face. Presently she realized from the full impact of his excited voice that he was looking at her and probably noticing her inattention. So she looked up at him with her jaw tightening and thereafter kept her eyes on him.

Surely he had never before been so handsome. As she watched him she found herself automatically relaxing, even taking an interest in whatever adventure he was recounting. But every now and then she caught herself up and her face took its set expression again. At last, after getting a gasp from his ma and a chuckle from the men with his account of the slide over the Erie Canal, he confessed to his broken ribs, and at that Tavie felt positive relief. Subconsciously she was glad there was something wrong with him, some helplessness in him; not maternally glad, not glad that there was some way in which she might solace him, but simply glad to have discovered a weakness in him, some ineffectuality behind the hurricane of his presence.

The others were instantly all solicitude and compelled Ike unwillingly to check his narrative. His ma must see at once how they had bound him up. As Ike started to take off his coat and waistcoat, he threw his old, world-inclusive smile at Tavie. His disrobing gave her the pretext she wanted, so she curtsied good night, turned into the kitchen, and went upstairs to the little spool bed that was now hers again.

An hour later Ike was alone with his pa over cigars and brandy-and-water in the north parlor, the Squire having led him in there because he thought matters might come up that he would prefer to keep even from the ears of his wife. All through the evening he, as well as Sarah, had been noticing a change in Ike, not only his high color and rough and chapped complexion—the results of exposure—but a new and unmistakable air of self-confidence, two or three new wrinkles at the corners of each eye, a new way he had of shifting his look suddenly to a new speaker or listener with an imperious air, an air of readiness for action, an air of command. The Squire felt, with a relaxation at first so expansive that it dwarfed misgiving, that here for better or for worse one of his life's jobs was done, that he was in the presence of the first of his sons to have grown to man's estate. And whatever else he might be, he was a man of force, a man who would make his mark, whether for good or ill.

For a minute or more after they settled over their drinks in the gilded chairs of the north parlor the Squire and Ike sat in congenial silence, the Squire luxuriating in these paternal vainglories and Ike's sensitive soul catching their reverberations, while each glanced alternately from his glass to the other, glanced sometimes shyly, sometimes frankly, communicating without words between those warm human centers that were almost identical in father and son. At last they broke simultaneously into unabashed grins at each other, lifted their glasses together, sipped, set them down, and were ready to talk.

"Sort of calculating to give me up for a bad job, are ye, Pa?" said Ike with a sly smile. "Perhaps," said the Squire with a chuckle, still holding to his relaxed mood though he knew it would not last. "True grit, Pa," said Ike after a pause, "were ye greatly concerned about my skedaddling off that way—your birthday and all?" "Not much," said the Squire, lying cheerfully for his peace. "Naturally, when we had no word from ye we grew concerned for your well-being. I blame ye for not writing to us." "So do I," said Ike. "There just ain't any excuse for me that way."

"I am delighted you were with John Fulton on this trip," said the Squire. "Of all men I know, he is most certainly beyond moral reproach." "That's right, sir," said Ike, scenting danger. From that moment the exuberance of both father and son evaporated, and the Squire's mien became at once serious and more confidential than was his wont with his children.

"Isaac," he said, "I want to talk to ye from now on more like a friend than like a father. What has occurred to me tonight is that all of a sudden you are a boy no longer but a man grown, and from now on I want to treat ye as a friend, and I want ye to treat me as a friend—a friend that's more than commonly concerned for your welfare."

"Thank ye, Pa," said Ike, loving his pa with all the human intensity of his soul. "Maybe I ain't old enough yet, but I think I understand what that means to ye, having had me—all of us youngsters—around the house so long. I promise ye I'll do my dangdest to deserve it."

"Now then," resumed the Squire, carefully controlling his emotion, "as I have indicated before, your interest in machinery has my hearty approval. It is only this business of your eagerness to make money that still sometimes troubles me. You give as a reason for it your belief that money instead of integrity and intelligence is going to be the criterion of authority in our community in future. You say that you desire to make money in order that we Lathrops may continue as influential in the affairs of the town as we have been heretofore. You once said that your chief aim is to be in a position to help John to the performance of public duties which without money it would be no longer possible for him to perform. Now I want to ask ye whether in your heart you are perfectly certain that these are the real reasons, whether there ain't perhaps some deeper cause for your anxiety to make money, some desire in yourself that has nothing to do with John or any of the rest of us."

Ike thought for a long time, turning his glass in his hand. "Yes, Pa," he said at last, "I guess there is another reason. I guess it's true I like making money anyhow, just for the fun of it. Ye know I've always been a great feller for hoss-swoppin', for that matter any kind of a game where I had a chance of getting the best of the other feller. True grit, I don't give a continental dang about having money. But I guess I do like a game like this railroad squabble we've been having. It's like pitching horseshoes, or swoppin' hosses—only more exciting.

"But at the same time," Ike added, sitting up vigorously and looking straight at his pa, "I doubt I'd go in for making money if I didn't have these other reasons. I'd figger it would be wrong to you and the rest. I ain't talking poppy-cock when I say I figger the Lathrops are going down hill if we don't get some more money in the bank. And I ain't talking poppy-cock when I say I want to help John in politics and put Ben through college. I ain't making up excuses when I say my aim's to help the family. It's just that everything seems to pull together for me and point the same way. I like to make money anyhow, and the time's come when the family needs some such feller as me out scraping round in the snow and busting his ribs to get a franchise ahead of somebody else who's minded like he is. There ye have it, Pa, and I don't figger I could tell John, or Jared Oxbow or Manuel Swift any more."

The Squire rose and straightened the candle. Ike pushed the little fire together. "Will ye fill your glass, son?" the Squire asked. "No, thank ye kindly, Pa, this'll do me nicely." The Squire was feeling pleased with Ike's candor. They sat down again, and again communicated for some time in silence.

"I must ask your forgiveness, Isaac," the Squire began again, "for continuing to catechise ye, but while we're on these subjects it would perhaps be wise to have it all out on the carpet. As I understand it your plans for making money will involve considerable—shall we say, competition?—of the kind you have just now engaged in, this rather than taking regular work at a salary and rubbing pennies together till you make them stick?" "Some of both, I figger," said Ike.

"And these deals necessarily involve some pretty sharp trading, do they not, very similar to the traditional methods of hoss-swoppin'?" "Just keeping quiet at the right times and putting in a word at the right time, as I see it. Nobody yet has ever accused me of lying in a hoss-trade—though I can't say as much for everybody in the world. Everybody knows the rules and fellers that break them—like Stark and Grabbot—and—Joe Kirkwood—sort of lose their standing."

"But some of the people you must deal with will break the rules sometimes." "Most likely," said Ike. "Well, are you not afraid of being affected by these sharp practices, being, as they say, blackened by touching pitch?"

"Well, Pa, I'll tell ye. If ever in a big deal I should catch anybody lying to me I'd figger to give him back as good as he gave, and I cal'late it wouldn't hurt my conscience greatly. But outside of that I figger to keep on playing clean, like I always have. Pa—since we're talking straight—ye mustn't get it in your head that I'm up to anything wrong! A feller may make a big mistake sometimes, but deliberately breaking the rules everybody knows is another sort of critter."

"All I am asking," said the Squire, "is that you always be sure of your own conduct. Since you are sure now, perhaps it is not unreasonable for me to make a request—a request that is no more than the right of a friend. If ever you find yourself troubled in conscience about anything you have done or anything you propose to do, I would take it as a kindness if you would bring it to me?" "Of course I will," said Ike easily. "Anything at all?" pressed the Squire. "Yes, sir."

Ike looked down for a moment, then up at his pa with a smirk. "Women too?" "Yes, by all means include that too," said the Squire with an easy smile, "though that wasn't precisely what I had in mind."

"What's Tavie mad at me about?" Ike threw out impulsively. "Hadn't noticed she was," said the Squire. "Well, she is—seems mad at me most of the time, scowling as if I'd swiped some taffy from her, and touchier'n a heifer."

The Squire lifted his eyebrows and said, "Ummmm—you'd better watch out, Isaac. Sometimes when women act that way it means they're setting their cap for ye." "That's nonsense, Pa." Then he added with casual bravado, "Why, I never even kissed Tavie in private but once—oh yes, twice." "Well, ye'd do well to keep your eyes open," said the Squire with a pleased smile, for he thoroughly approved of Tavie. "I will," said Ike. "I ain't figgering to get tied up yet a-while to anybody, not for a good long while."

The Squire took this statement indifferently, but Ike sank into a severe reverie. He'd best not monkey with Tavie any more. He remembered how she'd asked him to kiss her down in the glen. Something in him was flattered at the thought that she might be after him, and for a moment the perennial dream of fornication surged through his nerves. Then immediately something cold and much stronger possessed his will, something that had crossed the ocean with all his ancestors two hundred and more years before, something of indelible race, of a race that now for many generations had lived under the domination of the mind, something hard and healthy, something clean and joyful and lofty and touched with scorn.

The Squire watched his son's face with understanding. He saw that decisive manhood return that during the recent discussion had lapsed back into the boy. "Pa, ye mustn't fret about me," said Ike suddenly, turning straight to his father's gaze with that new air of authority he had acquired. "I've my job to do and I see it clear."

"I believe ye," said the Squire. "Shall we go to bed?"

CHAPTER XXXIX

T H E battle for the railroad franchise was won at Albany on the first. of February, when, after much lobbying on both sides, Squire Fulton's application for a charter for the Utica, Bloomington and Byzantium Railroad was granted, and by the same vote Senator Applemore's application was turned down. On the following Wednesday morning the Squire and Solon Samson stepped quietly from the coach at the Liberty, bringing with them the charter that both established Byzantium Falls as the future industrial center of northern New York, and paradoxically vested control of its principal industrial asset in the old group that, with the exception of Squire Fulton and Bub Tanofly, was not rich and, with the exception of Squire Fulton, Perez Price, Bub Tanofly and Ike Lathrop, was actually hostile to modern industry.

That afternoon at the Blackwater meeting Squire Fulton made his report, Ike being present but his pa not having come in. Among many other anecdotes of the railroad war the Squire told how one evening in Albany Applemore had called on him and Solon and tried to blackmail them. Applemore said he had a letter from the Honorable Bodacius Strong—Member of Congress from their district and Applemore's puppet. It appeared that the majority of Congress was still in favor of Clay's Compromise of last September. In consequence, more rigid enforcement of the Fugitive Slave Law was about to begin, and their district of northern New York was scheduled among those to be first attacked. Representative Strong said that, while he was powerless to prevent enforcement, he might for some months be able to divert it from the district to other regions. He sought advice as to whether public opinion in the district would be in favor of this diversion, or whether it would prefer to face rigid enforcement immediately and get it over with. Applemore had said "with his open smile" that he was seeking Solon Samson's and Squire Fulton's advice as to what he should write to Congressman Strong. Squire Fulton had suggested that the Honorable Bodacius Strong be left to exercise his own most statesmanlike judgment, and afterwards had proposed a toast to the hope that Applemore, Solon Samson and himself might have the pleasure of meeting in prison as soon as the new railroad could carry them there.

Following Squire Fulton's report, the Blackwater meeting fell into a long discussion of the Fugitive Slave Law and Clay's Compromise generally, Solon Samson maintaining that the Law should be opposed as unconstitutional, Squire Staunton advancing the view that the primary object was the preservation of the Union, and that to this end the Fugitive Slave Law and Clay's Compromise should be supported, whether the Law was constitutional or not. In a silence near the end of the debate Squire Sample asked, "And may it not be that one day these two issues of slavery and the Union may be joined and become a single issue between North and South?" "That," said Squire Staunton, "is precisely what we must struggle to prevent, for that single issue will be the issue of civil war."

"Then let us face it," said Solon Samson. Squire Staunton stared at him in weary sadness. He had seen his brother march off to die in the Revolution, and had himself been wounded in 1814 in the bloody Battle of Round Harbor. The little debate ended futilely, as thousands of other little debates had been ending for thirty years in every city and village and crossroads, as they would continue to end for ten years more during the trial of Clay's last effort at compromise, while the shadow of that "single issue of civil war" advanced and withdrew, advanced and withdrew, but at each advance was a little nearer, a little darker, over the nation.

After the meeting Solon and Ike rode home to the Hollow together, both under the genial influence of cider. As they were walking up the second hill they gradually overtook a yellow glow which turned out to be a lantern in the cutter of His Honor Justice Longcoat, being driven home by his hired man. Both Solon and Ike bade good evening to His Honor, giving their names, for they were in darkness whereas the Judge's mammoth face was illuminated by the lantern. He was clearly startled by their sudden advent out of the night, and, after he had mastered himself sufficiently to return their salutations, his face settled into a heavy scowl of angry suspicion.

Solon Samson cleared the suspense, his voice rich with well modulated sarcasm. "With regret, sir," he said, "I learn that I had the ill fortune to kill your dog on the evening of January thirteenth while passing your residence on my way to Byzantium Falls. I wish to convey my sorrow at this intelligence, for it was not my intention to compass the death of the animal, and I struck with no more violence than was reasonable under the circumstances, the dog being loose on the public highway and in the act of attacking me with great ferocity."

The Judge had suspected as much, but was now flabbergasted by the suddenness and candor of the confession, especially as he knew as well as Lawyer Samson did that he had been in the wrong in loosing the dog on the highway and had no legal leg to stand on. So he merely mumbled, "The animal was a bitch, sir," rolled up his big eyes in the lantern-light and fell silent. "I stand corrected, sir," said Solon. "And a good night to you, sir." Touching his hat, he kicked his skinny little mount and posted ahead, Ike following him into the darkness.

On the following Monday, the tenth of February, the coaches of Squires Fulton and Sample carried the subscribers from Blackwater County to the first stockholders' meeting of the Utica, Bloomington and Byzantium Railroad, which opened that evening in Bloomington, the non-subscribers Solon Samson and Isaac Lathrop also attending. That evening and the following day the corporation was formally organized, Squire Fulton being chosen president, and the vice-presidencies, the treasuryship and the corresponding secretaryship going to other towns. To Ike's astonishment, when these elections were completed, he heard someone from Utica nominating *him* for executive secretary. And the next moment he heard himself being voted a salary of $1,000, and being qualified to hold office bv a gift of seventy $100 shares of stock.

Ike had hardly collected his thoughts after this complete surprise—for Squire Fulton had kept Ike's prospect a secret from him—when he heard the meeting passing certain specific instructions for him. The executive secretary would proceed at once to invite representatives of engineering firms to a conference, and, as soon as an approximate route could be agreed upon, to invite bids for the construction of the road. Also, he was instructed to enter upon a study of the methods and costs of operation of railroads and to be prepared to report at the next stockholders' meeting, which was called at the same place for Tuesday, April 15th. Speaking to these instructions, Ike said that, while he believed he would be able to prepare a report on operations in time for the April meeting, he doubted if the engineers could supply bids before summer, since they would be unable to start their surveys until the snow melted.

The next day the Blackwater contingent set out homeward at dawn. Ike was glad to ride with the driver on the box of Squire Fulton's crowded coach. The sun came up gold on a dazzling white and blue winter day. For most of the morning he sat in silence, his chin in his mittened hands. In the center of the wide, empty landscape, it all seemed incredible to him, a dream that had not really happened. Two or three times he looked up at the old coachman, then back at the coach, and turned round to listen to the voices inside. Yes, they were undoubtedly there inside, undoubtedly returning from an event which had really happened. Besides his job in the bank, his interest in the Steam Engine Company, his share of stock in the Tanofly Paper Company, his mortgage on Redemption Quin's store, he now had a salaried job of $1,000 a year, was possessed of an interest in a railroad worth almost $7,500 now and potentially worth two or three times that. And most remarkable of all, he was the active head of the railroad, the fellow who was going to do the real work. He was already a wealthy man, already a power in the new, industrial Byzantium.

The next morning Ike went over his plans and his duties to the railroad with Howell Sherwood. Between them and his further duties to the Steam Engine Company, it seemed impossible for him to continue full-time work at the bank. At the same time, he wished eagerly to continue his banking education, learning more of mysteries of loans, collateral, the floating of bond issues, all the major business of a bank as a source of commercial credit in the community. It was agreed that for two hours each morning he would assist Philip with the accounting as he had been doing heretofore. In return he would receive no salary, but Master Sherwood would instruct him, at hours and places convenient to both, in the principles of credit, especially the financing of new industries.

After dinner at Master Sherwood's, Ike entered upon his new schedule which freed him from the bank in the afternoon, and walked with Alec Mathiesson across the river to the Engine Company. His immediate concern was the exciting necessity of installing himself where he could prosecute his two major interests at once, writing letters, holding conferences, studying, storing the papers that would accumulate. He and Alec decided that a front corner of the shop could be cleaned up, floored, and partitioned off. Buoyant at the prospect of the dignity of having his own office, Ike set out to find a carpenter and stopped on the way to report to John Fulton.

To his surprise the Squire disapproved. Because of the heavy responsibility involved in the affairs of the railroad, he felt that the president and the executive secretary should be under the same roof. He proposed to turn over to Ike the little room off the main office of the Fulton and Price Paper Mill, the little room where the men had left their things the night of the ball. He would charge no rent for it and, since the railroad was getting free quarters for its chief business, he suspected it would not object if the executive secretary prosecuted his other interests in the same office.

Ike was aghast at the magnificence of the proposal. The room was about fifteen feet square and had its own pot-bellied stove in the middle. Being at the southwest corner of the factory, it had two windows looking westward down the river and two southward at the level of the east end of the Mall, the buildings in the immediate prospect being successively The Liberty, Van Ness's block, the Baptist Church—with the dial of its clock visible at a narrow angle—and the Universalist Church.

Ike at once set out to furnish his new office. He betook himself to Van Ness's Cabinet Store, a block away, and within an hour he and Pete Van Ness had carried over a dull-stained, small cherry desk with three drawers under the top and compartments for ledgers in the sides, three second-hand tap-room chairs, and—inevitable mark of any forum for dignified discussion—a large cuspidor which Ike placed in the center of the room beside the stove. These major items being installed, Ike walked the length of the Mall to Ostrum Applemore's General Store—selecting this in preference to other emporiums for his own ironic amusement—and returned freighted with three ledgers, a quire of foolscap, envelopes, a standish with two inkwells, two quills, a box of nibs and a sand box, a bundle of rubbers, and half a dozen sticks of sealing wax.

It was after four o'clock before Ike had all this equipment put away and paused to sit at his empty desk in solitary glory. "Yes, it's true, sure grit!" he said in his mind. Here he sat, after less than three months, in a position of authority as great as that of any young man in town. "Yes, greater, by Jimminy!" he said aloud. There below him through its gorge roared the Kamargo—*his* Kamargo. A mile farther down, on the opposite bank, stood the Tanofly Mill—*his* mill. Across the river, out of sight from here, was the Engine Company—*his* Engine Company. Here, right here, was the office of the railroad—*his* railroad. Yonder, a little below the level of his eye, stretched the village—*his* village, among whose busy five thousand there were not two dozen men as influential as he was this minute. "By Jumpin' Juniper," he whispered to the emptiness of his office, "the Lathrops ain't dead yet."

CHAPTER XL

DURING the two weeks since Ike's return at the end of January, Tavie, now re-established at the Lathrops', had been stewing in hotter juice than she had bargained for. Several times she had been compelled by sheer faintness to show Sarah Lathrop her distress by pleading indisposition and retiring to her room in the midst of one of Ike's enthusiastic accounts of his doings. Ike, on the other hand, having determined, after the talk with his pa, to meddle no more with Tavie, kept the resolve easily, treating her again with the friendly and straightforward indifference which had characterized their childhood and which was in contrast to the self-consciousness he had recently felt and shown as a result of kissing her. Again he was breezy with her, strong, self-assured, full of gaiety, easy of manner, maddeningly unobservant, absolutely self-sufficient and without any need of her at all.

And, the more impregnably Ike resumed the armor of chastity, the more Tavie loved him and the more poignantly she became aware of precisely what that love meant. Perhaps if she had tolerated a veil of virginal self-deception between her mind and her desire, the fiend that persecuted her might have let her off with a little temporary hysteria, an occasional fit of inexplicable weeping, an occasional outburst of scorn for Ike. But Tavie was not of the stuff of hypocrisy, and her knowledge of the carnalities of life was not only clear but proudly clear. Not only did she know exactly what she wanted but she romanticized that knowledge and, with all the power of a fiery, fanatical imagination, heightened the power of the attraction even as she battled with it. She lived perpetually with a scream incipient in her throat. Of all forms of madness she suffered that most wretched form in which she knew she was mad and why, and in which the knowledge only increased the madness instead of soothing it. And the fiercer the fight became, the more furious became her determination not to turn and flee from it. She would defeat this monster now once and for all, in order that she might thereafter escape to the fulfillment of her great ideals for the betterment of the country and mankind.

To make the victory complete when it should come, she shut her full little lips upon every impulse to seek solace by confiding in her ma or in Sarah Lathrop. Sarah saw her predicament clearly enough, though she was unaware of Tavie's frankness in facing it. She gave the girl every opportunity to talk to her, but would have thought it at once bad taste and bad policy to shock Tavie's maidenliness by opening the subject.

The Squire also observed Tavie's state and discussed it, at first lightly, with his wife. Like Sarah he marvelled at Ike's easy indifference, but attributed it to his excitement in the novelty of his new adventures, and was satisfied that if Octavia did not leave for new employment before spring she would never leave. In their whispered conversations in bed the Squire playfully professed admiration for Ike's power of resistance. But before he went to sleep he usually lapsed into troubled wonder at his favorite son whose impulses seemed to be running counter both to family tradition in external affairs and to normal, healthy behavior in these more personal matters.

As the first half of February passed and Ike seemed to reward Tavie's increasing nervousness with nothing but increasing indifference, the Squire grew solicitous for her and more and more annoyed at Ike. And since he had shut his strong will upon his disapproval of the boy's business doings, that disapproval now reinforced his resentment of Ike's conduct toward Tavie. The Squire's own sense of responsibility became involved. He conceived that he had no right to keep his friend's daughter in the house to no end but her own discomfort and humiliation. Yet before speaking to Solon Samson he must be quite certain of Ike's attitude; and having talked with him so fully on the night he returned from Utica, and got his promise to tell him of anything that was troubling his conscience, he felt reluctant to bring up intimate matters again. So for a while yet the Squire simply took every opportunity to pet Tavie, and hopefully bided nature's good time.

During the three nights and days of Ike's absence at the Bloomington meeting of the railroad subscribers, Tavie brightened up considerably. Being essentially a sturdy person, her youth reasserted itself and she even looked back on the last two weeks of distress with something like amusement. She re-read her letters from Constant, from the President of Oberlin, and a more recent one from that peerless leader Mrs. Lucretia Mott. On the Wednesday when Ike was expected back she went about singing, and just before supper dashed up to her little room and reappeared in her best calico and her most fetching hair ribbon and rosette.

But instantly she came down to the kitchen again, a cold fright seized her, not desire, not consciousness of Ike, but simply meaningless panic. Sarah and the Squire observed that she was suffering a chill and that, keeping herself busy with unnecessary service, she ate nothing but a nibble of unbuttered bread and a sip of tea. When supper was over and it was apparent that Ike was not coming, her gaiety quite suddenly returned. After the dishes were put away and the kitchen mopped she stood with the Squire, Ben, Master Lane and Master Hawks behind Sarah at the harpsichord and contributed vigorously to the singing of "The Wounded Hussar," "Kate Kearney," "The Sea," and others of Sarah's favorites.

The next day Tavie kept reassuring herself that all would be well, that the trouble with her last evening had been that she had been silly enough to try to make herself attractive, that it was letting go in such little things that released the larger devil in her. Besides, it was the time for her to feel flighty and nervous anyway. It was nothing but the beginning of the usual discomfort that had made her want to dress up and appear gay, not for Ike's benefit but for her own. She would not make that mistake again. That evening she would not even put on a clean apron for supper. She didn't give tuppence whether Ike came home that night or not.

Thinking these determined thoughts, Tavie was mixing a bowl of Sally Lunn for supper, standing by the drip board at the sink in the kitchen. The big clock in the front hall chimed once for four-thirty, and Tavie beat the batter more vigorously, knowing it would require about an hour in the Dutch oven. Suddenly she was taken with a cramp and, pulling over a chair, she sat down and took the mixing bowl on her lap. Her ears began roaring like a heavy wind, and her heart began to thump as if it would jump out of her chest.

Presently, it seemed to her that the thumping was that of a horse's hoofs. Then she recognized it as Ike's horse Chesty, just now walking up the South Mall out of the Falls. She saw Chesty, and Ike on him, as if from some point close to them on Washington Street. She saw the people they passed, and Ike touching his plug hat to them. Now she was herself sitting on Chesty's haunches behind Ike, first sideways, then astride. When he began to trot each stride was like a knife in her, for she was somehow prevented from rising to the trot. And all this time she was still stirring the mixing bowl to the rhythm which was at once her heart and the gait of the horse. When they reached the Center she jumped down from Chesty with a sudden stab of pain and, while somehow running along beside Ike in the deep snow, was dimly aware of pouring the Sally Lunn into a baking tin, pushing the fire together, and setting the tin in the Dutch oven before it.

After that she continued her duties as if it were not herself but some other who was doing them, and she was but faintly conscious of what went on around her. She chopped up vegetables and threw them into the pot with the boiling chunks of venison haunch. She sliced the bread and the ham, fetched in the milk and the butter. She lifted out the table and set it. She did not realize that Sarah was giving her a hand at all these things and had spoken to her without getting a reply. She was but faintly aware of the men coming in from chores, the usual stamping, throwing off of wraps, blowing of fingers, washing of hands and faces in the basin.

All this time she felt herself in reality to be again riding behind Ike on Chesty, and trying to call to him, but he could not hear her for the noise of Chesty's hoof-beats and the roar of the wind in their ears. She did not know that her calls were mumbles and that Sarah Lathrop heard them and understood them. She was aware of riding up the hill and into the drive with Ike, but his actual entrance into the kitchen impressed her no more than the other activities there. She did not see Sarah Lathrop gesture him and all the men into the keeping-room, and close the door after them. All that impressed her was that now she was back in the Lathrop kitchen, that Ike was now somehow inside her and that she was about to give birth to him.

More clearly than the other recent happenings, she became aware of Sarah Lathrop before her, felt her take hold of her hands, and heard her say, "Octavia, dear, will you not go upstairs and rest?" At this, Tavie's will stiffened automatically, though her head was still confused about her actual condition. "No, thank you kindly, Sarah Lathrop," she said, "I am quite able to serve supper." "If you will not go up and rest," said Sarah, "then I must beg you to go home to your parents for supper and to visit them for some time. Your pa will have just reached home, and you have not seen him now for several days."

Something in this suggestion swept through Tavie's nerves like a clear, cool wind. Her conscious mind was still half-deluded by the notion that she was pregnant, but her whole unconsciousness surged to this hope of escape and rest, sweeping away for the moment any sense of guilt in running away from her battle. "That is very kind of you, Sarah Lathrop," she said with eagerness. "If it is your wish I shall indeed do it." And with that she seized her cloak from its peg and threw it around her.

"John Lathrop will be anxious to walk home with you," said Sarah a little tentatively, turning toward the closed keeping-room door. "Oh no, he must not do that!" whispered Tavie excitedly. "It will be a bright night. I am much better alone." Sarah was of the same opinion, so she did not press the matter. She merely kissed Tavie, looked lovingly into her eyes, stood in the open kitchen door after she stepped out and was lashing on her snowshoes, and waved her farewell as she started off, softly gallumping out the drive.

As soon as she was gone, Sarah opened the door of the keeping-room, beckoned to her husband and whispered to him. Donning only his coonskin cap, he went out the kitchen door, drawing it softly shut behind him. Gingerly he walked alongside the house where the snow was trodden and peeked around the great bank that contained the lilac bushes at the front corner. Although the moon was new and only an hour up, it was a brilliant, starry night, much lightened by an active borealis which was hidden from the Squire where he stood beside the house. In her dark cloak he could see Tavie against the snow as clearly as if it had been daylight.

It was a warm night, almost up to freezing, and she had not put up her hood, so that the Squire sometimes caught a glint of light on her golden hair and suffered wistful moments thinking what he would do if he were in Ike's situation. Having turned into the road, she had slowed her pace, until she actually stood still a moment between each forward step. At the fork in the roads she stopped completely and stood with bowed head, her two clenched hands against her breast. Suddenly the Squire saw her head straighten up, and she said, "Octavia Samson," in a loud, ringing tone. But a moment after she lowered her head again and raised one elbow across her face. Then she bent slowly forward and seemed to be letting herself down until only her head and shoulders were visible above the shallow snow bank on this side of the Lower Road.

The Squire stepped into full view and started to run to her through the two feet and a half of snow in front of the house. But after a few steps he checked himself, and returned quietly into hiding. She was only kneeling. Her attitude was voluntary. It would be cruel, unless it became clearly necessary, to let her know she had been seen.

Tavie continued for some time in an attitude of prayer, with her head bowed, and the Squire could hear her speaking softly, though he could not make out what she said. At length her head lifted and soon after she gave a sudden start backward as if falling. But she did not fall. In a moment she straightened up to her full kneeling height and spread her arms wide, holding this position for a long time. She was at a spot where the sky was open through the trees above her and the Squire noticed how the light of the stars or the borealis, striking her hair, glowed golden around her head.

Finally, she resumed her talking in a low tone, and shortly rose, continuing to hold her hands out before her. Then she laughed a gay, healthy laugh and started off, clump-clumping rapidly down the road. As she walked she broke into "The Son of God goes forth to war," singing it lightly and in double-time to her snowshoe stride. Her song grew faint in the distance, and her step faded away in the glen.

Hastily the Squire returned to the kitchen door, lashed on his snowshoes, and set out in stealthy pursuit. From the point where Tavie had knelt her tracks went regularly down the road and, holding himself concealed behind the trees short of Solon Samson's clearing, the Squire saw that they continued up to the front door beside which her snowshoes leaning against the clapboards gave conclusive evidence that she was inside.

"What a high spirited child she is!" he thought. And, trudging back up the road, he was so filled with compassion for her and with anger at his son that he did not once look around at the fine borealis that behind him was licking up from the northern horizon almost to the zenith, filling the atmosphere with little crackling sounds like fire. At supper he said the blessing as if he were extremely put out with God, and sat down to table in a state of silent rage such as was extremely rare with him.

It was a morose and taciturn meal, the Squire keeping his head bent over his plate, and Master Lane glancing up from time to time to scowl at Ike. Neither Henry Hawks nor Ben had any notion of the significance of Tavie's sudden disappearance, and if Ike had any faint suspicion it was painlessly strangled in his unconscious by the iron hands of his mental self which he had made his whole self during the past three weeks and in terms of which he proposed to continue to live untroubled.

After supper and prayers the Squire asked Ike with unnatural formality to accompany him into the north parlor. Although uninvited, Master Lane hitched after them with his angry, rheumatic gait and, having shut the door behind the three of them, shook his fist in Ike's face. "John Lathrop," he said, though actually addressing Ike, "I ain't practiced in nosin' into the affairs o' father and son. But I'm bound t' tell ye that girl's the image of her grandma. She's a true blue high-spirited youngster if ever I see one, and if I was half yer size and double yer age I'd hoss-whip ye within an inch of yer life." And with that he gave Ike a sharp slap in the face with the back of his knotty hand and waddled out of the room mumbling.

Ike got from this senile challenge only amazement, untouched by any twinge of conscience or flash of perception of the true condition of Tavie. When his pa had reclosed the door, he said simply, "Poor old duffer. I figger he's referring to the old story about him and Mistress Jolam." "I daresay," said the Squire icily, without any show either of amusement or compassion for Master Lane. Instead, he came directly to the point, without his usual offer of brandy and cigars, without even suggesting that they sit down.

"Isaac, I must ask ye whether you are entertaining any serious intentions toward Octavia?" "Why, no, Pa! Ever since ye gave me a word of advice a spell back, I've been particularly careful to let her strictly alone."

"And if ever it appeared that she *did* entertain serious feelings toward you, would you continue to let her strictly alone?" "Why, yes, sir, that would be my plan, at least for a good spell to come. Naturally, if I found that we were more than friendly interested in one another I'd have to think about marrying, but I'd like to avoid marrying for some time yet, at least until some of these things I'm poking into have got themselves turned into money in the bank."

"Very good," said his pa. "Now I must ask ye further whether Octavia has ever given ye any indication of entertaining any special feeling for you." "No, sir," said Ike quickly, but lifting his forehead with false surprise that was meant to convey to his pa that he was lying, that of course he could not make any such revelations respecting a woman. The Squire caught his meaning, and enjoyed a moment of partial satisfaction in realizing that at least Ike was adhering to the external code of decency. But whereas Ike was conscious only of lying in refusing to reveal the one time when Tavie had asked him to kiss her down in the glen, the Squire took it that he was virtually admitting an understanding of Tavie's passion for him, and was expressing his indifference to it and her feelings, her only too apparent suffering.

"Very good," said the Squire again, wheeling abruptly and opening the door. "But, Pa," said Ike, with a sort of cold panic flooding through him, "if ye figger anything of the kind 's troubling Tavie, then—likely one of us—should leave the house." "I shall attend to that," snapped the Squire, and he walked out, aware now of a gulf between him and his greatly loved son so deep that henceforth he must not even attempt to cross it openly, however much he might cross it in spirit and suffer from what he found on the other side.

CHAPTER XLI

A S S O O N as Tavie had turned from the Lathrops' drive into the road, before supper that evening, she had come fully to her senses. The recent delusions at once evaporated and she knew that she was showing the white feather; she was running away from Ike. Her palpitations and the ringing in her ears stopped, and nothing of abnormality remained but a heavy physical weakness in which her mind seemed to detach itself from her body and she saw things with extreme clarity. She paced slowly and thoughtfully along the road, wondering whether she should not go back and face the music, even if it drove her crazy, or whether she might not be able to carry on her fight better in the long run if she went home, as Sarah Lathrop obviously intended, for the duration of the present time, perhaps five days more.

As if in response to the mere thought of returning into her ordeal, a little spasm of pain stabbed her, and in reaction against it her defiant will instantly set her jaw. Then the cramp returned a little stronger, and the challenge of her will was a little more fierce. By the time she reached the fork in the road all her former physical agony had returned, but this time she enjoyed no escape into the recent delusions, nor did she hear any encouraging voices calling to her from the outer night. There was nothing in the world but dull weight and slow, meaningless, grinding pain.

In a desperate sally of spirit she stamped her foot and called out, "Octavia Samson." Immediately the world was all flickering lights, and each ray was a little knife-jab in her vitals till they fused again into the single, dull, heavy anguish. She felt her knees weakening and, shielding her eyes with her arm to shut out the cruel lights, she knelt down slowly on her snow-shoes. "O God," she prayed, "O God of women, must my ordeal be so hard? Can there be no end? Can there be no victory? O God, if there be a compassionate God anywhere, tell me now what I should do. I am not afraid, and I will do it, while I live."

She continued kneeling, opening her soul to whatever higher power there might be to help her. The weight of pain and depression lightened and her mind cleared again, as if detached from her flesh. All around her, as if from the trees and the sky, she heard little crackling noises, gentle, un-frightening trills, like children laughing. Then they became words, the old voices calling to her. "Tavie," they kept saying, "Octavia—Octavia—Octavia Samson." Slowly she straightened up on her knees and opened her eyes. The world was full of dancing light as before, but now there was no pain in it. It was outside her, flickering over the snow and the trees and across the sky. And it all seemed to be speaking to her, crackling in that gentle, soothing way.

She looked down toward the Lathrop cemetery and the ghostly birch, and as she did so a formless wave of light gathered there and swept up the hill toward her, changing color through the whole spectrum as it came. For a moment she fell back in terror, but even as she did so the wave passed harmlessly over her and a voice said more distinctly than ever, "Octavia Samson."

Slowly she straightened up again, half recognizing that voice. The wave of kaleidoscopic light returned across her and thenceforth continued to swing gently backward and forward like a shimmering veil, while a rustle like wind came near and retreated with it and presently was formulated again into that articulate, recognizable voice, rising and falling away:

"It is you," it said, "who are making your ordeal so hard—" Tavie raised her arms in happy consecration, for it was the voice of Lucretia Mott, the great leader of Reform whom she worshiped: "What is the love of a man that we should let it absorb us and turn our thoughts from those ideals to which we are consecrated? . . . What is it but something altogether in the course of nature, to be taken lightly and joyfully, even as men enjoy us. . . . Proceed into marriage and fulfillment, for that is your right and your natural way. Deny nothing when the denial grows more costly than the thing denied. . . . Take the love of man for what it is worth, which is little enough. Take it or refuse it as you will. If you are a-thirst, drink, but do not thereby dedicate yourself to drunkenness. . . . Let temperance be our motto in all things but devotion to our cause."

After the last words, "devotion to our cause," the veil of rainbow light faded, but the sky and the world continued to sparkle and rustle with gentle fire. Suddenly Tavie's soul was released as never before. "Take it for what it is worth," she repeated ecstatically over and over—"which is little enough! Why, of course," she continued speaking aloud, "I have known it always. I will do as I wish, even as men do, and take it lightly, and I need not worry about it any more." A fancy of herself in her grand-ma's bridal dress drifted across her mind, and she smiled in easy self-indulgence, neither denying the implication nor valuing it over-highly.

"Ike, my dear," she again said aloud, "you may have me when you want me now. And I shall no longer fear to make you want me. Only do not ask too much of me, my dear, and I shall not ask much of you either. If it is to be marriage, then let it be 'something altogether in the course of nature,' not a silly slavery of me or an equally silly mastery by you." She rose, still extending her hands forward in joy. "Let us meet as equals, Ike, you with your work and I with mine, and without any exaggeration. Let us take love and enjoy it for what it is worth, 'which is little enough.' "

With that Tavie laughed a wholly joyful laugh and arose. The present returned to her, and she decided that for many reasons, including her desire to see her pa, it would be sensible to sleep at home for the next few nights. Tramping off down the road, she found herself singing for joy, while the stars and the borealis flickered laughingly over the world.

And at that very hour on that very evening, February 13, 1851, Mrs. Lucretia Mott was writing a letter of advice to a young friend; and some of the phrases she wrote were identical with those Tavie heard in her vision.

CHAPTER XLII

DURING the night after Tavie's crisis in the glen it began to rain, and the thaw continued throughout the next day. After supper Squire Lathrop walked home with Tavie through the sodden snow, having an errand of painful delicacy to her pa. When the two men were alone in Solon's office, the Squire proceeded to notify his friend, with the utmost diffidence and indirection, that he saw evidence on Octavia's part of a more than friendly interest in Isaac. Furthermore, after conversation with Isaac, he felt obliged to confess, to his own distress, that the boy showed no evidence of serious intention in the matter. While it would be cause for deep disappointment to him and to Sarah if Octavia should leave their house, nevertheless he would fully understand Solon's position if he decided to withdraw her from a situation that might, if his observation was correct, lead her into embarrassment.

Actually, this revelation by his friend John Lathrop was far less disturbing to Solon Samson than it might have been to a different kind of father of a different kind of daughter. In general, he attributed women's frequent helplessness before their desires to the fact that their minds were uncultivated, that they had never been disciplined to the processes of logic and abstract thought. He had always asserted that women had naturally all the endowments of men, if only they could be developed. In the face of public prejudice, he had at great sacrifice helped Tavie to a college education which, until the progressive action of Oberlin, had been impossible for women. He felt vindicated in the fine standing she had attained, and had no doubt that one day she would make a record in the academic world comparable to that of any man.

Consistently with his general views, Solon considered Tavie as qualified as any man to order her desires, and, consequently, now took the news of her emotional involvement no more seriously than as if she had been a son. Indeed, while John Lathrop was embarrassed by the fear of injuring Solon's pride, Solon was equally put to it to conceal a certain condescension toward Isaac. For he was convinced that when Tavie married, she would choose someone of her own academic stamp.

When John Lathrop had finished his painful revelations Solon did his best to appear concerned. He put on his lawyer-like scowl, uttered the profound opinion that it might be wise to leave the young people to work out this delicate matter in their own way, stated that he had the utmost confidence in Octavia, and expressed the conviction that if she found herself bestowing an unrequited affection she would not long repine. Altogether, the conversation between these two old friends and first-rate minds was on the level of that of two hens discussing their chicks that had long since left the coop and were fending for themselves. Both were glad to escape into cigars and grog and to talk of other things.

After Solon and Charity and Tavie had seen Squire Lathrop out at about half-past nine, Solon walked back into his office, threw his cigar in the Franklin stove and for some minutes contemplated it in the embers with a countenance as savage as if it had been the Supreme Court of the United States in full bank. It was his duty, he decided, to include his wife in this confidence, to impart to her any intelligence he might have, nearly affecting his daughter. Accordingly, he now summoned both his women folks from the parlor, and both saw at once from his embarrassment that the matter was personal.

"I confess," he said, gesturing to them to sit down, and himself remaining standing by the mantel behind the stove, "I confess that the subject of John Lathrop's errand seemed to me somewhat unworthy of his usual acumen. He came to notify me, presumably as bearing upon Octavia's happiness, that Isaac had no present intention of marrying and that he hoped, while Isaac remained so minded, that Octavia would remain in an equal state of indifference."

At this Charity tossed up her hands and dropped them on her knees in dismay, but at the same time Tavie broke out into such a warm, rippling laugh that both parents looked at her startled, and her ma almost guessed the truth and more than the present truth. "Dear old John Lathrop!" Tavie said. "I hope you thanked him for warning me of my danger. And I hope you warned him also that I likewise am not in a marrying mood—having other bees in my bonnet—and that Ike also would do well to tend to his railroads and steam engine companies."

They remained silent for some moments, listening to the fast melting drip of icicles from the eaves outside. Solon and his daughter looked sympathetically at each other, being obviously of one mind in belittling the Squire's warning; but Charity looked at the floor, being as obviously disturbed by it. "Ah me," she said, lifting her hands again and dropping them on her knees, "it may be the change in the weather, but all this day I have suffered the most disturbing premonitions. The air seems heavy with mischance, and I cannot bring myself to disregard such warnings, foolish as they may seem to both of you."

At that moment there was a gentle tap on the front door and Charity barely suppressed a scream. "It has come," she said in a whisper, her gray eyes sinking into their hollows as when she was reading her crystal. But she did not move, knowing that whoever was at the front door could see them through the window if he chose.

"Go ye both into the parlor," said Solon in an authoritative mumble as he took the candle from the mantel. "Listen well, and if it proves to be anything untoward, lead the Negro quickly to Malachi Jolam while I entertain the company here." At this Charity and Tavie rose, crossed the little front hall into the parlor and closed the door to a crack. Master Samson followed with the candle and, when they had gone, opened the front door.

"I beg yo' pahdon, suh," said a quiet voice whose accent Solon instantly recognized, "but would you do me the kindness of directing me to the house of Mastuh Solon Samson?" "I am Solon Samson, sir. Will you step in? It must be inclement abroad after this rise in temperature. I see it is raining again." "Thank you, suh," said the stranger, coming in and removing his broad-brimmed black felt hat turned up on one side, Solon stepping back and standing between him and the parlor door. "May I take your coat?" said Solon, extending his hands as if to assist the blond youth remove his brown greatcoat that was spotted with rain. "Thank you, again, suh, but I'm mighty afeered when y'all learn my errand you may not feel so kindly toward me."

"Not at all, young man," said Solon jovially. "Am I not correct in guessing from your uniform that you are a Federal marshal? If so, I was honored by one of your colleagues less than three months ago and was most cordially treated. So you see I have no ill feelings toward ye and am of course interested to know what business fetches ye here at this hour." "Well, suh, I'm afeered you are right in thinkin' I'm a marshal, and I'm afeered I have some troublesome news fo' you hyah in my pocket."

"Come in, I beg of ye," said Solon, bowing and gesturing toward the open door of the office, being now satisfied that Charity had heard enough to send her about her duties. Keeping his cloak on, the marshal stepped into the office as indicated. Solon closed the door behind them and waved toward a chair. The marshal remained standing.

"Would you be good enough to tell me your name?" asked Solon. "Yes, indeed, suh," said the other. "I beg yo' pardon, suh. My name is

Swain, Corporal Swain, in charge of a new detachment of marshals assigned to this district fo' better enforcin' the Fugitive Slave Law." At this
they shook hands, and Solon stepped back and stood easily against the
mantel.

"And now, suh, I may as well tell you I have hyah a warrant to search
yo' premises fo' a passel o' nigrus bein' run through these pahts." "Will
you do me the honor of showing me the warrant?" said Solon, bowing.
"It appears that I am not without friends who are anxious to give accurate
accounts of my comings and goings." The marshal produced the warrant
and Solon, hearing minute sounds on the inside cellarway to the rear,
commented loudly on the document as he read it. "I observe," he said,
"that this warrant is signed by my old friend Justice Longcoat who is
seldom remiss in his zeal to reassure himself as to the propriety of my
conduct. However, I regret to inform you, Corporal, that the warrant is
improper, even under the so-called Fugitive Slave Law of last August, for
it fails to give the name of a particular, alleged fugitive or the name of
his owner. While I shall in no way resist the search if you insist on making it, I must warn you that I reserve my right to bring an action for
illegal search against either you or His Honor Justice Longcoat."

With this Solon handed back the warrant with a bow, meanwhile continuing to speak: "And even if this warrant complied with the requirements of the so-called Fugitive Slave Law, I would still feel compelled
to inform you, Corporal, that you will act at your peril, for the whole
law itself is unconstitutional on many grounds, and will undoubtedly be
held so when it reaches the Supreme Court of the United States—"

At this there were sudden footsteps in the other part of the house and a
shrill whistle. Corporal Swain sprang to the door, threw back his cape
revealing his revolver, and backed out of the room, closing the door after
him. Solon Samson immediately opened it and followed, just then hearing a strange voice in the kitchen saying, "Caught these hyah ladies
sneakin' 'im out the back do'." "That's fust-rate wuhk, Jones," said Corporal Swain. "Now suppose yo' leave them with me and search the rest o'
the house." "Kindly help yourself to a candle," said Solon, coming into
the kitchen and indicating the array of them on the mantel. "Yonder is the
cellar door, in case you wish to start your search there." "Thank you, suh,"
said Corporal Swain and Private Jones, both bowing, the latter then taking a candle and lighting it from another on the mantel.

"And now," said Corporal Swain, bowing successively to the ladies and
Solon, "I must trouble y'all to considuh yo'selves under arrest in the name
of the United States, and I reckon it's needful to have a little meetin' that

won't take much mo' of yo' time. Mastuh Samson, suh, may we use yo' office, or would you prefer that we sawt o' come to awduh hyah?" "Come into the office, by all means," said Solon.

The Corporal bowed to Charity and Tavie who led through the parlor and across to the office. "Mighty sorry, suh," he then said to Solon, "but it's regulations I walk behind y'all." "Illegal arrest, Corporal," said Solon, glaring at him. Then he bowed and strode across his hall, holding his head high, for the first time in his life under the ignominy of being in the position of a criminal, and all the fanaticism in his blood welling up to the long battle ahead, of which this was not even the first skirmish. "Git along, nigguh," said the Corporal to the old Negro who, clad in a torn overcoat and ashen in color, scuttled after Solon.

"Mastuh Samson, suh," Corporal Swain began when they were all in the office, "may I have the privilege of assuming that these ladies ah of yo' family?" "I beg your pardon, sir," said Solon. "Mistress Samson, my wife, I have the honor of presenting Corporal Swain of the Federal Constabulary. My daughter, Miss Octavia." "I assho you, ladies," said the Corporal, when he had made a courtly bow to their two stares of unflinching hatred, "that it is a privilege to meet you, and I beg of you to assist me to see to it that you receive the leniency to which you ah entitled. Will you honuh me by sittin' down while I conduct a little examination that is pewly a mattuh o' fawm but must be attended to, even wheah ladies ah involved?"

Charity and Tavie both stood firm, making no sign. Solon waved to them to be seated and Charity obeyed; but Tavie said, "Pa, for the first time in my life I must disobey you," and tossed her chin in the air. At this the Corporal gave her a look of real dismay, being embarrassingly touched by her defiant beauty. "I apologize, ma'am," he said simply, and himself sat down at the desk and took a roll of foolscap out of his blouse pocket. "May I use yo' quill, suh?" he asked of Solon, who nodded. During the examination that followed they could occasionally hear Private Jones thumping about the house in the course of his search.

Corporal Swain started with the Negro. "Boy," he said, "don' be skeert. You ah among friends and nobody's go'n' to switch you." "Yassuh," said the darkey, rolling up his eyes till nothing showed but the whites. "What's yo' name, Boy?" "Blue, suh, yassuh." "Well, Blue how do you like bein' a free nigguh?" "O gemmen, if this hyah's freedom 'tain't only bumpin' in cahts an' libin' in holes and shakin' wit de aag."

"Blue, who's yo' mastuh?" "Massah Will. Gawd's love, massah, ah's speculatin' all my days who's totin' breakfas' fo' he, and no nigguh on de whole plantation knows lak ah do how he lak he hominy and he juleps."

"House nigguh, ah you, Blue?" "Yassuh, gemmen." "How come, then, you run away from Massah Will? Didn' he treat you pretty?" "Oh, yassuh, 'deed he did. Nevah once switched me all ma laf. And nobody lak Blue knowd how to put he to bed most eb're night, and cussin' lak a fine gemmen if Blue wa'n't by to pull off he boots."

"How come you run away, then, nigguh?" "Gawd's truth, gemmen, ah nebuh run'd away. No, suh! Tell Massah Will Blue didn' run away. Po' white trash oberseer o' field nigguhs give me a cut wi' he big whip, an' ah fell to meditatin', and fo' bettuh meditatin' ah jes' stepped out pas' de ol' coon tree. An' raght soon come de soun' o' dem debbil dogs. And what, suh, could po' nigguh do but hoof out? So ah runned and swum, and puhty soon Blue bein' toted in cahts o' yams and co'n, and hyah ah is. Ah nebah run'd away, no suh, not dis hyah nigguh."

"What's Massah Will's name?" asked the Corporal. "Lawdy me, Massah Will, suh." "What's the rest of his name?—his last name?" "Gawd in heaven, gemmen, everybody know de Livin'stons. Fustest folks in de county." "What county, Blue?" "Lawd, ah jes' dunno. An't but one county, Ah reckon." "What state? Geo'gia—Alabama?" "Oh yassuh, Miss'ippi, suh."

Following the examination of Blue, that of the others was brief and perfunctory—names, residences, and—with great embarrassment—ages. At last the Corporal rose, rolled up and stowed away his sheaf of foolscap, thanked them all for their kindness and refused with regret Solon Samson's offer of a nip of brandy. "I must tell you, suh," he said, "that Justice Longcoat instructed me that if I arrested y'all I was at once to release you on yo' own recognisance. So kindly consider yo'self at lahge subject only to the awduhs o' the co't. And I will take it on myself to extend the same c'u't'sy to the ladies, who, I trust, will hyah nuthin' fuhthuh from this unfawtunate incident, though I cannot restrain myself from sayin' I hope fo' the honuh of bein' permitted to retuhn latuh, on some mo' agreeable and less troublesome errand. Thank y'all again, suh. It has been an honuh to meet you, and permit me to wish y'all the best of good fawtune, though it will be mah duty in some mattuhs to testify against you." And with a side-long glance at the rigid-faced Tavie he turned toward the door.

"Go along, nigguh," he said to Blue. "You on yo' way to Mississippi." "I should be happy," said Solon Samson, "to drive this unfortunate man to whatever destination you require. It is a wretched night for walking the highway. I assume you gentlemen have horses." "Fawgive me, Mastuh Samson," said Corporal Swain a little condescendingly, "but I be-

lieve that some day—and I hope it won't be too late—y'all will lun that
we know best how to take cyah of ou' nigguhs. Blue, tell this gentleman,
would yo' rathuh go fo' a ride with him in a carriage, aw would yo' rathuh
walk along holdin' onto my stirrup?"

"Lawd, gemmen," said Blue, "Ah an't nobody to rahd in no carriage
and Ah thank Gawd Ah's come on folks as has some medidation o' this
nigguh's ways." "You see, suh?" said the Corporal, smiling. "I see only
fear, sir," said Solon, and his black eyes burned the other's out of countenance. "Some day, suh, I hope y'all will see mo'," said the Corporal. And
with a peremptory jerk of his head, he sent the Negro out of the room and
out the front door before him. In the rainy darkness Private Jones, having completed the search of the house and found nothing, was waiting
for them.

Thus began the case of *United States* vs. *Samson* which in less than two
weeks became a nation-wide *cause célèbre.* Justice Longcoat proceeded
with the greatest consideration, the charges against Charity and Octavia
Samson being dismissed without indictment, and Solon's case being
brought to a speedy hearing, during the week following his arrest. On the
morning of the trial the defendant, the presiding justice and Senator
Ostrum Applemore were equally astounded to find a crowd of over a
thousand lining the South Mall to cheer Solon Samson as he rode to the
Court House, revealing—what no one had appreciated before—the degree to which the Fugitive Slave Law had increased the anti-slavery sentiment in the village. At Wheeler Corner they compelled Solon to stop
and make a speech from his horse, a speech that was never recorded but
might well have gone down as one of the great and futile speeches that
failed to avert the inevitable conflict. In it he admitted to having assisted
Negroes to Canada. But, he said, if the highest court of the land held the
so-called Fugitive Slave Law to be constitutional, he would thereafter abide
by it, and he plead with his fellow-citizens in that event likewise to abide
by it until the orderly processes of government should remove it from
the statute books.

In the trial Solon admitted to harboring the fugitive, dropped his technical objection to the form of the search warrant, and placed his whole
defense upon the unconstitutionality of the Fugitive Slave Law under
which he had been arrested. He merely read an outline of his legal defense and did not give Justice Longcoat the benefit of an argument on
any of the points in detail. His Honor had little choice but to find the
defendant guilty and to lay upon him the reasonable penalty of a $500

fine and four months in prison. Bub Tanofly—who had had much to do with assembling the triumphal crowd on the morning of the trial—raised $5000 to finance the appeal and if necessary to pay the fine. Because of the importance of the issue, the case was hurried through a formal affirmation by the Circuit Court of Appeals, and set on the calendar of the Supreme Court of the United States for March fourteenth.

In the appeal in the narrow courtroom, crowded with dignitaries of the government, the whole North spoke through Solon Samson, pleading against the law not only on a half-dozen technical grounds but on the broader principle that the Constitution could not give Congress power to make criminals of a large proportion of the population for doing what they were compelled to do by their deepest moral and religious feelings:

". . . I do not speak of a law which may interfere with the convenience, the comfort, the emoluments, the wealth, of a large section of the population. I speak only of an Act addressed to those deepest moral convictions, those promptings of conscience which we believe to be the voice of a Supreme Being, those moral impulses by which alone we can live proudly. . . . I do not contend that it is for the Court to examine into those convictions and to pass judgment upon them. But I do contend that the Court, where it finds them existent in fact, is bound to take notice of them and declare them inviolate.

". . . In this matter, touching closely the moral and religious feelings of millions of citizens, let the language of the Constitution be strictly construed. Let it not be interpreted to give the Congress power to make criminals of millions of citizens for harboring fugitives toward whom their deepest sympathies have been aroused. Let it not go farther, as this Act presumes to do, and compel those millions of citizens actively to assist in tracking down fugitives, making a legal duty of such a violation of religious duty as none of these millions could perform and afterwards look his fellow-citizens in the face or confront his God alone in his chamber. . . ."

A week later, after Solon had reached home, his conviction was affirmed, the news reaching Byzantium and the nation by telegraph. Immediately he put his affairs in order, turning his current law business over to Judge VanSanford in the village, and giving Tavie his general power of attorney, exactly as he would have done with a grown son.

On the 25th of March he was to set out to begin his four months' sentence in Fortress Monroe. Two evenings before his departure, Bub Tanofly and an impromptu committee rode out to the Hollow and kidnapped him for a mass meeting in the Arsenal where he was cheered by two thousand people for half an hour. He was continually interrupted with cheers throughout his speech, and few troubled to analyze his plea for obedience to the law as it had been finally declared, and his further plea against abolition as a proposal more vicious than the Fugitive Slave Law. All they knew was that this man was martyred for a cause in which they all believed.

And throughout the North similar mass meetings were being held and bonfires were flaring. That Yankee moral conscience to which Solon Samson had referred came fully awake and began to crystallize. Thenceforth, the infraction of the Fugitive Slave Law and the traffic of the Underground Railroad, never large, increased but little. But behind the restraint of the law, behind the sky-line of the future, the marching feet of a crusade began to gather.

CHAPTER XLIII

THE SIX WEEKS of Solon Samson's trial, appeals and commitment were a period of ecstasy for his daughter. To have this father, this mentor, martyred for a cause in which she believed, a cause which she hoped presently to serve, was a matter of almost mystical consummation for her, and her pride and admiration for him outweighed any feelings of compassion for his plight. The issue, to her understanding as well as to his, was too large, too significant for humanity, to be affected by personal concerns. Being a fanatic, indifferent to the opinion of the world, she suffered no shadows upon the pure glory of her father's sacrifice. It was only his earnest plea that she would be hurting his cause that kept her from making public speeches in his behalf. It was only lack of cash that prevented her accompanying him to Washington for his final appeal.

During this exciting period Tavie came in for some of the nation-wide publicity that fell, to his disgust, upon her father; for journalists easily got hold of the fact that this intrepid reformer—he was usually pictured as a rabid abolitionist—had likewise a fiery, reforming daughter who was of the Woman's Rights Movement, the friend of its leaders, and was, besides, that even more lurid thing, a woman graduate of Oberlin College. A cartoon had wide circulation portraying father and daughter gravely smoking cigars together, their feet on a table, a cuspidor between them, glasses in their hands marked "Pure Water," the father with long hair and cadaverous features, the daughter in short skirts that revealed, in that particular attitude, two buxom calves which were hardly suggestive of Tavie's shapely but slim legs.

During this period Tavie's correspondence with leaders in the various Reforms became voluminous and, although she hated the general publicity, especially the insulting cartoon, she yet knew, on her own part, that the notoriety would strengthen her credentials for a self-supporting position somewhere in the Reform Movement. She wrote confidentially to every judge before whom her pa appeared, stating that she was as guilty as he was and appealing for permission to serve his sentence for him, or at least to share his fate in prison; and the courtly replies she had to these letters were a source of angry humiliation to her. It was remarkable that in all her correspondence and agitation she never expressed a wish for her father's acquittal or contributed anything to the nation-wide effort to attain it.

Nor did the activities of these months of February and March, 1851, eclipse Tavie's interest in Ike. The erotic *vita nuova* she had entered at the instance of Lucretia Mott's voice in the glen only enriched this time of joyful release. In addition to her domestic and semi-public duties she managed, early in March, to make herself two new cambrics and three new rosettes and twisted ropes to set off her golden hair; and she undertook that vanity of vanities which theretofore she had decried, the training of a flight of long, golden curls in front of each ear. She flirted with Ike irresponsibly and continually, discovering in herself a talent for innuendo and half-invitation which she had never dreamed she possessed.

But, for several reasons, she now neither sought nor took advantage of opportunities to make him kiss her. Although she was stirred by him as much as ever and delighted in baiting him, her deepest devotion was now running to her pa and his cause. Her strong imagination being diverted into higher things, her carnal desires were less directly exigent and led to no such violent reactions as they had done before. Also, she was reticent of too obvious invitation because now, for the first time in her life, she was consciously assuming a purely feminine role toward a man, was taking pleasure in behaving like any little minx, and, as part of that behavior, had no impulse to direct candor. She was playing for bigger stakes than a kiss in the moonlight, and was far from certain that Ike was yet ready to be really captured; for, outside of an increasingly friendly response to her now usual gaiety, he showed no emotional signs of relenting from his provocative aloofness. Incidentally, in this irresponsible mood Tavie need not face the question of precisely what bigger stakes she was playing for, the difficult question of whether, after all, it was marriage with Ike that she really wanted.

Tavie was right in her perception that Ike was not ready to be captured, though on his part he delighted in what he considered her new friendliness and their increasing congeniality. Ever since she had gone home that Thursday night at the end of February—the day before Solon Samson's arrest—and his pa and Master Lane had given him his come-uppance over something about Tavie that he couldn't figure out, she had seemed to him a changed girl. Her moodiness that used to go against his grain was all gone. Even the business of her pa's trial didn't seem really to bother her. She was gayer than he had ever seen her, looked prettier, dressed better, was corresponding with all sorts of high muckamucks and would laugh with Ike over the pompous letters she got from them.

Moreover, she was taking an interest in Ike's own affairs—and that was more than he could say for the rest of the family! Almost every evening he and she sat up after the rest had gone to bed—for the Squire was lapsing from his usual winter habit of writing articles for the papers and essays in his journal. Quite as much as Solon's trial and Tavie's correspondence, they discussed the steam engine company or the railroad, which latter was now taking most of Ike's time. He had plunged deeply into a study of all the literature there was on railroads and railroading, and his pile of tracts, maps, drawings, designs, charts and monographs accumulated beside the big desk in the keeping-room almost as high as the desk itself. During the week after Solon Samson's original trial before Judge Longcoat he held a meeting of engineers, a tentative route was settled, and the competitors agreed to submit bids not later than August first.

And all these things Tavie went over with Ike almost every evening, showing, as Ike thought, an intelligent and impersonal interest. He figured that they were becoming friends in the best sense of the word, and his chaste attitude toward her accepted this status with enthusiasm. Whenever the time came to marry he would certainly be as glad to have it Tavie as any girl he knew. And for the present the nicest part of it was that he didn't have to think about that. Their friendship was perfectly frank and free of all kissing and such flirtatious nonsense.

On the evening of March first, after the meeting of the engineers, Ike and Tavie stayed up as usual after the family retired, and Ike took the occasion to tell her straight out that never until recently had he realized she had so much sense. "Oh, truly?" asked Tavie, turning her head slantwise and looking up at him archly and with an incipient laugh. "You are very flattering, Master Lathrop." "Oh, I didn't mean that," said Ike, flustered. "I just meant that we're such true grit friends now, and always before there used to be some sort of nonsense—or something—always coming up between us. Oh, you know what I mean, Tave." And Tavie smiled and nodded gravely, imparting that she understood perfectly what he meant.

"I wonder," continued Ike, hoping he wasn't getting on slippery ground, "why people can't always go on like this, just being good friends, and not having to get excited, and have spats, and get married, and all such." "That puzzles me too," she replied, knitting her brows very prettily.

"Sometimes I think it's because folks are—just—well—ninnies." "I guess that's it," replied Ike gravely, "just—ninnies." "Well, anyhow," he added, "we ain't ninnies—not for a while anyway!" And they smiled wisely at each other.

Fifteen minutes later, in his bed, Ike kept turning over in his mind the profound truth of what Tavie had said, that folks were somehow "just ninnies," and he wondered if he would ever get silly about Tave and lose this fine friendship they had now. And in her bed Tavie rolled this way and that, thinking about her pa and Ike all mixed up together, and—for all that she knew what she wanted and that she wasn't getting it—she felt mighty pleased with herself.

A few evenings later Tavie became aware of a particularly dangerous cloud darkening over her designs. Immediately after his selection as Executive Secretary of the railroad, Ike had risen, by unanimous vote of the females of Byzantium, to the unrivalled position of Catch Number One, so obviously so that gossip of the machinations in the village to ensnare him reached even Tavie's secluded ears, so obviously so that, at Jabez Munson's instance, he became known to the members of the Gang as "Stud Lathrop," a name which rose intermittently to plague him all his life. In the three weeks since his elevation in the railroad he had been invited to no less than fourteen select little supper parties.

In spite of his modesty and unsophistication where women were concerned, some suspicion of the meaning of this popularity at length penetrated Ike's indifference to it, and one evening when he was deciding he must cut down on his social activities he raised the question with Tavie. "Tave," he said shyly, dropping his eyes to the many-colored rag rug in the keeping-room, "don't think I'm getting stuck up, but do ye figger all these invitations I'm getting might have somewhat to do with the railroad and the chance I've got of coming by a little money?" "It's hard to believe they'd fall so low," said Tavie solemnly, "though you never can tell about those village folks, those Gadstons and Starks and the rest. They're not like us, you know, Ike."

"They sure ain't," said Ike, "excepting for the Gang and the old fellers at the Blackwater. Though to speak the truth," he added thoughtfully, "Pru Stark's most usually at the parties I've been to"—Tavie had feared as much—"and I'll give her credit, she's the only one of the pack of 'em that don't make a fool of herself trying to talk big about the railroad or the engine. I figger she's as ashamed of herself as I am about the holy show we made at the 'F and P'" [Fulton and Price] "ball. I got to allow she ain't half as bad as I used to figger, and I ain't half so bothered about

John's marrying her." "She's indeed pretty to look at," said Tavie. "No prettier 'n you, Tave," said Ike quickly, and they both smiled in the most frank and impersonal fashion.

This was on March fifth, the evening before the Applemore's annual ball in their stone mansion on Washington Street. Because of the combination of Tavie's poverty, her prolonged absence at college, and her pa's general avoidance of the new-rich of the village, she was not of what the next generation would call "the social set" there, and was never invited to the smaller parties. The Applemore's annual ball, as distinguished from that of Fulton and Price, was always small and select, and though Solon and Charity Samson had always been invited—and usually refused— Tavie had never before been honored. But this year, perhaps because of her current celebrity, the invitation had been addressed jointly to "Master and Mistress Solon Samson, Miss Octavia Samson." The fifth of March falling about midway between Solon's appearance in the Circuit Court of Appeals and his final argument in the Supreme Court, he was at home. And so, on that night, the senior Samsons and Lathrops rode in through the near-zero cold in the latters' big sleigh, and Ike and Tavie rode in together in the famous little shell cutter borrowed from Ike's grandparents who had decided not to go.

Between Tavie's own golden beauty, her ma's dexterity with a piece of tawny velvet that had appeared in several forms for three generations, some of the stiffest crinoline which Tavie gave Ike the money to buy for her in the village, the new, long, gold curls in front of her ears which no woman in Byzantium could equal, a copper rope round her headdress, gold eardrops, wide gold bracelets and other jewelry that had been her grandma's, Tavie looked prettier than Ike or anyone had ever seen her. Jingling in with her under the stars, he had never been more contented and easy with any girl, not even with sister Aggie. He was never more proud than when he escorted her from the hall into the brilliant glare of the chandeliers in the Applemore's ballroom—one whole side of the house thrown together by opening the sliding doors—and marched with her up to Senator and Mistress Applemore and their daughter Hannah, the center of all eyes. During the evening he led her out for more than half the figures—and quite voluntarily too, for she was a constant center both of young men, many of whom now met her for the first time, and of older men who wished to pay indirect respect to her pa.

It was in fact the first time in Pru Stark's career that she was given a close run, even surpassed, as the belle of the ball. Though only three years older than Pru, Tavie felt very mature in the presence of the famous little beauty and all the other young schemers. She took malicious pleasure in observing that Pru's big saucer eyes were seldom off her throughout the party, and that they grew wider as time passed. For Ike somehow didn't manage to lead Pru out once during the entire evening. As a climax, during the general departure when Tavie went up to Mistress Applemore's room for her wraps, the usually intrepid Pru paled visibly when she entered and stared at her for a long moment with blank, passionate and unconcealed hatred.

On the way home Ike told Tavie that, true grit, he hadn't meant to slight Pru. Did Tavie think she was put out? "Why indeed not," said Tavie gaily. "Why should she be?" "Well," said Ike, "I figger it looked sort of funny after the hurrah I gave her at the F and P ball. I meant to lead her out all keerect, but every time I had in mind to start after her somebody came up I had to be polite to, some friend of pa's or somebody trying to sell something to the railroad." "Of course," said Tavie thoughtfully, "you *were* the handsomest man there, and the best dancer. Naturally, I suppose Miss Pru would have enjoyed a figure with you. Any girl would. I was indeed grateful to you for leading me out as often as you did, though I knew it was only because we were friends, and since you'd brought me you wanted me to enjoy myself."

"Nonsense," said Ike. "You know you were the only one I true grit hankered to dance with." Tavie wanted to slip her arm through his under the bear robe, but she refrained. It was enough for now that she had won a smashing victory. Also, from that blank stare which she had received when she was getting her wraps, she had learned for sure what she wanted to know about Pru.

CHAPTER XLIV

I K E did not know that after the Applemore ball his comings and goings on the Mall were watched more closely than ever from the upper windows of the Liberty. Usually he reached and left his office in the Fulton and Price Mill by the diagonal path that slanted down from Applemore's Iron Block, thus shortening the walk and avoiding the east end of the Mall where the Liberty stood. But on Wednesdays when he went to the Blackwater, he walked straight up Mill Street and past the Liberty to the south side of the Mall. On Wednesday the twelfth, at four o'clock, he was thus passing Stark's tavern when a sash went up on the second story and Pru's voice called softly, "Ike, could you spare me a minute?"

He found her alone in her ma's parlor, bewitchingly costumed in a purple silk street dress with an old-fashioned lace fichu that made her look more than ever like her ma. As Ike came in she first cocked her head fetchingly on one side, then jumped up and gave him her prettiest curtsy. "Salutations, great man," she laughed. "I had begun to think I'd never see you again." "Honest, Prue," said Ike, as always a little discommoded by her beauty when alone with it, "I've been wanting to see ye all this week to tell ye how Applemore's ball was clean spoilt for me, being's I never got so much as a word with ye, let alone a figure."

Pru threw back her head in her trilling laugh. "Oh, Ike, thank you, but I never thought of it twice. I was so glad you gave most of your time to that Mistress Octavia, for she never comes to parties, does she?—though it shouldn't concern me for I guess she's nearly old enough to be my mother." "Tave's twenty," said Ike a trifle coolly, and Pru got bitter confirmation of her suspicions. At once she grew very serious, sat down, didn't invite Ike to sit down, put her lovely little hands in her lap and looked at the backs of them for a quarter of a minute.

"Ike," she said, "of course I'm really ashamed of having made you come up here. I know everybody's bothering you to death these days, so that somebody who just wants to be friendly dare not see you without seeming to be after you like all the rest, as if you were the greased pig at the fair. Well, I'm not after you, but I have something quite important to talk to you about—important at least to me. Perhaps it will take half an hour. I know you're in a hurry to get to the Blackwater now, and I know you hate being here like poison. And besides, I'd rather see you somewhere where we won't be interrupted. I wonder if you'd let me come to your office some time?"

"Why sure grit," said Ike, a little artificially, being embarrassed by this typical example of Pru's indifference to convention which she somehow carried off as the prerogative of her beauty. "Any time at all," said Ike, "that is—" "Some time when you are quite sure you will have no business on hand." "Would, say, half-past three tomorrow afternoon suit ye?" asked Ike. "That would give us an hour." "That would be splendid," said Pru, rising. "Do I have to pass many people in the office? Would you—?" "If ye'd leave here at exactly half-past three by the Baptist Church," said Ike, "I could sort of walk up and meet ye." "Oh don't bother to do that," she replied, "but if you could plan to be at the door of the Mill at half-past three, that would be just scrumptious."

Her mood grew suddenly playful. Extending her drooping fingers to him she said, "O Master Lathrop, you are so generous! I am so honored that you would give poor little me a jiffy of your valuable time!" Ike felt her attraction creeping through him and as he touched her fingers he stepped back toward the door, smiling awkwardly at her banter.

"And, Master Lathrop," she persisted, now with her characteristic, sudden gesture of pressing down her dress in front with both hands so it ballooned up behind like a pigeon's tail, "truly you must not think I am trying to marry you, for I know that the only talk of marriage there will ever, *ever* be between us, will be about how you can rescue your big brother from my wicked, wicked clutches." "All keerect, Pru," said Ike, and they both laughed easily. "See ye tomorrow, and sorry I must hurry on now."

As soon as Ike reached the office Thursday afternoon he was so embarrassed by the highly irregular prospect of a lady's calling on him— above all, Pru Stark—that he confided it to Squire Fulton. The Squire smiled a little censoriously and said, "Business and pleasure, ye know, Isaac." "I know, sir," Ike replied. "The fact is—well—anyhow it won't happen again."

At a quarter past three he grew very nervous, closed his ledger, put it away, and tidied up the room. He spat his quid of tobacco in the cuspidor and straightened his tie the best he could without a mirror. He began to take frequent deep breaths. At twenty-five past he put on his greatcoat and beaver and marched self-consciously out through the main office, being too preoccupied to notice that both the Squire and Master Price had absented themselves, and that no one remained but three old clerks. As he came down the stairs he observed for the first time that the frosted glass in the upper half of each of the double doors had a classical, nude figure of a woman in it.

He went out, started up Mill Street, paused as if he had forgotten something, returned, re-entered and stood in the vestibule, holding the door a crack open and peeping out. He was in a panic lest someone appear, either from without or from within. Years seemed to pass before the Baptist Church clock struck one. The stroke had hardly reverberated away to silence when he heard the rustle of Pru's dress, even before he could see her approaching on the footpath. He opened the door and she stepped lightly in, her padded cloak being forced open a little by the door which was too narrow for her spread of crinoline. Ike blamed himself for not opening both of the double doors to give her room.

"Ye're on the minute, all keerect," said Ike, bowing. "It's so kind of you to let me come at all," said Pru, glancing up and then down quickly, being obviously embarrassed and a little breathless. Ike offered her his arm and led her up the long stairs, down the hall with closed doors leading into the big drying room where they had danced, through the main office where no one of the clerks appeared to notice them, and so into his private domain. He closed the door and bowed, indicating the chair he had set for Pru across the desk from his own.

"Would it be dreadful if I took off my things?" she asked, whisking off her purple velvet bonnet with a frisk of her curls and revealing her sleek, black hair, parted Madonna-like and caught up behind in a knot decked with artificial pink roses. Ike took her cloak and bonnet without comment and hung them and his own coat and hat on hooks in the wall. Before sitting down Pru looked out at the view of the Mall. "What a lovely prospect you have, Ike," she said, "so much higher than ours." And without more ado she moved her chair to the side of Ike's desk so that she could look out the window. Then she sat down and leaned forward over the desk, putting her elbows on it. She had on the same purple silk dress as yesterday, but without the fichu, whose absence revealed that it was cut in a deep square in front so that, in Pru's present position, it was difficult for Ike to avoid seeing pretty far down inside her corset. He looked out the window and Pru looked at the back of her hands.

"Ike," she began presently, "what I want to talk to you about is that I'm mightily dissatisfied with the life I'm leading here, just gallivanting round from one senseless party to another. I was head of my class at the Institute, you know, and, even if I am a woman, there ought to be something I could do with myself besides—just—waiting around to get married. That's all it comes to, Ike, this life we lead here, we girls whose pas have enough money so we don't have to work in the kitchen. Oh, of course"—with this she threw up her little hands emphatically—"I've worked plenty in the kitchen. I suppose I'm ready to get married now, and probably some day I will. But even if I wanted to get married today, what could I do about it?" She made a wide gesture with one hand that ended pointing at Ike. "Take you. If I, or any girl, asked you to marry them, you'd run away farther than the north pole. And, anyway, a girl can't do that, for some reason known best to—perhaps—God. So I want to do something with myself till somebody I like well enough is ready to marry me."

From now on as Pru talked she alternately dropped and raised her eyes and each time they fell full on Ike he winced a little at their impact, as if someone had struck him softly in the solar plexus. "I've thought a good deal about your friend Miss Octavia," Pru continued, "and I think she's shown a lot of spunk. One thing I've wondered was whether you wouldn't drive her into the village some time and bring her to see me. I'd like to find out whether I could get into Oberlin College and how to go about it." Ike wondered, quite unsuspiciously, why Pru didn't write Tavie a note and invite her in, or even drive out herself to the Hollow to see Tavie some afternoon.

"But, Ike," she went on, and now her eyes rested on him in longer periods and she began to knit her pretty little brow, "I'm really very much more interested in business than I am in book-learning—that, as you probably know, is the real trouble between me and John. I'm not just thinking about money, the way pa does most of the time. I'm thinking about really *doing* something, like this mill or like this railroad of yours, or your steam engine. I know everybody has said it to you, but it's true that in really getting this railroad started you've done the finest thing anybody's ever done in all this country."

She looked at him suddenly with great eagerness, the lids drooping ever so little over her big blue eyes, the nostrils of her delicately arched nose a little dilated so that Ike could see the light through one of them, her thin, cupid's bow lips parted, showing the edges of her teeth, also slightly parted behind them. Ike felt a peculiar sensation, and his breath caught as he dropped his eyes.

Pru continued: "Ike, I don't pretend, as some do, to know anything about your railroad, but I know I'm not so stupid I couldn't learn. What I'd like best in the world would be to study to fit myself to have some kind of a position under you, no matter how humble, some position where

I'd have some little part in really important things that are going on, the things you are engaged in." A thought tried to form itself in Ike's mind to the effect that old Stark had sent Pru to spy on his doings; but he was now crumbling before her beauty, and no thought except that of her immediate presence had a chance of getting into his consciousness. Pru noticed that his color was rising and that he was breathing more rapidly.

"We could speak to the Squire or Master Price," he said hoarsely. "There might be something out there"—he moved his head toward the door—"or perhaps up in the printing house." "But, Ike," said Pru, leaning still farther forward on the desk so she was almost lying on it, "I'm not looking for a position 'out there' or anywhere but *right here,* under you—that is, in the work of the railroad."

Ike felt something like an enormous wave, much stronger and different from anything he had ever felt before, lifting and drawing all of his body involuntarily toward Pru, and he was unable to keep his eyes from hers for an instant. As if it were somebody else's voice, he heard himself saying, "There ain't any place for a clerk in the railroad yet, Pru. I could try, but I know they'd laugh at me. Maybe after the line gets running there might be something, but that won't be for a couple of years anyway. But—but—we—we might——"

He paused. Somehow this fierce attraction he was feeling had nothing to do with marriage, nothing to do with anything except this moment, here and now, that seemed to expand until it was all of life, all of hope and ambition, everything brought to a focus, the final secret about to be utterly revealed.

"But, Ike," Pru was saying, *"something* might come up, *something* for me—us—to do together. At least won't you show me some of those drawings of the line that all the men have seen, and the pictures of the engine and the carriages, and the figures about the cost of running them? I can really understand those things, you know." And she stood up and moved to the corner of the desk only a foot from him.

Ike found himself spreading out some of his drawings on the desk and weighting them so they wouldn't roll up. Pru moved over beside him and she was now releasing up at him her whole bag of smiles and feints and blushes as fast and as fatally as if he were standing in a nest of delicious hornets. She moved clean against him sideways as she leaned over the first chart, and he could feel her thigh rub against his as she straightened up and said, "Ike, that's really wonderful."

Automatically, unconscious of what he was doing, he reached around, took her by the shoulders, turned her to him and pressed her close, his hands moving hungrily all over her back and shoulders. When he pushed her from him a little so as to look down at her, she was still touching him from the waist down, and as he peered down into her face, her lips were parted as before and she slowly closed her eyes.

As he leaned to kiss her his eyes fell on an almost imperceptible pock mark at the corner of her mouth—

Suddenly that half-open mouth, those lips, were just mouth and lips. They had nothing to do with him or Prudence Stark or anything human. Something centuries older and wiser than Pru took possession of him, something that said that the world passeth away and the lust thereof, and that the wages of sin is death, something that had founded a civilization in terms of which Ike had been living contentedly most of his life. Suddenly what he held in his arms was strange and revolting to him. He pushed her slowly away, then turned from her to lean on the desk. "Pru," he said, hoarse and trembling, "we're making fools of ourselves."

Pru, finding herself unheld, opened her eyes and saw that she was no longer even being looked at. Instantly, through flaring anger, she began to cover her retreat. Rushing away to the window, she pressed her forehead against the frame and beat it with her little fists above her head. "O Ike," she half screamed, "you've been dreadful! Hateful! I didn't come here for that! I didn't—I didn't!"

Ike remained behind his desk with his head bowed, supporting himself with his arms on the sides of the desk, for he was still trembling like a leaf. "It's all spoilt now! You've spoilt it all!" he heard Pru carrying on. "Oh, I must get out of here! This dreadful place! I thought you were a gentleman!" At this Ike lifted his head and saw her run across the room and snatch down her wraps. He strode over to help her but she switched away from him and swung her cloak on alone. "No, Ike," she said more calmly. "You must not help me, you must not touch me. You have proven a deep, deep disappointment to me and I never want to see you alone again."

She looked directly up at him with a face tear-streaked, pale, and at the same time proud, fierce and menacing, with a deep sneer around the nose, a defiant expression compounded of her pa's malevolent arrogance and her ma's fineness and real independence of spirit. "There's still the railroad," said Ike weakly. "The railroad! Poof!" hissed Pru, snatched open the door for herself and sailed out, the three clerks like sheep all turning their heads to observe her, then returning to their ledgers without further sign. Ike closed the door and slumped into his chair.

Gradually he ceased trembling, but hot surges of thwarted passion boiled

up in him and subsided like geysers at slowly lengthening intervals. All
he could do was to cover his face with his hands and wait for calm. Presently, snatches of Pru's last words began to repeat themselves in his brain—
"The railroad! Poof!"—"I didn't come here for that!"—"You've spoilt
it all!"

After he had repeated these things in his mind a few times a thought
slowly gathered. "But I didn't spoil it all. What I did was to save it from
being spoilt! Certainly *she* wasn't going to stop me from kissing her and
getting into God knows what. 'Didn't come here for that?'—By God"—
he struck his desk with his fist and spoke aloud—"that's just what she did
come here for! You were a sap, Ike Lathrop, a god-danged suckling pig
being led out to butcher. All that talk of the kitchen and marriage! By
Holy Crimus, that's just what she *was* after."

His late passion, not yet subsided by any means, surged into anger at
Pru and disgust at himself, and he strode up and down the office. Finally
he sat down and tried to work. The Baptist Church clock struck four.
"Jiminy Crickets," thought Ike, "Pru was right—all that took less than
half an hour. And, by God!"—he thumped his fist on the desk again—
"it might have sewed us up for life."

He bent over a sheet of the new stationery he had had printed for the
railroad. "Gentlemen," he wrote so unsteadily that he tore it up and threw
it in the cuspidor. "Gentlemen," he started on another sheet, "Yours of
the twenty-fifth at hand and we are very much interested in your designs
of uniforms for railroad employees." That wasn't what he wanted to say.
They weren't a danged bit interested, wouldn't be for two years, and didn't
like these people anyway. He heard voices in the main office and presently
there was a rap on his door. "Come in," he shouted fiercely. Squire Fulton
came in and Ike, as he rose, dropped his eyes to keep from glaring at his
benefactor and the President of the Company. He walked over, shut the
door, strode to the window and stood with his back to the Squire.

"Excuse me, John Fulton," he said, "if I seem a little discommoded and
if I say to ye, 'By God, so long as I live that won't happen again.'" "Would
ye like a nip of brandy, Isaac?" inquired the Squire, not trying to conceal his amusement. "Thank ye, sir, I should be very grateful." The Squire
fetched it, a pitcher of water and cigars. So the President and the Executive
Secretary ended the day with their feet on the desk, tippling brandy and
smoking jovially together, discussing business only in so far as they exchanged a few humorous and unflattering pleasantries about some of
their associates in "the finest thing anybody's ever done in all this country."

CHAPTER XLV

W H E N Ike came into the kitchen that evening Tavie had never seemed so beautiful. Riding home in the sunset through the soggy but still snow-covered winter landscape, he had admitted to himself that Pru had a way of stirring him up as no other girl had ever done, but at the same time there was something mean and scheming in her, something of her pa, that had always soured him on her and still did. For all her being so pretty and so lively and independent, she just wasn't his sort of folks. So when he came home to Tavie in his own house, she by now so much a part of the family, he felt more than ever secure in her presence and friendship. When she smiled at him as he came in, she made his recent passage with Pru seem trivial and remote, and he even fancied he wanted to kiss her more than he did Pru.

And indeed all that evening there was a special glory about Tavie, though it happened to have nothing to do with Ike. The next day was the fourteenth of March, when her pa was to make his appeal to the Supreme Court of the United States in a great cause that was also hers. She was perfectly friendly with Ike, but her talk was mostly with the Squire, and was a series of eager questions about procedure in the Supreme Court. Would the President be there? And Senators Webster and Clay? Would the argument be reported in full? When nine-thirty came she rose, and all the family with her. The Squire took her in his big arms and kissed her most tenderly. She curtsied to Sarah, which was unusual since she had been helping there. She gave Ike a gorgeous, impersonal smile and a friendly squeeze as she shook his hand. Then she shook hands with Master Lane, Master Hawks and Ben, and went up to bed, leaving a feeling of lofty consecration behind her.

Tavie's transfiguration lasted a week, through her pa's return from Washington and until after the Supreme Court's affirmance of his conviction on March twenty-first. From then on she enjoyed diminishingly those feelings of glorious martyrdom which had been hers from the night of his arrest. Petitions to the President for his pardon were being widely circulated and hundreds of thousands of names being collected; but, curiously enough, Tavie took only a perfunctory interest in these efforts. She took more interest in the proud and ecstatic letters she continued to pen to Mrs. Mott, Mrs. Stanton, Master Garrison, and other leaders of abolition, letters in which she continued to celebrate their cause and her father's martyrdom, assuming as a matter of course that he would go to prison. When, on the day before his departure, he gave her his general power of attorney, she was little impressed by the personal responsibility it involved her in. All it meant to her was that he was now setting out nobly to endure the consequences of the responsibility he had assumed for the betterment of mankind.

And immediately thereafter there began a subtle change in her attitude toward Ike. No sooner was her pa out of town than she began, for the first time, to show an active interest in the minutiae of Ike's well-being and physical comfort. She found herself rushing to take his hat and coat when he came in at supper time. She observed with solicitude every detail of his bearing and manner, and any trifling change in his color or expression was enough to alter her mood. Feverishly she started to knit him a new pair of mittens, though winter was almost over. When, on the first of April—the very day her pa's sentence was to begin—Ike was trying to conceal the fact that he was coming down with a cold, she noticed the faint hollowness in his voice even before Sarah did, and had trouble suppressing her anger when Sarah preferred her own hot potions and unguents to Tavie's enthusiastic, random suggestions. For the first time she began to experience and to recognize in herself the devotion that was Aggie's love, and her ma's, and Sarah Lathrop's, the desire for ministration that had made Aggie angry with her when she had implied that all love, including Aggie's for Homer, was just a carnal business. She began to love Ike less, as she had said to Aggie, "like a cow," and more as if he were her little boy. And she failed to observe that under her ministrations Ike began to grow self-conscious, that his nonchalant friendliness began to give way to a meticulous courtesy and a calculated watchfulness for her wishes, which was not altogether natural on the part of a young man toward a girl he had known all his life, whom he had called his best friend, and whom he was certainly not courting.

On the third of April, two days after Solon's sentence was to have begun, Tavie and her ma received a letter from him written in Washington, stating that Senator Webster had obtained a pardon for him from President Fillmore, but that he had refused it on the grounds that he had been properly convicted and that there were no mitigating circumstances. Tavie was of course proud of her pa's fortitude; but something about the leniency implicit in the offer of pardon, the realization that it had resulted from a nation-wide petition, troubled her in a way that she could not explain. For the next few days she was moody at her work, and all of a sudden felt shy of Ike, afraid to offer him the numerous little offices that suggested themselves to her impulses.

Then, on the eighth, another letter arrived from Solon, this time from Fortress Monroe prison. Triumphantly Charity Samson bore it up to the Lathrops' that evening and read it to the assembled household. The letter was cheerful, entirely given over to describing Solon's comfortable situation —the pass he had received by Executive Order to leave and return to the prison at his convenience, the courteous offer of the freedom of the law library in the neighboring village of Hampton, the friendly letters that reached him in hundreds daily, his exemption from the usual stigmas of prison uniform and menial labor.

Tavie listened to the letter with a dreadful sinking feeling. When the reading was finished she felt dizzy and faint, retired hastily to her little chamber at the head of the back stairs, threw herself on the bed and gave way to hysterical tears. Unconsciously she had wanted her pa to suffer enough harsh treatment to be called persecution. The image she had carried of him as a martyr for justice was rudely swept away. The lofty love of that image that had supported her was suddenly meaningless. Her two months' balloon-flight of ecstasy ended in collapse.

Not having admitted to consciousness the hope of her pa's persecution, Tavie could not now understand her reaction. As she pressed her head into the pillow she said to herself that it was because she was beginning to be nervous again, and because the period of strain and excitement was now over and she had nothing further to do for her pa. She felt terribly alone. She was nobody, just the hired girl at the Lathrops and very much in love with Ike downstairs. Oh, how she wished he would come in with his quiet step and lift her in his arms!

But no sooner had she imaged this possibility than she began to tremble. She felt incapable of facing Ike, somewhat as she had felt before the vision of Mrs. Mott. Then, remembering the injunction of her great leader, she set her jaw. What must be must be. "If you are a-thirst, drink"— "Something altogether in the course of nature." She got up from the bed, smoothed down her pretty brown plaid cambric, flounced up her hair, straightened the lilac ribbon that bound it and the rosette on the side, rubbed her cheeks until the recent paleness disappeared, gave herself a supposedly gay smile in the mirror, and went downstairs.

During the winter Tavie's change in attitude toward Ike had of course not been wasted on the Squire and Sarah Lathrop, each of whom interpreted it in a different way. Working with Tavie daily in the kitchen and the loom-room, Sarah had the best chance for accurate observation. She guessed correctly that the girl's abrupt emergence from anguish into gaiety and ease after her pa's arrest had little to do with Ike but was due to the fact that Solon's plight was now filling her imagination.

The Squire did not entirely agree with his wife's diagnosis. He assured her that from the minute he had spoken severely to Ike about Tavie—on the night of her flight, twenty-four hours before Solon's arrest—Ike's attitude had changed. It was, in the Squire's opinion, this change in Ike, not the misfortune of her pa, that had brought on the girl's remarkable recovery into happiness and had instigated her coquetry which she no longer felt would be wasted to her humiliation. The Squire would whisper to Sarah in bed that he was sure the boy had decided in his own mind to marry her "as soon as he has us irresponsible old folks taken care of." When late in March Tavie's attitude toward Ike patently changed from one of blandishment to one of real tenderness, he decided, as he told his wife, that "something had happened," that now, "in the good old-fashioned way," they were mated for good and all, and that any day now Ike would declare their intention of being married.

But as the days dragged by and Ike made no sign, while Tavie's desperate attachment to him became more and more plain, the last worms of disillusionment began to nibble in the Squire's bosom. He ceased discussing the matter with his wife, as long since he had ceased discussing Ike's career. He began to face the probability that his favorite son, a Lathrop, the grandson of his own father, the great-grandson of his own grandfather, had been guilty of dishonor in an affair of the heart. And this not two months after promising his father to reveal to him anything that was troubling his conscience. Perhaps this gallantry was not even troubling his conscience! Perhaps, by God, the young rapscallion had no conscience! It began to look as if this boy of his was bad through and through.

It was against the background of these dark forebodings that the Squire observed Tavie's behavior on that evening of April eighth when Charity Samson walked up and read to them the letter from Solon. The news it brought must surely have been an occasion of joy for Octavia, had she been in a normal state of mind. But, on the contrary, the Squire observed that she not only showed little interest in her pa's comfortable situation but, after hearing the letter out, retired hurriedly to her room. A few minutes later, when she came downstairs again, her efforts at conversation were pathetically strained, especially when directed toward Isaac. As she sat in one of the straight chairs with her hands in her lap and her eyes lowered to the floor, she was a picture of a lovely and lovable wronged woman, if ever the Squire had seen one. After her ma had left and the household was going to bed he asked Ike to wait up.

The instant they were in the north parlor and the Squire closed the door with an air of gravity, Ike knew something was up. With a harshness which Ike had heard before only on that evening in late February, his pa demanded, "Isaac, I must ask ye to give me any explanation you can for the recent noticeable change in Octavia's behavior." "So far as I know, Pa, there ain't anything to explain," said Ike. "All I've noticed is that recently she hain't been quite as easy and friendly as she was. I've guessed that it might have something to do with Solon Samson's going to prison, though I ain't certain." "You will give me your word, sir, that you know no other reason?" "Why, yes, sir," said Ike, thoroughly flabbergasted.

"Good night, sir," said the Squire, turned abruptly, paced away into his room and closed the door softly. His soul was now burning with a new conviction that his son was a liar as well as a seducer. For an angry minute while he was undressing he considered turning him out of the house. But a few minutes later, as he lay feigning sleep for his wife's benefit, he regretted that he had broken his previous determination never to question the boy again. "By God, I am an old man!" he thought. "All I can do is wait!" He sighed a deep sigh that was half a groan, which confirmed Sarah's wakeful suspicion that he had been taxing Isaac with Octavia's behavior that evening.

Meanwhile Ike, alone in the north parlor, was helping himself to brandy. His pa's dishonorable implications had not only hurt but angered him, and over his first neat glass he considered proposing that he leave the house. Certainly the daily rides to and from the village were a waste of time there was no use making unless he was wanted at home. By the time he poured himself a second drink, watered it in the kitchen, returned and sat down in the big gilt armchair, his anger had subsided and he began, as often recently, to puzzle over the change in Tavie. Certainly he hadn't said or done anything to disturb her, and anyhow he knew she was against marriage, both from the promise she had made him make last fall and from their more recent, frank discussions.

Nevertheless, there was no doubt that during the past two weeks something had been bothering her. It seemed they just couldn't get started on any more of the good talks they had had a month ago, and she was forever pestering him by trying to do him foolish little favors. Several times she had made him late at the bank by insisting on rubbing out some danged little spot on his clothes that nobody could see anyway. And whenever it was stormy she acted like a fool, begging him not to go in to work—as if a feller's job was a sort of game he could play or not as he felt like.

As nearly as he could figger this all started after his wrastle with Pru-Stark. He wondered now if that little hen-hawk had somehow got word to Tavie that he had tried to paw her, and that this had made Tavie mad so that her recent fussiness was a way of paying him back. It was specially strange that she had begun to change at that time, because it had been from then that he had begun to think about her more seriously than before. Pru's antics had made him value Tavie more than he ever had. He remembered now how much he had been dreaming about her recently, and how his carnal desires were troubling him again these nights. "Perhaps," he thought, "there's nothing for it but to break my promise and try to get her to marry me." But in remembering his half-waking fancies of Tavie, Ike forgot that his deeper, wholly unconscious dreams, involving consummation, were usually mixed up with the image of Pru.

Ike poured himself a third drink and sat down determined to think the business through. Considering all sides of the matter, Tavie was a danged fine girl, and a pretty one, and he'd be a lucky feller to marry her. She did have these pernickety ways, of course, but he guessed all women were that way sometimes. She was a good worker, a good cook, and handy with her needle. She was far smarter than most, and when she was behaving naturally they'd never lack for plenty of good talk and plenty of fun. Ike was a little hazy about the Reform business, but he guessed that wouldn't interfere any more than it did with her helping here. She was a good dancer too, most as good as Pru. Considering the Samsons and the Lathrops together, they should have youngsters smart enough to come in when it rained. All in all, there was no objection to Tavie as a wife, and there was an uncommon lot in her favor.

"But, consarn it," Ike said to himself, "I don't want a wife yet a while. I hain't the means to set up a household without selling things that maybe'll triple their value in a few years. I don't figger we want to spend even the money to put a wing on this house—and besides, how do I know I may not have to move into the village one of these days, when the railroad really gets going? Much wiser to wait till a lot of things get straightened out."

Having thought himself around a circle, Ike continued to ruminate half-articulately: "I'll just have to quit thinking about Tave and get back on my feet, the way I was before Pru made a fool of me. If I could do it three months ago, no reason why I can't do it again. Just go along as I have, trying to be particular pleasant to Tave so as not to hurt her feelings, but at the same time doing nothing to imply we're more than friends. Why, consarn it, if we can't be easy friends like we were a spell back, we oughtn't to get married anyhow. Thing to do's to get over this woman itch I've been having lately and get some sense back. And if Pa don't like it, why, by Jumpin' Jiminy, Pa's wrong. If he lights into me again and won't talk sense, by dang, I'll move into the village!" Having concluded which, Ike realized that he had got himself a brick in the hat and rose. "At least," he snickered, "figger I'll do some sleeping tonight." He blew out the candle and made his way up the front stairs.

And upstairs in her bed Tavie likewise was turning the situation over and over in her mind. Desperately she admitted to herself that what she wanted most now was for Ike to be happy. If he wanted to be rich she wanted him to be rich. If he wanted the world, she wanted to get it for him. Yet during the past two weeks when she had been feeling that way it had seemed as though she was helpless to contribute anything to his happiness. When she had been flirting with him, it seemed easy to please him, but now she felt always that everything she did really displeased him, in spite of his nice manners and thoughtfulness. She knew that he had important doings afoot the next few days, the monthly accounts for the farm, and some meeting of railroad engineers he had to report on. Wasn't that in a day or two now? There you had it! She couldn't even remember a simple thing he'd surely told her many times!

Tavie concluded that the first thing she must do was to get back into that state that Ike had called friendship. She must be comrades with him again, no longer because that was the best way of holding his interest but because that was the best way she knew of making him happy. She must be gay, foolish and false as she had been before when she had pleased him. She must not show concern over his appealing little needs and boyish helplessness. Since he wanted her to be shallow, she would be shallow. By Heaven, she would be shallow if it killed her! Remotely she heard Ike's step going up the front stairs, and immediately fell into a nervous chill.

CHAPTER XLVI

THE NEXT DAY the first real spring rain attacked the snow that had been withering through March but still lay a foot deep on the level. Leaving the office in a downpour, Ike put on the woollen cap which he kept there to substitute for his beaver on such occasions. As he rode up the two hills to the Center, the ruts in the winter's ice were down to the planks of the pike and the whole countryside, still under its shallow, soggy white blanket, was alive with the soft thudding of rain and the music of hidden under-rushing waters.

"Looks like business," said peg-leg Elijy Harris at the Center as he came out with a blanket over his head and swung back the tollgate for Ike. "Figger it's the false spring," said Ike. "More 'n likely," said Elijy, "but I allus cal'late ye've to git through the false afore ye come on the' true." As Ike posted off in the dusk he heard some bluebirds murmuring somewhere in the rain, and there were more crows hollerin' in the woods than he had heard before.

When he crossed the stone bridge at Solomon Sloan's forge it was almost dark, but from the roar of the Lathrop River he knew there was a run of open water. "Funny Pa's been so slow hauling wood this winter, after he cut so early," thought Ike. "Ain't like him. Must be a good fifteen cord to draw yet." Anticipating the need of fast work before it was too late for the sledges, Ike had told Howell Sherwood and Squire Fulton that he might not come in tomorrow. Whether they hauled wood or not, he was himself a week late with his monthly farm account, and he'd have to cut dirt to get his report ready for the railroad meeting on the fifteenth, less than a week off.

A few moments—but not too quickly—after Ike stamped, dripping, into the summer kitchen, Tavie came casually out from the main kitchen and vouchsafed him no greeting. "Kind o' damp out, is it?" she inquired in an offhand way, stepping over to the sink and pouring off the water from some dried apples that had been soaking. "Surer'n bluebirds in April," said Ike, lifting off his woollen cap and shaking it over the hot little stove so that the drops spat and sizzled. "By Crimus," he continued, "this coat's soaked up a good ton of water," this as he took it off gingerly and held it up in both hands. "Figger I ought to ring it out before trying to hang it up."

This was the first time in weeks Tavie hadn't run to take his coat if she was present when he came in. She now started toward him spontaneously but checked herself by the stove as if she had only intended to poke the fire, which she proceeded to do. "Spread it on two hooks by the stovepipe," she said indifferently. "It'll dry out there as well as anywhere."

When Ike had hung his coat on the pegs in the wall behind the stove Tavie couldn't check herself from asking, "Are you wet anywhere inside?" "Only the seat of my pants, I figger," said Ike, putting both hands around to inspect that region. "Likely Ma won't let me sit on the furniture." At this they both forced great artificial smiles and chuckles.

Tavie now looked Ike up and down with her best effort at an easy interest. "Looks as if your collar had wilted too," she said, snickering. "Figger I'd best change it?" "Suit yourself," said Tavie, going back to the sink. "It doesn't matter to me." "Well, I may as well change it," said Ike, thinking that Tavie likely thought he ought to. "I suppose you've to change your pants anyway?" said Tavie, not looking at him. "Oh, likely," said Ike, though he saw no sense in it, the house being hotter than usual what with both kitchen and summer kitchen fires going and the temperature near fifty outside.

"Ike," said Tavie as he started into the kitchen. "Yep, Tave," he said, turning back. "Let me know if I can be of any help with that—railroad—document you have to prepare." "Thanks, Tave, I figger to reckon up the farm accounts after supper. Likely'll get at the railroad report tomorrow." "When's that engineers' meeting you spoke of a while ago?" Tavie continued. "Had it a spell back," said Ike thoughtlessly, then quickly revised his statement. "Likely ye mean the stockholders' meeting next Tuesday. That's a sort of engineers' meeting, too, for it's when I'm to put in my report on a lot of things I've picked up from engineers hither and yon."

Tavie was too distressed by her stupidity to answer, and Ike, after considering her back hesitantly for a moment, stepped into the kitchen. Immediately his ma rushed up to him and he gave her a squeeze and a kiss. "Isaac," she exclaimed, "you're wringing wet! Go change your clothes in the loom-room at once. There's a fire there and the rest of upstairs is clammy. You're hardly over your cold." "All right, Ma," said Ike. "I guess I'm wetter'n I thought." Going up the back stairs he thought to himself that after all it was a feller's ma that really knew how to look after him, though at the same time Tave was somehow easier than she had been and things might work out sooner than he'd expected.

In the loom-room he found Master Lane, Henry Hawks and Ben all like-wise putting on dry clothes, from red underwear out—the Squire using the keeping-room for the same purpose. They commented on the weather as they changed. All were impressed by Ike's report of open water at Sloah's bridge. "Be wagonin' in that fifteen cord of wood yet," said Master Lane. "Devil's got into this house this winter." The ladies' workroom was heavy with the stench of masculine sweat and damp masculine clothes. In the silence the rain pattered authoritatively on the roof and the dripping from the eaves was louder than the rain. A piece of loosened ice slid a little way down the shingles. "Ye're keerect, Ike," said Henry Hawks, "it means business." They carried their wet garments down to the summer kitchen and arranged them on chairs and racks. The smell of sweaty, rain-soaked wool was stronger through the house than the rich savor of chicken pie from the Dutch oven before the kitchen fire.

At supper the Squire was his usual jocular self. He said he could tell by thought-reading that Master Lane considered him a shiftless farmer for leaving fifteen cord of wood to rot up on the mountain, but that he relied on the Lord to perform a miracle in the morning by sending a regiment of stout fairies who would have it all piled in the shed before sundown. Just to give the Lord a hand they'd all plan to be at the cutting by day-break, with the three sledges, rain or shine—which would require every-body to turn out at four. To this proposal Master Lane grunted and Henry Hawks looked dubious. "But, gentlemen," protested the Squire, "you fail to take the Lord into account and the fact that nowadays we have such reliable communication with Him and other spirits, eh, Octavia?"

Tavie, who had been fighting her way through the meal in a tense, inar-ticulate haze, was at this moment helping Ike to more tea. Suddenly hear-ing herself named, she gave a little start, so that about a teaspoon of boiling tea slopped out of the kettle-mouth and lit fairly on Ike's blond scalp. "Hieee," he exclaimed, ducking, then looked up with a silly grin, fearing that Tavie would take it amiss if he gave vent to the witticism that rose in his mind. Tavie herself gave a dreadful little gasp. Throughout the rest of the meal everybody saw that her lower lip was trembling, and no one spoke to her again.

Tavie went to bed as soon as the kitchen was cleared up, and Ike spent the evening at the desk, bringing the farm accounts up to date. As he worked, he momently expected his pa to invite him into the north parlor and go at him again about Tavie's jumpiness. But instead, the Squire read quietly in his chair and went to bed with the rest at nine-thirty, first looking over Ike's shoulder at the accounts and bidding him a friendly good night.

As soon as the Squire had disappeared in his room, Sarah pulled up a chair beside Ike, put her long, slim hand over his big one, and looked lovingly into his eyes. Feeling troubled and helpless about Tavie, and supposing his ma had in mind to talk about her, Ike was not far from blubbering. He put his other hand over his ma's and they looked at each other without saying anything. Presently Sarah rose, leaned down and kissed him. "Good night, Isaac," she whispered. "You must bear with your pa." And she went off silently to bed beside her biggest boy who was beginning to seem like her youngest.

By four o'clock next morning it had stopped raining, and the five men set off in the darkness with the bobs and the two sledges drawn by the two pairs of oxen and Mol and Nancy. Up on the mountain they were already heaving the eight-foot sticks from the piles to the sledges, when the big virgin boles of the forest began to stand out in the dawn twilight. The woods were under that most spiritless silence of the year, the silence of absolute death just before spring breaks. Not even the chickadees were stirring, and the distant calls of a couple of crows sounded more like spectral voices than like the first return of life.

The Squire, who always worked harder than any of his help, was today exceeding himself. While the rest, conserving their strength in the usual way, threw up the sticks with two men to a toss, the Squire piled all alone, throwing up the hundred-pound logs like kindling wood and getting more work done than any two of them. On the trips in it was often necessary to give the animals a hand with the loads, for the snow was soggy and the going hard. Once, during the second trip in, when the underlying ice gave way and the rear bob dropped into a sink-hole, the normal thing would have been to hitch on the other pair of oxen. Not so the Squire. While everybody else pushed on the sides the best they could, he got behind the load and shouting, "Heow," seemed fairly to lift the ton of wood and, with Ben goading the oxen, they moved out of the sink-hole without delay. By dinner they had hauled ten of the fifteen cord. With ten cord that had been hauled earlier, twenty cord was already piled in the long shed behind the horse-barn, to season there for a year before any of it began to move to the utility pile in the courtyard.

At the dinner of steaming stew, with something in it from almost every bin in the cellar, the Squire was unusually silent and, when he spoke at all, did so in a strange voice that did not seem like his own. He refused Ike's offer of help in the afternoon, saying that he knew he had work enough to do for his report and they had plenty of hands. Sarah begged him to lie down, but he insisted on going out again with the rest.

Ike was glad of the chance to start his railroad report which he should finish by Saturday night, and he worked at it all afternoon with a concentration that was as unaware of Tavie as of everyone else in the house. At supper the Squire looked heavily pale, ate little, and after prayers consented to go in and lie down on his bed. He fell into a sleep so deep that he did not know when Sarah and Ben took off his clothes and rolled him under the covers.

CHAPTER XLVII

A L L D A Y Friday and Saturday Ike worked on his railroad report in the village and brought his manuscript and figures out to the Hollow at night. On Saturday he also brought out a letter from John which the Squire as usual read to the assembled household before supper. John said that he wished to remain in New Haven during the spring vacation which would begin next Wednesday, the sixteenth. He had almost decided to go into law next year instead of divinity, but whichever should be his final decision, he felt he should take advantage of what might be his last chance to do some further reading in the latter subject. As John had been prophesying this since Thanksgiving, the news of his decision was no surprise to the family.

Ike had now finished the main work on his railroad report, but there remained a few points about operations on which he and Squire Fulton had not entirely agreed. After supper he wanted to discuss these with someone. Tave was the natural one, since she had been over much of it during the winter and she had offered to help him a few days back. But Ike couldn't for the life of him decide whether she really wanted to talk with him or not. Certainly she hadn't been any more herself the last three or four days. Though she'd stopped fussing over him, and whatever she said to him was agreeable enough, yet she always spoke to him in a funny, stand-offish sort of way, as if she was really mad at him but was trying to put up a mighty front of still feeling friendly. Perhaps the truth was that for some reason she just didn't want any more of his company.

The men had had a hard week and were all out of the way by nine o'clock, leaving Ike sitting sideways at the desk, Sarah in the low rocker knitting, and Tavie in one of the straight chairs, looking at Ike in her set way that made him think she wanted to bite his head off. "Well, Ma," he said, "I finished my report and it wouldn't take much urging to make me talk about it." "You don't have to memorize it, do you?" asked Sarah easily, counting stitches. "Gosh, no," laughed Ike. "It's about thirty pages long. This ain't like a recitation in school, ye know, Ma. These fellers ain't

347

a bit interested in my rhetoric. What they'll listen to is what I've to say. All I've to do is read it so they can hear, and like as not they'll interrupt me every few sentences and tell me I'm talking through my hat."

"Aren't you nervous about it?" asked Tavie with unnecessary vigor. "Not about making the report," said Ike, "though I'm a-mighty nervous about some of the points in it."

"Octavia," said Sarah Lathrop, "we've all had a hard week. If you feel tired I hope you won't hesitate to go to bed, as I shall do myself very shortly." Tavie took this, not as an intimation that Sarah wanted to talk with Ike alone—which in fact she did not—nor as a piece of honest consideration for her obviously wrought-up state—which it was. Rather, in her determined mood she took it as a challenge.

"No, truly, Sarah Lathrop," she said with something like her usual spirit. "If Ike wants to talk about the railroad I would especially like to listen." "I'm mighty pleased if ye sure grit do, Tave," said Ike, "for there are two or three points I'd like to ask ye about, things to do with travelling in general, and that's something you've had more experience in than I have." Tavie threw a triumphant flash of her brown eyes at Mistress Lathrop, but dropped them hurriedly to her lap when she looked at Ike's now frank and absolutely dissolving smile.

Sarah Lathrop, having done her best to extricate Octavia, rose and said, "The fact is, Isaac, I understand so precious little about your railroad that I'd only ask silly questions and most of the time wouldn't know what you were talking about. So I'll bid you good night, and I urge you not to sit up late, for you both need rest." And with that she left the two together, each desperately determined on easy comradeship.

Tavie was immediately in a panic, for Ike was at his most beautiful, and she knew he wouldn't miss a trick to be polite to her. "Why don't you sit yonder in the big rocker?" he now said. "It's the only real comfortable chair in this room—if I did pick it out." "Why don't you sit in it yourself?" replied Tavie. "It's a man's chair." "Oh, I'm sort of reverent about it. It's Pa's, and I've never sat in it yet, except when I bought it from Pete Van Ness." "Well, I guess I'm superstitious too," said Tavie awkwardly.

Ike then relieved her by setting out on a long monologue about the railroad and his report, leading up to a few practical details about the convenience of travellers. How long should be allowed at stations where meals would be served? How much travel could be expected of a person without having a sleep in a bed? And how much sleep would they usually need then? How often"—and here Ike leaned forward and whispered naughtily —"should the train stop for ladies' convenience? I'm told that if ye figger often enough for men, that'll suit the ladies." Ike leaned back again and resumed his easy dignity. Tavie's head was swimming with the simple figures he had been quoting just before, her mind seeming unable to hold anything long enough to understand it. But she did manage to hear this last question. "Why, I'm sure you're right about that," she said with a nervous little smile that was trying to be both easy and faintly scandalized. As soon as she had spoken she could feel her lower lip trembling.

"Ye see," resumed Ike, "it ain't all as easy as it might seem, because it all has to do with the cost of operations and so in the long run the fare per mile. With good hickory and maple, as I told ye a spell back, they say ye get your most economical running at about twenty-five mile an hour. Faster or slower than that you're wasting fuel. Starting especially takes an uncommon lot of power and a hotter fire than is necessary for ordinary running. Of course stopping and waiting is sheer loss, and if ye stop for long and let your fire out there's an a'mighty waste of wood in getting up steam again. What ye've to do is hit a kind of medium between economy and the passengers' comfort. If ye make them too uncomfortable they'll prefer the horse coaches, and if ye stop too much to accommodate them, ye'll have to charge so much that they'll ride in the horse coaches anyway. There's a place in between we're bound to find. We've to charge a little more than the old coaches at best, but if we can take middling care of the travellers we can win out on account of our greater speed. The thing is to offer the conveniences that will persuade just enough folks to ride on the railroad to make it a paying business, and at the same time not offer so much ye'll have to raise the fare and scare 'em all out. I've found my answers to all these questions, but I thought maybe you might have some notions, coming at the thing fresh and having travelled on that Western railroad, that might be more useful than my notions that are mostly taken from books."

Ike paused, and it was as if Tavie had not heard a word he had said. Desperately she had seized on snatches of the questions he had raised, and had been trying to put the time of eating, the rate of burning without draught, the rate of burning at starting, and the cost of wood together in a single algebraic proposition. Her mind had even been trying to construct a set of elements that she could call w, x, y and z and put into some kind of an equation. But the result had been chaos, and from the moment she had attempted this calculation everything Ike had said had been an unintelligible jumble.

Now she dropped her face in her hands and felt herself trembling violently. She heard Ike saying, "Don't try really to figger anything, Tave. That takes quill and paper. It's only the general questions I thought might interest ye." She felt a drop on her hands and experienced some relief in the realization that now she couldn't avoid showing tears. "Ike," she said, looking up at him with shining eyes and speaking with increasing hysteria, "it's just no use. I just don't understand a thing about your railroad, any more than your ma does. Only she's honest and says so, and I've tried to pretend that I did understand something. Well, I just don't, and I never did. Back a month ago when we were such—such good friends—I was only fooling you to—please you, and I just can't do it any longer. I can't. I can't. I'm just no use to you at all!"

She dropped her face in her hands and let the sobs come. She looked up at Ike and saw his gentle, big eyes on her with such tenderness as she had never imagined a human being could show. Then, responsive to her glance, she saw that little pucker between his eyes, that look of unconscious appeal that was something like a hurt child's. Feeling herself about to faint, she rose and groped out of the room and across the kitchen. Ike came after her and took her by the shoulders.

"Tave," he said, "ye mustn't take on. We can't go on like this. Ain't I your friend? Ain't I entitled to see ye cry if ye're o' mind to, and to try to righten whatever's making ye cry?" Tavie turned around and put her wet face against his big chest, while he patted her shoulders so gently it was like the caress of summer wind. His touch stopped her hysterics. With his arm around her shoulder, and taking the candle from the kitchen mantel, he led her into the north parlor, sat her down in one of the gilt armchairs and pulled up another for himself.

"Can't ye tell me what's the trouble, Tave, whatever it is that's come between us the last few weeks? We were getting on so fine before. Can't ye tell me? Or if ye can't tell me, can't ye write it down and let me read it some time? There's no sense going on this way. Honest, Tave, I've thought about it more than anything—except maybe business—and I'm clean stumped. Likely as not I've done something"—at this Tavie, feeling much easier, shook her head emphatically—"but whatever it is, I can't get at it unless ye'll help me."

When Tavie was sure he had finished she said, "Well, Ike, my—friend, if you'll give me a little more time, maybe a week or two, I may be able to make you understand, or at least to stop behaving like such a—what did we call it?—a 'ninny.'" Here they both smiled in retrospect. "But, Tave, why can't ye give me just a little hint, something so I can be thinking about it too and maybe help ye, if it's you needs help? I'm as much in the dark as if all the candles and lamps in the world had gone out."

Tavie contemplated her toe for a long time, and gradually there came over her face a smile of combined fondness, pity and a sense of tragedy, the smile of a woman who is in love with a man who is not in love with her, who has no notion of her state, and isn't even giving her the emotional release of treating her badly, the smile of a captive who yet feels somehow stronger, the mistress of greater and deeper forces, than her innocent and ignorant captor, the smile of a tortured person who is yet grateful to her torturer for bringing her whole soul awake, and who pities him for his inability to share the awakening.

Presently, behind that smile, Tavie's fierce will set and she looked up at Ike without wincing. Then she looked away again, and when she spoke it was in a hesitant and tender tone. "Well, Ike," she said, "if you insist I can —perhaps—tell you—give you a hint—of part of it—just now—just these last few days. I don't know how much you know about—women. Had you ever heard that there are—times when—?" She glanced up at Ike with a hunted look, then turned away, biting her lip in shame.

Ike had never been so embarrassed in his life. He had heard of such things, but only in the coarsest way from men. Now he easily exaggerated what little knowledge he had. For him this was sufficient excuse to explain everything, and he certainly didn't want her to go into details. "I'm uncommon sorry, Tave," he murmured. "I've just been a danged fool!" He dropped his head and slowly ran one hand through his gorgeous blond mane. Tavie reached over and ran her hand slowly through it too, feeling relaxed for the first time in months, still smiling her consecrated, quiet smile.

Finally Ike reached up, took her hand down and pressed it gently between both of his. But he still kept his head down. Tavie rose, stepped over beside him, ran her hand through his hair two or three times again, then went quietly from the room and up to bed.

Ike stayed in his bent position a while longer, then straightened up. Slowly a great smile came over his face. He didn't want a drink now. Abruptly he rose, blew out the candles and marched up the front stairs to bed, suppressing an impulse to whistle a tune.

CHAPTER XLVIII

T A V I E'S unmaidenly confession cleared the air for Ike. He gloried in the restoration of the former feeling of congeniality, heightened now by the sense of sharing what seemed to him the most intimate and final of secrets. He was flattered to the depths·by Tavie's confession, and for about two weeks showed a sort of watchful possessiveness when he was about her, as if they were married and she pregnant.

For about a week things were almost as satisfactory to Tavie. A confession of something to somebody, even a distorted confession, was good for her soul. Also she saw at once on Sunday that, far from lowering herself in Ike's eyes, she had increased her importance to him, had even acquired a new sort of power over him. Amused as she was at his avuncular solicitude, she yet found repose in it, for it was obviously not feigned through politeness. Since she had never discussed such a thing with anyone but her ma, she too felt something of a new and important privacy with Ike. During his absence at the railroad meeting on Tuesday night, she was able to think calmly about the questions he had raised, and on Wednesday evening made him some intelligent, detailed suggestions, two or three of which actually found their way, years later, into the initial operations of the Utica, Bloomington and Byzantium Railroad.

But when a week and more had passed she began to realize wearily that her profession of indisposition could not long serve her. She gave Ike credit for more knowledge than he possessed, and presumed that shortly his credulity must lapse. She began to feel toward him exactly as she had before, the same fluttering timidity, the same irrepressible impulse to minister to him, made desperate by the same hysterical sense of helplessness to please him, now or ever. She did, however, carry away two permanent effects from her interlude of peace. One was the lesson that the confessional method worked with Ike. The other was a greater consciousness of specific, carnal desire than she had entertained of late. Her purely conversational intimacy had weakened the bars of reticence, and she now hungered consciously for a more realistic intimacy.

After worrying through another week, aided by Ike's continuing solicitude, Tavie got in the same post a letter from her pa and one from Mrs. Mott. Her pa's letter was divided as usual between professions of his own comfort, expressions of affection and inquiries as to whether she had any new hopes of the appointment in Oberlin. Mrs. Mott's letter was posted in Oberlin. That friend and leader said she was giving a course of lectures there and was taking advantage of the opportunity to further Tavie's case with the authorities. She had had agreeable talks both with President Mahan and with Dr. Finney, who was to succeed Dr. Mahan as president next term and would undoubtedly be responsible henceforth for any new appointments to the faculty. There was nothing specifically encouraging for Tavie in the letter, but, combined with her pa's, it drew her attention from herself to her larger loyalties and restored her perspective. The next afternoon, which was the first of May, she walked down to the lower meadow to think things out clearly. Spreading an old horse blanket on the muddy ground, she settled herself on a little point at a bend in the swollen Lathrop River, a situation hidden by alders from the house a half mile back up the hill.

Tavie was not one to be sentimental about spring and nature, but the steady, quiet, impersonal swirl of the brook immediately put her in the detached mood she had sought. Also, the sight of the meadows greening to the thrust of millions of young blades of grass; the pussywillows fully burst in tall clusters by the stream; the bright green skunk-cabbage rank along the bank; the streaking of the trout like shadowy, live arrows up the stream; the rich screaming and chatter of many pairs of meadowlarks, all busy at mating and play: all this helped to restore that sense of the basically biological significance of love to which she had held so stoutly until she began to fall in love with Ike in the submissive way that she knew kept women slaves to men.

She saw that her undoing had been the relaxing of her original conviction that love was simply an animal business, a too great indulgence of her tender impulses. Those impulses, she now concluded, were after all but manifestations of the single vital urge, no more than physical impulses in themselves, the impulses of motherhood. In letting them control her, she had been putting the cart before the horse. Henceforth she must keep her mind on the main chance, the chance of really attracting Ike, without thinking about taking care of him or even being casually friendly with him. She must overcome this present fatal tendency at once to serve him and to run away in terror if he so much as looked at her. She must play the minx as she had done back in the winter, only now with a more deliberate purpose of really capturing him. She must know the full experience of love for what it was worth—"which," the phantom of Mrs. Mott had told her last February, "is little enough"—"Something altogether in the course of nature"—"To be taken lightly and joyfully, even as men enjoy us." Tavie's breath caught, and she sighed deeply at the thought of taking this love "lightly and joyfully." Oh, Ike! If only you were as ready as I am! She lay back on the blanket and closed her eyes.

"Proceed into marriage and fulfillment." Tavie saw the flickering borealis and heard the phantom speaking these phrases as clearly as if it had been last night instead of months, ages ago. "Proceed into marriage." Ike did not want to marry her. And in truth did she want to marry him? Ike, the business man, blind to the needs of humanity—Reform, Woman's Rights, Temperance, Abolition. To be truly his wife would be to sacrifice her life's ambitions. Ah, she would sacrifice them quickly enough!

But Ike didn't want to marry her! Why should she lead him to it? Perhaps make him unhappy—make him regret it—make him hate her—perhaps wreck both of their lives. Were they not fortunate? He did not want to marry her, and marriage to him would be for her the greatest of mistakes. Oh, Ike, are we not fortunate? Again she sighed deeply. She felt a lump in her throat and the tears rising. She opened her eyes and sat up abruptly, in irritation at her weakness.

"Proceed into fulfillment"—"Deny nothing when the denial grows more costly than the thing denied." That was it. That was the solution for her and Ike. It was common enough certainly. A fair share of marriages started that way. That was what Constant had wanted, and certainly he loved her. Only with Ike it would be with no thought of marriage. Let that be a separate question, afterwards. Something to be avoided if possible, unless in its turn it became a thing whose "denial grew more costly than the thing denied." It would be the worst thing for both of them! Oh, Ike, would it be the worst thing? Again the lump in her throat—

"Shame on you, Octavia Samson," she said aloud, kicking the ground with her heel. "Ike does not love you. You ought to be glad. Ike does not love you, do you understand? Have you no pride? Ike does not love you. Remember that! He *does not love you!*"

Tavie stood up, clasped her hands behind her head and stretched back, looking defiantly at the blue sky. Who is Ike Lathrop? she thought angrily. I am Octavia Samson, daughter of Solon Samson who loves me and is in prison for breaking the Fugitive Slave Law! Octavia Samson, educated woman, graduate of Oberlin! Friend of many great men and women! Octavia Samson, reformer, worker for Woman's Rights! Who is

Ike Lathrop? Who is any man? "Proceed into fulfillment." She glanced at the orange sun low over Pond Hill, and knew it was time to be starting supper. She picked up the blanket and walked proudly up the hill, as she had walked down into the glen on that snowy night after she saw the vision.

At a quarter of six Ike came in fairly dancing with enthusiasm. Tavie felt the usual jump in her heart but, setting her teeth, she was able to say, "Good evening, Ike," lightly enough and to give him a direct smile that had more of insinuation than tenderness in it. After hanging up his coat he kissed his ma with more zest than usual, then came over to Tavie at the sink and whispered, "Tave, I've great news, sure grit! I'll tell ye alone if ye like, but I'm saving the general announcement for supper." Without waiting for Tavie's reply he skipped off into the keeping-room, where his pa, having cleaned up after chores, was reading in the big rocker.

"I've first-rate news, Pa!" said Ike irrepressibly, seizing his father's hand. "I hain't told a soul yet, and I'm figgering to make the announcement at supper!" "Good," said the Squire, smiling responsively to his son's enthusiasm. "Something about the railroad, is it?" "If ye don't mind, Pa, I'd like to tell ye all at once." "Is it perhaps something we might drink a toast to here before we sit down?" asked the Squire. "Why, yes, sir, it is," said Ike, but he added with a little pucker of his brow, "that is, if ye agree with me that it's important." "I daresay," said the Squire, "anything so important to you will be equally important at least to your ma and me. Suppose ye get the glasses and the brandy." And as Ike went out the Squire went back to reading the editorial in the last *Albany Argus*.

A moment after Ike's return with the potables Master Lane, Henry Hawks and Ben came in from chores, leaving their boots outside as always in this muddy season and stepping into their respective carpet slippers which Sarah always left arranged inside the kitchen door. As soon as each had had his splutter in the basin in the kitchen sink and had scratched his scalp with the comb before the little mirror, the Squire called out genially, "As soon as supper's ready, will the women folks honor Isaac and me by joining us? We've some fine news for ye." At this Sarah hastily finished slicing the boiled ham she had just forked from the pot, set the platter in a Dutch oven before the fire, left the biscuits in the other Dutch oven, and nodded to Tavie.

"Well, Isaac," said the Squire when all were assembled, "tell us the news before we explode with curiosity." "Well, sir," said Ike, looking from Tavie to his ma, "fact is we've just sold a Byzantium steam engine to Applemore and Bostwick for the *Democratic Union*. It's our first sale, but, more than that, it's the first time a steam engine has been used to run a press in the whole world, and if it works our fortune's made. We signed the contract and they've given a bond for payment upon satisfactory performance." And Ike beamed like a boy who had brought home the biggest trout anybody ever saw.

The Squire's first thought was that not only would Ike's fortune be made but Applemore's grip on the community would be strengthened. But he said, "That's capital, Isaac," and quickly turned to pour out six nips of brandy—Tavie of course wouldn't take any. "And now," he resumed, lifting his glass, "I propose a toast to the first steam engine in northern New York and to the continuing fortunes of the Byzantium Steam Engine Company."

Tavie felt a surge of anger at the formality and indifference with which this toast was proposed. For once she wished she had not signed a pledge not to drink. She was tempted to break her pledge, but instead she now threw a defiant look at the Squire and marched straight up to Ike. "That's great news, Ike," she said, reached up, drew his face down and gave him a smacking kiss on the lips. Then all of a sudden she felt a burst of tears rising, and fled into the kitchen. "I am very happy for you," said Sarah, likewise stepping over to Ike and kissing him.

But the Squire stood dumb, appalled by Tavie's brazen display of emotional commitment to Ike. There was a moment of awkward silence. "Well," said Master Lane, lifting his glass, "be ye drinkin' liquor, or ain't ye?" And he gulped his drink, followed by the others without unison.

At supper and thereafter Ike continued to monopolize the conversation, with his pa's acquiescence and his ma's and Tavie's encouragement. When they were settled in the keeping-room Ben asked, with the condescension of seventeen, whether these engines would be of any use on a farm—say, to turn a grindstone. "Indeed, they will," said Ike. "We're even working on a sort of locomotive that'll run without rails and can be steered by turning the axle like a wagon. We could even plow with that, or haul a load on tolerably even ground." And Ike rattled on, while Ben smiled a little dubiously.

When the conversation lagged Tavie asked Ike if he could draw a rough design of the engine that was going to run the press of the *Union*. Ike's eyes widened with delight, and turning to the desk, he fished out a piece of foolscap and started to draw with the quill, while Tavie pulled up a chair next to him.

This gave the others the chance they had wanted. The hired men bade a general good night and went up to bed, followed by Ben. "Well, Isaac," said the Squire, rising, "it's near ten. I shall be much interested to study your drawing in the morning, but in the meantime I believe a little sleep would sharpen my wits." Ike and Tavie said good night to the Squire, who vanished into his room. Sarah lingered for five minutes, looking over Ike's shoulder and asking sincere, irrelevant questions. Then she kissed Tavie . and Ike and went off to join her husband. The big clock in the front hall made Tavie jump when it started to strike ten.

As the house quieted down and Ike drew on and on, showing no sign that he even knew Tavie was there, she first lapsed from her nervousness into a kind of dream state, luxuriating in his proximity, his beautiful hair, his big, gentle profile and rosy cheeks, his obvious strength and self-sufficiency. Just now he was completely concentrated on the minute lines he was making, and Tavie felt a kind of maternal pride in watching over him, eager to help him if she could.

But when she glanced from his face to the multiplying complexity of the lines of the drawing, her dream state suddenly scattered. She knew that most of the drawing would be meaningless to her. From then on, every time he stirred his elbow a little spasm gripped her, fearing that he was through or even that he was going to speak.

As this terror increased, Tavie's will stiffened against it. Spiritually she withdrew from Ike, almost losing consciousness of his presence, engaging in an inward battle of which he was only the symbol of one of the forces. "Something altogether in the course of nature"— "To be taken for what it is worth, which is little enough," she said fiercely in her mind. "What say?" said Ike, suddenly looking at her, and her determination and inward battle went up in panicky smoke. "I thought ye said something," said Ike quietly, turning back to his work. "Likely I fancied it."

From then on Ike became aware of Tavie's nervousness and began to wonder how he could relieve her of it. He finished the drawing, put back the pen and rose. "There she is," he said lightly. "And now I figger it's time I turned in. We can look at the drawing in the morning." "But, Ike," Tavie managed to say, "I—I—want to see the drawing—*now*." "Pretty late, ain't it?" he said casually. "For me, I'm kind of tuckered out, with all the excitement of the afternoon." Tavie set her teeth, and all she could think to say, and that almost unintelligibly, was, "I want to see it—I want to see it."

Ike had walked away to the mantel, and now he came back dubiously. "All keerect, if ye say so," and his world-inclusive smile beamed down on her like a dissolving blow. She had to drop her eyes. Then she pulled up close to the desk—she did not dare to stand—and bent over it, apparently studying the unintelligible patchwork Ike had made. It was obvious to him that she was only trying to please him. As he stood over her, looking down at her back as she bent over the desk, the contrast flashed into his mind between Pru Stark looking at the railroad drawings in the office with her plan to bamboozle him, and Tavie here, who was really his friend and only wanted to be nice to him.

He sat down beside her and spent fifteen minutes going over the details of the proposed engine, being very careful not to pause so as to embarrass her and remembering, even when he got very interested, not to ask her if she understood. Tavie sensed his protective attitude and, as long as he continued to talk, felt reasonably secure again, even luxurious in his now close proximity. She had time to prepare herself for the end of his exposition, and when he had finished she said with real feeling, "It's a wonderful thing, Ike, though there are some details I don't fully understand." "There are plenty I don't," said Ike.

Tavie went on with her prepared speech: "I am so proud of you, Ike, so proud that you have really got the start you wanted, and that you got it while I was here and while we were friends. It will be one of my finest memories as long as I live and whatever becomes of me." While Tavie was speaking Ike was attacked by a desire to kiss her, a desire he had recently kept so well under control that he had thought it wouldn't trouble him again. She was indeed unusually desirable just now, the single candle from the desk sharply outlining her straight features, and throwing bright highlights on her brown eyes that now seemed black, and a shimmering glint on the waves of gold hair that swelled out from under the bronze rope, with the two curls trembling in front of her ears.

"Thank ye, Tave," said Ike when she had spoken her piece. "There certainly ain't anyone in the world I'd rather have pleased with me than you."

Instantly he realized he had said something amiss, for Tavie turned her head away. He determined on a plan that he thought would clear things up. Drawing his chair a little way from the desk, he sat down, clasped his hands and looked at them for a moment. Then he straightened up and threw one leg over the other.

"As a matter of fact, Tave," he said, "it's now a fairly good bet that our little engine company's going to make some money, and that sort of suggests something I've had in mind to speak to ye about for a good spell." He paused as if embarrassed, and Tavie was sure she was going to faint. She put her elbow on the desk, her hand covering her trembling lips.

"What I want to speak to ye about," Ike resumed, "has to do with that power of attorney your pa gave ye before he went away. Ye'll recollect that we bought a bull calf from him last Thanksgiving time and, whether ye know it or not, all we gave him for it was ten dollars. As I told him then, ten dollars was no more than a fair price for veal, and it's likely that's an exceptionally fine bull in the making—by our Xerxes out of your Clover. 'Tain't likely there'll be a better sire of milkers in the county than that little bull, and so your pa and I made a sort of contract. Either of us could value him at any time we like, and whatever he was worth over the ten dollars we'd owe your pa, less the cost of his feed. Fact is, that's a loose kind of arrangement all round, and I'd a'mighty like to get it straight and simple."

As soon as it was apparent that Ike was not leading up to the question of marriage, Tavie's near swoon of agitation had given way to the most abysmal sense of humiliation, due partly to the shock to her pride, but mostly to the realization that she, Octavia Samson, could be so dependent on any man as to hang trembling on the possibility of his declaring himself. She wanted to crawl in a deep hole somewhere, and as Ike went on mumbling about bulls and dollars she wanted to scream and scratch out her eyes for a trivial, helpless girl.

"Every day he lives," Ike was continuing his monologue, "it gets more likely the little feller's going to grow to a value of four or five hundred when he's a three-year-old. I think it'd be no more'n fair to value him at two hundred and sixty today, and that's allowing for his keep to date and his keep for another year before he starts to serve. I say just two-sixty because that happens to be a convenient figger. We allowed your pa ten dollars for him at the start-off. That reduces the figger to two-fifty. Then your pa's paid down to fifty dollars on a note he owes me. We cancel that and that leaves two hundred we owe ye on the bull calf. Of course we could let the agreement go as it is, and in two or three years, it's likely we'd owe your pa four hundred instead of two hundred. But I'm of the opinion that, as a result of this sale to Applemore, the engine company stock is going to do plenty better than double in value in a couple of years. What I propose is to give your pa two of my six shares, worth two hundred today and worth anybody's guess day after tomorrow."

Tavie wondered if Ike would never stop. "Now, I know your pa's mighty pernickety about taking anything that might turn out to be worth more than he paid for it. I can't promise ye he'd do as I'm suggesting if he was here. But to my way of thinking he's foolish that way and ought to enjoy some of the profits of a business he helped to start. If you and I put through this deal he'll likely accuse me of outwitting ye and all that. But he's a stickler about law and'll likely stand by the legal bargain. So, if we do this, he may in spite of himself turn up with a thousand or two one of these days.

"Of course, if I'm wrong about the engine company stock being bound to go up, I don't figger to trim your pa, so I plan to put in the transaction an undertaking to buy back the stock for five hundred, say, three years from now, and that'll be somewhere around the right figger for the bull at that time. What d'ye say, Tave? I'm uncommon certain it's a chance to do your pa a good turn."

With her elbow on the desk and her mouth in her hand, Tavie was biting the palm and taking a kind of fiendish joy in the pain. She understood nothing that Ike had said, and all of a sudden realized he had stopped talking. Angrily she turned her eyes toward him, without otherwise changing her position.

"I'm sorry I bothered ye with this, Tave," Ike said simply, lowering his head. "I should have had more sense. We can take it up another time." And he rose as if to go to bed. "What do you want?" Tavie asked fiercely. "Nothing now," Ike said. "We can take it up again whenever it's agreeable." "What do you want?" Tavie repeated. "Please tell me." "All I was thinking," said Ike, now looking worried, "was that ye might sign a bill of sale of the calf to me in return for the ten dollars paid, the cancellation of the note, and two shares of engine company stock." "Why, let's do it, then!" said Tavie. "Here—what—where do I sign?"

"Well," said Ike, "if ye want to do it I guess I can write out a bill of sale, but it'll take a minute." He sat down to the desk, took a piece of paper, and wrote out the bill. While he was doing it Tavie fell to trembling in her old way, and by the time he pushed the little document over in front of her, the first thing she did was to drop two great tears on it. "Where do I sign?" she stammered. "Write 'Solon Samson' there," said Ike, "and 'by Octavia Samson' under it." She wrote a wretched little signature that suggested but remotely her usually bold hand. "I'm plaguy sorry I brought this up, Tave," said Ike, sanding the document. "I sure grit think it's for the best."

He put the paper down and glanced sideways at her in embarrassment, then shifted round in his chair, put his arm on the desk, and faced her with that full gentleness of his—not now his big, omniscient smile, but his look of universal sympathy and solicitude, as if he were a sort of boyish god baffled by some intimation that everything was not well with the world he had made.

"I've been a fool tonight, Tave," he said. "Sort of lost my head, I guess, about the engine. I knew better, of course, but I near forgot that ye might not be feeling quite up to scratch and I had no business pestering ye." And with that he reached over, took her hand down from her face, and pressed it between his two big ones.

While Ike had been speaking to her his soft, baritone voice had acted as a charm on Tavie. She had stopped trembling, had lifted her gaze and dropped it several times until finally her eyes rested on his almost without effort. When he stopped speaking and took her hand, she started trembling again, but she kept looking at him. She saw a faint flush come on his face and that old pucker appeared between his eyes. She knew that in a moment he was going to kiss her. He took one hand from hers, put it on her shoulder and started to draw her toward him. Suddenly the tears welled up. With a little shriek she leapt from her chair and fled.

Upstairs on her bed, the tears of helpless love gradually changed to tears of rage at herself for a coward, a feeble, spiritless baby. As Pru Stark had done to the window frame in Ike's office some months before, now Tavie pounded the pillow with her fists. Finally, from sheer exhaustion, she lay still and began to think.

Downstairs Ike paced the room a couple of times, then sat down at the desk with his chin in his hands and gazed at the candle. "Dang stupid of me," he thought. "But she sure is a funny one. If all women are like that it's no wonder fellers take to drink. On the other hand, Tave's only been like this a little while, a month or some such, and she's bound to straighten out true grit one of these days. No use blaming her just because I made a slip myself. She'll be all keerect come morning, and I haven't anything further to bother her with so far as I know."

The clock in the little hall at his left began striking eleven. Ike didn't feel specially like bed. He sighed and looked down at the desk. He picked up the bill of sale, looked it over, folded it, and put it in his pocket. Then he looked over his design of the proposed engine again. He had omitted a good many features to make it simple. He thought he might as well finish it, showing the shaft, pulley and belt to the press. There was even room to draw in the press in outline, though he couldn't draw it in detail if he wanted to. He picked up his pen and went to work again.

The whole house was still but for the steady scratch of Ike's pen, the soft click as he dipped it from time to time, an occasional pop from the embers in the kitchen, the soft ticking of the big clock in the hall. Out in the barn one of the horses thumped his stall. Very faintly Ike could hear the rush of the swollen Lathrop River. Yes, he'd been a fool all right, he thought, after all she'd told him. Yet Tave was a sort of funny girl for all that—fine as they come—pretty, too—but sort of funny—maybe like her ma. When it came to that, Solon was a little peculiar himself. Ike had never seen Aggie behave like that, even when she was in love with Homer—and they say women are specially pernickety when they're in love.

The back stairs at the other end of the kitchen creaked twice before Ike noticed it. "Tave going outside," he thought, paying no particular attention and going on with his drawing. But presently he found himself listening for something he didn't hear, the usual creak of the boards in the summer kitchen when anybody went out back. From listening subconsciously, he began to listen consciously, but didn't look up. The house was as quiet as ever. The ticking of the clock in the hall. Master Lane's muffled snoring upstairs. Ike stopped drawing. Minutes passed. He heard his own heart thumping, and it seemed to grow louder. Suddenly he glanced up to the left. The doors through to the north parlor were open, and there was a glow there. He rose and walked casually across through the hall.

Tavie had set her candle on the little gilt mantel, and she was standing beside it. Her nightgown, with lace at the neck and wrists and down the button band, was turned open at the throat so a V of her chest was bare. She had on a little lace nightcap that let her hair wave out and down over her shoulders, and in front of the cap she had tied a band of tiny, artificial flowers. When Ike came in she put her hand on the mantel. Otherwise she did not move, but stood stock-still, staring at him.

As Ike stood, staring back at her eyes that seemed coal black in the candle-light, he had the feeling that he was looking at Solon Samson, not Tavie; not a woman at all but Solon Samson, tall, strong and severe. His only emotion was amazement. Then she leaned forward suddenly, so the inner curves of her breast showed, and extended her hand toward him in an inviting gesture. Desire rose sudden and warm through him. He stepped forward, and the next moment was holding her in his arms, kissing her. She clung close to him, then reached round, took one of his hands and pressed it against her breast. The next thing he knew his hand was inside her nightgown. Then he drew back suddenly and, holding both of her hands strongly in both of his, lifted his head and closed his eyes.

"Tave," he whispered huskily, "Tave, we mustn't——"

"Ike," whispered Tavie, looking down and putting her cheek against his chest. "Ike, I—I love you." She drew back to peer up at him with frightened appeal. He opened his eyes and looked down at her. The desire he had been fighting flooded with tenderness. He took her gently by the shoulders, kissed her on the lips and continued looking at her with that pucker between his eyes. Tavie lowered hers, and leaned lightly against him.

"I came down," she murmured, "to ask you to—to—come to my room— tonight." She clung to him, sobbing softly, and Ike, still holding her by the shoulders, pressed her against him till the sobs stopped.

"Tave," he said, now breathing rapidly, "if we did that, ye know, ye'd have to marry me."

"No, no, no," said Tavie, shaking her head violently against him, then drawing back and lifting her face defiantly, but not meeting his eyes. "You promised me you wouldn't mention that, and you must not. I—simply—I love you and I must—you must— Otherwise I must go away—far—soon—tomorrow."

"But, Tave—," Ike began.

"No, no," she said strongly, stamping her slippered foot. "You must not. Please—please don't mention—that—any more." Once more she put her face on his chest and began to sob.

"Tave," he said, speaking with difficulty while pressing her against him. "Tave, you know I love you." She gave a shudder, then stopped sobbing. "It shouldn't be long now," Ike continued, "before I can afford to get married on my own." Tavie's body stiffened. "In fact, I think it would be a good notion to get married right soon. Why not?"

Tavie thrust back from him strongly and looked straight up at him with that Solon Samson glare she had had when he first came in. "Then you refuse me, do you?" she said quietly. She relaxed and lowered her eyes. Ike felt her trembling. "I thought," she said faintly, "you'd do something to help me."

Ike drew her into a long embrace, more abandoned than before. In a pause, while Tavie's head hung back, her eyes closed and her lips parted, Ike whispered, "Tave—my darling—I guess I want this more than you do, but we can't do it without getting married—at least—at least some time." Tavie reached up with her hands, drew his face down to a kiss, then murmured so faintly he could hardly hear her, "My darling—just—promise me one thing—don't talk of it any more tonight. That's all I ask."

For answer Ike took her in his arms again, feeling her limp and utterly his. Finally, she reached out weakly and took the candle from the mantel, making as if to turn away. Ike half-carried her through the kitchen to the foot of the back stairs. He looked back at the glow of the candle in the keeping-room and hesitated. "Soon!" he whispered, releasing her. She leaned up to be kissed, then went slowly up the back stairs, staggering once against the side wall.

With the clumsiness of whirling impatience, Ike snuffed the candle in the keeping-room, then went out to the kitchen and crouched, scattering the fire. He felt detached, numb, suspended in the universe. A thought of caution flitted remotely through consciousness— It wasn't yet too late—

What was he doing?— Then he laughed at the notion of showing the white feather now.

The next thing he knew he was undressing in the dark in the back attic. When he got his nightshirt he managed to observe that Ben was sound asleep, seeming somewhere far off in that other world outside Ike, that inconsequential, forgotten world where Ike had lived ages ago. With the darkness spinning round him so he was afraid he would fall down the back stairwell, he groped his way to Tavie's door and scratched on it with his fingernail. "Come in," came a whisper which he could hardly hear for the pounding of his heart.

Slowly he drew open the door and entered. Tavie had shaded the candle and sat in the dim light, half-propped up in bed, wearing her little lace nightcap with the band of artificial flowers in front of it, and her hair tumbling down all over her bosom. For a long moment they stared at each other, their feelings mutual in combined shyness and desire. Gently Ike sat down on the bed and took one of Tavie's hands. Instinctively she drew the covers to her chin and turned her face away. Then on an impulse she looked back with a gay smile, released the covers and extended both her arms.

CHAPTER XLIX

F O R M O S T of May, Tavie and Ike were together every night without a shadow falling across their idyll. Sometimes they waited until the house was asleep, then went to Tavie's room. Sometimes, when they were supposed to be sitting up "gabbin'" after the family had retired, the gilt Louis XV furniture of the north parlor witnessed such scenes of abandoned impatience as it had shared, if at all, only in its youth eighty and more years before in France. During all this period Ike's conscience was clear, for every night he whispered to Tave of his plans for their forthcoming marriage. He proposed that they take a wedding trip to Oberlin, if that would please her, and afterwards it would likely be best to rent a little house in the village, for the business of the railroad would take most of his time after the middle of July when the bids of the engineers began to come in. To all of this Tavie would listen with an affectionate indifference and, drawing Ike's big head down against her neck, would whisper ecstatically, "Let's enjoy this happiness while we can, and not worry about that for a little while."

Together they floated in a warm flood of the present, and although Ike thought he was very circumspect, yet actually the external world was so unimportant and so far away, even from his eyes and ears, that unwittingly he took the most flagrant chances. And as if the gods were conspiring to protect the lovers, the external world kept its distance outside their secret circle, and miraculously not a person in the house had the slightest direct evidence of their meetings.

But without direct evidence, it was plain to everyone except Ben that some change had occurred. Tavie bloomed and sparkled and hummed at her work. Her thin cheeks seemed to fill out and their usual pallor gave way to a rosy glow. Sarah Lathrop, herself now very nervous and forlorn with her own change, took a secret delight in the realization that the fruitful life of the family was going on. The Squire was sure that, even if he had been mistaken before, there was now no doubt that Ike was taking liberties with Octavia. He had so far armored himself against the boy's misconduct that he kept the matter out of his thoughts. Yet the increasing certainty of an illicit connection going on in his house between his son and the daughter of his friend, with no prospect of a condoning marriage, gnawed like a cancer in his midriff.

As for Master Lane and Henry Hawks, they sank into that state of deliberately blind tolerance which was conventional in such cases unless and until there should be evidence of an imminent birth. Master Lane had said his say when he thought there was yet time; he now figured there was nothing more he could do about it. He ceased glowering at Ike and nipping him with sarcasm and became ceremoniously polite, as did Henry Hawks. Once when they were at morning chores Henry said, "Ike seems to be late this morning." "Yep," said Master Lane without changing the rhythm of his milking. And thus the matter was fully discussed, understood, and thereafter closed between the two old men.

The effects of Ike's union with Tavie were as evident in his changed manner and appearance as in hers. There was a new vitality in him, an air of certitude even greater than that which had come over him when he had first risen to authority in the world of affairs. His perceptions, especially of his mother's wishes, were quicker than usual, and his gaze, especially into his father's eyes, was more direct and penetrating. He was prepared, at the slightest challenge from his pa, to tell him that he was in love with Tavie and had asked her to marry him.

One afternoon near the end of the month two disquieting incidents occurred. Having dined as usual at Howell Sherwood's, Ike walked with Alec Mathiesson down Washington Street and along the west side of the Mall on the way to his office. At Grabbot's store Ike left Alec and turned in to make a purchase for his mother—till then represented by a rubber on his finger. And as he strode into the spacious store, without any premeditation on either side, he almost ran into Mistress Stark and Prudence just emerging from some shopping of their own.

Instead of the embarrassment which he would have anticipated had he foreseen this first meeting since the passage in his office, Ike was suddenly inflated with a sort of bravado which expressed itself in exaggerated courtesy. With a deep sweep of his hat, he touched Mistress Stark's ungloved hand with his lips—a form of salutation which had almost vanished from the code of Byzantium. Then, turning to Pru and taking her fingers in his, he gave them a little press and bowing over them, looked so magnanimously into her eyes that the arrogant flash vanished under drooping lashes and, quickly taking her mother's arm, she forced her on her way before any but the perfunctory mumbles of greeting had been exchanged. As they went down the steps of the little bluff to their waiting carriage Pru almost visibly shook herself, ruffling away a sensation which was new in her experience, not haughty resentment at this catch-of-the-town who had humiliated her, but the terrifying perception that here was a man who could completely possess and command her if he chose. By the time she had settled her skirts in the corner of the new brougham, she had recognized this new sensation, pronounced it intolerable, scotched it, and filed it away in the wise little cabinet of her mind. By the time the stable-boy had released the horses into a brisk trot up the Mall under the caressing sun, she was again her dignified, beautiful self, serene and unperturbable, smiling and nodding graciously at the passers-by on the foot-path and in other similar carriages.

The effect of this meeting on Ike was even more momentary. He did not pause to consider why he had enjoyed what he would have anticipated with discomfort. As he eagerly questioned the clerk about the health of himself and his family, while he cut off six and two-thirds yards of white lawn according to sample, Pru completely vanished from his consciousness. But he was exhilarated all the same, and a trifle flushed. Deep in the center of his being something had stirred whose immediate expression was playful and gay. With a lilting, exuberant gait he marched out of the store carrying his bundle, his coat-tails swinging, his mind turning to steam engines, his spirit sailing high on the caressing south wind of this beautiful near-June day. So absently joyful was he that at the door he almost collided with the tall, splendidly shawled Mistress Gadston and the dainty Mistress Tanofly. Gathering himself, he favored them with the same overflowing courtesy he had shown the Starks. Then he proceeded on his way with his feet somewhat nearer the ground.

The other incident of that afternoon was more immediately disturbing. Returning from the office at four, Ike was just crossing Wheeler corner when he saw Bub Tanofly coming up Court Street, as usual driving his own little empty brougham. But, as was unusual, he was walking the horses and was slumped forward on the box closely wrapped in his greatcoat though few were even carrying theirs today, his silk hat tilted so far forward that it threatened to fall off. Ike's first thought was that Bub was drunk, that he had never before seen him nearly so far gone.

Without seeming to notice him, Bub reined in his horses gently at the corner. He straightened back his hat, glanced away from Ike at the Wheeler House, and contemplated his horses' backs indecisively for a moment. Then, without looking at Ike, he said out of the corner of his mouth so Ike could just hear him, "H'ist yer carcass up here, or climb inside if it suits ye better." Ike stepped on the wheel and h'isted his carcass up on the box. Without comment Bub slumped with his elbows on his knees again, clucked softly to the team and resumed his slow way. All the way up Washington Street to Bub's big, square, brick mansion nothing was said, and Ike alone acknowledged the salutes of passing acquaintances.

After leaving the rig for the coachman to unharness, Bub led Ike through the kitchen, into the big hall, and so to the front parlor with the white marble fireplace, marble-top tables, heavy lace curtains, and two or three groups of white figures of Christian and bucolic personages disposed on ebony pedestals under glass domes. As Bub walked Ike noticed that his boots sloshed as if they were full of water.

"Set down," he said peremptorily, then disappeared and returned with a decanter of rum, a white china pitcher of water and tumblers. "Got any reason to refresh yourself?" he asked in a sarcastic tone as he closed the door. "Not unless to join ye," parried Ike, observing now that Bub was not drunk and looking up at him with concern. "Put down yer coat and fix yerself a drink," Bub commanded. Ike obeyed. Bub likewise threw off his coat and revealed the fact that his clothes were soaking wet below the waist. He kept his hat on, and while Ike was watering his own drink, put down a full tumbler of neat rum.

Ike sat down, Bub pulling up a little hair-cloth chair so as to face him closely, and fetching from the hearth a polished, brass cuspidor which he placed beside them. He was no sooner seated than two puddles of water began to spread round his feet on the costly carpet. "Seegar?" he inquired more gently, producing a handful from his breast pocket, and Ike took one. Bub lighted it and his own from a little perpetual lamp, sat down again and looked straight at Ike with his elbows on his wet knees, rolling his cigar from side to side in his mouth.

By this time Ike was tense and uncomfortable, but was suddenly and strangely relaxed when Bub demanded, "Recall Mattie Spencer, do ye?—about yer time at the Institute—smart girl—pretty—pa lost his farm—barmaidin' fer Stark at the Liberty?" To all this Ike nodded his clear recollection of Mattie, for he had danced with her at the Fulton and Price ball. "Tried t' drown herself just now," Bub muttered, flicking a non-existent ash from his cigar. "Keep yer mouth shut about it or I'll plug ye. Ought t' keep my own mouth shut, bein' nobody else knows it but Doc Daw, but figgered I'd have to tell somebody I could count on." There was a brief pause.

"Well, got anything to say? Can't ye make a noise? All keerect, is it, nice girl throwin' herself in the River?" Ike shuddered. "Made a rabbit jump over my grave," he said. He took a long drink of his grog, then tipped back in his rocker, looking straight at Bub, wondering if he was implicated in this attempted suicide beyond having apparently prevented it. As the silence continued, Ike felt uncomfortable again.

"Goin' to tell me more or ain't ye?" he finally demanded. "Come around, did she?" Bub's manner softened and he spoke so low as to be hardly audible, looking alternately at his feet and his cigar-end. "Jumped off the cliff about ten rod above the mill. Nobody on the bridge at the time. Lucky, I happened to be down on the shore lookin' at a pool o' dead water they tell me I ought to catch in a slantin' dam to increase the head. Mattie went under first off, then come up floatin' round this pool. Only up to my waist. Pulled her out easy. H'isted a lot o' water out o' her and rolled her on a bar'l in the cellar. Went upstairs and got Nick Forham's eye through the door without showin' my pants. Told him t' keep his mouth shet and hoof it fer Doc Daw, and after t' get the team harnessed. Nick'll keep mum. He's a good feller and knows I can whip him.

"By the time Doc come Mattie was mumblin' plenty. Doc said she was comin' round and we lugged her up through the bushes t' the coach. Pulled down the shades and drove her to Doc's. Doc promised t' tell me if she was knocked up. Figger he thinks I done it. Let him think so till I've learned what I want to—though I hain't no more doubt who done it than I have that you didn't."

During this account Ike had renewed his grog. "Nice pile of manure," he said emphatically. "Can ye figger who done it?" Bub leaned forward and his voice sank to a whisper coming out of the corner of his mouth. "Almost as quick as Mattie started breathin' she began mumblin', and between a-pumpin' her and a-rollin' her carcass on the bar'l I put my ear down. The first thing I caught was 'Joel,' and she kept sayin' it over 'n over most every time she fetched a little breath. Then she said, 'Joel, t'will be easier fer ye—easier fer ye'—by which she meant her bein' dead'd be easier fer Joe. And not long after, when she was breathin' clearer she kept whisperin', 'I want t' die—I want t' die—I want t' die'—like that," and Bub gasped in imitation of the way poor Mattie had said it.

He leaned back and paused again, now scowling as he had at the beginning. In spite of his two drinks Ike again felt uncomfortable and speechless. He could do nothing but sit forward in his chair, spit in the cuspidor, and gaze intently at the two puddles of water under Bub's pantlegs. Once more he was relieved when Bub resumed his monologue, now with fierce scorn, though still in a low tone, and glancing from time to time at the big walnut door with the arched frame.

"By Holy Jumpin' Jesus Christ!" he began, leaning forward toward Ike and thumping the arm of his rocker, "I figger nobody's a-goin' t' hang me fer no saint. Also I like Joe Kirkwood fer a hard fighter if he ain't always a square one. But by Holy Jumpin' Jesus, no married man's no call a-breakin' in virgins, ner anybody else fer that unless he's goin' t' light out with 'em. I know Mattie was a virgin six months back, fer I pawed her myself one night late at the Liberty and after we got lathered up I asked her flat was she or wan't she. And from the way she blushed and slid off my lap and blubbered and sidled out into the kitchen, there wa'n't no more doubt o' her bein' a virgin than that I ain't. And by Crimus, I never touched her again. T' my way o' thinkin', whores is one thing and virgins is another, and by God, Joe Kirkwood's a skunk if I ever smelt one."

"Keerect," said Ike, remembering how Joe had broken faith with him in Paris on the return from the railroad war. "And what's more," Bub resumed, "what call has a wise feller like Joe Kirkwood knockin' up a girl anyhow, specially a girl he knows don't know how t' take care of herself? There's plenty o' ways o' havin' yer fun without manufacturin' no brats, and Joe knows that as well as you or I do. Of course I figger Joe'll take care of her as fer as money goes, and anyhow Doc says ten to one she'll have a miscarriage from shock. Just the same I'd take per-tikler pleasure in turnin' up my cuffs with Joe, only everybody'd know it and they'd say we was a-fightin' over some woman, and likely Mattie's name'd come in soon or late. Ain't I right, Stud Lathrop, ye old whore-master?" And Bub smiled indulgently in using this nickname, being in fact convinced Ike was a babe in arms about women.

Ike had sunk into a deep reverie, and he came out of it at Bub's question with a visible start. "Yes, ye're right, righter'n molasses," he said with a sort of detached animation, then rose and stood looking out the window. Behind his back Bub eyed him with a sly twist at the corner of his mouth, and the image of that Samson girl at Applemore's ball crossed his mind. "By the way, Stud," he said casually, and for the first time in his usual loud tone, "when does old man Samson git out o' the stocks?"

At this Ike wheeled round and said menacingly, "August first, ain't it? He went in the first of April. Why'd ye ask?" "Just popped into my mind," said Bub with his old patronizing smile. "If ye recall, I bet a lot o' money on him and I figger t' git it back yet. Leastwise I figger t' git plenty o' ser-vice out o' him fer the benefit o' the niggers." "Best fergit the niggers, the lot o' ye," said Ike, walking over to his coat, "and leave it to those fel-lers in Washington." "Well, 't's a better game than knockin' up virgins, anyhow," said Bub with a sideways glance, and pulling his wet pants away from his legs so as to let him rise. Ike had his coat and hat in his hand.

"Sorry ye got t' git back t' pullin' yer cows' tits," said Bub. "I'm obliged to ye fer listenin' to my story. Likely tellin' ye so's t' bile over a little and keep from lightin' into Joe the next time I see him. And don't forget to keep yer mouth shut," he added as he opened the door for Ike. "No fear," said Ike with a smile that was almost an admission of Bub's recent, implied accusation. "Let me know if ye want me, for a second or anything. I wouldn't mind takin' a pot at Joe myself"—this in a whisper with his hand on the nickle-plated front door-knob. "That's another kettle o' fish," said Bub. "When it comes to business, man to man, you or I can trim him in his own 'tater patch." They both laughed easily. "Remember me kindly to Mistress Patience," said Ike, opening the door, and, touching his hat, he walked down the front steps and out of the portico that from the street looked so much like the jaws of hell.

As Ike rode out of Howell Sherwood's stable his chief thought was that it was after five and he'd have to press Chesty a little. So, turning up Washington Street, he kicked him into an unwilling trot, for Chesty was accustomed to walk as far as the edge of the village. Ike glanced at Bub's house in passing, but saw no sign of that chivalrous reprobate. Immediately thereafter when he looked ahead again, his stomach gave a convulsive jump. There was Joe Kirkwood up the street, walking easily homeward, swinging his stick.

Ike calculated that if he slowed Chesty to a walk Joe would be in his front door before he came abreast of him. Then he thought, "No use bein' a baby," and leaned forward to help Chesty up the muddy little grade. As ill luck would have it Joe looked back at his front gate, saw Ike coming, stepped out to the road and waved to him to stop. "I'm in a powerful hurry, Joe," said Ike as he drew Chesty in and touched his hat. "Thought you might be interested to know," said Joe, "I took an option for Horace Gadston on the Union Mills property at the Middle Falls." "You can have it," said Ike with his hoss-swoppin' smile.

"Also wanted to tell you Horace has come around and will lower his bid on that *Union* job." "Too late," said Ike. "Contract's all signed with Jerry Smart." "No use being enemies, is there, where there's no further cause?" said Joe with his wide, cat-like grin, showing his even, gat teeth." " 'Tain't us who are being enemies," replied Ike shortly. "Horace had his chance. No objection to giving him a bid on the next job if he wants it. Got to skedaddle now. Good night to ye, Joe." "Good night to ye, Ike," said Joe, still with his wide grin.

As he posted away, Ike felt a discomforting sense of fraternity with

Joe, as if they were partners in the same crime. This sensation presently gave way to a clear pang of conscience such as he had felt dimly at Bub's. Before he knew it he was deep in self-accusing contemplation and had let Chesty teeter down to a walk.

"By Crimus," he thought, "when ye come down to it I ain't any better than Joe. It's a danged flimsy excuse that I keep asking her to marry me, so long as she keeps shying away and I keep letting her shy. I've danged well got to *make* her marry me, else I'm as big a skunk as Joe is, no matter how straight my intentions. I guess all women are pernickety and a decent feller's consarn well bound to fetch 'em round. Only difference is I've been luckier'n Joe—so far." And with that his thoughts groped for a while around Bub's statement that there were "plenty o' ways of havin' yer fun without 'manufacturin' no brats.'" Ike could only guess at the ways, and the consideration of them violated his honorable intentions. So he cleared the cloud on his spirits with a strong determination to make Tavie marry him at once, and pressed Chesty on at a fast walk up the two hills.

Beyond the tollgate he kicked him into a run and held him there for the remaining two miles of level highway. With his mind made up, he exulted in his speed through the warm afternoon. The young green woods rustled as he galloped by. Far and wide in the fields the bobolinks, meadowlarks and field sparrows were jingling a silvery chorus. The sun was still high and Ike's conscience was clear as the glittering air. He was going to get everything settled right now! By God, they'd never couple his name with Joe Kirkwood's!

CHAPTER L

THAT EVENING there was a junket at the Swift's, and Ike and Tavie walked up together. The Doctor had a letter from Emmanuel dated two months before at Sante Fe, a long letter graphic with details of vast landscapes, minor brushes with Indians, and hardships on the desert, a vital letter teeming with the sense of enormous, groping populations on the move toward what goal they knew not, an exuberant letter, ending with the statement that 'Manuel was glad he had come even if he never saw an ounce of gold, and with a postscript that of course he expected to be home within the year. Instead of being read aloud, the letter was passed round from hand to hand, out of consideration for the Oakses, for Lem was chronically gloomy these days over Constant's having "laid down" at Oberlin, Ohio, and persisting in his refusal to come home where he belonged.

And all the time the letter was going quietly round, the dance in the kitchen was whirling to the jingle of Master Lane's harmonica and Jehu Jones's inimitable prompting, filled at this season with references to "The ice goin' out and water comin' in, and sprouts in the wheat field not too thin"—"And the finch on the wing and the hawk on the scream, and the meddy-lark a-whistlin' like a god danged dream"—"And the old cow freshnin', and the calf in the pail, and the ewe lamb a-friskin' of her stiff young tail"—"And the blossom goin' out and the lilac comin' in, and the young feller fiddlin' with the hair on his chin"—and so on without repetition all evening, a sort of pagan chant celebrating the return of Proserpine over the land.

And Ike and Tavie spun as if loosed from the earth, curving together for their turns with outstretched hands like two gusts of spring bending inward to unite in a single, rollicking whirlwind. Not a woman there, and scarcely a man, but guessed the approximate truth, and not one that did not either offer, or acquiesce in the covert remark, "What a handsome couple they'd make."

Ike and Tavie outstayed even the music and walked down the hill arm-in-arm, hand-in-hand, while the moon, as if to complete the setting of their stage, came up huge and white over their right shoulders. "Let's set awhile," said Ike as they passed the upper barn, half way down the hill. His determination and faith were still clear and strong, and he knew this night would help him. "Capital," said Tavie, then, glancing up and down the empty road, she drew his face down and held it in a long kiss while his arms lifted her. Then they climbed the wall, Ike spread his greatcoat, and they lay down in the presence of nothing but the moon, growing bright as day, the stars and the warm air rich with lilacs from every wall-corner.

Tavie threw back the hood of her party cloak, straightened up the edges of her hair, turned on her side so as to put her head on Ike's shoulder and waited, luxuriating, for him to take her in his arms. But instead he lay motionless on his back with his hands clasped behind his head and resting on a stone. Finally he said, so softly that it hardly violated the wide stillness, "Tave, ye know this is going to be our best night of all." Tavie nodded ecstatically against his shoulder, then snuggled closer to him, lifting her free hand and putting it gently on his cheek. "Do ye know why?" Ike murmured, and again Tavie's nodding head rubbed his shoulder, she thinking that he meant it was because this would be their first night out-doors. "It's because," Ike continued, turning his head enough to kiss the palm of her hand then straightening back, "it's because tonight we're going to get really betrothed and tell the folks tomorrow and in a couple of weeks we'll be married."

There was nothing new to Tavie in this proposal, but theretofore Ike had always put it in the form of entreaty. There was something in his manner now and in his putting it as a quiet, firm announcement that sent a little tremor of fear through her. She knew she must meet this issue before long, but she hoped to postpone it a little while yet. She pressed his cheek more strongly with her hand and said, "Oh, darling, let's not talk of that tonight, our first night outdoors under the sky." Then she added in a whisper, "I know this can't last forever, but let's not spoil it while it does last."

After a pause Ike said, "It won't spoil it but'll make it better, true grit, sweetheart. And there ain't any reason why it can't last forever, once we're married. It just ain't right going on this way any longer."

Tavie stiffened ever so little and lay perfectly still. Finally she said, "Why do you worry so, dear? You know it was I who started this, not you. I alone am to blame if there's anything wrong in it." Ike rolled his head back and forth in negation. "No, Tave. I guess I wanted it more than you did, and in the long run I'm the feller who's responsible." Without Ike's knowledge tears began silently to wet his shoulder.

Then, through a long silence, Tavie got herself in hand. She closed her eyes on the moon that now seemed to be racing up the sky, carrying away her dream at the moment of its greatest fulfillment. "You know, Ike, my dear," she spoke firmly and in a louder tone than before, "you know I love you, don't you?" "I hope so," said Ike with the faintest touch of sarcasm in his gentle voice. "But you know too," Tavie continued, "or you ought to know, that I have another love, perhaps a greater love, the love of the work I hope to do in the world—just as in your—friendship—I know I come second to the work you want to do in the world. I truly don't know yet which is the greater love for me, but I do know this is not the time and place to decide. I do know that I must not discard all my education and all my plans and Pa's plans for my life, until I have given them a fair try."

"Don't figger to tie ye up in a pen," said Ike.

"As you know," Tavie went on, ignoring Ike's remark, "as you know if you will only admit it to yourself, I brought all this on deliberately, and I'm not a bit sorry for anything. I fought it off until I had to either—do as I did—or leave the neighborhood. I gave in to you because I knew that if I went away the thought of you would plague me all my life. It may be—though I'm far from sure yet—that if I go away—soon now—I may be able to put you out of my mind. I know we can't go on this way forever. I've been happier this past month than I ever expect to be again—unless we can go on just a little longer. All I ask is a very little time to see if this beauty of it wears away a little or whether, as it may, it grows deeper and deeper and I know I shall never escape. As soon as I know that I promise you I shall not try to escape any longer. I will throw aside everything else and devote the rest of my life to trying to make you a good wife, as good a wife as you deserve, a better wife than I am ready to become now. If I pledged myself to you tonight, don't you see I might always feel there was something else I hadn't given a fair trial?—something for which I might have been better suited. I simply don't know yet, and I can't know until I have tried it away from you for a while."

Tavie felt Ike relaxing and she pressed her point. "We have years ahead of us, Ike. Married life at its happiest is sometimes hard. I could not make you as good a wife if I undertook it with the possibility of regret. By the end of July—before John comes home—I shall have almost a hundred dollars laid away—I know we can't fool John and I don't want to try. At the end of July—only two months off—we'll set a day if you choose—I am going somewhere—where, I don't know yet. If I can't by then find employment in the Reform Movement, I can at least work out as I am doing now, in the houses of any of a dozen girls I knew in college. It doesn't matter what I do or where I go—so long as it is a good way off. The main thing is to find out what happens to both of us—when we are separated for a few months. If by, say, September, I find that you are still more to me than my other plans—more to me than anything in the world—then, if you still want me, I'll return and—marry you—whenever you say."

Tavie paused, with her eyes still closed, and listened to Ike's breathing which now seemed ever so little faster than it was a few moments before. Her confession being over, she trembled at the feelings that crowded behind it, the fear that now at last she would have disgusted Ike and turned him against her, the knowledge deep in her heart that even now if Ike insisted he could scatter her plans to the night and make her promise anything he chose, the hope from the same deep source that he would do this, the hope, from another and perhaps stronger source, that he would not, and the conviction, from this same source, that if he did they would both regret it in years to come. "Don't you see, Ike," she said, now almost whispering again, "that all I ask is a very little time—make it less than six weeks if you want to—just to be happy, without any complications, as we—are now? Is that too much to ask? Is it, my dear?"

While Tavie had been talking two things had been happening in Ike. In the first place, his sensitive and responsive nature was going out to her and understanding completely everything she said. In the second place, the moment she said, "I am going away somewhere," some secret little devil in his midriff relaxed its grip with sensations of relief which—without remotely acknowledging their significance—Ike rationalized with some such thoughts as these:

"If I'm beholden to do the decent thing by Tave, figger I'm just as beholden to do what I can to make her happy— Sure grit she means what she says, and in the long run maybe she'll be happier if I let her have her way"— (Here conscience intervening) "Figger I could bring her round all right, spite of what she says, but" (Here, exit conscience) "as she says, maybe she'd regret it later— No real harm in going on a little longer, she says, and in the long run maybe she'll be happier if I let her have her plenty happy— Pity to stop right off short—especially on a night like this"— (Enter conscience.) "There'll be other nights." (Exit conscience.) "Might never have another such night— Figger I'd regret missing it more'n she would when it comes to that— Month or six weeks ain't very long— If we take a little more pains than we have, ought to get through it without anybody being the wiser— If anything serious happens we can always get married later as well as now."

And so the fish of Ike's righteous determination came nearer and nearer the net under the spell of the moon and the milky white meadow and the scent of lilacs and the silence and Tavie's overwhelming honesty. And deeper than any of these thoughts of Ike's or anything Tavie said was the suspicion, unacknowledged by Ike, but quite conscious in Tavie's mind, that it was he quite as much as she who needed more time.

When Tavie finished speaking Ike did not answer her question, but, after a pause, said softly, "Will ye give me your promise, Tave, to make a final answer by September?" At this Tavie raised herself with a little jump to her elbow so she looked into Ike's eyes. "I promise you absolutely that by the end of July I shall go hundreds of miles away, and if you won't write me all summer until September first, and if you write me then that you still want to marry me, I'll either come back at once and marry you or I'll say 'no' for good and all."

"You know it's funny, Tave," said Ike, turning his head toward her and crossing one arm to her shoulder, "but you've said what I guess I wanted to say all the time—about going on a while without getting things all mixed up—only, I just wanted to be sure that you wanted it too." And at this Tavie sank into his strong arms with a great feeling of release while somewhere—as yet unknown even to her—a wretched little weed took root, a weed of contempt for the man she loved.

Eager to prolong the rising ecstasy, she presently turned from a long kiss, pressing her cheek against Ike's chest and opening her eyes to the moon that was still low and now seemed to be rising so slowly that eternity would be realized and ended before it reached the zenith. In unshadowed bliss she felt Ike's ardent hands moving over her. "O my dear, my dear," she murmured, "this is the most beautiful night of all, as if all the others had been only preparation for this."

And ten minutes later, like nature saluting itself, on the edge of the silvery pine woods across the meadow a Vesper Sparrow awoke and sang to the moon. And at lengthening intervals he awoke and sang again and again, till at last Tavie slept, and Ike watched. A little east wind whispered down from the mountain, bringing mist that lay on the meadow in white, drifting pools. Very gently Ike reached over and drew his greatcoat over Tavie. And he continued to watch alone, his eyes lifted to the stars. And he thought that whatever the stars were doing was very like this, and that it was right, and that they understood and that whatever might happen in the future, this night was worth it and would never be forgotten.

CHAPTER LI

I K E had hardly settled in his bed, as the big clock below struck two, when, tired as he was, his conscience awoke to harass him. He lay staring at the sloping ceiling of the room that was half-lighted by the moon outside. He had failed. He had let Tavie wheedle him out of his determination to end this state of affairs that was wrong. He had known beforehand that she'd do something of the kind, yet when he was put to it he had failed to control her. Perhaps he was just no good. Well, he'd given her his word. He guessed he'd have to go on this way for two months, till the end of July. He recalled having promised his pa to tell him if anything was bothering his conscience. Well, it was bothering him sure grit, but what could Pa do more'n he himself had done already? His pa couldn't make her marry him. That was his own job. If he told him, Pa would only be more angry than he was now; if he told him the whole truth he'd think badly of Tavie; and nothing good could come of it. Nothing to do but wait. Maybe she'd get over her notions in the next two months and marry him without running away first.

His mind began to drowse into the escape of his business affairs. So Joe Kirkwood had taken an option for Horace Gadston on the Union Mills property— He and Alec should have done that long ago— They agreed it was the place they wanted— Should have taken Bub and a few others into the company to raise money to buy it— Now they'd have to build at some other site, and every good one was controlled by Gadston or Grabbot or some such— Maybe there might be a leak somewhere in the option— He'd have to keep his ears open— He'd see Zeb Milliken, lawyer for the Union Mills— Maybe Zeb was in cahoots with Joe— Joe was a slick one all right— Mattie Spencer— Danged sweet girl— Hoped she'd pull through— Joe was a skunk— No, he wasn't as bad as Joe, he'd asked Tave to marry him first off— Everything would come out O.K. . . . And nature, demanding rest, put Ike's conscience to sleep along with his body.

On the first Monday in June, more than a week later, at the regular dinner of the Gang at the Wheeler House, Bub Tanofly grew voluble about women. The youngsters, Nat Gadston and Tim Slocum, listened with concentrated, lascivious rapture, Jabe Munson and the two VanSanfords—Fred's older brother Medad was now a member of the Gang—interrupted Bub from time to time with questions implying their own sophistication. George and Alec were plainly bored by the discourse, half lewd, half medical, and Ike affected a like indifference. He was interested, however, to learn what Bub meant by "not manufacturin' no brats," also that women mostly wanted to be let alone at certain times, which was "an a'mighty good thing, bein's that's the time a feller's most likely to get 'em in trouble." While pretending to be indifferent to what Bub was saying, Ike thought back, realized that he had been regularly with Tavie through what must have been one of these times early last month, and that another such time must be due about now. Funny, Tavie hadn't seemed a bit queer a month back, not at all like she was in April when she told him about it.

After dinner Ike walked with Bub down Court Street as far as Trinity Church where he turned down the lane past the graveyard, and walked up River Street to the office. He learned that Mattie Spencer had had her miscarriage and had near bled to death, though Doc Daw said she'd pull through if there weren't any complications. He was keeping her in his house, having given her ma and pa a cock-and-bull story about intestinal poisoning. Doc had put the thing up to Joe Kirkwood flat, and told him who had pulled Mattie out of the river. "So I cal'late from now on I've got lawyer Kirkwood where I want him, and that's next best to givin' him the thrashin' he deserves."

Ike walked down Trinity Lane, putting women out of his mind and wondering whether one of these days they might have a chance to give Joe a different kind of thrashing. He had learned that Zeb Milliken, lawyer for the Union Mills, was not in cahoots with Joe about the option he had taken for Horace Gadston on the Mills property. Zeb had shown Ike the option, which was no great affair, having cost Horace only $100, and expiring on the ninth of July. Since Horace showed no sign of taking it up, Ike might still get the property for the Engine Company.

That night at home, Ike had in mind to talk a little common sense with Tavie in the north parlor after the folks had gone to bed. But instead of giving him the chance, she went up to bed before anyone else, which meant she would be expecting him in her room later. For a while he discussed the farm with his pa in the artificial manner which had become habitual with them. He noticed a letter from John on the desk and wondered why Pa had said nothing of it, it being the Lollapaloosa's habit to enclose some message for each member of the family, all of which the Squire would read aloud before supper. Presently Ike inquired casually what news there was of John, to which his father replied, "Indeed. I nearly forgot to show ye the letter which ye will see on the desk. I read it to the others at dinner. Do read it if ye wish."

John's letter was full of college, and debates, and national politics, and hopes of winning a *summa*. There were tender and humorous messages in it for every member of the household down to Henry Hawks, and even including the horses and old Tippie the dog; but there was not one word of reference to Ike. As he folded it there came over him that feeling of ostracism from the family which he had first felt more than six months before, after he sold Dandy. Only now it was stronger, more lonely. He felt a lump in his throat as he rose and replaced the letter on the desk, and, without turning back into the family circle, he walked across into the north parlor.

His ma followed quickly, thrust him down in one of the little chairs, and pulled up another, taking both his hands. "Can you explain it, Isaac?" she asked gently. "Has there been anything between you and John?" "Not a thing, Ma," Ike replied, "except the little squabble we had here Thanksgiving about my going to college, and he's always sent me messages since then, until now. You don't think Pa might have written him something to turn him against me, do ye?" Sarah thought a moment, then said, "No, Isaac, your pa would not do that. He'd be very scrupulous not to do that. There must be something else. Can't you think of some little disagreement, or some expression of yours that he might have taken amiss?"

Ike dropped his chin in his hands, and presently said, "It's true something has *happened* that might rub John the wrong way, but there ain't a way in the world he could know about it, and instead of writing it I figgered to wait till he was home and we could talk it out face to face." "What is it, Isaac?" asked Sarah. "It's about Pru Stark," said Ike, and he proceeded to tell her the whole story of Pru's attempt on him in the office last March. "That's it, of course," said Sarah softly. "But, Ma, how could he know?" "Mistress Prudence wrote him." "But, Ma, how could she? For I was right and she was wrong, and if I did anything to rub John the wrong way she did ten times as much."

"Oh, Isaac," his mother sighed, "you must learn more about women, especially little hussies like that. She was not interested in the truth. She was interested only in revenging herself on you. She may not even have referred to this particular incident at all. But whatever it was, you can be sure she is responsible for it. If it were anything else, I am sure John would have written to you before giving you this rebuff."

"I'll write him," said Ike. "You know best," said Sarah, "but it would seem to me unwise for you to put this rather delicate matter on paper." "Ye're right, Ma," said Ike. "I'll just write him something, and after he's home we'll have it out straight." They both rose, Ike kissed his ma, and they returned to the keeping-room with their arms around each other. Ike took quill and wrote: " 'Paloosa:—What's up?—Scamp," folded it, sealed it with the family seal, and put it in his pocket for delivery to the Post Office in the village in the morning.

Upstairs later, Ike discussed the farm with Ben as they lay in bed, and he enjoyed the innocent, juvenile companionship. Even if Ben did talk big these days, as if it were his farm and Ike a sort of relation, yet he was the only male member of the household who was still natural with him. Ike felt disappointed and alone when Ben's voice mumbled off into sleep, and he knew he had a duty to perform. This business of the 'Paloosa was somehow too deep in him to share with Tavie. He heard Ben's regular breathing and the snores of Master Lane and Henry from their respective rooms. Stealthily he slipped out of bed and crept out into the darkness of the back attic, carrying his carpet-slippers in his hand. His bare feet knew every crack and nail-head in the floor boards, and he had long learned to avoid the board that creaked at the top of the back stairs.

Tavie was lying awake for him as he expected, and the moon was visible diagonally through her window from the hard little spool bed. Ike sat down on the edge of the bed, kissed her and took her hand in both of his, but he made no move to join her. As always, their conversation was in whispers.

"Tave, I got a little information today. It's kind of embarrassing but I figger I better tell ye all the same. If I'm right in my calculations, the time ought to be pretty close when—you—ye'll be feeling sort o' nervous again." He looked at her for an acknowledgment, but got none. So he continued, now putting one hand across her and resting on it, but looking everywhere except at her face which was very clear and white in the moonlight. "They tell me, Tave, that that time, and a few days each way, is the most likely time to have—make—a baby. So it struck me it might be wise to—sort o'— be careful for a spell. Maybe it'd be best if I didn't come in for a few days."

Tavie, who had closed her eyes while Ike was talking, now merely put her hand lightly on his and whispered, "Why, my dear, if you don't want to come to me, just don't come. You don't have to make up a story about it." "I ain't making up a story, true grit, Tave. Ye know I want to come to ye, but since ye won't agree to marry me, I figger we've to be careful about such matters. That's horse sense, ain't it?"

"I suppose so," said Tavie, and she rolled her head to one side on the pillow so as not to see Ike's face, even in the shadow, and also partly to hide her own from the brilliant, cruel moon. Then she looked back with a gay smile. "And we both need sleep too," she said, "so go back to your bed, and I'll let you know as soon as ever it's over."

Ike reached down to lift her in his arms and at first she was limp. But gradually, as he pressed her close, she stiffened and met his kiss on the lips. Then he kissed her neck, her shoulder and her hand, patted her cheek, picked up his slippers and glided away. As Tavie saw her door close without any click of the latch she bounced over and buried her face. "It's all over," she thought. "He doesn't want me any more." With another jump she sat up in bed, flung off her pretty nightcap, and tugged at her soft hair with both hands. For the first time she faced the fact! She had skipped last month entirely!

Out in the back attic Ike did a clumsy thing. As he closed Tavie's door he heard his pa's step below, coming in from the summer kitchen to the main kitchen, the door at the bottom of the stairs being open. There was nothing unusual in the Squire's having to get up at night. But Ike had not heard him do it since he had been going to Tavie's room, so he paused startled and put his foot squarely down on the troublesome board that gave its usual loud squeak. Immediately the steps below stairs stopped.

Ike gathered his wits and executed a plan he had held in readiness. Creaking the board deliberately again, he started downstairs, reaching back at each of the first two steps to draw on his slippers, then proceeding openly down to the kitchen. "That you, Pa," he said, as he supposed in a natural tone, coming out into the candle-lantern light and blinking as if still half asleep. "Yes, Isaac," said the Squire, who was standing on the hearth. "Do ye require the lantern?" Thank ye, sir," said Ike, advancing to take it. "Chilly for June, ain't it?" "You don't need to whisper, Isaac," said his father. "We can wake no one here." "Didn't know I was whispering," said Ike in a husky, feignedly jocular voice. "Figger I ain't quite awake yet." "I see," said the Squire, handed him the lantern, and proceeded through the keeping-room to his own bed.

Out in the back-house Ike knew the bubble was bust now, sure grit. From now on he was a stranger, a branded scallawag, a sneaking seducer in his own house. But back in his bed he enjoyed a compensating thought. For a week he wouldn't have to go creeping round at night like a thief!

CHAPTER LII

ALONE in her room, the Solon Samson in Tavie gradually awoke and possessed her. Once the first moment of terror at Ike's leaving her and at her probable condition was past, the part in her that was not prepared to be a wife rose in ascendance over the part that was in love. Sitting up in her bed while the moon climbed above her window, she drew far back out of the current of mutuality in which she and Ike had been drifting, and was once more herself alone. For the hundredth time she returned to the conviction that this was only a fleshly business, that all the seeming spiritual transport and the excruciating tenderness were but derivatives of this one desire. Was it not possible that, knowing now the full satisfaction of this desire, she was prepared henceforth to forego it? She had let nature take its course, as the phantom of Mrs. Mott had advised her, and she knew now just how much, and how little, the demand of nature was worth. She was newly armed for her fight for women's independence and Reform generally, her work in the world. Yes, she would fight on, even in the face of this new and terrifying possibility to which Ike had referred. She concluded that her instinctive decision out in the field was right. She must try herself a little longer with Ike. Then she must try herself apart from him for a time. Above all, she must not marry him now.

The very next day she characteristically took the bull by the horns. Professing a desire to buy some stuff for a new dress, she left the Lathrops' after dinner, went down to her own house, told her ma the same lie, harnessed the horse to the cart, drove deviously to Dr. Daw's white-columned frame house in the village, tied her rig at the kitchen post instead of in front, was admitted by the Doctor himself, followed him into his office, and told him the essential facts. She was particularly careful to assure him that her lover—whom she did not name—was begging her to marry him, but that she refused on account of her own ambitions which she described.

The doctor, who was a friend both of Solon Samson and Squire Lathrop, listened with increasing concern. He was a stern-faced man, with strong,

383

regular features, a presence that was august without elegance of manner, no detectable sign of humor, and big, gentle blue eyes that reminded Tavie of Ike's. When she had finished her story he lifted his eyes to hers and said, "Miss Octavia, may I be so bold as to inquire whether you have any objection to marrying this gentleman other than your plans for an independent life?" "None, sir," said Tavie a little defiantly. "In fact I am in love with him." "You have had no quarrel?" "None, sir." "If I may be so bold, are you sure he loves you?" "No, sir, I doubt that he does, although he thinks he does." "Then, tell me, Miss Octavia, in your heart is not that the real reason for your refusal to marry him?" "No, sir, I assure you it is not. My reason is simply my own ambition, abetted by my father's ambition for me."

The doctor leaned back in his chair and considered. "If I understand you correctly, Miss Octavia," he said presently without looking at her, "you are prepared to have a child outside of wedlock rather than marry the father of the child whom you say you love and who wishes to marry you?" "Yes, sir," said Tavie with a little toss of her head. "I am prepared to do that if necessary, though I wish to do everything possible to avoid having the baby. That is why I came to see you."

"You understand that you are proposing to do yourself a wrong, which, justly or unjustly, will result in your ostracism from society and will thus stand in the way of your carrying out your ambitions in the Reform Movement?" Tavie lowered her eyes and nodded. "To marry a man, have his child, and afterwards leave him, that is a very serious matter, but it might eventually be condoned. But you are here proposing a course which will permanently destroy not only your own standing and influence but will make the possible child equally an outcast for life, condemned certainly to inescapable misery, probably to drunkenness and hatred of his mother, and very possibly to crime. Furthermore, I can assure you that if you persist in this course you will break your father's spirit as not the whole nation could otherwise do. I am your father's friend and I know whereof I speak. Had you considered these factors in your problem, Miss Octavia?"

Tavie had not. She had thought so far only of her own dilemma, and not at all of the child as a fact, a living person. As the doctor spoke she kept her head lowered and now her lip was trembling. "Please don't, Doctor Daw," she murmured, and looked up with tears running down her cheeks. "I have not considered these things. I am simply decided that I do not want to marry and do not want to have a child. That was all I came to ask you, whether there is any way of preventing it."

Doctor Daw was silent for a full minute. He knew of Solon Samson's ambitions for this girl, knew that he would undoubtedly be disappointed if she settled down to matrimony. Yet he could not break his life-long practice. "No, my dear," he said gently, "that is one thing we doctors are forbidden by law to do. If ever it became known that I had done such a thing I would be condemned both by my profession and by the community, and such usefulness as I have in wider fields would be destroyed."

At this Tavie took out from under her cloak and handed to the Doctor the latest copies of the *Byzantium Eagle* and of the *Democratic Union,* both folded back to the thinly veiled advertisements of alleged contraceptives and medicines to bring on miscarriage—advertisements so incongruous with the otherwise decorous tone of those respected periodicals. "I suppose, then," she said, smiling bitterly and wiping away her tears, "that I must do what I can with these, without hope of advice from you."

The doctor glanced at the papers and threw them on his desk. "Not one of these things," he said, "has the endorsement of a reputable physician. Many of them are dangerous, and few if any are effective. I can not advise you to try any of them." "Then, sir," said Tavie, rising, "I must try them without your advice. I am grateful to you for your warning about the future. May I pay you for it now, since I do not wish my parents to know that I have visited you?"

The doctor had risen with her and now motioned her back to the chair where she had been sitting. "One thing I can do," he said, remaining standing and looking down at her with a slight scowl. "If you purchase any of these patented prescriptions I would consider it a favor if you would bring it to me. Though I can not help you to the end you seek, I am greatly concerned for your general health. If you will bring me any purchase you make, I will analyze it for you, warn you of its dangers, and give you my opinion as to whether the prescribed doses are proper."

Tavie jumped up gaily. "Oh, thank you, Doctor! I knew you were kind and that you would help me." Then, as she swung lightly out through the kitchen her revived spirits fell again. At her entrance a pale-faced, shawl-clad figure, sitting in a chair stirring broth on the little stove, seemed to contract as if it had been struck, then lifted toward Tavie its hollow-socketed, gray-blue eyes. "Good day, Mattie Spencer," said Tavie, and had the presence of mind to suppress even formal inquiry as to her health. "Howdy, Tavie," said Mattie. Without words a flash of half understanding passed between the two old schoolmates. Mattie resumed her stirring and Tavie walked out and closed the door softly behind her.

Two hours later Tavie left Grabbot's store on the Mall and set out up Washington Street at a smart trot, having beside her on the seat a roll of gay muslin, and tucked inside her cloak a wrapped bottle labelled "The

Happy Home," which Doctor Daw had examined and pronounced harmless in the prescribed doses—and which he secretly knew was sometimes effective in such cases.

Tavie had just emerged from the avenue of trees and was clattering along on the plank pike under the blue sky when she heard galloping hoofs behind her. It was Ike. "Greetings, Tave," he shouted, pulling up alongside. "Why didn't ye let me do your shopping for ye? By Jiminy Juniper, we've sold another engine, a little one to Squire Sample at the Harbor, to run a sawmill with!" "Oh, Ike, I'm delighted," said Tavie, astonished to find herself lapsing into the irresponsible, flirtatious rôle she had played back in the winter during her father's trial. "Did you yourself persuade Squire Sample to buy it?" "Sure grit," said Ike, "and I didn't tell him a thing that wasn't true. It's the greatest sport I know, trying to sell something you whole hog believe in." Tavie beamed her admiration, and they chatted all the way home as gaily and impersonally as if it had been ten years ago.

And for a week thereafter Ike and Tavie were as easy in the house as in the old "friendly" days, Ike's integrity restored by the fact that he was now doing nothing he was ashamed of, Tavie exultant in her revived fanaticism, and full of faith in Doctor Daw and the medicine she was taking in overdoses that made her ears ring.

CHAPTER LIII

AFTER A WEEK, Tavie's hourly expectations lapsed into fatalism
—somehow Providence would bring everything right in Its mysterious
way. Her hope was still high, she was still able to avoid facing the dark
alternatives the doctor had outlined. Yet her exultant mood left her, and in
its place her desire for Ike beside her began to torture her again. She
realized that of all things she must not return to the hysterical state of six
weeks before. On the evening of Tuesday, the tenth of June, she threw him
a dazzlingly provocative look just before she went up to bed. And from
the way his face lighted in response she knew that he too was ready to
return to her.

Half an hour later Ike lay in his bed waiting for Ben to go to sleep, his
heart pounding with a deep, organic, involuntary rhythm. For the last
few days he, more than Tavie, had been frantic from the sudden starvation
after six weeks of fullness. Yet even now, as he lay in the sweet flames of
anticipation, shame also rose in him like thick smoke in a stove that
threatened to stifle its own fire. He knew that, being thus far freed from
Tavie, he should not return to her until she promised to marry him. Yet
he knew he would return, and again and again until the end of July—
six weeks more of weak, inexcusable conduct, six weeks more of feigning
indifference of decency to Tavie. And so like a slave, partly to lust but
mostly to what he fancied to be Tavie's happiness, he drifted out of bed
and down the back attic without a sound.

In the morning a change in Ike and Tavie communicated itself to the
household. Throughout the past six weeks their love, however immoral
and however shadowed latterly by Ike's misgivings, had yet been genuine
and had shed, in its own terms, an aura of authenticity through the house.
Now it was changed into stark lust mixed with considerations of policy on
the part of both principles, and on Ike's part with a twisted, half-hypocritical
sense of duty to Tavie. The false under-current immediately poisoned the
social air of the family. There began a sort of domestic reign of terror, a
period of increasing tension the most dreadful that ever had arisen in the

walls of any Lathrop homestead for more than two hundred years, a reign of nervous terror in which healthy affirmative values and gentle desires were stifled, and life and civilization continued in crass, external terms, like a grim machine, deprived at once of its natural power and its normal load, running aimlessly under the momentum of the centuries.

Tavie daily grew more panicky at her secret prospect and drew more and more into herself, giving Ike nothing of strength, nothing of real warmth and support that might partially have alleviated his own ordeal.

On Ike's part the mark of shame grew daily more visible upon him. In place of his old, springy gait he shuffled, almost slunk, when he walked, and seemed never able to stand for a moment without turning away to sink into a chair. Yet of all the people in the house, he still met everybody's eyes, except Tavie's, directly, with a sort of angry and hunted challenge.

Sarah was in a highly irritable state on her own account. Seeing her strong son bent under a weight which seemed more than he could bear, she blamed him not at all but identified all of his burden with Tavie. Obviously she had assumed the duty of cherishing him and, after giving him some moments of happiness, she had as obviously renounced her duty and was in process of destroying him. For the first time in her life Sarah became a shrew. Nothing that Tavie did in the house was right, and her husband and the hired men fared little better. Only Ike and Ben escaped her critical tongue, and when alone with either of them she was liable to give way to sobs which had no immediate cause.

The Squire lived under perpetual impulsion to pitch Ike out of the house without explanation or ado. Yet, although he had definitely given his son up for lost, there remained, while he and Octavia were in the house, the hope of a condoning marriage, and precipitate action might darken their lives, and that of the family, permanently. He decided to wait until John returned from Yale early in August, and took refuge in physical effort.

He undertook by himself to plow the side-hill pasture, which was a labor for a generation. With seventy years' erosion since the trees were cut down, the stones great and small had "grown" until the five acres was one great rock heap with a filling of earth. Every day the Squire went out alone with pick, shovel, crowbar, and the stone boat with the oxen or the mare Nancy. Often he lifted and rolled three and four hundred pound boulders without help of the bar. Always he came home to supper exhausted. But he kept his surface of civilization though his soul was stricken. More than ever he was attentive to his dress, sometimes changing completely for supper. More than ever he was courtly, and though he now often repeated his stories, it was he alone who kept the conversation alive at meals.

The hired men, who normally considered it their antique prerogative to jibe at all the members of the family, now moved through the house like silent, disapproving specters, and even between themselves the tension grew. One morning at milking Henry Hawks said with sudden exasperation, "I see that god-danged booby is lyin' abed again." Master Lane stopped milking, shifted his stool unnecessarily, and spat. Henry was so agitated that he rose and stood looking out into the barn-yard through a window of the shed. After contemplating him for a moment, Master Lane said viciously, "Wal, be ye milkin' or be ye gabbin'?" There was a clatter of tin. Henry had left his pail under the cow and she had kicked it over. He went back to his chores. Master Lane reserved his comment. It was evident that they were close to an explosion.

Ike's ordeal was made harder to bear by the fact that he had no important business to tend to during the last half of June. There was nothing of consequence to do for the railroad until the engineers' bids should begin to come in. Alec Mathiesson was busy building the engine for the *Union* and, with the Sample order to fill after that, there was no point in seeking new orders that couldn't be met for months. The future of the engine company must await the success of the *Union* order. Thereafter, when it had proved itself, they would raise money and buy or build a factory. There was nothing to be done now about the ideal site of the Union Mills, on account of the option Joe Kirkwood had taken for Horace Gadston and which still had a month to run.

For the first time in his life Ike now attended church with an interest that went beyond participation in the singing. Sunday mornings and afternoons and Wednesday evenings during the last three weeks of June, he entered those white portals as a self-acknowledged sinner, seeking some ultimate solution, some forgiveness, above all some direction in the darkness of soul in which he was groping. When the young Reverend Nathaniel Norcross virtually took as text a passage from the philosopher Emerson and pointed out that the freedom he was advocating was a freedom of opinion and not a freedom of indulgence, Ike, who six months before would have scoffed, took the viper to his bosom, admitted to himself that the sermon applied to him, and afterwards thanked the Reverend Nathaniel with a warmth so pathetic that half a dozen members of the congregation, as well as his parents, observed it.

But in church he found little comfort, and no permanent solution to his problem. He remembered what Aggie had told him about "love and God." He was making a sorry business of love—and he took all the blame to himself—but he yet believed that some day he would discover God. He prolonged his daily rides to and from the village, going up unknown wood roads and dismounting, letting Chesty nibble at shrubs and wintergreens. In the forest silence, broken only by the peaceful singing of vireos or thrushes, he found temporary escape from his burden. He had momentary fancies that when he found God, He would have something to do with this immense quiet of nature. Yet when Ike tried to force himself to reason it out, his mind only returned to his immediate cares and his guilt.

His situation with Tavie grew progressively worse. She stopped inviting him with looks, and waited for him to invite her. It seemed to him that she still wanted him to come to her, but whether she wanted him or not, he believed it was for him to keep her in love with him, aware that he stood ready to marry her any time. When they were together it became more and more a matter of getting love over with and separating to go to sleep. Their whispered words in the final calm that used to be so tender became as stilted and impersonal as if they were two strangers who found themselves together in somebody else's parlor and could hit on nothing to say. Sometimes for long, terrible minutes Ike felt just that way, completely strange and indifferent to what lay close to him in the little bed.

The climax came on the first of July. Ike had not visited Tavie for five days and was consequently a-whirl with desire. And yet, after a good half hour of mutual provocation, he rested in the realization that he was impotent.

"I guess I'm just no good, Tave," he whispered, clasping her again with a needless display of muscular strength. "I might as well quit ye for now." Tavie said nothing and Ike crept back to his own room and lay awake with strangely cool feelings. He smiled in the darkness at the thought that he might be permanently "no good"— "At least that'll be one thing out of the way." And he was pleased that tomorrow he would walk with a clear conscience.

CHAPTER LIV

THE NEXT MORNING Ike was not as calm as he had expected. Though unashamed, he was in a highly nervous state. At breakfast he upset his cup of tea which made everybody at the table jump. He stamped around the house looking for his beaver, then remembered he'd left it at the office the afternoon before when it looked like rain. In saddling Chesty he jerked the girth so the startled horse sidled against the stall and, for the first time in seven months, reached round to nip him. He was hysterical with desire now harder to control than before he took up with Tavie. It wasn't as easy to be "no good" as he had thought it would be.

The escape from the house and the exercise of riding calmed him somewhat. He ran Chesty almost to the Center, where he turned up a favorite woods road. He knew he'd be late to the bank, but, by God, he must think this out or he'd go crazy. He lengthened the reins, hitched Chesty to a sapling and walked up and down. Finally he sat on a mossy beech log where he had sat before. The silence of the forest did not soak up his worries as previously, but in the vacuum of it his practical thoughts grew clearer. He knew that the reason for his impotence had somehow to do with keeping up a thing that had come to be wrong, a thing that just went against the grain. He had a flash of churchly mysticism and wondered if some Higher Power had intervened to save him. Last night might have been sent as a warning.

Clearly he must not go to Tavie again, even when he was ready to, even if she thought he was quitting her. Sooner or later the failure of last night would be bound to recur—at least until they were married. For the first time he began to blame Tavie as well as himself. She was responsible for his feeling like a skunk, like Joe Kirkwood. He'd tell her so, consarn it, without trying to spare her feelings any more, and at the same time he'd tell her that whenever she was ready to marry him he was ready to marry her as he'd been all along. He rode out of the woods at least clear in his head, though he was still in an abnormal state, a belligerent mood in which he wanted nothing so much as to knock somebody down.

In the village Ike's contentious mood sought outlet in walking rapidly from place to place on supposed business. After dinner he walked with Alec over to the *Democratic Union* office where Alec was busy assembling the new Napier press and completing the stone foundation for the engine that was to run it from outside the main building. Being assured by Alec that all was going well, Ike walked over to the Tanofly Mill and conferred with Bub about Gadston's option on the Union Mills that would expire in a week now. They agreed that if old Horace didn't take it up Bub would put up four hundred dollars toward a new option for the Byzantium Steam Engine Company, in return for which he would get four shares of its stock. Having completed this arrangement, Ike walked to his own office where, as usual these days, he found nothing to do, though two of the engineers wrote that they expected to send in their bids for the railroad in about a week.

After pacing up and down the room to no·purpose for a few minutes, he went over to the regular Wednesday meeting round the cider barrel at the rear of the Blackwater Bank. Today he wanted neither cider nor talk. After performing the courtesies, he stood off by himself, feeling contemptuous of the conversation and taking no part in it. He thought to himself that Ostrum Applemore was not far wrong in the name he now publicly applied to these old grannies—the "Backwater Nestors." Shortly after four, Ike threw Master Marshfield a clandestine wave of farewell, and slipped out without interrupting the talk. He walked rapidly up to Howell Sherwood's stable, still feeling like a mad bull and wanting something to gore.

Before setting out for home he bethought him to see if there was any post for the Hollow, and so rode down across the Mall and hitched Chesty in front of the Post Office. There were a few miscellaneous letters for residents of the Hollow, the usual weekly letter from Constant Oaks to Tavie, the usual bundle of papers for the Squire. But besides, there was a letter for Ike himself from John, undoubtedly in reply to Ike's inquiry a month ago as to "What's up?" The sight of the letter agitated Ike and he was afraid to open it; so he did so at once to relieve the suspense.

Standing by one of the front windows in the little one-story building, he read:

Dear Scamp:—In asking me "what's up" I presume you refer to my failure to send any message to you in my last letter to the folks. Under the circumstances I simply could not think of anything honest to say, and I think you will agree that you and I should not undertake hypocrisy toward one another at this late date. I am sure you will believe me when I assure you that the matter has nothing to do with our little misunderstanding last Thanksgiving about your going to college or into "business." Suffice it to say that I have trustworthy information about your conduct that has wounded me deeply. Since you will undoubtedly recognize to what I refer, I am sure you will agree that it can not be discussed in a letter. If, on the other hand, you claim innocence, which you will have an opportunity to do when I come home at the end of July, I shall be badly put to it, for my information comes from a source I am bound to believe. Please postpone any explanations, for we must not grow angry at this distance. Yours, John.

Ike crumpled the letter in his fist and dropped it in the sawdust. "Angry!" He wanted to pick up the whole village and pitch it across the river! He wanted to pull up the nearest stone hitching-post and pound it on the ground! Ike's impulses in this kind of frustrated rage were physical, like his pa's. But whereas his pa was at the moment carrying a three-hundred-pound boulder upgrade to the stone-boat, Ike merely crumpled a piece of paper in his fist and stood still with the world reeling round him and the blood welling into his head so he thought it would blow up. And the next thing he knew he was quietly riding Chesty up Washington Street, giving no sign except to ignore the usual greetings from acquaintances on the way.

"So!" he finally began to think, "the whole god-danged tribe is against me, condemning me like a pup without hearing my case! They're just a god-danged litter of self-righteous, church-going hypocrites!—all except Ma and Runt, who's minding his own business." So great was his rage, so fundamental the quarrel, that Pru Stark and her petty villainy were too small to deserve his resentment or enter his thoughts. Nor did his silent cursing of his pa and beloved brother, and Tavie in passing, relieve his feelings. Very sedately he rode Chesty homeward, feeling light as a feather, relieved from all responsibility, making up his mind and settling it more firmly than he usually did where personal relationships were involved.

At supper and all through the evening Ike's rage was so great that it galvanized the household and suppressed even the usual jocularity of the Squire. Sarah and Tavie both noticed that his eyes were almost black, as they had never seen them since he was a boy and fighting with some other boy. His conduct was gracious to the verge of sarcasm, and his bearing graceful as polished steel.

After supper he smoked a cigar with the men, but refused his pa's proffer of brandy. When the women had the dishes put away he rose, bowed to his pa and excused himself from the room. Entering the kitchen, he bowed to Tavie and invited her into the north parlor with that steely look in his eyes that made her wonder if he was going to murder her.

But when he had closed the doors and they had seated themselves his manner became natural again. His anger at John made his task easier with Tavie.

"Tave," he said in a casual tone which made her fear it was audible in the kitchen, "it's clear that we must not be together again after last night. As I've told ye, I've felt it was wrong all along, and now it's come to the point where I'm no good to you or myself any longer. If you had agreed to marry me it would be different. If you would agree to marry me now it would be different. I am ready and anxious to marry ye as I have been for two months now, and as I shall be as long as I live for all I know to the contrary. In giving in so far, but continuing to refuse to marry me, you've done a wrong both to yourself and to me. I'm obliged to stop it."

It was more than evident to Tavie that he didn't love her any longer, if ever he had. This cold thing before her, the thing she had feared in Ike from the beginning, couldn't love anybody. And more terrrible than the admission of that was the realization that now swept over her that she was responsible for his being in this condition, that by making him violate his principles she had brought out and strengthened this cold thing in him that she feared. In the light of this personal realization, she forgot for the moment the burden of the last three days, the fact that the calendar had now turned again since she visited Dr. Daw.

Now Tavie wanted to cry, but could not relax so far under those calm, unnaturally dark eyes. She simply said, "I think you are quite right, Ike. It was evident last night that something was wrong. I shall remember what you say. I must have time to think. I promised you to leave by the end of the month, you know." With an attempt at tenderness which made her lip tremble but had small effect on Ike, she added, "If this is the end, Ike, let us never forget the sweet times we have had together, times that I believe will make the tenderest and happiest memories of my life." With that she rose and Ike, rising with her, replied, "Indeed, we must cherish them, Tave. For my part, also, I doubt I shall ever recapture them—unless"—this with a slight bow—"you give me the chance to recapture them on my own terms —that is, marriage."

"May we part friends, Ike?" Tavie asked, coming nearer to him. "Indeed we may, Tave," he said gently, leaned down, and they kissed each other ever so lightly on the lips. "Good-by," said Tavie, and turned and fled out of the room. As she went, Ike's eyes followed her with a rapidly softening look. He felt a little surge of desire, but it passed quickly, and in its place there rose through him a slow sensation as of great doors swinging open to the sky. His anger at his pa and John remained, but the nervous cause of its extremity was lessened. He crossed into the keeping-room and asked his father, with fitting deference, if he might speak to him in the north parlor.

"Pa," said Ike lightly, discarding his formal manner when they had seated themselves, "beginning next week when the engineers will get down to business, the railroad's going to take a mighty sight of my time. Also, we're planning to expand the engine company which will take some new financing, and it will be my lookout to see to that. If I'm to give these things the time I ought I can't afford to waste two hours a day riding back and forth between the house and the village. I've been thinking it over and I've about concluded, if ye make no objection, to take a room in the village somewhere so's I can stay in nights a good part of the time. I'd figger to come out Saturdays and spend Sunday as usual, likewise to come out and help hayin' when I could, or hire somebody else if needful."

"Does that mean," asked the Squire with a polite nod of interest, "that you propose to relinquish your interest in the financial side of the farm, the accounting and marketing?" "No, indeed, sir," said Ike quickly, though he had not thought of that side of it before. Then, after a short pause, he added, "At least not unless you wish me to. It's true Ben is coming on first-rate, and if ye wish I'll sort of begin breaking him into the bookkeeping and the marketing. He's already taken to marketing enough to argue with me that I lay too much stress on it, he figgering it'd be best to keep more in the old way of spending less money on machinery and increasing the dairy, and making less money from selling cheese and other produce. He tells me we're getting the place where it's dependent on city markets where we ought to keep independent of all markets. There's something to be said for his argument, though I'm for going on expanding as we've been doing. If Ben holds to his notion after he's a little more broke in to our whole situation, the difference between his ideas and mine will of course be something for you to settle, sir."

After a long pause the Squire said, with seeming ease, "As I've told ye many times, Isaac, you must decide these things for yourself. If it seems best to ye to move into the village, you have my permission to do it. And if you wish to initiate Ben in the methods you've been using on the farm, there surely can be no harm in it." "Thank ye, sir," said Ike with genuine relief, for he had feared opposition. His determination did not waver, and his anger against John was still strong, but his anger against his pa was lightened. With a place of his own to retire to, he could better bear his pa's suspicions and disapproval of him.

"I've been figgering," he resumed presently, "that unless things take a bad turn I'll have the means come fall to send Ben to college without having to sell any land off the place." "That is very considerate of ye, Isaac," said the Squire with ill-concealed iciness, and Ike dropped the subject. The Squire inquired politely whether Ike had yet selected a place of residence in the village. "No, sir," said Ike, his manner growing formal, "for I wished to discuss the matter with you first. I've a notion, though, of something I might try. Master Redemption Quin, the druggist—ye may remember I bought his property after the fire—is determined that he owes me a hundred dollars I helped him with when he bought his new place, and it has been on my mind to find some way of clearing his conscience for him. I looked over his new place once, since he gave me a mortgage on it, and as I recall he has an extra room upstairs, besides the one he lives in. It occurred to me I might rent it from him and let him work out what he claims he owes me in rent, without really costing him a penny. I believe I could board across the street at Mistress Jerry Stone's."

"That is very considerate of you," said the Squire again, but now quite honestly, and he suffered a twinge of hope that Ike still might turn out to be a decent citizen. Tempted by this hope, he presently said what he afterwards regretted. "Isaac, are these demands of business the only reason for your wish to move into the village?"

Ike looked away and gazed into the little, gilt fireplace, feeling his anger rise and setting his will for what still threatened to become a painful interview. "No, sir," he finally said abruptly, looking up at his pa with a challenge. "No, sir, it ain't the only reason, though I conceive it to be sufficient reason by itself. The other reason is a letter from John that I got this afternoon in which he accuses me, without explanation, of a serious wrong." It did not occur to the Squire that this accusation could pertain to anyone but Tavie and, though he was not surprised, he suffered a deep pang in the apparent discovery that the affair had become so public that some busybody had written John about it.

"I have always believed," Ike went on, "that John was not only my older brother but my best friend, and this accusation has hurt me so deeply that I don't want to be in the house when he comes home, and I want to stay out of it until he comes to me with some kind of amends. As I said, that ain't the chief reason of my wanting to take a room in the village. But this makes it easier, makes me give up resisting the notion as I have been doing for some time."

"And are you quite sure," pursued the Squire unwisely, "that John is unjustified in making this accusation—whatever it is?"

"Absolutely," snapped Ike. And the Squire sank back into that cold tomb inside himself whose walls were the conviction that Ike was a libertine and a shameless, deliberate liar. Indeed, he was glad he was leaving the house without having to be pitched out. "When do you plan to make this move?" he said, resuming an easy manner and rising to end the interview. "Likely Monday," said Ike indifferently, rising too and unintentionally glaring his father out of countenance. "You will be here tomorrow evening, then?" "Why, sir, I hadn't planned otherwise," said Ike, suspecting that his pa wanted to hasten his departure. The Squire looked at him with a forced but knowing smile which Ike at first could not understand. Then suddenly a genuine smile in return spread over his face.

"By Jiminy!" he exclaimed, now himself again, "Tomorrow's my birthday, ain't it? I'd clean forgot." "You arrived on July third, 'thirty-one, if my memory serves me," said his pa, opening the door.

Ike's combined twentieth birthday and farewell party was long remembered with enthusiasm by the dozen young people of his generation who remained in the Hollow, and with disapproval by their elders—for Deacon Victory Birdseye's perennial charge that junkets were "drunken revels" was then for the first time fully justified. In outline the party was a combined community supper, shower for Ike and a kitchen dance on a community scale. By six o'clock fifteen rigs and more than fifty inhabitants were assembled, dumping their gifts for Ike on the long keeping-room table and their baskets and heaped platters of food on the banquet tables arranged on three sides of a square in the summer kitchen. Already, with the sun still far above setting, full sixty candles blazed on the tables that were further adorned with potted geraniums. The door and window frames were heavily draped with buckeye daisies, day lilies and bee balm, and on the back wall of the room hung two sheets with life-sized red silhouettes stitched to them, which Sarah had sat up all night to make, one representing Ike riding a railroad locomotive which was bucking like a horse, the other a stationary steam engine in the act of exploding with Ike sailing through the sky above it in a graceful, angelic pose.

The Squire outdid himself with supplies of both cider and rum. He deliberately got himself tipsy before he made his farewell speech to Ike, which was at the same time expressly a farewell speech to the dozen youngsters who had gone to California last fall, and was by implication a farewell speech not only to the young generation but to the old days at the Hollow. Ike's reply—to the effect that his purpose in moving temporarily to the village was to learn enough to later build a factory in the Hollow and get a spur of the railroad there—got plenty of cheers and a tremendous toast, but it somehow didn't ring true. The ensuing meal was noisy throughout, and at the end of it Ike, stuffed with food and cider, was required to dance his famous "cricket" in the space between the tables, while the company roared and clapped. While Ike's presents were being inspected, the banquet tables and horses were carried outdoors. Jehu Jones began tuning his fiddle to Master Lane's best harmonica, and the bacchanalian business of the evening got fully under way.

Altogether, it was the gayest and noisiest junket ever held in the Hollow, the dance lasting until not only had the Fourth of July dawned but its sun was fully risen, and there were poppings round the hills from the firecrackers and torpedoes of the youngest generation. If the machine of the Lathrop tradition was running down, if both the motive power and the load were removed, the wheels rattled the more merrily for that. Subconsciously, almost everyone there knew that the machine of that whole country community was running down, and they were impelled to enjoy to the full what time of it was left them. Ike's departure had little importance in itself, for he was not undertaking either a dangerous adventure or one which appealed much to those self-sufficient and money-scorning farmers. Yet it was taken with a deeper and less articulate sadness than the departure of the famous eight last Thanksgiving, as a symbol of the true significance of that earlier departure. For it was now tacitly understood that not one of those eight, the backbone of the younger generation, would ever permanently return.

In the dancing that evening there were such drunken stamping and yipping and cutting of capers that even Jehu Jones was abashed. A great civilization that had built a nation was no longer sure of itself. The old certitude was giving way to pretense, and pretense took the form of excess in pleasure that for two hundred years had been more pleasurable in being more disciplined. There were signs of decay in Lathrop Hollow that night before Independence Day, 1851. A half century later the dancers at a gathering such as this would be like bare and frolicsome skeletons of the populations of a forgotten age, an age when millions of educated men in thousands of such country communities carried with self-assurance the responsibility of a world.

Soon after midnight the old folks began to depart, most of them bearing the promise of anguished heads for the more formal doings of Fourth of July. At last only Dr. and Mistress Swift remained, dozing in chairs in the keeping-room, while in the summer kitchen the Squire, Sarah and the young people carried on the revels through dawn and beyond.

Before leaving, the Doctor gave Sarah Lathrop something, with whispered instructions. Then he and his wife walked arm in arm up the hill, facing the bright sun. Their only comment on the party, the only word spoken between them all the way home, came from Mistress Swift. "John looks sick," she said.

And, awaking three hours after he had sunk into heavy sleep, and realizing it was time to be up, Squire Lathrop found himself unable to rise. Sarah, now having passed her second almost sleepless night, crawled out of bed and returned from the kitchen with a tumbler and a pill. "Reuben Swift left this for you," she said quietly and lifted his head to help him swallow the dose. Ten minutes later he was dressing, his complexion gray and pasty, his jowls heavy, his cheeks cavernous. At nine o'clock he drove his family down to the Independence Day celebration at the Corners, where he delivered the address of the day as usual.

CHAPTER LV

ON MONDAY MORNING, the seventh of July, Sarah insisted on driving in with Ike in the shay, and she spent most of the day in the good-sized slant-ceilinged room over Quin's drug shop, sweeping and mopping up the filth of what had been a commercial storeroom for fifty years. She spent five dollars on a rope bed, dresser, commode, mirror, chair, blue and white calico print curtains, two small rag rugs, two yards of towelling, a clothes whisk, a hairbrush and an ornamental hair wreath which she hung over the dresser. When Ike called for her to drive home at half-past four the place was ready for him to move in. The night before they had reached an understanding on all points, inarticulately about Tavie, articulately about the Squire and John. Sarah had got her tears over with then, and all the way home she was as gay as if she had been building her own nest.

On Tuesday Ike brought in a nightshirt, his carpet slippers and two clean collars, and thus established himself as a resident of the village of Byzantium Falls. All was as usual at the bank during the morning, but late in the afternoon in his office in the Fulton and Price mill a strange feeling of hollowness came over him and drained his energy. He gazed out his window over the Mall, the trees of whose central islands were now heavy with summer foliage, and it was as if he had never before seen anything in the panorama spread below him. In spite of his many friends in the village and his precocious importance in its business circles, he suddenly felt himself alone and a stranger there. Squire Fulton came in for a moment, and it was as if he had never encountered this portly, jovial man before. When he left, Ike looked out of the window again. The golden sun threw a line of light along the tops of the wide ridges beyond the village to the southwest. He felt a heavy lump rise through his throat and up behind his eyes as if he were going to cry. He forced himself back to the preliminary sketch of one of the engineering firms which was spread on his desk.

At half-past five he walked up Columbia Street toward his new abode. Fifty yards short of Quin's place he crossed the street to the farmhouse of old Jerusalem Stone who had the distinction of still cultivating ten acres within thirty rods of the Mall. Ike hoped to fix things so he could see Old Jerry every day, for just now he was the only person in the village he wanted to see. He walked round to the kitchen door and presented himself to white-haired, chalky-complexioned, gentle Mistress Abigail Stone, who received him civilly, not having a notion who he was. Old Jerry must have been following him up the street, for Ike was hardly in the kitchen when the tanner's fast, sturdy step came in the driveway, and there he stood glowering at him with his hands in his pockets.

"What ye up to, young Lathrop?" he demanded. "I've taken a room at Quin's across the street," said Ike. "Understand ye take boarders." "Quittin' the farm where ye belong, be ye?" said the old tanner. "For a few months," Ike replied. "Ha'n't a place for ye, young Lathrop," said Old Jerry. "Table's too full o' young smart alecs a'ready." Ike bowed, bade good evening to Mistress Abigail, and walked slowly up the middle of Columbia Street to the Spencers' house where poor Mattie's ma was delighted to take him as a boarder. She was a lugubrious lady, chronically downcast since her husband had lost their farm, and just now flutteringly suspicious about Mattie's recent alleged intestinal poisoning.

Ike ate little supper, then took a long walk in the sunset out Madison Street and the Round Harbor Road. When he was clear of the village he climbed a snake fence and a little hill on the left and sat down under a butternut grove. From here he could see Lake Ontario eight miles away, its long fringe of horizon now gilded by the low sun. The wide, empty scene only increased his loneliness, so he took off his hat, rolled over on his stomach and buried his face in his hands. Pa would be reading in the keeping-room now, Ma putting away the dishes, and Tavie mopping up. The lump in Ike's throat grew more than he could bear, and he let the sobs come.

A succession of thumps nearby penetrated his grief, and he looked up at a red bull glaring at him and pawing the ground on the ridge two rods away. He jumped to his feet, threw a stone that hit the bull in the head and ran at him, waving his arms. "Git along, ye god-danged varmint," he shouted. The bull swerved away, rolling a great white eye at him, turned back and watched him a moment with lowered head, then walked off down a cowpath toward the barn, throwing back his head once to lick his shoulder with his long tongue.

This encounter with something tangible partly dissipated Ike's sadness, putting him in a contentious mood. He walked back to his room, considering the plans he and Bub Tanofly had already made for the following day.

It might be an important day for the Engine Company, for at one o'clock Horace Gadston's option on the Union Mills property would expire.

Ike spent a restless night in his new bed, and in the morning got to the bank before Philip or Master Sherwood. At noon Bub called for him and they walked together to the Wheeler. To their satisfaction, they found Joe Kirkwood having his preprandial grogs, leaning half across the bar and twitting Job Wheeler about his billiard-ball head as that august politician permitted only his cronies to do. Instantly on entering, Bub and Ike put on their swopping smiles and Joe, turning half round as Job greeted them by name, as instantly assumed his. "Morning, boys," he said, showing his square, gat teeth. "Shadowing me, are ye, Ike?" "Every move ye make," said Ike as he and Bub stepped up to the bar beside him and nodded to Job for their usual respective ale and grog. "Well, you won't have much longer to do it," said Joe, glancing at the clock. "That gives me forty-five minutes yet." He looked at his watch. "My own clock makes it only forty-four. What does yours say, Ike, my lad?" "Don't figger I'm going to forget ye after forty-five minutes, do ye, Joe?" said Ike with his disarming smile, and he walked over to the kitchen door, pushed it open and held up two fingers to Mistress Wheeler.

As soon as Ike moved away, Joe and Bub severally contemplated their drinks, being uncomfortable together these days and each knowing the other knew why. When Ike returned he broke the silence by asking Joe how soon the Kamargo Mill figgered to import their Micks. Joe was a stockholder in the company and did some of its law business. "Probably not before July," he said indifferently. "Why don't you boys get some of them to lay your railroad? They say they're all-fired handy with a pick and they work for nothing, live on half a dozen potatoes, a slice of ham and a pint of whisky a day."

"Worst thing could happen to the community," said Ike candidly, "taking food out of good people's mouths." "Oh, you god-danged Backwater you," said Joe, smiling. "Business is no Sunday school, and nobody knows it better than you and I do." At this point Mamie Wheeler came in with plates of dinner for Ike and Bub, and they started after her into the adjoining dining room. "You fellows got something private to talk over, have you?" said Joe, coming after them and being a little drunk. "Not as I know of, have we, Bub?" said Ike, and Bub merely looked back and grunted. Mamie Wheeler placed them on one side of the table, and Joe lounged down on the bench on the opposite side.

"Well, Ike," he resumed, "you've trimmed me again. At least you've prevented me trimming you so far." "How come?" said Ike, attacking his dinner. "Oh, don't play Miss Innocent. I know you want the Union Mills.

How else would Zeb Milliken refuse to extend our option?" "Finest site in town," said Ike with his mouth full of cabbage, "if a feller's any use for all that power. Have ye taken up your option yet?" "No, and I don't want to, but Horace has given me his orders. Don't need it more'n a bull needs two pizzles. Could do as well with a place fifty feet downstream. But Horace figgers—this is my guess—you'll be bound to have it when you expand your Engine Company."

At this Ike looked up with eyebrows lifted in astonishment. "Horace is mighty flattering and I hope he's right, we with one order being built and one little one waiting after that. I'm uncommon pleased if he thinks we're worth gambling—how much is it?—fifteen thousand? I hope he wins." "I think all he wanted," Joe resumed in a confidential tone, "was to get you to buy off his option. Now that you don't seem to be doing it, he's bound to go through with it anyway. Going to put you in your place for giving that casting job to Jerry Smart." "Mighty expensive putting," said Ike. "His faith in us ought to put up the value of Alec's and my stock. How'd ye like some at two hundred?"

"Say, Ike, I've got to stop this bluffing and get down to my option as I was told to. What I wanted to say was, why don't you give Horace three or four hundred for it, let him think he trimmed you, and you control the property?" "Assuming we're so consummate important as to want two hundred and more horsepower," said Ike, "what's the difference between soothing Horace's rage by giving him a few hundred now and maybe mitigating his loss a little later by giving him, say, five thousand for the property when he can't get it off his hands? The way you say, Alec and I are trimmed certain, but if we wait we might do the trimmin'." "You know how much chance there is of trimming Horace," said Joe impatiently. "Like as not he wouldn't sell to you at all, once he was really mad by having been forced to buy." "All keerect," said Ike. "You know how much chance there is of our wanting a big place like that." "All right," said Joe, half-rising. "That's all I wanted to talk to you about. And now I've got to go down and buy the place. If you regret not having taken it when you could, don't blame me."

At this point a heavy tread came down the outside hall and into the bar. Dr. Daw appeared in the door of the dining room and, without greeting anybody, motioned peremptorily to Joe. Ike admired the way the guilty man pulled himself up casually and followed the doctor out. "Damned serious," muttered Bub. "Doc Daw don't get all brustled up fer nothin'. Most likely she's dyin'." Ike glanced at Bub quickly, then muttered, "I hope she don't die, but I hope she acts like she was dying till one minute after one."

Five minutes later, being a quarter of one, Bub and Ike separated at the door of the Wheeler to be prepared to take advantage of what opportunity poor Mattie Spencer's fate might throw in their way. Bub turned to the right and walked up to Sherwood's Bank, there to wait for Ike and put up four hundred dollars if Ike got a new option. Ike turned to the left and walked down the near side of Court Street till he was opposite Zeb Milliken's law office, a tiny clapboard building, next to Trinity Church, all one room, built originally for Judge VanWyck before he went on the bench. From the door being closed Ike concluded that Zeb was not back from dinner. He walked on till he was beyond the church, then crossed the street, walked around through the graveyard, and up to the back of Zeb's office, where he peered in through one of the windows at the neat little barrel-vaulted chamber entirely walled in books. It was empty, so Ike went back to a strategic point in the graveyard where he waited, one foot up on the iron picket fence round the VanSanford plot.

With a jump of his pulses Ike saw Zeb Milliken enter his office, and immediately walked out to the street and followed him in. The polite little lawyer with the red-glinting black hair, vertically oblong lean face, and horizontally oblong spectacles, was just hanging up his hat when Ike stood smiling behind him, waiting to hang up his. "I see you an't wasting any time, Isaac," said the young attorney for the Union Mills to whom Judge VanWyck had turned over his large practice. He stepped back of his desk at the rear and glanced over it as usual to be sure that every weighted pile of papers was where he had left it. Then he looked at Ike over his spectacles, motioned him to the client's chair opposite, and himself sat down. "No, sir," said Ike, "I'm here to take an option the minute Horace's expires. Hope ye won't mind my twiddling my thumbs for five minutes," he added, looking at his watch. "This office moves by Trinity Church time," said Zeb with his delicate smile. "I leave my watch at the bank."

The little lawyer grew suddenly serious and confidential. "Isaac, we have not felt it proper to intimate anything so long as the Gadston option was outstanding, but since it's so close to expired, we don't mind telling ye, though I hate to disappoint ye, that we an't interested in any more short options of that sort. We've already refused to extend Gadston's for a month. If you wish to consider buying that's one thing, but it isn't worth our fee to the company drawing these little options that don't come to anything." (Though Master Milliken had no partner, he always spoke of himself in his professional capacity as "we.") "What d'ye say to a year?" said Ike, tilting back in his chair and trying to be casual, though he wished that plaguy door was closed, and every step in the street outside made his pulse quicken.

"Well, Isaac," said the little lawyer, turning his head to one side like a bird about to drink, "that might be a little different. Can you say what your proposition would be?" "Four hundred for a year's option for $10,000," said Ike, letting his chair down and looking at Zeb eagerly. Zeb trilled a merry little childish laugh. "Ah, Isaac, I fear you think you're swoppin' hosses." Ike slumped in his chair and dropped his face in his hands.

"First, Isaac," said little Zeb, "let me make it quite clear that we have no discretion in price. That has been set by the company at $12,000, and cannot be reduced but by action of the Board of Directors. As to the option, on the other hand, we have some discretion. A year's option for a fair price would be worth considering. Now, then, let us consider a fair price. It seems to me that twelve hundred dollars for a year's option for twelve thousand would be reasonable."

Ike looked very glum, feeling really discouraged and believing it the best tactics to show it. Zeb shifted a paperweight. "I will tell ye what we might consider, Isaac. We might split it to six months and six hundred dollars. Would that suit ye?" Ike came instantly to life, but he continued to look glum. He took a bundle of checks and his bankbook out of his pocket and studied the latter, just as if he didn't know by heart every dot in it. "No," he said sadly, "your notion is too high," and he shook his head slowly and ruefully. He contemplated his book again for a few seconds, then looked up at Zeb with desperate appeal. "Could ye make it five hundred?"

Zeb rose and looked out the back window. Ike didn't dare stir. Zeb sat down again, and a maternal smile came over his face. "We might consider it. But remember, it is not yet one o'clock." All smiles left his face and, carefully removing a weight from a pile of papers, he began to read a document. Ike wanted to thump the table and say, "Done." But instead, he replaced his checks and bankbook in his pocket and waited, straightening up in his chair, crossing his legs and beating time slowly in the air with his free foot. He could hear his watch ticking the seconds away. Once Zeb glanced over his glasses, smiled faintly, and resumed his reading.

Suddenly there was a step on the path outside the open front door and Ike's heart stopped. He dared not look round as he heard the step on the doorsill and saw Zeb look up with his imperturbable smile. "See ye're busy, Zeb," said the voice of Dr. Jephthah Starbuck of the "Checkered Store" a few doors upstreet. "I wondered could ye lend me a quire o' foolscap till tomorry. I'll be back when ye're at liberty. Howdy, Ike. Can't ye speak t' old friends? See ye're still a-wearin' th' old meal-sack." "Howdy, Jepthy," said Ike, turning round. "I didn't recognize ye. Glad to see ye." Ike wanted to murder him with a paperweight. "I believe we could accommodate ye,

Jepthy," said Zeb. "Don't trouble now," said the firefighting doctor-merchant, perceiving that he had interrupted something. "Any time'll do. I'll be back." And he departed so softly that Ike had to look around to be sure he had gone. As he settled back in his chair the air all at once was filled with a faint wooden clatter, as of little sticks striking rapidly together. It lasted four seconds which seemed to Ike an hour, when there was a wooden blow harder than the rest, a pause, and the lovely alto voice of Trinity Church next door said "on-n-n-n-n-ne."

Without changing his position Ike turned his eyes on Zeb who finished the sentence he was reading, then put the paper back in its proper pile and looked gravely at Ike. He took a key from his waistcoat pocket and considered it for a moment through his spectacles. He opened one of the low doors in the side of his desk and took out a strongbox. He replaced the key to the door in his pocket. He took out the key to the strongbox from another pocket and opened the same. He took out his copy of the Gadston option and considered it briefly. Slowly he untied the ribbon, spread the option on the desk, weighting all the corners, dipped a quill, and spoke aloud as he wrote, "Expired, one o'clock, July ninth, eighteen hundred fifty-one."

Ike was still expecting Joe Kirkwood's step and again lifted his eyebrows at Zeb with an inquiring appeal. The lawyer took a piece of foolscap from the central drawer of his desk and dipped a quill. "Let me see,"—he paused, stroking his cheek with the feather—"did we say six hundred dollars for a six months' option to purchase for twelve thousand dollars?" "Five hundred," said Ike, smiling through his impatience. "Cash in full?" "Cash in full," said Ike, taking out a check from his pocket and reaching for another quill to make it out, then sitting back, smiling along with Zeb at his own impatience. "Very well," said Zeb, and started to write in his slow, beautiful hand. Ike rose and walked the cracks slowly round and round the room. Sometimes he paused and read the labels on the backs of the law books. He stared for a long time at one called "The Conscience of the Court."

It was almost two o'clock when Ike walked out with the option in his pocket. Immediately he felt like a skunk for having taken advantage of Mattie Spencer's condition. He wondered if she had really died. "Well," he rationalized to himself, " 't was no more than Joe's come-uppance." He was thinking not only of Joe's treatment of Mattie, but of the little lesson in business Joe had given him himself, that morning in Paris back at the end of January.

CHAPTER LVI

THAT evening, following the meeting of the "Backwater Nestors," George Fulton took Ike home to supper. Ike told him and Squire Fulton about the option he had taken on the Union Mills, but of course could say nothing about the condition of Mattie Spencer that made it possible to get it. After supper he and George sauntered down Factory Street in the hot summer evening, swinging their sticks, watching the dark, rolling surface of the Kamargo on their right, and pausing to look at the half-finished Irishmen's shanties that defaced the bank at intervals. There was a carnival out at Swain's Grove, and George and Ike had mumbled about it as their destination. But by mutual consent they walked along the north instead of the south side of the Mall, and so voluntarily exposed themselves to the irresistible social suction of the front door of the Wheeler.

As they stepped quietly into the bar they heard Joe Kirkwood in the dining room reciting with drunken enthusiasm what proved to be a poem of one Poe. Joe was the town authority on poetry, modern and, especially, Elizabethan. Having finished *To Helen,* he launched into something by some English poet whom he loudly described as "that prince of fornicators, P. B. Shelley." All the evening's company was in the dining room, for the bar was deserted, even by Job Wheeler. Apparently no one heard Ike and George come in, so they leaned quietly against the bar, out of sight, and listened.

Having finished with Shelley, Joe shifted the subject by an alcoholic, mental sequitur. "Now, take Ike Lathrop," he shouted, "there's another prince of fornicators if he'd only wake up and go to work. Yes, gentlemen, there's a youngster with some brains and some fight in him. A little while ago I gave him a small trimming——"

"On the railroad?" interrupted an ironic voice which Ike recognized uncomfortably as that of Jabe Munson.

"No, it was old John Fulton trimmed us on the railroad. This was only an incident of the railroad war, a little trimming on the side, just between Ike and me. Well, the boy learned his lesson and he's come on since then. He knew I had an option for Horace on the Union Mills and he knew it expired today. Furthermore, he knew I was going to take it up at the last minute, which was one o'clock, for I told him so at twelve-thirty. Incidentally, Horace, I may have had my own reasons for telling him the truth, for you've no more need for the Mills property than you have for the Court House." Ike and George heard Horace Gadston grunt.

"Anyhow," shouted Joe, "Ike knew all that, and not five minutes after I'd told him I was going down to take up the option, I was called away on unexpected, personal business. Ike knew it was personal and important, and if I'm not mistaken he knew what it was—but what it was isn't to the point. Anyhow, I got down to Zeb's as soon as I could, which was four o'clock, and discovered that Ike had taken a new option for his Engine Company at one o'clock, the second ours expired. What do you think of that for a smart one?" "Ummmm," Ike heard Ostrum Applemore's senatorial bass, expressing more admiration than censure.

"The stinkin' little varmint," said the gruff voice of Horace Gadston, whose own record was rich in similar transactions. "Stinkin' nothing, you old thief," bellowed Joe, and there was a loud slap of a hand on a fat shoulder. "There's a hard-fighting youngster with none of your sniv'ling Backwater Miss Nancy about him. There's a good gambler worth anybody's mettle." There was a silence in the other room, full of the soft stir of arms lifting cans to mouths, a silence of uncertainty tinged with disapproval. Ike wanted to sneak out and run as fast as he could, anywhere.

"That doesn't seem like Ike," said the voice of Fred VanSanford quietly. "It'd dang near kill the old Squire, or John for that matter, if they knew it." "They need never know it," said the soft voice of Editor Humility Halleck, and Ike knew that his being there meant the whole town would know it in twenty-four hours. What a skunk Joe was! This was as bad as if Ike should walk in there and tell the whole truth about Mattie Spencer. But he couldn't do that, even if Joe did deserve it.

"Know it?" Joe exclaimed in response to Master Halleck's comment. "Why in hell's pizzle shouldn't those high and mighty Lathrops know it? At last they've somebody with some gumption in their sniv'ling family . . ."

"That's a god-damned lie, Joe Kirkwood!" shouted Ike, rushing into the startled dining room and whipping off his coat. "What ye told of me's true, but I'll ask ye to step out back and I'll knock what ye said of my family back into your ugly mug." Swiftly and quietly Job Wheeler had risen when Ike rushed in, and as Ike stood there trembling, with fists clenched, aware of nothing but Joe Kirkwood's grinning face, he paid no attention to a simultaneous touch on both wrists until suddenly he felt a slight wrench and came to with both his arms pinned behind him. "Let him alone, Ike, he's drunk," Job's hoarse whisper said in his ear.

"But I ain't," snapped Ike, giving a mighty wrench which whirled Job around but didn't loosen his grip. "Leave me be, Job," said Ike more gently. "I ain't going to bust anything here, unless ye hold on and make me thrash round." Meanwhile Job was glaring fiercely over Ike's shoulder at Joe who had risen in his corner, under the close watch of Fred and Jabe who had risen likewise to prevent his exit from the bench. "Very well, Miss Nancy," Joe said quietly, "since you are so ashamed of being a man, I withdraw what I said and apologize. I didn't mean what I said of your family. I never said it. Is that sufficient?"

Ike relaxed a little and Job let him go. "All keerect," Ike mumbled, dropping his head and swinging out to lean on the bar with fury still boiling in him. "Have a drink, Ike?" said Job, bringing him out his coat and hat from the dining room where he had thrown them. "No, thank ye, Job. I'll be all right. Guess I'll take a walk. I'll be back." He put on his hat and walked out into the hall, pulling on his coat. Job stepped to the door of the dining room. "Help yerselves to drinks, fellers," he said, "all but Joe. He don't get any more. I'm stepping outside fer a minute." "O.K., Job," said Jabe Munson, rising again, and he took orders for a round for everybody, including George Fulton, and excepting Joe.

Job caught up with Ike, standing uncertainly at the door. "Do ye mind if I step out with ye, Ike? I'd like to talk to ye a minute." And so, under Job's guidance, they walked clean around the Mall, a circuit of ten minutes. "Ye must understand Joe," Job said in a confidential tone. "What he said of yer family is what he thinks of every family in town, and I know what I'm sayin', Ike. I've heard him say the same of the Fultons and the Stauntons, all the best." "Well, he's no danged call saying such things, whatever he thinks," snapped Ike. "I know it, Ike. I an't excusin' him and I an't blamin' ye fer gettin' yer dander riz. Any man would. I'm just tellin' ye that Joe didn't mean no special insult to your family. He'd a' said the same o' any leadin' family whose name happened to come up." "He wouldn't have said it of anybody's family who was there," grumbled Ike, still raging. "No, likely not. Joe wan't lookin' fer a fight. That's another thing. He didn't know you and George was there." They were rounding the corner by the Universalist Church. "That's no excuse," Ike rejoined. "Wal," said Job, "it an't much of one, I grant ye, but sometimes we all say things, especially in liquor, we wouldn't say to people's faces." Ike was silent, admitting the truth of this.

"Besides," Job pressed his advantage, "don't know how much ye heered, but fact is he was meanin' to praise ye personal to the skies." "I know," said Ike glumly, "that's the worst of it, praising me for the lowest thing I ever did in my life. Never would have done it but for the sneakin' trick Joe did me that ye heard him refer to. Figgered to get back at him and teach him manners next time." "Wal," said Job, "I cal'late ye succeeded. Joe likes ye now and when he's yer friend, he's yer friend fer keeps." "Well, I ain't his," grumbled Ike. "That's no matter to Joe," said Job with a chuckle. "Once he decides ye're all right, the wusser ye treat him the better he likes it. Lay ye a hundred to one—serious I will—Joe'll never trim ye again, no matter what ye do to him. I'm tellin' ye he's queer that way, not like anybody ye ever see. What he was sayin' about ye was honest praise. He meant every word of it, and once he talks like that about a feller he never changes his mind. It an't a bar-keep's business to tell no tales, but I've been a-watchin' Joe fer ten years, and ye'll find that what I'm a-tellin' ye's the truth." "Queer critter," said Ike in a natural voice, and they turned into the Wheeler.

Ike joined the group in the dining room quietly, and Ostrum Applemore made room for him on the bench. The talk was now on the everlasting South and slavery, and Ike's return to the room was as unacknowledged as if he had stepped out to the shed. Job broke his rule by bringing him a double grog and Ike drank it with only moderate speed, showing that all was calm now. Whenever Ike wasn't looking at him, Joe's big steel-blue eyes watched him from under his massive forehead. The cat grin was no longer there, and his face had an expression not far from sadness and tenderness. Ike caught the look sometimes and it made him uncomfortable, but it didn't revive his anger.

At nine-thirty George Fulton rose to go and Ike followed him out. "A'mighty sorry I made a row, George," he said at the door, "and thank ye for the supper." "I don't blame you," said George. They shook hands. "Good night to you," said George with a faint touch of formality, and he walked away. Returning to the bar, Ike met Jabe and Fred and Humility Halleck and they exchanged pleasantries about Joe and his loud voice.

Ike hesitated, thinking he should go too. But something like a mysterious magnet drew him back into the dining room and the company of the three men who were anathema to all decent folk. Gadston and Applemore left almost immediately, the Senator's last jovial remark being, "Now don't you two young bulls pitch into each other." Joe merely lifted his eyes in a faint smile and dropped them. There was an unembarrassed silence for half a minute. Then, "Job," called Joe to the host who was cleaning glasses in the bar, "will you trust me with another now?" Job walked slowly in and stood by the table, looking judicially from Joe to Ike and back to Joe again. "Ask Ike," he said finally. "All keerect," said Ike. Job brought one for Ike as well.

The twenty-five-year-old and the twenty-year-old sat silent again and did not drink until they had started talking. "Ike," Joe finally said in a quiet voice, "do you know why I got pickled this afternoon?" "Maybe—partly." "Did Bub tell you?" "Yep." Long silence. "Didn't tell anybody else, and I won't peep," Ike added. "I'm not afraid of that," murmured Joe.

"The truth is," said Joe after another pause, "I've been honestly in love with Mattie for half a year. Been an awful situation, worst I was ever in. I'd have lit out with her somewhere but for my youngsters. Fond of them too. I'm not soft about women, but this was different. Mattie didn't have a bit of whore in her. All my fault. Only thing I was ever sorry for in my life. Sweetest girl I ever knew. Ready to die for me. That's why she jumped in the river, to make it easier for me. Never thinks of herself. She perked up when I came in this afternoon. Held her hand for three hours."

Joe fell silent again, took a sip of his drink and looked at the table. "Ike," he said finally, "I'm truly sorry for what upset you tonight. Didn't know you were there, of course. Drunk as I was, I meant to praise you." "Peculiar way ye took to do it," said Ike with a smile, "picking out the dirtiest thing I ever did in my life." "You know, Ike, that's the only thing I don't like about it, or about you, being sorry for what you did." Ike chuckled ironically. "I'm afraid ye'll have to go on not likin' me, then, for I'm more ashamed of it than anything I've ever done"—"almost anything," he added, thinking of Tavie. Joe shook his head in wonder and paternal concern. Finally he looked up. "Well, anyhow, you can count on me from now on, whether you like it or not."

"Ye're a queer critter, Joe," said Ike, looking directly at him with a friendly smile. "Maybe I am," said Joe, and fell silent, his mind returning to Mattie. Ike didn't dare ask the question uppermost in his thoughts.

Finally Joe sat up, wearing his cat grin. "Time to turn in. I'm due for a headache tomorrow." They rose and put on their beavers. "Joe," said Ike, "you didn't tell me—Mattie?" "No," said Joe, thrusting his hands in his pockets and lifting his big head defiantly, "I told her not to die. Probably another dirty turn I did her."

CHAPTER LVII

I K E worried for more than a week about his skulduggery in getting the Union Mills option. At the meeting of the Gang on Monday it was plain that George, Jabe and Fred were uneasy with him, and everybody was careful to keep the talk away from the subject. Ike managed to get out to the homestead three afternoons to help with hayin', and though the rumor of his deal had not reached the Hollow, the atmosphere there gave him no comfort. His pa seemed mostly concerned to outpitch him in the hayfield, and after supper he would go out and work till dark at his everlasting stonin' of the side-hill pasture. Ike's own state of mind was made more hectic by his recent, abrupt return to celibacy, and, though Tavie was like a stranger to him, her presence increased his nervous tension.

Throughout the week he went round and round the same circle in his mind. The only person he had harmed was old Horace Gadston, trimming him out of the option he was going to take up as well as the hundred dollars he had given for it. But this was no more than Horace had done to plenty of folks, and it was certain he'd skin Ike out of his eye-teeth if he got a chance. Alone in his office, Ike would thump his fist on his desk and call himself a snivelling baby for even considering making amends to the old skinflint. But then he would slump back in his chair again and admit that there was something about the deal he was bound to get straight in his mind, or it would plague him as long as he lived. His conscience was troubling him, sure grit. This was the sort of thing he'd agreed to tell Pa, and he'd have to do it pretty soon unless he could get straightened out on his own hook.

On Friday afternoon, more than a week after he had taken the option, Ike walked into Horace Gadston's office in his foundry across Mill Street from the Union Mills property. The industrialist was sitting at his desk facing the window, his beaver on as usual, a long cigar slanting out of his mouth. For half a minute Ike contemplated his back, with mingled feelings of shame and contempt. He knew the old scalawag must have seen him pass the window and must have heard him close the door when he entered.

At last Gadston looked round with a start, as if he had been deeply pre-occupied and just now realized someone was in the room. "Evenin' Ike," he said cheerfully. "Have a cheer." And he hitched his own halfway round. Ike kept his hat on and remained standing, looking hard and straight at Gadston, who lowered his head till his rosy jowls rolled over his collar, while his good eye looked up at Ike sideways and his bad eye surveyed the ceiling.

"I came by," Ike said in a hard voice, "to tell ye I'm a'mighty sorry about the Union Mills deal and I want to make amends." Gadston snorted. "Think nothin' of it, my boy—think nothin' of it. All in a day's work—all in a day's work." Then he dropped his good eye to the floor and his bad eye to Ike, and added, "what's yer proposition?"

"Well, sir," said Ike, "I hain't a straight proposition yet, for I'd have to get the company's permission to make ye one. But I guess I can get the company's permission if I try. What I came to ask ye was whether, if I get the company's permission, ye'd care to take the property at our option figure, which is the same as yours was, twelve thousand. And besides, I'll make up to ye personally the hundred dollars ye lost on your option."

Gadston sniffed. "What's bitin' ye? Figger ye can't raise the twelve thousand?" "No, sir," said Ike, feeling anger rise in his cheeks, "hain't thought of that yet. I just want to make amends to ye for what I did." Gadston sniffed again, looked at the floor, and considered. "I might give ye, say, five thousand fer a controllin' interest in yer company," he finally proposed, not looking up. "No, Master Gadston," said Ike with dignity, "I ask ye to understand that nothing of that kind is in my mind. I simply want to give ye a chance to buy the property at the figger it would have cost ye if Joe had taken up the option in time." And after a pause he added, "If ye don't want it, that's the end of it. I ain't holding the offer open after I leave this office."

Gadston looked up at him with a smile. "I'll give ye seven thousand cash fer the property." Ike had expected something like this, but hadn't decided what to do. To raise the five thousand dollars' loss, he'd have to sell or pledge most of his stock in the railroad. His common sense rose in an angry flood and drowned the faint tendency of conscience to consider this proposal. "Ye ain't talking sense, Master Gadston," he said. "I didn't come to make ye a present, just to make amends for the trimmin' I gave ye. Since ye don't want the property I ask ye to take this check for a hundred, which I understand was what the option cost ye."

Ike took from his pocket the check he had drawn, stepped forward and dropped it on the desk. Gadston picked it up, looked at it and dropped it in the cuspidor. "Look here, young feller," he blustered, "do ye figger I'm a sort o' whore to be bought off with a piddlin' hundred?" Ike bowed and turned to the door. "Make it eight thousand," said Gadston. "Sorry ye ain't interested," said Ike, bowed again and went out. When he had gone Gadston had the decency to tear up the check, but he chuckled, deciding not to tell Ike he had done it, just to keep the young varmint pestered, wondering when it was coming in.

The effect of Ike's effort to clear his conscience with Gadston was to throw him into still deeper self-doubt that was the more upsetting because he could not now explain it. Where before he had at least the sense of having effected a smart deal, he now felt altogether out of the straight furrow. Where before he had suffered active shame, he now felt merely helpless and trivial. That very evening in the Wheeler he had a chance to confide what he had done to Bub Tanofly and Joe Kirkwood, but he couldn't bring himself to tell them, knowing how they would laugh at his Miss Nancy righteousness and feeling they'd danged well be entitled to. On the other hand, he had a chance to tell Jabe Munson and George Fulton of his attempt to square himself, but couldn't fetch himself up to that either. After all, he hadn't really squared himself, and he was certain that Jabe and George would figger he should have gone the whole hog and sold to Gadston at his figure, taking the trimming he deserved. He hadn't been wholly true to either side of his nature, and between them he stood alone and uncertain, stripped of any sustaining conviction. All he knew himself was that he now felt like an outsider with everybody. Desperately he was searching for some kind of assurance, and he could make no guess of where to look for it.

When he rode out to the homestead on Saturday he was in a pathetic state, between his spiritual helplessness and his bottled-up carnal desires. He figgered he had nothing to confess to Pa or Ma now, yet he wanted something terribly that they—or, for all he knew, anybody—might be able to give him. He was ashamed without knowing what he was ashamed of. After he reached home he wanted to please everybody, but didn't know how to do it. When they were pitching, he almost jabbed the shoulder of Ben who was making the load. After supper he tried to help his pa stonin' in the side-hill pasture, but they couldn't seem to work together, and Ike came near to dropping a boulder on the Squire's foot. It seemed to him that everything was working against him.

Tavie made him specially uncomfortable. She wasn't nervous at all, but hard and calm and remote. She didn't avoid him, but when they looked at each other her eyes might as well have been made of china, and it was Ike who dropped his. In bed Saturday night he knew that part of his trouble was wanting Tavie again, or, more likely, just any woman. He dreamed luxuriously of Pru Stark. Yet in the morning he knew it was more than that that he wanted. He remembered Aggie's advice—love—God—especially God, he thought.

At church he came nearest to being alive. Walking back up the hill after meeting, he said to his pa that whatever God was, he figgered he had something to do with permanent things that didn't change, like home and the church you were brought up in. At this the Squire's lip quivered, but he covered it with a smile, cleared his throat and said, "That's what I've always thought, Isaac." Ike's mind went off looking for something else to say, but he couldn't think of anything.

Riding into the village on Monday morning, he realized one thing that was bothering him beside the need of women. He must get back in the good graces of the Gang, especially Jabe Munson, Fred VanSanford and George Fulton. That noon at the Wheeler he would tell them he had done his best to make amends to Horace Gadston. That ought to fetch things at least into the clear. This hope partly revived his spirits during the morning. But on the way to the Wheeler he felt nervous and helpless again. At dinner they all were as needlessly polite as they had been the week before. As then, the subject of the option was avoided. Ike couldn't force himself to bring it up, and he left the group early.

The next day brought an event which normally would have kept Ike in an ecstasy for weeks. The steam engine for the *Democratic Union* was finished, and at three o'clock Ike and Bub Tanofly joined Alec at the flimsy little engine house painted red, with its woodshed on one side and on the other a tall brick chimney that Alec already had belching fire. It was a sizzling hot day outside, and inside the enginehouse the thermometer was a hundred and twenty even before Alec solemnly closed the door on the company of three. With a flourish he produced a bottle of champagne he had had sent from New York, lifted it, shouted, "I christen thee Big Byzantie," and smashed it against the side of the long steam drum while all three of them shouted, "Hurrah!" Then he produced a second bottle of champagne and tumblers and, after most of it had followed the cork to the ceiling, they toasted the engine and the company.

This ceremony over, Alec ran out the door, leaving his fellow stockholders a trifle nervous in the presence of this new and gigantic dragon, roaring in its firebox and crouching as if to spring through the flimsy roof.

In a minute he returned with Ostrum Applemore and Theophilus Bostwick, who had been waiting in the main building, owner and editor respectively of the *Democratic Union.*

"Anybody nervous?" Alec asked with his quick, shy smile, running his
hands through his black hair. "If so he is permitted to wait outside." Everybody, including Alec, was nervous, but each grumbled a show of courage
and held his ground. Like prisoners watching the clock for the minute of
execution, they all peered at the steam gauge that was now climbing with
increasing speed from twenty to twenty-five.

"Figure that'll do for a starter," said Alec. "Might as well begin at low
pressure till we're sure everything is working O.K. Ought to have thirty-
five. But we can try it this way first, and if it turns the press at all we can
speed it up afterwards as much as you wish. We mustn't be surprised if it
doesn't work first-off. You understand, Senator?" In answer Applemore
pointed an anguished finger at the steam gauge which was nearing thirty.
Alec laughed a little too lightly and said, "Very well, here goes the first
steam-driven press in the world." All wore sickly, nervous smiles. Alec
opened the throttle and there was a thunderous thump inside the boiler,
whereat everybody but Alec staggered back.

With a slow hiss the piston-rods thrust the connecting-rods and the wheel
and belt on its free pulley began to turn. In no time the engine was rattling
at terrific speed and the little building was filled with steam. The gauge
dropped, but immediately began climbing again. Alec gave a quick yank
on the chain of the safety valve that sent a squealing white column up to
the roof, and again the onlookers staggered back. When the pressure was
back to thirty Alec opened the firebox, threw in some more wood and
closed the drafts. Then with a magnificent gesture he pushed the big
wooden lever that shoved the belt from the free pulley over onto the shaft
pulley, and so much of the shaft as was in the enginehouse began to turn.

Ostrum Applemore was perspiring with steam and excitement. He
slapped his editor on the back and yelled, "B' God, Theophilus, there she
goes! Press goin' now, is she, Mat'son?" "Not quite yet, Master Applemore," shouted Alec. "There's another belt to throw on inside the office.
Ike, I'm going to ask you to be assistant engineer for a minute while we
see what's going on inside at the press. Best keep her down to forty." Ike
nodded courageously, instantly using his authority to yank the safety valve
and drop the pressure below thirty. Alec led the others out, leaving Ike
alone in the hiss and roar and the seething cloud of steam. Throwing off
his coat and waistcoat, he leapt back and stood perspiring in his plug hat

and shirt sleeves, tensely at the alert with his eyes on the gauge and his hand on the chain of the safety valve.

But the fresh wood and the closing of the drafts were already decreasing the pressure. In two minutes Alec returned and told Ike to go into the office, which he did at a run. Bub, scowling with concentration, was feeding folio sheets to the big press that was sedately slapping down and up, down and up, Master Bostwick at each upward swing snatching out the printed sheet on which appeared, in the largest type the *Union* could boast,

DEMOCRATIC UNION
NAPIER PRESS
BYZANTIUM STEAM ENGINE COMPANY
FIRST STEAM DRIVEN PRESS
IN THE WORLD

As Ike watched, the rate of slapping slowly diminished and finally stopped, to the obvious relief of Bub and Master Bostwick. Alec ran in. "Will that do for now?" he asked eagerly of the proprietor of the *Union*. "Perfectly," said Applemore with a delighted smile, "and I congratulate ye, young man."

Ike turned to Alec and took him in his arms.

On Thursday morning the *Democratic Union* gave half of its space to its new steam engine that had driven the new press on which this edition had been successfully printed. There was a flamboyant editorial celebrating the beginning of a new era in printing, and there were effusive biographical sketches of Alec and Ike, and even Bub. In the bank Ike glanced through what six months before would have been the record of a major triumph. But now it seemed more like a death warrant to him, a writ of ostracism from the world to which he had always belonged. It seemed to him that all this had not really happened. It was a sort of accident, and all that was truly going on was a quest for something inside himself, or for something outside he would call God, something more important than money or even friends. He was very polite in response to the congratulations he received from everybody who came into the bank, but he was not present in spirit and made several mistakes in counting out money from the till.

The following afternoon the Byzantium Steam Engine Company held a meeting in Ike's office, and, though the business was important, Ike sat indifferently by the window, letting Alec and Bub make all the decisions.

They voted him two shares of stock to replace the two he had given Solon Samson. And they voted to raise enough by an issue of new stock to take up their option on the Union Mills property, finance the move into the larger quarters, and purchase new equipment. It was agreed that only young men should be admitted to the company, and that George Fulton, Jabe Munson, and Fred VanSanford should be the first approached. As the Treasurer, Business Manager and chief diplomatist of the company, Ike was to solicit the subscriptions.

Climbing the dark stairs to Judge VanSanford's office, Ike expected failure and merely wanted to get it over with. After Fred and the big-bearded Jabe had congratulated him a little too warmly on the success of the *Union* engine, Ike, remaining standing, put his proposition brusquely, almost defiantly, without any effort to enlarge on the possibilities of the company. The proposition to each of them was to invest three thousand dollars in new stock. Having spoken his piece, he turned his back on them and looked out the window up Washington Street.

Fred immediately and cheerfully turned Ike down on the ground that he didn't have and couldn't raise the money, which Ike suspected was the truth. He nodded to Fred without comment, then looked at Jabe, wondering what his excuse would be. When it came it was so tenuous as to leave no doubt of Jabe's meaning. "Well, Stud, my boy," he said, "I could likely find yer three thousand, but I figger my business is lawin', not manufacturin' steam engines. Wouldn't want the worriment of it. Got plenty o' knittin' to tend to right here." There was a moment of embarrassed silence. "Well," said Ike, turning away suddenly, "no need to make a prayer meeting of it. A'mighty sorry you fellers don't want to jog along. Good evening to ye." And he swung on his hat and walked out. Down on the Mall he shuffled along the footpath in an aimless, tired way.

There was still time to walk up to the Fulton and Price bindery and see George Fulton, but Ike couldn't bring himself to it now. He knew George would turn him down, and George, in his cheerful, direct, untalkative way, was always so danged right. Ike knew he'd make him feel more ashamed and cast down than the others had. Besides, George would be the last of his friends in the village whose folks and ways were like his own, the friends whose families were his own family's friends. He'd still have Bub and Alec, but neither of them touched the old-fashioned, local thing in Ike that Jabe and George and the VanSanfords did. After George turned him down he'd be an outsider for good.

That evening Ike sat alone in a bar down Court Street where none of the Gang ever came. He saw that the big mistake he'd made was in drift-

ing away from Pa. Pa's being mad about his going into business, along
with the trouble with Tavie, had made him get his back up and be too pernickety and close-mouthed. At a time like this, the folks he wanted to be
with most were the family. The place for him was back at the Hollow.
Never should have left it. He'd move back next week. The railroad business would get heavier from now on, but he'd manage somehow, riding
back and forth every day. He'd make a clean breast of everything to Pa
and Ma, the way he'd trimmed Joe Kirkwood on the option and the trouble with Tavie. He'd tell Pa the truth, that he'd been asking Tave to marry
him for near three months. Pa'd be bound to forgive him then.

As he figured on these serious matters, sitting alone with a glass of ale,
Ike felt that his trouble with the 'Paloosa about Pru Stark didn't amount
to much. The big fellow would be home in a week or two. They'd clean it
all up quick enough, and after that the 'Paloosa would help him with Pa.
It wouldn't be so a'mighty hard, with Tavie out of the way. She'd agreed to
leave before the 'Paloosa came home. If she stayed, she'd have to marry
him. Whatever else happened, there'd be no more nonsense between them,
nothing more to be ashamed of. Altogether, it seemed as if things at home
ought to clear up now, even if he had lost his friends in the village. It all
seemed quite clear and easy. Ike's tense, frustrated nerves, coupled with
the little ale he drank, clothed the homestead and the family in a rosier
glow than they had had even when he was homesick at first. That night he
slept peacefully, like a child.

The next morning, which was Saturday, when Squire Fulton started
home for dinner Ike gave him a note for George, asking him to stop in
at the office early that afternoon. This would give George a chance to get
out of coming and so make things easier for both of them. But instead
of refusing, George walked into the office at two o'clock. "Hope I haven't
kept you waiting," he said cheerfully, hanging up his hat. He sat down in
a chair by the window, tilted back, glanced out over the Mall, then looked
at Ike with a faintly playful smile, as if he understood everything and
took it as a joke.

"Got a notion what I want to see ye about?" said Ike, clasping his
hands behind his head. "I think so," said George, crossing his legs, "if
it's the same thing you wanted to see Fred and Jabe about." Ike saw from
this that they'd been talking it over, though Jabe wouldn't talk straight
to him. "Well," he asked, "what d'ye say?" "Can't do it, Stud," said George,
"after the way you trimmed Kirkwood on that option."

They both smiled, and George added earnestly, "Please don't misunder-
stand me. Personally I am as fond of you as ever, and whatever made you

do that is none of my toad-puddle. But I just can't be associated with a company, yours or anybody's, that does things like that."

"Did ye know," said Ike, "I went to Gadston and offered to let him have the place at his option figger, which was the same as ours, and to pay him the hundred he lost besides? He laughed at me and offered to buy the place for eight thousand. Do ye figger I should have let him have it and stood the four thousand loss myself?"

George thought a moment. "No, maybe not. The trouble is that's just the kind of dilemma you find yourself in if you're a decent fellow, and then do a thing of that sort. The trouble was in the original deal. It seems to me that if you do a thing like that, that's against your nature, it does something to you that no amount of immediate atoning will take care of." "Ye're right," said Ike, dropping his eyes.

After a moment Ike looked up with a bitter smile. "It's your notion, then, that we remain friends personally, but in business ye'll have nothing to do with me, at least not for a spell till ye see how I behave from now on?" "Yes," said George. "That's a pretty fine line, George. Business is more'n half my life nowadays, and if a feller's against me in business he might as well be against me personally too."

"Perhaps that's where you're making a mistake," said George, looking out the window, "in letting business be more than half your life. To my mind business has nothing to do with life, except the little part that's personal, where a fellow's notions of right and wrong come in." "Maybe ye're right there," said Ike slowly. "Maybe I hain't enough life outside of business." To himself Ike thought, "Love and God," but he didn't say that to George. They fell into a long silence, Ike looking down.

Abruptly Ike rose and walked to the west window, where he stood gazing down the river. "By the way, Stud," said George, "will you come to supper tonight? I'm going to ask Fred too, and maybe Jabe." "Wish I could," said Ike, walking back and rolling up the engineers' papers on his desk, "but I figger I'd best go home on Saturdays always." "Will you come up to the house and have a drink now?" Ike looked out at the Baptist Church clock which he had learned to read at this narrow angle. "I'm afraid not now," he said. "As it is, it'll be four before I get home. I guess the hay's all in, but I have little enough time with the family these days anyhow."

They took down their hats and walked out silently together, parting at the street door, George to walk home, Ike to go to get the post before setting out for the Hollow. "Is everything O.K.?" said George, offering his hand. "O.K.," said Ike, taking it and returning the pressure, feeling that it was George, not he, who was being the hypocrite.

In spite of having foreseen George's reaction, Ike lagged as he walked up the slanting path to the Mall, as if he were carrying a great physical weight. This was the end of his personal life in the village. "Now," he murmured as he came up in front of Applemore's Iron Block, "there ain't anything for me but business." Then, "Business!" he snorted aloud, "Business be god damned!"—at which gentle little Hosea Hooper, son-in-law to Applemore, just emerging from his hardware store, staggered back and concealed himself in the doorway.

"Business!" Ike sneered again as he shuffled past. "By God, I'll sell out the whole caboodle now, and go back to the Hollow where I belong!" He lifted his head, but still walked slowly, and all the frustrated lust and affection in him lifted the homestead again into a sort of heaven, the end and reward of all his desires. He'd go back for good. Yes, by God, if Pa wanted him to, he'd go to college yet!

As he started down Court Street he began thinking about John. One thing was sure. Whatever happened, *they'd* always come back together. They couldn't ever be really apart, any more than he and Pa and Ma could. "By God," Ike thought, "I'll make things right with the 'Paloosa, if I have to knock Pru Stark clean out of his addled head!" He walked into the Post Office with a determined step.

As if answering his thoughts there was a letter from John in the post, besides two for Tavie from Oberlin—one from Constant and one from somebody else. John's was addressed to Pa, and the seal had been broken in transit. His letters were always for the whole family, so Ike had no qualm of conscience in whipping it out, stepping to the front window, and beginning to read like a famished soul.

There were two or three pages about the examinations just ended, how John must wait around for Commencement, and how with the new fast train service, he expected to reach Utica on Friday afternoon, the first of August, and get home the following day. "That's next Saturday!" thought Ike. Then he started the following paragraph:

"Indeed, what you say about Ike troubles me greatly. I must confess that certain unwelcome intelligence has come to me tending to corroborate your view. As for the homestead, I am delighted to hear that Ben is coming along so nicely. Frankly, I had always thought of the place as belonging to all of us jointly, with Ike as the guiding spirit, and I hope you will give the matter deep consideration before carrying out the intention you intimated. However, this is a matter in which your judgment must as always be paramount. . . ."

Ike dared not read any more. He was not angry now, as he had been before when he read John's curt note to him about the petty matter of Pru. He felt the world giving way under him, and for a moment he leaned against the window as if he had been struck. Pa had written John his adverse opinion of him, and John had agreed with him. Pa had proposed to cut him off, and John had made only a perfunctory protest.

There was no defiant reaction to this tearing away of Ike's whole foundation. Slowly and laboriously he walked up Washington Street to Howell Sherwood's stable. Slowly and laboriously he saddled Chesty, thinking nothing, forming no plan, numb in emotion. The first thing he knew, he saw his hand giving Peg-leg Harris his penny at the tollgate at the Center. Then he felt Chesty trotting under him. Time and the landscape drew far off again, and he rode in a vacuum.

Somewhere in the back of his conscious mind the image of Tavie fluttered. She, or at least his own weakness about her, was the cause of all this, starting with the time he kissed her eons ago last Thanksgiving. It was from then on that he had gradually moved away from the family until now he was a stranger shut out for good. He was alone in the world, on his own devices. Without formulating the thought, his unconscious mind gave him faint comfort in the realization that he was now free of Tavie. He had made his mistake. He had offered to do what was right. And now he was free.

This moment's faint reprieve faded into the image of buildings up on that hill, barns and a strange lilac-colored house, far off as a star, the house that had once been his, the place where he had lived long ago. He lapsed into mental and emotional numbness again. He had no volition, no plan. Chesty, bent on oats, stepped out in his long trot up the last half mile from the Corners, and Ike did not hinder him.

CHAPTER LVIII

TAVIE'S calendar had now turned for the second time since she saw Dr. Daw, and she was resigned to her fate. The medicine had not worked. There was no escape for her now. After supper on Friday evening—when Ike in the village was deciding to return to the homestead—she went upstairs and lay down, calm under a powerful sense of destiny that had been coming over her during the past month. She considered every possible and impossible course, and always came back to Dr. Daw's vigorous advice. Nothing would so disrupt her life and her ambitions as to have a child outside of wedlock in some obscure region, alone and without resources, dependent thereafter on the charity of friends for the most elementary social intercourse, useless to the Reform Movement, necessarily disclaimed by its leaders, even by Mrs. Mott. There was only one clear course, and so she made her plan, with a faint alternative plan, as yet unformulated, in the back of her mind. It was her cold, rational mind that made the plan. Yet, once it was settled, there was something else in her that awoke and glowed.

On Saturday Sarah observed that Octavia had her color back, that she was quick and responsive again, and that she hummed at her morning chores as she had not done for weeks. She concluded that Octavia's feelings for Ike were taking a new turn. She was sure of it when immediately dinner was put away Tavie flew upstairs and, after an inordinately long time, came down in her prettiest yellow calico, with her hair carefully flounced out in waves from under a yellow hair ribbon. At two o'clock Sarah told her that she was going to take her knitting over and spend the afternoon with Samantha. And she kissed Tavie before she left.

As Chesty carried Ike around the curve at the top of the hill and he was only ten rods from the house a faint sense of panic rose in him, a sort of pathetic apprehension at the prospect of meeting Pa, even Ma. They didn't want him. He wished he were somewhere else, but he hadn't the will to decide to go away. Anyhow, he thought, he must deliver the post,

and this simple dictate of habit was sufficient to overcome the more complicated impulse to flee. As he succumbed to it Chesty was already stamping into the barn, and afterwards Ike could remember not one thing that
happened after hearing that sound until some twenty minutes later when
the outer world suddenly and unexpectedly impinged on his consciousness again.

What happened was that as he swung down from the saddle Tavie
came running out to meet him. "Howdy, Ike," she said gaily, assuming
his semi-vernacular. "Howdy, Tave," replied Ike mechanically. "Glad to
see ye." Chesty, released, walked into his stall and Ike followed and un-
bridled and unsaddled him, while Tavie fetched him a bucket of water,
and afterwards threw a scoop of oats in his trough and a few forks of
hay in his manger.

"Thanks, Tave," said Ike as they met again in the main barn. "Ike,"
said Tavie, looking up at him, "I came out to meet ye to apologize for
having been so queer the past month. I've been worried about something
I'll tell you of later. It won't happen again." "Don't let it concern ye,
Tave. I figgered I understood." "No, you didn't, Ike—not for once. Come
in the house quick and I'm going to tell ye. Everybody's out."

She noticed that Ike was hardly seeing her and that he was deathly
pale. "Are ye feeling up to snuff, Ike," she said, taking his arm and bending forward to look up in his listless eyes. "Fitter'n a fiddle," said Ike.
"How are you feeling these days?" Tavie's announcement that nobody
was at home relieved the sense of panic in Ike's unconscious, but the
house and its furniture nevertheless seemed strange and stark to him, like
a place which he had visited once before in company but to which he was
now returning furtively as a trespasser or a thief. As for Tavie, she might
as well not have been present at all. She led him into the north parlor and
sat him down in one of the two gilt chairs she had set out for this interview.

"Ike," Tavie began, "aren't you a little glad to see me?" "Surer'n shootin'," said Ike. "Ye're looking pretty as a picture." And his social reflexes
turned on her a pale imitation of his big smile. Tavie decided that it was
his determination to let her alone that was making him so unnatural,
and she concluded there was nothing for it but to come to the point.
"Ike," she said, "I must tell you something." She dropped her gaze to the
fireplace, felt herself beginning to tremble, looked up again straight into
his face and said softly, "I'm going to have a baby."

This remark brought Ike back to earth, but not quite quickly enough.
At any other moment in his career he would have received the revelation with suavity and magnanimity. But in his present state the impact

of it struck first clean down into his unconscious that was equipped with nothing but the most elementary responses. Instantly his whole face dropped in such a look of horror and dismay as might have come over him bound to a stake and watching the torturer light the fagots. The look lasted no more than two seconds, when the news he had received flashed up into his conscious mind where all his store of social feelings and responses instantly awoke and took charge of his actions. The color poured back into his cheeks. His real smile spread over his face.

"That's capital, Tave!" he said with enthusiasm, leaned forward, took her trembling hand in both of his and pressed it to his lips. "Now we can be married at once! Today! No, tomorrow in church, right after meeting. Where's ma? Let's go tell her right now! Let's go down and tell your ma! Come on!" He half rose and leaned forward to take her in his arms, but she leapt up with a shriek, ran into the kitchen and up the back stairs. Ike rushed after her, but she dropped the catch on her door and he shook it in vain. "No, Ike," she sobbed against the other side of the door. "I could never marry you now, never, never, never!"

Ike sat down on the top of the back stairs and the board creaked as usual. In a moment Tavie spoke on the other side of the door, "Ike, was there any post?" "Yes, Tave, two letters for ye. O Tave, what's the matter with ye anyway? Why can't ye calm down and be natural? Let's get married and get all this nonsense over with. If I've been acting perculiar it's because I got some bad news today which I'll tell ye about later."

Coldly Tavie replied, "I'm both calm and natural, and I'm sorry you've had bad news. You've been kind and generous, but now I understand everything. Please put my letters outside the door and please"—here her voice rose hysterically again—"please go away!" Ike took out the bundle of letters, including the one from John, picked out Tavie's with difficulty in the dimness of the back attic, and set them by her door. Then he rose, took a step down and spoke again.

"Tave, I'm mighty sorry if ye don't like it, but I figger we can make out sure grit, and ye'd best give in. We can have all those fine times over again all our lives, only they'll be better. I'll wait for ye downstairs." But Tavie only screamed back, "I mean it, Ike! Don't you see? This is final! I'll never, never marry you! Oh, please, please go away! Leave the house! This is the last thing I'll ever ask you as long as we live. I mean it, Ike. *I mean it!*"

Ike heard her break into sobs, concluded there was nothing more he could do now, and walked downstairs. In spite of this crisis with Tavie, this major crisis in his own life, the moment he set foot in the empty

kitchen the sense of being an alien in this house he loved rose stronger
than the effects of the recent scene. Only now his mind was fully awake,
and his emotions were boiling. But thought and emotion alike were as
yet confused and unco-ordinated. All he knew was that he must get out
of here. He didn't need Tavie's orders to go away. Swiftly he glided
into the keeping-room, laid the package of post on the desk, returned
and hurried out the kitchen door without his hat.

Down in the back pasture he paused by Dandy's grave close under the ·
big boulder, and all the emotions of that earlier crisis poured back through
him. Less hurriedly now, he walked on down to the flat of the lower
meadow and, turning to the right, waded through the stubble of the
recently cut hay, scattering the grasshoppers. Once more his mind had
turned inward in self-concentration, but his emotions were now awake
and powerfully volitional, and when he perceived anything external at
all he perceived it in a frame of hot concentration that at once marked
its minute details and saw its significance as a whole.

Automatically he proceeded through an acre of uncut swale to a spot
he had marked often but where he had never paused before, a point
where the unfenced boundary between the lower meadow and Jolam's
Grove ended at the stream, a cool spot where there was a little mound
shaded from the sun by the last of the big hemlock trees, and beside it
a tiny hollow little larger than a man's body, both the mound and the
hollow carpeted deep and soft with hemlock needles. Across the stream
was a thicket of berry bushes and young birch, oak and maple. Ike threw
himself down on his stomach in the little hollow of hemlock needles
and rested his face in his clasped elbows.

As he lay there with closed eyes the first thing that crept in on him
was a sense of enveloping silence and, welling back to meet it out of his
own soul, a feeling of escape from his present troubles and the intimation of something more important beyond them. Tavie's recent revelation
that had stirred him out of emotional numbness; the terrible sense of
divorce from his family, his home and his friends in the village; even past
causes of misery like the death of Tom and the death of Dandy: all these
things seemed present and in a way identified, all troublesome impedi-
ments rising between him and some clear place beyond where he wanted
to go, like a berry bramble round his legs that he had to get through to
reach a cleared field, like a lot of foolish letters on his desk that he had
to answer before getting on to some business that interested him. These
brambles, these letters, all these personal troubles of his were now mingled
and unified, like some one thing askew with existence, some obstacle

or veil he must break through to come to some truth that he knew was not far beyond.

Something elemental in him was awake and struggling up toward consciousness. There was no sadness in him now; his recent sense of baffled hurt was translated into a sort of generalized volition, desperate, determined and affirmative. He could not weep. He could only lie there grimly waiting, listening with all the myriad sensibilities of his soul, listening and believing that he would hear a voice, that someone or something would speak a secret to him. Though there were sounds in nature around him he did not now hear them. He heard only silence, with a sense of obstacles between him and something ultimate in that silence.

Very clearly now, but without at first seeming to order themselves, the strong affirmations of his life thus far rose and paraded through his mind, each interrupted and inconclusive, each promising something, pointing somewhere, but never getting there, each seeming to have in it the promise of something permanent and final, yet each in turn arrested and falsified by something external and trivial: his love of John; his love of his brother Tom and of Dandy that were supposed to be dead; his love of his family and its tradition and of the place that had been his home and was his home no longer; his love of Aggie and her faith that he would find love and God. And without words his mind ordered itself in a questioning attitude which, if it had needed words, would have said, "Where now are all these things that were here yesterday and were going to last forever?" And he listened and heard at first only an infinite silence, while his mind found a word and kept saying it over and over like the beat of his pulses, "Where—Where—Where—Where?"

Then the sound of the questioning faded into the inclusive silence, and out of it, as if coming slowly nearer from a distance, his outer and inner ears heard the soft rushing of Jolam's Falls, and it seemed to say, "I am here—I am here—I am here." And a little gust of wind travelled through the needles of the hemlock above him and it seemed to whisper, "I am here—I am here."

Ike lay very still, his mind on tiptoe as if afraid to waken something, and his soul came close and whispered in his mind's ear, "Yes, the drops of water go over the falls and down to the big river and the lake and the ocean, but the falls are still here. And the wind comes by today and is lost in the sky tomorrow, but the wind is still here." Ike's soul was still again, listening, and he felt something like a knot begin to loosen within him. Across the stream he heard a yellow-throat sing in the thicket, and he heard the flutter of tiny wings in the hemlock above him. And again his soul whispered to his mind, "It is always a different bird that returns, yet the birds return every spring, and the spring returns, and the summer and the other seasons return. Everything is new, and everything is permanent and the same."

Ike sat up slowly in the little hollow under the hemlock and opened his eyes, but he yet was very still, watching and listening, and he did not know that he had moved, for the falls and the wind and the birds were still rustling around him and whispering, "I am here—I am here." And he saw a pair of fire-tails flitting through the hemlock branches in their restless way, flashing their yellow and orange and black feathers. And he knew that each one of them was moving as no fire-tail had ever moved before, yet he had seen many fire-tails every spring and summer of his life and they seemed the same as they had always been. And he saw the leaves hanging on the saplings across the stream, and he knew that each of them had veins and tints and tiny scallops that were different from those any leaf had ever had before or would ever have again. Yet there were the leaves, and they would fall in October and return again next spring and eternally thereafter. And the male fire-tail fluttered across the stream and trilled his song, and the female fluttered after him. And Ike knew that these birds were born and lived and had their young and died, yet the birds continued, and life went on forever without end.

Then a stronger wind gust moaned through the hemlocks and Ike saw it run out over the uncut swale of the meadow in swift-moving windrows like waves with silver tops on a green ocean. And he thought of the big Lake and the enormity of it, and all the changing life it contained, and how it was always really the same and eternal. And he glanced at the trunk of the hemlock tree beside him and it seemed to say, "I am here. I shall live and grow a hundred years, and I shall die, but there will be other hemlock trees like me here and nothing will be changed." And Ike reached out and touched the hemlock, and rose and walked softly from hemlock tree to hemlock tree in the grove, touching each with his hand, and each seemed to say, "Yes, I am really here."

He returned to the little hollow and sat down quietly again and watched and listened, and something like great doors began to swing open in his mind. He watched the sky, where enormous white clouds were floating slowly across the sun, their edges bulging like snow-buried mountains shining silver from the light behind them. And the doors of Ike's mind opened wide, and his soul spread its wings to include the clouds, and flew out beyond them to the endless space where the stars were at night. And his soul returned to him with all the stars and eternity in its hands. And his mind formed what his soul had told it, thinking in words, "There ain't any end to time or to space and they're all one, and there ain't any end to things inside them, though they change into new shapes, like when they die."

And Ike put his hands over his eyes and still listened, till very softly and clearly his mind said the word, "God." Then, "God is the whole shebang. He is what don't change in things, though the shapes of them change. Everything is part of God and can't die. Nothing that has existed can ever really die." And Ike's mind understood this that he had really known always. He rose and walked up and down beside the trees, and every now and then he blubbered tears of joy because he had found God and said His name and knew what it meant.

He sat down on the mound under the hemlock, and dropped his face in his hands again, and he knew as he had always known that Tom and Dandy were still around. Their bodies were changed into ground and the roots of things, but the God in them that the God in Ike loved was still around just as it had always been, like the falls and the wind and the birds. He clasped his hands together and moved them up and down in front of him and pressed them to his forehead, for he knew it was true, and he understood it more clearly than he had ever understood anything in his life, and he knew he would never forget it. He laughed and cried together, thinking what fun it would be to write Aggie that he had found God, and how glad she would be.

He straightened up then and put his elbows on his knees and his chin in his hands and began to think deliberately about people and the things that had been troubling him. He guessed that what friendship or love was was when this thing in him that was permanent and part of God saw the same thing in somebody else. "Maybe that's what ye call the soul," he thought, "and love is when two souls see each other and sort of talk together just like I've been talking to the whole of God. I figger that's the most important thing there is, and what's wrong is things that folks do to stop their souls talking with other souls or with the whole of God. I guess that's all there is to right and wrong. Love is right, and what interferes with love is wrong. Everything else, most of the things folks do most of the time, is just practical, to get enough to eat and wear, and to enjoy life, maybe to get the best of another fellow in a swop. All that is just practical. Ye may make mistakes, and get yourself in an a'mighty tangle, but ye ain't doing anything wrong unless ye interfere with love." Ike thought the worst thing he had ever done in his life was to sell Dandy, because he and Dandy loved each other and he turned him over to Gam

Stark who'd likely hurt him. " 'Twouldn't have been so bad," he thought, "if Dandy'd come back like I figgered, for I could have made it up to him. That's where I made a practical mistake. Figger most things that are wrong are mostly practical mistakes where a feller don't see that something he's up to is really going to hurt his love for somebody, or theirs for him."

He fell to thinking about John and he concluded sadly that what John had just done to him was the worst thing he could remember anybody doing, worse even than his having sold Dandy. First off, the Lollapaloosa had made a mistake in believing whatever it was Pru had written him. Then he did worse than that in turning around and denying his love for Ike, stopping their souls talking together like they had done almost since they were born. That, Ike figgered, to deny love straight off, was the worst thing a man could do.

He thought about the Union Mills option and the snarl it had got him into. He couldn't see that he'd done any wrong to the principal ones involved. He and Horace Gadston certainly didn't love each other. Any liking he and Mattie Spencer had for each other wasn't hurt by the deal. And if anything, Joe Kirkwood seemed to like him better after it than he did before. Only wrong was to Jabe and Fred and George who didn't have a plaguy thing to do with it, yet they turned out to be upset by it and not so fond of him as they had been before. He'd made a mistake that had stopped their souls talking to his, and that was wrong.

"Trouble is," he thought, "with these moral rules that people get all mixed up with their souls. If ye do so-and-so it's bad no matter what the consequences, and if ye do so-and-so it's good no matter what the consequences. Whether ye like the rules or not, ye're bound to have them in mind pretty sharp if ye value the friendship of folks that believe in them. Ye're bound to keep God, this thing that's everywhere and don't change, a'mighty close to your shoulder and be a'mighty quick to listen when He whispers that something ye figger on doing is going to cut ye off from somebody ye love that's all tied up in the rules.

"That's what I did to Pa about Tave," Ike thought. "No real harm in fornicating, in or out of marriage. Natural thing. Keeps life going. But I knew all the time that Pa believed the rule that it was wrong to do it without getting married straight off. And as things have turned out, that ain't such a bad rule anyhow. Trouble is that unless ye're a'mighty careful, fornicating is going to make a child, and that means ye've got to take care of the child which means ye've got to marry its ma."

Ike's mind shied off for a few seconds, but his mood quickly brought it back to his first real admission of the truth of his feelings about Tavie. "Fact is," he thought, "I don't want to marry Tave a god-danged bit, and I don't believe she wants to marry me either. Fact, Tave and I don't really love each other, like I love John and Aggie and Jabe. Our souls don't quite talk clear to each other, and that ain't anybody's fault. I've tried and I figger she has too. Might as well get that straight once and for all. Just got all itched up about her because she happened to be the pretty girl I saw most of, and made up a lot of nonsense about how I wanted to marry her. Would have done the same with Pru Stark if it wasn't for the Lollapaloosa—yes, I figger, and a danged sight quicker." Ike kicked the ground vigorously with his heel. "Just made a calf of myself. Made a mistake like selling Dandy—that is, if I'm looking for marriage to be like friendship with a man."

He paused in his mystical thinking and began to rationalize. "I guess it's mighty rare when women's and men's souls can talk together anyhow. The 'Paloosa's making a calf of himself about Pru, but one of these days he'll wake up to find she hain't any more soul than a female cat a-yowling for a tom. I guess even Ma and Pa have to play a sort of game with each other, and they get on better'n most. I guess it's rare a feller and a girl understand each other like Aggie and I do, even brother and sister.

"Marriage, I figger, is just one of those rules that come out of practical necessity. Chiefly a way of bringing up children. Just plain good sense. No soul or God in it for the most part. Best plan is to take a common sense view of it, marry somebody that's decent, smart, and ain't a-going to bother a feller over much. Find your God all by yourself, and your friendship with men. Fact is, I could marry plenty of girls—take Pru—who'd get my own soul a plaguy worse snarled up than it'll ever get with Tave. Worst mistake of all would be to crawl out of it now. That would give Tave's soul a twist it'd never get over, let alone Pa's and Ma's and Lollapaloosa's, and this youngster's she's going to have; and in the long run all this'd give my own soul the worst twist of all. Altogether, I'm lucky to have got hooked up with a first-rate girl. Likely I didn't make such a mistake after all. Figger I can manage it, after seeing things like I have today."

Ike leaned back on the mound, clasped his hands behind his head and closed his eyes. For the first time in his life he had a sense of permanent peace. He was sure he could meet anything now, including death. He was sure he would win back the love of his Pa and John and Jabe and George and Fred, and everybody whose soul was anything like his. As for folks in general, he'd just use common sense, try not to do anything

again that would come between him and this God he had found, or between him and any of his friends, or for that matter would hurt the God
in anybody's soul, even a stranger's. No use getting all brustled up and
quitting business in a hurry. He'd move back home when the railroad
business was over, and he'd quit business for good when he had enough
in the bank so the family could hold up its end in the modern world. No
harm in going on as he'd set out, only being more careful from now on
about other people's souls. He'd have it all out with Pa, and he knew he'd
come around. More than anybody but Aggie, Pa'd understand about this
God he'd found.

The wind was dropping, but there was still a murmur in the hemlocks
over him like a soft pipe organ with as many keys as there were needles
on the trees, and under it all was the eternal rustle of Jolam's Falls, forever changing, forever ringing little vanishing strains like elfin violins
and chimes, and yet forever the same. Three wood thrushes began to
jingle at each other, two from the woods behind him and one from the
thicket across the stream. "This beats Church," Ike thought. "It's enough
for me."

The sun came in sight under the big white clouds that were almost
down to the western horizon on Pond Hill across the Hollow. It was
fire red and the whole world was instantly aglow with its highlight on
every leaf and every blade of grass. With a start Ike realized it was after
eight. What would Tave be thinking of him? Now he'd have more of
a time than ever with her pernicketiness! He got up and walked back
along the meadow, first slowly, then increasing his speed. His problems
became real and practical in his consciousness, but he wasn't afraid of
them. None of them was as important as what he had found, and what
he had found would make him able to face them. He was eager to marry
Tavie at once, and he thought romantically of the child.

As he walked uphill through the back pasture in the rosy twilight and
came in sight of the lights in the house he realized that it wasn't going to
be easy. For the first time in his twenty years he saw life with people
as a challenge, like a game he was bound to win, like a business deal,
like a hoss-swoppin'. At the boulder over Dandy's grave he paused and
made a sort of vow. "Howdy, old boy," he said aloud. "We've another race
to run and the hardest of all. But it's for the biggest prize."

CHAPTER LIX

W H E N Ike entered the kitchen he was greeted by emptiness and silence. There was nothing on the big hearth but embers left from dinner, no sign of supper having been eaten or even prepared. Ike stepped to the keeping-room door. There sat Master Lane and Henry Hawks like two dummies reading by candle light, and neither of them so much as flickered an eye to acknowledge Ike's entrance. He heard footsteps in the front of the house above and, recognizing them as his ma's, hurried up the front stairs.

She was in the loom-room with a candle-lamp, remaking the bed in which Henry Hawks had been sleeping. When Ike came in she straightened up, gave him a look of challenge and pain, then leaned over again, tucking in the bed. "What is it, Ma?" he said softly. "Octavia has gone to Oberlin," Sarah said in a guttural tone that was near to tears. "Gone?" exclaimed Ike.

Sarah straightened up again, raised a hand to her forehead, then half collapsed on the foot of the bed, holding to a post as she spoke. "Your pa came in at four o'clock and found Octavia packing her things. She said she had a letter from the college offering her immediate employment. Your pa thinks it's a cock-and-bull story because they'd have made their arrangements for next year long before this." "I fetched out two letters from Oberlin," said Ike, "one from Connie Oaks and the other I didn't notice."

"Perhaps, perhaps," said his ma. "I hope it's true. She told your pa she must leave at once, that she would have her ma drive her as far as Berne tonight, where they have relations, and from there she'd make out to reach Utica in time for the Sunday night stage for the West. Your pa said he'd drive her—which I guess was what she wanted. They've been gone about two hours. Charity and Numa are coming up here. Ben's down with the cart for them now." Sarah lifted her hand to her mouth and looked away. "You must not see Charity, Isaac. She suspects something terrible has happened. So does your pa—I think that's why he was

433

willing to light out so fast—he didn't want to see you. O Isaac, what have you done?"

She looked at him again, with agonized doubt and half-accusation, her eyes shining with tears which did not fall. "I must take after them," said Ike quietly. "I don't know, I don't know anything," was all Sarah could contribute. "Oh, here's a note Octavia left for you." She snatched it out. of her waist and gave it to him. Ike broke the seal and bent to the candle, reading:

Dear Ike—

I beg you not to follow me. It would only make a dreadful scene— everything worse for both our parents—it's bad enough for them now —it wouldn't change my mind at all—I have no time to write now— will write you fully at first opportunity—perhaps tonight—will ad- dress the office—I promise to keep in touch with you and to call on you if I need help.

Good-by—T.
Burn this.

Ike crumpled the note, stuck it in his trousers pocket, and for a moment looked straight at his mother. Her strained expression softened, for she thought she had never seen him so beautiful. He walked across into his and Ben's room and stood at the window, looking up at the twilight road where Tavie had vanished over the hill a little while ago while he was finding God. A tremendous sense of fate came over him. Somehow—he couldn't figger how—this might be for the best. She'd keep in touch with him. A few days or weeks wouldn't matter. He felt closer to Tavie than he ever had in his life. He trusted her.

Ike turned and walked back to his ma, who was still sitting where he had left her. "Ma, I'd like to tell ye everything that's between Tave and me." His mother gave him a sad smile and he walked over and took her hands off the foot of the bed. "Yes, Isaac," she said, dropping her cheek on their joined hands, "I want to hear. I think I ought to know, for your pa's sake, and for yours too. But," she added, looking up ab- ruptly, "I'm afraid this isn't the time for it. Our first duty now is to Charity Samson, and it just occurred to me that I must ask you a ter- rible thing. I went down to Charity as soon as your pa and Octavia left. She was rocking back and forth, doing nothing except mumble, 'I saw it all in the crystal—I saw it all in the crystal—I knew it would come!'" "Yes," said Ike. "Back last Thanksgiving time she saw something about

Tave and me in her crystal, and whatever it was made her near faint away."

"You surely mustn't see her now, Isaac. Dreadful as it is for me to say it, I think it would be best for you to go back to the village tonight, just as quick as you can, before Charity Samson comes." Ike threw back his head, and his mother, looking up at him, knew he was stronger than his trouble, whatever it was. "You know I believe in you, don't you, Isaac?" she said. "Yes, Ma," he replied, and kissed her. After a moment he said, "I figger ye're right, Ma. Send me word when I should come out." "I will," she replied, "or I shall drive in some afternoon soon. I must insist on Charity's remaining here until Solon Samson returns. One sad thing about this is that he was liberated today. But he has to attend meetings all the way home and won't get here till August fourth." "That's ten days," said Ike. "Yes," said Sarah. "Now hurry, my boy!" She rose and laid her head on his chest a moment while he pressed her gently. And as he went downstairs, even though he was an outcast from his home, Ike felt that all this was right, and the words of the hymn, "God moves in a mysterious way," ran through his mind. Walking through the keeping-room, he noticed that the post was scattered on the desk, and pausing to finger it over, he observed that the letter from John was gone.

Ike spent a leisurely Sunday alone in the village, writing Aggie a long letter about the God he had found, taking a solitary walk out in Camilla, doing a little clandestine work in his office on the first bid on the railroad, that had come in last week. On Monday morning he was at the Post Office before little Loyal Hall returned from the Liberty with the bag. True to her word and Ike's faith, Tavie had written him from Berne. He had an hour before he needed to report at the bank, so he carried the letter to his office, for solitude, and read:

Uncle Philander's House
Berne, Sat. Eve., July 26, 1851

Dear Ike—

This is going to be an indiscreet letter and you must destroy it immediately you have read it.

If you will look in your heart you will admit that neither of us really wants to get married. I had brought myself to the point this afternoon, but I simply could not go through with it. The minute I was on the highroad I knew I had made the right decision, at least for now. We can be much better "friends," as you used to say, without it. It may be we shall have to marry yet, but if we do let's face the facts as friends, and not have any deception.

The story I told about the appointment to Oberlin was partially true. I am to tutor a group of girls in Greek from the fifteenth of August till shortly before the fall term opens. My only lie was in saying I must report in haste. Though President Mahan made no promise in his letter, he hinted plainly that if I proved myself in this work a college appointment would follow. It would be ironic if this chief ambition of mine should fall in my lap, and I should be prevented from taking advantage of it because of this personal complication! We shall see.   .

Practically, I do not yet know what I am going to do, though there are more possibilities than you probably realize. If you will look at the advertisements in any paper you will see one of them, and you don't need to caution me to be careful. I do not know whether I shall go as far as Oberlin. Since your kind pa has offered to drive me all the way to Utica tomorrow, I shall have to take the coach for the West, but I have friends in almost every town along the route. That is one encouraging thing. The moment I got out of Byzantium I began to feel like a personage. I am really known to a number of influential people, and quite close to a few of them, both men and women. And most of them are people of liberated ideas to whom I can talk quite freely.

Nevertheless, I do not yet know what my course will be. But two things I solemnly promise you. One is that I will notify you of any important move I make, and will appeal to you if I need money. The other thing is that neither you nor I nor any other human being who is or may become concerned in our doings will ever be permanently disgraced or forced to live outside the normal world. You can trust me for that, Ike, even though it involves my returning to Byzantium within a month or two. If I do return you will at least respect me for having done my best to free you.

(This last sentence was scrawled at a downward slant at the end of the paragraph, and was in an uneven hasty hand, quite different from the precise regularity of the rest of the letter.)

I shall be able to think more clearly when I am alone. Your kind father is a good deal of a burden. In his gentle way he has been cross-examining me about my supposed appointment at Oberlin, but I was ready for that. He is more troubled about you than I had realized, and it was apparent that, without crossing the bounds of propriety, he wanted me to talk about you. So I praised you to the skies, told him how honorable you were, and finally confessed that you had asked me to marry you. To that he merely said, 'Doubtless,' but didn't seem cheered by it. I told him that, fond as I was of you, I wasn't ready to marry yet, told him the truth—that is, the essential truth— pretty much the same things I said to you that night after the Swifts' junket last May. He smiled graciously but obviously was not impressed. I beg you to make every effort to regain his faith in you, for his sake more than for yours.

Good-by for now, Ike. Don't be disturbed if you don't hear again for two or three weeks. The West is a big place, you know!

T.

Ike read the letter twice, burned it in his stove, and walked up to the bank feeling more than ever that everything would come right. Tave was certainly as first-rate as they came, best girl he could possibly marry. If she could only stay the way she was when she wrote that letter they could be friends sure grit. He could love her always, the way he loved Aggie and the 'Paloosa.

At dinner with the Gang that noon Ike was subtly restored to the position of respect he had held before, his mien of quiet assurance seeming to include and understand them all and making Jabe, Fred and George ashamed of having judged him harshly. It was on the whole a silent session, yet somehow a comfortable one. Once Bub, with his usual blatancy, made everybody except Ike wince by throwing out, "Wal, I hope Joe's conscience is still settin' pretty over the loss o' that option." Ike looked straight at Bub, and, with a double meaning which only Bub understood, said, "Joe ain't a bad feller. I hope none of you fellers ever do anything you've occasion to be ashamed of." And everybody in the group except Ike and Bub dropped his eyes.

As they rose to go, Ike suggested that Bub and Alec come to his office for a meeting of the Company; he had something he wanted to propose. Jabe Munson said that he wanted to have a word with Ike, so he walked along with him, telling Alec and Bub he'd come after them in five minutes.

"Ike," said Jabe, "I want to tell ye I'm sorry fer the way I behaved toward ye last week about the engine company. It's true I an't much on things o' the sort, but I figger I could scrape up a thousand dollars if it'd be of any use." "That's a'mighty good of ye, Jabe," said Ike without hesitation, "but I figger your first notion was the right one. Ye don't want to have yourself mixed up in a concern that did a turn of that kind. Funny, all that bothers me about a thing like that is whether it bothers my friends, or whether it does any real hurt to anybody else. But you ain't made that way. I hesitate to advise ye against coming in, for I figger ye'd make a penny out of it. But ye'd best wait a spell. There won't be any more slippery tricks, but before anybody else comes in I want to see that Alec gets a bigger share than he's allowed now. The option's for six months and there ain't any lather about it. Think it over some more. I'll keep ye informed of what's going on, and I'll see to it that your opportunity to come in at par stands open a spell longer."

"All right, Stud, suit yourself," said Jabe. "But unless I notify ye to the contrary ye can count me in fer ten shares at par." "All keerect and thank ye," said Ike. And he hurried back to Wheeler Corner and down the path to Mill Street after the other two members of the engine company.

At the meeting Ike insisted that whatever stock they sold henceforth, Alec should receive free additional stock equal to a third of the amount issued, so that no matter where any of the rest of them stood, Alec would always have a one-third interest. He then reported that his approach to George, Fred and Jabe had produced only a thousand from the last, and he told how he had just advised Jabe to stay out until he saw whether he liked the way the company was going. At that Bub sniffed and proposed that they at once approach Joe Kirkwood who, he knew for a fact, was ready to come in for anything up to five thousand. He proposed that he and Ike likewise increase their subscriptions to five thousand and that "we git things a-goin' without lickin' no more unwillin' boots."

Ike agreed to this in general, saying that Joe's coming in would likely cure the black eye they'd got on account of the option. He figgered, however, that three thousand apiece would be all they'd need to put in. Twenty-six hundred more from Bub, twenty-four hundred more from Ike, and three thousand from Joe. Eight thousand, with the thousand profit on the *Union* job and Jabe's thousand if he came in, ought to be all they'd need for a spell.

"Figgerin' on puttin' off buyin' the Union Mills property, be ye?" asked Bub. "Nope," said Ike. "Givin' up the notion altogether?" sneered Bub." "Nope," said Ike. "Well," said Bub, "spit it out." "What's wrong with the banks?" asked Ike. "Assuming the business is going to make money, we might as well be paying interest as dividends. And once we'd settled up, the fewer the shares of stock the more each share'd be worth." Bub curled his lip. "And what bank d'ye figger is goin' to give us five or ten thousand. The Blackwater wouldn't risk it. Sherwood wouldn't do it on account o' your interest in his bank. D'ye figger on goin' to Grabbot at the Merchants fer money? God-danged fine creditor he'd be!" Ike smiled faintly. "Had it ever occurred to ye we might start our own bank?"

Alec immediately beamed, and Bub for a long moment looked both startled and dubious. Then he smiled too, chuckled, and made a long, enthusiastic brown spit into the distant cuspidor. "By God's holy breeches, Stud, there's no denyin' ye're the prize bull calf in this barnyard." Nothing more of importance was discussed at the meeting.

CHAPTER LX

EARLY Tuesday afternoon Henry Hawks came up to Ike's office and told him curtly that his ma was downstairs in the carriage. From the point of view of the business of the Utica, Bloomington and Byzantium Railroad, she could hardly have picked a worse time to interrupt the executive secretary. Nevertheless, Ike at once weighted the papers and maps on his desk, told Squire Fulton he'd make up for it by working that evening, and went down to the street. Fifteen minutes later Sarah and Ike alighted at Master Quin's drug shop and Henry Hawks, having hitched Mol to the hitching-post, settled down to whittling a long stick he'd brought along to serve in this eventuality.

Sarah was in a troubled mood, wherefore she held her arrogant nose high and her manner was artificially vivacious. The sight of Ike's untidy room eclipsed for the moment his involvement of the heart, and, throwing off her mitts, bonnet and jacket, she spent the first fifteen minutes striding competently about, licking it into shape, sweeping it, and eliciting from Ike a solemn promise that he would mop it that very afternoon. Then she sat down on the bed, motioned to Ike to pull up a chair, looked at him intently for a moment, smiled, patted his hand, straightened up primly, folded her hands in her lap, and said, "Now then."

Slowly, with much embarrassment, Ike told his ma the whole story of his relations with Tavie, from the first kiss last Thanksgiving to her announcement last Saturday, his mystical awakening down by Jolam's Grove, and Tavie's reassuring letter which he had destroyed. When he told her the initiative Tavie had taken in the improprieties he did not speak as if trying to exonerate himself, but stated the facts quite simply for what they were worth. When he had finished, the first thing Sarah said, observing her hands, was, "I was afraid that girl's ambition would disqualify her for love." Then she paused, and one by one stated her thoughts as she formulated them.

"There is not the slightest doubt, Isaac," she said, "that you have done wrong." "Not the slightest, Ma." "Nevertheless," continued Sarah, "I am glad for both you and Octavia that you are not now married and"—here she paused and very deliberately smoothed down her green silk dress, secretly arriving at a prophecy which she did not reveal—"may never be." "Whatever happens, Ma," said Ike, "I am as certain as I could be of any-thing that this will work out to the satisfaction at least of Tave and me, and I think of you too, though I ain't so sure of Pa. Maybe Tave'll—get rid of this—trouble, like she said in the letter. Maybe after a spell she'll come back and we'll be married. Maybe there'll be something else I ain't thought of. But I'd wage my last red that a year from now we'll be glad I didn't chase her and make a rumpus."

After a long pause Sarah spoke again, as if talking more to herself than to Ike. "No, you mustn't tell your pa all of it. I think you can tell him everything up to this last eventuality. But that, I believe, would give him such a shock as he might never recover from. You might marry and have a baby too soon. That would humiliate him, but he would re-cover. But to know that you were tolerating the present state of things, even approving it, that would be too much for him."

After another long pause in which she continued to smooth her dress, she looked straight up at Ike with that withering, arrogant look that meant only that she was not quite sure of her ground. "I do think, though, that you should have a good talk with your pa at the first oppor-tunity. Whether you should make a partial confession, or whether you should simply try to assure him that you are at peace with your own soul, I should make that depend on what he seems to want of you at the moment. Perhaps to assure him that nothing is troubling you would be sufficient, though I cannot say certainly as to that. Your pa's incon-sistent in some ways, Isaac—and I never said this to anyone before. He has spent his life preaching and writing what he calls liberal religion, the right of every man to find God and make his moral decisions in his own way. Yet, though his code is liberal enough, when it comes to his own conduct or the conduct of anyone close to him, he is as rigid as Dea-con Victory Birdseye. I can assure you that nothing but marriage would for him condone your present situation."

" 'Paloosa's that way, too," said Ike. "Yes," replied his ma, "but the relationship between brothers is very different from that between father and son. John will come as far to you as you will to him. Your pa thinks he will, but he really won't. You must remember, Isaac, that you have already wounded your father deeply in all this, that during the last win-ter he has become an old man at sixty. You must show great considera-tion for him." "It's that hauling rocks," said Ike, "that's hurting him more than anything I've done." "Perhaps," said Sarah, "but the reason he is hauling rocks is to tire himself so he can sleep at night instead of lying awake worrying about you." To this Ike said nothing, but looked long at his mother with his brow puckering in sudden understanding and fright.

"And now," said Sarah, smiling cheerfully, "I have some good news, which in the excitement last Saturday I forgot to tell you. John is arriving this Saturday, the second of August." Ike smiled warmly, but did not confess that he had already learned this from the letter with the broken seal. "I'll hire a gig and drive him out," said Ike. "No, Isaac," said Sarah tenderly, "not under the present circumstances, unless we send you word that Charity Samson has gone home. Let John rent his own gig—though," she whispered with a giggle, "you may have to pay for it! Or perhaps your pa will drive in for him. He should get back from Utica tomorrow." "Drat Charity Samson," said Ike. "All keerect," whispered his mother with another giggle. "But after all, Isaac, Solon is to arrive Tuesday, only a week from today, and she can't stay longer than that. Then we'll all be together again." And after renewed, solemn injunctions to mop his floor and keep his room in better order hereafter, Sarah gave Ike a cheerful kiss and departed to the auspices of Henry Hawks and her perennial gauntlet of greetings and calls when in the village. Ten minutes later Ike, whistling, was mopping his floor with Master Redemption Quin's mop, while the pressing business of the Utica, Bloomington and Byzantium Railroad lay neglected a half mile away on his desk.

At half-past three the next afternoon Ike walked hurriedly through the Blackwater County National Bank, saluting the antiquated Marshfield "boys" as he passed. It was his purpose merely to put in a formal appearance this Wednesday, and return in ten minutes to the business of the railroad. But when he stepped into the cider room at the rear his breath suddenly caught in his throat and he stopped with a start. Among the "Nestors," who were still standing greeting one another and filling their cider cans, the first thing he saw was his pa's back, towering above all but Squire Staunton with whom he was talking.

Even as Ike paused, his pa turned round as if he knew he was there, and though his face was flabby and gray he gave Ike a fine smile and raised his hand in salute. Immediately Ike crossed to him and shook his hand, equalling his father in the aplomb with which he carried off the meeting. "Glad to see ye back, Pa," he said easily. "Did ye have an easy journey?" "Very easy," said the Squire. "On the return I had the pleasure of stopping with two stockholders in your railroad. They seem to expect great things of ye." And, smiling up at Squire Staunton, he gave Ike a pat on the shoulder with a fine show of paternal pride.

As Ike left him to go the rounds of formal greeting to the others, Squire Lathrop beckoned George Fulton to him and told him that he thought he would be pleased to know that John would arrive in Byzantium on Saturday. And immediately thereafter George went to his own pa, and whispered something to which Squire Fulton nodded.

Presently Ike succeeded in isolating his father from the group and led him to one of the back windows. As Ike glanced out at the little orchard in the rear, it flashed through his mind as strange that the relations between father and son could not be as simple as that between those trees and their apples. "When the time comes for the apples to drop," thought Ike, "the tree won't hinder them." To his father he said, "Pa, I would greatly appreciate it if ye would have a private word with me before ye drive out to the Hollow."

Alone with Ike, the Squire's mien immediately changed to one of heavy weariness. "Not here, surely?" he said, without looking at Ike. "No, sir. I had planned to leave in a moment anyway, before they fairly sat down and began to talk, and I hope ye will consider coming with me to my office, where we can be alone." "Very well," said the Squire, so low it was hardly audible, and turned back to the company.

In five minutes more there began a shuffling of chairs. Squire Lathrop tossed off what remained in his can of cider, picked up his hat and stick from the table, and stepped out into the room, thus drawing attention. Addressing the company in the person of Squire Staunton, who had taken his usual position at the mantel, Squire Lathrop said, "Gentlemen, Isaac and I beg ye to excuse us, for we have a small matter to discuss and I must be off within the hour." There was a grumble of protest, for Squire Lathrop had not been in to one of the meetings in more than a month, but he and Ike merely bowed with a wave of farewell and turned toward the door.

"Before ye go," said Squire Fulton—and the Lathrops paused, looking back—"I desire to announce two coming events of interest to us all. On Saturday John Lathrop, junior, returns to us as a graduate of Yale College, and I have the pleasure to invite all those present, with their families, to my house that evening for a junket in his honor. Old style as usual"—this meaning that those who wished were invited to wear knee breeches in the fashion of their youth.

"My other news," continued the Squire, "I have only by rumor. It is that Solon Samson, being already liberated and in process of enduring a triumphal progress from city to city, plans to be among us on Tuesday next." In response to this there was a spontaneous cheer and a rising toast. "Of Solon's proper reception we shall talk later," resumed Squire

Fulton. "My purpose at the moment is to announce the junket on Saturday in honor of young John. And it will be expected," he concluded, addressing the Squire and Ike, "that all members of the family of the guest of honor will lodge with the host and hostess that night." "We are much honored, John," said Squire Lathrop, "and I know of no reason why I may not now accept with many thanks for myself and all of my family."

As soon as the Squire and Ike climbed into the shay in which the Squire had just returned from Utica, a terrible silence fell over father and son, not a silence of embarrassment but the deep fundamental silence of two great rocks that had once been one, cleft by an earthquake and now resting side by side with a fissure between. "Glad to hear John's coming home," said Ike as they trotted past the Liberty, and his voice sounded like something harsh and out of place in the universe. The Squire said nothing, having the letter in his pocket which Ike had brought home the Saturday before and which the Squire had found on the desk with the seal broken. Also the Squire was in possession of several devastating facts which Ike did not know had come to his attention. One of these had reached him that afternoon, just after arriving in the village and before going to the meeting of the Nestors. Horace Gadston had met him on the Mall and out of combined malice and embarrassment— for Horace felt really inferior to all the Nestors—had told him jocosely of the trimming Ike had given him in the matter of the option. In Squire Lathrop's state of mind this was no more than another straw on a load that was already heavier than he could long bear.

In Ike's office the Squire, who had never been there before, hung up his hat and accepted with a bow the chair Ike set out for him by the window. Ike sat down behind his desk and his mind was as empty as the cold, black stove beside him. Seeking to break the ice with a pretense of casualness, he tilted back in his chair and said, "Will it suit ye if I drive John out in a hired gig on Saturday? Or shall I have him ride out on Chesty?—he can ride him back for Fulton's junket and we can fetch out his baggage later." "If you don't mind," said the Squire, looking at Ike with a social smile, "I would greatly prefer to meet John myself on Saturday."

Ike's reaction to this was sorrow at the width of the gulf between them, and real pity for his pa. He let his chair back to a straight position, looked down at his desk and said with quiet sadness, "Very well, sir." When, after a silence, he spoke again, his voice was natural and full of warmth, yet it was insufficient to thaw his pa's frozen soul. "Pa," he said, "what I wanted to say to ye was about a promise I made ye last winter to tell ye if ever anything was bothering my conscience."

The Squire's big, gray face turned almost white, and Ike paused, feeling the time was inopportune and hoping his pa would either leave or ask him not to continue. But the Squire only threw one leg over the other and sat stone still, looking out the window. "Would ye join me in a nip o' brandy?" asked Ike in a subdued voice. "No, thank ye kindly," murmured the Squire. "What I've to say," Ike resumed, "can be put in a few words, and afterwards I can go into it more fully if ye wish. Since I made ye that promise I have done two things that have bothered my conscience and I h'ain't told ye of them at the time for two reasons. One reason was that in each case I'd have had to talk to ye about a woman in a way that ain't tasteful—one a woman with whom I was somewhat implicated myself, the other a woman with whom another party to the transaction was implicated. The other reason I didn't tell ye the two things I've done that were wrong was that in each case I did everything anybody could do to atone for them before I had a chance to talk to ye. If I had told ye what was troubling me, it would only have troubled you, and there wasn't anything ye could have told me to do that I hadn't done already. Maybe I was wrong, but I honestly don't think there was anything to be gained, and I figgered the notion of my telling ye things was so ye could give me advice if I needed it. If ye think I was wrong I'd be glad to tell ye now everything there is to tell. Only first off I want to assure ye that there ain't anything bothering my conscience at this moment. I'm a'mighty sorry for two things I did, but they ain't on my conscience in the sense that there's anything further I or anybody can do about them."

"Is that all?" asked the Squire, rising. "Unless ye'd like to hear me out on these two things I've done I'm sorry for." "Another time, perhaps," said the Squire, walking over and taking down his hat and not looking at Ike, for he did not wish to curse him and cut him off openly until he had talked with his eldest son in whom he had faith.

Ike rose, held the door for him and said as he went out, "Thank ye, Pa, for coming." Then he sat down and stared before him while the pent emotions boiled in him and slowly resolved themselves, not into anger or sense of personal hurt, but into a wide sadness and sense of injustice in the universe, that intended father and son should love each other and forgive each other, no matter what mistakes either might make.

Outside, Mol drew the Squire through the Mall and up Washington Street homeward, walking or shambling into an easy trot according to her own impulses. Letting the reins sag listlessly on the dashboard, the Squire's weary mind soon drifted away from the recent interview with Ike. From it he had carried only one new conviction, that the boy, having broken the seal and read the letter from John, and there discovering that he was to be cut off, had now merely attempted to ingratiate himself in order to prevent what to him would be only a financial loss. For the Squire had, like barbed spearheads in his heart, two unanswerable bits of evidence of which Ike was unaware. On Saturday afternoon when he had entered the house about half-past four he had had occasion to go up to the back attic and as he had started up the stairs Tavie in her room had suddenly screamed, "Please go away! For God's sake go away and never let me see you again!" A few minutes later she had emerged and come downstairs, and with great embarrassment had told the Squire the cock-and-bull story about the appointment to Oberlin. And an hour and a half later, when he went up to carry down her trunk, glancing automatically around the room to see if she had left anything, he saw something under the bed that Tavie had overlooked in her distraction, and picked up an empty bottle labelled "The Happy Home." Thrusting this in his pocket and afterwards in his satchel, he had carried it to Utica, where he had shown it to an obscure druggist and had learned that the implications of the directions on the bottle were as he had suspected.

That evening the Squire walked down to the lower meadow after supper, and happened to choose for his lonely contemplations the same spot Ike had chosen the previous Saturday. But instead of falling on his face as Ike had done, he knelt down by the big hemlock tree on the little knoll and, raising his clasped hands against the bark, closed his eyes and besought his God for guidance, asking Him if he were old and stiff-necked and guilty of the sins of pride and intolerance, asking Him wherein he had erred in rearing this child. His hands slid down the tree to the ground, and his great frame shook with heavy, convulsive sobs as if the earth were heaving, sobs that led to no resolution but exhaustion, until his legs straightened out and he fell into complete sleep for ten hours.

At ten o'clock Master Lane and Henry Hawks, sent out by Sarah with a lantern, found him there. And not wishing to disturb him, they sat down on either side of him and watched in silence, which was their manner of love. When half an hour had passed Master Lane beckoned Henry a little away from the Squire. "Trot up and tell Sarah we've found him," he said, "and come back with a nip of brandy."

After another half hour Henry returned with three blankets, a bottle of brandy, a jug of water, and extra candles for the lantern. Thereafter, knowing the order in which the stars went down behind Pond Hill, the two old men woke each other at two-hour intervals through the night. And when Henry woke Master Lane for his third watch, in broad daylight, the Squire stirred and opened his eyes.

CHAPTER LXI

AT SEVEN O'CLOCK on Friday evening, two days after the fruitless interview with his pa, Ike walked a rented gig and pair of bays into the yard of the Bull and Bear in Howeville, twenty-five miles from Byzantium Falls. After tending to the horses, he ate a cold supper in the tap-room in the company of the lanky, leathern host who was known as "Painter" Smith from the number of panther scalps he had taken in the nearby Adirondack wilderness. They discussed the railroad a few minutes—for Howeville had been one of the centers of the surveying operations of the last two months. Then Ike rose, said he must turn in, and asked about the coach from Utica in the morning. Painter said it pulled in between half-past two and half-past three and usually stopped about fifteen minutes. Ike asked him to wrap up a cold breakfast for two and leave it in the pantry, and to have tea boiling on the stove by half-past two. He settled his reckoning of three shillings for supper, stable, lodging and breakfast, had a short grog on the house, lighted the candle-lantern he had brought in from the gig, and Painter showed him to the best room in the house, as was appropriate to the Executive Secretary of the railroad. He threw off his coat, waistcoat, cravat, collar, cuffs, boots and pants, put his watch under his pillow and the shaded candle-lantern on a chair beside his bed, lay down and fell instantly asleep.

Ike awoke at two as planned, rolled out of bed, put a fresh candle in the lantern and proceeded to dress. As he had feared from the look of the west the evening before, it was raining outside, along with wind gusts that splattered the dark windows. With his lantern he went downstairs and out into the kitchen where the cook-stove was already roaring, throwing arcs of light on the ceiling from its leaky griddles, and Painter was just setting the big teakettle on. "Stormy mornin'," said Painter, fetching Ike his wrapped-up breakfast from the buttery. "Yep," said Ike, taking the bundle. "Figger 'twon't last beyond sun-up."

In the stable Ike took his topcoat from under the seat and stowed the breakfast there. As he harnessed the bays to the gig in the dim light, righteous anger began to boil in him till he was in a sort of releasing ecstasy in the nearness of an adventure that was to have final consequence, and to which, for the first time in three months, he was bringing an absolutely clear conscience. As he closed buckle after buckle on the horses, his indignation rose till he felt himself charged with the power of fate and shaping future events to his will. After finishing the harnessing, putting up the top of the gig, lighting the lamps, and haltering the horses, he put on his coat, and, carrying the lantern, stepped out into the gusty darkness. At that moment, as if answering the demand of his will, the coach horn sounded far away in the night. He went back to the kitchen, poured out two cups of tea to cool, and went to the front door, where he stood beside Painter Smith while the coach with its single lantern came creaking and groaning up the hill.

The coach did not enter the tavern yard but pulled up in front, the driver and Painter grunting their routine greetings to one another as the brake set and the big carriage wobbled to a stop. Before the driver had turned to throw down his post bag Ike asked him abruptly, "Do ye stop at Ice Creek, Byzantium?" " 'Tain't a reg'lar stop," said the driver, groping back for the Howeville bag. "H'ain't a fare fer it. Don't stop less'n someone's to git up there." "How much'd a fare be from Ice Creek to the Liberty?" demanded Ike. "Shillin', if I remember rightly," said the coachman, lifting his lantern to read the label on a bag. Ike fished in his pocket and handed up the coin. "This'll be for a passenger getting on at Ice Creek." The driver lifted his lantern so as to look down at Ike. "All keerect," he said, and dropped the post to Painter Smith, who was the local Postmaster.

Meanwhile the footman had descended and opened the coach door, and was trying to rouse a sleeping passenger for Howeville. So certain was Ike that events would turn as he willed that in paying the fare into the Falls from Ice Creek it had not occurred to him that John might have missed this coach. He now stepped round to the other side, opened the door, lifted his lantern, saw John asleep in the corner under his coat, and immediately began to shake him.

"That feller's fer Byzantium," said the footman angrily. "I know it," said Ike, continuing his shaking. "He's my brother and he's going to ride with me a piece. Take his baggage on to the Liberty. He'll be back with ye before ye git there." "Hi—Scamp," said John, coming slowly to consciousness and seeing Ike's face in the lantern light. "What's up?" "Plenty's up," said Ike abruptly. "Git out."

John sat up, yawned, put on his silk hat, looked inquiringly at Ike, and obeyed, wobbling clumsily into his coat as he stood outside in the rain.

"Where's this?" he asked vaguely. "Howeville," said Ike. "My baggage."
"Leave your baggage be. Ye'll be back with it before ye reach the Liberty.
Come along." He led John into the tavern and back to the kitchen, where
he handed him a big tea cup and took up his own. "Put that down ye fast,"
he commanded, and proceeded to drain his own, while John watched him
from over his cup, amazed and apprehensive at Ike's surly manner.

Without further remarks except Ike's monosyllabic commands, they presently splashed out in the gig through the mud of the drive, turned westward past the coach that was still at the front door, and at a fleck of Ike's
whip trotted away in the rain toward Paris. Ike reached down under the
seat and handed John the bundle of breakfast. "Here's some victuals," he
said. "Undo it and give me a fried cake." There was no sound but the rain
and the pounding of the horses' hoofs while John, his fingers all thumbs
from sleep, undid the bundle, handed Ike a fried cake, helped himself to a
slab of cold beef, and put the open package down between them on the seat.

Ike swallowed half of his fried cake, and threw the rest away. "Big doin's
round here since ye left," was his first comment. "Yes, I know," said John.
"George wrote me that you were recognized by everybody as the most
promising man of our age in town." Ike grunted. "Didn't drive out here
to get any of your compliments about what I know don't interest ye," he
said. "I drove out to talk over two or three important matters I want to get
straight before ye see Pa, who'll be at the Liberty. First off, what're these
god-danged lies ye've swallowed that made ye so uppity about me the past
month or so?"

"Lies?" said John, suddenly coming awake and his eyes blackening in
the light of the carriage lamps. "Ye heard what I said," snapped Ike. "Who
set ye against me—Pru?"

"Don't you think," said John, "that's a pretty abrupt way to bring up a
subject that has hurt me more than anything that ever happened to me?"
"Not a god-danged bit too abrupt for a feller like you who's turned against
his brother on the word of a filthy little slut that hain't no more decency in
her than one of her pa's swine wallerin' in the Mall."

"All right, if it's a fight you're after," shouted John, turning and grabbing
Ike's throat. "Do you know what you're saying?"

"Yes, I know danged well what I'm saying," said Ike, drawing his chin
down into his collar. "And if ye don't like it ye can get out and turn up
your cuffs and I'll leave ye lying in the mud and be done with ye till ye
come crawling back on yer dirty knees and beg me to forgive ye."

Something in the power and conviction of Ike's onslaught struck down
into John's nature where fairness and tolerance dwelt stronger than his

love for Pru or his fury at an insult. He lowered his hands and looked straight before him into the rain-slanted darkness, while his whole body trembled.

"A tarnal fine brother, you are," Ike went on. "You know I'd cut off my head for ye, and if anybody said a word against ye I'd lay 'em out and not believe it, or even if I did believe it I'd lay 'em out just the same and keep my mouth shut till I'd had it out with ye. God-danged fine brother you are to get moon-struck and turn against me on the word of a lying little hussy that ain't worth yer little toenail, or mine fer that, turn against me and get high a'mighty about how ye've got evidence 'from a source ye're bound to believe' and how it's caused ye 'great pain.' Well, ye can take your 'evidence' and your 'great pain' and take 'em plum to hell along with the rest of your sanctimonious and ignorant carcass. I've got plenty more to tell ye of things where I've likely done wrong, and I'll take what ye've got to say to me and likely do what ye tell me to. But, by God, I hain't done any wrong to you, and ye'll get that notion out of yer addled head before I say a word to ye of matters that have to do with grown-up people instead of lovesick puppies."

There was a long silence between them. Then, "I'm sorry, Scamp," said John, so low Ike could hardly hear it against the rain on the carriage top.

"All keerect," said Ike and continued more gently. "All keerect so far. But we're going to get this little matter cleaned up right now. What did Pru write ye?"

John dropped his chin in his hands and as Ike saw his face in silhouette against the carriage lamp, his forehead and fine arched nose looked exactly like their ma. "It wasn't much," he said softly. "She wrote that you invited her to your office."

"That's a lie," broke in Ike. "And she said that after she went there she couldn't possibly tell me what you had done, but it was such that she felt she ought to warn me that I could not trust you."

"Another lie," said Ike. "Is that all?"

"That's all," said John.

"Now, then," said Ike, feeling that if he could do anything to turn John against Pru, no matter how it might hurt him now, it would help him in the long run, "Now, then, whether ye like it or not, ye're going to hear what really happened." And Ike proceeded to tell in full detail the story of Pru's attempt on him, no longer in a vituperative tone, but quietly and taking care to be accurate; how, to begin with, he didn't deny that sometimes Pru was mighty pretty though he didn't like her; how he had danced with her too much at the F and P ball, and afterwards hadn't given her a thought until the incident in question; how she had summoned him into the Liberty and told him she'd like to go to college or get a position in the railroad or the engine company, and how she asked if she might come to his office where they could talk without interruption; how he foolishly and innocently had let her come; how she came there "half naked" and leaned over the desk "so as to be almost lying on me"; how she wanted to see the drawings for the railroad and how, when he had spread them out, she came around beside him and "rubbed up against me like a cat round yer leg"; how he lost his head for a second and put his arms around her; how he was just going to kiss her when he came to his senses and pushed her away and said, "Pru, we're making fools of ourselves"; how she took on then and shrieked and wouldn't come back to look at the drawings and said "Puff" when he mentioned it, and skedaddled out; and how he hadn't seen her since except at parties and on the street.

Having finished his account, Ike said, "Well, there's the truth of it. Ye can believe Pru or ye can believe me. Nobody else knows—except Ma. When ye left me out of that letter I was near crazy about other things and I asked Ma if she knew what was up—and she didn't—and she asked me to think hard—and I couldn't think of anything but this and I told her—and she said right away, 'That's it,' only she didn't think Pru would risk coming as near the truth as she did—figgered she'd written ye something made up out of whole cloth that Pru figgered would turn ye against me. Ma says all she was after was to make herself out sanctimonious and to get revenge on me for turnin' her down. That taught me something about women. By the way, Ma knows everything there is to know about everything, and she's the truest grit member of this family, and don't forget it. She ain't for me or you or Pa or any of us that's got troubles between ourselves. She's clean for all of us together and she's got more sense than any three of the rest of us—unless maybe Aggie. Well, there's the whole truth of it, and do ye believe me or don't ye?"

Unnoticed by Ike, John had been crying, for deep in his soul he believed Ike and loved him, yet that belief and that love were in conflict with his desire for Pru that he had romanticized and raised to a burning consecration now for five years, since at sixteen he had gone with his ma one afternoon to call on Mistress Stark and had been fed cookies by the lovely, delicate-featured, petal-like little girl of twelve.

"Scamp," John plead, "don't ask me to say in words whether I believe you or don't believe you. Give me a few days to come to that. I can say now that I'm sorry and ashamed of having turned against you, and I'm not against you now. Only—you know what it means to me—don't ask me, just yet, to say that I believe Pru has—lied to me—not that kind of a lie. Give me a little time! Good God! Give me a little time!" He dropped his face in his hands.

"All keerect, 'Paloosa," said Ike gently. "I'm sorry I had to tell ye that, but ye forced me to it, else it'd a' stood between us as long as we lived."

John nodded assent in his hands and Ike reached over and pressed his right hand against their backs. Without looking up, John reached out and took Ike's hand and they gripped each other with a power expressive of the deepest devotion in either of their souls.

Presently John released Ike's hand and sat up straight. They were just passing the big tavern in Paris where Joe Kirkwood had lied to Ike and where there was now a light in the tap-room in preparation for the arrival of the coach. Their discussion thus far had taken near three-quarters of an hour. There was less rain than there had been, but it was still gusty, and the way the wind sometimes buffeted the carriage top from behind them exhilarated Ike with a sense of being alone with his God of Nature. They heard the coach horn at the other end of the long street that was Paris, but Ike let the horses walk down the hill out of the village, knowing that the stage would change there and had regular stops thereafter at Bear River and Chalons. From now on they would easily keep ahead of the coach.

"First off," said Ike, resuming his attack on the controversial matters that stood between them, "I may as well tell ye, 'Paloosa, that I'm now feeling kind of sheepish about the way I lit into ye a while back. I guess the reason was that I'm pretty stirred up about a lot of things and that happened to be one where I was sure I was right and you were wrong. From now on I've to tell ye some things where I ain't so consarn sure I'm right, though I'm a plaguy sight righter'n Pa'll admit, he having refused to talk to me and planning to cut me off like he seems to have written ye."

Ike then told John about his having innocently read the letter with the broken seal, ending by saying, "I figger Pa thinks I broke the seal for some sinful purpose, though the fact is I didn't break it at all, and what I was after was to see if ye had anything decent to say to me. Until now your letters to Pa have always been for all of us, and if he wasn't there when they came Ma or I or somebody has always opened them." "I know that," said John.

Ike next told John the whole story of the Union Mills option, beginning with the account of how Joe Kirkwood had trimmed him right back there at the Paris Tavern, including the story of Mattie Spencer, and ending with his efforts to make amends to Gadston, and the reactions of George,

Fred and Jabe to his proposal to buy stock in the Engine Company. "I ain't certain Pa knows about that," Ike concluded, "though he likely does for it's public property in the village, all of it but Mattie's story, which is the only part of it I wish ye'd keep to yourself. I was going to tell Pa Wednesday afternoon, but he wouldn't listen and walked out of my office."

After a silence Ike added, "Well, 'Paloosa, there's something I did that wasn't right and concerning which ye've a right to judge me harshly if ye're o' mind to."

John considered for some time before replying. "Yes, Scamp, I'm afraid I do judge you harshly in that respect, but perhaps not in the way you judge yourself. The whole thing makes me feel sick, gives me a sense of hollowness, something without any truth in it anywhere. I don't think the particular sharp deal was so important. You didn't hurt Mattie any, and she seems to be the only real human being involved. And, furthermore, when you decided you were at fault you tried to make amends, which is all any man can do. No, it isn't the thing itself that bothers me. It's just the fact that if you involve yourself in that world they call 'business' you're bound to be rubbing shoulders with scoundrels like Kirkwood and Gadston, and you're bound to make sharp deals like this to keep your end up. To my mind your being in that world at all involves an apostasy against everything our family stands for, and the more successful you are the more of a disgrace you are to the Lathrop name. That's straight, Scamp, as straight as you were with me about the other matter."

"I know, 'Paloosa," said Ike sadly, "and ye've a right to your notion. I hope in ten years ye'll say I was right, though ye won't if I go on trimming folks like in that Union Mills option. I've a powerful lot to say to ye in that line, more'n we've time for now. For I've still the main confession to make to ye, the confession of the thing that has turned Pa against me even more than my doings in the village."

"How's Tave?" said John telepathically. "Wait," said Ike. "I'm going to tell ye all about how she is." And beginning with the first kiss last Thanksgiving, of which he had at that time secretly boasted to John, he gave a full but halting account of his relations with Tavie through the winter and spring, clarifying her hysterical actions in the beginning by saying, "It seems the real reason was that she was in love with me from the start-off, though I had no notion of it then."

He passed lightly over the turn his feelings had taken toward Tavie after the episode with Pru, merely saying that soon after that he figgered he'd ask Tavie to marry him as soon as his affairs were in shape. When he came to their first night together and the later period of terrible hypocrisy, when he kept going to Tavie though she wouldn't agree to marry him, his head hung forward in shame and his voice was a mumble so that John had to lean close to listen. He perked up when he came to his mystical awakening, and ended with an account of his interview with their ma last Tuesday and with their pa on Wednesday.

The whole account took over an hour and a half, and during it the light of a cloudy dawn had been growing around them. It had stopped raining and after the sun rose there were moments when its light behind them shone through a cloud rift and sparkled on the wet leaves in front. As Ike finished, they were passing their mother's girlhood home in Chalons, but neither dared to look at it, or at anything but the jogging backs of the bays in front of them.

At length John said in a husky voice, "You've done a terrible thing," and Ike nodded his drooping head very much as John had done when Ike was accusing him of being a bad brother. "Technically you seem to have behaved properly enough, since you proposed marriage from the beginning. As you said, the only slip you may have made was in not following her when you found she was gone, but, as you said again, with Pa present that might only have made a worse situation than ever."

"I could still take after her," said Ike, "but I feel so danged sure that it'll all come for the best this way. I can trust Tave, ye know. She ain't going to behave like—Mattie Spencer."

"No," said John, "she won't do that. She'll come back and marry you first. But I can't feel it will all come right. I can't help believing that you've done something that neither you nor Tave will ever get over, no matter what happens, whether you get married or not, whether this child of yours is ever born or not." "Maybe," said Ike.

What John was really thinking was that Ike and Tave had done something which he himself would never get over, and he had a terrible, alienating feeling that Ike might get over it if only the practical difficulties worked themselves out. "It isn't that you've done a technical wrong," he repeated. "It's deeper than that." Ike nodded assent. "The terrible thing is that you almost indifferently did this thing, assumed this responsibility to a girl you didn't love."

"I thought I did love her," said Ike, "but I know different now."

"My God, Scamp, how could you? Is there something missing in you? Don't you see?" Ike didn't in John's terms, but he did in his own, which told him that he had done wrong in failing to perceive that he and Tave were unsuited from the beginning. So he could answer quite sincerely, "I do now."

After a short silence he added, "I guess I don't know what love is." And in a moment John added wearily, "I guess I don't either." Which astonishing reflection made Ike's face light up as he glanced quickly at his brother, who was looking gloomily at the dashboard. In his heart Ike thought that he knew more about love than John did. At least he had had a woman and he knew two things that love wasn't, namely, lust, and pity for a woman who was in love with you. He did not formulate these thoughts, but merely felt instantly pleased when John showed this first doubt of the validity of his moon-sick desire for Pru.

"I suppose you know," resumed John, "that you've probably done something I'll never get over, even if you do. Way down inside I can't forget a thing like that, whether I do it myself or somebody I'm fond of does it. I may reason it away and think I forgive it, but there is something that always sticks. At the same time there's something else inside me that loves you and will stand by you no matter what you do."

At this Ike felt a great leap in his heart, for it was the thing above all else he wanted to hear, and above all people from John. He threw his arm over John's shoulder for a moment, then withdrew it and said, "Well, I'll do any consarn thing ye say, and I ain't fooling. If ye say I'll jump in the falls, or I'll take after Tave and pester her till she marries me, or I'll go away and change my name, or anything else." "Will you quit business?" asked John.

Instinctively Ike calculated that he already had property worth near thirty thousand. After a short pause he said, "Yes, 'Paloosa, I'll quit business." John thought a moment, then gave a little laugh that was half ironic and half affectionate. "No, Scamp, you won't do anything you don't believe in yourself. Perhaps another way of putting it is that you won't do anything you don't want to do yourself."

The implied charge of selfishness went completely over Ike's head, for his soul was glowing in the sense of nearness to John again, where he had feared he would curse him and quit him as his pa had virtually done. He felt acutely the pain he was causing John, but this vicarious discomfort, while sufficient to dampen any demonstration of his joy, was yet insufficient to scotch it. In his heart he was satisfied and happy for the first time since he greeted John last Thanksgiving. "Well," he said, pulling in the horses and putting his hand on the brake for the descent of the big Hampton hill, "what does it matter anyhow, so long as we're still fond of each other?" "I'm damned if I know," said John gloomily, looking far off over the enormous grove of elms and maples spiked with spires which was the village six miles away and below them.

All the way down the big hill they were silent, except once when Ike told John he could tell Pa anything he liked, only he'd best talk to Ma first. After Ike pulled the team off the road at Ice Creek to wait for the coach he grew animated and questioned John about college and his plans. Yes, John told him, he'd got his *summa*. Yes, he'd finally settled on law instead of divinity. Ike launched into local news, the junket for John at the Fultons' that night, Solon Samson's return next Tuesday. But John answered in monosyllables, and Ike gave up trying to make him talk, knowing what he was thinking. Finally he said, "Ye'd best talk to Ma before settling on anything about Pru. She's wiser than either of us." "I will," said John. Behind them they heard the jangling and creaking of the coach trotting down the road.

CHAPTER LXII

THE ANNUAL JUNKETS of the Nestors, their wives and surprisingly few descendants were always old style in manner and in dress. Most of the group having been young men in the years between 1790 and 1820, they delighted in these occasions to unfold their carefully preserved dress clothes of the last period before masculine vanity retired from bright into somber colors, from knee breeches, silk stockings and shiny slippers, into pantaloons and boots, and finally the nondescript sobriety of trousers. At the Fultons' junket on this Saturday night Squire Staunton, in powdered hair and crimson velvet—the waistband of the breeches having stood without lengthening for more than fifty years—harked farthest back in the tradition of sartorial splendor, while Squire Lathrop—the waistband of whose tight-fitting nankeen breeches had extended but little—represented the latest of the old styles, with his plum silk frock coat, yellow silk, low-cut waistcoat, and heavily ruffled shirt front and stock.

The Fultons' ballroom, comprising most of the third story of the house and still boasting its musicians' gallery and powder closets, was not only alive with masculine lace, velvet and silk, with mulberry, crimson, green and blue, but it moved to a stately tempo that was almost forgotten in this younger time. The music was harp, flute and violin, and the dances evinced that combination of severe elegance and communal gaiety which, in diluted form, was still characteristic of Yankee civilization. Minuets, and the older, more stately quadrilles—such as the waltz quadrille and the white cockade, alternated with country dances—Money Musk, Lady Walpole's Reel, Morning Star, the various hornpipes, and Hull's Victory. Throughout the evening not a lady was turned by the waist except in the waltz, not a single jig step rattled on the floor. To the rhythm of their youth, the Nestors came fully alive. With young John just returned and the guest of honor of the evening, Squire Lathrop seemed his old self again, vying with his host for popularity with the ladies and with Squire Staunton and Judge VanSanford for leadership in the talk when the men were alone.

Supper downstairs at ten o'clock, in the two south rooms thrown together

457

through their double doors, was unusually bibulous. While the extra help were clearing away the last of the oyster stew, shredded ham, cheese, jellies, nuts, oranges, etc., George Fulton and his pious older brother, Ed, were opening bottles of madeira on the sideboard and filling the third set of wine glasses. When this was done Squire Fulton, in his blue coat with white silk lining and borders, rose at the head of the long, improvised table covered with white damask. The chatter and laughter blended into a hum subsiding rapidly to a hush in which Squire Lathrop said audibly to the hostess at his left, "Egad, Lorinda, it's a pity your jealous husband won't let me look into your eyes untroubled for a half hour together." All the ladies of adequate age flitted their napkins and hissed, "Hush you, John Lathrop," then turned their decorous attention on the host.

"Not only would he steal my wife," retorted Squire Fulton, "but he deliberately brings here the means of interrupting me just as I was about to steal his," at which Sarah Lathrop on Squire Fulton's right glanced up at him and down, and composed herself, looking very arrogant indeed.

"Friends," said Squire Fulton, "I don't need to assure ye that it is the greatest pleasure of the year when Lorinda and I have the privilege of entertaining ye. And I dare boast that, difficult as the choice will be, when the time comes to select our company in Heaven most of us will prefer to be found seated together with our families rather than round our musty old cider barrel with our musty sawdust and our musty ideas." "Hear—hear," interrupted Judge VanSanford, lifting his glass of madeira with mingled enthusiasm and impatience to be at its contents.

Chuckling at his friend Robert, Squire Fulton resumed. "They call us the Backwater Nestors." Cheers. "But I'm not convinced that nowadays we haven't a little too much rapids and not quite enough backwater turning round in familiar pools, knowing where it is, and deciding where it's going next. Aye, I'm not at all certain that out of our own backwater we are not presently going to send out the strongest forces into the new currents." Prolonged applause.

"Now to speak truth, I never was much on giants." Laughter—none of the Fultons were over five feet eight and all the Lathrops, including their women, were six feet or better. "But I am still on moderately friendly terms with the Greek heroes, and as I recall it most of those youngsters who scampered around the plains of Troy were most appallingly tall. Loath as I am to admit that size of body has anything to do with size of soul, nevertheless I am persuaded that in the young generation those who will see farthest will be the ones who can look over the heads of the others in a crowd. And in one particular case I am convinced that we have with us tonight a young hero of Argos who began seeing over all of our heads from the minute I first looked at him some twenty-one years ago and remarked to his diminutive pa that he was the longest baby God Almighty ever sent to earth in these latter days."

Laughter and cheers, and poor John's head was swimming in a vacuum from which everything he had planned to say had vanished.

"For strength of character and steadfastness and clarity of purpose I pledge ye that Byzantium has not yet produced a champion the equal of the man that same long baby has grown to be. I give ye our newest graduate from Yale, John Lathrop, Junior."

With a roar the whole company, including the ladies, was on its feet with lifted glasses, and John, smiling round in agony, saw them drained one by one, then slowly, like the approach of the executioner, watched the guests reseating themselves, and realized that silence had fallen. He rose and, lifting his own glass, bowed to each as he said, "John Fulton, Mistress Fulton, Pa and Ma, and friends," sipped his madeira, set it down and felt his confidence returning.

With his fine, stately delivery and breadth of view, John immediately lifted the occasion beyond Byzantium to the nation. He outlined the changes he had seen in his short life, changes in dress and manners, in architecture and literature and religion, above all in the social and political implications of the Reform Movement and in the economic implications of the new mechanical inventions, and the factory system in industry. He thought that these changes were only beginning, that they were going much farther toward a new and better order which no one had yet the temerity to prophesy. "For my part," he said, "I have chosen the law." Flutter of approval and applause. "I propose to devote my life first of all to the nation and that branch of the Reform Movement which seems to me most significant, and secondly to this community and the guidance of it under the moral principles we and our ancestors have stood for, and against the new, threatening principles of sharp dealing and selfish greed." Cheers.

Squire Lathrop sat silent, visibly flushed with pride, glancing shyly from face to face and finding nothing but approval of this son whom he could trust. When the company was quiet again John continued:

"And now in conclusion I must touch on a matter which is dominant in my own hopes and ambitions, but in which I fear that some of you may hold views different from mine. I wish to declare openly my allegiance to the greatest aspect of the Reform Movement which travelled too long in darkness, under the stigma of lawlessness, and which our great fellow-townsman, soon to be welcomed with public honors, has already done so much to sanctify." He was interrupted by a sudden, spontaneous cheer like a cannon blast that rattled the chandelier and the bric-a-brac on the mantel and was prolonged in a rising toast to Solon Samson.

"I wish," resumed John, "to make the proudest boast of my life, a boast that in my small way connects my name with his. I wish to confess with pride that until the affirmance of Solon Samson's conviction by the Supreme Court I was an active participant in the Underground Railroad, and I care not who knows it. But now that the Fugitive Slave Law has been declared constitutional, I accept Master Samson's further view that adherence to law comes before private moral conviction."

John paused and the silence in the room became absolute. "The thing," he said slowly, "is now an open fight to the finish. No alternative is left us now but to struggle for complete abolition, abolition to be attained gradually, moderately, with adherence to law and with full compensation to those whom it might aggrieve, but abolition complete and final, to be sought unflinchingly and regardless of cost, till the blot of human slavery is forever removed from this land. To this end I have joined the Abolition Society, and I propose from now on to prosecute its ends in this community. I have taken this stand in full knowledge of the possible consequences, with full information of the extent to which the South is already disaffected, and of the extremity to which that disaffection may go. I solemnly believe that we must be ready, if need be, to face that extremity. Ladies and gentlemen," he raised his glass, "I pledge you our country, this Union of States, not yet the land of the free but which we, with God's help, will make the land of the free, one nation faithful to the trust of 1789, one nation under one free government, the beacon and the hope of the world."

In solemn silence everyone rose. Old Squire Staunton did not raise his glass but stood with bowed head. Squire Lathrop touched his glass to his lips when the time came, but his wife saw his face grow purple as he set it down untasted and thereafter his features grow rigid in something like terror. Ike's brow puckered, but he drained the toast out of love for John. The rest with silent accord lifted their glasses and drank the pledge. When they had done so Squire Fulton raised his empty glass, said huskily, "With apologies to the ladies," and shattered it on the floor, followed by all the men. Then, as they stood silent, the Reverend Ira Bentham lifted both his hands and, while all bowed their heads, said, "And may God grant that we are right in the pledge we have taken."

CHAPTER LXIII

ON SUNDAY the Lathrops went to the First Presbyterian Church with the Fultons, and it raised a lump in Sarah's throat to see how her husband deferred to John in the greetings that followed the service. Afterwards, all but Ike drove out to the Hollow and the dinner Charity Samson had prepared for them, she having declined to go in the evening before without her husband. All Sunday afternoon and evening the Squire was unusually quiet, but obviously happy and responsive to anything John might say. Nothing more personal came up than John's decision to study law, and he delighted his pa by saying that, with the foundation he had already laid, he believed he could qualify himself by reading in Byzantium, without being absent another year at law school. At nine o'clock the Squire said the gaiety of the evening before had been too much for him, and went to bed. Sarah and John sat up till Charity Samson and Ben and the hired men had retired. Then they went out and sat on the wide, stone doorstep under the stars, and had Ike and Tavie and Pa on the carpet until midnight.

In the morning the Squire was rested and his complexion had its old, healthy ruddiness. The hay being now in, he harnessed Nancy to the stone-boat and took John down to the side-hill pasture to exhibit his rocky achievements of the last three months. "This has become a kind of hobby with Nancy and me," he said with his old smile, pointing to the three acres of fresh holes where rocks had been and to the stone walls he had doubled to six feet in width. "By Heaven, Pa," said John with honest admiration, "that is a real achievement."

"In another two days," said the Squire, "this old pasture will be fit to plow, and you can set down in the record that the second Squire accomplished alone in three months what it would have taken the first Squire and his sons a year." He slapped Nancy with the reins and they started for the far corner, where numerous undermined boulders still in place indicated work in progress. "I haven't written a word all winter," said the Squire debonairly as they walked along. "They say that with old age the mind gives way before the body. But I agree with old Haz Flint up in Chalons, who, when he heard it was talked that he was losing his mind, said, 'Mebbe so, mebbe so, but anyhow I don't miss it.'" John laughed as lightly as he could.

"I fancy," continued the Squire jocosely, "that with you here I shan't be in quite such a hurry to lose my mind. I count on you to straighten out your old pa on a number of things I've lost faith in. But there'll be plenty of time for that. Well, here we are! Can ye still handle a crowbar, or have ye given it up as a weaker weapon than the pen?"

Both men stripped to the waist, revealing the Squire's wide, sunburned, iron-hard shoulders, and John's narrower ones as flabby and white as a girl's. Thenceforth, their talk was related only to the work of their muscles, the quick order to "hold her" when a great rock was balanced on a bar so that the chain could be passed round it, the drawled commands to the understanding Nancy, the "heave" when they lifted a rock between them and rolled it onto the boat, the "snub her" and "lower away" when the scissors and tackle came into play to drag up the two-log ramp the boulders for the upper tier of the wall. Once when John had failed to dislodge a stone and the Squire had then done it with great effort, so that the veins stood out on his forehead, and afterwards they both paused breathing, the Squire said chuckling, "Ah, my lad, two years from now we'll begin to put ye in proper Lathrop shape. The mind's well enough, but the strength of the body comes first. When that weakens we're on the downgrade for sure." John could only say, "That's right, sir," being appalled by such a speech from his father.

The last work of the morning was to dig deep round the largest stone in the pasture, an enormous slab lying slantwise in the ground and weighing, by the Squire's estimate, close to two tons. When they had cleared enough under it to take the chain and had placed next to it the ramp which would be needful to slide it up out of the deep hole, the Squire considered it and shook his head.

"Nancy," he said, addressing the mare, "I'm afraid this one is going to be too much for us. What do you say to asking our friends Daisy and Buttercup to come down with us after dinner and give us a hand?" He patted Nancy and glanced at the sun whose zenith he could spot to the minute by its position in relation to the biggest maple in front of the house. "Well, sir," he said to John, "that's our morning's work, and after dinner we'll tackle this last Herculean labor." He unhooked Nancy from the boat and led her back toward the bar-way, dragging her toggles. "How are you bearing up, son?" he said laughingly to John who was plodding up the grade beside him, hardly able to drag one long, lanky leg after the other.

After dinner the Squire lay down and John gratefully did the same, asking his ma to wake him as soon as the Squire stirred. Fortunately for John, who needed sleep, he did not stir until four o'clock. When John came down his pa, who had not put on his overalls, said good-humoredly, "Well, son, it is the prerogative of old age to sleep, and I have no doubt that in my absence ye have hoisted that pebble out of the earth." "I took it upstairs and slept with it under my pillow," said John. "I am afraid," said the Squire, "we must let it rest until the morning. In the meantime I suggest that we walk down and plan our tactics." So they went down to the pasture again, without horse or equipment.

The Squire sat down on the big slab and John sat on the ground below him. "Looks like a battlefield," he said, glancing over the pasture mottled with holes and piles of earth, then gazing absently northward to the gap where the Lathrop River and the highway ran through the hills toward the Center and the village beyond. "Yes, son," said the Squire, "it is the field of the hardest battle I ever had, a battle as I wrote ye, between right and my love of my own blood. The plain fact is that I undertook this work to escape from fruitless and maddening thought, and to tire myself so I would not lie awake to no purpose night after night."

"Is that why you gave up writing this winter?" asked John. "Partly that, partly the realization that I now had nothing to write, that that young fellow Emerson and I have been wrong in our faith that each man had in him the capacity to choose his own way. It took my son to teach me that a boy decently brought up could choose a way that violated most of the precepts of ordinary honor. I can speak of it to ye because I know you will support me in this trial. I cannot speak of it to your ma because I know she will be torn between her affection for me and that for her son. As I wrote ye, I shall leave the homestead to you and Benjamin. I shall cut Isaac off in my will. I have waited only for your return to execute the new will and thenceforth to forbid him the premises."

"Did you know, Pa," said John after a long pause, "that Ike has been passing through an ordeal almost as serious as yours? He honors your good opinion above all things in life and he feels he has lost it without his fault. Because you refused to let him drive me out from the village, he drove all the way to Howeville to meet me, simply to ask me to intercede for him with you."

"The young scoundrel!" murmured the Squire, trembling, "trying to steal a march on me." "Only trying to return to your good graces," said John. "Why can he not plead for himself, then?" mumbled the Squire angrily. "He told me he had tried to and that you left his office before he was fairly started in his explanation." "His 'explanation' consisted of assuring me that his conscience was clear in all matters." "So he said to me," said John. "In the light of my positive knowledge, that can mean only that he is either lying or has no conscience, that he is thoroughly bad."

"You know, Pa," said John, "that I dislike Ike's going into industry as much as you do. Yet during the winter, associating with many fine young men who are doing virtually what he is doing, I have somewhat changed my ideas toward the new industries." "You don't mean?" began the Squire with terror and fury in his face, followed by that rising purple tint in his complexion which Sarah had noticed on Saturday evening. "You don't mean—," he repeated, but was unable to proceed, and John hastened to reassure him.

"No, sir, I am not planning to go into business myself and I wish Ike were out of it. Yet I recognize the possibility—witness the Fultons—of these new enterprises being carried on for the general good with honesty and honor." "Are you aware of some of your brother's more notorious *honorable* doings?" "Of some of them, yes, sir," said John. "Specifically, I know that Ike immediately regretted his action in the matter of the option on the Union Mills and that he went to Master Gadston with a generous offer to surrender the advantage he had unfairly gained." "So it has come to a Lathrop making amends to an ignorant trimmer, has it?" said the Squire with a heavy sigh, his face still livid.

Defensively his mind now groped away from the terrible possibility that John was taking sides with Ike against him. For escape he turned the conversation to his other complaint against Ike to which he knew no defense was possible. "In addition to lowering himself by engaging in this degrading competition with men like Gadston and Applemore, I must tell ye further, as I implied in my letter, that there are other and yet darker counts against this young man in a field where there can be no excuse, no hope, as you seem to imply, of better conduct in the future. He has actually *done* already a thing for which many reprobates have been properly shot, and done it *in my own house, under my very nose,* flaunting disgrace in my face. It is a delicate matter which we need not discuss in detail, but I can assure ye that my evidence is complete. There is still a remote possibility of condonation, but it will not be voluntary on his part."

John saw that any defense of Ike in the affair of Tavie would only drive his father into a frenzy, so he said simply, "Of that I could only speak after the most complete information."

"Then," said his father, purpling again, "you refuse to accept my word on a matter which gentlemen do not customarily discuss together." "I mean nothing of the sort, Pa," replied John. "I merely mean that if you cannot discuss it with me I must naturally accept your word on it."

There was a long silence in which things rose in the Squire's mind which he could not face. "Well, son," he said lightly, "how does the old place look?" "Finer than ever," said John, also relieved. "Benjamin is coming on nicely," said the Squire, "and I believe he may be trusted one day to take the responsibility of running the farm. Your active presence, however, will be necessary for a number of years, especially while Benjamin is in college, and even after he returns you may find it necessary to take a part of your time away from your law practice and devote it to the farm. We can't afford to keep two hired men, you know, and Henry Hawks came with full understanding that his employment was temporary. It has occurred to me," he added suddenly with an artificially gay smile, as if revealing a surprise that would be received with joy, "it has occurred to me that we might build ye an office on the south slope beyond the barnyard. Since you are not going to law school, we might break ground this very summer!"

This suggestion, which was so far from John's own plans, gave him a swift sinking feeling in the midriff. He decided that now was certainly not the moment to break his pa's illusion. "Indeed that is most considerate of you, Pa," he said with a show of enthusiasm, then looked away and fell silent. Somewhere deep in the Squire's subconscious a final torturing suspicion raised its head. But he quickly turned from it in fear. "Well, my son," he said lightly, "no doubt you will wish to look in on chores." And he slid off the big rock that he planned to move in the morning and led John up to the cow-shed, enlightening him on the way as to the state of the dairy.

While the Squire and John had been asleep in the afternoon, Ben had taken Charity Samson and little Numa back to the Glen, in preparation for the return of Solon on the morrow. So there were only the family and the two old hired men at supper. The Squire talked incessantly in a light and artificial manner, interrupting John whenever he started to speak, seeming to take the words out of his mouth but really putting his own interpretation on what John was going to say, as if he were afraid to let himself hear his son's views on anything. He told the rest what a help John had been in clearing the pasture and how they expected to finish the work in the morning. "I am afraid," John began—"Oh, a trifle soft, no doubt," the Squire interrupted him, "but it was remarkable how little education debilitates a man who is really bred to the soil. I'll wage ye," turning to Master Lane, who went on eating, "that in haying John will prove the master of any of us—unless, of course"—with a smile at his youngest—"it is Benjamin." At the end of supper he suddenly placed his hands on the sides of the table and leaned forward as if to impart a great secret, seeming to look alternately at John and his wife, but actually avoiding both of their eyes.

"And now, my girl," he said, "John and I have a little surprise for ye. As soon as we have finished stonin' the pasture we're going to break ground south of the barnyard for what is to be the most up-to-date law office in town. John believes that with a proper equipment of books, which we shall provide, he can prepare himself there, and when he completes his studies he will be immediately established in practice, right here at home. In the meantime and thereafter, he will devote a part of his time to the farm. And so"—the Squire lifted his hands and rubbed them together with a gesture of satisfaction—"this long separation will be ended." John glanced sideways at his mother who immediately rose to end the meal.

At prayers the Squire thanked God for having united the family again, and confided in Him how happy they were all going to be in the future. The conversation was impersonal until ten o'clock, when all retired except the Squire and John, Sarah begging them both to go to bed soon, for they must still be tired from their exertions of the morning. "For myself, perhaps so," said the Squire, taking Sarah by the shoulders. "But, my girl, ye will be astonished henceforth at the strength of our boy here. At last he has come into his own."

As soon as they were alone the Squire assumed an air of ponderous gravity which was as little like his usual dignity as his artificial levity at supper had been like his usual playful manner. He motioned John to a chair, gave him a fresh cigar, lighted his own at the candelabra and sat down at the desk. With pompous deliberateness he took a key from his pocket, opened the little central cupboard of the desk and took out a document which he unrolled and weighted, adjusting the candle to suit him, and spent five minutes in reading, just as if every word of it was not engraved on his suffering heart. At length he rose and handed it to John.

"This," he said solemnly, "is the new will I mentioned to ye. I should be glad of any suggestions ye might make before I execute it." The Squire sat down in the hair-cloth rocker and watched John, as, laying aside his cigar, he leaned forward in his chair to get the light of the candelabra on the will which covered less than a page of foolscap in the Squire's small, scholarly hand. By the principal clause he devised the homestead jointly to John and Ben, but charging it with the support of his wife, his parents, and Aggie and her child, if and when they or any of them should occupy the homestead and should contribute the usual services to its maintenance. Then followed the clause cutting off Ike, then the residuary clause leaving everything not otherwise mentioned to John. John read it twice and attended particularly to the words of the clause cutting off Ike: "Inasmuch as my son Isaac has ceased to interest himself in the aforementioned Lathrop Homestead, and has taken up his residence elsewhere, and for other good and sufficient reasons, it is my intention to cut off my said son Isaac, and I do hereby cut him off, with a bequest of one dollar ($1)."

John rose, laid the will on the desk, walked over to the mantel, and remained standing, his blue eyes darkening to near black. For a full minute the clock in the hall ticked in the silence, John seeing his course with perfect clarity and hitting upon no way he could spare his pa in following it. At last he said, "Pa, since you have asked me to comment on the will I must do so honestly. This requires me to ask you a personal question. Is your reason for cutting Ike out of his share in the homestead chiefly his personal misconduct, or is it his having gone into business and moved into the village?"

"Oh, I daresay," said the Squire, pursing up his lips and gesturing with his hand as if it were quite obvious, "if he had been guilty of no personal misconduct, I would have mentioned him in the will, but since he would have still left the homestead I would still have felt that he had surrendered any just claim to share it with you and Benjamin."

"Then, Pa," said John with his jaw set, "I must tell you that I should fare no better than Ike in regard to the homestead. My ambitions in the anti-slavery movement may take me far afield. But aside from that, even as a lawyer I now feel that my wisest course would be to move into the village. Whether we like it or not, the modern world is moving away from the country districts. It is in the villages and cities that the great questions of the future are to be decided. I think I would be neglecting the opportunities of the times and condemning myself to insignificance if I failed to acknowledge this modern tendency and to take my part in it."

John did not dare look at his pa's face, but if he had done so he would not have seen what he feared. Instead of any purpling of his complexion or other sign of weakness, he would have seen a calm and genuine certitude settle on the big features, and he would have seen those big blue eyes looking at him with affection and admiration. In a moment the Squire rose, came over to John, laid his gentle hand on his shoulder, forced him to meet his eyes, and said quietly, "Don't be troubled, my boy, for the candor with which you have spoken. I know it was not easy, and I thank ye for it. To confess the truth, it was my suspicion that you might have some such feelings that made me delay executing this will until I had shown it to ye." "Thank you, Pa," was all John could say.

"And now," said the Squire, stepping back, "what you have told me will lead me again to alter this will in some respects, and while the matter is still fresh in my mind I would prefer to tend to it now and be done. I hope you suffer no lameness from the exertions I put ye to this morning. In any case a little sleep will not come amiss. And so I will bid ye good night."

John wanted to stay with his pa, but he now felt the full, integrated power of the man who was graciously dismissing him. He wanted to speak but could only stammer while his pa smiled understandingly at his confusion. At last he merely muttered, "Thank you again, Pa, and good night to you," and walked slowly up the front stairs. As usual he found Ben reading, and confided to him that he thought Pa was going to change his will and leave the farm to Ben alone.

It was dawn when the Squire finished copying the new will and signed it. He walked out to the summer kitchen, opened the northeast door and sat down on the step where Ike had sat when he was drunk last Thanksgiving and had made ill-considered love to Tavie. He watched the sun come up and pour its clear light down over his acres, and he thought that even though their work was done they had done well, that after all the strength of the family had not failed here, and, though the future was dark to him, yet he had no reason to say that the family would not continue as vigorously in some new location. His heart warmed to Isaac and faith in the time, perhaps some months hence, when he would embrace him and forgive him and be forgiven.

Down in the back pasture he heard Tippie the cow-dog barking, and Henry Hawks calling the cows, and soon after heard Benjamin and Master Lane rattling the milk pails outside the kitchen. When they were safely away he rose and walked back through the house to his room, where Sarah came wide awake as he entered.

"My girl," he said, "I have been a burden to ye for some months, but now it is ended." Sarah saw that this was the husband she had had for thirty-four years and had recently feared she had lost. She sprang out of bed and felt his strong arms around her. "O John," she murmured, "I am so happy. I too have hardly been myself for months, but I think it is over." "We can talk honestly now," said the Squire. "You need no longer care for me like a sick child. I have been proud and blind, and thought harshly of Isaac, and the thought poisoned me. I know he will prove himself honorable, and I shall tell him so, and will make full amends to him." "Did John do this for you?" whispered Sarah. "I knew he would." "Yes," said the Squire, patting her. "Yes—it was John."

The Squire slept until dinner where all noticed the change in him. After dinner they were to start harvesting wheat, Ben to run the mowing-machine, Master Lane and Henry Hawks to assist with their time-honored scythes. All were instructed to come back to the house immediately if they heard any unusual sounds from the direction of the Center. When they had gone the Squire said to John, "Son, before I go down to help Benjamin I am going to have a fling at that last stone in the side-hill pasture. I would be glad of your company. It is likely, as you know, that we shall be interrupted shortly."

So for an hour the two men and the white oxen, Daisy and Buttercup, wrestled with the two-ton slab. After many false starts they succeeded in crashing it over on the ramp, but the oxen were unable to slide it up out of the hole. "If I were anyone else," said the Squire, "I would make short work of this with the scissors and tackle, but as a personal indulgence, and because this marks the end of this task, I am tempted to try an old-fashioned method. When this field is cleared I should like to say I had a personal hand in the last of it." "I wish you wouldn't try it, Pa," said John, "if you are thinking of that old tump-line." The Squire laughed heartily. "Come, come," he said, "I'm not as old as I was yesterday. I dare boast I am still the strongest man in town."

At that moment they both looked suddenly down the Hollow where the highway came out of the gap to the north. Faintly but unmistakably the sound of music reached them, the sound of a band. "Hurray!"

shouted John impulsively, picking up a stick and throwing it in the air. "Hurray! There they come!" "Hip-hip," shouted the Squire, and together they bellowed, "Hurray! Hurray! Hurray!"

Unhooking the oxen from the rock, they goaded them into their slow trot up through the bar-way to the barn, put them in their stalls, and rushed into the house to don their best clothes. Ben had already swung up the mowing-arm and was jouncing up the back pasture behind Mol, while Master Lane and Henry Hawks were urging their rheumatics at a fast shuffle up from the far meadow.

And on every other farm in the Hollow, at Swifts', Emmenses', Oakses', Wilcoxes', Stones', Oxbows', and the rest, men and horses were running for their houses like chickens to feed, and wives, daughters and hired girls were throwing off their aprons as they ran to their rooms where their Sunday best clothes were already laid out. There was such a rattling of gear and banging of doors as echoed back and forth in the cup of hills above the still faint sound of the approaching band, and running men called half a mile to each other across the fields, "It's Solon!—Hurray! Hurray!—Here comes Solon!"

CHAPTER LXIV

SOLON SAMSON'S reception in the Falls had been organized by Bub Tanofly as Grand Marshal and Chairman of the Committee on Arrangements, and he had sworn that, by Jesus's britches, he'd turn out every man, woman and baby in the village, with a thousand from the county. The preliminary ceremony had occurred at the corporation limits at 6:30, where the horses of the coach from Utica were thrown into a near runaway and Solon himself was temporarily deafened by fanfare after fanfare aimed at him by the blue-coated Byzantium Brass Band on its gorgeous red and gilt carry-all; Captain Beezlebub Tanofly's brave company of Zouaves in their gay pantaloons and fezzes stood at an irregular present arms; and President VanWyck of the village adorned Solon's head with a laurel wreath and presented him with a huge golden key of the city.

After breakfast at Squire Fulton's, the conquering hero was conducted to the bannered and buntinged Mall by a parade comprising about a fifth of the men of the village, while an assembly of near four thousand, crowding the street and buildings at the western end of the big forum, welcomed him with a roar of cheering that kept up, with ceremonious intervals of silence, for three hours. After mounting the speakers' stand, gorgeous with flags and the national shield in red, white and blue flowers, Solon stood for half an hour in a Demosthenes-like attitude while the following organizations, comprising the parade, passed in review:

The Blackwater Sax-Horn Band, a pedestrian organization detailed to blare the rhythm for the review in competition with the Bunker Hill Fife and Drum Corps which squealed at the rear; Byzantium Lodge No. 289; Byzantium Commandery, No. 11, Knights Templar, in their plumes and sashes; Kamargo Lodge No. 217, I.O.O.F.; Iroquois Lodge, No. 161, I.O.O.F.; the three Hose and one Hook and Ladder Company of the Byzantium Fire Department; Montezuma Encampment No. 87; the Blackwater County Industrial Association, preceded by a two-staved banner with the words, "Fourier—the Union of Labor and Capital"; the Byzantium Mechanics' Association, preceded by a similar banner bearing the prophetic motto, "The Soul, the Mind, and the Machine"; The Young

Men's Association for Mutual Improvement in the Village of Byzantium Falls; The Blackwater County Temperance Society, preceded by
a single-staved banner on a yard, portraying a white waterfall on a blue
field; the Sons of Temperance in two divisions, Morning Star, 156, bearing an appropriate banner, and Meridian, 303, whose banner displayed a
gilt sun beating down from a silver sky on a brown desert; Company
D, 35th Battalion, 16th Brigade, 4th Division, National Guard, New York,
which drew a renewed cheer from the crowd for its passable marching,
after the straggling exhibition of its civilian predecessors; finally, the
Bunker Hill Fife and Drum Corps.

After an invocation by the Reverend Tremble Thomas, mass singing
under the leadership of the Byzantium Brass Band, and speeches by Senator Applemore and the Reverend Ira Bentham, Solon Samson was introduced by Judge VanWyck. As always since his conviction, Solon plead
for observance of the Fugitive Slave Law. But he devoted the greater
and more moving part of his speech to the illegality of secession and the
need of preserving the Union at any cost, thus furthering a change that
had already begun in the popular will, a fusion of two separate moral
emotions which would grow together during the next decade until they
were one and indistinguishable—the hatred of slavery, and the love of the
Union. Solon ended his speech with solemn words—"To that flag and
that Union let us dedicate our efforts, our honor, and if need be our
blood, from this time forward." And he sat down in a quiet that was
in ominous contrast to the thunderous cheering that had greeted him,
a quiet not at all derogatory of Solon, but a troubled, wondering silence
in which thousands of thoughtful people stood staring up at their leader
whom they were ready to follow.

Following a banquet at Perkins Hotel, Solon and Judge VanWyck
again mounted the Judge's florally adorned carriage which had served
throughout as the chariot of honor, and set out for Lathrop Hollow, followed by a cavalcade of volunteer riders and preceded by the gilt and
red carry-all of the Byzantium Brass Band which banged and whooped
all the way to the corporation limits. The cheering crowds thinned out
as they proceeded up Washington Street. Precisely at the village boundary
the bandmaster nonchalantly flicked his baton and the brass bedlam ceased
in the middle of a phrase. Solon was suddenly in silence beside his friend
Judge VanWyck, starting up the hills toward his home. He had survived
his ordeal and was no more troubled by his greatness, but for an occasional flag in a farmhouse or the wave of a farmer whom he knew. Ike
Lathrop galloped up out of the cavalcade following and, after leaning

down to welcome him personally, handed him a note which Charity had sent in for him the Saturday before, along with his formidable bundle of post which Ike had had the thoughtfulness to get from the Post Office.

Begging Judge VanWyck to forgive him, Solon read the note from his wife. It told of Tavie's sudden departure ten days before to accept an appointment at Oberlin, and plead so earnestly with Solon not to be troubled by it that he was troubled indeed. Scowling in disappointment and apprehension, he turned down the corners of his bundle of letters till he found a fat one from Octavia.

What Tavie wrote her pa revealed nothing respecting Ike or the expected child. But what it did reveal threw him into a confusion of mind and emotion which lasted most of the way to the Hollow. What she had done was at first a shock to the hopes and plans he had cherished for her. But after reading her letter again and again, and sinking into a half-hour's meditation, he perceived, as she argued, that she was now in a better position than ever to prosecute her life work. His initial disappointment gave way to pride in his daughter's decisiveness and courage. His passionate love for her, enhanced by her absence and his approval of what she had done, became once more the source of happiness it had been since her childhood.

The little procession trundled round a bend half a mile short of Sloan's Bridge that was the entrance to the Hollow. Solon came out of his reverie and his eyes had the black glitter that was his smile. His soul filled with the normal, untroubled emotions of home-coming, and he leaned out of the carriage for the first glimpse of the scene and the people he loved. The Byzantium Brass Band, silent since it left the village, crashed suddenly into the racket that, more than a mile ahead, sent the Squire and John and all the citizens of Lathrop Hollow scurrying in from their fields.

The snarl and clatter of the professional brass band would under any circumstances have been offensive in the human and natural quiet of Lathrop Hollow. It was especially inappropriate to the simple plan which Jehu Jones and Reverend Nathaniel Norcross had laid for the greeting of their friend. So when the brass uproar on wheels had passed Oxbows' house and was entering the grove below his mill, not forty rods from the Corners, skinny old Jehu took the matter in hand. With the authority of Master of Ceremonies, he laid hands on the nearest horse, which was bridled but unsaddled, sprang on it for all his near ninety years and blue knee breeches, and galloped down through the grove with the fury that could twist a drunken ballroom to its will.

Jouncing up to the carry-all he bellowed, "Stop that pesky racket or I'll hoss-whip every tarnal blue-jay o' ye," whereat the Master turned indifferently to his musicians, flicked his baton, and the thunder as usual stopped suddenly in the middle of a measure. "Howdy, Solon. God bless ye," called Jehu to the carriage following. "Howdy, Jedge. See ye in two jerks." And he wheeled and galloped back to the little crowd assembled at the Corners, dismounted, handed the horse to its owner, took a deep breath, and was composed. Back in the carriage Judge VanWyck, sensing the situation, stood up, got the eye of the Bandmaster and motioned to him to pull his equipage to the right of the road and stop, which the Master caused his driver to do, and the rest of the procession passed by it in silence.

Cleared of the obstruction of the carry-all of the band, the carriage, followed by some sixty mounted friends of Solon's, came in sight of the eighty-odd residents of the Hollow assembled by the hall at the Corners. In contrast to the village, there was here no cheering, no blare of trumpets, but, just audible above the noise of the stream, came the slender, sincere notes of Master Lane's harmonica and Jehu Jones's violin, playing "Home, Sweet Home." Old Judge VanWyck smiled to conceal his feelings, and Solon assumed that expression of great facial severity but with twinkling eyes which was his way of revealing the most profound pleasure.

There they all were, the people who were one with him in every tie that mattered, the people he loved more than the Blackwater fellowship or anyone else in the village, far more than any of the great men with whom he had become friendly during the last three months. There stood his wife and little son, and John Lathrop, old Professor Tom Lathrop, and Young John, back from college, and Lem Oaks, Eliphalet Emmens, Reuben Swift, Malachi Jolam, Joachim Wilcox, Jared Oxbow, Elisha Stone, Homer Haddock, the young Reverend Norcross, and a dozen others, even the old scarecrow Vic Birdseye, together with their wives and children, all in their Sunday best, all just standing there, just looking at him intently, making not a sound but the simple music, really glad to see him.

The carriage pulled up by the hall and the music stopped. Nobody could say anything. Solon jumped out and seized his wife in a long hug while she quietly cried. Then he picked up little Numa and kissed him. Next stood his closest friend, John Lathrop, in his best bib and tucker. Solon did the only thoroughly irregular thing he ever did in his life. Sedately he kissed John Lathrop. Then he kissed Sarah Lathrop. Then he went around and embraced every man in the Hollow and kissed every woman on the lips and every child on the forehead, all with great dignity. Then he walked proudly back and stood by the carriage, presuming that something was expected of him.

"Solon," said Squire Lathrop, "you and young Norcross and Jehu and I were supposed to make speeches. Let's not make 'em. There will be time enough for that later. Let's go home." "You all know what I have to say," replied Solon, looking around at those faces with his severe expression and dancing eyes. Then he put his foot on the step of the carriage, whereat Judge VanWyck stepped out the other side, went to Charity Samson and said, "Mistress Samson, I beg of ye," and led her to the carriage. She stepped up with quiet thanks, followed by Solon and little Numa who sat squeezed between them on the seat. The rest started ahead on foot up Lathrop Lane when Jehu Jones, his aplomb threatened for the first time in his recollection, remembered something that was to have been incidental to his speech.

"Whoa-up thar," he called. "We forgot some'at besides speeches." From the grass by the hall he picked up a bed pillow disguised under a silk table cover of Mistress Stone's and bearing a number of black objects. Advancing to Solon with this, Jehu bowed and said, "From the pocketbooks and needles of every woman in the Hollow," and presented him with the first real gifts he had received, two complete new best suits with embroidered waistcoats, a new pair of dress boots, and a new silk hat.

Solon laid the clothes on the seat in front of him and rose. "Ladies," he called out, extending his arms, "I'm giving ye back ten-fold the love that went into these welcome things." Then he made one of the few jokes in his record. "I hope ye didn't foresee I'd come home in stripes and would need them forthwith."

The carriage proceeded up the hill at a walk, surrounded by everybody on foot, and followed by the numerous riders from the Falls who hung back respectfully, all except Ike who swung down from Chesty, handed him to Bub Tanofly and ran ahead to be with his own. Everybody began asking Solon questions and assuring him that jail was the place for him, as he had never looked better in his life. Presently some of the youngsters in front began to snake-dance and sing songs of welcome. Among these was an old revival hymn, "Say, Brothers, will you meet us?" which made a stirring march, the words of the verses transitory enough but the chorus already fixed in its immortal form, repeating three times the words, "Glory Glory, Hallelujah."

The little parade moved up the hill, past Lathrops' and down the corduroy of the Lower Road to the glen. In passing the Lathrop cemetery Ike saw the owl that lived there rocket over the road, and he glanced

at the big, bent white birch that had startled Tavie and him in the moonlight last winter. He wondered if Solon Samson knew that Tavie had
skedaddled, and how he'd take it when he heard the whole truth about her.

When they reached Solon's house the Samsons got out of the carriage
without driving in, and Solon walked up to the open door with one arm
around his wife and the other hand down on Numa's shoulder. As he
entered he turned back and waved to the crowd, which was too much
for Jehu Jones and he shouted, "Three cheers for Solon"; and Jolam's
Grove was startled by more noise not of its own windy making than
it had ever heard. The Samsons disappeared for a moment, and Jehu,
followed by most of the men, including those who had ridden out from
the village and had by now dismounted and hitched their horses as they
could, walked up to the house. Solon returned and bowed them in, Jehu
leading him to the right into his office while as many as could crowded
in the door behind. The old, dilapidated books were undisturbed on
the shelves, but all round the floor, backs up, were ranged brand new
sets of Cowan's, Hill's and Derrio's *New York Law Reports,* along with
many books of legal reference which Solon had needed for years. "The
gift," said Jehu with a bow, "of all the men in the Hollow, all the fellers
of the Blackwater cider barrel, and numerous others from the township
and elsewhere whose names ye will find on that paper on yer desk."

Solon was overwhelmed. He stared at the faces in the door so savagely
that they feared he was really angry. "Gentlemen," he said, "I am speechless. It is no discredit to most of ye who are not of the profession when
I say that I doubt if ye know what you have done for me." "It's jail that
does it," called out Dr. Swift, and Solon dropped his eyes. The remark
was inappropriate. Solon was indeed wondering whether it was proper for
him to accept such a gift as a reward for an adjudged misdemeanor. But
he dismissed consideration of it for the moment and knelt down to read
some of the precious labels. "Come, Solon," said Squire Lathrop from the
door. "None of that now. Come into the parlor where ye have guests."

In the parlor was punch contributed by the Squire, and everyone par-
took for an hour, most of them overflowing back into the front yard
under the tall hemlocks. At four o'clock Judge VanWyck took his leave,
followed by the rest of the villagers, and soon after the residents of the
Hollow began to drift away. By half past four there remained in the
house only the Samsons, Squire Lathrop, Sarah, John and Ben, Dr. Swift,
Jehu Jones and Lemuel and Felicity Oaks.

Ike had been the last to leave, and he stood for some minutes uncertainly beside Chesty where Bub had left him tied to a fence-rail. He won-

dered if Charity would mind his presence at this time, wondered how much any of them knew. Spying him there, Solon called from the door, "Come back, Isaac, I beg of ye. That railroad will do without ye in the village tonight. Come back and we shall have one of those old-time confabs after the junket is over." Ike came back. He knew he deserved to be shot by Solon Samson, yet he was mighty fond of him. He'd done his best by Tavie, and things were at a pass where he couldn't do anything more just now.

The little group of neighbors and close friends was no sooner seated than Solon excused himself and Charity for a moment, led her into his office and showed her the letter from Octavia. As he expected, she was hysterically moved. But he assured her that the girl had done well, and just now Charity's life was so full of his return that she was soon quieted. They returned to the parlor, and ceremoniously Solon dipped out and distributed cans of punch to all. It was evident that something was coming, and the company fell silent. "Friends," said Solon, "this is a doubly happy hour for this house, and it may be that some of ye are not yet acquainted with our greatest cause of happiness. I take great pleasure in announcing to ye that on last Thursday evening our Octavia was married to Constant Oaks in Oberlin, Ohio."

The tremors in four sets of Lathrop nerves had a moment's grace when Lem Oaks jumped up, exclaiming, "By God, Solon, that's first-rate news! The boy's been in love with her since they were babies and he'll make her an honest husband if girl ever had one!" "I know that, Lem," said Solon, "and I also am inordinately pleased. My only regret is that these young people are not here with us now." Whereupon Lem, slopping over his punch, rushed over to the couch and kissed Charity, and Solon solemnly kissed Felicity, and Lem kissed Felicity, and Solon kissed Charity, and Jehu Jones kissed Felicity and Charity and Sarah Lathrop, and Dr. Swift, starting at the other end, kissed Sarah and Charity and Felicity, and the Lathrops came into action and kissed all the ladies, and Charity and Felicity on the sofa fell on each other's bosoms and cried.

Squire Lathrop, John, Ike and Ben all kept smiling their best smiles, and Sarah looked arrogant. The Squire lifted his can and said gaily, "Friends, this is a joyful day for the Hollow. I pledge ye health and eternal happiness to Octavia and Constant, as true and well matched a pair as ever came out of Byzantium." And they all stood and drained their mugs with varying degrees of difficulty, in the grip of widely varying emotions.

Half an hour later, leaving the Samsons', the Squire walked ahead up the corduroy with Sarah and Ben, and John and Ike followed, lagging back out of earshot. It was a hot afternoon, and the cicadas were buzzing from the thickets all around them. "Fine hurra's nest, eh, 'Paloosa?" said Ike. "By God, that's one way I never figgered things'd turn, and I can't see the right of it." "There isn't any," said John quietly, taking some comfort in the fact that Ike didn't seem to be enjoying a sense of relief at the news of Tavie's marriage. "Never figgered she'd do that to herself," said Ike. "And to poor old Connie," said John. "Think how he'll feel when he learns the truth of it." For reply Ike took a letter from his pocket and handed it to John:

Oberlin
Care of Aggie
Thursday, July 31

Dear Ike—

Connie and I were married three hours ago and I want you to know that I have not deceived him. The plan I had in mind, which I didn't reveal to you, was to get some down-and-outer somewhere on the frontier to marry me for money—that was why I said I would appeal to you if I needed money. The agreement would have been that he leave me after the ceremony and later I would divorce him in Indiana where it is easy.

After I left Buffalo it seemed to me that I ought to give Connie first chance at this unsavory arrangement, if it could be done without imposing on his chivalry. This appealed to me, of course, because I am really fond of Connie and would not require him to leave me at once. The marriage might even be a success!

So I came to Oberlin and put up with Aggie, and as soon as I arrived, wrote her a letter, heading it Byzantium. In it I told the whole truth, my being in love with you, my having instigated the whole business, and the complete results. I said I would not marry you, though you kept asking me, because I knew you didn't love me. I said nothing of my plan to go west, for that would have roused Connie's chivalry. Instead, I asked Aggie for advice in the letter. Should I marry you who didn't love me or Connie whom I didn't love?—assuming, of course, that Connie still wanted to marry me. Putting it that way seemed to give him a free chance to decide.

After I had finished the letter, Aggie sent Homer for Connie, and when they came back she got rid of Homer and showed it to him. I was hidden in the next room, and there was no doubt of what he wanted and hoped. So when I was sure of it I appeared, and we were married two hours later—now three hours ago—it is already dawn!

I am to live with Connie for a year, and at any time after that he will leave me if I ask it. With all due respect to you, I think Connie is the kindest, most unselfish man in the world. I didn't want you to think I had deceived him.

It is much better this way, Ike. You are free. If we had married, part of me would have been happy, and part of me would have regretted it, increasingly with the years. This way I can do my work in the world.

No regrets, mind you. I haven't any.

Good-by, my friend,
T.

As John handed back the letter Ike said, "That ain't the end of it."
"No," said John.

CHAPTER LXV

FIFTY YARDS ahead of John and Ike the Squire walked homeward in composure between Sarah and Ben. The presence of the boy made conversation impossible, but husband and wife knew they were in agreement that this was a major calamity. Yet the Squire felt strangely at peace. The worst had now happened and there was nothing further to hope or fear. His two most promising sons had deserted him and one of them was thoroughly, irredeemably bad. Nothing could surprise or hurt him now. He was ready to meet Ike and John with sympathy and forgiveness. They had killed the petty, personal thing in him that needed them.

In the house the Squire seemed to Sarah and to his sons to loom too large for the walls. In the keeping-room John, Ike and Ben stood together by the mantel, all in their best clothes, feeling more than usually a united family as they watched their pa through the open door to his bedroom. They knew what he was up to, and each of them proposed to help him if he would let him. It was half-past five and Master Lane and Henry Hawks, having left the Samsons before the family, were up at chores and could finish them alone. Sarah, comforted by the presence of all three boys for the first time since Thanksgiving, and by the obvious composure of her husband, was busy over the little stove in the summer kitchen. The kitchen fire was long dead on the great hearth, and the house was cool in comparison to the afternoon heat outside. As on every summer day, a vireo was singing monotonously in the maples in front of the house, and the cicadas never ceased humming.

Having stripped off his coat, waistcoat, cravat, collar and cuffs, and changed into his working boots, the Squire came out to his sons, rolling up his sleeves and having a playful grin in the wrinkles at the corners of his eyes. "I daresay you youngsters know what I'm about," he said, and they all nodded with their several versions of the big Lathrop smile. It was the first time Ike had felt easy in his pa's presence since last winter. "I'd be honored," the Squire continued, "if the three of ye would come out to witness my little experiment. You don't need to take off your duds, for I shall ask ye to do nothing but watch. We've but half an hour before supper."

Five minutes later the Squire, carrying a tump-line over his shoulder, goaded the yoked Daisy and Buttercup out of the ox-shed, and the boys walked beside him down to the little experiment. They crossed to the far corner of the side-hill pasture where he had left the chain round the two-ton slab, lying over on the ramp of logs in its hole. Halting the oxen in approximate position, he carried the chain forward between them and hooked it to the yoke-ring, then ducked out under the yoke and stripped himself to the waist. He tied the heavy tump-line through the yoke-ring and, walking straight out in front of the oxen, settled the tump comfortably on his forehead, leaning into it slightly, tautening the line and trying several angles of draught till he found the one that suited him. Then, still leaning into the tump, he said, "Benjamin, do ye goad the cattle, while I help as I may and we shall have it out in short order."

Ben did as he was bid, first flicking the oxen into position for straight draft with appropriate "Gee" and "Haw," while the Squire swung in front of them, keeping himself in the same line. Finally Ben, crouching tensely in close to the big beasts screamed explosively, "Hip-hyee-hyee-hip-hip." The chain and the tump-line to the Squire's forehead straightened out; the oxen snorted and leaned; the white beasts and the half-naked Squire all straining forward at the same angle in a splendid show of muscular power. "Hip-hyee-hyee-hip-hip," screamed Ben, and John and Ike saw the great veins standing out on their pa's neck and his face growing purple.

"Hip-hyee-hyee-hip-hip." The Squire heard Ben for the third time urging the oxen, and all the power of his life and his tradition strained forward into that band across his forehead. It was as if he were drawing the boulder of evil from the pasture of the world. It was his civilization, his country, all mankind he was lifting upward to a flickering light that he began to see dimly ahead. He felt his strength increasing as he drew, and he exulted in certainty that he would succeed. He had always been here drawing this boulder, for years.

Suddenly he heard a sharp report like a musket, and the weight came. On and on he dragged, he ran, with the load growing always lighter, till he seemed to leave the earth and to be rising easily upward through space toward that light that receded less rapidly than he gained on it, till it was near and dazzlingly bright. Now it was no longer mankind but his son Isaac whom he was drawing upward. He was back in a night blizzard when he had led the little boy up the back pasture from tending a line of traps, and they came in sight of the lantern Sarah had set out for a beacon in the lee of the barn. He was back in the time up in Chalons when he had ridden toward the light of Ian McLeod's windows on the night that Sarah became his betrothed. He was back on the summer night when he had stayed out till dark fishing and expected a whipping and came up through the side-hill pasture with a two-pound trout and saw Venus very bright on the eastern horizon. He was back to an earlier time when a candle bent down close over his cradle. He was back . . .

The stone had not moved. When their father fell John and Ike picked him up mumbling, and struggled with his two hundred and ten pounds up to the house. Ben ran ahead and in a moment clattered out the drive on Mol, without saddle or bridle, up the hill for Dr. Swift. As John and Ike came round the barn with their burden Sarah stood in the kitchen door, very tall, absolutely pale, absolutely quiet. In a moment they heard the Doctor galloping back down the hill. But when John and Ike laid him on the bed Sarah knew at once that he was dead. And she fell on his body and lay there for how many hours and days and years she did not know.

Two days later, in the presence of a thousand friends from the town and county, they laid him in the family cemetery near his grandfather, with room left for his parents and his wife between. The spot was just where his tall stone, when it should be set up, would eclipse the white birch tree that had frightened Ike and Tavie during the winter.

After dinner on the day following the funeral John asked Sarah if he might walk over to Grandpa's and Grandma's. When he had gone, Ike asked her if he might take a walk in the lower meadow for half an hour. Then Ben told her he should look at the barley in the south meadow, and asked if he might leave for twenty minutes. But each boy was bent on the same errand, and in each case the mission he stated was a lie.

Ike, taking the shorter route, arrived first, and John, going round by the upper road, and cutting back through the pine lot he and Ike had crossed last Thanksgiving, arrived soon after. As John drew near the wall he instinctively walked quietly, but Ike would not have heard him anyway. He was kneeling on the left side of the mound of fresh earth, the backs of his hands on the ground and his face in his palms. He was hearing the rustle of Jolam's Falls, and the wind in the hemlocks and birches, and the flutter of birds, and beyond these the roll of the seas and the outer winds and the rustle of the stars. He was knowing that his pa was one with all these eternal things, and that he could not die. But Ike was weeping because he knew that he had loved his pa and always would, and that he had killed him because he had concealed his love and had been wilful.

John heard Ike murmuring, "O Pa, Pa, speak to me. I love ye, Pa. I love ye and I know I killed ye. And you were right about Tave and I was wrong. I know ye ain't dead, but I killed ye."

"Scamp," said John quietly, and Ike looked up without surprise and with his face covered with tears. John came over the wall and knelt on the other side of the grave. "I killed him too, Scamp," he said, "when I told him on Monday I was going to the village." And John clasped his hands and lifted them to the sky. "Before God, Pa," he said, sobbing, "I know I killed you, but I think what I told you was right. Before God, I'll carry on your work in the world." And John threw his face down on the ground and sobbed more bitterly than Ike had done. Ike leaned across the grave and put his hand on his brother's clasped hands where they lay on the ground.

Meanwhile Ben had been standing at the lower wall and he now said, "Do you fellows mind if I come in too?" Both Ike and John looked up at their younger brother with love in their eyes, and he climbed over the wall.

So the new generation sat there, John on the right of the grave, Ike on the left, and Ben at the foot. And they were drawn together with a force that held them through life, so that whatever other tension might arise between them they always remembered that day when they came together, each by his own way, to their pa's grave. The coincidence was so strong and simple that grief left them and Ben did not weep at all, but lay on his stomach on the ground looking from one of his brothers to the other, and something like a warm smile rose behind all their eyes.

Finally Ike said in a natural and affectionate tone, "Runt, ye know 'twas Pa's wish that ye go to college, and I've the money to send ye and to spare. I figger ye're the feller of all of us should go, even more than the 'Paloosa." And John nodded with eager sincerity. There was a long silence in which they all listened to Jolam's Falls and the cicadas, and the vireo singing back home in the front yard maples, and Ben, the baby of the family, pulled grass blades one by one and tossed them away.

"No, fellows," he said finally, smiling back and forth from one to the other of his brothers—and they both noticed that his voice and way of speaking that had always resembled the Squire's were now indistinguishable from his, so it might have been their pa speaking to them. "No, fellows. I know pa wanted me to go to college. But beyond that he wanted that one of us should stay at the homestead. Since I haven't made the break yet, it's wisest that I should not make it now. I've been doing some thinking on my own account, and I own I'm not certain that college and the world are any different than Lathrop Hollow, or any bigger, for that, I believe if I could find any peace in the world I could find it here just as quick, and a deal surer, the way Pa did, and most of our folks have done. So I'll thank ye, Scamp, and I'll say here before Pa that I'm settled to take care of the homestead and of Ma if she's o' mind to stay here."

They sat quietly a few minutes longer at the grave, when Ben first showed a new authority they had tacitly conceded to him while he was speaking, the authority of host at the homestead and head of the family when they were assembled there. "We all told Ma we'd be back," he said, "and she's alone. We'd best be starting." So they rose and walked up the corduroy arm in arm, all silent in that phase of grief which is love and a sort of joy. And on Sunday, three days later, they opened the will and found that if Ben was disappointing their Pa in not going to college, he had yet declared himself in accordance with the Squire's broader intentions. The homestead went to him alone, and, after numerous personal bequests, John and Ike shared equally in the residual estate.

CHAPTER LXVI

A WEEK after the death of the Squire the entire business center of Byzantium Falls was destroyed by fire, the part that meant the village to the Blackwater group and all those whose tradition was older than the Industrial Age. By evening the twenty-four buildings from Daw Street along the west end of the Mall, and on both sides of Court Street down through Trinity Church, were gone. But all through that day, while the holocaust raged, the new factories along the river did business as usual, and in the destruction of the *Union* office the famous steam engine "Big Byzantie" stood unharmed while its flimsy shed wilted around it.

Due to the southeast gale that carried in the opposite direction the smoke and the thunder of buildings blown up in the path of the flames, the news did not reach the Hollow till early the following morning. Incredulous of the extravagant rumor, Ike and John set off at once with their buckets, leaving their ma for the first time since the Squire's death, while Ben stayed in from harvesting to keep her company. After running Chesty and Mol to the Center and beyond to the edge of the big hill, they saw that it was true. Enormous clouds of smoke, some black, some white, rolled up from the direction of the Mall, two miles below and before them, and drifted away northward on the now diminished wind, the underside of the clouds sometimes reddening and fading with the reflection of flames beneath.

The fact was so vast, so grim, that the fire terror and all sense of adventure faded from their minds. They merely glanced at each other, and let the horses edge down hill at a walk, in no hurry to verify this new death with their eyes. "All gone," each was thinking silently to himself. "The Wheeler gone, and Forest's Hat Store, and Small's, and Carter's, and Grabbot's, and Seth Marlow's, and Applemore's, and Walsh's, and the *Union* and the *Eagle,* and the Flatiron Building, and the Iron Block, and the Merchant's Bank, and Simons's, Dr. Starbuck's Checkered Store, and the Town Clerk's, and the Post Office, and Trinity Church. . . ." "All gone," they both kept thinking—"gone." It was the outer symbol of the inner change that had been the death of their pa but a week ago. Henceforth life would not only be new, it would be on a new stage. Everything that had been before seemed suddenly dim, like a book read long ago.

485

The same flaccid amazement pervaded the village, where nothing much seemed to be happening. There were no horses or vehicles moving, and the streets were almost empty of pedestrians. Those they passed were walking slowly, with heads bowed or lifted to look at them blankly, without greeting. Life was over and life had not begun again.

Ike and John left their horses at Howell Sherwood's and walked down to the scene of destruction, not bothering to bring their buckets. The western end of the Mall and Court Street beyond were still roaring and crackling as if alive, but the flames in the gutted buildings seldom shot higher than the brick and stone walls that still stood, and the worst of the heat had burned itself off during the night. The wide eastern footpath of the South Mall and all the main Mall to the eastward had been opened to foot traffic, and there they stood now, villagers and townspeople, perfectly silent, the eyes of each staring blankly at some particular bonfire, devoid of impulse, thinking absolutely nothing. Ike and John mingled in the rear of the crowd in front of Seth Marlow's stone house, on the unburned eastern side of the South Mall.

The fire was what was called "under control," which meant that it had burned everything it could reach. Just opposite where John and Ike stood was the big stone building containing, among other places of business, Howell Sherwood's bank. By the all-night effort of Neptune Company Number One, helped by the wind, the flames from the ruins of Goliath Walsh's Saddle Shop, blown up with gunpowder the day before, had been prevented from crossing Daw Street, and this one structure of the original line had been saved. As there was no activity, no greeting, no conversation among the crowd, so officially there was little going on. The hose of Neptune Company—handled by Jabe Munson, for they learned later that George Fulton had been badly burned early on the roof of the Flatiron Building—was playing alternately on the bonfire that had been Walsh's Saddle Shop and on the windows and cornices of the stone building that had probably been saved. The other two hose companies and the Hook and Ladder Company were continuing their all-night patrol elsewhere, out of sight at the Court Street end of the ruins.

Across there on Daw Street corner the little hose of Neptune Company, and Jabe and the others carrying it, looked pathetically small beside the gigantic spectacle of desolation that stretched away northward. The bare brick walls of Seth Marlow's General Store and Carter's Drug Store and Forest's Hat Store loomed larger in ruin than before, with their empty door- and window-holes showing nothing but fire and smoke and the unroofed sky behind. It was as if a battle of Titans had been fought there, great forces contending over issues that had in them the fate of mankind. People had lived there forgotten ages ago and had done noble deeds such as those who succeeded them could never equal. Ike took John by the arm and whispered with a dry mouth, "There's the end of old Byzantium." John nodded, glassy-eyed.

Soon after that, they heard a phrase behind them in a familiar voice, a sighed phrase not intended for anybody's ear. "All gone," it said, and again, "All gone." Ike and John looked around slowly and saw Seth Marlow sitting on the sill of his doorway that gave directly on the street, one leg bandaged and hoisted into a chair placed out for him on the broad step. Seth was the captain of the Hook and Ladder Company and was plainly a casualty of the fire. He stared from Ike to John and nodded to the latter, which was all the greeting anyone was capable of that day. John and Ike stepped up and leaned against the door frame on either side of him, saying nothing. Presently Seth lifted his hands in a shrug and sighed, looking across at the one wall which was the relic of his three-generation-old general store.

"No insurance?" asked Ike softly. Seth sighed again, and shook his head feebly. "Lose your stock, did ye?" asked Ike again. Seth nodded, then said in a weary whisper, "Had to be with the Company. They didn't git half my things out. Thousand worth or better." "Figger to open, don't ye?" asked Ike still more softly, almost inaudibly. Again Seth shrugged. "Nothin' to open with," he whispered hoarsely. "Might sell out my share here," with a gesture backward toward the inside of the house. "Lived here since I was born. My part wouldn't fetch much." "Need money do ye, Seth?" asked Ike, leaning down confidentially. "No, thank ye kindly, Ike," said the Hook and Ladder Captain. "I ain't the borrowin' sort."

Ike paused and looked across the street at the stark brick wall with nine oblong holes where windows and door had been, and the big flames licking around playfully inside from the debris in the cellar. Then he turned back to Seth. "How much did ye value the place at?" he asked. "Turned down four thousand two year back. Han't much idee o' such matters. All I've got's yonder, 'cept a share in this," indicating the house, "along with the rest o' the family. What ye see is all's left of Seth Marlow." "I'll give ye five thousand for her as she stands," said Ike quietly, and John threw him a look of anguish. "What say?" asked Seth, glancing up with interest. "Five thousand as she stands," repeated Ike, again almost inaudibly. "I'll ask ye a week to raise the money if ye'll take it. Figger Howell Sherwood's a mite discommoded today." Seth chewed his quid slowly for half a minute, then murmured casually, "Ye've bought 'er," adding, "if ye mean what ye say and ain't foolin' me, ye'll find paper and quill in yonder."

Ike went into the parlor and wrote out the contract, signed it, and fetched it out to Seth who duly signed. Ike carried the contract back, sanded it, folded it, put it in his pocket and returned to the door beside Seth. "What'd ye do to your leg, Seth?" he murmured. "Broke," mumbled Seth. "Fell off a ladder agin the Wheeler like I'd never seen one afore. Doc says it'll lay me up two months." "Figger t' open then, do ye?" "Ain't figgerin' nuthin'," said Seth, " 'ceptin' five thousand'll do me a long spell without sellin' pots and fabrics. Mebbe go back to farmin'. Better life 'n runnin' up ladders 'n bustin' yer limbs."

Ike nodded and was about to add something when, glancing over John's shoulder down the Mall, he swallowed inadvertently. There, in a close-fitting taffeta plaid with a Spencer jacket and fetching be-ribboned Leghorn hat, was Pru Stark, hanging on her ma's arm, and edging her in their direction, her little handkerchief pressed to her mouth and her face the picture of distracted, despairing beauty. She seemed to be trying to find a spot where she could see through the crowd, but she was not ten rods away and Ike divined that she had seen them and was going to join them. "What d'ye say to going home to ma?" he said to John, who nodded, not having seen Pru. "Hope your leg does first-rate," Ike said to old Seth as the brothers turned away and started up toward Howell Sherwood's.

They said nothing until they were on the road, walking the horses out deserted Washington Street. "Makes me kind o' sick," said Ike. "One thing I'm glad of. Pa didn't see it." "It didn't make you too sick to trim poor old Seth," said John bitterly. "Trim him? I didn't trim him," said Ike in astonishment. "If I hadn't bought the ruin ye can be a'mighty sure Grab-bot or Stark or Gadston would have bought it for half what I gave him. I'll wage ye fifty to one the old buzzards are out there counting hot bricks now and buying up uninsured places faster'n a pig gobbles swill. That's what I'm always telling ye. If we don't do it those fellers will. Only they'd really trim him and wash their hands of him. But me having bought it, ye can be mighty certain that if ever I turn a penny by the property and if old Seth comes to want, I'll take care of him—same as I will that Quin feller—same as we'll always look after Master Lane and old Henry. Can't ye see it ain't the same as Gadston and such?"

"Perhaps," said John with a sigh. "Furthermore," added Ike when they'd ridden a ways in silence and were coming out of the village in sight of the hills, "ye'll see that'll turn out to be the best piece of property that changed hands on account of the fire."

After another silence John asked, "What do you want that pile of bricks and ashes for anyway?"

"Figger to build a bank there," said Ike. "Lathrop's Bank."

Part III

JOHN

CHAPTER LXVII

DURING April, 1860, the cholera as usual crossed the Ohio River at Cincinnati and spread northward with the spring. The invader paused to make his grim calls mostly in the cities, passing swiftly as a dark cloud northward over the rural districts, spraying them but thinly with his shafts. The tribute from the little college town of Oberlin had never exceeded a dozen in a year, and the light visitation of 1860 left but two fatalities behind it; one of them, however, of such cruel pathos as touched the devout little town to the heart and put a hard burden on the four ministers to explain the mysterious ways of a just God. This was the second son of Mr. and Mrs. Constant Oaks, seven-year-old Constant, as studious and conscientious a lad as any in that grave, academic community.

Little Constant died during the night of April twenty-ninth, in the midst of the prolonged thunderstorm that marked the end of the epidemic for that year. Constant Oaks made the little pine box himself, and laid in it the black-haired relic which was the image of himself and the outward symbol of the central force of his being, his love for his wife. On Tuesday, the first of May, two hundred men, women and children walked out Lorain Street to the cemetery behind the little coffin, for the father, a clerk in Shad Stevenson's grocery store, was much beloved, and the mother, if not quite beloved, was greatly admired and respected as the leader of the Woman's Rights Movement in the state, a teacher in the Female Department of the college, and a national figure in the Reform Movement generally. After the funeral Shad Stevenson told Constant to stay away from the store as long as he liked, and everyone from the President of the College down urged him to go away for a spell. But instead of that, he sat by the grave under the cottonwood every day for a week.

Little Constant's death could hardly have come at a more embarrassing time for his mother, Octavia Oaks as she was properly known, though the press usually called her "Slavie" or "Slave"—these epithets having been settled on her through insulting rhymes affixed to cartoons. During the near nine years of their marriage and while teaching in the Female Department of the college, Tavie had more than carried out her contract with Connie, and now of all times she knew she should stay by him in

491

this loss of his passionately loved son, this only source of his slight and half-apologetic pride in the world. Yet the Republican Convention, now but two weeks off at Chicago, represented a crisis not only in the nation's affairs but also in the Woman's Rights Movement which, along with Mrs. Mott, Mrs. Stanton, Fanny Wright, Mary Ann McClintock, Miss Anthony and a few others, Tavie had led to victory in state after state up to this critical hour. Besides keeping up her teaching, Tavie was bound, during the next two weeks, to co-operate with the others in deciding whether and how the Movement was to inject itself into the boiling stream of national politics.

As its leading figure in the West, Tavie had sounded out the three possibilities for the Republican nomination in that region, each of whom had visited Oberlin in the past year. Mr. Bates she had cornered with difficulty; he had given her short shrift, and she had reported him as hopeless. Mr. Chase, Ohio's "favorite son," had treated her with polite but condescending evasiveness when she sat next to him at supper at the house of President Finney of the College. But Mr. Lincoln had accepted her own invitation to supper, and had listened with deep-furrowed dignity to her exposition of the unenfranchised position of women as a case of government without consent of the governed within the meaning of the Declaration of Independence, a case of chattel slavery indistinguishable from that of the Negroes.

When she finished her argument Mr. Lincoln said, "Mistress Oaks, since you're a teacher of Greek, I reckon you've seen a little piece called *Lysistrata* by that fellah Aristophanes."

"If you'll forgive me, Mr. Lincoln," said Tavie, "the comparison is unfair."

"Well, ma'm, that's a question of fact in which we may disagree, since it isn't proven yet. Now there are a lot of smart women in the town where I live, and I believe most of them have heard you and your friends speak there. I've taken the trouble to ask around, and I'll bet you a nickel against an old two-cent piece there ain't six women in the town who are hankerin' for the vote or would exercise it if they had it. Mind ye, in theory I can't find any particler answer to what you've been saying. But you've a powerful piece to go yet, Mistress Oaks, before you can persuade us cowardly politicians that the women of the country are specially fretful under being governed without their consent.

"Now there was a neighbor of mine called Nick Nevins, a smart fellah, good provider, and powerful stubborn, unconscionable stubborn about drinkin' green whisky on Saturday nights and causin' his good wife the most exasperatin' difficulties in gettin' him up for meetin' on the Sabbath. She was one of the ladies who got troubled about her rights, and she had a will of her own too. So one Sunday she left Nick snorin' and went off to church wearin' a pair of your bloomers she'd made herself on the sly. Someone must have hustled to tip Nick off before she came home, for when she got there she found him cookin' dinner in the kitchen, all dressed up in one of her best dresses, hoop and all. 'Now what in the world are you up to?' says she. 'Wal,' says Nick, 'since you prefer to wear the pants I'm callatin' to wear the petticoats. And I'll thank you to fetch in a box-ful of wood and be spry about it.' That was the first and last time bloomers were seen in Springfield, and Mistress Nevins has testified to me personally she don't want the vote, so I somehow haven't gone to much bother trying to get it for her."

"Mr. Lincoln," Tavie asked in irritation, "how many of the Negro slaves do you think want their freedom?" "Maybe two per cent, without great exaggeration." "And yet you are for abolition."

At this Mr. Lincoln scowled in an enormous and gentle sort of way that made Tavie feel ashamed of having somehow hurt him unjustly. "Mistress Oaks," he said, "I must ask you to pardon a piece of plain speaking, but I'd thank you to go right out yonder to all your fanatical orators and editors and tell them that what they say about me is a lie."

Suddenly his enormous scowl changed into an enormous smile which reminded Tavie of Ike's, though it was harder, older, and etched in deep furrows. "I must confess," he said, "that I'm mighty sick o' hearin' my voice, for it ain't a pretty one. It may be that I've dozed a little now and again when I should have been listenin' to it. But to the best of my observation it has yet to misquote me by saying that I am for abolition in the old states. In national politics I've just two strings to my bow. One is the restriction of slavery to the states where it now exists; the other is the preservation of the Union; and if I had to snap the first to keep the other squeakin' I'd do it quicker'n greased lightnin'.

"In the long run, I say, either slavery or freedom must go, but to abolish the first suddenly would be a crime near as great as to abolish the second at all. I wish you'd tell your friends that, Mistress Oaks, and ask them to stop flatterin' me with allegations of a lot of Christian sentiments I don't aspire to possess. Tell your righteous friends that, Mistress Oaks, for now you've touched me on a matter everybody in my home town is interested in. And if ever you can drum them up into as much interest in the slavery of women, you can count on my having something as precise to say in the matter. Until then, if you'll excuse the advice of a country politician, I'd say you'd be serving your country better if you'd keep your eyes on the issues of the hour.

"The Union is going to be divided at the next presidential election, or
it ain't. Slavery is going to be extended to the territories, or it ain't. Before
the bar of history those are the questions this generation will answer for,
and they're plenty. Not all the politicians in thirty-three states could introduce female suffrage now if they wanted to. That question may be a
big quarry some day, but just now it's a cottontail skippin' across the trail
of the buffalo herd. And that reminds me," the future President continued,
"of a neighbor of ours back in Kentucky, a sort o' humorous chap
named——"

All these opinions of Mr. Lincoln, Octavia Oaks had reported almost
verbatim to her colleagues in the East, adding that she was more impressed by him than by any statesman she had ever met, that while Ohio
would undoubtedly stand for Mr. Chase at the Republican Convention,
and while she personally would continue to support Mr. Seward because
of his clear stand against slavery in the "irrepressible conflict" speech, nevertheless she would feel that the country was secure in the hands of Mr.
Lincoln.

And only a month ago she had had a letter from Mrs. Mott saying
that the leaders in the East were agreed that what Mr. Lincoln had said
was not only good statesmanship but wise policy for Woman's Rights.
They had decided to concentrate all of their energies on Abolition until
after the presidential election; for, once the slaves were freed, their own
argument would be made unanswerable by the spectacle of ignorant black
men enjoying the vote while they, the enlightened white women, were
held in the penumbra of slavery. Let them turn all their strength to the
support of Mr. Seward who was nearest to an Abolitionist of any of the
leading candidates. Mrs. Stanton and Miss Anthony at least would attend
the Republican Convention. If Octavia and the ladies of the West were
one in these sentiments, let them also come to Chicago, not later than the
fourteenth of May, two days before the Convention, "and together we
shall march forward for righteousness, shoulder to shoulder, unflinchingly,
as we have done these many years."

On receiving this letter Tavie had bartered half her August vacation to
call a conference of Western women at Columbus to act on Mrs. Mott's
proposals, and herself thereafter to attend the Republican Convention. The
conference had been settled for Saturday, May fifth, Tavie to be chairman
of it and the conveyor of the important message from the Eastern sisters.
All this had been announced in Mrs. Bloomer's paper, *The Lily,* with lofty
editorial predictions of what was to be expected from "the dauntless Mrs.
Oaks" and "those great springs of freedom, the glorious states across the

Appalachians." And then, in the stormy dawn of May first, little Constant had died.

After the funeral the remaining three-quarters of the Oaks family sat together on their little parlor sofa, Tavie in the center with her head on big Connie's shoulder and her other arm around eight-year-old Solon, as perfect a rosy-cheeked, blond replica of his true pa as little Constant had been of his. Solon's lip quivered continuously and streams of tears ran down his face, but his teeth were set fiercely and he would not blubber. Suddenly he burst out, "Excuse me, Ma," jumped up, clicked his heels in a bow, and ran upstairs.

Constant and Tavie sat in silence, listening to the fast ticking of the clock in the kitchen, Tavie's eyes on an old scar Connie had got on his wrist when he broke a pitcher just after Solon was born. At last Connie said, "Tave." "Yes, Connie"—she reached over and put her hands on his. "Ye must go to that conference, like ye figgered." "Why speak of it now?" said Tavie. "Ye've done what ye could for us, girl," said Connie. "And from now on, more than ever, ye've to lead your own life." "We'll see," was all Tavie could say, for she was at once undecided about the conference and anxious to check this impulse of Connie's to rub old salt in this new and worst wound of all. "We'll see, only let's not talk of it now."

But Connie, far from wanting to sit quiet with Tavie and his grief, was obviously restless. He kept running his hand through his black mane as he had hardly done at all since little Connie was born. "Tave," he said finally, "I'm hungry. I han't et all day." Indecisively Tavie rose, went out into the kitchen and gingerly lighted the stove with one of the new-fangled sulphur matches. When she had gone, Connie stood up and looked for a long time at the life-sized engraving of his boy in the silvered frame where it hung on the wall beside a similar picture of Ike's boy. Then he knelt against the sofa, facing it. "O, God," he said simply, "the minister's true grit, but he han't a boy, and Tave's true grit but she don't love this one. I'm the feller can help him. Tell me where he is." Then he suddenly shouted in anger, pounding the sofa, "God, tell me where he is!" Tavie came running in. Connie staggered to his feet and towered above her with one elbow over his eyes. Then he fell on his knees and with his face on the floor sobbed in terrible, great convulsions. Tavie dropped beside him and put her arm around him, but he did not know she was there.

Homer and Agatha Hislip came in the front door without a sound and Tavie motioned out into the kitchen, where Aggie continued the preparation of supper. And half an hour later, when they all tried to eat soup in the kitchen, Connie kept insisting that Tavie should go to her conference Saturday at Columbus, until both she and Aggie concluded that he really wanted to be left alone. As soon as she had agreed to go Connie set down his bowl, strode out into the twilight, and spent the night by the grave, returning in time for a silent breakfast.

During Wednesday and Thursday, Aggie cut down for Tavie an eight-year-old black crepe dress which she had worn when her own second baby had died, fortifying the old buckram with a wire hoop which Homer improvised. On Thursday, in pursuance of Aggie's established custom of taking Tavie's children when she went on tours, little Solon took his nightshirt and slippers over to "Uncle Homer's" house across Pleasant Street and a few doors above, on the corner of Lorain. In order to reach Columbus by Saturday Tavie had to leave Oberlin before dawn Friday morning and drive the eighteen miles south to Wellington, for there was no connecting line between the Michigan Southern Railroad from Cleveland to Oberlin and points west and the Cleveland, Cincinnati, Chicago and St. Louis road which ran through Wellington. Connie insisted on driving her down, though Homer offered to do it and Tavie begged Connie to let her hire Frank Stevenson, the grown son of Connie's employer, to take her in his livery rig.

At the Wellington station Connie stood for half an hour with his arm tight around Tavie's shoulder, never saying a word, and Tavie not daring to straighten his wide bow tie. When the train came in sight miles away on the plain to the northeast Connie abruptly lifted her black veil back over her black bonnet, gazed desperately in her face for half a minute, then crushed her in his arms, lifting her on tip-toe, not kissing her but dropping his big head on her shoulder as he used to do back in the Hollow when she was refusing to marry him. Then he held her for minutes while the other half dozen travellers looked away with lumps in their throats and the little engine with its enormous funnel crept nearer, till it hissed, clattered and screamed to a stop, enveloping them in dust, wood-smoke and steam.

Connie pitched up Tavie's roll on the rear platform and when the train started off, snorting and stuttering, she stood there to wave and throw kisses. But Connie only stood watching her with both hands clenched in his hatless hair. When she had been carried off backwards a half mile from the station and the engine was rattling up to travelling speed, she saw through the whirling dust that Connie put his hands to his forehead to see her better. And so she watched him standing there, receding, his dimensions, like those of the station and the track, contracting toward nothing, till lengthening miles away he became invisible and the station, where she knew he still stood, remained for a long time a speck that finally vanished and blended in the sky line.

CHAPTER LXVIII

BECAUSE no trains ran on Sunday, Tavie could not get back to Wellington till shortly after noon on Tuesday, the eighth. Instead of Connie, she found Frank Stevenson waiting for her with his livery carriage. "Afternoon, Mis' Oaks," he said, picking up her roll. "Connie came over last evenin' and asked I should fetch ye." Tavie was glad Connie hadn't bothered, and made out a dinner of coffee, ham sandwiches and fried cakes in the little station. During the four-hour drive home Frank had the good sense to keep his mouth shut against either communication or spitting tobacco juice, and Tavie was left to her own emotions and reflections.

All the way down to Columbus she had fought to clear her mind of little Connie's last agony, and she had partly succeeded in replacing it by memories of his happy moments, the joyful glow of near tears in his black eyes when she returned from a tour, the only real exuberance the serious little lad ever showed when he came running home a year ago with a copy of *Evangeline,* the first prize for general excellence in the Third Grade.

But on the way back from Columbus his last agony had risen again to torture Tavie, and she wanted nothing so much as to pass straight through Wellington and not see Oberlin again for a long time. The last thing in the world she wanted to do was to visit that terrible little grave under the cottonwood tree, and nothing would ever take her out to that cemetery again. The conference in Columbus had endorsed Mrs. Mott's suggestions. Another lady from Ohio and one from Indiana had agreed to go to Chicago. But Tavie had said her decision as to going herself must wait until the last minute, and she would communicate it by telegraph.

On the drive home from Wellington the tenor of her feelings changed again, and a strange sense of comfort came over her. She had mothered big Connie so long that her duties toward him had become a part of the pattern of her life, like a career that had not been altogether pleasant at the outset but to which she had become wholly reconciled, so that she did not question its exactions any more and would hardly have known what to do with herself if its demands on her energies had been removed. As the carriage jogged along, the assurance of lapsing into routine duty dimmed the images of her dying boy and of that horrible, constricted place where they had laid him. Her feelings surged to make up to Connie for those five days' desertion. She would have another child, she hoped, and she could be spared at Chicago. She would study to adapt herself to Connie's grief, which she knew was more total than hers, for she still had the child of her love and he had nothing. So instead of the panic she had anticipated, it was with a sadder but deeper sense of homecoming, more consecrated than ever before, that she began to recognize the farms, then crossed the railroad and proceeded at a walk up Main Street to the Campus, then right on College, and left into Pleasant in sight of home.

With half-hysterical enthusiasm, as if undertaking a difficult but worthy task, Tavie entered the always unlocked door of her little house and told Frank to set her roll in the hall. She was not surprised that Connie was not there. He had spent all of last Wednesday and Thursday at the cemetery, and he probably would continue doing it for some time yet, would probably appear for supper about an hour hence. When Frank had gone she hung up her mourning bonnet and cape on the mirrored antler-rack in the hall and stepped into the parlor with that swift, authoritative, housewife's glance that took in the whole room instantly and knew if any dust had gathered anywhere, or if any article were a half inch out of place.

In that glance she observed two unusual things: little Connie's picture had been removed from the wall, Solon's remaining—doubtless Connie could not bear the little fellow looking at him, and she fully sympathized; and there was an envelope on the marble-top table addressed to her in Connie's handwriting, so neat and cultivated in contrast to his uncouth speech. With affectionate eagerness Tavie sat down in the low, hair-cloth rocker, broke the seal, unfolded the big sheet of foolscap and read:

Monday night—7th

Dear Tave—

Everybody was so nice to me that it made me mad. They were nice to me like they have always been, only more so. They are fond of me sure grit, but mostly they are sorry for me because you have this other life and everybody knows I love you more than you love me. We have done what we could for Con and there isn't anything more to do. I can't stand people being sorry for me any more. I'm going West on the cars Tuesday and it isn't likely you will ever see me again. Just to make it easier, Aggie told me walking home from church that she had a letter from John Lathrop and he's a delegate to the Republican Convention from New York after all and will arrive on the cars Wednesday. Though I've nothing against John, he is the next to the last fellow in the world I want to see. I might kill his brother yet— No, Tave, don't worry, I won't kill him so long as he stays east of the Mountains and don't bother you without marrying you. Anyhow, I'd rather not see John.

If ever there is anything I can do for you write me at the Chicago Post Office and I will get them to forward it. Don't write inside a month, for if you do I won't open it. Don't worry, I shan't be in Chicago, come the Convention. I don't know where I'm going, but it will be a good piece west or maybe south. I drew out the savings and took half, telling Caleb to deliver the other $200 to you. The only person knows I'm going is Shad. I asked him always to put some posies on Con on his birthday and funeral day. I figure Solon will never want, now his pa's so rich. But if ever you or he do want, write me. I figure you can divorce me easy in Indiana, like you talked first off. I am taking Con's picture with me from the parlor. I asked Ag and Homer not to come over to meet you Tuesday, making out I wanted to be alone with you. The real reason is I want you to do a lot of thinking by yourself before you tell Homer I'm gone. He'd get all brustled up and send telegrams all over and, being he's ex-Congressman Hislip and a delegate and a friend of Salmon Chase's and all, he'd likely catch me before I could get into the tall timber. That wouldn't be the straight of it, Tave, and you must stop him doing that. You know I'll come back quick enough if you need me.

I thank you, Tave, for the only joy I've ever known. You've done plenty more than you agreed to, plenty more than I had any right to ask. Now you are entitled to some joy of your own, besides doing good for people. If you find it, write me and I'll be happy true grit. I'll love you as long as I live, and after, if there's any after. It's amighty hard to stop writing so I'll just cut right off.

Connie.

During the next twelve hours Tavie's feelings ran with astonishing swiftness back to their origins, as if the sandglass of her life were reversed. Her first sensations were those she would have expected, and they lasted but a few moments. She laid the letter on the table and felt herself alone in a terrible emptiness in the little house, emptiness in the town outside where there was nothing to center her life but that grave she felt she could not face. What was there to do? What did it matter what she did? She heard the little pendulum clock rattling away in the kitchen. Connie had remembered to wind it! What difference did it make whether she ever wound it again? She sat perfectly still with her lips pressed tightly together. She rocked slowly backwards and forwards, and her rocking seemed to make no impression in the empty house that was now so strange and no part of her.

While these feelings possessed her she did not cry. But suddenly the image of little Connie in his grave and of big Connie going westward on the cars rose simultaneously in her mind. They were both so helpless now— gone where she could do nothing for them. Her lips trembled and she covered her face with her hands. Connie was so fine, so strong and yet such a child. He was sure to get in trouble out there by himself. He was so honest and quick-tempered. She rose and paced back and forth between the parlor and the sitting-room behind, and now the house seemed real to her again.

Yes, she must go out and put flowers on the grave every day until Connie came back. He had said not to write him for a month. She would write him anyway, and if he didn't come back she would write him again. She must get him back. She paused, impelled to go over to Homer and ask him to do what Connie had said not to do. No—Connie was right. That would spoil things, to hunt him like a criminal. She would induce him to come back voluntarily.

She went back to the sitting-room, sat down at the little roll-top desk and wrote him a desperately swift letter, telling him he must come back for his own sake and for hers. They would have another child. The last paragraph of the letter went more slowly than the body of it. She wrote it deliberately, saying that he was mistaken if he thought she hadn't been happy, saying she thought he had been happy too, and that she could not imagine going on without him. Very hesitantly she sealed and directed the letter to the Chicago Post Office, and wrote on the outside, "Connie, please read this. It is of the first importance."

The composition of the letter dispelled the sadness Tavie had felt, and left a sort of impatience in its place. Leaving the letter on the desk, she rose, paced once into the parlor and back again, bethought her of her duties at the College tomorrow, walked out into the kitchen, found that Connie had laid a fire for her to cook her supper, and had left a half-consumed roast of beef in the pantry. For the first time in a week she ate well, and as she was putting away the dishes her mind turned to the many practical decisions she must make.

If she had no reply from Connie by the thirteenth she would go to Chicago. She would go with Homer, who was a delegate and was going to take Aggie. John Lathrop would probably go with them too. She began to think of the passages from Xenophon and Hesiod she had assigned her students. During this last term before final examinations, she must work more closely with the girls individually. Starting tomorrow she must make each of them feel free to come to her. She must discard the mourning veil. She wondered if Solon could tend the garden under her direction. If not, she could probably get Frank Stevenson to help. Should she get in old Mrs. Benton to live with her and get Solon his supper when she was late? She'd leave Solon with Aggie a day or two till these things got straightened out. Yes, the Chicago Convention would be the important event of the year. The Southern delegates having deserted the Democratic Convention in Charleston made it almost certain that the Republican candidate would be elected. The Union party would surely not win. She believed the North was more interested in abolition than in secession. At least the women were. Strange that Mr. Lincoln had said he would prefer to see slavery extended than to see the Union dissolved. That position, if it were understood, would almost certainly eliminate him as a serious opponent of Senator Seward.

Thinking these impersonal thoughts, Tavie put the dishpan away and wiped out the copper sink. Then she paused, looking over the sink out the kitchen window, and her thoughts vanished in a sensation of peace which she did not attempt to analyze. Through the block and across the campus beyond Main Street, the sun was quietly disappearing behind the high cupola of Tappan Hall, the center of the College, making of its lofty shadow a special, early twilight in her garden while the rest of the village was still in daylight. Tavie's eyes fell affectionately on the rectangular border of orchard violets that little Solon had "helped" her set out when he was only three years old. She did not notice that the buds of some of the tulips inside the border had already burst into color. Connie had set out the tulips.

Under an impulse to go over to bring Solon home from Aggie's, Tavie walked through the sitting-room back to the parlor and paused to part the lace curtains and look out at the front yard where the many narcissuses were so gay along the broad sidewalk that she smiled faintly. Solon had set out the narcissuses all by himself just last fall. She turned back into the room and her eye fell on the rectangle, cleaner than the rest of the gray wallpaper, where little Connie's picture had hung. She had an impulse to move Solon's picture symmetrically over the middle of the wall space, and started back for the kitchen to get a wooden chair to stand on. Suddenly she stopped, and lifted a hand to her forehead in amazement.

"Tavie Samson!" she said in an audible whisper; "Tavie Samson, what are you doing, treating little Connie's picture as if it were any old picture that's gone?" Then, *"Tavie Samson!"* she whispered again in still greater amazement, touched with irritation. It was the first time she had pronounced her maiden name in almost nine years. "Tavie Samson—Tavie Samson"—she kept repeating it in excitement mixed with a rising sense of wrongdoing. She stepped back and sat down suddenly on the sofa where she had sat with Connie after the funeral. She felt uncomfortable there, jumped up and sat on the other little sofa opposite, planting her elbows ungracefully on her knees and her chin in her hands and gazing at the arches and columns of the carpet design.

Tavie was too honest-minded to deny the truth for long. It was as if these heavy mourning clothes were falling from her, as if all the years with Connie were sloughing away, leaving her without pretense what she had been before, what she had been at heart all the time. It was suddenly as if Connie had never been part of her life, as if she had never borne his child. Now she remembered the agony of that birth as if it had simply been an accident that had happened to her, without personal significance. It was as if that child had never been born at all. She had been no more than a professional mother for nine years to Connie, and for seven years to his son. The job that had seemed so deeply a part of her that she had returned to it with a sort of joy and without which she would not have thought she could have gone on, this task was now proving so thin a mantle that, in spite of her most generous intentions, it was slipping away in a few minutes.

"You are fortunate," her mind kept saying to her. "You had your great love and you have the child of that love without disgrace, and you are free! You are Tavie Samson again, and you are Octavia Oaks, instructress in Oberlin and nationally known Reform leader as you wanted to be, and your pa wanted you to be! You are free! The world is brighter before you than ever!" With a gasp she jumped up, ran out to the mirror between the antlers in the hall, and peered at her face, whose usual pallor was flushed now with an inward joy she could not control. "You are a beast," she hissed at her image in the glass. "You are an unnatural monster and a harlot." And she gave a little scream, stamped her foot and beat her forehead with her fists.

But when this theatrical effort was passed she lowered her hands, looked straight at herself in the mirror again and there were no tears on her cheeks. There she was, no doubt of it, Tavie Samson, aged but little in nine years, the complexion a little swarthier, but the same long, sensitive face, the same short mouth with the full, red lips, the same piercing brown eyes, and the same fluffy golden hair that would fall wavily now as it used to if she let it down, and still had the single wave all around the crown where it used to swirl out when she wore a rope round it, or a nightcap.

Her high forehead showed many shallow wrinkles, but it had been so when she thought deeply even when she was a girl. Now as she looked the wrinkles smoothed out, and there, inescapably, ruthlessly, was Tavie Samson just as she used to be, smiling, yes, *smiling* at her, impertinently, irrepressibly. "Oh, it's shameful, awful!" she cried, turning away in disgust and pacing back and forth again in the parlor. She heard a scratch at the front door and froze in terror. What if Connie should return now! For a long time she stood with the back of her hand at her mouth, impelled to flee out the back door. Then she heard the scratch again.

It was only Nippins the cat. She let him in. He was more little Connie's cat than Solon's. Tavie ran into the pantry and poured him out some milk. Then she ran into the garden and picked a handful of violets. She snapped off a half dozen near-opened tulips—they would be from big Connie. She ran back to the house, put on her black cape and bonnet, dropped the veil, went out the front door and picked three or four narcissuses—they would be from little Solon. Then she walked with restraint up Pleasant Street to the corner and out Lorain. And as luck would have it, neither Homer nor Agatha nor anyone else saw her, or if they did see her they didn't see fit to interrupt her obvious errand. And at the fresh grave in the well-kept cemetery she added her flowers to the still fresh ones Connie had put there in the morning. And then, for the first time since little Constant died, she knelt in the grass and really wept, not for her son who was dead but for any seven-year-old boy who had died and was down there so alone, without anyone nearby above ground who really loved him.

She prayed for the soul of little Connie and promised never to leave him untended; and she prayed for big Connie who was even more alone; and lastly she prayed for herself and for forgiveness for her selfishness and for strength and wisdom and love to go on caring for Connie if he wished it. But in praying for herself her thought words were only made up as in a speech, and she stopped sobbing. And as she walked home, she was ashamed of feeling faintly self-righteous for a deed of love that had no love in it.

In the house, she lighted the big globe oil lamp in the sitting-room and sat down in the spring rocker to think. Every time she rocked, the spring made a little ringing thump, and she was glad of the companionship of the sound. "Yes," she thought with her ruthless clarity, "it is true, I am glad Connie is gone. I am glad little Connie is dead. I am free as I always wanted to be." And she rocked for a while, with her lips contracted in their tight, fanatical line. "It is a disgraceful thing, and if I continue to feel this way I shall have to keep up the sham, though I shan't be able to deceive Aggie and won't try to. But perhaps it won't continue," and she paused in her thoughts again, rocking, denying in her mind the hope that rose that this sense of freedom would continue. "How do I know?" she rationalized, lifting her hands and slapping the leather arms of the chair. "Perhaps I'm just tired and overwrought and suffering hallucinations." She rocked again till the conviction that it was so, that she was glad, crept up once more into consciousness. "Well, anyhow," she thought, jumping up, "I *am* tired." So she went into the kitchen and brewed herself some weak tea. Then she fetched in some wood for the morning, put Nippins out, lit a candle, blew out the lamp in the sitting-room, and went to bed.

She was indeed exhausted, and deep sleep came instantly to release her from her shame in the sense of joy in her freedom. As if to soothe her for her faithlessness, her last conscious thought was of Connie and how, in that vague and satisfying way of half-dreams, she would somehow make him happy yet and restore his self-confidence.

Yet just after dawn, when the cotton curtains were glowing saffron, and a song sparrow was shouting his joy somewhere, and the bobolinks were tinkling in the open field across the road, and Tavie stirred dreaming and reached vaguely out beside her toward something human, she did not think herself in her dream to be in that big bed in Oberlin where she had never been alone before, but supposed herself in a narrow spool bed hundreds of miles to the eastward, and the pillow she touched was not the illusion of her black-haired, black-eyed husband but the image of that other with the tousled blond mane, the big, merry blue eyes, and that quick, sympathetic, querulous pucker between the eyebrows, the elusive one who had never loved her at all.

Slowly and luxuriously she awoke, her dream blending into the facts of consciousness. She knew it was so; she was glad to be free. She listened to the bobolinks with unashamed joy, then rolled over, closed her eyes again, and dozed. She thought about John Lathrop, coming today, and a deeper sense of peace flowed through her than any she had known in years, since that Thanksgiving eve when John had flirted with her and made her feel proud and secure, though she was already in love with Ike. She had never been in love with John. And yet—and yet—if the old folks only hadn't frightened them by saying they were a match made in Heaven! No, she wasn't in love with John, but of all the men of her age she had known he stood for something deeper, more permanent, perhaps, even than her love for Ike. He was home, and the old ways, and her own people. He had stuck to his ideals as her pa and his pa had, and had refused to take the rich for his law clients even while Ike was becoming one of the richest men in Byzantium. He was minded as she was about the nation, about Reform and abolition. She had not seen him in six years, since she last went back East taking little Connie—but not little Solon, because everybody at home knew there wasn't a blue eye anywhere among the Oakses or the

Samsons! She would see John today, with his big, stately walk, his proud, hawk nose, his steel-blue eyes wide apart, his sensitive nostrils and chin, and that big smile like all the Lathrops that included the world. There would be no unfaithfulness to Connie in seeing him, for she understood from Aggie that he was still in love with the Stark girl. He and she could never be anything but friends. Her thoughts veered off toward Ike, but she didn't want to think about him, so she opened her eyes, looked at her little watch under her pillow, and got up.

It was still only half-past six when she put the breakfast dishes away and she had an hour before her first class. She glanced at the Greek lessons for her classes that day, then sat down at the desk in the sitting-room. There was the letter she had written last evening. Yes, she could no longer deny it. She was glad to be free. Connie was right. The time had come for that separation which he had promised her any time after the first year. Deliberately, she picked up the letter she had written him, carried it into the kitchen, and burned it to the last white cinder. Then she put on her bonnet, purposing to go over to see Solon before he went to school. She wondered if Aggie had any mourning dresses simpler than this heavy crepe one.

It was like Aggie to come in the front walk just at this moment, bringing Solon with her. When Tavie opened the door he rushed in like sunshine, then paradoxically burst into tears with his yellow head against his ma's black bosom. Tavie beamed on him joyfully, knowing it would be impossible to deceive Aggie. When she looked up she saw that Aggie had an armful of black things, and embraced her, exclaiming, "Oh, Ag, trust you to take care of everything!"

Aggie was at first startled at her lightness, but two minutes later she had read Connie's letter and was looking at Tavie with her great, gentle, understanding smile. Tavie wrinkled her forehead, spread her hands and shook her head in a gesture of resigned negation, and Aggie nodded sorrowfully, conveying that it had to be so. "Where's Pa?" demanded Solon suddenly. "He went to Chicago yesterday on some business," said Tavie. "I shall explain it to you after school." "But, Ma, how will Con do without him while he's away?" Tavie pressed her boy to her and said with a trembling lip, "I shall explain that to you later too. It will be quite a long story." Then they went upstairs, and while Aggie crept around Tavie, with a mouth full of pins, fitting the dresses she had brought, her thoughts slipped apprehensively not only to Ike but to John also. It occurred to her that the latter was to have the precarious honor of arriving at an emotional and susceptible moment. His train was due a little after eleven. She told Tavie to come in for dinner.

CHAPTER LXIX

FOR ABOUT eight years now John had been practicing law in Zeb Milliken's office and nominally as his partner, though they kept their clienteles separate and Zeb's was much the larger, both because he was senior and because John's other activities left him but little time to devote to his law practice. In '55 he had become Principal of the Kamargo Religious and Literary Institute, and in '56, upon the organization of the Blackwater County Republican Committee, he had accepted the chairmanship. In '58 he had temporarily retired in favor of Bub Tanofly while himself running for Congress in the district, and had come close to beating Ostrum Applemore in spite of the Democratic boss's torchlight parades, his vested organization with its jobs and seegars, and his *Democratic Union*. Although the tension that had risen between John and Ike in '50 was now relieved and they shared Ike's old quarters over Quin's drug shop, yet John had consistently refused help from his now rich brother. As he had said in that argument long ago at the homestead, he could not accept help from an industrialist, even from Ike. And furthermore, in so far as Ike had any political feelings at all, they were sympathetic to the "Doughface" Democrats.

Now, in '60, back in the saddle as Chairman of the Republican County Committee, John had high hopes of victory. The Kansas-Nebraska Bill, the Dred Scott decision, the Southern threats of secession, the revival of *Uncle Tom's Cabin*, the execution of John Brown, had crystallized the anti-slavery and the Union feeling in Byzantium, and it began to look like a Republican landslide. Bub Tanofly as Secretary of the County Committee had at last organized an old list of Underground sympathizers into a working machine. Also he had headed a syndicate—John did not know that Ike had secretly supplied him with most of Bub's own large subscription—which had purchased the defunct *Eagle* from Humility Halleck, and, John having assumed the editorship in addition to his other duties, the paper had been reborn as a powerful organ whose subscription list was creeping up monthly on the *Union*. Furthermore, John had at last persuaded Solon Samson to run for Congress, and his standing as the first victim of the Fugitive Slave

Law, nine years ago, should be enough to elect him without outside help. Finally, John's own early abolitionism had now taken a moderate turn which brought him in line with Solon Samson's views, with the dominant, local, anti-slavery sentiment, and with the attitude of the national Republican leadership. There was no serious dissension in the party. And so it was with the self-confidence of one who had a district to deliver in November that John set out as a delegate to the Chicago Convention on Saturday morning, May fifth—the day of Tavie's Woman's Rights conference in Columbus, Ohio. In his gray frock coat and gray stovepipe—most men now wore black —he carried his carpet-bag to the station at seven o'clock and boarded one of "Ike Lathrop's hyenas," as the passenger coaches were called.

In that amusement-mad age, all the communities in the northern part of New York still applied the old taboo on Saturday night performances. So Saturday was the time for travelling actors, acrobats, all kinds of showmen, to crowd the southbound train to keep engagements in the larger and more depraved cities in the center of the state. When John stepped into the box-like "hyena"—the roof, except in the very center, was lower than his near six feet three, even without his hat—a quarter of its stiff board seats were already occupied by the miscellaneous personnel of Professor McCarthy's Greatest Show on Earth, a human menagerie of freaks, sharks, contortionists, and third-rate acrobats which had been taking tribute from Byzantium for the last fortnight. John squeezed into a seat at the rear of the car. The train filled rapidly with hoops, frock coats and plug hats. A minstrel show trooped into the car behind, immediately began to sing, and kept it up all the way to Utica.

Only ten minutes behind schedule, the locomotive shrieked and the brakemen on the platforms unwound the chain brakes. All the experienced travellers seized their hats and leaned forward to avoid having their necks broken, the Ladies and Gentlemen of the Greatest Show on Earth squealed and chattered, and in the car behind, the minstrel show cheered. The conductor's bellcord slapped taut and a gong rang. There was a lurch and a jolt with the force of a collision, then a great hissing of steam that enveloped the train as it moved a few inches; then another jolt and a lurch and a pause, another, and another, as if the engine were a terrier shaking its cars; till gradually the barn-like station slipped spasmodically backward; the jolting became more rapid and less violent; the engine released scalding jets of steam over Mill Street, and by the time they crossed Mechanic Street they were gliding at a fairly even ten miles an hour. John settled back in his seat and watched Factory Square slide past and afterwards the raging Kamargo. There was more impatient yanking by the engine till the speed was over thirty miles an hour and the laughter and singing of the show people were inaudible above the rattle, booming and banging of the train. John adjusted his hat and sat gazing out the window, stroking his perfectly trimmed, five-year-old mustache and Vandyke beard. Instinctively he verified the presence of his wallet in his breast pocket and his money belt around his stomach under his clothes. Then he took from his bag the currently popular *Knitting Work: Web of Many Textures,* by Ruth Partington, and settled down to chuckle over "Partington pearls."

At the notoriously sinful village of Bethlehem another bevy of entertainers invaded the train. These were the ladies of a burlesque show, unmistakable by their gorgeous apparel which they did not change even at the filthy prospect of a railroad journey. By their dress and deportment they fell into three groups: one with downcast eyes, chaste, be-ribboned habilliments and timid gestures, simulating the new maidenliness that was in vogue; one with direct, aristocratic bearing, gorgeous in low-cut evening gowns, big, plumed bonnets, enormous hoops, pounds of imitation gems, and wielding long-handled parasols or ribboned staves; and a third group of boisterous ladies of pleasure of the old school, dressed as provocatively as the police would allow, in tight-fitting skirts in defiance of mode.

In a stately procession a dozen of these show ladies entered John's car, already crowded to standing room, and began releasing volleys of sighs and sniffs of disgust at the horrid chance that had placed their superb persons under the auspices of a country railroad. Not a lady but spotted John's distinguished and apparently expensive person and paused by his seat in confused distress, peering far ahead in the desperate search for a place. When they were all in and jammed around him in the aisle, John rose, smiled genially at them all and offered his seat. One of the seeming maidens took it with an easy smile of thanks from under her yellow bonnet, then edged over to the window to make room and glanced up at one of the boisterous trollops in invitation to sit down.

"No, thankee, Maggie," said the other who was painted into complete disguise but for her youthful blue eyes. "There ain't room fer the likes o' me alongside them hoops o' yourn. Me and the tall feller here'll sort o' stand guard over ye, eh, Handsome?" And she gave John a dig with her elbow. The modest one gave her comrade a grateful smile as she settled her green-mitted hands in her yellow silk lap. "We can do turn about," she said in a soft, melodious voice. "Easy, Little Daffodil," said the trollop in a stage whisper. "How d'ye know the Senator here's up t' takin' care o' the two of us?" John grinned, and the seated girl looked up at him intently till he averted his eyes.

Though John had kept himself virgin to women, he was not at all averse to the companionship of ladies of entertainment, having often found them to be the wisest, the most generous and disinterested of friends. He had no sympathy with the current stigma on "fallen women," and as he stood now in the aisle, crowded in among hoops, bonnets, ruffles, legs and bosoms, he looked with contempt upon those of his fellow male passengers who, while glancing at the women with furtive smirks, yet affected a self-righteous indifference and kept their seats. Stooping under the roof, he was wedged between the painted little Jezebel who had addressed him and one of the heavily plumed, aristocratic ladies. Both now let their expensive shawls fall back to give him an aerial view of bosom. The maiden in the seat likewise threw open her green cloak, but her yellow waist was modestly buttoned to the throat.

Suddenly the engine shrieked and everyone braced himself for the ordeal of starting. At the first lurch the duchess on John's left fell bosom first against him, while at the same instant the familiar drab on the other side gave a yank at his arm that braced him on a seat back, and she squealed with delight when it almost buckled and he swayed against her. "Say, honey," she shrilled, "this ain't no place fer attackin' respectable ladies." John laughed and righted himself in time to pick up and restore with decent grace the reticule of the seated maiden that had slid from her lap. Then he gripped the seat back again against the half dozen dangerous yanks of the train that ensued.

While they were still moving at the ten-mile-an-hour village speed, John saw the little daffodil maiden gazing up at him with a kind of gentle candor from under her bewitching yellow bonnet. In general cut her round face was of the same doll type as his still hopelessly beloved Pru's, though her delicate complexion was pale—she wore no "false bloom"; her large eyes were a deeper blue than Pru's; her nose a little larger and more severe; and where Pru's lips were thin and bowed, this girl's were soft and full. As John returned her frank, unashamed gaze, he felt first a warmth like friendliness come over him, then the mounting impulsion of desire. At the same time the girl's eyebrows lifted delicately, she recoiled a little, and a look of surprise and fright came over her face. With a sudden gesture of panic, she put her hand to her mouth and looked out the window, her bonnet hiding her face. Not Pru had ever roused more hunger than was now surging out of John's eyes down around this lovely girl who could not be over twenty.

"Pretty, ain't she?" the trollop beside him startled his spell, and he half straightened up. "Maggie and I most gen'ly work together. Ye do yer lookin' at her, but ye talk business with Buffalo Bertha," pointing to her-self and giving John a big wink. The daffodil girl, so inappropriately called Maggie, turned around to give Buffalo Bertha a look of gentle reproof, then resumed her looking out the window where the landscape was now rattling by at a good thirty-mile clip.

John stood up as straight as he could in the car and gazed at the union of the walls and the roof, the prey of conflicting impulses. Of recent years, while Pru had continued to refuse him all but faint hope, he had found increasingly in women who resembled her the same attraction with which she held him, so much so, in fact, that he was beginning to attach some weight to Ike's argument that all he really wanted was any attractive woman. The Scamp said that he himself could get keyed up about Pru if he'd let himself, but nothing was easier than turning his thoughts from her to half a dozen other girls in town.

With his virginal idealism already weakened by Ike's argument, John now found himself right here with a lady of easy virtue who drew him in the same way Pru did. The train being now in full thunder, he leaned down and shouted in her ear a request for her name and where he might find her late that evening. The girl glanced up at him with something between pride and terror, then looked down and shook her head. Fairly aflame, John shouted in her ear, "I beg you. You are very beautiful." She looked up at him again, then down, and twisted her bag for a moment in her green-mitted hands. Then she rose, stood softly up against him, seized his lapels and reached up with one hand to draw down his ear.

John was swimming with desire as great as he had ever known. "Please do not ask me any moah," she said softly in a Southern accent, while he felt her breath on his cheek, and sometimes her lips touched his ear. To control himself he closed his eyes as he bent down to her, while he felt her bosom against him and her little hands tugging at his lapel. "You must not be kind to me, you hiah?" she said decisively, "faw I see you ah a gentleman and you look like my brothah. You must not ask me any moah." She sat down and stared fiercely in front of her, disregarding the tears that now ran from her open eyes.

John first lifted his head to control his emotion. Then he looked down at her where she sat staring straight ahead, one hand gripping her bag. And as he devoured her with his eyes he suddenly saw something through the lace of her mitt on the back of her hand, an ugly red sore.

Faintness and nausea seized him and, not seeing anything, he staggered through the other ladies to the back door of the car with its ominous sign, "Prepare to die, all ye who pass through this door when the train is in motion." The brakeman in the corner rose, offering his seat, and John took it, the brakeman then opening the door and wedging it back, admitting a little air to the fetid car. Once John glanced up and saw the painted "Buffalo Bertha" looking at him with her forehead wrinkled in a look of combined pity and interrogation—"Won't I do?"

John sat in a trance, while the nausea passed and the regular clatter of the car's trucks became a reassuring sound, something strong and healthy in the world. At last he could smile bitterly. And his first formulated thought was to wonder whether Pru, under the same circumstances, would have been as selfless. He still might talk to the girl, but he decided that she would probably honestly prefer not to see him again. At Bloomington, where they stopped for dinner in the station, he sought for companionship a male acquaintance in the car behind. And when he reached in his breast pocket for his wallet to pay for the meal, he found it was gone.

In angry certainty as to who had taken his money, John borrowed the twenty-five cents from the man with him and ran out of the station after the ladies of the burlesque, who were prudently boarding the train early in the hope of getting seats for the rest of the ride. Abruptly he touched his late flame on the elbow and she docilely followed him to one side, keeping her eyes down under her yellow bonnet. But when he addressed her she looked up at him with a look at once pleading, proud and helpless, and he found it incredible that she was involved at once in the horrors of disease and crime. "Someone," he said, trying to look coldly down at her, "has stolen my wallet. There is little money in it and that I shall not begrudge the clever thief. But there were papers in it which I need and which would be of no value to anyone but myself. If you could find the wallet and its contents I would be grateful and"—here his expression changed to an apologetic smile—"I would reward you if you would let me."

The girl looked up at him with an expression of pride which he never forgot. Slowly she turned away from him, busied herself for a while inside her copious green cloak, then turned back and handed him the wallet with a gesture almost haughty. "I kept the money, sir," she said, "and I ask you not to rewawd me fuhthah. You can have me arrested if you think best. I've been in jail befoah, sir." She dropped her eyes and looked away. "I'd rathuh you did that than have you think hatefully of me." "Don't worry, Miss," said John hoarsely, "I shan't have you arrested."

"Could I ask you one favuh?" she said with her lip now trembling, "for it ain't likely I shall see you again and I told you the truth when I said you looked like my brothah. Could I ask you one favuh, sir?" "Of course," said John, distressed to see that proud little face so wretched. "Will you try, for a little while—perhaps a year, perhaps two years—just as a kind-ness—not to forget me?"

John looked straight down into her beautiful eyes that looked back as straight at him, with some of their pride returning. Avoiding her hands, he took her strongly by the shoulders and said, "You beautiful child, if it will make you any happier I will tell you that I have fallen in love with you, and I shall surely remember you as long as I live." They walked slowly to the train side by side, turned from the platform into separate cars, and each looked back to stare at the other by way of saying good-by. John sat down in a daze, wholly unaware of the minstrel show that was whooping "Dixie" around him. Presently he had the presence of mind to slip his hand inside his waistcoat and shirt and run it along his money belt. He found it intact. But thereafter the passionate assertion he had made proved true. For he not only remembered this remarkable girl always, but he remembered her so well that she influenced, not many years later, one of the principal changes of his life.

CHAPTER LXX

HAVING spent Sunday in Utica, John started for the West on Monday morning, and on the train immediately found himself part of an increasing pilgrimage of cranks, fanatics and charlatans, each bearing his special variation of the single, crusading banner of Reform, all bound for Chicago in the conviction that their miscellaneous hopes for the perfection of mankind were somehow unified and embodied in the Republican Party. In the station John met Mrs. Elizabeth Cady Stanton, who had entertained him in New York in his college days and who was going to Chicago with Miss Susan B. Anthony in the interest of Woman's Rights. Once the train started, John left these ladies to join a conclave of men that gradually preempted half of a car, lounging on the seats, standing in the aisle, exhorting one another above the thunder of the train.

There were a few out-and-out Abolitionists from Massachusetts whose violent perfectionism supplied the only contentious element in the gathering. There were several ministers, including a Baptist revivalist who was determined to set up a tent tabernacle somewhere in the neighborhood of the Convention Hall and who, upon finding that John was a delegate, proceeded to instruct him in his duties as an emissary of the Lord. There were Temperance Workers, bound to effect the insertion of a dry plank in the Republican platform; Prison Reformers who saw a connection between their cause and that of the slaves; Know Nothings who sought a declaration against foreigners and the Roman Catholic Church; Workers for the Amelioration of the Condition of the Insane; members of the newly founded Society for the Prevention of Cruelty to Animals; a spiritualist of abolitionist leanings who had been informed by the spirit of John Brown that the Republican Convention would be the beginning of freedom in America; several Y.M.C.A. workers, including a gymnast; a hydropath, a dentist, a phrenologist, and several dispensers of patent nostrums, these practitioners all convinced that the minds and souls of delegates could function purely only after appropriate treatment of the body, and the dentist asserting that he proposed to examine the teeth of every presidential possibility.

These, and the followers of the numerous other movements of the hour, crowded together and bellowed to each other out of a genuine feeling of brotherhood, the sense of a common cause, Reform, the perfection of America, a cause that now for the first time was somehow single, more important than any of their individual causes, a cause that they all identified with the sanctity of the Union and the necessity of confining slavery within the old slave states. They all knew that the preservation of the Union and the limitation and eventual extirpation of slavery were conditions precedent to the introduction of an earthly Heaven. Once these difficulties with the South were attended to, the New Jerusalem would descend apace.

Just short of Rochester an unfortunate bull disputed the right of way with the locomotive and, at the sacrifice of his life, succeeded in derailing its front truck. In the hour's delay that ensued the Baptist revivalist did not miss the chance to hold a meeting, and John, being the only real delegate on the train, was duly required to address the assembled passengers from the rear platform. John was now an easy stump speaker, and he had been deeply impressed by the spiritual unanimity of these otherwise miscellaneous pilgrims. There was something significant in it, a picture that began to fill that frame of ideal, human perfection which he had carried in his mind since childhood. Standing on the rear platform, his gray hat resting on the brake wheel, his hands and face lifted from time to time in consecration, he outdid himself in eloquence:

"—This train is like a great river flowing westward across the country, and we who have joined this train, and our separate concerns, are so many springs and brooks, each pouring its little power into the central stream that, joining other such rivers in the coming Convention, can do no less than sweep all before it in an united flood. I have no doubt, my friends, that at last, out of all the separate reforms of this generation, we are rising in this united wave, called the Republican Party, to move on to our first positive and conclusive victory.

"And yet, my friends, we are in truth moving in a larger river than this, a river not bound for this victory immediately ahead, this pause in first triumph, this lake, this settlement of these questions of secession and slavery. We are borne on a greater river whose destination lies beyond these things, beyond all the lakes of reform which we shall reach in passing. The name of this greater river is the United States of America, and its course is not in space. It is not moving with this train across the reaches of this land. Its course is in time and in human history, its beginning two centuries and a half ago and its final outpouring into the ocean of perfection to occur, by God's will, before the end of the present century——"

John went on to list the great underlying freedoms that were the ancient currents of that River of America, and he discussed the reforms that had been boiling in it for the last thirty years. He ended his speech with a plea for moderation in dealing with the question of slavery. Immediate and complete abolition would be an affront to the South, a disruption of its economy which would create suffering as great as that of slavery itself. Abolition would come in due course, but it must be effected in co-operation with the South, on the principles of complete compensation to the slave-holders and gradual emancipation of the slaves, to keep pace with their education. This gradual and peaceful emancipation would be possible only when the present apprehensions of the South had been dispelled. The Republican platform should go no farther than to declare against slavery in the territories and in any new states that should be admitted. It should declare against secession, but it should declare just as emphatically against abolition in the present slave states.

John's plea for moderation was received with less enthusiasm than his eloquence about the River of America. But his earnestness and fine address held the audience, and even the Abolitionists suffered no doubt that the cause of humanity was in good hands while the Republican Party could produce such leaders as this splendid young man. When he finished, the Baptist minister swung the little crowd into the revivalist hymn,

> "We're traveling home to Heaven above—
> Will you go? will you go?"

They had barely got through a dozen verses when the locomotive squealed. The minister stopped the hymn, thanked God for the Republican Party, and said a benediction. Everybody climbed back on board, and the journey was resumed.

On Monday evening John attended conferences of delegates in Buffalo, and on Tuesday did the same in Cleveland. On Wednesday morning he left Cleveland for the sixty-mile ride to Oberlin, choosing the daily local train instead of the daily express in order to get a clearer impression of this western country which he had not visited before. Although Aggie had sent home engravings of the village and college of Oberlin, he had unconsciously assumed that it was an outpost of civilization in an otherwise unsettled wilderness. He half expected that the train would run mostly through primeval forests, broken by occasional unstumped clearings round log farm buildings, and that the stations would be trading posts where he would doubtless see Indians in native costume and a few settlers wearing buckskin and carrying muskets, desperadoes of the sort that were said to typify the frontier.

He was surprised, therefore, at first a little disappointed, to see his train in the station fill up with Yankee farmers scarcely distinguishable from those of Blackwater County, N. Y. To be sure, the frock coats which some of them wore tended to the meal-sack fit a little more extremely than was common in Byzantium. Their bow ties were usually askew or hanging untied outside their waistcoats like wide black or brown ribbons. Their untrimmed beards were universally stained with tobacco juice. Their hats were all of the broad, felt, "California" variety, John being conspicuous for the only plug hat on the car. Nevertheless, these were unmistakably his own people, suggestive less of the tight-lipped industrialists of the metropolis of Byzantium Falls than of the more open-countenanced neighbors of his boyhood in Lathrop Hollow. They differed chiefly in a more expansive and easy manner, as if everybody, including strangers, was everybody else's friend, and the car was noisy with laughter and back-slapping long before the whistle cautioned everybody to hold on against the shock of starting. Without exception the men who passed his seat nodded to him with a friendly smile, and at first he failed to notice that this usually changed to a glance of faint suspicion as they passed him by and spat tobacco juice on the floor.

John recalled Homer Hislip's discomfort in Byzantium, his charge that the folks there were "stuck-up" and ceremonious. For the first time now he understood what Homer meant, and he did not feel at all "stuck-up" in grasping the point. On the contrary, he felt uncomfortable, sitting alone and silent in his seat, while all the other passengers were chattering and laughing, many of them obviously strangers to each other. John felt that he was lacking in something fundamental, some instinct of friendliness that was essential to democracy, and he looked from one group to another, smiling at their jokes and hoping that someone would speak to him. But it was too late now. Everybody had chosen his seat and was content with his immediate company. Such glances as came John's way were furtive and, as it now seemed to him, indifferent. At first they had all greeted him as openly as they did one another, but now they all recognized something in him that set him apart.

John looked out the window at the dirty houses of Cleveland, taking no pride in the fact that he was a Lathrop of Lathrop Hollow. "What in hell," he thought, "do these people care about the Lathrops and their Hollow? These people are Americans and they are all equal. It is no concern of theirs whether I am above them or below them. What they feel is that I am not *of* them. These people are all Yankees. They are like our common ancestors who gave to the world and fought for the doctrines of individual independence and social equality. They have carried that old civilization with them while we have begun to take an unseemly pride in our family traditions, setting up a feeble imitation of the English aristocracy against which our fathers revolted. It is among these people that the real tradition of America will go forward."

John enjoyed a moment of self-justification in the thought that his family tradition was one of deserved intellectual leadership, that he was probably better equipped for public service than any man in the car. But this thought gave way again to the feeling of being disqualified for politics of national scope, the fear that his intellectual equipment was valueless if he was not at heart one with such people as these. He suffered from a sort of nostalgia for a way of life that had been real, he fancied, as late as his pa's youth, but which had lapsed in John into theory. Here in the West it continued as a living fact. Somehow he must make himself one with these folks and win their respect. But how? Alas, he must do it in his own way. He must wait. He must let them come to him. It would be impossible for him to assume their expansive manner over-night. So he sat self-consciously looking out the window at somebody planting peas in his little garden across from the Cleveland station. He looked forward to seeing Homer Hislip in his home domain. He wished the train would start.

The whistle blew, everybody grabbed a seat, and the train did start. The bonnet of an old lady across the aisle went askew and she dropped her parasol. Three farmers collided picking it up while John made only an impulsive, preliminary gesture. The train gave another jerk and the three farmers fell down amid the laughter of everybody, including the old lady, but excepting John, who found his face rigid in a sort of painfully social smile. His mind went back to his freshman year at Yale. Not even then had he felt so inept, such an outsider.

If the passengers in the train gave John a sort of idealistic nostalgia, his homesickness became real as soon as the train chugged out of Cleveland into the open country. Here was no wilderness, but wide fields fenced with rails and stone walls exactly as they were at home, in the background big, gently curving hilltops bulging like those of Byzantium against the sun-bright blue sky, and everywhere old, established farms of architecture only one stage younger than that of his pa's house, now his brother Ben's. John's vague expectation of crude, pioneering conditions quickly vanished in the recollection that after all this was the old Northwest Territory, settled almost as early as Byzantium was and by the same New England Yankees. This also was his country, where people did the same things they did back in the Hollow, where they thought and worshiped and laughed and drank and sang exactly as his forebears had done.

As he looked out over that wide landscape, familiar though seen for the first time, he felt a strangely pure sense of home-coming, of going back where he belonged. Here was no problem of modern manufacturing and a lot of irresponsible people coming into wealth and power. Here was the original, agricultural foundation of America. Everywhere oxen were swinging sedately from side to side, dragging the plows across the fields. Already whole bulging hills were furrowed as if a titanic, close-tined rake had swept in long, curving strokes across them, and many farmers were gracefully riding their harrows like careening rafts drawn swiftly over the glebe by horses. The farm houses, here more often painted than in the East, were abristle round the foundations with daffodils, narcissuses and other greenery not yet in flower. Everywhere the cattle were out in the meadows where the dead grass of winter was tinted over with green. At every stop, above the chatter of passengers, John could hear the meadowlarks singing a little way beyond in the open fields.

More than any other feature it was these crossroads villages that gave John the feeling of belonging to this western land. Every one, with its green, its church or two, its cluster of stores, its water mill, was exactly what all the villages of Blackwater County, N. Y., had been in his own early memory, when the Falls with its industrial promise had not risen to precedence and upset the balance of life. The train passed plenty of old-fashioned saw mills, grist mills, cider mills, distilleries and tanneries, but on the whole ride from Cleveland to Oberlin John saw not one factory, not one sign that anybody was materially richer than anybody else, not a single invitation to youth to leave the simplicity of the farm in the greedy and precarious pursuit of money. The pace of life was leisurely and sure, the ends known, as used to be true back in the Hollow. Storekeepers and postmasters sat tilted back against their door-jambs in the sun, often with a little senate of old men on the bench beside them. Everybody had time to think. The restless hurry that came with industry and the hope of wealth had not yet poisoned this land.

Outside on the landscape as inside in the personnel of the passengers, John saw the America of his convictions, an America that still aspired to a perfection beyond money. He considered the thousands of miles to the Pacific, and a great elation came over him. Byzantium, the whole East that was succumbing to industry, was but a little fringe of decay on the Atlantic seaboard. Centuries would pass, an ample age in which a perfect society would become settled and invulnerable, before that infection would attack these boundless regions. John saw no significance in the fact that the train twice took to village sidings and waited patiently for freight trains to crash by, headed eastward, one jammed with cattle on the hoof, the other loaded with grain from the elevators of Chicago.

He grew exuberant and joyful, even as his neighbors on the train were, irrepressibly optimistic and friendly. Impulsively he touched the shoulder of one of the men in the seat in front of him and motioned him back. He did not observe that the man first turned from his smile with a furtive half-sneer, then swung back with an exaggerated swagger. Immediately they began shouting politics above the racket of the wheels, and John found, as he expected, that his new acquaintance was a Republican. John did most of the talking, while his companion merely waggled his beard, chewing his quid judicially and occasionally spitting on the floor and splattering John's shiny boots. Thus he attributed to the man his own ideas and found him most stimulating and congenial. John was delighted. He was getting on with these splendid people, these true Americans. He was deeply flattered. It did not occur to him that the stranger beside him might be even more deeply and subtly flattered, that the more he listened to John's cultivated accent the more he felt himself superior both to this Eastern stuck-up and to the other people on the train.

This man got off at the last station before Oberlin, and immediately thereafter John was introduced to a new aspect of the West, an absolute flatness stretching to a level horizon broken only by farm houses, now more widely separated, and occasional clumps of trees. He had read of the great plains, but this beginning of them held him spellbound, aghast at the distances, the enormous dimensions, the romantic mystery of sheer, limitless extension. To him that great emptiness was an inspiration, a symbol of infinity, not a reminder of the littleness of man but an intimation of his strength that would go on across those reaches until he found his grail, his truth, his perfect world. He thought again of the vastness of the territory of this nation and of the insignificance of the East in comparison to what remained waiting to support great populations. He thought again of the figure of that great river of aspiration which he had used as a symbol of the nation in a speech two days before. He imagined that river flowing indomitably across this plain, which he knew stretched from here a thousand miles westward. There was room, there was time in which to fail and fight on again. With the convention in Chicago, America was beginning her greatest journey. Here was the real America, the America of the future. John had an impulse to jump off the train and run anywhere, to run as fast as he could until he dropped.

Meanwhile one of the clumps of trees on the horizon had been increasing in size, and buildings became visible around it. The train veered southward toward it. Presently the brakeman opened the door, letting in a refreshing cyclone of dust. "Oberlin!" he shouted through cupped hands. "Station's Oberlin!"

CHAPTER LXXI

H'OME R H I S L I P was waiting at the station, and John was immediately struck by the change nine years had wrought in his brother-in-law, nine years of which four had been spent in Congress and the last six as Chairman of the Republican State Committee and first lieutenant of the state boss, Governor Salmon P. Chase. Homer's former penchant for orange and green in dress had given way to a sartorial elegance which equalled John's in restraint if not quite in ease of carrying it off. His frock coat fitted him smartly and differed from John's only in being fawn-colored, with a stovepipe hat to match, where John's scheme was gray. Where John's waistcoat was green velvet, Homer's was of white satin. Instead of the conventional, wide black bow tie which John wore, Homer had a large brown cravat which matched his suit and was so copious that it almost obscured his high collar. In contrast to John's dark, pointed beard and mustache, Homer's beard was cut off straight like a turf-colored spade and his upper lip was clean shaven.

He greeted John with an exaggerated manner which had been practiced so long it was now automatic, his left hand swinging out his hat in a splendid curve while he bowed deeply, glancing upward with a smile, his right hand reaching far forward and up to clasp John's fingers lightly, the whole gesture giving the impression that he was greatly honored to meet his guest while at the same time he wished to keep his posterior person as far away from him as possible. Having completed this ceremonious greeting, he instantly stepped forward into an upright stance, slipping into a close pressure of the clasped hand, while the other hand seized his friend's elbow, his honest blue eyes gazed profoundly into the other's, and he said with fervor, "By God, old fellow, it's a great pleasure to see ye!"

This ritual being over, Homer backed off, still holding John's hand, and looked him up and down with a most hospitable smile. "Well, I see ye're the same old swell. After all, we don't change much, do we, eh?" John was put to it, for he had never dreamed anyone could change so much in nine years as Homer had. "You are looking splendidly, Homer," he said. "Politics certainly becomes you. This is a pleasure I have looked forward to so long that it's hard to believe it has truly arrived." "Well, sir, we've got ye now and we figger to keep ye as long as we can," said Homer, picking up John's bag and leading off around the little station, his open coat swinging. John followed, wondering where the old Homer was, the boisterous crudity with a chip on his shoulder, the scion of this wide, simple, unspoiled country. For better or for worse, Homer had certainly come on!

"I fetched the new buggy," he said, stowing John's carpet-bag in the rear under the seat, "figgerin' to drive ye round the campus before dinner. Jump in. Folks all well at home?" As John reported on the good health of his ma and Ike and Ben, they jogged out onto the Main Street and Homer began pointing out the houses of divers leading citizens, while explaining grandly that most of the newer and finer houses were on the other side of town. After two long blocks they turned left beside the original village green, now the college campus. "Well, my boy," said Homer with a nonchalant effort at understatement, "here's our little college." And he held the horse to a walk, himself gazing at the cluster of buildings judicially, as if he were now appraising them for the first time, while inwardly he awaited the word of authoritative approval.

John had seen many engravings of Oberlin, and he understood its significance in the educational world far better than Homer did. He had expected just what he saw, a well-kept set of college buildings, similar to any of several institutions in the East. Yet he felt something was expected of him, and duly exclaimed, "That's an all-fired fine college, Homer, as handsome as any I ever laid eyes on!" Whereto Homer replied, "Not a bad lot of shacks." And the atmosphere glowed with the temporary nourishment of his pride. They turned right round the campus into Professor Street, Homer pointing out Ladies Boarding Hall on the corner, where Tavie taught, then the Chapel, French Hall, Tappan Hall, the Union School, and the new hall, as yet unnamed.

As they turned right again into Lorain Street, Homer suddenly fell silent and stared straight ahead with a statesmanlike scowl. John was afraid he had somehow offended him and quickly inquired about the fine church ahead on the left. "First Congregational," said Homer in a remote voice. "Best in town. We go there." Then he stopped the horse opposite the church and continued to scowl through an impressive pause.

At last he said, "I regret that the time has come when I must tell ye some bad news. A week ago Tavie's second boy, little Constant, died of the cholera. As if that wan't plenty, a few days after the funeral Connie set out fer the West, leaving a letter for Tavie that he was gone fer good. I offered to telegraph the Governor to have him stopped and to go fetch him back myself, but Tavie argued if he didn't want to come back by himself she didn't want him. An't sure yet I done right. Tavie's true blue. Outside of wearin' mournin', ye wouldn't know her heart's likely breakin'. She don't know yet what she's goin' to do about the house and Solon and all. Maybe nothin'. They're comin' to our house fer dinner. It's only a block down yonder. Ye can see the wing on the corner." He pointed with the whip. "Aggie said I should warn ye."

John's first thought was a moral one, the perception of a sort of bitter justice in this as far as Tavie was concerned—secretly, he had always felt that that second child was a mockery, and now he was not astonished that a just Fate had taken it away. His next impulse was one of fear for the other boy, Ike's little Solon; the prospect of seeing him for the first time had been his happiest anticipation on this trip. Then his mind veered to poor Connie, the little son he had lost, and his sympathy went out to that honest, tortured soul. John stared at the dashboard, feeling that he would never see him again, regretting that the last time he had seen him, nearly ten years ago, he had made Connie jealous by frolicking with Tavie.

"Tavie'll be coming along any minute now," Homer interrupted John's thoughts. "We'd best git along, so ye can sort o' git settled before dinner." "Thanks for warning me," said John. "It's powerful sad," said Homer with a sigh, then clucked to the horse and held him down to a funeral walk. It was plain to John that Homer knew nothing of the real situation. "Hope ye'll like our house," he now changed the subject, having performed his unpleasant duty. "Picked out the ironwork at Cleveland. Best in town . . ."

John heard him murmuring on, but noticed little of what he said. In his own soul a new unquiet was stirring, a faint fear, a new form of the old self-consciousness with Tavie that had been established by their parents' untimely conviction that they were made for each other. Defensively, the image of Pru rose in his mind, and was immediately obliterated by that of the little burlesque girl on the train. For some moments he ruminated on her lovely image.

As they turned into Homer's drive John was hardly aware of the trim white house with its symmetrical wings, each with its porch and elaborate iron trellises, the whole yard surrounded by an intricate iron fence. As they passed the kitchen he heard a cry and jumped out of the buggy in time to catch Aggie in his arms and kiss her with an almost lover-like passion. Here was something substantial indeed. But his delight passed as quickly as it arose. Not even Aggie was substantial enough. As he walked to the kitchen door with his arm around his sister his only thought was that Tavie would appear any minute now. He would as lief have been somewhere else as just there at this moment. Tavie bereaved and entitled to his sympathy. Above all, Tavie eligible again. It would be the same as it had always been—only worse.

In the kitchen Aggie stood John off and appraised his six feet three, not at all disconcerted by that big smile beaming down at her, that smile so like Ike's and yet so relatively vacant, so much more detached and less immediately interested in her on whom he was bestowing it. "Your beard is scrumptious, 'Paloosa," she said. "And it scratches more than most," she added, rubbing her face. "It's capital to be here, Sis," he replied. "Where are the children?" "Homer gets back from school about a quarter-past twelve," she replied, pointing to the busy, pendulum clock which thereupon rapidly struck off noon. "He'll likely bring Solon—Oaks" (with a faint, sly smile) "along with him. Tavie and Solon are dining with us. Did Homer tell you?" "Yes," said John, and he suddenly avoided her eyes, swinging round to appraise the large, immaculate kitchen, redolent with dinner and sunlight tinted by four windowfuls of geraniums and green and white curtains.

Aggie guessed the reason for his nervousness, and at the same moment the comfort of the house began to dispel it. "By Jiminy, Ag," he said, putting his arm round her again, "you've made a home here that Ma'd be proud of." And Aggie glowed to what was the first sign of her brother having really arrived.

"Where's Sarah?" he said. "She was with me when you drove in," said Aggie, looking around. "Sally, come out from behind the wood-box. This is your Uncle John I told you was coming." John followed Aggie's look to where his three-year-old, golden-curled, round-cheeked niece stepped tentatively out from behind the wood-box and stood in her blue cashmere dress and white apron tied on the shoulders with blue ribbons, appraising him with head tilted on one side, the picture of unembarrassed, conservative curiosity.

John caught his breath in unfeigned amazement. Instantly sensing her conquest, the child's mood changed quick as the flash and flare of a match, and in a visible glow of gold she dashed headlong toward John, holding up a wooden doll and exclaiming, "See! See! See!" John would have caught her up but she rebuffed him, thrusting the doll full in his face and repeating, "See! See! She's my baby!" "I see," said John. "She's a nice baby." And again he reached out to take her, but again she drew back with little stamps of her feet, shaking her curls, and held up the doll again, commanding, "Kiss it! Kiss it!"

John solemnly took the doll and kissed it, saying, "Nice dollie, nice baby," then handed it back to little Sally, who snatched it, pressed it to her bosom, and jumped up and down, emitting squeals of joyful laughter, which she continued to do as John swung her high, then settled her against his shoulder whence she drew back and, with a captivating smile, began to stick her finger into one of his features after another. "That's your nose," she said, giggling. "That's your eyes. That's your ears. That's your mouth." And when John closed his teeth softly on her finger she drew it out, danced in his arms, squealing with joy again, then stuck it back in his mouth and said, "Do it again." Then more squeals—more, "Do it again"—more squeals—more, "Do it again." And this game would have gone on through eternity had there not been a sudden step on the kitchen porch whereat Aggie saw John visibly stiffen and forget the child in his arms.

"I want down," said Sally abruptly, and John set her down as Homer came in carrying John's coat and bag. "Forgive me, Homer," he said, "for not helping you unharness. I was led astray by this young lady," and he nodded down at Sally, who was now showing her baby the stove, perfectly oblivious to the undependable male world. "All keerect, John," said Homer. "Ye ain't allowed to do a lick o' work on these premises." Then he added, turning to Aggie, "Ain't Tavie come yet? Come along, John. I'll show ye yer diggin's."

John felt strange and uncomfortable again. He was glad to move, to retreat, to follow Homer through the bright dining room and dark front hall into the best guest room, which was on the ground floor in the north wing, heavy with mahogany, gloom, and the stuffy, dry odor of perennial newness. The big, door shutters on the porch, having been opened but yesterday, admitted a little light through the outer trellises and vines, a little light which the gray, embossed wallpaper received as reluctantly as the unworn, Chinese-patterned black, red and white carpet now received the feet of the intruder. Aggie had put a bowl of violets on the black marble-top table and another on the enormous dresser, but their color was not enlivening and their scent seemed rancid in the dry stuffiness of the room.

"Well, my boy," said Homer, setting John's dirty roll and coat on the immaculate, heavy lace counterpane, "this is the finest room in the house—fact is, though I wouldn't repeat it, it's the best in Oberlin. An't seen it beat, not even t' Washington." John nodded and smiled his approval. "It's an all-fired fine room," was all he could say. "Only room in the house, outside the kitchen 's got runnin' water, hot and cold. See?" And he ostentatiously turned on the two faucets in the arched marble recess that held the washstand.

"Figger next year t' put in a bathroom. Meantime ye'll have to do with the old backhouse. That's an outside door yonder. Well, my boy, come out when ye're o' mind to. I figger dinner's ready now and only waitin' fer the boys and Tavie. There she comes now, by Cracky," he added, pointing out through one of the French doors. But instead of looking, John merely swung off his coat, hung it on one of the line of black and white glass-headed hooks beside the washstand and busied himself with the straps of his bag. He wished Homer would leave, or bring him a drink, or both. But instead he merely stood uncertainly behind him, murmured something about the "best portieres west of Buffalo," and at long last said, "Well, my boy, come out when ye're ready." And John heard him close the door.

Mechanically he brushed his clothes, washed, changed his collar, tie and cuffs, brushed his hair, beard and mustache, went out to the backhouse, and returned. He did all this in the sort of hectic daze he remembered having felt years ago when he first visited in strange houses in New Haven and New York and was afraid of doing something awkward. He wasted time over everything, though he knew perfectly Aggie was waiting dinner for him. He arranged his razor, shaving brush, and soap stick on the washstand. He took out his black evening suit and hung it up. He went out to the backhouse again.

Annoyed at himself, he strode impatiently to the dresser and, leaning forward to the mirror, looked closely from one to the other of his darkened, steel blue eyes in an effort to plumb his own soul. "What's up with you, John Lathrop?" he whispered. "Don't you know how to behave? Tavie's supposed to be bereaved and you think she isn't. You're bound to sympathize with her, and you don't feel any sympathy. Well, what of it? In God's name, what of it? Can't you carry off a simple thing like that?" He turned away, pushed his hands in his pockets and looked out the side window. "Certainly you're not in love with Tave," he thought. "Haven't seen her in six years. Weren't in love with her then. Weren't ever in love with her. Good friend. All-fired glad to see her. In mourning. Husband living. What's the hurra's nest?"

There was a feminine tap on the door, and he swallowed hard. It opened a crack and Aggie said, " 'Paloosa, when you come out go straight across the hall into the parlor. There's somebody—two people—waiting to see you there." "Be right there, Ag," John called cheerily. "Hope I haven't kept you waiting." She closed the door. John turned with a sniff of self-disgust, crossed the room, re-opened the door, crossed the hall and walked into the parlor with the long, stately stride he always assumed to reassure

himself in going forward to speak on a public platform, while his face
set in a conventionally sympathetic smile and his mind imaged the friendly
kiss he would give Tavie and the kindly words he would say.

Tavie instantly altered all that. Like a golden sunbeam, for all the
world like his little niece Sally, framed in a black bonnet and flouncing
black skirt, she leapt up from the hair-cloth sofa and came running to
him with hands outstretched and a joyful smile. The first thing he knew,
he had given her not one but three great warm kisses on the lips and
was pressing her close to him, holding her under the elbows, and beaming down into that rich, open, quite un-Tavie-like smile that made not
the slightest picture of sadness.

Her black bonnet was cut far back so that her golden hair waved out
from beneath it over her ears. She had always been pretty, but now, for
the first time in John's observation, she was beautiful. There was a glowing, mellow, relaxed maturity about her, a sureness that was in contrast
to the old Tavie who was forever tense and harassed by her ideals, either
for herself or for the world. She was greatly changed even since her visit
home six years ago, when Ike and John had agreed that for all her importance in the Reform Movement and at Oberlin, she was as far from
contentment as she had ever been.

As John looked fondly down at her now, his sensations were as different from anything he had anticipated as they were from the hungry desire with which he looked down at Pru on the rare occasions when she
let him kiss her. He felt comforted and at peace, as if he had come home.
For the first time he was happy to be here. How absurd that he should
have been nervous at the prospect of seeing her! This was better than
love surely. This was like seeing your long lost sister—"Yes," he thought,
"even better than seeing Aggie." As if countering his own thoughts,
Tavie now leaned back a little, took his arms in her hands and shook
him affectionately, then paused and spoke the first word either had
uttered—"Oh, *ohhh,* I'm so happy! And I thank God it's you who have
come, and not Ike." And she threw her head back, closed her eyes
ecstatically for a moment, then thumped her head forward again on
John's chest and held it there affectionately while her hands tugged at
the lapels of his coat. John remembered how his wallet had been lifted,
and chuckled. Tavie leaned back and cocked her head on one side.

"What are you laughing at you—big—galumpus?" she said mockingly.
"Nothing I can tell you now," he said, still chuckling. "But, Tave"—his
face grew eager and serious—"if you're glad to see me, think how glad
I am to see you and to be here just now when you need"—quickly she

thrust up a hand and pressed it to his lips. "Not a word of that now. There will be plenty of time. Here"— She turned away quickly—"Here's Solon. Solon, this is Mr. Lathrop, your Uncle Ike—I mean John—I told you about."

Eight-year-old Solon, who had been watching them with faintly contemptuous dignity from the window-niche, came forward with assurance, extending his hand, and said, "I am most happy to meet you, sir." John, still holding his hand, crouched down and looked straight into his own childhood, his own blond, dancing-blue-eyed brother when they were that age. He was pure Ike, not a sign of Samson or Oaks about him. John looked up at Tavie and she nodded quickly, looking more like her old, nervous self. Then she whipped up her handkerchief, stuffed it against her mouth and turned away.

John jumped up and said, "Come, Solon, I have something to show you," and led him across the hall into his bedroom whence Solon emerged in a moment with a small bow and arrows and dashed down the hall, shouting, "Hi, Home, look-it this!" John came out, bearing another bow and arrows destined for eleven-year-old Homer, and a China doll with real hair destined for Sally. Tavie came forward to meet him, smiling her way out of brief tears, and stood looking up at him inquiringly. "He's perfect," John said, whereupon Tavie lowered her head for a moment again, wiped her eyes, smiled up cheerfully, and said, "Forgive me, John." They walked down the hall together, with their arms about each other's waists, lengthening and shortening their strides respectively in order to keep in step.

Dinner went off with unseemly hilarity, until Homer gave Tavie a glance of dignified reproof, and the deep lemon-pie was eaten in solemn silence.

CHAPTER LXXII

THE BOYS had to run for school, and the moment they were out of the house Aggie's love of intrigue overcame her apprehensions for John. While he went to his room to fetch remembrances for her and Homer from home, she got and persuaded her husband's disapproving ear, and the rest was easy while he was showing John the house and the barn and she and Tavie were doing the dishes. When the men returned from their tour of inspection, Aggie was already putting on her bonnet. Fifteen minutes later Sally was tucked away for her nap and Mr. and Mrs. Hislip rattled out in their double carriage, the back seat covered with linens and sweets for certain widows and orphans in and outside the village.

"Aggie left us so we could talk," said Tavie. "The parlor's the most comfortable place. Have you cigars or whatever you want?" Presently they settled themselves in the parlor, Tavie on the sofa with some knitting, John in a big, blue plush chair with a saucer for ash tray. "You see," Tavie said, while John was lighting up, "this is probably the only time we shall have to talk, my present situation being what it is. Oberlin is liberal enough in its *ideas,* but extremely strict in practice. I shall be on virtual probation merely because my husband has left me, shall probably have to board with some respectable family. And if it were known that I were entertaining a man while I am in mourning, even with Aggie and Homer present, I might well be dismissed. By now, the whole village knows a handsome man is visiting the Hislips, and they know I often dine here." "Perhaps you'd better go now," said John. "No," replied Tavie. "Village gossip takes a few days to reach the college. There is little danger in this one indulgence, but we must not do it again."

There was a short silence which Tavie broke. "How's Ike?" she asked without raising her eyes. "Same as ever," said John. "Question whether he or Gadston or Lem Grabbot is the richest man in town, and Ike only going on twenty-nine, though he looks much older. Virtual president of the railroad now, though his title is Executive Vice-President, old Squire

Fulton being still nominally the President. Ike's bank was the only one came through the panic three years ago, because he had the genius to sell the bank's bonds of western railroads while they were still high. Saved Bub Tanofly and Kirkwood from bankruptcy by buying their stock in the bank, so he's sole owner now. Coining money with the Engine Company——"

"But, John," broke in Tavie impatiently, "I didn't ask about Ike's finances. How *is* he? Is he happy? Does he ever—seem to miss me?"

John blew a lot of smoke before replying. "Tave, Ike's probably closer to me than anybody in the world, but I can't make him out. Sometimes I'm convinced he's the most independent and courageous of any of us, as when he gives off without shame that he's an atheist as far as church goes and so gets the village down on him, or when he holds out against most of us on slavery and secession. Says that if we drum up trouble with the South he'd see the Union split in two before he'd go to war. You have to admire that in him, for everybody knows he's not a coward.

"But at the same time, though he's got over the sharp dealing that used to distress us, I can't see that he has any real object in life except to make money. He can't even say any more that he's doing it for the family, for neither Ben nor I will let him help us, outside of presents and such. I know this hurts him, though we all have a clear understanding now."

"But do you think he's happy?" persisted Tavie. "Hasn't he some connection with the world, or with people, that enriches his life?" "None of importance that I can find," replied John. "He's generous. Gives away plenty of money to needy people, and to all his employees whether they're needy or not. He's popular with most of the village, always has a kind word for everybody. But he cares nothing for politics, Reform, the country. Thinks I'm 'barkin' up an empty tree,' though I think he's more fond of me than of anybody alive—yes, even more than he is of you." "That's not much," said Tavie almost indifferently.

"Funny," continued John, "Ike's attitude toward me is almost the same as Pru's—only, alas"—this with an ironic smile—"he's a thousand times more attached to me than she is. They both think I'm wasting my time because I refuse to take clients and causes that would enrich me, and have persuaded Zeb Milliken to the same policy. Sometimes I think Ike is better suited to Pru than I am. They agree on most everything. The three of us go to parties together mostly. Everybody knows that Pru won't have me. Ike and I are getting to be as hopeless bachelors as the old Marshfield boys." John paused and smoked a moment, then resumed.

"The important thing in Ike is something he has all by himself, something he calls God and won't talk about often. I think he's happiest when we ride out to the homestead Sundays, and he spends most of the time alone down in the lower meadow." "I know," said Tavie. "Aggie has tried to make me understand Ike and his religion, but I can't. Maybe that was the trouble from the beginning." "I don't understand it either," said John, "though there's something strong in it I honor without understanding it." After a pause John continued, "Anyway, I think I'm more attached to Ike in a permanent sort of way than to any person in the world, perhaps more even than to Pru." "I'm glad of that," said Tavie, shifting a needle. "I hope you don't forget it." "Please don't lecture me about Pru," said John, with a pleading tone. "I shan't," said Tavie. "That would be unseemly, since I'm jealous of her." "On whose part," asked John with a smile, "Ike's or mine?" "Both," said Tavie candidly, not looking up.

John smoked a few moments, then shifted a leg. "But, Tave, you're the important person just now. Homer told me what's happened. I wanted to see if I could do anything for you, something besides just talking about Ike—though I know that's important. Do you want to talk about yourself? Do you want to know that I sympathize as only your almost oldest friend can? Or do you want to avoid the subject?" "I want awfully to talk," said Tavie, "but it isn't easy, you know." "I know," said John; "then don't try." "I must," said Tavie. "It's our only chance." She laid down her knitting, but kept her eyes down, and John noticed the color leaving her face. "There's one subject, however," she said, speaking distinctly and with lips compressed in her old, tense way, "one subject which I would prefer to avoid. That is—the boy. I wish no sympathy on that score, and I do not wish to discuss my own feelings, even with you." She looked up with a hard expression, and John's gallantry made him close his mind against all deductions. "Very good," he said simply.

Tavie picked up her knitting again, and the color came slowly back into her face. John was wondering what she did want to talk about, and how to make it easier for her, when she looked up again and began speaking easily and earnestly. "To begin with," she said, "as I told you at first, I can hardly tell you how grateful I am that you turned up just at this time, you instead of Ike. I need your comfort more than anybody's right now, because we are so alike in some ways. I have never really known what you thought about—everything, and I've honestly worried more about your attitude than anybody else's, you and Aggie being the only ones who know the whole story. Ike *has* told you the whole story, hasn't he?"

"I think so," said John, "and please don't think I blame you a bit, Tave. There was, of course, a serious wrong back in the very beginning, and that was Ike's fault, not yours."

"Oh, no, it wasn't," said Tavie, looking up smiling. "It was all my doing, every single bit of it. John, my dear, you must know the world well enough to realize how easy it is for a woman who isn't positively loathesome to capture almost any man, *in the way I captured Ike*. To make a man really love you is another matter. Sometimes I think a woman's artifice can have nothing to do with that. I was young and determined and in love with Ike. It seemed that if I could only once—love him—that way—I might get over it. Perhaps in my silly, conceited little heart I hoped that if I could get him in that way he would really be in love with me. But he never was in love with me, and if I had married him we would both have been miserable." "I'm not so sure of that," said John. "Yes, we would, both of us, because we would have had nothing in common to compensate for the fact that Ike didn't love me."

John shifted his knees again, thinking of Pru, as Tavie continued, taking up her knitting: "I learned my lesson, that nature's provision is wise. A man should make all the advances, for a woman must be sure a man is in love with her before she gives in. If ever I fall in love with another man—which is very doubtful—he'll never know it until after we're married, and there will be no marrying until after a long chase. No. Ike was not in the least to blame. A man with a speck of gallantry could not have refused me, and Ike never stopped asking me to marry him even though I at least knew he was not in love with me. Don't blame Ike for that. And I don't think you should blame me either. I took a crazy chance, and I think I can say I have taken my medicine." "No," said John, "I certainly never judged you harshly for that, Tave. I shall always admire the courage you showed, believing as you did that marriage would have made one or both of you unhappy."

"But Connie"—Tavie looked up anxiously—"Connie, I take it, is another matter with you? Do you think I wronged Connie? You know I didn't deceive him?" "Yes, I know that," John nodded with assurance. "Well," continued Tavie, "which do you think would have been fairer to Connie? To marry some nonentity elsewhere, come here apparently deserted, have a child, and live in the same town with Connie? Or to do what I did—marry him without loving him, be a good wife to him,

and have his child which was a great joy to him and would have continued to be so if fate had not intervened? I was fond of Connie, would
have done anything possible for him. I didn't and don't love him, and of
recent years he has grown bitter about that, though the boy was a great
compensation. The whole thing with Connie will be a doubt in my soul
as long as I live. I am not arguing that I did right. I don't know. There
are only two people in the world whose opinion might reassure me. My
pa is one—and I dare not talk to him. And you are the other."

Tavie looked straight at John with a sort of eager anguish, and he
looked back as straight and said, "Tave, I know you did right. Connie'll
never love anybody but you. He's that kind. You gave him almost nine
years and you had his son. If anything happens to him now, it was bound
to happen anyway, only otherwise he would have had no happiness, no
compensation at all. It seems perfectly clear."

Tavie dropped her knitting, jumped forward, sank in her hoops at
John's feet, rested her elbows on his knees and looked up with tears
shining.

"Do you really mean that, John? Are you convinced of it?" "Absolutely," said John, and he leaned forward and kissed her forehead. "And
I don't need to tell you how much I appreciate your wanting my opinion."

Tavie went back on the couch and knitted silently for a moment. "Poor
old Connie," she sighed. "Poor old Connie," John echoed. "He's certain
to get in trouble," Tavie said. "He's so quick, and fearless, and honorable." "I know it," said John, "and too restless to settle down." "And
doesn't give twopence," added Tavie, "for Reform or anything that might
occupy his mind. He's not stupid, you know?" "I know it," said John.
"I feel as if he were here now, listening to us," said Tavie, and she glanced
apprehensively around the room, looking longest at the portico over the
window niche six feet behind John.

"And now," she began again with a sigh, "you long-suffering old thing,
can you stand one more confession? You know I have only you and Aggie
to talk to." "The fact is," said John, "I feel more at home this minute than
at any moment since—well, since Pa died." Tavie gave him a quick, troubled look which he did not catch, then dropped her eyes and resumed
her knitting. "The next confession," she said slowly and with determination, "is that I am glad Connie has gone."

"I rather assumed that," said John, smiling a little crudely till Tavie
caught him up with a flashing look. "And I have determined that if he
comes back I will not have him. The only real thing I could do for him
would be to have another child, and, John, I just can't do it. Just in the

twenty-four hours since he has left I have come to look back with a sort of horror on the falsity of the last nine years. If this break hadn't come, I might never have known it. I would have gone on with my work, and that would have seemed enough. But now, just in the last twenty-four hours, Connie has quite suddenly seemed *loathesome* to me. I can't, John. I can't." She was crying.

"It seems that for the first time in my life I am really a human being and am entitled to be one. If Connie came back I would run away, from everything—College, Reform, everything but Solon—if I lost *him* I'd kill myself—I'd run away rather than go back into that, that—sort of righteous prostitution. Connie agreed before we were married"—she quieted down now—"to leave me any time after a year. Well, the time has come. It was sometimes hard before, but from now on it would be absolute torture. Hell could be no worse. Is that wrong, John? It is against the *Bible,* perhaps, but it isn't against humanity. I have fought for the freedom and decency of other women. Haven't I earned a little for myself? Haven't I, John?"

"Tave," said John after a half minute's deep consideration, "that is a point on which I dare not pass judgment. If Connie had mistreated you, there would be no question about it. Since he has not, on broad moral grounds there is no doubt that your place is with him, as his is with you. I don't think you are obligated to pursue him, but I cannot say surely what you should do if he came back. There is the important special circumstance of your pre-marital agreement, though I doubt if a court of law would honor it."

"Stop being a lawyer," Tavie said sharply without looking up. "What *ought* I to do as a human being?"

"Tave, I don't know, though God knows I sympathize. Let's hope the poor fellow won't come back." "I'm not made that way," said Tavie a little coolly, "at least not as far as Connie is concerned. Either I shall get Homer to have Governor Chase fetch him back, or I shall send him away if he comes back by himself." John smiled, and Tavie looked up and smiled too. "I suppose you're thinking I'm the same old bossy Tavie. Well, what else can I do and be honest? Connie surely can't boss me, no matter what happens. With Ike, of course, if he had really *wanted* to boss me it would have been different. Likely still would."

Tavie paused, and John looked away, gazing absently at the floor, thinking of poor Connie. When he glanced up, her face was chalky white, and her eyes seemed glazed, as if they had lost their pupils. She looked like her ma. John leaned toward her and started to speak. Suddenly she screamed, "Look out, John! There he is, back of you!" John jumped up, wheeled round, whipped back the portiere, and saw nothing. He took a step toward the door, then stopped, feeling ridiculous. If Connie had been in the room he could not have got out in the instant between Tavie's scream and his own jump to his feet. He looked round at Tavie. She was panting violently, sitting straight upright on the sofa, both hands clutching its edge, her head raised, her eyes closed, her face still colorless. John remembered something about its being dangerous to break in on Charity Samson when she was in one of her trances.

For some moments he stood hesitant. Then Tavie said, without opening her eyes, "John, would you come here and sit by me and put your arm tightly around me?" He quickly complied, feeling her breath coming and going so rapidly it was a sort of vibration, and her body trembling so much more rapidly that it seemed like a tingling sensation in his arm. Very slowly the trembling was reduced to spasms with quiet between, and her respiration fell to ordinary fast breathing. She laid her head on John's shoulder and grasped his knee tightly, digging in with her fingers. "At least I didn't faint," she finally whispered. "It's Ma in me. They say I'm a medium and I've been to meetings at the college. I fear it, but they say it's my duty." "Pshaw!" said John.

"It was probably nothing," Tavie continued, in a whisper. "Or if it was anything, it was something happening to him somewhere else. But I did see him come out from behind that curtain and raise something in his hand over you—a club—it looked more like a bottle."

"Some believe in it," said John in a strong, normal tone which made Tavie snuggle against him, "but I don't, and none of the doctors at home do. You were simply over-wrought, after all you've been through." "I hope so," whispered Tavie, and John felt her relaxing rapidly. He drew her back so she rested easily against him, and at the same time loosened the grip of his arm and held her gently. Her hand now lay limp on his knee. A full minute passed.

"O John," said Tavie at last, her voice now regaining its normal quality, "I am so glad you were here when that happened. To see me, you wouldn't think I was somebody in the world, would you? Fighting for the proposition that women should be equal to men in all things?" She sighed and John said, "That has nothing to do with it." "You know," she continued, disregarding his polite remark, "I am more contented with you than with any person in the world. You and Aggie are my only friends, who really know me; and I love Aggie but she isn't like a man, like this"—and she gave his knee a little squeeze. Tavie felt John withdraw from her a little and added hastily, "Don't be afraid of me, John. You know I love Ike, and I know you're in love with Pru. But let's keep this friendship we have together, and never, never spoil it. It may be possible, you know—if I don't see too many visions!"

In token of binding the agreement John removed his arm from Tavie's waist and laid his big right hand on his knee, palm up. Tavie's hand went into it, then their other two hands joined in the pact that was sealed by quiet pressure on both sides. Tavie looked up at John, radiant again as she had been when she sprang to meet him, but quietly radiant now, waiting, responsive. For the first time in his life he longed to take her in his arms and kiss her passionately, without the excuse of greeting or parting. But Tavie lowered her head and shook it slowly.

"After all," she said tenderly, "we're still man and woman, aren't we?" "But," said John a little huskily, "we both know the dangers." "And how easy it is to deceive ourselves," said Tavie. "And how very easy it is to deceive ourselves," agreed John with emphasis. "And to deceive each other," added Tavie, and she glanced up playfully and saw John nodding gravely like a dear, big, ingenuous boy who was getting a little beyond his depth.

They both laughed and John raised her hands and kissed them severally, then stood up. "Oh, but don't leave me!" exclaimed Tavie. "Sit there." She pointed to the far end of the sofa and hastily took up her knitting. John lit a fresh cigar a little pompously and complied. For a long time they sat in comfortable silence. At last Tavie said, "Chicago." "Yes, Chicago," John replied with an easy sigh. "Are you going, Tave?"

And so they swung out from themselves into that consecrated stream where they belonged, both separately and together, that river of aspiration which John had named as an image of the nation progressing toward perfection. And in the talk that followed, their blood stirred more than it had to their friendship or to one another's persons, Tavie arguing for absolute abolition, and John for the preservation of the Union.

And the stream rolled on through the afternoon, and through that evening when Homer took John to call on some of the faculty of the College and some of the local Republicans. It continued the next afternoon when John addressed a Republican rally arranged by Homer; and that evening, when he was the guest of honor at a supper given by President Finney of Oberlin, and Tavie was there and spoke, and John heard her for the first time, and appreciated her importance as a public figure, his peer or his superior in a realm that was higher than friendship.

The stream rolled on through Friday when Tavie telegraphed Mrs. Stanton and others that she would go to Chicago, and Homer telegraphed

Governor Chase in Columbus and Republican Headquarters in Chicago that there would be two ladies in his party. It widened when they went to Columbus on Saturday, arriving there Sunday morning, and were entertained as the guests of the Governor. It became a march when they pulled out of Columbus on a special train on Monday, while cannon boomed and thousands at the station cheered off the "favorite son" of Ohio.

It became a thunderous whirlpool when they were part of forty thousand others pouring slowly into Chicago, then milling in the mud along the ill-defined shores of Lake Michigan and singing to the crash of forty bands that left no moment of silence from Monday evening until the morning of Wednesday, the 16th, when ten thousand enthusiasts jammed into the huge wooden "Wigwam," each wearing a badge, Homer's proclaiming his adherence to Chase and John's to "Old Irrepressible" Seward.

The stream narrowed into concentrated power when John sat up all Wednesday night with the Resolutions Committee, and on Thursday saw the Convention adopt the three important planks respectively declaring against the extension of slavery to new territory, denying the right of the Government to interfere with slavery in states where it already existed, and denying the right of secession from the Union.

And on Friday it narrowed again for its final plunge when, after Lincoln had passed Seward on the third ballot and lacked but one and a half votes for the nomination, Homer Hislip mounted his chair and shouted the release of four Ohio votes from Chase to Lincoln. Then the stream roared into the widening leap of its Niagara as bedlam broke loose in the "Wigwam" and cannon boomed on the roof, and other cannon took up the sound across the city, and the telegraph wires began to release hundreds and thousands of cannon in every city and crossroads of the North, proclaiming the first solidarity of region against region, the first political campaign of section against section.

And the thunder of that river was never absent from men's ears during the months that followed, until the cannon roar of the political campaign swelled into the rumble of a threatened military campaign, and those who had directed the great river away from the rocks of abolition found themselves swept with redoubled power into the struggle to preserve the Union, with or without slavery. And no one knew where the river was leading tomorrow, but all knew they would gladly die for their country. And they believed that not far ahead, under God's direction, lay victory and peace, and the first perfect nation in the world.

CHAPTER LXXIII

BUB TANOFLY, Jabe Munson, Joe Kirkwood and Zeb Milliken spent all of Election Tuesday, November 6, 1860, playing poker in the rooms of the Byzantium Young Men's Association, which was the old Gang slightly expanded and formalized into a club—the "Young Asses," Ostrum Applemore delighted to call them. Fred VanSanford was in and out of the game, while his older brother, Medad, spent most of the day reading at one of the two windows that looked out over the Mall. The two rooms were on the third floor of the sprawling Grabbot Buildings, which occupied the sites of four smaller blocks destroyed in the Great Fire of '51. Throughout the day Fritz, the German factotum, kept the poker players and the rest supplied with cold beef, relish, bread, cheese and liquor from the combined tap-room, kitchen and dining-room behind. As always, the air was blue with tobacco smoke. The plug hats and frock coats of the poker players were variously disposed on the gas jets and the backs of the comfortable tavern chairs. By noon, Bub and Joe were surly drunk.

Soon after dinner George Fulton came in and, after watching the poker game a while, got himself a grog and pulled up a chair beside Medad Van Sanford at the window. Five years ago George had married one of the daughters of Squire Sample of Round Harbor, and they were settled in a small house on Hamilton Street, near the new big one Squire Fulton had built in the center of five acres of park. Today, George had dined with his parents, along with Sarah, John, Ike and Ben Lathrop, and Solon, Charity and Numa Samson; the visitors from Lathrop Hollow were to spend the night with the senior Fultons. After dinner Ike had gone to his bank, and John to the *Eagle* office to see to the setting of the "extra" that must be ready to appear some time before the next morning, whenever the telegraphic news of the national election seemed conclusive.

In mid-afternoon Tim Slocum came into the club, Tim just turned twenty-eight, the baby of the association, perennially mild and oppressed with a sense of inferiority because that tough industrialist, Orion Slocum, his pa, had flatly refused to send him to college and make him "more of a god-danged milksop than ever." Soon after Tim, Alec Mathiesson entered and, as Secretary and Treasurer, repaired to the back room and went into executive session with Fritz, the barkeeper-chef. The members of the club were to sup early at the long table in the back room. Afterwards, with the wives of six of them, they were going to Mrs. Horace Gadston's *soirée* to await the local election returns, chiefly the results of the congressional contest between Republican Solon Samson and the Democratic boss, Ostrum Applemore.

Nine of the twelve members of the club were now present, and the most noticeable effect that the years had wrought in them lay in their all being now bearded or mustached or both. Jabe Munson was more deeply concealed than ever behind the full, reddish thicket which he seldom troubled to trim. Joe Kirkwood's bushy sideburns were thicker on his puffy jowls. Zeb Milliken now also wore sideburns, stiff ones that extended down into walruses on either side of his delicate, oblong jaw. Bub Tanofly had an enormous mustache across his round, red face; Tim Slocum a slighter edition of the same. Fred VanSanford still had a blond Vandyke and mustache, while Medad, George Fulton and Alec Mathiesson all wore neat variations of the common chin beard. To an observer not accustomed to the current mode, they would have seemed older, more august, than their years implied. Joe Kirkwood, thirty-six, was the oldest of the group.

Alec Mathiesson came in from the back room and demanded, "Anybody like to breathe?" "Up, ye three," growled Bub Tanofly, for the stakes were high. Alec started to open the other window, the one where George and Medad were not sitting. "Shut 'at window," muttered Joe Kirkwood. "See you, by God!" George Fulton arose and got grogs for himself and Medad. Alec stood at the fireplace, checking over accounts on the imitation black marble mantel.

Ike Lathrop came in with his quiet step, and it was as if everybody sensed his presence without seeing or hearing him. "Hi, Ike"— "Hi, Ike"— "Hi, Ike," they all said in a general murmur without looking up from what each was doing. Ike went out to the bar, exchanged greetings with Fritz, tossed off a straight whisky and lit a cigar. He walked back to the window Alec had proposed to open, opened it, and sat down so as to look out over the Mall on one side and into the room on the other. This was Ike's particular corner, and if anyone else was sitting there when he came in he usually found some excuse to vacate it. Setting his silk hat on the floor, Ike tilted back against the wall, crossed his knees and rested his silver-headed, straight cane against them. It was a cane which the President of the New York Central Railroad had brought him from Alaska—for Ike at twenty-nine was a director of the "Central" and a financial power in the state, in addition to his local importance in Byzantium.

Of all the members of the Young Men's Association, nine years had marked Ike most deeply. His swirling mane of formerly golden hair was now widely streaked with pure white, giving him an even more striking aspect than formerly. His chin beard was a duller blond than his hair, and it was streaked with a darker gray. His complexion, always florid, was now more so, and at close range numerous red curlycues of blood vessels were visible in his cheeks. The big, pure blue eyes were even gentler than before, gentle almost to the point of sadness; but the little lines around them now seemed always on the verge of stiffening into something hard, something between indifference and defiance. The old vertical pucker between the eyes, a little off center to the left, had become a permanent furrow, but it was still an expressive feature, and it was deep with concern at this moment. As he sat alone by the window, there was no sign of the old, world-inclusive, Lathrop smile. Rather, his whole person seemed diffused with warmth. As soon as he sat down the atmosphere of the room was composed, as if the club had been waiting for him before feeling itself a unit and at home.

Ike looked out on a Mall that retained few reminders of the old one of 1850. The big shadow of the Grabbot Buildings and the adjoining American Hotel—pretentious successor to the old Wheeler, put up by Job Wheeler after the Great Fire of '51—had already crept out past the watering-trough to the nearest island where two cannon of the War of 1812 had been installed under the trees for the purpose of proclaiming political news that evening. Diagonally southeastward, where Perkins Hotel had stood before it burned in '52, a crowd of Y.M.C.A. youths sat on the recessed, two-story grand stairway of Washington Hall, whence the returns would be shouted to the crowd throughout the night, while in the auditorium on the third floor its capacity of two thousand would be dangerously exceeded in a rally to honor the new congressman from the district, whether Applemore or Samson. On the corner of Gadston Street stood the brick Tanofly Block that Bub had near broke himself building just before prices dropped in '57. Farther down on the south side of the Mall was the new Hall House, an enormous frame structure with double verandas. Beyond it rose the two wooden towers of the new Universalist Church, compounded of Notre Dame and a hay barn. On the north side of the Mall, that used to be open to the river, stood the Gadston House, the biggest hostelry north of Albany, splendid with crenellations along its roof line and overhanging, fake turrets at the corners. It was a new Mall, even to its topography. The roadway had been graded and the old swale on the north side was drained away. The bluffs that used to surround it had been cut back for the foundations of the new buildings which were entered from street level, instead of by the stairways of the old time. The Mall was new, and around it lay a new village that had doubled its population to ten thousand since Ike and the railroad had become part of it.

It was a mild, Indian summer afternoon, the sky sleepily hazy and the air rich with the incense of burning piles of leaves. The wide, dusty market place was aglow with a mosaic of red and yellow leaves drifted down from the neighboring streets and from the three central islands of the Mall itself where the trees had now grown to respectable size. At the far end, the old Baptist Church clock struck four, and Ike looked nostalgically at its white tower, the only considerable landmark left from the Mall of only ten years before. On the corner north of it, Stark's Liberty Tavern also remained from the old days, and Ike fancied that Pru and her ma were sitting there in the upstairs windows now. Pru had told him she was going to buy a telescope to keep tabs on the doings in the club. She was twenty-seven now, still the prettiest girl in town, and showing no sign of marrying either John or Nat Gadston, her principal suitors. Ike listened to the music of an accordion coming from the American House next door. Somewhere in the distance up Washington Street a hand organ was warbling. A dozen saddle horses and carriages stood at some of the hundreds of hitching-posts round the Mall, but for the moment none of them was moving. As always, Ike was conscious of the rumble of the Middle Falls at the Mill Street Bridge, now a new suspension bridge which the corporation had employed Alec to build. It was a peaceful scene, life seeming as secure as ever in the changed village.

"Hand, Ike?" asked Jabe Munson, and Ike saw that Joe Kirkwood had slumped into alcoholic slumber. "Thank ye, no," said Ike. "What y'up to?" growled Bub, who wasn't far behind Joe. "Figgered it wasn't a bad time to lay in a little gold," said Ike, and looked out the window. "H'much?" "Fifty thousand." " 'T's lot." "Yep." " 'Dye sell?" "Southern railroads." "Better'n gold." "Won't be worth a red after tomorrow." "Ye're a liar, Ike Lathrop," muttered Bub, wagging his head and banging the table clumsily with his fist. "B' God, ye're a liar. B' God, I say ye're a liar. Jabe, gimme a hand. Dollar 'thout a draw." "Done," said Zeb Milliken. Bub hiccuped as he picked up his cards one by one with difficulty.

John Lathrop strode in, looking pale and harassed, nodded to the room, went to the back room, threw off his coat and vest, sprawled on his back on the long table and closed his eyes. "Up all night, was he?" asked George Fulton. Ike nodded. It was already near dark in the back room.

Nat Gadston came in wearing a sour smile. He was the beau brummel of the club, having always a certain sartorial dash to him, an excess of perfection illustrated now in the slight angle of his hat, revealing the curly ends of his sandy red hair, the fancy beading round his lapels, the carnation in his buttonhole. He and Tim Slocum represented the second generation of new wealth in the club, neither of their pas having any claim to eminence but their industrial success. As distinguished from Tim, however, Nat was a personage, a college graduate, universally considered a good fellow and able in his pa's foundry. His first activity outside of business had been in the campaign now ending, when he had been doing some electioneering for Ostrum Applemore and the Democrats.

"Well, Ike," said Nat, "now it's all over, there's not much doubt Long John wins, and Heaven help us all! Hope he'll be satisfied when we're all dressed in rags and virtue." "Figger Heaven won't help ye much so long as ye ain't helpin' yerself," said Ike. "Have ye collected your Southern accounts?" "Haven't had time, Ike. Don't see any need to be hurried about 'em. I'm not so bothered about the accounts as about future business." "Better'n gold, b' God," murmured Bub Tanofly. "Better'n gold." "It's no secret," continued Nat, "that we've a big order for rails from the Western and Atlantic Railroad for construction in Alabama. We don't know whether to accept it or not." "Lick 'em in a week," murmured Bub. "Take over their buggerin' railroads and make 'em pay." "It's the darned uncertainty," said Nat. "That's what Long John and his slang-whangin' rail-splitters are doing to us. Everybody's on pins and needles and business'll stop."

"For God's sake," called John in irritation from the back room, "can't you money-grubbers forget your measly pennies for a minute? Not even when human slavery and the Union are at stake?"

There was an embarrassed pause. Ordinarily Nat would have overlooked this remark, but now he was startled and put on the defensive, not having known "Long John" was there. "All right," he called with a faint sneer in his voice, then walking back into the gloom where John was. "Come on, then. Have a drink to your gosh-darned victory of virtue, and the devil with the country! Light the gas, Fritz."

Fritz went round with matches, lighting the unglobed jets in the back room during the beginning of the conversation that followed, then retired behind the bar.

"No," said John, swinging off the table and standing against the bar in his shirt sleeves, "I'll be damned if I'll drink with any such attitude as that. You and all your god-damned pack are out to ruin the country as fast as you can, so long as you get your profits."

"Business *is* the country," said Nat, growing icy.

"It wasn't twenty years ago," shouted John, who was tired, exasperated and belligerent. "And for two centuries before that we got on all-fired nicely without it."

"I suppose you and your snivelling reformers want the country to eat virtue, eh?"

"It isn't enough," John went on, "for you and your kind to keep the niggers in slavery. You're making slaves of white men as fast as you can in your god-damned prisons of mills. Why don't you admit it? The only honest one in the lot of you is that New York swell—a friend of your ma's, I suppose—who said what the whole tribe of you feel, 'To hell with the people!' By God, we'll——"

"Look here, Long John, for some time I've heard about enough of your highty-tighty jibing at my family. Everybody knows my papa isn't handy with his napkin. But, by gracious, he's one of the men that made this town, where if your self-righteous old man and all his grannified Nestors had had their way we'd all still be shov'ling manure and heaving swill to the hogs."

John stood perfectly still. "I'll ask you to apologize for that remark about my pa," he said quietly, but his voice trembled. Nat turned away with a sneer and ostentatiously started to take off his coat. There was a scraping of chairs in the front room and the two drunken members, being nearest the door, got in first. "Soak 'im one for me, Nat," rumbled Joe Kirkwood, still blinking from recent sleep. "Knock the namby-pamby liver out of 'im and if ye don't I'll do it for you," and he leaned on the table, swaying. Bub was less drunk and in better control of his legs. "By Jesus, ye'll take back what ye said of the old Squire, ye flimsy squirt," and he lunged at Nat. But at that moment Ike's hand caught him on the shoulder and pitched him back into the front room so hard he gashed his scalp on a chair as he fell. Then Ike likewise hove big Joe out through the door, said to the rest, "Set on 'em," shut the door, locked it, put the key in his pocket, and jumped between John and Nat.

"If there's to be any boxing," he said quietly, though his eyes were steel black, "I'm going to take on both of ye, and I ain't taking my coat off, either. I ain't talking to the merits of your argument, fer ye're both right. But ye're a consarn pair of babies if ever I see one. Stand up here, Nat. Fritz, set us out three ponies."

Nat paused, glaring at John, then stepped up to the bar as Ike commanded and leaned over it, breathing hard, his anger complicated by his secret sense of inferiority to the Lathrops.

On the other side of Ike, John towered above them both like a great arrogant eagle, never taking his eyes off Nat, perfectly sure of himself, perfectly determined to beat an apology out of Nat, but acceding for the moment to the place and the sense of unfairness in being now two to one against the contemptible dandy. " 'Paloosa," said Ike, looking up at John, "to begin with, ye insulted Nat's ma and pa and ye shouldn't have done it." "I did not," said John. "I said that every rich man in the nation who puts his profits above public service is a swine. If anyone wishes to take the definition to himself, I am prepared to repeat it specifically."

"But ye didn't have anybody special in mind, unless that feller in New York? Ye weren't thinkin' special of me or Nat or his pa or ma or anybody else in Byzantium?" "I was not," said John.

"That suit ye?" said Ike to Nat, who glanced sullenly up at John, then down again and nodded. "And now, you polecat," said Ike, lowering his voice and facing Nat squarely, "ye've two shakes to apologize for what ye said of our pa or ye're going head first through that wall," and Ike closed his fists and stepped back to swing. "My quarrel," said John savagely and thrust Ike back, crowding up next to Nat.

"I apologize," said Nat. "I didn't really mean it." And he dropped his head in his arms on the bar. Ike looked up at John, and they both nodded with a look of contempt that registered at once their own basic unanimity and their mutual opinion of Nat.

At this moment Alec Mathiesson succeeded in picking the lock on the door, and everybody crowded in except Joe Kirkwood, who had gone to sleep on the floor. "Lemme have a poke at 'im," Bub Tanofly shouted; but Jabe Munson grabbed him and Ike said, "Shut up, Bub." Then he turned to the bar and said, "Set 'em up, Fritz." Eight more ponies of whisky appeared instantly on the bar, as instantly seized by the members, who lifted them and waited for Ike. Nat remained with his head in his arms on the bar till Ike was through his little speech.

"Fellers," he said, "there's some different ideas between all of us here, and anybody who's in this club ought to be a good feller and not too a'mighty lodged in his views. For my part I want to tell ye there ain't a better feller in this club than Nat Gadston, and here's to him and God bless him."

They tossed off their drinks with a cheer and Nat straightened up with a shy smile. Lifting his glass, he said a little shakily, "I can't say anything but 'thank you,' Ike, and here's to you and"—looking up challengingly at John—"here's to you, John." And he tossed off his drink.

Ike motioned everybody but the late contestants back to the other room. "If you two cockerels start turning back yer cuffs again," he said, "we'll have the fire hose on ye." And he walked out after the rest. "Two more whiskies," said John, and Fritz hastily complied. He knew how to handle fighting drunks, but had been at a loss with three angry and powerful sober men.

Nat considered his drink for a long time, rolling the little glass in his hand and organizing his thoughts. At last he said earnestly, without looking up, "John, I'm truly darned ashamed of myself for what I said. I guess the real reason was that for a long time I've been sort of jealous of you, and Ike, for having had the kind of a papa you had, somebody everybody respected and knew was a gentleman. You know, the fact is it's sometimes humiliating to know your papa still eats peas off his knife, and can't carry on an elegant conversation with genteel people. It makes a fellow have a chip on his shoulder, I guess. Here's to you." And he tossed off his drink.

John sipped his and said, "Nat, honestly, I can't follow you. It's true, our pa was respected, but it certainly had nothing to do with his table manners, the kind of manners a few of you have nowadays. Did you ever see my pa eat?" "Not to remember it," said Nat. "Well, he wasn't finicky about the way he handled his napkin or knife either, and, for that, neither are any of us in this club except you, and maybe Tim. Our manners are not what you call 'genteel' nowadays, and I don't know that any of us specially want them to be. The fact is, you will remember, that all this business of table manners and wearing the right kind of clothes, and calling people 'ladies and gentlemen' or 'vulgar' according to these standards, all that only started about—about the time you went to college." "And high time," said Nat cheerfully.

"We were taught another basis of good manners," continued John, "or rather what was called 'politeness' when we were children. Both Pa and Ma used to fill us with such injunctions as to 'make people feel easy' and 'never to tread on people's toes.' But I can't remember as a boy being taught much of what you'd call 'good manners' today." John tossed off the rest of his drink.

Nat was following his own line of thought without really listening to John. "Papa never taught me much one way or the other," he said. "But from the time I was a baby Mamma was forever teaching me how to bow and talk to people, and what to do with my hands and how to behave at table. And the great thing was that I must grow up to be a fine gentleman like Squire Fulton and Judge VanSanford and, above all, Squire Lathrop. I guess, as I said, this put a kind of jealousy in me that boiled over just now."

"And you mean to say," said John, "that in your way of thinking a man should be judged, not by his intellectual attainment or his service to the community, but by what are now called his 'manners'?"

"Why, thunderation," said Nat, "I've never thought of a better way, at least not an easier way of judging a man." "It's an easy way, that's sure," said John, and he gave a big, disgusted sigh.

"Besides making life pleasant for ourselves," said Nat, "we set a genteel example for the common people. Fritz, two more."

"Good God, Nat!" exclaimed John, thumping the bar, "that's even worse than I thought. I had always believed that Ike was at least partly right, that the people who have made money in the last thirty years or so would at least give lip service to the old standards of public service—the way, say, your friend Ostrum does—and that after a while, when the money-chasing was over, at least some of them would settle down to be responsible citizens. And here you come—and I know you're a mighty sight more conversant than I am with the way the rich think and talk in New York and Saratoga —here you come telling me that our new aristocracy of wealth is a class apart from 'the common people,' without any responsibility except to have 'good manners.' Why, good God, Nat, any skinflint can get good manners with a little instruction and money enough to buy clothes and flowers and all that nonsense. But it takes real character to maintain public responsibility, and it takes some learning besides to apply that responsibility wisely. The old Nestors knew they were leading citizens who were allowed to run things as long as the people trusted them. But what concerned them was the duties that implied, not the privileges. I doubt if a single member of the old Nestors ever used or even thought the phrase 'the common people.' "

"John," said Nat, "did you ever stop to think that to run a big business, like Papa's, really takes more work than, say, running a farm, tires you out more? A fellow can get some education and some manners when he's a boy, but once he gets into the harness of business, he has little more time to bother with learning or public responsibility, outside of giving away a little money now and then. When Papa comes home from the foundry at supper time, he's tuckered out. I'm getting the same way myself. All I want is to go upstairs and lie down—Mamma won't let us lie on the downstairs sofas, and she's right. Why, thunderation, John, I haven't *time* any more to indulge in high thoughts and profound reading. It puts me to sleep. I want to be amused.

"But, gracious," continued Nat after a pause, "let's not get too serious again. Goodness me, life's too short. Here's to Abe Lincoln." And he lifted his glass. "Here's to Old Abe," said John, lifting his. "May the Republicans win, and may they ruin for good and all every factory and railroad in the country." He drained his glass and set it down with a bang, turning then to Nat with a big, ironic smile. "Well, it's war between us,

Nat. Only see you don't take it personally any more. I'm against the whole lot of you, maybe even including Ike. But no more insults and brawls, eh, Nat? It's too big for that." "Thunderation, yes," said Nat, and they shook hands and walked into the front room.

It was almost dark there, for everyone had been listening to the talk at the bar and no one had bothered to light the gas. John and Nat paused in the door, adjusting their eyes to the gloom. Out on the Mall the shadow of the Grabbo Buildings had eclipsed everything, and the sky above was a darkening purple. At his window, Ike was watching the stars peeping out, and the gas lamps on the Mall flaring one by one as the lighter went his rounds with his long taper. "Ye're all keerect, 'Paloosa," he said. "It's war, and I hope ye ain't biting off a bigger quid than ye can manage."

There was a short silence, livened by distant singing from some of the half dozen saloons on the Mall. The Baptist Church started to strike five. "Gracious!" exclaimed Nat, "the polls are closing and I'm to count votes. See you this evening. Mamma said I must have supper at home with our guests." "See ye count them votes 'cordin' t' principle, young feller," said Jabe Munson in the darkness as Nat departed. Tim Slocum murmured that he also had promised his mamma to come home for supper, and he followed Nat out.

John sat down in the chair Tim had occupied. In the back room Fritz began to clatter about, preparing supper. Everyone was content to leave the front room in half-darkness broken by the glow from the back room, the fainter glow from the two windows and the occasional red spot of a drawn cigar. Joe Kirkwood still lay sprawled on the floor, breathing heavily in drunken sleep.

"Long John," said Jabe Munson, "I was sorry to see ye omit the gallingest twist ye could have given Nat's well-mannered tail. Did it ever occur to ye that the elegant mansion our breaths are to desecrate tonight is a house run by a woman? Did it ever occur to ye, further, that Mehitabel Gadston, instead of George's pa, or Fred's, or any of the Nestors, is gettin' to be the sovereign and mentor of fashion and manners in this town?" "Likely because she's the one who works at it most," suggested Medad VanSanford. "No, that ain't the real meaning of it," drawled Jabe. "John and Nat between 'em set up the real reasons, though nobody stated the fact. These great business men like Horace and Ike h'ain't the time or ideas to devote to livin' outside the two-ringed circus o' their gamblin' enterprises. They're glad to leave all that to their women and toe any chalk line they're told to, so long as they don't have to waste any thinkin' on it."

"You mean," said Zeb Milliken, "that we're coming into a woman's civilization?"

"Ain't it so, Zeb?" said Jabe, "with all this nursery jabber about what's genteel and good taste,.and bein' careful to shy off what takes a little deeper head-scratchin' than most ladies like to devote to a matter." "And all this nonsense about 'prominent people' depending on the way you tie your necktie," said Fred VanSanford. "This god-damned vain-gloriousness about some people bein' 'important' without countin' how much or little they've done in the world," said Jabe. "In place of the principles that men have worked out through the years, this new myth about woman being mysterious and inspired and always right above reason," said Zeb.

Ike broke the silence that followed. "Figger you fellers don't like women over much," he said. "Not a-runnin' the show, no sir-ee," said Bub Tanofly. "And furthermore, I'll lay ye a hundred they don't like it either inside their gigglin', empty little curly-heads." "But ain't we right, Ike?" asked Jabe. "Ain't Zeb hit 'er a-tween the eyes when he says we're easin' into a woman's civilization?" "Mebbe," said Ike, "but I figger we've still something t' say if we're o' mind to." "It seems to be a case," said Zeb in his careful way, "of the women being driven to assume an authority they don't want because the men are no longer able to assume it."

In the darkness George Fulton chuckled, then said, "I was only thinking of poor old Horace and what a figure he cuts, now he's getting respectable. He don't drink or chew or smoke any more in his own house, and he chews bread or grass or something to freshen up his breath before he goes home." "And Nat said," put in Fred VanSanford, "Mehitabel won't let him stretch out on the sofa downstairs." "And I'll bet," said John, "Wash Wycomb and J. Ludlow and Ory Slocum aren't far behind him." "Horace is a length ahead of the rest," said Medad VanSanford. "He's getting so he can bow and smirk mighty pretty. At the cotillion I heard him tell Fanny Ludlow her dress was elegant, and she blushed like a virgin, though Horace said it about as graceful as an old bull snuffin' round a cow's tail."

"Oh, I tell ye, fellers, we're in fer it," said Jabe. "We're a-runnin' like chickens to corn along with the rest of 'em. They say Mehit's to have some o' her Saratogy friends to show off this evenin', and we'll all behave like little gentlemen, and the first thing ye know we'll wake up some mornin' and find we're prominent folks with manners most as good as Horace's— all except mebbe Joe here, eh, Joe?" Joe Kirkwood mumbled. "And me, by God," growled Bub. "And me"—"And me"—"And me," everybody else echoed chuckling, ending in an inconclusive pause.

"Jabe," said Ike, "I was sort of figgering on something when I said a spell back we might still have something to say in the matter if we were o' mind to." "You mean," asked Jabe, "we might draw up a sort o' Declaration o' Independence o' inspired petticoats?" "In the.*Eagle,* eh?" said John. "I wasn't particularly thinking of the *Eagle,*" said Ike. "You mean—?" said Jabe. "Tonight!" said George Fulton. "Capital, Ike!" "Capital!" repeated Fred VanSanford. "We'll put on a show of our own!" "Wasn't figgering on any special show," said Ike, "just sort of—" "Just sort of behave like we were in our own homes, eh?" said Jabe. "Maybe with a wee mite o' trimmin', by cracky!" and Jabe slapped his knee in the darkness. "By Jesus' britches, Ike, ye're a genius and we'll do it!" shouted Bub, banging the table. "Fritz, fetch us some liquor."

"No, ye don't, Bub," said Jabe. "We're all liquored plenty a'ready. We're goin' t' behave a little better'n ever our mas learned us to, and it'll take bein' just a drop on the sober side. We've t' be a'mighty polite from beginnin' t' end, and anybody that's full, come seven-thirty, is just sorry he's too damned sick to go to this elegant soiry." "All k'rect," muttered Bub. "Fritz, fetch me some coffee."

"God-damned fine plan," muttered Joe Kirkwood, laboring to his feet. "So ye were a-listenin', were ye, ye god-darned soak," said Jabe. "Well, ye're one who's a'ready too sick fer a real genteel soiry." "Mind yer namby-pamby business," mumbled Joe. Half falling over Medad VanSanford, he stumbled to a window, thrust it up, stuck his head out and his finger down his throat and let fly on the wooden sidewalk two stories below. Then he stood up unsteadily and said, "Trouble with you milksops, you've never learned alcohol was the apple of Eden and the quintessence of knowledge. S'pose you never heard of Kit Marlowe 'n John Ford 'n John Webster 'n Rob Green 'n George Peele 'n two dozen others who set down a few words I'd recommend to you. 'N bear in mind not one of 'em ever trusted any inspiration 'cept women—real women—and liquor. 'N Shakespeare too, most likely. 'N right now I'm the only one o' the pack o' you's qualified t' do this right. 'N I'm goin' t' Mrs. Gadston's sumptuous soirée, if I have t' whale the whole god-damned village. Fritz, fetch me some coffee too! Make her stinkin' strong. Light the god-damned gas, somebody."

CHAPTER LXXIV

MEHITABEL GADSTON'S attack on the old masculine civilization on election night, 1860, was the climax and test of a labor of near forty years. This lifework had begun back in the twenties when Mehitabel Plank, with the red hair, black eyes, coarse complexion and slightly twisted nose, was the virtuous, unbeautiful and commanding barmaid at the old Perkins, memorizing by night all the etiquette books she could lay hands on, and practicing their lore by day and evening on unsuspecting sots in the taproom. In '30 the imperious lift of her shoulder took a coquettish turn and captured the rich founder Horace Gadston, twenty years her senior and three inches her inferior in height. During the next ten years she suffered two great disillusionments, and in the bitterness that ensued there germinated a new order of things for Byzantium. She learned that neither her husband's wealth nor her own matchless decorum would admit them to the intellectual oligarchy of the town, the then young "Nestors." And she learned that Horace, already absorbed in business, was both unqualified to act as the preceptor of a family and incapable of any but the most crass and perfunctory duties as a husband.

Taking the fate of herself and her children in her own hands, Mehitabel thereafter led her family in annual progress to Saratoga and New York where her ambitions took passionate root in strange and sentimental earth, just then being imported from abroad for the benefit of thousands of newly rich ladies in precisely Mehitabel's predicament. For twenty years her soul and the souls of her daughter Gloriana, and presently little Olympia, became impregnably padded in the new feminine code of manners, ethics, and deep, mysterious assumptions. They learned that they were of "finer clay" than the male of the species, and they learned how finer clay behaved under every conceivable circumstance. They learned to sigh and fetch a tear without grief, to lift their handkerchief to conceal a decorous smile without humor. They learned the mysteries of the salts bottle and how to near-faint at the prospect of embarrassment. They learned the use of powerful and competent claws, while keeping them cushioned under sweetness and light. They learned to fall into profound and sad pauses out of which their finer sensibilities would whisper forth inane "intuitions" to a wondering circle of the new school of sex-starved and frightened young men. They learned that ladies had no sexual feelings or real emotions of any kind, only sentiments and intuitions. They learned to starve themselves into the pallor of purity and to dabble at expensive dishes at table, while maintaining life by secret orgies of cake and solid cold cuts. They learned that convention was God and that they, with their appendaged males, were his chosen people, now known as his "best people." By 1860 neither fifty-five-year-old Mehitabel, thirty-year-old Gloriana nor fifteen-year-old Olympia was capable of a thought or impulse that was out of pattern. The last shreds of humanity in seventy-five-year-old Horace expressed themselves in secret drinking "for his stomach's sake," and in titillating bouts in expensive brothels which he and his like enjoyed on nights in New York when they went to the club to talk business together.

And as fast as Mehitabel mastered the new lore, she applied it to the mustering and training of an army of unhappy females in Byzantium. As a suitable headquarters she required Horace to buy her the fine stone mansion on the corner of Washington and Hamilton Streets; and she proceeded to disguise it, outside with a labyrinth of jig-saw work, a glass conservatory, a porte cochère and a four-story tower, and inside with tons of mahogany, imitation marble, velvet, lace, brass and multi-colored glass. Through Gloriana's perennial presidency of the Young Ladies' Sewing Circle she secured to herself the rising female generation. She personally enlisted and trained as her lieutenants most of the newly rich ladies of her own age, clinching their loyalty by informing them that they, not the Nestors and their families, were now the "best people." By the autumn of '60 she felt ready to join open battle with the forces of tradition. She chose election night, not because she knew or cared anything about politics, but because it gave her a festive pretext and because her New York friends, the Strongs and VanStrucks, would then be visiting her and would observe and assist her triumph. She bade to a formal *soirée*—a word theretofore unknown in Byzantium—the dozen new "best families," with a fringe of aspirants, to whom were added for slaughter the Fultons, the VanSanfords, the Samsons, the old bachelor Howell Sherwood, the widowed Mr. Marshfield and the widowed Mrs. Lathrop and Ben, all that was left of the glory of the Nestors, together with all the members of the Young Men's Association and their wives. By eight o'clock some eighty people had gone down the "receiving line"—another innovation in Byzantium—and were scattered through the green and lavender parlor and the walnut and mahogany sitting-room under the soothing light of gas chandeliers with their rose, ochre and cream-colored glass globes.

During the early phase of the battle, the tall and now white-haired Mehitabel stood for purposes of command by the pink mantel in the parlor, armored in social omniscience and thirty or forty pounds of hoops, brilliant white satin and Brussels lace, tiara, stomacher, miscellaneous diamonds and emeralds on throat, arms and hands, on one wrist her reticule, on the other the white bow dangling the long ribbon of her *porte-jupe* or "dress elevator." And during this first phase of the engagement, Mehitabel felt far from satisfied with the turn things seemed to be taking. The old Nestors with their natural courtliness—and complete ignorance that they were fighting for their lives!—and the young dandies of the Young Men's Association in their conscious conspiracy of naturalness were everywhere making easy and delighted prey of the ladies of the best people. Mehitabel was forced to overhear snatches both of badinage and earnest and flattering conversation which were heavy blows at the chaste foundations of her Temple of Female Superiority of a quarter-century's building. There old Mr. Fulton, and there Mr. Samson were respectively centers of admiring groups of her best trained soldiers who were obviously hanging on their every word. There young John Lathrop and George Fulton were flattering her ablest lieutenants, Mrs. Ludlow and Mrs. Slocum, into the most indecorous idiocy, causing them to blush and cut their sixty-year-old eyes in a fashion that was little short of vulgar. There young Isaac Lathrop was all but making open love to her guest, Mrs. Strong, discussing the similarity between love and religion, till Mehitabel felt forced to walk over and interrupt to prevent a most shameful capture. Similarly, that outrageous young Kirkwood was discussing poetry with her guest Mrs. VanStruck; and again Mehitabel was compelled graciously to step in and put an end to a positively indecent recitation of something called *Venus and Adonis*. And, on the other hand, old Lorinda Fulton and Sarah Lathrop were centers of groups of the gentlemen of the best people, all standing round them and chuckling like the most gauche and ill-tutored little boys.

But while all this was going on, Mehitabel did not realize that the forces of finer clay were in fact dealing far deeper wounds than they were receiving. On election night everybody of the old order, both old and young, wanted above all things to talk intelligently about the great issues of the hour; and to talk intelligently about anything was both forbidden and impossible in the society of the new order. While the forces of tradition were everywhere taking the affirmative and holding the floor, yet almost from the beginning they began to stagger under a suffocation of boredom far more fatal than any lapses from decorum they might be inflicting on the insipid enemy. Early in the party Squire Fulton tried to get round to something worth talking about by saying what an agreeable way this was to introduce an evening that was fraught with such momentous consequences for the country. "Did you know, Mr. Fulton," asked Mrs. Lowell with a sweet smile—in the new code you said neither "Squire," "Master" nor "Mistress," but "Mister" and "Missiz"—"did you know, Mr. Fulton, that Mrs. Gadston has been so thoughtful as to arrange for the returns to be brought here by a special messenger as they come in?" "Indeed?" said the old Squire. "I understand there is to be a mass meeting in Washington Hall as soon as the congressional returns from the district are in. The two candidates, Solon and Ostrum here, and I fancy young John Lathrop, will have to go there to make speeches, and I had supposed that we all were to go along to listen to them and to hear the rest of the returns as they come in." "Oh, dear me no," said Mrs. Hall a little reprovingly. "Dear Mrs. Gadston has fixed it so we won't have to mingle at all with the common people on the Mall." "I see," said the Squire; and from then on he felt increasingly uncomfortable as he lapsed into badinage so shallow that he was ashamed to hear the silly words his own tongue was saying.

In another corner Solon Samson characteristically introduced the major issue of disunion, but Mrs. Plum immediately interrupted him. "Indeed, Mr. Samson, we are fortunate in Byzantium that some of the gentlemen of the best people are interested in these things. But don't you think truly that most of the men in politics are a boorish and ungenteel crowd, not fit for polite society?" And Solon's courteous soul suddenly found itself in an agony of loneliness as he launched upon a discussion of the "handsome and tasteful objects to be found in this house."

More deliberate in their attack than their elders, the young men of the conspiracy regaled the ladies they cornered with the most courtly flirtation and serious and elegantly phrased discussions of religion, philosophy and literature. But after a few minutes of amusement at the confused and simpering effects they achieved, they too found the game too costly. It was worse than talking in a vacuum. They were spending their best efforts on grown human beings from whom they momently expected something more than juvenile, elementary response. But the heavy minutes dragged by, bringing nothing but the same eternal succession of giggles and squirmings and sighs. They were wasting their ammunition on a padded wall whose depth was infinite. The enemy was absolutely invulnerable. The glances of the Gang at each other that were meant to convey amusement, in fact conveyed mortal distress. The very walls seemed to be closing in.

The rose-scented air grew unbreathable, and the rooms reeled round the attacking lines. The courtly flirtations and the elegant discussions lapsed. By nine o'clock the silence of eighty people was seldom broken. The forces of finer clay were as chipper and genteel and smug as ever, prepared to go on sighing and being shocked forever. But it was with gratitude that the members of the Gang heard Mehitabel announcing something, and listened for ten minutes to an excruciating cornet solo by Professor somebody-or-other. The charge of the old order had been repulsed with awful slaughter.

Following the cornet solo and encore, supper was announced in the heavy, mahogany dining-room, library and the space of the wide hall between. Mehitabel had intended this to be the final routing of an enemy already broken and humbled by the onslaught of chastity and decorum. But, fancying as she did that she had been worsted in the early encounter, she was now determined as a last resort to bring on a general engagement. As she had foreseen, she suffered a minor triumph in the dexterity with which all her cohorts handled her several innovations in cutlery, while she saw Mrs. Lathrop and Mrs. VanSanford frankly staring at her for instruction in the uses of the butter knife and the ice cream spoon. When it came to the fruit knife and fork old Lorinda Fulton—who, with her husband the Squire, was the special object of Mehitabel's murderous intentions—held them up from her place down the table and said, "Mehit, ye'll have to tell me what this rig's for." "Oh, they're hardly necessary, dear Lorinda," said Mehitabel with a sweet smile round the corners of her long, twisted nose. "We sometimes use them for fruit." For a few moments she sat nibbling tiny slices from her apple, while fat Mr. Fulton beside her gobbled his pear *au nature,* spitting the skins on his plate. For the first time that evening she felt that the initiative in the battle had passed to her. But remembering that hour of seeming reverses in the parlor and sitting-room, she felt that the issue was still uncertain, that the *coup de grace* was yet to be struck. Around her the Knights of the old order sat glassy-eyed with boredom. But it was not in Mehitabel's code to know that boredom could be an anguish and a defeat.

It was Mehitabel's plan that, following supper, everyone should remain informally in the dining-room and library to hear the election returns until after the announcement of the congressional election when Messrs. Applemore, Samson and Lathrop would unhappily depart for the rowdy mass meeting in Washington Hall, all the others presumably to remain. She had timed her refreshments nicely, for she was just ending her public demonstration of the proper use of the fruit-knife and fork when the first returns arrived. The mechanical gong on the front door sounded, and Mattie

Spencer the "second-girl" skipped out of the room. In a moment she returned with a paper which she handed to Nat Gadston, who studied it for a moment, then rose, while everybody watched and the dining-room and library fell silent but for the soft whistling of the gas chandeliers.

"Ladies and gentlemen," said Nat, "I have the results of the village election which, I am sure, will be of interest to all of us. President of the Board of Trustees, Mr. Theophilus Bostwick." There was decorous applause, the ladies of the Democratic best people smiling and drooping their faces to their shoulders right and left, exactly as they would have done in admiring somebody's baby with murmurs of, "How sweet!" At the same time cheering became audible on the Mall, only a long block away. Bostwick was Applemore's man and had held the position of village President ever since the death of Judge VanWyck five years ago. There was a single cannon shot on the Mall, the signal of news favorable to the Democrats. "The other trustees," resumed Nat, "in order of the votes received: Mr. Washington Wycomb, Mr. Zebulon Hall, Mr. Zebulon Milliken and Mr. Medad VanSanford." This meant the now usual Democratic control of the next village government, Zeb and Medad being the Republican minority.

As soon as Nat sat down John Lathrop, the Republican Chairman, rose, for the first time that evening escaping into a realm where enthusiasm was possible. Lifting his sherry glass—one glassful per guest had been the only potation of the evening—he waited for silence, while Mehitabel looked at him with uncertainty as to the propriety of his intentions. "Ladies and gentlemen," he said in a much too hearty tone, "I give you the new Board of Trustees and the continuing President, Master Theophilus Bostwick. Here's godspeed to them and confidence in their integrity and ability!" At which all the men rose and sipped their sherry while the Democratic ladies looked disapprovingly and the Republican ladies of the old order again applauded. Theophilus Bostwick rose to respond but, catching an unmistakable scowl from both his wife and his hostess, merely said, "Thank you, gentlemen," and sat down awkwardly. There was a moment of uncertain silence. Then Squire Fulton, sitting beside his hostess and properly concluding that the refreshments were over, gave Mehitabel the opportunity of her lifetime. He pushed back his chair, scratched a match on the sole of his boot, and lit a cigar.

Like the great general she was, Mehitabel instantly saw her opening, and she did not hesitate to pour in her last reserves at the point where the enemy was giving way. First turning to the old Squire with a smile so sweet her twisted nose seemed to coil under it, she then rose and, leaning forward as if imparting a confidence, said in a well-modulated voice that was audible through both dining-room and library, "Ladies, it seems that the gentlemen would prefer to be alone." She pushed back her chair, at the same time executing her characteristic lift of a shoulder, and, while everybody else was rising, proceeded out of the room, followed first by the ladies of her army and afterwards stragglingly by those of the uncomprehending enemy.

The hostess led her forces clean through the sitting-room and hall into the parlor, as far as possible from masculine contamination; but Lorinda Fulton, emerging last, hobbling rheumatically on her cane and kindly assisted by Ruth Kirkwood, stopped in the sitting-room and sat down on the sofa. She conceived the possibility that Mehitabel's sudden withdrawing of the ladies might have had something to do with John's lighting a cigar. But even if it did not, she was still irritated by the sarcastic manner of it. She smoothed out her heavily brocaded gown and sat a little grandly, inwardly cursing herself for having come, for she had always known Mehitabel was a shallow, silly woman who didn't love her husband. Around her rallied instinctively the wives, sisters and daughters of the Nestors, living and dead, and the wives and sisters of the members of the Young Men's Association, except the Gadston girls. In the parlor the rest of the ladies assembled, under the immediate command of their general.

In the dining-room Squire Fulton continued to smoke his cigar, faintly conscious that he was the only man in the room doing it, but unable to see any relation between this perfectly natural act and the obviously sudden change in the plan of the party. The men from the library came in to occupy the chairs left by the ladies, and the Squire grew aware that almost everyone was looking at him and smiling, while his friends, Sherwood and VanSanford, after receiving muttered information from neighbors who knew the Gadston house, frankly burst out laughing. The roseate old man began to grow self-conscious and wondered if his cravat was askew or if he had dropped something on his shirt. Finally his friend Wash Wycomb called out, "Enjyin' yer sccgar, John," whereat he took it out of his mouth and looked at it suspiciously, but saw nothing wrong with it and replaced it, thus drawing a loud laugh of general delight.

While he was doing this Nat Gadston got up and whispered to his papa who then walked round to the Squire with a silly smile, leaned down to him and whispered, "A'mighty sorry, John, but Mehit don't like us to smoke in the house." "Dear me, dear me," chuckled Squire Fulton and put down his cigar, while all the men clapped and cheered. "No fool like an old fool," he said cheerily, while Lorinda in the drawing-room observed it all, gave an audible sniff, and all of her surrounding cohort rustled.

There was another clang of the front-door gong. Mattie Spencer opened it and received another paper which she took back to Nat in the dining-room. It was complicated, and he studied it for a good half minute before rising in the tense silence, broken only by tittering in the parlor. "Gentlemen," he said, "I have several returns here which I shall venture to give in proper order, though the later ones plainly include the former. With your permission I shall first give you what purports to be the complete returns from the village of Byzantium Falls and the Township of Byzantium in the congressional election." "Yeaaa," yelled Bub Tanofly. Immediately the pall of boredom began to lift, and all the men in the dining-room came alive.

Nat continued: "Village of Byzantium Falls: Mr. Ostrum Applemore, 1254 votes; Mr. Solon Samson, 1126 votes." Cheers and applause from the Democrats. Waiting for them to subside, Nat resumed: "Town of Byzantium, including the village: Mr. Solon Samson, 3017 votes; Mr. Ostrum Applemore, 2971 votes." There was a general whistle at the closeness of this, followed by loud applause from the Republicans. Ostrum Applemore looked across at Solon Samson with a laugh and a wag of his head, then clasped his two hands together in a gesture of congratulation. Solon returned the gesture while his black eyes twinkled in his severe face.

Nat cleared his throat, looked around, and continued: "I have what purports to be conclusive but not complete returns from the entire congressional district, certain remote townships being yet missing." The house was so silent that the distant murmur of the crowd on the Square was audible. Out of suffocation the great national issues arose and pounded in the heart of every man there. In the parlor Mehitabel said, "But as I was saying, my dear—" Then Nat announced: "For Congressman, Mr. Solon Samson, 21,473 votes; Mr. Ostrum Applemore, 15,917 votes." There were two successive cannon shots on the Mall, which was the signal of news favorable to the Republicans. Half a dozen of them in the dining-room shouted "Hooray," and jumped up to congratulate Solon, who waved them back and pointed to Nat who was waiting to continue.

"For Presidential electors," called Nat, and the absolute silence returned: "for Mr. Lincoln, 22,347 votes; for Mr. Bell, 8,768 votes; for Senator Douglas, 7,527 votes, for Senator Breckinridge, 262 votes." There was a roar from the Republicans all of whom now jumped to their feet; but Ostrum Applemore rose also, raised his hand for silence and got it. He lifted his sherry glass, which had a single drop in the bottom, and looked at it dubiously, turning it in his fingers, which got a loud laugh from everybody. "Gentlemen," said Ostrum, assuming his Websterian manner, "it is now my great and sincere pleasure to give ye Solon Samson,

than whom, though I disagree with him in politics, I can assure ye that this
district and this township have never set a more honest, a more fearless
and a more able statesman in any office that it is within our power to fill."
This from the usually sarcastic Applemore brought a unanimous cheer,
and the toast was sipped in sherry, followed by a prolonged roar of applause during which Solon, now sixty-eight years old and as straight, lean
and eagle-eyed as ever, rose and waited.

At last everybody sat down and it was Solon's turn to lift his now perfectly empty glass. There were two cannon shots on the Mall, and volleys
of cheers that continued audible while Solon spoke and throughout the
developments that followed.

"Gentlemen," said Solon, "it is my great pleasure to give ye Senator
Applemore than whom, in the recent campaign, no man could have asked
a more courteous and honorable opponent." Applause from everyone for
Solon's diplomacy, for they all knew it was a lie. "And now, gentlemen, I
regret that some of us must leave this agreeable gathering for the meeting
in Washington Hall. But at least I can assure ye, Democrats, Unionists and
Republicans alike, that if I am victorious in this election the full power of
this district in Congress will be thrown at once and equally against disunion and abolition, and I pray humbly to Almighty God that the pursuit
of neither of these courses may lead to the abandonment of the other."

He sat down to a repetition of the former roar of applause, but as usual
he had disappointed the zealots among his supporters. John Lathrop leapt
at once to his feet, shouting, "Gentlemen, gentlemen, we have yet to
drink the greatest toast of all. In the gravest crisis of this nation since it
became a nation, I give ye old Abe Lincoln and freedom and the Union."
The Republicans and most of the rest raised their glasses, drank the liquor-
less toast in pantomime and banged their fists down on the table in lieu
of breaking their glasses—which all, being cold sober, had the foresight
not to do. But the table, even the floor, trembled under the blow, after
which the cheering and applause scattered into loud talking as the men
reseated themselves. From the parlor came the exasperated voice of the
hostess, clearly audible in the sitting-room, "Mathilda, please ask Mr. Gadston to come here." "All right," said Mattie Spencer and scurried off to
the dining-room, returning in a moment in the wake of old Horace who
trotted up to his wife, the very picture of pathetic, senile apology.

Not a woman in either parlor or sitting-room but revealed the fact that
she was straining an ear. But they needn't have troubled. "Mr. Gadston,"
said Mehitabel in a cooing tone that had a snarl in it, "be so good as to ask
your friends to postpone their boorish actions to a more fitting time and

place." "But, Mehit—" protested poor Horace, but she would not listen. "Kindly do as I say, Mr. Gadston," she commanded stridently, looking down at him with a terrible smile that made him visibly shrink as he stood hesitant for a moment, then returned slowly to the dining-room with his beard flattened down against his shirt.

At this every woman in the sitting-room stiffened, and Lorinda Fulton, as the wife of the Squire whom she suspected had already been insulted, assumed her prerogative of command. As she rose all her cohorts rose with her and Sarah Lathrop and Ruth Kirkwood flanked her as she proceeded at her own hobbling speed across to the parlor and straight up to Mehitabel who stood as it were with fixed bayonet in front of the pink mantel awaiting this charge. "Mehit Gadston," said Lorinda, looking up at her hostess who towered a foot over her, "ye've become a silly and an ill-natured female, and if I were your husband I'd give ye a tanning ye wouldn't forget in a hurry. For my part I'm done with ye till ye mend your ways. I'm going downstreet where a person can take an interest in important happenings without being pestered by a lot of fiddle-faddle. As for John Fulton, I daresay he's old enough to take care of himself. Good night to ye, ladies." And she turned, hobbled back into the hall and started up the stairs. Half a dozen young women ran after her and begged her to let them fetch her things. The rest of her friends who had accompanied her advance into the parlor were already nodding good night to the silenced Mehitabel and her guests, Sarah Lathrop and Anastasia VanSanford, snickering uncontrollably at the glassy stares they received. Within a minute all the ladies of the old order were upstairs except Lorinda herself who stood alone at the parlor door, still looking very cross for her usual gentle self.

When Horace returned to the dining-room with his instructions from Headquarters he stood uneasily for a few seconds gazing round the room with his squint eye while, to his discomfort, the loud talk quieted down and everybody looked at him. "Fellers," he mumbled, "Mehit says we should be more quiet." Then he added as an afterthought, "at least while we're here." Immediately the pall of boredom descended again, and against it a rebellious grumble went round the room.

"Does that mean, Horace," asked the Squire, "that it might be better if we all went somewhere else to get our news, after all the kindness Mehitabel has been to in getting this messenger?" "Oh, no, John," said Horace, waving his hands helplessly, "not at all, not at all. You know Mehit. Let's all set down and fergit it, says I."

"What exactly did she say, Horace?" asked Judge VanSanford, frankly scowling. "Well, Bob, I don't know as I could jest repeat it rightly—something about a more proper place, somethin' of that sort." "And what do you say, Horace?" "Who? Me?" said Horace. "Fer my part I wish we could get in some good likker and enjoy ourselves here a-plenty." "Why don't we then?"—"Why not, Horace?" laughed half a dozen voices. But Horace only shook his hands deprecatingly again and mumbled, " 'T's impossible, fellers, 't's clean impossible. God dang it, ye know Mehit. Set down and fergit it, and let's be a little quieter."

By this time Squire Fulton realized that he had been affronted in the matter of the cigar, and at the same time he was honestly torn between politeness and the habit of a lifetime that called him to the Mall and the mass meeting where he would surely be one of those called on for a few informal remarks, "Well, Horace," he said cheerfully, rising, "Ostrum and Solon and John here are on the point of leaving us anyway, and for my part I guess it's time I left too. I've upset the lot of ye already this evening about a cigar, and I can't promise I might not give a little yip sometime from now on, or perhaps do something else that Mehit might find troublesome. I guess I'm the bull in this china shop, and it'll likely feel a deal more secure if I'm down with the fellers on the Mall where I belong. No offense to ye, Horace."

"To speak true, John," said Horace confidentially, "I don't blame ye a speck. Go along and enjy yerself, and maybe later I'll git a chance to skin out and jine ye." Squire Fulton gave Horace a pat on the shoulder and walked into the sitting-room, followed in a great surge toward escape by precisely the masculine counterpart of the ladies who had already bade their adieus and were now gathered in the hall, hooded and cloaked for the street.

"What's your hurry, girls?" Squire Fulton inquired as he came out among them. "I thought best to go down to Washington Hall for the speaking," said Lorinda, "and I guess the rest are of the same notion." Her eyes met her husband's and they both gave the long-accustomed secret smile of understanding which was utterly imperceptible to anyone else. "We'll wait for ye outside," said Lorinda, and they filed out the front door as Squire Fulton, followed by the Nestors and the men of the Young Men's Association, went in to their hostess in the parlor.

"A good night to ye, Mehitabel," said the Squire, bending over her hand without kissing it, then smiling in a perfect imitation of his usual cordial manner. "Ye've made it a more than usually pleasant election night and I'm most grateful for your hospitality. Unfortunately, some of our foolish citizens may call on me for a few remarks in the Hall tonight, and I dare not disappoint them. Before going I want to apologize to ye for my old fogy stupidity in lighting a cigar. It was quite inexcusable, as was likewise the unseemly racket we've been up to in the dining-room since you ladies released us from your restraining and charming hands. But I trust you will forgive us, and please take consolation to your heart that at least you have given us a pleasant time." And he gave Mehitabel's hand a little squeeze and passed on to her guests. Behind him filed the rest of the Nestors and all of the Gang but Nat Gadston and Tim Slocum, all with equally elegant and even more transparent excuses.

Ike had promised John to take Pru home from the party, and while his friends were saying good night he walked over to her where she sat alone in half a sparking sofa in the corner of the parlor. "Funny evening," he said *sotto voce,* giving her his personal smile. Pru flashed up a look of disgust at him, then dropped her eyes. "May I walk home with ye?" asked Ike. "Of course," said Pru, "if you really want to." "Sure grit, I do," said Ike. "Ye know I always do. Figgered I'd best be going along with the rest of the Gang." "Don't be a silly," said Pru. "Sit down and be comfortable. You haven't spoken to me all evening. They're going to dance."

Ike remained standing, leaning against the wall. His friends were going out the front door, successively Bub, Fred, Zeb, Joe, Medad, Jabe, John, Alec and George. As George pulled the door to behind him, Ike glanced round the parlor and felt something like a premonition, something like fear. The gentlemen of the best people were strolling in self-consciously from the dining-room. Ike was alone with the people like himself, the men who had got rich in the village; and all of his friends were gone. He was neither one thing nor the other.

"Figger I gotta go now," he said quietly to Pru. "If ye want to stay, tell me when to come back for ye." "Don't trouble," murmured Pru, rising without looking at him. "I'll go if you insist. But you're making a serious mistake." And together they walked over to say good night.

The heavy walnut front door closed on Ike and Pru, and this first pitched battle was over. The old, intellectual, masculine order had been defeated by nothing but stupidity and insolence. But it had been defeated all the same, and its army had withdrawn from the field. The years and the generations stretched ahead. In the election that had been held that day the nation had engaged in a different battle that would lead to something that would be called in terms a war. But it in turn would be only a battle, an ironic episode in the longer conflict between two civilizations.

CHAPTER LXXV

O N T H E way home Pru didn't want to mingle with the "rowdyism" on
the Mall that was now roaring with drunkenness and lurid with torches;
so she and Ike took the long way round by Staunton Street and Stark's
Lane. After they crossed Washington, Ike paused to light a cigar and,
as they started off, walked on the inside of Pru that the wind might
carry the smoke away from her. For a few steps she hung back as if
troubled, then said seriously, "Ike, I wish you'd throw away that cigar."
"Smoke bother ye, does it?" he asked, taking it out of his mouth. "You
know as well as I do that smoke doesn't bother me," said Pru impatiently.
"What's more, you know as well as I do that it's improper to smoke with
a lady on the street, and you know that the proper place to walk is on the
outside of a lady." "A'mighty sorry to be improper," said Ike with mock
gravity, and retained both his position and his cigar.

There was no street lamp on Staunton Street until you came to Gadston,
and the foot-path was webbed with extruding roots. Ike took Pru's arm
instinctively but she drew it away, having indeed small need of help, for
she knew every root on every footpath in the village as well as Ike did.
He put his hands in his pockets and walked along whistling softly. When
they had proceeded a minute or two in silence he said, "Bright night for
no moon, ain't it?" Pru did not reply.

As they turned down Stark's Lane she said with an air of profound
thought, "You boys think you're still running this village, don't you?"
"No, ma'am," said Ike lightly. "Don't you realize that Mrs. Gadston is the
social leader now, not Mrs. Fulton or Mrs. VanSanford?" "Very likely,"
said Ike, "if ye mean the one that gives the showiest junkets." "Don't you
know that if you keep on behaving as you did this evening, making open
and outrageous love to ladies two or three times your age, she won't ask
you to her parties any more?" "Good riddance," said Ike. "Then we might
have some fun." "But *I'm* going to continue to go to Mrs. Gadston's parties." "Don't figger anybody'll stop ye, though maybe John'd like to." "The
only reason she keeps asking you now is that she still hopes to catch you or

John or both of you for her daughters." "We're uncommon flattered," said Ike. "O Ike, you can have such beautiful manners when you're o' mind to. Why did you have to behave like a boor tonight?" "Didn't figger I did." "Don't you know that the refined ways Mrs. Gadston has brought back from New York are going to be the mark of a gentleman in the future?" "If ye're talking about politeness, I hain't ever seen any in the Gadston house." "Nat has the best of manners. In another ten years you and the whole old set will be out of things for good unless you change your ways." "Pru, ye're a fool!" "Do you think *that's* polite?" "No, ma'am." "Perhaps you'll find some day I'm not such a fool." "Likely."

As they turned at the Baptist Church corner, Pru slipped her hand into Ike's arm. A cannon flashed and boomed at the other end of the Mall where red lights were drifting in the crowd like fireflies. They stopped to look, and in a moment a second cannon went off.

"More good news for the Republicans," said Ike. "Hope this feller Lincoln knows what he's bit off." There was a steady roar from Washington Hall up there beyond the red lights. "What's he in for?" asked Pru, drawing Ike along toward the Liberty. "Secession, sure 's shootin'. Won't be so bad if he'll let them go peaceful. I voted the Unionist ticket, preferring to see them stay in peaceful, keeping their slaves till they find their own way to get rid of them." "Does John know you voted for Bell?" "Of course he does. George did too. Rest of the Gang voted Republican, except of course Nat and Tim." "Nat was mad when the whole Gang left tonight." "Likely." "I like him," said Pru, measuring her steps out to Ike's. They turned into the Liberty.

The furniture in Mistress Stark's upstairs parlor in the Tavern had had no accession in ten years except a globe of wax flowers on the mantel which Pru had wheedled out of her pa. When Pru and Ike came in, pretty Susan Stark was sitting as usual on her little hair-cloth sofa, diagonally backing the front window farther from the door. Old Gam occupied one of the straight chairs, and was making the rare concession of reading a newspaper, Applemore and Bostwick's *Democratic Union*. Mrs. Gadston had not asked them to her *soirée* because Susan was hopeless as material for her army, and Gam's meanness and ignorance had always disqualified them for the fellowship of the Nestors whom she had invited in order to proscribe them.

As Ike was helping Pru off with her hooded and embroidered cloak Gam rose and shook his hand with almost pathetic cordiality. Gam's respect for Ike had risen in exact proportion to the latter's wealth, and he was himself a permanently saddened man as a result of his failure to have disposed of the Liberty before the railroad supplanted coaches and the Gadston House took away most of his local trade. Ike's contempt for Gam, on the other hand, had not lessened, though there was a kind of sour, standing joke between them on account of Ike's acknowledged desire to buy Gam's ten-acre lot on State Street which was now his most valuable single asset. Gam could not think clearly in political terms, and his financial understanding was hazy outside the realm of personal trading. But he was vaguely apprehensive these days that trouble with the South might somehow reduce the value of his real estate, and he didn't want to get hooked again.

So he was specially glad to see Ike tonight and, feeling no compunction about the presence of ladies, he said, "Ike Lathrop, ye've clean tuckered me out holdin' onto the old piece, and ye can have her fer a fair figger." "What's yer notion of a fair figger?" asked Ike, looking straight at him, for he had outgrown his old hoss-swoppin' technique of feigning indifference. "Thousand an acre," said Gam with his old sneer and a shrug, bespeaking his willingness to sell for a song. Ike continued to look at him, and Gam dropped his eyes. Ike knew this meant he could have the piece for seven fifty an acre. It was still more than the land was worth, but Ike was tempted, his guess being that trouble with the South might send the dollar down and prices up. That was why he had laid by fifty thousand in gold. He took a couple of fast puffs on his cigar, and concluded that if the dollar went down the price of real estate would not go up in proportion. "Ain't interested," he murmured, and turned to Mistress Stark. There was still a sort of inter-generation love affair between them.

"Had a high time tonight," Ike said, beaming at Susan. "Sort of game between Mistress Mehitabel's crowd and the rest of us. Pru says Mehitabel won't ask us any more. She tells me I hain't any manners." Pru lowered her eyes and rocked a little irritably in the low hair-cloth rocker which was as much her place as the sofa was her ma's.

"Won't you take off your things, Isaac?" said Susan. "Yes, do," said Pru. Ike readily complied, for John had said he would appear after the two main speeches in Washington Hall, and had asked Ike to keep Pru up till he came. After a decent delay, Susan and Gam said good night, the former reminding her daughter of cordial and other refreshments in the upstairs pantry. Pru brought out the fine ivory set of dominoes John had given her, telling Ike she was now an expert. Ike moved up the low sewing table and they settled down to a silent, solemn game. One of the windows was open a few inches and they could hear the shouts and applause in Washington Hall, surging and falling like distant surf. Twice double cannon shots reported further good news for the Republicans. The Baptist Church nearby struck eleven, and while it was still reverberating Pru laid down her last domino. There was a roar from Washington Hall, louder and more sustained than ever, and before it died down there were two more cannon shots. Ike rose and stood by the mantel a moment, then sat down on the sofa and leaned back, throwing one leg over the other.

"Pru," he said in his most serious vein, "I figger that from now on ye'll be making a worse mistake than ever." "Not marrying John?" asked Pru, pushing the sewing table away, then reaching over to the side table for her knitting basket, setting it on her knees, and rummaging for her crochet work.

For several years everything—or almost everything—had been perfectly in the open between John and Pru and Ike, a permanent impasse that had become an accepted way of life between them, something at once much more and much less than a family relationship. Pru and Ike were in pretty fundamental agreement against John on many things, but the only openly avowed sentiments were John's. Ike's settled position was that of the ally of his brother, substituting for him at times like the present, usually accompanying the pair of them to parties, and occasionally pleading John's cause with sincerity. And Pru understood so well the firmness of Ike's self-imposed ineligibility that she carefully abstained from flirtation with him, playing consistently the sisterly role. So long as John was in the field she knew her strategy must be one of waiting. And if she cut John off herself she was sure she would lose Ike also. In the meantime, to have both Lathrop boys in tow was no small potatoes in Byzantium society.

So now she said, "Not marrying John?" quite easily and a little wearily, picking up her crochet work and waiting for Ike to say something new on the subject if that were possible. "Yes," he said. "From now on he's going to be the biggest feller of our age in town." "In politics, you mean?" "If ye call it that. I'd lay a thousand he'll be in Washington come another ten years, maybe sooner." "Ike, how many times must I tell you that I would not marry a poor man if he were President of the United States?" "The 'Paloosa'll never be poor, I figger." "But he'll never be rich either, not rich in the way one must be nowadays if they're to raise a family and give them a chance in the world." "When it comes to that," said Ike, "I figger Paloosa'd let me help in the education of his children. That wouldn't be like taking my money for politics when he figgers he's fighting what I stand for. He tried hard to get Ben to let me send him to college."

"It isn't education I'm thinking of," said Pru. "It's lots of other things that only money can give, a person's standing and importance in the community." "That's what I was just thinking of," said Ike. "Right tonight he's licking all of us who have lots more money than he has, and it's likely he'll go on licking us." "So long as he has the *Eagle,* perhaps," said Pru with a smile, not looking up, "and *somebody* put up the money to buy the *Eagle.* No, Ike, I don't believe you've changed your colors so quickly. If I thought you had, I do believe I should be disappointed in you." Ike really hadn't, but he was troubled that Pru did not share his pleasure in John's success so far, and in the probability that a Republican victory would mean a position for him in the government at Washington. But since Pru was obviously not interested, he fell silent. That was the way their talks about John always ended.

Bending over her work so as to show her sleek, perfectly parted hair, Pru smiled at her own thoughts for a while, then broke the silence. "Ike, there's one thing we've never talked about and I've never quite dared bring it up. You remember the time I came to your office almost ten years ago and you hardly spoke to me for over a year?—not until John fairly dragged you round to see me?" Ike's eyes had flickered when she first raised the matter, but his manner quickly grew easy and he chuckled, "Was it as long as that?" "A year, three months and nine days, to be exact," Pru said, cocking her head on one side in amusement at her own preciseness, then returning to her crocheting. "Have you ever forgiven me?"

"Let's see," said Ike, "at that time you were just seventeen and I was nigh twenty. Don't figger there's much forgiving in order for whatever those two babies did, do you?" "Did it ever occur to you," continued Pru, "that perhaps that little girl told the truth when she said she was interested in what you were up to? It's true, she was so mad at your snubbing her that she forgot everything else at the time, but afterwards she was even more mad at herself for having failed to carry out the real object of her visit which, as I recall it, was to get some kind of a position helping you. Didn't it ever occur to you, Ike, that perhaps that silly child really wanted what she said, besides wanting—to marry you or whatever it was that you thought she wanted?" And Pru went off in one of her rippling gales of laughter, threw Ike a round, blue-eyed glance of amused and indifferent friendliness, and went rocking back to her crocheting.

"Don't figger I ever thought much of it, one way or the other," said Ike a little uncertainly, then added with a smile, "but since ye've raised the question, Pru, there ain't no denyin' I did think that girl made a pretty little fool of herself." "Oh, there's no doubt of that," said Pru. "But I just wondered if you hadn't ever thought that besides being a pretty little fool she was really interested in the sort of thing you were doing—has in fact remained interested ever since, though she hasn't dared say so. Don't worry! I'm not trying to marry you now, or even to get a position in the bank or the railroad. I just have a natural curiosity, and since you brought up the subject of John I wondered if I mightn't think up some more original topic of conversation."

"Well," said Ike, "come to think of it, I guess ye're the only female in town I ever take any pleasure discussing business with, and more'n likely it's because, as ye say, ye have some interest in such matters." "Thank you, sir," said Pru, and she went on rocking and flicking her hook with a round cat grin. As often, Ike felt her attraction swim through him and rose to look out the window, shifting his thoughts to his brother in the way that had become automatic with him.

At the other end of the Mall a tall bonfire was billowing. Ike saw the flashes of another double cannon shot, and a moment after was relieved to hear three blows of the knocker downstairs. That meant John. He went down to let him in. John ran up the stairs ahead of him and when Ike followed him into the parlor he already had thrown off his coat and was patting Pru gently on the shoulders, while she looked up at him with her lovely, tolerant smile.

"My girl," he was saying excitedly, "do you know this is one of the greatest nights in the history of this country! You hear those cannon? Do you realize that cannon like them are going off all over the North and everybody is sure that Lincoln is winning! The last news before I left was that he has carried New York State! It's the only state we've heard from entire, but we'd all conceded New York to Douglas! He's carried Boston, too, and that was the only doubtful part of Massachusetts! Oh, my girl, I'm very happy tonight, and being here with you is part of it, and you must let me kiss you if I never do it again!"

Pru rose and yielded, but out of the corner of her eye she saw Ike turn and look out the window as John held her too long and passionately. Neither she nor Ike—nor indeed John himself—knew that through a moment the image of a little burlesque girl on a train passed in and out of his subconscious mind. At last Pru stirred in his arms and he released her. Then he ran over and slapped Ike on the back. "It's great news, Scamp, whether ye like it or not!" Ike turned, seized his hand and said, "I'm danged pleased, big feller, and don't forget it." And John said eagerly, "Here, Pru, we must have a toast. Where's that fine cherry cordial? In the pantry? Stay here! I know where it is!" And he ran out with flying coat-tails. Ike looked at Pru and she was exultant to see that his eyes were darkened. "Ye shouldn't let him do that," he said. "It ain't best for him." And he turned back to the window.

When John ran back with the little decanter and three cordial glasses, he was delighted to see that Pru now seemed as excited as he was. He filled the glasses and proposed a solemn toast, "To the three finest people in the world, Abe Lincoln, Pru Stark, and Ike Lathrop!" And when he had drained the little glass Ike raised his and said, "Here's to ye, Lollapaloosa, and to Old Abe, and may ye hold the country together." He and Pru drank, and she sat down.

John launched into a rapid account of the rally, how Solon Samson had come out of his shell and given a rousing talk for the preservation of the Union at any cost, how Ostrum Applemore had astonished everybody by speaking just as generously as he had at Gadstons', how when the news of New York State came in, the crowd had called for him, John himself, and how he thought he had done tolerably well. And he rattled on and called Pru a damned pretty little Democrat and smacked her on the lips. According to plan, but somewhat hesitantly, Ike said he figgered he'd go home to Redemption's and go to bed. He said good-night to Pru with a touch of self-consciousness, swung on his coat, told John to wake him when he came in, and vanished downstairs. He and John were in fact to meet later at the club.

As soon as Ike left the room, there rose between John and Pru that glass curtain of misunderstanding to which they were now long accustomed, through which they could see each other's surfaces but not each other's souls, on one side of which John exulted in his romanticized desire for Pru's now mature beauty, and on the other side of which she sat smiling in weary complacence. She now rocked slowly in her low rocker. John stood by the mantelpiece. Ike had hardly closed the front door when he threw back his great head and closed his eyes.

"You know, Pru," he said, "it may sound foolish and I suppose I don't really mean it; but sometimes I feel glad that you won't marry me. I fancy it makes a better man of me, and I begin to understand some of the great renunciations men have made, and in consequence have accomplished things of value to the world. I feel that all this strength of my love for you comes out in my work for the truth as I see it, giving me what wisdom I may have as Principal of the Institute, and above all driving me on in this campaign of Reform, fortifying my faith in the future of the country, even my faith in the existence of a just God." "I am glad I can give you that much anyway," said Pru.

"You know," John continued, again lifting his head and closing his eyes, "I feel as if I were right now in the finest possible heaven, right here: to be consecrated to a cause which takes all my mind and my faith, and to love you and to have you sitting here near me, a perpetual inspiration that, because of your very inaccessibility, can never fail." "You mean," asked Pru, "that you are happier if I remain always as I am?" "No, I don't mean that. I merely mean that whatever you do, there will always be some compensation, that if you can't give me personal happiness you are bound to give me spiritual happiness just by existing. I mean that Emerson is so right, just as Pa always said he was. He's the real great man of our time. What he says will last when all our little deeds are forgotten." What Pru thought was, "What Emerson thinks and what you and your Lincolns do are equally far from real life." But she only rocked and said nothing.

"You know, my dear," John resumed, "I'm going to ask you again to give me that little ambrotype, at least to lend it to me indefinitely, and when you want it back you shall have it. If I could only carry that, it would be like having you with me always. In fact," he added with a laugh that had no bitterness in it, "the likeness would be just about as valuable to me as you yourself, eh?" And Pru laughed too. "Well," she said, "I'd be hard indeed, wouldn't I, if I didn't let you take it on such a night and after such elegant speeches? But mind you, it isn't a pledge." "Oh, I know that only too well," said John. "If you were to give me a pledge now I doubt if I could stand it. The thought of it makes me giddy."

Pru got up, fetched the little ambrotype of herself when she was seventeen, and handed it to John, lowering her face as he took it. She knew he would insist on kissing her again, and he did, fairly lifting her off her feet, which she knew raised her hoops shoulder high behind and must make, to any mouse who might be looking, a most deplorable spectacle. John let her down, kissed the ambrotype, and put it in his breast pocket with a flourish. And as he did so there rose suddenly and paradoxically in his mind the image of the beautiful little harlot who had so attracted him and had stolen his wallet from that very same pocket.

They both sat down, and John leaned forward in his chair, his elbows on his knees and his eyes looking at Pru with a sort of vapid, gloating expression which she always saw there when she did him some little favor, and which she definitely disliked. He straightened up and patted the ambrotype through his coat. "I must go to the *Eagle* office now," he said, "and this makes me feel as if I were marching off to war." "Perhaps you are," said Pru. "Oh, no, no," laughed John, "only a political war to preserve the Union and at the same time stop the spread of slavery. But a great war at that! A great crusade! What I sometimes call in my speeches a great river of aspiration whose sources were far back in the beginnings of the country and whose destination is a wide ocean of peace, the first perfect nation in the world." The pulses of that river were now stronger in John's veins than the pulses of desire, and Pru was no more a living person to him but a symbol of his own strength that was identified with the strength of that stream. As he rose to go he merely closed his eyes and pressed Pru to him gently, without kissing her. Then he threw on his coat and rushed out, patting his breast pocket and calling back, "Your favor, madam." And even before the door closed downstairs Pru set about straightening up the room.

Out on the Mall, John felt the tumbling rapids of that river in the mael-strom of more drunkenness and fights and bonfires and red torches than he had ever seen on an election night. He felt the power of it at Washington Hall corner when the crowd "shushed" itself with difficulty into silence, and the voice of the megaphone from the steps bellowed, "Ohio goes for Lincoln," and the crowd exploded like a single gigantic gun that made the following boom of two cannon almost inaudible. He felt the thrill of rushing with the current when some drunken Republicans recognized him and picked him up on their shoulders and bore him in a short triumphal parade in which he lost his new hat. He felt the deep ominousness of that river when he went up to the club and, instead of a poker game or a loud argument, found Ike and Jabe and Joe and Bub and George sitting quietly together at the big table in the back room, talking earnestly and agreeing that if Lincoln really won, it undoubtedly meant secession and the likeli-hood of war. "And the sooner the better," said Bub, and Joe echoed him with emphasis.

John felt the nation-wide flow of that river all through the ensuing night as he went back and forth between the telegraph office in the Grabbot Arcade and the *Eagle* office behind, carrying more and more convincing returns, along with reports of the celebrations in various cities, the salutes of a hundred guns, the bonfires, the parades, the aerial bombs, until he could fairly hear the shouts and the songs of millions proclaiming their allegiance to Lincoln and freedom and the Union. He felt the exultation of faith in that great river's destiny when at six in the morning his tabula-tion showed that the election was assured, and he told his assistant to go ahead with the extra with the Lincoln head-line and the Lincoln editorial he already had in type, and soon after in the dawn twilight the two cannon on the Square began to boom a hundred times in slow alternation, while the whole village seemed to be shouting.

And all that winter John heard the sound of that river of national aspira-tion, growing monthly more insistent, more like the tramp of millions of marching feet. He felt the deepening thunder of it when on December 20th South Carolina seceded; and on January 9th, 10th and 11th Mississippi, Florida and Alabama followed; and a week later, Georgia; on the 26th, Louisiana; and on February 1st Texas; and on February 4th a convention met in Montgomery, Alabama, and formed a new government and elected a President and Vice-President of the Confederate States of America; and all the seceding states set about seizing the property of the United States within their borders; and soon thereafter the term "Rebel" drifted into town without benefit of the newspapers; and among the more hysterical and less educated citizens, it became common knowledge that all Rebels owned, beat, maimed and murdered slaves, and fed their flesh to bloodhounds; and this intelligence became so pervasive that the educated strata was at last prejudiced by it, and John remembered the intolerant attitude which the Southerners at Yale had held toward Negroes, and seriously pondered the possibility of their being guilty of such inhumanities.

And meanwhile the militia was drilling three days a week; and Bub had doubled the size of his company of Zouaves, and Joe was his first lieutenant; and most of the young Republicans bought drill hand-books; and when John himself received from the Republican National Committee an inquiry as to his willingness to accept a position in the State Department, he felt forced to reply that his acceptance would be upon the understanding that he would resign in case of a call to arms to enforce the laws of the United States; and even while he declared in the *Eagle* that there would be no war, he himself bought a copy of Viele's *Handbook for Active Service* and began to study it evenings.

He had a few days of hope that the river of aspiration would yet flow peacefully into the ocean of perfection when the President-elect, on his triumphal progress to Washington, said everywhere that there would be no war, that the crisis was artificial and without foundation, that he intended only to enforce the laws as he was sworn to do and otherwise would coerce no state, and confirmed the determination in his inaugural address when he said, "There will be no bloodshed unless it is forced on the government."

But in application of the President's own words the river began to roar again when almost every paper in the North shouted for the relief of Major Anderson who was besieged in Fort Sumter in defiance of Federal authority. And on the twelfth of April, like a stroke of the clock of fate, came the news that Charleston had begun the bombardment of the fort; and on Sunday the fourteenth in the churches of Byzantium, as in every other village and township in the North, prayers were offered for the defenders of Sumter, and the services were closed with the singing of the "Star-Spangled Banner." And after service the news of the surrender arrived, and flags appeared, and most Unionists and many Democrats joined the Republicans in declaring for the Union, and volunteer companies began to form and drill.

On the next day came the President's call for seventy-five thousand volunteers, and on the same day the Legislature of the State voted $3,000,000 to raise and equip thirty thousand militia for three years. A week later the local militia companies entrained with every flag in town flying and every band, fife and drum corps, and cannon booming; and Bub Tanofly and Joe Kirkwood stayed drunk for three days because they wouldn't let them go with the first. And the roar of the river of aspiration became the whole sound of the nation when every one of ten thousand towns, villages and cities in seventeen states rose in arms in defense of the Union that was to be the first perfect government on earth. And when a committee of young men asked John to raise a company of volunteers and be captain of it he accepted, and got indefinite leave from the School Board, resigned from the Republican County Committee, and persuaded seventy-year-old Squire Fulton to take over the editorials of the *Eagle*. George Fulton became his first lieutenant and Medad VanSanford his second, and Jabe and Zeb and Fred became his sergeants. By the first of May, all but four of the members of the Young Men's Association were in uniform. Nat Gadston and Tim Slocum believed that the South should have been reconciled at all costs. Ike Lathrop believed that the South should be allowed to go without a fight. Alec Mathiesson wanted to enlist, but Ike persuaded him to hold out a little, having other than military ideas about the war.

Throughout the North millions of peaceful men awoke out of moderation and united for War. Their old, moral resentment of slavery and the Fugitive Slave Law burst from its long restraint. The soul of John Brown began its march, and they sang with him between the two oceans.

CHAPTER LXXVI

B Y T H E middle of May, Bub and Joe, with their company of parti-colored Zouaves, were part of McDowell's army in Washington, and John's company had become "C" in a raw regiment, the 50th New York, raised exclusively in Blackwater County and training in Monroe Barracks at Round Harbor. Although it was now twelve miles each way, John continued to ride back to the homestead every Saturday, as he and Ike had done ever since they lived in the village. Two months passed, till the first storm of rumor died down to disgust among the soldiers, and the civilian population settled into the opinion that it was all a tempest in a teapot. Then on Monday, July 22, came the news of Bull Run.

Lathrop Hollow did not learn of the battle until Tuesday, and throughout the ensuing week Sarah Lathrop prepared herself for the ordeal of John's departure, rehearsing again and again the calm with which she would receive the news, augmenting the already excessive bundle of socks, underwear, jellies, medicines, a daguerreotype of the Squire and the prized locket of her own which were to be her parting gifts to him. On Friday she cleaned the house hysterically, and on Saturday morning filled it with every rose, phlox, and nasturtium in the posy bed.

After dinner she broke a plate in putting away the dishes, and fairly splintered the kitchen floor mopping it. Then she went to her bed-room, now the old loom-room, put on her best blue silk gown, labored long over the curls in front of her ears, put a rose jauntily over one of them, and donned a gold and jade set of brooch, bracelets and ear-rings that John had given her. At four o'clock he rode in on his black horse in complete regalia, with gold-braided black felt hat, epaulets, gauntlets, spurs, pistol and sword and chain. Sarah ran out to him, and when he dismounted soberly and embraced her more tenderly and longer than usual, she knew the long dreaded moment had come. For a moment she glanced away with her arrogant look, then asked lightly, "Any news, other than this unfortunate defeat?" "Yes, Ma," said John. "Last night we got orders to entrain on Tuesday, and I must return to camp tonight."

Sarah merely looked interested, even losing the haughty expression she had worn before the ax fell. When she spoke, her voice was lilting. "We must have a junket! I shall blow the horn for Ben and he'll go out to announce it at once." "No, Ma," said John, taking her hands and smiling down at her while she looked up at him with seeming eagerness. "I must be back by two in the morning. Suppose I ride round now and say good-by to the neighbors." "Do whatever you think best," said Sarah, feeling close to breaking down out of gratitude to him for wanting to save the last hours for the family. As soon as he rode out the drive, she flew upstairs to her bedroom and fell on her knees before her God and the portrait of her husband which Ike had had painted for her.

In the detached excitement of departure, John found little to sadden him in saying good-by to the dozen neighboring families in the Hollow. Outside his own home his personal ties to the community were almost gone. Both of his grandparents, along with Master Lane and most of his pa's friends, were dead. Dr. Swift had had a stroke and was an almost speechless, drooling old man. Jehu Jones, in sight of the century mark, was spry as ever, but he was senile and unable to disassociate the present hostilities from those of the Revolution. Solon Samson was in Washington. The news of Connie Oaks's disappearance and the death of little Constant had settled Lem into a sullen, hopeless existence—though his wife Felicity kept up a show of spirits because of letters continually reaffirming Connie's well-being which came from some anonymous person in St. Louis who signed himself, "A friend." The only old friends of near John's age remaining in the Hollow were the Reverend Nathaniel Norcross and his wife, who had been Diodema Swift. All the rest, down to ten years younger, had gone West or to some industrial center, or were now in the Army, most of them in John's own company.

When he had completed his circuit and started up the now broken corduroy from the Samsons', looking across at Pond Hill over the lower meadow shimmering golden in the heat, John for the first time felt a lump in his throat. The thought occurred to him that he might be seeing all this for the last time. He set his jaw against the weakness, but the restless excitement that possessed him was gone. He sank into his consecrated mood, conscious of a readiness to die for his country.

At the little Lathrop cemetery, immaculate under Ben's care, he dismounted and walked up to his pa's grave. Taking off his hat, he dropped on one knee beside the now sunken mound with the big headstone. "Good-by, Pa," he said softly. "I'm going because I believe it's right. I want you to be proud of me, and I want you to comfort Ma." He closed his eyes and lowered his head. The robins were singing everywhere in the glen. "Goodby, Pa," he said again in a whisper. He imagined the Squire was there, standing over him, giving him his blessing, and it was like the whole past of America blessing him. He stood up quickly and walked back to his horse.

When he rode into the barn, Ike was unsaddling. He gave John no greeting, and avoided his eyes. When John told him of his orders he merely mumbled, "Likely." As they started across to the kitchen his manner became easier, and he threw his right arm round John's shoulder. John's sword began to bang back and forth, hitting their legs alternately with each stride. "God danged toy," murmured Ike. Then he smiled, for Ben stood in the back door waiting for them.

All evening Sarah and the three boys sat in the now kerosene-lighted keeping-room. After the hot day, thunder kept rumbling in the distance, and a gusty wind rose through the maples outside, with occasional flurries of rain. The air cooled, and Ben made a small fire in the fireplace, "just to remember home by, 'Paloosa." Sarah kept a plate replenished with biscuits, and the boys consumed two bottles of port Ike had brought out.

When the clock in the front hall began striking midnight the tension increased. All knew that John's departure was now imminent. Every minute must be enjoyed and remembered. The silences grew long and freighted. Sitting beside John on the settle, Sarah's dark blue eyes watched him perpetually, and in the rain flurries that spattered the windows her ears identified every separate drop as important. No one said what they all were thinking—When shall we four sit here like this again?

At half-past twelve John rose, and his brothers after him. "I'll ride with ye a spell," said Ike and went for his coat. "Well, Ma," said John, turning to her and taking both her hands to lift her from the settle. Girlishly Sarah put her arm around John and laid her cheek against his shoulder. "Come upstairs," she said and, taking a lamp, she led him up to the loom-room where he and all her children had been born.

Five minutes later they all went out through the summer kitchen to the barn, Ike and Ben carrying candle lanterns. Amid the long, barn shadows that swung with the lanterns, John and Ike saddled their horses, John unstrapping his military cape from the cantle, putting it on and strapping Sarah's bundle of gifts in its place. Nothing was said, and Sarah stood tall, arrogant and motionless by the doors.

When everything was ready Ben held John's big, fidgety black horse, while he tossed off his hat and opened his arms to his ma, throwing back his cape with a faint jangle of his side arms. Sarah came to John slowly and held back from his embrace. "John," she said, speaking very distinctly and without a quaver, "I have saved till the last what I most want to say to you. We know that your pa is alive and watching us, and we know that his blessing goes with you wherever you go and whatever you do. But we must face the truth that, were he here in the flesh, he would disbelieve in this— war." "I know that, Ma," John murmured almost inaudibly. "I want to say to you," Sarah resumed, "what I believe your pa would say if he were here in the flesh— Since you believe this war is right, you must give it your full devotion. For my own part, I want you to know that my heart is with your cause as much as with you personally, that I shall pray hourly, not only for your safety, but for your complete victory." In saying this her head went up and she was more beautiful than her sons had ever seen her. Then she stepped slowly into John's embrace and was completely enveloped in his cape. Both Ike and Ben turned away.

When John released her he was crying, but she was not, and, though she was pale, she looked like a girl. John turned to take both of Ben's hands, said, "Good-by, old boy," kissed him, threw the reins back over his big black horse's head, and mounted. Ben swung open the doors and John rode out into the rain, followed by Ike with one of the lanterns. As they started out the drive John looked back and, waving his hat, gave the long "Yeaaa" the Lathrops always gave on important arrivals and partings. And up the road till he dropped out of sight over the rise, he stood in his stirrups looking back, watching Ben where he stood in the barn door with his arm around their ma, holding up the lantern beside her face, where she stood absolutely straight, absolutely pale, not shedding a tear.

Down the hill and through the Four Corners John and Ike rode in silence through the rain and darkness, holding their horses to a walk, neither of them able to say anything. Besides the thud and splash of their horses' steps and the rustle of rain on the fields, there was no sound but the faint clinking of John's gear and the frequent hiss of raindrops on the top of Ike's candle lantern. John finally broke the near mile of silence as they were climbing Pond Hill past Haddock's house. "There's only one Ma, isn't there?" he said. "It may sound funny from me, but it seems like sacrilege to mention Pru after what we've just heard."

They splashed along in silence till John spoke again. "But in spite of that, I must ask you to drive Pru down to the Harbor tomorrow. There's to be a final review in the afternoon. I couldn't both see her and come home tonight." "I figgered ye'd want something of the sort," said Ike, "so I've asked her already. She says she's going riding with Nat." "Won't he come too?" asked John. "Likely," replied Ike, "if ye want to ask him that kind of favor. He's easy enough these days, but I guess he's still pretty sore inside about our leaving his ma's party last fall, and his resigning from the club and all." "I guess you're right," said John after a pause.

"I had another notion," said Ike, "and I mentioned it to Pru. I likely know as much about your entraining as you do, being as the arrangements have been made with the railroad. Ye're to entrain at the Cochran Street crossing in the Falls at half-past nine Tuesday morning. I asked Pru to drive down there with me, and what with one thing and another ye can likely get a spell with her alone." "That's top notch, Scamp," said John.

They rode in silence again. "Danged funny," John said, "she'd do a thing like that at this time." "Hope ye don't forget it in a hurry," said Ike. After a long silence John replied, "No, Scamp, I don't think I shall." His mind turned to the image of the beautiful little burlesque girl on the train, and afterwards to the image of Tavie who had recently written him a magnificent letter. She was going to be a nurse.

They reached the top of the hill. The rain had let up somewhat, returning only occasionally with the gusts that were stronger here, rustling over the fields and through the bushes, making the horses snort. John was now in his mood of consecrated patriotism. He found himself imagining those gusts were Rebel cavalry, and he exulted in the hard contact of his sword against his thigh.

In a lull in the gusts Ike said, so low John could hardly hear him, " 'Paloosa, are ye sure grit going?"

"Yes," said John.

"Bub's dead," said Ike.

"Dead?" said John softly, coming down from his dreams. "At Bull Run?"

"Get off your horse," said Ike.

They dismounted, and with their horses' reins looped through their arms, crouched over Ike's lantern in the rainy darkness, while the gusts rushed through the bushes round them and John read in Joe Kirkwood's letter to Ike how at Bull Run Bub had refused to retreat when the major ordered them to; how he had called them all a "pack of lily-livered bastards" and had run out to meet the Rebels alone; how Joe, who was trying to keep the Company together, had looked back and had seen Bub surrounded by "I guess twenty Rebels" with bayonets pointed at him; how instead of surrendering he had come one of them a clip with his sword and "a dozen of them shot him at once;" how Joe, by falling down and playing possum, had stayed on the field and had managed that night to haul Bub's body back and get it carried to Washington by a "cemetery squad"; and how they had buried him on Meridian Hill with taps and a firing squad from the Company. The letter went on into ghastly details of the shambles at the stone bridge after the rout that began there, and ended with the comment, "We're bound to admit the Rebels showed more grit than we did."

John handed back the letter and they both stood up while Ike watched his brother's face that had no exaltation in it now. " 'Paloosa," said Ike again, now in a whisper, "are ye sure grit going down yonder to get blown up to show those fellers how to run their business?" "Yes," said John strongly, "more than ever now." In the candle-light the brothers looked straight into each other's eyes. In a single impulse they were in each other's arms like lovers, their heads on each other's shoulders, and Ike dropped the lantern that went out. When they straightened up they could not see the tears on each other's faces, and they shook hands with a grip that would have broken most men's hands. Without further words John swung into the saddle, and at once put his horse into a gallop in the muddy darkness. In his soul there had come a change. The last thread of tolerance of the Rebels was broken. At last he was really ready for war. He was become an animal, no longer eager to die for his country, but to kill.

Ike stood by his horse's head till John's receding clatter merged into the rustle of the wind by the roadside. Then he shouted with all his strength to the darkness, "Give 'em hell, 'Paloosa!"

By nine o'clock the following Tuesday Ike and Pru were sitting in a hired buggy facing the back road to Round Harbor, about ten rods below the Cochran Street railroad crossing. The train that was to take the 50th as far as Utica stood on the siding south of the crossing, the locomotive already getting up steam, its enormous funnel rolling up clouds of white smoke into the still air. The crowd up at the crossing was small, for the only announcement had been of the hour when the troop train would pass through the station a mile away, and the main crowd was gathered there. Here there were only a few hundred relatives and friends who had got wind of the entrainment, and the usual committee of flower girls from the Young Ladies Sewing Circle whose red, white and blue bonnets and sashes and laden baskets were a lightsome and refreshing sight under the dull, gray sky.

In spite of there being no sun this morning, Pru kept up her green parasol, for it matched her mitts and prettily framed her new bonnet and dress of pink-flowered, white organdie. Ike's conversation was monosyllabic to the point of rudeness, and Pru had at last retorted by lapsing into a huffy silence, sighing occasionally in criticism of him for having brought her out earlier than was needful. Morosely he smoked two cigars while a half hour passed after the time the soldiers were supposed to arrive. Irrelevantly the thought passed through his mind that the engine was wasting a powerful lot of wood in waiting.

It was well after half-past nine, and Pru had settled into a permanently serene and sarcastic smile, when at first faintly like the distant bell-cry of hounds, then in increasing waves and with a momently more insistent rhythm, a sound reached them from the west and made squirrels run up and down Ike's spine. The 50th was coming down the Cochran Street hill a mile away, and as more and more of the long column came into earshot over the crest the music swelled as if joined by more and more pipe-organs, and the under-rhythm grew heavier. Five minutes passed, at the end of which Ike inadvertently bit through his cigar and threw it away. Five minutes more passed and his breathing quickened and waves of emotion ran through him like a strong, warm wind.

They were marching at a good four-mile clip and were now so close that the words of the song were distinguishable, though no one in the waiting crowd needed to know the words. Ike had been hearing the song for weeks, but never before had he heard it sung in unison by over a thousand men to the *thud, thud, thud* of their marching, a thousand men who were his friends and who were marching away to fight for the idea of the song. He leaned forward with his hands on his knees, his jaw set and his heart pounding, while the great chorus swelled toward him like a tidal wave to engulf him:

> *John Brown's body lies a-mouldering in the grave—*
> *John Brown's body lies a-mouldering in the grave—*
> *John Brown's body lies a-mouldering in the grave—*
> *His soul is marching on.*
> *Glory, Glory, Hallelujah!*
> *Glory, Glory, Hallelujah!*
> *Glory, Glory, Hallelujah!*
> *His soul goes marching on.*

Ike suddenly grunted, realizing that tears were running down his face. "God danged babies!" he exclaimed, but he said it because he loved these boys. The head of the blue column was now almost abreast of Ike and Pru, first the Colonel on a white horse, with his bugler behind him and followed by his mounted staff, then the colors and regimental standard, with the color guard, then the band on foot, carrying their instruments and singing with the rest, then the ten companies with their captains leading on foot, the whole column stretching back a good three hundred yards, shouting their song and swinging freely at route order in perfect step.

When the Colonel was passing Ike and Pru he turned and spoke to his bugler who turned in his saddle and sounded a flurry of notes. The singing shredded away and stopped. All the captains shouted, "Company—attention." A thousand men stiffened, eyes to the front, and a thousand muskets swung up to the shoulder arms, rising and falling like a gigantic, steel-matted carpet, as they all kept step to the song still echoing in every boy's soul.

And the suddenly silent marching was even more moving to Ike than the singing had been. As they climbed the little grade up to the crossing, each blue-coated soldier laden with musket, knapsack, haversack and canteen, there was a grim, plodding shuffle to their heavy stride that had more power and fate in it than the free lilt with which they had marched and sung before. Ike did not share the feelings John had often expressed, the sense of a nation marching with invincible power to its destiny. But suddenly he was struck by the thought that here was old Byzantium and old Blackwater County moving out of his own background into some future foreshadowed by Bub's fate, the end of everything and everybody he had known. Nine-tenths of them were boys from the old homesteads. Ike knew most of them intimately, and all of the thousand by name. They were the names of his childhood, the names of his whole life. He knew these boys and he knew not one in a hundred would come back until he had done the job he was setting out to do. "By God!" he thought with a surge of emotion that choked him, "my place is with the Gang, right or wrong! Who am I to lord it with my ideas? To hell with ideas!"

As Company A, mostly from Rumford township, marched past, he stood up, waved his hat and yelled at the top of his voice, and the crowd at the crossing above took up his cheer. Not an officer or man of the Company shifted an eye to his salute. Company B, mostly from Camilla township, shuffled by, and not one of those hundred fellows he knew looked at him. Then came John and Company C, one hundred per cent from Byzantium township and including his best friends. Ike redoubled his yells and all the time Pru was waving her silly little lace handkerchief. But not John, not one of those boys he loved, relaxed his rigid attitude to turn his head toward him. Ike felt a terrible loneliness possess him. He was ostracized, shut out from his world. Then, as they passed him, Ike noticed that George Fulton, marching nattily with his sword at his shoulder, had his eye closed in an enormous wink, and Jabe Munson, treading along like a bearded giant, was showing his teeth in a horrible, blood-thirsty grimace. "By God!" thought Ike, "George and Jabe would go off with a joke!" And he yelled to them both by name.

By this time the head of the column had turned in beside the train. As Company D, Houston township, started by, the band, having halted, let loose with "The Girl I Left Behind Me," and the men quickened their step to keep time. Ike stood with his hat raised till the last of the regiment had passed, then jumped down and said to Pru, "Ye'd best get out. I'll send the 'Paloosa back." He helped her down, and himself ran up the grade to the crossing beside the supply wagons which brought up the rear.

By the time he got there the regiment was fallen out and most of the boys were sitting down, biting off quids of tobacco and getting them stowed. The flower girls were having a great time passing among them and throwing flowers in all directions in response to their calls. Many of the soldiers were cutting off buttons and giving them to the girls for souvenirs. As soon as Ike arrived, John turned Company C over to First Lieutenant Medad VanSanford and trotted back to where Pru was waiting. The officers were all wearing "monkey caps" today, instead of black felts.

During the next fifteen minutes Ike said good-by to the members of the Gang and so many others that he had to take out his note-book to set down the messages for relations and sweethearts. At last the regiment was ordered to fall in again and the companies were allotted to their cars. "Good-by, Ike"— "Take care o' chores, Ike"— "See ye t' Richmond," came the chorus of yells as the boys swarmed up on the platforms and disappeared in the train. Ike's last injunction to First Sergeant Jabe Munson was, "Don't be too god-danged brave"; and Jabe whispered back, "By Jiminy, I'm the fastest sprinter in the regiment." John came up, and as they shook hands Ike said, "Give 'em hell, 'Paloosa, since ye're going, and I mean it." John gave him a grateful smile and a final pressure of his hand. "You'd better go back to Pru," he said. "She's down there alone." As Ike started off, John stepped up on the platform and watched him.

Ike was so full of emotion that he scarcely heard Pru's first remark as they climbed into the buggy—"I think that foolish little cap of John's is most unbecoming." He slapped the livery horse with the reins and drove up to the crossing, pulling in a rod short of the track. The conductor yelled, "All aboard!" Steam streaked out of the engine's cylinders, and as the train moved slowly onto the crossing Ike had a sensation of something enormous being drawn upward and out from his body. The little crowd beside the train was cheering, and the flower girls, now massed in a tableau, were all waving their handkerchiefs. But Ike stood in silence with his hat lifted, watching A Company pass, then B, then C, with John on the platform, and every soldier at the windows waving and shouting to Ike; then more rapidly D, E, F, G, I, K, L. In the leading coaches, already far down the track and receding fast, the regimental band struck up,

> *Glory, Glory, Hallelujah!*
> *Glory, Glory, Hallelujah!*
> *Glory, Glory, Hallelujah!*
> *His soul is marching on.*

When the sound of the train and the music had faded round the curve, Ike started the horse up the street at a walk. He felt more loneliness than he had ever known. Suddenly he heard Pru beside him say, "Silly, silly boys! Silly, silly little boys." And Ike glanced at her with what was a new experience for Pru in the world of men, a look of unmitigated hatred. On the Mall a mile away the two cannon were beginning their hundred-gun salute, and there was the roar of a crowd cheering at the station. Pru slipped her hand through his arm. "Everybody is sure they'll be back in just a jiffy," she said sweetly.

CHAPTER LXXVII

A F T E R taking Pru home to the Liberty and delivering the rented buggy to the stable boy, Ike walked slowly up the Mall toward his bank. He still felt the half-frightened hollowness which had come over him when the troop train pulled out. The Mall seemed a new place, and he touched his hat to acquaintances with curiosity in his eyes, as if they were strangers he had just met, strangers who from now on were to be his friends. At the corner of Gadston Street he stopped and looked up at the big Tanofly Block Bub had near ruined himself in building. For the first time he saw it simply as a building, so much brick, mortar, glass and wood, instead of what it had always been before, a part of Bub. It was a thing without a soul now, because Bub did not exist any more. Ike walked along rapidly, no longer looking earnestly into the faces he greeted. He knew he was alone. All these good people were strangers to him and would remain so. The village was empty.

At Washington Hall corner he paused and stood for a moment indecisively. He was impelled to turn round and walk back to Factory Street, for old Jerusalem Stone was one man in the village he would like to see. But he decided he must first get his own notions squared off, so he crossed the South Mall and entered his bank. He learned from the clerk that Old Jerry Stone had come in shortly before, looked around, and walked out without saying anything.

Ike went into his office, sat down, and looked out the back window. He saw Ostrum Applemore come out of the *Democratic Union* office, and soon afterward Squire Fulton entered the *Eagle* office; but much as Ike despised the one and loved the other, they both seemed equally strange to him, like wooden figures that had no human meaning. Lem Grabbot came in to talk about the Kamargo Woollen Mill trying to get a government contract for uniforms—Ike was now a small stockholder and a director in old Lem's mill with its Irish employees. After Lem went, Ike tried to figure on the things he'd have to do as Bub's executor and the only outside stockholder in the Tanofly Mill. He decided there was no sense in doing anything until he gave out the news of Bub's death, and it would be best not to do that till the folks had a chance to calm down after the departure of the 50th. The only important new business Ike had afoot had to do with the engine company. Alec Mathiesson had gone to Washington yesterday, and there was nothing Ike could do about that till Alec got back. He looked at his mail, but couldn't think straight enough to answer anything. At half-past eleven he got up and went to the club rooms, determined to think out this yearning he had to go after the fellers and enlist in the 50th. The place was deserted, for Fritz the factotum was in John's company. Ike sat down in his usual place and tilted back his chair against the wall.

Ike had four contacts with the world, like four trees rooted in his life and lifting their branches and leaves outward to mingle with existence. One was a practical tree, his industrial and financial preoccupations. One was a spiritual tree reaching out through the stars and the winds to touch what he called God. One reached wistfully far away toward the little son he had never seen. One spread its sensitive leaves among his friends. It was this last tree that had seemed to draw out of him, roots and all, when the 50th's train started off round the curve this morning. As he sat here now among the chief associations of ten years, and many of the associations of his whole life, this tree of friendship seemed to slip back into place and for a little while everything seemed as real as ever. Bub especially was an active presence there in the chair at the end of the table where he always sat playing poker, with his hat tilted forward over his forehead. Ike lit a cigar and postponed the ordeal of decision, indulging himself in the nearest thing to repose he had known in three days, only rolling his cigar a little too frequently from one side of his mouth to the other, and spitting at the cuspidor a little too often and too inaccurately.

But after a few minutes, like a child who had run to bed from the terrors of the dark and buried his head in the covers, he began to feel the outer emptiness pressing in on him with all its perils. When the distant Baptist Church clock started to strike twelve, the sound was an abrupt reminder of actuality, and Ike tilted up his cigar with a jerk, knocking off the ashes on his waistcoat. A moment afterward a gust of wind rattled a window, and the sound shocked him into sudden loneliness, reminding him that the false animation of that window was his only companionship here.

Again the tree of Ike's love for his friends drew out of him and left a frightening void. The rooms were no longer peopled with warm ghosts. They were absolutely empty. Only the things the friends of some former life had touched, long ago. There was where Bub used to sit; but Bub was not there now and would not be again. There Joe Kirkwood used to sit, and he always chose that stretch of floor to go to sleep on when he was drunk; but Joe wasn't there now and perhaps never would be again. Yonder at the dark, empty bar Ike had stood for many drunken hours, arguing religion and women and politics with Jabe and Medad and Fred; but Jabe and Medad and Fred were gone, and it wasn't likely that all three of them would come back. There at the other window George used to sit and pass pleasantries about the people they didn't like in town; but George wasn't there now. Nobody was there—only the window rattling in the wind. Right here in this window John used to sit, and they shared every secret either of them had; but John was gone off to the war where Bub had gone, and he wasn't there any more than Bub was. There was the table in the back room where they had all had supper together hundreds of times; but there was nothing there now but the table made of wood, and the table didn't give a damn that the fellers had gone away.

"To hell with ye," Ike said suddenly, addressing the empty rooms and everything in the world that was indifferent to him and his friends. In a flight from fear he rose, walked out into the hall, locked the door that hadn't ever been locked before, ran down one flight of stairs to Lem Grabbot's office, gave him the key, said the lease was over for now and he'd have the things moved out whenever Master Grabbot said. Then he walked down the second flight of stairs to the sidewalk, went up to Mary Spencer's and said he wanted to be her boarder. Mistress Spencer's drunken husband —Mattie's pa—had died a few years back, and his change into a blessed memory had somewhat lightened her spirits.

After forcing down a little dinner without exchanging a word with any of the boarders, Ike set out into the country on the main Round Harbor Road. Twenty minutes later he climbed the steep little hill where he had sat more than ten years before when he was upset about Tavie and about John's having turned against him as a result of Pru's lying letter. Since then the former pasture on top of the hill had been stoned and plowed and it now carried a six-foot stand of corn. But on the edge of the plateau the butternut grove remained as it was, and Ike sat down on the thin grass under the trees exactly where he had sat before. He laid aside his hat, put his elbows on his knees, his bearded chin in his hands, and considered without thought the wide prospect of fields and woods, ending in the long and immutable line of Lake Ontario. Over the lake there was a band of blue sky round the western horizon.

After the activity of walking, the silence of the scene began to assert itself and the vast peace of Nature began to pour into Ike's empty soul.

Behind him the wind whispered of it through the corn, and above him in the leaves of the butternut trees; and he knew it would have whispered with the same eternal intimation if he had not been there. He sank gradually into his mood of prayer, his communion with the inclusive God that contained death and change and rendered them insignificant. The worshipful part of him, the mystical tree rooted in his own spirit, came alive and rustled its leaves.

Yet, while this offered escape from the void where the other tree had been, the void remained in its own region, and the vacuum drew on his soul and mind to be filled with some faith having human application. As hundreds of times before, he began to grapple with the problem of what the eternal truth of God had to do with man and his petty actions for good or for ill, with this war and the way hundreds of thousands of men were marching out to fight for something they thought they understood, with himself and whether he should or should not go out with his friends as he was now impelled to do.

Ike reviewed his long-standing convictions from the beginning. A man must worship God in his own way, and the same thing in him that worshipped his God would love his friends, could even love people who were not his friends, could love everybody and everything in the world because he saw in them the same thing that he had, the spirit that could worship and love. And the only guide he could find for conduct was to do nothing which would dry up that worship and that love, either in himself or in other people. A man's business was to stay where he belonged and be fond of people, and outside of that to do whatever interested him or whatever seemed needful, so long as it didn't hurt anybody else or interfere with anybody else's business.

In his sensitized mood Ike pondered once more this business of slavery in the South, and he could not get by the conviction that you hadn't any call to meddle in another feller's affairs, even if you figgered he was doing wrong, unless the wrong he was doing was interfering immediately with the peace of your community or the peace of somebody you were fond of. It might be all keerect to help the South get rid of slavery by offering to buy the slaves and thus setting them free, but that shouldn't be done unless they consented to it first. It was clear they were going to fight for it, and that meant that before we got through we'd cause a danged sight more suffering than slavery ever did, killing off the smartest youngsters on both sides. Of Ike's two friends who had got into it, one was already dead. What would it come to if they went on shooting each other for a long time? The fear of some of the Gang—perhaps John—getting killed made

Ike set his jaw and put his face in his hands, until gradually the silence around him reassured him again and he was able to pick up the thread of his thought where he had left off.

After all, everybody except Bub and Joe had agreed with him about abolition. It was this business of preserving the Union that got under their skin and made wild men of them. For the life of him, Ike couldn't get any more excited about preserving the Union than he could about abolishing slavery. The Union and States couldn't eat or die or get hurt or worship God or be fond of people. To Ike's way of thinking the Union and the States didn't exist at all. They were just words. What existed was the folks, and if the folks in one place wanted to live in one way and the folks in another place wanted to live in another way, they ought to have separate governments. Ike couldn't see any point in just having a big government. If, as the 'Paloosa was always saying, we were figgering to make the best government the world had ever seen, we could do it quicker and better with a few states that agreed than we could with a lot of states that disagreed so much they were minded to fight each other. Ye can't make a feller like ye or get along with ye by knocking him down, thought Ike.

He felt so strongly about this that he came out of his mystical mood and took to throwing stones angrily at nothing down the hill. He'd thought all this out before, and there was nothing in the Gang's going away that changed his ideas. He really agreed with Pru when she blurted out, "Silly, silly boys." What had made him mad was that she said it at the wrong time. The fact was, she didn't give a god dang about John or any of the fellers. That was the whole trouble with Pru, even if she was right in most of her notions.

"With me it's different," thought Ike, and he stopped throwing stones and sat quietly again. "I'd as lief be dead as alive without the fellers around, especially the 'Paloosa. It seems as though I'd rather go along with the Gang and get blown up with them, even if I do figger their notions are twisted.

"And yet, by God"—he threw another stone—"there ain't a shake of sense to that feeling, once ye figger it out. My being there won't stop their getting blown up. It's just a matter of staying with them a little longer, maybe getting peppered myself. If I got peppered, what good would that do anybody? And if I didn't, how'd things be different than as if I'd stayed at home where I belong? When ye come down to it, it's more than likely some of them—maybe most of them—will come home anyway, for the war can't last past autumn, that's certain. Ye're just being a baby, Ike Lathrop. Ye're lonesome, and ye're scared, after what's happened to Bub. There's nothing for it but to take it on the chin and mind your own business!" In hopeless exasperation he threw himself back on the ground and tried to stop thinking. The void in his soul was not filled at all, and in escape from it, his subconsciousness returned to the feeling of huge, peaceful nature around him. And so desperate was his need of escape that it carried him all the way into sleep.

As Ike slept, the sky slowly cleared and the sun moved down toward supper time, while the wind freshened and rustled steadily in the corn. The low branches of the biggest butternut tree shaded him from the sun's direct rays, but the increased light half woke his consciousness into a state that was partly dream and partly thinking. He felt the universe round him like an endless forest living in the summer sun, with birth and death going on quietly and without pain, as easy as the rain on the leaves or the snow melting in the spring.

Then through the forest there came a feeling of uncertainty, something like fear, and everything was troubled and seemed to be moving this way and that, it didn't know where. Then the fear and uncertainty became a sound, at first a rustling, then a yelling and a screaming that was a pack of thousands and millions of wolves hunting through the forest, chasing everything that lived, killing everything and fighting each other. And Ike knew that the wolves were men, and he felt a deep sadness, knowing that it was men who went about like wolves, destroying things and throwing everything out of kilter, when they were the critters in all nature that had the most sense, likely the only critters that had the sense to appreciate and enjoy what they had, this big, peaceful universe to live in. And men did these things figgering somehow they were going to make things better, which meant each according to his own special ideas; only their ideas didn't agree, so they had to keep fighting each other.

It seemed to Ike that the only real wrong in the world was this wolfish thing that made folks want to change things and make them what they called better, this talk of making a perfect country. It was this thing they called idealism, this hollering and working yourself into a lather about righteousness that was really wickedness, like old Deacon Vic Birdseye trying to keep folks from dancing or drinking good liquor; like these youngsters now setting out to tell those Southerners how to run their affairs. Ike guessed his pa had understood that, which was why he had always been against abolition and the Underground Railway. He felt closer to his pa than he had ever felt before.

Ike came fully to consciousness and opened his eyes; but the vision of the universe and of men's wolfish ways held as a new conviction in him, a perception that made him pity the wolves and feel a tremendous pity for the world. The void, left when the tree of love had been drawn out by the roots, was filled; but it was filled with sadness, a true and spiritual substance but without joy. Out of the sight of the distant lake with the sun now golden on it, and out of the sound of the wind in the corn, he got happiness and eagerness to live; but out of thinking of mankind he got only this heavy sadness that he knew would stay with him always. He was as lonely for the Gang as ever, but his loneliness was universal now, and he knew he must wait for fate that was beyond any man's control. His loneliness was for mankind, for what mankind ought to be, what they were born to be and were not. He'd have to go on being lonely. His duty, as Pa always said, was to follow the truth as he saw it.

Back at Mistress Spencer's for supper Ike was cheerful and easy with the boarders, quite different from the way he was at dinner. After supper Mattie came in for a few minutes off from the Gadstons. She kept looking at him and was flustered about something. Ike bet it was about Joe, for he knew Joe had told her that Ike knew about things. So he stayed around until they were alone in the parlor. Mattie whispered that she had a letter from Joe, and they hadn't been in that battle at all.

Ike went back to his and John's rooms over Quin's drug shop, and the place was so alive with John that he felt a sort of comfort there, exactly the opposite of what he had felt in the clubrooms before he went out in the country. For the first time that day Ike wanted a drink, and he sat alone with a bottle of port until after eleven o'clock. He thought a lot about Joe and Mattie, what a tender, motherly girl she was, and how Joe was certainly shooting straight with her, had been for ten years. Telling her those lies about not having been in that battle! Mattie was a mighty pretty girl when she wasn't blue about something. Ike wondered if the celibacy in which he had lived these ten years was worth all the trouble he had had in settling into that state and the occasional battles he still had with his desires. It wasn't so bad with the 'Paloosa around living the same way, but it was going to be harder sledding alone. It would be nice to have somebody like Mattie, but none of the easy ladies he knew were as sort of peaceful and kind as she was. He thought of Pru, and the notion of Pru as an easy lady made him chuckle to himself, the first time he had smiled that day.

The next afternoon right after dinner at Mistress Spencer's, Ike set out for Factory Street and the tannery, saddlery, and carriage shop of Jerusalem Stone. During the last ten years Old Jerry had modified his original, harsh judgment of Ike. In fact, one day during Ike's second year in the village one of the older apprentices had told him that he had heard Old Jerry say, "If any of them rich upstarts is to make anything of himself, it might be young Lathrop." Ike had taken this as an invitation, and thereafter had formed the habit of dropping into the Factory Street shop two or three times a month, just for the pleasure of tilting back in a certain chair, watching Old Jerry work, and sometimes gleaning pungent opinions on current affairs and the leading citizens of the town. The high priest of youth rarely criticized Ike directly, but it was always plain when some conduct of his was under suspicion. The surest sign was the location of his special chair. If it stood where Ike had himself originally placed it against the post between the two sets of double doors, he knew that all was well with him. But if it was farther back in the shop where he had first found it, he knew it was time to review his recent activities.

When Ike arrived that afternoon, the old man, now over eighty, sat in his usual place in the open double doors, sewing a breeching. "Afternoon, Old Jerry," said Ike, sticking his silver-headed cane under his arm and touching his silk hat. "Howdy, Young Lathrop," was the harsh reply. Ike knew he was in good grace. His chair was in its hospitable place, and it was rare for Old Jerry to vouchsafe more than a grunt of greeting. Ike offered him his plug of tobacco and stood while the old man cut off a slice. Then he did the same for himself, sat down, and tilted his chair back against the doorpost.

"A'mighty sorry to miss ye at the bank," he threw out after a minute's silence. Old Jerry grunted, spat, bit off a thread, started sewing again, then said, "I see yer brother set out on the cars yesterday morning." Ike said nothing. He knew he had been right. Old Jerry had dropped into the bank for no reason except that he figgered Ike might be feeling lonely. It was the surest sign Ike had ever had that he was definitely accepted into the flock.

After another long silence Ike said, "Still figger not to go to war. Come tarnal near enlisting after the fellers left." Old Jerry lifted his eyes in a quick, suspicious look. "Afterwards," continued Ike, "I recollected what Pa used to say about every man judging for himself. I figger 't ain't right, the war." Old Jerry grunted, then mumbled, without looking up but trembling a little with emotion, "Half my colts gone off, hankerin' t' git peppered. No tendin' t' business any more. Told 'em if they went they needn't come back. Didn't do no good. Half-baked little smart alecks! Makes a feller feel old, Young Lathrop." "Yep," said Ike, sinking far down into his own loneliness and knowing that in those few phrases Old Jerry had covered everything he had himself thought out yesterday. Old Jerry felt about his apprentices exactly as Ike felt about the Gang. They had loneliness and sorrow in common.

They both felt embarrassed at the revelation of their profoundest feelings, and the older man quickly sallied out of it. "See yer partner's gone t' Washington," he said in his harshest tone. "Yep," said Ike, wondering how anybody had found out where he was going. "What ye up to?" demanded Old Jerry. "Likely nothing," said Ike, and, far from resenting the rebuff, the old man instantly respected Ike's privacy. They sat silent for five minutes, feeling comfortable again with something unrevealed between them. Without preamble Ike rose and said, "Good day, Old Jerry." "Good day to ye, Young Lathrop," said the old man without looking up from his sewing. And Ike set off down Factory Street, feeling a glow of comfort in his sadness.

And immediately Ike did one of those things expressive of the deep paradox in his nature between impulsive, human warmth and the coldness that used to frighten his ma and Tavie, the absolute, almost thought-proof separation between his emotions, mystical or personal, and his practical calculations and activities, the divorce in him between the religious and moral impulses which had been united and indistinguishable from each other in all his forebears for eight generations. Without the slightest hesitation he walked across Fleet's Island and Alec's new Middle Falls Bridge to the Steam Engine Company. He entered Alec's office, locked the door, opened the safe, took out a roll of drawings and estimates, spread them on the large drawing table and fell to studying them intently. They were the results of Ike's having persuaded Alec to defer enlisting for a spell, and had been laboriously compiled during the last two months. They had to do with Alec's business in Washington at the present moment, where he was looking into certain patents as well as the present needs of the Government. They were drawings and estimates of the cost of manufacture of various types of cannon.

CHAPTER LXXVIII

N O W the lonely months of the war began to drag over Ike with the slowness of years. The newspapers and the letters from John and the rest brought no indications of military activity, but enthusiasm in the village rose into a continuous thunderstorm whose crashing and flashing it was impossible to escape anywhere. A recruiting tent, with its flagpole higher than the young trees, stood permanently on the westernmost of the three islands in the center of the Mall. New companies were always being formed. The Square blazed with posters proclaiming the virtues of this righteous crusade. Mass meetings were held two or three times a week on the Mall, inspiringly addressed by ministers, visiting politicians and other fire-eating patriots. Awkward squads were forever drilling there, and the dead of night was the only time not violated by the squeal of fifes and the rattle of drums.

Saddening as all this was to Ike, he was even more revolted by the obstructionist activities of the Copperhead Democrats, who, until the suspension of the writ of *habeas corpus* throttled them, held anti-recruiting mass meetings under the forensic leadership of Applemore and Judge Longcoat and with the financial backing of Horace Gadston and most of the industrialists. Their arguments were lofty, but Ike knew their only real concern was for their Southern markets which the war was destroying. Nat Gadston was the only one of the lot Ike respected, for Nat made no bones of any but business motives. In September Nat formed a new and pretentious club, the Byzantium Club, which bought Seth Marlow's house on the South Mall—thereby throwing old Seth pretty much on Ike's support during his few remaining years. The surviving Nestors refused to join the new club, but Ike and Alec Mathiesson did, and immediately regretted it. The atmosphere was dominantly Democratic, and there was too much and too forced good fellowship, too much parading of superiority over the Republicans, too much thumping of the bar and noisy damning of the war, and too unmistakable embarrassment when anybody in uniform came into the room. Ike felt something false and hypocritical that drew the heads of these

men together in their secret den. There was not one among them who
shared his honest and quiet pacifism that needed no loud declaration. At
heart they were as wolfish as the Republicans, as deeply impressed by the
idealism that was sending men out to die for the betterment of the world.
Only, for purposes of private gain, these men were not risking their lives
and were making up reasons to justify themselves. After the first week of
the Byzantium Club's establishment in its big house, Ike gave up going
there except as required to meet people on business.

Meanwhile, the Byzantium Steam Engine Company proceeded to the
manufacture of cannon for the Army. In mid-August Alec returned from
Washington with a contract for a trial lot of a dozen three-inch, rifled
ten-pounders. Ike wrote about the proposal to the other stockholders, Solon
Samson and Jabe Munson. Jabe sent back his approval from camp; but
Solon wrote that he could not be identified with an enterprise for profit out
of the war, that if the plan were carried through he must withdraw from
the company. The plan was carried out, and Ike negotiated the sale of
Solon's stock to Nat Gadston. He got Solon's permission to put the $5,000
proceeds into gold, and tucked it away for him in a safe deposit box. Ike's
own $50,000 in gold was not tucked away, but he kept it available as part of
the general reserve of the bank.

Alec, with his usual inventive zeal, accelerated by desire to get the business going so he could enlist, went to work on the new installations required,
while at the same time carrying out experiments which produced what he,
Ike and the Ordnance Department agreed would be the strongest—and
the most expensive—material ever used in field artillery. On December 1st
the first gun was completed. And so faithful to Ike's order of secrecy had
the employees of the engine company been that not until the gun was being
drawn out Mill Street to the open country for proving did the news leak
out of what the engine company was up to.

The next day, when Ike dropped by Old Jerry's, his chair was removed
from its usual place, and the wrinkled oracle did not greet him or ask him
to sit down. "Gone to making cannon for the Government," said Ike, suspecting that was the trouble, though he'd long ago thought it all out and
was easy in his conscience. Old Jerry made no sign. "Figger no wrong in
it," continued Ike, tapping his boot with his cane. "Ain't furthering the war,
for if we don't make them somebody else will. Government's going to take
just so many anyhow. Might as well see that they're good ones, so they
won't bust and hurt the gunners." Old Jerry stirred angrily. "Take it ye
ain't overly pleased with my scheme," Ike persisted. "Young Lathrop,"
snapped Old Jerry, laboring to his feet and glaring at him, "ye're just where

ye was when ye sold that late-cut gray to Stark and afore that when ye didn't git no hidin' fer yankin' Bashan." And with that he waddled back into the shop, by way of dismissal.

On the 5th of January the Engine Company shipped off a dozen three-inch rifles to Washington. Already the Government had ordered a further consignment on the same specifications, and an Ordnance Officer was stationed in the village to oversee the manufacture. Alec concluded that he had done all he could, and through John's efforts succeeded in enlisting in Company C of the 50th in place of poor Hate-evil Wilcox, who had died of fever in camp on Meridian Hill, Washington. Before setting out, Alec left Ike his proxy to vote his stock in the company.

The departure of Alec completed Ike's isolation in the village, for the new enterprise of the engine company had thrown a polite but unmistakable reserve over the previous friendship of the surviving Nestors. Inwardly he was secure in his convictions, and in his midriff there still lived the triple glow that was the love of his God of Nature, the love of his unknown son out in Oberlin, and the universal sadness that was the new form of his love for John and his other friends. But the sadness was a heavy thing, and Ike's sociable nature could not quickly adjust itself to living upon inward convictions alone. His withdrawal into himself had a withering effect on his outward appearance. His previously golden mane of hair almost completed its change to pure white. By the end of January his old swinging walk had lapsed into a slow, slightly stooping gait, as if he were bearing along the snowy sidewalks the whole weight of the gray sky. Not yet thirty, from having been considered a prodigy of youth, he began to be referred to as "Old Lathrop," even by men who were twenty years his seniors.

What feminine solace Ike might have found was shut out by his loyalty to his friends. He loved to sit with Mattie Spencer in her ma's little parlor whenever she got off from Gadstons'. Mattie long since knew the truth about Bub's death and how Joe had lied to her, and Ike could tell that she felt mighty close to him. When he was with her he felt surrounded by a tenderness such as he had never known with anyone but Aggie, and there were times when he was sure she would let him kiss her. About once a week he dropped in on Pru, and it was she, not Mattie, who kept him awake nights and bothered his dreams. Yet Pru must be saved for the 'Paloosa, as Mattie must be saved for Joe. Ike continued the battle with his desires that was harder than ever now. He suffered the more for knowing that Nat Gadston was seeing Pru two or three times a week, taking her to all the parties, and that Pru was flirting with him as only she knew how to do. And when he wrote John of this and asked for instructions, he got small comfort from his brother's reply. "—If I didn't know how distasteful it would be to you, I would suggest that you plunge in and take her away from Nat."

During all these months from mid-summer, '61, through the winter of '62, Ike found his only contentment in his Saturday evenings and Sundays out at the homestead; for Ben agreed with his pacific ideas. He wanted to move back there for good, and decided to try taking care of business by riding in two or three days a week. Accordingly, he stayed out one Monday in the middle of February, and enjoyed going back to chores and working out in the snow with Ben. But on Tuesday when he came into the bank he got the worst start of his business career. The day before, the first bundle of "greenbacks" had arrived from Washington, a week earlier than they were scheduled. Ike had not yet instructed his clerk in the proper use of this new form of currency, and in the afternoon there had been a mild run on gold. The clerk had passed it out innocently, while the other three banks were refusing their depositors anything but the new notes. In this way about ten of Ike's hoarded fifty thousand in gold had slipped away while he was mending fence in the lower pasture.

Other things combined to make him give up the notion of going back to the homestead for a while yet. There were signs that a business boom was beginning, and the new currency required readjustments in prices and wages in all of his concerns. Incidentally, on the question of wages Ike was as independent and cranky as he was in other matters. Throughout the rise in prices that began now and continued until the end of the war, the three companies that he managed—the railroad, the engine company and the Tanofly mill—were the only ones in Byzantium, beside the Fulton and Price mill, that kept increasing their wages in proportion with the cost of living.

One reason for the revival of business was the optimism that followed the capture of Forts Henry and Donelson in February. Ike shared in the general jubilation, and was ignorant enough in military matters to share also in the general belief that at last a decisive blow had been struck and the South would soon surrender. But this naïve credulity was soon shaken by a change in the tone of the weekly letters which John had all this time been sending to the *Eagle*, always with enclosures for Ma and Ben, and usually for Ike. It was soon plain that the 'Paloosa did not share the civilian belief that the war was almost over.

At first, after reaching Washington, the letters had been enthusiastic, celebrating the virtues of "over a hundred thousand brave fellows camped in and about the city. . . . I have not heard of one who is here for any other purpose than to see to it that the Union of States shall be preserved, and, in some cases, that slavery shall be abolished also." . . . "It is inspiriting to realize that there is no single mean motive behind the Union cause, whereas the whole movement of secession is based on the fear of the Rebels that they may lose their pitiful, human property." And, in the private enclosure for Ike, "Ah, Scamp, you should be with us."

By January John's letters showed that he was sharing the impatience of the country at the continued inactivity of the Army. "We are trained now if ever an army was. . . ." "Mud, mud, mud, mud, mud. . . ." "The hospitals are full of the 'casualties of the camp,' colds and pneumonia. . . ." "I must report the sad demise of Hate-evil Wilcox from fever. He had just become a corporal, and I know would have been an unusually gallant soldier. It is disgraceful that he should have died in his bed through no fault of his own—" "At last Alexander Mathiesson has joined us!"

Privately John wrote to Ike, "So you have really started manufacturing artillery! I take it this means that at last you are with us." He said he had had a splendid letter from Tavie, who had quit the college, was studying to be a nurse, and was shortly to go to the Army of the West. John said he had written her a warning that as soon as he was wounded he would issue a "special order" that she come to nurse him.

In the middle of February John did not even mention the victories at Henry and Donelson that everybody thought were going to end the war! Instead, toward the end of the month, his reports took an ominous turn. "The regiment is in charge of the Long Bridge over the Potomac . . . Company C was on guard day before yesterday. I was Officer of the Day and did not sleep. I took pride in imagining the hundreds, perhaps thousands, of other such pickets running all the way from the Atlantic to the Mississippi, supported by half a million trained men, all defending the Union and eager to fight for it——"

Then a week later, the dreaded news, "We had our 'baptism of fire' today." The "baptism" consisted of a skirmish between a picket and some Rebel cavalry in which John did not participate, although he was in support and came up in time to hear a few pistol balls whistle and to share in the capture of a Rebel whose horse had been killed and had fallen on him, breaking his leg. John was exuberant: "After the long wait it was exhilarating, I tell you, to charge the real enemy, even though we didn't get there in time to do any firing. We're in it at last! Hooray!"

John was not too exhilarated to write Ike privately: "I find it hard to reconcile your professed disapproval of the war with your manufacturing artillery, presumably at a profit. Scamp, let us hope this will not open up that old misunderstanding."

The next report brought news of a more formidable action. John and his Company C had captured a house which contained a large, isolated, Rebel picket. The Rebels put up a real fight and lost ten men before they surrendered. At the end of the letter John gave the first casualty list for Byzantium, the first impact of the reality of the war, the beginning of that long debit column which the community henceforth would grimly keep, as it were, with its patriotic right hand, while with its left it totalled its financial gains, the first two names, after Bub's and Corporal Wilcox's, of the two hundred odd that would later be graven on the Soldiers' Monument on the Mall. John wrote that the "sad price" of this "victory" was two killed, Corporal Hosea Hunter and Private Matthew Simons, and eight wounded, including Lieutenant George Fulton and Sergeant Frederick VanSanford. George's wound, John wrote, was a mere "graze," a scratch that didn't even take him off duty. But Fred was still unconscious in the hospital, and they feared his skull was broken from a blow of a musket butt.

In his private enclosure for Ike, John made no further mention of Ike's manufacturing guns. Instead, he went at length into his own feelings during this "Affair at Clancy's Farm"; how when he was giving his orders in the woods before the attack his teeth chattered so he could hardly be understood; how in the attack he heard none of the shooting and remembered nothing except breaking down a door with his shoulder; how when they were marching the prisoners back his knees trembled so he thought he'd fall down, and how afterwards Jabe told him that his trembled too, "figgerin' t' obey orders and do what the cap'n did"; but how "I seem to have behaved properly enough, for the Adjutant told me the Colonel had cited me." Near the end of the letter John wrote, "I forgot to say that I got a bullet clean through my cap without touching a hair—don't tell Ma. There is a superstition that if that happens to you, you will never be killed."

Thus John enlarged upon his own feelings and vicissitudes during this "affair." But his only comment on Fred's cracked skull was indirect and rhetorical: "We live now with only one thought—Johnny Reb must pay for Bub, Fred, Hate Wilcox, Hose Hunter and the rest. You know, Scamp, if there is a Heaven I am sure those boys are there. On to Richmond!"

The *Eagle* got out an extra on the day this report arrived, but Ike went to his room and drank a solitary half bottle of whisky. The danged tin soldiers! The "half baked little smart alecks," as Old Jerry had called them! The 'Paloosa talked as if he were playing soldiers and Indians with a lot of five-year-olds and had to pretend he enjoyed it as much as they did. When he tried to get serious, he only used flowery phrases that didn't mean a danged thing, like the Reverend Tremble Thomas. Why in hell didn't he go into the real questions? What was the point of it all? What was the good of killing two men and maiming ten to take some old ramshackle house from the Southern fellers? It seemed like the 'Paloosa couldn't face the real issues any more. Perhaps, when ye got in, the truth was so bad ye danged well couldn't face it! Ye had to make-believe and think about whether ye were being brave or not, like a boy. The whole caboodle of them playing tin soldier, with their lives at stake! They'd all gone clean out of their senses, and for all ye could tell they might stay there, playin' tin soldier the rest of their lives!

Ike started to write John a letter, but soon realized he was too drunk for it. He couldn't sit still, so he went out and started down Columbia Street. There was a mass meeting gathering in the Methodist Church to celebrate this "great victory" of "Byzantium's own Company." Ike went in and stood in a back corner.

During the prayer and the hymn he wished he hadn't come, but there were a lot of people round him and he couldn't get out without making a disturbance. When the Reverend Tremble Thomas began waving his arms and bellowing, Ike felt his blood rising up into his head:

"Lo, now, the great red dragon, having seven heads and ten horns, and seven crowns upon his heads, is loosed in the land for a season of destruction! But, hearken, I say unto ye that he that rideth on the white horse goeth forth to battle, and out of his mouth there goeth a sharp sword. And the great red dragon will be cloven in twain and cast into everlasting fire!"

Ike heard the redoubtable minister start speaking of the boys Ike knew and loved, young men the Reverend Thomas scarcely knew by name: "Lo, my children, let us bow down and humble ourselves before the wonderful works of the Lord. For these young men have turned from the ways of sin"—Ike presumed he was thinking of Bub. "Even from the depths of the pit they saw the gates of pearl shining on high, and, girding themselves with the sword of righteousness, they stood up and climbed thither by the golden stairway where angels do ascend and descend forever. And, lo, they have come to their reward, and even now look pityingly down on us from the right hand of the Lamb!"

Suddenly Ike realized he had said aloud, "God-danged jack-in-napes," and that everyone near by was looking at him. But instead of checking himself he let go. "I beg your pardon, Mr. Thomas," he called out, "but you happen to be speaking of my friends, and I must tell ye that not one of them ever laid any store by your pearly gates and your golden stairway. They are brave fellers and that's an end of it, and neither you nor I are worthy to open our mouths a-blattin' about them till we've gone down there and got blown up alongside 'em." And with that he thrust his way out of the church, while voices in the outraged congregation whispered, "It's Old Lathrop!" "He's an atheist!" "His brother's t' the war but he don't dast go!" "He's makin' money a-sellin' guns t' the Gov'ment!" "He's a disgrace t' Byzantium!" Ike waited outside on the sidewalk, hoping someone would come out and fight him.

But the only one who came out was Mattie Spencer, whom he hadn't known was there. "Oh, Ike," she whispered, looking up at him with her big, gray-blue eyes, "ye're right, and I'm so grateful to ye." And in the public highway in broad daylight he put his arm around her and they walked up and across the street to the door of Redemption Quin's drug shop, both of them tense and Mattie shedding tears. Ike swung open the door and stepped aside for her to precede him, but as she started in he said softly, "Mattie." "Yes, Ike," she said, stepping outside again and looking straight up at him with adoring eyes. "Mattie, I figger you and I have need of one another these days." Mattie bowed her head. "But we mustn't, my girl. We hain't the right, that's all. Ye've to wait for Joe and it's for me to help ye." In a tiny voice, without looking up, Mattie replied, "Ye're right, Ike." Slowly she took his big hand, raised it to her lips and kissed it. Then she turned and walked flaccidly on up the street to her ma's house.

Ike went up to his room, drank the rest of the whisky from the bottle and got himself weeping drunk. When that passed he fell to laughing aloud, being pleased with what he had done to the Reverend Tremble. "Thank God, had a skinful," he chuckled. Then, "Th' pearly gates— Figger th' bottle's th' only pearly gates Bub ever saw. 'R Fred, fer that. 'R any of 'em's th' gumption t' do things, place o' yappin' 'bout 'em." Alternately he laughed at the Reverend Tremble and wept over the danged little tin soldiers, till at last he fell asleep in his chair. He didn't know that already his other chair was set out again, by the post between Old Jerry's double doors.

CHAPTER LXXIX

A FEW DAYS later a letter from Aggie in Oberlin brought Ike the opportunity he had been waiting for for ten years. There was still no word from Connie Oaks—Ike knew that the letters that used to come to Connie's parents, signed "a friend," had stopped at the beginning of the war. Tavie was now with the Army of the West, in Nashville to Aggie's last knowledge. Little Solon was settled with Aggie. It was the chance Ike had wanted, to go out and see his boy without running the risk of upsetting Tave and Connie. In spite of the demands of business, he decided to go. On the 18th of March he set out, light-hearted as a boy himself. His joy was made poignant by being mixed with terror at the prospect of seeing the little fellow he had carried so long as an idea in his mind.

In general Ike did not share John's enthusiasm for the westerners. As he told his ma and Ben afterwards, he figgered their over-friendliness was due to "an itch to make ye think they're good fellers, being they ain't quite sure of it themselves." On the other hand, he did find among them a more realistic attitude toward the war than at home. This was because the western regiments had been engaged in major operations now for near two months, and there were long casualty lists every week. In Cleveland Ike neither saw a bonfire nor heard any speeches or bands, although recruiting was going on. Riding out across Ohio, he sat beside a man who said, "York state, be ye? They tell me yer fellers is a-settin' round Washington eatin' sugar candy."

Aggie met Ike at the Oberlin station alone. He was secretly delighted when she told him that Homer, who was a colonel in the state Adjutant General's Office, was on duty in Columbus. She had not taken little Solon out of school, for she thought best that Ike should not see his son for the first time in public.

Three hours later when the boy walked into Aggie's kitchen, all the nervousness Ike had felt at the prospect of seeing him instantly vanished. Never as long as he lived did he get over that first wonder of looking

599

into his own identical eyes, the reflection of his own identical feelings, in this bundle of young life. There was nothing of Tavie in his appearance, and in his manner only a little of the Samson tenseness. They were like brothers from the start. In the first five minutes they found themselves smiling at each other over nothing in particular, in the way of old friends.

That evening Solon voluntarily climbed up on "Uncle Ike's" lap and they told each other stories. When Aggie began to intimate the wisdom of bed, Solon delayed to tell Ike about his pa, how he had gone away on business after Con died, and how they hadn't heard from him—"how long is it, Aunt Aggie? Yes, two years." The boy pondered. "Say, Uncle Ike," he exclaimed, "why don't you be my pa? Jiminy, that would be fun. Ye'd like Ma too. She's first rate, isn't she, Aunt Aggie? Maybe you know her, though, do ye, Uncle Ike?" Ike nodded, not trusting his voice.

Every day Ike took Solon to school, and in the afternoons they played catch in the muddy yard. A few evenings after he arrived, the boy almost dissolved him by showing the fundamental likeness of their minds. "Say, Uncle Ike," said Solon suddenly at supper, "what's the idee of folks shooting each other the way they say they're doing down south. Jiminy, I'm for freeing the Niggers and all. But it seems to me the Rebels are just as good as the Niggers and I can't understand why we want to shoot them all dead. I guess if it comes to the Niggers being slaves or the white folks all dead I'd ruther see the Niggers slaves. That's what I tell the fellows, and sometimes I have to fight about it. What do you think about it, Uncle Ike? Aunt Aggie only says I'm too young to understand." And he gave Aggie a defiant flash of his blue eyes, as if to say, "Here's somebody knows I have sense."

"Well, Solon," said Ike a little huskily, "since ye've asked me I must tell ye that I feel exactly as you do about it. Our notions are like as two peas in a pod, and for the life of me I couldn't put it any better than you have. To tell the truth, that's why I ain't in the Army like your Uncle Homer and Uncle John, and likely your—pa."

On the 1st of April, having conferred with Aggie, Ike wrote Tavie the following letter:

Dear Tave,

    After all these years this is likely a funny time to write you as I'm going to. As you have likely guessed, I haven't wanted to make another move until we were both perfectly sure of our notions for the rest of our lives. I may as well tell you at the beginning what you're certain to find out soon or late, that my ideas on some matters are different from yours. I admire you no end, the same as I do the Lollapaloosa, but I don't take much more stock in your Reform than I did before, and I think this war is likely to prove a worse mistake even than slavery or the breaking up of the Union.

For all that, I've been thinking about you and young Solon most of the time these eleven years, and for some time now I've had a sort of plot with Ag to let me know when I could come to Oberlin to see him when you and Connie were both away. I wanted to do it this way so as to avoid trouble, and I think you will understand that.

Even if I had gone to college I don't think I could find words to say what a first-rate boy the little fellow is. All in all, he's just about the finest youngster I ever saw or ever hope to see. Incidentally, you'll probably want to have my scalp for having done what I could to . settle him in his ideas about the war and not killing people. I could hardly believe my ears when I heard the little shaver saying things I have thought all along.

But all that is beside the point. Seeing Solon has finally settled my notions about what you and I ought to do. More than anything else I know of I want you to marry me and come back home and we will settle down on the farm, or on some other farm, or even in the village if you would rather. Ag tells me you can divorce Connie anywhere for deserting you, and I have arranged with her about hiring a lawyer as soon as you say the word. I think we would be making a straight start not to see each other until that is over.

I suppose you are under some kind of a contract to finish a term of nursing, but I can't help telling you that I hope you get out of this war as soon as you can and come home and settle down. I may say there is plenty of reforming to be done these days, right in Byzantium. The Micks some of the factories have hired live more like pigs than like men, and even an old toper like me would like to see something done to keep them away from the bottle. I'm a director in the factory that hires most of them and I do what I can, though I haven't much to say. You may be pleased to know that Squire Fulton and I are the only employers in the village who have raised our men's wages so they can keep up with the rising prices. Not that I'm uncommon proud of it. It's only decent.

Your folks and mine were all well to my last knowledge. Likely you know already that Numa has enlisted, just when he was about to get through college. Your ma told my ma that they had promised him his degree, however. I guess he's as smart as his pa and sister.

I don't need to tell you how glad I am to get my mind settled on this at last, and I certainly hope you will feel the same way. You may be pleased to know that one of the first things Solon said to me was, "Uncle Ike, why don't you be my pa?" And soon after he said, "You'd like ma too." I figure that ought to persuade you, if I can't. I am staying here until the tenth of April, and hope to have a reply from you before that. If it doesn't arrive in time Ag will forward it to me at home.

My love to you, Tave—
Ike.

Ike walked around the college campus and past the Post Office twice before he dropped this letter in the box. Then he went back to Aggie's and had a hooker by himself from the bottle he kept in his bed-room drawer.

On the tenth there was no word from Tavie, but the town was tense with the news of the Battle of Shiloh, the first great battle of the war. The telegraph office had become a sort of grim club, and on the way to the train Ike stopped on the edge of the crowd of five hundred that now overflowed it out onto the campus. A boy came out and held up a bulletin scrawled with big letters: ESTIMATED CASUALTIES, 13,000. The crowd stood in stolid silence. Ike didn't dare look at any of them. Slowly, he walked on to the station. Thirteen thousand! More than the whole population of Byzantium Falls!

Ike got home the evening of April 14th and went first to his office in the bank. He lit the gas and found, beside the pile of business mail and telegrams on his desk, an unstamped letter addressed to him in John's hand. He slit it open and read:

At home
March 21, 1862.

Dear Scamp,

On Saturday the fifteenth the Colonel told me we had confidential orders to be prepared to move on the twenty-eighth "for a destination not stated," and that I might have ten days leave, starting that evening. I didn't telegraph because I wanted to surprise you all, and consequently missed you. Ben wanted to telegraph you to come back, and if it had meant only cutting off a day or two of your visit I would have let him. But this would have meant your turning around immediately after or even before your arrival at Aggie's. Feeling that I knew more of the circumstances than Ben, I asked him not to telegraph, and Ma supported me.

It was splendid of course to see Ma and Ben, the homestead and the folks at the Hollow, but I can't say as much for the Falls. I spent most of yesterday there and addressed one of the recruiting meetings. They made a great show of me. I understand you made quite a stir in the Methodist Church! Of course my oratory is not up to the Reverend Tremble's, but I could not help wondering what you would have said or thought when I told the people that, in spite of the dangers, I believed this the noblest opportunity that had come to us since the Revolution, and that personally I would be proud if I were told that I was to die for the Union.

I also told them that there was no glory in battle, but only madness and fear. There seem to be plenty of fifes and drums and speeches, but I would be glad to see on the part of the young men a little more serious consciousness of what they are going in for when they enlist, a little more quiet moral determination and not so much cheering. But I suppose we all have to go through that phase.

There is an under-current of rapacity in the Falls which revolted me even more than it used to. I found it in Nat's new club which I inadvertently entered. I am glad to hear you do not frequent the place. Squire Fulton had previously told me of the profits the Kamargo, the Byzantium Cotton and the Ludlow Woollen are making out of government orders, and I saw signs of it in the wise-acre glances and forced cordiality of Jones Ludlow, Ory Slocum and the rest. If I were to rewrite *Army Regulations* I would provide that anyone who increases his profits in war is guilty of treason, and shall be shot. Altogether, the village seemed empty and meaningless. On the one hand, hysterical enthusiasm, with no understanding of what war really is. On the other hand, these swinish business men making money out of our danger.

Tim Slocum told me he would enlist, but he could not bring himself to defy his old man who has threatened to cut him off if he does. Poor little shaver!

I called on Pru the minute I arrived and found Nat there. Pru seemed to warm up to me more than usual, but Nat was obviously embarrassed. I think you are right that there is something afoot between them. All I can ask of you is that you keep me posted as to what you observe, especially if an engagement seems likely. I don't know what I could do, but I would want to know anyway. After my first resentment, the image of Pru came back on me stronger than ever. But I still think often of that little burlesque girl I told you about and half expect to run into her among the droves of whores in Washington. The night after we took the Clancy house George and Medad and I got drunk in Washington, and I came nearer to falling than I have so far. I am beginning to accredit more than ever your advice that what I need is to experience the thing and perhaps get these dreams out of my mind. I make no more promises.

Besides the Fultons, I called on the families of the men we have lost. Judge VanSanford is still in Washington. When I left, Fred was conscious, but his talk was jibberish and one leg was paralyzed. If he stays that way it would be better if he had been killed. The judge is going to stay with him until he is well enough to bring home.

The only place I have been comfortable on my leave was right here at the homestead. And yet my soul, the thing in me that is really alive, is down there on the Potomac fighting the Rebels. That is real life and real death. It has occurred to me that the village will never seem the same to me again. Already I feel that those of us in the Company will have something in common that will set us apart from other people all of our lives. O Scamp, as I have said so many times, you ought to be with us! I am afraid you will regret having stayed at home. I must continue to believe in your sincerity and integrity in this artillery manufacturing. I cannot tolerate the thought that this or anything will ever come between us. Perhaps beneath all this there is something in me that is glad you are at home, no matter what you are doing. Perhaps in my heart I am more content in the knowledge that you are not in danger.

God bless you, my brother—
John.

P.S. Please write me a full report of your investigations and conclusions in the metropolis of Oberlin, O. And don't forget to keep an eye on Pru and Nat.

After reading this letter Ike did not ride out to the homestead as he had planned to. Instead, he tended to the rest of his mail, then went up to his room at Redemption Quin's and spent the night there. John's letter upset him on several scores, and he couldn't have said which bothered him most. Chiefly, there was the fear John mentioned of their growing apart as a result of the war. Knowing his brother, he did not miss the menace in the statement, "I must continue to believe in your sincerity and integrity." As he lay awake in bed he realized that he could do without anybody in the world, even young Solon, better than John. For the thousandth time he re-fought the question of enlisting, and came back to the same conclusion.

Then there was the new military attitude shown in John's letter. He seemed to be over the tin-soldier prattle, but instead of coming out of it into his senses, he had gone into this even more dangerous attitude of quiet determination, with full knowledge of what he was up against.

Finally, there was John's corroboration of his suspicions that there was something up between Nat and Pru. Why this should bother him so he couldn't figure out. He knew he had an itch for Pru himself, but in the long run he'd be glad to see her married to Nat and the 'Paloosa saved from her, wouldn't he? "Well, wouldn't ye?" he whispered to the darkness. "Ye're danged keerect ye would!" came the determined reply. He forced his mind upon sweet little Mattie Spencer, and so went to sleep.

In the morning Ike waited till church was out, then called at the Liberty, at the risk of being late for dinner at the Hollow. Mistress Stark as usual left him alone with Pru. She was very sprightly and curious about his trip to Oberlin and dreadfully disappointed that he had missed seeing that Mrs. Octavia—was it Oaks?—she had always admired so. After he had risen to go he said with an agitation that annoyed him, "Pru, I want ye should promise me something, and I figger we're old friends enough to give me the right to ask it." "Why, of course!" said Pru, opening her eyes as wide as blue saucers. "I want ye should promise me if ever ye're thinking of marrying Nat ye'll tell me before ye settle on it."

Pru threw back her head in her gay, rippling laugh. "Well, I declare! Now just what in the world would I want to marry Nat for?" "Well," said Ike awkwardly, "he's rich, like you always say ye want, and he's the kind of namby-pamby manners ye take a shine to, and ye told me straight once ye liked him. But, however all that may stand, I want ye to promise me ye'll tell me if ye cal'late to marry him."

Pru trilled again and ended by sighing, "Oh me, Oh my." Then she grew grave and said, "But seriously, my old friend, I wish you would tell John that if he wants to spy on me he'd better do it himself." This made Ike bluster with fury, while Pru looked up at him with an angelic smile. "But there, there," she said, reaching out and touching his hand with a pretty impulse. "If ever I was seriously interested in *anyone* you can be sure John would be the first one I'd tell and—if it is true you are so *awfully* interested"—this with a droop of her long lashes—"I think I might be willing to tell you too."

"Ye'll promise, then?" asked Ike. "Why, of course, you old silly," she said, looking up with her most direct and friendly candor. "Now trot along or you'll keep your mamma holding Sunday dinner for you." As Ike went down the little front stairs Pru pressed her bosom and cheek lovingly against the door post. "Thanks for coming to see me," she said, and gave him her most fatal, sure-fire smile of languishing loneliness. Ike carried it like a sword in his vitals for days.

So preoccupied was Ike with the effects of John's letter and his interview with Pru that the following Wednesday, when his mail was brought to him, he was at first oblivious to the significance of a letter addressed in Tavie's hand and forwarded by Aggie. Then suddenly the importance of it dawned on him and all feeling drained away, leaving an emptiness touched with fear. He shut his office door, slit the envelope, and started to read, the pucker in his brow unusually deep and the blood receding from his cheeks. The letter was written in pencil, on both sides of a piece of wrapping paper.

> Pittsburg Landing,
> Tennessee.
> April 11, 1862.

Dear Ike,

Your welcome letter of the first followed me here from Nashville, arriving on the first day of the battle. At another time I would probably be delighted by it and the question you put. Just now I cannot even consider it. It comes from another world, so far away that it hardly seems real.

I am writing this on a cracker box in a large barn where there are, or were, over a thousand wounded, both Union and Confederate, lying round on the bare floor, most of them without bandages other than those made from tearing up their shirts. Over three hundred have been carried out dead already.

At the other end of the barn is what the soldiers call the chopping block, an improvised operating table. Only today we have succeeded in getting the cover from a smashed wagon to curtain off the sight there, and today is the first time the operating with the groans and yells from that end have not been continuous. They would not let me assist in the operating, but I usually go there when they carry the poor creatures to their places on the floor. So over-worked were the doctors that they literally threw arms, legs, feet and hands out the door as fast as they amputated them. Outside, there is a pile of limbs I can only compare to a huge heap of manure. The stench and the flies are terrible. Most of the men are too weak to walk, even if they have their legs, so you can imagine the filth. My own hands are coated with dried blood because the orderlies are late today with the water cans from the river and I don't dare take water from the men to wash myself. They are unbelievably brave, and only a few groan when they are conscious. Hundreds are in delirium, so the terrible noise never stops. They call incessantly for water.

I had to stop here and go the rounds with the cups. Just now they are carrying out a dead man to whom I gave water not five minutes ago. When I walk round, the men all follow me with their great, suffering eyes, for I am the only woman here. They are my love now, Ike, all of them, and I can't even guess what it would be like to read your letter somewhere else. I believe this experience will make a lasting change in me of some kind. It can't seem that anything, not even Solon, will seem as important as it used to.

Some hours later—night.

I had to stop. There were too many calling for me. Many of them are asleep now and I have a candle. Nothing I say now is final, but I think if I were to write you a real answer, it would sound like this: You say you have got your mind settled on this at last. I am afraid I am less concerned with your having your mind settled than I am with your having your feelings settled. The only way in which I need to get my mind settled is in deciding how much you really care for me and whether you really want to marry *me*, outside of wanting to be with Solon and settle down. Once I knew that, I would have no trouble knowing how I felt about it. It wouldn't be a matter of getting *my* "mind settled."

Back from my round again. That might be a snap answer, Ike. But right now I haven't any feelings for anything but my boys here. I thank God I am here where I ought to be. This is my world, and I am sorry to say, my dear, that you seem miles away on some other planet, a place I may never see again, and certainly shall not until the war is over. When you speak of my leaving this service you are talking the most childish nonsense—like you and Solon talking about being peaceful, if you will forgive the sarcasm. It is as if you had never been born. Forgive me, Ike, for I am truly grateful for your letter. I simply must stop. A dozen of them are calling again. Most of them laugh. They call me "sister" and "darling," and it breaks my heart. No one who has not seen it can know what courage is. This must go as it is, for I can't steal any more time from my poor "vintage of the grapes of wrath."

The letter wasn't even signed, but it was Tavie's all right. In the midst of tears rising to stand in his eyes at the picture she drew, Ike felt a sense of personal relief. As if in escape from the horror of the letter, his emotions quieted, and his mind grew clear and perceptive. The agitation of the last few days disappeared. Outside his back window he noticed the crocuses in front of the *Democratic Union* office. Everything would go on as usual. He saw Pru in clear perspective again. She had flirted with him, that was all—the danged pretty little hussy! She likely wouldn't keep her promise, but he'd done what he could for the 'Paloosa anyway.

The full horror of Tavie's letter returned and translated itself into anger. He banged his tilted chair down on the floor and pulled up to the table. By God, he'd publish all of it in the paper but the personal part, even if it did upset the families. They'd see what they were twiddling fifes about! Thirteen thousand in one battle! And John and the 50th already off for "a destination not stated"!

CHAPTER LXXX

IMMEDIATELY after his return from leave in early April, '62, John and the 50th New York became part of McClellan's army of about 100,000 starting up the Peninsula of Virginia against Richmond. John's letters to the *Eagle* resumed their rhetorical, what Ike called their "tin-soldier," quality. The enclosures for Ike were, as before, mostly descriptions of John's own feelings, and confidences about his military achievements and aspirations:

"I am glad to say that, though I was taken with the old trembling of the knees before and after this battle" (In his letter to the *Eagle*, May 6, he had described the engagement before Williamsburg) "I was able to think with some clarity while under fire. . . . Last evening Colonel Mc-Naughton sent for me. He first praised me for 'gallantry'—a word we have heard so often that it has little meaning. . . ."

"Last evening Colonel McNaughton invited me to have supper with him in his tent, and he talked throughout the meal about the management of a regiment in battle. After supper he called the first officers' meeting we have had in two weeks and announced a new order of rank among the captains. Heretofore our rank has been in order of the dates of our commissions, so I have been third ranking captain. The Colonel made me first ranking captain, which means that old Company C now goes on the right of the line, and if the Colonel or Lieutenant-Colonel or Major is put out of action I become acting Major. . . ."

In these letters to Ike there was no personal word, no mention of what to Ike were the realities of the war, no news about Fred VanSanford lying in Washington, nothing about George Fulton, although in his letter to the *Eagle* John had said that "Lieutenant Fulton" had received his second "slight" wound, and three of the privates had been more seriously wounded. After the honest letter the 'Paloosa had left for him when he was home, this resumption of a soldier-boy attitude infuriated Ike. He had delayed publishing Tavie's letter about the slaughter in the Battle of Shiloh, but now he published it and sent John a copy, along with a plea to "write us a few letters as if you were a human being, the kind you know how to write well enough if you want to."

To this Ike got the following icy reply:

"Received your copy of the *Union* containing Tavie's letter and your comment, along with your notation that Squire Fulton had refused to print it in the *Eagle*. Shall write the Squire, suggesting that henceforth he publish anything offered respecting the war that seems true, provided only that it be accompanied, where desirable, by an appropriate statement to offset the effort of you or any person to impair the support of the Army and the war. I believe you will find that the effect of such truth will be to deepen the moral determination of the country. We are not a nation of cowards."

After reading this, Ike decided that since the 'Paloosa couldn't think of anything but himself and his high-falutin notions, he'd give him a dose of his own medicine. He wrote him a long letter in which he mentioned nothing but his business affairs, being perfectly aware of malicious intent in this paragraph:

"We have just sent off our third shipment of guns. The Ordnance Department writes that our last shipment was the best they have received from any factory. I am glad to say we have again raised the wages of our men. Also, though our costs are not yet all footed, it looks as though we might make a penny for ourselves. One way or another the Lathrops may yet make a good thing out of this war, you playing it at one end and I at the other. That's always good business, I'll tell you."

After this Ike did not hear personally from his brother for more than eight months, and John's reports to the *Eagle* became curt, military, stenographic, heartless in their record of the suffering of the men, and presently of the mounting casualty list.

As far as news went, John's letters to Ike were more than compensated for by a series he got from Jabe Munson, beginning after the Battle of Williamsburg John had mentioned, and going on through the campaign. Outside of his Saturdays and Sundays at the homestead and his talks with Old Jerry, these letters were Ike's only solace, indeed his only companionship, during those weeks of terrible suspense. At the outset Jabe forbade Ike to publish them, and because of many details in them he could not share them with Ma. He took the first few of them up to show to Old Jerry, but the tanner was so put out with the war that he wouldn't look at them or let Ike read them to him. Finally, near the end of June, Ike marked excerpts from the batch he had, walked up to Old Jerry's, sat down in his chair between the double doors, and persuaded the old fellow to listen, on the dual plea that if he didn't read them to somebody he'd explode, and that it was good to know there was one of the "half baked little smart alecks" who had kept at least a twisted sort of sense.

While Ike read, Old Jerry never raised his eyes from the bridle he was sewing, and his only comment was an occasional grunt that was close to a groan. Ike read the excerpts in the full vernacular in which they were phonetically written—for Jabe was addicted to *The Biglow Papers* and evidently aimed to compile a chronicle of the war in the rustic idiom:

". . . It's agin reggulations I should give you cowardly sivillians an accurit head count o' the fellers takin' this walkin' trip, fer it's well known if I did ye'd send on the information to our friend this Reb General Johnson that's unreasonably concerned with our affairs. But ye kin git some idee when I tell ye I seed five acre o' steers pasturin' alongside the highway, likely five thousand head that's no more'n a middlin' breakfast fer Capn Long John and his officer friends, bein' this hard tack and pork and coffee's plenty good victuals fer sergents and sech. . . ."

" . . . Fer yer eddication's sake ye'd ought to know what a battle is. A battle's a sort o' contry dance where all the Rebs stand in one line, only hid in trenches, then ye march out in another line till ye're, say, a hundred rod from 'em. Then some o' them cannon ye're a-manufacturin' start shootin' this grape shot at ye, bein' uncommon big and healthy grapes, and soon arter the line where they're a-hidin' sort o' catches fire with a beller. Two or three fellers fall down and wiggle on the ground, and ye go runnin' for'd in a nachrul hurry to turn yer partner, when yer bugle behind ye blows a tune ye call retreat. Then ye sort o' balance the enimy fer a minit and start backin' off, keepin' in line, and lookin' mighty fierce at the Reb and shootin' off yer fowlin' piece now and again. And purty soon ye're back where ye set out, only ye're carryin' some o' yer friends that started out with ye and got sort o' wore out with the exertion o' the dance. . . ."

In spite of Jabe's humor, his letters soon began to show the suffering of the Army from weather and disease:

". . . I can think o' nuthin' t' set down savin' it's rainin' mighty purty. And strickly speakin' that ain't news either, bein's it's been doin' nuthin' else fer two days we been takin' t' conquer about fifteen mile o' secesh mud. . . . It seems fer this promenade ye wait fer the cussedest downpour ye kin ketch, then ye set out with them wagon trains leadin' the procession so's to mix the highway into a perticler edifyin' kind o' puddin', composed o' this gray mud and water and manure, and no bottom to it that any o' them wagons has settled onto yet. Fact, arter mixin' up this puddin' they most usually stop up to their axes in the middle of it and kind o' set there afloatin' while the brave infantry go swimmin' by, totin' what they ain't throwed away o' their seventy-odd pound of equipment. . . ."

". . . As fer Company C, and most o' the 50th fer that, yer big brother and the President has been mighty thoughtful in seein' that jest at this time most everybody's shoes give out fer good—though most of 'em ain't a month old—so's a feller can proceed barefoot which as ye know's the only keerect method o' swimmin'. Some o' the fellers ties rags and strips o' leather onto their feet, but fer me it's more agreeable jest t' let yer toes swash round naked in this fine cool puddin'. . . ."

". . . I ain't tuckered with chasin' Mr. Reb or absquatulatin' away from him, but from ploddin' slow in the mud about thirty mile the past week, and swimmin', and liftin' them supply wagons out o' their sink-holes, and sleepin' three nights in that swamp down yonder with the air so thick and wet Lake Ontary water'd be preferable in the lungs, and drivin' the poor cusses that come here to fight t' cut down oak trees instead, with axes that'd serve better fer hammers, and lug 'em a half mile through that pestilenshul swamp fer them engineers with the orange stripes t' use buildin' corduroy bridges, and finally marchin' over one o' them bridges in bare feet gettin' cut deep with oak splinters instead o' swimmin' the equivalent mile through the swamp and the river that'd be less exasperatin', and then comin' up here yesterday on this sort o' desolate plateau lookin' over the swamp that instead o' improvin' a fel-ler's spirits only sets ye lower by showin' ye all thar be o' the sky which is nuthin' but rain and fog that sometimes splits as much as a quarter mile only t' show ye more rain and fog 'n how there ain't no end onto it. I'm tuckered with all that and with these ticks and lice and this god-darned camp fever has crawled into us outta the swamp and makes our poor devils keel over with a few rod o' marchin' 'n has already took a dozen to horspital a-poopin' blood and has more'n less got into all on us so this quinine's preferable to the leetl' musty pilot bread and bacon we git fer fixin's outta them consarned wagons. . . ."

Jabe's news was but little lightened by the revelation that they could hear the bells of Richmond five or six miles away, or by his report of the 50th's marching fourteen miles to watch, without participating in, the successful action at Hanover Court House. For after that victory, "I figger them Reb Gawds got spiteful at us, fer that night they let us have it prettier'n ever with a storm like it wuz all the waterin' troughs in Heaven droppin' tons o' solid water onto us in the dark like the Red

Sea closed on them Egyptians. And they wan't satisfied t' pound us all that night but kep' it up all through the ensuin' day when we learnt agin that whippin' the enimy ain't no wise related t' winnin' these battles, fer we wuz ordered t' swim all the way back t' this same camp we'd started from, takin' now a hul day t' the fourteen mile and natchully findin' every wedge tent down when we got here at nite and all the fixin's floatin' and spoilt, so we slept in our frog pond hungry. . . . The river down yonder in the swamp is a'mighty roarin' and they say them bridges is all busted out proper. . . ."

Jabe described the observation balloon, "with its name 'Intrepid' wrote on it so the Rebs kin read it t' Richmond," that was let up not far from camp on the property of one "Doc Gaines who's the first feller I've seed in this ignorant, savage, shiftless country ye might come some wise nigh callin' personable folks t' home. Though he ain't nuthin' edifyin' t' visit with and jest sets on his back steps whittlin', I can see it ain't all ways incomprehensible he's likely somat put out at havin' a balloon in his front yard and I figger nigh a divishun o' Yankee soljurs camped in his posies and his corn."

Jabe described with sardonic humor the distant roar and smoke of the Battles of Fair Oaks and Seven Pines on May 31 and June 1, four or five miles southeast of the plateau where the 50th and its Division and Corps were camped. "And I want t' tell ye the bladders o' the 50th N. Y. Inf., Army of the Potomac, did uncommon competent work beginnin' arter supper last night and clean up t' now, like they wuz tryin' t' git rid o' all that water the Rebs a' been pourin' into us now fer two weeks stiddy, so's t' be in light marchin' order in case we wuz called on t' show our famous courage. . . ."

But thereafter the letters revealed a lapse into the struggle against the weight of rain, fever, vermin and inaction:

". . . It ain't news to ye t' say it's rainin'. . . . The camp fever's increasin', some o' the fellers was sick first now comin' back, and some not comin' back, and always some fresh ones faintin' and poopin' blood and off t' th' horspital with the yaller flag, so they was 21 absent sick this mornin' report. . . ."

"O yes, we got them shoes, but at the same time the clothes, that's now got more wood-ticks than material in 'em, is wearin' out uncommon fast, includin' them o' the 1st Sgt. . . . Likewise we got these dawg tents that's somethin' new the Pres. and yer big bro. has devised to add to this seventy pound and more the soljers is told to tote, though most of us has whittled it down to fifty-odd and I cal'late the trail o' blankets and overcoats this Army has left behind it'll take care o' the ignorant savages hereabouts unto their skinny third and fourth generations. . . ."

This was from a letter dated June 22:

"This missive is bound t' be so sad I hesitate t' commit it t' writin'. All there is to it is everything is the same only worse and honest a'mighty, Isic, I figger this army's jest a-goin' t' fade away like a May snowbank. Co. C has lost 9 men from honest cashulties, and this mornin' report, by A'mighty, there's a round 30 absent in horspital with this Chickahominy fever, leavin' us 65 fellers outta the 104 we took outta Byzantium and every god durned one on 'em includin' the orficers is sick more or less so they drag theirselves round mighty difficult and it's hard fer me to pencil this instead o' droppin' off into dreams o' sunshine and buckeye daisies. . . ."

"I got some new duds from a heap they dumped in the regimental street, but they don't no wise fit and I han't the gumshun t' go t' dressmakin' myself and the pants is a'ready tore fer no good reason and muddied and crumpled up worse than my old ones that did me a year. But I figger it's no great taters what kind o' pants ye put onto a corpse that's lyin' out here in the mud, bein's a feller can't take his pants to hell with 'im.

> Yrs from the grave
> Him that was J. Munson,
> Citizen o' Rumford Township, Byzantium Falls,
> Washington and the Peninsula o' Virginia,
> Lawyer and Lover o' good whisky, all of
> which seems so fer back it was likely in
> one o' them Hindoo previous incarcerations."

This was the last of the excerpts Ike had insisted on Old Jerry's hearing, it being in fact the end of the last letter he had got from Jabe. When he had finished reading, the wrinkled tanner looked up with his mildest expression. "Take some comfort in such trash, do ye?" he asked. "Best I have," said Ike. "Thanks for listening." "What about yer brother?" said Old Jerry. "Don't write often," said Ike evasively. "When he does he tries to make sense of it. That's worse." "Ye're right," said Old Jerry.

CHAPTER LXXXI

ON THE day after Jabe dragged himself up to drop in the regimental mail-bag his despairing letter to Ike of June 22, events began to take a turn which restored the morale of the Army of the Potomac. On Monday, June 23, the sun came out and stayed out during the activities of the next nine days. With a quarter of the Army's original 100,000 men already dead or in hospital with the Chickahominy fever, the number of new cases began to fall off. On the 24th and 25th there were undeniable signs of reviving military activity. Along the seven miles of line held by four corps south of the Chickahominy River, unusually heavy artillery fire. Along the four miles of line held by Porter's Fifth Corps north of the River, the continuous *whack-whack-awhack-whack* of cavalry; the slower thump and creak of artillery lumbering westward on the road to Mechanicsville; the clatter of generals with their staffs going out on reconnaissance and returning; the galloping traffic of aides and orderlies bearing orders from Corps Headquarters down to the three divisions, from the division headquarters to brigades, from the brigades to the regiments; in the regiments the suspension of drill routine and the substitution of inspections and the issuance of reserve ammunition to cram cartridge cases and haversacks; and finally, on the morning of the 26th, the sure promise of a move, the issuance of three days' individual rations to the men.

In the thirty-acre, muddy-white, dog-tent city of Morell's 1st Division, camped on the plateau above its Headquarters in a brick mill belonging to the Dr. Gaines Jabe had mentioned to Ike, the signs of activity were translated into a tornado of rumor whirling this way and that through the fancies of those 12,000 boys. In Griffin's 2d Brigade two stories prevailed: one that the cavalry had captured Stonewall Jackson personally—his being the only Rebel name beside that of Jeff Davis generally known to the Yankee soldiery—and that in consequence they were going to march straight into Richmond; the other story that General Porter was up in the observation balloon "Intrepid" over yonder, and as soon as he spotted the cannon doing all that bellerin' south of the river, he was going to take one of the regiments of the Brigade and go capture the caboodle of them—the particular regiment he was to take varying according to whether the story was told in the 50th New York, the 4th Michigan, the 9th Massachusetts, or the 62d Pennsylvania. And among the field officers and the few line officers—such as John Lathrop—who had friends down at Division Headquarters, it was known that an attack was expected on the right of the line near Mechanicsville, and that Jackson had joined the Rebel Army around Richmond and was now somewhere north of them on a flank movement with his Corps.

The wind of rumor stopped in dead suspension when, late in the morning of the 26th, the general call was heard rolling over in Martindale's 1st Brigade across the road, then in Butterfield's 3d Brigade next to it, and the scene for a mile over there became a huge swarm of bees, bugles tooting the assembly, orderlies and officers galloping, companies forming, and thousands of voices mingling in a murmurous undertone. The expectation of rumor was belied not long after by a different and unmistakable sound a few miles to the west—*rat-tat-tat, rat-tat-tat, tat, tat, rat-t-t-t-t-tat*—then, *Bam-b-b-b-bam-b-bam-b-bam*. This firing lasted only a few minutes. Like an anti-climax came mess call. But when the officers of the 50th were walking back from dinner they saw Martindale's Brigade with its three stands of regimental colors swing out into the road and head westward. Then Butterfield's Brigade belied both rumor and latest knowledge by marching out and heading eastward, away from where the firing had been.

For two hours Griffin's Brigade grumbled under the hot sun and the buzzards wheeling in the blue sky—"We're in reserve again"—"Why in hell don't they give us a chance?"—"If we ain't goin' t' whip the Johnnies we'd best be home at chores where we belong"—"Don't make a red's difference. When we whip 'em we're sartin' t' retreat arter, anyhow"—"Shut up. Little Napoleon knows his taters." Then at two o'clock came the roll of the general from their own Brigade Headquarters.

As under a hurricane, fifteen hundred tents went down together on that gray plain. An hour later Griffin's Brigade, with the 50th New York leading, marched off to take part in the bloody repulse of the Rebels at Mechanicsville, and the following day in the great battle and defeat of Gaines's Mill, where the line of Porter's Fifth Corps, after an all-day fight against more than twice its number, broke at Butterfield's Brigade, and that night the 22,000 survivors of the Corps retreated southward across the Chickahominy River, burning the bridges that had been built for the capture of Richmond.

Some time in the morning of June 28th Captain John Lathrop rolled over on his stomach. Something red and hot—the sun—was scratching his eyes. He rolled over on his face and continued to enjoy his first rest after two terrible days and the night between, but the melee of battle still seething in his subconscious mind began to shoot up little spurts of connected images:

Bam-b-b-b-bam-b-b-bam, brrroom-boom, brrroom-boom, brrrrroom-brrrrroom-brrrrroom, the undertone of the deep, infernal, bass viol sawing of the artillery at Mechanicsville— The 50th forward at a run toward the smoke-curtained ridge where the guns were—*brrrr-boom—grrrroom—grrrroom—grrrroom*— Caissons swerving back and forth across the field at a gallop, one skidding over, killing the man that was riding it— Rebel shells bursting in front of the running 50th— The voice of Nolan, the politically appointed Lieutenant-Colonel, "McNaughton, we can't go in there!"— The shout of Colonel McNaughton, "Colonel Nolan, go to the rear under arrest and report to me after this action"— The slide down the ridge into the breast-high rifle pits, a man on the slope with his skull lying open in two oozing halves like a walnut— *Brrrrack-rack, brrrrack-rack, brrrrrrack, brrrrrrack, brrrrrrack,* the metallic slapping of the mile-long line of musketry under the guns thundering canister over them from the ridge— *Grrrrroom, grrrrroom, grrrrroom, grrrrroom,* all noises lost in that steady drone made resonant in the sounding box of the little valley, the flashes flickering out level like instant red bars through the solid smoke— The fire lessening— The unbreathable, acrid smoke drifting off— The sight of that steep-sided death valley, fifty feet deep, two hundred yards across at the top— The marshy swale at the bottom checkered with red-blotched, gray and brown bodies— The shrubbery twitching over others that crawled— A white horse trying to rise, his hind quarters mincemeat, his lungs screaming like the concentrated terror of the world— The little stream in the valley dammed with heaps of bodies, the current pinkish— A wounded Rebel working his way laboriously, hand-over-hand, across the remaining span of a blown-up bridge, both legs dangling useless in the current— The cheer for him, "Go it, Reb!" "Tell yer friends to lay off and we'll come help ye"— The Reb slowly losing his grip and dropping into the current.

"Yipiyipiyipiyipiyipiyipiyipiyipiyipiyipiyipiyipiyipiyipiyipiyipiyipiyipi . . ." the wild, falsetto, Rebel yells— Another crowded attack coming down through the woods on the opposite slope— Half a dozen criss-cross flags— "Load, grape and canister, target troops to appear at edge of trees opposite, range one hundred and fifty"— "Yipiyipiyipiyipiyipiyipi-yeh-yeh-yipiyipiyipiyipi-

yipiyipi-yeh-yeh . . ." *Rat-t-t-crrrack* from the Rebel line— "Fire at will,"
"Fire at will," "Fire at will"—*b-b-b-bam, brrrrrrrack-rack, brrrrrrack,
b-boom-brrrrrroom-grrrrrroom-grrrrrroom-grrrrrrroom-grrrrrroom*— Rebel
shells— Through a break in the smoke, a gun crew scattered into flying
meat on the ridge over the 50th— John scrambling up and shouting an
offer of infantrymen to the regular artillery lieutenant who salutes stiffly
and walks away— Down in the pits, the 50th loading and firing like
clockwork, the rammers up-down-up-aim-fire-prime-load—rammers up-
down-up-aim-fire— Half a dozen wounded— Alec Mathiesson faints dead
away without being hit— The brown masses piling deeper in the valley,
none reaching the pits— *Grrrrroom-grrrrroom-grrrrroom-grrrrroom-grrrr-
room*— Somewhere bugles— The Rebs retreating, scrambling up the slope,
hundreds plastered against it by the canister— Silence— Powder mist—
Twilight— A blond, little wounded Reb working his way up the bank
opposite, up ten feet, losing his hold and sliding back, up ten feet, losing
his hold and sliding back. . . .

Night and the moon— Marsh mist, the stench of blood rising— The
swelling medley of moans from the wounded in the valley— John on
watch— Three generals inspecting the line— Griffin, the fatherly Brigadier
of John's brigade— Reynolds, in command of this end of the line— Meade,
studious, imperturbable face with one eye slightly wall— John alone
again— The moans of the wounded sinking to whimpers— A chill in
the mist— Croaks and a hiss in the valley— A sudden rustle and something brushing John's hat, a buzzard dropping on a body just below him
on the slope— The increasing stench of blood turning to carrion— The
cries of the wounded diminishing.

John relieved at midnight— A whisper, "Wake up, Lathrop. March
orders. Silence. Not a word above a whisper."— "Yes, sir"— The night
retreat back on the road whence they had come— The voices of the men—
"Up-tailin' ag'in." "Whipped 'em ag'in, so we're sneakin' away ag'in."
"What feller's t'blame, anyhow?" " 'Tain't Little Nap?" "Likely it's the
President wants to git us peppered fer nothin' "— The voice of First
Sergeant Jabe Munson, "Put yer opinions in writin' and hand 'em in at
revilly"— Silence— Tramp-tramp-tramp-tramp-scrape-scrape-scrape-scrape-
tramp-tramp-tramp-tramp— The undertone of memory, *b-b-b-boom, grroom, grroom, grroom, b-b-b-boom, grroom, grroom, grroom.*

The stone John's cheek was on bothered him. He put his hands under
his face and turned the other way. The images faded. For a brief eternity
he sank into absolute sleep again.

Other images, from the battle yesterday—the jam at the bridge by

Gaines's Mill at dawn— The new position, steamy hot, jungle-like basin of a dry creek— Small oak trees and big pines, waist-deep honeysuckle, poison ivy and cat-briar with tough thorns— Major Donahoe in command of six right companies, A on the flank bent back up a little hollow, C next— Back up the slope four companies in support— Donahoe, John's friend, slight figure, face like the pictures of Alexander Hamilton, Greek scholar, West Point— A few fence rails for barricade, padded with knapsacks and dirt— Can't get axes from the artillery to cut trees— The men trying to whittle down little oaks with their jack knives—John standing by an oak at the left of his company— Can't see other troops in the jungle— The 4th Michigan somewhere on the left— The 62d Pennsylvania in support on the top of the slope behind— On the right the shallow hollow— Beyond, the vines and the forest— The 9th Massachusetts is on outpost and is to fall back there— Silence, all sounds far away— Heat— no feeling of an army around— Sun through the oak leaves— Cardinals singing— Flies— Peace— The men eating their rations— Playing cards— Some singing softly in harmony— A wailing cry coming nearer— *"Philadelphia Press* and *New York Tribune* only five cents"— Bare-foot, twelve-year-old boy— "Sonny, ye ought to be home helpin' yer ma"— "Aw, I ain't afraid of the Rebs. I'm a friend of Little Napoleon's"— *Tat-tat-rat-t-t-tat.*

Tat-tat-rat-t-t-tat— "Yipiyipiyipiyipiyipiyipi . . ." The 9th Massachusetts running out of the woods across the creek and floundering through the vines to their position—*Rat-t-t-tat*— Ripley's regular sharpshooters coming back as skirmishers— One of them jumping over C Company's barricade, panting, sweating, shouldering John from his tree, watching his dress right and left, dodging back up the bank— "Yipiyipiyipiyipiyipiyipiyipiyipi . . ." Yelling Reb companies come out of the trees chasing the 9th Massachusetts, plunging down into the cat-briar—*brrrrrrack* from the 9th, like an enormous blow on a tin pan echoing down the little valley— The Rebs skeddadling— Silence— Reb voices hidden in the woods not fifty yards away above the opposite bank of the dry creek— "Thirty-fifth Georgia ready, suh," "Foteenth Joja ready, suh"— "Fawty-ninth Jawja ready, suh"—A Rebel drum— "Yipiyipiyipiyipiyipiyipi-yeh-yeh-yipiyipi-yeh-yeh-yipiyipi-yeh-yeh . . ." Three criss-cross battle flags— "Fire"—*brrrrrrrrrrr-rrrrrrrrack*——

Minutes—hours—blur— Rebs, flags and horses down in the vines— Rebs uptailing— Rebs coming on again— *Brrrrrrrrack-brrrrrrrrack-brrrr-rrrrack*— Bayonets— Knifing, grunting at the barricade— *Brrrrrrrrack-brrrrrrrack* from the support companies— C Company catching it— Ben Hanks down— And Peace Martin— Noah Prentice falling back with blood spouting from his heart round a bayonet, dragging the musket and the Reb with him over the barricade, and Jabe Munson sticking his bayonet clean through the Reb into the ground— John's revolver going off inaudibly in Rebs' faces— A pause— Jabe Munson methodically lifting the dead and wounded back from the line— Donahoe sending George Fulton hobbling to the rear— Nick Cochran still fighting with one of his eyes dangling from its socket, pouring blood down his face— Alec Mathiesson cowering behind the line and John shoving him into a prick from a bayonet coming clean through Hannibal Strong— The first sergeant of F Company reporting to John its only two officers out of action and John ordering it into closer support— In a pause ordering F to give C's front line ammunition— C Company paying no attention, crouching behind their barricade and the dead, looking over at the Rebs who were killing their friends, snarling at them to come on, trusting their bayonets— Another charge, heaviest over to the right, up the little hollow between the 50th and the 9th Massachusetts— The Rebs pouring in— The 62d Pennsylvania charging down the hill behind its colors— Colonel Cass falling— The charge rolling over him— The Rebs crowding over toward the 9th Massachusetts— Donahoe yelling, "Lathrop, take F, cut in behind them and we'll get them"— "F Company, follow me! There they are!"— No fight— "Ah surrenduh, Ah surrenduh, Ah surrenduh,"— Two companies of the 62d crowding in front of John, herding the remains of the Reb regiment up the slope— Back by his oak tree— Pause— That same studious face with the big, beak nose, the slightly wall eye, the big bumps on the forehead— General Meade— "We are going to relieve you, Captain."

Up on the curved plateau behind the woods and the line— Open, gray fields— A farmhouse with high brick foundations and long steps— Horsemen coming and going— Headquarters— Guns beside it— More guns over there beyond it— All the boys of the 50th dead asleep— Captain Flint the Surgeon sewing up their cuts without waking them— Fussing at John's wrist— "Thank you, Doctor"— Hours fighting to keep awake— Ears hearing nothing but eyes seeing gun smoke rolling up over two miles of woods along the creek— Wounded straggling by— Ambulances— Ammunition carts galloping— Sunset over the thick trees— The plateau in shadow with bluish white mist drifting.

Roar of a new attack faintly audible— John looking through his glasses at the left of the Corps line over yonder under the sun— Two Yankee soldiers backing out of the woods with bayonets at point and running in again— A larger group doing the same— "Yipiyipiyipiyipiyipiyipiyipiyipiyipiyipiyipi-yipi . . ." A company backing out of the woods, then another, a whole regiment— Men starting to run for the guns up beyond the farmhouse— Officers beating them with their swords— Rebel line appearing, firing on the rout— John seeing through his glasses their criss-cross battle flag (not suspecting that these were Hood's famous Texans and that one day he would see that flag closer)— More Rebels appearing, the break in the Yankee line scattering back right and left *bam-b-b-bam*—the guns ,firing a little up there beyond the farmhouse, but not like Mechanicsville— General Griffin riding by, stopping to speak to Colonel McNaughton— The Brigade coming up out of the 'woods, the regiments in column, the men carrying their wounded— "50th New York, fall in"— Dusk, dust and powder-smoke— Impossible to tell Rebel from Yankee at fifty yards— Bedlam on the plateau—*b-b-b-bam*—"yipiyipiyipiyipiyipiyipi . . ." Men, horses, artillery carriages whirling in every direction— Yells of a cavalry charge over there where the rout is— Rumble of the repulsed cavalry, followed by limbered artillery, stampeding between the 50th and the rest of the Brigade— Nervous yells of John's men, "Hey, Cap'n, time to go," "Time fer a little sprint, eh, Cap'n"— Colonel McNaughton, "Forward march"— C Company at the rear— A column in the near darkness coming up out of the woods where the 50th had fought.

Up by the farmhouse— The artillery there wheeled round to face the rout at the left— "Yipiyipiyipiyipiyipiyipi . . ."— *B-bam*— The cannoneers up-tailing it through C Company— Jabe Munson knocking down somebody who started to run— General Griffin, "McNaughton, protect those guns"— Colonel McNaughton, "Target those Rebs. Fire at will." "C Company, fire."— The company crowded together— The straggling volley— Artillery limbers galloping through them— From the right a sudden Rebel whoop, right on them, and a regimental volley flashing in the dusk— The rout of C Company and A next to it with artillery swerving among them, herding them right and left like cattle— John running downhill after them— "Halt, you cowardly bastards!"— The company piled up getting over a rail fence— John out in front of them with drawn revolver— "Halt, you cowardly bastards!"— The company huddled together— "Company C, fall in. Right dress"— The quiet valley of the Chickahominy below them to the south, the moon glowing in a purple sky— Half a dozen fugitives pausing and looking back from fifty yards down the hill— "Sergeant Munson, collect those brave men and form them on the left of the Company"— Jabe Munson, "Hey, you citizens of Byzantium, New York! The Reb says ye kin come back now if ye'll be good boys."

The sullen march back to fall in at the rear of the retreating regimental column— The sudden quiet and moonlight— Feet shuffling in the dust—

"Colonel McNaughton, I wish to report that C Company was routed, but is now at the rear of the column, all present or accounted for"— The Colonel's square-jawed, pugnacious grin under his mustache— "Don't worry, Lathrop. No company ever did better than yours did today. If they hadn't run they'd have been captured. I am going to propose them for a company citation."

John rolled over on his back—again the hot, red sun scratched his eyes. "Halt, you cowardly bastards! Halt, you cowardly bastards!" He woke himself up, though he didn't know he was yelling. He rolled on his side and opened his eyes, saw his company bivouacked in a rough line before him in a meadow of green grass instead of a gray waste. Most of the men were still sleeping, but a few were boiling coffee and grinning at him. Jabe Munson was alternately scratching his lice and polishing his musket. John hadn't a notion where he was. Not an image from the past two days remained in his consciousness. Last evening—actually it was three evenings before—he had a letter from Ike: "Wish you would write to me. . . . The Ordnance Department seems to like our guns. They are getting us a Government subsidy to enlarge our plant. . . . It seems too good to be true. We have soldiers guarding our factory, so spies won't blow it up. So we are 'at the front' too. I wish you would figure to have yourself ordered here." John had torn up the letter and thrown it in his camp fire. He had stopped writing Ike because he didn't want to hear such news of his greed and hypocrisy. It might force him to break with him.

John sat up in this strange, pleasant place. Looking at Jabe, he noticed his pants, the cloth rubbed into little rolls of fuzz, leaving big patches of nothing but fish net through which Jabe's filthy drawers and hairy legs were visible. He observed that the pants of several others were in the same condition. This was the new issue of clothing, less than a week old—"Shoddy." Last evening—actually three evenings before—after he read Ike's letter he had walked down to Division Headquarters to see his friend, Captain Henshaw, one of General Morell's aides. Henshaw had told him they were expecting an attack somewhere out toward Mechanicsville. Why are so many of the men bandaged? There is Medad asleep, and Zeb Milliken frying hardtack. Where is George Fulton?

CHAPTER LXXXII

AFTER John's negro servant had brought him some beef and coffee, a blurred, composite picture of the action of the last two days stood somewhere far off in his mind. Captain Green, the Regimental Adjutant whose little mustache always had a sarcastic twist, came by with an order for a detailed report of the losses of the last two days in men and equipment, in addition to the morning report which Jabe had already turned in. John, Medad, Jabe and Zeb Milliken took a section apiece and held an informal inspection of the battle-shredded company. A third of the remaining forty-eight men were slightly wounded. More than half of the blouses, caps and knapsacks had stayed up there at the shambles of the barricade. There was not an overcoat, not an extra pair of shoes and only ten blankets in the company. The only items of equipment that almost universally remained were the foul, ragged garments they had on, the canteens, muskets, cartridge boxes, and the haversacks where they carried their rations.

The spirits of the boys were as savage as their outward appearance, sullen to the verge of mutiny. When John had finished inspecting the section he had taken and was starting to leave it, someone growled, "Cap'n, were we whipped yesterday?" "No," said John, "Company C wasn't whipped, not by a jugful, nor the 50th either." "So we're sneakin' away ag'in, eh?" said somebody else out of the corner of his mouth. "I guess somebody else got whipped somewhere else," said John, "so the whole Corps had to retire." "Tigger that means we oughta go for'd," said a voice from the neighboring section. "Rule seems t' be when ye whip the Reb ye retreat. Oughta be turn about—when ye get whipped ye advance." John laughed, but nobody else did.

"Cap'n," said Dave Walsh, who went barefoot by preference and liked to be detailed company cook, "we come here t' fight and whip Johnnie and take this Richmond. Well, we fit and we've whipped Johnnie plenty, three times. And every time we whip 'em we retreat a little further. Fer me, it don't add up and make sense. What we're wanting to find out is, why ain't we advancin' against this place Richmond?" "All that's in the hands of the generals," said John. "Our only duty is to do as we're told. We've done it the best we could, and that's the end of it." "Little Nap's O.K.," growled Luke Clock, barefoot like Dave Walsh, and there was a series of grunts in assent.

After the inspection was over and John lay on the ground alone, troubled by the attitude of the men, and at the same time sharing it against his will, Alec Mathiesson marched up and saluted rigidly. "Sit down, Alec," said John. Alec remained standing at attention, and he spoke in a hesitant, excited way, not looking at John.

"Cap'n, I know I've been a coward so far, and I ask you to bear me in mind for some dangerous mission—" John's olfactory memory was the smell of powder and blood, and he had a faint, visual image of pushing Alec into a struggling line somewhere. "I want to prove," continued Alec, "that I can act like a man even if I'm not one." John slapped the ground with his scabbard. "Alec, you're talking like a damned fool. There's not a finer, cleaner man in the Army than you are." "Thank you," said Alec. "I ask you, then—will you—bear me in mind?" "Yes," said John. "Thank you, sir," said Alec, and he walked away stiffly, forgetting to salute. John noticed the ugly way the lounging men looked at him as he went back to his place and sat alone, staring in front of him. "Poor Alec," thought John. He knew he would not trust him with a mission that was both dangerous and responsible.

Early that afternoon the drums in every Brigade in Porter's Corps began rolling the general, and by three o'clock that tattered fifth of the Army of the Potomac was on the march. The pace was slow and the sullen spirit John's company had shown in the morning was evident everywhere. There was no singing, almost no talking. The men shuffled under their now light loads, never looking at their officers, rarely even at each other. The direction of march was southeastward. Everybody knew that was away from Richmond. Something like a solid mass of lead was weighing down on that whole six-mile column. John felt it as much as the rest. Why were they always retreating, whether they won or lost?

Major Donahoe rode down the column. John saluted and stepped out into the grass to ask him a few questions in an undertone. "Pat," he said, "didn't our Corps engage most of the Reb Army up there north of the river yesterday, Jackson and all?" "Seems so," said Donahoe. "And our engineers burned the bridges last night after we retreated?" "Yes," said Donahoe. "Then we're between the Reb and Richmond. Why aren't we marching straight there instead of in the opposite direction?"

Donahoe laughed, unconvincingly, as John had done under his man's questioning in the morning. "John, you're still a volunteer soldier, aren't you?" "Well, can you answer my question?" "Well, if we must be insubordinate, it may be that the rest of the Army is already in Richmond." "If they were even near it," said John, "we'd have heard some artillery before now, instead of the little sputtering we heard this morning." Donahoe rode away. John listened for firing in the west, not really expecting to hear it. The only sound was the shuffle and rumble of the Corps in motion.

At about half-past six Griffin's Brigade crossed a railroad, and shortly thereafter halted near a four corners. For three hours the soldiers nibbled what was left of their rations, grumbled, dozed, and watched an endless procession of supply wagons trundling past the corners, and at one point the 3,000 head that remained of the famous herd of steers. What they were watching was part of McClellan's change of base from White House to Harrison's Landing. At nine o'clock the Brigade marched again, turned right and crept along under the stars in column of twos in the grass beside the supply trains. At about midnight they crossed a long bridge over a swamp, and soon thereafter turned into an open field and bivouacked.

The next morning, Sunday, the spirit of the Corps revived a little when they marched westward and spread out in battle formation apparently facing Richmond. But then they lounged all day in the hot sun, hearing to the north of them the roar of two battles—one in the morning to be known later as Allen's Farm, one in the afternoon to be called Savage Station.

At officers' call that day Colonel McNaughton praised the regiment for its work at Gaines's Mill, and said he had recommended C Company for a citation. He announced promotions which he had recommended, among them Major Donahoe to Lieutenant Colonel, John to Major, Lieutenant VanSanford to Captain, Second Lieutenant Fulton—who was supposedly somewhere among the wounded—to First Lieutenant. These officers would immediately take up their new duties. Several of the companies, including C, would recommend one sergeant for a commission.

Immediately after the meeting John and Medad called up Jabe, and John begged him, as often before, to accept a commission. "No, fellers, my place is with the company. Once ye start totin' that useless hardware, ye're done for. Long John's quittin' us now, and Medad'll be next. Before this war's over you feller's 'll all be dead or generals, and I'll be pluggin' along with the company." John and Medad next offered the commission to little Zeb Milliken, who stroked his side whiskers a while before saying he would accept it.

That evening John called the hungry company together and made them an earnest, farewell speech which evoked an enthusiastic response for him personally but made little effect on the deeper, sullen spirit of the men. When John walked away, Jabe, who had contributed nothing to the send-off, went with him and put his enormous arm around his shoulder, both of them being near six feet three and Jabe wide as two of John. When they had walked a couple of rods Jabe's hand tightened on John's shoulder and they stopped. For a moment they stood limply in the moonlight not daring to look at each other. Then Jabe's hand squeezed John's shoulder again. "Good-by, Cap'n," he murmured. "Good-by, Jabe." They didn't even shake hands as they turned and walked in opposite directions, Jabe back to the company, John up to his new station with the field officers and the regimental staff.

During the night the men got one day's rations, having already been without food for twenty-four hours and getting no more till two days later. In the morning they started a slow, galling, five-mile march to the south through typical gray wastes of oak scrub and pine. They still moved in a straggling column of twos in the grass beside the road, crowded off by the endless wagon trains, and halting frequently for long periods in the baking sun.

At about ten o'clock the 50th came out of the sparse woods and started up an open slope speckled with stubble and dead cornstalks. It was a field about a quarter mile wide, rising gently and with remarkable evenness for near a mile to a height of forty or fifty feet. To the east and west this slightly tilted plane was bordered by woods, and at the western edge a sharp declivity was indicated by the tops of pine trees evidently standing on lower ground beyond and close to the hill. It was as if a thin slice of a titanic cheese here lay on its side on the lower plain. Major Donahoe rode back to John, handed him a map and said General Griffin wanted them to observe this terrain. John studied the sketch map as he walked. The place was called Malvern Hill.

John got the names on the map in his mind and handed it back to the Major. That large stuccoed house with the Mansard roof and the two tall chimneys over to the right on the west end of the crest was called the Mellert house. There was a sharp drop behind it marked "bluffs," and there was a farm track running out from it to the road. As John walked up that long, gradual rise remarkable for its openness and evenness, its absolute lack of cover, he thought what a concentration of guns along the crest could do to infantry advancing up it in the direction they were now marching. He felt a stir in his stomach when, as he reached the crest, he saw a line of guns already in position there, half concealed in the edge of a wheatfield back of the farm track that ran along the crest. God help the Rebs if they tried it here!

Beyond the crest the road descended again gradually southward for about another mile through the ubiquitous oak scrub and pines. Here the western valley cut in closer to the road, and they passed another long line of artillery trained out over the bluffs in that direction, perpendicular to the one trained northward in the wheat on the crest of the hill. Beyond these guns the ground fell off more rapidly to the south and through openings in the trees John saw increasing vistas of the wide, peaceful James River, with two boats, which he presently recognized as gunboats, anchored near shore, flying the stars and stripes. Overlooking the green valley of the James, the Corps was drawing up for a halt on the scrubby hillside.

Here the 50th, along with the rest of Griffin's Brigade, ate its 543 individual dinners, and while this was going on, George Fulton mysteriously appeared, hobbling on a board for a crutch. He had gone absent without leave from the horde of wounded collected at Savage Station and had managed with a bribe to stow away among boxes of crackers in one of the supply wagons, where for two days he had been fattening, as he said, "like an overfed rat." He defied Medad and John to arrest him and, to show his fitness for duty, threw away his board and ran about hippety-hop at a great rate.

At three o'clock Griffin's Brigade was wakened from its nap by the general roll, and marched back northward by the road it had come. Colonel McNaughton divided the regiment into two battalions, the leading six companies under Major Donahoe, the rear four companies, successively F, E, A and C, under John. Once more they passed behind the line of thirty guns trained out over the valley to the west, and shortly beyond them turned west on a crossroad, then north again cross-country through the oak scrub and out on an open western shoulder of Malvern Hill back of the tall-chimneyed, stuccoed Mellert house. Here the Colonel halted the 50th and made his preliminary dispositions.

The shoulder was like an enormous, natural bastion, making about two-thirds of a circle two hundred and fifty yards in diameter, extending the line of the crest out into the valley. To the east of it along the crest stretched the line of artillery John had seen in the wheat. To the south of it was the other line of artillery trained westward from the bluffs. A little north of the center of this natural turret, on its base line where it merged in the main hill, stood the Mellert house, the ground sloping down gently from the house to the edge of the shoulder, and thereafter falling off more steeply into the valley. To the west and southwest the view was unobstructed over the half-mile-wide valley that was speckled golden with shocks of wheat, but the view to the north was cut off by the tops of pine trees growing on the lower slope.

The Colonel sent Major Donahoe to post his six companies along the southwestern edge of the shoulder, an attack being expected from that direction across the valley, and he had John place his little battalion in support fifty yards behind Donahoe. Back in the oaks, off the shoulder, the 4th Michigan lay in reserve. Beyond it along the crest the other two regiments of Griffin's Brigade—the 62d Pennsylvania and the 9th Massachusetts—were in support of the artillery in the wheat. The 50th lay about two hundred yards diagonally to the rear of the 62d Pennsylvania and facing almost in the opposite direction. Between them the bastion-like shoulder swelled out westward, treeless, flanking both the eastward and southward lines of Yankee artillery, plainly the key to the whole position, and all but the 50th's 100-yard arc of its six hundred yards of circumference entirely unoccupied.

The 50th had just settled into position when they enjoyed grandstand seats at a stage battle in the wide valley below them to the west. Two Rebel batteries galloped out from the foot of the opposite slope, followed by a small brigade of infantry scattering out into line of battle. The batteries unlimbered in plain sight in the middle of the valley and immediately opened fire, one shrapnel going off on the bluffs below the 50th, and another whizzing over and bursting in the 4th Michigan. With a roar the thirty guns lined up to the south opened and in less than five minutes performed the remarkable feat of unwheeling all the guns in one battery and two in the other and exploding two caissons. Meanwhile a brigade of Yankee infantry—Warren's regulars—came out from the bluffs as skirmishers, while the Rebel line was hesitating behind its doomed artillery. Above the roar of the guns John heard from the south what seemed a single, slow clap of thunder, then another, and he just had time to glance that way and see the big wreaths of smoke spinning up over the Yankee gunboats when the two ten-inch shells went off with explosions that shook the hill where he was lying almost a mile away. But where they struck was just behind the support line of Warren's Brigade and when the volcanoes of dust and smoke cleared, John could see casualties lying there. The regulars moved on without wavering. When the gunboats *Aroostook* and *Galena* respectively thundered again John watched the sky, for he had heard you could see the high-trajectory "lamp-posts" in flight. He saw one of them, like a passing shadow just at the turn at the top of its trajectory, but the image had hardly time to register when—*bow*—*bow*—the two giants went off too close for comfort in the valley below, heaving up fifty-foot columns of dirt and wheat. This time they were no nearer the Rebel lines than before, but were over instead of short. The "moral effect" was immediate. The brigade of Rebels turned and ran, and no more enemy was seen that afternoon. Warren's two attack regiments advanced at the double and wheeled in by hand the two guns and six caissons, all that was left of the two Rebel batteries. A cheer from the watching Yankee troops ran along the bluffs. It had all been like clockwork.

It was now about five o'clock. In front of his little four-company battalion John sat on the ground with his hands clasped around his knees, watching three guns of Weeden's 1st Rhode Island Battery go into position a little to the left of the 50th, a point from which they could cover both the southwestern slope of the shoulder and the lower part of the western slope. Colonel McNaughton was posting two pickets from Donahoe along the edge at hundred-yard intervals out to the right. There was a rattle of wheels and one of the mule-drawn carts from the ammunition train appeared with orders to leave three boxes with Captain Lathrop. John told the ammunition corporal to unload them over by F Company on the right of his battalion.

Colonel McNaughton came up on foot and told John he was in charge of the ammunition. After he had put a detail over it he would report to him at Donahoe's position. John posted a section under a sergeant from Company F over the three sacred boxes. Then he walked back to Captain Johnson of E Company, who was next junior to himself in the regiment, left him in command of the battalion, and hurried forward to join Colonel McNaughton and Major Donahoe down on the edge of the shoulder. As they stood together, the field officers of the 50th made a pair of steps in inverse order to their rank, the Apollo-faced Donahoe being three inches shorter than John, and the bull-dog-faced Colonel, broader shouldered than either of them, being three inches shorter than Donahoe.

The Colonel now led them round the whole curve of the shoulder, first northward along the western edge. Here the slope was open down about a hundred yards to a line of bushes beyond which there seemed to be a sharp drop or terrace which would give attacking troops good cover under which to form. Beyond this drop the slope continued mostly open for another two or three hundred yards down to the valley.

The right-most picket the Colonel had placed was at the point where the edge of the shoulder turned eastward along the top of the steeper northern slope that was mostly covered with pines. When they had walked along here a few steps the Colonel stopped and grinned at his field officers. They were all thinking the same thing. All the Reb had to do was walk up here unopposed and take them in the rear. A hundred yards to the east of them, a long ravine ran in another hundred yards from the north almost to the Mellert house, sharply cutting the shoulder from the main hill. Beyond the Mellert house they could see the track that ran straight east from its door along the crest to the Quaker Road by which they had marched up the hill in the morning, and along this track the two-hundred-yard-long line of gun muzzles sticking out of the wheat, covering the gentle, even main slope. The nearest battery was in the Mellert barnyard and was trained down the ravine.

The Colonel led on up to the Mellert house, behind Gibbon's Battery in the barnyard, and walked out a little way in front of the main line of guns. On that mile of even slope down to the north there wasn't a stick of cover but a few scattered cornstalks and Mellert's barn on the west edge of the slope, near the drop into the ravine. John asked Donahoe if he thought the Rebs would be crazy enough to try it here. "They seem to like to attack us where we want them to," said the Major. "Listen, gentlemen," said the Colonel.

There had been occasional heavy firing from the north all day, and now it was gathering into the steady, deep sawing of a major battle. It was the beginning of the last and most desperate Rebel attack of what had been virtually a single army rear-guard action lasting all that day, and which would be divided in the final record into the battles of Fraser's Farm, White Oak Swamp, Newmarket Crossroad and Glendale. From this time until dark the horizon about five miles northward was never quiet, a low white haze of powder smoke rolling up continuously from that region where they and the rest of Morell's Division of Porter's Corps had lain inactive all yesterday. "When they get through up there," said the Colonel, "the next show may be right here. Pity we shan't be able to see it"—for this crest was just above the eye-line from down on the shoulder, and the Mellert buildings intervened. "But who knows?" added the Colonel. "We may have the big show out there." And he pointed toward the shoulder. Then he turned and started back.

Just then General Morell, with all three of his brigade commanders and their staffs, rode up from the shoulder to the front of the Mellert house, all looking northward toward the distant cannonade and the line of smoke rolling up over the trees. General Griffin spotted Colonel McNaughton and rode out to meet him. "McNaughton," he said, returning the salute, "I am to command this artillery and the infantry in support of it. My Headquarters, as well as Division Headquarters, will be in that house. As this main line will require continuous attention, I wish to detach you and put you in independent command of the bluffs out there on the left, directly under the Division Commander. Please report to General Morell for further orders."

"What troops shall I have available?" asked McNaughton. "For the present only your regiment. The entire army of the enemy, with the exception of Holmes's Division, of which Wise's Brigade attacked this afternoon, is now engaged with the corps of Heintzelman, Sumner and Franklin in the vicinity of Newmarket Crossroad. We shall not be attacked tonight. I believe it is General Morell's intention to reinforce you in the morning."

"Very well, sir," said Colonel McNaughton. He saluted with a formality which showed he was not reassured, and walked along toward the Mellert house. He told Donahoe and John to go back to the regiment, and himself disappeared amidst the dismounted cavalcade of generals, staff, aides and orderlies that were massed round the front door. As John passed, Captain Henshaw, General Morell's senior aide and the Headquarters mess officer, stopped him to tell him that all field officers were to mess here at Division, and that his recommendation for promotion had already gone up to Army.

A quarter of an hour later John, Major Donahoe, Captain Flint the Regimental Surgeon, Captain Green the Adjutant, and the Quartermaster were lying under the little oaks at 50th Headquarters, located back of John's support battalion about two hundred feet from Division Headquarters and marked by the regimental colors and standard, a pile of knapsacks, two sergeants-major, a clerk, four orderlies and two musicians, all asleep, the Surgeon's big, leather kit-bag, the Adjutant's strongbox, and a bench made of three old boards got from a pile alongside the Mellert house. John was lying on his side, his elbow supporting his head, looking over the fat Surgeon at that unoccupied near horizon, not a hundred yards away to the northwest, where the shoulder dropped off into the valley. As he watched he saw Colonel McNaughton come round the other side of Division Headquarters with none other than General Morell in tow. They went straight out on the shoulder, and it was apparent from his gestures that the Colonel was speaking plainly. Presently they came back, this time passing within earshot.

"Quite so, quite so," the General was saying in his harsh voice, "*if* you are attacked in force, I say, *if you are attacked in force,* McNaughton. The enemy must approach us either by the Quaker Road we followed to this position or by the River Road where Wise appeared this afternoon. He will attack from either the north or the west, possibly from both. In neither case is he likely to extend his line as far as this point. If he does we shall have ample warning, both from Ripley and his sharpshooters and from direct observation. I purpose to move the 4th Michigan out to that ravine in the morning, but their mission will be to protect the left of the artillery, specifically Gibbon's Battery. After your work last Friday I have every confidence in you and your regiment. If you are surprised in force before morning you may call on Woodbury"—he was the Colonel of the 4th Michigan. "But that is quite inconceivable, McNaughton, quite inconceivable." And the General walked away.

As Colonel McNaughton came over to John and Donahoe his grin was almost savage. But when they rose to greet him, his kindly voice was in contrast to his expression. "Donahoe," he said, "take all your officers up there on the right and show them the ground. Tell them they may have to move there by the flank in a hurry, probably under fire. Lathrop, take your officers farther to the right, up there as far as the outer picket at the bend of the shoulder, and tell them the same thing."

John led the officers of Companies A, C, E and F out as far as the northwest bend of the shoulder, feeling for the first time the importance and authority of a field officer. Standing in the hundred-yard interval between Donahoe's two pickets, they all looked down that hundred-yard slope to the west, unobstructed by even a fence, with the line of bushes and sharp drop at the bottom which obviously could give shelter to a large body of troops. When Donahoe came out with his officers he and John apportioned the western edge of the shoulder between them, the present location of Donahoe's inner picket marking the division between Donahoe's right and John's left, in case the 50th had to move to the right to cover the entire two hundred yards of the western slope the Colonel had indicated. As they were walking back to the battalion, John showed the officers a new position they would take if necessary, facing northwestward to be prepared to move into line beside Donahoe as they had arranged. John then showed the sergeant in charge of his reserve ammunition a new point, farther to the right, where he would move in case the battalion advanced in that direction.

Back at Regimental Headquarters, Colonel McNaughton was sitting on the ground, smoking his pipe. "Well, boys," he said, as Donahoe and John came up, "we're in command of this corner, and we're going to show them something tomorrow." It was the first time John had ever heard the Colonel speak boastfully.

CHAPTER LXXXIII

A L T H O U G H for two months the Army of the Potomac had floundered in mud and wasted away in sickness, and now for five days—or, more exactly, five nights—had been retiring successively from eight fields of battle on only one of which it had been defeated, its morale was not yet broken, its optimism of a volunteer army not yet wholly killed. The soldiers were still able to half-believe the campfire Nestors, who on the 29th began to assure them that all they were doing was to lead the old fox Stonewall Jackson into a trap where they would finish him for good. But when on the 30th, Keyes's and Porter's Corps saw the broad James River across their southward line of march, and when Franklin's, Heintzelman's and Sumner's Corps, having marched all night after their hard and successful battles on the 30th, likewise saw it at dawn on the 1st of July, and there was no sign of any provision for crossing it, every ragged, amateur tactician in the ranks saw that the trap was here, if anywhere. Henceforth they must do one of three things. They must advance on Richmond to the west; they must hold their position; or they must retreat to the east or southeast. And whichever of these courses they pursued was bound to have a decisive effect upon their morale, that sensitive "Spirit of the Army," which was so different from the spirit of the individuals, yet mysteriously controlled them all.

So great was the confidence in General McClellan that the men were sure to accredit him with any victory they might win, but if they retreated again they would take the fault to themselves. They were prepared for the cynical belief that, however well they might fight as individuals and regiments, yet victory was not for them. One more retreat, whether from victory or defeat, and their spirit might break for good.

The Army was, therefore, in a mood at once nervous and ugly on that 1st of July, 1862. It was at bay on the line of its own integrity, its own manhood, desperately determined not only to win this fight but to chase the Reb all the way to Richmond, or, if it did not, to lose faith in itself. Its angry, crusading spirit, its peculiar morale as a volunteer army, was never higher, in spite of its Commander's consistent disregard of its costly victories.

The spirit of the Army at Malvern Hill was a spirit of victory. But, here, as previously in this campaign, it was neither the spirit nor the behavior of the Army, certainly not the larger tide of history, that was to determine the outcome of the battle. That was to be settled by the judgment of one man, General McClellan, "Little Napoleon."

John was now close enough to Division Headquarters so that he immediately heard the news, brought in by dispatch riders during the evening of the 30th, of the final and decisive repulse of the Rebels at Glendale. He was filled with an elation that would not let him sleep, where he lay on his blanket on the gray dust and dried oak leaves on the right flank of his little battalion. All night he heard the pickets changing out there on the shoulder he was to guard, and, what strained his attention even more, the perpetual shuffling and murmur of marching hosts an eighth of a mile behind him out there on the Quaker Road beyond that long line of artillery on the crest.

He knew those were the corps of Franklin, Sumner and Heintzelman marching back from their victorious fight whose rumble he had heard in the afternoon. He knew they were going into position somewhere behind Morell's and Couch's Divisions. He persuaded himself that the retreat all the way from Mechanicsville to this powerful position had been for the best. The Rebels had been lured here where the artillery and a little infantry of the old 5th Corps would shatter their whole army. Then Franklin's, Sumner's and Heintzelman's Corps, having rested for a day, would march out in counter-attack. The Rebel Army would be routed for good and the war would be over. John arranged all these matters in his hectic, half sleep, but in his waking moments he had no such spectacular hopes. All he knew was that the 50th must hold that shoulder of the bluff on the left of the line of guns, and that somehow, in the unpredictable future, their holding it would contribute to the winning of the war.

Breakfast was at 5:30 in Dr. Mellert's dining-room, and, as always when action was imminent, it was a silent meal. As John was walking out of the hall with Colonel McNaughton they overheard the Chief of Staff dictating an order that involved the 4th Michigan. The Colonel walked on by, not deigning to eavesdrop, but his sardonic grin widened and held, so that from then on all through the day, his wide teeth were almost always visible.

In front of the house he pointed to Mellert's barn on the northern slope near the head of the ravine and told John to send an officer with two runners there to establish a look-out at the hay-door. He told John to go personally when he posted him and point out a hill less than a mile to the northwest that was as high as the one they were on. The officer was to watch this hill and its slopes particularly and continuously until he was recalled, and was to report in detail any activity there. The Colonel said that if the enemy was smart he would put artillery there, but, what was more important, any force moving round to attack their own left by way of the valley must at some time appear on the left slope of that hill.

Fifteen minutes later John was at the door in the hayloft of the sizable barn, giving his instructions to Lieutenant Holman of Company A whom he had detached for the purpose. The hill in question was apparent enough, and the clear view of the valley up along its western side for a great distance. John saw why the Colonel had established the look-out here—the view of this region was cut off from the shoulder by the growth of pines on its northern slope. The only obstruction of the view from the hay-door of the barn was a thick line of bushes, apparently marking a stream flowing southwestward into the valley between the hill in question and Malvern Hill. This line of bushes and the ground for some distance beyond it was now mostly under mist that would presumably vanish when the sun reached it. Just as John was leaving, a Division look-out, a sergeant major, arrived to watch in the same direction.

Returning from this duty, John walked through the barnyard where Gibbon's Battery was posted, then paused back of the Mellert house and looked westward down into the valley. The big shadow of the shoulder was just drawing down the opposite slope and the sun was beginning to shine on the shocks of wheat that dotted the half-mile-wide valley for its entire visible length.

As John was reporting to Colonel McNaughton beside the colors at their headquarters, the 4th Michigan behind them was falling in. While it was doing so its dapper, florid Colonel Woodbury came over to speak to McNaughton. "Jim," he said with his rosy smile, "it's plain you're too good to need support, so they're sending me out there to watch that ravine. I am to keep close contact with the 62d Pennsylvania and protect Gibbon's Battery at all costs. I am to keep 'so much contact as possible' with you. It is plain you are an incidental consideration." "Perhaps I'm worth a line of pickets?" suggested McNaughton. "I'll do better for you than that," said Woodbury. "I'm going to extend my left from the ravine all the way out along that northern edge of the hill to your picket yonder. It will make a thin two-hundred-yard line and the Reb will be able to get up close through the pines. If I'm attacked in force both from the ravine and on that slope I'll have to draw back my left to help support Gibbon's guns." "Then they'll get you in the left rear," said McNaughton. "And you in the right rear," said Woodbury. "Anyway, I'll thank ye to put up a good rumpus for me and I'll mention it in my memoirs."

McNaughton slapped Woodbury on the shoulder with his gloves and Woodbury walked over to his regiment whistling. "My room-mate at the Point," said McNaughton to Donahoe a little sentimentally. Then, "Green, what was the morning report?" "Forty at sick call for dressings, sir—off duty. One new case of fever—evacuated. For duty, 29 officers, 474 men." The 4th Michigan was now marching off past the Mellert house in column. Colonel McNaughton lit a cigar. The northern and northeastern two hundred yards of the six-hundred-yard circumference of the shoulder were now to be thinly held by the 4th Michigan. The southwestern two hundred yards could be covered by Weeden's battery if they weren't directly attacked. In covering the remaining two hundred yards, the western slope of the big bastion, the 50th was to have no support at all.

The 4th was just stringing out its line from the ravine to the 50th's picket when another column appeared through the oaks from the rear, marching without colors. They were Ripley's regiment of Berdan's sharp-shooters, the same that had acted as Corps skirmishers at Gaines's Mill. They disappeared beyond the Mellert house and the Colonel told John to watch where they went. John walked around the house and saw them going down the ravine in front of the 4th Michigan, between the main slope of the hill and the shoulder. A little later they could see them through their glasses stringing out in a long line westward across the valley, the men in pairs ten to twenty yards apart, each pair taking position on the south side of one of the shocks of wheat. John concluded from this that Headquarters now knew the main attack was coming from the north. That meant the 50th would probably have to move up into the positions he and Donahoe had agreed on yesterday. It meant the worst.

John walked down the line of his four support companies, verifying with the company commanders the position the battalion was to take when they moved to the right, and the one they would take on the edge of the shoulder if there was an attack there. He shifted Captain Johnson with E Company to the right of the line. Then he sat down with Medad Van-Sanford and George Fulton in front of C Company, which was next to E Company, the right center of the four companies in the battalion. "Men feeling better this morning?" John asked Medad. "Yes," said the new company commander, "as well as could be expected without breakfast. Dave Walsh has decided after all that we'd best give the Johnnies one more lickin' before going to Richmond." The three were all out of tobacco, so they flaked dried oak leaves by rolling them in their hands and burned their tongues from the resultant conflagrations in their pipes.

Seven—eight—nine o'clock passed, the soldiers all lounging in that indifference at the prospect of attack which a week ago was a pose and now was a habit. First Sergeant Jabe Munson had stolen a piece of burlap somewhere and was sewing it onto the net skeleton of his evaporated "shoddy" pants. Zeb Milliken came up and squatted beside the recumbent officers.

"Gentlemen," said Zeb, smiling his delicate smile and pulling his side whiskers, "I've been having bad dreams. Saw Pa last night, talked with him right here beside me." "So it's come to you, has it?" laughed George Fulton. "Yes, sir," said Zeb. "Hez Plum saw it and so did Noah Prentice, and they caught it right afterward." "How many men in the company, including the brave officers, do you think haven't 'seen it'?" asked George Fulton, lying on his back with his hands under his head and his eyes closed. "I don't know, George," said Zeb. "There's likely nothing in it, but I see no harm in taking precautions. I just wanted to tell the big acting major here that in my will I have expressed the wish that he succeed to my personal law practice, as well as our joint practice."

"That's capital of you, Zeb," said John. "I appreciate the thought." But there was a touch both of impatience and annoyance in his smile. By now it was tacitly recognized as a sort of bad taste to refer to the shadow of death that hung over all of them. "And if you don't mind," pursued Zeb, "for old friendship's sake, I want to shake hands all around." They stood for this unmilitary ceremony, and each smiled with indulgent indifference as he shook Zeb's hand. "Thanks, fellows," said Zeb with his gentle voice, then went over to Jabe and repeated the ritual. Jabe did not look up from his sewing till the time for hand-shaking came. "Bet ye a dollar I beat ye t' hell," he said, then swung his great, bearded head around, winked at the officers, and pulled his forage cap a little farther on one side.

The day was getting hot now, sultry in the shadow of the oaks behind them, though a breeze frequently rattled softly through their leatherlike leaves. One by one, the letters and card games in the company were wound up in favor of sleep. Sergeant Munson sent a canteen detail to the Mellert house to beg some water, and they returned with a gallon for the entire company. It was ten o'clock. Very innocently, from far over beyond the right of the Corps line, came *Tat—rat-tat—Rat-t-t-tat*.

John got up, walked slowly to his headquarters at the ammunition dump behind E Company and looked through his glasses down at the line of sharp-shooters in the valley. One man at each shock of wheat was on watch, looking northward, but there was no indication that they saw anything. He sat down. The intermittent rattle of skirmishing continued in the distance beyond the Mellert house. Then it stopped. For a moment John thought he heard very faintly the Rebel yell. Then *boom—b-boom—b-b-boom,* more than half a mile to the eastward.

The artillery fire grew heavier, but it was not the line of artillery along the near crest. It was nothing that concerned the 50th. John listened indifferently, at the same time alternately watching the valley, where nothing happened, and Division Headquarters where the usual succession of galloping aides and orderlies were already arriving and departing. One of the runners John had posted under Lieutenant Holman in the barn came down with a message for the Colonel who was sitting on a bench twenty yards away at Regimental Headquarters. The Colonel read the message, dismissed the runner, and handed the piece of paper to Adjutant Green for filing.

The cannonade over on the right stopped for five minutes, then set up again for two minutes, then stopped for good. John observed one thing about this preliminary action, wherever it was. After the first flutter of shots that marked the retirement of skirmishers, there was no musketry at all. This meant the guns had driven off the Rebels before they came into musket range. John believed this would happen every time they were foolish enough to attack along that northern slope. But there was no artillery but that section of Weeden's Battery over here on the left, and even if those three guns were swung around from southwest to northwest they could cover only the lower part of the slope. John felt a grim elation, a sense of isolated determination and certainty, something he had caught from the Colonel. The 50th was going to catch it alone.

Not long after the end of the preliminary action at ten o'clock John's vain-glorious feelings were somewhat dampened by the appearance of a new column coming up from the rear through the oak trees. As it came nearer John saw a General and a brigade pennant leading. This was no regiment to support the 50th. This was an entire brigade! John felt superficially reassured, and at the same time resentful, jealous. The 50th was being shorn of the heroic possibilities he had built up in his mind. After all, it was merely to be one of many regiments out here on the shoulder.

But John lost both his feeling of reassurance and his jealousy when the head of the column turned right at about what had been the left of the 4th Michigan line and marched away eastward, till, when the brigade finally halted, its left was a good two hundred yards back of the 50th and faced perpendicular to it. "Martindale's Brigade," McNaughton called across to John and made a shrugging gesture. It was plain it was to support the main line in front. The 50th New York was still isolated on its big turret behind the Mellert house.

After Martindale's 1st Brigade halted there was a good deal of marching farther to the rear whence it came. Still more troops were coming up into reserve. But none of these had anything to do with the 50th. It was evident that Division Headquarters was expecting action only on the main slope. General Morell apparently still thought it "inconceivable" that McNaughton could be attacked in force. Again, one of the runners John had posted in Mellert's barn reported to the Colonel. Again he handed the report to Green indifferently.

Another hour passed during which John went heavily asleep. He was awakened in a sweaty daze by renewed artillery firing, and as he stood up, gathering his wits, he realized that, though it was farther away than before, it was now straight north of their end of the line, in the region cut off from view by the pine tops along the northern edge of the shoulder. *Bang*—a shell went off somewhere up there to the right of the Mellert house. It must be Rebel artillery firing on the main line of guns from somewhere in the vicinity of that hill he had told Lieutenant Holman to watch. This might mean business. *Bang—b-b-bang*—a volley of shells burst up there near the guns. Then, from the same direction, *Bam—bam—b-bam—bam*—four or five of the Yankee batteries ranging deliberately, piece by piece. In half a minute they settled into their range—*Boom—b-b-b-boom—b-b-b-boom*—the bass viol sawing of Mechanicsville again, but this time not so resonant, the sound not confined in a narrow valley but scattered from the open hilltop.

A runner arrived from the look-out in Mellert's barn and John walked over to the Colonel to hear the report. The Colonel sent the runner back and handed John the note:

"11:54—Rebel battery—four guns—opened on our artillery from hill one mile northwest—bursts short—no damage—Rebel infantry in force—likely two brigades—at east foot of same hill— No infantry visible on left slope of hill or in valley—our guns beginning to reply—Holman."

John handed the note to Adjutant Green. Abruptly the artillery fire stopped, and at the same moment the Rebel yell and the sound of musketry became audible to the north. The artillery on the crest opened again, first ranging slowly as before, then letting go with volleys. John wished he might go up there on the crest and see what was going on.

The other runner arrived:

"12:01—Rebel battery being pulled off hill one mile northwest—two guns left silent—likely damaged by our fire— Infantry attack coming up left of main slope—brigade in line of three regiments with two regiments in support—another brigade forming behind— Our skirmishers retiring toward the left— Attack more than half a mile away— Some of our batteries being pushed out from wheatfield to crest to meet it— Opening now— No Rebels in sight west of hill—Holman."

As John read this note he swallowed involuntarily. His mouth was dry. Colonel McNaughton flicked the ashes impatiently from his cigar and looked out at Donahoe, standing on the edge of the shoulder on the right flank of his battalion, studying the valley with his glasses. Donahoe dropped his glasses and did not even glance in their direction. Colonel McNaughton flicked his cigar again, having nothing to flick.

The roar of the artillery on the crest was now steady, the intervals between shots rarely perceptible. For a few seconds it slackened, then rose again. A runner arrived:

"12:11—Attacking brigade stopped at 700 yards by five batteries pushed forward from wheatfield to crest—heavy casualties—three regiments retiring, two of them routed—two support regiments lying down— Supporting brigade now advancing through them— No activity on hill to northwest or west of it—Holman."

The artillery fire grew faster. Gibbon's Battery, in the Mellert barnyard on the left of the line of guns, theretofore silent, opened. *Rat-t-t-t-tat*— there was a light volley from the right of the 4th Michigan along the ravine. "Go up to Headquarters, Lathrop," said the Colonel, "and report what you see."

John ran around the left side of the Mellert house. Just as he came in sight of Gibbon's Battery it ceased firing, and the cannoneers started to sponge the three of the six guns that had gone into action. To the left of it along the ravine the 4th Michigan was lying on its six hundred stomachs, not firing at all. The cannonade of the main line of guns on the crest slackened. John could see the level bars of flame, the guns jumping back into the road when they were fired, the cannoneers running with them and rolling them up into position again. Other cannoneers were running back and forth between the guns and their caissons in the wheatfield, some of them bringing up ammunition, most of them carrying water buckets. All but a few of the guns had ceased firing and were sponging. Beyond those that had moved forward into action, John could see plenty of muzzles that had not fired at all, still sticking out of the wheat over on the right. The rich smell of black powder and the little white clouds from the near-by discharges, some of them still holding their ring shape, drifted by him on the light east wind. On the east slope of the ravine there lay a few Rebel casualties.

The main slope of the hill was above John's eye-line. Unless he went farther than Headquarters it was certain he had little to report. The artillery ceased firing entirely. There was only the remote sputtering of outposts and patrols that always marked the fringes of a battle. One of the 50th's runners came past the rear of Gibbon's Battery. John intercepted him, sent him back, and himself ran with the report to the Colonel:

"12:14—Second attacking brigade started charge bayonets at line where other brigade stopped—this attack stopped at 600 yards by same artillery fire—estimate 2500 in two attacking brigades—casualties now visible on the field more than 500— Both brigades retreating full tilt, regiments running in masses, not yet re-formed— Runner watching from rear window of barn reports 62d Pennsylvania and 9th Massachusetts moved up into wheatfield to support artillery, but they did not fire— 4th Michigan on the left one volley on flank of the attacking line— No activity on the hill to the northwest or west of it— No enemy in sight except brigades retreating—Holman."

For two hours now there was only sporadic firing, mostly far away on the right, brief rattles of musketry and an occasional single shot from a field gun. Lieutenant Holman sent in a few reports of patrols observed and once "a reconnaissance party of officers on hill a mile to northwest where Rebel battery was." John walked down in front of his battalion, where a few men were chewing the last of their hoarded rations. He went out to Donahoe's position and inspected the valley with his glasses.

A mile and a half to the south was the James River, with the gunboats *Aroostook* and *Galena* swinging slowly at anchor in the current a little way from shore, strange, toad-like monsters with their heavy shoulders of side paddlewheels, no one visible on their sun-baked decks but the watch officer on the bridge and the bluejacket on watch aloft. Half a mile nearer, to the southwest, was the scene of the comic opera action of yesterday, marked by five broken guns and two caissons and the four craters where the "lamp-posts" from the gunboats had struck. To the northwest the line of sharpshooters stretched reassuringly across that glittering valley of shocked wheat, one of each pair of them now obviously asleep under the sizzling, direct rays of the sun. Up on the bluffs where John was the east wind was blowing cooler.

At one o'clock the Colonel, Donahoe, and John were summoned to mess at Division Headquarters where, in the glaring white dining-room, they were served with all they wanted of the miracle of ice-water. After dinner the officers lounged for half an hour in Dr. Mellert's parlor, whence they could see most of the slope of the hill where the noon attacks had occurred and where three or four white flags now marked hospital details from either or both armies collecting the Rebel wounded. General Morell came in and told Colonel McNaughton that the cavalry reported no force of the enemy in the valley to the northwest or on the higher ground beyond it. All talking was in low tones and everybody assumed there would be plenty of action before night, the two attacks of the morning having been only feelers.

At two o'clock all talk stopped. The bursts of musket-fire over on the right grew rapid. A dispatch rider galloped in from General Couch. General Morell showed the message to General Griffin who scribbled an order and gave it to an orderly: "Show this to all battery commanders at once unless they are already engaged."

Over beyond the Quaker Road to the right three or four batteries began to range and the musket fire stopped. As the field officers of the 50th stepped out the front door to return to their command they could see dozens of guns being rolled forward from the wheat to the crest over on the right of the line across the Quaker Road. As they walked out of sight back of the Mellert house these guns also began to range, and in a few seconds the steady roar of firing at will was rising again, though this time the guns at their end of the line were taking no part in it. As Colonel Mc-Naughton sat down on the bench at 50th Headquarters he said, "Well, gentlemen, this will show the enemy everything we have for him, though I guess he'll pay plenty for the information."

For two hours, until four o'clock, they listened to a desultory battle half a mile away on the right, the firing being mostly light with long intervals of comparative silence, there seeming to develop no single attack as violent as the brief sharp one on the left at noon. And again they heard not a single infantry volley. It looked as if the infantry, certainly the infantry in support of the guns, was going to have an easy time of it. At precisely four o'clock this third attack stopped abruptly.

The sudden complete silence of the artillery was ominous, as if the enemy were gathering all of his strength for a final assault. It lasted an hour and a half. John passed through a state of excited impatience into one of indifference. They weren't going to be attacked today after all. The sun swung down toward the hills across the valley. John observed that if they should be attacked on that western side of the shoulder they would have to fight with the sun in their eyes. The breeze was refreshing. A haze began to rise and hang low over the valley.

At 5:30 there was not a sound on Malvern Hill. Morell's and Couch's Divisions were drowsing, along with the two-hundred-yard lines of artillery in front of each of their positions. The Mellert House was as quiet as if its proper owner and all his servants were there and taking their naps. Not an aide, orderly or runner moved anywhere. John had forgotten all about the war in the adventures of one David Copperfield, contained in a book by an English novelist Ike had given their pa more than eleven years before and which Ben had sent him. Even the Colonel was asleep.

Suddenly, and without any preliminary musketry, a gun in one of the batteries near them on the crest fired, followed at once by another, and in succession by the rest of a six-gun battery. Four or five other batteries chimed in and for half a minute John listened incredulously, doubting that anything of importance could be going on, suspecting that the guns were merely "registering" on some point to the north. But his sense of unreality was abruptly dissipated when he heard a distant volley of Rebel guns followed instantly by four or five shell-bursts over back of the 50th where Martindale's Brigade was, and soon after another batch nearer, the smoke of some of the bursts being visible among the oak trees.

The Colonel woke up from his nap so startled that he drew both his sword and revolver. The usual rushing of messengers began around Division Headquarters. Automatically everybody in John's battalion was lying down, most of them facing those shell bursts, though technically they were behind their line. The artillery on the crest thundered up into a heavier unison than it had shown all day.

The earth began to shake steadily. A runner dashed down to the Colonel from Lieutenant Holman:

"5:35—Rebel batteries going into position same hill northwest— Our batteries open on them while going into position— But Rebel batteries open, shells going over our guns and bursting among infantry behind crest— More Rebel batteries opening about a mile to northeast along low ridge, visible only from their smoke— Estimate four Rebel batteries to northwest and six to northeast— Cross-fire— Watcher reports casualties among two of our gun crews— All our artillery formerly in wheatfield now on crest and firing, with other guns farther to east beyond Quaker Road—heaviest firing of campaign— Large bodies enemy infantry—five or six brigades—forming battle line base of northern slope on both sides of Quaker Road— Our skirmishers retiring to left— No infantry on hill to northwest and none visible in valley west of it, but mist rising there now makes visibility bad, as well as heavy smoke drifting from our guns— Believe general attack coming— All but one battery on hill to northwest now silent—good work our guns—Holman."

Colonel McNaughton dismissed the runner who raced back into that infernal roar behind the Mellert house. He handed John the message and while he was reading it wrote a request to Lieutenant Waterman commanding the three guns of Weeden's Battery to swing them from southwest to northwest so as to cover the slope in front of the 50th. Having dispatched one of his orderlies with this, he took Holman's report from John, scribbled on it, "Move right in your own discretion if you see anything warranting it," and sent this by another orderly to Major Donahoe.

Five long minutes passed, with the earth shuddering under that volcanic roar on the crest and white smoke-clouds rolling up over the Mellert house, bending westward and shredding into long, thinning fingers a mile out over the valley and beyond. Headquarters was now a beehive of aides and messengers coming and going, mounted and unmounted. On the left of the 50th Lieutenant Waterman was swinging his guns around as requested. An orderly ran down from Headquarters asking Colonel McNaughton to report any activity in the valley. John and the Colonel, watching there through their glasses, could see nothing themselves nor any activity among Ripley's sharp-shooters to indicate that they saw any enemy. There were now patches of mist in the valley, in addition to the clouds of smoke drifting over it. The other runner from Lieutenant Holman arrived:

"5:43—Big attack on slope east of ravine—heavy slaughter at 600 yards but five brigades coming on on front reaching east beyond visibility— Can see no activity hill to north or valley west of it though visibility now bad from smoke and mist in the valley— Enemy brigade near me coming inside artillery fire— Watcher reports 62d Pennsylvania coming out through guns to meet them— Shall I stay position if surrounded?— Advance brigade near barn now—under fire 4th Michigan on flank—Holman."

"Go up there, Lathrop," snapped the Colonel. "Have Holman stay unless he's sure to be captured. Look over that hill and report back at once. I will have Johnson form your battalion."

John trotted up to the Mellert house with the runner, and as he rounded its corner it was like stepping over the edge into the quarter-mile-wide crater of an erupting volcano. He looked along the line of fifty guns he had last seen half-hidden in the wheat but now all in action almost wheel to wheel along the crest, with as many more guns continuing that roaring line to the eastward the other side of the Quaker Road.

The noise was not resonant as at Mechanicsville nor metallic as at Gaines's Mill. It was one continuous, unbroken roar as if the earth were a living thing at bay and that hill its head, a dragon that never paused to breathe but rolled out the steady thunder without interval, rhythm or change in quality. So fast was the fire from that quarter mile of near a hundred guns that a single sheet of flame parallel to the earth seemed to stand out level in front of them all, and individual flashes were not perceptible, while the big wreaths from the separate discharges merged quickly in a single white cloud that rose slowly, leaning to the west like the smoke of a quarter-mile line of burning brush. Behind the firing line of the guns, they were continually leaping back in pairs, threes, fours and dozens, then rolling forward again with the men at their wheels, all so regular that it was like an enormous steam engine with a hundred pistons all turning the heavy shaft of the battle line. Between the guns and down the ravine to John's left there was plenty of infantry in action, but musket-fire was inaudible. As Gaines's Mill had been the infantry's battle, this was the artillery's. Behind that display of vulcanism John felt infinitesimal, lilliputian. He was not only frightened in the usual, involuntary way that left his conscious mind clear, but he was dazed, buffeted by enormous power, bewildered, hardly aware of his mission.

Now he and the runner were dashing behind Gibbon's Battery in the Mellert barnyard, and John could not have told, then or afterward, whether it was firing or not. The trail of a gun in recoil snaked back just where his running foot had been and he never knew it. Men were running and shouting in the smoke all around him and several cannoneers cursed him, but he heard none of it. They were approaching the barn and he did see twenty or thirty Rebels running alongside it straight toward him. The nearest ones all went down together, but John did not know that the canister from two of Gibbon's guns had streaked past him, along with the continuous fire of the 4th Michigan from across the ravine, the balls shattering the lower siding of the barn and splintering its oak posts.

The first thing John knew he was up in the hayloft, crouching to the left of the door, looking out northeastward over the shambles on that long gentle slope. Here it was as if they were in the mouth of that bellowing earth monster, for they were in front of the line of the guns. John no longer heard the roar which was here one of the set conditions of life. He was in a world where all sound was obliterated, where the ears were useless organs. Smoke continuously rolled into the haydoor as if the lower story were on fire, and the air was purplish and chokingly acrid. The big barn vibrated hugely as if two or three giants were beating it with trees. Immediately below and in front were hundreds of Rebels, a few score huddling under the flimsy protection of the barn within ten feet of John's pistol, not bothering with him nor he with them, about half the others running, kneeling, firing, loading, fixing bayonets, and the remainder lying on the slope, some writhing slowly, some quiet.

Beyond these John saw for an instant to the eastward the panorama of that field of slaughter, the remnants of four brigades with fourteen regimental battle flags still staggering up toward that earth monster inside the fatal 600-yard range of its grinding iron jaws, the whole slope hummocky behind them with their dead and wounded, each regiment rolling on with its front rank continually falling under and unrolling out behind like a carpet of bodies while the colors went down and up, down and up with the same regularity as that engine of guns rumbling along the crest.

The brigade attacking the Yankee left, the one just in front of the barn, was the farthest advanced. With the exception of those who ventured round the right of the barn into the muzzles of Gibbon's Battery, it was inside the artillery fire and dangerously threatening the flank, though continuously decimated by the cross-fire of the 4th Michigan from across the ravine and the 62d Pennsylvania from the right of the barn. John's glance of a moment saw an officer with his hat whirling high on the point of his sword, causing two standards and all the near men to rally behind him in a ragged line; but the bulk of them remained scattered, fighting alone. Having been in the barn perhaps twenty seconds, John for the first time heard a volley of musketry close enough to be audible, like a faint grating under the bellow of the artillery. Then he saw blue coats in a good line move out round the barn with a bristle of bayonets in front of them, and at the center of the line the colors and standard.

It was the 62d Pennsylvania advancing on the remnant of Armistead's Brigade that still outnumbered them but was scattered and shattered by the long attack. The Rebel General shouted something and the little line he had gathered turned tail down the slope. At the same instant John saw the Captain leading the 62d run out in front of the regiment, heard their cheer and their shouts, "Remember Black!"—their Colonel who had been killed at Gaines's Mill where their other field officers had been wounded—and the line did a wheel to the left at a dead run.

General Armistead and the hundred and more with him escaped, as did hundreds of others outside the line of the 62d's charge. But those near the barn and in the ravine were caught between the 62d and the 4th Michigan whose flanking companies closed in behind them and cut off their retreat. For seconds they fought and added a few more to the windrows of dead. Then the muskets began to go down and the hands to go up and about a hundred prisoners were hustled back through the barnyard to the rear.

The retreat from the Yankee left, where the Rebels had been farthest advanced, infected the rest. About half of the men in the four brigades that had come yelling up that slope ran back with the canister still scything them till they were beyond its range, when shells followed with their pettier harassment as they formed and disappeared into the distant woods.

The battle was not over. It continued on the right beyond the Quaker Road, and would soon be renewed on the left. But the slope between the Mellert house and the road was for the moment cleared of the enemy. The nearer guns slackened into occasional single shots. The usual shrieks of the wounded became audible. John became aware of a body lying in blood just behind him. It was the Division Sergeant Major, killed by a dozen canister balls from a shot of Gibbon's Battery fired too high through the siding of the barn.

John had been in the barn little over a minute. He stepped over to Lieutenant Holman who had been watching from the other side of the hay-door, stolidly continuing his mission of observing that hill a mile to the northwest. John raised his glasses on it. The smoke around them was clearing and the visibility of the hill itself was good, one Rebel gun being visible there, lying on its side. But between the foot of the hill and the beginning of the Malvern slope the mist was even heavier than it had been in the morning, lying low along the bushes that marked the stream, but high enough, John and Holman agreed, to conceal troops moving in column.

John lowered his glasses and saw with the naked eye a fresh line of Rebels forming along the bottom of the near slope. "The danged fools ain't satisfied yet," said Holman and spat tobacco juice with a calm John admired. "You'd better stay on watch a while yet," he said. "But if the smoke gets so bad again you can't see anything I'd go to the rear of the battery out here until you think it's cleared. In other words, stay while you can see anything, but don't get yourself captured for nothing. Let me take one of your runners with me, in case the Colonel has any further message for you."

John took a look through his glasses at the new Rebel line forming for suicide at the bottom of the slope. He could make out a dozen standards of regiments, but had no way of knowing whether they were fresh ones or not. The shelling of the artillery began to speed up again and John happened to have his glasses on a point where three men fell from a shell burst. "Looks no worse, anyway," he said to Holman. "I hain't et," was the lieutenant's comment. "I'll send back something by the runner," said John. "Lookit," said Holman, with his glasses on the suspicious hill.

John looked. Above the mist along the stream, on the other side of the line of bushes, a small thing like a head was moving along, probably that of a mounted man. It teetered southwestward at a trot and disappeared behind the pines at the bottom of the long ravine. They continued to watch but that was all they saw. "I'll report it," said John and, followed by the runner whose turn it was, he climbed down the ladder to the main floor. As he was passing the door of the Mellert house a soldier sprinted by him, panting. To the guard at the door he gasped, "Message from Colonel Ripley for General Morell." The guard took the message which the runner produced from his shirt and called, "Message from Colonel Ripley." The messenger sat down and wiped his forehead with his sleeve. He was one of the sharpshooters. John ran the remaining five rods to the 50th Headquarters.

The Colonel was not there. John saw his own battalion sitting down in formation, with Captain Johnson out in front in command. He asked Captain Green where the Colonel was. The Adjutant replied with irritating facetiousness as usual, "Seems to be a little something of interest in the valley," and he twisted his mustached lip. "Perhaps a little quarrel among the sharpshooters." John looked down at Donahoe's position and there were the Colonel and Donahoe, both looking down the slope at something so close they alternately raised and lowered their glasses.

John could see from where he was that there were no more sharpshooters out in the center of the valley. In spite of the cannonade, here slightly muffled, that was rumbling up into full power again on the crest, he could hear carbines firing down beyond the edge of the shoulder. He started to run down to the Colonel when he heard someone dashing up behind him. It was Captain Henshaw of Division Headquarters. "Lathrop," he yelled hurriedly, "can you tell Colonel McNaughton at once that Colonel Ripley of the sharpshooters reports a column of the enemy—at least a brigade—marching southwestward around the north of this shoulder into the valley? Say that they should appear opposite him any moment. Tell him I am going with orders from General Morell for the 13th

New York, on the left of Martindale's Brigade, to move left in support of you. All clear?"

"Yes." John sprinted the fifty yards down to the edge of the shoulder and relayed Henshaw's message as more important than the report of his own observations at the barn. The Colonel was wearing his bulldog grin and was watching the sharpshooters who had closed into what looked like two companies of close skirmishers four or five hundred yards down there at the foot of the slope, retiring alternately through each other, backing off southward down the valley. They were firing rapidly with their repeaters into that hidden region behind the pine trees below the northern slope, although showing no sign of being under fire themselves.

The Colonel seemed not to hear John's message from the General, but kept looking alternately with his glasses up to the right and with his naked eyes down into the valley. Suddenly three or four companies of Rebels ran out from the northern cover of the shoulder and formed line of battle facing and pursuing the sharpshooters southward. When they opened fire it was inaudible for the roar up on the crest, but a few of the sharpshooters dropped, and their line, in retreating down the valley, began to bend back toward the hill. Then a Rebel column appeared, led by a group that looked like a general and his staff. "Mahone's Brigade," said McNaughton, looking through his glasses. "Lathrop." "Yes, sir." "Tell Major Schoeffel to halt his 13th in column, the head about where your battalion is. You make room for him. Tell him Mahone's Brigade is appearing and I will notify him as soon as an attack develops. Tell him if Donahoe moves to the right to put four companies in Donahoe's present position to support Weeden's guns. Hold the rest in reserve. When you have delivered the message report to me." At that moment they all looked to the right. *Crrrrrrack*—against the cannonade on the crest they heard the left of the 4th Michigan open fire, and saw its small support running out on the shoulder behind it.

John started to the rear on the run and had just reached his own battalion when he saw the 13th coming at the double through the little oak trees. Running up to Captain Johnson, he said, "Move the battalion by the right flank far enough to let that regiment halt here. Don't take that diagonal position until further orders." Then he ran on to meet the major commanding the 13th, and delivered the order from Colonel McNaughton. Over on the left Weeden's three guns opened. The fire of the 4th Michigan was now heavy on the northern edge of the shoulder, shooting down into the pines.

As John started back to the Colonel a runner from the 4th Michigan dashed up with a written message for Colonel McNaughton. "Give it to me," said John, dismissed the soldier, and read it as he ran:

"Brigade attacking my left. Mahone opposite you. Armistead in main attack on crest. Probably Wright attacking me. Can hold left unless pressed on right in the ravine.   Woodbury."

John gave the message to McNaughton and crouched beside him, looking down the slope. The Rebel brigade was forming line of battle a quarter of a mile down in the valley, heading diagonally up the hill toward Weeden's guns, two battle flags already advancing and two more regiments running out to form line in support. Weeden's battery was already firing canister, and with every bellow of its gun a few brown shirts toppled. Suddenly there was a heavy explosion at the battery and three or more men fell there. John saw Lieutenant Waterman send off a runner. Some of the reserve artillery had taken his guns for Rebels and were firing on them. The guns continued in action.

Now the Rebel line was edging to the right, and they extended in that direction until the four regiments were coming straight up the hill toward the line of bushes a hundred yards below the 50th, where they would be out of the field of fire of the battery. Their two-hundred-yard line broke into a run, and like distant crickets John could hear them yelling. "All right, Donahoe," said the Colonel. "By the right flank into position." "Lathrop, get your men ready to move to the right." The first line of the Rebels was already coming under cover of the line of bushes and the drop in the ground a hundred yards below them.

John ran back, wheeled his battalion into the diagonal position facing the right, and crouched in the furious restlessness of waiting in support. He saw Donahoe's six companies scuttling the hundred yards to the right, ducking to keep cover behind the edge of the shoulder. As they moved up into the new line some of the men showed themselves. There was an impromptu Rebel volley and the 50th got its first casualties of the day.

Four companies of the 13th formed line and moved into the position Donahoe had left. The rightmost picket of the 50th that was to be John's right when he went in, swung round from watching the northern slope in front of the 4th Michigan and lay with muskets pointed down the hill to the west. The 4th was now hotly engaged.

The fire of Donahoe's companies ripped out and continued. Never had John felt such an exultant eagerness for the battle in immediate prospect. He wanted to fight. The Rebs were four regiments against the 50th. He wanted to chase them down that hill. He wanted to kill. He realized that

Holman's runner was yelling something to him. "Tell Lieutenant Holman," he shouted, "to join his company."

The volcano up on the hill was now in full roar again, but John scarcely heard it. He saw his friend Donahoe's six companies firing their fastest, the front rank prone, the rear rank kneeling. He felt his own four companies behind him, including his own special C Company and five friends with whom he would as soon die as he would with anybody. As never before in the two major battles he had seen, the cause of the Union, his country, his ideals, his army fighting for them, came alive in his consciousness.

He looked round at his men with a tense smile and from most of them got back similar, reassuring looks. It was an unbeatable army, an unbeatable cause, that waited there on Malvern Hill, an army crouched and eager not only to wipe out the defeat of Gaines's Mill, but then to press on at the double all the way to Richmond, to take the offensive from the Rebels and win the war. The spirit of the volunteer army was still alive. "God damn it, Captain—Major—whatever ye be," shouted an irrepressible, "let's go after 'em!" "Yipiyipiyipiyipiyipiyipi"— From over the crest they heard the Rebel yell against the roar of the artillery and the crash of the infantry. *Rat-t-t-tat—crrrrrack—rat-tat-tat—crrrrack—crrrrrr-rack,* from Donahoe's battalion fifty yards in front of them. And the Rebel bullets in brigades of mosquitoes whizzing over—*bimm-b-b-b-bimm—b-b-b-bimmm—bimmmmmmmmmmm—zzzzz—bimmmmmmmmmmmm.*

John saw things minutely, as if he were all eyes. He saw Old Glory and the colors a rod behind what had been the inner picket on Donahoe's right that was to be his left. He saw the Colonel alternately standing up and squatting behind the ten men of the picket who were now all lying down, firing down the slope with the rest of their battalion. He saw Major Donahoe running back and forth behind his line, sometimes stepping up into it, generally staying near the right where he could watch the Colonel. A hundred yards farther to the right, John saw Donahoe's rightmost picket, also lying down and firing, like a little island out there bounding the long gap in the line that he was to fill, the critical point of contact at an angle with the 4th Michigan, the point where if either gave way both regiments would be taken in rear and the Rebels would sweep down the whole line on the crest, capturing the guns, defeating, perhaps routing the Army. Nine or ten regiments against the 4th and the 50th. He glanced over at the 13th New York. Six companies in reserve. By God they wouldn't need them!

John looked hungrily at the Colonel and Donahoe. Why didn't they send for him? There seemed to be no change in Donahoe's line, its front rank still in position prone, its rear rank ducking to load and rising to the kneeling position to fire—no change except that a few figures that had been in the rear rank were now lying still, and some of the prone figures in the front rank were not firing. A dozen wounded men were dragging themselves back toward his position, and the stretcher-bearers were running out from Regimental Headquarters. At the left, where Donahoe had been before, the four companies of the 13th were in action. Beyond, they were wheeling Weeden's guns forward. But the Rebel brigade was now all covered by the curve of the shoulder, and those guns did not fire again.

Colonel McNaughton was sending a man to the picket out there on the right flank, and when he had run along, crouching Indian fashion, and delivered his message to the sergeant in charge, the whole picket of ten men likewise scuttled back and took the position of support line behind the other picket where the Colonel was. Now the Colonel was standing up and suddenly John saw him shout something to the men of the two pickets round him. Then he ran toward Donahoe, making a sign with both hands like corking a bottle, and Donahoe ran along behind his line shouting through cupped hands. The Colonel ran toward John making the same sign, and pausing to shout to the Color Sergeant as he passed him. The men were already loaded and John turned and yelled, "Fix bayonets."

The rattle of Donahoe's line ceased for a moment, then, as the Colonel rushed up, it began again, and John saw the men now firing with bayonets fixed. There was a momentary lull in the noise of the 4th Michigan. Up over the edge of the shoulder into that hundred yards of unguarded stretch where he was to go into position, rose first the emblems on the staves of two Rebel battle-flags, then the criss-cross flags themselves, then a couple of officers waving swords, then a few more officers, all running up on the shoulder, then, in close formation, showing they had not been in action, the fronts of six or seven companies, obviously the assault lines of two fresh regiments.

John jumped up, whipping out both his sword and his revolver, unconscious of details or danger, unaware of anything but uncontrollable force surging through him toward those Rebels. A voice that was his own shouted, "All right, boys, here goes Blackwater County!" Then he felt a weight on his shoulder and there were words in his ear which he afterward remembered— "No, Lathrop, you're a young man—this is my job"—

then louder words— "Stay here— Watch your ammunition— Tell Schoeffel
to get in line where you were, ready to support us or the 4th."

Then something of self-domination from a long inheritance gripped
John in the vice of military discipline. He stared at the Colonel with
senseless, bulging eyes, while his teeth sheared clean through both edges
of his tongue. Then he heard his boys yelling past him, saw them charge
away from him, saw the swords of the Colonel and all the company commanders high out in front, beyond them heard a heavy Rebel volley, saw
twenty or thirty spaces open and close in the line, heard the unique, heavy
thump and clatter as a hundred front line bayonets and bodies collided
in unison with as many Rebels in the furious momentum of that charge,
saw the line pause an instant, then race on, the Rebels and their two
standards disappearing down the slope before it, saw the 50th's colors
and standard go forward at a run, heard Donahoe's line cheer and jump
in with bayonets on the left of McNaughton's, saw the whole line disappear down over the edge of the shoulder, felt his knees trembling like
palsy, and remembered he was there alone with an order to carry out.

He still heard heavy jostling, thumping, shouting and irregular firing
down there out of sight over the edge of the hill, then a rising cheer running along the two-hundred-yard front the 50th had covered. It had all
taken perhaps thirty seconds. McNaughton's famous bayonet charge was
over, when one regiment of 503 men, unsupported, without firing a shot,
drove from this key position four assault regiments of the enemy all in
line.

In the seventy-five yards John's battalion had covered in its rush to the
edge of the hill three of the four company commanders now lay among
twenty-six of their men, Captain Hart of A and Lieutenant Hutchins of
F stone dead, Medad VanSanford trying unsuccessfully to rise. John signalled to his ammunition sergeant to bring the reserve boxes to the point
where he was, raced past Headquarters, shouting to the Surgeon that
three company commanders were down over there, then ran up to Major
Schoeffel of the 13th and gave him the order to swing his remaining companies in line in that diagonal position where John's battalion had been,
ready to support either the 50th on the west slope or the 4th Michigan on
the north.

John ran back to his former station where the reserve ammunition now
awaited him. When he got there the 50th was all back along the edge of
the shoulder, his battalion in position on the right, lying down as Donahoe's men had been before, apparently awaiting another attack. John ran

forward to Medad who had slumped into unconsciousness. He lay in a pool of blood from a hole in one side just under his ribs. John pulled out his shirt, ripped off the tail and stuffed it into the wound, then carried him up to Regimental Headquarters and turned him over to the Surgeon.

Conscious of irregularity in having left his post to give Medad personal attention, John hurried back just in time to issue a box of ammunition to the detail Donahoe had sent up for it, the sergeant in charge having already pried open the tightly nailed box with his bayonet. This matter being disposed of, John raised his glasses to see how his battalion, and particularly C Company, had fared.

The wounded from Donahoe's battalion had all been removed, and the dozen dead laid side by side behind the line. But the stretcher-bearers had not yet got around to John's battalion that the Colonel had led in. Their eight dead and eighteen wounded, except for Medad, still lay there in a rough line, marking the place where the battalion had run straight into the Rebels' volley at thirty yards. Company C had got off lightly, only the barefoot Luke Clock being among the dead, and only Ebenezer Gorham and Corporal Zebedee Adams, beside Medad, among the badly wounded. But as the forty-four men remaining in the company lay there in their double line, the marks of the charge were on them, the slashes of shirts and pants from Gaines's Mill being doubled and most of the rents being dark stained. George Fulton, now the only officer with the company, was kneeling at his defense post in the center behind it, straightening up every few seconds to look down the hill; he had got another of his close shaves, this one being literally that, a slash on the cheek from a bayonet or saber.

Jabe Munson, now commanding the right platoon and lying behind it, had an ugly streak of red from his thigh all the way down his burlap pants to his boots, and as John studied him through his glasses, he thought he could see blood still oozing out of his thigh at the top of the streak. Zeb Milliken, behind the left platoon, had lost a sleeve of his shirt, but showed no sign of a wound. John wished George would order Jabe to the rear with that bleeding thigh of his.

He ran his glasses over the rest of the battalion and the regiment, and saw them all in the same shredded condition. Donahoe's right arm hung limp, and John could see that his jaw was set against pain as he sometimes turned in profile, lying at the right of his front line, watching down the slope. Miraculously the Colonel, who had led the most daring part of the charge, appeared to be unmarked, his uniform hardly ruffled. He was the only man now standing up in the regiment, a pace behind the line of battle, where the Rebs could surely see at least his head. John wondered if he knew about Donahoe's arm and if he did whether he would put John down there in command of the left. He felt a surge of hatred for the Colonel. He had compelled John to be an onlooker. He remembered his words—"You're a young man, Lathrop—this is my job." It made him burn with humiliation.

While he was thus glaring at his commanding officer the Colonel turned and walked rapidly toward him. John stood at his stiffest attention, saluting being dispensed with in action and even standing at attention being a rare formality. As he came up the Colonel saw the anger in the look of his tall young subordinate. "Never mind, Lathrop," he said, putting his hand on his arm. "One of us had to stay back here, and that was something I would never ask a man to do unless I was leading it myself. Go on up there now and take your battalion. You'll have plenty of work yet."

John reported the state of the ammunition and pointed out the six companies of the 13th that were crouching in general reserve just south of them. Then from over the edge of the shoulder came the Rebel yell like a hundred packs of hounds taking the scent. Ten Company commanders shouted "Fire!" *Crrrrack-rrack-rrack—crrrrrack—rack—crrrrrrrrrrrrrack* ripped all along the front of the 50th. John lost his personal feelings, dashed down to his battalion, ran along whacking each of the company commanders on the shoulder, ran back to the left and touched Donahoe to let him know he was there, saw that classical face turned savage with pain, then stood up to look down at the Rebel charge. He was unaware of the racket of the 4th Michigan to the right and behind him, where another attack of Wright's Rebel Brigade was in progress.

Again four regiments were attacking the 50th in close formation, each with about four companies in line and the rest in support. They were not charging bayonets up the hill, but had sent back a volley in return for the one they got when they jumped up into attack, had run up a little way, lain down, and were just now ripping out a second volley, followed by a second rush.

By these intrepid tactics they were keeping formation, but were giving the 50th the full advantage of its settled, partially concealed position along the top where each one of its shots had five times the chance to be effective that the hurried ones of the Rebels did. In a long minute they had advanced only half way up the hill and had fired only twice, while every man of the 50th had got in four or five aimed shots.

The original attack companies had withered away and were being absorbed in the support companies moving in. The attackers' advantage of numbers was now far under three to one, and the Yankees still had the advantage of position. The four Rebel flags were going down as fast as they bobbed up. A colonel dashed out to lead his regiment in a bayonet charge, but went down before his men saw him, and they never rose from their partial concealment lying down. Another colonel made the same gallant attempt and was out in front, his regiment rising with a cheer, before he fell dead. They then took a dreadful volley from some of Donahoe's companies and wavered.

Two or three companies did charge bayonets and a remnant reached the top where, after a brief melee, some of them were taken prisoners and the rest ran down the hill. This started the retreat. In another minute the four regiments were back under cover of the low ground behind the line of bushes, leaving almost three hundred of the thirteen hundred that had started the fight, crawling and moaning on the slope.

John went back to the center of his battalion where all of the company commanders were signalling for ammunition, and two men of the ammunition detail were already fetching it. In this second attack John's battalion had suffered only ten casualties, C Company having lost three wounded and none killed. The men were still on edge and there were insubordinate shouts of, "Let's go at 'em again!" "Ass t' this still huntin'!" The fight over in the 4th Michigan was sputtering off into another repulse.

John paused behind Company C where Jabe was now standing up and George Fulton was kneeling beside him, examining the hole in his thigh. Jabe was as gray as the dust underfoot, but he smiled as John came up. "Hadn't you better order Jabe to the rear?" he said to George. "If ye do it," said Jabe in a weak, savage voice, "it'll be the last order either o' you feller's 'll give. It ain't anything but a flesh wound, anyway, see?" And he walked around to show them, thereby starting a gentle flow of blood. "You'll be all right if you'll tend to your job and not race round," said George. John walked toward his station at the rear of the center of the line, and as he passed the left platoon of Company C little Zeb Milliken, commanding it, turned from watching down the slope and winked at him. John winked back, stepped up to the line and looked over. A little way down the slope, the face of one of the dead Rebel colonels was turned toward him. The name didn't come to him, but his mind went all the way back to his class at Yale. Just then the Rebel yell sang out in gathering volume, and for the third time the brown lines surged out of the bushes a hundred yards below.

This time the fifteen or so assault companies climbed up, gave their hurried volley, took the deadly one that crashed along the line of the

50th, dropped another fifty of their number, and then came on at charge bayonets without stopping to load. At a dead run they were up the hundred-yard slope in a half a minute, having taken two more volleys, then closed right in with bayonets, being now reduced to less than a thousand men against the 50th's more than four hundred remaining. The chances of attack forced the remnant of one of the regiments into a wedge or phalanx shape with its battle flag near the point which now happened to drive right between C and A Companies at the center of John's battalion, between Zeb Milliken's left platoon and the right platoon of A Company, all immediately in front of John. Dave Walsh was at the left of C's line and his bare foot went up and then down as he drove his bayonet into the first Rebel, yanked it out, lunged up at the second with his musket butt, then himself went down with his whole lower jaw carried away by a shot from an officer's revolver.

The men from the threatened flanks of both companies were now closing in round the point of the wedge and for a few seconds the fight was all weight and pressure, grunts, panting, thumps, the whack of metal and wood, the contact being so close at the point that weapons were presently useless and it was all knees, fists and fingers on throats. Then the outer flanks of the two threatened companies, being themselves free of attack by the extreme congestion of the Rebel regiment, began pouring lead into the mass of it pressing behind.

To meet this the rear of the wedge opened out and the weight at the point was lightened to fifteen or twenty Rebs, with their battle flag in their midst, fighting in the closest of contact with about the same number of Yankees, the Rebs having already pushed back the line a little, though it was holding with the immediate force of shoulders, arms, fingers and teeth, and for ten seconds the only serious casualties were when Alonzo Small lost his footing and fell and three or four Rebs stumbled right over him on their faces and were immediately dispatched by as many shots from John's revolver.

Just at this moment E Company on the right, having forced another small Rebel regiment to give a little ground, did a foolhardy thing. It charged bayonets diagonally across the front of C, driving its own immediate attackers down the hill along with the few who were engaged with the right of C. This left the rear of the remnant of the wedge outflanked, and individuals from it began to give way and join in the retreat of the left of their line.

Zeb Milliken, who had been behind the straining line of his men, clubbing in with his musket as he could, suddenly saw the Rebel color-bearer through the spreading ranks, drove into his side with the bayonet, grabbed the staff, and got out just as the whole point of the wedge was giving ground and more and more of its supporters were taking to their heels. John at that moment was realizing that E Company had charged without orders, was swinging far out in front, and the first thing Johnson knew he would be down at the foot of the hill and captured. The straight way for John to the runaway company was right through the now scattering wedge, and as he started he saw Zeb standing there seemingly hesitant, holding up the Rebel battle-flag.

Just then three Rebs who had passed Zeb realized what had happened and turned back on him with their bayonets in the now clearing field. Just behind Zeb was Alec Mathiesson who was crouching as if under the protection of Zeb's little body, and John had a flashing thought that here was the chance Alec had wanted. He himself had twenty feet to go and as he jumped forward his revolver missed fire twice and he threw it away. He saw Zeb throw down the flag and face the three Rebs with his bayonet.

Just then from somewhere Jabe staggered in front of John, lunged forward and collapsed on the ground beside Dave Walsh who was blowing blood bubbles from his jawless throat, his eyes wide open. As John jumped over Jabe he saw Alec make a retiring, girlish jab with his bayonet as the three Rebs closed on Zeb who drove at one of them and missed, the other two getting him together, then the third, and down went Zeb on the flag he had captured, much of his blood and most of his intestines spilling out over it.

The Rebs tugged at the flag, which gave John his chance. He dropped his saber, grabbed Alec's musket, at the same time kicking him forward over Zeb, spitted one of the Rebs by surprise, jumped clean inside the second's bayonet as he rose to meet him and carried him to the ground with his knees, and leapt up to see somebody from E Company clubbing the third Reb down and saving his life. In more fury at Alec's cowardice than at Zeb's death, John ran blindly on down the hill in the midst of E Company till he heard someone shout, "Halt, for God's sake, E Company, halt," and came to his senses, hatless, weaponless, having lost all contact with his command.

It was Captain Johnson himself shouting, and John ran out in front to help him, spreading his arms as if to turn cattle. They succeeded in herding together the remaining seventy men of this large company and starting them in a formless mass double-timing back up the hill toward their position, the two senior captains trotting behind them.

Over in front of Donahoe the fight had been less spectacular but was now having the same outcome. As John looked that way there was a heavy but irregular volley. The fighting line up at the edge of the shoulder broke, and the two Rebel regiments that had been there started down hill with their battle flags, keeping a good line as they ran. Seeing that the right of the line was safe, and the issue in front of Donahoe undecided, McNaughton had played his last card. He had marched in the six reserve companies of the 13th, and ordered them to fire on the Rebs as they could through the openings in the fight. John saw the retreat coming, shouted to Johnson, "Chance for some prisoners," pointing at the left of the retiring Rebel line that was going to pass right by E Company. Johnson halted his company, got them in two ragged lines and, himself leading at a walk, marched out by the flank so as to intercept the flank of the retreat. Most of the Rebels saw what was in front of them and swerved over to the right, but a score or more ran blindly right into the bayonets of E, fetched up with a start, and a moment later were being prodded back up the hill, while the rest of the regiment on the crest cheered.

John went back as he had come, first heading for Zeb. Alec was on his knees bent clean over that oozing bundle, fairly screaming in his sobs, while the rest of the platoon stood menacing round, men most of whom were not Zeb's friends in civil life but who had learned to love him as a brave leader. John felt an impulse of pity for poor Alec, but he also realized the real danger in this hour of animal rage from those fifteen men standing in silent hatred, either their own or somebody else's blood already smearing most of them.

Grabbing Alec by the collar, he jerked him to his feet, saying harshly, "To your post, Mathiesson. All the rest of you, to your posts." Alec staggered to what had been his place near the left of the rear rank and collapsed on the ground. George Fulton was bending over Jabe who looked dead. "He's alive," said George, glancing up as John approached, "and I think I've stopped the blood."

John looked away down the hillside over those hundreds of bodies. It was clear that no further attack was preparing at the moment. One of the men brought him his sword, his pistol and his hat. As he took the last he noticed without emotion that it had three new bullet holes in it. Then he began to break with the relief of the strain. Zeb dead and Jabe and Medad near it. He looked at his four companies and they seemed to be in order. He went back to Jabe and saw no stretchers in sight. He knelt by the big, silent hulk, held the long beard aside and listened to his chest.

His heart was beating lightly. "Ask Captain Flint to send us a stretcher—my personal request," he said to somebody, and the boy ran for Headquarters.

While John waited he looked westward over the valley. The battle was still rumbling behind him up on the crest, and the firing of the right of the 4th Michigan a hundred and fifty yards behind him was heavier than it had been all day. But John did not hear it. He was watching the quiet sunset across the valley and thinking how at that moment it was setting just so over the Rumford Hills where Jabe was born, and over the Chalons Hills where Zeb was born, over behind Fire Chief Obid Plum's House on Washington Street opposite where Medad and Fred were born, and over Pond Hill across the Hollow where he was born and his pa's grave was. Irrelevantly he remembered helping Ike butcher a hog when they were boys, and the sight of the blood spurting out as Ike withdrew the knife.

The stretcher arrived and the bearers set it down beside Jabe. Four of the boys lifted him gently onto it and the bearers went to the ends and stooped down. "Never mind, men," said John, standing up. "Lieutenant Fulton, take the other end." Nobody laughed as the two officers bore the big sergeant up through the twilight to the dressing station at Headquarters, not even the boys of the 13th, most of which they passed on the way. "Friend of ours, Flint," said John to the Surgeon, who looked at them cynically, wearing an apron which, with his bare arms, was entirely covered with blood. There was a wet, meaty smell around the doctor and the dressing station, though no amputations were performed there.

Suddenly John became aware of thunderous action all along the line of the 4th Michigan. He saw the support that had been at the left backing out, then going by the right flank at the double, disappearing behind the Mellert house. He saw the leftmost platoon of the 4th crowding over to the right and firing diagonally backward. He saw Captain Johnson on the right of his own battalion peer down the northern slope into the pines, then glance back as if wanting instructions. He saw the line of the 13th wheeling to the right so as to face the rear of the 4th. John and George sprinted back for their posts. John almost ran into Colonel McNaughton who was looking for him, and gave him an angry reprimand.

"This is war, Lathrop, and you are not at your post. The 4th Michigan is engaged front and left and its left will retreat. Move your battalion immediately by the left flank behind Donahoe, then fifty yards up the hill. Make way for the four companies of the 13th that will join their regiment from their position on the left of Donahoe. Keep watch there.

You are in support both of Donahoe and the 13th. If your battalion is in motion when the enemy appears you will be tried for it."

John ran on in a panic, for the 4th Michigan's left was backing off toward the right as they loaded. "Battalion, fall in in place," he bellowed, running up to the center of it, "By the right flank, march," and he indicated the direction by waving his sword toward the left, which was right for the men as they faced him in hasty formation. But the Second Lieutenant now commanding F Company on the end of the line got confused and headed in the wrong direction, starting an altercation with Company A behind them. In terror and fury John rushed at F Company, shouting, "F Company, about face, follow me, double time," and he led them off behind Donahoe's right, where B Company was loudly laughing at this hay-foot-straw-foot demonstration.

Having got them started, John turned and ran backwards at the head of the column, saw—thank God—that Johnson was at the tail of E Company, keeping it closed up. Then ignominiously he tripped over one of his own empty ammunition boxes and sat down hard, at which none of his battalion quite dared to laugh. He got up, shouting frantically, "Battalion, halt," for F Company, having been infected by John's panic, was engaged in something of a stampede. Their lieutenant and non-coms got them halted in a straggling way, well beyond the left of Donahoe's battalion, and the other three companies closed up in a series of collisions. The four companies of the 13th double-timed past him to join their regimental line which suddenly delivered its second volley of the day, and thereafter continued to fire occasional volleys, but without settling into fire at will.

John feared the enemy had indeed appeared while his little column was in motion and he was done for. But he composed himself, the immediate danger being over, gave them "About face—forward, march" for about a rod, then, "Battalion, halt—right face. Right dress." He had the companies re-form in proper order, and presently marched them up the hill in column of sections and counter-marched, heading them toward Donahoe behind the support of the 13th, a position from which they could swing immediately into line facing either north or south and could almost as quickly go right front into line in support of Donahoe. He ordered Johnson of E Company to detail ten men under a sergeant for picket duty, and told the rest to sit down in place.

While John was posting the picket on Donahoe's left, Donahoe's battalion fired, and John saw what at first seemed like a new attack coming in the dusk from the line of bushes. But after Donahoe's volley, so much of the Rebel line as John could see dropped back out of sight. As he was running back to his battalion Donahoe's right companies fired again, but thereafter they were silent.

John walked up to Captain Johnson and explained his orders, confiding the pickle he had got into, carrying Jabe up to the dressing station. Johnson laughed, being a humorous, easy-going farmer in spite of his black hair and flashing black eyes, and the fact that John's recent defalcation almost got him captured or annihilated. Three or four minutes passed, the 13th occasionally firing a volley, and the racket beyond being heavy. Captain Flint passed them, going down to Donahoe, where they watched him slit off the Major's right sleeve and bind up his arm. John stopped the Surgeon on the way back and learned that a minie ball had gone clean through Donahoe's upper arm, grazing the humerus, that there had been little hemorrhage and it was only a superficial fracture. He was suffering severe pain but could not be given morphine while he insisted on remaining on duty. The Surgeon walked on back to his dressing station.

The artillery along the crest was again in full rumble, and in the dusk the flashes of the discharges were perceptible like continual, flickering lightning through the oak trees. John and Captain Johnson stood listening to it and to the heavy musketry over on the north end of the shoulder, a hundred and fifty yards away. But they could see none of the action, due to the gathering darkness and the fact that the 13th was in front of them. Johnson drew John a little apart from the men and they squatted down. "John," he said, "if we win this fight do you figger the big fellers'll let us advance on Richmond?" "I don't know, Zach," said John. "I'm afraid to think about it." "If we don't," said Johnson, "I'm afraid of a mutiny." John made no comment. Johnson pointed out an enormous bank of black cloud bulging up into the sky from the east.

The twilight phase of the battle did not involve the 50th New York. The 4th Michigan, which had been holding off Wright's Brigade while the 50th was holding off Mahone's, had been attacked by a new force on its right from across the ravine, which required the left of its line to be drawn in. The fire of the 13th New York prevented Wright's Brigade from coming up in rear of the 4th, but instead it attacked the new flank, coming up through the ravine. Meanwhile Mahone's Brigade had started another attack on the 50th, but, seeing Wright's Brigade moving eastward, had suspended it and followed Wright through the pines in the attack on the 4th. The 4th was driven back, Colonel Woodbury was killed, and the Rebels came up the ravine almost to the Mellert house. Gibbon's Battery limbered up and got away just in time to avoid capture. At the same time other Rebel brigades penetrated the artillery on the main line along the crest, most of the batteries being now out of ammunition. One gun was captured and turned around.

But as a result of his niggardliness of support for the 50th New York and the 4th Michigan, General Morell still had Butterfield's Brigade in reserve, the only fresh troops of either side on the field. Advancing through the lines of Griffin and Martindale, they easily drove back the Rebels, and the gallant brigades of Wright and Mahone tenaciously bivouacked for the night at the foot of the ravine just under the Yankee lines.

There was a moment's threat in the darkness when Ransom's Rebel Brigade marched up unopposed on the northwest curve of the shoulder where John's right had been, got a mixed volley from the 13th New York and others, countermarched in good order, disappeared whence it had come, and was not heard from again. The Battle of Malvern Hill was over.

Sitting in the dark at the head of his column, John heard shouting and marching for a quarter of an hour, as Butterfield's Brigade relieved all of Morell's line except the 50th and 13th New York. Then suddenly he realized it was still. Not a field piece firing. Only an occasional musket in the distance that might have been someone hunting. The sky was coal black from the east up to the zenith. The seeming stillness was for a time overwhelming, and John got up and moved about to retain a sense of reality. Then ordinary sounds that had been inaudible, part of the sudden hush that fell after that day-long volcano of battle, began to penetrate his consciousness. Men were talking near by in a low tone. There was the clatter of a mounted detachment somewhere up on one of the roads. A friendly shout at Headquarters. The cries of the wounded out there in the night were rising toward the peak of their terrible symphony, always reached just before death began to impose its rapid diminuendo. Back among the oak trees a few camp fires began to glow. A gust of wind rippled the leaves with an intimation of rain. In the sky there was a gentle rumble of natural thunder. West of the zenith there were stars.

CHAPTER LXXXIV

" W A K E U P, Lathrop— Wake up— We're going to take a walk." It was
Adjutant Green shaking John where he had dropped into heavy sleep after
posting the pickets last evening. "The Colonel wants to see you. May as
well take your things. No more sleep tonight." John got up, still half asleep,
then leaned down groping for his sidearms and hat. "What time is it?"
"Two-fifteen." "Order to advance?" "Ask the Colonel." John's face and
equipment were wet, and he could hear the rain pattering on the oak leaves
back of him. Hooking his belt buckle with his blouse clumsily turned up
under it, he stumbled down to Headquarters and reported.

The Headquarters personnel was already astir. It was raining in a steady
drizzle, without any more thunder. The Colonel, who had laughingly forgiven John at mess last evening for having quit his post, was sitting on the
bench, studying a paper. His grin in the lantern light was replaced by a
cynical twist of his heavy mouth and a sad, pouchy droop of the skin under
his eyes. His hat was on the ground beside the bench and the rain had
plastered some of his hair down on his forehead. He looked more dishevelled than at the end of his charge the afternoon before. "Read this," he
said. John read:

> Headquarters 2d Brigade,
> 1st Division,
> 5th Corps,
> Army of the Potomac.
> July 2, 1862. 2 A.M.

1. The Brigade, as part of the Division, will proceed at once to Harrison's Landing in heavy march order.

2. Regiments will report to the Brigade Commander when ready to
march and will then receive their routes.

3. Regiments will maintain pickets until they march.

4. It is of the utmost importance that quiet be maintained. The men will not talk. Orders will be conveyed in whispers. Lanterns will not be lighted till troops are on the highway.

> By order of
> Charles Griffin
> Brevet Brig. Gen.
> Cmdg 2d Brigade.

As John handed back the order the Colonel spoke to him with a confidential snarl out of the corner of his mouth. "It's retreat, Lathrop. No need to go all the way to the base to guard communications. This is my job, Lathrop. You have nothing to do but march at the rear and keep the column closed up. You can ride Donahoe's horse if you're o' mind to. I've sent for it, along with mine." Donahoe had walked back to the Field Hospital last evening after the fighting was over. "Yes, sir," said John. "Tell the companies to form at once with full packs, and if I hear a sound or see a light somebody will go to the brig." The Colonel went on with the details of his verbal march order.

Half an hour later, the 50th crept off that field where it had fought so well. Being stationed at the rear of the column, near where C Company had fought, John had the satisfaction before starting of seeing that Zeb's body had been removed, which meant that he had been buried and his grave marked with a stick. Before mounting Donahoe's horse John stood a moment at the spot where Zeb and Jabe had fallen, and where he had himself plunged into the melee. The pickets had already joined the column that was shuffling away in the darkness that shut off visibility at ten feet. John was alone in the rain. He took off his hat and said softly, "Good-by, Zeb, old fellow." Then in sudden anger, "O God, if you are a just God, see to it that these boys did not die in vain." Then with a great effort—for the retreat order had drained his reserve energy and left only exhaustion—he drew himself up into the saddle and followed the column.

In his heart John now believed that Zeb and the rest had indeed died in vain, that the war was lost, the Union was lost, the perfect nation he had striven for was lost. Everything was in vain. They were marching round in foolish, murderous parades. Ike and his money-grubbing represented all the meaning there was in life. The unlighted lantern strapped to his pommel made the little sorrel restless, and John yanked the curb angrily, then apologized— "Forgive me, little fellow"—and he patted his wet neck.

The column jammed up when they were passing the place where John's support companies had been, and Captain Loftus, the Officer of the Day, who was marching the pickets at the rear, spoke to John in a hoarse whisper: "Where are we going, Lathrop? The men are grumbling worse than usual. They think we are sneaking out again." "I don't know where we're going," lied John. "We must keep them quiet."

The rain was now settling into a downpour. The column moved again, turning south so as to avoid the oak trees beside the Mellert house, then east in the road by which they had marched into position two afternoons before. At this point the road was in a cut, and as John's horse stepped gingerly down the shallow, invisible bank he began to hear a strange, hoarse murmur mingling with the rustling of the rain. The column jammed again, and the murmur spread back through the dark mass like the mingled, low rumbling of a herd of restless bulls. It had nothing to do with the usual talking, singing, cheering or jeering of the soldiers. It was not so loud, lower in tone, more ominous. It was a mob murmur.

As the sound reached the troops at the tail of the column John could make out some of the myriad, mumbled words that composed it— "We're headin' east— We're sneakin' out agin— We're licked agin— What's the way to Washington— By God! I'm done!— By God! I've had enough!— Me, too— Me, too— Me, too—" And as the murmur ran up and down the column John heard a series of whacks and clatters in the darkness as of metal striking the road.

He saw lights ahead and got one of the men in the pickets to light his lantern just as the column moved again. As his horse danced forward to catch the column it trod on something and sidestepped, then did it again with a snort. In the lantern-light John saw muskets in the road that had been thrown away, in one place a pile that looked as if a whole platoon had dropped them together.

Above the grumbling there was loud jeering ahead, and presently John reached a crossroad where another column was halted, with a lantern at its head, to let the 50th pass. On the other side was the rear of a third column halted, and the three regiments were having it back and forth— "Hey, Reb"— "Howdy, Reb"— "We kin beat ye runnin' any day— Great soldiers you be— Licked 'em, did ye?" And there was a loud laugh from all three columns. "Silence," John shouted and the men trudging over the crossroad into the byway looked round at him at first startled, then with leers that were not only insubordinate but menacing.

From now on they were on a strange, little travelled road, and the march became unreal, eerie. The steady, soft hammering of the downpour on the men, the road, the fields and the occasional trees and clumps of bushes, the

low, mob-murmur of the troops, the *squash, squash, squash* of wet shoes
and the scrape of wet clothing, all mingled in a steady rumble like the
rapids of a river. The little yellow light from John's lantern threw the
shadow of his horse's head huge on the right of the road and on the other
side yellowed the fringes of the ghostly mass of troops, bent forward, every
man soaked to the skin, dripping from noses and visors, the muskets carried at all angles, a few of them missing. And all round in the near distance
were similar dots of yellow lanterns and the same rumble of surly, soaking, marching men—for this was a country of many little farm tracks and
a dozen brigades were using them.

All round there were voices in the dark, some loud and authoritative,
most of them low and furtive. Continually John saw faces peering at him
from bushes and knew they were stragglers, deserters from this army that
had set out to save the Union. He challenged the first half dozen of them
and they ran off over the fields where he had no chance to follow them
without failing in his difficult duty of keeping his own column closed up.
Many brigades had passed this way before and the track was littered with
discarded equipment—muskets, bayonets, knapsacks, belts, cartridge boxes,
blankets, caps, canteens, blouses—that tripped the men as they walked and
kept John in danger of being unseated by his skittish mount. Bitterly it
occurred to him that this was his first experience as a mounted field officer.
With a remnant of pride he assured himself that most of this equipment,
most of these stragglers, were from other organizations that had preceded
the 50th.

Suddenly in the last formed company there was a commotion, and in
the darkness John saw something like heavier darkness dash off the road
to the left. He took after it, his horse clattering over a dozen muskets that
this mutinous platoon had discarded. Ahead of him in a field they were
shouting to each other— "Hurray!"— "Com'on, fellers!"— "This way to
Washington!" He got ahead of the bulk of them and yelled, "You damned
fools, you'll be captured by the Rebs or shot for desertion. Get back there
in ranks." He had drawn his saber but had no intention of using either it
or his revolver. His lantern flared and went out. There was a sudden series
of thumps and curses and John's horse stopped dead, almost throwing him
over its head. When he got back in his seat he groped out with his saber
and touched something solid, a rail fence.

"Get together, the bunch of you," he shouted, "and double back to the
regiment." "Who be you?" someone jeered. "Cap'n Lathrop, and you're
going back with me where you belong. You can march at the rear where
I can keep an eye on you." "Where are we goin'?" someone asked can-

didly. "I don't know any more than you do," said John persuasively. "All
I know is we're bound for a rest while other brigades keep after the
Johnnies. We've done well and we're not going to end in disgrace if I know
it. If you don't get back there at once you'll either be shot for desertion or
tortured by the Rebs. Come on, no more nonsense." "All right—all keerect,
Cap'n," said a few surly voices, and John could just make out a huddle of
men by the fence.

Riding behind them and making them double-time, he managed to get
them back to the road in the dark, and drove them stumbling up to the
rear of the column, though he knew that the seven or eight he finally got
there were not all of the crowd that originally had broken. Stopping in the
road, he managed to light his lantern. For a moment he let his horse stand.
He became aware of himself, John Lathrop, alone there in the midst of the
scattered fragments of an army.

He felt the spirit of defeat pouring down on them with the rain all over
that unseen countryside. It enveloped him like the chill of his own soaking
clothing. Where now were Zeb and Bub and Fred and Jabe and Medad,
and scores of others he knew almost as well? Where now were the high
hopes, the high dreams they had had for years, and which they carried
down here into this gray land? He sympathized with the boys. He had an
impulse to be free, to light out anywhere across those dark fields. Then he
kicked his horse into a canter and splashed up to the rear of the column.

Now a new rumor murmured back through the troops from the regiment ahead, and it particularly unnerved the 50th, marching as it was at
the rear of the Brigade. The new rumor whispered that the Rebs were
chasing them. They had got around the flank somehow and were heading
them off. Any minute now they would walk into an ambush. Any minute
now the muskets would crack and they would be surrounded. Angry discouragement and disillusion changed to fear. The men crowded together
in the road like cattle pelted by the storm.

The march slowed up all the way back from the head of the brigade
column. A cry came back from the front: "The Rebs are coming," and
the men at the rear pressed forward, jostling, treading on each other's heels.
The occasional lights, the frequent shouts, the shuffling of thousands of
soaked shoes in other columns became Rebs, evil, relentless spirits, ghostly
personifications of the army's own fear swooping down to annihilate it in
the darkness. Then like certain death came the real clatter of a mounted
detachment galloping up behind them.

John heard it first and was himself so infected by the spirit of panic that
he turned and stopped in the road with drawn saber and revolver while his

horse snorted and danced. Then from behind him in the column came a medley of yells and a clatter of feet, and as he turned he could dimly see the whole rear of the column scattering out on both sides of the road.

The cavalry detachment galloped up, and the lieutenant who was leading, seeing John's belligerent attitude in the light of his lantern, saluted with a laugh, swerved his troop off the road beside the infantry column and cantered by, while every company sidled off the road and a few panicky soldiers raised their unloaded muskets. The Colonel had no choice but to halt the disorganized regiment while the frantic officers of the rear companies ran shouting out into the fields regathering their men.

When the column was re-formed the Colonel rode up and down it, delivering a flood of profane billingsgate that did much to restore a sense of reality. The mob murmur was hardly audible any more, and there was no more breaking ranks. At least once some soldier made a joke that drew a general laugh in the darkness above the pelting rain and the *squash-squash-squash* of the marching feet.

But the phantom of panic still hung over the 50th, over that whole retreating army. Everywhere in the by-roads it was marching in huddled formation, the soldiers leaning forward, stumbling, fleeing from what behind them none could have said, hurrying as though the raindrops were Rebel bullets to which they were incapable of replying. When, after another half hour, the Brigade came out on a main highway, the River Road, it was evident that they were part of a routed army, routed after victory by its own broken spirit without menace from the enemy.

The highway was in places completely carpeted by equipment. Every few rods there were full wagons in or beside the road, some broken, some simply abandoned by the drivers and guards in order to join in the rout of the foot soldiers. Once the 50th passed a field piece all hitched up beside the road, without an artilleryman in sight. A lead horse was down and they had not waited to cut him out of the traces, but had rushed to mingle with the hurrying infantry.

Something was dying in that seven miles between Malvern Hill and Harrison's Landing, a powerful physical and moral force in the world, something that less than ten hours before had been alive and had won one of the greatest battles of history. What was dying was the spirit of the volunteer army, killed by futility at the top to which it had contributed nothing. The spirit of the old Army of the Potomac that had marched out to save the Union and to make men free was killed by this retreat and laid away in the tomb of memory. In mockery of the song it sang less frequently from now on, its soul lay moldering in the grave while its body went marching on. Once only, a year hence, that soul would be re-embodied and for four days would march again, before soul and body alike would disappear for good, the soul into history, the body dismembered and scattered among a hundred thousand graves and invalided old men.

The retreat in panic from Malvern Hill was the death agony of the volunteer army and the birth agony of a new army that succeeded it, a trained, professional army in which the single soldier was interested only in doing his own job, with little concern for the cause, or the victory or defeat of the army as a whole. In place of the volunteer's high, crusading spirit and expectation of early victory for the Right, the idealism became a quiet, dogged thing, like the spirit of these men's ancestors who had conquered the wilderness slowly with their hands. The war henceforth became their way of life, its routine and hardships, its childish pleasures, the pattern of existence as they found it and as it had to be lived.

Out on the main River Road to Harrison's Landing this change was going on rapidly as the feeling of panic gave way to a sense of approaching the destination. The rain lessened and the visibility improved so that the men could see each other five or six ranks away. The mutinous murmuring stopped and the straggling became only that of physical exhaustion no longer stiffened by tense nerves. The men trudged doggedly, most of them falling into step in the mechanical, energy-saving way of veteran troops. The remarks of the irrepressible spirits in every regiment sounded normal again, like the banter of any march, though the substance of them expressed a new stoicism such as would have been impossible a week ago.

The comment in the 50th New York was typical of that heard all along the road— "Wal, fellers, back home must be nigh time t' turn out 'n twiddle the old cow's tits"— "Keep yer ginger up, Hank, ye're still livin', ain't ye"— "Hitch up yer pants, Ezry, no use t' die on yer feet cause the Reb licked us—oughta be glad t' give him a leetle enjoyment"— "Shet yer mouth, I ain't stewin' over nuthin'"— "Arter all, sez I, walkin' round ain't so bad"— "Strikes me it's only a new manner o' livin'"—etc., etc.

And after a few minutes of these observations, sallying at intervals above the rhythm of shuffling feet, the interest of the regiment turned to the practical consequences, the only thing that remained of the night of disgrace. The bulk of the men who had not thrown away any of their gear began to bait the few who had, while the latter were busy convincing themselves of the truth of the lies they were going to tell their officers— "Say, Job, ye old hero, where's yer blunderbuss ye was so proud of?" "Shet yer mouth—it slipped out o' my hands up yonder a-clubbin' them half dozen Rebs come onto me sudden."— "Swopped in yer knapsack, did ye, Zeke?— What d'ye git fer it?"— "Shet up or I'll swat ye—laid it down up yonder while we wuz haltin' and couldn't find it arter"— "Give yer bagnet to a girl in bed last night, did ye, Henry?"— "Feller snatched it off me in the dark up yonder 'n couldn't tell fer life which way it went to."

Having joked itself back to its senses, the 50th fell silent, as did gradually the Brigade, the Division and the rest of the Army that was still on the march. For miles ahead and miles behind there was only the occasional word of an officer above the stolid tramp-tramp-tramp of that horde, winding down to Harrison's Landing with its back to the enemy. There was no dawn ahead in the east, but the graying light under a heavy sky was a new day. On the right, between little headlands and groves of luxurious trees there were glimpses of the broad James River. On the left were low hills covered with green, green suggesting home to the few tired men who raised their eyes to notice it, green in contrast to the gray uplands where they had fought and where two-fifths of their fellows had been wasted to no end.

It was a reborn army that dragged itself down to rest at Harrison's Landing. But John Lathrop in that army was not reborn to stoicism or defeat, then or ever. There was in him no seed of worldliness, no possibility of adaptation to the unidealized actualities of this or any other phase of existence. Life was fanaticism for him from beginning to end, his single impulse to go on fighting to make the world better. The immediate emergencies of the panic being over, he smiled sourly at the share he had had in it, in feelings if not in action. Then he lapsed into the pessimism of the previous night, the despairing search for a reason for this retreat—for he took no stock in the chance stab he had made in telling the stragglers they alone were bound for a rest. He fought against irrepressible suspicion of the higher command— Was it General Porter?— Was it McClellan?— Was it the President?— The Secretary of War?— Should he write Solon Samson in Congress about it? From exhaustion his eyes closed and he sank into a grateful stupor.

Donahoe's horse sidestepped and John opened his eyes, startled. It was gray twilight and the rain had stopped. Under the impulsion of duty he did the only thing that occurred to him that might prove useful. He cantered forward to look over the regimental column, and his futile fury rose as he drew nearer to the cased colors behind the Colonel at the head, those colors that had led so many of his friends to death and were now retreating without defeat. He slowed down to a walk behind C Company, and from detailed familiarity with it he verified with satisfaction that no one had straggled and at least not a musket was missing.

He rode up alongside it and when the men called cheerfully, "Hi, thar, Cap'n Lathrop," he felt a lump in his throat. As he looked more closely, he saw what the downpour of the night had done to that new issue of clothing that arrived just before Mechanicsville. The dozen pants and the half dozen blouses that remained were no longer garments but netting. In the rain the unwoven fabric had dissolved away and nothing remained but the skeleton, the coarse net, like poor Jabe's pants—"shoddy." The work of some of those god-damned war contractors! John's anger and humiliation at the retreat now had something specific to chew on, something that was neither futile nor insubordinate. He could write Solon Samson about shoddy clothes, and he would. By God, somebody would suffer for the profits they had made out of the soldiers' suffering!

He exchanged salutes with George Fulton, blew out his lantern and returned to his post at the rear. He felt better for his rage at the manufacturers piling up money back in the North. In his anger he hardly saw the green hills on the left or the peaceful James River on the right. Presently he did notice on the low ground ahead along the river a city of tents. It meant a permanent camp, compulsory rest. All the aspiration, the tension, the fury of the last two months collapsed in him. There remained only fatigue.

Late in the afternoon of the next day, the 50th was settled in what was to be its camp for a month, and John got time to go and look for Jabe and Medad in the section of the canvas metropolis that was the Army Hospital. He found Medad first. The minie ball that hit him had only cut a big vein in his side and had not touched a vital organ. His recovery was certain.

John had more trouble finding Jabe, but finally ran him down among seven other non-commissioned officers in one of the big conical tents for slightly wounded. In spite of two days of all the roast beef he could eat, Jabe was still deathly pale above his reddish beard, for he had lost a third of the blood from the great reservoir of his body. The bullet that had cut the artery in his thigh had not touched the bone or a tendon. He had been told he would be back on light duty in two weeks unless the wound became feverish, which was unlikely at this late date. When John came in, Jabe was dressed and sitting up on his cot. Every minute or so he got up and walked around, "just to remind this pesky leg she's to learn to walk without limping."

Through some of the later wounded in the Field Hospital Jabe had learned about Zeb's death. Neither he nor John wanted to talk about it, but when John was about to go Jabe showed him a letter he had just written to Ike, a letter in a very different tone from his previous ones:

Army of the Potomac
July 2, '62

Dear Ike—

They tell me that in our last scrimmage little Zeb was done for. He and I were getting particularly close, being sergeants together, and generally sleeping in the same dog tent. I've seen a lot of fellows killed and hurt bad, but when it comes to losing your best friend it's time to stop and take stock of the whole shebang. We don't talk about such things much in the Army, so I'm writing my notions to you.

All in all, I've concluded that going into this war is the best thing Jabe Munson ever did, and I'd say the same if I knew I was going to be done for and that the Reb was going to whip us. I'm doing something it isn't likely I'd ever have done if I'd stayed at home. I'm living for something I believe in that's bigger than Jabe Munson, or his friends or his town, and I figure there isn't any way of true grit living for a thing except to go out and risk dying for it. Losing your best friend is the next thing to getting potted yourself, so I guess you won't question my sincerity when I set this down, knowing little Zeb is up there under the mud not so far away.

Yours,
Jabe.

They were both embarrassed as John handed back the letter, and they parted as usual without any salutation.

CHAPTER LXXXV

B A C K in Byzantium, with no contact with his friends except through Jabe's letters, Ike continued to watch what Theophilus Bostwick in the *Democratic Union* called the "dread vulture of war spreading its gigantic shadow over the country till its red wings eclipsed the free sky over every hamlet and home." Cut off from John yet perpetually fearful for him, alien both to the war-mongers and the profit-mongers, his personal loneliness made heavier by his larger sense of the failure of humanity, Ike nevertheless determined to hold to the pacific stand he had taken. Almost the only recent act of the government he had approved was the Homestead Act of May, 1862, under which any citizen or prospective citizen could obtain title to 160 acres of good Western land by occupying it as a farm for five years. While this had no personal interest for Ike, he saw in it the only answer to the growing problem of underpaid labor in cities and large villages. He wrote letters to that effect to both papers, and arranged for the exodus of half a dozen "Micks" from Grabbot's Kamargo Woollen Mill, although he was a director of it.

In the middle of June the second great national loan had appeared, and more greenbacks poured from the Government printing presses. By the first of July the premium on gold was more than a hundred per cent, and Ike was on the point of converting his hoard into greenbacks, when the failure of McClellan's Peninsula Campaign convinced him the war had an indefinite period to run and that legal tender would go still lower.

Small change was passing out of existence, and daily mercantile transactions were becoming difficult and ridiculous because of the currency of "shin-plasters," tickets issued by stage lines, taverns and merchants, and finally—the most satisfactory—postage stamps carried in little folders that appeared for the purpose. Along with some eight thousand other banks throughout the country, Ike had helped increase the chaos of currency by issuing his own private bank notes.

His only companionship was now that of Old Jerry and Jabe's letters. Then, on the tenth of July, came the brief, idealistic one written from hospital, and a day or two later the *Eagle* published John's curt report of the three big battles in which the 50th had been engaged. Zeb Milliken and half a dozen others were dead, Jabe, Medad, and more than a dozen others wounded. And in spite of all this, Ike saw that Jabe was still filled with that moral fervor which he knew was taking the Gang steadily farther from him. He found little consolation in the letters thereafter, and in fact Jabe henceforth wrote him less frequently.

Ike had brief hope of waning enthusiasm for the war when the July call for 300,000 new volunteers met at first an apathetic response, and on August 4, the Secretary of War announced that there would be a draft on the states to fill the deficiency. But whether due to the threat of the draft or to the end of the harvest, there was a sudden spurt in recruiting, and Blackwater County filled its quota handsomely.

After Malvern Hill, the only news from the 50th during July and August was of the promotions of Major Donahoe to Lieutenant-Colonel, John to Major, Medad VanSanford to Captain, George Fulton to First Lieutenant, and Henry Daw to Second Lieutenant. On September second came John's cryptic report to the *Eagle*, of Second Bull Run: "Battle three days ago. Defeat. 50th on Provost Guard and not in action. Afterwards formed part of large rear guard, but enemy did not attack." From Jabe's humorous letter Ike gathered the facts: the rout of the Army, the horrible condition of the wounded, the macabre fiasco of drunken male nurses setting out from Washington to find them and getting lost in the rain, the disorganization of the Army, the state of panic in the national capital.

Then came the news of Antietam, which brought out extras of both papers on September eighteenth, and kept the village crashing with bands and crackling with bonfires for two days. And five days later John's report to the *Eagle,* always awaited with terrible suspense, brought the good news, "50th in reserve. No casualties." A week later came the Emancipation Proclamation, more bands and parades, and the incorrigibly wishful belief throughout the village that the war was now practically over.

The balloon of optimism continued to swell through October, November, and December, and was deflated but little by the guarded reports of the bloody repulse at Fredericksburg; for in that battle the 50th was but lightly engaged, Company C suffering no casualties, and the whole 50th losing only three wounded and ten missing, a patrol having been captured. Byzantium continued in momentary expectation of Lee's surrender; but Ike saw no real sign that the South was licked.

There was more than military hope and the Emancipation Proclamation beneath the buoyancy of that autumn, for business was prospering as never before. To be sure, the financial condition of the government was none too rosy, the cost of the war being $2,500,000 a day, and the national debt being close to $500,000,000. But prices were sky high, and Ike's industrial and railroad stocks had increased in dollar value more than fifty per cent. He was making more money than he ever dreamed of from everything except the engine company where, between high wages and a few bad estimates of costs, the profits had proven illusory. However, the new addition under government subsidy was more than half built, and Ike and Nat Gadston figured they would recoup in the spring.

Altogether, the optimism in the air during those closing days of '62 was difficult to escape, for it was made up of several elements and almost everybody in town was susceptible to at least one of them. Antietam had shown the honest patriots that the Rebels could be licked, and they were convinced that it would be a matter of only a few weeks now before that licking would be made final. Secondly, the Emancipation Proclamation gave the now rapidly increasing Abolitionists the proud assurance that their cause was an aim of the war, second only to the preservation of the Union. And finally, the industrialists were now finding the war a profitable thing after all and, whatever their pious professions, they were secretly not averse to seeing it drag on.

Everybody was satisfied with the moment and hopeful—if somewhat paradoxically hopeful—of the future. The *Democratic Union* began to hedge from its original opposition to the war, and in their New Year's editions both it and the *Eagle* prophesied certain victory in the coming year. Both newspapers ran glowing résumés of the services to date of the regiments containing companies from Blackwater County, featuring the 50th Infantry which had been wholly recruited there. The *Eagle,* however, retained its supremacy as the authoritative war organ of the county by running beneath the roll of honor a signed article sent from camp near Fredericksburg by Major John Lathrop, "whom we dare call the most distinguished soldier and citizen of Blackwater County, our beloved editor and friend."

Ike's bank being closed for New Year's, he took the *Eagle* into his office to read John's article in peace:

"At the end of this first full year of war it is fitting that we once more examine our aims in the conflict, once more decide whether the pursuit of them is worth the cost in suffering, and, if we decide that the aims are worth that cost, then to reconsecrate ourselves to their realization. I wish to speak as a soldier, for since it is the soldiers who are bearing the chief burden of the war it is the soldiers' opinion that should be determining on the questions whether and to what end that burden should continue to be borne.

"In the beginning we took up arms to preserve the Union of the States, not asserting anything sacred in a union merely as such, but believing that this particular Union under this particular Constitution gave promise of building on this continent the first perfect government on earth. . . ." Ike knew all this by heart. He began to skim through the other familiar arguments:

"In our farthest vision we believe our cause to be just, and we must, therefore, prosecute the war to final victory or defeat. . . ." Ike's mind slumped into its universal sadness.

"At the beginning most of us considered slavery an evil which must eventually be removed from the nation, yet we believed it contrary to the principles of our government to interfere with another man's property, and we would not have enlisted in a war whose aim was abolition. . . .

"I believe that on this point the experience of the war has changed our view. We appreciate more fully than before the determination of the South to preserve slavery at all costs, and we believe that if the question is not settled now once and for all it must again at some future time lead us into armed conflict between the sections. . . .

"We must remember that the Emancipation Proclamation is legal only as a military measure, and must be followed not only by a fitting constitutional amendment but by just compensation to all those slave-holders whose property has thus been taken away. . . .

"But deeper than the evils of disunion and slavery there is another which is becoming daily more apparent throughout the nation, an evil so insidious that I believe its extirpation should be made one of the aims, even the paramount aim of this conflict. . . ." From here on Ike read with increasing concentration, and the return of that sense of something being torn from his vitals which he had felt when the 50th pulled out a year and a half ago.

"In this country, as in every great country in human history, there are two broad categories of citizens. There are those, on the one hand, who attempt to govern their own lives and their communities and the nation upon moral principles. On the other hand there are those who govern their lives in the interest of their private advancement, for the most part financial or economic. . . .

"To our record as a freedom-loving people we may justly add the boast that we undertook this greatest of wars upon moral issues only, without any greedy purpose or prospect of gain. For, let it always be remembered, it was the money-grubbing industrialists who opposed the war, fearing some disruption of their greedy practices, fearing some interruption of the flow of gold from the South into their miserly safe deposit boxes.

"But now that the war is protracted, these same timid money-grubbers have learned to practice their cupidity in new ways. They are cheating the Government and the country with adulterated products. . . . They are lining their pockets with the blood and the lives of the soldiers. We marched out against greed in the South, and a new army of greed arises in our rear. It is as yet a contemptible army, small in number and composed exclusively of cowards. To the best of my knowledge it has not yet invaded the Government, and I believe it will not do so. Nevertheless, it should be scotched before it has insinuated itself further through the veins of the nation. Its members should be exposed and pilloried where they lurk in their factories and banks. Every profit they have made should be taken from them more utterly than the slaves should be taken from the southern planters. Slavery is an ancient evil for which its present defenders are not responsible. Financial greed in the North was an insignificant evil until the recent rise of modern manufacturing; now for the first time it is being pursued widely and openly by yellow dogs who, if they were in the Army, would be shot for desertion or espionage.

"If I had my way I would say to the Rebel soldiers who have had the courage to meet us openly in the field: 'Let us now turn our backs on one another. You go home and destroy your money-grubbers and we will go home and destroy ours'— What a lark that would be after facing brave men!— 'Then let us return and confront each other, and I think we shall find that we have nothing more to kill one another about. You were first deceived and misled by your money-grubbers, and now we are beginning to be deceived and misled by ours. While they are behind us, our disagreement cannot be made clear. When they are no longer behind us it may not exist——"

Ike could not finish John's diatribe. He took it to be aimed directly at himself. It was his brother's way of writing him a letter for the first time in almost eight months. His own conscience was clear. No mill that he controlled was making adulterated products. The engine company's guns were the best the Army was receiving. But all that was beside the point. It was plain the 'Paloosa was done with him.

Ike looked long out his back window at the hard, frozen ground. Every impulse was drained out of him. He did not want to see Old Jerry now. He did not want to get drunk. He did the only thing he could do. He labored into his greatcoat, walked slowly out to the hill on the Round Harbor Road, and sought escape in his god of Nature under the gray and lifeless sky.

CHAPTER LXXXVI

ON THIS same New Year's Day, '63, when John's article appeared, the Battle of Stones River was in progress near Nashville, where Tavie was on duty in the Base Hospital. During the previous summer she had managed to follow fairly close upon Grant's Army in its advance into southern Tennessee and had been in as quick touch with the wounded at Corinth and Iuka as she had been at Shiloh. But her presence had been tolerated rather through the ignorance than the approval of the authorities. Just before Grant moved his base from Corinth down to Holly Springs, Headquarters seemed for the first time to discover her and her two assistants who had been recently sent down from Ohio. She got a polite communication from the Chief of Staff informing her that "no women would be allowed to accompany the army on a move then contemplated"—she was apparently considered, not as a nurse, but as a "woman," like any camp follower. She and her two helpers went over to Memphis where General Sherman's army was based. But they fared no better there. In December Tavie heard of renewed operations in Kentucky and northern Tennessee, and in the middle of the month she led her little command to Nashville.

There she found that a large tavern had been commandeered as a base hospital and that it was equipped with such unheard of services as running water and gas. Knowing the conditions that would surround the wounded in the main Army of which she had come to consider herself a part, Tavie felt like a deserter at the prospect of such luxuries. Nevertheless, she understood that the Rebels were concentrating at Murfreesboro, thirty miles to the south, and that might mean action. She obtained an interview with General Rosecrans and found him sympathetic. He assigned her to the Base Hospital and authorized the Medical Colonel Commandant to give her the authority of a corporal "if he found it expedient."

He did not at first find it expedient, and Tavie and her two subordinates suffered the usual arrogance and salaciousness on the part of the enlisted men of the Hospital Corps. Two weeks passed. Then, on December thirty-first, began the bloody, four days' battle of Stones River whose wounded overflowed the hospital into neighboring houses and sheds. By New Years' morning, Tavie having worked all night, the Commandant had seen what she was good for. He gave her a corporal's authority and put her in charge of the largest ward, the old ballroom on the top floor.

Due to the glut of wounded, the five hundred-odd crowded into the old tavern were only the most serious cases, and as rapidly as they died their places were filled by others brought in from outside. Tavie was busier than ever before, because with two spigots of running water in the house it was possible actually to wash the hands, faces and most deeply encrusted limbs of as many of the men as you could find time for. Also there were bottles and canvas pads provided for the patients, and with so much sanitation as a basis it was possible to introduce a little elementary cleanliness into the room. Altogether, it was a palace after mud and ruined shacks. And not the least among its luxuries resulted from the Commandant's determination to experiment with ether, he having seen it used in Boston before the war. He asphyxiated plenty of wounded, but most of them would have died anyway, and the morale of the place was improved by the fact that there were fewer screams from the "chopping block" downstairs.

By the evening of the fourth of January the first maelstrom of deaths and operations was over. Most of the men who remained had a fighting chance of recovery. What Tavie always called the "after-battle" passed into its second phase when, as she had learned, the presence of a woman in the room often stimulated the men's vitality and assisted their cure. As usual, everybody was calling her "darling." Only now, three-quarters of a year after Shiloh, this attention no longer "broke her heart." It merely called forth a certain professional attitude, the habit of smiling in a frank and friendly way, combining this responsiveness with an indifference which would keep the men from getting over-excited. By the evening of January fourth the worst of the physical work of the "after-battle" of Stones River was over. Tavie had not slept for three days and two nights, and after supper, as she was going her rounds, she did something new in her experience. She fainted dead away.

The orderlies laid her on a couch under the sputtering gaslight in the big hallway outside her ward. When water on her forehead did not bring her to, they notified the Colonel who came up and looked her over. He put one of the girls from downstairs in charge of the ward, and gave orders that Tavie was to be allowed to sleep as long as she wanted to. For almost five hours she remained in a deep stupor.

Some time around midnight Tavie became slowly conscious of cursing in a Rebel accent, very loud and close to her and in a voice that seemed somehow familiar. "Set me down, you gawd-damned Yankee white trash or I'll kick you down stayahs! You hyah what I tell you? I know this lady and I'm bound to tell her somethin' o' fust value to her, if I have to whup every gawd-danged Yankee in this hawspital."

Coming slowly to consciousness, Tavie heard the tone of the voice suddenly change. "Honey," it said softly, "Mis' Oaks, I got to tell you somethin' private y'all want to know. Honey, Mis' Oaks, I'm mighty sorry to distuhb you, but it's special impawtant faw you, and I reckon maybe if you'll open yo eyes you'll recollect havin' seen me befo' and 'll let me speak to you private. Honey, Mis' Oaks, I'm mighty sorry but I'm askin' y'all to wake up."

Tavie opened her eyes slowly, then came quickly to consciousness and stood up in confusion, running one hand over her forehead, then shaking down her dress and looking round. She saw four privates of the hospital staff with a man on a stretcher whom they apparently had just brought upstairs and had now set down on the floor. By his uniform and insignia he was a Rebel captain of cavalry. One leg of his breeches had been slit off and his thigh was dressed. He had propped himself up on one arm and was looking at Tavie intently. "Y'all recollect me, Mis' Oaks?" he asked gently.

Tavie now had herself collected, and suddenly as she looked at the man in the gaslight something remote inside her stirred with hatred, hatred not of Rebels, for she was long over that as far as individuals went, but hatred of this particular man. Bearded and filthy as he was, she recognized the Federal marshal who had arrested her pa almost twelve years ago. "What is it, Evans?" she addressed one of the stretcher-bearers professionally. "Cavalry skirmish, ma'am, this arternoon somewhere north'ard. Musket ball. Colonel probed it. Orders to put 'im in the dance-hall, ma'am."

"Very well," said Tavie. "Bring him along. I believe we can place him without turning up the gas and disturbing the men." "But, Mis' Oaks, honey," persisted the ex-marshal, now paling rapidly and speaking with difficulty, "you ain't huhd what I'm bound to tell y'all private." Tavie was used to hearing something of the sort from most of the wounded. "You must be quiet now," she said with professional gentleness. "You are wounded and must rest. You will have plenty of time to tell me when you are stronger." The man fell back on the stretcher out of weakness.

Suddenly Tavie was struck with a strange suspicion. "Wait," she said to the stretcher-bearers. Then she dropped down beside the man and whispered into his ear, "How did you know my name was Oaks? It was Samson when—we met before." "That's it, honey," whispered the man. "Now you see it, I reckon. I've news faw you from somebody— somebody impawtant." "Keep him here till I return," said Tavie to the men and ran down the two flights of circular stairs to the Colonel's quarters. She was used to coming into his room at all hours, and now, though in bed, he wasn't asleep after probing this Rebel captain's thigh.

Tavie turned up the gas as usual and spoke with an almost personal eagerness which was unusual in her now. "I am very sorry to trouble you, sir, on a personal matter. A Rebel captain was just brought upstairs"— "Ball passed clean through, grazed the femoral artery," interrupted the Colonel methodically. "Carbolic syringe again in the morning. Should pull through." And he rolled over. "Sir," persisted Tavie, "this is a personal case for me. I must tell you that my husband deserted me two years and a half ago, and I have heard only indirect news of him since. This man says he has news of my husband and I would like to talk to him without disturbing the other men or seeming to show favoritism. As a personal matter I request that you put him for a short time in the field officers' room. It is empty since this morning. The man is too weak to talk now, but doubtless he will be stronger tomorrow. I assure you I shall not over-tax him."

"Very well," mumbled the Colonel, and pulled up his blanket in sign of dismissal. Upstairs, Tavie had the men put the captain in one of the five beds in the small field officers' room, the only beds for patients in the hospital. He had fallen into a deep sleep and there was fresh blood soaking the bandage on his thigh.

For an hour Tavie watched him in the low gaslight with more tenderness than she had bestowed on any individual wounded man since the early days. He was obviously sincere, and was identified with the only person, outside of little Solon, who could draw her interest to the outside world. Along with the generalized tenderness and the heightened sense of duty that had come with her work, Tavie had concluded that her conduct in letting Connie go had been selfish. She had determined to find him and take him back after the war. And here before her lay someone who was identified with him. Although this Rebel was blond where Connie was dark, yet something in his features, or perhaps his impulsive manner, reminded her of Connie. As she watched him sleeping she had a confused feeling that she was back in Oberlin watching Connie when he was down with a cold.

When an hour had passed and it was evident that his wound had stopped bleeding, Tavie fetched a basin of water and sponged off the sleeping man's hands and what of his face wasn't bearded. Then she went in for a brief tour through the usual hog-pen bedlam of snores and groans in the ward. There were only two death-rattles, and her assistant had already notified the stretcher-bearers. Tavie returned to the field officers' room and went to sleep on a bed near the representative of her husband.

The next day Captain Swain was stronger, and Tavie contrived to find time to sponge him above the waist and clean the mud from his hair and beard. In the course of these operations she learned what he knew of Connie's story.

Captain—then Federal marshal—Swain had been off duty one afternoon in St. Louis in the spring of '60 and had fallen into talk with Connie, then a stranger, at a bar, "where, I reckon, honey, we had a few too many." Captain Swain continued: "Con had just come in from Chicago and he was down in the dumps, sho' enough. Befo' long he'd told me about y'all and the boy and how he reckoned to set you free from him. When I asked him wheyah he was from and he said Oberlin, but befo' that Byzantium, N. Y., I asked about you, honey, and that's how I come by the straight of it. Natchully I got mighty excited, bein's I ain't evuh stopped bein' in love with you, honey, since that night I 'rested yo' pa and you eyed me so sassy."

"Captain Swain," interrupted Tavie, "if you don't mind, don't you think we'd get along better if you didn't make love to me? You see all the soldiers do that, so it doesn't greatly bother me. But it's bad for you, and I shall have to leave you if you keep it up. Forgive me. I am truly grateful to you, and I do want to talk to you because—well—your turning up here really means a lot to me."

"Have it yo' way, honey," said Captain Swain. "Reckon yo' right. Mebbe a felluh makes himself so't o' ridiculous makin' polite speeches when he's tied togethuh with a piece o' cloth. Have it yo' way, honey, but I'm sho' glad yo' glad t' see me." Tavie gave him a quick, human smile and propped him up while he put his foul shirt back on. Then she covered him with a blanket, set to work on his beard and he resumed his tale. She saw that her touching him stirred him up more than was good for him, so she worked very slowly and mostly just listened, avoiding his very blue eyes which were undoubtedly honest in their admiration of her.

"Well, honey, after a little anothuh bunch o' felluhs wuh standin' theyah beside us at the bah, and I'm mighty sorry t' say they wuh all South'nuhs. They wuh talkin' politics an' Abe Lincoln an' Yankees—that was jest befo' the Chicago convention you'll recollect. 'Twas all usual enough till all of a sudden one of 'em began talkin' of Yankee women and not too respectful. I saw Con gittin' nervous, and just then one of 'em says—fo'give me, honey, but I must tell you the straight of it—he says, 'All Yankee women ah whoahs an' lookin' fo' nuthin' but money.'

"Well, honey, I always reckoned I was quick on the trigguh, but Con, he's quickuh, and that's why I liked him from then on. 'That's a gawd-damn lie,' he yelled, and spun the felluh round and knocked him th' whole length o' the bah wheyah he toppled over a table and lay mighty still. With that anothuh of 'em come on and I fixed him, bein' just as mad as Con was and thinkin' o' y'all, honey, same as he was. But bein' a mahshal, I had the habit o' keepin' my head in a rumpus, so when I see Con grab a bottle was standin' on the bah and lift it to the next felluh was comin' at him I grabbed the bottle off him in the ayah and let the felluh have it with my fist.

"By that time—and it wan't mo'n ten seconds—I was gettin' mighty worried about what might come of it, tho' I luckily wan't in unifawm. So when I saw the bah-tenduh comin' I just pulled my gun an', grabbin' Con with the othuh hand, I says, 'Make tracks outta hyah.' So we backed out and I put up my gun and we hoofed it down the street——"

Tavie interrupted him, "Can you remember what date that was, Captain?" "Yes, ma'am, that I can, faw my promotion came through the day aftuh. It was May 9, 1860, and it was a Wednesday." "Can you remember what time it was when Connie raised the bottle to strike the man?" "Not that precisely, I can't, no ma'am, but the whole row was close around one-thuhty in the aftuhnoon." He paused, noticing Tavie's set expression. "I saw him raise that bottle," she said, "in a vision, plain as day, in broad daylight, just at that hour. In my vision he stepped from behind a curtain in the house of a friend and raised the bottle over a man I was talking with. The bottle had a fancy label." "That's it, ma'am," said the Captain, "good old Monongahela whisky. Well, I declayah! See things like that sometimes, do you, honey?" "Nothing before I ever corroborated as closely as that," said Tavie.

She made her patient try to sleep for a while, and later in the day got the rest of the story. He and Connie had not been pursued, and Connie spent the night in the marshal's room which was on the other side of the city. The next day his promotion came through and with it orders to Chicago for the Republican convention. He thought Connie ought to get out of town too, and since he wouldn't go to Chicago he had persuaded him to go down to Louisiana to visit his folks for a while and to get a job in the near-by village if he wanted to. The upshot was that Captain Swain's family had liked Connie and he had liked them, and in spite of being a Yankee he had got a job in the grocery store in the village and didn't get in any more fights. From then on it was Captain Swain who had sent Lem and Lorinda Oaks occasional letters about Connie signed "A friend," though Connie had made him promise not to write Tavie. When Louisiana seceded in January, '61, Captain Swain had gone home, resigned from the Federal Constabulary, and enlisted in a local regiment that wasn't called until September.

"Aftuh Bull Run," he concluded his story, "Con got awful jumpy. He nevuh was much on politics, but he said he wouldn't fight against his own folks, no mo' would he fight against us who had befriended him. Theyah wan't any stoppin' him but after Bull Run he must light out faw the West wheyah nobody'd catch him and make a soldyuh of him. It was some time in the end of July he set out, with about two hundred dollahs in Federal money, and from that day yo' ma- and pa-in-law ain't had any letters from me, faw I hain't no mo' notion wheyah Con is than they have, mebbe not so much." "I don't think he's dead," said Tavie. "I hope he ain't," said the Captain, not looking at Tavie.

The second day, Captain Swain continued to gain strength, though the wound high in his thigh was pussy and inflamed when it was dressed and showed no sign of healing. In the afternoon his face became slightly flushed, and he begged Tavie "faw jest ten minutes mo' confab," which she contrived to give him. "Honey," he said, "you ask me not to make love to you. I wan't bo'n a gentleman, honey, but we ah good folks and not fah from gentle folks."

"Of course you're a gentleman," said Tavie indignantly. "That's one trouble with you Southerners. You don't take people for what they are but for what they were born." "Mebbe, honey," he said, "but that's no mattuh. Anyhow, what I'm goin' t' say to you is spoken like a gentleman that knows a lady when he sees one and ain't thinkin' no dishonah. Fuh-thuhmo', I ain't altogethuh like those othuh soldiuhs, faw I have known you a long time. It's the truth, honey, I've been crazy in love with you from the fuhst minute I saw y'all back yonduh in yo' pa's office. I just want to tell you that now, an' that I love Con faw a friend too, an' I hope y'all get back togethuh and make out fine. But if evuh we find out Con's dead, I want you to know I'm waitin' to suhve you and I want to marry you. Maybe you don't love Con and maybe you do, but if evuh you reckon on anybody else I want you to know I'm waitin'. That's all, honey. You've been mighty kind to me and I an't goin' to pestuh you any mo'. Run along now, and thank you."

During this speech Tavie felt tears coming to her eyes, and all of her generalized tenderness for the soldiers seemed to draw together and concentrate in this man. She wasn't in love with him, but she had no interest now in whether she was in love or not, or in marriage that was supposed to be related to love in that other life. What mattered was that here he lay, not only suggesting Connie to her in a mysterious way, but being a man of the same purity and devotion in his own right, a man just as truly and selflessly in love with her as Connie was, and one who, like Connie, had asked nothing of her. Impulsively she lifted his hand in both of hers and kissed it. Then she stood back, frightened at this breach of duty and at the effect it might have on the wounded man. His breathing grew heavy, and the vitality seemed to leave his eyes as he stared at her. "Thank you, honey," he murmured, "thank you, thank you." "You must sleep," Tavie whispered, backing off to the door. A look of agony came over his face, and he turned his head away from her.

During that night and all the following day Captain Swain's fever mounted and the wound looked uglier and more pussy. A severe infection had set in. On the fourth day he was delirious with fever and his pulse was dangerously high. The Colonel considered an amputation, but gave up the idea when he became convinced that the poison was already in the blood and that the man could not survive the operation. Tavie lost her head and confessed to the Colonel that she had tolerated his attentions. She said she knew she deserved to be dismissed, but she swore it was the first time she had been guilty of anything of the kind and begged to be kept on. The Colonel laughed and said if she killed half the men in the hospital he still could not get along without her. He seemed hard and hateful to Tavie, though his professional attitude was exactly what hers would have been a few days before.

All that night she sat by Captain Swain's bed, watching his face in the faint, yellow glow of the gas jet behind her. Occasionally she rose to sponge his burning forehead. The rest of the time she sat with her fingers on his wrist, feeling the pulse that pounded steadily faster, while remaining strong and countable. About four o'clock he began to mumble unintelligibly and grew restless. Tavie looked under the blanket and saw that the thing the Colonel feared had happened. The great femoral artery that had been grazed by the bullet had been finally punctured by the infection and the resulting hemorrhage, driven by the fevered pulse, was gushing like a spring. Tavie jammed in the lint she had ready and called the orderly. In five minutes they had him downstairs on the operating table, and in twenty minutes more the Colonel had completed the difficult hip amputation. There was no time for anesthetic, but Swain was deeply unconscious and his screams were only gurgles in his throat.

They carried what remained of him back upstairs, already shrunken and colorless as a corpse. He had lost half of his blood. Tavie still sat beside him in the gray of dawn, eerie against the low gaslight. There was still a pulse, but she felt it gradually weakening to a flutter. It began to skip. The pauses grew slowly longer. It had stopped.

Tavie continued to hold the wrist and to look at the dead face. Suddenly she realized it was not the body of the man who had been there before. The hair that had been blond was now coal black and the open eyes were black and Connie's. She felt a bump on the wrist she was holding and looked at it. Even in the dim light, there it was, the familiar scar. It was Connie dead there on the bed beside her. The filthy army shirt was gone. Instead he had on a nightshirt, and instead of the army blanket he had a sheet and a quilt over him. She lifted the cover and the nightshirt. There was the hip amputation, but instead of being neatly bandaged it was bound in old rags. Tavie replaced the covers, dropped her head on the bed and dug her fingernails into her palms. She remained so for some minutes, then straightened up in her chair. It was the body of the Rebel captain on the bed again.

Tavie got up and walked to the window in the gray dawn light, and her old life came back strongly. She was sure Connie was dead. She was herself once more and belonged to no man. She was Octavia Oaks, instructor at Oberlin College, Abolitionist, leader in the Woman's Rights Movement, lecturer on Reform. But even as she felt her independence again, Ike came into her mind. They said his hair was white now. She believed she was now completely free to marry him, yet she was equally sure she never would. He had written her with obvious relief that they would think no more about it until after the war.

Tavie thought of John. He was like her big brother whom she would trust to the last ditch. He had written her every month since they went out, begging her to get transferred to Washington. He kept saying that his luck could not hold always, and he wanted her to nurse him if he got hit badly enough to be evacuated. He described the hospital sheds they were building in Washington. They were not handsome apparently, but were splendidly appointed, with a bed for each patient. Tavie had about decided that as soon as things quieted she would write Mrs. Dix to ask if she ould be of service in Washington. But she would write nothing of this o John till it was certain. John had written her more than was needful for friendship. Tavie wondered if he was waking up. If she had a chance to spoil that little Stark hussy's game, she would not scruple to do it.

Tavie walked back to the dead man and closed the great, staring eyes, picked up the limp hand between both of hers and said softly, "Good-by, Connie." She felt the tears coming, turned away quickly and put out the gas. By the time she got downstairs the lump in her throat was gone, and she reported the death to the Colonel in her usual professional manner. He rose from his breakfast, put his arm around her, pressed her to him sideways and gave her a fatherly pat on the shoulder. She gave him the guarded, friendly smile she gave the patients. He invited her to sit down to breakfast, but she asked to be excused. An hour later the body upstairs was underground, Tavie having walked out to stand beside the overworked Chaplain.

CHAPTER LXXXVII

J O H N ' S New Year's article in the *Byzantium Eagle* was widely copied, and a week later it got him an invitation to the White House, summoning him all the way up from camp near Fredericksburg. When the guard stood aside, admitting him to the President's office, the tall, awkward heart of the Union cause rose from his writing table to meet him, and for a moment looked straight at him while John stood at salute. John had never seen a face so deeply furrowed, and the dark eyes that were focussed on him seemed rather to be looking wearily at something a long way off behind him.

This was the impression of an instant. Then, "Come in, Major Lathrop," he said cheerfully, waving in return to John's salute, and at the same time swinging round his writing table and coming toward him to shake his hand with a slow, pump-handle motion. "It was good of you to drop in, for I wanted to have a look at the feller who said a lot of things I wish I'd said first." As he greeted John thus, his face was completely encircled by a horseshoe-shaped furrow with his beard in the open end. This was his official smile. Suddenly it vanished as their eyes met level with that sense of delighted recognition which all abnormally tall men feel in meeting one of their kind.

"Nicolay!" the President bellowed suddenly, making John jump. "Nicolay!" Then, "Here—what's your name?— Lathrop, take off your hat and stand back to back with me." John complied nervously and Secretary Nicolay came in and winked at him. "I told ye, Nicolay," said Lincoln, pressing his head back against John's, "the feller that wrote that article would measure longer than I do and ought by rights to be in my place. Now I'll bet you a dime on it." Very gravely Secretary Nicolay fetched a chair and stood on it studiously looking over the heads of the two giants. "You lose your dime, Mr. President," he said finally, stepping down and replacing the chair. Lincoln sighed, fished in his pocket for the dime, tossed it to Nicolay, sat down again at his table and waved John into the chair opposite him.

"I can give you a choice," said he, putting his big hand on a box on his desk, "between some fine seegars I keep here for the foreign diplomats and some others I carry in my pocket that they say aren't so good, though my friends use 'em by preference." "I believe, Mr. President," said John, "your friends' preference would be mine." Lincoln passed him a cigar from his vest pocket, scratched a match before John could and reached enormously across the writing table to give him a light. Then his face settled with an abrupt change into that sad, far-away look that made John wonder if he had forgotten his presence.

"As I see it," he said at last, now speaking with a slow and deliberate drawl, putting on his spectacles and leaning forward to look at one of three papers on his table, "as I see it, we've just four alternatives. One is, as you seem to suggest, we might shoot every last one of these army contractors and good riddance—though it has always seemed to me that you can't enforce virtue against individuals with a gun. Another thing we've thought of was to put up this income tax progressively so as to leave them no more than what we figure out to be a healthy, living profit. Or again, we might confiscate all of their profits above a certain amount.

"The trouble with all of these propositions is the same. If we shot 'em or took away their profits they'd stop running their factories, and you fellers would get even less to eat and to wear and to shoot than you do now. The fourth method proposed is that the Government buy every factory making anything useful in the war and run them as we do the Post Office. That would be a big job, Major, and a lot of my friends in Congress wouldn't stand for it for a number of their own reasons. Nevertheless we're considering it, and I think before long we shall at least get as far as making all of our small arms in Government arsenals.

"I was wondering, Major, whether you had any private notion of your own that you didn't see fit to set down in that fine article, any practical notion how to stop these contractors trimming us and debauching the country, and at the same time keep the war going."

John lowered his eyes and said, "I am sorry, Mr. President, but you have mentioned the only specific courses that had occurred to me." Then he rose, feeling his audience was at an end, and stood in military fashion. "Set down," said the President, with a little wave of his hand, leaning back and tilting his spectacles up on his forehead while his face became animated again, as when he had discovered that John was tall.

"Y' know, Major, we fellers in Washington are powerful good at snoopin', and when I asked Nicolay to write you that note I asked him at the same time to do a little snoopin' about you. I hope you'll forgive the impertinence. The best source of information turned out to be our mutual friend Congressman Samson from your home district, along with a few figgers from various departments of the Government. I just wanted to express the hope, if you'll forgive me, that you won't be too hard on that brother of yours. Master Samson and I both thought you might have had him partly in mind when you wrote that article."

John's face stiffened at the mention of Ike and he flushed faintly. "It is possible, sir," he said in a soft tone, but stiffly, "though I trust it did not appear that I had raised a private matter into a national issue." "Not at all, Major, not at all," said the President. "I just wanted to tell you what I have found out and what you may or may not know, that this"—he lowered his spectacles again and looked at the paper on his desk—"this Byzantium Steam Engine Company is making us the best quality of field guns we're getting for the Army, even from our own arsenal. Their guns are the only ones not one of which has burst, although about fifty of them have seen hard action. Furthermore, we're paying no more for 'em than for guns that have given us trouble and the Ordnance Officer stationed there writes us that, between paying good wages and turning out first-rate guns, your brother and his company are making little if anything out of the enterprise, if in fact they ain't running a little behind. I just wanted to be sure you knew that and that the Ordnance Department thinks mighty highly of your brother's company. So it may be some of the things you said in your article, while more true than you likely know about many a contractor, don't precisely fit your brother."

"I am very grateful to hear it, sir," said John eagerly, while his eyes that had darkened at first returned to their normal blue. "I'm afraid you and Solon Samson may have accused me justly of having had my brother in mind, along with several others. Now I shall take the first opportunity to write him that I was mistaken, and I shall take pride in telling the source from which I learned of my mistake."

"You know," continued the President, "one of the sad things in life is that a powerful good feller may sometimes find himself caught in a powerful rotten system. That, as I see it, is the situation of a lot of our rebellious friends down yonder." "I am glad you feel that way, Mr. President," said John, "for I have felt so more and more as the war progressed. I daresay the same may be true of many who find themselves caught in this rotten, modern financial and industrial economy of the North." "I profoundly hope so," said Mr. Lincoln with no great conviction. "Anyway, the evidence is that it is true of your brother, and we must always remember that, North or South, it is the system we are fighting and not the individuals." "That is true, sir," said John, his voice soft with emotion.

The President now turned his attention to the second paper before him. "There was one other little matter I had in mind that might interest you, Major," he said, and his tone for the first time became severe. "Some of my generals—and they always know everything—tell me that in saying the soldiers' opinion ought to decide whether we continue the war or not you were guilty of a flagrant and dangerous breach of Army Regulations, bordering on sedition. For this, as I understand it, they're figgerin' to have you shot.

"Now, as you may have gathered, I like your article and if I had my way I'd sooner give you some kind of a reward than this supposedly unpleasant penalty for having written it. It occurred to me that the best way was somehow to have you disappear on paper, for those fellers can't do a thing unless it's on paper in half a dozen different colors of ink. What we've to do is somehow to get Major John Lathrop off the documents for good and all. We've got to sort o' kill him in our way before they have a chance to kill him in theirs. Now in this connection I told Nicolay to get your record from the War Department across the street, and here it is. Did you know you've been cited for bravery three times?" "No, sir," said John, his heart jumping, "I only knew of once." "Well, here it is, three times, plain as paper can make it, and if you'd skedaddled from the Rebs every time you saw 'em that wouldn't change the fact once it's on paper. That means that one of these peerade days I'll have to pin a medal on you, that is, if the General Court Martial don't get you first. Incidentally, Major, while I do the pinnin' of medals I have nothing to do with the awardin' of them. That's for the clerks who understand these records."

The President looked down at John's record again. "Furthermore, Major, did you know also that you've been recommended for a Lieutenant-Colonelcy?" "No, sir," said John in astonishment. "Well, you have—although they're so busy across the street that I understand they're postponing promotions for a spell. Well, now it happens that, although I haven't much say about medals, I have authority to issue commissions on my own hook, and I sort o' reckoned it wouldn't confuse the War Department much if I just issued this one a little ahead of when it was coming anyway. So I had Nicolay—who's more President than I am—make out a Lieutenant-Colonel's commission for you. Here it is, and if you like I'll sign it now and you can take it away with you."

"Thank you, sir," said John in an emotionally hoarse tone. "That will mean more to me than a dozen medals." "It struck me that would sort of get Major John Lathrop out of the way, so they couldn't shoot him,"

said Mr. Lincoln, looking at him over his spectacles. "Suit you, will it?"
"Indeed it will, sir," said John. Very deliberately the President read the
commission, just as if he hadn't signed thousands of them. He dipped a
pen and for about a minute wrote a careful interlineation. Then he signed
it and pushed it across to John, who, without looking at it, thrust his
hand impulsively and improperly across the desk to grasp the big bony
hand of his Commander-in-Chief. He was unable to speak.

Secretary Nicolay came in and said, "Mr. President, General Halleck
has been waiting for ten minutes and he seems to be impatient." "Come
in, Halleck," roared the President, again making John jump as when he
first called in Nicolay. John rose and stood at rigid salute. Lincoln waved
acknowledgment and, without rising, reached over again and shook his
hand. "Drop in again when you're o' mind to," he said. "If I happen to be
busy I'll tell Nicolay to tell you some of his stories, which are better'n
mine."

When John turned he confronted General Halleck standing at salute.
John saluted him and walked to the door, leaving him still standing with
his hand to his forehead waiting for the President to acknowledge him.
Maliciously John stood at the door, peeking back into the room under
the suspicious eye of the guard. Mr. Lincoln at his desk was writing something on his military record, neither welcoming nor acknowledging the
salute of the General of all his Armies.

Presently, without looking up, he said, "Halleck, that was the young
feller that wrote that seditious article. I thought you might be interested
to know that I've fixed him so you'll never catch him now." With an impatient gesture General Halleck dropped his hand, but still stood waiting.

Out on Pennsylvania Avenue John for the first time looked at his new
commission. After the usual recitation about "reposing faith" in his
patriotism, etc., the President had interlined, "and for conspicuous bravery
in the field and for writing a certain article."

CHAPTER LXXXVIII

ON THAT same afternoon, just about the time John was leaving the White House, Ike got a letter from Joe Kirkwood. Since Bub's death Joe had been in command of his Zouaves and had been campaigning mostly in the Shenandoah Valley, apart from the 50th and the rest of the Gang in the Army of the Potomac. This was the first letter Ike had had from him since the early days. It was brought to his office by one of the soldiers in Joe's company who was home on furlough.

Jan. 3, '63

Dear Ike—

Since I shall send this personally by a trustworthy lad, I'm going to say what I damn please in spite of censorship.

I'm getting mighty sick of wallowing round in the mud and getting licked by the Rebs about twice for every once we give them a licking. I've had a good chance to find out what the Rebs are like, because one of my jobs has been to examine prisoners. The officers are always haughty and stand with folded arms and won't talk. I have come on a number who have been north to college, but with two or three exceptions they have been ashamed of it, taking a swaggering pride in their ignorance of everything but their violent and ornamental social code. They consider themselves great aristocrats and vastly superior to all Yankees, whom they persuade themselves are something lower than their poor whites. They live entirely for show and for the moment, being interested only in gallantry and swagger, hard fighting, hard drinking and, I presume, hard wenching. They make a drama of the war and never come out of their parts, the swash-buckling parts of old-time buccaneers.

All this, as you may imagine, I like. Don't ask me to be consistent. I like my books, but I like hard living better, which incidentally was the case with most of my favorite authors. I guess the thing I like best about the Rebs is that they make no namby-pamby pretense about a moral crusade. All they want is to teach the god-damned Yanks

694

a lesson and send us skedaddling out of their cow-pasture. In my opinion, they are going to do it, and you know how I always respect a fellow who trims me.

All of which is leading up to the announcement that I am going to disappear. Long before you get this I shall be somewhere "over the hill." I am writing to ask you to take care of Mattie. I don't mean to put any frills on her, but just see that she never comes to want. I enclose a check for five hundred, and I have named you executor of my will. If the five hundred isn't enough, I wish you would look after Mattie anyway. After seven years you can prove me legally dead and reimburse yourself out of my estate. It won't cost you much, won't cost anything so long as she has a good position like the present one with Mehitable Gadston. I just want to feel sure you will be standing back of her in a time of need. This is probably the last favor I will ask you.

I am asking you this because you and Bub were the only two I ever really gave a damn about, and you are the only one I have ever thought had any understanding of both Mattie and me.

When I ask you to take care of her I don't mean that you should confine yourself to any namby-pamby self-righteousness. Do anything you want with her and I hope you can make her happier than I have done. Or leave her alone if that suits you better.

As my agent and banker I assume that you will continue to pay my income to my family, retaining your commissions.

Well, my friend, it's a short life and I get awfully nervous when it's not a merry one. I would like to see you and Mattie and my young ones, but otherwise I have no desire to enter the great city of Byzantium Falls again. I never really belonged there, or for that matter anywhere I have yet found. The war is a great eye-opener.

Regards always,

Joe.

Ike looked heavily out the back window at the snow that had been falling almost steadily since New Year's. Another member of the Gang gone. But perhaps, Ike thought with a sigh, it was best this way for Joe. Through the falling flakes Ike could just make out Theophilus Bostwick shovelling off the footpath in front of the *Democratic Union*. Joe, who had some gumption, was gone; but Theophilus and all the other old duffers stayed on.

That evening Ike was purposely late for supper at Mistress Spencer's, so it would seem natural for him still to be there when Mattie arrived for one of the three evenings a week she was now getting off from the Gadstons'. Ike and Mattie helped her ma with the dishes, then she said good night to them, gave Ike a sad, piercing look, and went up to bed. Ike had scarcely seen Mattie in two weeks, and it was plain to him that she also had something on her mind. They sat down in the north parlor, and after he had put a chunk in the stove he asked her if she'd had any word from Joe recently.

At this she put her hands to her face and sobbed softly, and Ike went over, sat down beside her on the sofa and put his arm around her. When she was quiet she fished inside her waist and produced a letter from Joe which she said a soldier had brought her at supper time at the Gadstons'. She gave it to Ike to read:

Jan. 4, '63

Dearest Little Mattie—

I sent you a Christmas letter two weeks ago. I hope you received it.

As you know, I always like things going on, and in spite of occasionally getting shot at down here, there isn't enough going on to suit me. Outside of seeing you there is nothing to take me back to the Falls, and anyway I couldn't come there now without being caught and punished, maybe very badly. So I've a notion to go away somewhere else, perhaps a very long way off. If you don't hear from me again within about a week you can know that I have gone. I will probably be safe, but I shan't be able to write you, and it may be we shall never see each other again.

I hope you find somebody who will make you happier than I have. I am sure you will get over missing me after a while, and I hope it will be sooner than I get over missing you, for that will be never. I don't expect ever to find anyone who will take your place, although I hope to find a better life than the one in this Army or the one at Byzantium.

If ever you are in trouble or in need, call on Ike. He is the only person in the Falls I would trust to be as gentle with you as you deserve. I have written him to keep an eye on you and to see that you never want. I know we can trust him.

Good-by, my little sweetheart. Many thanks for the happiest times I have known.

Joe

Ike handed back the letter, and Mattie replaced it in her bosom. For almost half an hour they sat without saying anything, Ike's arm around her waist and her cheek in the hollow of his shoulder, her blue-gray eyes staring wide and straight ahead at nothing.

At last she said softly, "Ike, ye ain't comfortable," put a pillow behind him and returned to her former place, this time snuggling a little closer. "He may not be gone yet," Ike said. "There ain't time yet to be certain." "Oh, yes, he's gone right enough," whispered Mattie, hardly louder than breathing. "I knew it would come and now it has come. He's gone. He's gone." She closed her eyes tightly and tears oozed out between the lashes onto Ike's lapel.

Presently Ike said, "I guess we're in the same boat, Mattie. I figger that piece John wrote in the *Eagle* was aimed at me. You know I'm plaguy attached to him." Instantly it was as if Mattie completely forgot her own trouble. Her hand came up and pressed soothingly against Ike's cheek, and he felt himself enclosed in the warm, maternal aura that was Mattie's personality. He held her strongly, but he did not kiss her.

Half an hour later Mattie had to go back to Gadstons', and Ike walked with her through Benson's Lane all the way to Hamilton Street. The snow had stopped, and it was a sharp, white, starlight night. Their feet crunched cheerfully on the trodden footpaths, and when they stopped to say good-by at the corner of Hamilton Street the village was as silent under its frozen trees as if it had been the deep forest. Ike kissed Mattie three times on the lips very gently, holding her just as gently in his arms. He knew it was not time yet, but he knew he wouldn't have very long to wait, and he knew she knew it too.

It turned out that Ike had to wait only until Mattie's next evening off from the Gadstons'. And the morning after this tender consummation he got his first letter from John in over eight months.

Washington

Jan. 10, '63

Dear Scamp—

By this time you have probably read my article in the New Year's edition of the *Eagle,* and have no doubt gathered why I have been unable to bring myself to write you for so long. At last the time has come when I see that I have been stiff-necked, arrogant, blind, stupid. I apologize not only with sincerity but with joy in throwing off the burden this estrangement has been to me. It has been intolerable,. Scamp, and all my fault. I can well appreciate that it may not be easy for you to forgive me so quickly, but I know you will in the long run.

The occasion of my awakening was in itself no small event. The President liked my article and invited me to Washington to talk about it. I have just come from the White House. Scamp, if ever there was wisdom in humanity it is all in that man. And humor! To put me at ease he wasted five minutes making a to-do about our both being tall!

But to get on. It seems that in contemplation of this interview the President asked Solon Samson—whom he calls "our mutual friend"— about me, and he learned not only all about me but pretty much all about you and the Engine Company. He even sent to the Ordnance Department and got a full report on the company. He told me in effect that I should be inordinately proud of my brother, that you are making the best grade of guns the Army is receiving, and at the same time are paying high wages and realizing no profit for yourself. I know you wrote me these things, but I confess I underestimated their importance and did not appreciate the patriotic motive behind them. My apology is abject.

I have some bad news. Joe Kirkwood has apparently deserted. Just before I came to Washington I had a letter from Loyal Hall who succeeds to the command of Bub's old company. Loyal said that a few nights before he wrote me, Joe went out past one of his own pickets, saying he was going to "get him a nice, fat Reb for break- fast." And he hasn't been heard from since.

But to get back to the chief subject of this letter. I want publicly to wipe out any inference in my recent article that might seem to include you among the "money-grubbers." I am going to write an- other bit for the *Eagle* in which I shall praise those manufacturers who are serving the government for no profit. Oh, how well I under- stand now what you meant when you wrote months ago, "You see, I too am at the front!" I also now understand what you meant when you said that you and I between us were "playing the war at both ends." When I read this I was stupid enough to think you meant that we were playing it for some kind of gain for ourselves. Now I see what you meant was that we are both *serving* the war in our different ways,. and I see also that, practically speaking, your way is the more valuable.

Well, Scamp, I'm still virgin. I came near falling a few days after

Fredericksburg when I got Washington leave, and a lot of us went
to an elegant place that is run for officers only. The women were
superior and I almost went over. I imagine now I'll jog along in the
old celibate rut without much trouble. I am always both hoping and
fearing I'll run into that tragic burlesque girl I told you of. The one
who said she had a brother who looked like me.

I guess that's all for now. I am entitled to a month's leave some
time this winter, but at present I don't know when I shall get it.

My devotion as always,

'Paloosa

The nervous scowl with which Ike began to read this letter became a
broad smile of affection and amusement as he proceeded. He saw clearly
enough through the big 'Paloosa's effort at self-deception. He knew that
he really disapproved of the gun-making as much as ever. But on the
other hand, he saw that John was eager to seize any opportunity to down
his disapproval and persuade himself that Ike was doing something he
could call patriotic. This meant that at bottom the attachment between
them was still as strong on John's part as on Ike's own. He was sure
now that John's complaint of him would disappear when the war was
over. Immediately he loved the whole world and must have company.
He went over to the Byzantium Club for dinner and had three whiskys
with Wash Wycomb even if it was in the middle of the day. And though
it was in the middle of the week, he rode out to the Hollow for supper
and spent the night at home.

So began for Ike a sort of Indian Summer of the war period. For the
first time in his life he knew what it was not only to be loved by a woman
but to be spoiled by her. Under Mattie's meek exterior there was a quick
wisdom which understood his every whim before he did, and had sense
enough not to pester him about wraps and his health. The Ordnance Officer assigned to the Engine Company was a bachelor, and for his own
purposes had rented an isolated house on River Street which was easy
to reach without being seen. He had told Ike before that he might use
the house at any time, so Ike now rented a room there. It became home
to him and Mattie, and he bought pretty things for her to fix it up—
though she wouldn't let him give her personal presents. They met there
on Mattie's nights off, she telling her ma that Mistress Gadston was keeping her in most of the evenings these days.

Ike continued to drop in on Pru Stark about once a week, and he now enjoyed his calls on her more than at any time since John left. The edge being off his carnal desire, he felt a comfortable nonchalance in Pru's presence, a nonchalance so comfortable indeed that frequently during his visits he would glance up and catch her gazing at him curiously. But no one ever caught on to his and Mattie's secret.

Most important of all, Ike was now squared with the 'Paloosa. They wrote each other every week and John published his conciliatory article in the *Eagle*. One evening Ike and Mattie were in their room, Ike standing by the mantel, Mattie knitting and rocking slowly in the rocking chair. "Mat," said Ike, "ye know the fact is I'm sort of stalling in my letters to the 'Paloosa, figgering to let him keep his high-minded notions and enjoy 'em while he can. Do ye figger I ought to tell him the truth, that there ain't any love of the war in our running the factory at a loss, that we'd take a profit quick enough if we knew how?"

Mattie glanced up at him blankly for an instant, then dropped her eyes and resumed her rocking. "I'm afraid I can't help ye there, Ike," was her soft reply.

CHAPTER LXXXIX

AFTER the fiasco of General Burnside's "mud march," near the end of January, '63, the Army of the Potomac retired to Washington, and under discouragement, sickness and weather the morale sank to the lowest ebb of the war. Colonel McNaughton was now a brigadier and Colonel Donahoe, commanding the 50th, met the situation by granting three weeks' furloughs wholesale. He let three whole companies go at a time, with co-extensive leaves for the officers.

The turn of Companies A, B and C came on March second. Immediately all the complaints of the last two months were forgotten. In their freight wagons provided by the War Department, they pulled out of the capital singing, and every man was hilariously drunk before they reached Baltimore. Late at night they debouched yelling from the New Jersey ferry, their boyish nerves rebounding from the contraction of a year of discipline, and their wills long apprenticed to irresponsibility by the constant threat of death. The brilliant and crowded city was used to such invasions and absorbed this one without astonishment. After two days of roistering—including a riot at the popular play, *The National Guard,* where the portly Statue of Liberty rendered the "Star-Spangled Banner"—and three nights of stupor in the beds of fancy ladies or on bar-room floors, or billiard tables, or in the brig of the Military Police, the heroes of the 50th, now stripped of money, managed to take the cars for the north country.

Meanwhile, Alec Mathiesson had returned to his family, and John, Medad, George and Jabe were being entertained by Mrs. Elizabeth Cady Stanton and her husband. They were as exuberant as the men to be freed of the tension of the real war, and were delighted, instead of being revolted, by the gala spectacle of war prosperity in full roar. The city's normal population of about a million was now swelled by hordes of merchants, contractors, speculators, and their camp followers, gamblers, harlots, public entertainers and miscellaneous charlatans and criminals from all over the country and abroad. While the city's vitals stank and whimpered with poverty and seethed with drunkenness, brawls and crimes of violence, its surfaces glittered with extravagance and luxury that saw fit to make their display while the artificial sun of a debased currency yet shed its precarious light of war profits. On the muddy streets John and the rest saw women like walking stores of gold, jewels, and the most costly imported silks and laces. At the theater and opera they saw them again in full, bare-bosomed glory, the sparkle of their armor capped with dust of gold or silver on their hair, while their men swaggered with large diamonds for cuff-links, shirt-studs and waistcoat buttons. Somewhere in the bones of the city the original crusading spirit still lived: in the families whose last sons had enlisted, whose daughters were studying to be nurses, whose fathers, rich or poor, stinted themselves to buy Government bonds when they were issued, not waiting for them to depreciate; in the conscientious co-operation with the Government in the newly established Freedmen's Bureau; in the great, life-saving work of the United States Sanitary Commission; in the bloodthirsty but still sincere haranguing of the pulpit and the press; and in the more substantial secret prayers of hundreds of thousands for victory. In the bones of the city the original war for the Union still moved with undiminished strength, but on the surface all was profiteering, speculation and display, the glare, the costumes and the whirling hubbub of a vast, tawdry circus.

John and the rest chose to see only the circus, and it delighted them. They heard their hostess and her husband speak with angry contempt of the "sybarites of shoddy," but even John's spirits were too high to remember the sufferings of the Army from bad clothing, shoes, food and powder that had raised these sybarites to power. He and Medad and George and Jabe flirted with the young ladies—not "shoddy"—Mistress Stanton had in for dinner, but they had more fun in the public dance halls, and at one of the shoddy "Victory Balls" of the new rich which they furtively attended against Mistress Stanton's orders. They did their best to talk profoundly with Master Greeley and other worthies who came in to congratulate John on his article, but they enjoyed themselves more when displaying their wisdom to whores and other bar-room acquaintances. They stayed an extra day, starting northward on the sixth. They played poker all the way home, and in the twilight of the next afternoon not one of them bothered to look out the car window at the increasingly familiar country, still a foot deep in snow.

Byzantium had seen each of its surviving soldiers at least once since the beginning of the war, but it had not before received them in force. Consequently a season of carnival was planned for the two weeks that Company C would be at home. The festivities were to begin on this Saturday evening, the seventh of March, when it was learned by telegraph that the officers would at last arrive.

It was after five o'clock and dark when the train pulled in, its whistle, as on each of the last four afternoons, announcing its heroic freight with a shrieking waste of steam all the way from the Cochran Street crossing, where they had originally entrained, to the station a mile beyond. A bonfire of tar barrels was sizzling in the snow beside the station, illuminating on the wall a white banner proclaiming in red and blue letters, "Welcome, Heroes." As the train quaked to a stop the two cannon on the Mall began booming their hundred times. Then a mob poured onto the train and dragged out John, Medad, George and Jabe one by one, each of them being cheered by the crowd of four or five hundred people as he appeared on the platform. John felt a momentary, old-fashioned surge of joy at home-coming—the first for almost a year—and he embraced Ike with unmixed emotion. The next thing he knew he was teetering on three or four pairs of shoulders, being carried up through the archway under the Gadston House to the Mall, preceded by a band.

The official welcome was a supper at the Byzantium Club, where the fifty-odd surviving members of Company C, along with such members of Companies A and B as had come in from the outlying townships, and with one male relative of each soldier, were the guests of the village. The club was crowded and noisy and there was no doubt now of the support of the war by all parties. John was amused at the effusive greetings he received from Wycomb, Slocum, Ludlow, and their arch-spokesman, Ostrum Applemore, just as if he hadn't openly insulted them as cowards in his article. He learned from Applemore that the draft had passed Congress last Tuesday.

Supper in the crowded dining-room was opened with singing of the "Battle Hymn of the Republic," and after that, because it was doubted whether the crowd, once fed, could be held together for the ceremonies, the ceremonies were put ahead of the meal. Theophilus Bostwick, who was appropriately President both of the village and the club, had to get a cane to rap silence into the stifling, shouting, back-slapping room, after which he delivered the address of welcome, none of which John heard, engaged as he was in drinking silent toast after toast of greeting at long range with almost every person in the room. The first thing he knew he realized he was being cheered and was required to stand up while old Theophilus read a flowery and inaccurate account of his valiant exploits. At the end of it there was a great cheer and everybody rose and toasted him. To his relief he was not urged to make a speech, merely lifted his own glass in acknowledgment and sat down. Thereafter the same compliment was paid in succession to every member of Company C, dead, wounded, sick or present, each of the last in turn standing up and receiving his cheer. The gathering of this data had been a formidable, patriotic labor, and the delivery of it took more than an hour.

This worthy business being over, Theophilus Bostwick banged for order again, and said that he was privileged to make an announcement on behalf, not of the village, but of this "splendid club." In honor of this occasion and of "our heroic young friends" it was to be known from this moment, "no longer as the 'Byzantium Club' but as the 'Union Club.'" Another cheer shook the erstwhile house of old Seth Marlow—not a member of the organization—as everyone stood and toasted "The Union Club," "The Army," "Victory," "Hang the Rebels," etc., etc. Then they were allowed to eat.

By the end of supper, and in spite of the fact that he had a skinful, John was in a glassy, semi-anesthetized state of boredom. Automatically the soldiers, after running gauntlets of foolish and sententious questions, gravitated together in the front room, where John had his first pleasure of the evening in greeting on equal and inebriate terms the men he had been bossing and who had been treating him with enforced servility for nearly two years. "Well, fellows," he shouted, after half an hour, "in my opinion I at least am dismissed." As he started out the men shouted with proud familiarity, "Let's see summat of ye, John," "Let's learn what sort of a feller ye be, John." "Keerect," shouted John. "What do you say to Headquarters at the American bar for the next two weeks?" "O.K.," "O.K.," went around the company. Some naïve enthusiast proposed, "Three cheers for Colonel Lathrop," but John raised his hand and shouted, "To hell with Colonel Lathrop!" "Three cheers for old Long John," came the counter proposal from another corner, and the cheers were enthusiastically given. "At the American!" John shouted back, turned to Ike, swung on his cape and campaign hat, and they walked out.

At the Liberty, John thrust in the front door without knocking, raced upstairs, lifted Susan Stark high off the floor and kissed her, did the same to Pru, and greeted old Gam like a long lost friend. "Well, it's great to be in and it's great to be out," he said with impersonal enthusiasm. "Gam Stark, how's the hotel business these days?" Gam grumbled, and John turned to Pru, "Well, my kitten, I suppose there will be parties and you're ordered to go with me to all of them." He seized Pru's hands, kissed them, dropped them abruptly, turned to her ma and told her she was younger and prettier than ever. Then he said to Ike with the same zest, "Now then, Scamp, I suppose we've a long drive ahead of us. Good night to all of you. It's mighty fine to see you." And he led Ike down to the bar for "just one more to get us home."

Upstairs Susan and Pru looked at each other and looked away. For the first time in her twenty-nine years Pru suspected that she might not occupy the full extent of John Lathrop's horizon. Also, in his uniform and detached exuberance he was certainly the most beautiful man who ever drew breath. For the first time in her twenty-nine years she thought there might be, there just might be, the faintest possible chance.

Ike had stabled the cutter at the Liberty, and the first thing John said as they jingled down the Mall was, "Pretty minx, isn't she?" "Come prettier in Washington, do they?" said Ike, having his suspicions. "Oh, I daresay," said John indifferently, and Ike figgered that after all he was still virgin to women.

All the way home John chattered about the glories of New York and the details of what he, Medad, George, Jabe and Alec had done there. Not a word about the Army, the war, or shoddy, not the remotest personal innuendo. Ike might as well never have seen this light-headed person, and he didn't open his mouth except to cluck occasionally to Tim, the carriage horse.

John greeted Sarah with a hoist, a smack and a hug, exactly as he had greeted the Starks, mother and daughter, and when she clung to him and began to cry he looked confused. Then he came to his senses for a moment and patted her tenderly. But thereafter for an hour the four Lathrops made conversation of the most banal and trivial sort. Finally, Ben yawned and announced he was going to bed. Sarah caught Ike's eye and he went to bed also. Then she took John into the north parlor, sat him down, and looked straight at him in silence, but smiling in a happy, gloating way. "How are you, Ma?" he said finally in a normal, relaxed tone, now smiling naturally himself. "I was never in better health," said Sarah. Then demurely, "And how are *you*?" "I'm fine, Ma. Haven't had a moment's sickness or more than a scratch. But—Ma—let's not talk about the war." "I understand," said Sarah, reaching over and taking his hand. And as far as his ma was concerned, John was at home.

He stayed out at the homestead throughout his two weeks. Delighting at first in civilian clothes, he rode into the village every afternoon for an hour or two with the soldiers under the ministrations of Job Wheeler at the American, usually followed by a party in the evening. Sometimes Ike rode back home with him after the parties, but usually he had to be at the bank early, and so stayed in town.

Gradually the first exuberance wore away. John, Medad, George, Jabe, and sometimes Ike, exhausted Byzantium's dens of iniquity, and Jabe began to tire of the woman with whom he was cohabiting out at the Polar Bear. Gradually the strangeness of the village John had felt a year before began to oppress him. He wasn't consciously homesick for the Army, but he wanted to be anywhere but where he was, some place with novelty and surprises. He shied away from thinking about the rich and their war contracts, the shoddy he suspected Grabbot's Kamargo Mill was making. Yet the feeling of these people round him, the triviality of them, of everything here except the homestead, became a weight on his subconscious mind. Once, four or five days after their return, when he was alone with Jabe in the American, sitting in one of those silences that were becoming more frequent with them, he said, "Jabe, can you imagine yourself settling down after it's over?" "Nope," said Jabe.

Meanwhile Ike was feeling in a different way than he had anticipated the gulf that now separated him from John and the rest of the survivors of the Gang. Their first boisterousness was unnatural and childish, and it annoyed him. He could understand their not wanting to talk about the war, but he couldn't understand their not wanting to talk about anything. Their chatter was as trivial as that of boys in their naughty 'teens. As grown men in their middle thirties, they would sit around giggling over dirty stories, and whenever they grew serious, it was to discuss nothing but women, liquor and gambling.

When the first boisterousness wore off, in the middle of the first week after their return, Ike found the apathy that ensued even harder to bear. He would come on Jabe and the rest in the American, just sitting, smiling in an empty, idiotic sort of way, giving no more evidence of having anything on their minds than when they had been telling dirty stories. If they enjoyed some deep, mutual understanding in these silences, Ike couldn't make it out. Certainly he didn't share it. He began to feel like a stranger with his old friends, and ill at ease. On the surface he was increasingly irritated, but deep in him the old, lonely sadness and terror that had disappeared in the last two months began to return.

On Saturday a week after they came home, Ike came on the four of them sitting as usual at a table in the American bar. They stopped talking when he came in, and, though he knew danged well they hadn't been saying anything important, yet he felt as if he had interrupted a private conversation. He sat down and the silence continued, his four old friends looking at him with those remote, idiotic smiles. Job brought him his ale and he drank it noisily, then banged his can down on the table. "Danged talkative bunch, eh, Job?" All four of the soldiers looked mildly at Job and said nothing. Job wagged his head and went to washing glasses.

After another long silence Ike said, "Maybe you fellers would be interested to know we've arranged a special train for ye next Saturday, the twenty-first, when they tell me ye're going back." The four looked at each other, and Jabe said, "We were just talkin' of mebbe lightin' out, say, Thursday, before the Comp'ny. Got a little official business in New York to finish up."

"Thursday, eh?" said Ike indifferently. "Well, it's all one with me, but I suppose ye 'know the patriotic folks have arranged a big fair in Washington Hall Wednesday, Thursday and Friday for the U. S. Sanitary Commission. A few hayloads of lint and bandages to be collected, and a tarnal lot o' money, I cal'late. Big event Friday night, a farewell ball for ye, with all manner of doin's before it. I ain't certain, but I've been told they're counting on the 'Paloosa for a few remarks. Figger they'll be disappointed if ye ain't there, though it's nothing to me."

"Come to think of it, Pru did tell me something of the sort," said John. They all looked at each other and smiled in their vapid way. "Well, ye ought to decide," said Ike with disgust in his voice, "for I figger they'll be counting on you fellers more than anybody." They all looked at Ike blankly. "Figger it's orders," said Jabe.

CHAPTER XC

ON WEDNESDAY of the next week, the first day of the "Mercy Fair," there was no party in the evening, and Ike rode out with John to the homestead. When John rose to go to bed early, Ike asked him flatly to stay up a spell, and shortly thereafter Sarah and Ben left them alone. Ike led John into the north parlor, provided them both with grog and cigars, and sat down himself in one of the gilt armchairs. John stood with his back to the unlit fireplace, his eyes staring at the opposite wall, obviously not interested.

" 'Paloosa," said Ike, "ye're to make a speech day after tomorrow night in Washington Hall before a good part of the county, and knowing what I do of your feelings on some things, I don't want to see ye make a jackass of yourself." John looked at him blandly and began the regular nodding of his head, the sign of polite boredom which he inherited from their pa. Ike was determined to shake him out of it if he had to fight him to do it.

"I'm o' mind," he continued, "to tell ye a few things ye can put in the next article ye write and make it say something useful." John's eyes flickered at the mention of the article. He stopped nodding, set his tumbler on the mantel, put his cigar in his mouth, clasped his hands behind him, and gazed blankly at the portrait of their great-grandpa across the room.

"Had ye ever got through your head," Ike went on, "why Applemore and Gadston and all have turned so patriotic all of a sudden and gone to slapping ye on the back and hollering for the war? Ye don't figger, do ye, that calling them yellow-livered cowards in that article made them fall in love with ye? Ye don't cal'late, do ye, that they give a counterfeit shin-plaster fer any of your lofty notions?" "I suppose," said John, shifting his cigar, "that if they're behind the war now it's because they're making money out of their shoddy."

"All keerect," said Ike. "I'm glad ye see about a quarter of the truth, but I figger ye ain't even come anywhere near glimpsing the whole of it. These industrial and financial fellers hain't any notion the war can go on over long, for if it did the country'd go broke and they along with it. What

708

they're doing is to take a good long look into the future. They're stacking their cards for *after* the war and doing a mighty slick job of it. They've come to see a way they can keep up their profits if the North wins, but they know they'll be in for a trimming if the South gets out of the Union. They've mostly lost the Southern market now—though there's plenty selling secretly to the Confederacy—but they're set on getting the Southern market back to make up for what they lose when they stop selling things to the Army." John flicked the ash from his cigar, took his tumbler from the mantel, sat down, threw one leg over the other and listened, his eyes darkening as Ike proceeded.

"As ye may recall, between '57 and '60 there wasn't enough tariff for anybody to squabble about. In '61 Congress put on a sensible tariff for revenue, along with putting up taxes on everything else, but it wasn't enough to keep the Government and the states from keeping on buying guns and all from England and France where they could get 'em cheaper. The patriotic manufacturers here began to holler about what a shame it was to send money out of the country, and they talked mighty pathetic about their infant industries and how with just a little protective tariff to get started they'd soon be able to turn things out cheaper than the English, and after that the tariff could be repealed. So the innocent Congress, likely for the most patriotic reasons, passed last year's tariff which gave up the notion of revenue for the notion of helping our home industries get going. The upshot is that ye've by now a lot of money invested in new plants selling things to the Government a little dearer than England could have done it, and incidentally making plenty of money, mostly by adulterating their output in various ways, like you said in your article.

"This year or next ye're going to see this protective tariff still higher, and out of their profits ye're going to see the manufacturers footing the bill for the Republican political campaign and in consequence getting hold of the Government, all with the purpose of seeing to it that their high tariff is here to stay. From having been Democrats and ag'in the war at the start off they'll all turn into patriotic Republicans in control of the whole shebang and nobody'll be able to get rid of 'em." John's face wore a sneer now, and he finished his drink. But he let Ike continue.

"All this," Ike went on, passing John the decanter, "gives them a fine prospect of skimming the cream off the South if they can win the war. With the tariff, England can't put goods down there any cheaper than Lem Grabbot or Ory Slocum can, but if the South should win and get free the North wouldn't sell them a red of goods for many a long year. So your friends the industrialists are bound to see the North win and their notion of winning'll be a plaguy sight more drastic than yours. They'll figger not only to keep the South in the Union, but to sure grit conquer and control the whole country down there, just to be sure those fellers don't figger out a way to manufacture their own goods or trade with anybody else but them. They'll see to abolishing slavery all keerect, not on account of any fine notions of humanity, but just to keep the South from making things with cheap labor at less cost than they'll have to pay the North.

"Yes, 'Paloosa ye can count on the rich being sure grit behind ye from now on, and they'll win your war for ye. Ye're going to hear them hollering about the wickedness of the South a deal louder than you fellers ever did. The Union'll be preserved and the slaves'll be freed, like ye said. But instead of this fine, free country ye've figgered on after these righteous things are done, ye're going to find a new country more under the thumb of the rich than it's ever been before. They'll be able to tell folks how patriotic they were for a long time to come. And while they're telling ye that, they'll be putting the finishing touches on the old decent folks from the farms, like all our friends, and they'll be doing it in the North just as sure as they'll be doing it in the South. The farmers are doing a pretty war business right now, but that's only because the industrial folks ain't got around to getting control of their markets. But one of these days ye'll see 'em do it, and from that time the fellers on the farms, in the North as much as in the South, will be mighty lucky if they can scratch together enough to eat.

"I want ye should get it straight, 'Paloosa, that from now on it's the Grabbots and the Gadstons and the Slocums that are waging this war. They hain't got the President yet, and they likely won't get him. But already they're coming on powerful strong in Congress. Applemore dang near beat Solon last fall, and he did it by going patriotic and talking like a Republican. I'll bet ye ten dollars in gold that within a year he and the whole caboodle of his backers will be in your righteous party, and the next thing ye know they'll be your bosses, not Master Lincoln with his fine ideas. Ye can set the turn pretty well at that Conscription Act they passed in Congress the other day. That means the high ideas have shot their bolt. From now on they've to *buy* the boys to go down and get shot. It's the rich who are footing the bill and ye can be sure they're going to get well paid for it. Now get this through your head, 'Paloosa." Ike lowered his voice and spoke slowly, *"At the start-off ye were sure grit fighting for what ye thought ye were, and the rich were against ye. But from now on ye ain't fighting any more for your perfect Union and for the slaves. Ye're down there fighting for us fellers that stay home and get rich."*

John had been fidgeting and drinking fast. Now he exploded. "That's a god-damned lie," he bellowed, jumping up, crashing his tumbler into the hearth, then turning on Ike and fairly snarling as he spoke. "If you had the slightest understanding of what war really is, instead of sitting back here getting fat on other men's blood, you'd know that not a man of us would stay in it if we didn't know we were fighting for the Right, and the same will be true of the new men in the draft." Ike looked straight back at John and spoke quietly, "At least I know enough about the war to have opposed it from the start. As for the boys in the draft, they'll be fired up all keerect with all these notions ye'll still think ye're fighting for. Likely they'll get fellers like you to make recruiting speeches like ye've done before, and Slocum and Ludlow'll cheer for ye louder'n any. The boys'll think they're fightin' to make men free all keerect. I'm telling ye what they and you'll be *really* fighting for, whether you like it or not."

John sniffed in disgust, paced the room twice to get control of himself, then asked, "What are you going to do if they draft you?" "I'm going to get out of it, buy myself out as ye're allowed to. I'm settled for good against the war, even if I am getting pretty dividends out of my Kamargo Woollen Stock." "With us enough to make guns but not enough to fight for us, eh?" said John huskily, his rage now giving way to his underlying bitterness at Ike's occupation. "Well," said Ike, "I figger we've had that out before. I've told ye many times I wouldn't be making guns if it in any wise increased the number of them being used to slaughter folks with. The only difference our making guns makes is that ours are a little better'n most so they don't blow up the fellers firing them."

Again John paced the room, trying to turn his mind from this intolerable subject. But he succeeded only in touching a different phase of it and his voice was still husky. "Nat Gadston told me he was going to enlist. At least he's consistent. When he comes around to us he's willing to go out and fight for what he believes." "What he believes is just what I told ye," said Ike. "Nice thing about Nat is he's frank. He says he's for the war now in order to get the South as a market after the war, which'll be possible with the tariff, as I said. As for his enlisting, I think ye can thank Pru for that. We were both there the other night discussing these matters, and Pru began to twit him about not going out since he was for the war now. It was mighty mean of her, Nat being most as crazy about her as you are, and she not giving a god-dang about him or anybody."

At this John smiled sourly, for, though he had not fully admitted it to himself, Pru's actions during this leave, added to the memory of her conduct when he first went to the war, were throwing increasing shadows on the romantic image of her he had carried for twenty years. The reference to a matter in which he no longer wholly disagreed with Ike calmed him for the moment. His mind took a turn toward something that might lead to practical action.

Standing quietly at the mantel, he said, "You know something of Grabbot's Kamargo Woollen Company, do you?" Ike nodded. "Are they making shoddy?" "Yep." "The dirty bastards," snarled John. "I'm a director," said Ike quietly. "Good God," shouted John, throwing his cigar in the fireplace and turning on Ike, with scorn putting ice in his returning fury. "Well, I can assure you you won't be for long. Don't think I'll treat what you just told me as confidential. Perhaps you don't know I was the fellow who started Solon Samson's Congressional investigation of this rotten traffic. He's had contracts with a dozen factories cancelled already. Now I'll tell him about you and Grabbot and I'll tell him where I got my information." "All keerect," said Ike quietly. "I can sell out easy at a fine profit tomorrow. I've only stayed in till now, figgering to use my minority influence to get Grabbot to quit making this pesky stuff."

John didn't listen. He paced the room a dozen times, then made a last, desperate effort to make peace with his brother by bringing up the one point on which he had persuaded himself that Ike was behaving with honor and patriotism. He spoke quietly, with an effort at casualness, but he did not look at Ike, and there was a pleading tone in his voice.

"Anyway," he said, "it is true, is it not, that you are making no profits on the guns you are selling to the Government?" "Yes, it's true," said Ike. He considered his cigar for a moment, then went on slowly, and with reluctance. "But since we're talking straight, 'Paloosa, right there's another matter I figger I ought to set ye clear on. Ye mustn't go on believing, like ye seem to, that I wouldn't turn a fair profit for the engine company if I knew how to. So far, I can't see but two ways. One is to get the Government to pay us more, and they write that they've got the price of guns set so they can't do that. The other way would be to reduce the wages of the men, and I'm dead set against that, it being a notion of mine that industry has got to be run so as to take care of its employees the same as townships take care of people on the farm who are in trouble. But without going into details, ye may as well understand straight that if I can figger out a way to make this gun business pay, I'm going t' do it. So I thank ye and Solon and Master Lincoln for your flattering thoughts, but the truth is——"

"Please stop," John broke in quietly. "Please don't tell me any more of that. In spite of a good many things you've said, and a few you've done,

I've managed to hold on to the conviction that at heart you're a decent citizen and out, not to make money, but, as you claimed at first, to keep up the Lathrop fortune in order that we may continue to serve the community. If I thought your life was primarily devoted to making money I'd be through with you, and I mean it. But I don't think that and I don't propose to. Whatever you *say*, what I see you *doing* is to sell to the Government at no profit, and in that you have my admiration. I still believe in you, Scamp"—John's voice began to tremble—"and God help me if ever I stop believing in you. So let's have no more talk about the rotten side of the war, and no more talk about your hoping to make a profit out of it. Perhaps I'm a coward, but if ever you do make a profit out of your guns, I pray to God I don't know it."

Ike stared for half a minute into the fireplace, then looked up into John's tense face, his own brow now puckered with distress. "I'd have to tell ye, 'Paloosa," he said simply. John turned slowly out of the room and went upstairs.

CHAPTER XCI

THE CULMINATION of the "Mercy Fair" on Friday evening, the twentieth of March, was to be a pageant, followed by certain other ceremonies and a "Victory Ball." The great auditorium of Washington Hall, with a capacity of 2,000, was, but for its gothic windows, completely lined with bunting, flags and tissue paper, the motif red, white and blue. From the lighted central chandelier thirty feet above the floor, with its twelve-foot circle of a hundred gas jets, festoons looped out to the walls and the remote corners of the enormous room, while beneath the chandelier there hung a curious sphere, four or five feet in diameter, wrapped in red, white and blue cloth and exciting the wonder of all but the few who knew its secret. Around the big central floor space between the tiers of seats that rose against the walls there were some two dozen open booths tastily decorated. Here the young ladies of the "best families," variously arrayed as stars, angels and the several virtues, had for three days collected money for the United States Sanitary Commission in payment for predictions of the patron's happy future, or a reading of his head, or for miscellaneous treasures of pastry, porcelain, embroidery, glass, knitting, shell, feathers, and human hair, all these enticements to generosity being contributed to the cause, along with their winsome smiles, by the young ladies in charge. It was rumored that the collection had already run high in the thousands, and it was further rumored that Horace Gadston and Squire Fulton had agreed between themselves to double whatever the collection should prove to be. The counting of this evidence of the village's practical patriotism was to be one of the features of the evening's entertainment. Opposite the main entrance, in the center of the west side of the room, was the speakers' platform, entirely covered with flags, while above it a real stuffed Baldheaded Eagle with wings outspread hung by a long wire, a trifle off balance by the port quarter and swaying gently in life-like fashion to the upper breezes of the auditorium.

By seven o'clock the tiers of benches round the four sides of the room were filled, the most expensive of the reserved seats being well placed under the strong wall lights at the ends of the hall so as to reveal Byzantium's somewhat pale effort at shoddy, metropolitan glitter. Mrs. Ludlow indeed was so far in the mode that a little gilt dust shone on her graying black hair, the result suggesting rather an accident of some kind than the hours of art she had spent on it. On the rest of the benches crowded the common herd, including Mistress Fulton, Mistress Lathrop, the Samples from Round Harbor, the VanSanfords and Howell Sherwood. The crowd overflowed the seats onto the central floor where marshals with badges emblazoned with the golden words, "Mercy and Victory," kept them back against the booths.

At half-past seven a bugle sounded the assembly at the head of the grand stairway outside the entrance doors, and immediately a fife and drum corps at the same point rattled into "Yankee Doodle." The pageant was beginning.

First came the fife and drum corps, then Mrs. Horace Gadston, the Chairwoman of the Mercy Fair and Victory Ball Committee, on the arm of Squire Fulton, who was to be Master of Ceremonies. Then came the other members of the Committee, all female, and so happily adjusted in number that they exactly used up for escorts the village President and Trustees, plus Ostrum Applemore. Then came three lovely female infants as flower girls, decked with cherubic wings and bearing baskets from which they periodically threw on the floor little handfuls of colored paper that simulated flowers. These got the first real ovation of the parade in the form of universal sighs and exclamations of endearment with scattering applause which swelled into a roar of cheers at the wonders that followed.

Behind the flower girls came Miss Olympia Gadston, clad airily as a hooped "Winged Victory" and bearing a lofty staff with a gilded eagle at the top, dangling in its beak an enormous laurel wreath. Then came Lieutenant Colonel John Lathrop, in full dress but lacking his sword—for the officers had been asked not to carry them on this peaceful occasion. On John's arm, almost equalling him in height, came Columbia, clad and capped voluminously in flags, in the person of Miss Gloriana Gadston. Then, at a well-kept interval, unarmed and looking very little and sheepish under the artillery of applause they evoked, marched the veterans of Company C commanded by Captain Medad VanSanford, and behind them such others of the 50th as had come in from the outlying towns.

The parade circled the hall once, then the leaders, from Squire Fulton and Mehitabel Gadston to John and Gloriana, mounted the speakers' platform, leaving the fife and drum corps to squeal its way back to the entrance and so out. At Medad's command the soldiers swung into line with their backs to the speakers' platform, halted, and stood at attention. Everyone else stood. A bugle sounded a note, after which thirteen-year-old Patience Ford, daughter of a brand-new family in town—said to be rich—sang "The Star-Spangled Banner" inaudibly. Then Reverend Tremble Thomas did a long and reverberatingly audible prayer, and everybody sat down, the soldiers on benches prepared for them, leaving a passage to and from the speakers 'platform.

Old Squire Fulton advanced from his place in the center of the semicircle on the platform, and spoke briefly and with feeling of the service of the 50th, of the pride the county took in them, of the humility and joy their presence gave "to those of us no longer able to be with ye in the flesh," and the hope that the offering of the community represented by the Fair would be a measure of the unanimous support they were receiving at home. He said that everything of value about their heroism and about the war generally had been recounted many times and needed no repeating, but he wanted "you, our boys, to know that wherever ye go the love of your homes and of your village, township and county goes with ye." The fat, florid, jolly, and now obviously moved old man threw an air of dignity over the assembly which lasted throughout the evening, even surviving the next two events on the program.

First of these was the collection of the money from the booths and the gate. Four little girls in red, white and blue held out by the corners a large flag in the center of the hall under the big chandelier and the enigmatical globe suspended by a rope beneath it. Into this flag the fair occupants of the booths and the ticket-seller, advancing from their stations with extended aprons they had donned for the occasion, dumped the jingling and rustling contents of the same. Someone had appropriately cautioned the little girls holding the flag that it must not touch the floor. But it and its weighty contents were too much for them. It did touch the floor; one of the little girls dropped her corner hysterically and began to cry; and the end of it was that the girls from the booths wrapped it in a bundle round its treasure and bore it to the speakers' platform and Squire Fulton. The count had in fact already been made. Squire Fulton gave the heap a dignified look, then announced from a paper that $5,647.73 had been collected, and that he was informed that this amount was to be doubled by certain citizens.

When the self-congratulatory applause over this munificence had died away the Squire raised his eyes to the enormous, lofty globe, said, "And now for this many-colored moon," and a hush of expectant curiosity fell over the up-gazing hall. While Columbia stood at the head of the steps at the front of the speakers' platform, with hand upraised, a group of men laid hold of an unnoticed rope in a corner of the auditorium. There were mumbled commands, a scraping of feet, the moon stirred, descended a few inches, and stopped. There was an impatient consultation, then an authoritative person strode over to the ropeholders and gave the audible command, "Heave 'er up ag'in." It was obvious that something had jammed.

The men hove and the moon rose a good yard into the circular chandelier. "Ease 'er," commanded the voice, and at that it dropped, jerked, broke soundlessly from its celestial moorings and hit the floor with a half-ton, padded jolt that shook the building. The momentary consternation turned to laughter when Squire Fulton said, "We seem to have survived that Rebel bomb, anyhow." Then some twenty ladies, obviously plebeian, marched across the hall in a determined way and rolled the five-foot monster to Gloriana Gadston, who still stood with hand upraised.

One of the ladies then read in a shrill voice from a paper: "We are the Blackwater County Lint and Bandage Committee. This ball of lint and bandage, O Columbia, is our humble offering to thee in thine hour of need." Whereto Columbia replied, "For the brave soldiers, O sisters, I accept this gift in the spirit in which it is given." Most of the soldiers snorted irreverently. Squire Fulton said, "It is my understanding that a freight wagon is waiting to take this heavenly object to Washington in its present form. Is that right, Ike Lathrop? Where are ye?" "That's right, sir," shouted Ike from where he and Nat Gadston were sitting with Pru Stark. "On the contrary, Squire Fulton," said the intrepid and indignant Chairwoman of the Lint and Bandage Committee, "we're to unroll it ourselves and pack it properly and we're proud to do it." And meanwhile many ladies round the room were dabbing handkerchiefs at their eyes, feeling that the sadness and sanctity of this gift were being outraged by frivolity. At the Squire's suggestion, the moon was rolled in behind the soldiers to one corner of the speakers' platform, where it remained ingloriously all evening, like a theater property stripped of its illusion by too close familiarity.

"And now, ladies and gentlemen," said the Squire in a loud voice to center attention again, "we come to the happiest, surely the proudest, event of the evening. And to this end I take pleasure in retiring in honor of our honored citizen, ex-Senator Applemore, who needs no introduction." Ostrum Applemore had meanwhile picked up from behind his chair a long, loosely wrapped, paper package, and he now came forward, laid it on a table by the rail at the front of the platform, and waited with one hand in his waistcoat for the applause to subside.

Ex-Senator Applemore fully knew that he had a delicate job on his hands. He had clashed with young John Lathrop on the platform many times.

He knew himself and his cronies to be detested by him, and he had a healthy respect for John's inflammability and for his persuasive sincerity when aroused. Also, he conceived that he had an important political task to perform this evening, the task of uniting discordant forces for the better prosecution of the war. Accordingly, he had prepared his speech carefully. He spoke more candidly, with less rhetorical flourish than was his wont. And if he did not speak the whole truth, yet he made what proved to be the mistake of saying nothing that was in itself false or exaggerated.

"Mr. Master of Ceremonies," he said, "and ladies and gentlemen of Blackwater County. It is not so much my mission to speak to ye tonight as to speak *for* ye, and I sincerely hope that in what I have to say I shall express our collective sentiments, as well as my own as an individual citizen. Particularly tonight I wish to address our most distinguished soldier of Blackwater County, Lieutenant-Colonel John Lathrop." There was a prolonged burst of applause as he turned to bow to John, then moved over to the corner of the platform so that henceforth he could face both John and the crowd. "Colonel Lathrop," Mr. Applemore repeated, "and through him every officer and man of the 50th New York Infantry, and every other soldier from Blackwater County, wherever they may be tonight." Another burst of applause interspersed with cheers, and the soldiers for the first time turned round on the benches so as to face the platform. Ex-Senator Applemore continued:

"In a sense it ain't proper that I should be the one to address Colonel Lathrop this evening, for the occasion of the address is one which frankly I did not propose, though I quickly fell in with the proposal when it was brought to my attention. But in another sense it is peculiarly fitting that I, or some other member of the Democratic Party in the county, should address ye, Colonel, and I feel happy and honored to be standing before ye this evening, bearing witness that all former differences of opinion are now healed and together we present a united front to the common enemy." (Applause and cheers.)

"Ever since Colonel Lathrop took up residence in the village, now more than eleven years ago, he and I have found ourselves in disagreement on political matters, and this disagreement, while never reaching a personal misunderstanding, became serious in the election of 1860, and still more serious upon the issue of the war which, as I had predicted, followed upon that election. Let no one accuse me now of recanting the position I took then. Though I have now taken a different position, I have in no detail changed the basic views I had in the beginning. I opposed the war then as a needless waste of lives and money. If I were now to be put back in April,

'61, with the further knowledge gained from the terrible experience we have had in these two years, I would be even more strongly against the war than I was at that time. I would then have let the 'erring sisters go in peace,' and if we were at peace now and faced with the same prospect again, I would say again to let them go." (This drew a few determined handclaps which were promptly drowned in a storm of hisses.)

"But we are not at peace, and the war has now proceeded to a point where it is folly for any man to conceive that it will not be fought to a finish, to a final victory, aye, a conquest by the one side or the other. And that man would be mean and spineless indeed who, seeing his beloved country beleaguered in a conflict from which there is now no hope of withdrawal, would not offer his last drop of blood, his last cent of money, in her defense. It is the crisis in which our country stands that has primarily led me, and many other Democrats, to change our position, and join with the Republicans in support of this righteous crusade to preserve the Union and abolish slavery from this land." (This, uttered fervently and with finger pointed to heaven, drew applause and cheers as heavy as when he had mentioned the soldiers.)

"That, my friends, is the moral, the patriotic side of this great question. Beyond that, and incidental to it, there is the economic side. The country has invested its millions, and this village has invested its hundreds of thousands, in equipment for the manufacture of supplies for the Army. If the North does not prevail, to the end that these new plants may be gradually adjusted to the uses of peacetime life under the protection of an adequate tariff, then, added to the gigantic cost of the war, we shall find ourselves in national bankruptcy and our people subjected to widespread suffering almost as dreadful as that of the war itself. It therefore behooves us to prosecute the war to victory in defense of our economic life as well as upon patriotic motives.

"First, then, on the patriotic issue, and, secondly, on the economic issue, I hold that the time has now come when every citizen of the North, whatever his views in the past, must put his shoulder to the common wheel. We who were Democrats and lost our cause at the polls must say to you who were Republicans, 'From this time forward we are with you, no longer Democrats, no longer Republicans, but Americans fighting for our lives, our families and our country. It is no longer *your* war. It is *our* war now, and we are one for victory.'" (Again universal applause and cheers.)

"And so, Colonel Lathrop, I say to you proudly that it is *our* war and that I am with you heart and soul. You and the rest of the brave boys at the front are now as much my representatives as you are the representatives of those who supported your valiant undertaking from the beginning." (At this he picked up the paper package from the table and inserted his hand in one end of it.) "And in token of this support, I am honored and touched by the privilege granted me to present you, on behalf of Blackwater County, with this sword, and may it lead you, your regiment, and the cause of the North, forward into speedy victory." Amid an increasing and sustained roar of cheering he slipped the paper from the scabbarded sword—which was a costly one with a carved ivory hilt—and held it across his arm, the hilt toward John.

John rose and came forward, hesitated, took the sword below the hilt, laid it on the table, and seemed not to see Ostrum Applemore's hand extended to shake his. For more than two minutes he stood facing the room, and it seemed plain that the continued cheering was for him, not Applemore. This eased the difficult thing he had quickly decided to do. It seemed to show that, whatever Ike might say of the rich running the war from now on, the mass of the people were still with him, the Army, and the original, moral aims of the war. When the cheering had almost stopped, he began, and throughout he spoke quietly, with restrained and passionate earnestness, as if he were addressing personally each separate individual there. He used no tricks of oratory at all. It was like a tense, private conversation. The great hall fell absolutely quiet to hear him.

"Master of Ceremonies, Master Applemore, ladies and gentlemen. First let me thank you on behalf of all the members of the 50th for the splendid reception you have given us throughout our two weeks' leave, and especially tonight. Perhaps we should be most grateful for the fine ovation you have just given us, for I know that was not for me personally. It was for what I am here to represent, the 50th, the Army, and more than the Army, the Union cause. We shall remember that, my friends, and we shall know that you are with us when we return." (There was an attempt to cheer, but John's tense and personal manner made it seem inappropriate, and it died away.)

"I thank you, too, for this beautiful sword that has been offered tonight and I would like to take that, too, as a token of your belief in the Union cause. I did not know it was to be offered. I was told simply that I was to make a few remarks on a subject of my own choosing. The offer of the sword and some of the things Senator Applemore has said require me to speak differently than I had intended.

"Master Applemore has said this is now *our* war, and he generously offers his support to the cause of the North. I cannot but wonder whether when he says 'our war' and 'the cause of the North' he means what I mean

and what the soldiers mean who are prosecuting the war. Our war and the
cause for which we propose to continue fighting is very simple, and exactly
what it was in the beginning. We believe that this Union and this Government should be preserved, and we believe that slavery should be abolished.
These are the things we are fighting for. We in the Army are not interested
in conquering the South as if it were a foreign nation and making it tribu-
tary to us. We are not only disinterested in economic motives, we despise
them." (Here loud applause started among the soldiers, spread rapidly
through the room, then stopped abruptly.)

"We are not even greatly interested in patriotism that contains no moral
faith in the cause we are fighting for. It is very easy to cheer and follow a
parade. It is something else to really believe in a cause and be faithful to it.
Nineteen members of Company C, and a hundred and five members of
the 50th are dead down there because they believed in something enough
to be willing to die for it, and there are two or three times as many wounded
and sick in hospital. These are our friends who believed in the cause we
believe in. We want to be very sure that we keep faith with them, that we
continue to fight for what they died for, not for something else they would
not have understood." (At this three or four soldiers jumped to their feet
and shouted, "Keerect"— "Ye're speakin' the truth, Colonel"— "We're
with ye, Colonel." And there was an angry hubbub starting among them,
till John raised his hand and stopped it.) "And what they died for was not
simply 'victory' that anybody can shout for. It was the aims of the victory,
the preservation of the Union and the abolition of slavery. That is our war,
the soldiers' war. It is very simple and exactly what it was in the beginning.
For us there isn't any other war.

"But Master Applemore has said with an honesty that I admire that this
is not his war. He was not for the cause of the Union in the beginning, and
he is not now. He is for some other war that we do not fully understand,
something that he calls a patriotic war and an economic war. I do not want
to do Master Applemore an injustice for I am not sure of his personal
motives, but some of the things he said cannot but raise pictures of what
such another war might be.

"He mentioned factories that are making supplies for the Army. I happen to know on credible authority that one of the largest factories in this
community is turning out an infamous material for uniforms called
'shoddy.' I understand there is some slight effort within the directorship to
stop this dastardly practice. When I return to Washington I shall make it
my first duty to report what this factory is doing, to the President if necessary. It is needful that such factories sell nothing more to the Government.

The cause of such factories might be the cause of Master Applemore's economic war, and we of the Army consider such factories more our enemies than the Rebels. We do not want the support of criminals who are cheating the Army for their profit. Their war is not ours." (Again loud cheering started among the soldiers and spread through much of the audience, but it did not yet break from the spell of solemnity John had cast, and it was not sustained.)

"Master Applemore also used the word 'conquest' in relation to the South, and he mentioned the protective tariff. All of these things carry unsavory suggestions of self-seeking that have nothing to do with our war, with the war for the Union and the abolition of slavery. If I believed we were fighting for any of these things I would do what I could to lead my regiment in revolt. I think I would sooner die fighting these economic causes than I would fighting the Rebels." (Loud and brief applause from the soldiers.)

"Master Applemore has generously offered me a sword, saying that we are fighting together now, that his cause is ours. I am sorry to say that I am not persuaded that this is so. I shall not do him an injustice by presuming to name his cause, but I am sure it is not mine, for he has said so. Therefore, I must regretfully decline the sword." (The soldiers broke into cheers and John raised his hand.) "To you others, to you who I believe are still most of the people here at home, I say for myself, and I say for the 50th, that we shall continue as we began and you can trust us. We will save the Union and we will abolish slavery."

John turned away, not knowing whether he had finished or not, but the cheering stopped him. Starting with the soldiers, it climbed back through more than half the audience, as group after group broke out of the reverent mood into which he had thrown them with his quiet, earnest delivery. As he stood uncertain he saw the sword lying on the table beside him, and the rigid control he had been exercising suddenly broke. He whipped it out of its scabbard, raised it in both hands and would have snapped it across his knee, but behind him Squire Fulton called, "John, my boy, don't," came forward and put his hand on his shoulder. Then he reached round, took the sword from him by the hilt and laid it on the table while John stood looking at him in bewilderment.

This action on the part of Squire Fulton, who was personally beloved by all parties, added the applause of Applemore's supporters to the loud cheering of the rest. Then everybody watched attentively to see what would happen next, and the applause and the cheering rapidly died away. The Squire started speaking to John personally, but in a clear voice that showed he was conscious of the audience that returned to its former, tense quiet.

"John, I knew your great-grandfather, and your grandfather well, and your pa was my nearest friend. I was at your house the night ye were born and stood with him when the mid-wife brought ye out to show to him. Since then ye have become my own son's best friend, and I believe we are as near to kin as it is possible for those to be who are not of the same blood. And all of us of both families, of all generations, have stood and worked together to the same ends, the good of the community irrespective of private gain. That motive, I dare boast, was the only one in the little gathering that until about ten years ago used to meet round the cider barrel at the rear of the Blackwater County Savings Bank. Doubtless many of those here never heard of that gathering. Many more, I daresay, have forgotten the authority it used to wield in the town and the county. Toward the end it lost greatly in influence, and Senator Applemore and others used to refer to us humorously as the 'Backwater Nestors.' There are four or five of us left, all but one here tonight." (A burst of applause for Congressman Samson.)

"Latterly, as we declined in influence we saw a younger group, composed in part of our sons, growing up, as we believed and as the event proved, to carry on the principles of public service which we stood for. That younger group, with, I believe, two or three exceptions, went out in response to the President's first call. Two of them have been killed in battle and three others wounded.

"In going out to preserve the Union ye did not do anything that to me seemed remarkable. Ye were merely keeping faith with us, your fathers, as we tried to keep faith with our fathers and our grandfathers. It would have been surprising only if ye had not acted as ye did, and as ye are continuing to act. Ye have done the bravest thing any of your ancestors have done since the Revolution, only because the opportunity to do it fell to you and not to them. Ye have acted in the spirit of us who reared ye, exactly as if we were one body. Your cause is ours exactly as if we were beside you in the lines.

"Now, about this sword"—here he put his hand on it—"I must tell ye that we of the old 'Backwater Nestors' were the ones who started the subscription for it. We are old men, and when Master Applemore and others offered to join us in the gift we saw a chance of closing the rupture of many years, and we welcomed them. To us it meant peace at last. I do not know whether we were mistaken or not, but since ye think we were I must tell ye that this gift does not come from them but from us who are of your blood and your faith and your cause. The subscriptions for this sword have not yet been paid in, but we, not they, are in charge of the collection. I can promise ye, since ye wish it, that no single person will contribute to this gift who was not for the war from the beginning, and for the cause of the Union which is ours. You must accept it and wear it proudly, knowing it to be the symbol, not only of this present cause, but of the tradition of many generations that have sought to make this a better country under a righteous God, the tradition to which you young men are being faithful. Accept it as a final cementing of those ties with us which are so strong that they can only break with death. As between us we can say with truth, 'It is *our* war.'"

He handed John the sword and John took it and embraced the old Squire as if he had been his father. The audience broke out in a wild roar that held while John dropped the ring over the hook on his saber-belt and stood flushed and grinning with his hand on the hilt. Somewhere in the far corner of the room the thunder of cheering and applause began to throb in rhythm, till throughout the hall two thousand voices merged in the music of the original crusade of the Union:

Mine eyes have seen the glory of the coming of the Lord:
He is trampling out the vintage where the grapes of wrath are stored;
He hath loosed the fateful lightning of His terrible swift sword:
His truth is marching on.
Glory, glory, hallelujah,
Glory, glory, hallelujah,
Glory, glory, hallelujah,
His truth is marching on.

He has sounded forth the trumpet that shall never call retreat;
He is sifting out the hearts of men before His judgment-seat;
Oh! be swift, my soul, to answer him! Be jubilant, my feet!
Our God is marching on.
Glory, glory, hallelujah,
Glory, glory, hallelujah,
Glory, glory, hallelujah,
Our God is marching on.

At the end of the last chorus John whipped out the sword, did a saber salute, and grounded it. The song merged back into wild cheering that held while the soldiers of the 50th jumped up, dragged John from the platform and carried him on their shoulders round the hall.

CHAPTER XCII

ONE THING that had contributed to John's restlessness throughout his leave had been a change in Pru Stark's bearing toward him. Traditionally, her role in his presence had been one of dignified calm, the role of divine beauty brooding upon the travails of mankind: the downcast eyes that forebore to entice him, while rising occasionally in tender sympathy with something he might say; the resignation that accepted his adoration humbly, while sorrowing that it could not be returned in kind. But all through this leave of '63 Pru had seemed unnaturally animated, alternately baiting him by speaking flippantly of matters of concern to him and flirting with him in a silly, diminutive way that was quite as aggravating. In vain he looked for the outward semblance of that image of absolute beauty which he had carried for so long.

On Friday of his first week at home John was going to a supper for officers and non-commissioned officers at the Club, and for the first time during his leave Pru was going to a party with Nat Gadston. A little after five, being already restless and weary of the village, he dropped in at the Liberty, as always expecting at last to find what he now thought of as the old Pru, the Pru of his dreams.

At first it seemed indeed that he had found her. For the informal party that evening she had on a blue figured white taffeta dress, with very wide ruffles all the way up, moderately low neck, small hoops, an enormous bow behind and a smaller one at the bosom—for since Pru had passed twenty-five she had been dressing more youthfully than when she was really young. She was indeed bewitching now and, knowing it, she stood before John quietly with downcast eyes as she used to do. John stepped forward impulsively to kiss her, but she lifted her hand and retreated modestly, fearing to disarrange her bows. "You're lovelier than ever," said John. "By Heaven, I wish I had got out of that supper." Pru colored faintly, sat down, and looked up at him complacently. John stood as he usually did in front of the fireplace.

"Do you like my dress?" said Pru. John nodded. "I would have worn a prettier one if you had condescended to take me this evening," she said, dropping her eyes. "But, alas, it isn't much fun dressing up for you now, when you have that scrumptious uniform and won't even wear it, no matter how hard I try to make you." At this she shook her head sadly and John saw the silly, coquettish mood returning. "Don't be absurd, Pru," he said. "Don't you know I have to wear that thing, or something like it, all the days of the year except when I'm home? I don't think it's unfair to ask that you indulge me that much without complaining about it."

Pru looked down, pouting, and when she spoke her voice had that wheedling, sorrowful, diminutive quality that John was so sick of. "Excuse me if I seemed complaining. I was only hoping that, just to please me, just this once, you would wear that gorgeous, gorgeous uniform at the Wycomb's party tomorrow evening." "Piffle," said John impatiently.

Pru jumped up girlishly and stood before him with her white-gloved hands folded in front of her little bosom, her head cocked on one side, and her eyes looking up at him sideways with the utmost coyness. "Are you always going to be so mean to poor little me?" she asked. John stepped forward again to kiss her, but she ducked her head and he stood back against the fireplace with a shrug that resolved into a smile compounded of friendliness, contempt and malice. Prettily Pru jumped forward two steps to him, reached up, took the lapels of his frock coat in her little hands, and, leaning fairly against him, looked up with a smile calculated to draw the gods from their thrones. But what she said was, "Just this once, just this only, only once, aren't you going to be my big, beautiful, brave soldier boy?"

For a moment's hesitation John's eyes glittered in a strange way that frightened Pru. He gave a gay laugh, picked her up by the middle, swung her face down over one arm, and gave her a good spanking in spite of the hoops that bobbed forward at every whack. Then he set her down on her ma's little sofa, where she remained curled up with her face pressed into her hands against the haircloth back. John returned to the mantel and stood, at first pleased with himself, then startled at what he had done and torn between the desire to face it out and the impulse to go over and kneel by her and beg forgiveness.

Pru, meanwhile, under cover of her abject posture, was suffering a more serious conflict of emotions. In spite of the humiliation, she had actually enjoyed the most delicious feelings in John's manhandling of her. No one in her life had ever treated her so irreverently, and she liked it. She knew she ought to punish John and that would be easy. At the same time, she knew instinctively that with the merest gesture of honest endearment she could really capture him now, really bring him to her feet, and she was greatly worried by the independence he had been showing all through the past week. There wasn't a soul in the family part of the house. The reconciliation might be extremely important and final. They might become really engaged. They might even be married next week because of his going back to the war. She began to wonder if she could find a wedding dress in town that would be tolerable.

She thought of Ike. She had wanted him all these years and couldn't get him. But she could yet get John, and John was now by all odds the catch of the town. She thought of the easy things she could do. She could look around with a sad and suffering smile. She could simply extend one of her hands backwards without looking around at all. It would be very simple. She grew frightened. At the critical moment, she failed. What she did do was to stand up with dignity, go over and sit down in her low rocker, smooth out her ruffles and say, "I see they make boors in the Army."

This use of a word from Mehitabel Gadston's vocabulary merely angered John and dissipated his apologetic and sympathetic impulses. He looked at his watch. Quite unexpectedly to both of them Pru began really to cry. John stepped over to her, took one of her hands from her face, patted it and said, "Truly, I'm sorry, Pru, and I apologize." But it was a conventional apology, such as he might have given any stranger toward whom he had committed some trivial inadvertence. "Oh, it doesn't matter," said Pru, looking up with a sickly smile, ashamed of herself for having cried.

"I hope I didn't—didn't—break anything," said John with an air of artificial concern. "Nothing that can't be mended," said Pru, with a bitter *triple entendre* only part of which John understood, for it was aimed more at herself than at him. "You'd better go now," she added. "You'll be late for your party." "Are you quite all right?" he asked, understanding that she would want to fix herself up before Nat came. "Quite," she said.

John did not wear his dress uniform at the Wycomb's party, or at any other time until the grand pageant and Victory Ball at the end of the Mercy Fair the following week. For a few days he and Pru were constrained and formal with one another. But at the Ford's party on the Monday after the spanking she resumed her kittenish ways. On Thursday when he went to the Stark's for supper before going to the Bostwick's charade party, John had the, for him, remarkably acute suspicion that what she really wanted was another spanking. This occurred to him when they were alone together in the parlor after supper, and it made him smile to himself. "What were you thinking?" demanded Pru, suddenly coming out of her winsome role. "Oh, nothing," said John, "merely that my little indiscretion last Friday didn't matter so much after all." "Don't you dare to try it again," snapped Pru with a stamp of her foot. "Don't worry, I shan't," said John, laughing.

Then came the big doings on Friday night at the end of the Mercy Fair, the night before the soldiers were all to entrain for Washington. Ike took Pru to Washington Hall, and John was to take her home after the Victory Ball. Following John's public snub of Ostrum Applemore, and the other ceremonies, the ball was a gorgeous affair, with a military band and a string orchestra alternating. Ike had filled out John's program and inadvertently sought about half the dances from the wives and daughters of the rich industrialists and financiers. So John had an alternately hot and cold evening, though he made a point of going up to Ostrum Applemore and expressing the hope that he wouldn't take his action personally. To this Ostrum laughed heartily, shook his hand and said he didn't blame him but he'd make him change his tune when he saw the practical support he was going to give him. Whereat John concealed his contempt with difficulty. He remembered what Ike had said about Ostrum turning Republican before long.

Altogether the ball seemed to John an empty and pompous show. The gowns were rich beyond anything he had ever seen in Byzantium, and the whole atmosphere, from decorations to supper, was lavish. Yet everything was scraping and ceremony. You could fairly feel the self-consciousness of Mehitabel Gadston's ladies of the "best people" as they said just the right thing or made just the right gesture with their heads or their fans; and the reverent services the gentlemen crowded to bestow on them evinced not so much courtesy as competitive nervousness for their own standing in the eyes of final authority. There was no spontaneity to it. The old freedom was gone, the gaiety of the old cotillions when the dresses were prettier and less costly, the ladies more sprightly, everybody tuned up with hard cider, Jehu Jones or some such master prompting, and some genius at the accordion, the harmonica or the fiddle. John was glad when at midnight it was over and he went down the great stairway through the admiring crowd with Pru on his arm, she lovely with pride in her "soldier boy." But once they were outside she fell strangely silent. It had been thawing for two days and the Mall was deep in mud. As John handed Pru along the stone crosswalks her arm seemed unusually rigid.

Pru had decided to change her tack with John. She wore a plain, purple silk dress, which, although it admitted her age, gave her that stately beauty which as a girl she had sought but which latterly she had eschewed. When they had taken off their wraps, she sat on the sofa where she had been humiliated, and John accepted the implied invitation to sit beside her. "Well," said John, "I told off Ostrum, didn't I? To tell the truth, I was pleasantly surprised that I got more applause than he did. It shows the town is still right at heart, even if a few rich upstarts are trying to make the war over into a business venture." And he slapped his knee gently in satisfaction.

"John," said Pru, laying her hand on his knee and withdrawing it decorously, "I want to talk to you very seriously." John looked at her intently, finding her utterly desirable, but he made no move, for he liked this return of her old straight-forward manner and wanted to hear what she had to say.

"I'm afraid," she said, "that what I have to say may hurt you, but I would not be honest if I did not say what I think. To begin with, you don't suppose, do you, that all that cheering was for your ideas, your ideals, about the war?" John merely listened. "Not for a minute," Pru went on. "What they were cheering was just what they always cheer, the uniform, the music, the excitement, and especially in your case a real soldier who had been in the real war. There were a few, of course, who understood what you said and cheered for it, just as there were a few who understood what Mr. Applemore said and cheered for that. But what they most applauded was a real, live colonel who had been in battles."

"That's not true of the fellows in the regiment," said John sourly.

"Perhaps not," said Pru. "I am speaking of the village, and the village is more important because it will be where you live long after the regiment is forgotten. So long as the village can see soldiers and hear bands and patriotic speeches it will shout its head off, and it will shout just as much for what you call Mr. Applemore's war as it will for what you call your war." "I don't believe it," said John, but his thoughts returned to Ike's talk of two nights before, and he felt depressed.

"What I really want to say," Pru continued, "is that I think you are making a very serious mistake in alienating Mr. Applemore and the people he represents. He and Mr. Gadston and Ike are the leading men in town now, and Mrs. Gadston is undoubtedly the leader of society. It is true Ike is considered queer, and he has hurt himself some by being an open atheist. But a good many people agree with him about the war, if only they had the courage to admit it, and they admire the way he goes about his own business, merely making what he can out of the war, the way any smart man should out of any opportunity that comes his way."

At this John curled his lip under his mustache, and his eyes blackened, but he continued to listen. "What the people in the village respect now, John, is the man who can rub two pennies together and make them stick. It is true they don't like Mr. Grabbot because he is surly and selfish and won't speak to anybody. But if a man is only pleasant and knows how to get around people the way Ike does and Mr. Applemore and Mr. Gadston, then they honor him for making money because it is what they all would like to do if they could. The rich men run the village now, John, and they're going to do what they like with it.

"Now, what all this comes to is that you have a position to maintain in this town, but I am afraid it isn't due to what you think it is. It isn't due to your education and your high ideas. It isn't due any more to your being a Lathrop, at least not a Lathrop of Lathrop Hollow. At the moment it is due to your being a soldier who has been promoted and all that. But in the long run it is due to your being Ike Lathrop's brother, the brother of one of the three most respected men in town. For Ike's sake if not for your own, you should stop opposing everything he stands for. You should be grateful that Mr. Applemore and the rest are supporting you in——"

"Please stop," interrupted John. Abruptly he rose and swung on his cape. He unbuttoned his blouse, stuck his hand in his breast pocket, drew out the ambrotype of Pru he had carried nearly two years, and laid it on the mantel. "Good-by," he said, bowed, and went downstairs and out of the tavern, closing the door softly behind him.

For a long time Pru stared straight in front of her. She had decided to make this issue clear, and if the result were satisfactory she would seize the next chance to yield to the not very deep attraction John had had for her since he came back. She smiled to herself a little bitterly. She presumed she had lost John for good, but at the same time she enjoyed the sensation of having spoken honestly. And besides . . . She began to wonder what the effect of this break would be on Ike. After years of hesitation she had at last crossed her Rubicon.

Four evenings later, immediately upon his arrival in Washington, John went to the "elegant place" for officers only, and with feelings so mixed as almost to thwart his purpose, ran into Buffalo Bertha, who had been the companion of the lovely little burlesque girl on that train ages ago in '60. For their several diplomatic purposes neither he nor Bertha mentioned her that evening, nor through the night. But in the early morning when John, having to report at reveille, was dressing by lamplight in Bertha's luxurious room, she sat up in bed, clasped her hands around her knees and said, "Colonel, ain't ye concerned fer news of somebody?"

John stopped pulling on his boot and looked up at her. "Very much concerned," he said. "I wanted to ask you——"

Bertha rolled over on her big bed, took a little envelope from a drawer in the stand and handed it to him. It was sealed with a crest and inscribed to John Lathrop, Esq., Byzantium Falls, New York, in a small, cultivated hand. "She didn't want I should post it," said Bertha, "until I'd tried to find ye and hand it to ye personal. She was afraid it might bother ye."

John looked hard at Bertha. "Dead?" he whispered. Bertha nodded. "Ran out past the sentry and jumped off the Long Bridge the night after she wrote that to ye. Poor child! She was sick bad. Wan't no help fer her."

John read:

Washington
May 5, 1861

My dear Mr. Lathrop,

Perhaps you will remember that the date on this is an anniversary for you and me, a greatly treasured one for me.

Virginia has seceded and my place is across the Potomac, but this sorry state of affairs only serves to remind me how worse than useless I would be to my people, or to anybody.

You may wonder how I know your name. I got it from your wallet.

I must write you this, even though you never receive it. You have been the last thing I have loved in this world, you and, in a different way, Buffalo Bertha. I was not made to exist without love.

You said you fell in love with me and I believed it. I still believe it. I know you have kept your promise to remember me for a year or two. It is only a year now, but it seems an eternity. You may forget me now. But I want you to know that for a year you brought happiness to a life that otherwise was quite wretched, entirely through its own fault.

It is strange that one of the last sentiments left me is pride, pride in a name to which I no longer have the slightest claim. I want to sign this to you in my own name, which I relinquished. Not even dear Bertha knows it, and she must not, for the sake of others. I trust you, of course. My oldest brother looks like you. I am proud to sign my true name to you, because I believe that if we had met under other circumstances I would have been your bride. And I believe, my true love, that we shall meet again.

Oh, forgive me.

Devotedly,

Anne Stoneweather

The surname was of one of the leading families of Virginia. John had known Guy Stoneweather well, at Yale. He remembered the Rebel colonel he had seen dead on Malvern Hill, with his face turned toward him. Yes, they had looked alike.

John found that Ike had been right in his persistent predictions of twelve years. Like little Anne, Bertha, in her different, hard, coarse-complexioned way, was of the same physical stamp as Pru. The old, excruciating dream of Pru vanished from his mind. When he thought of her now, it was in a new and quite unromantic fashion. She was almost thirty, near the point where she would be fair game. How she would squeal and squirm! With amusement John would sometimes speculate on the possibility, when he was in bed with Bertha, during the month he remained in Washington.

But while the experience with Bertha served to dethrone Pru from her seat on the hill of John's idealism, it was the little burlesque girl who replaced her there. And from that time she reigned there as long as he lived, whatever his other relationships, a tender and pure image, not torturing him as Pru had done but strengthening him, keeping his faith in the perfectability of mankind.

Soon after he returned to Washington John called on Solon Samson and reported that the Kamargo Woollen Mill was making shoddy. While there he learned for the first time that Tavie was seeking a transfer from the West to one of the hospitals in the capital. The news gave him a start of something like fear.

CHAPTER XCIII

IN THE spring of '63 the Army of the Potomac was a trained machine. It was still in fact the old volunteer army, for the new drafted quotas were not·to arrive till July; but it was a veteran volunteer army, with all the wisdom and stability of professional soldiers. The first, crusading spirit, the determination on early victory, all that had been laid to rest after Malvern Hill. There was but little consciousness left even of the causes of the war. To be killed, to be wounded, to advance, to retreat, that was the real day's work and sufficient to the day. Idealism was an immediate thing, to do your job a little better than your neighbor, your company a little better than the neighboring company, your regiment, brigade and corps than the neighboring regiment, brigade and corps. The only other realities were your feet, the commissary, the hope of cigars, whisky, women and a furlough. Victory and defeat—those were words for the newspapers and the generals. This was a veteran army, with no "spirit" but the quiet, fatalistic determination of the Yankee civilization that sent it out. As nearly as is humanly possible, the seven corps of the Army of the Potomac in the spring of '63 were so many enormous and reliable chess men, dependent for their behavior upon nothing inherently unpredictable, but solely upon the decisions of their commanders in relation to the decisions of the enemy.

On April twenty-seventh, Fighting Joe Hooker put this Army in motion from Fredericksburg, and five days later at Chancellorsville, its right flank was rolled up like a carpet through the decision of Generals Jackson and Lee operating upon the indecision of Generals Hooker and Howard. From that chessboard it retired well, unbroken, undiscouraged, and waited for what next should be asked of it. In that battle the 50th New York was but lightly engaged, though Captain Medad VanSanford of Company C got a piece of his skull nicked out by a minie ball, and was evacuated to Washington.

A month later this grim army found itself once more on the move, now northward and westward, not knowing nor caring whither it was being led. As always, the men took not the slightest interest in the long familiar oak scrub and gray or red baked soil of the worn-out tobacco land of eastern Virginia, but marched with the slouching, strength-saving shuffle of veterans, their heads hung forward, one eye instinctively watching the road for stones that meant foot-bruises.

But when they had passed by the scenes of their former defeats near Manassas and Centerville and came into a country where the hills had real grass on them and there were green forests of real trees, something like animation began to ripple in little gusts up and down those eight-and nine-mile corps columns. The cynical jokes, the exchanges of discourtesies between regiments and with the natives they passed, became more frequent, and it was not unknown during the morning marches for regiments to sing a little as they used to do.

Then, after they crossed the Potomac at Edward's Ferry and knew they were in Maryland, they began to glance at the landscape and each other with quick, inquiring looks, and their shuffle livened into something approaching the eager tread of green troops. Nobody thought of Maryland as northern soil, yet it was technically so. Now every boy in the ranks knew that, for the second time in the War, Lee was trying to invade the North, and that they were either chasing him or marching to head him off. Round every campfire in that Army of ninety thousand the perennial Nestors became voluble in their opinions. "Looks like the Old Fox ain't learnt his lesson t' Antietam." "Got it straight from my brother who's the Colonel's orderly we're a-closin' in on Lee and he's likely to surrender without a fight." "Well, fellers, I cal-late there's t' be no mistake about it this time." Every one of those ninety thousand boys knew there would indeed be no mistake about it this time. Something like the early crusading spirit began to tremble through those seasoned, cynical troops. The Rebs 'd be danged sorry fer what they were up to, "the consarned, yippin' little varmints."

The 50th New York was now part of Weed's 3d Brigade of Ayer's 2d Division of the 5th Corps, the Corps having been under the command of General Meade since Fredericksburg. On June twenty-eighth, when the bulk of the Army was in the vicinity of Frederick, Maryland, Fighting Joe Hooker resigned and the command was given to General Meade, General Sykes succeeding him in command of the 5th Corps. With the exception of a few officers like John who had felt Meade's quiet power, that modest general was unknown in the Army. Mostly, the soldiers still dreamed of McClellan. The change of commanders gave the Army nothing because of Meade himself. Yet everybody knew that Fighting Joe had been licked, and any change, even thus in mid-stream, was sure to have a good effect on the men. As always, the veterans took the appointment of any new commander, whether of company or higher, as a challenge to their prowess. They would show him, by God, how real soldiers behaved!

On the twenty-ninth something happened to the Army more important for its spirit than a change of Commander. On that day it spread out in a great fan northward and northeastward from Frederick, Buford's cavalry and the 1st, 11th and 3d Corps toward a place called Emmitsburg, the 12th and 2d Corps and Army Headquarters toward Taneytown, the 5th Corps toward a hamlet called Union Mills, and the 6th Corps still farther eastward toward Manchester. And on every one of those roads the troops underwent the same change.

They came into country that was not only green, it was dairy country, where there were fields of timothy, wheat and barley, and fat herds of cattle grazing in rich pastures. The fences were not of stone, but their rails were thriftily kept. The barns were bigger than Yankee barns and they had an unfamiliar overhang on one side, but they were dairy and hay barns and they were painted red. The houses were different in detail from Yankee houses and they were painted every color but white, but they were neat all the same and had window boxes of geraniums and roses. After the shacks of eastern Virginia, they were farmhouses where human beings could live. Not only that, but many of them now began to show a diminutive Old Glory strung from a window or between trees on the lawn, and often the farmers in the fields would lean on their rakes to swing their hats and cheer as the soldiers tramped by.

On the night of June thirtieth, the 5th Corps camped at Union Mills on Pipe Creek. After supper John walked down to the big brick mill that gave the place its name, and for half an hour he stood by a gigantic sycamore tree talking with the miller, a Mr. Shriver, who, but for a faint flattening in some of his syllables, might have hailed from anywhere back in the hills at home. He took out a flask of raw cider brandy from under his coat-tails and insisted that John take a long swig to Abe Lincoln and the Union. He said it was only five miles from here to the Pennsylvania line. This intelligence was already running through the Corps, so that the twilit hills that cupped the mill were already singing, and later, at tattoo, John had to go round to shoo the boys of the 50th away from their campfires to whatever strip of ground each had chosen to sleep on under the bright stars.

During the night the regiment got its first bundle of post in two weeks. After breakfast at sunrise, July first, just as the general was sounding to form to resume the march northward, John's negro servant brought him, along with his roan mount, a letter from Tavie. He stuck it in his belt and sat his horse beside Colonel "Pat" Donahoe while the march order blew, and the 50th, following a battery of artillery that was now attached to the Brigade, swung out into the Hanover Pike at a faster quick-step than usual. All the soldiers now had the red maltese cross of the 5th Corps sewn on their forage caps. Today it was John's turn to bring up the rear, and he took his place there, holding his horse to a walk in the grass beside the regimental mule, driven by a contraband and buried from ears to tail to hoofs in officers' baggage and Headquarters' equipment.

The sun was already up, and it gave promise of being another balmy summer day, warm but not sultry, the sun gold without glare. The sky was fading from purple to clear, light blue, with peaceful, monumental white clouds hanging motionless, like the suspended smoke of giant mortars whose thunder had been absorbed into silence before the memory of man. The road, mostly shaded under a vault of heavy maples, went straight up and down big, fertile hills that reminded John of Blackwater County. The first of these began at once, and as the column was crawling up it John took out Tavie's letter and tore it open with something like irritation.

The letter was posted from Washington, and, as John inferred from the postmark before he opened it, it said that she had got her assignment there. She was to be assistant to the woman in charge of nurses at the Armory Square Hospital—the place where John hoped he'd be evacuated if he got badly hit—and she described its virtues at length, each ward a separate building and very comfortable with iron beds and all conveniences.

John looked up and smiled at his own·hypocrisy. Feeling more friendly toward Tavie than toward any girl he knew, and having urged her for two years to get a position in Washington, he now wished she were not there! When he got back to the capital he wanted to see Buffalo Bertha, and he felt bored at the prospect of confronting Tavie's earnestness and essential purity. He had a lively thought of how much fun and how absurd it would be to climb into bed with Tavie, how they would both laugh about it. However friendly they might be on other terms, there was certainly nothing of that between them. But after all, he concluded, he'd be all-fired glad to have Tave take care of him if he "got a ride"—that is, in an ambulance. He glanced at the column that was still leaning forward up the hill, under its sixty pounds per man of arms, ammunition, knapsack, haversack, canteen and their contents. If anything, the men were crowding each other a little. Even the regimental mule and the little squad of negro servants at the tail of the column were well closed up. John returned to Tavie's letter.

As usual in the letters of people in the service, the somber news was mentioned last and with sharp brevity. Tavie had gone to see Medad in hospital. John read her news, stuck the letter in his belt and cantered forward to Company C that was leading the regiment and was just now spilling up over the top of the hill. As he overtook it he motioned to Jabe Munson and George Fulton, now in command of the Company, both marching at the rear. When they had run out to John's horse and saluted he leaned down and said, "Medad's dead."

They merely looked at each other in an accustomed, quiet, hard way. Their emotion was not civilian emotion, nothing about the passing of another member of the Gang, very little thought of "poor old Medad" or of poor old Judge and Mistress VanSanford who had now lost two of their three boys, Fred being hopelessly idiotic. Their feelings were the simple ones of soldiers. The Reb had got one of their close comrades, and every Reb they could draw a bead on would pay. George Fulton, in one of his typical lapses from military ceremony, ran midway up the company, cupped his hands and called softly to the fifty-one men now in Company C. "Fellows," he said, "Medad's dead." Nobody made any comment or turned an eye, but the step of the company quickened visibly. John rode back to his post, took out his revolver and tried the action. It had jammed at Chancellorsville.

For two hours the Corps marched northward with frequent halts on the hilly road for the benefit of the artillery, scattered through the column, and the mule-drawn supply wagons at the rear. They passed half a dozen prosperous farms, the houses painted green or yellow, the big barns red. In the front yards of most of them the stars and stripes were displayed, and at some of them women came out on the front porch, holding their babies, to watch them go by. Most of the way the trees and shrubbery were so thick along the rail fences that the soldiers caught only fleeting glimpses through them of vistas of golden wheat and stubble fields against a background of intensely green, wooded hills. Twice they came out upon magnificent, almost mountainous panoramas of gold and green spread far below them. During the march the color of the roadway changed. Down in Virginia it had been bone gray. Through most of Maryland it had been red. Around Union Mills it was purple. Now it was paling into brown and dark gray, the color of good, rich, familiar ground. In the greenery over and around the road cardinals, thrashers and vireos sang continuously.

From the second hilltop with a panorama they dropped down into a wide valley and proceeded for a level stretch through woods on both sides. John rode absently, his eyes mostly on the road or his horse's ears, his thoughts on Tavie and his mistress. Suddenly he came out of reverie with a faint start, something like the sense of Rebs in the offing, something communicated from his regiment marching along in front of him. The men were growing talkative, and somewhere ahead, in the artillery perhaps, or in the leading infantry regiment, there was cheering.

As John looked up he was emerging from the woods into open, sunny farmland, and the road went up a gentle slope to the near horizon from beyond which the cheering was rising. Instead of fences, the road now ran between stone walls. Instead of the thick trees and shrubs that had made it an arcade before, there were here but half a dozen trees all the way to the hilltop and they were whopping, feather-duster elms! On both sides of the road the stone walls checkerboarded the slope into open golden wheatfields, green pastures where cattle were drowsing under nut trees, and rich meadows bright with buckeye daisies and devil's paintbrush and musical with bobolinks fluttering and jingling over them. From the tall grass across the wall from John a real, northern meadowlark sang, rose and flew away chattering.

He felt a catch in his throat. Something like a strong, cool wind was blowing down the length of that five-mile column. There was yet no shouting among the near troops, but the officers were stepping out beside the column, waving their hats or their swords to each other, and John joined in this exchange of greetings. Everybody understood, and at first it was too deep for shouting. To every boy in that column, whether he came from New England, New York, Pennsylvania, or Michigan, that simple summer landscape with its stone walls and its elms meant the same thing. God help the Rebs now!

John touched his horse with his spurs, galloped up to the head of the regiment, saluted Pat Donahoe and asked if he should ride up to the hilltop to see what the rumpus was about. It might be General Sykes, or even General Meade. As always when they were together, the men all looked at their young colonel and lieutenant-colonel with affectionate eagerness. John being six inches taller than Pat, either afoot or horseback, the men called them David and Goliath, and were ready to follow either of them through hell. Donahoe beamed at John out of his straight, classic

features and said, "Go ahead, John, if you're o' mind to." John saluted Pat
and the colors, touched his horse and started up the half-mile slope at a run.

As he overtook Hazlett's Battery of the 5th U. S. Field Artillery the
slope became steeper, and he let his horse lapse into an extended trot
as he passed the two hundred-and-fifty-yard-long battery, the big axles
of the guns, caissons and limbers creaking and thumping to the acci-
dents of the road, the iron tires and the horses' hoofs striking sparks on
the stones. The artillerymen, most blasé of soldiers, sat slouching on their
limbers and caissons, or rode like hunched-up dummies on the nigh horses
of their three-pair teams, many of them side-saddle for change of posture, all
swaying forward and back like part of their animals, giving them no more
than an inaudible cluck as they leaned into their collars for the grade,
their riders showing no sign of separate, human existence except occasionally to spit tobacco juice out of the corners of their mouths without
turning their heads.

John reached the top of the hill that was level for thirty rods before
it dropped off again. In spite of the cheering and singing beyond the
drop, and in spite of two years in the Army, John was struck by the
magnificent view, and for a moment he let his horse down to a walk.
In one sweep he could see, not only the 2d Division but the whole 5th
Corps, like a single organism five miles long and two wide, undulating
slowly over the earth on its myriad of unseen, individually busy feet.
Northward to the hazy limit of sight, like the sensitive tentacles of the
blind, crawling Corps, he could see little detachments of the independent
cavalry playing between the clumps of woods, visible only by their puffs
of dust, or like shadows of bird-flocks scurrying over the pastures and
fields. Two miles westward through openings in the woodlots he could
see without field glasses long sections of the other half of the Corps on
its parallel road, the whole column marked by the long, gray snake of
its dust cloud that sometimes let through the morning sun to glint on
its muskets by whole regiments, on the "brass Napoleons" of its artillery,
on the specks of its cavalry guidons like bobbing primroses, on its artillery standards like buttercups, on the occasional unfurling flash of its
colors. Three miles ahead marched the advance guard of his own column, then a mile of open road, and the solid main body, blue beneath
its dust: Corps Headquarters; Division Headquarters; the 2d Brigade;
the leading regiment of John's own 3d Brigade; the Battery of the 5th
Field Artillery disappearing down into the narrow, hidden, near valley;
then, stretching backward two miles on the straight road in the valley
behind, the rest of John's own Brigade; the carts of the Engineer Regi-

ment; the white, divisional supply wagons; the little black ambulances with the yellow guidons of the hospital corps; the dark masses of the Corps Artillery with its siege guns and howitzers; and the long column of the rear guard, the 3d Division, the Pennsylvania Reserves.

John had never before seen a whole corps in motion, a whole, self-contained army in itself, five miles of soldiers on each of two roads so near together the two halves could see each other. He knew that somewhere within reach of the cavalry six other such units were moving similarly, all making together a single, controlled body that was the Army of the Potomac. It gave him a feeling of power, such as he had not known since he first heard the guns at Mechanicsville.

The battery and forge wagons at the rear of the artillery were now passing John, and his own Regiment was coming up into sight. He galloped ahead to the drop of the hill whence the roar of cheering and singing was rising and where the blasé artillerymen, as they dipped out of sight, came successively alive, the drivers and cannoneers of each carriage in turn standing up in their stirrups or on their foot-boards to crane their necks to look at something ahead and below, then waving their caps and shouting. When John reached the drop, he first saw in the hollow a white farmhouse—the first white one he had seen!—with its red barn beyond, its grove of elms, and its flower-beds glowing in the sun. The friendly farmer was at his gate, waving to the artillerymen as they passed, but they hardly noticed him for cheering and pointing at something where the singing began and roared off over the little rise beyond and so away into the long, panoramic distance. John cantered down the slope, cut through the artillery, saw what it was, rode round it and halted his horse, with a swelling sensation in his chest. It was a stone post about a yard high, bearing on one side the boldly cut word "Maryland" and on the other "Pennsylvania."

John tried to sing with the artillery as they lumbered by, but they were notoriously the worst singers in the Army. The 50th, now cheering, was coming down the hill, and as they approached John dismounted and, looking at them, patted the stone with one hand and pointed to it with the other. Donahoe rose in his stirrups and, turning, called the regiment sharply to attention. When they fell silent he gave them "Eyes Right," then, as he was passing the marker, he himself opened the song, and the regiment in step took it up in perfect concert so that it rolled forward up into Pennsylvania, back over the hill through the Brigade, and finally clear back through the Engineers, the Supply and into the 3d Division.

For five minutes three miles of soldiers were shouting together the song
of the original crusade for the Union:

Glory, glory, hallelujah,
Glory, glory, hallelujah,
Glory, glory, hallelujah,
His soul is marching on.

John resumed his place at the rear of the regiment and for fifteen
minutes more the Brigade went singing on. A great change had come
over Sykes 5th Corps, the first great change since the retreat from Malvern Hill, when they finally learned that war was not flags and parades
and victory, but mud and disease and filth and retreat and individual
helplessness. Twenty miles to the east the same change was coming over
Sedgewick's 6th Corps at a place called Manchester, and ten miles to
the west over Hancock's 2d Corps and Slocum's 12th Corps at a place
called Taneytown, and ten miles farther west over Sickles's 3d Corps at
a place called Emmitsburg; and a little north of that over Howard's 11th
Corps on the way to a place called Gettysburg; and still farther north
over Reynold's 1st Corps making a forced march to this same Gettysburg; and just west of that village over Buford's cavalry which at that
moment was beginning one of the heroic stands of the war against overwhelming odds, holding off Heth's Rebel Division until Reynolds should
arrive.

All through Meade's Army a change had occurred in the last few days.
In the hearts of 90,000 boys the spirit of the first crusade awoke from its
year's sleep. It was still a veteran army whose units would act in concert
as only veteran troops could do. But beneath that, it was the old volunteer army again, determined under its discipline to do a little more than
could be expected of it, once more certain of victory as it had been in
the beginning, once more eager to die for its civilization that for two centuries had been striving to create a perfect world.

And north of this old Army of the Potomac on this first of July '63, from
Chambersburg, from Carlisle and York, the Rebel Army of Northern
Virginia was likewise concentrating on Gettysburg, an army equally veteran, equally alive with the spirit of its civilization, equally fighting for
its homes and, fresh from Chancellorsville, equally certain of victory. As
the two most powerful living forces then on the earth, each unopposable
except by the other, those two great armies moved toward each other,
the one bearing the spiritual restlessness of man that must move forward

toward the dream of a better condition, the other bearing the rational conservatism of man that is content to rest in a condition already achieved; the internal struggle of every nation; the internal struggle of every man.

Equal in numbers, almost equal in equipment, equal in training, equal in spirit of victory, these two great armies crawled toward each other, the result of their meeting to depend in no wise on a difference in the troops, but on the chessboard decisions of their generals. Already one of these decisions had been made. Though without contemplation of immediate battle, Lee had ordered a concentration of his corps at this place called Gettysburg where the map showed a meeting of eleven roads. Already Hancock, sent by Meade, was on his way thither from Taneytown, riding in an ambulance in order to study the maps preparatory to making the second great decision, the counter decision to Lee's.

At noon the halt sounded back through the 5th Corps. John as usual rode forward to C Company, dismounted, gave his horse to his servant who ran up, and lounged in the grass under a maple tree with George and 2d Lieutenant Henry Daw. Regimental details were already going out in search of wood and water, and 526 men were kindling their little fires along the roadside. Jabe joined George and Henry, and for a minute or two nobody seemed to have anything to say. Colonel Donahoe and Major Johnson came by together and stopped. Jabe started to get up, and Donahoe said, "Keep your seat, Sergeant. May we sit down, Fulton?"

There were startling contrasts between the six men there beside the road. Long, slender John with his eagle beak, wide mustache and Vandyke beard, lying back full length with his campaign hat off and his eyes closed. Little Henry Daw, sitting up, very pale and intense, being barely twenty, silkily bearded, an infantile and slimmer replica of his humorless, doctor father. Big, broad-shouldered Jabe sprawled out on one elbow, his cap as usual stuck on as if glued to one side of his head, smoking a cigar, gigantic in any posture with his enormous, fleshy, red-veined face and his full beard which he nowadays shortened occasionally with horseclippers. Dark, smiling Major Johnson, lanky and always seeming a trifle awkward with his big bones. Blond little Donahoe with his pale, classical nose, forehead and cheeks, his thin but mobile lips under his drooping mustache, and his spotless uniform. George Fulton with his black eyes, soft, black beard and his uniform as spotless as the Colonel's but negligently worn, both his blouse and his waistcoat now open, his hat off and his collar unbuttoned.

George told his negro boy to bring him that bottle of Taylor's. When it came he uncorked it and handed it first to the Colonel who flourished it with a toast, "To Pennsylvania and good whisky." Which was echoed with variations and such zest as the bottle went round that only half of its contents got back to George. This loosened the tongues. "I feel like a recruit," said John, having lapsed back on the ground and closed his eyes again, "ready to die for the Union." Henry Daw glanced at him impatiently, as if marvelling that he could speak irreverently of so sacred a topic. "So do I," said Johnson. "Me, too," said George. "Men in good shape, Sergeant?" asked the Colonel. "Yes, sir," said Jabe. "First time in a year I hain't heard a growl all day. All seem keyed up proper, like the early days when we figgered we were to enter Richmond every time we went on patrol." The Colonel's mouth curved in his gentle smile. "Beats all," he said, "what that state line did for us." "It's a wonder," said Johnson, "General Ayres was able to keep us down to so slow a pace. Must be saving us for something." "Any news, Colonel?" asked John improperly. "No," said Donahoe. "From the map my guess would be that we're as far north as anybody." "Maybe we're to establish contact," said George. "That means a big rumpus." "I hope so," said Henry Daw. Presently the officers' servants arrived with soup and coffee, and Jabe got up to go fetch his own from one of the little fires.

And just then, while the 5th Corps was indolently consuming its soup and hardtack and coffee, the second great decision of the generals went into effect. Hancock had reached Gettysburg, finding the 1st Corps hotly engaged west of the town, Reynolds and Buford dead and Doubleday in command, Howard's 11th Corps going into action on the right of the 1st, just in time to meet Ewell's Rebel divisions that were arriving rapidly from the north. Knowing no more Yankee troops would arrive for many hours, Hancock selected Cemetery Hill for the 1st and 11th to retire on if outnumbered and flanked, and he posted there all the artillery not already in action. Then he reconnoitered the fish-hook ridge from Culp's Hill to Round Top and sent a dispatch rider to Meade in Taneytown, recommending that the Army be ordered up and battle offered on this line. At one o'clock Meade got Hancock's decision and immediately accepted it. Dispatch riders galloped across to Emmitsburg after Sickles's 3d Corps which he had already started for Gettysburg. From Taneytown the 2nd and 12th Corps were put in motion for the concentration point, and dispatch riders clattered out eastward with orders for the 5th and 6th.

While these orders were still far off the 5th Corps finished its dinner, and at two-thirty resumed its leisurely march, so leisurely that the over-eager infantry jammed up and reduced the length of the column by a quarter.

At four o'clock John heard cheering ahead, and half an hour later the 50th marched into Hanover where for the first time in a campaign a whole village was turned out to meet them, cheering and hand-clapping rippling continuously up and down the street that was packed with people, others leaning from windows in houses and business blocks, and the stars and stripes waving everywhere. This indeed was like home, and John smiled and saluted, catching the eye of girl after girl. As he rode he was thinking that the people of the North were all right. What did these folks care about money and factories? Where now were Ike and his money-grubbers, and Pru and her Mehitabel Gadstons?

As John was passing through the center of the town a dusty dispatch rider clattered up from the rear, halted in the street and shouted, "Where's Corps Headquarters?" "Here," yelled a military police in front of a hotel. The cavalryman dismounted and ran for the door, his trained horse following at a sedate walk.

Four hours later the 5th Corps was again on the road, under forced march orders for Gettysburg. It was a fine night for marching, a live, ghostly night with a cloudless moon laying snowy high lights on the black tree masses and stone walls, and sheets of silver over the fields of ripened wheat. About midnight there was a halt when the 50th was in Bonneauville. For an hour the sound of the 5th Corps was the munching of 2000 horses and mules in the grass by the roadside, the buzz of eight miles of boys sleeping in the moonlight, the whir of night wind through the trees, and where John and Donahoe and Johnson slept on the steps of Bonneauville church, the soft tapping of a wind-blown rope in the belfry above them.

CHAPTER XCIV

D A W N at Gettysburg, July 2, '63. Another clear blue and white summer day. The cattle out in the pastures between Cemetery Ridge and Seminary Ridge, almost parallel, a mile more or less apart, the village spreading between their northern ends. From the village the five-mile fish-hook Yankee position, running two ways: the bend curving back eastward two miles round Cemetery Hill to the barb at Culp's Hill; the shank running straight south three miles on Cemetery Ridge to the eye of the fish-hook at the Round Tops, the left-flank of the Yankee position. Dawn, the sun striking first on the wooded crest of Big Round Top, commanding the view of the line northward but not commanding the line, too high, too steep to get field-guns up to the summit. Dawn, the sun striking next on the crest of Little Round Top, a hundred feet lower, symmetrical giant rock-pile scrubbily wooded, commanding the view of the line and also commanding the line, not too high, not too steep to haul field-guns up to its summit. Dawn. Still in twilight, a herd of steers grazing the soggy glen between Little Round Top and the Devil's Den, a lower knoll of titanic boulders five hundred yards in front of it. Sunrise. The farmers already out cutting their wheat in the golden acres between Cemetery Ridge and Seminary Ridge. They are troubled. Too many soldiers trespassing, trampling the wheat. There was a battle yesterday west of town and thousands of bushels ruined. Who knows? They might fight in my wheatfield yet. Sunrise. Another blue and white summer day. Thousands of bobolinks jingling.

Slow, mammoth activity. Big, white, rainless clouds bulging slowly into the sky. Big army corps moving slowly, the gigantic chess pieces advancing under the hands of the generals. Ten, twenty . . . forty, fifty . . . seventy, eighty thousand Yankee boys moving in in the form of veteran chess pieces. Ten, twenty . . . forty, fifty . . . seventy, eighty thousand Rebel boys moving in in the form of veteran chess pieces. The Northern dream of two centuries and a half taking visible form, the dream of a civilization to make a better world moving in to its trial with the Southern fact, the fact of a civilization content with the present.

They say the fact or the dream will be ended here. They say that if Lee wins here England will recognize and support the Confederacy. They say that if Meade wins, the strongest chess piece of all, starvation, will move henceforth in the hands of the Yankee generals. They say the struggle of history will end here, that the fact or the dream henceforth will prevail forever. Are there any other forces gathering over the land? Behind the skyline of the future any unseen armies waiting to attack the victor in the coming battle?

At Gettysburg only the slow, mammoth activity of summer clouds and army corps moving into position. The chess pieces of dream and of fact advancing under the hands of the generals. No fate, no forces of history to determine this game here. Just the generals moving their veteran pieces, equal in numbers, equal in equipment, equal in spirit of victory: the six huge Yankee pieces—Newton, Hancock, Sickles, Sykes (Sedgewick is still far away on his famous march from Manchester), Howard, Slocum; the three huge Rebel pieces—Longstreet, Hill, Ewell (a Rebel corps is the equal of two Yankee corps in numbers). Yesterday Lee moved first to concentrate at Gettysburg, not to fight there. Next, Hancock's decision yesterday, turned to a move by Meade, to concentrate at Gettysburg and to fight on the five-mile fish-hook position, the left at the Round Tops. The first bloody exchange of pawns yesterday, and Meade driven back to the prepared line. No move in the game since. Only the gigantic posting of corps as decided. Lee in the Seminary directing the game. Meade in the cabin on the Taneytown Road, behind Cemetery Ridge, directing the game.

Seven o'clock by the bells of Gettysburg. Only the *rat-t-t-tat* of patrols, the low rumble of army corps moving into the lines. Facing each other, hidden along the opposing ridges, the eyes of thousands of boys watch two vultures drifting high in the sunlight. Must be some farmer's old cow is dead. On Cemetery Ridge the boys from New England are at home with the stone walls. They are mending them, building others. They are stone beavers.

Eight o'clock by the bells of Gettysburg. It is going to be hotter than yesterday. Not a shot all along that five-mile line from Culp's Hill to Little Round Top. The outposts from both ridges are out and in touch and agreed on their stations. Between them the calls of veteran enemies, knowing their code—"Hi, Yank, have ye got any wahtuh?"— "Hi, Reb, have ye got any baccy?"

Nine o'clock by the bells of Gettysburg. *Lee moves.* Ewell will attack the Yankees' right at Culp's Hill for a strong diversion. For the main attack Longstreet will circle the Yankee left and surprise it and roll up the flank like a carpet. Longstreet starts Generals Hood's and McLaws's Divisions on the long wheel of three miles under cover of woods. Two brigades from Hill's Corps follow to support them. It will take some hours for the 18,000 men and fifty-seven guns to get into the new position.

Ten o'clock—eleven o'clock—noon, by the bells of Gettysburg. On the five-mile, fish-hook Yankee line from Culp's Hill to the left at Little Round Top, not a shot. Eighty thousand boys sleeping, playing poker on blouses spread behind stone walls, chewing tobacco and spitting across the wall toward the Rebs, munching their late breakfasts or early dinners of individual rations. Behind the ridge, the creaking of wagons and artillery carriages, the reserve artillery parking on picket lines; the clatter of aides, orderlies, details marching, picking reserve entrenchments; traffic of drummer-boys, musician-litter-bearers, war correspondents, civilians with passes, sutlers; on the Baltimore Pike, the thumping and hammering of field hospitals raising their tents for yesterday's toll and heavier toll expected; the hundreds of little black, four-patient Rucker ambulance carts with the beautiful, soothing springs, lining up into park and unhitching. Some already have trotted off with yesterday's freight. It is seventy-nine miles to Washington.

One o'clock by the bells of Gettysburg. General Sickles on the Yankee left believes his Corps cannot hold his mile of difficult line and at the same time stand off a flank attack against Little Round Top. But by moving out to that rocky diagonal ridge facing half left from the Devil's Den out to a peach orchard, he thinks he could stand off a flank attack and protect the main line behind him. A strong reconnaissance party makes contact with a Rebel column moving out to the left in the woods— *Rat-t-t-tat-t-t-tat*—it reports the column to Sickles.

Two o'clock by the bells of Gettysburg. *Sickles moves.* His Corps swings like a mile-long gate half-opening out to the left, the pivot not Little Round Top but the Devil's Den five hundred yards in front of it. Little Round Top, commanding Sickles's new line and the main Yankee line on the Ridge northward, Little Round Top is left untenanted.

Two-thirty. In the soggy pasture between Little Round Top and the Devil's Den the herd of horned steers is huddled for shade under saplings. Its owner is harvesting fiercely in the quarter-mile-square wheatfield farther out behind the Devil's Den Ridge—already Sickles's Corps in its swing is trampling down hundreds of bushels. Meade has word that the head of Sedgewick's Corps is at Bonneauville, six miles away—two hours will bring him, and with him superiority to Lee in numbers. Sedgewick is doing well, already the fastest corps march on record—twenty-seven miles in thirteen hours. They say Sedgewick's a god to his soldiers.

Three o'clock. Sickles's move is complete and Meade receives word of it. With his staff he gallops two miles and confronts him. "General Sickles, your orders were to hold Little Round Top. You have disobeyed orders." Sickles retorts hotly he could not hold the line from Hancock to Little Round Top without reinforcement. Meade to Sickles—"Return at once to your former position"—*Bammmmm*, one of Longstreet's guns echoes over the ridges—*Bammmmm*, one of Sickles's replies from the Devil's Den. Meade accepts the situation. "General Sickles, I will send you the 5th Corps. If you need you may call on Hancock." And he wheels and gallops away.

Three-thirty. A mile on the other side of the Devil's Den Ridge a long line of tawny midgets comes out of the woods with their rosy flags. The sun glints on their muskets. Then a second line. They come on, keeping their dress. *B-b-bam*, from the Devil's Den. *B-b-bam*, from the Peach Orchard. The cotton-puff bursts of shrapnel open and fade above them. A third line, a fourth. It is Hood's Division of Longstreet's Corps, four brigades. On their left McLaw's Division will follow in echelon. The fire of Longstreet's artillery quickens. A shell goes off in the wheatfield behind Devil's Den Ridge. The farmer runs for his house. His steers are stampeding backward and forward in the glen below Little Round Top.

Four o'clock. General Hood rides out to his right, sees around the Devil's Den, sees through his field glasses that Little Round Top is empty—only some Yankee signalmen waving a semaphor. *Hood moves.* He swerves Law's Brigade off to the right; General Law himself to lead two of his regiments unseen over Big Round Top and down to occupy Little Round Top; his other three regiments and Robertson's Texas Brigade to go straight for Little Round Top unless needed to help Anderson's and Benning's Brigades to carry the Devil's Den. That will flank both the Devil's Den Ridge and the main Yankee line. A battery on Little Round Top will finish it. Law sets out with 800 men, two regiments, starts the mile swing, keeping concealed, across difficult country toward Big Round Top. His other three regiments and Robertson's four continue in battle line straight toward Little Round Top and the Devil's Den. The Yankee battery on the Devil's Den cliff is finding their range with shrapnel. They are still beyond musket and canister range. Benning's and Anderson's Brigades are deployed on their left, coming up in line with them. Robertson's Brigade are those same Texans that broke Butterfield's Brigade at Gaines's Mill a year and a week ago. That Yankee Brigade, now commanded by Colonel Vincent, is at rest with the 1st Division of the Yankee 5th Corps, two miles away on the Baltimore Turnpike.

Shortly after four, the 5th Corps, ordered up to support General Sickles, got under way from its all day rest in reserve on the Baltimore Turnpike. Colonel Vincent's Brigade of the 1st Division was leading. The way was a narrow by-road, two miles to the line. In the jam the 2d Division would hardly move before five. General Weed's 3d Brigade was the last of the 2d Division, the 50th New York now leading the Brigade, C Company the last of the 50th. Donahoe sent John ahead to reconnoiter this Little Round Top of which there had been much talk among brigadiers and field officers who had ridden the line in the morning. Setting out, John fell in with Lieutenant Hazlett, a regular officer commanding the battery of the 5th Field Artillery that would move behind the 50th. Hazlett was a friend of General Weed's. He was bound for Little Round Top on a little private reconnaissance.

John and Hazlett cantered along in the grass beside the by-road, passing the organizations of the 1st Division that were already moving. Soon they were up to the head of the leading brigade and exchanged waves with Colonel Vincent—a close friend of Donahoe's, a big man with a big round face and an almost Christ-like strength and purity of expression. When they had passed him they let their horses into a run on the open farm road, now cluttered with no more than aides, orderlies and other reconnaissance parties.

Big Round Top was plain in front of them, and when the road veered to the right they saw the lower, symmetrical hill, Little Round Top. The artillery beyond was barking into battle excitement. But no musketry was yet audible.

When the road began rising to cross the right shoulder of Little Round Top, they saw that its near slope was heavily timbered with big hickories and maples and free of underbrush. Hazlett said, "Let's cut in here." At a walk they went diagonally off the road up the slope that rose about a hundred feet in five hundred paces. The hill was a pile of enormous rocks. Under these old trees, there was soil from the leaves, but not enough to bury the form of the boulders that bulged everywhere from a foot up to three or four feet, with dangerous holes between them and between the tree-roots. "Lieutenant," said John, "could you get guns up here?" "We could try, Colonel. Suppose I trace out a course if I can. I'll join you up there on the crest." He went off on a gentler diagonal, and John rode up through the boulders under the trees.

On the summit the trees ended, and as John rode out on the bare, flat little table, his mind winced with a startled, familiar feeling. He knew he had been there before and he knew every rock and scrub tree on the downward slope to the front and the left. He knew the titanic boulders piled in a lower knoll five hundred yards to the front and left, with the thread of a stream in the valley between where a herd of steers was grazing— From the talk in the morning he knew that the knoll was called locally the Devil's Den and the little stream Plum Run. Running out from the knoll, he knew that low, wooded ridge diagonally out to the right; and to the right of the ridge a quarter-mile square golden wheatfield. And spreading off to the right three miles to the hazy village, he knew the wide panorama, the ridge they were on and the other parallel, with the mile-wide strip of farmland between them.

When John rode out on the summit of Little Round Top, the plank-piling rumble of Sickles's and Longstreet's artillery was suddenly nearer, the gun-blasts visible a mile out there at the Peach Orchard, and Rebel shell-bursts over there on the Devil's Den Ridge, two or three a second. And there to the left of the Ridge he could see the brown, Rebel battle lines coming. But these sights of a battle beginning were nothing strange. What struck with a stir in his stomach, a stir of old recognition, was this hilltop quiet here in the heat, with the grasshoppers singing. He had seen it all before. Was it once in a dream? Was it back in the Hollow? Out west when he went to Oberlin and the Chicago convention? John knew he was coming home. He had always been here.

He dismounted and stood by the little maple. He remembered it well, and the comfortable rock at its base to sit on. He sat down on it now and took off his black felt hat in the heat. Down there to the right on the forward slope of boulders and scrub some Signal Corps men on the largest boulder were wagging their big white semaphor. John remembered that ten-foot boulder. In his mood of dream he looked to the left, his eye fixed on a low maple thicket fifty yards off, a thicket blighted by something, the leaves turning. He had seen that before too. His eyes travelled down the slope—the rocks, the scrub trees and the thickets. His conscious mind barely formed the thought— "What a hell of a place to keep men in line of battle, especially charging!" But his unconscious mind had been here before, not fighting. A hundred yards down the slope was a rock that was specially familiar. He raised his glasses on it—a big rock with a flat top sloping up to the left—when was it he had lain there? Was it some time out hunting partridge?

Lieutenant Hazlett appeared on foot and stood by John and the maple. A tall, dark man, for a flash he fitted into John's mood of recollection.

Then he seemed strange. "By Jove, Colonel," said Hazlett, "if we can get guns up, this is a fine position, this level top made on purpose for a full battery. The left gun precisely here beside you, and a field of fire almost a semi-circle." John thought he remembered a three-inch rifle standing there beside him. When had it happened before? "Shall we look over here at the left?" said Hazlett. John hitched his horse and walked down the slope of the crest to the dip of the shallow valley between Little and Big Round Top. Here the trees were big saplings, more tall than the scrub on the front, not so tall as the forest behind. "No place for artillery," John said. "Not worth it," said Hazlett. They walked back to the summit.

Over on the Devil's Den Ridge musketry ripped into action and sawed unseen to John and Hazlett on Little Round Top. Over the Ridge the familiar mist of powder began to rise. Far out to the left of the Ridge, the Rebel lines were coming in musket and canister range, some of them halting, firing, running like tiny dolls, halting, firing, advancing more slowly. John and Hazlett raised their glasses. "Looks like two brigades," said Hazlett. "And more on the right, from the firing," said John. "That means a division," said Hazlett. "It means it's a real attack. My God! This hill should be held. They've only to come here and take it. With a single battery here they could clean out everything yonder." With a wave he included everything held by Sickles—the Devil's Den, the diagonal ridge, the Wheatfield, the distant Peach Orchard where Sickles's guns were barking. John and Hazlett looked at each other with terror. It was not for them to give battle orders. "Well, Colonel," said Hazlett, "I must get back to my battery." John looked at his watch. It was half-past four. "In passing," he said, "would you report to General Weed what we've seen? And please tell Donahoe I'll wait to see what develops, unless he sends for me. In any case I'll return before he can reach the place back there where we left the road." Hazlett saluted and left. In the sky over the Devil's Den Ridge and far out over the Rebels, the vultures were thickening and wheeling lower.

John sat down again on the stone by the little maple, conscious of the ghostly field gun there beside him where Hazlett had said it should be, where he thought it had been before. Out there to the left the battle was grinding. But here he was alone but for that squad of signalmen. Here on Little Round Top the grasshoppers were still buzzing untroubled. John lapsed in a moment's detachment. He had a feeling of rightness. Perhaps the war would be settled here, the Union preserved or broken. That was the simple question. He thought of Ike and his prophecies. Could it be that greed, these banks and factories would make use of the victory? If that were to happen John hoped he would die today, right here on this little familiar hill. He heard hoofbeats whacking the stones coming up the hill from the right.

Four horsemen appeared. John rose, whipping on his hat, and stood at salute. He recognized General Warren who had commanded the Brigade for a time last winter. He was now a staff major-general, Chief of Topographical Engineers of the Army. "How do you do, Lathrop? What do you think of this corner? Nice place for a picnic?" "I believe it should be held, sir," said John. "I agree with you," said Warren. He walked down to the biggest boulder where the signalmen were still waving. John went with him.

"Keep on talking," said Warren as he mounted the boulder and the semaphor man jumped down to make room. "If you've nothing official to wig-wag, then say out of code, so the Rebels out there can read it, that we've here a division in place and another supporting." And with that he stood on the boulder and raised his glasses on the Rebel lines out there to the left coming in on the Devil's Den. John raised his too. For a moment they looked in silence. Thin through the rumble and crash of the battle they could hear like distant bells the Rebels beginning their hungry singing.

"Do you see it, General?" said John. "Yes," said Warren. Far behind the Rebel line, working out toward Big Round Top, two shadowy masses were moving, half hidden by walls and bushes. "Two stands of colors," said Warren, talking to himself, "two regiments, a thousand men perhaps, will come over Big Round Top to seize this hill." Then to John, "See those other regiments—seven battle flags I make it—the balance of two brigades—moving to support the attack on the Devil's Den, or to come here, or both." He lowered his glasses and pointed to the Devil's Den Ridge. "Ward has two thousand men over there. Probably two enemy brigades over there out of sight already attacking. They can add a brigade if they need it. That will be six thousand against two thousand. We've only one battery there. They will carry it quickly. Then—" He pointed to the crest behind them.

A moment he stood, deciding, looking back to the right. Just then, no more than a quarter mile below them, a blue column with a red and white, divisional headquarters flag began to crawl out into sight beyond Little Round Top. Warren knew what it was. He had been with Meade when he ordered the 5th Corps up. *Warren moved.* "Lathrop," he ordered, "stay here and watch those seven Rebel standards. I'll be back." He jumped from the boulder, clanging his saber against it and mounted. His staff followed him clattering down through the boulders.

Back on the summit John watched for fifteen minutes the pawns moving to carry out the decisions of the generals. Two Yankee regiments marching back through the wheat from the Peach Orchard and climbing up to reinforce the Devil's Den. Another regiment moving in farther off to the right on the Ridge. The Wheatfield and woods around crawling with blue columns and standards, aides and orderlies riding hard, artillery galloping into position and opening. Rebel shells whizzing over the Ridge to burst in the wheat and the valley below Little Round Top— one burst among the huddled steers; their blood reddened the smoke; the surviving half of them scattered. The Rebels now swarming in close to the Devil's Den, yelling like panthers. Two Yankee guns unlimbering in the little valley to cover the flank of the Den. "Two guns," thought John, "and two Rebel Brigades—4000 men—attacking! and"— He raised his glasses— "Those seven other battle flags—two other brigades—moving in!" He saw from those seven, three standards bear off to the right to join the attack on the Devil's Den, the other four coming straight on, but slowly as skirmishers, under fire from the Devil's Den. The three broke into a run—John could hear them yelling—swarming in round the Den, mostly flanking it up the near valley, not four hundred yards below him. The two Yankee guns opened down Plum Run with canister, but a Yankee regiment charged down in front of them, blocking their fire. Before this regiment fired, the three criss-cross Rebel flags closed hand-to-hand into the boulders. The fight in the Den was screams and snarls like animals.

Through his glasses John watched the remaining four battle flags. Were they coming to further support the assault on the Den? or— The visibility was bad through the trees— But no sign of their swinging in toward the Devil's Den— There they were, coming straight on— Six hundred yards— They were coming for Little Round Top!

John seized his horse's bridle—but Warren had told him to stay. Suddenly the shouts and screams over at the Den changed to a heavy rumble like a mob murmur that moved off up the ridge to the right. John knew what that meant. The Den had been carried! A shrapnel burst high over him, then another lower. First spatter of lead on Little Round Top. He raised his glasses again. Those four Rebel battle flags were passing the Den, working up the valley between Little and Big Round Top. They would join with the two that had gone over Big Round Top. That would mean a brigade and more—perhaps 2500—to occupy Little Round Top. Where was Warren? He'd told him to stay. Lead spattered the rock John was sitting on, and another buzzed over. He saw the puffs from the Devil's Den—Rebel sharpshooters—they had telescopic sights. John rose to un-hitch his horse and move back into cover. He heard hoof rattles off to the right and behind them a rhythmed murmur of panting. Five horsemen came up, Warren and his staff, and with him Colonel Vincent. Behind them a Yankee stand of colors bobbing up through the rocks. John ran to report to Warren.

"Three standards of those two brigades turned into the Devil's Den. They have carried it. The other four regiments are coming straight here, not five hundred yards away. Artillery ranging, and sharpshooters in the Devil's Den." Warren disregarded this last warning. He and Vincent rode up to the summit, passed over and down in the valley this side of Big Round Top.

John moved his horse into the trees, and when he ran back to the summit the color guard of the 20th Maine was dashing across it, with the regiment laboring up behind through the rocks at the double. Two shrapnel burst high—sharpshooters' bullets spatted—and three men fell— first blood on Little Round Top. John watched while the 20th Maine passed over, and the 83d Pennsylvania came on, then the 44th New York and the 16th Michigan, all panting, not yelling, swarming over the summit, keeping close formation, bent low for cover. John waved his hat and cheered them all as they passed, but they did not see him. They were veterans, thinking of their ammunition, how to use these boulders and trees to fire from. The last of Vincent's Brigade disappeared down the slope out of sight of the sharpshooters. John heard the field officers yelling down there, then the captains and lieutenants posting the line. For a minute the hubbub faded to distant calls and the crackling of bushes. It almost stopped. Then, "Load"— "Load"— "Load"— "Load"— "Load," came the commands of the captains. That meant the Rebels were in sight and forming for battle.

Forgetful of sharpshooters' bullets, John stood in excitement and uncertainty by the little familiar maple. Now he should go back to the regiment. The 2d Division would be almost up to the point back there where he said he'd meet Donahoe. Should he wait for Warren? As he hesitated the General clattered up and stopped on his horse to look over at the Devil's Den.

The four Rebel regiments were now swarming up through the trees, going over the lower slope of Big Round Top and down toward Little Round Top. A Rebel battle flag came down from the Devil's Den, the regiment following, heading up the cut between Big Round Top and Little Round Top. The Yankee regiment in the valley fired at its flank, and they broke in a run for the cover of rocks and bushes— John could hear them yelling. Warren raised his glasses on a group of horsemen.

"That's Robertson," he said. "Some of those troops are his famous Texans. The other brigade is Law's— I saw Law coming down through the trees from Big Round Top." *Thud.* Warren jerked his head to one side. Blood streaked on his neck. "Go down and tell Vincent," he said in a husky voice, "he's both Robertson and Law to cope with. Another regiment is crossing from the Den against him. I will get reinforcements." He clattered away with his aides. John ran down in the woods toward the Yankees. *Crrrrrrrrack*—he saw the smoke rip out, marking the long four-hundred-yard line. The fight of Vincent's Brigade was beginning.

Ten minutes John stayed with Vincent, watching that fight that more than another decided the Battle of Gettysburg. He saw that brigade with every musket in line, 1200 against 2500 on almost equal ground—not a man in support anywhere—if one of those boys broke, the line broke and Little Round Top was taken. With Vincent he walked up and down that long double rank, one prone behind stones and trees, one kneeling, Vincent telling them quietly every man must hold to the end where he was. There would be no retreating. And not one of those Yankee boys looked round at Vincent, but they shifted their quids, settled lower for better sighting, and looked at the Rebels.

Twice the mass of Rebels howled in on the center, and the grinding saw-teeth of the Yankee fire ripped them at seventy-five shots a second, a thousand farm boys firing who knew how to hammer out five aimed shots a minute—and anyone of those boys would be mad if he missed a crow's head across a big cornfield. Twice the butternut line swarmed up to bayonet range and the Yankees did what only veterans could do— the front rank held fire—when the Rebels closed in they got it point blank and solid—they wavered and fell to the sweep of the scythe and crept back to the roll of their drums.

Twice they tried the center in mass and left five hundred wounded and dead at the foot of Little Round Top. The odds were reduced now, 2000 against 1000. Then they tried the left flank, the extreme left flank of the Yankee Army, sent two Alabama regiments against the 20th Maine, now about 300 in number. John ran over with Vincent, saw the 20th far outflanked, Colonel Chamberlain bending back three companies in a right angle; saw him stand off a bayonet charge that almost surrounded him; got his report by a runner that his ammunition was gone; when the next charge came heard him order a counter charge; saw the left three companies wheel up into line cheering and the regiment chasing the Rebs down the valley where they captured 300. Later that evening the Brigade's patrols picked up a thousand Rebel muskets left from the fight against Vincent.

All this John saw, moving back of the line with Vincent. And even while the 20th Maine was chasing back two regiments, he saw four more moving off to the right. That meant they were going to try the other flank, the 16th Michigan. Four regiments on the 16th Michigan on the front of the hill. John ran back to the summit. He met Warren just riding up. John pointed—two regiments coming in sight in the valley in files, working out round the front of the 16th Michigan, two more appearing behind them. The two started up the hill at diagonal, the other two starting up straight for the 16th Michigan. They were going to march up round the flank without fighting. That would be the end of it, Vincent's Brigade surrounded and the hill taken. Warren raised his glasses. "Those two flanking regiments," he said hoarsely, "are the Texans."

A moment John looked at Warren while the sharpshooters' bullets pecked at them. The General was pale from the wound in his neck, his coat-collar soggy with blood. He had been all over the field and got no help, for the battle was hot out there now, McLaw's Rebel Division crushing in Sickles at the Peach Orchard, and Hill's Rebel brigades moving in. All of the Yankee 5th Corps that was up was pouring out into the Wheatfield. Warren had not got a regiment.

A moment he looked at John blankly. Then John ran to his horse, mounted, raced past the moans of Vincent's dressing station and down through the big trees on the back of Little Round Top. He galloped out of the woods down onto the road precisely as Donahoe came up at a walk at the head of the 50th.

"Thought you were hit," said Donahoe. "We must go up there now!" shouted John wildly. "Are you our new brigadier?" said Donahoe, laughing. John put an insubordinate hand on his pistol. "You hear that!" he shouted so the whole regiment heard him. Up over the hill musket fire was beginning, and the yipping of Rebels. "You hear that!" John yelled. "Vincent up there with two brigades against him! That's one brigade opening now on his right, that's the 16th Michigan! And Robertson's Texans are climbing the hill on the flank to take it without fighting!" "John," said Donahoe quietly, "take your hand off your pistol. Please try to act like a soldier." John glared at him, and mumbled, "I'm sorry, sir." They both looked round. Warren and his aides came galloping recklessly down through the trees and the boulders.

Warren's voice rasped from his throat wound but he shouted as wildly as John, "Donahoe, take your regiment up here at once." Donahoe rode out to meet him and saluted. "General Warren, my orders are to follow General Weed." "Never mind that," rasped Warren. "I'll take the responsibility. Go up there at your fastest double. Go over the top on the right

of Vincent and drive back a flanking brigade. It is Robertson's Texans."
"Come on, 50th, at the double," shouted Donahoe, and he diagonaled up
under the big trees where Hazlett and John had gone earlier. With a yell
the 50th broke in a run up the slope behind him. Warren spurred his horse
back down the column to see what was following the 50th. "Lead them up,"
Pat Donahoe said to John beside him. "I'll be back by the time you get
there." And he rode up ahead at a springing gallop from mould-padded
boulder to boulder.

John led the regiment up through the trees at a trot, Major Johnson
beside him, keeping just ahead of the colors. They had four or five hundred yards to go. Beyond the summit the musketry slackened. Was the
Michigan regiment breaking? Each second John heard more plainly the
Rebs yelling. He drew his sword, turned in his stirrups, and shouted,
"Come on, boys, we've got to beat them there! If we don't, they'll lick
us!"— Then from behind on the left came a rumble and rattle and clatter of hooves and whips and a medley of voices— "Come on, ye beautiful bastard!" "Come up, Columbus and Cabot!"— "Come, Powder and
Shrapnel!"— "Lunette and Handspike!"— "Come up, Lanyard and Brim-
stone!"— "Watch that hole, Philadelphia, ye big-bellied clodhopper!"—
"That's better!"— "Can ye bust that trace, Elephant?"— "That's it, my
beauty!"— *Crack-crack*— *Crack-crack*— The panting of maddened horses.
It was Hazlett's battery! "On that limber, ye white-livered boobies!" "Now
—heave!"— "Thar she clears!"— "Watch that slide, ye god-damned gos-
lings!"— *Crash*— "Did mamma's boy bust his leg?"— *Crack-crack-crack-
crack*— "Oh, there's oats in the bin and there's hay in the mow. Can ye
get me home now?" "Look out, George Washington, ye off son-of-a-
bitch!"— "Come 'ere, Goliath."— "All right, Minnie May, lift 'er!"—
Crash—crack-crack. On they came up the hill, rearing, snorting, clattering
the rocks into sparks, bursting roots, balking and plunging, bending upward enormous muscles into straining collars, lifting tons of steel pounding and reeling up over the boulders, while the gunners like monkeys ran
round and hove on the wheels, the non-coms sat on their horses and pointed
and bellowed, and, quietly leading them, Lieutenant Hazlett picked the
way he had marked in the morning.

The first section, the second, the third and the fourth reached a place
where the soil and leaves almost buried the boulders. With no sound but
the jingle of chains and the rattle of axles, the creaking of leather and
the juggernaut panting of horses, they came up past the rear of the 50th,
then veered right toward its column. "Make way there," yelled Hazlett.
The companies of the 50th opened for each six-horse carriage in turn,
then slipped through behind it and hurried up after the column.

They had only a hundred yards now to the summit. Below and above on the right, the hubbub of the climbing battery. Straight above and beyond the crest, the firing and the Rebels singing. Were they already there?— Through the trees John could see the bare top. He looked back— the column was free of the battery. He was about to turn back and yell, "Bayonets," when Donahoe came clattering down on his foam-covered chestnut. "No time for bayonets!" he shouted. "Those god-damned Texans are almost to the top and the 16th Michigan's breaking! I'll lead the boys up. Johnson, you stay with me. John, drop back and as the companies come up send them right into line on the run. Keep out on the flank yourself and swing the boys in in a wheel. Don't let them flank you." And he drew his sword, yelled, "Come on, boys!" and leaned up hill on his horse, pointing the regiment forward. "Come on, boys. It's our first fight since the Peninsula and we'll do it again!"

The pace of the column quickened as they came stumbling and panting up over the boulders. John rode out to the right and beckoned to the second company to form right into line and come toward him, then the same to the third, and the fourth, all the time trotting higher up toward the crest. He rode out on the open summit abreast of Donahoe, rode out into the clock-work racket of Hazlett's battery unlimbering into action, the left two guns already in place and loading—the left gun there by the maple sapling where John had dreamed it—and Hazlett yelling, "Double canister— Fire at will when you see them."

John bellowed, "We'll have to go through you, Hazlett." "Go at them," yelled Hazlett. "We're with you—hold fire." It was all in an instant— John saw Donahoe there by the maple jump from his horse, throw the reins to the Sergeant Major— Heard shrapnel and sharpshooters' bullets peppering the rocks, saw four or five cannoneers crumple— Heard Donahoe shout, "Come on, boys, there they are!"— Saw him wave his sword and lead down at a run where the hats of the Texans were just bobbing up past the last of the boulders— Saw three rods to the left Vincent swinging his hat, shouting, "God bless you, Donahoe!"— Saw Pat run ahead of the troops as far as the blighted thicket— In the very same second saw Donahoe and Vincent drop— Donahoe dead, Vincent mortally wounded. The men saw it too and the shout went back, "They've got Donahoe!"

Then the wrath of the crusade of centuries broke— No more shouting— Only terrific silence and the shuffling of five hundred animals coming up out of the forest. John's mind was as clear as a wedge splitting rock— Johnson knew Donahoe's plan— John waved to him to lead on, and Johnson ran down where Donahoe had started. The first company poured after him down into the rocks, without loading, without bayonets, down into the rocks and the Texans, their musket-butts swinging. The second drove in on the right. No firing. The air was all slugging muskets. The next company in. Then the fourth, as John had directed. He had fixed on the flank of the Rebels—he could circle it easily. The companies rolled up on the top and John sent them down there in echelon. No thought of support—he'd get them in line—then he'd lead them. C Company came last. John dismounted and let his horse go, ran ahead down the hill by George Fulton. And then Hazlett opened above them with brain-splitting blasts like the power of God's anger behind them.

As John ran down through the rocks and bushes with C, there was no musketry up there behind them—only the roar of the battery, and furious motion. The Butternuts had got Donahoe!— Arms swinging up out of the rocks and bushes, muskets sweeping upward and falling— Grunts, groans, the thump and crunch of wood and metal on bone and flesh, men jumping on boulders and catapulting down on the Texans, surprising them round the rocks, heading them back, clubbing them, kicking them, stabbing them, using their bayonets as knives, no time to fix them. No melee John had ever seen was like it, nothing so fast, so elemental, so everywhere.

Those two Texas regiments—the other two facing the 16th Michigans were from Law's Alabamans—had marched all the previous night and had taken half an hour's hell from Vincent. They were caught by surprise when they thought they were getting there easily. They gave ground. They started to run, to crowd over into the Alabama regiments that were bending back the flank of the 16th Michigan. They infected them with panic and they too retreated a little. The 16th rushed back into line and their fire power steadied.

John got C a hundred yards down the hill, told George to guide on him, looked up the hill at his seething line pouring over the rocks, saw it already almost at right angles to the 16th Michigan, saw the Texans retreating, put his hat on his sword-point and floundered out through the bushes in front of C Company, then back up the hill in front of D, A, E, L, H and stopped, his hat high on his sword, jumped up on a boulder, glanced toward the enemy, failed to notice a light touch like a hand on his shoulder, spread his sword arm—his left wouldn't spread though he felt no pain. The 50th halted. John bellowed to right and left, "Hold the line here for Donahoe." The Captains passed on the command. John ran back to the right at C Company, jumped up on a rock, and looked toward the Rebels.

He realized the 50th's staff was behind him. He sent Adjutant Green to tell the captains of the three right companies to be ready to swing either back or forward as ordered, then to go and tell Major Johnson to post himself back of the center—for the present he, Lathrop, would stay with the right. They were to hold now, not to advance.

Just after Green went, John heard a voice behind him, "Ye're bleedin', 'Paloosa." It was Jabe. John looked at his left arm. Even through the blouse it was pumping out blood from above the elbow, running down in a stream off his hand. Jabe twisted a tourniquet on it and the bleeding lessened.

Slowly, oppressed by heaviness, John walked up behind the line, conferred with Johnson, and returned to his watch on the rock. He felt the world growing silent around him. For the first time that day he noticed the constant humming of bullets. Somewhere up the hill he heard a quiet voice say distinctly, "Pleasant evenin'." Subconsciously and without surprise he sensed that he was standing on that rock he had seen from the top in the morning. Then he heard the Rebs coming.

Back at two hundred yards they had rallied. John saw their four crisscross standards advancing above the bushes. They were heading just as before diagonally up to the summit. They were not trying to flank him. He would not have to draw his right companies back. As if he were someone else watching, he found himself running along through the rocks behind the companies and shouting, "Let them have it by company when you see them—keep cover till they're on you."

Now the regiment was ready, their muskets loaded and bayoneted, every man behind cover and sighting. Beginning company by company, the wheel of their fire rattled out and ground up to its twenty a second, ripping those tired Texans in front and in flank as they reeled blindly upward. John ran back to the right in the valley, saw the attack was all inside his flank, felt himself jump out in front, heard himself yell to the three right companies to charge bayonets behind him, felt himself rush forward, blind through the bushes, not knowing he was stumbling, felt dimly around him the commotion of shooting and grunting and thumping and cursing, saw a Rebel flag bobbing over the bushes, saw it start to go back— for a flash his mind saw the flag of the Texans coming up from the woods at Gaines's Mill, came round a big boulder, saw a Rebel colonel turn toward him, heard his own revolver go off first, saw the Rebel tumble, paused and took bearings by the hilltop. He was too far advanced. With difficulty he mounted a boulder and spread his good arm to halt the three companies. The Rebels were in full retreat now. Up the hill they had not come to bayonets. They had dropped into cover. They could not advance. Now their drums were rattling them back, scuttling brown through the bushes like wood-chucks. The firing was lessening. John shouted to the companies to return to their former positions.

John felt giddy. The artery in his arm was pumping again. He was standing by the slanting rock at the right of the regiment. He was lying on it, chin in his good hand, watching in the direction the Rebs had retreated. He heard himself say, "Green, give that tourniquet a twist." He heard himself mumbling to Green about the companies sending out skirmishers. Green left with his orders. John knew he was weak from loss of blood. Should he relinquish the command of the regiment? He looked at his arm. The bleeding had stopped. He resumed watching.

For a time John was aware of the usual business of the line to the left of him— The wounded boys helping each other— There was old Fritz, the cook of the club, holding his side and staggering— The skirmishers going out in front— Alec Mathiesson, the miserable coward, with his bayonet belligerently stuck out though there wasn't a Reb in two hundred yards. For a time John listened to Hazlett up there shelling the Devil's Den. He heard Yankee sharpshooters up the hill behind him, potting the Rebel sharpshooters. Somewhere off to the right was the rumble of heavy action. Then it merged in a whir receding far off. His mind said, "Why are they doing it? We held the hill and the Butternuts have skedaddled. The fight is over."

At that moment Sedgewick's Corps was filling the line that Sickles had left in the morning. It was held more strongly than ever. At that moment General Weed was leading the rest of his Brigade up on Little Round Top. As the General rode up, a sharpshooter's bullet found him and he fell from his horse, dying. Hazlett, his friend, leaned over him, and slumped dead across him. Vincent, Donahoe, all but one of Vincent's colonels, Weed, Hazlett. But the hill was held strongly now. John in his half-conscious dream was right. The fight of Vincent's Brigade and the 50th New York had settled the battle.

Slow, mammoth movement of clouds in the summer sky. Slow drifting of battle mist over the field of Gettysburg. Slow movement of army corps. An hour and a half ago Warren's move meant checkmate at Gettysburg, checkmate of the Confederacy. But Lee does not know it. Meade does not know it. For an hour and a half more out there in the Wheatfield, for a day more at Gettysburg, for two years more across the nation, they will move their pieces before checkmate is complete and acknowledged.

Out there in the Wheatfield was boiling the Whirlpool of Gettysburg,

Lee pouring in regiments, brigades, Meade pouring in regiments, brigades, driving forward in thousands, being driven back in hundreds, men falling like leaves from the autumn tree of their civilizations, four falling a second, the wheat all sodden and red and buried in bodies. The sun touched Seminary Ridge. It was twilight in the valley below Little Round Top. They fought on till dark in the Wheatfield and through the neighboring forests, till all concert of action was lost. The wheel of firing slowed to the rattle of patrols and skirmishes. The yells of the fight merged in the single, multitudinous wail of fifteen thousand wounded. The Yankees at last held the Wheatfield and the Rebels the Devil's Den and the Peach Orchard. But no matter who won out there, the original fish-hook line was held more strongly than it was in the morning. Warren had seen to that. The moves of the army corps had been made. The two civilizations had come up to their hour. Was there other silent artillery riding the clouds above Gettysburg? Did the sun, dropping behind Seminary Ridge, set on more than the Rebel Army?

John heard someone speaking his name. Someone was shaking him. He looked round heavily. It was Green. He read him an order from Colonel Garrard, now commanding Weed's Brigade. The 50th would move by the flank up the hill and occupy a short fifty-yard line on the right of the 16th Michigan. Slowly John understood. He started to rise and couldn't. It was like a man's muscles trying to lift the body of an elephant. He told Green to take the order to Johnson and tell him to take command of the regiment.

When Green had gone John managed to strain to his feet by the rock. As from a great distance he heard the order come down to C Company, "By the left flank by double file," and he started to stagger after them. Someone came to him—Jabe— "George says I can help ye up, Lollapaloosa. Ye ain't over steady." "I know it," John mumbled, "but the thing's stopped bleeding. I can get there alone. Go along with the Company. That's orders." Jabe went ahead and watched John from the bushes till he was almost up to the summit.

John started up the grade, lurching from boulder to boulder, using his good hand. He felt no pain, felt nothing, thought nothing, drew off into an empty, silent world where he moved mechanically. He did not hear another regiment chattering by him, nor its Colonel say, "Wait for a litter, Lathrop," nor his own voice murmuring, "No, thanks, I'll manage. I'm not hit badly. Just bled some of the ginger out of me." Where the grade was steep John crawled on his knees and his good hand. He did not know when he passed through the sharpshooter regiment and again refused a litter. It took him fifteen minutes to creep up that hundred yards, but he had no sense of time.

He forgot that there was a war and that he was wounded. But he knew that all was well with him. He was going somewhere for certain—it was all very easy.

When he reached the new line, though well to the 50th's right, Jabe figgered John was all right now and left off watching him and joined the regiment. Crawling up round the big top boulders, John heard a faint and remote disturbance—it was the battery just over him, now booming four shells a minute per gun at a new target, the far edge of the Wheatfield. He just missed being decapitated by the leftmost gun as he loomed up unexpectedly in front of it—the concussion was a faint wind to him. He walked past the gun slowly and sat deliberately on the stone at the foot of the maple where he'd sat alone earlier.

The concussion of every shot of the battery shook him, but he didn't know it. He was unaware of the roar, but his sight was minutely clear—the motion of the guns, jumping back a rod, rolling up and firing again, fascinated him childishly. As before, his mind failed to hear someone shouting at him—it was Lieutenant Rittenhouse, now commanding Hazlett's battery— "May I help you, Colonel? The dressing station is near. Will you have a litter?" John felt faint annoyance, like a fly pestering him. Inaudibly to himself his voice was saying, "No, thank you. I'm not hit badly. Just bled some of the ginger out of me."

Everything his eyes fell on was fresh and exciting. On that left gun that ran back and forth beside him he watched a corporal "thumbing the fire." The gun was almost glowing hot. In that shape it was impossible to load it with the vent at the breech open—the charge would go off immediately. So the corporal kept closing the vent with his thumb while the men loaded, then jumped back opening the vent—the gun leapt to its shot and recoiled past John. For minutes he watched this corporal, his thumb blackened to gristle and smoking each time he pressed down on the vent. John wanted to tell him to stop, that he'd burn his thumb. The act was complete in the thought. His attention wandered in the direction the guns were shooting. It was only a half mile out there in front and below to that Wheatfield. For almost an hour he watched it blankly, like a child seeing someone parade toy soldiers. He did not know it was war, that he was in command of a regiment. He did not know he was sitting there on a stone with a three-inch rifle tearing the sky to pieces beside him. He was nothing but eyes seeing images.

Slowly he understood those were people out there in that field running and crowding together with bursting shells and lines of smoke all across them. Somewhere under his empty consciousness there formed a surprised thought— They were fighting! Why were men fighting there? He could see them—thousands knocking each other down, shooting each other, bayoneting each other, killing each other. Why should so many men be angry at each other? Why should so many men be killing each other like animals? As the minutes passed his blood-drained mind took slowly the shape of incredulity, then of horror. There arose a memory of his early boyhood when he first saw his mother cry— There was something wrong in the world— That was not the way things were intended. Faintly there came a more recent memory—Ike—the Scamp—he said men should not kill each other. The Scamp was always right——

Thinking of Ike was a stir of emotion, and John's mind grew a little stronger. Dimly he knew where he was—he was somehow in it. All this commotion beside him had something to do with the fighting out there. He saw that corporal thumbing the fire—that gun had something to do with it. They were firing it to kill people. What was he here for? What was he doing here where men were killing each other? He must stop them—he must stop that gun firing. He must go down there and tell those people to stop fighting. He got to his feet and stood wavering.

Then someone was in front of him, his arms around him supporting him— Over a big shoulder he saw that gun fire again and dart back on its wheels, then roll forward with the men on the spokes and the corporal with his thumb on the vent. He straightened back and looked at the bearded face near his— It was good old Jabe— Remotely, like a whisper, John heard him saying, "Got worried about ye and been clean down in the valley with a detail and searchin' the hul hill fer ye. Now ye're goin' t' hospital." John didn't know what he said, but he knew Jabe, and he smiled— Jabe was not killing people. Over the big shoulder he saw the corporal lift his thumb from the breech——

The world roared open in crimson, at its center that bursting gun, its red-hot rents bending back to release a volcano—a painless sledgehammer struck John in the side— Saw Jabe double back, the trunk lying flat on the legs, the face an expressionless grin— Lunged forward across it, hung over the broken wheel of the gun— For an infinite second bulging, unconscious eyes with no mind behind them stared with minute clarity at the burst breech— Tiny flames licking— On a bent-out strip of steel an elliptical plate with some printing on it—

BYZANTIUM STEAM ENGINE COMPANY,
BYZANTIUM FALLS, NEW YORK.

Someone was meddling with his side . . . very far away . . .

CHAPTER XCV

THERE was a gap in time that might have been minutes or centuries. Then there was motion in great waves that rose easily to incalculable height, and settled easily again to warm and comfortable depths. And sometimes going up there was an inner rotation like the rolling crest of the wave, round and round, round and round and returning, all very slow and easy and satisfying. There was no place in the motion, no person, no name, no John Lathrop, only the comfortable waves that were everywhere and nowhere, the universe where everything was just as it ought to be. Then the waves would stop, and there would be other blanks in time. Then the waves again and more rolling. The motion was hot now, as if the waves were of air over fire, and the hotter they were the more comfortable and soothing they were. Then there was color and the rolling waves of the hot universe were red and purple and orange, all just as they ought to be.

Then there was a place in the waves, and an awareness of the waves going round outside the place, and a pleasure in watching them roll as they ought to. Then there was something nearby, and yet outside the place, something like a faint prick and a tug like a fish-hook that had gone clean through the skin and was being drawn away by a line, sometimes steadily with a sort of itch, sometimes in yanks that were like little blows. Then there were long blanks again that would end in the itch again that was a half delicious and half uncomfortable pain in the hot waves. Then the little yanks again, and the place was rolling on a point where it was impaled high up on the weather vane of Dr. Swift's barn and turning round and round in the sweet, hot wind. And there were other faint discomforts like fumblings near the place and hard crockery interfering with lips, and a pricking like a needle nearer to the place than where it was impaled. Then a rhythm, a strong thump-thumping, thump-thumping in the waves. Then more blanks in time, and afterwards the vast and comfortable hot waves again.

And the waves resolved into two curves rising in the universe, and one was something absolutely perfect and the other was the United States of America. And they were trying to meet, rising symmetrically and bending toward each other. But to make them meet was an effort and ended in the thump-thumping that became an audible sound. Then the tuggings of the fish-hook that grew more and more uncomfortable and the prickings nearer the place. Then a blank in time again, and out of the blank the curves again trying to meet in the universe. Then there was a sound that was perfect and for an instant the curves met, though the words of the sound were incomprehensible— "It is draining well. The fever cannot last long at this height. He must take nourishment." John opened his eyes to a bright white light, and far off like a glass reversed yet filling the universe . was the face of Tavie smiling down at him from the white light. His lips tried to say, "Howdy do, Tave," and he closed his eyes and the curves were absolutely together.

In the terribly hot, white dryness he was unaware of pressure on his hand or of the icepack on his forehead. But the place that had rolled in the waves and risen with the curves became a self that was in its bed at Lathrop Hollow, and Tavie was there and was both herself and Sarah Lathrop, and Ike rode Dandy through the room and out the window. All this was exactly as it ought to be, but then there were joltings and fumblings at his head and lips, and Sarah and Tave whispered, "Try to drink this, John." He tried to tell Ike to bring Dandy back, but it was something hard at his lips. Then there was another blank in time.

· He was milking with Pa, and after supper Pa heard his Greek lesson for tomorrow, and he was mending wall with Brother Tom who had died. And Ike was married to Tave, and there was Abraham Lincoln, who had always been a member of the family and was married to Ma and Grandma and Tave. Ike was President of the Gang, and they all lived round the Hollow and met two or three times a week at our house. Ike said nobody must ever sell Dandy. Pru Stark was a pure white cow with beautiful, blue eyes; she came into the kitchen and drank cream from a saucer like a cat and was no trouble to anybody. And the little burlesque girl was a virgin and they would be married pretty soon. And they were married and John got in bed with her at Utica, but instead she was in Richmond. Tave was President of the United States and she had freed the slaves and destroyed all the factories and banks. She was the same as that perfect curve rising through the universe that the curve of the United States was trying to meet. They were going to meet now, and John was lying with his face on one of Tave's breasts. Then he had her very easily, very easily, and the burlesque girl said "my true lover," and the curves met—John heard the thump-thumping, thump-thumping.

Then the hot waves were too hot for comfort, and John tried to turn over but was held down. There were the fish-hook tuggings that were now in his side and terribly painful, and he heard the man's voice again, though he did not understand the words— "It is fortunately placed for drainage, just above the diaphragm. If the fever continues to go down and he takes nourishment, he will have a good chance of recovery." Then John felt uncomfortable prickings in his left shoulder and the same voice saying, "This one is still clean and will heal rapidly."

John heard his own voice ask for water, but he had forgotten that he asked for it when the jolting at his head and the fumbling at his lips wakened him and he swallowed some water, and he thought he was swallowing Dandy. Then he fell back with his eyes open and saw whitewashed beams under a whitewashed roof. He moved his eyes and saw a white plaster wall opposite and other iron beds with men in them, and bright windows and bright sunlight on the wall. Then he moved his eyes again and saw Tavie clearly, smiling down at him in the relaxed and tender way he had seen at Oberlin, her hair towsled and shining like pure yellow gold in the sunlight.

"Hello, Tave," he said with a feeling like smiling, then he tried to raise his arms in an impulse to give her a kiss, but at once had a terrible pain in his right side and his left shoulder and Tave seized his arms and held him down and kissed his dry lips. "How did you get here?" he murmured as he closed his eyes. "They let me come to take care of you," whispered Tave, looking away impatiently at the door of the ward that led into the front of the wooden building and the kitchen. "Good," said John faintly. Then he opened his eyes and asked, "Where are we?" "You were hit, John, and we're in hospital. You're doing nicely." "Armory Square Hospital?" murmured John. "Yes," said Tave. "I'm assistant to Mrs. Thomson, who is in charge of the women nurses, and I can see you whenever you want me." "Good," whispered John and he pressed her hand with all his strength, which was hardly perceptible to her.

He felt her arm behind him and her shoulder under his head. "John, you must eat this." He opened his eyes and saw another nurse, a freckled, red-haired girl, holding a bowl of something. "Howdy do," he said faintly and tried to smile, but his heart was thumping at a great rate. "This is Miss O'Malley," said Tave. "She's your nurse. You must eat this soup." The nurse gave him a few spoonfuls and he swallowed them. Tavie felt his pulse, said that would do for now, and let him down gently. "Now you must sleep," she whispered close to his ear. John was very uncomfortable in the hot bed and tried to roll over, but he felt Tavie holding him down irresistibly. "Whatever you do," she whispered, "you must not move. If you lie perfectly still you are out of danger."

John understood and lay still, feeling his heart thumping dreadfully, the terrible pain in his side and a sense of being suffocated. Gradually the suffocation and the beating of his heart subsided. He knew he was in the Armory Square Hospital and that Tave was with him. His mind raised no image connected with the Battle of Gettysburg. The last he remembered was getting a letter from Tave. He went back into the world of the curves and the waves.

That was in mid-afternoon on July fourth. The next day John's fever was lower, as the General Commandant had hoped, and his first crisis was past. He lay conscious with his eyes open for two or three half-hour stretches, and ate milk toast and a little stew. He smiled at the General, but gritted his teeth and fainted when he dressed his side. Across the aisle he recognized a colonel he had known somewhere—he had had a hand amputated and waved to John with the other. Rolling his head to one side, John saw someone beside him who breathed with horrible gurgling sounds—he learned afterwards that a shell fragment had torn out his esophagus. On the other side John recognized a Rebel colonel. His mind bore no image of his charge in the valley below Little Round Top. He merely knew it was a Rebel colonel and he'd seen him somewhere. He asked Tavie to give him his compliments. When Tavie delivered the message the Rebel colonel moved his lips but could not speak. He was already almost unconscious, with his eyes open, having an infection, from a revolver shot in the intestines, which was spreading rapidly. He died that night.

On the 6th John's fight with hemorrhage, shock and fever was so far won that Tavie propped him up in bed a little for change of position. She told him the truth of his condition. The musket wound in his shoulder was healing nicely. Although the ball had severed the main artery, there was nothing serious in the wound after the hemorrhage had stopped. The wound in his right side was the bad one. Most of the seventh, eighth and ninth ribs had been carried away and the lung had collapsed. His shirt had been kept well stuffed into the hole all through his twenty-four hours' ambulance ride, and that probably had saved his life. The chest cavity was infected, but the location of the open wound was ideal for drainage. The General was certain that if he remained quiet so as not to bring on another hemorrhage, he would recover. He would be in bed for months, and out of service for at least a year. In two or three years the ribs would grow back and he would be as good as ever.

John heard this with a sense of relief. In his feverish state he had been getting nervous about not being back with the regiment. Now he realized that he was not going back to the regiment for a long time, that this doctor general was now his commanding officer and that Tavie would be near him. He belonged just where he was. Still no image of the battle or any detail of it crossed his thoughts or dreams. His delirium was over, but from his earlier mutterings Tavie had gleaned several items that intrigued her.

On the 7th John's fever was much reduced and he ate a normal meal. On the 8th his fever was gone and he was strong enough to take an interest in the room, which had sun all day on one side or the other. The glare of the white walls, roof beams and roof was relieved by dark purple bunting wound and festooned among the beams, by window curtains of the same material, by a green carpet in the wide aisle between the beds, and on the walls by numerous restful chromos of bucolic scenes and engravings of ships and the heads of horses and dogs. About a dozen of the general and field officers were fully conscious and sufficiently free from pain to nod and smile to each other. There was a feeling of peace in the place. A few of the officers in adjoining beds conversed in low tones and chuckled, but no one mentioned the war.

Besides Miss O'Malley there was a male nurse called Smith in the ward, a conscientious and physically powerful middle-aged man from Wisconsin whose principal duties were to bring the patients their urine bottles and the pans for their stools, and to roll or move them gently so Miss O'Malley could change the sheets. There was a double door between the ward proper and the vestibule in front that was flanked by the office on one side and the kitchen on the other. Through the double doors stretcher-bearers occasionally carried out a corpse or carried a new patient in. At the doors there was a guard with fixed bayonet.

On the 8th Tavie got a letter from George Fulton, who was still with the regiment. He enclosed a report of Gettysburg for the *Eagle* such as John might have written. He said that if a report did not come from John soon after Gettysburg, the people at home might infer that something had happened to him. Ike would probably come to Washington to look for him, and as Tavie probably knew, that might not be wise. He suggested that Tavie copy the report and send it "either to Ike or to my father, saying that John was wounded in the right hand, that he dictated the report to you, that his wound will be healed in a week or two, that meantime you and he are enjoying yourselves in Washington, etc., etc." George told Tavie how John was wounded and Jabe killed. But in the report for the *Eagle* he gave no details, merely naming the casualties of Company C in the impersonal style John would have used; the dead including First Sergeant Jabez Munson, and the wounded Lieutenant-Colonel John Lathrop. That night Tavie copied the report as if John had dictated it to her, and sent it to

Ike, along with a letter containing a fictitious statement of a wound in John's hand and an equally fictitious message from John for his ma which gave Tavie some qualms in the composing.

On the next day, the 9th, a week after John was wounded, there arrived a letter from Ike which was written before Gettysburg and had been delayed, going first to the regiment. Recognizing the hand, Tavie had some doubt as to the wisdom of giving it to John. So she waited until late afternoon when he had slept two hours and seemed strong and cheerful, and stayed by him while he read it.

June 30, '63

Dear Paloosa—

X tells me that you haven't written her and she figures you're done with her. If it's true, I figure I ought to be both glad and sorry. I'm glad for your sake and sorry for my own, for with you out of the picture I'd likely think about her more than is healthy for me. I wish you would write me whether it is true or not.

We're still losing money on our guns and I haven't been able to get a better price for them from the Ordnance Department. I may have some news for you pretty soon about the Engine Company. After the way you talked when you were here I feel I'm bound to report to you as if you were a judge sitting over me. I figure your disapproving of my wanting to make a little profit out of guns is only part of your disapproving of the whole way I'm running my life. I hope some day to please you better by quitting business, but the time to quit hasn't arrived yet, and as long as I am in business I must go on running my affairs in my own way. I figure this damned war keeps both of us in an unhealthy state of mind.

I am more and more convinced that your enemies, the rich, will get hold of the Government and the war at the elections next year. Ostrum Applemore says he is going to the next State Republican Convention "just as an observer," which means that he's probably going to run against Solon again next year, and is already looking for some Republican votes. He continues to be full of praise for you, and has got himself clean round to the notion that the war was a righteous affair from the beginning.

The draft is going on, and it's the fashionable thing in Mehitabel Gadston's set to buy a substitute, what they call "having your representative at the front." By doing this you appear mighty patriotic and you don't run any danger of getting peppered. Thank God, I am buying a "representative" because I don't believe in war, not because I'm afraid of being peppered. I got a boy from out in Camilla whose pa needed the $800.00, of which I pay $300.00 and the state and the nation the rest as bounty. Applemore got Nat Gadston a commission and he's off in camp somewhere.

Well, I'm sicker of the war every day, and will be glad when you begin to get some sense about it. Ma and Ben send their love.

Don't forget to tell me about X.

Scamp.

While John read this Tavie watched the artery in his forehead pulsing faster and his respiration increasing. She put her hand on his wrist, but he paid no attention to it. When he had finished the letter he crumpled it in his hand and closed his eyes. Then he opened them, smiled at Tavie and whispered, "Could I have a little whisky?" Tavie brought him a teaspoonful in water. When he had drunk it he squeezed her hand and said softly, "Thank God, you're here, Tave." "Close your eyes," she whispered. He did, and his pulse and respiration both returned toward normal. After about a minute he opened them again and said, "Nothing to bother about. He didn't know I'd been hit. You'd better not read the letter." And John looked straight at Tavie with the love in his eyes she was long used to from the wounded, but which, coming from John and after having heard him mumble her name in delirium, made her drop her own eyes. When she looked up John was asleep. She carefully detached her hand from his, then took the crumpled letter from the other, carried it out to the kitchen and burned it without reading it. She told Miss O'Malley to give John no more letters without showing them to her first, but she omitted to mention the matter to Smith or the General, so it did not become part of standing orders for the ward.

That evening the General told Tavie that John was doing remarkably well, that he had reached the point where he would remain for anywhere from one to six months, as long as the empyema in his chest cavity was active and draining. While that remained, there was always danger of hemorrhage, but barring that there was every chance of complete recovery. Even a hemorrhage might not prove fatal, although it would set him back some weeks.

Tavie visited John five or six times every twenty-four hours and usually managed to sit with him for an hour in the afternoon. She saw the color come back in his face and his smile grow strong and generous as it used to be. His fever rose a little every evening, but this would continue until the infection in his chest was dried up, a matter of months. Every time she sat with him now she expected he would start making love to her, and she did her best to talk or read to him continuously. She saw his look toward her change from the helpless, adoring appeal that was typical of the wounded to an intent stare, as if he were studying her. Sometimes she thought his look was indecent, and she wondered what the war had done to his attitude toward women.

John grew tense whenever Tavie mentioned Ike. He said he must continue to make himself believe that the Scamp's greediness for profit was more talk than fact. Tavie gave up speaking of Ike. She brought her pa to see John, having first coached him. John asked Solon if he thought Applemore was going to try for the Republican nomination next year and Solon, managed to show amusement at the suggestion. John asked him if the pressure for a still higher tariff was getting too strong in Congress. At this Solon looked very severe for a moment, then chuckled with his best attempt at hypocrisy and said he had no doubt they would be able to take care of that. On that same afternoon, Sunday, the 12th, President Lincoln came through the ward on his frequent rounds and remembered John distinctly, though he now seemed more remote and sad than ever, and John didn't see him smile once as he went from bed to bed, holding one limp hand after another.

Still John's mind raised no single image of the battle of Gettysburg, and something in his subconscious prevented him from asking about it, or about the regiment. He thought mostly about Tavie. He was perfectly sure they would be married after he got well, and it seemed to him that she knew it too. His dreams and half-waking dreams became lascivious, usually of the four women he had known best. His subconscious would start off in bed with Buffalo Bertha or Pru. Then he would see the little burlesque girl far off, and his lust would change to an abstract yearning for some absolute perfection. This yearning would change into the diagrammatic dream of the curves meeting. The curves always merged back into the image of Tavie and met in her. The dream of Tavie would return to the original, lascivious impulse and usually ended in consummation.

And these dreams had their counterpart in his waking thoughts from day to day. In spite of Tavie's desirability to him now, he knew they had at last reached that point only because the rest of the curves of their lives coincided so exactly. They were already one in every important aspect of existence, already had all of their experiences in common except carnal relationship. He was glad that had come last, as the expression of their identical idealism, rather than as an original thing which, as in the case of

Pru, would only have built up a feverish, false, and transitory state of things. Now when he thought of Tavie carnally, he felt as if he were mating with the whole world, with his mother, with God. It was the inevitable part of his whole life, not merely a separate, pleasurable act in itself. And this did not mean that his specific desire for Tavie was any the less. On the contrary, it was stronger than any desire he had known, strong with absolute certainty, a quiet kind of strength that included everything and did not force him into romanticizing contrary to fact.

From day to day John put off speaking to Tave about his love for her, enjoying the suspense and suspecting that she did not want him to yet. But on the afternoon of Thursday, the 16th, he had no pain at all in his side and his spirits were too high to be repressed longer. Tavie had been admiring him for the last few days, believing that he of all the soldiers she had nursed was not going to say anything to her he'd later be sorry for. So she was both surprised and pleased at his manner of approach. He did not take her hand or try to get her to kiss him. He merely rolled his head on the pillow, looked at her with a kind of gentleness that reminded her of that far-off image of Ike, and said, "Tave, when am I going to get well so we can be married?" Tavie was taken unawares and blushed as she dropped her eyes. "Of course, I mean," John added, "if you're not going back to Connie, if you're going to divorce him, as you may now, for desertion."

Tavie had heard nothing more of Connie, but since her vision at the death of the Confederate captain she was convinced that he was dead, and did not take him into consideration in anything she said to John or thought about him. She quickly mastered the flurry of confusion John's question had raised and looked up at him appealingly. "John, you must not think or say such things at this time." "Why not, Tave?" said John with his clear, untroubled look. "Because it's liable to excite you and that's very bad for you, even dangerous." "I'm not excited," said John. "I know it's a long way off. I just wanted to tell you how happy I am to know that you are the only person in the world I love, except Ma, and maybe Ike. I thought it might please you too.

"All I want," John persisted, "is for you to say you feel the way I do and that we will be married as soon as it's possible, between my condition and whatever you plan about Connie. Just say, 'Yes, as soon as we can get everything arranged.' That's all I want now, Tave. Why, God A'mighty, you don't even have to kiss me. That *would be* exciting!" Tavie saw that his breathing was getting faster, and determined to finish this once for all.

"John, you know I feel closer to you in most ways than to anybody except Pa. There is no question about our being as good as brother and sister now.

But when you talk of marriage, you are talking of something in that other life that we can't think of sanely now, either of us. We should not even dream of such matters until long after the war is over and we're settled back in our normal ways again. We're both heart and soul in the war. This is our life now, but it won't always be, and we would be very foolish to commit ourselves about that other life which probably will last longer."

"You know, Tave," said John, and she was glad to see him look away and his breathing return to normal, "I've been thinking that as far as you and I are concerned this life is our only life, will be from now on. It's based in all those dreams of Reform and hopes for the country we have had together since we were babies. The war has solidified those dreams. It has made them concrete, like chains binding us together that we shall never be able to break, even if we try. I am perfectly sure of it, Tave. To be here with you is something stronger even than being at home. We shall carry this out with us. There isn't any other life. Two years of hell for what we believe is something we shall never get over.

"The war," John went on, "will destroy a lot of nonsense we used to take stock in. I mean specially Ike and Pru. I don't think it's unfair to them to say that the way we got wrought up about them was due to the fact that we couldn't sort of have it out with them and get it over with. They attracted us and that seemed mighty important. I'm speaking certainly of myself, but since I've been watching you around here I've been thinking it's probably true of you too. I honestly can't see now what it was about Pru that held me so long. That isn't a very gallant way to talk, is it? But I'm talking to you, the girl I really love. As far as Pru goes, I could be almost as well pleased with any healthy lady of the streets in Washington, and I may as well tell you that I know what I'm talking about." Tavie dropped her eyes. She had thought so, and she was glad for John's sake.

"As for you," John continued, "that's entirely different. I want you these nights with a hunger that probably isn't good for me at all. If you're worried about your duty, you can say to yourself that it's better for me to tell you and stop stewing about it. Once it's out, I don't expect anything of you, not until after we're married. We can be perfectly peaceful here, and maybe I won't dream as much as I have. Just say to me that if we feel the same after the war as we do now we'll be married as soon as we can. At least you can say that much, and truly it will make me feel easier."

Tavie saw John was tired from talking. But his breathing was normal. She put her hand on his and spoke very tenderly, for in a deep, quiet way she was more moved than she had been by any man since she left Ike twelve years ago.

"John, a great deal that you say is true, and I think I do love you now, probably in the same way you love me. But I can't share your confidence in the unimportance of that other life. I must ask you not to make me promise anything now. It would be easy to promise, but I cannot lie to you, even for your own good. Once or twice in the past two years things have happened to me that seemed to put me back temporarily in the old world that I am afraid will turn out to have been not very different from the new world after the war. And when that happens to me, there is only one dream of love in me, and I can't blot it out, much as I sometimes wish I could. I know I shall never marry Ike, no matter how much he asks me to, for he doesn't love me a tenth as much as he loves his railroad or his bank or his engine company. Yet there he is inside me like a live coal. Just as sure as I go back to Oberlin or Byzantium or anywhere at all after the war is over, I know he will become, after little Solon, the most important personal thing in my life, even if I never see him again. I can tell you that all of me loves you except some essential thing that is the center of my life and is all Ike's. If I knew how to get over it I would, but I don't think it will be as easy as it was for you to get over Pru. I will do anything in my power for you, perhaps more than I would do for Ike. But I cannot marry you or say I love you entirely."

John had closed his eyes and now merely murmured, "Tave, I must sleep." Tavie withdrew her hand and watched him for a long time, feeling as if he were her son.

After John's nightly fever subsided, about midnight, he came clean awake. For more than an hour he stared at the guard standing in the cone of light from the gas jet outside the door in the vestibule. He did not think about himself but about Tavie and Ike. He thought what hard luck it was for Tave, how unfair that she should be bound to a man who didn't love her and who, even if they were married, would stifle everything that made her the most perfect woman in the world. How much easier it was for men than for women! By and large a man got rid of a woman by going to bed with her, but a woman was liable to be caught for good. Tave was certainly the bravest and most independent woman he knew, yet here she was caught like any little Mattie Spencer. Poor Mattie! John knew she was Ike's mistress these days, but from the way he spoke about Pru, he was evidently not taking Mattie very seriously. He'd write him he could have Pru, and God bless them. God! What a marriage that would be! They'd meet only on the lowest side of both of them.

Alone there in the darkness, staring at the hissing gas jet and the guard out in the vestibule, John admitted to himself that he was at the end of his rope with Ike. He couldn't afford to go through life hoping, half hypo-critically hoping, blinding himself to the truth. That last letter showed that Ike was as irresponsible as ever. It was perfectly clear that he was making money out of the war generally, and that he was trying to make it out of selling guns. In his inward struggle John's love of his brother still clung to the single fact that so far he had actually not made money out of selling guns. That became a symbol, the sole criterion of Ike's decency. Even though he tried to make the gun business profitable, so long as he did not succeed in fact John would go on believing in him. Everything depended on that. The first recollection from Gettysburg drifted across his mind. He was sitting on a quiet hill where grasshoppers were buzzing. Far out to the left and below him he saw Rebels deploying. His side began to ache and his heart was thumping. He called Smith and got an opiate. In the morn-ing, Friday the 17th, he woke slowly for breakfast, and once awake felt strangely restless.

After breakfast Smith distributed the mail instead of Miss O'Malley and brought John a letter from Ike. It had been written after Tavie's and George Fulton's forged report of the Battle of Gettysburg had arrived, but before any news had leaked home as to how Jabe had been killed or that John had anything but a slight wound in the hand:

July 14, '63

Dear Paloosa—

So old Jabe is gone. Now you have got rid of everybody in the Gang except yourself and George and Alec, and likely they'll go next. I think the lot of you, from the President down, are no better than murderers. It sounds queer to say it, but I'm glad you have a wound in the hand. Maybe that will keep you from committing suicide a while longer, and maybe by the law of averages you won't be as likely to be shot again.

At first everybody thought that after this "great battle" (great mur-der) the South would surrender. Greenbacks started up and I came near to selling my gold. But now we hear that Lee is safe in Virginia and as spry as ever, so the rest of you will get another chance to get killed and crippled and driven loony over a lot of nonsense that's none of your business. Greenbacks are off again, which means the country doesn't believe in your man-hunt any more than it did before.

I have to tell you what I said I would. We made a little money on our last shipment of guns that went out early in May. We had to decide between four things—going out of business, reducing the wages of the men, getting more money out of the Government, or reducing the qual-

ity of the metal in our guns to that used by all the other factories making them. I was set on keeping the men employed, which meant both
staying in business and paying wages they could live on at present
prices. The Government wouldn't give us any more money. So we
saved on the metal going into our guns. I was sorry to hear by this
morning's post that the thing happened I was afraid of. We are the
only company making guns to whom it hasn't happened before, and
they say that in both these cases the guns were overheated from too
much firing, more than they're guaranteed for. They say that in this
"great battle" two of our guns burst and killed some men. It is a pity,
but it was business necessity, for you see - - - - -

John's heart was already pounding, and the page and the letters were
reeling before his eyes that now closed involuntarily. For an instant he saw
with minute clarity the image of Jabe in front of him holding him up,
heard the roar of the burst gun, saw Jabe doubled back over his legs, his
face in that ghastly dead grin, felt himself lunge forward and thump across
the gun wheel, where the eyes of his mind now read and understood that
lettering on the plate on the burst-out, smoking breech—

BYZANTIUM STEAM ENGINE COMPANY,
BYZANTIUM FALLS, NEW YORK.

Then there was a blank in time.

On the very afternoon of the day Ike had written this letter to John and
posted it, the first batch of mail reached Byzantium from the surviving
members of Company C. Three people stopped Ike on the mall to ask
how John was, and showed him their letters which revealed not only that
John was seriously wounded but that he had been wounded and Jabe killed
by a burst field gun. Convulsed by sudden apprehension, Ike forgot the
bitterness he had just shown in his letter. After supper he rode out to the
farm and told Sarah and Ben he had to go to New York on business. Privately he told Ben the truth and asked him to warn the neighbors to keep
it from Ma. Then he rode back to the village and packed up to catch the
morning train.

All the way down on the cars he sat looking out the window in a kind
of a trance. He tried to be sensible, but could not down the sickening fear
that one of his guns had done it, that he had killed Jabe and maybe killed
John, the two men nearest to him in the world. In his mind he didn't feel
he was responsible. The war and the Government were really responsible.

Yet there was something askew and frightened deep in him, frightened not only for John but for himself.

To the rattle of the trucks he half drifted off into his mystical state but he found no warm peace there. It was as if the doors were closed to him. It was only an idea in his mind. The more he tried to escape from the world, the more he felt something wrong in him, torturing him and holding him to the world. He remembered the letter Jabe had written him a year ago from the Peninsula, saying that he was glad he was in the war even if it killed him. Ike knew he had meant that, and, in a strange, half-mystical way he could not get hold of, he now understood Jabe and honored him above all people he had known.

What was it that Jabe and the 'Paloosa and the rest understood that he didn't? He could not see that he had done anything wrong. Yet whatever it was he had done had set him apart from his friends. He could not see it, not for all his contact with the great, quiet secret of the universe. For the first time in his life he was overwhelmed by self-doubt that he could not escape. There was something in life he didn't understand, something the rest of these people were willing to die for. Frantic with these thoughts, he sat up all night between New York and Washington, while his fellow travellers snored in the racket of the swaying, dimly lamp-lit car. The more he searched, the further he seemed from the truth. Nothing that he had ever believed helped him. He reached Washington at eight o'clock on the morning of Friday, the 17th, just as John was fainting from the effect of his letter.

Miss O'Malley had not seen John's head slump over as he dropped the letter, nor had she seen him lunge up in bed as he unconsciously re-enacted his falling across the broken field gun. But she did pass a few minutes later and saw him lying in a faint, tried his pulse, found it high, and ran for the General, who was fortunately in his office. He came at once, pulled out the old packing and let the hemorrhage run a few seconds unobstructed to clean out the pus present, for he had not dressed the wound yet that morning. Then he stuffed the wound with arnica-soaked packing and sat with John's wrist in his hand, while looking round the room and occasionally gesturing to Miss O'Malley with his forceps to attend to one or another of the patients. After half an hour he carefully pulled out a corner of the packing in John's side and only a little blood followed. Then he took out all the packing. The hemorrhage had stopped. He thought this man had more resistance than any patient he had ever seen.

He put in fresh packing, told Miss O'Malley to let him sleep as long as he would, and not to change his bedding until he was fully awake.

Half an hour later Tavie came in, saw John unconscious in his bloody bed, picked up Ike's letter, read it and understood. She learned from the General that the hemorrhage had not been a bad one and that, with his constitution, he would recover if it didn't start again. Then she went and sat by him, feeling his pulse that was terribly rapid. After an hour he spoke without moving, and Tavie didn't know whether he knew she was really there or not. "Tave," he whispered. "It's the god-damned system. 'Business necessity'! My God! A Lathrop! Caught in the 'business system'! Money grubber! Irresponsible! No different from the rest." Then he slept again and his pulse began to drop.

At noon John came fully awake. He was pale as he had been eight days ago, his eyes steel black in the big white face and his untrimmed beard and mustache black against the fold of the sheet over the blanket. Miss O'Malley and Smith changed his bedding and he ate a little dinner. After eating he could not sleep as usual, but lay staring in front of him. For all his outward pallor he felt inwardly strong with a kind of fierce moral joy, his mind clear and unburdened of a weight which, consciously or unconsciously, it had carried for more than twelve years. He was remembering clearly the details of the charge at Gettysburg. But he now saw it in large perspective as part of that other war, that greater war against the industrial rich. This whole war with the slaveholders was only the advance guard action that must be won in military terms in order to clear the stage for the larger conflict.

It was now the quiet time of the day when most of the patients were asleep, Miss O'Malley off duty, and the General snoozing in his quarters. Beside the guards, no one was on duty in the ward except Smith. Suddenly John heard Smith's voice, saw him standing by his bed, and his mind came back to the present. "Colonel Lathrop," the male nurse repeated, "Mr. Isaac Lathrop is here to see you."

John saw the world swimming in front of him but he set his teeth and fought against fainting. "Ask Master Lathrop to come in," he said. "Yes, sir," said Smith. John felt his heart pounding so he thought it would break through his ribs. When he knew Ike was there he did not at first look at him, but stared straight ahead as before. "If you have come to finish me," he said distinctly, "then stay. Otherwise please go away and stay away. I wish never to see you again." With this he turned his great dark eyes directly on Ike, who stared back as directly. "But, 'Paloosa—," he started to speak tenderly, but stopped. There was nothing of John but those big black eyes against the white face and the white pillow, eyes that had nothing in them but strength, the kind of strength Ike could not understand. Before their superhuman, impersonal gaze he backed away, stumbled out of the ward, through the vestibule and out the front door, where he sank on a little bench in the sunshine, letting his hat and stick fall to the ground beside him. Inside, John had fainted, and Smith was waking up the General, who ran in to John with his emergency kit.

While Ike sat outside, hunched over on the bench, his plug hat and stick on the ground beside him, Tavie came round the corner of the building. At first she ignored the bent, civilian figure there, but as she was going in the door Ike looked up, recognized her, rose, and stood staring down into her eyes in a frightened, hunted way. Tavie felt her heart thumping while something deeper than her heart was welling up into her eyes, struggling to recognize and respond to this image she loved and had not seen for nine years. "Tave," he murmured hoarsely. "The 'Paloosa won't see me—says he's done with me." And with that he sank down on the bench again.

Through the whirl of her emotions Tavie felt some loyalty in her switch from Ike to John, and her jaw set in the old, fanatical way. "I think I understand," she said, her voice sounding remote to her own ears.

Ike looked up at her with more pathos than she had ever seen in the face of a human being, a strange, twisted look that had no relation to her memory of him. It was Ike's body sure enough. There were the powerful shoulders, bent over now. There was the magnificent mane of hair, now pure white, and a gray beard she had not seen before. There was the old florid complexion that used to mean all vitality to her, but now it was dry and scaly. There were the big, blue eyes, looking up at her with their old direct gaze, yet the face was turned only half up toward her and the gaze was sideways as if ashamed and concealing something. There was the old pucker between the eyes that had been the center of his charm, but it no longer expressed eager curiosity and concern for something out there Ike didn't understand. Instead, it was now a deep furrow bespeaking worry, worry about himself alone, uncertainty, no interest in her but self-centered timidity, terror before something outside that was bothering his inward complacency. It was the shell of the old Ike, not the giant who had occupied all of Tavie's sky. With rising panic she saw him as something remote, tiny, dwarfed, something that had contained what she had loved long ago in childhood but within which the thing she had loved had shrivelled beyond recognition, remaining a child still playing at existence and blind to mature reality. She felt she was looking down from a height at that pathetic figure and, what was worse, she felt no pity for it at all, only something like loathing and hatred.

She felt that she was going to faint, stepped inside and sat down in the General's reception room. She did not faint, but felt her face burning instead. She closed her eyes, and her mind knew it was true, while her feelings still battled against the truth. The old Ike she loved, the father of her child, was gone. He was not in the world. He was more surely dead than if he were under the ground. This love was not even an unattainable ideal. It was a memory. John was right. The old life was gone. This was the real life here, and would continue to be, perhaps had always been. The worst of it was, she knew she would have to see Ike again and that he would be a stranger to her. She would have to look at the man she had loved and see absolutely nothing.

Tavie set her slim jaw, took a sip of whisky from the General's decanter and went outside. She asked Ike to call for her at the nurses' quarters at six that evening, and she would make everything clear. She watched him as he walked away. There was not even the old springy step, simply a kind of bent shuffle, and he leaned on his cane as he walked. Tavie went in to John and the General.

John was asleep, the General holding his wrist. Tavie felt her lower lip trembling beyond control, and the tears coming. "Will he survive this?" she managed to whisper to the General. The gray-bearded old doctor nodded sympathetically. "There has been no hemorrhage," he whispered. "It is a powerful heart."

Part IV

ARTILLERY OF TIME

CHAPTER XCVI

IN A DAZE Ike returned from Washington that mid-July of '63. In a daze he rode out to the homestead, and with the hard impersonality of a stranger reported to Ma and Ben the facts of John's condition and of his own dismissal by his brother. The next day Ma and Ben set out for Washington. Ben returned in two weeks, but Sarah stayed until November, when the infection in John's chest was clear and the wound healed. Then she and Tavie took him to Oberlin for Thanksgiving, whence Sarah did not return to Byzantium till December.

Meanwhile, throughout that summer and fall, Ike struggled to adjust himself finally to a life of loneliness. He dared not tolerate any hope of reconciliation with the Lollapaloosa, who took his place in Ike's mystical world along with Pa, Brother Tom, Dandy, his own happy childhood, and, on a little lower plane, Jabe, Bub, Joe Kirkwood, Fred, Medad and Zeb. Of the old inner circle only Alec and George Fulton remained, and Ike knew George had secretly disapproved of him ever since he trimmed Joe in the sale of the Union Mills. Nat Gadston and Tim Slocum had never meant much to him anyway. He gave up all hope of companionship such as he had enjoyed before the war.

He avoided reminders of the old life and interested himself only in what was new. He stopped calling on the Fultons and the few other survivors of the Nestors. He delighted in the current building boom that was wiping out the last landmarks of the old village. The old, stone Presbyterian Church was being replaced by a bigger one of brick in some fancy style. Between it and the Mall, half the old mansions of Washington Street were coming down in favor of the now fashionable box-like houses with cupolas, of which Bub Tanofly's had been the first. On the Mall, bandstands were being put up on the two end islands where Ike used to sell his produce, and on the central island an elaborate, cast-iron fountain wasted water all day from the new reservoir. On Columbia Street the new Court House was nearing completion. Across the street from it Old Jerry Stone had just sold his little farm to the State, and a big armory was going to be built there.

785

Old Jerry had bought a small stone house on Factory Street opposite his tannery. Ike shared the general enthusiasm for these new and monstrous structures, not because he liked them but because they meant the burial of the past.

The thing was too deep in him, too permanent for active sorrow. He lived alone with his mysticism, while, like the village, he built a new shell around his soul. He grew sociable for the first time since the war began. Indiscriminately he squired half a dozen girls who meant nothing to him, from Gloriana Gadston down to the daughters of Bub Tanofly and Joe Kirkwood, who were half his age. He became once more the fondest hope of every mamma in town. No one but Ike himself suspected that in this harmless promiscuity he was fleeing the one shadow, the one threat of fate, that had not yet overtaken him and that he still feared.

Though John had not replied to his inquiry whether he was done with Pru, Ike strongly suspected that he was, and with the lifelong cap of fraternal loyalty lifted a little from his emotions, such a volcano of desire for her was seething in him as bid fair to occupy his whole sky. His opinion of her as a person and a possible wife had not changed, and he often thought ironically of that love—"love 'n God"—that Aggie long ago had prophesied he would find. He stopped going to see Pru and struggled to keep her image out of mind. He reminded himself continually that he had not yet heard from John. Yet she became the single end of his will, sleeping or waking. He suffered nights of agonized indecision as to what he would do if she became engaged to Nat Gadston. Nat, having obtained a political captaincy through the efforts of Ostrum Applemore, was happily absent during that whole summer and fall of '63.

The one vital connection Ike maintained with the past was Old Jerry Stone, whom he still visited once or twice a week in the tannery. Curiously enough, although Ike confessed to him the tragic incident of the burst gun, Old Jerry still set out his chair for him, partly, as Ike knew, because of his continuing to pay his workmen well, contrary to the practice of the other industrialists, and partly, as Ike guessed, because the old man's powers were failing. He enjoyed the presence of anyone who stood for the old village he had loved and over whose youth he had so benignly tyrannized. But in September Old Jerry fell down in his shop with a stroke, was carried home to his little house across Factory Street, and the village and the surrounding hills did not again tremble to the tolling of the red and gold Bull of Bashan. Ike continued to go to see him in his house. The old man became less and less articulate, and more and more prone to inexplicable rages. But Mistress Abigail often told Ike that Jerusalem had been asking for him.

And by seeing indirectly to large purchases of the harness which the 'prentices in the shop continued to turn out, Ike took some pleasure in adding Old Jerry to the increasing number of people in the village he was helping to support without their knowledge.

Ike kept his sanity by remaining an attentive, indeed an over-attentive lover to Mattie Spencer in the hired room that was their secret menage down on River Street. Against her protestations he was forever turning up with little presents. Nevertheless, Mattie became increasingly troubled by his seeming detachment, the over-formal, almost mechanical nature of his attentions. Sensual as she was, this yet wasn't enough for her fundamentally motherly nature. One night in October as they lay in bed she said, "Ike, please don't stay with me because ye think ye ought. Sometimes I think any other girl would do ye as well." Whereupon Ike merely laughed and discovered twenty new places to kiss her.

In November Pity VanSanford was married to Numa Samson, who got a two weeks' furlough for the purpose. Medad being dead, Fred idiotic, young Robert away in the Army, and Solon Samson in Washington, Ike stood up with Numa as best man, the old Judge giving Pity away. The wedding was in the cheerful parlor of the stone house on Washington Street where he had gone so often with his pa. Present were only the remaining Nestors, their near relations, and those of the dead Nestors. Young Numa, only twenty, meant the Hollow to Ike, and everybody said he was going to be a worthy successor to his pa. Ike could feel Medad's presence in the house, and over in the corner Fred muttered about mumblety-peg all through the service. The past Ike had been fighting down surged over him, and he had to set his jaw to keep his lip from trembling. After the youngsters rolled away in the creaky old VanSanford coach, he went to his room over Quin's drug shop and for the second time in his life got dead drunk alone.

Early in December Sarah came home with the news that John was out of danger, though he would be a long time recovering his strength. In spite of Ike's studied nonchalance, she saw his pathetic eagerness for hopeful news beyond that of John's physical condition. But she had none to give him.

Just before New Year's, '64, Ike got a letter from John in Oberlin, written in an irregular, uncertain version of his old big hand:

Dear Ike:—

Forgive me for not writing you all these months. I have been very weak, and had to devote what strength I had to arranging Zeb Milliken's law practice, which he left me and which was large and mostly independent of mine in spite of our being partners. Perhaps it was cowardly of me to come out here to recuperate instead of going home. But it seemed to me that my first duty was to get well, and that would certainly have been delayed by the active continuance of our misunderstanding.

First, to reply to the question you asked about X in one of your last letters. Yes, that is over and done with. I am glad to say that I found you had been right all along, both as to the nature of my feelings and as to the cure for them. The field is yours!

The fact that our break occurred at a time when I was ill, and under peculiarly aggravating circumstances, is not ultimately important. It was bound to come soon anyway. I am sorry to disappoint Ma, but I must stick to my position. After thirteen years of hoping, I am finally convinced that at heart you have no more moral sense than the others who have got rich in the new industries before and especially during the war. I shall welcome any valid pretext to take back these words and apologize. But until I have such a pretext you are, as between ourselves, in the position of a stranger to me. The more clearly we understand that the break is final, the easier it will be, I think, to maintain a natural front in public.

Let us hope that when we are old men and through with active life, we can look back and laugh at all this, enjoying our second childhood together as we did our first. Sometimes I wish that time were near.

Finally,

John.

This letter did not make Ike get drunk. For a week it put him back in the stunned condition in which he had left Washington almost six months before. Then, as the shock of it wore off, he realized that it was no more than he had expected and prepared himself for. He must go on as he had before Numa's and Pity's wedding upset him, his true life in the world of deathless Nature where Pa and the rest were alive, and for the immediate world, just indifference and common sense, tending to business, finding what diversion he could, continuing the struggle with his desire for Pru.

But the consciousness, the hope, of John's possible continuing interest in Pru had been a stronger defense against her than Ike realized. With that last barrier gone, her image became a terrible, hot engine turning in his midriff, compelling him to action. He passed weeks of wakeful nights before he was able to order his thoughts and isolate four things he greatly wanted.

First, he wanted to get married to somebody he could trust and with whom he could settle down without the humiliating secrecy of clandestine carryings-on. Second, he wanted to get his little son Solon Oaks to live with him permanently. Third, he wanted to move back to the homestead and keep only a finger in business in the village. And finally, he knew he could never find any peace unless he carried on with Pru for a spell without marrying her—that would be the only possible way of getting her out of his system.

One of these objectives, the withdrawal from business, was immediately put beyond the range of present feasibility. At the end of January, Solon Samson told him that the majority of Congress was undoubtedly for a still higher tariff, that the new law would abandon the principle of revenue for the principle of protection, virtually prohibiting many imports. Ike recollected that this would be the tariff which he had predicted to John that the war profiteers would get the Republicans to pass for them. It meant the certainty of more profit than ever in all of his enterprises, and he concluded that it would be childish to pick this time to quit.

Over and over Ike considered the possibilities for marriage—Glory Gadston, Tavie, Mattie. It amused him to think of Glory's gigantic demureness, and of Mehitabel for a mother-in-law—that was easy to think about, for he knew he would never do it.

Mattie was a more serious problem. She had the first claim on him now, and she understood his ways. She was loyal and loving, had common sense, and took no stock in the airs she saw in the Gadston house among Mehitabel's friends. Ike enjoyed thinking how mad Mehit Gadston would be if one of Glory's supposed suitors married their hired girl.

But, after all, Tavie was still the best proposition. By marrying her he could pull together all the loose ends of his life. He would get little Solon under his roof. He would wipe out the remnant of his original sense of guilt about her. Her congeniality with John would work toward a reconciliation with the 'Paloosa. And perhaps the strongest reason for his trying Tavie first was that subconsciously he didn't believe he could get her. Quite aside from the problem of her divorcing Connie, Ike suspected there was something afoot between her and the 'Paloosa. Learning from Ma that she was back in the Washington hospital, he wrote her a candid letter, a better letter than he had written to her early in the war. He did not profess more than he felt, nor did he rest his appeal transparently on his desire to get little Solon. He merely said that "the longer I live, the more certain I am that I shall never find any contentment in life until you are my wife."

The reply was as candid and unequivocal: ". . . When I wrote you after the battle of Shiloh I spoke only for the moment and could not predict what my feelings would be after the war. In Washington we were both too troubled about John to pay much attention to each other. Now, my dear Ike, I am afraid I can and must say finally that it can never be. . . ."

When he finished Tavie's letter Ike could not deny to himself that he was relieved. But the relief was only momentary. He was now faced squarely with the problem of Mattie, with Pru torturing him all the time, even when he was in his mistress's arms. He concluded again and again that Mattie was the wife for him, but never could bring himself to a declaration. Paradoxically, the more seriously he thought of her in that way, the more restless and dissatisfied he became with their existing relationship. He grew more and more detached when he was with her. His attitude in their semiweekly meetings became one of impatience to get it over and go back to his bachelor bed, where he would find himself dreaming desperately of Pru. It was exactly what had happened with Tavie almost thirteen years before when he began mixing the pleasure of going to her room with notions of marrying her. As then, things came presently to a pass where, lying beside Mattie in bed, he could hardly make love to her at all. And, as long ago with Tavie, a night came at last, early in March, when he found himself absolutely impotent. As he lay in wretched self-consciousness, Mattie said softly, "Ike, don't ye think ye'd best leave me be for a spell?" "Likely," he said. About a week later he saw Mattie on the street with Loyal Hall, who was out of the Army for good, having lost his left arm at Gettysburg. Again, as when he got Tavie's letter, Ike admitted to himself that he was relieved.

Now there happened to Ike exactly what he used to lecture John about. Suddenly cut off from a year's vigorous life with Mattie, his desire for Pru became as romantic and helpless as that of a boy of sixteen. He had not gone to see her alone since his break with John, and a short time back he had decided that when he did so it would be with outright immoral intentions. But now when he thought of carrying out his plan he fell into a panic of shyness. She became the very image of burning, unattainable perfection. He had sense enough left to know that if he approached her now he would end up by marrying her. But this knowledge did not alter the fact of her, a perpetually oncoming flood of fire pouring into his body and mind.

As the terrible nights and days of frustration dragged by, Ike grew more and more frightened. He made excuses to stay away from parties where he knew Pru would be. He walked around blocks to avoid meeting her on the street. Once he saw her in the bank and fled out the back door. He came into a state of frozen detachment, as if he were encased in glass through which he could see everything but could touch nothing. He grew absent-minded at his work, could not even add a column of figures, and lost $3,000 by a foolish investment in response to a swindler's circular. He dropped a thoughtless remark to Ostrum Applemore to the effect that he was figgering to close up shop and go back to the homestead, and this caused a small run on his bank, till he came out to the line at the window and dispelled the rumor by a flat denial and a fit of hysterical laughter. The ladies of the town began to whisper guesses as to what was happening to Isaac Lathrop.

On April Fool's Day Nat Gadston came home for a leave of a week. Knowing he was with Pru every minute, Ike experienced suicidal agonies of jealousy, and whenever he had to talk to either Nat or Pru he was incoherent, being literally unable to hear what they said. Late in the afternoon of the day Nat left, which was Saturday, April 9, 1864, Gam Stark's hired man brought Ike at the bank a note from Pru. He went to an obscure saloon on Court Street and had a drink before daring to read it.

Dear Isaac:—

You have seemed so distant for the last nine months that I am afraid you will be displeased at my writing you, but I feel I must.

You have probably forgotten that on Sunday morning, April fifteenth, 1862, two years ago next Friday, you made me promise to let you know if ever I was seriously considering a certain person. Well, I am, and I trust you to keep the secret. I have promised to write an answer within a week, and I think it will be, "Yes."

I am certain that neither John nor you will be the least bit interested now. I am simply keeping my promise.

Ever yours,

Pru.

Instantly Ike's pent-up feelings were released in a sense of irresistible power, like one of those new express engines lighting out with the throttle wide open. It was almost six o'clock, but he never thought of supper. Instead, he half ran home to his room and labored a long, joyful and clumsy time over a meticulous toilet. At seven he strode down the lamp-lit north side of the Mall with his old springy step, swinging his cane, without a plan or thought of any kind.

Although he had forgotten to warn Pru that he was coming, it had not occurred to him that she would not be ready for him. And indeed she was, wearing a low-cut, hooped dress of blue ruffled foulard, her turquoise earrings, and a band of artificial flowers round the back of her head, the scent of her powder filling the room, her mamma indisposed and in bed and her papa downstairs in the tap-room—both under unusually strict orders. Ike could scarcely wait to throw off his coat before he had her in his arms, for the first time in his life abandoning himself to his desire for her. "My darling," he kept whispering hoarsely as his kisses ran over her face and neck and down on her bosom. In a moment he carried her to the couch, laid her there, and himself stretched out beside her, drawing her up against him with a grip such as she had never felt from a man. She was terribly frightened, but tingling with excitement. She was determined to go through with this if necessary, not fail as she had with John a year ago. She didn't trust Ike to marry her, but it was her one chance. She clung close to him, pressing her face against his shirt front.

"My darling," she heard him whisper, "I've wanted ye all these years, and now I'm going to have ye." She felt his hand go down inside her dress and play all over her little breast, then he bent down and she felt him kissing her there. Involuntarily she began to sob, and with tears running off her cheeks looked up at his excited, unnatural face. At this he lifted her, kissed her long on the lips, and she closed her eyes. Then she opened them, reached up with her free hand and stroked his hair. "Isaac, my darling," she whispered, "will you do me just one favor? Will you let me up for just one minute? I won't run away. I promise. Just one minute?"

The thought flashed through Ike's mind that she was going to do something expeditious about all those petticoats and things. "Yes, dear," he whispered and rose. Pru stood up and leaned against him, looking up into his eyes. "Please keep holding me close," she whispered, "I'm not going to run away." Ike took her in his arms and looked down at her more gently now, with tenderness beginning to flow through his lust. She gazed up at him through her tears with an adoring and helpless look of appeal which he remembered all his days. "Isaac, dear," she said very softly and earnestly, "I shall do whatever you say. But tell me truly, do you really believe this is the right way?"

Ike felt tenderness flooding him completely. With one hand he pressed her little head gently against his chest while above her he raised his own head and closed his eyes. Fleetingly, like something in another world, he remembered all the mean and selfish things he knew Pru had done. Then he thought of her here in his arms, certainly the most desirable woman in the world who had put herself in his hands and had promised she would do as he said. He remembered his determination not to marry her. Then he remembered his affairs with Tavie and Mattie, the unpleasant furtiveness of them, and how, although they were both fine girls, that way of doing things had brought the whole business to nothing. Perhaps there was something twisted in him that had made things turn out that way, whatever it was the 'Paloosa called immoral. Perhaps he had been showing the white feather all his life and it was that that had cut him off from the 'Paloosa and the Gang. He didn't want this with Pru to peter out and leave him the way he had been the last month, this that was certainly the deepest of them all.

These thoughts flashed through his mind in perhaps five seconds. Then he said simply, with less hoarseness in his voice, "No, it ain't." Under his hand he felt Pru lift her head while her hands clung still closer to his coat lapels. He looked down and she was peering up at him with lips parted and something like worship in her eyes. His tense expression relaxed and he smiled his old, inclusive, easy smile. "Let's get married," he said.

CHAPTER XCVII

UPON her engagement at thirty to the man she had always loved, Pru's qualities fused into the woman she remained henceforth, the woman that essentially she had always been. The kittenish ways of her recent uncertain years disappeared for good. Likewise the demure affectations of Mehitable Gadston's set, which airs and graces she had assumed only as a precaution, facing the possibility of one day being Mehitable's daughter-in-law. In external demeanor she fell into her ma's pattern, that of an easy and gracious lady of what was already the old school. She did not hesitate to burn her bridges and throw in her lot exclusively with the traditional people who no longer enjoyed what was coming to be called "social prominence." In the two months of her engagement her intimate associates became Patience Tanofly, Ruth Kirkwood, and Lydia Fulton— George's wife. She delighted Sarah and the other surviving wives of the old Nestors, and became of their fellowship as her mother had always been.

On the other hand her pa in her moved out from petty scheming into larger fields. Penurious about the expenses of the forthcoming wedding and matrimony, she was none the less determined to get everything she considered necessary. Gracious and tactful in her demands, she was none the less explicit and arbitrary, and her arrogant nose could go up to good effect. She persuaded her pa to give them for a wedding present the center acre of his ten-acre lot on State Street, the one Ike had always coveted, fetching round old Gam—who was losing money on the Liberty and couldn't sell it—with the telling argument that she was marrying a man who was richer than he was and, if treated well, would see that he never came to want. Before the wedding the cellar and foundations of the house were finished, taking in the cellar-hole where the original Stark house had stood, likewise the cellar and foundations of the new barn, covering the site of the old barn which had been standing in ruins in '50 and under which Dandy for a week had found shelter against the November sleet. Pru told Ike that she wanted a decent, modern brick house, but no castle to rival the Gadstons', the Fords'—the new, wealthy family in town—or anybody else. She found the original estimate of $5,000 too much and herself reduced it to $4,000. Ike said this suited him first-rate, as he wanted to be able to get his money out when things quieted down after the war, so that they might dispose of the new place then and move back to the farm. To Ike's frequent expression of this intention Pru never made any reply.

Sarah gave them the best wedding present she could, the old Lathrop coach, carefully repaired, refurbished and gaily painted by Ben. Pru did her best to head off this present, for she knew what it meant to Sarah, and they would have little use for it. But at last there was nothing to do but accept it, with genuine tears of gratitude. Handsome presents came from Oberlin, including a big silver coffee urn from John which he first had had sent to Oberlin all the way from New York. John sent the most affectionate congratulations and good wishes, along with sincere regrets that the doctor had positively forbidden him to travel—so he could not come to stand up with Ike as Ike had requested. He addressed him as "Scamp" in the letter, and begged him to believe him, assuring him that "there is no room at such a time for personal misunderstandings, however serious." Tavie, back in the hospital in Washington, was also unable to come, being denied leave because the "Grand Advance" of the Army was beginning.

Ike and Pru were married at noon on June first in the new First Presbyterian Church. In the personnel of the guests, it was a unique wedding in the history of Byzantium. Ben stood up with Ike and Lydia Fulton with Pru, old Gam giving her away. The guests included all the near kin of the old Nestors, most of the residents of Lathrop Hollow, and all of the employees of the four institutions in which Ike was chiefly interested—the Railroad, the Bank, the Steam Engine Company, and the Tanofly Mill. Invitations also went to the few girls Pru liked in her old Sewing Circle, including Gloriana and Olympia Gadston. But not one of the older generation of Mehitable Gadston's set was bid. Thus Pru cut herself off forever from "social prominence," and Ike was delighted.

After the ceremony Pru "went away" privately and without guests from the Liberty, and afterwards they gave an old-fashioned dance in the hall at the Hollow, with Jehu Jones, now a centenarian, officiating. The real "going away" was at seven o'clock in the Lathrop coach from the Lathrop homestead, amid cheers and showers of rice and blossoms, the "handsomest couple Byzantium ever saw" both sitting on the box and waving, and ancient Henry Hawks—unseen and "not sartin sure what he thought of this match"—jostling comfortably inside. Henry was to drive the coach back from Utica, after which they would take a three months' tour to Saratoga, Boston, Newport and New York. Pru said it would be their last chance and they might as well spend the money, since they could afford to.

While they were enjoying themselves that summer, and Grant, Lee, Sherman and Johnston were slaughtering their thousands, events occurred that were significant for Byzantium and Ike and Pru. One day in August Squire Fulton climbed a long ladder to cut an offensive limb from one of his maples, fell, broke his neck and died instantly. Later, John wrote Loyal Hall from Oberlin, asking him to take over the editorship of the *Eagle*. On the day of Squire Fulton's death Ostrum Applemore captured control of the Republican County Committee, which insured his nomination for Congress over the now veteran Solon Samson. Ostrum, with all of his cohorts, had come over in a body to the Republican Party, and he was now able on a moment's notice to weep in public over his early folly that had not seen the righteousness of the war. Business now owned the party that had been consecrated to human liberty and had undertaken the war as a selfless crusader. The past was officially dead.

Tim Slocum was drafted that summer, and when his pa ordered him to buy a substitute on pain of being cut off, Tim enlisted all the same. In spite of Ike's feeling about the war, he was pleased when he heard that the most insignificant member of the old Gang had at last shown some gumption.

One market day at the end of August, Ben dropped into Ike's bank to deposit some cash. The clerk showed him a telegram from Ike who was back in Saratoga on his return journey from Newport: "Have sold forty thousand gold at two hundred sixty to VanStruck New York deliver gold to messenger from New York on delivery of one hundred and four thousand green-backs likewise deliver five thousand Solon Samson's gold to same messenger on delivery of thirteen thousand more green-backs—Lathrop." "'That means," said the clerk, beaming, "that we're going to win the war. Ike knows." As Ben walked out of the bank he was thinking that now Ike had got what he set out after, and he wondered what good it would do him.

Ike and Pru returned early in September, and put up temporarily at the Liberty. The day after their arrival Pity VanSanford Samson bore a boy to Numa who, having been recently promoted captain from the ranks, was unable to get leave. When Ike was shown the squirming midget he felt a lump in his throat, wondering what kind of a world he would grow up in, this little fellow who certainly would stick by the old-fashioned ways of both his grandpas with the fierceness of all the Samsons.

Two days later Pru told Ike that they also were expecting an heir.

CHAPTER XCVIII

BY THE MIDDLE of September Pru and Ike had settled into their new brick house with its lofty ceilings and inside shutters on the plate glass windows, shedding cool privacy and comfortable gloom, its solid mahogany stairway, its lace curtains, heavy portieres, and upholstered and mahogany furniture which Pru had picked out and had had shipped from New York. With little friction their life settled into routine. Pru began to entertain a good deal, but always informally, and her parties often escaped notice in the papers. The personnel of her guests was usually mixed, but they had a certain reality in common, ranging from old Howell Sherwood and the VanSanfords down to promising youths from laboring families, many of whom thereafter found themselves unaccountably offered scholarships at the now flourishing down-state colleges, Hamilton, Cornell, Colgate. These parties suited Ike to a T. Though he had never regretted his own lack of education, yet he rarely respected anyone else who lacked it. Altogether, Pru behaved as Sarah Lathrop would have done in her situation and with her resources, as Lorinda Fulton had always done when her husband was alive, as her daughter-in-law Lydia, Pru's friend, and Pity Samson would presently be doing when their husbands returned from the Army.

Pru further identified herself with the old school by adopting a practice which only the Fultons and the Tanoflys, among the local industrialists, had carried out before. During the first two months of her residence she managed to call—not merely leaving a card—on the wives and mothers of every one of Ike's two hundred-odd employees. She arranged with the various managers to notify her when any member of these families was sick, and thereafter, whenever notified, she would leave them presents and see to medical attention where necessary.

But in all of Pru's hospitality and generosity there was a difference between her attitude and that of the older generation, an important difference of which only she and Ike were aware. The women of the older leadership would have shown the same social responsibility, but without any sense of established superiority, merely the consciousness that their husbands, through ability, had attained to importance in the community and were subject to certain Christian duties accordingly. But to Pru, wealth itself was a sort of escutcheon, irrespective of whether its possessors enjoyed either ability or leadership. Its privileges came before its duties, and, quite aside from her conduct, she assumed that by right of Ike's money she was a creature apart and above the common herd. Her arrogance with servants and shopkeepers differed from Mehitable Gadston's only in that it was more graceful and therefore more effective. She distinguished herself from the prominent set only in that she had one generation of what she called "blood" —she meant money—behind her, while Ike had many generations both in Byzantium and before—Pru did not take into account the fact that before Ike's day the richest Lathrop had never been "worth" over ten thousand dollars more than his poorest neighbor. Because Pru's conviction of her prerogative was mixed with a sense of *noblesse oblige,* causing her to perform real service to the community and win its respect, she did more than anyone else to fix those new class distinctions which Mehitable Gadston had more ostentatiously drawn.

The old Gam in Pru appeared in her immediately establishing a penurious tyranny in her own house, a tyranny which was in extreme contrast to her social graciousness. For miserly reasons she kept only one "girl,"—with additional help for parties. She paid her wretched wages and worked—even starved—her as near to death as possible. No Yankee girl would stay with her, but she found ready victims among the daughters of the Irish laborers. It was not rare for her in the morning to flay her servant with quiet sarcasm for having helped herself too generously to gruel, and in the afternoon to deliver a basket of fruit to the same girl's ailing mother.

From the outset Pru's gently but firmly expressed "wishes" restricted Ike's freedom in the house to that of a piece of furniture. In wet weather his carpet slippers were at the front door and he must remove his boots before entering. He must not lean clear back in his new spring rocker for fear of weakening the spring, nor must he sit always in one spot in his easy chair, lest it wear unevenly. He was forbidden to chew in the house, and— final affliction—he must not smoke there, for smoke poisoned the air, permeated the upholstery and discolored the curtains.

Ike fled to the garden and the big red barn. Outside his marriage bed, he found his only content at home sitting with old Henry Hawks—he hired a second man to do the heavy chores—in the harness room, smoking and spitting in or on the stove. He interested himself actively in laying out a spacious garden behind the house, and before snow flew in November had a wide lawn sprouting. He got Pete Van Ness to find him a comfortable garden seat which you could tilt back without breaking, and here, under the gray sky, bundled up in his greatcoat, wearing a comfortable, broad, black felt hat in place of his old plug, and with his hands clasped over the silver head of his cane, he would sit and smoke after dinner under one of the big apple trees that had been the orchard of the original Stark homestead. In the foreground stretched the diminutively hirsute promise of lawn; beyond, the big rectangle of plowed and staked ground where he and Henry were going to see to a posy and vegetable garden, come spring; then the young orchard they had already set out; and a hundred yards away, across the rear of the property, the fenced area where the two Jersey cows were still out to pasture. At one corner of the pasture stood the red carriage house, the repository for sleighs in summer, carriages in winter, and, Ike feared for all seasons henceforth, the old Lathrop coach, now carefully covered with cheesecloth like a shroud.

In this little domain Ike soon grew to feel intimately familiar, not only with the cows and his four fine horses that thumped in the barn, but with the clods and ridges in the plowed garden, the very blades of grass, the twists and crotches of the apple trees, the birds that fluttered down to take toll of his grass seed, the barn cats that appeared after the winter's hay with its mice was in. He even felt as if the sky over the place and the first snow-flakes that fell into it were somehow part of him, as they all together were a part of the bigger universe around. His spacious backyard became a mystic place to him, a private temple close where he could shut his eyes and imagine himself in Jolam's Grove back in the Hollow where his inner life had begun.

Behind Ike's tolerance of Pru's domestic tyranny there was more than his own gentleness and hatred of a row, more than his satisfaction in Pru's outward social behavior. There was the central, the one genuine fact of their married life which in large part compensated him for his superficial slavery. This was their perfect physical mating. The real basis of the difference between Pru's easy dignity and the fluttering affectations of the newly-rich ladies of the village lay in the fact that all of them—along with their husbands—were accrediting and applying the fashionable superstition that creatures of "finer clay" were too rarefied for base desires. Pru knew this was all poppycock. As always, she was worldly and realistic. As she had been continent and steadfast in pursuit, so she was passionate and abandoned in possession. Not in his most voluptuous dreams had Ike conceived of such a complete mating. He knew he could never tire of the continually mounting and richly resolving chemistry of their two desires that were one.

Sometimes in those first months, when he was sitting in the garden, a virtual exile from his own house, he might miss the gentle, motherly solicitude of Mattie, or it might occur to him that he had not found the understanding which Aggie had wanted for him. But, he would conclude, a man couldn't have everything, and in those days if he could have chosen again he would have taken what he had in preference to the rest. He sometimes wondered patronizingly if Aggie knew as much about love as he and Pru did. He wondered if anybody in the world did! As during the months of agony before his marriage, Pru continued to be the motive power of his life. As then, she was with him even when he was at work. But now, instead of the agony, he lived in a glow of memory and expectation. He believed if she should die, that carnal memory would suffice him as long as he lived, and he would never desire another woman.

This monogamous conviction of Ike's was put to the test early in January. Pru was almost up to her sixth month and Dr. Daw advised Ike to obstain. With the tenderest regrets, as if Ike were setting out on a voyage round the world, they parted, Ike leaving Pru's bed and installing himself in the second-best guest-room across the hall. And thereafter he found that his conviction had been true. As before, his sexual vitality arose in Pru and returned to her, but now without need of a physical channel. His affections for those around him were quickened, but instead of fixing on women or any woman, his lust faded away. It was as if his strength, like Pru's, were pouring back into their child.

CHAPTER XCIX

FOR SEVERAL months after Ike's marriage Mattie Spencer and
Loyal Hall had continued to keep steady company, and Ike had hope it
would lead to marriage. But during the fall Ike noticed that they weren't
going together any more. In December he learned that Mehitable Gadston
had given Mattie the gate. Then, during a week in January, not long after
the beginning of his own period of enforced continence, he twice saw
Mattie on the street in the company of some of the young Irishmen of the
town, and with too much "false bloom" on her cheeks. When he had just
about made up his mind to interfere, he got a letter from Joe Kirkwood.

Joe wrote in high spirits from somewhere in Arizona Territory. He told
how, after having just missed being shot by the Rebels for a spy, he had at
last got free and operated for a time with a guerrilla band in the West.
Then, about a year ago, he had run away from them and ended up "in this
region that is, I believe, the most soul-inspiring of any on earth, where I am
living by my sinful wits, moving from place to place and usually leaving a
bounty on my carcass, dead or alive. If they don't string me up in the next
few years I may buy me a few thousand acres and settle down, but there is no
prospect of it just now. Life is too much fun with my gang of Elizabethan-
American cut-throats, none of whom trust each other."

The letter ended as follows:

If the five hundred I sent you has not been enough to take care of
Mattie, write me as "Henry Smith," P. O., Virginia City, Nevada Territory. If I'm alive I plan to inspect that silver metropolis peaceably
some two or three months hence, and will then respond to any request
of yours with a draft on some bank under some name which in the
meantime I shall devise. If ever I settle down I may send for Mattie,
but don't tell her that, for it's extremely unlikely.

To hell with the old Gang, Ike, my boy! To hell with everything
but this vast country, this open sky, these big stars, and this gang of
drunken thieves of mine!

May you prosper legitimately or illegitimately,

Joe.

Ike wrote "Henry Smith" a cheerful letter at the Nevada address, daring him to try his new gang on the old Gang in Byzantium, revealing his own marriage, and reporting the good health of Joe's family. At the end he stated that Mattie was well settled, that no outlay had been necessary on her account, and that he did not expect there would be any. That evening he sent his clerk up to Mistress Spencer's house with a note for Mattie, asking her to drop in at the bank early the next day.

In the morning Ike left the door of his office open, and when he saw Mattie enter the bank he strode out, greeted her cordially, brushed the snow from her rubbers with the broom behind the door, and led her back to his office under the uplifted nose of Fanny Ludlow and the mild eyes of Ruth Kirkwood. He closed the door, took Mattie's old cloak, sat her down, sat down himself and looked at her for a few seconds with honest and troubled affection, while she kept glancing up at him, then down, with her big, blue-gray eyes. He observed that she had left off the "false bloom." Presently he said, "I've some news for ye, Mat. I got a letter from Joe. He's some place out in Arizoney Territory and seems to be having an a'mighty high time, farming or something of the sort. He seems to be pretty well settled."

During this statement Mattie perked up and stared at Ike wide-eyed, with something like happiness in her face. Ike smiled back, then took on a troubled expression, hesitated, and resumed: "Besides wanting to tell ye about Joe, I wanted to say, Mat, that I'm a'mighty sorry ye've left the Gadstons', and I've been more than a little bothered to notice ye on the street two or three times recently with young fellers for whom I can't bring myself to believe ye've any particular fondness. I hope ye'll quit it, Mat, and I'm here to help ye out if ye're in any sort of trouble."

At this Mattie fidgeted in her chair, rose, started for the door, half turned back and said, "Ike Lathrop, ye've no call to talk so." Ike jumped up, took her gently by the shoulders, felt her shudder to his touch, and sat her down again. "Yes, Mat," he said, "I figger I have. I've every call to. Don't ye realize that, after your ma, I'm likely the best friend ye have in town? I ain't stirring up any dead ashes. I'm talking about what ain't dead. In the way of friendship I'm just as fond of ye as ever I was, and that's likely fonder than ye give me credit for. I figger it gives me the right to look after ye if I can whenever ye need looking after, same as I would for Joe or Joe for me, same as you would for either one of us."

Mattie was now staring straight at Ike again, but instead of the faint elation that had been in her face when Ike spoke of Joe, two little streams of unattended tears were running off precisely the center of each lower eyelid, in exactly the same volume, jetting and stopping together, as if they were turned on and off together by the same delicate faucet somewhere behind her eyes. "I ain't trying to dictate," Ike went on gently, "who ye should keep company with and who ye shouldn't. All I want to make sure is that if ye keep company with some feller ye're doing it because ye want to and not for any other reason."

After a pause in which they both dropped their eyes, Ike looked up again and continued: "Now it happens that for some time I've been wanting somebody, likely a smart girl, to work in the office over at the Tanofly Mill where I'm sort of President, somebody to be there all day, tell fellers when they come in where they can find me, and keep all the post and the business papers in order. I don't know what the pay'll be but it'll be middling good."

"I couldn't do that sort o' thing, Ike," said Mattie, looking scared, "I han't the book-learnin' fer it." "Ye can read and write, can't ye?" said Ike with a laugh, "and ye can foot a column of figgers? Ye can say, 'Good mornin'' to a stranger, can't ye, and 'Did ye want to see Ike Lathrop?' and 'Ike's over at the bank,' or 'Ike's likely at the Railroad office,' or 'Ike'll likely be here after dinner about three'—" "Not 'Ike,' but 'Mr. Lathrop,' " Mattie broke in. "Ye can have it Mehitabel's way if ye prefer it," said Ike, "but that's all there'll be to it—at the start off, except to open the post and get it in some shape on my desk, and after a while learn to throw out what's of no account. Maybe later ye'll learn the ledgers so ye can look up the accounts. Don't concern yourself for a spell about anything but learning the business slow and easy."

Mattie was now looking down, twisting her brand new white kid gloves —the mark of the garish, and presumably fallen woman. "The trouble is, Ike," she finally said in her old meek voice, "I'd feel ye were just doing me a kindness I could never repay. If I could sure enough do something for ye in return it'd be different." And she looked at him with her tender smile, not leaving any doubt as to what she meant.

Ike's eyes never wavered. He spoke very softly now, but with friendliness rather than tenderness in his voice, "Mat, we may as well settle now at the start-off, that whatever happens, the old days are done and finished. But in the way of friendship, I want to tell ye that the biggest favor ye could do me would be to let me do this for ye, with nothing more. It's true as gospel I need a sort of clerk over there. And it's true, too, that I'm asking you first because I'm as fond of ye as most anybody I know and I couldn't sleep nights if ye weren't comfortable. If ye don't let me do this for ye, ye'll be doing me a mighty unkindness, and don't forget it, Mat."

"Ike," said Mattie, turning her head away and speaking through little sobs, "it ain't all ways fair of ye to stir me up like this, knowin' me as ye do. Ye know I'm a one-man girl and not a slut. Ye know there's only two fellers in the world I could care fer, and you're one of 'em. And here ye come bein' gentle to me and sayin' at the same time I'm to see ye likely every day, only I'm not t' be able to do anything really fer ye. It ain't fair of ye, Ike. It ain't like ye." And she turned her head away, taking a little handkerchief from her muff and lifting it to her trembling lips.

Ike replied almost harshly: "Mat, ye're acting like a nincompoop, and it's time ye quit it. Ye're a one-man girl, all keerect, and ye'd do well to settle from now on ye're going to act like one. Ye've had uncommon hard luck and I'm not forgetting it. It's sort of got ye down, but your back ain't broke yet, and it ain't going to break. Ye're a brave, first-rate girl and ye're going to stay one. It ain't too much to say ye've the chance of a job here that most any girl in town would envy ye. It's high time ye quit sniv'lin' and looked life straight in the face. This job ain't going to fetch ye into Heaven. It ain't even going to fetch ye much happiness in itself—likely it will seem funny for a spell, us being together in just a business way. But this job's going to support ye pretty and set ye on your two feet. Ye'll be seeing the smartest folks in town instead of the good-for-nothings. One of these days, if the right feller comes along ye'll be ready for him. If he don't, anyway ye'll be better off than walking the streets with a reputation ye don't deserve. Now straighten up and run along and be over at the Tanofly Mill at three this afternoon and I'll start ye off."

While Ike was speaking Mattie had been pulling off her white gloves and stowing them in her muff. Now she did straighten up as he told her to and smiled with more animation than he had seen in her since their first days together. They both rose, Ike put her cloak on her, and she sailed out of the bank with her head as high as any lady of the "first families" waiting to cash a hundred-dollar check at the counter.

And so began a relationship, new in Byzantium, that lasted as long as Mattie and Ike both lived, for Joe Kirkwood was heard from only once again, and then by neither Ike nor Mattie, nor in relation to anything that directly concerned them. Mattie made herself indispensable to Ike, the Mill, and afterwards the Railroad. She became again the smart girl who had been the best speller in John's class at the Institute. Her motherliness expanded to include all of Ike's business concerns, whether he was active in them or not, and all of the people employed in them. She was the only woman in town in such a position. Paradoxically, it was the kind of position Pru had sought back in the spring of '51 when she came to Ike's first office in the Fulton and Price Mill.

CHAPTER C

AS THE WEEKS of celibacy passed, Ike came to realize that his marriage was more a diversion from his deepest concerns than a solution of them. He could not even talk to Pru about John, for the mention of him only made her smile as if Ike were a little boy who had to be humored. He had not heard from the 'Paloosa since his wedding. The first heat of his romance with Pru had burned away the shell he had built around his hurt in order to go on living. Now that the romance was inactive, the wound was uncovered. The integration of his carnal desires and his expected child gave him a point of sure contact with the actual world which prevented him from reconstructing his shell and compelled him to face his wound and admit it. He could not escape from it now but carried it with him. The fear that had come over him when he was going to Washington to see John, the fear that there was something wrong with him, woke in him again. At the center of that fear was the break with the 'Paloosa. Now he could no longer deny his terrible hunger for a reconciliation. Pathetically each morning, he first looked through the post on his desk for his brother's big writing. Secretly he showed the hired girl a sample of it—if a letter came that looked like that, Henry Hawks was to bring it to the bank.

Ma and Ben always told him what news they had, and Aggie sometimes wrote him. Soon after the first of the year John had been pronounced cured and had rejoined the Army of the Potomac. He had been immediately promoted to Colonel and put in command of a new regiment. One market day in February Ben brought Ike a letter, saying, "Here's one at last that's more for you than anybody."

> Armory Square Hospital
> Washington, D. C.
> Feb. 5, '65.

Dearest Ma and Ben—

Don't be disturbed by the superscription. I am not wounded again and am quite well. I will explain it presently.

Ever since I rejoined the Army I have had something to say to Ike,

but since we have broken it seemed wiser not to write him. I hope you
will show him this letter.

I want to give Ike his full due in an important matter. I want to
admit that he was right in his prophecy two years ago that the conduct
of the war would pass from the idealists who first undertook it into
the hands of the industrialists. They have control of Congress now
and call themselves Radical Republicans. I wish it were possible to
enjoin them from using the sacred name of that glorious old party.
The poor President!

This new crowd is not only going to keep up the tariff, but they
are shouting about conquering the South as Ike predicted, and taking
control of politics down there, to be sure the Niggers vote and everything stays Republican. They are preparing amendments to the Constitution to free the slaves without compensation, which is an outrage,
and to give the Niggers the vote at once, which is extremely unwise.
I have been listening to them in both houses of Congress and had the
pleasure of hearing the Honorable Ostrum Applemore hold forth.

The old 50th N. Y. is gone, like the rest of the veteran, volunteer
regiments. The 370 men who remained of it after Gettysburg were
split up to form the nuclei of three of the new draft regiments.
Though it is improper for me to write it, this new army is a sorry thing
in comparison to the Old Army of the Potomac. They say that in the
advance of last summer they usually put the veterans in support, in
order to keep the drafted men facing the enemy. This horde of mer-
cenaries will win, through sheer weight, being superior in numbers,
supplies and equipment. But there will be small glory in it.

Solon Samson wrote me what he has undoubtedly told you, that he
is going to accept Judge VanSanford's offer to go into that fine old
partnership with young Robert, and Numa when the war is over.
The Judge has also invited me to join them, and I have transferred
Zeb's practice to them, as well as the little I had. Solon Samson wrote
that it was only Numa's wish that had made them decide to move into
the village. There goes the last strength from the Hollow, except for
Ben.

I suppose you know that Tim Slocum was killed in a night attack
at Petersburg. He should be honored along with the bravest of our
boys, because those night attacks are always volunteer affairs.

The news about myself is that I am resigning for good. It seems
that I should never have been let back into service. I commanded one
of the raw, draft regiments for about two weeks at Petersburg, and

though I did not get into action I did persuade the General to send me on a five-mile ride with a dispatch, in order to test my strength. I never thought I'd finish it for the pain in my side, and when I got back they said that the pain would continue indefinitely and was probably caused by severe adhesions. I carried my own resignation to Washington, with the Surgeon's endorsement that it was submitted at his request. I am only nominally in hospital, under temporary observation, and am free to go and come as I choose. It is a disappointment not to be in at the end, which is not far off, for after all, the two original aims of the war are still alive. But there is some consolation in knowing that I shall not share in a victory that is likely to be used disgracefully, so as to make every decent Northerner ashamed of his cause.

I ran into Alec Mathiesson in the hospital grounds and he, like me, is being discharged for good. That wound he got in his foot as Spottsylvania has left him with a permanent limp. Have you learned how gallantly Alec at last vindicated himself? After remaining an apparent coward through Gettysburg, he won the Congressional Medal of Honor, the highest honor the country can give, for "heroism" at Spottsylvania. I have only recently learned from George that he penetrated the famous salient alone, got behind the Rebel line, surprised and killed three Rebel guards who were leading off about twenty prisoners, and led them all back into our lines. Like Jabe, he will not accept a commission. He is greatly changed and I am afraid for him. He is hysterical when he talks and doesn't seem to be able to keep his attention on anything. He is already discharged and expects to go to New York in a day or two.

My discharge should come through in about a week. As I am not feeling quite up to snuff, I believe I shall go out to Oberlin to rest for a few weeks before deciding what I am to do. Frankly, it will be an ordeal to meet Ike, probably for him too. I am afraid it will be an equal ordeal to see what Byzantium has become.

My own ideas will not change. I feel like a man without a country, with Applemore in control of the Republican Party. I wish you two would come out to Oberlin.

Tavie left Washington just before I arrived. She is the head of the female nurses at this hospital now, but there are so few patients these days that she is going home for a rest of two months or until there is a major engagement.

My dearest love to you two always,

John.

Ike took small comfort in this letter. It looked as if John were considering staying out in Oberlin. He knew what it meant when he wrote, "My own ideas will not change." He knew that if he was to get squared with the 'Paloosa he'd have to meet those set ideas. He fell to dreaming of the plan he had for doing it, the plan that must wait at least until the war was over, maybe a year or so longer, till his greenbacks rose to parity with gold. Then he could afford to retire from active business. He would build Pru and the youngster—"John Lathrop," of course—a fine house on the hilltop above the old homestead. He would buy back all the land in the Hollow he could get his hands on and restore the Lathrops to the position they had held in the days of their great-grandpa, before they whittled their holdings away to send five of them to college. Perhaps the 'Paloosa would marry Tavie, and with little Solon they would come back to live either with him and Pru, in the homestead, or maybe in another house they would build alongside. The 'Paloosa would be the "Squire." They would persuade the Samsons to stay in the Hollow and they could all practice law together. They would make the Hollow of some consequence again. Everything would be re-established as Ike had planned it when he moved into the village.

Ike showed John's letter to Pru and outlined his plan to her. She listened with her smile of pregnant dignity and when he had finished, gave him a long, loving look. "Isaac," she said, "must we discuss these things now?" Ike didn't want to bother her with details in her present condition, so he dropped the matter for the present.

A few days later Pru's flashy brother Jonathan arrived from the West. He chose to stay with them instead of with his parents at the Liberty, and as a result of his visit Ike got first-hand confirmation of the plot of the Radical Republicans against the South. One evening he didn't know what to do with Jonathan, so he took him down to the American House bar where Job Wheeler showed them part of a confidential letter he had got from Ostrum Applemore:

"The South cannot possibly hold out until summer. Tell the members of the faithful, or any youngsters who look promising, that there are going to be some ripe opportunities soon after the end of the war. We are going to give the Negroes the vote and shall want a lot of patriotic young men to go South as party agents to organize them into good Republicans. The business may be dangerous, though the plan is to place sufficient garrisons in the South to keep the Rebels in their place. Send me a list of possible candidates, preferably young men with nerve who would appreciate an opportunity to skim some valuable cream. . . ."

After reading the letter Ike said that any feller who would do such a thing was a "danged scallawag" and ought to be hoss-whipped. Jonathan Stark, who had his father's unscrupulous slyness plus plenty of nerve, said he was in for a hoss-whippin' then, for the notion "hit him between the eyes." He asked Job to send his name in to Ostrum. Job said that after forty years of bar-keepin' he figgered he'd earned his diploma and he was thinking of going himself, "jest to see the country before retirin'." In the course of two hours two others were enlisted from the young ruffians who lounged in.

In the morning Ike wrote John of this at length, feeling elated that he was able sincerely to agree with John in indignation at this recruiting of an army of "danged worthless pirates who haven't anything to recommend them except their shiftlessness and the possession of a carpet-bag." He took the occasion to outline in detail his plan for quitting business and for their all returning to the Hollow, only omitting his hopes respecting Tavie and little Solon.

But to this letter he got no reply.

CHAPTER CI

DURING THE NIGHT of February twenty-fifth, one of Ike's problems in connection with his plan to retire from business was miraculously solved for him. About eleven o'clock fire was discovered in the engine company, and by dawn the building was destroyed. Having summoned Henry Hawks to sit in the hall outside Pru's door, Ike got there in time to save the ledgers, strong boxes and some of the more delicate tools before the heat drove everybody from the building. Thereafter the hose companies could do nothing but soak down Gadston's Foundry across the street and put out the embers that from time to time lit on its slate roof.

With mingled relief and sentimental memories Ike stood with Constable Haverstraw on the suspension bridge that Alec had built and watched this his first business venture go up in high, curling flames, their crackle and roar inaudible against the thunder of the Middle Falls whose deep tumbling curtain and shore-line border of ice they lighted with an infernal orange glow. Ike thought how the invincible and eternal power of the Falls went rumbling on through the years, while the works and lives of men rose and vanished like the seasons around them.

About dawn the roof and two floors of the old main building collapsed together into the cellar, and the tin roof of the long, one-story addition the Government had built was sagging like a metal blanket supported by a few burning posts. The place, with all its gun lathes and other valuable machinery, was a total loss.

One of Ike's worries of many months was now over. The plant, long adapted exclusively to making guns, would have been useless after the war. The old machinery for making parts of steam engines was already obsolete, and former competitors and successors in that field had taken the trade from the Byzantium Company. To go back to that would be to start all over, and Ike for his own part had no intention of launching a new venture now. The company had justified itself, even if they wrote off the plant as valueless. But it hurt Ike's sense of good business to do that, and now the fire had solved the problem for him. The Company would collect $40,000 insurance, and the site was still the best in town for a factory. Ike figured that the property as it stood was worth $30,000, giving the Company a capital balance, including the insurance money, of about $70,000— this in addition to total dividends of about $250,000 in fourteen years, all on an original investment of less than $20,000. The Company had certainly made a good thing for all of them, all of them now being Alec, Nat Gadston, Ike, and Bub's and Jabe's estates, of both of which Ike was executor.

By another piece of good fortune, Nat arrived the following evening for a two weeks' leave. Ike had trouble concealing his pleasure a few days later when Nat came into the bank with a proposition from his pa to buy the ruin for $20,000. "What use'd your pa have for it?" asked Ike, looking up from his desk with apparent surprise. "He believes that after the war he can maintain his present volume of business which is about double what the old plant can handle." "What about Alec?" asked Ike. "Papa says he'll hire him," said Nat. " 'Twon't do," said Ike. "Alec's bound to be his own boss." "I guess you're right, Ike. That's something we'll have to talk over. What do you think of the price?" "Couldn't consent to less than thirty thousand," said Ike.

Three days later they drew up a contract of sale for $25,000 with certain personal conditions. If and when Gadston needed more hands he was first to employ the men on the engine company's payroll at the time of the fire. Alexander Mathiesson was to have the option to pay all or any part of the purchase price for which he was to be compensated with stock in the Gadston Company at par—which would give him, if he exercised his full rights, almost a third interest in the foundry. Alec was to remain an independent agent as to any inventions he might make in the future.

Ike sent the contract unsigned to Alec's New York address, along with a letter calling attention to the advantages for Alec which it contained, explaining that he had authority to vote Alec's stock under the power of attorney he had left, but that he would not do it without Alec's consent. He pointed out that he held on deposit for Alec more than $5,000, his share of the war dividends, and that if the deal went through Alec would be entitled to over $20,000 more in the winding up of the old Engine Company. Ike said that if he preferred not to go in with Gadston, this total of $25,000 would be sufficient for him to set up a new shop of his own. Ike closed the letter with an invitation to come to visit him soon for old time's sake, whether anything came of the proposed deal or not.

Five days later Ike got a reply from Alec's father, whom he had visited several times in New York:

March 7, 1865

Dear Isaac:

Alexander is at our house in New Jersey with a gentleman whom we call his friend. He has been very badly shattered by the war. He is perfectly sane, but prone to fits of sudden excitement, and I am sure it will be months before he can get down to work. I am taking the liberty of opening his post and answering it where necessary. I expect him back within a week, but even then I shall try to keep anything from him that might excite him. Your proposal is, I fear, of that nature.

I infer from the tone of your letter that you favor this sale, and if that is the case I heartily agree with you. As to whether or not Alexander should take advantage of this opportunity to buy stock in the Gadston Company, I have my own opinion, but I believe we should wait until the last possible moment to let Alexander exercise his own judgment. I would suggest that you revise the contract giving him at least three months, and more if possible, in which to exercise his option. With this proviso I suggest that you sign the contract. I believe that you and I between us are qualified to act in Alexander's best interests.

I trust we may have the pleasure of seeing you in New York before many months have passed. As soon as Alexander has got possession of himself you may trust me to notify you. Kindly give my warmest regards to my old friend Howell Sherwood. And my respects to your mother and your wife, both of whom I am looking forward to meeting and entertaining here as soon as they will vouchsafe me that privilege. Believe me,

Sincerely yours,

Stephen Mathiesson.

The day after Ike received this letter he signed the contract of sale, having written in a provision giving Alec four months in which to take up his option to purchase stock in the Gadston Company. Ike did not think Alec would want to go into business with the Gadstons. What he would probably do would be to set up a small, well equipped experimental station where he could devote all his time to study and invention. Ike knew that this had been the dream of Alec's life, and here Providence had given him the opportunity to realize it.

Not long after signing the contract Ike got a telegram from Alec's father: "Alexander returned yesterday disappeared this morning telegraph any information." By telegraphing conductors and station masters along the line Ike located Alec in Utica that evening and telegraphed Mr.

Mathiesson, making the railroad wires available to him if he wished to have Alec apprehended. In the morning he got another telegram from Stephen Mathiesson: "Thanks assistance Alexander coming to you probably good for him."

That evening Ike met the seven o'clock train from Utica, and Alec was the first to jump off in the dim light outside the station, wearing a fine greatcoat, but hatless and without baggage of any kind. He gave Ike no formal greeting, but began talking to him with enthusiasm while they were yet twenty feet apart. He limped deeply as they walked along together. "Had to come to see you and the old place, Ike. Want to get down to business. Had to sneak out of the house without anything, or Pa would have made a row. But after you discovered me in Utica he telegraphed his blessing. Let's go over to the old plant now. Can't wait to get to work. I've a dozen ideas for patents that I think will give us a monopoly on field guns and keep us going after the war, besides some notions about repeating rifles that'll make them better than the present carbines. Come on. Let's go over the old bridge now. Has it fallen down yet?"

They had reached the corner of Mill and Factory streets. It was plain that Alec had no suspicion of the fire or sale of the property. "No," Ike said, "let's not bother tonight. It'll be cold in the old place and it'll stay as it is till morning. Besides, Pru has supper for ye."

"Oh, that's right, isn't it? You married Pru after all. Well, congratulations! There's none prettier." And he limped along toward State Street without further objection. "Got a child coming," said Ike, feeling on the defensive. "Well, well, that's fast work. Congratulations, you old Scamp." And he shook Ike's hand for the first time.

Almost immediately he began to talk about the war and, unlike all other soldiers who had seen real action, he seemed to enjoy recounting his own exploits. He talked in detail of his achievements at the Wilderness, Cold Harbor, Spottsylvania, not in a personally boastful way but with a strange detachment as if he were talking about the gallantry of a brother or some mutual friend of his and Ike's. "That was something, eh?"— "Not bad for the young cuss, eh?"— "Three Rebs together with only a scratch in the foot—fast work, eh?"— "Best bagnet man in the comp'ny— not bad for the young feller, eh, Ike?" This boastfulness made Ike question Master Mathiesson's statement that Alec was "perfectly sane," Alec, who was normally modest to self-effacement about his real achievements in engineering. All the way up the street he never ceased talking about himself, and showed no interest in seeing either Ike or the village for the first time in over three years.

Pru had the door hospitably ajar for them and, heavily belaced in her maternity gown, now came out into the hall, smiling and extending her hand. Alec kissed it in the old-fashioned way, Pru noticing that his hair and fingernails were even more filthy than they used to be. "Ike is indeed a lucky man," he said, having forgotten how really beautiful Pru could be. "And what about me?" she replied, opening her lovely eyes wide. "Oh, anyone who goes into partnership with Ike is in for it. I should have warned you if I had known you were in danger." And he glanced round at Ike with the first objective and affectionate look he had given him. By the dim light of the parti-colored gas lamp in the hall Ike noticed that the old pallor of Alec's lean face had changed to a sallow swarthiness, and that its nervous lines were deepened into heavy creases. His black tangle of hair was the same, and he ran his hand through it two or three times while he was exchanging courtesies with Pru. His black eyes had the same quick, eager look, but they roved as they talked now, never resting on their object. When Ike took his coat he saw that he was the same as ever in dress. He wore a fine, new, black frock coat, but it already was creased and spotted, looking as if it had been part of him for ten years.

After supper Pru remained standing in the sitting-room. "I do hope you will excuse me, Alec," she said, "but I keep early hours these days," giving him a frank smile. "And besides I know you boys have at least a night-full of talk which you can manage without any help. I think, my dear," turning to Ike, "that in honor of Alec's return we might treat this as a party"—this meant they might smoke. "You will find a pitcher of iced water in the pantry—that is, if you have need of any such effeminate liquid!" Alec kissed Pru's hand and Ike, taking her arm securely, conducted her slowly up the long, straight, mahogany staircase.

When Ike came down he first closed the big double doors of the sitting-room, as he had been commanded while upstairs, in order to keep the smoke out of the parlor. Then he supplied whisky, glasses and ice water. They settled themselves in the spring rocker and the easy chair, and Ike kept interrupting Alec's chatter till he had his attention. Then he proceeded to tell him the whole story of the fire and the sale of the property.

As long as Ike talked about the fire itself and the forty thousand insurance, Alec listened with interest, once throwing in the comment, "Now we can rebuild the shebang as it should have been in the first place." But when he told about the sale and Alec's option to buy about a 30% interest in the Gadston plant Alec understood nothing and his attention wandered. As always, legal and business matters were only confusing to him. He understood that Ike wanted to retire from business. Also he heard Ike say that he, Alec, now had plenty of money to put up the experimental laboratory he had always wanted, and that Ike would be glad to advise him about the business end of it. But what Alec really gathered was that somehow Ike wanted him to go to work for Horace Gadston. Whether through some essential defeatism in his nature or because Ike's behavior during the war had made him suspicious of him, this became a fixed idea. He remembered his eternal debt to Ike for having given him his start, and his essential courtesy made him decide instantly that he would do what Ike seemed to want him to. Once he interrupted Ike with, "Why old Horace and I always got on first-rate, and I could think of much worse bosses!" Or again, "I see what you're up to, Ike Lathrop. You're trying to marry me off to Glory Gadston, and I might surprise you one of these days by showing you I can do it without a step-ladder."

As to "the said Mathiesson's" right "to re-imburse the said purchaser in the amount of all or any part of the said purchase price, and to receive in return therefore capital stock of the said purchaser in the amount of the said re-imbursement at an agreed valuation of one hundred dollars ($100) per share of the said capital stock," etc., etc., of all this Alec understood absolutely nothing. All he understood was that somehow Ike and his pa and Horace had fixed it up that he was to take a job with the latter, and out of long-standing gratitude to Ike he was going to do his best to carry out the plan.

After he was in bed, being drunk, Alec began to laugh out loud at the prospect, and so long and hilariously that Pru with a candle came in to Ike who was dead to the world, woke him with difficulty, and asked him to silence his crazy friend. This Ike did, half believing she was right in calling him crazy. Pru then asked him abruptly if he had aired out the sitting room as she had requested, first closing the register so as to waste no heat. Ike had forgotten to do this and duly complied, Pru waiting imperiously at the top of the stairs.

In the morning when they walked downstreet together, Alec would not go with Ike to the bank or even to get a hat before going over to see the ruins, and Ike decided it would be best to go with him. All the way across Fleet's Island Alec was looking straight ahead and when they came out on the bridge he had built he noticed neither it nor the big falls to the right, but fixed his eyes on the quadrangle of stone walls at the other end of it, roofless, windowless and empty inside.

As they stood looking in where the big side doors had been he gave no evidence of sentiment at the spectacle of ruin heaped in the cellar. His eyes did not rest on the second window from the corner opposite, where his office had been, nor did he seem to see prominently in the pile of debris in the cellar a safe lying with its face slantwise up toward them with the still legible initials "A.M." All he said was, "There's still width enough, Ike." He walked off to the end of the building where had stood the Government addition which he had never seen, and showed little interest in what remained of the frame and sagging tin roof of its cheap construction. He returned to the shell of the main building and again paused looking in at the big doors. At last he said, "We could still use three walls and lengthen the building up-river by about thirty feet."

When they were out in Mill Street again Alec stood for a moment looking across at the Gadston Foundry that was already clanging. Then he ran his hand through his hair two or three times, looked round curiously at Ike, glanced away, glanced back and laughed. "Well," he said, "I may as well start business with old Horace," and he swung off across the street, Ike following. At the door Ike mumbled to him, "Whatever ye do don't commit yourself to anything now or for a good spell yet." "All keerect," said Alec with a meaningless toss of his head, and they went in. While Alec interviewed Horace, Ike walked around the plant, observing that they were indeed busy.

"C'm in," bellowed Horace in response to Alec's gentle knock. "Well, I'm uncommon glad to see ye, Alec," rising and shaking hands as the returned hero entered nervously. "Have a seegar?" "Thank you," said Alec, lit it and sat down. "Leetle hard luck ye come back onto, eh?" said Horace with a rosy, patronizing smile. "That's true," said Alec. Then, "I came in, Master Gadston, to talk with you about this arrangement you seem to have made with Ike about my taking a position with you." "Suit ye, does it?" said the magnate with an air of generosity. "I think so," said Alec, "but I'm afraid I don't understand it yet. How much did you plan to pay me?"

At this Horace involuntarily looked at Alec with his bad eye, a sign of surprise. Could it be possible that this boy would settle for a job, that he might not have to give him the shares in the Company? Wishing neither to lose this opportunity if it was genuine nor to appear such a fool as to take Alec seriously if he was joking, Horace waved his hand in a non-committal arc and said in a jocular tone, "Oh, as to that, I figger ye're a likely lad and we could start ye at twenty-five a week, maybe make it thirty-five if ye'd agree to give the Company any o' them bright idees they say ye fetch out o' yer head sometimes."

"Maximum eighteen hundred and twenty a year, eh?" asked Alec so frankly that old Horace began to believe he was as simple as he seemed.

"Seems to me pretty good pay for a starter," said Horace, still with his non-committal smile. "Of course, there's no telling how we might raise ye after ye learned the business. My boy Nat's been here over ten year now and we give him fifty a week."

"Thank you, sir," said Alec, rising. "If ye've any objection to my proposition, let's hear it," said Horace, with a munificent wave of his cigar. "If ye hain't, why let's put 'er in writing and she's done." He tilted back in his chair, stuck his thumbs in his suspenders, and watched Alec with a friendly smile. He figured this would let him out of the contract and square up the old grudge he had against these boys for having prevented him from buying the little shop where they started business, and afterwards getting the better of him on the Union Mills purchase.

"I'm afraid I shall have to think it over," said Alec apologetically. "All keerect, take yer time," said Horace without rising, looking back at the papers on his desk. "Only don't think too long." And he turned back to his own affairs.

Alec closed the door softly and paused. "Eighteen hundred to start with, and an ultimate hope of twenty-five hundred," he thought. "And to work under that swine." He laughed at his fancied predicament.

Ike came up and touched his shoulder, at which he jumped and afterwards avoided Ike's eyes. "Great old duffer," he shouted above the roar of the falls as they crossed the bridge, then laughed the loud way he had last night. When they were across the bridge he had built he paused as if confused, then walked on a few steps to examine the anchorage of the big cables in the limestone there. "Seems sound yet," he shouted to Ike, then turned and ran back across the bridge and examined the two anchorages there, while Ike waited for him. He started back at a normal pace, paused at the center of the bridge, walked over and leaned on the cables at the low point of their loop in the center, gazing at the falls. Then suddenly, without taking off his overcoat, he vaulted over the cables and dropped into the whirlpool fifty feet below. That afternoon they grappled the body out of the racks of the flume of the Tanofly Mill.

CHAPTER CII

A L E C ' S death was the most shattering blow Ike ever received. Not only had Alec been one of his two or three closest friends, but Ike felt that he had killed him directly, without the interposition of any chance that he should not have foreseen. He dismissed the old voice of temptation— "It was only a mistake in judgment"—with the flat self-accusation, "That's the sort of mistake decent folks don't make." Why had he revealed the Gadston arrangement so quickly?—Alec had four months in which to make up his mind. Why hadn't he insisted more urgently on the experimental station? Ike accused himself of most heinous intent. He thought what he'd had in his bonnet was that through Alec's getting a 30% wedge into the Gadston plant he was some day going to trim old Horace out of control. Way down inside he hadn't cared what happened to Alec. So he saw it now.

The day after the funeral and Mr. Mathiesson's departure for New York with the body, Ike went out to the Hollow and spent most of the afternoon sitting on the big castle rock above Dandy's grave. At first the quiet of the snow-covered Hollow, the soothing sound of Jolam's Falls, the hollering of some crows down in Jolam's Grove, all this for a time took him out of himself into the great impersonal universe where these private concerns—even death—were of no more importance than a drop of snow melting on the rock beside him. When he glanced up at the house, there he knew Ma was; there was Ben down in the far pasture mending fence; and they in personal terms were also part of this big, inclusive peace that would not change.

But Ike's pantheism did not long serve him now, any more than it had done when he was on the way to Washington when he had learned of the burst gun. After a few minutes' escape into it from the distress of the last few days, it faded before the stark immediacy of the facts of his life. Here, six feet under this rock were Dandy's bones, and he had killed him. Then there was Pa over there in the cemetery, and he had killed him. Then he'd almost finished Tavie in one way, and almost finished 'Paloosa in another. He had sure grit finished Jabe, and now Alec. These were the people who had been fondest of him. You couldn't explain it by saying in each case there was a mistake in judgment, not when there was this whole string of them.

More finally and quietly now than in that frightened ride to Washington, Ike concluded that there was something wrong inside him, something missing that somehow poisoned people when they got too close to him and found he didn't have it. What he'd always wanted more than anything else was friends, and now he hadn't a friend in the world except Ma. Ben had always suspected him in his quiet, untalkative way. He wasn't even sure of Aggie any more. There was something he didn't understand, something missing in him without which he didn't deserve to have friends. "No, Ike"—Aggie's words rose in his mind from that Thanksgiving time back in '50—"No, Ike, . . . I'd hate to see you . . . at the Falls. . . . I'd be afraid you'd wake up years later and find you had lost something you couldn't ever get back." "Love and God," Ike thought to himself. What did the God he had found amount to now? What did the kind of love he had found amount to, with all his friends dead or quitting him? He remembered his visit with Susan Stark back on that morning just after he'd sold Dandy. "Isaac, . . . you have too fine an inheritance to throw away. . . . Even if you get rich as Croesus it will mean nothing to you unless you have something else to live for . . . as your father has, and your grandfather, and your brother John will have. . . . You have something that money can't give you, but . . . money might take it away."

Ike drew up his knees and dropped his chin in his clasped elbows. Yes, whatever it was that was missing in him was something he'd lost when he moved into the Falls and went to making money. That was when he first sure grit got out of the straight furrow, and he'd always half known it when he talked of coming back to the homestead. The first thing for him to do now was to carry out that plan, move back to the Hollow where he understood the old ways and knew how to behave without hurting folks—"where ye belong," as old Jerry Stone had told him fourteen years before. An hour later he rode back to the village full of desperate impatience to complete this difficult move. As he touched his hat to people he looked at them hard, wondering what it was they understood about life and folks that he didn't, what it was that kept him outside the human pale.

During the ensuing weeks Ike set about winding up his business affairs, no longer as a means of winning John back, but entirely on his own hook, as a condition of saving his own soul. He decided not to wait for the end of the war to give him a profit of $64,000 in greenbacks, which was about what he figured he needed to carry out his plan to buy up most of the Hollow. He'd gamble on that. He got Patience Tanofly to agree to promote Nick Forham from Manager of the Paper Company to President, with a fat block of stock which he had sure fire earned, Ike remaining merely as the representative of the majority Tanofly interest, along with his own. He approached Howell Sherwood on a proposition that had been in his mind since the National Bank Act of '63, a proposal that they consolidate their banks into one National Bank which would be the largest in town, each putting in an equal amount of assets and operating as partners. Their voting power would be equal, but Master Sherwood would actively run the business and in return would take two-thirds of the profits. In this way Ike would avoid the run on his bank that would occur if he sold it outright and withdrew completely.

Howell Sherwood said that, since he was getting on, he had thought of some such scheme himself, though he would be better pleased if Ike remained active in the village and they shared equally in the profits. He finally agreed to Ike's plan, however, and they set Solon Samson to work drawing up articles and an application for a charter. They employed the old founder Watchful Smart as secret agent to begin negotiations with Ostrum Applemore for the purchase of his block which adjoined Ike's, the plan being to throw the two street floors together into what would be physically as well as financially double the size of any other bank in town.

The problem of the bank being the most difficult in his plan of retirement, Ike postponed his resignation as Executive Vice-President of the railroad and from his several directorships until after he had moved to the Hollow. These matters could be tended to privately at any time and need not cause any shock to the businesses involved.

During the last week of March he rode out to the Hollow three times and tramped around in the crusted snow on the hilltop, staking out the house he would build and another he would get the 'Paloosa to build alongside. He delegated Solon Samson to sound out the Swifts, Emmenses, Oakses and Wilcoxes about selling their places, the stipulation to be that the old people were to occupy them as their own while they lived, paying in every case a rental lower than the return on the purchase price if invested in government bonds. The proposal seemed likely to be accepted, since all the young men from each of these families had now moved away permanently, and the old folks were having a hard time to make ends meet.

Of all these active plans and preparations during March Ike said nothing to Pru. If she were against the plan he must not argue with her now, and if she were for it he knew from experience that she would take a more active interest than was good for her at this time. The baby was due in the middle of April.

On Monday, April third, Mistress Abigail Stone came into the bank and told Ike Jerusalem would like to see him. At four o'clock Ike walked up Factory Street to the little house and went into Old Jerry's presence almost timidly, feeling he didn't deserve to talk to him till he'd sure grit got back in the straight furrow, instead of just figuring about it.

The ancient tanner was sitting in a rocking chair, wrapped up in shawls. His leathern face was now gray instead of the tan it used to wear, and the myriad wrinkles of his face seemed softer, as if the vitality that held them stiff were relaxing.

But there was little relaxing of either Old Jerry's will or his wits. "Set down," he said in the weak high pitch his voice had taken on since his stroke. After a long silence during which Ike mostly looked out the window, he said, "Hear yer friend jumped off the bridge. Miss him, do ye?" "Yes, sir," said Ike, crossing his legs, glancing at Old Jerry, then looking down. "Why don't ye look at me?" demanded the old man. Ike did then, and all his recent self-accusing came into his face, the big, sad eyes, the pucker in his brow set deep with trouble. "Figger I killed him," he said, then uncrossed his legs and looked at the floor. "Figger there's something missing in me. Started back yonder when I sold that gray, like ye told me. Killed him. Then killed my pa. Nigh killed my brother. Did kill one friend. Last off killed my nigh best friend. Bothers me. Didn't figger to tell ye of it."

"Young Lathrop," squeaked Old Jerry, "ye're a god-danged liar." Ike looked up at him curiously, half-amused. The harassed look left his face for a moment, then returned. "Feel responsible for it all," he said. "Something wrong inside me." "Likely," grunted the old man. "Never seed human yet didn't have suthin' amiss in 'im."

Ike resumed looking at the floor, but the pucker in his brow was not so deep, "Who ye missin'," demanded Old Jerry suddenly, "oth'n yer crazy friend jumped off the bridge?" "Brother," said Ike, looking up with all his self-doubt in his face again. "Figgered 's much," said Old Jerry. "Jedgin' ye, be he?" Ike nodded. "What call's he got jedgin' ye?" "That ain't the point," said Ike. "He's quittin' me, and he's good cause to. He's right." "Goin' some place else?" "Don't know," said Ike. "Missin' him 'cause he's agin ye, eh?" "Yes, sir, when it's my fault." "Who says it's your fault?" "He does, and so do I." "No, ye don't. Ye're lyin' t' me. Best mind yer own jedgin' and tell him mind his'n." "I don't judge anybody," said Ike. "That makes ye better'n he be," said Old Jerry; and Ike looked at him a little angrily on John's account. "Tell him t' save his jedgin' till he's some brats t' fetch up, and be mighty close with it then."

They sat silent a few moments. "Figgering to move back to the Hollow," said Ike. "Goin' back 'cause ye're o' mind to?" piped Old Jerry. "Yep," said Ike. "Speakin' true, be ye, or lyin' to me like when ye said ye figgered ye killed them fellers?" "Speaking true," said Ike. "Young Lathrop, ye're a god-danged fool besides a liar," squeaked Old Jerry. "Ye're too old to be doin' things ye ain't o' mind to." Ike smiled. "Fact is," he said, "I'm o' mind to all keerect, only I'm doing it a little quicker'n I figgered— partly to please my brother, but mostly because of what happened at the bridge. Want to get hold of something I've lost—maybe something I never knew."

They sat silent again for a while. "Trouble with you is," said Old Jerry, "I never give ye that hidin' fer yankin' Bashan." Ike's face grew slowly tense again. "Old Jerry," he said slowly, "ye recollect the day I sold the gray I asked ye why ye never gave me a hidin' and ye said ye weren't quite certain there was that in me worth your hidin'?" "Mebbe I did," said Old Jerry indifferently. "Do ye still figger ye were keerect?" said Ike with an earnestness almost pathetic. "Young Lathrop," said the old man, trembling with emotion— Ike had a sudden fear he was going to kill him too by giving him another stroke— "Young Lathrop, to answer that I'd have to be you." He raised a knotted finger and shook it at him. "Ye're a man grown now and ye're bound to do yer own jedgin' without troublin' about no brothers and no Old Jerries." Ike looked up. Slowly his face relaxed into the old, broad smile it had hardly worn since John and the Gang went to the war. He was thinking not of himself but of this old oracle, and loving him with all the bottled up warmth of his nature.

For perhaps half a minute Ike looked straight into those old blue eyes with quiet adoration while Old Jerry scowled terribly and his wrinkles stiffened. Suddenly he croaked, "Abigail." "Yes, Jerusalem," said his gentle, chalky white complexioned wife, coming in from the kitchen. "Fetch me that old raw-hide from the cellar-way." When she brought it he stood up on one leg, the other being paralyzed, and thrust his wife back when she tried to support him. "Young Lathrop," he squeaked, "bare yer ass." Ike took off his coat and leaned over. Six times he heard the raw-hide whistle, and the half dozen strokes were plenty smart for him to remember the rest of his life.

When they stopped, Ike peeked around and saw Mistress Stone helping

Old Jerry down into his chair and wrapping the shawls back around him. He put on his coat in some embarrassment, feeling this was the time to make a hasty exit. He looked at Old Jerry and saw the wrinkled face horribly contorted in a kind of gigantic monkey grimace, while an unmistakable tear was in the corner of each eye. Ike knew what he was thinking —this was the last time in this world he would ever hide a youngster for yanking Bashan. Suddenly he started trembling and squeaked with almost inaudible weakness, "Git yerself a ginger out o' the tin box on the shelf and skedaddle afore I hide ye agin."

Ike walked out into the kitchen where Mistress Stone hastily gave him a slab of ginger. Then, chewing it, he half ran back past Old Jerry into the hall, picked up his hat, coat and stick, glanced back at the old man who had closed his eyes, and went out the front door, mumbling a prayer to any God that it hadn't killed him. He walked up High Street with the feelings of a triumphant fifteen-year-old. He was sure grit one of Old Jerry's boys now. His mature conviction of a deep flaw in himself was not dispelled. But his perspective was restored. There must be some good in him. At least he had one valued friend. He would have something to start life over with when he got back to the Hollow.

Ike decided to drop in on Old Jerry every day. The next day when he called he was asleep, but Mistress Abigail said she knew he'd be pleased when she told him Ike stopped by. As he went down the stone walk from the little house he looked across at the tannery and saw that Bashan, the red and gold bull's head that had been part of Byzantium and Blackwater County for longer than Ike had, had been removed.

CHAPTER CIII

ON MONDAY the tenth, a week after Ike's accolade in the Order of Old Jerry, he and Pru were sitting at breakfast when they both looked up inquiringly at the same moment. Muffled by their thick brick walls, the sound of bells was audible, not the fire alarm from either the Universalist Church or Fire Company Number One on Factory Street, but fast ringing bells from all over the village. Shortly there were two explosions that made the chandelier rattle. "Sounds like the guns on the Mall," said Ike. "Likely up to recruiting again. Grant wants some more boys to butcher." The guns always frightened Pru, so Ike went around to her, patted her shoulder and kissed her. Then he walked out to the front door and opened it.

At the foot of State Street he heard the Baptist Church clanging rapidly, and the Universalist Church with its richer, more melodious tone, the sedate heavy boom of the First Presbyterian Church, the musical, distant alto of Trinity, the nasal whanging of the Columbia Street Methodist Church, and faintly from Madison Street the slower toll of the Catholic St. Patrick's. As Ike stood in the door the two cannon on the Mall went off again, and the new Court House, the new French Catholic Church, Fire Company Number One on Factory Street, and just below him the Congregational Church all joined in the lively ringing.

It was going to be a clear day with a suggestion of spring. The ice was all gone from State Street that was a good foot deep in mud. Everybody from upstreet was running past, for it was near seven o'clock anyway. "What's the racket?" Ike yelled to several, but they all shouted they didn't know and hurried on by. Ike grabbed his hat, coat and cane, told Pru he'd find out what it was, and joined the stream of running men.

On the Mall the old 1812 cannon kept booming as fast as they could. There was continuous cheering there, and by the time Ike got down with the crowd from State Street the big plaza was a seething bedlam, a dozen flags already waving and more appearing at windows and slipping up flagpoles every minute. Ike found himself in a jostling melee, everybody shouting unintelligibly. Then someone clipped him hard in the back and ran by shouting, "Lee's surrendered to Grant!— Lee's surrendered to Grant!— The war's over!— The war's over!"

For long seconds Ike stood dazed, while all the hopes, fears, loves and hatreds of four years poured from their suppressed recesses into his midriff, as if it were a cannon that had stood loaded a long time and was at last to be wholly discharged. Finally, understanding poured through him and his first paralyzing amazement was swept away. Something snapped in his will and he was released into the first popular hysteria he ever shared. Faintly he heard his voice yelling, howling and laughing. Dimly he was aware of his body running and capering, banging people on the head with his hat, throwing it into the air till at first he had smashed it, then lost it. He found himself carrying two or three people on his back till, the load increasing, they all went down together. He found himself being carried high in the air, waving his stick, and the next instant with a thump he was down in the mud again, and up again running. He found himself in one of the impromptu parades, wading round and round the Mall for what might have been a moment or an hour, bursting his lungs shouting "The Battle Hymn of the Republic" and all the war tunes one after another.

The three bands of the village were out, and many excruciating soloists were blaring and tooting from office windows. A lot of red flares appeared, to be thrown in the air as soon as lighted, and many coats were singed. The fire companies appeared and took precautionary positions at hydrants. One of the new companies for the Army formed with its wooden, practice guns and tried to march round behind a fife, but they were jeered and broken up by spontaneous mobbing parties. Old Theophilus Bostwick was rushed up Washington Hall steps whence he made a long speech and was cheered continuously, so that no one heard anything he said. Ike found himself being hoisted up the big steps also, and heard himself shouting things no word of which he ever remembered. The three bands apportioned the village between them and led parades respectively up Washington and State and down Court Streets. Ike bethought himself to join the one going up State and dropped out to tell Pru the news. She sobbed hysterically for an hour while Ike himself, holding her, calmed down a little.

When Pru said she was all right and felt no ominous intimations—it might be any day now—Ike changed his muddy suit, went downstreet again and had a drink in every saloon down the Mall. He stepped into the bank and found a telegram from his broker in New York saying that greenbacks had shot up to 150. He had already made $50,000 on them, but without an instant's hesitation he decided not to sell. It was already noon, and he made his way as fast as he could back up the Mall and homeward. He was drunk with more than whisky. The war had been the whole trouble, a long nightmare from which he was now waking. Now he and Pru would move back to the Hollow with their boy! 'Paloosa would marry Tavie and they would return with little Solon! Everything would go on as before. His carpet slippers were not at the door, and he tramped in joyfully with his muddy boots.

Pru and dinner were waiting for him and he put his arm around her as they walked into the dining-room, talking all the time as he seated her and sat down himself. "It's over, my girl! The whole danged, murdering shebang is over and we can come back to our senses! Greenbacks up to one fifty! Figger that makes us the richest folks in town! The 'Paloosa and George'll be back and we can settle down to the old life! Back to the Hollow as soon as the baby's born, eh! Hain't wanted to bother ye, but I've been squaring off to get ready for it. Solon Samson's buying back all the land Great-grandpa owned! Selling the bank to Howell Sherwood! Contract likely ready to sign this afternoon!"

Ike paused. The hired girl was out of the room. Pru was looking at him with her saddest, most beautiful expression. She had wanted to postpone this till she would be able to compensate him properly, but now she was afraid he would do something they would both regret. "My dear," she said softly and with every bit of appeal she could summon, "we are not going back to the Hollow. You can have the Hollow or you can have me, but you can't have us both. My child will not grow up in that backwater."

At one o'clock Ike sat down at his desk in the bank. The hubbub on the Mall had quieted for the noon hour and had not started up again. His dinner had sobered him, and the meaning of what Pru had said came over him as a stark fact, like death, the death of everything he still counted on in the world. More than he had realized, the return to the Hollow had been his central dream for fourteen years, the more recent agonized hunger for a reconciliation with John but a part of that single, inclusive ideal. As when he had seen the 50th pull out for the war, but now without any emotion, he felt as if everything inside him that was alive were being drawn out and away forever, leaving nothing in its place. He was a shell sitting here, without animation or purpose, incapable of escape into the universe, incapable even of grief.

He gave a weak, ironic chuckle. "You can have the Hollow or you can have me, but you can't have us both." He knew Pru meant that. She wasn't a Mattie Spencer to concern herself first with his wishes. He knew that when he married her. His face took on a sad, twisted smile. "Great feller ye are, Ike Lathrop—big banker—same as president of the railroad—everybody licking your boots. Can't even control your wife. No more master in your own house than Horace Gadston. Might as well have married Mehitabel!"

He straightened up a little in his chair and looked out the back window where the sparse grass was turning green and a song sparrow was at it in a little tree he had planted. For a good ten minutes he looked at nothing, his brain a void. Then, far off, he heard his mind saying, "And yet—and yet." "My child will not grow up in that backwater." That backwater. Lathrop Hollow. That backwater. Ike put his elbows on the desk, his gray-bearded chin in his hands, and closed his eyes.

In a waking dream he went back to the Hollow that night more than fourteen years ago when Dandy had just died. He was sitting outside the hall in the Conestoga wagon under the stars, while inside the dance was going on for the folks who were setting out for California. He remembered how he had guessed then that this was the beginning of the end for the Hollow, that these and others would go West, and he and others would go to the village and other places where the factories were starting. He heard the sound of the stream under the ice, then Jehu Jones's fiddle and the hundreds of voices—"O Susanna—don't you cry for me—For I'm off for Cal-i-for-ni-a—with my banjo on my knee." He heard the fox yelp up on Swift Mountain.

He remembered thinking how the Hollow had been before the Lathrops and the other white people came there. Now he dreamed that it had all gone back to that wilderness. He was still there at the end of the hall in the starlight, with the sound of the stream down behind him. But there was no fiddle now, and no voices. The hall was empty and fallen in. The church yonder was empty and unpainted, the lilac bushes up to its eaves and the roof buried in creepers. Nat Norcross's and Jehu Jones's houses were just cellar holes, the graveyard lost under lilacs and sumac. Beyond, up Lathrop Hill, stretched the reconquering forest under the stars. The fox on Swift Mountain was a wolf howling. The Lathrop homestead—Ike's mind refused the image of its desolation.

He opened his eyes and was back at his desk in Lathrop's Bank in Byzantium Falls. "Yes, by God," he whispered, "Pru's right. The Hollow is done for. Something stronger than I am is doing it, something not I nor anybody can get the best of. The young folks are shiftless already and they'll get more so. Whatever it is that used to be there, the thing I'm looking for, just ain't there any more. If I went back now I'd only get shiftless myself, and my boy after me."

Now Ike knew he would never go back. The 'Paloosa would stay out in Oberlin. Young Solon would grow up out there in the West. This new boy, to be called John Lathrop, would grow up in the village. The house up on State Street was the nearest to a homestead now.

He stood up and walked to the window. Looking out into the little back yard of the bank, hearing faintly the distant rumble of the Middle Falls, he felt his strength returning. He'd seen it all along, that the Hollow was going backwards. That was why he'd joined with the money power that had built the village. At the same time he'd known he was turning his back on something important in the old life. That was why he kept talking about going back to the Hollow, while he kept putting off doing it. He'd been trying to straddle two horses that couldn't be made to team up, and he was bound to choose one or the other. "Ye're a man grown and ye're bound t' do yer own jedgin'." He'd chosen his real horse in the beginning. The other horse, the life at the Hollow, was as good as dead anyway. He'd let it go now and ride on alone.

"Yes, alone," he thought. His look of sadness came over his face and his brow puckered. He'd go on alone, with whatever it was in him that had lost him his friends. In talking of going back to the Hollow he'd only been trying to run away from his trouble, running home to Ma like a baby. He'd pretended that the thing he was missing was back in the Hollow, like his old flint-lock hanging in the summer kitchen. That was too easy. He saw now that whatever was wrong with him was inside himself, and it didn't matter where he was. It would go back with him to the Hollow, same as here. If he couldn't get at the truth in the village, he couldn't anywhere. Mixed with the settled sadness in Ike's expression there came over his face the old, sure calm. The troubled pucker between his eyes was deep, but if Tavie could have seen it then she would have seen in it the old, searching eagerness she had loved, not the twisted, self-doubting worry she had seen in Washington. He'd a fight to make now, all alone, right here in the village, with things just as they were. He did not know whether he would win, but he knew the fight would be long.

At five o'clock Howell Sherwood came in with the articles of partnership for the merged bank. "We'll have to change that, Howell," said Ike. "If ye don't mind, I'll work with ye and take my share of the profits. I ain't going back to the Hollow."

CHAPTER CIV

B E N brought Sarah in the next day, to stay with Pru until after the baby was born. Susan Stark was there most of every day, and the two prospective grandmothers who had always been friends took great joy in finishing up all the lace and pink and blue preparations. In spite of her continuing excitement, Sarah noticed that Ike was more like his old youthful self than she had seen him in years, more warm and responsive on the surface, but behind his gentle eyes more of that hard thing in him that used to frighten her. Pru saw it too and understood. She told Sarah of the fight she knew Ike was making, and they both wept. Pru never loved him more than right then, in her own critical time, because she knew what he was giving up for her.

Ike walked home every day by way of Old Jerry's. The old fellow was getting visibly weaker, and never did understand about the war being over. Ike got the habit of walking in quietly without knocking. On Friday he found Mistress Abigail rocking steadily in the kitchen, sitting straight up, crying with her eyes open. Old Jerry was in a coma. Dr. Daw had told her there was no hope. She held on to Ike's hand for a long time. Then he started supper for her and fetched in some wood. After his own supper he came down again, with a basket of victuals Pru had the girl put up. He sat by the old man till after midnight. Then he woke Mistress Abigail as they had arranged and departed, promising to be down before breakfast.

The next morning, Saturday the fifteenth of April, Ike awoke to the sound of the village bells ringing again. He dressed hurriedly, went down and opened the front door. All the churches and the Court House were tolling, but this time very slowly, as little like the fire alarm as the fast ringing had been on Monday. There were people hurrying downstreet, but not so many as on Monday because it was only half-past six. The street lamp on the corner was still lighted, for it was not yet full daylight. Ike went back upstairs and found Sarah dressing Pru. "Sounds like a funeral," he said. "Must be Old Jerry's dead and the word's got round. I'd best go down and see." Once he was outdoors, he lit out and ran all the way down to the little stone house on Factory Street.

It was true. Mistress Abigail sat beside the dead man, quietly rocking. Ike put his hand on her shoulder, but for a long time she didn't know he was there. In another month they would have been married seventy years. When he got her attention he whispered that he would tend to everything, tip-toed out, and got one of the men from Jerry's old tannery across the street to come and stay in the house. As he walked back up High Street he thought about the undertaker, and the funeral—probably tomorrow. He must tend to a cemetery plot, for he knew that Old Jerry had never bought one. He'd get a monument later. He must get both papers to print an extra to let people know about the funeral. They ought to be willing to do that, for anything important enough to ring all the bells in town about.

The tolling continued, slow, ominous as doom. Ike thought how mad Old Jerry must be if he knew they were making all that fuss over him. He ate his breakfast hurriedly and joined the people going downstreet. There was a crowd on the Mall, but no cheering. The half-dozen flags that flew regularly were at half mast. A few windows had black crepe hanging out. Lincoln had been shot the night before and was dead.

Again Ike shared the feelings of the crowd, the terrible solemnity that at that moment was falling over the whole North like a cloud, the panicky incredulity, the sense of personal bereavement as if everybody individually had lost his father, the feeling of startled helplessness at being suddenly cast loose from the leadership which everyone had assumed to be permanent, like God. Hundreds of people merely stood staring at each other, and many men were openly sobbing. Ike was standing near the Universalist Church and, seeing a number of people going in, he followed them, joined in a hymn and a prayer for the President's soul and for the welfare of the nation. A number of people left the service, blubbering. Ike's reaction was more realistic. Most of the mourners were Republicans, followers of Ostrum Applemore, ignorant adherents of the new Radical Republicanism which had here lost its greatest enemy. "Yes," Ike thought, looking at Job Wheeler praying, "the jig's up now. The wild men in Congress will walk rough-shod over the South now—over the North too, for that matter."

Ike went outside. Yes, Lincoln was a great man, even if he had butchered a half million boys and maimed twice as many. It took a great man to affect people this way. Old Jerry was a great man too. Only they weren't tolling bells and hanging out crepe for him. Nobody had even heard he was dead, and for a long time Ike couldn't bring himself to spread the news. All up and down that great Mall nobody spoke above a whisper,

and by now the whole village was that way. It was as if they were standing at the Crucifixion. At last Ike slipped out of the crowd and went
about his business on Old Jerry's account. He saw the undertaker, arranged
for the funeral, and got the announcement in the extras of both papers.

And at three o'clock the next afternoon, Sunday the sixteenth, the bells
that had stopped tolling for Lincoln the night before tolled again for Lincoln
and Old Jerry together. And the crepe in every window of the Mall was
there for Lincoln, but it was Old Jerry's too. Over a thousand people overflowed the lawns of the houses next to his on Factory Street. Over five
hundred people walked behind the hearse all the way down to the old
Columbia Street Cemetery where Ike had provided a plot. Those people
came from every walk of life in Byzantium. Many of them did not know
each other. But every one of them felt privately that in Old Jerry he had
lost his best friend. Their thoughts of him were all mixed up with their
thoughts of Lincoln. Together they represented the end of something.

CHAPTER CV

T H E F O L L O W I N G Monday late in the morning the younger of Ike's two hired men came running into the bank and told him he'd best come home. Dr. Daw had started up already. Ike ran all the way up State Street, and after he had come in closed the door softly and waited till his panting quieted. His ma came half way downstairs and motioned to him to come up, which he did on tip-toe. Dr. Daw was sitting by Pru, holding her pulse. Susan Stark was standing on the other side of the bed. The place was a litter of basins, pitchers, syringes, sheets and towels.

Pru gritted her teeth and closed her eyes as Ike came in. But in a moment she opened them and gave him a brave, trusting smile. When another of the pains had come and passed she glanced at her ma, then at the doctor. He rose, took Ike by the elbow and led him out and across the hall into his room. "Isaac," he said, "I must tell ye that women usually don't like to have their husbands in the room at this time, though ye should stay on the place. Everything seems normal. It will be at least an hour, more likely two or three. Maybe more. Hold on to yourself, boy. You've a brave little wife." "I'll be out in the garden," whispered Ike with a dry mouth. "Tell Ma and Susan Stark."

He tip-toed downstairs, found his dinner waiting, and managed to drink half a glass of milk. Then he went out to the barn, exchanged a glance with Henry Hawks, carried his garden-seat outside and sat down under the big apple tree. His mind was empty of everything but futile, fluttering nervousness, gathering momently into waves of terror. Pru was going to die. The baby was going to die. They were both going to die. He'd killed Pru too. The baby would be a girl. All keerect! All keerect! Anything, so long as Pru didn't die.

He forced his mind to consider his garden in prospect. It was a warm midday. He'd forgotten to bring his hat and greatcoat, but he didn't need them. The frost was out of the ground. There were patches of green in the grass. Henry Hawks had plowed and manured the big round central bed as Ike had told him to. The sun looked warm on the clods and a few

little white butterflies were fluttering and lighting on one spot. Henry had
staked out the other beds afresh, triangles, crescents, long, narrow rec-
tangles. Pretty soon they could set out the line of rose bushes clean across the
back. He'd get Henry to whitewash the cobblestones that he was going
to use for borders round the beds. Henry was taking the two cows back
to the pasture at the rear of the property. They'd get nothing there but
sun. The one with the diamond must be almost ready to freshen.

Ike couldn't stand it. He got up and paced round and round the big
central bed that Henry had plowed. He came back and sat down and tried
to think about the annual railroad meeting next week. Proposal to merge
with the New York Central. They were going to make him President in
Squire Fulton's place. He'd figgered to resign when he was counting on
going back to the Hollow, but he'd take it now. He'd go crazy in the
village if he wasn't occupied.

He heard a step on the back stoop and jumped up so quickly he stumbled.
It was Ma and he ran to her and grabbed her. She smiled in a remote,
omniscient way. "It will be a long time yet, Isaac. You must be patient."
Then she left him so abruptly that he started involuntarily after her,
paused and stood foolishly, then went and examined the bark of the big
apple tree, not even seeing it.

He sat down and grew more composed. Ma had said it would be a long
time yet. He got to dreaming about the baby—John—after Great-grandpa
and Pa and the 'Paloosa who hadn't answered the letter he wrote him two
months ago about going back to the Hollow. Fetch up the brat right, just
as if he were back at the homestead in the old days. None of Pru's airs
about money, making out it made ye better than other folks. Nat had
talked like that back in '60 when the 'Paloosa had told him off and they'd
taken off their coats. Hadn't settled yet whether making money was wrong,
the way Susan Stark had said back in '50. But it was sure grit wrong getting uppity about it. He'd agreed with the 'Paloosa about that in '60, and
he still did. Fetch the boy up to be an American, not whatever sort of
British duke Pru figgered their money entitled him to be.

His dry mouth tried to swallow. What in hell was he thinking about?
Pru was in there suffering, maybe going to die, and he was complaining
of her. What in hell did it matter what happened if they got through this?
He looked at his watch. More than an hour had somehow got past. He
walked all the way down to the carriage house and ran back for fear
somebody might have come out. Everything was the same. He heard that
new second girl he'd got in giggling in the kitchen. It didn't occur to him
she was giggling at him. He sat down again. Another eternity passed.

He began to hear strange sounds at near intervals. They came from beside the house and he walked round to investigate, moving cautiously as if somebody was going to jump at him. They were terrible, deep guttural groans, hardly human, and they were coming from Pru's open window. Ike couldn't stand it and turned back. The next thing he knew he was clear back in the pasture. He called himself a danged coward and forced his legs to walk back and sit down on the bench, turning it round so he could watch the house. The groans continued, sometimes hoarse, unnatural screams. He thought he would go crazy but he sat there and faced it. Pru was doing this for him. This was more important than the Lollapaloosa, or his boy Solon, or the Hollow.

Suddenly he realized that the groans had stopped. He listened, his diaphragm convulsing. Was she dead? Had he killed her? He got up, ran to the side of the house, listened under Pru's window. There were no more groans, but he could hear mumbling in the room and people moving around.

He ran back and into the back door. In the sitting-room he met his ma coming for him. She fell into his arms and wept on his shoulder. "It's a beautiful little girl," she whispered, "Oh, Isaac!" As he petted his mother the suspense of the last two hours scattered and left a kind of embarrassed disgust. He had thought he was prepared for it to be a girl, but now he felt indifferent, empty, false, and ashamed of himself for feeling so. "How's Pru?" he asked softly. "Splendid," Sarah said. "She will sleep for a good while. Oh, Isaac, she's such a beautiful little thing!" "Pru?—no—yes, of course—ye mean the baby." Ike gave a foolish grin. Sarah went back upstairs.

Ike sat down on the sofa. He wanted a big drink, to see a man, to go to the Club. But instead he sat like a bad boy on the sofa. In a few minutes Susan Stark came down and in her turn wept on his shoulder. Then she said he might come up and see the baby, though he must take only one look. And she kissed him again and led him upstairs.

The baby was in its bassinet in Pru's dressing room, which Susan and he entered from the back hall, so as not to go through Pru's room. Sarah was in there too and stood back proudly, giving the maternal grandmother the honor of the official showing. The bassinet was by the window and Susan drew down the shutter for light. Then with an expert and tender gesture of waist, elbows and wrist she bent down and uncovered the little face, and Ike bent over his red, wriggling, faintly mewing, eight-pound daughter.

Something powerful in his stomach seemed to fuse, like the ends of two beams coming perfectly together, like a gun in the engine company sliding onto its carriage and settling into a perfect fit. Looking at the exquisitely formed little face, something happened to Ike that he had been waiting for unconsciously all his life. He loved this little thing absolutely and selflessly. Here was something he would like to fight and die for. The stifled love that had been John's in childhood re-awoke and attached itself to this creature who would never violate it with notions about conduct. The love that had been scattered between Tavie and Mattie and Pru concentrated upon this little girl in whom it would never get complicated by lust or worldly considerations. This was simple, absolute, final. The conventional hopes, the essentially selfish plans and ambitions Ike had been indulging for his wished-for son evaporated joyfully and left a single, immutable fact—love. He wanted to pick up this fact, this whole little world, right now, and he put his hands impulsively on the sides of the bassinet. His ma drew him away with a warning finger. Susan gave him a proud smile, covered up most of the little face, closed the shutter again, and followed him and Sarah out into the hall to get the paternal judgment.

"I'm glad it's a girl," said Ike with a dazed, triumphant smile, and he hugged and kissed both grandmothers. "How's Pru?" "She's sleeping," said his ma. She and Susan exchanged quick executive glances. Sarah returned to the baby and Susan walked with Ike up the two steps to the front hall. Then she opened Pru's door and vanished soundlessly into the room, closing the door unceremoniously in Ike's face.

Ike went downstairs, glowing with contentment. The big house he had considered as temporary took on meaning for him. It was home. The doctor came down and they congratulated each other. Ike offered him a drink but he declined in his serious, humorless way. He said all was well. Susan would let Ike know when Pru woke up and he might see her for a moment, "only a moment, mind ye, Isaac." The doctor departed, promising to return. Ike decided he could do without a drink. Instead, he got the second girl to bring him half a cold roast and ate it all. Then he went out back again, this time taking an old overcoat, his black felt hat, and his indispensable, silver-headed cane.

He turned the bench around, lit a cigar and sat facing the garden in his typical attitude, his cane leaning against his crossed knees. He felt fully and simply alive, integrated, his mind and feeling fused and clear. He thought of the Love and God Aggie had told him he would find. He had found God soon after, and now he could write Ag that he'd found love too, not just the kind she'd figgered for him, but better as he saw it.

It was a warm afternoon, the sun still high on his left, the sky clear blue. Some juncos were pecking at the manure on the big circular bed.

Down in the back pasture a meadow lark sang. Henry Hawks must be asleep, for it was quiet in the barn. Everything was quiet, the village sounds far away, emphasizing the stillness. Ike felt the big, peaceful universe pouring into him. It was the same as out at Jolam's Grove, with the village sounds taking the place of Jolam's Falls. They were part of Nature. They were alive. God was here, the same as out there. Only now that little girl in there was the center of it instead of Ike himself. She tied it up to the world. Love and God were the same thing now.

A locomotive began puffing down on Factory Street. It was a peaceful, lazy sound, part of it all too, but it reminded Ike of other things. It was his railroad, he had made it. In making it he had got rich, and in getting rich he had lost every friend he had, all the old ways, the Hollow, everything that had been his foundation in the world. But now it seemed to him that he was starting over. That little girl was his new cornerstone. It would be his job to fight for her, to work to make her happy, to shield her from pain, to compensate her for the pain that would come, all through the years. It didn't matter what happened to him except as it affected her. It seemed to him that he had found the secret, the thing missing in him that he had been looking for.

Ike thought and felt all these things easily, without strain. The complications of the past were resolved in the simple fact of existence, of being fully alive. He was as simple as the sunlight, the ground, the juncos pecking out there. Like them he was impelled to be about some simple, natural industry. He got a spade from the barn, took off his things, and for an hour spaded the smaller beds, his conscious mind dormant, his nerves in equipoise. Every now and then he rested for a moment and looked at the house with the old light in his eyes, between them the old eager pucker of passionate curiosity.

The sun got low and the west salmon-colored. Henry Hawks came out and stood for a time, dubiously inspecting Ike's spading. At length he looked up. "Hear ye've a daughter," he said. "Yep," said Ike. "Not a bad thing," said Henry, and walked off to get the cows.

At five o'clock the second girl came out for Ike, and his heart began to beat like sixty. At the head of the front stairs Susan was waiting for him. She said Pru was awake and she was going to bring the baby in to show her. He should stand outside the door and not come in till she signalled him. She left the door ajar, and Ike could hear the muffled activity inside. Then he heard his daughter squeak like a kitten and he almost exploded with pride.

After what seemed hours Susan came to the door and motioned him in.

Pru was propped up in bed, holding the swaddled little red thing in her arms. She raised her eyes as Ike entered and dropped them again, apparently not seeing him, but Ike knew it was because she was in a haze of happiness. She was pale, but Ike could feel the glow of her love, like something rich and sweet, filling the room. The two grandmothers stood on either side of the bed like enormous, responsible goddesses, completely concentrated on the fretting mite of humanity. At last they gave each other judicial glances and agreed it was enough. Susan lifted up the baby that squeaked again in its deep shawl. Ike went to Pru, dropped beside the bed on his knees and gently took her limp hand in both of his.

Weakly Pru turned her head toward him on the pillow and looked straight into his eyes with a smile both tender and inquiring that made him want to cry. "She's beautiful, darling," he whispered, "the most beautiful thing that ever lived." Pru did not change expression but she gave his hand a barely perceptible squeeze.

His ma touched him on the shoulder and he rose to go. Pru turned her hand over and crooked a finger in signal to him to put his head down. When he did she whispered in his ear, "She'll be fit for a prince." Ike touched her forehead with his lips, and tip-toed out. Alone in the hall, he muttered, "Like hell she will."

CHAPTER CVI

THE NEXT DAY Ike wrote Aggie, and he also wrote a note to John, as follows:

Dear 'Paloosa:

Since you haven't answered the letter I wrote you two months ago I presume you are not greatly concerned with my doings. But in case it might come into your plans, I want to tell you that I have changed my mind and am not going back to the Hollow. Naturally, I hope you come home anyway, whether you settle in the Hollow or in the village.

We had a daughter born yesterday, and she is certainly first-rate. Her name will be Sarah, if Ag don't mind. Pru is doing nicely and sends love.

Yours ever,

Scamp.

To Ike's astonishment he got a cheerful reply to this by return mail:

Dear Scamp:

Forgive my long delay, which has been due to uncertainty. It is great news about the daughter, especially all you say in Aggie's letter, which she showed me. We have many things to talk over, and I have some news for you too, but let's wait till I see you. Love to Pru.

Ever your brother,

L'p'loosa.

This stirred Ike up so that on that evening he forgot to bring home his daily presents for Pru and little Sally. He could hardly sleep for a week and whistled most of the time in the bank. Was the 'Paloosa really going to marry Tave and come home? It was too good to be true.

But then the weeks dragged by again without a word. Ike's lonely sadness, his sense of something missing in him that shut him off from friends, began to return. He had been too quick, too unwise, to respond with hope to a word from the 'Paloosa. There was still a void in him that had not been filled by his love for his little girl.

One Sunday evening in the middle of June Ike, Pru, Ma and Ben, with little Sally in her bassinet, were sitting out in the garden under the big apple tree, Ike on his bench and the rest in chairs. It was their habit now to alternate visits, one Sunday at the homestead, the next in "town" as the village was now generally called, the original town having lost its political importance and the village being close to the twenty thousand population that would make it a city. It was a soft summer evening, almost hot, the sun still up but a nighthawk already growling about the sky. A yellow warbler was exclaiming occasionally in the lilacs behind the line of rose bushes. In the lower orchard two robins and a wood thrush were ringing their peaceful bells at each other. A cat walked the top of the tall fence along the side of the property. The two girls clattered softly in the kitchen. It was so quiet the rumble of the Middle Falls was audible. Sarah and Pru were knitting. Ike and Ben were smoking. Nobody had said anything for several minutes. Sarah and Ben must start back to the Hollow soon.

Remotely they heard the mechanical front door bell clang. Ike uncrossed his legs. "Let her go," said Pru without looking up—she resented this second girl whom Ike had made her promise to keep until the baby was weaned. The bell clanged twice. Pru kept on knitting—this would give her a pretext to discharge the girl. There was a shuffling of feet on the back stoop and everybody looked round. Down the steps with a jump, a yell and a run came successively John, Aggie, Tavie and Homer.

After holding Ma in his arms a long time and Pru just as long, John turned to Ike, took him strongly by the shoulders, said nothing, and while the rest of the kissing and crying was going on somewhere outside the consciousness of both of them, looked down into Ike's eyes in the direct, old, affectionate way, as if nothing had happened. Then he jumped to the bassinet and made Pru let him pick up the baby. Ike stood numb, with a lump in his throat for joy and wonder. The 'Paloosa had really come home! Paradoxically, he felt a wave of sadness—here they were, he and the 'Paloosa, just as before, only Bub and Jabe and Fred and Joe and Alec were gone. Then he bethought himself, and went into the house for more chairs, assisted by Homer. "The old place has indeed changed," said Homer to him, "and yer new house is a beauty. Ye're lookin' first-rate yerself, Ike." Ike hadn't seen his brother-in-law in over ten years. Anyhow, he was more tolerable with these genteel affectations than he had been without them, and Aggie had written Ike that Homer had paid John the hundred dollars he'd lost on some bet about the war way back at Thanksgiving in '50.

When the clatter of greeting was over, and little Sally had been thoroughly admired and everybody was settled down, they all sat speechless with too many things to ask and say. John was thin and pale but animated, boyish, beaming, as if four years of hell didn't stand between him and his family. Sarah and Pru both made covert observations.

Ike finally broke the silence. "Well, what ye up to?" In answer John and Tavie stood up and John stepped over and kissed her, then stood with his arm around her, she showing her ring, while looking down and blushing as if she hadn't been twice a mother, a political leader accustomed to public insults, and nurse to thousands of mangled male bodies. Sarah fairly screamed as she jumped and had Tavie in her arms, while Pru was almost as quick with John, clasping his hand tight in a comradelike grip and looking up without coquetry—"O John, I'm so glad and so happy for you!" When Sarah was through with Tavie Ike stepped up and kissed her tenderly, held her hand and beamed down into her eyes, unable to say anything. Then he went back and sat down on the bench beside Aggie who reached over and took his hand. Unconsciously Ike had given Tavie the old tenderly inquisitive look that once would have made her swoon. She was glad the test was over. She felt no impulse to swoon. That was now finally in the past and done.

"Is Nat Norcross still a chaplain?" asked John. "Yes," said Sarah, "but he's at home. When?—." "Why, tomorrow!" said John, "just as soon as we can get out there! Only family and the neighbors in the Hollow. Afterwards we'll have a kitchen dance, with old Jehu." "He's a hundred and two," said Ben, "and as melodious as ever—probably will be going strong when we're all gone—and," he added as an afterthought, "when what we stand for is gone too."

This roused a flurry of self-consciousness. "You must have supper," said Pru, putting down her knitting and rising. "Thank you, Pru," said Homer, who had never called her by her name before, "we had loads at the station." She started for the house all the same. "Wait a minute, Pru," said John. "We've truly had supper. Please sit down again. I've something I want you to hear." Pru looked at the baby, sat down again and took up her knitting.

"There's a sad side to this too," said John. "Tavie has conclusive evidence that Connie Oaks died in a place called Virginia City, Nevada Territory, at six o'clock in the morning, January eighth, 'sixty-three. He was shot in the leg in a Yankee-Rebel altercation. An old doctor amputated the leg at the hip, and Connie died soon after. The evidence is conclusive, but Tavie must keep the source of it secret. So that's the end of old Connie. He was too good for this world, for my part the purest-souled man I ever knew."

As no one said anything, John resumed: "There's a strange side to it that shows Tavie has inherited Charity Samson's remarkably accurate"— he glanced at Ike—"gift of prophecy. During the war, she once nursed a Rebel captain, wounded in the thigh, who turned out to be the Marshal who arrested Solon Samson in 'fifty for running slaves in the Underground. His leg had to be amputated at the hip, and he died of the operation. As he lay dead he seemed to Tavie to change into Connie, likewise lying there before her, dead from an amputation of the hip. She now learns that the time the Rebel captain died was exactly when Connie died, six o'clock in the morning of January eighth, 'sixty-three."

Tavie was obviously embarrassed, and Sarah reached over and patted her hand. As if to change the subject Ike rose and said, "'Paloosa, come in and see my horses before it gets dark." When they were in the barn Ike whispered, "Was that from Joe Kirkwood?" John nodded. "I thought so," said Ike; "I had a letter from him saying he was bound for that place. Is he still Henry Smith?" John nodded again.

They walked on to the shed part of the barn, with its animals in their four stalls and two stanchions. "Do you remember Charity Samson's prophecy back in 'fifty?" said John. "You to do something harmful to Tavie, I to go through fire and suffering and the like, and afterwards to do something good for Tavie?" "Never forgot it," said Ike. "Funny, ain't it? By the way—young Solon—is he to be Solon Lathrop now?" "Indeed he is," said John with his big, genuine smile. "But don't feel too set up—his hair's getting darker!—almost like mine!" As John looked at Ike his expression grew suddenly strained, and he dropped his eyes. After a moment's hesitation he paced forward out of the barn, Ike following.

Ike fetched whisky and cordial from the house, and toasts were drunk to Tavie, to John, to Tavie and John together, to little Sally, to peace, to Grant, to everything in the world except what the home folks were most curious about and would have liked also to have drunk to. The talk grew animated, a little too animated, avoiding the one question that everybody wanted to ask Tavie or John. Pru skirted closest to it when she said sweetly, "I only wish you had brought young Solon on, for I have never seen him." Tavie's parry of this raised hopes— "Later perhaps. Just now he is studying for a special

examination the school is to allow him for having missed the last month."
"Was he ill?" asked Sarah anxiously—for she had seen little Solon and had
no doubt of his paternity. "No," said Tavie—she looked up inquiringly at
John. "I took him on a little trip round the West," said John with artificial
casualness. "Had to go—law business for a friend. Thought he might never
have a better chance to see the country."

Against Pru's protests Sarah and Ben said they must go, but Sarah first
insisted that she would see to the beds. All the women went in the house,
taking the baby. They settled that Homer and Aggie were to have the best
guest room, Tavie to take Ike's recently re-instated place in Pru's bed, and
Ike and John to sleep together in the other room— "They'll sit up all night
gabbing, anyway." Pru laughingly let her three in-laws take the baby upstairs
and tuck her away, also opening the beds, while she set out a cold supper
in the dining-room which they could eat or not as they chose. She also set
out in the sitting-room a tray with whisky, glasses, a pitcher of icewater,
and—sign of a gala occasion—Ike's box of cigars. She knew how much the
forthcoming talk with John was going to mean to Ike.

Outside in the twilight the men skimmed over the usual political and
business subjects. When at last they heard the women re-gathering in the
kitchen Ben stood up and quietly tried the unbroken ice, "Well, 'Paloosa,"
he said, "for my part I can't hold in any longer. Are you coming home or
ain't you?" John drew strongly on his cigar, so that by its glow Ike saw
that same strained expression that had come over his face in the barn. But
he replied easily, "Well, Runt, that's something we've to talk a lot about
when we've more time for it." Ben grunted, "You're no better than Ike.
You both say you prefer the old life, but when it gets right down to coming
home where you belong and showing you mean what you say, all you do is
talk, talk, talk. In my opinion you're a pair of butterflies. All you sure
enough want is to drift where the wind is blowing."

John and Ike looked at each other, but they couldn't see one another's
eyes in the dusk, and each laughed by himself. "Runt," said John, cheerfully, "you may like acting better than talking, but when you do say something you hit the nail on the head. I guess no one of us ever said a truer
word." Ben and Ike went into the barn to harness the buggy.

Left by themselves for a moment, Homer said to John, "You and the
Scamp could likely talk better alone, couldn't ye?" "Do you mind, old
man?" John asked affectionately. "Not in the least, old boy," said Homer
heartily, "not in the least, I assure ye."

Five minutes later Sarah and Ben rattled out the drive with everybody's
promise to appear for dinner at the homestead tomorrow. It was to be the

first complete family dinner Sarah had spread in more than ten years, since '54 when Aggie and Homer were last on from the West. She and Ben kept nothing like the larder of the old days, and Pru was under instructions to come out early, bringing a suckling pig, a turkey and two roasts. Ben was to arrange with Nat Norcross to have the ceremony in the old church at two o'clock, and immediately afterward a dance in the summer kitchen with Jehu Jones fiddling and prompting and Elijy Harris from the Center on the jew's-harp—Elijy was still vigorous, having barely turned eighty. In the morning Tavie and John would first go round to see Solon and Charity Samson in the little house on Academy Street they had just bought with the money Ike had made for Solon in greenbacks. Then Henry Hawks would fetch them out to the Hollow in the old Lathrop coach. After the wedding and the junket he would drive them away in it, "just for a little jaunt of a week or two," John said,—this probably meaning the Thousand Islands. Besides arranging the other details, Ben was to invite everybody in the Hollow to the wedding, but the only guests from the village were to be near relations, the Solon Samsons, the Numa Samsons—Numa was home on leave, awaiting discharge—and the Starks. Pru already had in mind a subterfuge by which she'd get her ma away for the day without her pa—she'd rather not go herself than have him there on this intimate occasion!

As soon as Ma and Ben had driven down State Street with everybody blowing kisses from the front steps, Aggie and Tavie, being tired from their three days' train ride, had to go up to bed, and Homer professed cheerfully that he too felt "like he'd been drawn through a knot-hole." Ike lit the gas in the sitting-room and Pru lit it and turned it down in the dining-room, reminding Ike and John of the supper there which no one had touched. The good nights were said. Ike closed the door to the hall and the double doors to the parlor, and opened the two big windows. He supplied John and himself with whisky, waved to the easy chair, and himself sat down in the spring rocker. John remained standing by the black marble fireplace. The brothers were alone.

Immediately it was as if Ike had not seen John before. A complete change came over his appearance, a change that had been intimated by that strained expression Ike had seen fleetingly in the barn and which harked back to the last time he had seen him, in the fateful interview in Washington. He seemed taller, longer-boned than ever as he stood with one arm stretched out along the mantel, the other hand holding his whisky glass. He was terribly thin, his chest flat, his neatly bearded face pale to cadaverousness, accentuating the fine lines of his arched nose, accentuating above all the blue-black eyes that, not looking at Ike now, seemed nevertheless enormous. Wide streaks of his dark hair were following Ike's into premature whiteness. The mark of the invalid was on him, but like a thin disguise upon invincible, nervous power.

"To begin with, Scamp," he said, "I want to apologize utterly for the years of injustice I have done you, starting with that night in 'fifty when we talked with Pa after you'd sold Dandy and proposed to go to work for Howell Sherwood. We both saw the writing on the wall then. We both knew that the old ways were doomed. We both knew that the nut of the change was in this new way of working to make money instead of working to live and after that serving the community. We both knew that the change was contrary to the hatred of money which we had been taught from infancy, which we inherited from our ancestors from, I guess, the first minute they set foot on this continent. We both knew that the change was wrong, but we proposed to meet it differently. I thought we ought to stand inflexibly against it and die in the last ditch—as Ben is doing in his simple, direct way, God bless him! You thought we ought to accept the inevitable, set ourselves at the head of the change and adapt it to our convictions. You were right. You took the wise way, the strong way. You faced the facts as they were, as the generals must do in the Army. You retreated a little in order to advance more strongly afterward. I took the weak way, what for my nature was the easy way. When I thought I was facing the facts I was really running away from them. Perhaps I am continuing to run away from them, though I don't think I am. Be that as it may, I was wrong. I am beaten."

"Like hell you are," said Ike, gulping down his whisky. John fingered his glass on the mantel and continued:

"But I'm not apologizing to you because I am beaten. I am apologizing because I wronged you, did you as great an injustice as a brother ever did a brother, and we have both suffered for it. You have shown in your actions that you were not greedy like those others with whom I, in my stiff-necked ignorance, compared you. You had an itch for competition, for swopping. You made two or three early mistakes, like selling poor old Dandy and afterwards trimming Joe Kirkwood about the Union Mills—and God knows Joe had it coming to him. But after that you learned your lesson—I know more about your affairs than you think, for I haven't corresponded about the *Eagle* with Squire Fulton and Loyal Hall for nothing. You learned your lesson and put into practice the one principle that might have justified the new industrial economy. You took the same neighborly responsibility for your men that we would have taken back in the Hollow for

folks who were less fortunately situated than we were. I know what you
have done for your employees—or I know some of it. I know some of the
things you have done secretly for other people in the village."

"Don't amount to a hill o' beans," said Ike. John disregarded him and
went on:

"And one of the finest things you did was the very thing that killed Jabe
and almost killed me. At that time most of the manufacturers of war supplies were getting rich out of the high prices they were getting from the
Government and the low wages they were paying their men. You and
Squire Fulton and Perez Price were the only exceptions I ever heard of,
and Fulton and Price were never faced with the issue you were faced with.
You had to choose between reducing your men to starvation wages, shut-
ting down and throwing them out of employment, or depreciating the
quality of your guns. Feeling as you did about the war—and Heaven
knows you were right about the scoundrels getting control of it!—feeling
as you did, you did the only honest thing you could do. It was less important to you that two or three soldiers might get killed than that forty or
fifty families you were responsible for should suffer. Fate set an ugly trap
for us, but I, not you, was the one who swallowed the bait when I broke
with you. The only mistake you made was in talking so danged much
about making money in your letters. That broke me down."

"Likely was on my conscience as far as you were concerned," said Ike.
"Had to confess everything to ye. Likely wanted to plague ye a little, too,
for being so danged sure of yourself. I ended up by plaguing myself plenty.
Don't know whether I was right or wrong otherwise, but I was wrong
there, that's certain."

"I see now," said John, "that the reason I was so severe with you was
because you were so close to me. It was as if I was doing wrong myself,
and I had to be as forceful with you as I would be in trying to overcome
something in myself. As between you and me, I guess that was the greatest
mistake I made. It took Aggie to point it out to me. She said you would
understand." For the first time John looked directly at Ike, with all his
power in the appeal of his eyes. "Do you?" he said.

Ike couldn't speak for his emotion, but he smiled and John knew he
understood. John couldn't speak either, so he looked away, noticed his drink
for the first time, and swallowed it. Ike replenished both glasses and sat
down again. "Why don't ye sit down?" he said, again waving toward the
easy chair. "Feel like standing up," said John. "Been sitting down for three
days."

"And now for the future," said John, "and that takes us back over familiar ground. I guess we're agreed on what's happening. It's what Pa pointed out in that same talk back in 'fifty when you and I set out on our different tacks. The old civilization—what I used to call in my speeches 'the River of America'!"—John made a rhetorical gesture and smiled—"has split in two directions, separate currents. One is going into the cities, the new industries and the new money economy. The other is going to the West. You have joined the first, and now all my personal inclination is to join that too. I could go into the VanSanford office and make a comfortable living. I could join you in a fight for responsibility among the financially powerful. I could do business only for you and George Fulton, and perhaps Watchful Smart and a few others. I could preach what I believed, in the *Eagle*. I could do all that and keep my integrity.

"But, however completely I may have changed my opinions about you, I still feel the same about the money economy. By and large I believe that it, and most of the people running it, are greedy, predatory and ruthless, and that sooner or later they will ruin the country. I know there are fine men in it. I believe that Thaddeus Stevens himself is a sincere and misguided idealist. I know that for a long time there will be a smattering of preachers, editors and others minded as I am, and they will continue to preach against the money motive. But I know, too, that most of the people who pay solemn attention to them will then go right out and continue to do their bit toward destroying the nation. Being convinced of this, I could not in the largest sense keep my integrity while living in the midst of it, even though I did nothing unprincipled myself."

"Thought ye said ye saw some point after all in my trying to look after my men," said Ike.

"I certainly do," said John, "as far as you individually are concerned, but I am perfectly sure you are going to lose your fight, just as I have lost mine so far. I am telling you honestly that my whole inclination is to join you in it. I would enjoy it. I know everybody involved, both friends and enemies. I would enjoy having at Applemore here for a few years. I would enjoy the fight almost as much if I lost it. But the point—at least one of the points—is that I *know* I would lose. I would be doing just what I did with you. I would be standing stiff-necked for my principles down to the dotting of an 'i,' when a little concession, a little compromise, might have won my battle for me elsewhere."

"Ye mean the West?" said Ike, slumping a little in his chair.

"Yes," said John, looking away. They both drank. John continued, speaking very quietly:

"You see, Scamp, there's more involved than anything we've mentioned yet. There's the whole question of this democratic government we've been trying in New England and the North for pretty near two centuries and a half. It's the first great experiment of the kind in human history. Before the war we used to talk of making this the first perfect nation on earth, and I can't entirely let go of that dream. Under this money economy democracy is doomed, any way you look at it. The employees in factories and other big businesses are not free agents. They depend on their employers for everything. Living in a dirty hovel with no garden and no critters, no way of looking out for themselves, destroys their independence. They are not in a position to stand up and say what they think. They are sure, most of them, to vote as their employers want them to. As things are now, this gives the employers the power to run the Government pretty much as they like. With their money they can finance the campaigns of demagogues like Applemore, who will go to Washington and tend to their tariffs and other interests for them."

"Figger I have more faith in mankind than you have," said Ike. "Nowadays they'll likely vote for what their bosses want because they figger that some day they'll be bosses too. They like this new way of things because they figger it gives them a chance to rise themselves. But if the time ever comes—and I think it's far off, I grant ye—when smart fellers can't rise to be bosses themselves, then I think ye'll see them stand up and vote your Applemores out quick enough, whether they vote for going back to the old homestead and supporting themselves, or for some of this socialism that ye hear talked at the Mechanics' Institute, or for something else we've no notion of. I don't think they're so danged helpless as you do."

"They're either helpless," said John, "or they're mighty gullible. If they're not afraid of their employers, then they're mighty quick to fall in behind a band and some torch-lights and some weeping from a soap-box draped with a flag. You used to say that yourself, when you planned to make money so you could buy me bands and torches. Do you remember?"

"My notion," said Ike, "was that we'd lead them into voting for something that was good for them instead of voting for Applemore and what is good for Horace Gadston and Lem Grabbot. I still think we could do it. It would be pretty hard to beat you and me and the Samsons and the VanSanfords and Howell Sherwood and George Fulton, and quite a few more, with the *Eagle* to do our hollerin' for us."

"That's the other side of it," said John. "We might win here for a while. I don't think we could stay ahead for long. I know we could never win in New York or in any of the big centers. But even suppose we could.

Our experiment in democracy would be just as dead. What we would do at best would be to build up a sort of aristocracy of rich families who would look after their people and in return would hold their loyalty. That might be a satisfactory state of society, but it would be turning back to the feudal world. I want to see this experiment in democracy go forward.

"As I see it, democracy can only survive where everybody, or every family, owns property enough to keep itself fed, clothed and housed, no matter what happens. And that means owning your own farm, as almost everybody in America did until the factories and the cities started herding them together. That is still the condition in the West and will be for generations to come, perhaps always will be. It may be that some day the money system will capture the West too. I know that many western farmers are already selling produce to New York City. But they still raise their necessities on their own farms, and it will be a long time before the factory system comes out there to make them dependent on wages. When it comes I shall want my children—yes, even yours—to retire before it as we would do before an Army that was too strong for us. I shall want them to retire before it as long as they are unable to beat it, until the last Lathrop homestead is on the Pacific where we will take our last stand and die quietly, as Ben is doing.

"There are thousands of greedy people in the West, land speculators and gamblers of all kinds. But there are millions of people who are not, people just like ourselves, who see things as I do. I think it is my duty, I think Pa would say it was my duty, to throw in my lot with these people. After I got your note about the birth of little Sally, Homer and young Solon and I took a long trip up into Wisconsin, and Homer and I have staked out our hundred and sixty acres apiece under the Homestead Act. Our places are adjoining and Homer has bought three thousand acres besides, of which I am to have half if you'll lend me the money to buy it. The country is beautiful, the hills about the size of those around the Hollow, only very little of it is cleared yet. What we have taken up is a sort of cup in the hills too, and Homer is insisting we must call it Lathrop Hollow. Tavie is giving up teaching, but she will keep up her Reform activities in the West, with me helping her. I am going to clearing my land and farming, but even in the two weeks we were in the region there was a movement started to send me to Congress in 'sixty-six—so fast do things move in that new country. The district of course is enormous and thinly populated, but there are a good many people from Oberlin there and they seem to think well of me. The chance of going to Congress and meeting Applemore head on is not the real reason for my deciding to move out there, but it's an additional reason. Here my only chance in politics would be to join the Democratic Party which opposed the war. I still believe in the war, even though the victory is to be brutally prostituted—as you predicted."

"Young Solon?" said Ike, who was sitting up straight now, his face that combination of gentleness in the eyes, troubled uncomprehension in the pucker of the brow, and behind them both quiet strength, that expression which never left his face again but momentarily, as long as he lived.

"That is for you and Tavie to settle between you," said John, "but I'm afraid Tave won't give him up."

"Naturally not," said Ike.

"I'm almost as fond of him as you are," said John, "and it will be a joy to have him with me. Only I'm afraid my influence will be in my way instead of yours."

"I ain't afraid of that," said Ike. "The war's the only thing we ever sure grit disagreed on."

They looked straight at each other now. The house and the night outside were perfectly still, but for the soft hissing of the gas and the distant rumble of the Middle Falls. "I guess," said John, "we were born to go different ways, and we've no choice but to follow our destinies, whether we want to or not."

"It's something stronger than we are," said Ike, "that's driving us apart, something like the falls yonder that no man can stand up against, like the river that splits in two channels at the head of Fleet's Island whether it likes it or not."

"And we're both sure of our ways," said John, "and the man isn't living who can tell either of us he is wrong."

"I ain't sure of anything in the world," said Ike softly, "except that baby girl upstairs that I'm bound to live up to. There's something missing in me that all of our folks had and you and Ben still have. I figger I've gone as far as most in religion, but when it comes to acting I still can't see but the only way is to look to the practical results, without any right and wrong about it. I've even thought it was these moral principles that are what's wrong, driving folks to kill each other, like in the war. But I know I'm missing something, for, even looking at it in my practical way, this twisted thing in me has hurt my friends and driven them away from me.

"I used to think I'd find what was missing in me if I went back to the Hollow, but I see now that if I did that I'd only be sneaking out of the fight. Whatever is wrong is clean inside me, and I can't lose it by running away. I'm about ready to admit you and Pa were right in the beginning, figgering I was wrong to try to make money. But just quitting business without seeing what else I'm going after wouldn't solve anything, as I see it. I'm bound to see where I'm going first, then I can get rid of what stands in my way. I ain't sure of anything any more. But I aim to go on trying as long as I live."

"I guess," said John, "that what is missing in you is faith, faith in the old way of life, or in some way of life. That's what is missing everywhere in the East, pretty much everywhere in the whole modern world for that matter. Everything now must be measured by laws and practical results. There's a man in England who has published a book claiming that the animals and plants weren't created by any Higher Power but have evolved under certain laws through a vast period of time. Perhaps they'll say next that man has nothing to do with any God, that he's subject to practical laws along with the rest of nature. All this new science, from the mechanics of factories to these strange notions of the origins of things, is like an island that has risen in the river, and a large part of our civilization is splitting off around it to make a new channel. People are forgetting ultimate things, and are listening to the engineers and the scientists who must see everything proven, and who call faith superstition. For my part, I have to be sure of something. I have to have faith, else I wouldn't want to live."

"Well," said Ike, rising, and his voice was easy and clear, "you and I've got back together, and that's one thing that's ultimate and more important than where we live." "And no matter what happens," said John, "we'll never be really separated again." "As I see it," said Ike, "we never were." "The mistake was mine," said John. "Let's have some supper," said Ike.

They ate supper, then went back into the sitting-room and both sat down with the bottle between them. All of the past came out of its remotest crannies and hiding places, Tavic, Pru, Pa, Mattie, the burlesque girl, brother Tom, Grandpa and Grandma, every member of the old Gang, the earlier gang in the Hollow who had gone to California and none of whom had returned, boyhood, the early dances and bees and showers, the childhood loves and tragedies and triumphs, the old Thanksgiving parties of which the one in '50 was the last real one, the old order of life that had seemed as if it must last forever. These two had curved far apart on the currents of the times and for tonight were curved back and running as one again, as before Dandy died. Those two great divisions of the river of America that were parting flowed as one through that night, while time that was separating them flowed inevitably outside in the darkness.

At two o'clock John fell asleep, and Ike sat quietly drinking, watching him. He noticed how frail he looked when his big eyes were closed, and thought how it likely wasn't good for him to sit up all night drinking liquor. Overhead he heard Pru picking up little Sally to nurse. It was quiet again. Ike was alone with the night, with the dead he believed were not dead, and the living things he loved most, all near at hand. Through an opening in the maples in the yard he could see the stars.

In the low rumble of the Middle Falls and the hissing of the gas above him, in the rustle of the blood in his ears and of the sap in myriad growing things outside, Ike could hear the irresistible force of time and growth and change, like a still cannonade destroying the things men had loved and built, that new men might build and love new things in their places. And beyond the rustle of change his spirit flew out and was one with his God of Permanence beyond the stars.

But even as Ike reached out to his faith in a God that was beyond life and death, he knew that that same God must somehow include a faith in some way of living on the earth. He knew, as the 'Paloosa had said, that it was this faith that was missing in him. The mistake he had made was in seeing only the God that was eternal beyond what men did, and in measuring what men did by nothing but the practical results. Even though the old rules were based on practical sense, yet a man must feel some such rules as part of his God, else he couldn't live among folks and didn't deserve to have any friends. Ike didn't know how to come by the kind of faith the 'Paloosa had except to wait. Perhaps some time it would come to him, the way he had first found God down in the lower meadow.

Sitting there alone in the night, he felt the big earth rolling among the stars, carrying along the village and the hills out at the Hollow and the hills out at the new Lathrop Hollow in Wisconsin, and mountains and rivers, and billions of trees thrusting their roots, and billions and billions of blades of grass, all stirring and thrusting their roots. He thought how all over half of the rolling earth men were sleeping, each alone with simple dreams and wants that wished no one any harm. And how over the other half of the earth men were awake and struggling to adjust their simple wants to the simple wants of their neighbors. And how out of these struggles their simple wants got changed into great faiths and visions, and great hates and wars, and how these myriads of simple wants struggling made, all together, the silent forces of change that divided brothers and nations and brought them together again. And Ike knew that the River of America would never run contentedly again in one channel unless it was in the 'Paloosa's channel, and everybody had the same faith in some way of living. It might not be the 'Paloosa's way now, but it would have to be some single way.

As Ike watched through the window he saw the high western sky grow purple behind the stars. Outside in the heavy summer leaves a robin began to sing softly, and the light in the room was grayish against the yellow flare of the gas. The 'Paloosa mumbled something and opened his eyes that immediately met Ike's. They both smiled in the old sure way. "Ye had a nap," said Ike. "I still want to sleep most of the time," said John. "I guess I'm a good way from cured." He got up unsteadily, walked to the window and stood looking out. "But they haven't finished me yet," he said without looking round. "I'm not going to die."

"Ye're danged right ye're not," said Ike. He got up and turned out the gas.